THE POLDARK OMNIBUS

Winston Graham

THE POLDARK OMNIBUS

Ross Poldark
Demelza
Jeremy Poldark
Warleggan

THE BODLEY HEAD
LONDON

This edition first published 1991
The Bodley Head, 20 Vauxhall Bridge Road, London SW1V 2SA

Ross Poldark
All rights reserved
First published in Great Britain 1945

Demelza
All rights reserved
First published in Great Britain 1946

Jeremy Poldark
All rights reserved
First published in Great Britain 1953

Warleggan
© Winston Graham 1953

Winston Graham has asserted his right under the Copyright,
Designs and Patents Act 1988 to be identified as the author of this work

A CIP catalogue record for this book
is available from the British Library

ISBN 0-370-31654-1

Printed in Great Britain by
Mackays of Chatham PLC

Contents

ROSS POLDARK

A Novel of Cornwall 1783–1787

Prologue

JOSHUA POLDARK DIED in March 1783. In February of that year, feeling that his tenure was becoming short, he sent for his brother from Trenwith.

Charles came lolloping over on his great roan horse one cold grey afternoon, and Prudie Paynter, lank-haired and dark-faced and fat, showed him straight into the bedroom where Joshua lay possed up with pillows and cushions in the big box bed. Charles looked askance round the room with his small watery blue eyes, at the disorder and the dirt, then lifted his coattails and subsided upon a wicker chair which creaked under his weight.

'Well, Joshua.'

'Well, Charles.'

'This is a bad business.'

'Bad indeed.'

'When will you be about again, d'you think?'

'There's no telling. I fancy the churchyard will have a strong pull.'

Charles thrust out his bottom lip. He would have discounted the remark if he had not had word to the contrary. He hiccupped a little – riding always gave him indigestion these days – and was heartily reassuring.

'Nonsense, man. The gout in the legs never killed nobody. It is when it gets up to the head that it is dangerous.'

'Choake tells me different, that there is other cause for the swelling. For once I misdoubt if the old fool is not right. Though in God's truth, by all appearance it is you that should be lying here, since I am but half your size.'

Charles glanced down at the landscape of black embroidered waistcoat spreading away from under his chin.

'Mine is healthy flesh. Every man puts on weight in his middle years. I would not wish to be a yard of pump water like Cousin William-Alfred.'

Joshua lifted an ironical eyebrow but said no more, and there was silence. The brothers had had little to say to each other for many years, and at this their last meeting small talk was not easy to find. Charles, the elder and more prosperous, who had come in for the family house and lands and most of the mining interests, head of the family and a respected figure in the county, had never quite been able to get away from a suspicion that his younger brother despised him. Joshua had always been a thorn in his flesh. Joshua had never been content to do the things expected of him: enter the

Church or the Army or marry property and leave Charles to run the district himself.

Not that Charles minded a few lapses, but there were limits, and Joshua had overstepped them. The fact that he had been behaving himself for the last few years did not score out old grievances.

As for Joshua, a man with a cynical mind and few illusions, he had no complaint against life or against his brother. He had lived one to the limit and ignored the other. There was some truth in his reply to Charles's next comment of, 'Why, man, you're young enough yet. Two years junior to me, and I'm fit and well. Aarf!'

Joshua said: 'Two years in age, maybe, but you've only lived half as fast.'

Charles sucked the ebony tip of his cane and looked sidelong about the room from under heavy lids. 'This damned war not settled yet. Prices soaring. Wheat seven and eight shillings a bushel. Butter ninepence a pound. Eh, well, it's no hurt to us. Wish the copper prices was the same. We're thinking of cutting a new level at Grambler. Eighty fathom. Maybe it will defray the initial outlay, though I doubt it. Been doing much with your fields this year?'

'It was about the war that I wanted to see you,' said Joshua, struggling a little farther up the pillows and gasping for breath. 'It must be only a matter of months now before the provisional peace is confirmed. Then Ross will be home and maybe I shall not be here to greet him. You're me brother, though we've never hit it off so well. I want to tell you how things are and to leave you to look after things till he gets back.'

Charles took the cane from his mouth and smiled defensively. He looked as if he had been asked for a loan.

'I've not much time, y' know.'

'It won't take much of your time. I've little or nothing to leave. There's a copy of my will on the table beside you. Read it at your leisure. Pearce has the original.'

Charles groped with his clumsy swollen hand and picked up a piece of parchment from the rickety three-legged table behind him.

'When did you last hear from him?' he asked. 'What's to be done if he don't come back?'

'The estate will go to Verity. Sell if there are any purchasers; it will fetch little. That's down in the will. Verity will have my share in Grambler too, since she is the only one of your family who has been over since Ross left.' Joshua wiped his nose on the soiled sheet. 'But Ross will come back. I've heard from him since the fighting ceased.'

'There's many hazards yet.'

'I've a feeling,' said Joshua. 'A conviction. Care to take a wager? Settle when we meet. There'll be some sort of currency in the next world.'

Charles stared again at the sallow lined face which had once been so handsome. He was a little relieved that Joshua's request was no more than this, but slow to relax his caution. And irreverence on a deathbed struck him as reckless and uncalled-for.

'Cousin William-Alfred was visiting us the other day. He enquired for you.'

Joshua pulled a face.

'I told him how ill you was,' Charles went on. 'He suggested that though you might not wish to call in the Rev Mr Odgers, maybe you would like spiritual consolation from one of your own family.'

'Meaning him.'

'Well, he's the only one in orders now Betty's husband's gone.'

'I want none of them,' said Joshua. 'Though no doubt it was kindly meant. But if he thought it would do me good to confess my sins, did he think I should rather tell secrets to one of my own blood? No, I'd rather talk to Odgers, half starved little hornywink though he is. But I want none of them.'

'If you change your mind,' said Charles, 'send Jud over with a message. Aarf!'

Joshua grunted. 'I shall know soon enough. But even if there was something in it with all their pomp and praying, should I ask 'em in at this hour? I've lived my life, and by God I've enjoyed it! There's no merit to go snivelling now. I'm not sorry for myself and I don't want anyone else to be. What's coming I'll take. That's all.'

There was silence in the room. Outside the wind thrust and stirred about the slate and stone.

'Time I was off,' said Charles. 'These Paynters are letting your place get into a rare mess. Why don't you get someone reliable?'

'I'm too old to swap donkeys. Leave that to Ross. He'll soon put things to rights.'

Charles belched disbelievingly. He had no high opinion of Ross's abilities.

'He's in New York now,' said Joshua. 'Part of the garrison. He's quite recovered from his wound. It was lucky he escaped the Yorktown siege. A captain now, you know. Still in the 62nd Foot. I've mislaid his letter, else I'd show it you.'

'Francis is a great help to me these days,' said Charles. 'So would Ross have been to you if he was home instead of coosing around after Frenchmen and Colonials.'

'There was one other thing,' said Joshua. 'D'you see or hear anything of Elizabeth Chynoweth these days?'

After a heavy meal questions took time to transmit themselves to Charles's brain, and where his brother was concerned they needed an examination for hidden motives. 'Who is that?' he said clumsily.

'Jonathan Chynoweth's daughter. You know her. A thin, fair child.'

'Well, what of it?' said Charles.

'I was asking if you'd seen her. Ross always mentions her. A pretty little thing. He's counting on her being here when he comes back, and I think it a suitable arrangement. An early marriage will steady him down, and she couldn't find a decenter man, though I say it as shouldn't, being his sire. Two good old families. If I'd been on my feet I should have gone over to see Jonathan at Christmas to fix it up. We did talk of it before, but he said wait till Ross came back.'

'Time I was going,' said Charles, creaking to his feet. 'I hope the boy will settle down when he returns, whether he marries or no. He was keeping bad company that he should never have got into.'

'D'you see the Chynoweths now?' Joshua refused to be side-tracked by references to his own shortcomings. 'I'm cut off from the world here, and Prudie has no ear for anything but scandal in Sawle.'

'Oh, we catch sight of 'em from time to time. Verity and Francis saw them at a party in Truro this summer . . .' Charles peered through the window. 'Rot me if it isn't Choake. Well, now you'll have more company, and I thought you said no one ever came to see you. I must be on my way.'

'He's only come quizzing to see how much faster his pills are finishing me off. That or his politics. As if I care whether Fox is in his earth or hunting Tory chickens.'

'Have it as you please.' For one of his bulk Charles moved quickly, picking up hat and gauntlet gloves and making ready to be gone. At the last he stood awkwardly by the bed, wondering how best to take his leave, while the clip-clop of a horse's hooves went past the window.

'Tell him I don't want to see him,' said Joshua irritably. 'Tell him to give his potions to his silly wife.'

'Calm yourself,' said Charles. 'Aunt Agatha sent her love, mustn't forget that; and she said you was to take hot beer and sugar and eggs. She says that will cure you.'

Joshua's irritation lifted.

'Aunt Agatha's a wise old turnip. Tell her I'll do as she says. And – and tell her I'll save her a place beside me.' He began to cough.

'God b' w' ye,' said Charles hurriedly, and sidled out of the room.

Joshua was left alone.

He had spent many hours alone since Ross went, but they had not seemed to matter until he took to his bed a month ago. Now they were beginning to depress him and fill his mind with fancies. An out-of-doors man to whom impulse all his days had meant action, this painful, gloomy, bedridden life was no life at all. He had nothing to do with his time except think over the past, and the past was not always the most elegant subject matter.

He kept thinking of Grace, his long dead wife. She had been his mascot. While she lived all had gone well. The mine he opened and called after her brought rich results; this house, begun in pride and hope, had been built;

two strong sons. His own indiscretions behind him, he had settled down, promising to rival Charles in more ways than one; he had built this house with the idea that his own branch of the family of Poldark should become rooted no less securely than the main Trenwith tree.

With Grace had gone all his luck. The house half built, the mine had petered out, and, with Grace's death, his incentive to expend money and labour on either. The building had been finished off anyhow, though much remained unrealized. Then Wheal Vanity had closed down also and little Claude Anthony had died.

. . . He could hear Dr Choake and his brother talking at the front door: his brother's rusty thickened tenor. Choake's voice, deep and slow and pompous. Anger and impotence welled up in Joshua. What the devil did they mean droning away on his doorstep, no doubt discussing him and nodding their heads together and saying, well, after all, what else could one expect. He tugged at the bell beside his bed and waited, fuming, for the flip-flop of Prudie's slippers.

She came at last, looking ungainly and indistinct in the doorway. Joshua peered at her shortsightedly in the fading light.

'Bring candles, woman. D'you want me to die in the dark. And tell those two old men to be gone.'

Prudie hunched herself like a bird of ill omen. 'Dr Choake and Mister Charles, you're meaning, an?'

'Who else?'

She went out, and Joshua fumed again, while there was the sound of a muttered conversation not far from his door. He looked around for his stick, determined to make one more effort to get up and walk out to them. But then the voices were raised again in farewells, and a horse could be heard moving away across the cobbles and towards the stream.

That was Charles. Now for Choake . . .

There was a loud rap of a riding crop on his door and the surgeon came in.

Thomas Choake was a Bodmin man who had practised in London, had married a brewer's daughter and returned to his native county to buy a small estate near Sawle. He was a tall clumsy man with a booming voice, thatch-grey eyebrows and an impatient mouth. Among the smaller gentry his London experience stood him in good stead; they felt he was abreast of up-to-date physical ideas. He was surgeon to several of the mines in the district, and with the knife had the same neck-or-nothing approach that he had on the hunting field.

Joshua thought him a humbug and had several times considered calling in Dr Pryce from Redruth. Only the fact that he had no more faith in Dr Pryce prevented him.

'Well, well,' said Dr Choake. 'So we've been having visitors, eh? We'll feel better, no doubt, for our brother's visit.'

'I've got some business off my hands,' said Joshua. 'That was the purpose of inviting him.'

Dr Choake felt for the invalid's pulse with heavy fingers. 'Cough,' he said. Joshua grudgingly obeyed.

'Our condition is much the same,' said the surgeon. 'The distemper has not increased. Have we been taking the pills?'

'Charles is twice my size. Why don't you doctor him?'

'You are ill, Mr Poldark. Your brother is not. I do not prescribe unless called upon to do so.' Choake lifted back the bedclothes and began to prod his patient's swollen legs.

'Great mountain of a fellow,' grumbled Joshua. '*He'll* never see his feet again.'

'Oh, come; your brother is not out of the common. I well remember when I was in London —'

'Uff!'

'Did that hurt?'

'No,' said Joshua.

Choake prodded again to make sure. 'There is a distinct abatement in the condition of our left leg. There is still too much water in both. If we could get the heart to pump it away. I well remember when I was in London being called into the victim of a tavern brawl in Westminster. He had quarrelled with an Italian Jew, who drew a dagger and thrust it up to the hilt into my patient's belly. But so thick was the protective fat that I found the knife point had not even pierced the bowel. A sizeable fellow. Let me see, did I bleed you when I was last here?'

'You did.'

'I think we might leave it this time. Our heart is inclined to be excitable. Control the choler, Mr Poldark. An even temper helps the body to secrete the proper juices.'

'Tell me,' said Joshua. 'Do you see anything of the Chynoweths? The Chynoweths of Cusgarne, y' know. I asked my brother, but he returned an evasive answer.'

'The Chynoweths? I see them from time to time. I think they are in health. I am not, of course, their physician and we do not call on each other socially.'

No, thought Joshua, Mrs Chynoweth will have a care for that. 'I smell something shifty in Charles,' he said shrewdly. 'Do you see Elizabeth?'

'The daughter? She is about.'

'There was an understanding as to her between myself and her father.'

'Indeed. I had not heard of it.'

Joshua pushed himself up the pillows. His conscience had begun to prick him. It was late in the day for the growth of this long-dormant faculty, but he was fond of Ross, and in the long hours of his illness he had begun to wonder whether he should not have done more to keep his son's interests warm.

'I think maybe I'll send Jud over to-morrow,' he muttered. 'I'll ask Jonathan to come and see me.'

'I doubt if Mr Chynoweth will be free; it's the Quarter Sessions this week. Ah, that's a welcome sight! . . .'

Prudie Paynter came lumbering in with two candles. The yellow light showed up her sweaty red face with its draping of black hair.

''Ad your physic, 'ave you?' she asked in a throaty whisper.

Joshua turned irritably on the doctor. 'I've told you before, Choake; pills I'll swallow, God help me, but draughts and potions I'll not face.'

'I well remember,' Choake said ponderously, 'when I was practising in Bodmin as a young man, one of my patients, an elderly gentleman who suffered much from strangury and stone . . .'

'Don't stand there, Prudie,' snapped Joshua to his servant. 'Get out.'

Prudie stopped scratching and reluctantly left the room.

'So you think I'm on the mend, eh?' Joshua said before the physician could go on. 'How long before I'm up and about?'

'Hm, hm. A slight abatement, I said. Great care yet awhile. We'll have you on your feet before Ross returns. Take my prescriptions regular and you will find they will set you up. . . .'

'How's your wife?' Joshua asked maliciously.

Again interrupted, Choake frowned. 'Well enough, thank you.'

The fact that the fluffy lisping Polly, though only half his age, had added no family to the dowry she brought, was a standing grievance against her. So long as she was unfruitful he had no influence to dissuade women from buying motherwort and other less respectable brews from travelling gypsies.

II

The doctor had gone and Joshua was once more alone – alone this time until morning. He might, by pulling persistently on the bell cord, call a reluctant Jud or Prudie until such time as they went to bed, but after that there was no one, and before that they were showing signs of deafness as his illness became more clear. He knew they spent most of each evening drinking, and once they reached a certain stage, nothing at all would move them. But he hadn't the energy to round on them as in the old days.

It would have been different if Ross had been here. For once Charles was right, but only partly right. It was he, Joshua, who had encouraged Ross to go away. He had no belief in keeping boys at home as additional lackeys. Let them find their own stirrups. Besides, it would have been undignified to have his son brought up in court for being party to an assault upon excise men, with its associated charges of brandy running and the rest. Not that Cornish magistrates would have convicted, but the question of gaming debts might have been raised.

No, it was Grace who should have been here, Grace who had been snatched from him thirteen years back.

Well, now he was alone and would soon be joining his wife. It did not occur to him to feel surprise that the other women in his life scarcely touched his thoughts. They had been creatures of a pleasant exciting game, the more mettlesome the better, but no sooner broken in than forgotten.

The candles were guttering in the draught from under the door. The wind was rising. Jud had said there was a ground swell this morning; after a quiet cold spell they were returning to rain and storm.

He felt he would like one more look at the sea, which even now was licking at the rocks behind the house. He had no sentimental notions about the sea; he had no regard for its dangers or its beauties; to him it was a close acquaintance whose every virtue and failing, every smile and tantrum he had come to understand.

The land too. Was the Long Field ploughed? Whether Ross married or not there would be little enough to live on without the land.

With a decent wife to manage things . . . Elizabeth was an only child; a rare virtue worth bearing in mind. The Chynoweths were a bit poverty-stricken, but there would be something. Must go and see Jonathan and fix things up. 'Look here, Jonathan,' he would say, 'Ross won't have much money, but there's the land, and that always counts in the long run . . .'

Joshua dozed. He thought he was out walking round the edge of the Long Field with the sea on his right and a strong wind pressing against his shoulder. A bright sun warmed his back and the air tasted like wine from a cold cellar. The tide was out on Hendrawna Beach, and the sun drew streaky reflections in the wet sand. The Long Field had not only been ploughed but was already sown and sprouting.

He skirted the field until he reached the furthest tip of Damsel Point where the low cliff climbed in ledges and boulders down to the sea. The water surged and eddied, changing colour on the shelves of dripping rocks.

With some special purpose in mind he climbed down the rocks until the cold sea suddenly surged about his knees, sending pain through his legs unpleasantly like the pain he had felt from the swelling these last few months. But it did not stop him, and he let himself slip into the water until it was up to his neck. Then he struck out from the shore. He was full of joy at being in the sea again after a lapse of two years. He breathed out his pleasure in long cool gasps, allowed the water to lap close against his eyes. Lethargy crept up his limbs. With the sound of the waves in his ears and heart he allowed himself to drift and sink into cool feathery darkness.

Joshua slept. Outside, the last trailing patterns of daylight moved quietly out of the sky and left the house and the trees and the stream and the cliffs in darkness. The wind freshened, blowing steadily and strongly from the west, searching among the ruined mine sheds on the hill, rustling the tops of the sheltered apple trees, lifting a corner of loose thatch on one of the barns, blowing a spatter of cold rain in through a broken shutter of the library where two rats nosed with cautious jerky scraping movements among the lumber and the dust. The stream hissed and bubbled in the darkness, and above it a long-unmended gate swung *whee-tap* on its hangings. In the kitchen Jud Paynter knocked the neck off the second bottle of gin and Prudie threw a fresh log on the fire.

'Wind's rising, blast it,' said Jud. 'Always there's wind. Always when you don't want it there's wind.'

'We'll need more wood 'fore morning,' said Prudie.

'Use this stool,' said Jud. 'The wood's 'ard, twill smoulder.'

'Give me a drink, you black worm,' said Prudie.

'Wait on yourself,' said Jud.

. . . Joshua slept.

Book one

October 1783–April 1785

Chapter one

IT WAS WINDY. The pale afternoon sky was shredded with clouds, the road, grown dustier and more uneven in the last hour, was scattered with blown and rustling leaves.

There were five people in the coach; a thin clerkly man with a pinched face and a shiny suit, and his wife, fat as her husband was thin, and holding to her breast a confused bundle of pink and white draperies from one end of which pouted the creased and overheated features of a young baby. The other travellers were men, both young, one a clergyman of about thirty-five, the other some years his junior.

Almost since the coach left St Austell there had been silence inside it. The child slept soundly despite the jolting of the vehicle and the rattle of the windows and the clank of the swingle bars; nor had the stops wakened it. From time to time the elderly couple exchanged remarks in undertones, but the thin husband was unwilling to talk, a little overawed by the superior class in which he found himself. The younger of the two men had been reading a book throughout the journey, the elder had watched the passing countryside, one hand holding back the faded dusty brown velvet curtain.

This was a small spare man, severe in clerical black, wearing his own hair scraped back and curled above and behind the ears. The cloth he wore was of fine quality and his stockings were of silk. His was a long, keen, humourless, thin-lipped face, vital and hard. The little clerk knew the face but could not name it.

The clergyman was in much the same position over the other occupant of the coach. A half-dozen times his glance had rested on the thick unpowdered hair opposite, and on the face of his fellow traveller.

When they were not more than fifteen minutes out of Truro and the horses had slowed to a walking pace up the stiff hill, the other man looked up from his book and their eyes met.

'You will pardon me, sir,' said the clergyman in a sharp vigorous voice. 'Your features are familiar, but I find it hard to recall where we have met. Was it in Oxford?'

The young man was tall and thin and big-boned, with a scar on his cheek. He wore a double-breasted riding coat cut away short in front to show the waistcoat and the stout breeches, both of a lighter brown. His hair, which had a hint of copper in its darkness, was brushed back unpretentiously and tied at the back with brown ribbon.

'You're the Rev Dr Halse, aren't you,' he said.

The little clerk, who had been following this exchange, made an expressive face at his wife. Rector of Towerdreth, Curate of St Erme, Headmaster of Truro Grammar School, high burgess of the town and late mayor, Dr Halse was a personage. It explained his bearing.

'You know me, then,' said Dr Halse with a gracious air. 'I usually have a memory for faces.'

'You have had many pupils,'

'Ah, that explains it. Maturity changes a face. And – hm. Let me see . . . is it Hawkey?'

'Poldark.'

The clergyman's eyes narrowed in an effort of remembrance. 'Francis, is it? I thought –'

'Ross. You will remember my cousin more clearly. He stayed on. I felt, quite wrongly, that at thirteen my education had gone far enough.'

Recognition came. 'Ross Poldark. Well, well. You've changed. I remember now,' said Dr Halse with a glint of cold humour. 'You were insubordinate. I had to thrash you at frequent intervals, and then you ran away.'

'Yes.' Poldark turned the page of his book. 'A bad business. And your ankles as sore as my buttocks.'

Two small pink spots came to the clergyman's cheeks. He stared a moment at Ross and then turned to look out of the window.

The little clerk had heard of the Poldarks, had heard of Joshua, from whom, they said, in the fifties and sixties no pretty woman married or unmarried was safe. This must be his son. An unusual face with its strongly set cheekbones, wide mouth and large strong white teeth. The eyes were a very clear blue-grey under the heavy lids, which gave a number of the Poldarks that deceptively sleepy look.

Dr Halse was returning to the attack.

'Francis, I suppose, is well? Is he married?'

'Not when I last heard, sir. I've been in America some time.'

'Dear me. A deplorable mistake, the fighting. I was against it throughout. Did you see much of the war?'

'I was in it.'

They had reached the top of the hill at last and the driver was slackening his bearing reins at the descent before him.

Dr Halse wrinkled his sharp nose. 'You are a Tory?'

'A soldier.'

'Well, it was not the fault of the soldiers that we lost. England's heart was not in it. We have a derelict old man on the throne. He'll not last much longer. The Prince has different views.' The clergyman took a pinch of snuff and nodded complacently.

The road in the steepest part of the hill was deeply rutted, and the coach jolted and swayed dangerously. The baby began to cry. They reached the bottom and the man beside the driver blew a blast on his horn. They turned into St Austell Street. It was a Tuesday afternoon and there were few people about the shops. Two half-naked urchins ran the length of the street begging for a copper, but gave up the chase as the coach swayed into the mud of St Clement's Street. With much creaking and shouting they rounded the sharp corner, crossed the river by the narrow bridge, jolted over granite cobbles, turned and twisted again and at last drew up before the Red Lion Inn.

In the bustle that followed, the Rev Dr Halse got out first with a stiff word of farewell and was gone, stepping briskly between the puddles of rainwater and horse urine to the other side of the narrow street. Poldark rose to follow, and the clerk saw for the first time that he was lame.

'Can I help you, sir?' he offered, putting down his belongings.

The young man refused with thanks and, handed from the outside by a postboy, climbed down.

II

When Ross left the coach rain was beginning to fall, a thin fine rain blowing before the wind, which was gusty and uncertain here in the hollow of the hills.

He gazed about him and sniffed. All this was so familiar, quite as truly a coming home as when he would reach his own house. This narrow cobbled street with the streamlet of water bubbling down it, the close-built squat houses with their bow windows and lace curtains, many of them partly screening faces which were watching the arrival of the coach, even the cries of the postboys seemed to have taken on a different and more familiar note.

Truro in the old days had been the centre of 'life' for him and his family. A port and a coinage town, *the* shopping centre and a meeting place of fashion, the town had grown rapidly in the last few years, new and stately houses having sprung up among the disorderly huddle of old ones to mark its adoption as a winter and town residence by some of the oldest and most powerful families in Cornwall. The new aristocracy too were leaving their mark: the Lemons, the Treworthys, the Warleggans, families which had pushed their way up from humble beginnings on the crest of the new industries.

A strange town. He felt it more on his return. A secretive, important little town, clustering in the fold of the hills astride and about its many streams, almost surrounded by running water and linked to the rest of the world by fords, by bridges, and by stepping-stones. Miasma and the other fevers were always rife.

. . . There was no sign of Jud.

He limped into the inn.

'My man was to meet me,' he said. 'Paynter is his name. Jud Paynter of Nampara.'

The landlord peered at him shortsightedly. 'Oh, Jud Paynter. Yes, we know him well, sir. But we have not seen him to-day. You say he was to meet you here? Boy, go and ascertain if Paynter – you know him? – if Paynter is in the stables or has been here to-day.'

Ross ordered a glass of brandy, and by the time it came the boy was back to say that Mr Paynter had not been seen that day.

'The arrangement was quite definite. It doesn't matter. You have a saddle horse I can hire?'

The landlord rubbed the end of his long nose. 'Well, we have a mare that was left here three days gone. In fact, we held it in lieu of a debt. I don't think there could be any objection to loaning her if you could give me some reference.'

'My name is Poldark. I am a nephew to Mr Charles Poldark of Trenwith.'

'Dear, dear, yes; I should have recognized you, Mr Poldark. I'll have the mare saddled for you at once.'

'No, wait. There's some daylight yet. Have her ready in an hour.'

Out in the street again, Ross turned down the narrow slit of Church Lane. At the end he bore right and, after passing the school where his education had come to an ungracious end, he stopped before a door on which was printed: 'Nat. G. Pearce. Notary and Commissioner of Oaths.' He pulled at the bell for some time before a pimply woman admitted him.

'Mr Pearce bean't well to-day,' she said. 'I'll see if he'll see you.'

She climbed the wooden stairs, and after an interval called down an invitation over the worm-eaten banisters. He groped a way up and was shown into a parlour.

Mr Nathaniel Pearce was sitting in an easy chair in front of a large fire with one leg tied in bandages propped upon another chair. He was a big man with a big face, coloured a light plum purple from overeating.

'Oh, now this is a surprise, I do exclaim, Mr Poldark. How pleasant. You'll forgive me if I don't rise; the old trouble; each attack seems worse than the last. Take a seat.'

Ross grasped a moist hand and chose a chair as far from the fire as was polite. Insufferably hot in here and the air was old and stale.

'You'll remember,' he said, 'I wrote you I was returning this week.'

'Oh yes, Mr – er – Captain Poldark; it had slipped my memory for the moment; how nice to call in on your way home.' Mr Pearce adjusted his bob-wig which, in the way of his profession, had a high frontlet and a long bag at the back tied in the middle. 'I am desolate here, Captain Poldark; my daughter offers me no company; she has become converted to some Methodist way of belief, and is out almost every night at a prayer meeting. She talks so much of God that it quite embarrasses me. You must have a glass of canary.'

'My stay is to be short,' said Ross. It certainly must, he thought, or I shall sweal away. 'I am anxious to be home again, but thought I'd see you on my way. Your letter did not reach me until a fortnight before we sailed from New York.'

'Dear, dear, such a delay; what a blow it would be; and you have been wounded; is it severe?'

Ross eased his leg. 'I see from your letter that my father died in March. Who has administered the estate since then, my uncle or you?'

Mr Pearce absently scratched the ruffles on his chest. 'I know you would wish me to be frank with you.'

'Of course.'

'Well, when we came to go into his affairs, Mr – er – Captain Poldark, it did not seem that he had left much for either of us to administer.'

A slow smile crept over Ross's mouth; it made him look younger, less intractable.

'Everything was naturally left to you. I'll give you a copy of the will before you go; should you predecease him, then to his niece Verity. Aside from the actual property there is little to come in for. Ouch, this thing is twinging most damnably!'

'I have never looked on my father as a wealthy man. I asked, though, and was anxious to know, for a special reason. He was buried at Sawle?'

The lawyer stopped scratching and eyed the other man shrewdly. 'You're thinking of settling at Nampara now, Captain Poldark?'

'I am.'

'Any time I can do any business for you, only too pleased. I should say,' Mr Pearce hastened on as the young man rose, 'I should say that you may find your property a little neglected.'

Ross turned.

'I have not ridden over myself,' said Mr Pearce; 'this leg, you know; most distressing, and me not yet two and fifty; but my clerk has been out. Your father was in failing health for some time and things are not kept just so neat and tidy as you'd like when the master's not about, are they? Nor's your uncle so young as he used to be. Is Paynter meeting you with a horse?'

'He was to have done so but has not turned up.'

'Then my dear sir, why not stay the night with us? My daughter will be home from her praying in time to cook me a bite of supper. We have pork; I know we have pork; and an excellent bed; yes, it would suit me well.'

Ross took out a handkerchief and mopped his face.

'It's very kind of you. I feel that, being so near my home to-day, I should prefer to reach it.'

Mr Pearce sighed and struggled into a more upright position. 'Then give me a hand, will you? I'll get you a copy of the will, so's you may take it home and read it at your leisure.'

Chapter two

DINNER WAS IN progress at Trenwith House.

It would normally have been over by this time; when Charles Poldark and his family dined alone the meal seldom took more than two hours, but this was a special occasion. And because of the guests the meal was taking place in the hall in the centre of the house, a room too large and draughty when the family had only itself to victual.

There were ten people sitting at the long narrow oak table. At the head was Charles himself, with his daughter Verity on his left. On his right was Elizabeth Chynoweth and next to her Francis his son. Beyond them were Mr and Mrs Chynoweth, Elizabeth's parents, and at the foot of the table Aunt Agatha crumbled soft food and munched it between her toothless jaws. Up the other side Cousin William-Alfred was in conversation with Dr and Mrs Choake.

The fish, the poultry, and the meat dishes were finished, and Charles had just called for the sweets. At all meals he was troubled with wind, which made female guests an embarrassment.

'Damme,' he said, in a silence of repletion which had fallen on the company. 'I don't know why you two doves don't get married to-morrow instead of waiting for a month or more. Aarf! What d'you lack? Are you afraid you'll change your minds?'

'For my part I would take your advice,' said Francis. 'But it is Elizabeth's day as well as mine.'

'One short month is little enough,' said Mrs Chynoweth, fumbling at the locket on the handsome encrusted lace of her dress. Her fine looks were marred by a long and acquisitive nose: on first seeing her one felt a sense of shock at so much beauty spoiled. 'How can one expect *me* to prepare, let alone the poor child? In one's daughter one lives one's own wedding day over afresh. I only wish that our preparations could be more extensive.' She glanced at her husband.

'What did she say?' asked Aunt Agatha.

'Well, there it is,' said Charles Poldark. 'There it is. I suppose we must be patient since they are. Well, I give you a toast. To the happy pair!'

'You've toasted that three times already,' objected Francis.

'No matter. Four is a luckier number.'

'But I cannot drink with you.'

'Hush, boy! That's unimportant.'

Amid some laughter the toast was drunk. As the glasses clattered back upon the table lights were brought, tall candles in shining silver candlesticks which had been taken out and specially polished for the occasion. Then the housekeeper, Mrs Tabb, arrived with the apple tarts, the plum cake, and the jellies.

'Now,' said Charles, flourishing his knife and fork over the largest apple tart. 'I hope this will prove as tasty as it looks. Where's the cream? Oh, there. Put it on for me, Verity, my dear.'

'I'm sorry,' said Elizabeth, breaking her silence. 'But I'm quite unable to eat anything more.'

Everyone at once looked at her, and she blushed.

Elizabeth Chynoweth was slighter than her mother had ever been, and there was in her face the beauty which her mother had missed. As the yellow light from the candles pushed the darkness back and up towards the high raftered ceiling, the fine clear whiteness of her took one's attention among the shadows of the room and against the sombre wood of the high-backed chair.

'Nonsense, child,' said Charles. 'You're thin as a wraith. Must get some blood into you.'

'Indeed, I—'

'Dear Mr Poldark,' said Mrs Chynoweth mincingly, 'to look at her you would not credit how obstinate she can be. For twenty years I have been trying to make her eat, but she just turns away from the choicest food. Perhaps you'll be able to coax her, Francis.'

'I am very satisfied with her as she is,' said Francis.

'Yes, yes,' said his father. 'But a little food . . . Damme, that does no one any harm. A wife needs to be strong and well.'

'Oh, she is really very strong,' Mrs Chynoweth hastened on. 'You would be surprised at that too. It is the breed, nothing more than the breed. Was I not frail as a girl, Jonathan?'

'Yes, my pet,' said Jonathan.

'Hark, how the wind's rising!' said Aunt Agatha, crumbling her cake.

'That is something I cannot understand,' said Dr Choake. 'How your aunt, though deaf, Mr Poldark, is always sensible to the sounds of nature.'

'I believe she imagines it half the time.'

'That I do not!' said Aunt Agatha. 'How dare you, Charles!'

'Was that someone at the door?' Verity interposed.

Tabb was out of the room, but Mrs Tabb had heard nothing. The candles flickered in the draught and the red damask curtains over the long windows moved as if a hand were stirring them. The walls of this hall were lined with an oaken wainscot which let in more than a necessary amount of ventilation.

'Expecting someone, my dear?' asked Mrs Chynoweth.

Verity did not blush. She had little of her brother's good looks, being small and dark and sallow with the large mouth which came to some of the Poldarks.

'I expect it is the cowshed door,' said Charles, taking a swill of port. 'Tabb was to have looked to it yesterday but he rode with me into St Ann's. I'll thrash young Bartle for not attending to his work.'

'They do thay,' lisped Mrs Choake to Mrs Chynoweth, 'they do thay as how that the Prince is living at an outwageous wate. I was weading in the *Mercury* as how Mr Fox had pwomised him an income of one hundred thousand pounds a year, and now that he is in power he is hard put to it to wedeem his pwomith.'

'It would seem unlikely,' said Mr Chynoweth, 'that that would worry Mr Fox unduly.' A smallish man with a silky white beard, his was a defensive pomposity, adopted to hide the fact that he had never in his life made up his mind about anything. His wife had married him when she was eighteen and he thirty-one. Both Jonathan and his income had lost ground since then.

'And what's wrong with Mr Fox, I'm asking you?' Dr Choake said deeply from under his eyebrows.

Mr Chynoweth pursed his lips. 'I should have considered that plain.'

'Opinions differ, sir. I may say, that if I . . .'

The surgeon broke off as his wife took the rare liberty of treading on his toe. To-day was the first time the Choakes and the Chynoweths had met socially: to her it seemed folly to begin a political wrangle with these still influential gentlefolk.

Thomas Choake was turning ungratefully to squash Polly with a look, but she was saved the worst of his spleen. This time there could be no mistake that someone was knocking on the outer door. Mrs Tabb set down the tray of tarts and went to the door.

The wind made the curtains billow, and the candles dripped grease down their silver sconces.

'God help me!' said the housekeeper as if she had seen a ghost.

II

Ross came into a company quite unprepared for his arrival. When his figure showed in the doorway, one after another of those at the table broke into words of surprise. Elizabeth and Francis and Verity and Dr Choake were on their feet; Charles lay back grunting and inert from shock. Cousin William-Alfred polished his steel spectacles, while Aunt Agatha plucked at his sleeve mumbling, 'What is it? What's to do? The meal isn't over.'

Ross screwed up his eyes until they grew used to the light. Trenwith

House was almost on his way home, and he had not thought to intrude on a party.

First to greet him was Verity. She ran across and put her arms round his neck. 'Why, Ross dear! Fancy now!' was all she could find to say.

'Verity!' He gave her a hug. And then he saw Elizabeth.

'Stap me,' said Charles. 'So you're back at last, boy. You're late for dinner, but we've some fine apple tart left.'

'Did they lame us, Ross?' said Dr Choake. 'A pox on the whole war. It was ill-starred. Thank God it's over.'

Francis, after a short hesitation, came quickly round the table and grasped the other man's hand. 'It's good to see you back, Ross! We've missed you.'

'It's good to be back,' said Ross. 'To see you all, and . . .'

The colour of the eyes under the same heavy lids was the only mark of cousinship. Francis was compact, slim and neat, with the fresh complexion and clear features of handsome youth. He looked what he was, carefree, easygoing, self-confident, a young man who has never known what it was to be in danger or short of money, or to pit his strength against another man's except in games or horseplay. Someone at school had christened them 'the fair Poldark and the dark Poldark.' They had always been good friends, which was surprising, since their fathers had not.

'This is a solemn occasion,' said Cousin William-Alfred, his bony hands grasping the back of his chair. 'A family reunion is more than name. I trust you are not seriously wounded, Ross. That scar is a considerable disfigurement.'

'Oh, that,' said Ross. 'That would be of no moment if I didn't limp like Jago's donkey.'

He went round the table greeting the others. Mrs Chynoweth welcomed him coldly, extending a hand from a distance.

'Do tell us,' lisped Polly Choake: 'do tell us thome of your experwiences, Captain Poldark, how we lost the war, what these Amewicans are like, and—'

'Very like us, ma'am. That's why we lost it.' He had reached Elizabeth.

'Well, Ross,' she said softly.

His eyes feasted on her face. 'This is most opportune. I couldn't have wished it different.'

'I could,' she said. 'Oh, Ross, I could.'

'And what are you going to do now, my lad?' asked Charles.

'It's high time you settled down. Property don't look after itself, and you can't trust hirelings. Your father could have done with you this last year and more—'

'I almost called to see you to-night,' Ross said to Elizabeth, 'but left it for to-morrow. Self-restraint is rewarded.'

'I must explain. I wrote you, but—'

'Why,' said Aunt Agatha; 'Lord damn me if it isn't Ross! Come here, boy! I thought you was gone to make one of the blest above.'

Reluctantly Ross walked down the table to greet his great-aunt. Elizabeth stayed where she was, holding the back of her chair so that her knuckles were whiter even than her face.

Ross kissed Aunt Agatha's whiskery cheek. Into her ear he said:

'I am glad to see, Aunt, that you're still one of the blest below.'

She chuckled with delight, showing her pale brownish-pink gums. 'Not so blest, maybe. But I wouldn't want to be changing just yet.'

The conversation became general, everyone questioning Ross as to when he had landed, what he had done and seen while away.

'Elizabeth,' said Mrs Chynoweth, 'fetch me my wrap from upstairs, will you? I am a little chilly.'

'Yes, Mother.' She turned and walked away, tall and virginal, groped with her hand for the oak banister. Her movements held an extraordinary unstudied grace for one so young.

'That fellow Paynter is a rogue,' said Charles, wiping his hands down the sides of his breeches. 'If I was you I should throw him out and get a reliable man.'

Ross was watching Elizabeth slowly going up the stairs. 'He was my father's friend.'

Charles shrugged in some annoyance. 'You won't find the house in a good state of repair.'

'It wasn't when I left.'

'Well, it's worse now. I haven't been over for some time. You know what your father used to say about coming in the other direction: "It is too far to walk and not far enough to ride."'

'Eat this, Ross,' said Verity, bringing a piled plate to him. 'And sit here.'

Ross thanked her and took the seat offered him between Aunt Agatha and Mr Chynoweth. He would have preferred to be beside Elizabeth, but that would have to wait. He was surprised to find Elizabeth here. She and her mother and father had never once been to Nampara in the twelve months he had known her. Two or three times he glanced up as he ate to see if she was returning.

Verity was helping Mrs Tabb to carry out some of the used dishes; Francis stood plucking at his lip by the front door; the others were back in their chairs. A silence had fallen on the company.

'It is no easy countryside to which you return,' said Mr Chynoweth, pulling at his beard. 'Discontent is rife. Taxes are high, wages have fallen. The country is exhausted from its many wars; and now the Whigs are in. I can think of no worse a prospect.'

'Had the Whigs been in before,' said Dr Choake, refusing to be tactful, 'none of this need have happened.'

Ross looked across at Francis. 'I've interrupted a party. Is it in celebration of the peace or in honour of the next war?'

Thus he forced the explanation they had hesitated to give.

'No,' said Francis. 'I—er—— The position is——'

'We are celebrating something far different,' said Charles, motioning for his glass to be filled again. 'Francis is to be married. That is what we're celebrating.'

'To be married,' said Ross, slicing his food. 'Well, well; and who—'

'To Elizabeth,' said Mrs Chynoweth.

There was silence.

Ross put down his knife. 'To—'

'To my daughter.'

'Can I get you something to drink?' Verity whispered to Elizabeth, who had just reached the bottom of the stairs.

'No, no. . . . Please no.'

'Oh,' said Ross. 'To . . . Elizabeth.'

'We are very happy,' said Mrs Chynoweth, 'that our two ancient families are to be united. Very happy and very proud. I am sure, Ross, that you will join with us in wishing Francis and Elizabeth all happiness in their union.'

Walking very carefully, as if a little afraid of her step, Elizabeth came over to Mrs Chynoweth.

'Your wrap, Mama.'

'Thank you, my dear.'

Ross went on with his meal.

'I don't know what your opinion is,' said Charles heartily after a pause, 'but for myself I am attached to this port. It was run over from Cherbourg in the autumn of '79. When I tasted a sample I said to meself, it is too good to be repeated; I'll buy the lot. Nor has it been repeated; nor has it. And these are the last dozen bottles.' He put down his hands to ease his great paunch against the table.

'A pity,' said Dr Choake, shaking his head. 'It has a bouquet rare in any wine. Fff-um . . . Rare indeed.'

'I s'pose you'll be settling down now, Ross, eh?' said Aunt Agatha, a wrinkled hand on his sleeve. 'How about a little wife for you, eh? That's what we've to find next!'

Ross looked across at Dr Choake.

'You attended my father?'

Dr Choake nodded.

'Did he suffer much?'

'At the end. But the time was short.'

'It was strange that he should fail so quickly.'

'Nothing could be done. It was a dropsical condition that was beyond the power of man to allay.'

'I rode over,' said Cousin William-Alfred, 'to see him twice. But I regret that he was not – hm – in the mood to make the most of such spiritual comfort as I could offer. It was to me a personal sorrow that I could be of so little help to one of my own blood.'

'You must have some of this apple tart, Ross,' said Verity in an undertone behind him, glancing at the veins in his neck. 'I made it myself this afternoon.'

'I mustn't stop. I called here only for a few minutes and to rest my horse, which is lame.'

'Oh, but there's no need to go to-night. I have told Mrs Tabb to prepare a room. Your horse may stumble in the dark and throw you.'

Ross looked up at Verity and smiled. In this company no private word could pass between them.

Now Francis, and to a less degree his father, joined in the argument. But Francis was constrained, his father halfhearted, and Ross determined.

Charles said: 'Well, have it as you wish, boy. I would not fancy arriving at Nampara to-night. It will be cold and wet and perhaps no welcome. Pour some more spirit into you to keep out the chill.'

Ross did as he was urged, drinking three glasses in succession. With the fourth he got to his feet.

'To Elizabeth,' he said slowly, 'and to Francis . . . May they find happiness together.'

The toast was drunk more quietly than the others. Elizabeth was still standing behind her mother's chair; Francis had at last moved from the door to put a hand beneath her arm.

In the silence which followed, Mrs Choake said:

'How nithe it must be to be home again. I never go away, even a little way, without feeling gwatified to be back. What are the Amewican colonies like, Captain Poldark? They thay as how even the thun does not wise and thet in the thame way in foreign parts.'

Polly Choake's inanity seemed to relieve the tension, and talk broke out again while Ross finished his meal. There was more than one there conscious of relief that he had taken the news so quietly. There had always been something unpredictable in Joshua's son.

Ross, however, was not staying, and presently took his leave.

'You'll come over in a day or two, will you not?' said Francis, a rush of affection in his voice. 'We've heard nothing so far, nothing but the barest details of your experiences or how you were wounded or of your journey home. Elizabeth will be returning home tomorrow. We plan to be married in a month. If you want my help at Nampara send a message over; you know I shall be pleased to come Why, it's like old times seeing you back again! We feared for your life, did we not, Elizabeth?'

'Yes,' said Elizabeth.

Ross picked up his hat. They were standing together at the door, waiting for Tabb to bring round Ross's mare. He had refused the loan of a fresh horse for the last three miles.

'He'll be here now, that's if he can handle her. I warned him to be careful.'

Francis opened the door. The wind blew in a few spots of rain. He went out tactfully to see if Tabb had come.

Ross said: 'I hope my mistimed resurrection hasn't cast a cloud over your evening.'

She looked at him a moment. The light from indoors threw a shaft across her face, showed up the grey eyes. The shadows had spread to her face and she looked ill.

'I'm so happy that you're back, Ross. I had feared, we had all feared—— What can you think of me?'

'Two years is a long time, isn't it. Too long perhaps.'

'Elizabeth,' said Mrs Chynoweth. 'Take care the night air does not catch you.'

'No, Mama.'

'Good-bye.' He took her hand.

Francis came back. 'He's here now. Did you buy the mare? She's a handsome creature but very ill tempered.'

'Ill usage makes the sweetest of us vicious,' said Ross. 'Has the rain stopped?'

'Not quite. You know your way?'

Ross showed his teeth. 'Every stone. Has it changed?'

'Nothing to mislead you. Do not cross the Mellingey by the bridge; the middle plank is rotten.'

'So it was when I left.'

'Do not forget,' said Francis. 'We expect you back here soon. Verity will want to see more of you. If she can spare the time we will ride over to-morrow.'

But only the wind and the rain answered him and the clatter of hooves as the mare sidestepped resentfully down the drive.

III

Darkness had fallen by now, though a patch of fading light glimmered in the west. The wind blew more strongly, and the soft rain beat in flurries about his head.

His was not an easy face to read, and you couldn't have told that in the last half hour he had suffered the worst knock of his life. Except that he no longer whistled into the wind or talked to his irritable mare, there was nothing to show.

At an early age he had caught from his father a view of things which took very little for granted, but in his dealings with Elizabeth Chynoweth he had fallen into the sort of trap such an outlook might have helped him to avoid.

They had been in love since she was sixteen and he barely twenty. When his own high-spirited misadventures caught up with him he had thought his father's solution of a commission in the Army a good idea while the trouble blew over. He had gone away eager for fresh experience and sure of the one circumstance of his return which would really matter.

No doubt was in his own mind and he had looked for none in hers.

After he had been riding for a time the lights of Grambler Mine showed up ahead. This was the mine round which the varying fortunes of the main Poldark family centred. On its vagaries depended not merely the prosperity of Charles Poldark and his family but the subsistence level of some three hundred miners and their families scattered in huts and cottages about the parish. To them the mine was a benevolent Moloch to whom they fed their children at an early age and from whom they took their daily bread.

He saw swinging lights approaching and drew into the side of the track to let a mule train pass, with the panniers of copper ore slung on either side of the animals' backs. One of the men in charge peered up at him suspiciously, then shouted a greeting. It was Mark Daniel.

The main buildings of the mine were all about him now, most of them huddled together and indeterminate, but here and there the sturdy scaffolding of headgear and the big stone-built engine houses stood out. Yellow lights showed in the arched upper windows of the engine houses, warm and mysterious against the low night sky. He passed close beside one of them and heard the rattle and clang of the great draught bob pumping water up from the lowest places of the earth.

There were miners in groups and a number of lanterns. Several men peered up at the figure on the horse, but although several said good night he thought that none of these recognized him.

Then a bell rang in one of the engine houses, a not un-mellow note; it was the time for changing 'cores'; that was why there were so many men about. They were assembling to go down. Other men now would be on their way up, climbing ant-like a hundred fathoms of rickety ladders, sweat-covered and stained with rusty markings of the mineral rock or the black fumes of blasting powder. It would take them half an hour or more to come to the surface carrying their tools, and all the way they would be splashed and drenched with water from the leaky pumps. On reaching grass many would have a three- or four-mile walk through the wind and rain.

He moved on. Now and then the feeling within him was so strong that he could have been physically sick.

The Mellingey was forded, and horse and rider began wearily to climb the narrow track towards the last clump of fir trees. Ross took a deep breath of the air, which was heavy with rain and impregnated with the smell of the sea. He fancied he could hear the waves breaking. At the top of the rise the mare, all her ill nature gone, stumbled again and almost fell, so Ross awkwardly got down and began to walk. At first he could hardly put his foot to the ground, but he welcomed this pain in his ankle, which occupied thoughts that would have been elsewhere.

In the coppice it was pitch black and he had to feel his way along a path which had become part overgrown. At the other side the ruined buildings of Wheal Maiden greeted him – a mine which had been played out for forty years; as a boy he had fought and scrambled about the derelict windlass and the horse whim, had explored the shallow adit that ran through the hill and came out near the stream.

Now he felt he was really home; in a moment he would be on his own land. This afternoon he had been filled with pleasure at the prospect, but now nothing seemed to matter. He could only be glad that his journey was done and that he might lie down and rest.

In the cup of the valley the air was still. The trickle and bubble of Mellingey stream had been lost, but now it came to his ears again like the mutterings of a thin old woman. An owl hooted and swung silently before his face in the dark. Water dripped from the rim of his hat. There ahead in the soft and sighing darkness was the solid line of Nampara House.

It struck him as smaller than he remembered, lower and more squat; it straggled like a row of workmen's cottages. There was no light to be seen. At the lilac tree, now grown so big as to overshadow the windows behind it, he tethered the mare and rapped with his riding whip upon the front door.

He had scarcely expected an answer. There had been heavy rain here; water was trickling from the roof in several places and forming pools upon the sandy overgrown path. He thrust open the door; it went creaking back, pushing a heap of refuse before it, and he peered into the low, irregularly beamed hall.

Only the darkness greeted him, an intenser darkness which made the night seem grey.

'Jud!' he called. 'Jud!'

The mare outside whinnied and stamped; something scuttled be side the wainscot. Then he saw eyes. They were lambent, green-gold, stared at him unwinkingly from the back of the hall.

He limped into the house, feeling leaves and dirt underfoot. He fingered his way round the panels to the right until he came to the door leading into the parlour. He lifted the latch and went in.

At once there was a scuffling and rustling and the sound of animals disturbed. His foot slid on something slimy on the floor, and in putting out his hand he knocked over a candlestick. He retrieved it, set the candle back in its socket, groped for his flint and steel. After two or three attempts the spark caught and he lit the candle.

This was the largest room in the house. It was half panelled with dark mahogany, and in the far corner was a great broad fireplace half the width of the room, recessed and built round with low settles. This was the room the family had always lived in, large enough and airy enough for the rowdiest company on the hottest day, yet with warm corners and cosy furniture to cheat the draughts of winter. But all that was changed. The fireplace was empty and hens roosted on the settles. The floor was filthy with old straw and droppings. From the bracket of a candle sconce a cockerel viewed him with a liverish eye. On one of the window seats were two dead chickens.

Opening out of the hall on the left was Joshua's bedroom, and he next tried this. Signs of life: clothing which had never belonged to his father, filthy old petticoats, a battered three-cornered hat, a bottle without stopper from which he sniffed gin. But the box bed was closed and the three captive thrushes in the cage before the shuttered window could tell him nothing of the couple he looked for.

At the farther end of the room was another door leading into that part of the house which had never been finished, but he did not go in. The place to look was in the bedroom upstairs at the back of the house where Jud and Prudie always slept. Perhaps they had gone up early.

He turned back to the door, and there stopped and listened. A peculiar sound had come to his ears. The fowls had settled down, and silence, like a parted curtain, was falling back upon the house. He thought he heard a creak on the shallow stairs, but when he peered out with the candle held high he could see nothing.

This was not the sound he was listening for, nor the movement of rats, nor the faint hissing of the stream outside, nor the crackle of charred paper under his boot.

He looked up at the ceiling but the beams and floorboards were sound. Something rubbed itself against his leg. It was the cat whose bright eyes he had seen earlier: his father's kitten, Tabitha Bethia, but grown into a big grey animal and leprously patched with mange. She seemed to recognize him, and he put down his hand gratefully to her enquiring whiskers.

Then the sound came again, and this time he caught its direction. He strode over to the box bed and slid back the doors. A powerful smell of stale perspiration and gin; he thrust in the candle. Dead drunk and locked in each other's arms were Jud and Prudie Paynter. The woman was in a long flannel nightgown; her mouth was open and her varicosed legs asprawl. Jud had not succeeded in getting properly undressed, but snored by her side in his breeches and leggings.

Ross stared at them for some moments.

Then he withdrew and put the candlestick on the great low chest near the bed. He walked out of the room and made his way round to the stables at the east end of the house. Here he found a wooden pail and took it to the pump. This he filled, carried it round the house, through the hall and into the bedroom. He tipped the water into the bed.

He went out again. A star or two were showing in the west but the wind was freshening. In the stables, he noted, there were only two half-starved horses. Ramoth; yes, one was still Ramoth. The horse had been twelve years old and half blind from cataract when he left.

He carried the second bucket round, through the hall, across the bedroom and tipped it into the bed.

The mare whinnied at his second passing. She preferred even his company to the darkness and unfamiliarity of the garden.

When he brought the third bucket Jud was groaning and muttering and his bald head was in the opening of the box door. Ross allowed him this bucket to himself.

By the time he returned with the fourth the man had climbed out of the bed and was trying to shake the streaming water from his clothing. Prudie was only just stirring, so Ross devoted the water to her. Jud began to curse and groped for his jack knife. Ross hit him on the side of the head and knocked him down. Then he went for another supply.

At his fifth appearance there was more intelligence in the eyes of the servant, though was still on the ground. At sight of him Jud began to curse and swear and threaten. But after a moment a look of puzzlement crept across his face.

'. . . Dear life! . . . Is it you, Mister Ross?'

'From the grave,' said Ross. 'And there's a horse to be seen to. Up, before I kill you.' By the collar of his shirt he lifted the man to his feet and thrust him forward towards the door.

Chapter three

A WET OCTOBER evening is depressing, but it drapes some soft shadows on the rough edges of ruin and decay. Not so the light of morning.

Even at the height of his mining Joshua had always had a few fields under care, the house had been clean and homely, well furnished and well stocked considering the district. After a tour which lasted from eight until ten Ross called the Paynters out of the house and stood with legs apart looking at them. They shuffled and were uneasy under his gaze.

Jud was four inches the shorter of the two. He was a man in the early fifties to whom bow legs gave a look of horsiness and bulldog strength. During the last ten years satirical nature had tonsured his head like a friar. He had lived in this district all his life, first as a tributer at Grambler Mine, then at Wheal Grace, where Joshua took to him in spite of his weaknesses.

Prudie Jud had picked up at Bedruthan ten years ago. Their first meeting was one of the things that Jud held his tongue about even in his cups. They had never married, but she had taken his name as a matter of course. She was now forty, six feet in height, with lank Spanish hair incurably lousy; and wide shouldered, with a powerful body which bulged everywhere it aesthetically shouldn't.

'You're tired after a hard morning's work,' said Ross.

Jud looked at him uneasily from under hairless brows. With Joshua he had always had to mind his P's and Q's, but of Ross he had never been at all afraid. A harum-scarum, highly strung, lanky youngster – there was nothing in him to fear. But two years of soldiering had changed the boy.

'Tes as clean as a new-scrubbed place can be,' said Jud on a grudging note. 'We been at un for two hour solid. Splinters I got in me 'and from the old floor, drat un. Blood-poisoned I shall be maybe. Runs from your 'and to your arm, it do. Up yer veins and then *phit* – ye're dead.'

Ross turned his sleepy but unquiet eyes on Prudie. 'Your wife has not suffered from her wetting? As well not to forget the feel and taste of water. Very little is used in gaol.'

Jud looked up sharply. 'Who says gaol? Prudie an't going to gaol. What she done?'

'No more than you have. A pity you can't share the same cell.'

Prudie sniggered. 'You will 'ave yer jest.'

'The jest,' said Ross, 'was yours last night and for fifty nights before.'

'You can't get neither of us convicted fur bein' a bit tiddley,' said Jud. 'Tedn't law. Tedn't right. Tedn't just. Tedn't sense. Tedn't friendly. Leave alone all we've done for you.'

'You were my father's personal servant. When he died you were left in a position of trust. Well, you may have a guinea for every field you find that isn't choked with weed and lying fallow, the same for a barn or a stable that is not falling down for need of a timely repair. Even the apples in the orchard are mouldering amongst the dead leaves for lack of someone to gather them. . . .'

'Twur a poor summer for frewt. Down come the apples rottin' away wi' wasps in un. Shockin' twas. You can't do nothing to an apple when thur's a drane in un. Not except kill the drane and eat the apple, an' thur's a limit t'what two bodies can eat.'

'Twas a nice chanst I didn' swaller one of they wasps,' said Prudie. 'Thur was I munching away as clever as you like. Then sharp, just as I has me teeth in un, I hears a 'vuzz-vuzz.' And, my ivers, there 'e is! You can't see the front end, but the back end is there wavin' about like a lamb's tail, all 'is legs agoing and striped like a flag. If I 'adn't just urd——'

'Get one of they in yer ozle,' said Jud gloomily. 'Out come their sting an' *phit* – ye're dead.'

'Lazy in everything,' said Ross, 'but the search for excuses. Like two old pigs in their sty and as slow to move from their own patch of filth.'

Prudie picked up her apron and began to dab her nose.

Ross warmed to his theme. He had learned abuse from a master and had added to it while away. Also he knew his listeners. 'I suspect it must be easy to convert good stock into cheap gin,' he ended. 'Men have been hanged for less.'

'We thought – twas rumoured——' Jud sucked his gums in hesitation. 'Folks said——'

'That I was dead? Who said it?'

'Twas common belief,' Prudie said sombrely.

'Yet I find it only near my own home. Did you begin the story?'

'No, no; tedn't true. Not by no means. Tis we you should thank for giving the lie to such a story. Nail it, I says. Nail it to the bud, I says. I've got the firmest faith, I says; and Prudie can bear me forth. Did we b'lieve such a wicked lie, Prudie?'

'Dear life, no!' said Prudie.

'My uncle has always thought you wastrels and parasites. I think I can arrange for your case to come before him.'

They stood there on shifty feet, half resentful, half alarmed. He had no understanding of their difficulties and they had no words to explain. Any guilt they might have felt was long since overgrown by these explanations which they could not frame. Their feeling now was one of outrage at being so harshly attacked. Everything had been done, or left undone, for a very good reason.

'We've only four pairs of 'ands,' said Jud.

Ross's sense of humour was not working or he might have been undone by this remark.

'There is much gaol fever this year,' he said. 'A lack of cheap gin will not be your only hardship.'

He turned and left them to their fears.

II

In the gloom of the Red Lion Stables he had thought his hired mare had a damaged fetlock, but the light of day showed the lameness to be no more than the result of a very bad shoeing. The mare had an open flat foot and the shoe was fitted too short and too close.

He rode into Truro next day on the almost blind Ramoth to see if he could do business with the landlord of the Red Lion.

The landlord was a little doubtful whether enough time had passed to give him the right to dispose of his surety; but legality was never Ross's strong point, and he had his way.

While in the town he drew a bill on Pascoe's Bank and spent some of his slender capital on two young steers which he arranged for Jud to collect. If the fields were to be worked at all there must be an outlay upon working animals.

With some smaller things slung over his saddle he arrived back shortly after one and found Verity waiting for him. For a sudden leaping moment he had thought it was Elizabeth.

'You did not come to visit me, Cousin,' she said; 'so I must wait on you. That I have now been doing for forty odd minutes.'

He bent and kissed her cheek. 'You should have sent word. I have been to Truro. Jud will have told you.'

'Yes. He offered me a garden chair but I was afraid to sit on it lest it collapse under my weight. Oh, Ross, your poor house!'

He glanced up towards the building. The conservatory was smothered with giant convolvulus, which had swept over it, flowered and was beginning to rot.

'It can be put right.'

'I am ashamed,' she said, 'that we have not been over, that I have not been over more often. These Paynters——'

'You've been busy.'

'Oh, we have. Only now that the crops are in have we time to look round. But that is no excuse.'

He glanced down at her as she stood beside him. She, at least, had not changed, with her trim little figure and untidy hair and big generous mouth. She had walked over from Trenwith in her working dress with no hat and her dove grey cloak pulled carelessly about her shoulders.

They began to walk round to the stables. 'I have just bought a mare,' he said. 'You must see her. Old Squire is beyond recall and big Ramoth has no eyes to avoid the stones and ruts.'

'Tell me about your wound,' she said. 'Does it pain you much now? When was it done?'

'Oh, long ago. At the James River. It is nothing.'

She glanced at him. 'You were always one to hide your hurt, were you not?'

'This is the mare,' he said. 'I have just paid five and twenty guineas for her. A great bargain, don't you think?'

She hesitated. 'Does *she* not limp too? Francis was saying . . . And that right leg, which she holds——'

'Will get better more quickly than mine. I wish you could heal any injury by a change of shoes.'

'What is her name?'

'No one knows. I am waiting for you to christen her.'

Verity pushed back her hair and frowned with one eyebrow. 'Hm . . . I should call her Darkie.'

'For any reason?'

'She has that pretty black streak. And also it is a tribute to her new owner.'

He laughed and began to unsaddle Ramoth and rub him down, while his cousin leaned against the stable door and chattered. Her father often complained that she was 'lacking in the graces,' meaning that she was incapable of the flowery but agreeable small talk which added so much to the savour of life. But with Ross she was never tongue-tied.

He asked her to dinner, but she refused. 'I must go soon. I have far more to see to now that Father is not so nimble.'

'And enjoy it, I suppose. Walk with me as far as the sea first. It may be days before you come again.'

She did not argue, for it was pleasant to her to have her company sought. They set off linking as they had done as children, but this way his lameness was too noticeable and he loosed her arm and put his long bony hand on her shoulder.

The nearest way of reaching the sea from the house was to climb a stone wall and drop down upon Hendrawna Beach, but to-day they climbed the Long Field behind the house and walked the way Joshua had walked in his dream.

'My dear, you'll have some hard work to get things shaped up,' Verity said, looking about her. 'You must have help.'

'There is all winter to spend.'

She tried to read his expression. 'You're not thinking of going away again, Ross?'

'Very quickly if I had money or were not lame; but the two together——'

'Shall you keep Jud and Prudie?'

'They have agreed to work without wages. I shall keep them until some of the gin is sweated out of them. And also this morning I've taken a boy named Carter, who called asking for work. Do you know him?'

'Carter? One of Connie Carter's children from Grambler?'

'I think so. He has been at Grambler, but the underground work was too heavy. There's not enough air in the sixty-fathom level to clear the blasting powder, and he says he started coughing black phlegm in the mornings. So he has to have outdoor work.'

'Oh, that will be Jim, her eldest. His father died young.'

'Well, I can't afford to pay invalids, but he seems an acceptable boy. He's starting to-morrow at six.'

They reached the edge of the cliff where they were seventy or eighty feet above the sea. On the left the cliffs slipped down to the inlet of Nampara Cove, then rose again more steeply towards Sawle. Looking east, upon Hendrawna Beach, the sea was very calm today: a smoky grey with here and there patches of violet and living, moving green. The waves were shadows, snakes under a quilt, creeping in almost unseen until they emerged in milky ripples at the water's edge.

The gentle sea breeze moved against his face, barely touching his hair. The tide was going out. As they looked the green of the sea quickened and stirred under the crouching clouds.

He had not slept well last night. Seen from this side with the pale blue-grey eyes half lidded, and the scar showing white on the brown cheek, his whole face had a strange disquiet. Verity looked away and abruptly said: 'You would be surprised to learn – to learn about Francis and Elizabeth——'

'I had no option on the girl.'

'It was strange,' she went on haltingly, 'the way it happened. Francis had scarcely seen her until this summer past. They met at the Pascoes'. Then he could – could talk of nothing else. Naturally I told him you had been – friendly with her. But she had already told him that.'

'Kind of her——'

'Ross . . . I'm certain sure that neither of them wished to do anything unfair. It was – just one of the things that happen. You do not argue with the clouds or the rain or the lightning. Well, this was like that. It came from outside them. I – know Francis, and he couldn't help himself.'

'How prices have risen since I went away,' said Ross. 'I paid three and three a yard for Holland linen to-day. All my shirts have been eaten by the moths.'

'And then,' said Verity, 'there was the rumour of your having been killed.

I do not know how it came about, but I think it was the Paynters who stood most to gain.'

'Not more than Francis.'

'No,' said Verity. 'But it was not he.'

Ross kept his tortured eyes on the sea. 'That was not a pretty thought,' he said after a moment.

She pressed his arm. 'I wish I could help you, my dear. Will you not come over often? Why do you not have dinner with us every day? My cooking is better than Prudie's.'

He shook his head. 'I must find my own way out of this. When are they to be married?'

'November the first.'

'So soon? I thought it was to be more than a month.'

'They decided last night.'

'Oh. I see . . .'

'It is to be at Trenwith, for that suits us all best. Cusgarne is nearly falling down and full of draughts and leaks. Elizabeth and her mother and father are coming in their carriage in the morning.'

She chattered on, aware that Ross was hardly attending but anxious to help him over this difficult period. Presently she was silent and followed his example in staring out to sea.

'If,' she said, 'if I were sure not to get in your way this winter I would come over when I could. If——'

'That,' he said, 'would help more than anything.'

They began to walk back towards the house. He did not see how red she had gone, flushing up to the roots of her hair.

So it was to be November the first, less than a fortnight forward.

He went a little way with his cousin, and when they parted he stood at the edge of the pine copse and saw her walking quickly and sturdily in the direction of Grambler. The smoke and steam from the mine was drifting in a cloud across the desolate rubble-scarred moorland towards Trenwith.

III

Beyond the rising ground which made up the southeastern rib of Nampara Combe was a hollow in which lay a cluster of cottages known as Mellin.

It was Poldark land, and in these six cottages, built in the form of a friendly right angle so that everyone could the more easily watch everyone else's comings and goings, lived the Triggses, the Clemmows, the Martins, the Daniels, and the Viguses. Here Ross went in search of cheap labour.

The Poldarks had always been on good terms with their tenants. Distinction of class was not absent; it was understood so clearly that nobody needed to emphasize it; but, in districts where life centred round the nearest mine, polite convention was not allowed to stand in the way of common sense. The small landowners with their long pedigrees and short purses were accepted as a part of the land they owned.

On his way to the Martins Ross had to pass three of the cottages, before the door of the first of which Joe Triggs sat sunning himself and smoking. Triggs was a miner in the mid-fifties, crippled with rheumatism and supported by his aunt, who made a bare living fish-jousting in Sawle. It did not seem that he had moved since Ross went away twenty-eight months ago. England had lost an empire in the west; she had secured her grip upon an empire in the east; she had fought single-handed against the Americans, the French, the Dutch, the Spaniards, and Hyder Ali of Mysore. Governments, fleets and nations had grappled, had risen and been overthrown. Balloons had ascended in France, the *Royal George* had turned on her beam ends at Spithead, and Chatham's son had taken his first Cabinet office. But for Joe Triggs nothing had changed. Except that this knee or that shoulder was more or less painful, each day was so like the last that they merged into an unchanging pattern and slipped away unmarked.

While talking to the old man Ross's eyes were straying over the rest of the cottages. The one next to this had been empty since the whole family had died of the smallpox in '79, and it had now lost part of its roof; the one beyond, the Clemmows', looked little better. What could one expect? Eli the younger and brighter had gone off to some lackey's job in Truro, leaving only Reuben.

The three cottages of the opposite angle were all in good repair. The Martins and the Daniels were his particular friends. And Nick Vigus looked after his cottage, for all that he was a slippery rogue.

At the Martin cottage Mrs Zacky Martin, flat-faced and bespectacled and cheerful, showed him into the single dark room downstairs with its floor of well-trodden earth on which three naked babies rolled and crowed. There were two new faces since Ross left, making eleven in all, and Mrs Martin was pregnant again. Four boys were already underground at Grambler, and the eldest daughter, Jinny, was a spaller at the mine. The three next youngest children, aged five and upwards, were just the sort of cheap labour Ross needed for clearing his fields.

This sunny morning, with the sights and sounds and smells of his own land about him, the war of which he had been a part seemed unsubstantial and far off. He wondered if the real world was that one in which men fought for policies and principles and died or lived gloriously – or more often miserably – for the sake of an abstract word like patriotism or independence, or if reality belonged to the humble people and the common land.

It seemed that nothing would stop Mrs Zacky talking; but just then her daughter Jinny came back from her shift at the mine. She seemed out of breath and about to say something when she pushed open the half door of the cottage, but on seeing Ross she came forward and curtsied awkwardly and was tongue-tied.

'My eldest,' said Mrs Zacky, folding her arms across her wide bosom. 'Seventeen a month gone. What's to do, child? Have ee forgotten Mister Ross?'

'No, Mother. No, sur. Tedn't that at all.' She went to the wall, untied her apron and pulled off her big linen bonnet.

'She's a fine girl,' said Ross, inspecting her absently. 'You should be proud of her.'

Jinny blushed.

Mrs Zacky was staring at her daughter. 'Is it that Reuben that's been playing you up again?'

A shadow fell across the door, and Ross saw the tall figure of Reuben Clemmow striding towards his cottage. He still wore his damp blue miner's drill coat and trousers, the old hard hat with its candle stuck to the front by clay, and he carried four excavating tools, one of them a heavy iron jumper used for boring.

'He follow me every day,' said the girl with tears of annoyance in her eyes. 'Bothering me to walk wi' him; and when I walk he say nothing but only looks. Why don't he leave me alone!'

'There now, don't take on so,' said her mother. 'Go tell they three young imps to come in if they d' want anything t' eat.'

Ross saw his opportunity to leave, and got up as the girl ran from the hut and called out in a shrill clear voice to three of the Martin children who were working in a potato patch.

'Tes a prime worry to we,' said Mrs Martin. 'He do follow her everywhere. Zacky's warned 'im twice.'

'He keeps his cottage in an uncommon bad state. You must find the stench very poor when the wind is that way.'

'Oh, we don't creen nothing 'bout that. It is the maid we're consarned for.'

Ross could see Reuben Clemmow standing at his cottage door watching Jinny, following her with his small pale eyes and his disconcerting stare. The Clemmows had always been a trouble to the neighbourhood. Father and Mother Clemmow had been dead some years. Father Clemmow had been a deaf mute and had fits; children had made fun of him because of his twisted mouth and the gobbling noises he made. Mother Clemmow had been all right to look at, but there had been something rotten about her; she was not a woman content with the ordinary human sins of copulation and drunkenness. He remembered seeing her publicly whipped in Truro market for selling poisonous abortion powders. The two Clemmows had been in and out of trouble for years, but Eli had always seemed the more difficult.

'Has he given trouble while I have been away?'

'Reuben? Naw. 'Cept that he scat in Nick Vigus's head one day last winter when he was tormenting of him. But we hold no blame to him fur that, for I could do it myself oftentimes.'

He thought: by returning to the simple life of the peasant one did not escape. In his case he exchanged the care of his company of infantry for this implicit concern for the welfare of people living on his land. He might not be a squire in the fullest sense, but the responsibilities did not determine.

'Do you think he means harm to Jinny?'

'That we cann't tell,' said Mrs Zacky. 'If he was to do anything he'd never get into no court o' law. But tes worrying for a mother, my dear, as you'll acknowledge.'

Reuben Clemmow saw that he in his turn was being watched. He stared blankly at the two people in the doorway of the other cottage, then he turned and entered his own cottage, slamming the doors behind him.

Jinny and the three children were returning. Ross looked at the girl with more interest. Neat and trim she was; a pretty little thing. Those good brown eyes, the pale skin slightly freckled across the nose, the thick auburn hair; there would be plenty of admirers among the young men of the district. Little wonder that she turned up her nose at Reuben, who was near forty and weak in the head.

'If Reuben gives further trouble,' Ross said, 'send up a message to me and I'll come and talk to him.'

'Thank ee, sur. We'd be in your debt. Maybe if you spoke to him 'e'd take some account of it.'

IV

On his way home Ross passed the engine house of Wheal Grace, that mine from which had come all his father's prosperity and into which it had all returned. It stood on the hill on the opposite side of the valley from Wheal Maiden, and, known as Trevorgie Mine, had been worked in primitive fashion centuries ago, Joshua having used some of the early workings and rechristened the venture after his wife. Ross thought he would look over it, for any concern was better than moping the days away.

The next afternoon he put on a suit of his father's mining clothes, and was about to leave the house, followed by mutterings from Prudie about rotten planks and foul air, when he saw a horseman riding down the valley and knew it to be Francis.

He was on a fine roan horse and was dressed in a fashionable manner, with buff-coloured breeches, a yellow waistcoat, and a narrow-waisted coat of dark brown velvet with a high collar.

He reined up before Ross, and the horse reared at the check.

'Hey, Rufus; quiet, boy! Well, well, Ross.' He dismounted, his face smiling and friendly. '*Quiet*, boy! Well, what's this? Are you on tribute at Grambler?'

'No, I have a mind to examine Grace.'

Francis raised his eyebrows. 'She was an old strumpet. You don't hope to re-start her?'

'Even strumpets have their uses. I'm taking a stock of what I own, whether it is worthless or of value.'

Francis coloured slightly. 'Sensible enough. Perhaps you can wait an hour.'

'Cut down with me,' Ross suggested. 'But perhaps you no longer care for such adventures – in that attire.'

Francis's flush became deeper. 'Of course I'll come,' he said shortly. 'Give me an old suit of your father's.'

'There's no need. I'll go another day.'

Francis handed his horse to Jud, who had just come down from the field. 'We can talk on the way. It will be of interest to me.'

They went indoors, and Ross searched among such of his father's belongings as the Paynters had not sold. When suitable things had been found Francis stripped off his fine clothes and put them on.

They left the house, and to overcome the restraint Ross forced himself to talk of his experiences in America, where he had been sent as a raw ensign after only a month with his regiment in Ireland; of those hectic first three months under Lord Cornwallis when almost all the fighting he had seen had taken place; of the advance towards Portsmouth and the sudden attack by the French while they were crossing the James River, of the routing of Lafayette; of a musket ball in the ankle and his being drafted to New York as a result, so escaping the siege of Yorktown; of a bayonet cut in the face during a local skirmish while the articles of the preliminary peace were being signed.

They reached the mine and the engine house, and Ross poked about among the tall gorse for some minutes; then he went over to his cousin, who was peering down the shaft.

'How deep did they drive it?' Francis asked.

'No more than thirty fathoms, I believe; and most of that will be under water. But I have heard my father say that most of the old Trevorgie working drained itself.'

'We have begun an eighty-fathom level at Grambler, and it promises big things. How long since this ladder was used?'

'Ten year, I suppose. Shelter me, will you.'

The strong breeze hindered the lighting of the hempen candles. With one candle in the front of each hard hat they began to descend the ladder. Francis would have gone first, but Ross stopped him.

'Wait. I'll try it out.'

The first dozen rungs seemed stout enough, and Francis began to follow. This was a fairly wide shaft, the ladder nailed to the side and supported with wooden platforms at intervals. Some of the pumping gear was still in position, but farther down it had fallen away. As they left the daylight the strong dank smell of stagnant water rose to meet them.

The first level was reached without incident. By the smoky flickering light on his hat Ross peered into the narrow opening of the tunnel; he decided to try for the next level. He called this up to the man above him and they went on down. Once Francis dislodged a stone, and it clattered upon the next platform and fell with a sleek plop into the unseen water below.

Now the rungs began to prove treacherous. Several had to be missed altogether, and then one gave just as Ross put his full weight upon it. His foot caught in the next rung, which was sound.

'If ever I open a mine,' he called up, his voice echoing round and round the confined space, 'I shall put iron ladders down the main shaft.'

'When times are better we intend to do that at Grambler. Bartle's father was lost that way.'

Ross's feet went cold. He bent his head to peer at the dark oily water which barred his way. The height of the water had dropped during the last months, for all round him the walls were covered with green slime. His breath rose steamily to join the smoke from the candle. Beside him, some two feet deep in water, was the opening of the second level. This was the lowest part of the old Trevorgie Mine.

He took two more steps down until the water was above his knees, then stepped off the ladder into the tunnel.

'Faugh! what a stench,' came from Francis. 'I wonder how many unwanted brats have been dropped down here.'

'I think,' said Ross, 'that this level runs east under the valley in the direction of Mingoose.'

He moved off into the tunnel. A splash behind him told him that Francis was off the ladder and following.

The walls here were streaming with brown and green stained water, and in some places the roof was so low that they had to bend to get through. The air was foul and dank, and once or twice the candles flickered as if about to go out. Francis caught up with his cousin where the tunnel widened into a cavern. Ross was peering at the wall where an excavation had been begun.

'See this,' Ross said, pointing. 'See this streak of tin showing between the mundic. They chose their level wrong. We know how big the jumps have been at Grambler.'

Francis wet his finger in the water and rubbed the rock where the faint dark mottling of tin showed.

'And what then? You haven't seen our cost sheets at Grambler since you returned? The profits have a shy fancy to leap to the wrong side of the ledger.'

'At Grambler,' said Ross, 'you have driven too deep. Those engines were costing a fortune when I left.'

'They do not burn coal,' said Francis. 'They eat it as a donkey would eat strawberries. "Munch," and they're braying for more.'

'Here a small engine would do. This level is workable even without pumping.'

'Don't forget it is the autumn.'

Ross turned and stared down at the black foul water above his knees, then looked again at the roof. Francis was right. They had only been able to come this far because of the dryness of the summer. The water was rising now. In another few days, perhaps even hours, it would not be possible to get back.

'Ross,' said the other man. 'You heard, did you not, that I was to be married next week?'

Ross gave up his peering and straightened. He was about three inches taller than his cousin. 'Verity told me.'

'Um. She said too that you didn't wish to attend the wedding.'

'Oh . . . it isn't that in so many words. But with one thing and another . . . My house is like the Sack of Carthage. Besides, I was never one for ceremonies. Let us go on a little. I wonder if it might not be possible to unwater all these old workings by means of an adit driven from the low ground beyond Marasanvose.'

After a few seconds Francis followed his cousin.

The flickering light of the two candles bobbed about, throwing back the darkness here and there, drawing smoky shadows to follow and casting odd grotesque reflections on the bottle-dark water.

Soon the tunnel contracted until it became egg-shaped, about four feet six inches high and not above three feet across at the widest part. It had in fact been cut just big enough to allow the passage of a man pushing a wheelbarrow and bending his head over it. The water came to just below the widest part of the egg, and here the walls were worn smooth with the rubbing of long forgotten elbows.

Francis began to feel the need of air, the need to straighten his bent back, the weight of thousands of tons of rock above his head.

'You must, of course, come to the wedding,' he said, raising his voice. His candle was sputtering with a drop of water which had fallen on it. 'We should be greatly upset if you did not.'

'Nonsense. The countryside will soon tire of talking about it.'

'You're damned insulting to-day. It's our wish that you should come. Mine and——'

'And Elizabeth's?'

'She especially asked that you should.'

Ross checked a sentence on his tongue. 'Very well. At what time?'

'Noon. George Warleggan is to be my groomsman.'

'George Warleggan?'

'Yes. Had I known that you——'

'You see the ground is rising a little. We're turning north now.'

'We don't intend to have a big wedding,' Francis said. 'Just our families and a few friends. Cousin William-Alfred will officiate and Mr Odgers will assist him. Ross, I wished to explain——'

'The air is improving here,' Ross said grimly, pushing his way round an awkward corner of the confined tunnel and bringing down a shower of loose stones plop-plopping into the water.

They had climbed a few feet and were almost free of water. Ahead was a glimmer of light. Climbing still, they reached an air shaft, one of the numerous winzes driven down to make working conditions just supportable. Like the main shaft, this went deeper; it was full of water to within a few feet of them and was crossed by a narrow bridge of planks. There was no ladder up this shaft.

They peered up at the small circle of daylight above.

'Where is this?' said Ross. 'It must be the one beside the track to Reen-Wollas——'

'Or that at the edge of the sand hills. Look, Ross, I wished to explain. When I first met Elizabeth this spring past there was no thought in my head of coming between her and you. It was like a stroke from the blue. Both she and I——'

Ross turned, his face high-strung and dangerous. 'In the *devil's* name! Isn't it enough to——'

Such was his expression that Francis stepped back upon the wooden bridge crossing the shaft – the bridge broke to pieces like a biscuit, and he was struggling in the water.

This happened so quickly that for a moment nothing could be done. Ross thought: Francis cannot swim.

In the semidarkness he came to the surface anyhow, an arm, fair hair, and the hard hat floating, his clothing a help before it became waterlogged. Ross fell on his stomach, leaned over the edge, nearly overbalanced, could not reach; a despairing face; the water was viscous. He pulled at a piece of the rotten bridge; it came away; he swung it down and a big iron nail caught on the shoulder of his cousin's coat; pulled and the coat tore; a hand grasped the end of the wood and Ross pulled again; before the wood crumpled they made contact.

Ross tensed his muscles on the slippery rock floor and hauled his cousin out of the shaft.

They sat there in silence for some moments, Francis gasping and spitting out the foul water.

'By God! what was your reason to flare up so?' he said in anger.

'By God, why don't you learn to swim!' Ross said.

There was another silence. The accident had released emotions within them; these for a time hung in the air like a dangerous gas, impossible to name but not to be ignored.

While they sat there Francis took sidelong glances at his cousin. That first evening of Ross's return he had expected and understood Ross's disappointment and resentment. But in his casual, easygoing way he had had no idea of the extent of the emotion behind the fine-drawn expression of his cousin's face. Now he knew.

He also sensed that the accident of his fall had not been the only danger in which he had stood . . . in which perhaps he still stood.

They had both lost their candles and had not brought spares. Francis glanced up at the disc of light high above them. A pity there was no ladder here. It would be an unpleasant journey back all the way they had come, groping in the dark. . . .

After a minute he shook some water off his coat and began the trip back. Ross followed him with an expression which was now half grim, half ironical. For Francis the incident might have betrayed the extent of his cousin's resentment – but Ross felt it should also have shown him its limitations.

It had done that much for himself.

Chapter four

IN THE WEEK before the wedding Ross left his property only once: to visit Sawle Church.

Joshua had expressed a wish to be buried in the same grave as his wife, so there was little to see.

'*Sacred to the memory of Grace Mary: beloved wife of Joshua Poldark, who departed this life on the ninth day of May, 1770; aged 30 years.* Quid Quid Amor Jussit, Non Est Contemnere Tutum.'

And underneath Charles had had carved: '*Also of Joshua Poldark, of Nampara, in the County of Cornwall, Esqr., who died on the eleventh day of March, 1783, aged 59.*'

The only other change was that the shrubs Joshua had planted had been uprooted and the mound was thinly grown over with grass. Beside this on a small headstone adjoining was: '*Claude Anthony Poldark, died 9th January, 1771, in the sixth year of his age.*

Four days later Ross returned to the church to bury the hopes he had carried with him for more than two years.

All the time at the back of his mind had been the half conviction that somehow the wedding would not be. It was as hard to believe as if someone had told him he was going to die.

Sawle Church was half a mile from the village of Sawle at the head of the track leading to the village. To-day the main altar had been decorated with golden chrysanthemums, and four musicians scraped out the hymns on fiddles and bass-viols. There were twenty guests; Ross sat near the front in one of the tall pews so convenient for sleeping, and stared across at the two figures kneeling at the altar and listened to the drone of William-Alfred's voice forging the legal and spiritual bond.

Soon, it seemed in no time at all for so vital a matter, they were out in the churchyard again where were gathered about four dozen villagers from Sawle, Trenwith, and Grambler. They stood at a respectful distance and gave out a thin little unrehearsed cheer when the bride and bridegroom appeared at the door.

It was a bright November day with areas of blue sky, intermittent sun, and grey-white monuments of cloud moving unhurriedly before the fresh wind. Elizabeth's veil of old lace blew in billows about her figure, making her seem unsubstantial and ethereal; she might have been one of the smaller clouds which had lost its way and been caught up in the human procession. Soon they were in their coach and were bumping off over the rough track, followed by the rest of the wedding party on horseback.

Elizabeth and her father and mother had come out from Kenwyn in the Chynoweth family coach, rattling and lurching along the narrow rutted lanes and throwing out behind a fog of grey dust which settled evenly upon the staring people who gathered to watch it go by. For the appearance of such a vehicle in this barren countryside was an event of the first import-ance. Horseback and mule train were the unvarying means of travel. News of its coming moved faster than its large red iron-rimmed wheels could carry it, and tinners panning tin in nearby streams, cottagers and their wives, farm labourers, miners off duty, and the flotsam of four parishes turned out to see it pass. Dogs barked and mules brayed and naked children ran shouting after it through the dust.

As the drive was reached the coachman set the horses at a trot. Bartle on the back seat blew his horn, and they arrived before the front of Trenwith House in fine style with several of the following riders trotting and shouting alongside.

At the house a banquet had been prepared which put all other feasts in the shade. All were here who had been here on the night of Ross's return. Mrs Chynoweth, beautiful as a well-bred female eagle; Dr Choake and his silly pretty wife; Charles, rising to the occasion in a large new wig, with a brown velvet coat finely laced about the cuffs, and a red waistcoat. Verity spent less than half her time at the table, being constantly up and down to see that things were going right, her fluffy dark hair becoming untidy as the afternoon advanced. Cousin William-Alfred, thin and pale and unapproach-able, lent some solemnity and restraint to the proceedings. His wife Dorothy was not present, being ill of her old complaint, which was pregnancy. Aunt Agatha, taking her usual place at the foot of the table, wore an old-fashioned velvet gown with a whale-bone hoop, and a cap of fine lace on her dusty wig.

Among the newcomers was Henshawe, captain of Grambler, a big young man with the lightest of blue eyes and small hands and feet which allowed him to move easily for all his weight. Mrs Henshawe was out of her depth here and paused now and then in her over-genteel eating to glance uneasily at the other guests; but her husband, though he had been down a mine since he was eight and could neither read nor write, was used to mixing with any class and was soon picking his teeth with the two-pronged fork set for the sweetmeats.

Opposite them, trying not to notice this, was Mrs Teague, the widow of a distant cousin with a small estate near St Ann's; and dotted about the board in diminished thirds were her five marriageable daughters, Faith, Hope, Patience, Joan, and Ruth.

Next to her was a Captain Blamey, whom Ross had not met before, a quiet presentable man of about forty, master of one of the Falmouth-Lisbon packets. During the whole of the long meal Ross saw the seaman speak only twice, and that was to Verity thanking her for something she brought. He drank nothing.

The other clergyman did not help Cousin William-Alfred with the dignities of the day. To the Rev Mr Odgers, a desiccated little man, was entrusted the cure of the village of Sawle with Grambler, and for this the rector, who lived in Penzance, paid him £40 a year. On this he kept a wife, a cow, and ten children. He took his seat at the feast in a suit going green with constant wear and in a faded horsehair wig, and he was constantly stretching out a hand, on which the dirt was ingrained and the nails broken, for another helping from some dish, while his narrow jaws worked to be rid of what was still before him. There was something rabbit-like in the quick furtive movements: nibble, nibble, before someone comes to frighten me away.

Making up the company were the Nicholas Warleggans, father, mother, and son.

They alone stood for the new-rich of the county. The elder Warleggan's father had been a country blacksmith who had begun tin smelting in a small way; the smelter's son, Nicholas, had moved to Truro and built up a smelting works. From these roots all the tentacles of their fortune had sprung. Mr Nicholas Warleggan was a man with a heavy upper lip, eyes like basalt and big square hands still marked with their early labour. Twenty-five years ago he had married a Mary Lashbrook from Edgecumbe, and the first fruit of the union was present to-day in George Warleggan, a name which was to become famous in mining and banking circles and one which was already making itself felt where the father's was not.

George had a big face. All his features were on the same scale: the decisive nose drawn back a little at the nostrils as if prepared for opposition, the big intent brown eyes which he used more often than his neck when looking at what was not in front of him – a characteristic Opie had caught when painting his portrait earlier that year.

When the great feast was at last over the big table was pushed out of the way and the exhausted guests sat round in a circle to watch a cockfight.

Verity and Francis had protested that this form of entertainment was not suitable, but Charles had brushed them aside. One seldom had the chance of a tourney in one's own home; usually it meant riding into Truro or Redruth, a devilish fagging business he was becoming less and less inclined for. Besides, Nicholas Warleggan had brought down Red Gauntlet, a bird with a reputation, and was willing to match him against all comers. Charles's own cockerels would become soft without fresh blood to meet them.

A servant of the Warleggans brought in Red Gauntlet and another bird, and a moment later Dr Choake returned with a couple of his own fancies, followed by the boy Bartle with three of Charles's birds.

In the confusion Ross looked about for Elizabeth. He knew she hated cockfighting; and sure enough she had slipped away to the end of the hall and was sitting on a settle beside the stairs drinking tea with Verity. Cousin William-Alfred, who disapproved of the sport on advanced Christian grounds, had withdrawn to a recess on the other side of the stairs where the Bible was kept on a three-legged mahogany table and family portraits frowned down over the scene. Ross heard him discussing with the Rev Mr Odgers the distressing condition of Sawle Church.

A faint flush coloured Elizabeth's skin as Ross came up to her.

'Well, Ross,' said Verity, 'and does she not look sweet in her wedding gown? And has it not all been a great success until now? These men with their cockfighting! Their food doesn't settle in their bellies unless they see blood flowing in some foolish pastime. Will you take tea?'

Ross thanked her and refused. 'A wonderful feast. My only wish is to sleep after it.'

'Well, I must go and find Mrs Tabb: there is more to see to yet. Half our guests will be staying the night, and you have to be sure that each room has its bedding and each bed its warming pan.

Verity left them, and they listened a moment to the arguments and discussions going on about the space which had been cleared. With sport in prospect the company was quickly recovering from its food exhaustion. This was a vigorous age.

Ross said: 'Are you among those who will stay?'

'To-night we are to stay. To-morrow we leave for Falmouth for two weeks.'

He stared down at her as she gazed across the room. Her fair hair was short at the nape of the neck, with the ears bare and a single wisp of a curl in front of each. The rest was curled and piled on her head, with a small headdress in the shape of a single row of pearls. Her dress was high at the neck with huge tufted sleeves of fine lace.

He had sought this encounter and now didn't know what to say. That had often been the way when they first met. Her fragile loveliness had often left him tongue-tied until he came to know her as she really was.

'Ross,' she said, 'you must wonder why I wanted you to come to-day. But you hadn't been to see me and I felt I must speak to you.' She stopped a moment to bite at her lower lip and he watched the colour come and go in it. 'To-day is my day. I do want to be happy and to feel that all those about me are the same. There's no time to explain everything; perhaps I couldn't explain it if there were. But I do want you to try to forgive me for any unhappiness I may have caused you.'

'There's nothing to forgive,' said Ross. 'There was no formal undertaking.'

She glanced at him a moment out of grey eyes which seemed to show a hint of indignation.

'You know that was not all . . .'

The first cockfight was over amidst shouting and applause, and the defeated bird, dripping blood and feathers, was rescued from the arena.

'Why, it was no fight at all,' said Charles Poldark. 'Aarf! Rarely have I seen five guineas earned so quick.'

'No,' said Dr Choake, whose bird had beaten one of the Warleggans'. 'Paracelsus underrated his opponent. A fatal mistake.'

'Eathily done!' said Polly Choake as she smoothed down the head of the victor while their manservant held it. 'Conqueror looks none so vithious until hith temper be roused. People thay as how I am like that!'

'He has not come through unscathed, ma'am,' said the servant. 'You'll soil your gloves.'

'Well, now I thall be able to afford me a new pair!' said Polly.

There was laughter at this, although her husband lowered his brows as at a breach of taste.

Charles said: 'It was a poor show all the same. There's many a youngster could have done better. My Royal Duke could swallow either of 'em, and he little more than a stag!'

'Let us see this Royal Duke,' said Mr Warleggan politely. 'Perhaps you would like to match him with Red Gauntlet.'

'With who? With what?' asked Aunt Agatha, wiping a dribble from her chin. 'Nay, that would be a shame, it would.'

'At least we should see if his blood were really blue,' said Mr Warleggan.

'A battle royal?' said Charles. 'I am not averse. What is the weight of your bird?'

'Four pounds exact.'

'Then they fall in! Royal Duke is three pounds thirteen. Bring them in and let us see.'

The two birds were brought forward and compared. Red Gauntlet was small for his weight, a vicious creature scarred and toughened with twenty fights. Royal Duke was a young bird which had fought only once or twice and that locally.

'And the stakes?' said George Warleggan.

'What you will.' Charles glanced up at his guest.

'A hundred guineas?' said Mr Warleggan.

There was a moment's silence.

'. . . And the whole range of columns supporting the roof,' said Mr Odgers, 'are held together only by iron bars and clamps which are constantly in need of reinforcement. The east and west walls are virtually tottering.'

'Yes, yes, I'll back my fancy,' shouted Charles. 'Get on with the fight.'

Preparations were begun with slightly more care for detail than usual. Whatever might be the habits of Mr Nicholas Warleggan, it was not the custom of local squires of Mr Poldark's financial status to put so much on a single combat.

'. . . You know that was not all,' Elizabeth repeated in an undertone. 'Something was understood between us. But we were so young——'

'I don't see,' said Ross, 'in what way explanations will help. To-day has made it——'

'Elizabeth,' said Mrs Chynoweth, coming on them suddenly. 'You must remember this is your day. You must join in, not isolate yourself in this manner.'

'Thank you, Mama. But you know I've no taste for this. I am sure I shall not be missed until it is over.'

Mrs Chynoweth straightened her back, and their eyes met. But she sensed the decision in her daughter's low voice and did not force an issue. She looked up at Ross and smiled without warmth.

'Ross, I know you are not uninterested in the sport. Perhaps you will instruct me in its finer points.'

Ross smiled back. 'I feel convinced, ma'am, that there are no subtleties of combat on which I can offer you any useful advice.'

Mrs Chynoweth looked at him sharply. Then she turned. 'I'll send Francis to you, Elizabeth,' she said as she left them.

There was silence before the opening of the fight.

'What is more,' said Mr Odgers, 'the churchyard is worst of all. So full of graves is it that the ground can scarce be opened without turning up putrid bodies or skulls or skeletons. One is afraid to put in a spade.'

'How dare you say that to my mother!' Elizabeth said.

'Is honesty always offensive?' Ross answered. 'I'm sorry.'

A sudden sharp murmur told that the fight had begun. From the start Red Gauntlet had the advantage. His little eyes gleaming, he flew in three or four times, finding his mark and drawing blood and knowing just when to withdraw before the other bird could use his own spurs. Royal Duke was game enough but in a different class.

This was a long fight, and everyone watching it became excited. Charles and Agatha led a chorus a encouragement and counter-encouragement. Royal Duke was down in a flutter of feathers with Red Gauntlet on top of him, but miraculously avoided the *coup de grâce* and was up again and fighting back. At last they separated to spar for an opening, heads down and neck feathers out. Even Red Gauntlet was tiring and Royal Duke was in a sorry state. Gauntlet could do everything but finish him off.

'Withdraw!' yelled Aunt Agatha. 'Charles, withdraw! We have a champion there. Do not let him be maimed in his first fight!'

Charles plucked at his bottom lip and was indecisive. Before he could make up his mind they were at it again. And suddenly, quite surprising everyone, Royal Duke took the initiative. He seemed to have drawn fresh reserves from his triumphant youth. Red Gauntlet, winded and taken unawares, was down.

George Warleggan grasped his father's arm, upsetting his snuffbox. 'Stop the fight!' he said sharply. 'The spurs are in Gauntlet's head.'

He had been the first to see what they now all saw, that the Duke, by sheer staying power and some luck, had won the fight. If Warleggan did not at once intervene Red Gauntlet would fight no more. He was wriggling round and round on the floor in a desperate and weakening effort to throw off the other bird.

Mr Warleggan motioned back his manservant, bent and took up his snuffbox and put it away. 'Let them go on,' he said. 'I don't encourage pensioners.'

'We've got a champion!' crowed Aunt Agatha. 'Ecod, we've got a champion, sure 'nough. Well, isn't the fight over? The bird's done for. Lor' bless us, he looks dead to me! Why wasn't they stopped?'

'I'll give you my draft for a hundred guineas,' Warleggan said to Charles with an evenness which did not deceive anyone. 'And if you wish to dispose of your bird give me the first refusal. I believe something could be made of him.'

'It was a lucky stroke,' said Charles, his broad red face shining with sweat and pleasure. 'A rare lucky stroke. I seldom saw a better fight or a more surprising finish. Your Gauntlet was a game bird.'

'Game indeed, 'said Mr Chynoweth. 'A battle royal – um – as you said, Charles. Who is to fight next?'

'He that fights and runs away,' said Aunt Agatha, trying to adjust her wig, 'lives to fight another day.' She chuckled. 'Not against our Duke. He kills ere ever they can be separated. I must say you was all mortal slow. Or peevish. Was you peevish? Poor losers lose more'n they need.'

Fortunately no one was attending to her, and two more cockerels were brought forward.

'You have no right,' said Elizabeth, 'no right or reason to insult my mother. What I have done I have done willingly and of my own mind. If you wish to criticize anyone you must criticize me.'

Ross glanced at the girl beside him, and the anger suddenly went out of him and left only pain that everything was over between them.

'I don't criticize anyone,' he said. 'What's done is done, and I don't want to spoil your happiness. I've my own life to live and . . . we shall be neighbours. We shall see something of each other. . . .'

Francis withdrew himself from the crowd and dabbed a spot of blood from his silk stock.

'Someday,' Elizabeth said in a low tone, 'I hope you'll come to forgive me. We were so young. Later . . .'

With death in his heart Ross watched her husband approach.

'Not following this?' Francis said to his cousin. His handsome face was flushed with food and wine. 'I don't blame you. An anticlimax after the other bout. It was an astonishing performance, that. Well, my dear, are you feeling neglected on your wedding day? It is shameful of me and shall be remedied. May I shrivel and waste if I leave you again to-day.'

II

When Ross left Trenwith much later that evening he mounted and rode for miles, blindly and blackly, while the moon climbed up the sky, until at last Darkie, not yet sound from her earlier injury, showed signs of lameness again. By then he was far beyond his own house in bare wind-swept country unfamiliar to him. He turned his mare about and allowed her to find her own way home.

This she lamentably failed to do, and the night was far gone before the broken chimney stack of Wheal Grace showed that he was on his own land.

He rode down into the valley and unsaddled Darkie and entered the house. He drank a glass of rum and went up to his bedroom and lay there on the bed fully clothed and booted. But his eyes were not closed when dawn began to lighten the squares of the windows.

This was the darkest hour of all.

Chapter five

FOR ROSS THE early part of the winter was endless. For days on end the driving mists filled the valley until the walls of Nampara House ran with damp and the stream was in yellow spate. After Christmas the frost cleared the atmosphere, stiffening the long grass on the cliff edges, whitening the rocks and heaps of mining attle, hardening the sand and painting it salt-coloured until licked away by the unquiet sea.

Only Verity came often. She was his contact with the rest of the family, bringing him gossip and companionship. They walked miles together, sometimes in the rain along the cliffs when the sky was hung with low clouds and the sea drab and sullen as any jilted lover, sometimes on the sand at the sea's edge, when the waves came lumbering in, sending up mists of iridescence from their broken heads. He would stride on, sometimes listening to her, more seldom talking himself, while she walked swiftly beside him and her hair blew about her face and the wind stung colour into her cheeks.

One day in mid-March she came and stayed an unusual time, watching him hammering a support for one of the beams of the still-room.

She said: 'How is your ankle, Ross?'

'I feel little of it.' Not quite the truth, but near enough for other people. He limped scarcely at all, having forced himself to walk straight, but the pain was often there.

She had brought over some jars of her own preserves, and these she now began to take down from their shelves and rearrange.

'Father says if you are short of fodder for your stock, you can have some of ours. Also that we have seed of radish and French onion if you would like it.'

Ross hesitated a moment. 'Thanks,' he said. 'I put in peas and beans last week. There's room enough.'

Verity stared at a label of her own writing. 'Do you think you can dance, Ross?' she said.

'Dance? What do you mean?'

'Oh, not the reel or the hornpipe, but at a formal ball such as they are holding in Truro next Monday week, Easter Monday.'

He paused in his hammering. 'I might if I were so inclined. But as I am not the need doesn't arise.'

She considered him a moment before speaking again. For all his hard work this winter he was thinner and paler. He was drinking too much and thinking too much. She remembered him when he had been a high-strung, lighthearted boy, full of talk and fun. He used to sing. This gaunt brooding man was a stranger to her for all her efforts to know him. The war was to blame as well as Elizabeth.

'You're still young,' she said. 'There is plenty of life in Cornwall if you want it. Why don't you come?'

'So you are going?'

'If someone will take me.'

Ross turned. 'This is a new interest. And are not Francis and Elizabeth to be there?'

'They were, but have decided not.'

Ross picked up his hammer. 'Well, well.'

'It is a Charity Ball,' Verity said. 'It is to be held at the Assembly Rooms. You might meet friends there whom you have not seen since your return. It would be a change from all this work and solitude.'

'Certainly it would.' The idea did not appeal. 'Well, well, perhaps I'll think it over.'

'It would not – it would not perhaps matter so much,' said Verity, blushing, 'if you did not want to dance a great deal – that is, if your ankle is painful.'

Ross was careful not to notice her colour. 'A long ride home in the dark for you, especially if it is wet.'

'Oh, I have the offer of the night in Truro. Joan Pascoe, whom you know, will put me up. I will send in to ask them to accommodate you also. They would be delighted.'

'You move too fast,' he said. 'I haven't said I would go. There's so much to do here.'

'Yes, Ross,' she said.

'Even now we're late with our sowing. Two of the fields have been under water. I cannot trust Jud to work alone.'

'No, Ross,' she said.

'In any case, I couldn't stay the night in Truro, for I have arranged to ride into Redruth to the fair on the Tuesday morning. I want more livestock.'

'Yes, Ross.'

He examined the wedge he had thrust under the beam. It was not secure yet. 'What time shall I come round for you?' he asked.

That night he went line fishing on Hendrawna Beach with Mark and Paul Daniel and Zacky Martin and Jud Paynter and Nick Vigus. He had no zest for the old ways, but the drift of circumstances was leading him back to them.

The weather was cold and unsuitable, but the miners were too used to wet clothes and extremes of temperature to pay much heed to this, and Ross never took any notice of the weather. They caught no fish, but the night passed pleasantly enough, for out of the driftwood on the beach they built a big fire in one of the caves and sat round it and told stories and drank rum while the dark cavern echoed with the noise they made.

Zacky Martin, father of Jinny and the other ten, was a quiet, keen little man with humorous eyes and a permanent grey stubble on his chin which was never a beard and never a clean shave. Because he could read and write he was known as the scholar of the neighbourhood. Twenty odd years ago he had come to Sawle, a 'stranger' from Redruth, and had overcome strong local prejudice to marry the smith's daughter.

While they were in the cave he drew Ross aside and said Mrs Zacky had gone on and on at him about some promise Mister Ross had made when he was over at their cottage soon after he came home. It was only about Reuben Clemmow and the way he was frightening young Jinny, making her life a misery, following her about, watching her, trying to get her away from her brothers and sisters to speak to her alone. Of course, he hadn't *done* anything yet: they'd deal with him themselves if he did; but they didn't want for that to happen, and Mrs Zacky kept on saying if Mister Ross would speak to him perhaps it would bring him to see sense.

Ross stared across at Jud's bald head, which was just beginning to nod with the effects of the rum and the hot fire. He looked at Nick Vigus's pockmarked face glowing red and demonic through the flames, at Mark Daniel's long powerful back as he bent over the fishing tackle.

'I remember the offer well,' he told Zacky. 'I'll see him on Sunday – see if I can get some sense into him. If not I'll turn him out of his cottage. They're an unhealthy family, the Clemmows; we should be better without the last of them.'

II

Easter Monday came before Ross had faced up to his other promise. But on impulse he had undertaken to be Verity's escort at the ball and out of affection for her he must go through with it.

The Assembly Rooms were full of people when Ross and Verity arrived. Many of the elite of Cornish society were present to-night. As Ross and Verity entered, the band was already tuning up for the first dance. The room was lit by scores of candles ranged along the walls. The murmur of voices met them, borne on a wave of warm air in which scents and perfumes were strongly mingled. They threaded their way across the room among talking groups and tapping heels and clicking snuffboxes and the rustle of silk gowns.

As was his custom when he went among the people of his own class, Ross had dressed with care, in a suit of black velvet with silver buttons; and Verity too, a little unexpectedly, had taken pains with herself. The bright colour of her crimson brocade frock lit up and softened the tan of her plain pleasant face; she was far prettier than he had ever seen her. This was a different Verity from the one who in breeches and a smock ploughed about in the mud of Trenwith indifferent to rain and wind.

Mrs Teague and her five daughters were here and were members of a party organized by Joan Pascoe, to which Ross and Verity were expected to attach themselves. While polite greetings were in progress Ross turned his brooding gaze from one to the other of the five girls and wondered why none of them was married. Faith, the eldest, was fair and pretty, but the other four grew progressively darker and less attractive, as if the virtue and inspiration had gone out of Mrs Teague as she produced them.

For once there were enough men, and Mrs Teague, in a new frizzled wig and gold earrings, gazed over the scene with complacent eyes. There were half a dozen others to the party, and Ross was the senior among them. He felt it: they were so young with their artificial manners and parrot compliments. They called him Captain Poldark and treated him with a respect he did not look for – all, that is, except Whitworth, a swaggering beau who was doing nothing at Oxford with a view to entering the Church, and who was dressed in the extremity of fashion with a cutaway coat embroidered with silk thread flowers on the cuffs, round the seams, and on the tails. He talked in the loudest voice and clearly wished to take charge of the party, a privilege which Ross allowed him.

Since he was here to please Verity he decided to enter into the spirit of the evening as much as possible, and he moved about from one girl to another offering the expected compliments and receiving the expected replies.

He found himself talking to Ruth Teague, the youngest and least attractive of Mrs Teague's quintet. She had been standing a little apart from her sisters and for the moment had drifted out of range of her overpowering mother. It was her first ball and she looked lonely and nervous. With an air of preoccupation Ross raised his head and counted the number of young men the Teagues had brought. There were, after all, only four.

'May I have the pleasure of the two second dances?' he said.

She went scarlet. 'Thank you, sir. If Mama will permit me . . .'

'I shall look forward to it.' He smiled and moved off to pay his respects to Lady Whitworth, the beau's mother. A few moments later he glanced at Ruth and saw she had now gone white. Was he so fearsome with his scarred face? Or was it the reputation of his father which clung to his name like an odour of unsanctity?

He saw that another man had joined the party and was talking to Verity. There was something familiar in that stocky quietly dressed figure with the hair done in an unpretentious pigtail. It was Captain Andrew Blamey, the Falmouth packet captain, whom he had met at the wedding.

'Well, Captain,' said Ross, 'a surprise to see you here.'

'Captain Poldark.' Ross's hand was gripped, but the other man seemed tongue-tied. Eventually he got out: 'No dancing man, really.'

They talked for some moments about ships, Captain Blamey mainly in monosyllables, looking at Verity. Then the band at last struck up and he excused himself. Ross was to partner his cousin. They formed up to begin, the titled people in some order of precedence.

'Are you dancing the next with Captain Blamey?' he asked.

'Yes, Ross. Do you mind?'

'Not at all. I am promised to Miss Ruth Teague.'

'What, the littlest of them all? How considerate of you.'

'The duty of every Englishman,' said Ross. Then as they were about to separate he added in a gruff and very passable imitation: 'No dancing man, really.'

Verity met his eyes.

The formal dance went on. The soft yellow candle light trembled over the colours of the dresses, the gold and cream, the salmon and the mulberry. It made the graceful and the beautiful more charming, the graceless and the ungainly tolerable; it smoothed over the tawdry and cast soft creamy-grey shadows becoming to all. The band scraped away, the figures pirouetted, moving and bowing and stepping, turning on heels, holding hands, pointing toes; the shadows intermingled and changed, forming and reforming intricate designs of light and shade, like some gracious depictment of the warp and woof of life, sun and shadow, birth and death, a slow interweaving of the eternal pattern.

The time came for his dance with Ruth Teague. He found her hand cold through its pink lace glove; she was still nervous and he wondered how he could put her at her ease. A poor plain little creature, but on examination, for which she gave him every opportunity by keeping her eyes down, she had some features to merit attention, a surprisingly wilful turn to her uptilted chin, a glow of vitality under her sallow skin, an almond shape to the eyes, which gave a hint of the original to her looks. Except for his cousin she was the first woman he had talked with who had not relied on a strong scent to drown the odours of the body. In finding a girl who smelt as clean as Verity he felt a impulse of friendship.

He summoned such small talk as he had and was successful at once in making her smile; in this new-found interest he forgot the aching of his ankle. They danced the two third together, and Mrs Teague's eyebrows went up. She had expected Ruth to spend most of the evening beside her, as a dutiful youngest was under every obligation to do.

'What a genteel assembly!' said Lady Whitworth, sitting beside Mrs Teague. 'I'm sure our dear children must be enjoying themselves. Who is the tall man distinguishing little Ruth? I missed his name.'

'Captain Poldark. A nephew of Mr Charles.'

'What, a son of Mr Joshua Poldark? And I never recognized him! Not at all like his father, is he? Not as handsome. Still . . . strikin' in his way – scar an' all. Is he taking an interest?'

'Well, that's how interest begins, isn't it?' said Mrs Teague, smiling sweetly at her friend.

'Of course, my dear. But how embarrassin' for your two eldest if Ruth were to become attached before them. I always think it such a pity that the etiquette of comin' out is not more strictly followed in this county. Now in Oxfordshire no girls would be permitted by their parents to make themselves so free as Patience and Joan and Ruth are doin' until Faith and Hope were happily settled. I do think it makes for bitter feelin' within the family. Well, imagine that bein' Mr Joshua's son and I never recognized him. I wonder if they are alike in their ways. I remember Mr Joshua well.'

After this dance Ruth came to sit beside them. Her face, from being so pale, was now flushed. She fanned herself rapidly and her eyes were bright. Mrs Teague was itching to question her, but so long as Lady Whitworth was irritatingly within hearing nothing could be said. Mrs Teague knew Joshua's reputation just as well as Lady Whitworth. Ross would be an excellent catch for little Ruth, but his father had had such a deplorable habit of snapping up the bait without getting caught on the hook.

'Miss Verity is quite forthcoming to-night,' said Mrs Teague to distract Lady Whitworth's attention. 'I believe she is more vivacious than I have seen her.'

'The young company, no doubt,' said her friend dryly. 'I see Captain Blamey is here also.'

'A cousin of the Roseland Blameys, I understand.'

'I have heard it said they prefer it to be known as a second cousinship.'

'Oh, really?' Mrs Teague pricked up her ears. 'Why is that?'

'One hears these rumours.' Lady Whitworth waved a gloved hand indifferently. 'One does not, of course, repeat them when there are young ears to hear.'

'What? Er – no, no, of course not.'

Captain Blamey was bowing to his partner.

'Warm in here,' he said. 'Perhaps – some refreshment?'

Verity nodded, as tongue-tied as he. During the dancing they hadn't spoken at all. Now they went into the refreshment room and found a corner sheltered by ferns. In this seclusion she sipped French claret and watched people passing to and fro. He would drink only lemonade.

I must think of something to say, thought Verity; why have I no small talk like those girls over there; if I could help him to talk he would like me more; he's shy like me, and I ought to make things easier not harder. There's farming, but he would not be attracted by my pigs and poultry. Mining I'm no more interested in than he. The sea I know nothing of except cutters and seiners and other small fry. The shipwreck last month . . . but that might not be a tactful thing to discuss. Why can't I just say, la, la, la, and giggle and be fanciful. I could say how well he dances, but that isn't true, for he dances like that big friendly bear I saw last Christmas.

'Cooler out here,' said Captain Blamey.

'Yes,' said Verity agreeably.

'A little overwarm for dancing in there. I don't believe that a breath or two of night air would do the room any harm.'

'The weather, of course, is very mild,' she volunteered. 'Quite unseasonable.'

'How graceful you dance,' said Captain Blamey, perspiring. 'I've never met anyone so, well – er – hm——'

'I greatly enjoy dancing,' she said. 'But I get little opportunity for it at Trenwith. To-night is a special pleasure.'

'And for me. And for me. I never remember enjoying anything . . .'

In the silence which followed this breakdown they listened to the laughter of the girls and men flirting in the next alcove. They were having a most agreeable time.

'What foolish things those young people are saying,' Andrew Blamey got out abruptly.

'Oh, do you think so,' she answered in relief.

Now I've offended her, he thought. It wasn't well framed; I meant no reflection on her. How pretty her shoulders are. I ought to take this opportunity of telling her everything; but what right have I to imagine she would be interested? Besides, I would tell it so clumsily that she'd be affronted at the first words. How clean her skin looks; she's like a westerly breeze at sunrise, rare and fresh, and good to get into your lungs and your heart.

'When do you next leave for Lisbon?' she asked.

'By the afternoon tide on Friday.'

'I have been to Falmouth three times,' she told him. 'A fine harbour.'

'The finest north of the equator. A farsighted government would convert it to its proper use as a great naval base and depot. Everything is in its favour. We shall need such a harbour yet.'

'For what?' asked Verity, watching his quiet brown face. 'Aren't we at peace?'

'For a little while. A year or two, maybe; but there will be trouble with France again. Nothing is properly settled. And when war comes, sea power will decide it.'

'Ruth,' said Mrs Teague in the other room. 'I see Faith is sitting out this dance. Why do you not go and keep her company?'

'Very well, Mama,' The girl rose obediently.

'What sort of rumours do you mean?' asked her mother when she was out of earshot.

Lady Whitworth raised her pencilled eyebrows.

'About whom?'

'Captain Blamey.'

'About Captain Blamey? Dear me, I don't think it kind to lend too much credence to whispered stories, do you?'

'No, no, certainly not. I make a point of paying no attention to them myself.'

'Mind you, I heard this on good authority, otherwise I should not consider repeating it even to you.' Lady Whitworth raised her fan, which was of chicken-skin parchment delicately painted with cherubs. Behind this screen she began to speak in an undertone into Mrs Teague's pearl earring.

Mrs Teague's black button eyes grew smaller and rounder as the tale proceeded; the creases in her eyelids moved down like little venetian blinds which had come askew. 'No!' she exclaimed. 'Is that so! Why, in that case he should not be allowed in the room. The scoundrel! I shall consider it my duty to warn Verity.'

'If you do so, my dear, pray leave it until another occasion. I have no wish to be drawn into the quarrel that might ensue. Besides, my dear, perhaps she already knows. You know what girls are these days: man mad. And, after all, she's twenty-five – the same as your eldest, my dear. She won't get many more chances.'

On her way to join her sister Ruth was intercepted by Ross. It was to ask her for the dance which was about to begin, a gavotte, that variation on the minuet which was now rivalling the minuet in favour. One lifted the feet, so, and so, instead of slurring them . . .

He found this time that she smiled more easily, with less constraint. From being slightly scared by his attentions it had not taken her long to become flattered. A girl with four unmarried sisters does not come to her first ball with overweening expectations. To find herself singled out by a man of some distinction was heady wine, and Ross should have been careful with his doses. But he, in a good-natured way, was only pleased to find pleasure in making someone's evening a success.

Rather to his own surprise he found he was enjoying the dance; there was a pleasure in mixing with people although he had tried to despise it. As they separated and came together again he continued without break his whispered conversation with her, and she giggled abruptly, earning a glance of reproof from her second sister who was in the next square and dancing with two elderly gentlemen and a titled lady.

In the refreshment room Captain Blamey had produced a sketch.

'Now, you see, this is the foremast, mainmast, and mizzenmast.

On the foremast is the mains'l, the——'

'Did you draw that?' Verity asked.

'Yes. It is a sketch of my father's ship. She was a ship o' the line. He died six year back. If——'

'It's uncommonly well drawn.'

'Oh, that. One gets used to the pencil. You see, the foremast and the mainmast are square-rigged; that is to say they carry yards at – um – across the run of the ship. The mizzenmast is part square-rigged, but she carries a gaff and a spanker boom and the sail is called the spanker. It was called a lateen in the olden days. Now this is the bowsprit. It is not shown in this sketch, but a sprits'l is set beneath it, so . . . Miss Verity, when can I see you again after to-night?'

Their heads were close together and she glanced up briefly into his intent brown eyes.

'That I couldn't say, Captain Blamey.'

'It is all that I plan for.'

'Oh,' said Verity.

'. . . hrrm! . . . On the foremast, this is the mains'l. Then comes the lower tops'l and then the upper tops'l. This attachment to the bowsprit is called the jackstaff, and – and——'

'What is the jackstaff for?' Verity asked, short of breath.

'It is the – er – Dare I hope that – if I could hope that my interest was in the smallest way returned – If that were possible——'

'I think that is possible, Captain Blamey.'

He touched her fingers for a moment, dumb with emotion. 'Miss Verity, you give me a hope, a prospect which would – which would inspire any man. I feel – I feel—— But before I see your father I must tell you something that only your encouragement would give me strength to venture . . .'

Five people entered the refreshment room, and Verity hastily straightened up, for she saw it was the Warleggans – with Francis and Elizabeth. Elizabeth saw her at once and smiled and waved and came across.

She was wearing a dress of peach-coloured muslin, with a white crepe turban close-fitting about her curls.

'We'd no intention of coming, my dear,' she said in amusement at Verity's surprise. 'How pretty you're looking. How do you do, Captain Blamey.'

'Your servant, ma'am.'

'It was really George's fault,' Elizabeth went on, excited and therefore radiantly beautiful. 'We were supping with him and I believe he found our entertainment difficult.'

'Cruel words from kind lips,' said George Warleggan suavely. 'The fault is with your husband for wishing to dance this barbarous *écossaise*. For my part I don't like the prancing.'

Francis came across to them. His face was slightly flushed with drink, and the effect also with him was a heightening of his good looks. 'We've missed nothing that matters,' he said. 'All the fun's to come. I could not be sedate to-night if all England depended on it.'

'Nor I,' said Elizabeth. She smiled at Captain Blamey. 'I hope our boisterous spirits don't jar on you, sir.'

The sailor took a deep breath. 'Not in the very least, ma'am. I have every reason to be happy myself.'

In the ballroom Ruth Teague had returned and Lady Whitworth had gone.

'So Captain Poldark has left you at last, child!' said Mrs Teague. 'What explanation did he offer you for such conduct?'

'None, Mama,' said Ruth, fanning herself brightly. Her almond eyes carried a fluttered, excited expression.

'Well, it is gratifying to be distinguished by such a genteel man, but there is reason in all things. You should know your manners if he does not. People are talking already.'

'Are they? Oh, dear. I cannot refuse to dance with him; he is most polite and agreeable.'

'No doubt, no doubt. But it is not becoming to make oneself too cheap. And you should think also of your sisters.'

'He has asked me for the next dance after this.'

'What? And what did you say?'

'I promised it for him.'

'Uff!' Mrs Teague shuddered fastidiously, but she was not as displeased as she sounded. 'Well, a promise is a promise; you may dance it now. But you must not go into supper with him and leave Joan to her own devices.'

'He has not asked me.'

'You're very free with your answers, child. I think his attentions must have gone to your head. Perhaps I shall have a word with him after supper.'

'No, no, Mama, you mustn't do that!'

'Well, we shall see,' said Mrs Teague, who really hadn't the slightest intention of discouraging an eligible man. Hers was a token protest to satisfy her sense of what was right and proper, of how she would behave if she had only one daughter and that one with a fortune of ten thousand pounds. With five on the books and no dowry for any of them, it deprived one of scope.

But they need not have concerned themselves. By the time the supper interval came Ross had unaccountably disappeared. In his last dance with Ruth he had been stiff and preoccupied, and she wondered furiously whether in some manner her mother's criticisms had reached his ears.

As soon as the dance was over he left the ballroom and walked out into the mild cloudy night. At the unexpected sight of Elizabeth his make-believe enjoyment had crumbled and fallen away. He wished more than anything to get out of her view. He forgot his obligations as Verity's escort and as a member of Miss Pascoe's party.

There were two or three carriages with footmen outside, and also a sedan chair. Lights from the bow windows of the houses in the square lit up the uneven cobbles and the trees of St Mary's churchyard. He turned in that direction. Elizabeth's beauty struck him afresh. The fact that another man should be in full enjoyment of her was like the torture of damnation. To continue to flirt with a plain little pleasant little schoolgirl was out of the question.

As his hand closed about the cold railings under the trees he fought to overcome his jealousy and pain, as one will to overcome a fainting fit. This time he must destroy it once and for all. Either he must do that or leave the county again. He had his own life to live, his own way to go; there were other women in the world, common clay perhaps, but charming enough with their pretty ways and soft bodies. Either break his infatuation for Elizabeth or remove himself to some part of the country where comparisons could not be made. A plain choice.

He walked on, waving away a beggar who followed him with a tale of poverty and want. He found himself before the Bear Inn. He pushed open the door and went down the three steps into the crowded taproom with its brass-bound barrels piled to the ceiling and its low wooden tables and benches. This night being Easter Monday, the room was very full, and the flickering smoky light of the candles in their iron sconces did not at first show him where a seat was to be found. He took one in a corner and ordered some brandy. The potman touched his forelock and took down a clean glass in honour of his unexpected patron. Ross became aware that at his coming a silence had fallen. His suit and linen were conspicuous in this company of ragged underfed drinkers.

'I'll have no more of such talk in 'ere,' said the bartender uneasily, 'so you'd best get down off of your perch, Jack Tripp.'

'I'll stay where I am,' said a tall thin man, better dressed than most of the others in a tattered suit sizes too big for him.

'Leave 'im stay,' said a fat man in a chair below. 'Even a crow's not denied its chimney pot.'

There was a laugh, for the simile was apt enough.

Conversation broke out again when it became clear that the newcomer was too deeply set in his own thoughts to spare time for other people's. His only sign of life was to motion to the tapster from time to time to refill his glass. Jack Tripp was allowed to stay on his perch.

'It is all very well to say that, friend; but aren't we all men born of women. Does it alter our entry into the world or our exit out of it that we are a corn-factor or a beggar? Talk of it bein' God's devising that some should wallow in riches and others starve is so much clap-trappery. That is of man's devising, mark ee, the devising of the rich merchants and sich-like, to keep them where they be and other folk in chains. Tis fine and pretty to talk religion and bribe the clergy with food and wine——'

'Leave God alone, ' said a voice from the back.

'I've naught to say against God,' croaked Jack Tripp. 'But I don't hold with the God of the corn-factor's choosing. Didn't Christ preach justice for all? Where's justice in starving women and children? The clergy are stuffed wi' food while your womenfolk live on black bread and beech leaves, an' your children shrivel and die. And there's corn in Penryn, friends!'

There was a growl of assent.

A voice spoke in Ross's ear. 'Buy a drink for a lady, will you, me lord? Unlucky to drink alone, y' know. The devil gets in brandy when you sup alone.'

He stared into the bold dark eyes of a woman who had moved her position to sit beside him. She was tall, gaunt, about twenty-four or -five, dressed in a mannish blue riding suit which had once been smart but now was very shabby; it had perhaps been picked up at second or third hand. The stock was dirty and the lace front awry. She had high cheekbones, a wide mouth, bright teeth, wide bold uncompromising eyes. Her black hair had been clumsily dyed copper. For all her mannish attitude and stare there was something feline about her.

Indifferently he motioned to the barman.

'Thanks, me lord,' she said, stretching and yawning. 'Here's to your health. You're looking wisht. Down in the mouth, y' know. Bit of company would do you no harm.'

'Aye, there's corn in Penryn!' said Jack Tripp hoarsely. 'And who be it for? Not for the likes of we. Nay, nay, sell the food abroad: that's the latest notion. They're not concerned wi' keeping us alive. Why is there no work in the mines? Because the tin and copper prices are so low? But why are they so low, friends? Because the merchants and the smelters fix the prices among theirselves to suit theirselves. Let the tinners rot! Why should the merchants care? Same wi' the millers! Same with all!'

Ross shifted on his elbow. These taproom agitators. His audience liked to be talked to in this manner; it gave mouth to grievances they had hardly begun to form.

The woman put her hand on his. He shook it off and finished his brandy.

'Lonely, me lord; that's what ails you. Let me read your palm.' She put out her hand again and turned his up to examine it. 'Ye-es. Ye-es. Bin disappointed in love, that's what it is. A fair woman has been false to you. But there's a dark woman here. Look.' She pointed with a long forefinger. 'See, she's close to you. Right close to you. She'll give you comfort, me lord. Not like these dainty maids who're afraid of a pair of breeches. I like the looks of you, if ye don't mind the expression. I'll wager you could give a woman satisfaction. But beware of some things. Beware o' being over partic'lar yourself, lest these dainty maids betray you into thinking that love's a parlour game. Love's no parlour game, me lord, as you very well know.'

Ross ordered another drink.

'Well, what of poor Betsey Pydar?' Jack Tripp said, shouting to drown the murmur of talk which had broken out. 'What of that, I ask you, friends? What, *you* haven't heard of Widow Pydar? Hounded by the overseers and dying of starvation . . .'

The woman drained her glass at a draught but she did not release his hand.

'I can see a snug little cottage by the river, me lord. Neat and proper as you please. I like the look o' you, me lord. I feel an uncommon taking. I think you're the type of man who knows what's what. I've a talent for reading character, as you can see. A rare judge of a man, I've been told.'

Ross stared at her, and she met his gaze boldly. Although they had only just set eyes on each other, it was as if a tremendous desire for him had flamed up in her. It wasn't all a matter of gold.

'And what did Parson Halse say when he was told?' asked Tripp. 'He said that Betsey Pydar had brought this on herself by disobeying the laws of the country. That's all the sympathy she got from he! He said that the overseers in the wisdom of Providence had sent her back to her own parish and she had only herself to blame. That's your clergy for ee! . . .'

Ross got up, pulled his hand away, put down a coin for the pot-man and threaded his way towards the door.

Outside the night was very dark and a light drizzle was falling. He stood a moment irresolute. As he turned away he heard the woman slip out of the inn.

She caught up with him quickly and walked tall and strong by his side. Then she took his hand again. His impulse was to wrench it away and have done with her importuning. But at the last moment his loneliness and dismay caught up with him like a slow-poisoning fog. What followed the rebuff? What was there for him to follow the rebuff? A return to the dance?

He turned and went with her.

Chapter six

IT WAS FORTUNATE that Verity had arranged to spend the night with Joan Pascoe, for Ross saw no more of the ball. From the cottage of the woman Margaret he rode straight home, reaching Nampara as the first threads of daylight were unpicking the clustered clouds of the night.

This was Tuesday, the day of the Redruth Fair. He stripped off his clothes, went down to the beach and ran out into the surf. The cold boisterous water washed away some of the miasms of the night; it was biting and tonic and impersonal. As he left the water the cliffs at the far end of the beach were losing their darkness and the east sky had brightened to a brilliant cadmium yellow. He dried himself and dressed and woke Jud and they had breakfast with the first sun slanting through the windows.

They came to Redruth just before ten, slid down the steep greasy lane into the town, reached the chapel, crossed the river and climbed the other hill to the fields where the fair was being held. The business of the day was already in progress with the buying and selling of livestock and farm and dairy produce.

It took Ross some time to find what he wanted, for he had no money to throw about, and by the time the various purchases had been made it was afternoon. In the second field every tradesman in the district had put up a stall. The better class and larger tradesmen, with their saddlery and clothing and boots and shoes, clung to the upper part of the field; as the slope increased one came to the gingerbread and sweetmeat stalls, the rope maker, the chair mender, the knife sharpener, the miscellaneous tents offering lanterns and brimstone matches, sealingwax and silver buckles, bracelets of braided hair, secondhand wigs and snuffboxes, bed mats and chamber pots.

It would take Jud some hours to drive home the new oxen, so with time to spare Ross wandered round to see all there was to be seen. From the third field the substantial tradespeople were absent: this was the province of the professional rat catchers, the pedlars, the ha'penny peepshows. One corner of this field belonged to the apothecaries and the herbalists. Men squatted on the ground and shouted before ill-spelt notices advertising their wares, which were the latest and most infallible cures for all the diseases of the flesh. Pectoral drops, Eau de Charm, nervous drops, spirit of benjamin, pomatum, fever powder, jesuit drops. Here you could buy plantain and salad oil, angel water, hemlock for scrofulous tumours, and burdock burs for scurvy.

In the last field, which was the noisiest of all, were the side shows and the hurdy-gurdies, the Lilly-banger stall, where you cast dice for an Easter cake. In some sort of reaction from the bitterness and excesses of last night he found a relief in mingling with his fellow men, in accepting the simplicity of their pleasures. He paid his ha'penny and saw the fattest woman on earth, who, the man next to him was complaining, was not as fat as the one last year. For another ha'penny she offered to take you behind a screen and put your hand on a soft spot; but the man next to him said it was once-bitten-twice-shy, because all she did was put your hand on your own forehead.

He stood for fifteen minutes in a darkened booth watching a company of guise players performing a mime about St George and the Dragon. He paid a ha'penny to see a man who in infancy had had his hands and feet eaten off by a pig and who sketched quite amazingly with a chalk in his mouth. He paid another ha'penny to see a mad woman in a cage tormented by her audience.

After he had seen the sights he sat down at a drinking booth and sipped a glass of rum and water. The words of Jack Tripp the agitator came to him as he watched the people pass by. For the most part they were weakly, stinking, rachitic, pockmarked, in rags – far less well found than the farm animals which were being bought and sold. Was it surprising that the upper classes looked on themselves as a race apart?

Yet the signs he had seen of a new way of life in America made him impatient of these distinctions. Jack Tripp was right. All men were born in the same way: no privilege existed which was not of man's own contriving.

He had chosen the last of the drinking booths, at the extreme end of the ground. The noise and smell here was less overpowering; but just as he was ordering another drink an uproar broke out behind the shop, and a number of people crowded to the corner to see what was on. Some of them began to laugh, as at a free entertainment. The uproar of squeals and barks went on. With a frown he rose to his feet and peered over the heads of the people standing near.

Behind the gin booth was a clearing where earlier some sheep had been quartered. Now it was empty except for a group of ragged boys watching a confused bundle of fur rolling over on the ground. This resolved itself into a cat and a dog, which the boys had tied tail to tail. The two animals were not much different in size, and after a fight, during which neither had the advantage, they now wanted to part company. First the dog pulled and the cat sprawled, spitting; then the cat with difficulty got to her feet and with slow convulsive movements, digging her claws into the earth, dragged the dog backwards.

The spectators roared with laughter. Ross smiled briefly, but it was not really a pretty sight. He was about to sit down when a smaller boy broke away from two others who were holding him and ran towards the animals. He dodged one of the other boys who tried to stop him and reached the creatures, knelt down, and tried to loosen the knotted twine about their tails, ignoring the scratches of the cat. When it was seen what he was about there was a murmur from the crowd who perceived that they were to be robbed of a free entertainment. But this murmur was drowned in a howl of fury from the other boys, who at once rushed in and fell upon the spoil-sport. He tried to put up a fight but soon went under.

Ross reached down for his drink but remained on his feet while he sipped it. A big man as tall as himself moved up and partly obscured the view.

'Sakes alive,' said someone; 'they'll maim the lad, a-kicking of him like that. Tis past a joke, the young varmints.'

'And who's to say them nay?' queried a little merchant with a shade over one eye. 'They're wild as cats. Tis a disgrace to the town the way they roam.'

'Break your windows if you complain,' said another. 'And glad of the excuse. Aunt Mary Treglown, her's got a cottage over to Pool——'

'Ais, I knaw . . .'

Ross finished his drink and ordered another. Then he changed his mind and moved into the crowd.

'God preserve us!' said a housewife suddenly. 'Is it a girl they're bating up? Or I'm mistook. An't any of ye going to stop 'em?'

Ross took his riding crop from his boot and walked into the arena. Three of the urchins saw him coming; two fled, but the third stood his ground with bared teeth. Ross hit him across the face with the whip and the boy shrieked and fled. A stone flew through the air.

There were three other boys, two sitting on the figure while the third kicked it in the back. This last youth did not see the approach of the enemy. Ross hit him on the side of the head and knocked him out. One of the others he lifted by the seat of his breeches and dropped into a neighbouring pool of water. The third fled and left the figure of the spoil-sport lying on its face.

The clothing was certainly that of a boy: a loose shirt and coat, trousers too big and falling loosely below the knee. A round black cap lay in the dust; the dark tousled hair seemed overlong. A stone hit Ross's shoulder.

With the toe of his boot he pushed the figure upon its back. Might be a girl. The child was conscious but too winded to speak; every intake of breath was half a groan.

A number of the townspeople had filtered into the clearing, but as the stones became more frequent they sheered off again.

'Have they hurt you, child?' Ross said.

With a convulsive wriggle she drew up her knees and pulled herself into a sitting position.

'Judas God!' she was at last able to get out. '. . . rot their dirty guts . . .'

The hail of stones was becoming more accurate and two more struck his back. He put his whip away and picked her up; she was no weight at all. As he carried her towards the gin shop he saw that crofters had joined together and were going after the boys with sticks.

He set her down at the end of the trestle table he had recently left. Her head sank forward on the table. Now that the danger from missiles was over people crowded round.

'What did they do to ee, my dear?'

'Scat un in the ribs, did they?'

'She'm fair davered, poor maid.'

'I'd lace 'em . . .'

He ordered two glasses of rum. 'Give the child air,' he said impatiently. 'Who is she and what is her name?'

'Never seed she afore,' said one.

'She do come from Roskear, I bla',' said another.

'I know she,' said a woman, peering. 'She'm Tom Carne's daughter. They d' live over to Illuggan.'

'Where is her father, then?'

'Down mine, I expect.'

'Drink this.' Ross put the glass against the girl's elbow and she picked it up and gulped at it. She was a thin scarecrow of a child of eleven or twelve. Her shirt was dirty and torn; the mop of dark hair hid her face.

'Are you with someone?' Ross asked. 'Where is your mother?'

'She an't got one,' said the woman, breathing stale gin over his shoulder. 'Been in 'er grave these six year.'

'Well, that edn my fault,' said the girl, finding her voice.

'Nor never said twas,' said the woman. 'And what you doing in your brother's clo'es? Young tomrigg! You'll get the strap for this.'

'Go away, woman,' said Ross in irritation at being so much the focus of attention. 'Go away, all of you. Have you nothing better to gape at?' He turned to the girl. 'Is there no one with you? What were you about?'

She sat up. 'Where's Garrick? They was tormentin' him.'

'Garrick?'

'My dog. Where's Garrick? Garrick! Garrick!'

' 'Ere 'e be.' A crofter pushed his way through the others. 'I got un for you. It was no easy job.'

She got to her feet to receive a wriggling black bundle, and collapsed on the seat again with it in her lap. She bent over the puppy to see if it was hurt, getting her hands more bloody than they were. Suddenly she looked up with a wail, eyes blazing amid the dirt and hair.

'Judas God! The dirty nattlings! They've cut'n off his tail!'

'I done that,' the crofter told her composedly. 'Think I was going to get me 'ands tored for a mongrel cur? Besides, twas 'alf off already, and he'll be better placed without it.'

'Finish this,' Ross commanded the girl. 'Then if you can talk, tell me if you feel any bones broke in their handling.' He gave the crofter sixpence, and the crowd, aware that the show was over, began to disperse, though for some time a ring of them remained at a respectful distance, interested in the gentleman.

The dog was an emaciated mongrel puppy of a muddy black with a long thin neck and covered sparsely about the head and body with short black curls. Its parentage was unimaginable.

'Use this,' said Ross, holding out his handkerchief. 'Wipe your arms and see if the scratches go deep.'

She looked up from fingering her body and stared at the linen square doubtfully.

'Twill foul it,' she said.

'So I can see.'

'It mayn't wash out.'

'Do as you're bid and don't argue.'

She used a corner of the kerchief on one bony elbow.

'How did you come here?' he asked.

'Walked.'

'With your father?'

'Fathur's down mine.'

'You came alone?'

'Wi' Garrick.'

'You can't walk back like that. Have you friends here?'

'No.' She stopped suddenly in her perfunctory wiping. 'Judas, I feel some queer.'

'Drink some more of this.'

'No . . . tis that atop of nothin' . . .'

She got up and limped unsteadily to the corner of the gin shop. There, for the diversion and reward of the faithful spectators, she painfully lost the rum she had drunk. Then she fainted, so Ross lifted her back into the stall. When she recovered he took her into the stall next door and gave her a square meal.

II

The shirt she was wearing had old tears in it as well as new; the breeches were of faded brown corduroy; her feet were bare and she had lost the round cap. Her face was pinched and white, and her eyes, a very dark brown, were much too big for it.

'What is your name?' he said.

'Demelza.'

'Your Christian name, though?'

'Please?'

'Your first name.'

'Demelza.'

'A strange name.'

'Mother were called that too.'

'Demelza Carne. Is that it?'

She sighed and nodded, for she was well filled; and the dog under the table grunted with her.

'I come from Nampara. Beyond Sawle. Do you know where that is?'

'Past St Ann's?'

'I am going home now, child. If you cannot walk I'll take you first to Illuggan and leave you there.'

A shadow went across her eyes and she did not speak. He paid what he owed and sent word for his horse to be saddled.

Ten minutes later they were up and away. The girl sat silently astride in front of him. Garrick followed in desultory fashion, now and then dragging his seat in the dust or peering suspiciously round to see what had become of the thing he had sometimes chased and often wagged but now could not locate.

They cut across the moors by a mining track worn deep and hard and pitted by the passage of generations of mules. The countryside hereabout was entirely abandoned to the quest for minerals. All trees, except an occasional ragged pine, had been cut down for timber, every stream was discoloured, patches of cultivated land struggled among acres of mine refuse and mountains of stone. Engine sheds, wooden derricks, wheel stamps, windlasses and horse gins were its adornment. Trenches and adits grew in the back gardens of the tiny cottages and huts; potatoes were hoed and goats grazed among the steam and the refuse. There was no town, scarcely even a hamlet, only a wide and sparse distribution of working people.

It was the first time he had been to Illuggan this way. With the improvement in the pumping engine and the new lodes of tin and copper available, Cornish mining had been going ahead until the slump of the last few years. People had migrated to these fortunate districts where the veins were richest, and the home population had increased rapidly. Now in the growing depression of the early eighties many of the breadwinners were out of work and the doubt arose as to whether the population could be maintained. The danger was not immediate but the spectre was there.

The girl in front of him gave a wriggle.

'Could ee let me down 'ere?' she said.

'You're but halfway to Illuggan yet.'

'I know. I doubt I shall be going 'ome yet awhile.'

'Why not?'

There was no answer.

'Does your father not know you've been out?'

'Yes, but I was lended my brother's shirt and breeches. Fathur says I must go to fair whether or no, so he says I can borrow Luke's Sunday fligs.'

'Well?'

'Well, I ain't got what I went for. And Luke's clothes is all slottery. So I reckon——'

'Why did you not go in your own clothes?'

'Fathur tored 'em last night when he give me a cooting.'

They jogged on for some distance. She turned and peered back to be sure Garrick was following.

'Does your father often beat you?' Ross asked.

'Only when he's bin takin' too much.'

'How often is that?'

'Oh . . . mebbe twice a week. Less when he 'an't got the money.'

There was silence. It was now late afternoon and needed another two hours to dark. She began to fumble with the neck of her shirt and untied the string. 'You can see,' she said. ''E used the strap last night. Pull me shirt back.'

He did so, and it slipped off one shoulder. Her back was marked with weals. On some the skin had been broken and these were partly healed, with dirt smeared on them and lice at the edges. Ross pulled the shirt up again.

'And to-night?'

'Oh, he'd give me a banger to-night. But I'll stay outdoors and not go 'ome till he's below again.'

They rode on.

Ross was not oversensitive to the feelings of animals: it was not in his generation to be so, though he seldom hit one himself; but wanton cruelty to children offended him.

'How old are you?'

'Thirteen . . . sur.'

It was the first time she had sirred him. He might have known that these undersized, half-starved waifs were always older than they looked.

'What work do you do?'

'Looking after the 'ouse and plantin' taties an' feeding the pig.'

'How many brothers and sisters have you?'

'Six brothers.'

'All younger than you?'

''Es-s.' She turned her head and whistled piercingly to Garrick.

'Do you love your father?'

She looked at him in surprise. ''Es-s . . .'

'Why?'

She wriggled. 'Cos it says you must in the Bible.'

'You like living at home?'

'I runned away when I was twelve.'

'And what happened?'

'I was broft back.'

Darkie swerved as a stoat scuttered across the path, and Ross took a firmer grip on the reins.

'If you stay out of your father's way for a time, no doubt he'll forget what you have done wrong.'

She shook her head. 'He'll save un up.'

'Then what is the use of avoiding him?'

She smiled with an odd maturity. ''Twill put un off.'

They reached a break in the track. Ahead lay the way to Illuggan; the right fork would bring him to skirt St Ann's whence he could join the usual lane to Sawle. He reined up the mare.

'I'll get down 'ere,' she said.

He said: 'I need a girl to work in my house. At Nampara, beyond St Ann's. You would get your food and better clothing than you have now. As you are under age I would pay your wages to your father.' He added: 'I want someone strong, for the work is hard.'

She was looking up at him with her eyes wide and a startled expression in them as if he had suggested something wicked. Then the wind blew her hair over them and she blinked.

'The house is at Nampara,' he said. 'But perhaps you do not wish to come.'

She pushed her hair back but said nothing.

'Well then, get down,' he continued with a sense of relief. 'Or I will still take you into Illuggan if you choose.'

'To live at your house?' she said. 'To-night? Yes, please.'

The appeal, of course, was obvious; the immediate appeal of missing a thrashing.

'I want a kitchenmaid,' he said. 'One who can work and scrub, and keep herself clean also. It would be by the year that I should hire you. You would be too far away to run home every week.'

'I don't want to go home ever,' she said.

'It will be necessary to see your father and get his consent. That may be hard to come by.'

'I'm a good scrubber,' she said. 'I can scrub . . . sur.'

Darkie was fidgeting at the continued check.

'We will go and see your father now. If he can be——'

'Not now. Take me with you, please. I can scrub. I'm a good scrubber.'

'There is a law to these things. I must hire you from your father.'

'Fathur don't come up from 'is core till an hour after cockshut. Then he'll go drink afore he do come 'ome.'

Ross wondered if the girl were lying. Impulse had prompted him this far. He needed extra help as much in the house as in the fields, and he disliked the idea of handing this child back to a drunken miner. But neither did he wish to cool his heels in some bug-ridden hovel until dark with naked children crawling over him, then to be confronted by a gin-sodden bully who would refuse his suggestion. Did the child really want to come? A last test.

'About Garrick. I might not be able to keep Garrick.'

There was silence. Watching her closely, he could plainly see the struggle which was going on behind the thin anaemic features. She looked at the dog, then looked up at him and her mouth gave a downward twist.

'Him an' me's friends,' she said.

'Well?'

She did not speak for a time. 'Garrick an' me's done everything together. I couldn't leave 'im to starve.'

'Well?'

'I couldn't, mister. I couldn't . . .'

In distress she began to slip off the mare.

He suddenly found that the thing he had set out to prove had proved something quite different. Human nature had outmanoeuvred him. For if she would not desert a friend, neither could he.

III

They overtook Jud soon after passing the gibbet at Bargus, where four roads and four parishes met. The oxen were tired of their long trek and Jud was tired of driving them. He could not ride comfortably on blind Ramoth because four large baskets crammed with live chickens were slung across the saddle. Also he was deeply annoyed at having to leave the fair before he was drunk, a thing that had never happened to him since he was ten.

He looked round sourly at the approach of another horse and then pulled Ramoth off the track to let them pass. The oxen, being strung out in single file behind, followed suit quietly enough.

Ross explained the presence of the urchin in three sentences and left Jud to work it out for himself.

Jud raised his hairless eyebrows.

'Tes all very well to play uppity-snap with a lame 'orse,' he said in a grumbling voice. 'But picking up brats is another matter. Picking up brats is all wrong. Picking up brats will get ee in trouble wi' the law.'

'A fine one you are to talk of the law,' Ross said.

Jud had not been looking where he was going, and Ramoth stumbled in a rut.

Jud said a wicked word. 'Rot 'im, there 'e go again. 'Ow d'you expect for a man for to ride a blind 'orse. 'Pon my Sam, 'ow d'you expect for a 'orse for to see where he's going when he can't see nothin'. Tedn't in the nature o' things. Tedn't 'orse nature.'

'I've always found him very sure,' Ross said. 'Use your own eyes, man. He's uncommonly sensitive to the least touch. Don't force him to hurry, that's the secret.'

'Force 'im to 'urry! I should be forcin' meself over 'is 'ead into the nearest ditch if I forced 'im to go fasterer than a bullhorn leaving 'is slime twixt one stone and the next. Tedn't safe. One slip one tumble, that's all; over you go, over 'is ears, fall on your nuddick, and *phit!* ye're dead.'

Ross touched Darkie and they moved on.

'And a dirty bitch of a mongrel.' Jud's scandalized voice followed them as he caught sight of their escort. 'Lord Almighty, tes fit to duff you, we'll be adopting a blathering poorhouse next.'

Garrick lifted a whiskery eye at him and trotted past. There had been talk concerning himself, he felt, at the fork roads, but the matter had been amicably settled.

On one point Ross was decided: there should be no qualifying of his position in the lice and bug battle. Six months ago the house, and particularly Prudie, had been alive with most of the things that crawl. He was not fussy but he had put his foot down over Prudie's condition. Finally the threat to hold her under the pump and give her a bath himself had had results, and to-day the house was almost free – and even Prudie herself except for the home-grown colonies in her lank black hair. To bring the child into the house in her present state would knock the props away from the position he had taken up. Therefore both she and the dog must be given a bath and fresh clothes found for her before she entered the house. For this duty Prudie herself would be useful.

They reached Nampara at sunset – a good half hour ahead of Jud, he reckoned – and Jim Carter came running out to take Darkie. The boy's health and physique had improved a lot during the winter. His dark Spanish eyes widened at sight of the cargo his master brought. But in a manner refreshingly different from the Paynters he said no word and prepared to lead the horse away. The girl stared at him with eyes already wide with interest, then turned again and gazed at the house, at the valley and the apple trees and the stream, at the sunset, which was a single vermilion scar above the dark of the sea.

'Where's Prudie?' said Ross. 'Tell her I want her.'

'She's not here, sur,' said Jim Carter. 'She left so soon as you left. She did say she was walking over to Marasanvose to see 'er cousin.'

Ross swore under his breath. The Paynters had a unique gift for not being there when wanted.

'Leave Darkie,' he said. 'I'll attend to her. Jud is two miles away with some oxen I've bought. Go now and help him with them. If you hurry you will meet him before he reaches the Mellingey ford.'

The boy dropped the reins, glanced again at the girl, then went off at a rapid walk up the valley.

Ross stared a moment at the piece of flotsam he had brought home and hoped to salvage. She was standing there in her ragged shirt and three-quarter length breeches, her matted hair over her face and the dirty half-starved puppy at her feet. She stood with one toe turned in and both hands loosely behind her back, staring across at the library. He hardened his heart. To-morrow would not do.

'Come this way,' he said.

She followed him, and the dog followed her, to the back of the house where between the still-room and the first barn the pump was set.

'Now,' he said, 'if you are to work for me you must first be clean. D'you understand that?'

'Yes . . . sur.'

'I cannot allow anyone dirty into the house. No one works for me if they are not clean and don't wash. So take off your clothing and stand under the pump. I will work the pump for you.'

'Yes . . . sur.' She obediently began to untie the string at the neck of her shirt. This done, she stopped and looked slowly up at him.

'And don't put those things on again,' he said. 'I'll find you something clean.'

'P'r'aps,' she said, 'I could work the 'andle meself.'

'And stand under at the same time?' he said brusquely. 'Nonsense. And hurry. I have not all evening to waste over you.' He went to the pump handle and gave it a preliminary jerk.

She looked at him earnestly for a moment, then began to wiggle out of her shirt. This done, a faint pink tinge was visible under the dirt on her face. Then she slipped out of her breeches and jumped beneath the pump.

He worked the handle with vigour. This first rinsing would not get rid of everything but would at least be a beginning. It would leave his position uncompromised. She had an emaciated little body, on which womanhood had only just begun to fashion its design. As well as the marks of her thrashings he could see blue bruises on her back and ribs where the boys had kicked her this afternoon. Fortunately, like her, they had been barefoot.

She had never had such a washing before. She gasped and choked as the water poured in spurts and volumes upon her head, coursed over her body and ran away to the draining trough. Garrick yelped but refused to move, so took a good deal of the water at secondhand.

At length, fearing he would drown her, he stopped, and while the stream of water thinned to a trickle he went into the still-room and picked up the first cloth he could find.

'Dry yourself on this,' he said. 'I will fetch you something to put on.'

As he re-entered the house he wondered what that something was to be. Prudie's things, even if they were clean enough, would smother the child like a tent. Jim Carter would have been the nearest choice for size if he had owned any other cloths but those he was wearing.

Ross went up to his own room and ransacked the drawers, cursing himself for never thinking more than one move ahead. One could not keep the child shivering there in the yard for ever. Finally he picked out a Holland shirt of his own, a girdle, and a short morning gown of his father's.

When he went out he found her trying to cover herself with the cloth he had given her, while her hair still lay in wet black streaks on her face and shoulders. He did not give her the things at once but beckoned her to follow him into the kitchen, where there was a fire. Having just succeeded in shutting Garrick out of the house, he poked up the fire and told her to stand in front of it until she was dry and to put on the makeshift garments in what manner she chose. She blinked at him wetly, then looked away and nodded to show she understood.

He went out again to unsaddle Darkie.

Chapter seven

DEMELZA CARNE SPENT the night in the great box bed where Joshua Poldark had passed the last few months of his life. There was no other room where she could immediately go; later she could be put in the bedroom between the linen cupboard and the Paynters' room, but at present it was full of lumber.

To her, who had slept all her life on straw, with sacks for covering, in a tiny crowded cottage, this room and this bed were of unthought luxury and unimagined size. The bed itself was almost as big as the room she and four brothers slept in. When Prudie, grumbling and flopping, showed her where she had to spend the night she guessed that three or four other servants would come in later to share the bed, and when no one came and it seemed she was to be left alone, a long time passed before she could bring herself to try it.

She was not a child who looked far ahead or reasoned deep; the ways of her life had given her no excuse to do either. With a cottage full of babies she had had no time at all to sit and think, scarcely any even to work and think; and what was the good of looking for to-morrow when to-day filled all your time and all your energy and sometimes all your fears? So that in this sudden turn in her fortunes her instinct had been to accept it for what it was, gladly enough but as philosophically as she had taken the fight at the fair.

It was only this sudden luxury which scared her. The drenching under the pump had been unexpected, but its roughness and lack of concern for her feelings had run true to type; it fell in with her general experience. Had she then been given a couple of sacks and told to sleep in the stables she would have obeyed and felt there was nothing amiss. But this development was too much like the stories Old Meggy the Sumpman's mother used to tell her: it had some of the frightening, nightmare temper of those and some of the glitter of her mother's fairy tales, in which everyone slept in satin sheets and ate off gold platters. Her imagination could gladly accept it in a story, but her knowledge of life could not accept it in reality. Her strange garments had been a beginning; they fitted nowhere and hung in ridiculous lavender-scented folds over her thin body; they were agreeable but suspect, as this bedroom was agreeable but suspect.

When at length she found the courage to try the bed, she did so with strange sensations: she was afraid that the big wooden doors of the bed would swing quietly to and shut her up for ever; she was afraid that the man who had brought her here, for all his air of niceness and kind eyes, had some Evil Design, that as soon as she went off to sleep he would creep into the room with a knife or a whip or – or merely creep into the room. From these fears her attention would be turned by the pattern of the tattered silk hangings on the bed, by the gold tassel of the bellpull, by the feel of the clean sheets under her fingers, by the beautiful curves of the bronze candlestick on the three-legged wicker table by the bed – from which candlestick guttered the single light standing between her and darkness, a light which by now should have been put out, and which would very soon go out of its own accord.

She stared into the dark chasm of the fireplace and began to fancy that something horrible might at any moment come down the chimney and plop into the hearth. She looked at the pair of old bellows, at the two strange painted ornaments on the mantelpiece (one looked like the Virgin Mary), and at the engraved cutlass over the door. In the dark corner beside the bed was a portrait, but she had not looked at it while the Fat Lady was in the room, and since the Fat Lady had left she had not dared to move out of the circle of the candlelight.

Time passed, and the candle was flaring up before it went out, sending smoky curls like wisps of an old woman's hair spiralling towards the beams. There were two doors, and that which led she-didn't-know-where held a special danger, although it was tight shut every time she craned to look.

Something scratched at the window. She listened with her heart thumping. Then suddenly she caught something familiar in the noise, and she jumped from the bed and flew to the window. Minutes passed before she saw how to open it. Then when a six-inch gap had been slowly levered at the bottom a wriggling black thing squirmed into the room, and she had her arms round Garrick's neck, half strangling him from love and anxiety that he should not bark.

Garrick's nearness changed the whole picture for her. With his long rough tongue he licked her cheeks and ears while she carried him towards the bed.

The flame of the candle gave a preliminary lurch and then straightened for a few seconds more. Hurriedly she pulled across the hearthrug and another rug from near the door, and with these made on the floor an improvised bed for herself and the puppy. Then as the light slowly died from the room and one object after another faded into the shadows she lay down and curled herself up with the dog and felt his own excited struggles relax as she whispered endearments in his ear.

Darkness came and silence fell and Demelza and Garrick slept.

II

Ross slept heavily, which was not surprising, as he had had no sleep the night before, but a number of odd and vivid dreams came to disturb him. He woke early and lay in bed for a time looking out at the bright windy morning and thinking over the events of the past two days. The ball and the gaunt wild Margaret: the aristocratic commonplace and the disreputable commonplace. But neither had been quite ordinary for him. Elizabeth had seen to that. Margaret had seen to that.

Then the fair and its outcome. It occurred to him this morning that his adoption of yesterday might have troublesome results. His knowledge of the law was vague and his attitude towards it faintly contemptuous, but he had an idea that one could not take a girl of thirteen away from her home without so much as a by-your-leave to her father.

He thought he would ride over and see his uncle. Charles had been a magistrate for over thirty years, so there was a chance he would have some views worth hearing. Ross also gave more than a thought to the violent court being paid to Verity by Captain Andrew Blamey. After the first, they had danced every dance together up to the time of his leaving the ballroom. Everyone would soon be talking, and he wondered why Blamey had not been to see Charles before now. The sun was high when he rode over to Trenwith. The air was exhilaratingly fresh and alive this morning, and all the colouring of the countryside was in washed, pastel shades. Even the desolate area round Grambler was not unsightly after the greater desolation he had seen yesterday. Darkie, as susceptible as anyone to the moods of the weather, tossed her head and pranced and without urging held to a fine lively trot even up the hill to the woods of Trenwith.

As he came in sight of the house he reflected again upon the inevitable failure of his father to build anything to rival the mellow Tudor comeliness of this old home. The building was not large, but gave an impression of space and of having been put up when money was free and labour cheap. It was built in a square about a compact courtyard, with the big hall and its gallery and stairs facing you as you entered, with the large parlour and library leading off on the right and the withdrawing room and small winter parlour on the left, the kitchens and buttery being behind and forming the fourth side of the square. The house was in good repair for its age, having been built by Jeffrey Trenwith in 1509.

No servant came out to take the mare, so he tethered her to a tree and knocked on the door with his riding whip. This was the official entrance, but the family more often used the smaller door at the side, and he was about to walk round to that when Mrs Tabb appeared and bobbed respectfully.

'Morning, sur. Mister Francis you're wanting, is it?'

'No, my uncle.'

'Well, sur, I'm sorry but they're both over to Grambler. Cap'n Henshawe come over this morning and they both walked back wi' him. Will ee come in, sur, while I ast how long they'll be?'

He entered the hall and Mrs Tabb hurried off to find Verity. He stood a minute staring at the patterns made by the sun as it fell through the long narrow mullioned windows, then he walked towards the stairs where he had stood on the day of Elizabeth's wedding. No crowd of bedecked people to-day, no raucous cock-fight, no chattering clergymen; he preferred it this way. The long table was empty except for its row of candlesticks. On the table in the alcove beside the stairs stood the big brass-bound family Bible, now seldom used except by Aunt Agatha in her pious moments. He wondered if Francis's marriage had yet been entered there, as all the others had for two hundred years.

He stared up at the row of portraits on the wall beside the stairs. There were others about the hall and many more in the gallery above. He would have had difficulty in picking out more than a dozen by name; most of the early ones were Trenwiths, and even some later portraits were unnamed and undated. A small faded painting in the alcove with the Bible, where it should not get too much light, was that of the founder of the male side of the family, one Robert d'Arqué, who had come to England in 1572. The oil paint had cracked and little was to be distinguished except the narrow ascetic face, the long nose, and the hunched shoulder. There was then discreet silence for three generations until one came to an attractive painting by Kneller of Anna-Maria Trenwith and another by the same artist of Charles Vivian Raffe Poldarque, whom she had married in 1696. Anna-Maria was the beauty of the collection, with large dark blue eyes and fine red-gold hair.

Well, Elizabeth would be a worthy addition, would grace the company if someone could be found to do justice to her. Opie might be too fond of the dark pigments . . .

He heard a door shut and a footstep. He turned, expecting Verity, and found Elizabeth.

'Good morning, Ross,' she smiled. 'Verity is in Sawle. She always goes on a Wednesday morning. Francis and his father are at the mine. Aunt Agatha is in bed with the gout.'

'Oh yes,' he said woodenly. 'I had forgotten. No matter.'

'I am in the parlour,' she said, 'if you would care to keep me company a few minutes.'

He followed her slowly towards the parlour door; they entered and she sat down at the spinning wheel but did not resume what she had been doing.

She smiled again. 'We see so little of you. Tell me how you enjoyed the ball.'

He took a seat and looked at her. She was pale this morning, and her simple dress of striped dimity emphasized her youth. She was a little girl with all the appeal of a woman. Beautiful and fragile and composed, a married woman. A black desire rose in him to smash the composure. He subdued it.

'We were so pleased that you were there,' she went on. 'But even then you danced so little that we hardly saw you.'

'I had other business.'

'We had no intention of being there,' she said, a little put out by the grimness of his tone. 'It was quite on impulse that we went.'

'What time will Francis and Charles be back?' he asked.

'Not yet, I'm afraid. Did you see how George Warleggan enjoyed the *écossaise*? He had sworn all along that nothing would persuade him to attempt it.'

'I don't remember the pleasure.'

'Did you wish to see Francis on something of importance?'

'Not Francis – my uncle. No. It can wait.'

There was silence.

'Verity said you were going to Redruth Fair yesterday. Did you get all the stock you wanted?'

'Some of it. It was on a question of unexpected stock that I wished to see my uncle.'

She looked down at the spinning wheel. 'Ross,' she said in a low voice.

'My coming here upsets you.'

She did not move.

'I'll meet them on the way back,' he said, rising.

She did not answer. Then she looked up and her eyes were heavy with tears. She picked up the woollen thread she had been spinning and the tears dropped on her hands.

He sat down again with a sensation as if he was falling off a cliff. He had not seen her cry before.

Talking to save himself, he said: 'At the fair yesterday – I picked up a girl, a child; she had been ill treated by her father. I needed someone to help Prudie in the house; she was afraid to go home; I brought her back to Nampara. I shall keep her as a kitchenmaid. I don't know the law of the matter. Elizabeth, why are you crying?'

She said: 'How old is the girl?'

'Thirteen. I——'

'I should send her back. It would be safer even if you had her father's permission. You know how hard people are judged.'

'I shall not come here again,' Ross said. 'I upset you – to no purpose.'

She said: 'It's not your *coming*——'

'What am I to think, then?'

'It only hurts me to feel that you hate me.'

He twisted his riding crop round and round. 'You know I don't hate you.

Good God, you should know that . . .'

She broke the thread.

'Since I met you,' he said, 'I've had no eyes and no thought for any other girl. When I was away nothing mattered about my coming back but this. If there was one thing I was sure of, it wasn't what I'd been taught by anyone else to believe, not what I learned from other people was the truth, but the truth that I felt in myself – about you.'

'Don't say any more.' She had gone very white. But for once her frailness did not stop him. It had to come out now.

'It isn't very pretty to have been made a fool of by one's own feelings,' he said. 'To take childish promises and build a – a castle out of them. And yet – even now sometimes I can't believe that all the things we said to each other were so trivial or so immature. Are you sure you felt so little for me as you pretend? D'you remember that day in your father's garden when you slipped away from them and met me in the summerhouse and let your head lie on my shoulder? That day you said——'

'You forget yourself,' she whispered, forcing the words out.

'Oh no I don't. I remember you.'

All the conflicting feeling inside her suddenly found an outlet. The mixed motives for asking him in; the liking, the affection, the feminine curiosity, the piqued pride: they suddenly merged into indignation – to keep out something stronger. She was as much alarmed at her own feelings as indignant with him; but the situation had to be saved somehow.

She said: 'I was wrong to ask you to stay. It was because I wanted your friendship, nothing more.'

'I think you must have your feelings under a very good control. You turn them about and face them the way you want them to be. I wish I could do that. What's the secret?'

Trembling, she left the spinning wheel and went to the door.

'I'm married,' she said. 'It isn't fair to Francis to speak as you – as we are doing. I'd hoped that we could still be good neighbours – and good friends. We live so close – could help each other. But you can forget nothing and forgive nothing. Perhaps I'm expecting too much . . . I don't know. But, Ross, ours was a boy-and-girl attachment. I was very fond of you – and still am. But you went away and I met Francis, and with Francis it was different. I *loved* him. I'd grown up. We were not children but grown people. Then came the word that you were dead. . . . When you came back I was so happy; and so very sorry that I'd not been able to – to keep faith with you. If there'd been any way of making it up to you I'd gladly have done it. I wished that we still should be close friends, and thought . . . Until today I thought that we could. But after this——'

'After this it's better that we shouldn't be.'

He came up to the door and put his hand on it. Her eyes were dry enough now and exceptionally dark.

'For some time,' she said, 'this is good-bye.'

'It's good-bye.' He bent and kissed her hand. She shrank from his touch as if he was unclean. He thought he had become repulsive to her.

She went with him to the front door, where Darkie whinnied at the sight of him.

'Try to understand,' Elizabeth said. 'I love Francis and married him. If you could forget me it would be better. There's no more I can say than that.'

He mounted the mare and looked down at her.

'Yes,' he agreed. 'There's no more to say.'

He saluted and rode away, leaving her standing in the dark of the doorway.

Chapter eight

WELL, HE TOLD himself, that was over. The subject was closed. If that queer perverted pleasure which came from striking with his barbed tongue at her composure – if that were satisfaction, then he had found some in the interview.

But all he felt was an ashen desolation, an emptiness, a contempt for himself. He had behaved badly. It was so easy to play the jilted lover, the bitter and sarcastic boor.

And even if he had upset her by his attack, yet her defence had more than levelled the score. Indeed, their positions being what they were, she could in a single sentence strike more surely at him than he at her with all the ingenuity his hurt could devise.

He was past Grambler and nearly home before he realized he had not seen either Charles or Verity, and the two questions he had gone to Trenwith to ask remained unanswered. He had not the heart to turn back.

He rode down the valley, too full of a deadly inertia of spirit to find satisfaction in the sight of his land, which was at last beginning to show signs of the attention it was receiving. On the skyline near Wheal Grace he could see Jud and the boy Carter busy with the six yoked oxen. At present they were not used to working as a team, but in a week or so a child would be able to drive them.

At the door of Nampara he climbed wearily down from his horse and stared at Prudie, who was waiting for him.

'Well, what is it?' he said.

'Thur's three men to see ee. They stank into the 'ouse without so much as a by-your-leave. They're in the parlour.'

Uninterested, Ross nodded and entered the living-room. Three working-men were standing there, big and square-shouldered and stolid. From their clothes he could tell they were miners.

'Mister Poldark?' The eldest spoke. There was no seemly deference in his tone. He was about thirty-five, a powerfully built deep-chested man with bloodshot eyes and a heavy beard.

'What can I do for you?' Ross asked impatiently. He was in no mood to receive a delegation.

'Name of Carne,' said the man. 'Tom Carne. These my two brothers.'

'Well?' said Ross. And then after he had spoken, the name stirred in his memory. So the matter was to resolve itself without Charles's advice.

'I hear tell you've gotten my dattur.'

'Who told you that?'

'The Widow Richards said you took her 'ome.'

'I don't know the woman.'

Carne shifted restlessly and blinked his eyes. He had no intention of being sidetracked.

'Where's my dattur?' he said grimly.

'They've searched the 'ouse,' came from Prudie at the door.

'Hold your noise, woman,' said Carne.

'By what right do you come here and talk to my servant like that?' Ross asked with malignant politeness.

'Right, by God! You've slocked my dattur. You 'ticed her away. Where is she?'

'I have no idea.'

Carne thrust out his bottom lip. 'Then you'd best find out.'

'Aye!' said one of the brothers.

'So that you may take her home and beat her?'

'I do what I choose wi' me own,' said Carne.

'Her back is already inflamed.'

'What right ha' you to be seein' her back! I'll have the law on you!'

'The law says a girl may choose her own home when she is fourteen.'

'She's not fourteen.'

'Can you prove it?'

Carne tightened his belt. 'Look 'ere, man; tedn't fur me to prove nothing. She's my dattur, and she'll not go to be plaything to a rake-helly dandy, not now, nor when she's forty, see?'

'Even that,' said Ross, 'might be better than caring for your pigsty.'

Carne glanced at his brothers.

'He ain't going to give 'er up.'

'We can make un,' said the second brother, a man of about thirty with a pockmarked face.

'I'll go fetch Jud,' said Prudie from the door, and went out flapping in her slippers.

'Well, mister,' said Carne. 'What's it to be?'

'So that's why you brought your family,' said Ross. 'Without the spunk to do a job yourself.'

'I could 'a brought two 'undred men, mister.' Carne thrust his face forward. 'We don't 'old wi' cradle thiefs down Illuggan way. Scat un up, boys.'

Immediately the other two turned; one kicked over a chair, the other upended the table on which were some cups and plates. Carne picked up a candlestick and dashed it on the floor.

Ross walked across the room and took down from the wall one of a pair of French duelling pistols. This he began to prime.

'I'll shoot the next man who touches furniture in this room,' he said.

There was a moment's pause. The three men stopped, plainly thwarted.

'Where's my dattur?' shouted Carne.

Ross sat on the arm of a chair. 'Get off my land before I have you committed for trespass.'

'We'd best go, Tom,' said the youngest brother. 'We can come back wi' the others.'

'Tes my quarrel.' Carne plucked at his beard and stared obliquely at his opponent. 'Will ye buy the girl?'

'What d'you want for her?'

Carne considered. 'Fifty guineas.'

'Fifty guineas, by God!' shouted Ross. 'I should want all seven of your brats for that.'

'Then what'll you give me for 'er?'

'A guinea a year so long as she stays with me.'

Carne spat on the floor.

Ross stared at the spittle. 'A thrashing, then, if that's what you want.'

Carne sneered. 'Tes easy to promise from behind a gun.'

'It is easy to threaten when it's three to one.'

'Nay, they'll not interfere if I tell 'em no.'

'I prefer to wait until my men arrive.'

'Aye, I thoft you would. Come us on, boys.'

'Stay,' said Ross. 'It would give me pleasure to wring your neck. Take off your coat, you bastard.'

Carne peered at him narrowly, as if to decide whether he was in earnest. 'Put down your gun, then.'

Ross laid it on the drawers. Carne showed his gums in a grin of satisfaction. He turned on his brothers with a growl.

'Keep out o' this, see? Tes my affair. I'll finish him.'

Ross took off his coat and waistcoat, pulled off his neckerchief and waited. This, he realized, was just what he wanted this morning; he wanted it more than anything in life.

The man came at him, and at once by his moves it was plain that he was an expert wrestler. He sidled up, snatched Ross's right hand and tried to trip him. Ross hit him in the chest and stepped aside. Keep your temper; size him up first.

'I don't love you,' Elizabeth had said; well, that was straight; discarded like a rusty ornament; thrown aside; women; now badgered in your own parlour by a damned insolent red-eyed bully; keep your temper. He was coming again and taking the same grip, this time swiftly with his head under Ross's arm: the other arm was round Ross's leg and he was lifting. Famous throw. Fling your whole weight back: just in time; side-slip and push his head up with a snap. Good, that was good; break his damned neck. The hold slipped, tightened again; they both fell to the floor with a clatter. Carne tried to get his knee into Ross's stomach. Knuckles on his face; twice; free now; roll over and on your feet.

The second brother, breathing heavily, pulled the overturned table out of the way. Fight him afterwards. And the third. Carne on his feet like a cat grasped at the collar of Ross's shirt.

The stuff held: they stumbled back against a tall cupboard which rocked dangerously. Good Irish cloth was bad now. Mooning about an assembly ball like a lovesick calf; going off bleating at the sight of his mistress. Seeking the squalid . . . Stuff would not tear. Hand up and take the man's wrist. Left elbow violently down on Carne's forearm. The grip broke, a grunt of pain. Ross took a hold on the man's side: the other arm gripped his own right to increase the strength of it. Butted his head low. Carne tried to jab with his own right elbow, but they were too close together. In time the miner kicked with his boots, but all the same he was swung off the ground and flung three feet against the panelled wall of the room. Seeking the squalid he had found the squalid: drink and whores. God, what a solution! This was a better. Carne was on his feet again and rushed. Two full punches did not stop him: he tackled Ross about the waist.

'Now ye've got un!' shouted the second brother.

Man's greatest strength was in his arms. He did not try to throw now, but ever tightened his hug and bent Ross back. He had injured a number of men this way. Ross grinned with pain, but his back was strong; after a moment he bent no further at the waist but at the knees, hands on Carne's chin, toes just off the ground – as if kneeling on Carne's thighs. Solid straining. Black spots danced across the walls; Carne lost his balance and they again crashed to the floor. But the grip did not relax. Letting blood of this drunken bully; thrashing his own child till her back bled; spots and blood; he'd get his lesson; break the swine; break him. Ross convulsively jerked his knees up; thrust sideways; was free. On his feet first: as Carne got up he swung on him with the full weight of his body to the side of the jaw. Carne went staggering back and collapsed into the fireplace amid a clatter of irons and kindling logs. A little slower getting up this time.

Ross spat redly on the floor. 'Come, man, you're not beat yet.'

'Beat!' said Carne. 'By a simpering young sucking bottle wi' a fancy mark on his face. Beat, did ye say?'

II

'All right,' growled Jud. 'I can't walk no fasterer. An' what's to do when we git there? Tes only three agin three, then. An' one of us is a slit of a boy, as thin as a stalk o' wheat an' delicut as a lily.'

'Here, leave off,' said Jim. 'I'll take my chance.'

'Ye don't think to count me, an?' said Prudie, rubbing her big red nose. 'Thur's no man born o' woman I can't deal with if I've the mind. Puffed up pirouettes, that's what men are. Hit 'em acrost the 'ead wi' a soup ladle, an' what happens? They crawl away as if you'd 'urt 'em.'

'I'll run on,' said Jim Carter. He was carrying a leather whip, and he broke into a trot to take him down the hill.

'Whur's the brat?' Jud asked his wife.

'Dunno. They searched the 'ouse afore Cap'n Ross come home. A wonder to me ye didn't see 'em and come down. And I wonder ye didn't 'ear me just now when I was shouting. 'Oarse, I am.'

'Can't be every place at once,' said Jud, changing shoulders with his long pitchfork. 'Tedn't to be expected of mortal man. If there was forty-six Jud Paynters poddlin' about the farm, then mebbe one of 'em would be in the right place to suit you. But as there's only one, Lord be thanked——'

'Amen,' said Prudie.

'All right, all right. Then ye can't expect 'im to be within earshot every time you start cryin' out.'

'No, but I don't expect 'im to be deaf on purpose, when I'm only one field away. The knees of your britches was all I seen, but I knew twas you by the patches on 'em and by the factory chimney puffin' smoke hard by.'

They saw Jim Carter emerge from among the apple trees and run across the garden to the house. They saw him reach it and enter.

Prudie lost one of her flapping slippers and had to stop to retrieve it. It was Jud's turn to grumble. They reached the plantation of apple trees, but before they were through it they met Jim Carter returning.

''Tis all right. They're . . . fighting fair. . . 'Tis a proper job to watch . . .'

'What?' snapped Jud. 'Wrastling? 'Ere, 'ave we missed it?'

He dropped his pitchfork, broke into a run and reached the house ahead of the other two. The parlour was in ruin, but the best of the struggle was over. Ross was trying to get Tom Carne out through the door, and Carne, though too spent to do further harm, was yet fighting fanatically to save the ignominy of being thrown out. He was clinging partly to Ross and partly to the jamb with a wicked, mulish will not to admit himself beaten.

Ross caught sight of his servant and showed his teeth. 'Open the window, Jud . . .'

Jud moved to obey, but the youngest brother instantly stepped in his path.

'No, ye don't. Fair's fair. Leave 'em be.'

With the respite Carne abruptly showed more fight again and took a wild grip of Ross's throat. Ross loosed his own hold and hit the man twice more. The miner's hands relaxed and Ross swung him round, grasped him by the scruff of the neck and below the seat of the breeches. Then he half ran,

half carried him through the door, across the hall, and out through the
farther door, knocking Prudie aside as she panted upon the scene. The
brothers waited uneasily, and Jud grinned at them knowingly.

There was a splash, and after a few moments Ross came back gasping
and wiping the blood from the cut on his cheek.

'He will cool there. Now then.' He glared at the other two. 'Which of
you next?'

Neither of them moved.

'Jud.'

'Yes, sur.'

'Show these gentlemen off my property. Then come back and help
Prudie to clear up this mess.'

'Yes, sur.'

The second brother relaxed his tense attitude slowly and began to twist
his cap. He seemed to be trying to say something.

'Well,' he got out at last. 'Brother's in the right, mister, and you be in the
wrong. That's for sartin. But for all that, twas a handsome fight. Best fight
ever I saw outside of a ring.'

'Damme,' said the youngest, spitting. 'Or inside of one. Many's the time
'e's laced me. I never thought to see 'im beat. Thank ee, mister.'

They went out.

Ross's body was beginning to ache with the crushing and straining it had
had. His knuckles were badly cut and he had sprained two fingers. Yet his
general feeling was one of vigorous, exhausted satisfaction, as if the fight
had drained ugly humours out of him. He had been blooded, as a physician
blooded a man with fever.

'Aw, my dear!' said Prudie, coming in. 'Aw! I'll get ee rags and some
turpletine.'

'None of your doctoring,' he said. 'Doctor the furniture. Can you repair
this chair? And here's some plates been broke. Where is the child, Prudie?
You may tell her to come out now.'

'Gracious knows where she's to. She seed her fadder a-coming and
scuddled to me all of a brash. I have a mind she's somewhere in the house
for all their searchings.'

She went to the door. 'Tes all clear now, mite! Yer fadder's gone. We've
drove un off. Come out, wherever you be!'

Silence.

The cut on his cheek had almost stopped bleeding. He put on his
waistcoat and coat again over his torn and sweaty shirt, stuffed the
neckerchief in a pocket. He would take a drink, and then when Jud came
back to confirm that they were gone he would go down and bathe in the
sea. The salt would see that no harm came of the scratches and strains.

He went to the big cupboard which had rocked so perilously during the
fight and poured himself a stiff glass of brandy. He drank it off at a

draught, and as his head went back his eyes met those of Demelza Carne, very dark and distended, staring at him from the top shelf of the cupboard.

He let out a roar of laughter that brought Prudie hurrying back into the room.

Chapter nine

THAT NIGHT ABOUT nine o'clock Jim Carter came back from visiting Jinny Martin. There had been some friendship between them before he came to work here, but it had ripened quickly during the winter.

He would normally have gone straight to his stable loft to sleep until dawn, but he came to the house and insisted on seeing Ross. Jud, already in the know, followed him unbidden into the parlour.

'It's the Illuggan miners,' the boy said without preliminary. 'Zacky Martin's heard tell from Will Nanfan that they're a-coming to-night to pay you back for stealing Tom Carne's girl.'

Ross put down his glass but kept a finger in his book.

'Well, if they come, we can deal with them.'

'I aren't so sartin 'bout that,' said Jud. 'When they're in ones an' twos ye can deal wi' 'em as we dealt wi' 'em to-day, but when they're in 'undreds they're like a great roarin' dragon. Get acrost of 'em and they'll tear ee to spreads as easy as scratch.'

Ross considered. Shorn of its rhetoric, there was some truth in what Jud said. Law and order stood aside when a mob of miners ran amok. But it was unlikely that they would walk all this way on so small a matter. Unless they had been drinking. It was Easter week.

'How many guns have we in the house?'

'Three, I reckon.'

'One should be enough. See that they're cleaned and ready. There's nothing more to do beyond that.'

They left him, and he heard them whispering their dissatisfaction outside the door. Well, what else *was* there to do? He had not seen that his casual adoption of a child for a kitchen wench would produce such results, but it was done now and all hell should crackle before he retracted. Two years abroad had led him to forget the parochial prejudices of his own people. To the tinners and small holders of the county someone from two or three miles away was a foreigner. To take a child from her home to a house ten miles away, a *girl* and under age, however gladly she might come, was enough to excite every form of passion and prejudice. He had given way to a humane impulse and was called an abductor. Well, let the dogs yap.

He pulled the bell for Prudie. She shuffled in ponderously.

'Go to bed, Prudie, and see that the girl goes also. And tell Jud that I want him.'

'He's just went out, just this minute. Went off wi' Jim Carter, the pair of 'em, he did.'

'Never mind, then.' He would soon be back, having probably gone no farther than to light the boy to his loft. Ross got up and went for his own gun. It was a French flintlock breechloader, one his father had bought in Cherbourg ten years ago, and it showed a greater reliability and accuracy than any other gun he had used.

He broke the barrel and squinted up it, saw that the flint and hammer were working, put powder carefully in the flashpan, loaded the charge, and then set the gun on the window seat. There was no more to do, so he sat down to read again and refilled his glass.

Time went on and he grew impatient for Jud's return. There was little wind to-night and the house was very silent. Now and then a rat moved behind the wainscoting; occasionally Tabitha Bethia, the mangy cat, mewed and stretched before the fire, or a billet of wood shifted and dropped away to ashes.

At ten-thirty he went to the door and peered up the valley. The night was cloudy and out here the stream whispered and stirred; an owl flitted from a tree on furtive wings.

He left the door open and went round the house to the stables. The sea was very dark. A long black swell was riding quietly in. Now and then a wave would topple over and break in the silence with a crack like thunder, its white lip vivid in the dark.

His ankle was very painful after the horseplay of this afternoon, his whole body was stiff, his back aching as if he had cracked a rib. He entered the stables and went up to the loft. Jim Carter was not there.

He came down, patted Darkie, heard Garrick scuffle in the box they had made for him, returned the way he had come. Devil take Jud and his notions. He surely had sense enough not to leave the property after the boy's warning. Surely he had not ratted.

Ross went into the downstairs bedroom. The box bed was empty to-night, for Demelza had been moved to her new quarters. He mounted the stairs and quietly opened the door of her bedroom. It was pitch dark, but he could hear a sharp excited breathing. She at least was here, but she was not asleep. In some manner she had come to know of the danger. He did not speak but went out again.

From the room next door came a sound like a very old man cutting timber with a rusty saw, so he had no need to locate Prudie. Downstairs again, and an attempt to settle with his book. He did not drink any more. If Jud returned they would take it in two-hour watches through the night; if he did not, then the vigil must be kept singlehanded.

At eleven-thirty he finished the chapter, shut the book and went to the

door of the house again. The lilac tree moved its branches with an errant
breeze and then was still. Tabitha Bethia followed him out and rubbed her
head in companionate fashion against his boots. The stream was muttering
its unending litany. From the clump of elms came the rough thin churring
of a nightjar. In the direction of Grambler the moon was rising.

But Grambler lay southwest. And the faint glow in the sky was not pale
enough to reflect either a rising or a setting moon. Fire.

He started from the house and then checked himself. The defection of
Jud and Carter meant that he alone was left to guard his property and the
safety of the two women. If in truth the Illuggan miners were on the
warpath it would be anything but wise to leave the house unprotected.
Assuming the fire to have some connection with these events, he would
surely meet the miners if he went to look and they were on their way here.
But some might slip around him and gain the house. Better to stay than risk
its being set afire.

He chewed his bottom lip and cursed Jud for a useless scoundrel. He'd
teach him to rat at the first alarm. This desertion somehow loomed larger
than all the neglect before he came home.

He limped up as far as the Long Field behind the house and from there
fancied he could make out the flicker of the fire. He returned and thought
of waking Prudie and telling her she must care for herself. But the house
was as silent as ever and dark, except for the yellow candlelight showing
behind the curtains of the parlour; it seemed a pity to add needlessly to
anyone's alarm. He wondered what the child's feelings were, sitting up
there in the dark.

Indecision was one of the things he most hated. After another five
minutes he cursed himself and snatched up his gun, and set off hastily up
the valley.

Rain was wafting in his face as he reached the copse of fir trees beyond
Wheal Maiden. At the other side he stopped and stared across to
Grambler. Three fires could be seen. So far as he could make out they
were not large, and he was thankful for that. Then he picked out two
figures climbing the rising ground towards him, one carrying a lantern.

He waited. It was Jim Carter and Jud.

They were talking together, Carter excited and breathless. Behind them,
emerging out of the shadows, were four other men: Zacky Martin, Nick
Vigus, Mark and Paul Daniel, all from the cottages at Mellin. As they came
abreast of him he stepped out.

'Why,' said Jud, showing his gums in surprise, 'if tedn't Cap'n Ross.
Fancy you being yurabouts. I says to meself not five minutes gone: now, I
says, I reckon Cap'n Ross'll be just going off to sleep nice and piecemeal;
he'll be just stretching his feet down in the bed. I thought, I wished I was
abed too, 'stead of trampling through the misty-wet, a mile from the
nearest mug of toddy. . . .'

'Where have you been?'

'Why, only down to Grambler. We thought we'd go visit a kiddley an' pass the evening sociable . . .'

The other men came up and paused, seeing Ross. Nick Vigus seemed disposed to linger, his sly face catching the light from the lantern and creasing into a grin. But Zacky Martin tugged at Vigus's sleeve.

'Come on, Nick. You'll not be up for your core in the morning. Good night, sur.'

'Good night,' said Ross, and watched them tramp past. He could see more lanterns about the fires now and figures moving. 'Well, Jud?'

'Them fires? Well, now, if ye want to hear all about un, twas like this——'

'Twas like this, sur,' said Jim Carter, unable to hold his impatience. 'What with Will Nanfan saying he'd heard tell the Illuggan miners was coming to break up your house on account of you taking Tom Carne's maid, we thought twould be a good thing if we could stop 'em. Will says there's about a hundred of 'em carrying sticks and things. Well, now then, Grambler men owes Illuggan men a thing or two since last Michaelmas Fair, so I runs along to Grambler and rouses 'em and says to 'em——'

''Oo's telling this old yarn?' Jud said with dignity.

But in the excitement Jim had lost his usual shyness.

'—and says to 'em, "What d'you think? Illuggan men are coming over 'ere bent on a spree." Didn't need to say more'n that, see? 'Alf Grambler men was in the kiddleys, having a glass, and was fair dagging for a fight. While this, Jud runs down to Sawle and tells 'em same story. It didn't work so well there, but he comes back wi' twenty or thirty——'

'Thirty-six,' said Jud. 'But seven o' the skulks turned into Widow Tregothnan's kiddley, and still there for all I d' know, drowning their guts. Twas Bob Mitchell's fault. If he——'

'They was just there in time to help build three bonfires——'

'Three bonfires,' said Jud, 'and then——'

'Let the boy tell his story,' said Ross.

'Well, now then, we builded three bonfires,' said Carter, 'and they was just going pretty when we heard the Illuggan men coming, four or five scores of 'em, headed by Remfrey Flamank, as drunk as a bee. When they come up, Mike Andrewartha mounts on the wall and belves out to 'em, "What d'you want, Illuggan men? What business 'ave you hereabouts, Illuggan men?" And Remfrey Flamank pulls open his shirt to show all the hair on his chest and says, "What bloody consarn be that of yourn?" Then Paul Daniel says, "Tis our consarn, every man jack of us, for we don't want Illuggan men poking their nubbies about in our district." And a great growl goes up, like you was teasing a bear.'

Jim Carter stopped a moment to get his breath. 'Then a little man with a wart on his cheek the size of a plum shouts out, "Our quarrel's not wi' you, friends. We've come to take back the Illuggan maid your fancy gentleman stole and teach 'im a lesson he won't forget, see? Our quarrel's not wi' you." Then Jud 'ere belves out, " 'Oo says there's aught amiss wi' hiring a maid, like anyone else. And he took her in fair fight, ye bastards. Which is more'n any of you could do back again. There never was an Illuggan man what——" '

'All right, all right,' interrupted Jud in sudden irritation. 'I knows what I says, don't I! Think I can't tell what I said meself . . .' In his annoyance he turned his head and showed that one eye was going black.

'He says, "There never was a Illuggan man that wasn't the dirty cross-eyed son of an unmarried bitch wi' no chest and spavin shanks out of a knacker's yard." I thought twas as good as the preacher. And then someone hits him a clunk in the eye.'

Ross said: 'Then I suppose everyone started fighting.'

'Nigh on two hundred of us. Lors, twas a proper job. Did ee see that great fellow wi' one eye, Jud? Mark Daniel was lacing into him, when Sam Roscollar came up. An' Remfrey Flamank——'

'Quiet, boy,' said Jud.

Jim at last subsided. They reached home in a silence which was only once broken by his gurgling chuckle and the words, 'Remfrey Flamank, as drunk as a bee!'

'Impudence,' said Ross at the door. 'To go off and involve yourselves in a brawl and leave me at home to look after the women. What d'you think I am?'

There was silence.

'Understand, quarrels of my own making I'll settle in my own way.'

'Yes, sur.'

'Well, go on to bed, it's done now. But don't think I shall not remember it.'

Whether this was a threat of punishment or a promise of reward Jud and his partner could not be sure, for the night was too dark to see the speaker's face. There was a catch in his voice which might have been caused by a barely controlled anger.

Or it might have been laughter, but they did not think of that.

Chapter ten

At the extreme eastern end of the Poldark land, about half a mile from the house of Nampara, the property joined that of Mr Horace Treneglos, whose house lay a couple of miles inland behind the Hendrawna sand hills and was called Mingoose. At the point where the two estates met on the cliff edge was a third mine.

Wheal Leisure had been worked in Joshua's day for surface tin but not at all for copper. Ross had been over it during the winter and the desire to restart at least one of the workings on his own land had, after consideration of Wheal Grace, come to centre upon this other mine.

The advantages were that drainage could consist of adits running out to the cliff face, and that in some of the last samples taken from the mine and hoarded by Joshua there were definite signs of copper.

But it needed more capital than he could find; so on the Thursday morning of Easter week he rode over to Mingoose. Mr Treneglos was an elderly widower with three sons, the youngest in the navy and the others devoted fox hunters. He was himself a scholar and unlikely to care for mining adventures; but since the mine was partly on his land, it was the smallest courtesy to approach him first.

'Seems to me you've got so little to go on; almost like digging virgin ground. Why not start Wheal Grace where there's shafts already sunk?' shouted Mr Treneglos. He was a tall heavily built man whom deafness had made clumsy. He was sitting now on the edge of an armchair, his fat knees bent, his tight knee breeches stretched to a shinier tightness, his buttons under a strain, one hand stroking his knee and the other behind his ear.

Ross gave his reasons for preferring Wheal Leisure.

'Well my dear,' shouted Mr Treneglos, 'it is all very convincing, I believe you. I have no objection to your making a few holes in my land. We did ought to be good neighbours.' He raised his voice. 'Financially, now, I'm a bit costive this month; those boys of mine and their 'unters. Next month perhaps I could loan you fifty guineas. We did ought to be good neighbours. How would that do?'

Ross thanked him and said that if the mine were started he would run it on the cost-book system, whereby each of a number of speculators took up one or more shares and paid towards the outlay.

'Yes, excellent notion.' Mr Treneglos thrust forward an ear. 'Well, come round and see me again, eh? Always glad to help, my boy. We did ought to be good neighbours, and I'm not averse to a little flutter. Perhaps we shall find another Grambler.' He rumbled with laughter and picked up his book. 'Perhaps we shall find another Grambler. Ever read the classics, my boy? Cure for many ills of the modern world. I'd often try to get your father interested. How is he, by the way?'

Ross explained.

'Why, damn me, yes. A poor job. It was your uncle I was thinking of. It was his uncle I was thinking of,' he added in an undertone.

Ross rode home feeling that a half promise from Mr Treneglos was as much as he could expect at this stage; it remained for him to get some professional advice. The man to approach for this was Captain Henshawe of Grambler.

Jim Carter was working in one of his fields with the three young Martin children. As Ross passed, Carter ran over to him.

'I thought I'd tell ee a bit of news, sir,' he said quietly. 'Reuben Clemmow's runned away.'

So much had happened since their meeting last Sunday that Ross had forgotten the last of the Clemmows. The interview had not been a pleasant one. The man had been shifty but defiant. Ross had reasoned with him, trying to get at him through a sort of blank wall of suspicion and resentment. But even while doing it he had been conscious of failure, and of the enmity towards himself – something that couldn't be met or turned by good advice or a friendly talk. It was too deeply rooted for that.

'Where has he gone?'

'Dunno, sur. What you said to him 'bout turning of him out must have frightened him.'

'You mean he isn't at the mine?'

'Not since Tuesday. Nobody's seed him since Tuesday.'

'Oh well,' said Ross, 'it will save trouble. He has been making things unpleasant for Jinny.'

Carter looked up at him. His high-boned young face was very pallid this morning. 'She d' think he's still hanging around, sur. She says he hasn't gone far.'

'Someone would surely have seen him.'

'Yes, sur, that's what I d' say. But she don't believe we. She says, sur, if you'll excuse it, sur, to look out for yourself.'

Ross's face creased into a smile. In Jim Carter he had evidently found a permanent bodyguard.

'Don't worry your head about me, Jim. And don't worry about Jinny, neither. Are you in love with the girl?'

Carter met his gaze and swallowed.

'Well,' said Ross, 'you should be happy now you've lost your rival.

Though I doubt if he seriously competed.'

'Not in that way,' said Jim. 'Tes only that we was afraid——'

'I know what you were afraid of. If you see or hear anything, let me know. If not, don't see bogles in every corner.'

He rode on. Very well for me to talk, he thought. Perhaps the lout has run off to his brother in Truro. Or perhaps he has not. No telling with that type. It would be better for the Martins if he was under lock and key.

II

Although he went to Truro several times Ross saw nothing more of Margaret. Nor had he the desire to. If his adventures with her on the night of the ball had not cured him of his love for Elizabeth, it had proved to him that to seek lust for its own sake was no solution.

The child Demelza settled into her new home like a stray kitten into a comfortable parlour. Knowing the great strength of family ties among the miners, he had been prepared after a week to find her curled in a corner weeping for her father and his thrashings. Had she shown any signs of homesickness he would have packed her off at once; but she did not, and Prudie gave her a good character.

The fact that within three hours of her coming Demelza had found her way into the good graces of the monstrous Prudie was another surprise. Perhaps she appealed to some half-atrophied mother instinct, as a starving duckling might to a great auk.

So after a month's trial he sent Jim Carter – Jud would not go – to see Tom Carne with two guineas for the hire of the girl's services for a year. Jim said that Carne threatened to break every bone in his body; but he didn't refuse the gold, and this suggested that he was going to acquiesce in the loss of his daughter.

After their one large-scale invasion the miners of Illuggan made no move. There was always a chance of trouble when the next feast day came, but until then the distance between the places would save accidental clashes. Ross suspected for a time that they might try to take the child away by force, and he told her that she was not to go far from the house. One evening, riding home from St Ann's, a hail of stones was flung at him from behind a hedge, but that was the last sign of public disfavour. People had their own concerns to think of.

Turning over the lumber in the library, Prudie came upon a piece of stout printed dimity, and this, washed and cut up, made two sacklike frocks for the girl. Then an old bedspread with a deep lace edge was cut up into two pairs of combinations. Demelza had never seen anything like them before, and when she was wearing them she always tried to pull them down so that the lace showed below the hem of her skirt.

Much against her will, Prudie found herself enlisted in a campaign in which she had no personal belief: the war on lice. It was necessary to point out to Demelza at frequent intervals that her new master wouldn't tolerate dirty bodies or dirty hair.

'But how do he know?' the girl asked one day when the rain was trickling down the bottle-green glass of the kitchen window. 'How do he know? My hair's dark and there an't that change whether you d' wash it or no.'

Prudie frowned as she basted the meat, which was roasting on a spit over the fire. 'Yes. But it d' make a powerful difference to the number of cra'lers.'

'Cra'lers?' echoed Demelza, and scratched her head. 'Why, everyone's got cra'lers.'

'He don't like 'em.'

'Why,' said Demelza seriously, '*you've* got cra'lers. You've got cra'lers worser than what I have.'

'He don't like 'em,' Prudie said stubbornly.

Demelza digested this for a moment.

'Well, how do you get rid of 'em?'

'Wash, wash, wash, ' said Prudie.

'Like a blathering duck,' said Jud, who had just entered the kitchen.

Demelza turned her head and gazed at him with her interested dark eyes. Then she looked again at Prudie.

''Ow is it you an't got rid of 'em, then?' she asked, anxious to learn.

'An't washed enough,' said Jud sarcastically. 'Tedn't right fur human beings to 'ave skins. They must scrub theirselves raw as a buttock of beef to please some folk. But then again it depend 'pon how cra'lers do attach theirselves. Cra'lers is funny, kicklish creatures. Cra'lers like some folk better'n other folk. Cra'lers 'ave a natural infinity wi' some folk, just like they was brother and sister. Other folk, God makes 'em clean by nature. Look at me. You won't find no cra'lers on *my* head.'

Demelza considered him.

'No,' she said, 'but you an't gotten any hair.'

Jud threw down the turfs he had brought in. 'If you learned her to hold 'er tongue,' he said pettishly to his wife, 'twould be a sight betterer than learning 'er that. If you learned 'er manners, how to speak respectable to folk and answer respectable an' *be* respectable to their elders an' betters, twould be a sight betterer than that. Then ye could pat yourself on the 'ead and say, "Thur, I'm doing a tidy job, learning her to be respectable." But what are ee doing? Tedn't 'ard to answer. Tedn't 'ard to see. You're learning her to be sassy.'

That evening Jim Carter was sitting in the Martins' cottage talking to Jinny. With the family of Martins he had become fondly familiar during the winter of his work at Nampara. As his attachment for Jinny grew he saw less and less of his own family. He was sorry for this, for his mother would miss him, but he could not be in two places at the same time, and he felt more at home, more able to expand and talk and enjoy himself in the easygoing cottage of these people who knew him less intimately.

His father, an expert tributer, had earned good money until he was twenty-six, and then the phthisis with which he had been threatened for years became the master, and in six months Mrs Carter was a widow with five young children to bring up, the eldest, Jim, being eight.

Fred Carter had gone to the lengths of paying sixpence a week for him to attend school at Aunt Alice Trevemper's, and there had been talk of the child staying there another year. But necessity blew away talk as wind blows smoke, and Jim became a jigger at Grambler. This was 'grass' or surface work, for the Cornish miners did not treat their children in the heartless fashion of the up-country people. But jigging was not ideal, since it meant sieving copper ore in water and standing in a doubled-up position for ten hours a day. His mother was worried because he brought up blood when he got home. But many other boys did the same. The one and three pence a week made a difference.

At eleven he went below, beginning by working with another man and wheeling the material away in barrows; but he had inherited his father's talent and by the time he was sixteen he was a tributer on his own pitch and earning enough to keep the household. He was very proud of this; but after a couple of years he found himself losing time through ill health and saddled with a thick loose cough like his father's. At twenty, with a deeply laid grievance against fate, he allowed his mother to bully him into leaving the mine, into throwing away all his earning power, into handing over his pitch to his younger brother and applying for work as a *farm labourer*. Even with the fair wages paid by Captain Poldark he would earn less in a quarter than he usually made in a month; but it was not only the loss of money, not even the loss of position which upset him. He had mining in his blood; he liked the work and wanted the work.

He had given up something that he wanted very much. Yet already he was stronger, steadier. And the future had lost most of its fear.

In the Martins' cottage he sat in a corner and whispered to Jinny, while Zacky Martin smoked his clay pipe on one side of the fireplace, reading a newspaper, and on the other side Mrs Zacky nursed on one arm Betsy Maria Martin, aged three, who was recovering from a perilous attack of measles, while on the other arm their youngest, a baby of two months, grizzled fitfully. The room was faintly lighted by a thin earthenware lamp or 'chill,' with two wicks in little lips at the sides of the well. The well contained pilchard oil and the smell was fishy. Jinny and Jim were seated on a homemade wooden form and were glad of the comfortable obscurity of the shadows. Jinny would not go out after dark yet, even with Jim for escort – the only sore point in their friendship – but she swore she hadn't a minute's peace when every bush might hide a crouching figure. Better here, even with all the family to play gooseberry.

In the dim light only portions of the room showed up, surfaces and sides, curves and ends and profiles. The table had just been cleared of the evening meal of tea and barley bread and pease pudding: the yellow light showed the circle of wet where the ancient pewter teapot had leaked. At the other end was a scattering of crumbs left by the two youngest girls. Of Zacky could be seen only the thick brush of his red-grey hair, the jutting angle of his pipe, the curl of the closely printed *Sherborne Mercury*, grasped in a hairy hand as if it was in danger of flying away. Mrs Zacky's steel-rimmed spectacles glinted and each side of her flat face with its pursed whistling lips was illuminated in turn like different phases of the moon as she gazed first at one fretful child and then the other. The only thing to be seen of the infant Inez Mary was a grey shawl and a small chubby fist clasping and unclasping air as if asserting her frail stake in existence. A shock of red hair and a freckled snub nose slumbered uneasily on Mrs Zacky's other shoulder.

On the floor Matthew Mark Martin's long bare legs glimmered like two silver trout: the rest of him was hidden in the massive pool of shadow cast by his mother. On the wall beside Jinny and Jim another great shadow moved, that of the tawny cat, which had climbed upon the shelf beside the chill and blinked down on the family.

This was the best week of all, when Father Zacky was on the night core, for he allowed his children to stay up until nearly nine o'clock. Use had accustomed Jim to this routine, and he saw the moment approaching when he must leave. At once he thought of a dozen things he still had to say to Jinny, and was hurrying to say them, when there came a knock on the door and the top half swung open to show the gaunt powerful figure of Mark Daniel.

Zacky lowered his paper, unscrewed his eyes and glanced at the cracked hourglass to reassure himself that he had not overstayed his leisure.

'Early to-night, boy. Come in and make yourself 'tome, if you've the mind. I've not put so much as foot to boot yet.'

'Nor me neither,' said Daniel. ''Twas a word or two I wanted with ee, boy, just neighbourly, as you might say.'

Zacky knocked out his pipe. 'That's free. Come in and make yourself 'tome.'

''Twas a word in private,' said Mark. 'Asking Mrs Zacky's pardon. A word in your ear 'bout a little private business. I thought mebbe as you'd step outside.'

Zacky stared and Mrs Zacky whistled gently to her fretful charges. Zacky put down his paper, smoothed his hair, and went out with Mark Daniel.

Jim gratefully took advantage of the respite to add to his whisperings: words of importance about where they should meet tomorrow, if she had finished mine work and housework before dark and he his farming . . . She bent her head sweetly to listen. Jim noticed that in whatever shadow they sat some light attached itself to the smooth pale skin of her forehead, to the curve of her cheeks. Light, there was always light for her eyes.

'Tes time you childer was all asleep,' said Mrs Zacky, unpursing her lips. 'Else you'll be head-in-the-bed when you did ought to be up. Off now, Matthew Mark. And you, Gabby. And Thomas. Jinny, m' dear: it is hard to lose your young man s'early in the day, but you know how tis in the morning.'

'Yes, Mother,' said Jinny, smiling.

Zacky returned. Everyone gazed at him curiously, but he affected to be unaware of their scrutiny. He went back to his chair and began folding the newspaper.

'I don't know,' said Mrs Zacky, 'that I holds wi' secret chatter between grown men. Whispering together just like they was babies. What was you whispering about, Zachariah?'

'About how many spots there was on the moon,' said Zacky. 'Mark says ninety-eight and I says an hundred and two, so we agrees to leave it till we see the preacher.'

'I'll have none of your blaspheming in here,' said Mrs Zacky. But she said it without conviction. She had far too solid a faith in her husband's wisdom, built up through twenty years, to do more than make a token protest at his bad behaviour. Besides, she would get it out of him in the morning.

Greatly daring among the shadows, Jim kissed Jinny's wrist and stood up. 'I think it is about time I was going, Mr and Mrs Zacky,' he said, using what had come to be a formula of farewell. 'And thank ee once again for a comfortable welcome. Good night, Jinny; good night, Mr and Mrs Zacky; good night, all.'

He got to the door but Zacky stopped him there. 'Wait, boy. I d' feel like a stroll, and there's swacks of time. I'll take a step or two with you.'

A protest from Mrs Zacky followed him into the drizzling darkness. Then Zacky shut the doors and the night closed in on them, dank and soft with the fine misty rain falling like spider's webs on their faces and hands.

They set off, stumbling at first in the dark but soon accustomed to it, walking with the surefootedness of countrymen on familiar ground.

Jim was puzzled at his company and a little nervous, for there had been something grim in Zacky's tone. As a person of 'learning,' Zacky had always been of some importance in his eyes: whenever Zacky took up the tattered *Sherborne Mercury* the magnificence of the gesture struck Jim afresh; and now too he was Jinny's father. Jim wondered if he had done something wrong.

They reached the brow of the hill by the Wheal Grace workings. From there the lights of Nampara House could be seen, two opal blurs in the dark.

Zacky said: 'What I d' want to tell you is this. Reuben Clemmow's been seen at Marasanvose.'

Marasanvose was a mile inland from Mellin Cottages. Jim Carter had a nasty feeling of tightness come upon his skin as if it were being screwed up. All his sense of contentment left him: he was instantly prickly, on edge.

'Who seen him?'

'Little Charlie Baragwanath. He didn't know who twas, but from the describing there's little room to doubt.'

'Did he speak to un?'

'Reuben spoke to Little Charlie. It was on the lane twixt Marasanvose and Wheal Pretty. Charlie said he'd got a long beard, and a couple of sacks over his shoulders.'

They began to walk slowly down the hill towards Nampara.

'Just when Jinny was getting comfortable,' Jim said angrily. 'This'll upset her anew if she d' get to know.'

'That's why I didn't tell the womenfolk. Mebbe something can be done wi'out they knowing.'

For all his disquiet, Jim felt a new impulse of gratitude and friendship towards Zacky for taking him into his confidence in this way, for treating him as an equal, not as a person of no account. Somehow it tacitly recognized his attachment for Jinny.

'What are ee going to do, Mr Martin?'

'See Cap'n Ross. He did ought to know.'

'Shall I come in with ee?'

'No, boy. Reckon I'll do it my own way.'

'I'll wait outside for you,' Jim said.

'No, boy; go to bed. You'll not be up in the morning. I'll tell ee what he advise to-morrow.'

'I'd rather wait,' said Jim. 'That's if it is all the same with you. I've not the mind for sleep just now.'

They reached the house and separated at the door. Zacky slipped quietly round to the kitchen. Prudie and Demelza were in bed and Jud was up and yawning his head off, and Zacky was taken in to see Ross.

Ross was at his usual occupation, reading and drinking himself to bed. He was not too sleepy to listen to Zacky's story. When it was done he got up and strolled to the fire, stood with his back to it staring at the little man.

'Did Charlie Baragwanath have any conversation with him?'

'Not what you'd rightly call conversation. It was just passing the time o' day, as you might say, till Reuben seized his pasty and ran off with un. Stealing a pasty from a boy of ten . . . !'

'Hungry men feel different about these things.'

'Charlie says he went off running into the woods this side of Mingoose.'

'Well, something must be done. We can get up a man hunt and drive him out of his burrow. The moral difficulty is that so far he has done no wrong.

We cannot imprison a fellow because he is a harmless idiot. But neither do we want to wait until he proves himself the reverse.'

'He must be living in a cave, or mebbe a old mine,' said Zacky. 'And living off of somebody's game.'

'Yes, there's that. I might persuade my uncle to stretch a point and make out an order for his arrest.'

'If you thought we was doing right,' said Zacky, 'I think twould satisfy folk better if we caught un ourselves.'

Ross shook his head. 'Leave that as a last resort. I'll see my uncle in the morning and get an order. That will be the best. In the meantime, see Jinny does not go out alone.'

'Yes, sur. Thank you, sur.' Zacky moved to go.

'There's one thing that might lead towards a solution so far as Jinny is concerned,' Ross said. 'I've been thinking of it. My boy who works here, Jim Carter, seems very taken with her. Do you know if she also likes him?'

Zacky's weatherbeaten face glinted a little with humour.

'They're both bit wi' the same bug, I bla'.'

'Yes, well, I don't know your view of the boy, but he seems a steady lad. Jinny's seventeen and the boy's twenty. If they were married it might be for their good, and there is the likelihood that it would cure Reuben of his ambitions.'

Zacky rubbed the stubble on his chin; his thumb made a sharp rasping sound. 'I like the boy; there's no nonsense about him. But tis part a question of wages and a cottage. There's small room for raising of another family in ours. And for labouring he gets little more than enough to pay the rent of a roof, wi'out vittles for two. I had the mind to build a lean-to to our cottage, but there's bare room for it.'

Ross turned and kicked at the fire with the toe of his boot.

'One cannot afford to pay mining wages to a farm boy. But there are two empty cottages at Mellin, in the other row. They bring in nothing as they are, and Jim could live in one for the repairing. I should ask no rent from him so long as he worked for me.'

Zacky blinked. 'No rent? That d' make a difference. Have you mentioned it to the boy?'

'No. It's not my business to order his life. But talk it over with him sometime if you're so disposed.'

'I will to-night. He's waiting outside. . . . No, I'll wait till to-morrow. He'll be over to our place, reg'lar as clockwork.' Zacky stopped: 'It is very handsome of you. Wouldn't you like to see 'em both together, then you could tell 'em yourself.'

'No, no, I'll have no hand in it. It was a passing suggestion. But make what arrangements on it you please.'

When the little man was gone Ross refilled his pipe and lit it and turned back to his book. Tabitha Bethia jumped on his knee and was not pushed off. Instead he pulled her ear while he read. But after turning a page or two he found he had taken nothing in. He finished his drink but did not pour himself another.

He felt righteous and unashamed. He decided to go to bed sober.

III

The wet weather had put him out of contact with Trenwith House during the last few weeks. He had not seen Verity since the ball, and he sensed that she was avoiding him so that he should not twit her on her friendship with Captain Blamey.

The morning following Zacky's call he rode over in pouring rain to see his uncle, and was surprised to find the Rev Mr Johns there. Cousin William-Alfred, his scrawny neck sticking well out above his high collar, was in sole possession of the winter parlour when Mrs Tabb showed him in.

'Your uncle is upstairs,' he said, offering a cold but firm grasp. 'He should be down soon. I hope you're well, Ross?'

'Well, thank you.'

'Hm,' said William-Alfred judicially. 'Yes. I think so. You *look* better than when I last saw you. Less heavy under the eyes, if I may say so.'

Ross chose to pass this. He liked William-Alfred for all his bloodless piety, because the man was so sincere in his beliefs and in his way of life. He was worth three of the politically minded Dr Halse.

He enquired after his cousin's wife, and expressed polite gratification that Dorothy's health was improving. In December God had given them another daughter, the blessing of another lamb. Ross than asked after the health of the occupants of Trenwith House, wondering if the answer would explain William-Alfred's presence. But no. All were well, and there was nothing here to bring William-Alfred all the way from Stithians. Francis and Elizabeth were spending a week with the Warleggans at their country home at Cardew. Aunt Agatha was in the kitchen making some herb tea. Verity – Verity was upstairs.

'You have ridden far on so unpleasant a morning,' Ross said.

'I came last evening, Cousin.'

'Well, that was no better.'

'I hope to leave to-day if the rain clears.'

'Next time you're here, venture another three miles and visit Nampara. I can offer you a bed, if not quite the accommodation you have here.'

William-Alfred looked pleased. It was seldom that he received open gestures of friendship. 'Thank you. I will certainly do that.'

Charles Poldark entered, blowing like a sperm whale with the effort of coming downstairs. He was still putting on weight and his feet were swollen with gout.

'Ho, Ross; so *you're* here, boy. What's to do: is your house afloating out to sea?'

'There's some danger if the rain keeps on. Am I interrupting you in important business?'

The other two exchanged glances.

'Have you not told him?' Charles asked.

'I could not do that without your permission.'

'Well, go on, go on. Aarf! It is a family affair and he is one of the family, even though an odd one.'

William-Alfred turned his pale-grey eyes to Ross.

'I came out yesterday not so much to pay a social call as to see Uncle Charles on a matter of outstanding import to our family. I hesitated some time before intruding upon ground which was——'

'It is about Verity and this Captain Blamey fellow,' Charles said briefly. 'Damme, I couldn't ha' believed it. Not that the girl should——'

'You know, do you not,' said William-Alfred, 'that your cousin has become friendly with a seafaring man, one Andrew Blamey?'

'I know that. I've met him.'

'So have we all,' said Charles explosively. 'He was here at Francis's wedding!'

'I knew nothing of him then,' said William-Alfred. 'That was the first time I had seen him. But last week I learned his history. Knowing that he was becoming – that there had been a considerable talk linking his name and Cousin Verity's, I came over at the earliest opportunity. Naturally, I was at pains first to verify the information which reached me.'

'Well, what is it?' said Ross.

'The man has been married before. He is a widower with two young children. Perhaps you know that. He is also, however, a notorious drunkard. Some years ago in a drunken frenzy he kicked his wife when she was with child and she died. He was then in the Navy, the commander of a frigate. He lost his rank and lay in a common prison for two years. When released he lived on the charity of his relatives for a number of years until he obtained his present commission. There is, I understand, an agitation afoot to boycott the packet he commands until the company discharges him.'

William-Alfred finished his unemotional recital and licked his lips. There had been no animosity in his tones, a circumstance which made the indictment worse. Charles spat through the open window.

Ross said: 'Does Verity know?'

'Yes, damme!' said Charles. 'Would you believe it of the girl? She's known for more than two weeks. She says it don't make any difference!'

Ross went to the window, bit his thumb. While he had been concerned with his own day-to-day affairs this had been happening.

'But it must make a difference,' he said, half to himself.

'She says,' William-Alfred observed judicially, 'that he will touch no drink now at all.'

'Yes, well . . .' Ross paused. 'Oh yes, but . . .'

Charles exploded again. 'God's my life, we all drink! Not to drink is unnatural in a man. Aarf! But we do not become murderous in our cups. To kick a woman in that condition is beyond forgiveness. I don't know how he got off so light. He should have been hanged from his own yardarm. Drunk or sober makes little difference.'

'Yes,' said Ross slowly. 'I'm inclined to agree.'

'I do not know,' said William-Alfred slowly, 'if marriage was his intention; but if it was, can we let a gentle girl like Verity marry such a man?'

'By God, no!' said Charles, empurpled. 'Not while I am alive!'

'What's her attitude?' Ross asked. 'Does she insist on wanting to marry him?'

'She says he has been reformed! For how long? Once a drunkard always a drunkard. The position is impossible! She's in her room and will stay there until she sees reason.'

'I've been very friendly with her this winter. It might help if I saw her and we talked things over.'

Charles shook his head. 'Not now, my boy. Later perhaps. She's as pigheaded as her mother. More so, in truth, and that's saying volumes. But the association's got to be broke. I'm mortal sorry for the girl. She's not had many admirers. But I'll not have any wife-kicking skunk bedding with my flesh and blood. That's all there is to it.'

So for the second time that spring Ross rode home from Trenwith having done nothing that he had set out to do. Last time Elizabeth. This time Verity.

He felt restless and uneasy at the thought of her misery. Very well for Charles to say 'that's all there is to it'; but he had come to know Verity better than her own father and brother did. Her affections were slow to take and hard to break. He was not even sure that this one would be broken by Charles's veto. It might be that she would defy everyone and marry Blamey, and that only then would the affection break.

That was the worst prospect of all.

Chapter eleven

'EVERYTHING ARRANGED NOW, Jim?'

It was a week later, and they had met in the stable. Jim Carter's gratitude was dumb. Two or three times before he had struggled with his tongue, but it wouldn't move. Now at last he got out:

'Tis what I d' want more than anything. I'd not thought to hope for it, hardly begun to. An' I've to thank you for it.'

'Oh, nonsense,' said Ross. 'Don't owe your happiness to anyone. Tell Zacky to-night that the warrant for Clemmow's arrest has been issued. As soon as he is located we can put him away for a space to cool his head.'

'It is the cottage I have to thank ee for,' Jim persisted, now that he was at last launched. 'That d' make all the difference. You see, if we had no hope for that——'

'Which have you decided on?' Ross asked, to cut short his thanks. 'Reuben's or the one next door?'

'The one next door, the one next to Joe and Betsy Triggs. We reckoned, sur, if twas all the same to you, that we'd not go into Reuben's cottage. It don't seem too comfortable, if you follow me. And the other's clean 'nough for five year. Smallpox have gone long since.'

Ross nodded. 'And when are you to be married?'

Jim flushed. 'Banns will be called for the first time next Sunday. I can't hardly . . . We're startin' repairing the roof to-night if the weather clears. There's little enough to do. Jinny would dearly like to come and thank you herself.'

'Oh, there's no need of that,' Ross said in alarm. 'I'll call and see you when you are nicely settled.'

'And we'd like,' Jim struggled on, 'if we d' get on, to pay you a rent . . . just to show——'

'Not while you're working for me. But it's a good thought.'

'Jinny d' hope to stay on at the mine, at least to begin. With my two brothers doing well for theirselves, Mother hasn't the same need of my help . . . So, I believe twill work . . .'

A sneeze attracted Ross's attention and he saw Demelza crossing the yard with a pile of logs held in her pinafore. It was raining and she was without a hat. Behind her Garrick, grown tall and ungainly in midpuppyhood, black and tailless and sparsely curled, gambolled like a French poodle. Ross wanted to laugh.

'Demelza,' he said.

She stopped instantly and dropped one of the logs. For a moment she could not see where the voice came from. He stepped out of the darkness of the stable.

'You're not allowing Garrick in the house?'

'No, sur. He come no further than the door. He come that far just to keep me company. He's awful sore at not coming no further.'

He picked up the log and put it back upon the bundle in her arms.

'Perhaps,' she said, 'he could come in just so far as the kitchen when he's rid of cra'lers too.'

'Crawlers?'

'Yes, sur. The things that crawl in your hair.'

'Oh,' said Ross. 'I misdoubt if he ever will be.'

'I do scrub him every day, sur.'

Ross eyed the dog, which was sitting on its haunches and scratching its floppy ear with one stiff hind leg. He looked again at Demelza, who looked at him. 'I'm pleased that Prudie is directing you so well. I believe his colour is a thought lighter. Does he like being scrubbed?'

'Judas God, no! He d' wriggle like a pilchard.'

'Hm,' Ross said dryly. 'Well, bring him to me when you think he's clean and I'll tell you then.'

'Yes, sur.'

Prudie appeared at the door. 'Oh, there you are, you black worm!' she said to the girl, and then she saw Ross. A faint sheepish smile creased her shiny red face. 'Miss Verity's here, sur. I was just going to tell 'er to go seek ee.'

'Miss Verity?'

'Just come this inster. I was rushin' out for to tell ee. Hastenin' I was, and no one can say different.'

He found Verity in the parlour. She had taken off her grey cloak with its fur-lined hood and was wiping the rain from her face. The bottom of her skirt was black with rain and splashed with mud.

'Well, my dear,' he said. 'This is a surprise. Have you walked in this weather?'

Her face had become sallow under its tan, and there were heavy shadows below her eyes. She looked as if she had been ill.

'I had to see you, Ross. You understand better than the others. I had to see you about Andrew.'

'Sit down,' he said. 'I'll get you some ale and a slice of almond cake.'

'No, I mustn't stay long. I – slipped out. You . . . came over on Thursday last, did you not? When William-Alfred was there.'

Ross nodded and waited for her to go on. She was out of breath, either

from haste or from the press of her feelings. He wanted to say something
that would help her, but couldn't find the right words. Life had clutched at
his kind little Verity.

'They – told you?'

'Yes, my dear.'

'*What* did they tell you?'

As close as he could remember, he gave William-Alfred's account.
When he finished she went to the window and began pulling at the wet fur
of her muff.

'He didn't kick her,' she said. 'That is a lie. He knocked her down and –
and she died. The rest – is the truth.'

He stared at the trickles of water running down the windowpane. 'I'm
more sorry than I can say.'

'Yes, but . . . They want me to give him up, to promise never to see him
again.'

'Don't you think that would be for the best?'

'Ross,' she said, 'I love him.'

He didn't speak.

'I'm not a child,' she said. 'When he told me – he told me the day after
the ball – I felt so sick, so ill, so sorry – for him. I couldn't sleep, couldn't
eat. It was so terrible hearing it direct from him, because I had no hope that
it wasn't true. Father doesn't understand me because he thinks that I am
not revolted. Of course I was revolted. So much so that for two days I was
in bed of a fever. But that – that doesn't make me not *love* him. How can it?
One falls in love for good or ill. You know that.'

'Yes,' he said. 'I know that.'

'Knowing him, knowing Andrew, it was almost impossible to credit. It
was terrible. But one cannot turn one's back on the truth. One cannot wish
it away, or pray it away, or even live it away. He did do such a thing. I told
myself again and again the thing he had done. And the repetition, instead
of killing my love, killed my horror. It killed my fear. I said to myself: He
has done this and he has paid for it. Isn't that enough? Is a man to be
condemned for ever? Why do I go to church and repeat the Lord's Prayer if
I don't hold to it, if there is no forgiveness? Is our own behaviour higher
than the Founder of Christianity, that we should set a higher standard for
others? . . .'

She had been speaking quickly and fiercely. These were the arguments
her love had forged in the quietness of her bedroom.

'He never touches drink now,' she ended pathetically.

'Do you think he will keep to that?'

'I am sure of it.'

'What do you intend to do?'

'He wishes me to marry him. Father forbids it. I can only defy him.'

'There are ways of coercion,' Ross said.

'I am of age. They can't stop me.'

He went across and threw another log on the fire. 'Has Blamey seen Charles. If they could talk it over——'

'Father won't consider seeing him. It is . . . so unfair. Father drinks. Francis gambles. They're not saints. Yet when a man does what Andrew has done they condemn him unheard.'

'It's the way of the world, my dear. A gentleman may get drunk so long as he carries his drink decent, or slips beneath the table with it. But when a man has been sent to prison for what Blamey did, then the world is not at all prepared to forgive and forget, despite the religion it subscribes to. Certainly other men are not prepared to entrust their daughters to his care with the possibility of their being treated in like manner.' He paused, struggling to find words. 'I am inclined to agree with that attitude.'

She looked at him painfully a moment, then shrugged.

'So you side with them, Ross.'

'In principle, yes. What do you wish me to do?'

She picked up her wet cloak, stood with it between her fingers, looking at it. 'I can't ask anything if you feel like that.'

'Oh yes, you can.' He walked over and took the cloak from her and stood beside her at the window. He touched her arm. 'For me, Verity, the winter is over. That and much more. Without you I don't know what the end would have been. Not this. If – your winter is to come, am I to refuse to help you because I take another view in principle? I don't bring myself yet to like the idea of your marrying Blamey; but that's because I care so greatly for your welfare. It doesn't mean I'll not help you in any manner I can.'

For a moment she did not answer. Suddenly he despised himself for what he had just said. Qualified help was weak and timid. Either come out dead against the attachment or else help without reservation, without giving the impression of reluctance and disapproval.

Very difficult. Because of their special friendship the first was impossible. The second was against his better judgment – for he had no personal love or belief to sustain him, except his belief in Verity.

But it was not good enough. The choice was difficult, but he must see more clearly than he had done. What would Verity have done if positions were reversed?

He released her arm. 'Forget what I said. There's no question of my disapproval. None at all. I'll do whatever you wish.'

She sighed. 'You see, I have to come to you, for there is no one else. Elizabeth is very understanding, but she cannot openly side with me against Francis. And I don't really think she wishes to. Besides – I thought—— Thank you.'

'Where is – Andrew now?'

'At sea. He'll not be back for two weeks at least. When he comes . . . I thought if I could write him telling him to meet me here——'

'At Nampara?'

She looked at him. 'Yes.'

'Very well,' he said instantly. 'Let me know the day before and I will make arrangements.'

Her lips trembled and she looked as if she was going to cry.

'Ross dear, I am indeed sorry to implicate you in this. There is enough—— But I could not think——'

'Nonsense. It's not the first time we shall have been conspirators. But look, you must put a stop to this worrying. Or he will not wish to see you when he comes. The less you fret, the braver will things turn out. Go home and go about your normal life as if nothing was to do. Make a show that you have nothing to worry over and it will be easier to carry. God knows, I have no licence to preach, but it's good advice nevertheless.'

'I'm sure of it.' She sighed again and put a hand to the side of her tired face. 'If I can come here and *talk* with you, that will help more than you know. To be contained within my own thoughts all the day, and surrounded by hostile ones. Merely to talk to someone with understanding is like——'

'Come when you like. And as often. I am always here. You shall tell me all there is to know. I'll get you something warm to drink while Jud saddles Darkie. Then I'll ride you back.'

Chapter twelve

JIM CARTER AND Jinny Martin were married at 1 p.m. on the last Monday in June. The ceremony was taken by the Rev Mr Clarence Odgers, whose fingernails were still black from planting his onions. As he had kept the party waiting a few minutes while he donned his vestments, he thought it only right to keep them no longer than strictly necessary over the actual ceremony.

He therefore began:

'Dearly beloved, we are gathered together here in the sight of God, anin the face this congregashun nay – num – num this man and this woman holy matrimony; which is an – num – state – num signifying unto us a mystical union – num – nite – murch – num – nar duly considering the causes for which matrimony is ordained. First it was ordained for the procreation of children to be brought up in the num – nur – cher – num. Secondly it was ordained for a remedy against sin nar – num fornication nar – nar undefiled members of Christ's body. Thirdly it was ordained for the mutual society, help, comfort, num – num – perity – versity – nar – num – man – shew – num – or else hereafter for ever hold his peace.

'I require and charge you both – num – num – num . . .'

Jinny's red-brown hair was brushed and combed until it glistened beneath the homemade white muslin bonnet set well back on her small head.

She was far the more composed of the two. Jim was nervous and halted several times in his responses. He was self-conscious in his own splendour, for Jinny had bought him a bright blue kerchief from a pedlar, and he had bought himself a secondhand coat almost as good as new, of a warm plum colour with bright buttons. This would perhaps have to last him as a best coat for the next twenty years.

' . . . and live according to thy laws; through Jesus Christ our Lord, Amen. Those whom God hath joined let no man put asunder. Forasmuch as N. and N. – er – forasmuch as James Henry and Jennifer May have consented together in holy wedlock and've nessed – name – no – given – nar – nar – reeve – ring – hands – I pronounce that they be man and wife together. In the name Far, Son, Holy Ghost, Amen.' Mr Odgers would soon be back with his onions.

A meal was provided in the Martins' cottage for all who could attend. Ross had been invited, but had refused on a plea of urgent business in Truro, feeling that the gathering would be likely to enjoy itself more freely in his absence.

As there were eleven of the Martins without the bride and six of the Carters not counting the groom, the accommodation for outsiders was limited. Old Man Greet doddered and creaked in a corner by the fireplace, and Joe and Betsy Triggs kept him company. Mark and Paul Daniel were there, and Mrs Paul, and Mary Daniel. Will Nanfan and Mrs Will were there as uncle and aunt of the bride; Jud Paynter had taken the afternoon off to come – Prudie was laid up with a bunion – and somehow Nick Vigus and his wife had managed to squeeze in – as they always managed to squeeze in when anything was going free.

The room was so full that all the children had to sit on the floor, and the juveniles, those from nine to sixteen, were arranged two by two up the wooden ladder to the bedroom – 'just like the animiles in the ark,' as Jud benevolently told them. The wooden bench that Jim and Jinny had used during most of the dark quiet evenings of the winter had been raised to the status of a bridal chair, and on this the married couple were perched like love birds where, for once, everyone could see them.

The feast was a strange mixture of food designed to tempt the appetite and upset the digestion, and port and home-brewed mead were in lavish supply to wash it all down and make the company more boisterous.

When the feast was over and Zacky had made a speech and Jim had said thank you for all your good wishes and Jinny had blushed and refused to say anything at all, when even with the door open the room had become insufferably hot and sticky and nearly everyone was suffering from cramp, when the babies were becoming fractious and the children quarrelsome and the grownups sleepy from heavy food and lack of air, then the women and children went to sit outside, leaving the men room to stretch their legs and light their pipes or take their snuff, and freedom to drink their port and gin and yarn contentedly about how the tamping got wet on the 120 level, or the chances of a good pilchard season.

The preparations of the men to finish up the celebrations after their own fashion were much frowned upon by Mrs Martin and Mrs Paul Daniel; but Zacky, although he agreed that he had found the Lord at a revival meeting at St Ann's a couple of years ago, still refused to lose his toddy as a consequence, and the others took their cue from him.

The port was cheap stuff for which Zacky had paid 3s. 6d. a gallon, but the gin had quality. On a quiet evening in September eight of them had taken a Sawle cutter round to Roscoff, and among the cargo they brought back were two large tubs of fine gin. One tub they had divided among themselves at once, but the other they had decided to keep for a feast. So Jud Paynter, who was one of the eight, had hidden the tub by lowering it into the broken rainwater barrel beside the conservatory at Nampara, where it would be safe from the prying eyes of any suspicious revenue man who might come around. There it had remained all through the winter. Jud Paynter and Nick Vigus had brought it along for this occasion.

While the women, having for the most part been barred from the new home, were now shown over it, with broods of children dragging at their heels, the men prepared to drink themselves into a comfortable stupor.

'They do say,' came the thin sleek voice of Nick Vigus over the top of his mug, 'that all the mines'll be closed down afore long. They do say as a man called Raby 'as bought all the big slag 'eaps in the county, and there's a process as he can treat the attle with as will give all the copper England d' want for a hundred year.'

'Tedn't feasible,' said Will Nanfan, hunching his big shoulders.

Zacky took a swig of gin from his mug. 'It won't need that for to put us in poor shape if things go on as they be going now. United Mines of St Day showed a loss of nigh on eight thousand pounds last year, and gracious knows what Grambler will show when tis next accounted. But this edn fitty talk for a wedding feast. We've got our pitches and our homes, and money d' come in. Mebbe it edn so much as we should like, but there be swacks of folk ready to change——'

'Mortal strange gin, this, Zacky,' said Paul Daniel, wiping his moustache. 'Never have I tasted gin like un. Or mebbe once . . . Mebbe once——'

'Well now,' said Zacky, licking his lips, 'if I 'adn been so con-centred on what I was saying I might have thought the very same. Now you call it to mind, it d' taste more like – more like——'

'More like turpentine,' said Mark Daniel.

'Mortal fiery,' said Old Man Greet. 'Mortal fiery. But in my day twas expected that a nip of gin should bite ee. Twas expected. When I was on Lake Superior in '69, when I was thur 'specting for copper, there was a store that sold stuff as'd take the skin off your 'and . . .'

Joe Triggs, the doyen of the party, was given a mug of it. Everyone watched him take a draught and watched the expression on his deeply corrugated old face with its sprouting side whiskers. He pursed his lips and opened them with a loud smack, then drank again. He lowered the empty mug.

'Tedn't near so good as what ee got from Roscoff back last Septemby,' was his growling verdict.

'But that's what tis,' two or three exclaimed.

There was a moment's silence.

'A different tub,' said Jud. 'Tastes all right to me, but tedn't so mature. That's what's amiss with un. Did ought to have been kept awhile longerer. Like Uncle Nebby's old cow.' He began to mumble a little tune to himself:

> *'There was an old couple and they was poor,*
> *Tweedle, tweedle, go twee . . .'*

It seemed that the same terrible suspicion had leapt unasked into everyone's mind. They all stared silently at Jud while he went on humming and trying to look unconcerned.

Eventually the little song gave out.

Zacky'looked down at his glass. 'It is powerful strange,' he said quietly, 'that two tubs of gin should have such opposite flavours.'

'Powerful strange,' said Paul Daniel.

'Damnation strange,' said Mark Daniel.

'Mebbe we was swindled,' said Jud, showing his two big teeth in an unconvincing smile. 'Them Frenchies is as cuzzle as a nest o' rats. Can't trust 'em no furtherer than ye can spit. Wouldn't turn me back on one nohow. Cross one and turn your back, and he outs with his knife, and *phit!* ye're dead.'

Zacky shook his head. 'Who's ever been cheated by Jean Lutté?'

'He always do do the straight thing by we,' said Will Nanfan.

Zacky rubbed his chin, and seemed to regret he had shaved that morning. 'He told me they was two proper tubs of gin; and both same brand, mark ee. That's what's powerful strange. Both same brand. Seems to me as someone's been tampering wi' this one. I wonder who could be?'

'I've a damnation thundering good notion,' said Mark Daniel, who had already drunk three pints of port and had just been ready to get down to the serious work of the evening.

'No need to get in a pore about un,' said Jud, sweating. 'Tes naught to do wi' me. There an't no proof o' nothing. Nobody can't say where the fault do lay. Anybody could 'ave tankered with un – that's if so be as somebody 'as, which if they 'as I doubt. But I suspicion tis the Frenchie. Never trust a Frenchie, say I. That Frenchie at Roscoff, he d' look all right, he d' talk all right; but do he act all right? He d' look ee in the eye like a Christian; but what do that surmount to? Only that he's two-faced like the rest, but more so.'

'When I was a tacker,' said Old Man Greet perseveringly, 'they had some proper gin down to Sawle Village where Aunt Tamsin Nanpusker lived. She that died in '58, fell down a shaft she did when she was well gone in liquor. An' not surprising when——'

''S, I well remember old Aunt Tamsin, said Nick Vigus, incautiously. 'She as rode down Stippy-Stappy Lane one day on the back of her old sow, wi' all the little uns wagging away be'ind. Regular procession, twas. Some drink old Aunt Tamsin had to put away——'

'Damme!' roared Mark Daniel. 'Ef I don't see it all now! That's where I tasted un before. It is Nick's doing. It is all Nick's doing! We're suspicioning the wrong man. You call to mind that poison brew Nick Vigus did hatch in his own back kitchen out o' devil knows what to sell to the poor fools wi' money to burn last Michaelmas Fair! Gin, he called it, ye recollect. Well, it was near enough the taste o' this to be brother an' twin to un.'

'Aye,' said Will Nanfan. 'Aye, that's truth. God's truth, for I drank some meself and wished I never touched un. It give a twist to yer innards, a twist like a reefer knot. Nick Vigus has cheated we!'

Vigus's sly pockmarked face went red and white by turns as the accusing stares focussed themselves on him. Mark Daniel took another sup to be sure, and then went to the window and sprayed it about the vegetable bed.

'Pah, the very same, or I'm a heathen. Nick Vigus, ye're a damnation crawling cheat and it is time ye was learned a lesson.' He began to roll up his sleeves, showing his great hairy forearms.

Nick backed away, but Paul Daniel blocked his escape to the door. There was some horseplay, then Mark Daniel took a firm grip and turned Vigus upside down and stood him on his head.

''Twas none o' my doing,' Nick shouted. 'Jud Paynter wur the one! Jud Paynter come to me last week and said to me, 'e said——'

'Don't ee believe a word of un!' Jud said loudly. 'I'm a honest man as ye all d' know, not given to tankering wi' the word o' truth. But Nick's a greasy liar as ye all d' know, and would sell his mother to save the skin off his nose. And as – as ye all d' know——'

'Shake un up, Mark,' Zacky said. 'We shall be getting at the truth by and by.'

'——Jud come to me last week and says to me, 'e says, "Can ee make us some o' your gin, boy? Cos that there tub I was keeping, all the gin 'as runned away into the ground——" Turn me right face up, Mark, or I shall sh-mother . . .'

Mark gripped his victim more firmly round the middle, and with a great heave stamped his kicking feet upon one of the beams of the cottage ceiling.

'Come, my dear,' he said gently. 'Speak up, for else ye may die unshrived. . . . '

''E says all the gin 'as runned away into the ground on account of the rats had gnawled away a 'ole in the tub – ah, ah . . . And on account of he didn't want to disappoint ee, would I make – would I make——'

'Catch 'im, Paul!' Will Nanfan shouted, as Jud Paynter, like an obsequious bulldog, tried to leave unnoticed.

They caught him in the doorway, and a great deal of heaving and muttering went on before the elder Daniel and Will Nanfan came back with him.

'Tedn't true!' shouted Jud, toothless with indignation. 'You're barking up the wrong door. What for do ee want to take that man's word 'fore mine. Tedn't fair. Tedn't just. Tedn't *British*. I dare swear if the truth be known that he stole 'alf the tub fur his self. Why blame a man ye know wouldn't rob——'

'If I had the 'alf, you 'ad the rest,' came from the upended Vigus.

'Let me get at un!' swore Jud, suddenly struggling. 'I'll tear 'is britches off. Let me face un and have un out. Ye pack of cowards: two to one! Let me get at un. I'll face ee one by one, ye cowards. Take yer 'ands off me and I'll poam ee. I'll poam ee——'

'Wait awhile and I'll poam ye myself,' said Mark Daniel. 'Man to man as ye'd like, see. Now out o' the way, boys . . .'

He carried Nick Vigus still inverted to the door. Unfortunately at this moment some of the women, hearing the uproar, had left the other cottage and reached this door led by Mrs Vigus. On seeing her husband presented to her at an unusual angle, she let out a piercing scream and rushed forward to the rescue; but Mark fended her off and carried Nick across to the cottage of Joe and Betsy Triggs. At the back of this was a slimy green pool which contained among other things most of their sewage. Since Reuben Clemmow had disappeared, this had held pride of place for smells in the neighbourhood.

At the brink of the water Mark sharply upended the half-choked man, grasped him again by the seat of his breeches and flung him on his face into the middle of the pool.

Mark breathed deeply and spat on his hands.

'Now for the next of un,' he said.

And thither also Jud Paynter went in his turn.

II

As Ross rode home from Truro that evening in the gathering windy dusk he thought of the two young people who were starting life together. That he had grown to like the boy, and the girl too, was his only excuse for concerning himself with their future. If the mine were started he would offer Jim a surface job, some sort of clerical work perhaps which would give him a better chance.

His outing to-day had been to do with Wheal Leisure. After buying things for the house, flour and sugar, mustard and candles, huckaback linen for towels, a new pair of riding boots for himself and a brush and comb, he had called on Mr Nathaniel Pearce, the notary.

Mr Pearce, as effusive, as purple, and as gouty as ever, sitting in an armchair poking the fire with a long iron curtain rod, listened with interest. Mr Pearce said, well now, and how pleasant, and I declare a most takable suggestion. Mr Pearce scratched at a louse under his wig while his eyes grew speculative. Was Captain Henshawe investing some of his own money? Dear, dear, now Captain Henshawe's reputation was high in the Truro district. Well now, dear sir, speaking as an indigent notary, he personally had only a little free capital, but there were, as Captain Poldark suggested, a certain number of his clients who were always on the lookout for a good speculative investment. He would be willing to give the matter his further consideration and see what could be done.

Events were moving slowly, but movement there was, and the momentum would increase. In a couple of months they might be sinking the first shaft.

As he led the mare into the stable and unbuckled the saddle he wondered whether to offer Charles and Francis a share.

He had come home at a good pace to reach the house before dark, and Darkie was steaming and sweaty. She was unsettled too and did not want to keep still while he wiped her down.

For that matter, the other horses showed the same uneasiness. Ramoth kept tossing his old head and whinnying. He wondered if there was a snake in the stable or a fox in the loft above. The pale square of the stable door still let in some light, but he could see nothing in the shadows. He patted Ramoth's soft old nose and returned to his task. This done he gave Darkie her feed and turned to leave.

Near the door were the steps to the loft where Carter had slept. As he glanced up these something grazed past his head and struck him a numbing blow on the shoulder. He fell to his knees and there was a thud on the straw of the floor. Then he got quickly to his feet again, staggered to the door, was through it and leaning with his back to it, holding his shoulder.

For a few seconds the pain made him feel sick, but it began to pass. He felt his shoulder and could find no broken bone. The thing which had struck him still lay on the floor inside the stable. But he had seen what it was, and that was why he had moved so quickly into the open. It was the rock drill, the iron jumper he had last seen in the hands of Reuben Clemmow.

III

They were all in the kitchen when he went in. With a piece of coarse thread and a large bent needle Demelza was trying to mend a tear in her skirt; Jud was sitting back in a chair with a look of patient suffering upon that part of his face which was not hidden by a large bandage; Prudie was drinking tea.

'Why, Cap'n Ross,' said Jud in a weak and trembling voice, 'we didn't hear ee come. Shall I go and wipe down the 'oss?'

'I have done that. Why are you back from the wedding so soon? What is wrong with your face? Prudie, keep my supper for ten minutes. I have something to see to.'

'The wedding is over,' said Jud. ''Twas a poor affair, a more poorer affair never I saw. Naught but Martins and Carters, the whole dashed danged blathering boiling of 'em, and a few o' the riffraff of the mines. I thought better o' Zacky than to invite such a poor lot of folk. Out o' my element I was——'

'Is aught amiss, sur?' Demelza asked.

Ross stared at her. 'Amiss? No, what should there be?'

'An' on the way back,' Jud said, 'hard by Wheal Grace I turned my heel 'pon a stone an' fell——'

But Ross had walked through into the house.

'You'd best keep yer tongue still when he's in one o' them moods,' Jud said severely to Demelza, 'or twon't be only your father you'll be gettin' a cuff from. Interrupting of your elders shows you been bad brought up . . .'

Demelza gazed at him wide-eyed but did not reply.

Ross could not see his gun in the parlour but found it in his bedroom. There he carefully loaded and primed it and pulled back the hammer to half cock. He had bolted the door of the stable so there should be no escape this time. He felt as if he had cornered an animal, a mad dog. There was only one way out of the stable.

In the gathering darkness he lit a storm lantern, and this time left the house by the front door, making a circuit of the building to reach the stable. Better not leave the man too long or he might do some hurt to the horses.

Quietly he drew the bolt of the door and waited for a gust of wind to die before lifting the catch. Then he pushed the door wide, entered, put the lantern down just out of the draught, and stepped away into the shadows of the stalls.

Darkie whinnied at his sudden entry; wind blew in, disturbing the straw and leaves; a bat fluttered away from the light; there was silence. The iron bar had gone.

'Reuben,' Ross said. 'Come out. I want to talk to you.'

No reply. He hadn't expected one. You could hear the fluttering of the bat's wings as it circled in the darkness. He went on into the stable.

As he reached the second horse he thought he heard a move behind him and turned swiftly, his gun up. But nothing stirred. He wished now he had brought the lantern farther, for its feeble light did not reach the deeper shadows.

Squire moved suddenly, stamping his hooves on the floor. All the horses knew there was mischief about. Ross waited five minutes, tense by the stall, knowing that now it was a test of patience, of whose nerve would stand the longest. He was sure of his own, but as time passed he found that sureness urging him to go on. The man might have gone back to the loft with his weapon. He might be cowering there, prepared to see the night through.

Ross heard Jud come out of the house and tramp across the cobbles. He thought at first he might be coming here, but heard him enter the earth closet next door. Presently he went back to the house and the door was shut. Still no movement in the stable.

Ross turned to go back for the lantern, and as he did so there was a hum of air behind him and a crash as the jumper was swung and hit the partition where he had been standing. Wood splintered and he turned and fired straight into the figure which came up in the darkness. Something hit him across the head and the figure was making for the door. As the man was outlined he pulled the trigger again. But this time the touch powder did not ignite; before he could pull back the cock Reuben Clemmow was gone.

He ran to the door and stared out. A figure moved beside the apple trees and he discharged the second barrel at it. Then he wiped a trickle of blood from his forehead and turned towards the house, from which Jud and Prudie and Demelza were just issuing in alarm. He was angry and frustrated at the man's escape, even though there was every likelihood of his being found in the morning.

It would be very difficult for him not to leave a trail.

Chapter thirteen

HE WAS OUT at dawn following the bloodstains which Clemmow had left behind; but just before they reached Mellin they turned north towards the sand hills and he lost track of them. In the days that followed nothing more was heard of the man, and the most reasonable conclusion was that he had lain down somewhere in that waste of sand and died of weakness and exposure. It was well to be finally rid of him, and nobody asked any questions. The fact that he had ever reappeared became a secret kept by the four members of the Nampara household and Zacky, whom Ross told.

During all the months of that summer the house of Nampara was seldom without flowers. This was Demelza's doing. She was always up at dawn and, now that the dread of being kidnapped and taken home for a thrashing had left her, she wandered at will in the fields and lanes, the lolloping Garrick trailing at her heels, to return with a big bunch of wild flowers, which found their way into the parlour.

Prudie had tried to break her of the habit, since it was not the duty of a kitchenmaid to brighten up the house with her gleanings; but Demelza went on bringing in the flowers, and her obstinacy and Prudie's inertia won the day. Sometimes it was a bunch of meadowsweet and ragged robin, sometimes an armful of foxgloves or a posy of sea pinks.

If Ross ever noticed these he made no comment.

The child was like a young animal which had spent fourteen years in blinkers, narrowing her gaze to the smallest domestic circle and the most primitive purposes; the first nine years linked closely to her mother in a succession of illnesses and ill treatment and poverty and childbirths, the last five facing all except the last alone. It was not surprising now that she expanded in body and in mind. She grew an inch in four months, and her interest in flowers was a symbol of her widening outlook.

She had taken to combing her hair and tying it back, where it sometimes stayed, so that her features had come out into the open. She was not an ill-looking girl and had a good clear skin and a quick mobility of expression; her eyes were intelligent and very frank. In another couple of years some young miner like Jim Carter would be courting her.

She was a very quick learner and something of a mimic, so that she began to add words to her vocabulary and to know how to pronounce them.

She also began to lose some. Ross had consulted Prudie – always a flattering way of approach – and Prudie, who could outswear a trooper when she chose, found herself committed to the reduction of Demelza's curse words.

Sometimes, faced by Demelza's probing questions, Prudie felt as if she were in a trap. Prudie knew what was right and proper, and Demelza did not. And it might be possible to teach some girls to behave themselves without taking care of your own behaviour, but Demelza was not one of them. She was much too quick in her conclusions; her thoughts raced ahead and met one on the rebound. So the process became not merely the willing education of Demelza but the unwilling regeneration of Prudie. It was not possible, she found, even to get drunk decently these days.

Ross looked on with amusement. Even Jud was not immune, but he bore the situation less graciously than his wife. He seemed to consider it an added grievance that she had not hit him with a broom handle for more than two months.

It was not a question of their being reformed by contact with the pure and lovely spirit of a child, for the child had as much original sin as they had.

If Demelza grew and developed, Garrick was a beanstalk. When he came he had been more of a puppy than anyone thought, and with proper food he enlarged so rapidly that one began to suspect the sheep dog in his ancestry. The sparse black curls of his coat remained, and his lack of tail made him curiously clumsy and unbalanced. He took a great fancy to Jud, who couldn't bear the sight of him, and the ungainly dog followed the bald old rascal everywhere. In July Garrick was pronounced free of parasites and admitted to the kitchen. He celebrated his entry by bounding across to Jud at the table and upsetting a jug of cider in his lap. Jud got up in a flood of cider and self-pity and aimed the jug at the dog, which scuttled out again, while Demelza fled into the dairy and covered her head with her hands in a paroxysm of laughter.

One day, to Ross's surprise, he received a visit from Mrs Teague and her youngest daughter, Ruth.

They had ridden over to Mingoose, Mrs Teague explained, and thought it sociable to call in at Nampara on the way home. Mrs Teague had not visited Nampara for nearly ten years and was so interested, she said, to see how Ross was managing for himself. Farming was such an engaging hobby, Mr Teague had always said.

'More than a hobby with me, ma'am,' Ross said. He had been mending the fence which bounded part of his land, and was dirty and dishevelled, his hands scarred and soiled and rusty. When he greeted them in the parlour the contrast with Mrs Teague's over-bright riding costume could not be ignored. Ruth too was got up to kill to-day.

Looking at her while they drank the cordial he ordered for them, he saw what it was that had taken him at the ball: the latent prettiness of the slightly rouged mouth, the unusual oblique set of her grey-green eyes, the lift of her wilful little chin. With some last despairing effort Mrs Teague had put a vitality into her youngest daughter that the others lacked.

They talked prettily about this and that. They had really been to call at the invitation of Mr John Treneglos, the eldest son of Mr Horace Treneglos of Mingoose. John was master of the Carnbarrow Hunt and had expressed supreme admiration for the way Ruth rode. He had invited them over so often that at last they felt impelled to gratify his request. What a noble house Mingoose was, was it not? The Gothic style and so very spacious, said Mrs Teague, looking round. Mr Treneglos was a most charming old gentleman; one could not help but notice how frail he had become.

How disappointing that Captain Poldark did not ride to hounds! Would it not do him a great matter of benefit, the mixing with other people of his own station and the thrill of the chase? Ruth always rode; it was her abiding passion; not of course that she was not highly accomplished in the gentler arts; one had to taste her syllabubs to know their richness; she had always believed, Mrs Teague said, in bringing up her children to be accomplished about the house; this piece of lace which she wore as a fichu had been made entirely by Ruth and Joan, though Joan had not the industry of her younger sister.

During all this Ruth looked uncomfortable, pouting her mouth and glancing obliquely about the room and tapping her riding whip against one of her small well-shod feet. But when her mother was otherwise occupied she found the opportunity to send him some knowledgeable and inviting looks. Ross thought of the few hours of daylight left and realized he would not complete the repair of the fence to-day.

Did he see much of the rest of the family? Mrs Teague asked. There had not been a single Poldark at the Lemon ball. Of course, one could not expect Elizabeth to go about so much as usual, now that she was expecting a confinement. Ruth blushed, and a sharp stab of pain went through Ross.

Was it true, Mrs Teague wondered, that Verity was still meeting that man, that Captain Blamey, somewhere in spite of her father's veto? One heard the rumour. No, well, of course, Ross wouldn't know, with being so much out of touch with the world.

At five-thirty they rose to go. They thanked him but would not stay to supper. It had been agreeable seeing him. Would he come over to visit them if they wrote fixing a day? Very well, one day at the beginning of next month. He had made Nampara most comfortable again. One felt, perhaps, that the touch of a woman's hand was needed to set it off, to give it graciousness and gentility. Did he not ever feel that way?

They moved to the front door, Mrs Teague chatting amiably, Ruth sulky and sweet by turns, trying to catch his eye and re-establish the flirtatious companionship of the ball. Their manservant brought their horses forward. Ruth mounted first, lightly and easily. She had the grace of youth and of the born horsewoman; she sat in the saddle as if made for it. Mrs Teague then mounted, satisfied with his approving glances, and he walked with them as far as the boundary of his land.

On the way Demelza passed them. She was carrying a basket of pilchards from Sawle, where the first catch of the season had just been landed. She was in the better of her two frocks of pink printed dimity and the sun shone on her tousled hair. A child, a girl, thin and angular with a long-legged stride; and then she raised her unexpected eyes.

She blinked once, curtsied awkwardly, passed on.

Mrs Teague took out a fine lace handkerchief and flicked a little dust from her habit. 'I heard you had – um – adopted a child, Captain Poldark. That is she?'

'I have adopted no one,' Ross said. 'I needed a kitchen wench. The child is old enough to know her own mind. She came. That is all there is about it.'

'A nice little thing,' said Mrs Teague. 'Yes, she looks as if she would know her own mind.'

II

The affairs of Verity and Captain Blamey came to a head at the end of August. It was unfortunate that this should occur on the day Ross had accepted Mrs Teague's invitation to return her call.

Verity had met Andrew Blamey four times at Nampara during the summer, once each time he was ashore.

Ross could not bring himself to dislike the seaman, for all his history. A quiet man with no small talk, a man with self-possessed eyes offset by an unusual modesty of bearing; the word one would instinctively choose to describe him was 'sober.' Yet sober was the last thing he had once been, if one merely accepted his own confession. Sometimes it was possible to sense a conflict. He had the reputation, Ross knew, for being a driver aboard his ship; and in the deliberate self-control, the self-containment of all his movements, one caught the echo of past struggles and guessed the measure of the victory won. His deference and tenderness towards Verity were obviously sincere.

If there was anyone he could dislike, it was himself and the role he was playing. He was abetting the meeting of two people whom common sense would emphasize were better apart. If things went wrong, he would be more to blame than anyone else. One could not expect clear-sightedness from two people deeply in love.

Nor was he at all comfortable about the progress of events. He was not present at their interviews, but he knew Blamey was trying to persuade Verity to run away with him, and that so far Verity had not brought herself to the point of agreement, still hoping that there might be a reconciliation between Andrew and her father. She had, however, agreed to go with him to Falmouth sometime soon and meet his children, and Ross had a suspicion that if she went she would not return. One could not go so far in a few minutes and be back without anyone being the wiser. This would be the thin end of disobedience. Once there he would persuade her to marry him rather than come back and face the storm.

The week before, Mrs Teague had sent a letter by one of her grooms inviting him to 'a small afternoon party' they were holding next Friday, at four. Heaping abuse on himself, he wrote out an acceptance while the man waited. The next day Verity came over to ask if she might meet Andrew Blamey at Nampara on Friday afternoon at three.

There was no need for Ross to be in while they met, except a convention which, knowing Verity, he didn't subscribe to; so he raised no objection, and only delayed long enough to welcome them.

Having seen them into the parlour and left word they were not to be disturbed, he got his horse and rode up the valley, casting regretful eyes about at all the work he might have been doing instead of riding away to play at foppery with a half-dozen silly young men and women. At the head of the valley, just beyond Wheal Maiden, he met Charles and Francis.

For a moment he was put out.

'A pleasure to welcome you on my land, Uncle,' he said. 'Were you thinking to pay me a visit? Another five minutes and you would have found me away.'

'That was our intention,' said Francis shortly.

Charles jerked his horse's head up. They were both looking flushed and angry.

'There's a rumour afoot that Verity is meeting that Blamey fellow at your house, Ross. We are riding over to discover the truth of it.'

'I'm afraid I can't offer you my hospitality this afternoon,' Ross said. 'I have an engagement at four – at some distance.'

'Verity's at your house now,' said Francis. 'We intend going down to see if Blamey is there, whether you like it or not.'

'Aarf!' said Charles. 'There's no need to be unpleasant, Francis. Perhaps we are mistaken. Give us your word of honour, boy, and we'll ride back without the need of a quarrel.'

'Well, but what is she doing there?' Francis asked truculently.

Ross said: 'Since my word of honour would not remove Captain Blamey, I can't give it.'

He watched Charles's expression change. 'God damn you, Ross, have you no sense of decency, no loyalty to your family, leaving her down there with that son of a whore?'

'I told you it was so!' Francis exclaimed, and without waiting for further talk turned his horse at a trot down the valley towards Nampara.

'I think you misjudge the man,' Ross said slowly.

Charles snorted. 'I think I have misjudged you.' He followed his son.

Ross watched them nearing the house with an unpleasant premonition of ill. Their words and looks left no doubt of the attitude they would take.

He pulled at Darkie's head and followed in their wake.

III

When he reached the house Francis was already in the parlour. He could hear the raised voices as Charles slid laboriously from his horse.

When they got inside Captain Blamey was standing beside the fireplace, one hand on Verity's sleeve, as if to stop her from coming between him and Francis. He was in his captain's laced coat of fine blue cloth with a white wing collar and black cravat. He wore his most self-contained look, as if all unruly passion were locked away, bolted and unreachable, guarded by all the controls of his own choosing and testing. He looked sturdy and middle-aged against the flushed handsome arrogance of Francis's youth. Ross noticed that Charles was carrying his riding whip.

'. . . no way to speak to your sister,' Blamey was saying. 'Any hard words you've a mind to speak can come to me.'

'Dirty skunk!' Charles said. 'Sneaking behind our backs. My only daughter.'

'Sneaking,' said Blamey, 'because you would not meet to talk over the matter. Do you think——'

'Talk it over!' said Charles. 'There's nothing to talk over wi' wife murderers. We don't like 'em in this district. They leave a nasty stink in the nostrils. Verity, get your horse and go home.'

She said quietly: 'I have a right to choose my own life.'

'Go, dear,' said Blamey. 'It's no place for you now.'

She shook off his hand. 'I stay.'

'Then stay and be damned!' said Francis. 'There's only one way of treating your sort, Blamey. Words and honour don't count. Perhaps a thrashing will.' He began to take off his coat.

'Not on my land,' said Ross. 'Begin any brawl here and I'll throw you off it myself.'

There was a moment's nonplussed silence.

'God's name!' exploded Charles. 'You have the impudence to take his side!'

'I take no one's side, but you won't change the issue with horseplay.'

'One skunk and another,' said Francis. 'You're small matter better than he is.'

'You heard what your sister said,' Captain Blamey interposed quietly.

'She has the right to choose her own life. I have no wish to quarrel, but she is coming away with me.'

'I'll see you in hell first,' Francis said. 'There'll be no cleaning of your boots on our family.'

Captain Blamey suddenly went very white. 'You insolent puppy!'

'Puppy, is it now!' Francis leaned forward and smacked Captain Blamey with an open hand across his cheek.

The red mark showed, and then Blamey hit Francis in the face and Francis went to the floor.

There was a brief pause. Verity had backed away from them both, her face small and sick.

Francis sat up and with the back of his hand wiped a streak of blood from his nose. He got to his feet.

'When will it be convenient for you to meet me, Captain Blamey,' he said.

Having found outlet, the seaman's anger had ebbed. But somehow his composure was not the same. If only for a moment, the controls had been broken.

'I leave for Lisbon by to-morrow's tide.'

Francis's expression was contemptuous. 'That, of course, is what I would have expected.'

'Well, there is still to-day.'

Charles stepped forward. 'Nay, there's no call for these damned Frenchy methods, Francis. Let's thrash the beggar and then go.'

'There'll be none of that, neither,' said Ross.

Francis licked his lips. 'I demand satisfaction. You can't deny that. The fellow once laid claim to be a gentleman. Let him come outside and meet me – if he's got the guts.'

'Andrew,' Verity said. 'Don't agree to anything . . .'

The sailor glanced at the girl distantly, as if her brother's hostility had already separated them.

'Fight it out with fists,' said Charles stertorously. 'The skunk's not worth the risk of a pistol ball, Francis.'

'Nothing else will discourage him,' said Francis. 'I'll trouble you for weapons, Ross. If you refuse them I'll send over to Trenwith for my own.'

'Send over, then,' snapped Ross. 'I'll be no party to your blood-letting.'

'They're on the wall behind you, man,' said Blamey, between his teeth.

Francis turned and took down the silver duelling pistols with which Ross had threatened Demelza's father. 'Will they still fire?' he said coldly, addressing Ross.

Ross did not speak.

'Come outside, Blamey,' Francis said.

'Look, boy,' said Charles. 'This is stuff and nonsense. It's my quarrel and——'

'Nothing of the sort. He knocked me down——'

'Come away and have no truck with the varmint. Verity will come with us, won't you, Verity?'

'Yes, Father.'

Francis looked at Ross. 'Call your man and get him to see these pistols are properly primed.'

'Get him yourself.'

'There are no seconds,' said Charles. 'There's no suitable arrangements.'

'Formality! One needs no formality when stalking a crow.'

They went outside. It was easy to see that Francis was determined to have his satisfaction. Blamey, white about the nostrils, stood apart, as if the business didn't concern him. Verity made a last appeal to her brother, but he snapped at her that some solution to her infatuation must be found and he had chosen this one.

Jud was outside, so there was no need to call him. He was visibly interested and impressed by the responsibility thrust on him. He had only seen such a thing once before and that thirty years ago. Francis told him to act as referee and to count out fifteen paces for them; Jud glanced at Ross, who shrugged.

'Yes, sur, fifteen did ye say.'

They were in the open space of grass before the house. Verity had refused to go indoors. She held to the back of the garden seat.

The men stood back to back, Francis an inch or more the taller, his fair hair glinting in the sun.

'Ready, sur?'

'Aye.'

Ross made a movement forward but checked himself. The headstrong fool must have his way.

'Then go. One, two, three, fower, five, six . . .'

As Jud counted the two men paced away from each other, and a swallow dipped and swerved between them.

At the word fifteen they turned. Francis fired first and hit Blamey in the hand. Blamey dropped his pistol. He bent and picked it up with his left hand and fired back. Francis put up a hand to his neck and fell to the ground.

IV

Ross's thought as he went forward was, I should have stopped them. What will this mean to Elizabeth if Francis . . . ?

He turned Francis over upon his back and ripped away the ruffles of his shirt. The ball had gone into the base of the neck by the shoulder but had not come out again. Ross lifted him and carried him into the house.

'My God!' said Charles, following helplessly with the others. 'The boy's dead . . . My boy——'

'Nonsense,' Ross said. 'Jud, take Mr Francis's horse and ride for Dr Choake. Say there has been a shooting accident. Not the truth, mind.'

'Is the hurt – serious?' Captain Blamey said, with a kerchief about his hand. 'I——'

'Get out of here!' said Charles, empurpled. 'How dare you come into the house again!'

'Don't crowd about him,' Ross urged, having laid Francis on the sofa. 'Prudie, get me some clean rags and a bowl of hot water.'

'Let me help,' said Verity. 'Let me help. I can do something. I can——'

'No, no. Leave him be.'

There was silence for some moments until Prudie returned in haste with the bowl. Ross had kept the wound from bleeding excessively until now by pressing on it with his own coloured kerchief. Now he lifted this and pressed a damp cloth in its place. Francis winced and groaned.

'He'll be all right,' said Ross. 'Only give him room to breathe.'

Captain Blamey picked up his hat and left the room. Outside he sat a moment on the seat beside the front door and put his head in his hands.

'God's blood, that gave me a fright,' said Charles, wiping his face and neck and under his wig. 'I thought the boy was gone. A mercy the fellow didn't shoot with his right hand.'

'Perhaps then he would have missed more cleanly,' Ross said.

Francis turned and muttered and opened his eyes. It took some moments for full consciousness to return. The rancour had left his eyes.

'Has the fellow gone?'

'Yes,' said Ross.

Francis grinned wryly. 'I winged him. It was your pesty duelling arms, Ross. Their sighting must be awry. Ach! Well, this will save the leeches for a week or two.'

Outside in the garden Verity had rejoined Andrew Blamey.

He had withdrawn completely within himself. In the space of fifteen minutes their relationship had been irrevocably changed.

'I must go,' he said; and they both at once noticed the pronoun. 'It's better before he comes round.'

'Oh, my dear, if you could have – shot wide – or not at all . . .'

He shook his head, oppressed with the complex struggles of his own nature and with the futility of trying to explain.

She said: 'This – I know it was his seeking – all this quarrel. But he is my brother. It makes it so *impossible* for me . . .'

He struggled to find the hope to argue. 'In time it will cool, Verity. Our feelings can't change.'

She did not answer but sat with lowered head.

He stared at her hard for some seconds. 'Perhaps Francis was right.

There has been only trouble. Perhaps I shouldn't ever have thought of you – have looked at you.'

She said: 'No, Francis wasn't right. But after this . . . there can never be any reconciling . . .'

After a minute he got up.

'Your hand,' she said. 'Let me tie it.'

'It's only a scratch. A pity his aim wasn't better.'

'Can you ride? Your fingers——'

'Yes, I can ride.'

She watched him walk round the house. He held his shoulders like an old man.

He came back mounted.

'Good-bye, my love. If there's nothing else, give me leave to keep the memory.'

She watched him cross the stream and ride slowly up the valley until the image in her eyes was suddenly misted and smeared.

Chapter fourteen

THE WHOLE PARTY was back at Trenwith. Francis, temporarily patched, had ridden his horse home, and now Choake was with him, making a showy job of the dressing. Charles, belching wind and the remnants of his anger, had stumped off to his own room to take a vomit and rest until supper.

Elizabeth had almost fainted at the sight of her husband. But recovering herself, she had flown up and downstairs to hasten Mrs Tabb and Bartle in supplying Dr Choake's needs and in tending to the wounded man's comfort. As would be the case all through her life, she had a store of nervous energy, unavailable at ordinary times but able to serve her in sudden need. It was a fundamental reserve which a stronger person might never know.

And Verity had gone to her room . . .

She felt herself detached from this household of which she had been a part for twenty-five years. She was among strangers. More than that, they were hostile strangers. They had drawn away from her, and she from them, for lack of understanding. In an afternoon she had shrunk inside herself; there would grow up a core of friendlessness and isolation.

She pushed the bolt across the door and sat abruptly in the first chair. Her romance was over; even though she rebelled against the fact, she knew that it was so. She felt faint and sick, and desperately tired of being alive. If death could come quietly and peacefully she would accept it, would sink into it as one sank into a bed wanting only sleep and self-forgetfulness.

Her eyes moved round the room. Every article in it was familiar with the extreme unseeing intimacy of everyday association.

Through the long sash window and the narrow window in the alcove she had looked with the changing eyes of childhood and youth. She had looked out on the herb garden and the yew hedge and the three bent sycamores in all the seasons of the year and in all the moods of her own growth. She had seen frost draw its foliate patterns upon the panes, raindrops run down them like tears on old cheeks, the first spring sun shine dustily through them upon the turkey rug and the stained oak boards.

The old French clock on the carved pine chimneypiece, with its painted and gilt figures, like a courtesan from the days of Louis XIV, had been in the room all Verity's life. Its thin metallic bell had been announcing the hours for more than fifty years. When it was made Charles was a thin strip of a boy, not a breathless empurpled old man breaking up his daughter's romance. They had been together, child and clock, girl and clock, woman and clock, through illness and nightmare and fairy stories and daydreams, through all the monotony and the splendour of life.

Her eyes went on, to the glass-topped display table with the carved legs, to the two pink satin bedroom chairs, the cane rocking-chair, the stumpy brass candlesticks with the candles rising in steps, the pincushion, the embroidered workbasket, the two-handled washing urn. Even the decorations of the room, the long damask curtains, the flock wallpaper with its faded crimson flowers on an ivory ground, the white plaster roses of the cornice and ceiling, had become peculiarly and completely her own.

She knew that here in the privacy of her own room, where no man except her brother and her father ever came, she could give way, could lie on the bed and weep, could abandon herself to sorrow. But she sat on the chair and didn't move at all.

There were no tears in her. The wound went too deep, or she was not so constituted to give way to it. Hers would be the perpetual ache of loss and loneliness, slowly dulled with time until it became a part of her character, a faint sourness tinged with withered pride.

Andrew would be back in Falmouth by now, back in the lodgings she had heard of but never seen. Through his quiet talk she had seen the bleakness of his life ashore, the two rooms in the lodging-house by the quay, the drab woman who looked after him.

She had thought to change all that. They had planned to rent a cottage overlooking the bay, a place with a few trees and a small garden running down to the shingle beach. Though he had scarcely ever spoken of his first marriage, she had understood enough to be certain that much of the fault of the failure lay with her – however inexcusable on his side the end might have been. She had felt that she could make up for that first failure. With her busy hands and managing ability and with their mutual love she would have made for him a home such as he had not had before.

Instead this room which had seen her grow to maturity would see her dry up and fade. The gilt mirror in the corner would bear its dispassionate testimony. All these ornaments and furnishings would be her companions through the years to come. And she realized that she would come to hate them, if she didn't already hate them, as one hates the witnesses of one's humiliation and futility.

She made a halfhearted attempt to shake herself out of this mood. Her father and her brother had acted in good faith, true to their upbringing and principles. If as a result she remained at their beck and call until she was old, it was not fair to blame them for the whole. They thought they had 'saved her from herself.' Her life in Trenwith would be more peaceful, more sheltered than as the wife of a social outcast. She was among relatives and friends. The long summer days were full of interest about the farm: the sowing, the haymaking, the harvesting; butter and cheeses to superintend, syrups and conserves to make. The winter ones were full too. Needlework in the evening, making curtains and samplers and stockings, spinning wool and flax with Aunt Agatha, brewing simples; playing at quadrille when there were guests, or helping Mr Odgers to train the choir at Sawle Church, dosing the servants with possets when they were ill.

This winter too there would be a newcomer in the house. If she had gone, Elizabeth would have been doubly lost; Francis would have found the well-run routine of the house suddenly out of joint, Charles would have no one to arrange his cushions or see that his silver tankard was polished before each meal. For these and a hundred other small needs the household depended on her, and if they did not repay her with overt thanks they showed her a tacit affection and friendship she couldn't disregard.

And if she had not found these duties irksome in the past, was it not just the first flush of disappointment which said they must be so in the future?

So she might argue, but Andrew said no. Andrew sitting now with his head in his hands in the dismal lodgings in Falmouth, Andrew next week in the Bay of Biscay, Andrew tramping the streets of Lisbon by night, or next month back in his lodgings, Andrew eating and drinking and sleeping and waking and *being*, said no. He had taken a place in her heart, or taken a *part* of her heart, and nothing would be the same again.

Last year she had drifted on a tide of custom and habit. She might so have drifted, without protest, into a contented and unambitious middle age. But this year, from now on, she must swim against the stream, not finding stimulus in the struggle but only bitterness and regret and frustration.

She sat there in the room by herself until darkness came and the shadows of the room closed about her like comforting arms.

Chapter fifteen

WHEAL LEISURE WAS not started that summer.

After some hesitancy Ross invited Francis to join them. Francis refused rather brusquely; but something more imponderable than this held up the project. The price of copper in the open market fell to £80 a ton. To begin a new seeking venture at such a time would be asking for failure.

Francis mended rapidly from his neck wound, but Ross's part in Verity's love affair still rankled with him and his father. Rumour had it that Poldark and his young wife had been spending money at an extravagant rate, and now that Elizabeth did not go out much Francis went everywhere with George Warleggan.

Ross saw little of Verity, for during the rest of the summer she scarcely left Trenwith. He wrote to Mrs Teague apologizing for his default, 'owing to unforeseen and unavoidable circumstances.' There was very little else he could say. He did not receive a reply. Later he learned that the 'small party' was Ruth's birthday party, at which he was to have been the guest of honour. It was by then too late to implement his apology and the damage was done.

After the postponement of the Wheal Leisure venture Jim Carter left his employment. He was not the sort of young man to be a farm labourer all his life, and Grambler reclaimed him.

He came to Ross one evening in August after they had spent all day cutting a field of barley, and explained that Jinny would not be able to work at Grambler after Christmas – at least not for the time – and they could not afford to be without her earnings. So, as he had never felt better in his life, he had taken a tribute on the forty-fathom level.

'I'm proper sorry to be leaving, sir,' he said. 'But it's a good pitch. I know that. Wi' luck I shall make thirty or thirty-five shillings a month, and that's what we've got to think on. If we could stay on at the cottage, we'd like to pay rent for it.'

'So you shall,' said Ross, 'when I think you can afford it. Don't be so generous with your money till you see if it goes round.'

'No, sir,' said Jim inarticulately. 'Twasn't exactly that——'

'I know, boy; I'm not blind. Nor, by the way, am I deaf. I heard it whispered that you had been out poaching the other night with Nick Vigus.'

Jim went crimson. He stammered and seemed about to deny it, then abruptly said, 'Yes.'

'It's a dangerous pastime,' Ross said. 'Whose land did you go on?'

'Treneglos.'

Ross suppressed a smile. His warning was, in fact, deadly serious, and he had no wish to weaken it.

'Keep away from Nick Vigus, Jim. He'll lead you into trouble before you know it.'

'Yes, sir.'

'What does Jinny say?'

'The same as you, sir. I promised her not to go again.'

'Then keep your promise.'

''Twas for 'er that I went. I thought something tasty——'

'How is she?'

'Proper, sir, thank you. We're that happy, just the two of us, that I wish, in a manner o' speaking, that there weren't going to be another. Still, Jinny's happy about that too. It isn't she that's afraid.'

II

Subtle changes were continuing to take place in the relationship between Demelza Carne and the rest of the Nampara household. Her mind having outstripped the Paynters, she turned elsewhere for information, and this brought her more into contact with Ross, who found some pleasure in helping her. He wanted to laugh at her remarks much more often than he allowed himself.

At the end of August, during the week the corn was being ricked, Prudie slipped and hurt her leg and had to lie up.

For four days Demelza flew about the house, and although Ross was not in to see what she did, the midday meal was always brought out in time and the larger evening meal was always ready when they came wearily home. Demelza did not cling to her new-found authority when Prudie got up, but their relationship was never again that of housekeeper and scullery maid. The only comment on the change came from Jud, who told his wife that she was getting as soft as an old mare.

Ross did not speak to Demelza about her efforts on those four days but when he was next in Truro he bought her one of the scarlet cloaks which were so fashionable in the mining villages of West Cornwall. When she saw it she was speechless – an unusual symptom – and bore it off to her bedroom to try it on. Later he caught her looking at him in a peculiar manner; it was as if she felt it only right and proper for her to be aware of his likes and wants – that was what she was here for; but for him to know hers was not quite in the bargain.

In place of Jim, Ross took an elderly man called Jack Cobbledick. He was a saturnine man, slow of thought and speech, with a ginger-grey drooping moustache, through which he strained all his food, and a long heavy-legged gait, as if he was always mentally striding through tall grass. Demelza nearly got into trouble several times when walking across the yard lifting her own long legs in imitation.

In September, when the pilchard season was at its height, Ross rode into Sawle now and then to see the fish brought in or to buy a half hogshead for salting down when the quality was good. In this he found Demelza, with her experience of catering for a large and poor family, a better judge than himself, so she sometimes rode behind him on his horse or walked on half an hour in advance. Sometimes Jud would drive over with a couple of oxen yoked to a rickety cart and buy up a load of the broken and damaged fish for half a guinea to dig into the land as manure.

From the church of Sawle you went down Stippy-Stappy Lane, and at the bottom was a narrow humped bridge and a green square surrounded by sheds and cottages, which was the nucleus of the village of Sawle. From here it was a few yards to the high bar of shingle and the shallow inlet of the bay.

Just clear of the bar were two gaunt fish-packing houses, and about these the summer industry of the village centred. Here the fish were picked over and packed into cellars for a month or so until the oil and blood had drained off them and they could be preserved and exported in hogsheads to the Mediterranean.

III

Elizabeth's child was born at the end of October. It was a difficult and protracted birth, but she stood the strain well and would have rallied more quickly had not Dr Choake decided to bleed her the day afterwards. As a result of that she spent twenty-four hours going off into dead faints which alarmed everyone and from which it needed any number of burnt feathers held under the nose to revive her.

Charles was delighted at the event, and the news that it was a boy roused him from his after-dinner stupor.

'Splendid!' he said to Francis. 'Well done, my boy. I'm proud of you. So we have a grandson, eh? Damme, that's just what I wanted.'

'You have Elizabeth to thank, not I,' said Francis pallidly.

'Eh? Well, I expect you did your part?' Charles quivered with subterranean laughter. 'Never mind, boy; I'm proud of you both. Didn't think she had it in her. What are you going to name the brat?'

'We have not yet decided,' Francis said sulkily.

Charles prised his great bulk out of the chair and waddled into the hall to stare around. 'Well, we've a fine variety of names in the family without going farther afield. Let's see, there's Robert, and Claude . . . and Vivian . . . and Henry. And two or three Charleses. What's wrong with Charles, eh, boy?'

'It must be for Elizabeth to decide.'

'Yes, yes, she'll do that, I expect. Anyhow, I hope she doesn't choose Jonathan. Infernal silly name. Where's Verity?'

'Upstairs now, helping.'

'Well, tell me when the brat's open to receive its grandfather. A boy, eh? Well done, both of you.'

Elizabeth's weakness delayed the christening until early December, and then it took place on a quieter scale than Charles would have liked. There were only eighteen present including the immediate family.

Dorothy Johns, Cousin William-Alfred's wife, had been caught between her pregnancies and was with him. She was a dried-up, prim little woman of forty with a reserved, sub-acid smile and inhibitions ahead of her outspoken age. She never used the word bowels even in private conversation, and there were subjects which she did not mention at all, a matter for astonishment among most of her women friends. Her last two confinements had told heavily on her, and Ross thought that she looked drawn and wrinkled. Would Elizabeth someday come to look like this? Her first child seemed even to have improved her looks.

She lay upon the couch where Francis had carried her. A great log fire was blazing and the flames leapt up the chimney like chained hounds. The big room was warm and people's glances were lit by the reflection of the fire; outside the grey cold day curled in a thin fog about the windows. There were flowers in the room, and Elizabeth lay among them like a lily while everyone moved around her. Her fine clear skin was waxen about the arms and throat, but in her cheeks there was more colour than usual. She had the hot-house bloom of the lily.

They named the child Geoffrey Charles. A bundle of blue silk and lace, with a small round fluffy head, deep blue eyes and Aunt Agatha's gums. During the christening he made no protest and afterwards he went back to his mother, uncomplaining. A model baby, they all agreed.

Over the meal which followed, Charles and Mr Chynoweth discussed cockfighting, and Mrs Choake talked to anyone who would listen of the latest rumours about the Prince of Wales. It was all over the country that he had been so driven to distraction by Mrs Fitzherbert's refusal to become bis mistress that one morning this month he had attempted to cut his throat with a razor. Mrs Fitzherbert had been summoned at once to Carlton House in great secrecy, but what had happened there one could only *guess*.

Mrs Chynoweth talked to George Warleggan and monopolized his attention, much to Patience Teague's annoyance. Aunt Agatha munched crumbs and strove hard to hear what Mrs Chynoweth was saying. Verity sat silent and stared at the table. Dr Choake pulled his eyebrows down and from under them told Ross some of the charges which ought to be preferred against Hastings, the governor general of Bengal. Ruth Teague, embarrassingly near Ross, tried to carry on a conversation with her mother as if he were not there.

Ross was faintly amused at Ruth's attitude, but a little puzzled at a constraint towards himself in one or two of the other ladies – Dorothy Johns and Mrs Chynoweth and Mrs Choake. He had done nothing to offend them. Elizabeth went out of her way to be kind.

And then in the middle of the luncheon Charles climbed laboriously to his feet to propose a toast to his grandson, spoke for some minutes breathing like a bulldog, then banged his chest, exclaimed impatiently, 'This wind, this wind,' and slid sideways to the floor.

With clumsy-handed care they upended the mountain of flesh, levering him first upon a chair, then bearing him step by step upstairs to his bedroom: Ross and Francis and George Warleggan and Dr Choake.

Once upon the massive four-poster bed with its heavy snuff-brown hangings, he seemed to breathe more easily, but he did not move or speak. Verity, roused from her lethargy, hurried about doing the doctor's bidding. Choake bled him and listened to his heart and straightened up and scratched the bald patch at the back of his own head, as if that might help.

'M' yes,' he said. 'I think we will do now. A heart stroke. We must be left perfectly quiet and warm. Have the windows kept shut and the curtains of the bed drawn so that there is no risk of a chill. He is so very big, hm; one must hope for the best.'

When Ross returned to the subdued company downstairs he found them settling to wait. It would be impolite to leave until there was some more definite word from the doctor. Elizabeth was much upset, they said, and had asked to be excused.

Aunt Agatha was gently rocking the cradle and plucking at the white hairs on her chin. 'A bad omen,' she said. 'On little Charles's christening day for big Charles to go down like that. Just like an elmin tree strick by lightning. I hope nothing will come of it.'

Ross went into the large parlour. There was no one there and he moved to the window. The gloomy day had grown heavier and darker, and there was a freckle of rain on the glass.

Change and decay. Was Charles, then, to go so soon the way of Joshua? He had been failing for some time, getting purpler and looser and more unwieldy. Old Agatha and her omens. How would it affect Verity? Little enough except for her bereavement. Francis would become master of this house and all the land. He would have a free rein to go the pace with Warleggan if he chose. Perhaps responsibility would sober him.

He moved out of the parlour into the next room, the library, which was small and dark and smelt of mildew and dust. Charles had been no more of a reader than his brother; their father, Claude Henry, had done most of the collecting.

Ross glanced over the shelves. He heard someone come into the parlour talking, but took no particular notice, for he had found a new edition of Dr Burns's *Justice of the Peace*. He had turned to the chapter on lunacy when Mrs Teague's voice, coming through the open door, took his attention.

'Well, dear child, what else can one expect? Like father like son, I always say.'

'My dear ma'am' – it was Polly Choake – 'the tales one hears about old Jothua! Most comical. I only do wish as I had been in these parts then.'

'A gentleman,' said Mrs Teague, 'knows where to draw the line. Towards a lady of his own class his intentions should be most strictly honourable. His attitude to a woman of a lower class is different. After all, men are men. It is very disagreeable, I know; but if a thing is gone about in the right way and the wench is provided for, there is no reason for anyone to come to harm. Joshua would never face up to the distinction. That was why I disapproved of him; that was why all the county disapproved of him and he was always fighting with fathers and husbands. He was too *loose* with his affections.'

Polly giggled. 'Pwomithcuouth, as you might thay!'

Mrs Teague warmed to her subject. 'The tales I could tell you of the hearts he broke! Scandal followed scandal. And like father like son, I always say. But even Joshua kept his own house free from sluts and queans. Even he did not kidnap a starveling beggar wench before she had reached the age of consent and seduce her on his own hearth. And to keep her openly for what she is: that is the worst part! It would be different if he kept her in her place. It's not good for the vulgars to know that one of their sluts is living in a position of equality with a man of Ross's standing. It puts ideas into their heads. To tell the truth when I was last over to see him – just a passing call, you understand, and that many months ago – I saw the creature. A hussy. Already beginning to put on airs. You can tell the type anywhere.'

'Hardly a day patheth,' Polly Choake said, 'but what he comes widing into Thawle, with she behind on the same horthe, all fligged up in a scarlet cloak.'

'It isn't good enough at all. It isn't good for the family. I wonder they don't tell him it must stop.'

'Maybe they don't fancy to.' Polly giggled. 'They do thay as how he ith a quick-tempered man. Mythelf, I shouldn't like to do it, for he might stwike one a blow.'

'Charles has been too easygoing,' came a fresh voice. So Mrs Chynoweth was there. She sounded annoyed. 'When Charles is gone Francis will take a different line. If Ross refuses to listen he must accept the consequences.' There was the sound of a door opening and shutting.

Polly Choake giggled again. 'No doubt she would dearly like to be mistreth of Trenwith 'stead of Elizabeth. P'waps then she would weform Francis too. My husband, Dr Choake, tells me as how he lost a hundred guineas on the turn of a card last night.'

'Gambling is a gentleman's pastime, Polly,' said Mrs Teague. 'Possibly——'

Polly's giggle became louder. 'Don't tell me bedding ith not!'

'Hush, child; you must learn to moderate your voice. It isn't——'

'That ith what the doctor always thays——'

'And very rightly. Especially is it unseemly to raise one's voice in laughter in a house of sickness. Tell me, child, what are the other rumours you have heard about him?'

Chapter sixteen

CHARLES WAS INCONSIDERATE enough not to gain his senses in time to satisfy the christening guests. Ross's parting picture of the unusually quiet house was of Aunt Agatha still rocking the baby and a thin bead of saliva trickling down one of the wrinkles of her chin as she muttered, 'Tis an omen, for sure. I wonder what will come of it.'

It was not, however, of Charles's illness or Geoffrey Charles's future that Ross thought on the way home. . . .

At Nampara they had been preparing for the winter by lopping off some of the branches of the elm trees for kindling wood. One tree only was condemned, whose roots, in the soft ground by the stream, were uncertain after the autumn gales. Jud Paynter and Jack Cobbledick had a rope tied to one of the higher branches and were using a two-handled saw on the trunk. When they had worked for a few minutes they would walk away and tug at the rope to see if the trunk would snap off. The rest of the household had come out in the afternoon twilight to watch. Demelza was dancing about trying to help, and Prudie, her muscular arms crossed like the knotted roots of the tree, was standing by the bridge giving unwelcome advice.

She turned and bent her heavy brows at Ross.

'I'll take the mare. And 'ow went the christening, an? Did ee get a nice drop of bed-ale? And the brat, dear of 'm; like Mr Francis, is 'e?'

'Like enough. What is the matter with Demelza?'

'One of 'er moods. I says to Jud, that girl, I says, will come to mischief in one o' them moods. She's bin like that ever since her fadder left.'

'Her father? What was his business here?'

'No more'n a 'alf hour after you'd left, he come. By 'is self this time, and in his Sunday britches. "Want to see my dattur," 'e says, quiet like an old bear; and she come tripping over 'erself out of the house to meet him.'

'Well?'

'Ye want for to draw at the old tree from the other side,' Prudie advised in a voice like a pipe organ. 'He won't come down just by playin' maypole with un.'

Jud's reply was happily carried away down-wind. Ross walked slowly towards the men, and Demelza came running to meet him, running with an occasional hop as she did when excited.

So absence had made the heart grow fonder and there was a reconciliation between father and daughter at last. No doubt she would want to return home, and the silly malicious gossip would lose its point.

'He won't come down,' she said, turning as she reached him and pushing back her mop of hair to gaze at the tree. 'He's strongerer than we suspicioned.'

Silly malicious gossip. Wicked empty dirty gossip. He could have wrung Polly Choake's useless little neck. He might not have got Elizabeth but he had not yet sunk so low as to seduce his own kitchenmaid. Demelza of all wenches, whose dirty skinny little body he had deluged with cold water when she came, not so many months ago it seemed. She had grown since then. He supposed that the gossips of the countryside could not conceive of the son of Joshua living a celibate life. Some women had minds like addle-gutters; if there was no stench they had to create one.

Demelza shifted and glanced at him uneasily, as if aware of his scrutiny. She reminded him of a restive foal, with her long legs and wayward eye. When she was in one of her moods, as Prudie called them, there was no foreseeing what she would do next.

'Your father has been here,' he said.

Her face lighted up. 'Yes-s-s! I've made en up with him. I'm some happy 'bout that!' Her look changed as she tried to read his expression. 'Did I do wrong?'

'Of course not, When does he wish you to return?'

'If 'e'd wanted that I couldn't have made en up, could I?' She laughed with pleasure, an infectious bubbling laugh. 'He don't want for me to go back, for he's wed again. He was marre'd again last Monday! So now he's ready to be friendly an' I don't have to feel every night, what's Brother Luke doing and do Brother Jack miss me. The Widow Chegwidden will look after him betterer than ever I could. Widow Chegwidden is Methody, and she'll look after they all right.'

'Oh,' said Ross. So he was not to be rid of his charge after all.

'I believe she think to reform Fathur. She believe she can make him tee-tottle. That's where she'll be mistook, I reckon.'

The two men, having sawed for a few minutes, solemnly walked away to the end of the rope and began to pull. Ross joined them and added his weight. He was pleased at the girl's loyalty to himself, pleased too at her pleasure. A perverse spirit within him was glad that he was not to have the easy way of meeting the scurrilous gossip. Let them talk till their tongues dropped out.

But surely Elizabeth wouldn't believe such a story. He must make the matter plain to Elizabeth.

He gave an extra hard tug on the rope, and it snapped where it had been knotted to a branch of the tree. He sat down with the other two men. Garrick, who had been out on a private rabbit hunt and missing the fun, came rushing down the valley and gambolled about the three men, licking Jud's face as Jud got to his knees.

'Dang the blathering whelp!' said Jud, spitting.

'It's poor stuff you rely on,' said Ross. 'Where did you find it?'

'In the library——'

''Twas soggy at one end,' said Demelza. 'The rest is sound.'

She picked up the rope and began to climb the tree like a playful cat.

'Come back!' Ross said.

'She put en up thur first time,' said Jud, aiming a kick at Garrick.

'She had no business to. But now . . .' Ross went nearer. 'Demelza! Come down!'

She heard him this time and stopped to peer through the branches. 'What's to do? I'm all but there.'

'Then tie it at once and come down.'

'I'll loop en over at the next branch.' She put her foot up and climbed a few feet higher.

'Come down!'

There was an ominous crack.

'Look for yourself!' shouted Jud.

Demelza paused and looked down, more than ever like a cat now which had found its foothold insecure. She gave a squeak as the tree began to go. Ross jumped out of the way.

The tree fell with a drawn-out noise exactly like the tipping of a load of slates. One second it was all noise, and the next there was complete silence.

He ran forward but could not get very near because of the far-flung branches. Right in the middle Demelza suddenly appeared, climbing with pawing movements among the branches. Prudie came flapping across from the stables, shouting, 'My ivers! My ivers!'

Jack Cobbledick reached the girl first from his side, but they had to cut away some of the smaller branches before they could get her clothing free. She crawled out laughing. Her hands were scraped and her knees bleeding; the calf of one leg was interlaced with scratches but otherwise she had come to no harm.

Ross glowered at her. 'You'll do as I tell you in future. I want no broken limbs here.'

Her laughter faded before his glance. 'No.' She licked the blood off one palm, then glanced down at her frock. 'Dear life, I've breeked my dress.' She screwed her neck round at an impossible angle to see the back.

'Take the child and give her something for those cuts,' Ross said to Prudie. 'She's beyond me now.'

II

In Trenwith House the evening moved towards its close.

When those guests had gone who were not staying the night a flatness and lethargy fell on the house. The absence of wind and the glowing ashes of the great log fire made the hall unusually cosy, and five high-backed well-padded chairs supported a semicircle of relatives drinking port.

Upstairs in his great curtained bed Charles Poldark, at the end of his active life, took short and anxious gasps at the vitiated air which was all medical science allowed him. In another room farther along the west passage Geoffrey Charles, at the beginning of his active life, was taking in the nourishment his mother could offer him, with which medical science had not found a means to tamper.

During the last month Elizabeth had known all kinds of new sensations. The birth of her child had been the supreme experience of her life, and looking down now at the crown of Geoffrey Charles's fluffy pale head so close to her own white skin, she was filled with a frightening sense of pride and power and fulfilment. In the instant of his birth her existence was changed; she had accepted, had seized upon a life-long commission of motherhood, a proud and all-absorbing task beside which ordinary duties became void.

After a long period of great weakness she had suddenly begun to pick up, and during the last week had felt as well as ever in her life. But she was dreamy, indolent, happy to lie a little longer and think about her son and gaze at him and let him sleep in the crook of her arm. It would have distressed her very much to feel that by staying in bed she was putting more responsibility on Verity, but she could not yet summon up the resolve to break the spell of invalidism and move about as before. She could not bear the separation from her son.

This evening she lay in bed and listened to the sound of movement about the old house. During her illness, with her very quick ears, she had come to identify every noise; each door made a different sound when opened: the treble and bass creak of unoiled hinges, the click and scrape of different latches, the loose board here and the uncarpeted patch there, so that she could follow the movements of everyone in the west part of the house.

Mrs Tabb brought her supper, a slice of capon's breast, a coddled egg and a glass of warm milk, and about nine Verity came in and sat for ten minutes. Verity had got over her disappointment very well, Elizabeth thought. A little quieter, a little more preoccupied with the life of the household. She had wonderful strength of mind and self-reliance. Elizabeth was grateful for her courage. She thought, quite wrongly, that she had very little herself, and admired it in Verity.

Father had opened his eyes once or twice, Verity said, and had been persuaded to swallow a mouthful of brandy. He did not seem to recognize anyone, but he was sleeping more easily and she had hopes. She was going to sit up in case he wanted anything. She would be able to doze in his armchair.

At ten Mrs Chynoweth came upstairs and insisted on saying goodnight to her daughter. She talked in so determined a voice about poor Charles that she woke her grandson; then she stayed on talking while he was fed, a thing Elizabeth hated. But at last she was gone and the child asleep, and Elizabeth stretched her limbs in the bed and listened happily to Francis moving about in the room next to hers. Soon he would come in to say good night and then there would be a great stretch of darkness and peace until the early morning.

He came in, stepping with exaggerated care and pausing a moment to peer at the sleeping child, then he sat on the edge of the bed and took Elizabeth's hand.

'My poor wife, neglected as usual,' he said. 'Your father has been talking for hours without a break on his grievances against Fox and Sheridan, while you have been up here alone missing all the delights of conversation.'

In his banter there was a certain amount of true feeling – he had been a little annoyed that she had come to bed so early – but at the sight of her his grudge vanished and his love returned.

For some minutes they talked in low tones, then he leaned forward to kiss her. She offered him her lips unthinkingly, and it was only when his arms went about her that she realized that tonight the friendly little salute would not do.

After a minute he sat back, smiled at her in rather a puzzled way.

'Is something wrong?'

She made a gesture towards the cot. 'You'll surely wake him, Francis.'

'Oh, he's new fed. He sleeps heavy then. You've told me so yourself.'

She said: 'How is your father? Is he any better? Somehow one does not feel . . .'

He shrugged, feeling himself put in the wrong. He was not happy at his father's collapse; he was not indifferent to the outcome; but that was something quite separate. The two conditions existed at the same time. Today he had carried her downstairs, liking the weight of her, sorry that she was not heavier but happy to feel the substance under her frailty. From that moment the scent of her seemed to cling in his nostrils. Pretending to busy himself with the guests, he had really had eyes for no one else.

She said: 'I'm not well to-night. Your father's illness upset me very much.'

He struggled with his feelings, trying to be reasonable. Like all proud men, he hated to be rebuffed in this way. It made him feel like a lascivious schoolboy.

'Sometime,' he said, 'will you feel well again?'

'That's not fair, Francis. It isn't my choosing that I'm not very strong.'

'Nor mine.' Recollection of his restraint during these months bubbled up in him. That and other things. 'I notice you didn't frown or look faint at Ross this afternoon.'

Indignation flickered in her eyes. From the very beginning the things Ross had said to her had found excuse and justification in her mind. She had seen nothing of him and was sorry for him; during the months while her baby was coming she had thought a good deal of Ross, of his loneliness, of his pale eyes and wild scarred face. Like all human beings she could not refrain from idly comparing what she had with what she might have had.

'Please leave him out of this,' she said.

'How can I?' he rejoined, 'when you will not.'

'What d'you mean? Ross is nothing to me.'

'Perhaps you're beginning to regret it.'

'I think you must be drunk, Francis, to speak to me like this.'

'A splendid fuss you made of him this afternoon. "Ross, sit here beside me." – "Ross, is my baby not pretty?" – "Ross, take a piece of that cake." – Dear, dear, what a to-do.'

She said, almost too angry to speak: 'You're being utterly childish.'

Francis got up. 'Ross, I am sure, would not be childish.'

She said, deliberately trying to hurt him back: 'No, I'm sure he would not.'

They stared at each other.

'Well, that's pretty straight, isn't it?' he said, and left her.

He flung into his own room, slamming the door without regard to the sick man or the sleeping child. Then he undressed anyhow, leaving his clothes on the floor, and got into bed.

He lay with hands behind his head and eyes open for an hour or more before he went to sleep. He was consumed with disappointment and jealousy. All the love and desire in him had turned to bitterness and aridity and desolation.

There was no one to tell him that he was wrong in being jealous of Ross. There was no one to tell him that another and more powerful rival had recently arisen. There was no one to warn him about Geoffrey Charles.

Chapter seventeen

IN THE GROWTH of Demelza's intelligence one room at Nampara played a distinctive part. That room was the library.

It had taken her a long time to overcome her distrust of the gaunt and dusty lumber room, a distrust which derived from the one night she had spent in, or beside, the great box bed. She had found afterwards that the second door in that bedroom led through into the library, and some of the fear of that first hour stuck to the room beyond the second door.

But fear and fascination are yokefellows, oxen out of step but pulling in the same direction, and once inside the room she was never tired of returning to it. Since his return Ross had shunned the place because every article in it brought back memories of his childhood and of his mother and father and their voices and thoughts and forgotten hopes. For Demelza there were no memories, only discoveries.

Half the articles she had never seen before. For some of them even her ingenious brain could not invent a use, and so long as she could not read, the piled yellow papers and the little signs and labels scrawled and tied on certain articles were no help.

There was the figurehead of the *Mary Buckingham*, which had come ashore, Jud told her, in 1760, three days after Ross was born. She liked tracing the carving of this with her finger. There was the engraved sea chest from the little fore-and-aft schooner which had broken its back on Damsel Point, drifted upon Hendrawna Beach and darkened the sands and sand hills with coal dust for weeks afterwards. There were samples of tin and copper ore, many of them lacking labels and all useless anyhow. There were spare strips of canvas for patching sails, and four ironbound chests at whose contents she could only guess. There was a grandfather's clock with some of its inside missing – she spent hours over this with the weights and wheels, trying to discover how it could have worked.

There was a coat of mail armour, terribly rusty and antique, two rag dolls and a homemade rocking horse, six or seven useless muskets, a spinet which had once belonged to Grace, two French snuffboxes and a music box, a roll of motheaten tapestry from some other ship, a miner's pick and shovel, a storm lantern, a half keg of blasting powder, a sketch map pinned on the wall of the extent of Grambler workings in 1765.

Of all the discoveries the most exciting to her were the spinet and the music box. One day, after an hour's tinkering, she persuaded the music box to work, and it played two thin trembling minuets. In excitement and triumph she danced all round the instrument on one leg, and Garrick, thinking this a new game, jumped round too and bit a piece out of her skirt. Then when the music was over she hurriedly went and hid in a corner lest someone should have heard it and come and find them there. A greater discovery was the spinet, but this had the drawback that she could not make it play a tune. Once or twice when she was sure there was no one about she ventured to try, and the sounds fascinated her even when they were discordant. She found herself perversely taken with such sounds and wanting to hear them again and again. One day she discovered that the farther her fingers moved to the right the thinner became the sound, and this seemed to give the puzzle away. She felt it would be much simpler to conjure tunes out of this than to make sense of the horrible spidery trails that people called writing.

II

Charles Poldark made an obstinate recovery from his heart attack, but was confined to the house for the rest of the winter. He still put on weight. Soon it was all he could do to struggle downstairs in the afternoon and sit panting and eruptive and purple before the parlour fire. There he would remain scarcely speaking for hours, while Aunt Agatha worked the spinning wheel or read the Bible to herself in an audible undertone. Sometimes in the evenings he would talk to Francis, asking him questions about the mine, or he would tap a mild accompaniment on the arm of his chair when Elizabeth played an air on the harp. He seldom spoke to Verity except to complain that something was not to his liking, and usually dozed off and snored in his chair before he would allow himself to be supported up to bed.

Jinny Carter's child was born in March. Like Elizabeth's child, it was a boy; and he was christened, by permission, Benjamin Ross.

A fortnight after the christening Ross had an unexpected visitor; Eli Clemmow had walked in the rain all the way from Truro. Ross had not seen him for ten years, but he instantly recognized his loping walk.

Unlike his elder brother, Eli was built on a narrow economical scale, with a suggestion of the Mongol in his features. When he spoke he slopped and slurred with his teeth, as if his lips were waves washing over half-tide rocks.

To begin with he was ingratiating, asking about his brother's disappearance, enquiring if no trace at all had been found. Then he was complacent, mentioning with satisfaction the good position he had got. Personal servant to a lawyer; a pound a month and all found; snug little room, light work, drop of toddy every Saturday night. Later, when he brought up the question of his brother's belongings, and Ross said candidly that he was welcome to what he found in the cottage but doubted if there was anything worth the effort of carrying away, Eli's eyes betrayed the malice which had all the time been hiding away behind his obsequious manner.

'No doubt,' he said, sucking with his lips, 'all the neighbours will have took anything of value.'

'We don't encourage thieves,' Ross observed. 'If you want to make remarks of that kind, make them to the people you accuse.'

'Well,' said Eli, blinking. 'I shouldn't be saying more'n I've the right if I said brother 'ad been drove out of his home by lying tongues.'

'Your brother left his home because he couldn't learn to control his appetites.'

'And did 'e do anything?'

'Anything?'

'Anything wrong.'

'We were able to prevent that.'

'Yes, but he was drove out of his 'ome fur doing nothing at all, and mebbe starved to death. Even the law don't say ye can punish a man before 'e do do a wrong.'

'He was not driven from his home, man.'

Eli fingered his cap. 'Of course tis common knowledge that ye've always had a down on we. You and father. Your father had Reuben put in the stocks for next to nought. Tis 'ard not to remember that.'

'You're fortunate,' Ross said, 'not to receive something else to remember. I give you five minutes to be off my land.'

Eli swallowed something and sucked again. 'Why, sur, ye just said I could go down fur to take anything of Brother's away that's worth the carrying. Ye've just said so. That be common justice.'

'I don't interfere with the lives of my tenants unless they interfere with mine. Go to the cottage and take what you choose. Then go back to Truro and stay there, for you're not welcome in this district.'

Eli Clemmow's eyes gleamed and he seemed about to say more, but he changed his mind and left the house without a word.

So it came about that Jinny Carter, nursing her baby by the upstairs window, saw the man come over the hill in the rain with his slow dipping stride and go into the next cottage. He was inside for about half an hour, and then she saw him leave with one or two articles under his arm.

What she did not see was the thoughtful expression on his sly Mongolian face. To one of Eli's peculiar perceptions it was clear that the cottage had been inhabited by someone less than a week ago.

III

That night the wind got up with violence and blew unabated through the following day. The next night about nine news came that a ship was in the bay and drifting ashore between Nampara and Sawle.

Demelza had spent most of the afternoon as she was coming to spend many afternoons when heavy rain stopped all but the most urgent outdoor work. Had Prudie been of an industrious turn of mind she would have taught the girl something more than the neat but primitive sewing she now understood; and there was weaving and spinning to learn, the drying and dipping of rushes for making rushlights. But these things were beyond Prudie's idea of housecraft. When work was inescapable she did it, but any excuse was good enough to sit down and take off her slippers and brew a dish of tea. So soon after dinner Demelza had sneaked off to the library.

And this afternoon by the purest chance she made the greatest discovery of all. Just as a premature dusk was falling she found that one of the big chests was not really locked but only held by a trick clasp. She lifted the lid and found the box full of clothing. There were dresses and scarves, three-cornered hats and fur-lined gloves, a periwig and red and blue stockings, a pair of lady's green lace slippers with blue heels. There was a muslin neck scarf and an *ostrich feather*. There was a bottle with liquid in that smelt of gin, the only intoxicant she knew, and another half full of scent.

Although she had already stayed longer than usual, she could not bring herself to leave, and went over and over the velvet and the lace and the silk, stroking it and shaking out the crumbs of dry lavender. She couldn't put down the slippers with the lace and the blue heels; they were too dainty to be real. The ostrich feather she sniffed and pressed against her cheek. Then she tried it round her neck and put on a fur hat and pirouetted up and down on her toes, pretending to be a great lady, with Garrick crawling at her heels.

With darkness closing in on her she lived in a dream, until she woke and found she could no longer see and was alone in the sombre room with the draught blowing cold and rain seeping through the shutters.

Frightened, she rushed to the box, pushed in everything she could find and shut the lid and slipped through the big bedroom and thence to the kitchen.

Prudie had had to light the candles, and delivered an ill-tempered lecture, which Demelza, not yet anxious to go to bed, adroitly steered round until it became a continuation of the story of Prudie's life. Hence the girl had only just gone upstairs and was not asleep when Jim Carter and Nick Vigus called in to say there was a ship in distress. When Ross, disturbed from his book, made ready to go with them he found Demelza, a kerchief about her hair and two old sacks on her shoulders, waiting to ask that she might go too.

'You're better in bed,' Ross said. 'But as you please if you want the wetting.'

They set out, Jud carrying a strong rope in case there should be a chance of giving help.

The night was so black as to be sightless. Out of the shelter of the house the wind struck a blow that was not temporary but enduring. They tried to overcome it, taking steps forward that should have been an advance. One of the storm lanterns went out, the other swayed and flickered, thrusting out a hoop of light which danced along with them clownlike and showed their heavy boots squelching across the dripping grass. Once or twice the force of the wind was so great that they were all brought to a stop, and Demelza, struggling voicelessly beside them, had to clutch Jim Carter's arm to hold her ground.

As they neared the cliff top the rain came again, drenching them in a few seconds, splashing into their mouths and eyes. They had to turn their backs and crouch behind a hedge until it was over.

There were people at the edge of the cliff. Lanterns winked here and there like glowworms. Below them, about a hundred feet down, more lights gleamed. They went down a narrow path until they came to a group of people on a broad ledge all staring out to sea. Before they could learn much a figure appeared from the lower path, coming out of the darkness like a demon out of a pit. It was Pally Rogers from Sawle, naked and dripping with his hairy body and great spade beard.

'It's no manner of good,' he shouted. 'They struck not fifteen minutes since . . .' The wind bore his voice away. 'If they was farther in we could get them a rope.' He began to pull on his breeches.

'Have you tried to get out to them?' Ross shouted.

'Three of us 'ave tried to swim. The Lord was agin the venture. She'll not last long now. Caught beam on she be, wi' water spouting over 'er. By daylight she'll be driftwood.'

'Any of the crew come ashore?'

'Two. But the Lord God had taken their souls. Five more there'll be afore sun-up.'

Nick Vigus sidled between them, and a gleam from the lantern showed up his shining pink face with its toothless pockmarked innocence. 'What cargo do she carry?'

'None for you, for tis agin the law.' Pally Rogers screwed the water out of his beard and scowled. 'Paper and wool from Padstow they do say.'

Ross left them and with Jud went farther down the cliff. Not until they were near the bottom did he find that Demelza had followed.

Here they were sheltered from the wind, but every few seconds a wave would hit a ridge of rock and deluge them in spray. The tide was coming in. Below them, on the last few square feet of sand, was a cluster of lanterns where men still waited for any slackening of the sea to risk their lives and swim to the wreck. From here it was possible to make out a dark lump which might have been a rock but which they knew was not. There were no lights on it and no sign that anyone still lived.

Ross slipped on the greasy path, and Jim Carter grasped his arm.

Ross thanked him. 'There's nothing to be done here,' he muttered.

'What d'you say, sir?'

'There's nothing to be done here.'

'No, sir, I think I'll be getting back. Jinny may be getting narvous.'

'There's another un coming in,' screamed an old woman nearby. 'See 'im there, bobbin' 'bout like a cork. First head, then tail. There'll be a pretty find for the morning tide! There'll be driftwood for ee!'

A flurry of spray fell on them like a swarm of insects.

'Take this girl back with you,' Ross said.

Demelza opened her mouth to protest, but wind and spray came together and took her breath.

Ross watched them climbing until they were out of sight, then went down to join the little group of lanterns on the sand.

Chapter eighteen

Jinny carter stirred in her bed. She had been dreaming, half dreaming that she was baking starry-gazey pie, and all the fishes had suddenly blinked their eyes and changed into babies and begun to cry. She was wide awake now but the cry was still in her ears. She sat up and listened for her own baby in its wooden box that Jim had made, but there was no sound at all. It must have been her imagination working on the beat of the rain against the tight-closed shutters, on the howl of the gale as it whirled past the cottages and roared inland.

Why had Jim left his comfortable bed and gone out into the wild night just in the hope of picking up some bit of wreckage? She had asked him not to go, but he had taken no notice. That was the way: always she asked him not to go, and always he made an excuse and went. Two or three nights every week he would be absent – to return in the small hours with a pheasant or a plump partridge under his arm.

He had changed a good deal these last few months. It had really begun in January. One week he had been away from the mine and laid up, cough, cough, cough. The next he had gone out two nights with Nick Vigus and returned with food for her that the loss of his earnings would have made impossible. It was no good to tell him she would rather do without the food any number of times over than that he should be caught breaking the law. He didn't see it that way and was hurt and disappointed if she didn't seem delighted.

She slid out of bed with a shiver and went to the shutters. She made no effort to open them, or the rain would have burst full into the room; but through a crack where the rain was trickling she could tell that the night was as dark as ever.

She fancied there was a noise in the room below. All the woodwork in the cottage creaked and stirred under the strain. She would be glad when Jim was back.

Almost she would have been glad if Benjy had cried, for then there would have been excuse to take him into her own bed for comfort and to feel the clutch of his tiny predatory hands. But the child slept.

She slipped back into bed and pulled the blanket up to her nose. Jim's bad habits were really all Nick Vigus's fault. He was the bad influence, with his evil baby face. He put things to Jim that Jim would never have thought of, ideas about property and the right to take food for one's belly that was not one's own. Of course Nick used such arguments only as an excuse for any of his sly doings that took him outside the law. But Jim accepted them seriously, that was the trouble. He would never have thought of robbing to feed himself, but he was beginning to feel himself in the right in stealing to feed his family.

A heavy squall buffeted against the shutter; it was as if an enormous man was leaning against the house and trying to push it over. She dozed for a minute, dreaming of a happy life when food was plentiful for all and children grew up laughing, without the need to work as soon as they could walk. Then she started into wakefulness, aware that there was a light somewhere. She saw three or four nicks coming through the floor and felt a warm pleasure that Jim was home. She thought of going down to see what news he brought to be back so early, but the warmth of her bed and the draughtiness of the room robbed her of the will. She dozed again and then was wakened by the noise of something falling in the room below.

Jim had perhaps brought back some prize and was stacking it in a corner. That was why he had returned so soon. Strange there was no one with him, no voices of Nick or her father. Perhaps they had stayed on. But the best chance of salvage would come with the morning light. She hoped they had all been careful. It was less than two years since Bob Tregea had been drowned trying to get a line out to a ship – and left a widow and young children.

Jim did not call up to her. Of course he would think her asleep. She opened her mouth to call down, and as she did so suddenly wondered with an unpleasant prickly sensation round her heart if the man below really was Jim.

Some heavy movement had induced the doubt. Jim was so light on his feet. Now she sat up in bed and listened.

If it was Jim, then he was searching for something, clumsily, drunkenly. But Jim had touched no more than a mug of light ale since he was married. She waited, and an idea which had blown from somewhere into her mind suddenly germinated and grew. . . .

There was only one man, it seemed to her, who would come in like this while Jim was away, who would move about so clumsily, who might at any moment come creeping up the ladder – and he had disappeared months ago, was thought dead. Nothing had been seen of him for so long that the cloud in her mind had gone.

She crouched there and listened to the gale and to the movements of the visitor. She didn't move an inch for fear of making a noise. It was as if her stomach and her lungs were slowly becoming frozen. She waited. Perhaps if there was no sound he would go away. Perhaps he would not come up, to find her here alone. Perhaps very soon Jim would really be back.

. . . Or perhaps he was still down there by the rocks watching the efforts made to save men he had never seen before, while at home his wife lay like a stone in bed and a half-starved lustful madman lumbered about the room below.

. . . And the child began to cry.

The fumbling below stopped. Jinny tried to get out of bed, but she had lost every bone in her body; she couldn't move and she couldn't swallow. The child stopped, began again more confidently: a thin wail competing against the buffeting of the wind.

She was out of bed at last, had picked him up, almost dropping him from her fumbling hasty hands.

The light below quivered and winked. There was a creak on the ladder.

She no longer had words to pray, nor resources to turn and hide. She stood at the side of the bed, her back against the wall, the child stirring feebly in her tightened arms, while the trap door slowly lifted.

She knew then, as soon as she saw the hand grasping the knotted wood of the floor, that her instinct had not been mistaken, that now she had to face something she had never known before.

II

By the light of the candle he carried it was possible to see the changes that months of living in lonely caves had brought. The flesh had shrunk from face and arms. He was in rags and barefoot, his beard and hair straggling and wet as if he had come from some underwater cave. Yet it was the same Reuben Clemmow she had always known, with the pale self-centred eyes and the uncertain mouth and the white creases in the sun-reddened face.

She fought down a wave of illness and stared at him.

'Where's my fire pan?' he said. 'Stole my fire pan.'

The child in her arms wriggled and gasped for breath and began to cry again.

Reuben climbed up the steps, and the trap door slammed back into place. For the first time he saw the bundle that she clutched. Recognition of her was slow in dawning. When it came all the rest came with it, remembrance of the injury done him, of why he was forced to shun people and frequent his cottage only at night, of the ten-month-old wound still festering in his side, of his lust for her, of his hatred for the man that had got her this squealing infant, Ross Poldark.

'Lily,' he muttered. 'White lily . . . sin . . .'

He had been so long apart from people that he had lost the faculty of making them understand. Speech was for himself alone.

He straightened himself awkwardly, for the muscles had contracted about the wound.

Jinny was praying again.

He took a step forward. 'Pure lily . . .' he said, and then something in the girl's attitude sent his brain clicking over upon an old forgotten rhythm of his childhood. ' "Why standest thou so far off an' hidest thy face in the needful time o' trouble. The ungodly for 'is own lust doth persecute; let 'im be taken in the crafty wiliness that they 'ave imagined. For the ungodly'th made a boast of his heart's desire, an' speaketh good of the covetous." ' He took out his knife, an old trapper's knife, with the blade worn down to about four inches from years of sharpening and use. In the months of isolation desire for her had become confused with revenge. In lust there is always conquest and destruction.

The candle began to tremble and he put it on the floor, where the draught blew the light in gusts about the room and swealed tallow on the boards. ' "He sittest lurkin' in the thievish corners o' the streets, and privily in 'is lurkin' dens doth 'e murder the innocent." ' Jinny lost her head and began to scream. Her voice went up and up.

As he took another step forward she forced her legs to move; she was halfway across the bed when Reuben caught her and stabbed at the child; she partly parried the blow, but the knife came away red.

The girl's scream changed its note, became more animal in sound. Reuben stared at the knife with passionate interest, then recovered himself as she reached the trap door. She turned as he came rushing up. He stabbed at her this time and felt the knife go into her. Then inside him all that had been tense and hard and burning suddenly ran away through his veins: he dropped the knife and watched her fall.

An extra gust of wind blew the candle out.

He shouted and groped for the trap door. His foot slipped on something greasy and his hand touched a woman's hair. He recoiled and screamed, banged on the boarding of the room; but he was shut in here for ever with the horror he had created.

He pulled himself upwards by the bed, blundered across the room and found the shutters of the window. He fought shouting with these but could not find the bolt. Then he thrust forward his whole weight and the fastenings gave way before him. With a sense of breaking from a prison he fell forward out of the window, out of the prison, out of life, upon the cobbles below.

Book two

April–May 1787

Chapter one

ROUND THE DINING table of the parlour of Nampara House one windy afternoon in April 1787 six gentlemen were seated.

They had dined and wined well, off part of a large cod, a chine of mutton, a chicken pie, some pigeons, and a fillet of veal with roasted sweetbreads; apricot tart, a dish of cream, and almonds and raisins. Mr Horace Treneglos of Mingoose, Mr Renfrew from St Ann's, Dr Choake from Sawle, Captain Henshawe from Grambler, Mr Nathaniel Pearce the notary from Truro, and their host, Captain Poldark.

They had met to approve the preliminary work which had been undertaken at Wheal Leisure, and to decide whether good gold should be risked by them all with the aim of raising copper. It was an important occasion which had lured Mr Treneglos from his Greek, Dr Choake from the hunting field, and Mr Pearce from his gouty fireside.

'Well,' said Mr Treneglos, who from his position and seniority occupied the head of the table, 'well, I'm not going to go against expert advice. We've been hummin' and ha'ing for more'n two years; and if Captain Henshawe says we should begin, well, damme, it's his money being risked as well as mine, and he's the one as did ought to know!'

There was a murmur of assent and some qualifying grunts. Mr Treneglos put a hand behind his ear to gather up the crumbs of comment.

Dr Choake coughed. 'Naturally we all defer to Captain Henshawe in his experience of working mines. But the success of this venture does not depend on the working of the lode, otherwise we should have begun a twelvemonth since. It is conditions in the industry which must determine our course. Now only last week we had occasion to attend upon a patient in Redruth who was suffering with an imposthume. In fact he was not our patient but Dr Pryce called us in for further advice. The poor fellow was far gone when I arrived at his considerable house, which had a fine drive and a marble staircase and other evidences of good taste and the means to gratify it; but between us we were able to alleviate the condition. This gentleman was a shareholder in Dolly Koath Mine, and he let fall the information that it had been decided to close all the lower levels.'

There was silence.

Mr Pearce, purple and smiling, said: 'Well now, in fact I heard much the same thing; I heard it only last week.' He stopped a moment to scratch under his wig, and Dr Choake said:

'If the largest copper mine in the world is reducing its work, what chance has our small venture?'

'That doesn't follow if our overheads are smaller,' said Ross, who was at the other end of the table, his bony distinguished face a shade flushed with what he had eaten and drunk. By growing longer side pieces he had partly hidden his scar, but one end of it still showed as a paler brown line across his cheek.

'The price of copper may fall still lower,' said Dr Choake.

'What's that you say? What's that?' asked Mr Treneglos. 'I couldn't hear him,' he explained to himself. 'I wish he'd speak up.'

Choake spoke up.

'Or it may equally well rise,' was the reply.

'I look at it this way, gentlemen,' said Ross. He drew at his long pipe. 'The moment is, on the face of it, a bad one for the starting of ventures large or small. But there are points in our favour which must be borne in mind. Supply and demand rule the prices of ore. Now two large mines have closed this year, and any number of small ones. Dol Koath may soon follow Wheal Reath and Wheal Fortune. This will halve the output of the Cornish industry, so supply to the markets will be less and the price of copper should rise.'

'Hear, hear,' said Captain Henshawe.

'I agree wi' Captain Poldark,' said Mr Renfrew, speaking for the first time. Mr Renfrew was a mine chandler from St Ann's, and therefore had a double interest in this venture; but so far he had been overawed by the presence of so many gentlemen at the meeting.

The blue-eyed Henshawe had no such diffidence. 'Our costs wouldn't be one half what Wheal Reath's was, ton for ton.'

'What I should like to know,' said Mr Pearce deprecatingly, 'speaking of course for the parties I represent, Mrs Jacqueline Trenwith and Mr Aukett, as well as for myself, is what figure we should have to obtain for our crude ore in order to show a profit at all. What do you say to that?'

Captain Henshawe picked his teeth. 'It is so much a lottery what the blocks do fetch. We all know that the copper companies are out to get the stuff dirt cheap.'

Ross said: 'If we get nine pounds a ton we shall come to no harm.'

'Well,' said Mr Treneglos, 'let's see your plan on paper. Where's the map of the old workings? We can follow better then.'

Henshawe rose and brought over a big roll of parchment, but Ross stopped him.

'We'll have the table clear for this.' He rang a hand bell, and Prudie came in followed by Demelza.

This was Demelza's first appearance, and she was the object of a number of curious glances. Everyone, except Mr Treneglos, who lived in his own private world, knew something of her history and of the rumours which surrounded her presence here. The talk was old talk now, but scandal died hard when its cause was not removed.

They saw a girl of just seventeen, tall, with dark untidy hair and big dark eyes which had a disconcerting glint in them when they happened to meet your own. The glint suggested unusual vitality and a latent mettlesomeness; otherwise there was nothing special to remark.

Mr Renfrew peered at her with puckered astigmatic eyes, and Mr Pearce, while keeping his gouty feet ostentatiously out of danger, ventured to raise his quizzing glass when he thought Ross was not looking. Then Mr Treneglos eased off the top button of his breeches, and they bent to peer over the map which Captain Henshawe was unrolling on the table.

'Now,' said Ross. 'Here we have the old workings of Wheal Leisure and the direction of the tin-bearing lode.' He went on to explain the situation, the angle of the shafts to be sunk, and the adits which would be driven in from the face of Leisure Cliff to unwater the mine.

'What's this here?' Mr Treneglos put a stubby snuff-stained finger on a corner of the map.

'That's the limit of the working of Trevorgie Mine so far as it is known,' said Ross. 'All accurate maps have been lost. These workings were old when my great-grandfather came to Trenwith.'

'Um,' said Mr Treneglos. 'They knew what they was about in those days. Yes,' he agreed *sotto voce*, 'they knew what they was about.'

'What do you mean, sir?' enquired Mr Renfrew.

'What do I what? Well, damme, if the old men was working tin here and here they was working the back of Leisure lode before ever it was discovered on my land. That's what I mean.'

'I think he's right,' said Henshawe, with a sudden quickening of interest.

'In what way does that assist us?' asked Mr Pearce, scratching himself.

'It only means,' Ross said, 'that the old men would not have driven all this way under such conditions for nothing. It was their custom to avoid all but the shallowest underground work. They had to. If they went this far they must have found some good return as they went along.'

'Think you it is all one great lode, eh?' said Mr Treneglos. 'Could it run so far, Henshawe? Has any been known to run so far?'

'We don't know and shan't know, sir. Looks to me as if they was following tin and struck copper. That's how it seems to me. It is very feasible.'

'I've a very great respect for the ancients,' said Mr Treneglos, opening his snuffbox. 'Look at Xenophanes. Look at Plotinus. Look at Democritus. They were wiser than we. It is no disgrace to follow where they led. What will it cost us, dear boy?'

Ross exchanged a glance with Henshawe.

'I am willing at the outset to be manager and head purser without payment; and Captain Henshawe will supervise the beginnings at a nominal salary. Mr Renfrew will supply us with most of the gear and tackle at the lowest margin of profit to himself. And I have arranged for Pascoe's Bank to honour our drafts up to three hundred guineas for the buying of winches and other heavy equipment. Fifty guineas each would cover the expense of the first three months.'

There was a moment's silence, and Ross watched their faces with a slight cynical lift of his eyebrow. He had cut down the opening figure to the lowest possible, knowing that a big demand would result in another stalemate.

'Eight fives,' said Mr Treneglos. 'And three from Pascoe's, that's seven in all. Seven hundred on an outlay of fifty each seems very reasonable to me, what? Expected a hundred at least,' he added to himself. 'Quite expected a hundred.'

'That's only a first outlay,' said Choake. 'That's only the first three months.'

'All the same it is very reasonable, gentlemen,' said Mr Renfrew. 'These are expensive days. You could hardly expect to become interested in a gainful venture for less.'

'Quite true,' said Mr Treneglos. 'Well, then, I'm for starting right away. Decide by a show of hands, what?'

'This loan from Pascoe's Bank,' said Dr Choake heavily. 'That means we should put all our business through them? But what's wrong with Warleggan's? Might we not get better terms from them? George Warleggan is a personal friend of ours.'

Mr Pearce said: 'A matter I was about to raise myself, sir. Now if——'

'George Warleggan is a friend of mine too,' Ross said. 'But I don't think friendship should come into a matter of business.'

'Not if it be detrimental to the business, no,' said the doctor. 'But Warleggan's is the biggest bank in the county. And the most up-to-date. Pascoe's has old-fashioned ideas. Pascoe's has not advanced in forty years. I knew Harris Pascoe when he was a boy. He's a stick-in-the-mire and always has been.'

Mr Pearce said: 'My clients, I b'lieve, quite understood it would be Warleggan's Bank.'

Ross filled his pipe.

Mr Treneglos unfastened another button of his breeches. 'Nay, one bank's the same as another to me. So long as it's sound, eh? That's the point, eh? You had a reason for going to Pascoe's, Ross, I suppose, what?'

'There is no grudge between the Warleggans and me, father or son. But as a banking firm they own too many mines already. I do not wish them to come to own Wheal Leisure.'

Choake bent his heavy eyebrows. 'I should not care to let the Warleggans hear you say that.'

'Nonsense. I say nothing that everyone does not know. Between them and their puppet companies they own a dozen mines outright and have large shares in a dozen others, including Grambler and Wheal Plenty. If they chose to close Grambler to-morrow they would do so, as they have closed Wheal Reath. There is nothing underhand in that. But if Wheal Leisure is opened, then I prefer to keep such decisions in the hands of the venturers. Big combines are dangerous friends for the small man.'

'I quite agree, gentlemen,' Mr Renfrew concurred nervously. 'There was bad feeling in St Ann's about the closing of Wheal Reath. We know it was not an economical mine to maintain; but that does not help the shareholders who have lost their money, nor the two hundred miners who have lost their work. But it helps Wheal Plenty to offer only starvation wages, and it gives young Mr Warleggan a chance of showing a tidy profit!'

The issue had touched some sore point in Mr Renfrew's memory. A wrangle broke out, with everybody talking at once.

Mr Treneglos banged upon the table with his glass. 'Put it to the vote,' he shouted. 'It is the only sensible way. But first the mine. Let's have the faint-hearts declare themselves afore we go any further.'

The vote was taken and all were for opening.

'Good! Splendid!' said Mr Treneglos. "Αρης στυγεῖ μέλλοντας. We're getting on at last. Now this question of the bank, eh? Those in favour of Pascoe's . . .'

Renfrew, Henshawe, Treneglos, and Ross were for Pascoe's; Choake and Pearce for Warleggan's. As Pearce carried with him the votes of his nominees, the voting was even.

'Damme,' mumbled Mr Treneglos. 'I knew that lawyer fellow would baulk us again.' Mr Pearce could not miss hearing this and tried hard to be offended.

But secretly he was looking for a share in Mr Treneglos's estate business; and finding Mr Treneglos firm on his course, he spent the next ten minutes tacking round to the old man's point of view.

Left alone, Choake gave in, and the absent Warleggans were defeated. Ross knew their adventure was so small as to be hardly worth the attention of a large banking firm, but that they had received it he was in no doubt. George would be annoyed . . .

Now that the chief hurdles had been taken, the rest of the business went through quickly enough. Captain Henshawe stretched his big legs, got up and, with a nod from Ross, passed the decanter round the table.

'I don't doubt you'll pardon the liberty, gentlemen. We've sat round this table as equals, and we're equal partners in the venture. Nay, though I'm the poorest, my share stands biggest in the general pool, for my reputation's there as well as my fifty guineas. So here's a toast. Wheal Leisure.'

The others rose and clinked their glasses.

'Wheal Leisure!'

'Wheal Leisure.'

'Wheal Leisure!'

They drained their glasses.

In the kitchen Jud, who had been whittling a piece of wood and humming his favourite tune, raised his head and spat expertly across the table into the fire.

'Something's moving at last. Dang me if it don't sound like they're going to open the blatherin' mine after all.'

'Dirty ole black worm,' said Prudie. 'You nearly spit in the stew pot that time.'

Chapter two

WHEN HIS NEW partners had gone Ross left the house and strolled across his land towards the site of his mine. He did not go down to the beach and across the sand hills, but made a semicircular detour which kept to the high ground. Wheal Leisure was on the first promontory midway along Hendrawna Beach, where the sand hills gave place to rock.

There was as yet little to see. Two shallow tunnels slanting down and a number of trenches, all made by the old men; a new tunnel with a ladder, and a few turfs cut to show where the new work was to be. Rabbits dodged and dipped their tails as he moved about; a curlew cried; a strong wind murmured through the coarse grass. Little to see, but by the end of the summer the view would be changed.

During the years of planning and frustration this idea had grown on him until it took first interest in his mind. The venture would have been started eighteen months ago if it had not been for Mr Pearce, who felt a natural care for the safety of his nominees' money, and the hesitances and pessimisms of Choake, whom Ross was now sorry to have brought in. All the others were gamblers, ready and eager to take a chance. Despite all the fine arguments to-day, there was really no improvement in prospects over a year ago; but old Mr Treneglos had happened to be in boisterous spirits and had carried the others with him. So the gamblers had at last had their way. The future would decide the rest.

He stared across to where the chimneys of Mellin Cottages were just visible in the valley.

He would be able to help Jim Carter now, help him without suspicion of charity, which the boy would never accept. As assistant purser at the mine he could be brought in to relieve Ross of some of the supervision, and later, when he had learned to read and write, there was no reason why he shouldn't be paid forty or more shillings a month. It would help both Jim and Jinny to forget the tragedy of two years ago.

Ross began to pace out again the position where the first shaft would be sunk. The irony of that tragedy at Mellin Cottages was that, physically, actually, it could have been so much worse. In the end only one life had been lost, that of Reuben Clemmow himself. The baby Benjamin Ross had suffered a cut on the head and cheek, which would never be more than a minor disfigurement, and Jinny had escaped with a stab which closely missed her heart. She had been in bed for weeks, with internal bleeding, which her mother, eventually forgetting her Methody scruples, swore she cured with a lock of her grandmother's hair. But that was long ago, and Jinny was well and had had a baby girl, Mary, since then.

It could have been so much worse. But just as baby Benjamin would always show the marks of the attack on his face, so it seemed Jinny was to carry them on her spirit. She had become listless, silent, unpredictable of mood. Even Jim was often not sure what she was thinking. When Jim was at the mine her mother would trot over and stay for an hour amiably prattling about the happenings of the day. Then she would kiss her daughter and trot the few steps back to her own kitchen with an uneasy feeling that Jinny had not been listening at all.

Jim too had lost his buoyancy because of the sensation of guilt that he could not be rid of. He would never forget the moment when he came back to find Reuben Clemmow dying on his doorstep, and the entry into his own bedroom with his child crying in the darkness and a weight that had to be pushed off the trap door. He could not escape from the fact that had he not gone out the tragedy would not have happened. He gave up his association with Nick Vigus, and no more pheasants made their appearance in his kitchen.

In fact these were no longer needed, for the whole neighbourhood took their case to heart. A public subscription was raised and all manner of presents were sent them, so that while Jinny was laid up and for some time afterwards they enjoyed a bounty they had never known before. But it was a bounty Jim privately disliked, and he was relieved when it tapered off. His pitch at Grambler was yielding good results and they had no need of charity. What they had need of was something which would wipe out the memory of that night.

Ross finished his pacing and stared down at the sandy earth. The eternal enigma of the prospector faced him: whether this acre of ground held under its surface riches or frustration. Time and work and patience . . .

He grunted and looked up at the sky, which promised rain. Well, if the worst came to the worst, they would be giving a few miners the chance of feeding their families. Conditions, everyone agreed, could hardly be worse throughout the county, or indeed throughout the country as a whole.

II

Conditions could hardly be worse, they thought, with the three per cents at 56.

The whole nation felt down in the mouth after the unequal struggle against France and Holland and Spain, the perverse unbrotherly war with America, and the threat of further enemies in the north. It was a spiritual as well as a material slough. Twenty-five years ago she had been on top of the world, and the fall had been all the greater. Peace had come at last, but the country was too weary to throw off the effects of war.

A tenacious prime minister, at 27, was holding his uneasy position in the face of all the coalitions to upset him; but the coalitions had hopes. Money had to be found, even for peace and reform; taxes had gone up 20 per cent in five years and the new ones were dangerously unpopular. Land tax, house tax, servants' tax, window tax. Horses and hats, bricks and tiles, linens and calicoes. Another impost on candles hit directly at the poor. Last winter the fishermen of Fowey had saved their families from starvation by feeding them on limpets.

It would take fifty years, some people said, before things righted themselves. . . .

Even in America, Ross had been told, disillusion was no less. The United States had so far been united only in a dislike for overlordship: and with that gone and all the after-war problems in train they seemed on the point of breaking up into local self-governing republics quarrelling endlessly among themselves like the cities of medieval Italy. Frederick of Prussia, tapping away with gouty fingers on his piano in the Sans Souci Palace at Potsdam, had been heard to say that the country was so unwieldy that now they had got rid of George the Third the only solution was to set up a king of their own. The remark even found its way into the fastnesses of Cornish society.

Other things too the Cornish knew, or sensed, with their constant illicit traffic between the French ports and their own. England might be down in the mouth, but things were even worse in Europe. Strange whiffs of a volcanic unrest came to them from time to time from across the Channel. Dislike for an old enemy as much as idealism for a new friend had tempted France to pour out her gold and men to help American freedom. Now she found herself with an extra war debt of fourteen hundred million livres and a knowledge of the theory and practice of revolution bred in the minds and blood of her thinkers and soldiers. The crust of the European despotisms was being weakened at its weakest spot.

In two years Ross had seen little of his own family and class. What he had overheard in the library on the day of Geoffrey Charles's christening had filled him with contempt for them, and though he would not have admitted to being influenced one way or the other by Polly Choake's gossip, an awareness of their clacking tongues made him dislike the idea of going among them. Monthly, out of common courtesy, he went to enquire after the invalid Charles, who refused either to die or get better, but when he found company there his conversation didn't touch on the popular subjects. He was not as concerned as they about the return of Maria Fitzherbert from the continent or the scandal of the Queen of France's necklace. There were families in the district without enough bread and potatoes to keep them alive, and he wanted these families to be given gifts in kind, so that the epidemics of December and January should not have such easy prey.

His listeners felt uncomfortable when he was speaking and resentful when he had finished. Many of them were hard hit themselves by the slump in mining and the increased taxes. Many were helping those hard cases with which they came in contact, and if that barely touched the fringe of the distress they did not see that Ross was doing any more. What they were not prepared to accept was that they had any sort of liability for the hardships of the day, or that laws could be framed to offer some less soul-destroying form of relief than the poorhouse and the parish cart. Even Francis could not see it. Ross felt like another Jack Tripp preaching reform from an empty tub.

. . . He topped the crest of the hill on the way home and saw Demelza coming to meet him. Garrick was trotting at her heels like a small Shetland pony.

She hopped from time to time as she came up.

'Jud d' tell me,' she said, 'that the mine is to open at last!'

'Just as soon as we can hire the men and buy the tackle.'

'Hooray! Garrick, go down. I'm real pleased 'bout that. We was all disappointed last year when we thought twas all set, sur. Garrick, be quiet. Will it be as big as Grambler?'

'Not yet.' He was amused at her excitement. 'Quite a little mine to begin.'

'I'm sure twill soon be a big un wi' great chimney stacks and things.'

They walked down the hill together. Normally he took her very much for granted, but the interest of the others to-day made him steal a sidelong glance at her now. A well-grown and developing girl, barely recognizable as the scrawny half-starved urchin he had swilled under the pump.

More changes had come about during the last year. Demelza was now a sort of general housekeeper. Prudie was far too indolent to wish to manage anything if there was a way out of it. Her leg had given trouble two or three times more, and when she came downstairs again it was easier to potter about the kitchen brewing tea for herself and doing a little light work than contriving the meals and cooking them, which Demelza so much seemed to enjoy. The burden was off her shoulders; Demelza never dictated, and was quite willing to continue doing her own work as well, so what was there to object to in that?

Apart from one violent quarrel, life in the kitchen was more peaceful than when Jud and Prudie shared it alone; a rough camaraderie had grown up between the three, and the Paynters did not seem to resent Ross's friendship with the girl. There were plenty of times when he was lonely and glad of companionship. Verity no longer had the heart to come over and Demelza took her place.

Sometimes she even sat with him in the evening. It had begun with her going to ask him for orders about the farm, by her staying to talk; and then somehow she was sitting in the parlour with him two or three evenings a week.

She was, of course, the most amenable of companions, being content to talk if he wanted to talk, or to persevere with her reading if he wanted to read, or willing to slip out at once if her presence was unwelcome. He still drank heavily.

She was not quite a perfect housekeeper. Though she came near enough to it for normal needs, there were times when her temperament played a part. The 'moods' of which Prudie had spoken still took her. Then she could outswear Jud, and once had nearly outfought him. Her sense of personal danger was at all times non-existent; but at such times even her industry was misdirected.

One dark rainy morning of last October she had chosen to clean out part of the cattle shed, and began pushing the oxen around when they got in the way. Presently one resented this and she came out boiling with indignation and wounded in a manner that made sitting down impossible for a week. Another time she chose to move all the kitchen furniture while Jud and Prudie were out. But one cupboard was too much even for her energy, and she pulled it over on herself. Prudie came back to find her pinned underneath, while Garrick barked his appreciation at the door.

The affair of the quarrel with Jud had a more serious side and was now discreetly forgotten by all. Demelza had tasted the bottle of spirits in the old iron box in the library, and, liking the taste, had finished the bottle. Then she went prancing in to Jud, who by mischance had also been having a private sup. She so tormented him that he fell upon her with some indistinct notion of slaying her. But she fought back like a wildcat, and when Prudie came in she found them struggling on the floor. Prudie had jumped instantly to the wrong conclusion and had attacked Jud with the hearth shovel. Ross's arrival was only just in time to prevent most of his staff from being laid up with serious injuries.

A frozen equanimity had fallen upon the kitchen for weeks after that. For the first time Demelza had felt the acid sting of Ross's tongue and had curled up and wanted to die.

But that was twelve months ago. It was a grisly spectre buried in the past. . . .

Without further speech they passed through the apple trees and walked towards the house, through the garden on which Demelza had put in so many extra hours last summer. All the weeds had been cleared, leaving much bare earth and a few straggling remnants of the plants Ross's mother had grown.

There were three lavender bushes, tall and ungainly from the press of weeds; there was a bush of rosemary, freed from its tangle and promising flower. She had also unearthed a damask rose with its bright splashed flowers of pink and white, and a moss rose and two monthly roses; and in her quest about the countryside she had begun to bring home seeds and roots from the hedgerows. These were no easy things to rear: they had all the waywardness of wild things, ready to luxuriate in desolate places of their own choosing but apt to pine and die when confined within the luxury of a garden. But last year she had had fine spurs of viper's bugloss, a patch of sea pinks, and a row of crimson foxgloves.

They stopped now, Demelza explaining what she proposed to do here and here, suggesting that she might take cuttings from the lavender bush and try to root them to make a hedge. Ross looked about him with a tolerant eye. He was not really interested in flowers, but he admired the neatness and the colour; and herbs which could be cooked or infused were useful.

Recently he had given her a little money for her own use, and with this she had bought a bright kerchief to wrap round her head, a pen to learn to write, two copy books, a pair of shoes with paste buckles, a big cloam mug to hold flowers, a sunbonnet for Prudie and a snuffbox for Jud. Twice he had let her mount Ramoth and ride with him into Truro, once when he had promised to visit the cockpit and watch Royal Duke fight for a fifty guinea purse. This entertainment, to his surprise and amusement, quite disgusted her. 'Why,' she said, ''tis no better than Fathur do do.' She had expected something more refined of a cockfight patronized by the nobility and gentry.

On the way home she had been unusually silent. 'Don't you think animals d' feel hurt like we?' she got out eventually.

Ross considered his answer. He had been led once or twice before into pitfalls by making unthinking replies to her questions.

'I don't know,' he said briefly.

'Then why do veers squeal like they do when you put rings through their noses?'

'Cockerels aren't pigs. God made it their nature to fight.'

She did not speak for a time. 'Yes, but God didn' give 'em steel spurs to fight with.'

'You should have been a lawyer, Demelza,' he commented, and at that she had been silent again.

He thought of these things while they talked in the garden. He wondered if she knew what Nat Pearce and the others had been thinking when they stared at her in the parlour a couple of hours ago, and whether she agreed with him that no idea could be more ridiculous. When he wanted that sort of pleasure he would call for Margaret in Truro, or one of her kind.

It seemed to him sometimes that if pleasure lay in the unsubtle sport that a harlot afforded, then he had not quite the normal appetites of a normal man. Well, there was an odd satisfaction in asceticism, a cumulative self-knowledge and self-reliance.

He thought very little about it these days. He had other interests and other concerns.

Chapter three

BEFORE SHE LEFT him Demelza said she had seen Jinny Carter early that day, and Jim was sick with a pleurisy. But Jim with his uncertain health was often laid up for a few days, and Ross did not take account of it. All the next fortnight he was busy with matters concerning the opening of the mine, and he put off seeing Jim until he could offer him certain cut-and-dried duties. He did not want this to seem a made-up job.

The library at Nampara was to serve as a mining office, and the domestic life of the house was disrupted while part of this was cleared and repaired. News that a mine was to open instead of close spread quickly, and they were besieged with miners from up to eighteen miles distant, anxious to take the work at any price. Ross and Henshawe tried to strike bargains fair to both sides. They engaged forty men including a 'grass' captain and an underground captain, who would be responsible to Henshawe.

At the end of the fortnight Ross met Zacky Martin and enquired about Jim. Jim was up, Zacky said, though not yet back at the mine, being troubled with his cough.

Ross thought over the arrangements so far as they had gone. Next Monday eight men would begin the adit from the face of the cliff, and another twenty would be at work on the first shaft. It was time for the assistant purser to be brought in.

'Tell him to come round and see me to-morrow morning, will you?' Ross said.

'Yes,' said Zacky. 'I'll see Jinny to-night. I'll tell her to tell him. She won't forget.'

II

Jim Carter was not asleep and heard the faint tapping on the door almost as soon as it began.

Very cautiously, so as not to wake Jinny or the babies, he slid out of bed and began to gather up his clothes. Once he trod on a loose floor board, and he stood still for some seconds suppressing a cough, until the girl's regular breathing reassured him. Then he pulled on his breeches and shirt and picked up his boots and coat.

The hinge of the trap door usually groaned when it was moved, but he had put grease on it earlier in the day and it opened now with no noise. He was halfway through when a voice said:

'Jim.'

He bit his lip in annoyance but did not reply; she might yet be only speaking in her sleep. There was silence. Then she went on:

'Jim. You're going out with Nick Vigus again. Why didn't you tell me?'

'I knew you'd only make a fuss.'

'Well, you needn't go.'

'Yes, I do. I promised Nick yesterday.'

'Tell 'im you've changed your mind.'

'I haven't.'

'Cap'n Poldark wants you in the morning, Jim. Have you forgotten that?'

'I shall be back long afore morning.'

'Maybe he'll want ee to take a pitch at the new mine.'

Jim said: 'I couldn't take it, Jinny. Tis a speculation, no more and no less. I couldn't give up a good pitch for that.'

'A good pitch is no good if you've to wade to your chin in water going forth and back to it. No manner of wonder you cough.'

'Well, when I go out to get a bit of extry, all you do is complain!'

'We can manage, Jim. Easy. I don't want more. Not that way. It fair sticks in my throat when I think how you've come by it.'

'I aren't all that Methody.'

'No more am I. Tis knowing the danger you've been in to get it.'

'There's no danger, Jinny,' he said in a softer tone. 'Naught to fret about. Honest. I'll be all right.'

A faint tapping was heard on the door again.

He said: 'Tis only while I'm not earning. You know that. I shan't be up of nights when I'm back on my pitch. Good-bye now.'

'Jim,' she said urgently, 'I wisht you wouldn't go to-night. Not to-night.'

'Hush, you'll wake the babies. Think on them, and the other one coming. We got to keep you well fed, Jinny dear.'

'I'd rather starve . . .'

The three words floated down into the dark kitchen as he descended, but he heard no more. He unbolted the door and Nick Vigus slipped inside like a piece of rubber.

'You been some long time. Got the nets?'

'All ready now. Brrr . . . tis cold.'

Jim put on his coat and boots and they went out, Nick whispering to his dog. Their walk was to be a fairly long one, about five miles each way, and for some time they tramped in silence.

It was a perfect night, starlit and clear but cold, with a north-westerly breeze thrusting in from the sea. Jim shivered and coughed once or twice as he walked.

Their way lay southeast, skirting the hamlet of Marasanvose, climbing to the main coaching road and then dropping into the fertile valley beyond. They were entering Bodrugan land, profitable country but dangerous, and they began to move with the utmost caution. Nick Vigus led the way and the thin lurcher made a second shadow at his heels. Jim was a few paces behind carrying a stick about ten feet long and a homemade net.

They avoided a carriage drive and entered a small wood. In the shadow Nick stopped.

'They blasted stars are as sharp as a quarter moon. I misdoubt if we'll have as fair a bag.'

'Well, we can't go back wi'out a try. It 'pears to me——'

'Sst . . . Quiet.'

They crouched in the undergrowth and listened. Then they went on. The wood thinned out, and a hundred yards ahead the trees broke into a big clearing half a mile square. Fringing one side was a stream and about the stream a thicket of bushes and young trees. It was here that the pheasants roosted. Those in the lower branches were easy game for a quick man with a net. The danger was that at the other end of the clearing stood Werry House, the home of the Bodrugans.

Nick stopped again.

'What did ee hear?' Jim asked.

'Somethin',' whispered Vigus. The starlight glistened on his bald pink head and made little shadows of the pits in his face. He had the look of a perverted cherub. 'They keepers. On the prowl to-night.'

They waited for some minutes in silence. Jim suppressed a cough and put his hand on the dog's head. It moved a moment and was still.

'Lurcher's all right,' said Nick. 'Reckon twas a false alarm.'

They began to move again through the undergrowth. As they neared the edge of the clearing it became a question not so much of disturbing the keepers, who perhaps had not been there at all, but of not flushing the pheasants until it was too late for them to fly. The brightness of the night would make this difficult.

They whispered together and chose to separate, each man taking one net and closing in on the covey from an opposite side. Vigus, who was the more practised, was to make the longer detour.

Jim had a gift for stealthy movement, and he went on very slowly until he could see the dark shapes of the birds, podlike among the branches and in the low forks of the tree just ahead. He unwound the net from his arm, but decided to give Nick another two minutes lest he should spring the trap half set.

As he stood there he could hear the wind soughing in the branches above him. In the distance Werry House was a dark alien bulk among the softer contours of the night. One light still burned. The time was after one, and he wondered about the people who lived there and why they were keeping such late hours.

He wondered what Captain Poldark would have to say to him. He owed a lot there, but that made him feel he couldn't accept any more favours. That was, always supposing he could keep his health. It would be no benefit to Jinny to do as his father had done and die at twenty-six. Jinny made a to-do about him having to wade through water to his working pitch every day, but she didn't realize that they were all wet and dry most of the time. If a man couldn't put up with that he wasn't fitted to be a miner. At present he was free of the blasting powder, and that was something to be thankful for.

An animal stirred in the thicket near him. He turned his head and tried to see but could not. The tree beyond was gnarled and misshapen. A young oak, one would guess from the dead leaves on its branches. They hung there rustling in the breeze all the winter through. A peculiar swollen shape.

And then the shape changed slightly.

Jim screwed up his eyes and stared. A man was standing against the tree.

. . . So their visit of Saturday had not gone unmarked. Perhaps every night since then there had been keepers waiting patiently for the next visit. Perhaps he had already been seen. No. But if he moved forward he was as good as caught. What of Nick coming round from the north?

Jim's mind was frozen by the need to make an instant choice. He began to move slowly away.

He had not taken two steps when there was the sound of a broken twig behind him. He twisted in time to avoid a grasp on his shoulder and plunged towards the pheasants, dropping his net as he ran. In the same second there was a scuffle at the other side and the discharge of a musket: suddenly the wood came to life – with the cry of cock pheasants and the beating of their startled wings as they rose, with the stirring of other game disturbed, with men's voices shouting directions for his capture.

He came to open ground and ran flatly, skirting the edge of the stream and keeping as much as possible in the deep shadow. He could hear running footsteps behind and knew that he was not outdistancing them; his heart pounded and his breath grew tight.

At a break in the trees he swerved and ran amongst them. He was not now far from the house and he could see that this was a formal path he followed. In here it was darker, and the undergrowth between the trees was so dense that it would be hard to force a way through it without giving them time to catch up.

He came upon a small clearing; in the middle was a circular marble pavilion and a sundial. The path did not go beyond this point. He ran towards the pavilion, then changed his mind and made for the edge of the clearing where a big elm tree leaned out and away. He scrambled up the trunk, scratching his hands and breaking his nails on the bark. He had just reached the second branch when two gamekeepers pounded into the clearing. He lay still, drawing thinly at the air.

The two men hesitated and peered about the clearing, one with head bent forward listening.

'. . . not gone fur . . . Hiding out . . .' floated across to the tree.

They walked furtively into the clearing. One went up the steps and tried the door of the pavilion. It was locked. The other stepped back and stared up at the circular domed roof. Then they divided and made a slow circuit of the open space.

As one of the men approached his tree Jim suddenly felt that peculiar stirring in his lung which he knew meant an attack of coughing. The sweat came out afresh on his forehead.

The gamekeeper slowly went past. Jim saw that he carried a gun. Just beyond the leaning elm the man stopped at a tree which looked more scalable than the rest and began to peer up through its branches.

Jim gasped at the air and choked and got a breath and held it. The second man had made his tour and was coming to rejoin his companion.

'Seen aught of 'im?'

'No. Bastard must've escaped.'

'Did they catch the other 'un?'

'No. Thought we'd got this un though.'

'Ais.'

Jim's lungs were expanding and contracting of their own accord. The itch welled up irresistibly in his throat and he choked.

'What's that?' said one of the men.

'Dunno. Over yur.'

They came sharply towards the elm but mistook the direction by twenty feet, frowning into the tangled undergrowth.

'Stay thur,' said one. 'I'll see what I can find.' He forced his way through the bushes and disappeared. The other stood against the bole of a tree with his gun at the cock.

Jim grasped at the branch above him in a frantic effort to hold his cough. He was soaked now with sweat, and even capture seemed little more fearful than this convulsive strain. His head was bursting. He would give the rest of his life to be able to cough.

There was a trampling and a cracking and the second gamekeeper came out, cursing his disappointment.

'He's gone, I reckon. Let's see what Johnson's done.'

'How 'bout getting the dogs?'

'They've nought to go on. Maybe we'll catch 'em proper next week.'

The two men moved off. But they had not gone ten paces when they were stopped by a violent explosion of coughing just above and behind them.

For a moment it alarmed them, echoing and hollow about the trees. Then one quickly recovered himself and ran back towards the elm.

'Come down!' he shouted. 'Come down out of there at once, or I'll shoot the life out of you.'

Chapter four

ROSS DID NOT hear of the arrest until ten o'clock, when one of the Martin children brought the news to him at the mine. He at once went home, saddled Darkie and rode over to Werry House.

The Bodrugans were one of the decaying families of Cornwall. The main stem, having scored a none-too-scrupulous trail across local history for nearly two hundred years, had given out in the middle of the century. The Werry Bodrugans were following suit. Sir Hugh, the present baronet, was fifty and a bachelor, undersized, vigorous and stout. He claimed to have more hair on his body than any man living, a boast he was ready to put to the proof for a fifty-guinea bet any evening with the port. He lived with his stepmother, the Dowager Lady Bodrugan, a hard-riding, hard-swearing woman of twenty-nine, who kept dogs all over the house and smelt of them.

Ross knew them both by sight, but he could have wished that Jim had found other preserves to poach on.

He wished it still more when he came to the house and saw that the Carnbarrow Hunt was meeting there. Conscious of the stares and whispers of the people in their red coats and shining boots, he got down and threaded a way among horses and yapping dogs and went up the steps of the house.

At the top a servant barred his way.

'What do you want?' he demanded, looking at Ross's rough working clothes.

Ross stared back at him. 'Sir Hugh Bodrugan, and none of your damned impudence.'

The manservant made the best of it. 'Beg pardon, sir. Sir Hugh's in the library. What name shall I say?'

Ross was shown into a room full of people drinking port and canary sack. Conditions could hardly be more difficult for what he had to ask. He knew many of the people. Young Whitworth was here and George Warleggan and Dr Choake, and Patience Teague and Joan Pascoe. And Ruth Teague with John Treneglos, eldest son of old Mr Horace Treneglos. He looked over the heads of most of them and saw Sir Hugh's squat form by the fireplace, legs astraddle and glass raised. He saw the manservant approach and whisper in Sir Hugh's ear and heard Bodrugan's impatient,

'Who? What? What?' This much he was able to hear because there had been a temporary dropping off in conversation. Someday he might come to accept this as a natural event when he entered a room.

He nodded and half smiled to some of the guests as he walked through them towards Sir Hugh. There was a sudden outburst of barks and he saw that Constance Lady Bodrugan was on her knees on the hearthrug tying up a dog's paw, while six black spaniels licked and lurched about her.

'Blast me, I thought it was Francis,' said Sir Hugh. 'Your servant, sir. The hunt starts in ten minutes.'

'Five is all I need,' Ross said pleasantly. 'But those I should like in private.'

'There's nowhere private in the house this morning unless it be the Jericho. Speak up, for there's too much noise for anyone to eavesdrop on your private affairs.'

'The man who left this bloody glass about,' said his stepmother. 'I'd horsewhip him, by God.'

Ross took the wine offered him and explained his mission to the baronet. A poacher had been taken on Bodrugan land last night. A boy known personally to himself. Sir Hugh, being a magistrate, would no doubt have something to do with the hearing of the case. It was the boy's first offence and there was strong reason to believe that he had been led away by an older and more hardened rogue. Ross would consider himself under an obligation to make good any loss if the boy could be dismissed with a severe warning. Moreover, he would be personally responsible . . .

At this stage Sir Hugh burst into a roar of laughter. Ross stopped.

'Blast me, but you come too late, sir. Too late by half. I had him up before me at eight o'clock this morning. He's on his way to Truro now. I've committed him for trial at the next quarter sessions.'

Ross sipped his wine.

'You were in haste, Sir Hugh.'

'Well, I didn't want to be delayed dealing with the fellow when it was the day of the meet. I knew by nine o'clock the house would be in a pandemonium.'

'The poacher,' said Lady Bodrugan, struck with the idea as she released the dog. 'I suspicion it was he who dropped the glass. I'd have him flogged at the cart wheel, by God! The laws are too easy on the varmints.'

'Well, he'll not be troubling my pheasants for a week or two,' said Sir Hugh, laughing heartily. 'Not for a week or two. You must agree, Captain Poldark, it's a standing disgrace the amount of good game that's lost in a year.'

'I'm sorry to have intruded on your hunting time.'

'Sorry your mission ain't a happier one. I've a nag to lend you if you've a mind to join the hunt.'

Ross thanked him but refused. After a moment he made his excuses and left. There was no more he could do here. As he moved away from them he heard Lady Bodrugan say:

'You don't mean you'd have let the varmint go free, Hughie?'

He couldn't hear her stepson's reply, but there was a ripple of laughter among those who did.

The attitude of the Bodrugans to his idea of letting a poacher off with a warning was, he knew, the attitude all society would adopt, though they might dress it in politer phrases. Even Cornish society, which looked with such tolerance on the smuggler. The smuggler was a clever fellow who knew how to cheat the government of its revenues and bring them brandy at half price. The poacher not only trespassed literally upon someone's land, he trespassed metaphorically upon all the inalienable rights of personal property. He was an outlaw and a felon. Hanging was barely good enough.

Ross came up against the same attitude a few days later when he spoke to Dr Choake. Jim was not likely to be brought up for trial before the last week in May. He knew that Choake, in his capacity of mine surgeon, had treated Jim as recently as February and he asked him his opinion of the boy.

Choake said, well, what could you expect with phthisis in the family? By auscultation he had detected a certain morbid condition in one lung, but how far it had developed it was not possible to say. Of course the complaint had various forms; mortification of the lung might set in early or late; he might even live to be forty, which was a fair age for a miner. One couldn't tell.

Ross suggested that the information would be of use at the quarter sessions. Evidence of serious ill health, together with a plea from himself, might possibly get the charge dismissed. If Choake would give evidence at the trial . . .

Choake knit his brows in a perplexed stare. Did he mean . . .

Ross did mean. Choake shook his head incredulously.

'My dear sir, we'd do much for a friend, but don't ask us to testify on behalf of a young vagrant who's been caught poaching. We couldn't do it. Twould come unnatural in us, like mothering a Frenchie.'

Ross pressed, but Choake would not budge.

'To tell the truth, I haven't a deal of sympathy for your aims,' he said at length. 'No good will come of being sentimental about such folk. But I'll set you out a note of what I've said about the boy. Signed with my own hand and sealed like a writ. That will be just as good as going there and standing in the box like a felon. We couldn't do that.'

Ross grudgingly accepted.

The following day Wheal Leisure had its first official visit from Mr Treneglos. He stumped over from Mingoose with a volume of Livy under his arm and a dusty three-cornered hat stuck on top of his wig. There was mining blood in the Treneglos family.

He saw what there was to be seen. Three shafts were being sunk, but it was hard going. They had struck ironstone almost at once. This in places meant working with steel borers and then blowing with gunpowder. The layer ran east to west and seemed to be of some size, so the next few weeks were likely to be tedious for all.

Mr Treneglos said, well, that would mean more expense, but the circumstance was not discouraging. Rich lodes of copper were often found in ironstone. 'Nature's safe,' he said. 'She keeps her treasures under lock and key.'

They went to the edge of the cliff and stared over the edge to the flimsy wooden platform halfway down, from which eight men in twelve-hour cores of four had begun driving an adit into the cliff. They had long since gone from view, all that could be seen from the cliff top was a boy of twelve who appeared from time to time with a barrow whose contents, the refuse of the four tunnelling beetles, he emptied onto the sand below. They too, Ross said, had met ironstone and were trying to find a way round it.

Mr Treneglos grunted and said he hoped those two old women Choake and Pearce wouldn't start whinnying about the expense at the next meeting. How long had they reckoned on it taking them to bring home that adit to the mine, eh?

'Three months,' Ross said.

'It will take all of six,' said Mr Treneglos to himself. 'It will take all of six,' he assured Ross. 'By the by, have you heard the news?'

'What news?'

'My son John and Ruth Teague. They've made it up together. They are going to be wed, y' know.'

Ross didn't know. Mrs Teague would be in transports.

'She's done well for herself,' the old man said, as if for once he spoke Ross's thoughts instead of his own. 'She's done well for herself getting John, even though he is a small matter boisterous in his cups. I could have wished for some maid with money to her name, for we're none too easy set for our position. Still, she takes a fence well and she's suitable enough other ways. I heard of a fellow the other day who was carrying on with his kitchen wench. I can't remember who twas. Serious, I mean, not for a lark. It all depends how you treat a thing like that. I well remember John put one of our serving girls in the straw before ever he was eighteen. Cost me a pretty penny.'

'I hope they'll be happy.'

'Eh? Oh yes. Well, I shall be glad to see him settled. I shan't last for ever, and there hasn't been a bachelor master of Mingoose for eighty year.'

'You're a magistrate,' Ross said. 'What is the sentence for poaching?'

'Eh? Eh?' Mr Treneglos clutched at his old hat just in time to save it from the wind. 'For poaching? It all depends, dear boy. All depends. If a man is caught with a whippet and snare in his keeping, then if tis a first conviction he may be given three or six months. If he's been convicted before or has been caught in the act, as the saying is, then no doubt he'll be sent for transportation. You have to be strong on the rogues, else we'd have no game at all. How's your uncle, boy?'

'I haven't seen him this month.'

'I doubt if *he* will go magistrating again. I s'pose he takes it easy? Perhaps he pays too much heed to the physical profession. I mistrust 'em myself. Rhubarb's my cure. As for the doctors: *timeo Danaos et dona ferentes*; that's my motto. That's my motto,' he added to himself. 'Should be Charles's.'

II

The trial took place on the thirtieth of May.

It had been a cold and unsettled spring with strong winds and days of chilly rain, but in the middle of the month the weather began to clear and the last week was quiet and suddenly very warm. Spring and midsummer were telescoped into one week. In six days of blazing sunshine the entire countryside grew and set into its richest green. The delayed spring blossoms came out overnight, bloomed as in a hothouse and were gone.

The day of the trial was very warm, and Ross rode into Truro early with the songs of the birds all the way. The courtroom would have been gloomy and decrepit at the best of times. To-day the tunnels of sunlight streaming in through the dirty windows fell on the gnarled old benches and showed up the big cobwebs in the corners of the room and hanging from the rafters. It picked out the emaciated clerk of the court bending over his papers with a pendulous drop glinting from his nose, and fell in patches upon the ill-kempt spectators crowded together whispering and coughing at the back.

There were five magistrates, and Ross was pleased to find that he had some acquaintance with two of them. One, the chairman, was Mr Nicholas Warleggan, George's father. The other was the Rev Dr Edmund Halse, whom Ross had last met in the coach. A third he knew by sight: a fat elderly man called Hick, one of the gentry of the town, who was drinking himself to death. During most of the morning Dr Halse kept his fine cambric handkerchief before his sharp thin nose. No doubt it was well soaked with extract of bergamot and rosemary, a not unwise precaution with so much fever about.

Two or three cases were got through quickly enough in the heavy airless atmosphere, and then James Carter was brought into the box. In the well of the court Jinny Carter, who had walked the nine miles with her father, tried to smile as her husband glanced towards her. During the period of his remand his skin had lost its tan and the thick smudges below his dark eyes showed up plainly.

As the case began the usher glanced up at the big clock on the wall, and

Ross could see him deciding there would be just time for this case before the midday break.

The magistrates were of the same opinion. Sir Hugh Bodrugan's gamekeeper had a tendency to wander in his evidence, and twice Mr Warleggan sharply instructed him to keep to the point. This gave the witness stagefright, and he mumbled through to the end in a hurry. The other gamekeeper bore out the story, and that completed the evidence. Mr Warleggan looked up.

'Is there any defence in this case?'

Jim Carter did not speak.

The clerk got up, pushing away a dew drop with his hand. 'There's no defence, Your Worship. There's been no previous conviction. I have a letter 'ere from Sir Hugh Bodrugan complaining of how much game 'e's lost this year and saying as how this is the first poacher they has been able to catch since January.'

The magistrates put their heads together. Ross quietly cursed Sir Hugh.

Mr Warleggan looked at Carter. 'Have you anything to say before sentence of this court is passed?'

Jim moistened his lips. 'No, sir.'

'Very well, then . . .'

Ross got up. 'If I might ask the indulgence of the court . . .'

There was a stir and a mutter, and everyone turned to see who was disturbing the magisterial dust.

Mr Warleggan peered through the shafts of sunlight and Ross nodded slightly by way of recognition.

'You have some evidence you wish to give in this man's defence?'

'I wish to give evidence of his good character,' Ross said. 'He has been my servant.'

Warleggan turned and held a whispered conference with Dr Halse. They had both recognized him now. Ross continued to stand up, while people shifted their positions and peered over each other's shoulders to get a view of him. Among those just to his left he saw a face he recognized, one it was impossible to mistake: the moist, prominent mouth and slant eyes of Eli Clemmow. He had perhaps come to gloat over Carter's downfall. That Ross might be coming to share it was something he had not expected.

'Will you take the witness stand, sir,' Warleggan said in his deep careful voice. 'Then you may say what you have to say.'

Ross left his seat and walked across the court to the witness box. He took the oath and made a pretence of kissing the greasy old Bible. Then he put his hands over the edge of the box and looked at the five magistrates. Hick was blowing as if asleep; Dr Halse was dabbing lightly with his handkerchief, no trace of recognition in his eyes; Mr Warleggan was looking through some papers.

He waited until Warleggan had finished, then began.

'No doubt, gentlemen, on the evidence you have heard, you will see no reason to look for anything exceptional in this case. In your long experience there must be many cases, especially at a time of distress such as this, when there are circumstances – of hunger, of poverty, of sickness – which extenuate the offence in some degree. But naturally the laws must be administered, and I should be the last to ask of you that the ordinary poacher, who is a trouble and expense to us all, should be allowed to go unpunished. I have, however, a close knowledge of the circumstances of this case which I should like to put before you.' Ross gave them a summary of Jim's vicissitudes, with particular stress on his ill health and the brutal assault made upon his wife and child by Reuben Clemmow. 'Living as he does in poverty, I have reason to believe that the prisoner fell into bad company and was persuaded away from certain promises he had made direct to me. I personally am sure of this boy's honesty. It is not he who should be in court but the man who led him astray.'

He paused and felt that he had the interest of his listeners. He was about to go on when someone sniggered loudly in the well of the court. Several of the magistrates looked across, and Dr Halse frowned severely. Ross had no doubt who it was.

'The man who led him astray,' he repeated, trying to regain the wandering attention of his listeners. 'I repeat that Carter has been led astray by a man much older than himself who has so far escaped punishment. It's he who should bear the blame. As for the prisoner's present health, you have only to look at him to see what it is today. In confirmation of that I have here a statement from Dr Thomas Choake of Sawle, the distinguished mine surgeon, that he has examined James Carter and finds him to be suffering from a chronic and putrid inflammation of the lung which is likely to prove fatal. Now, I am prepared to re-engage him in my employment and to stand surety for his good behaviour in the future. I ask for the consideration of these facts by the court, and that they should be taken into careful account before any sentence be passed.'

He handed to the clerk the piece of notepaper on which, in watery ink, Choake had scrawled his diagnosis. The clerk stood hesitantly with it in his hand until Mr Warleggan impatiently beckoned him to pass it to the bench. The note was read and there was a brief consultation.

'It is your contention that the prisoner is not in a fit state of health to be sent to prison?' Warleggan asked.

'He is very gravely ill.'

'When was this examination made?' Dr Halse asked coldly.

'About three months ago.'

'Then he was in this state when he went poaching?'

Ross hesitated, aware now of the unfriendly nature of the question. 'He has been ill for some time.'

Dr Halse sniffed at his handkerchief. 'Well, speaking for myself, I feel that if a man is – hm – well enough to go stealing pheasants, he is – hm – well enough to take the consequences.'

'Aye, true 'nough,' came a voice.

Mr Warleggan tapped on the desk. 'Any further disturbance . . .' He turned. 'You know, Mr Poldark, I'm of a mind to agree with my friend, Dr Halse. It is no doubt a misfortune for the prisoner that he suffers these disabilities, but the law gives us no opportunity to draw fine distinctions. The degree of a man's need should not determine the degree of his honesty. Else all beggars would be thieves. And if a man is well enough to err he is surely also well enough to be punished.'

'Yet,' Ross said, 'bearing in mind the fact that he has already suffered nearly four weeks' imprisonment – and bearing in mind his good character and his great poverty, I cannot help but feel that in this case justice would be best served by clemency.'

Warleggan thrust out his long upper lip. 'You may feel that, Mr Poldark, but the decision rests with the bench. There has been a marked increase in lawlessness during the last two years. This, too, is a form of lawbreaking both difficult and expensive to detect, and those who are apprehended must be prepared to bear their full share of the blame. Nor can we apportion the guilt; we can only take cognisance of the facts.' He paused. 'In view, however, of the medical testimony and of your own testimony as to Carter's former good character, we are willing to take a more lenient view of the offence than we should otherwise have done. The prisoner is sentenced to two years' imprisonment.'

There was a murmur in the court, and someone muttered a word of disgust.

Ross said: 'I trust I may never have the misfortune to have the leniency of the court extended to me.'

Dr Halse lowered his handkerchief. 'Have a care, Mr Poldark. Such remarks are not entirely outside our jurisdiction.'

Ross said, 'Only mercy enjoys that privilege.'

Mr Warleggan waved a hand. 'Next case.'

'One moment,' said Dr Halse. He leaned forward, putting his finger tips together and pursing his thin lips. He disliked this arrogant young squireen afresh every time they met: at school, in the coach, in court. He was particularly gratified at having been able to put that sharp little question about dates which had turned the other magistrates to his own way of thinking. But even so the young upstart was trying to have the last word. It would not do. 'One moment, sir. We don't come here and administer justice according to the statute book without a considerable sense of our privileges and responsibilities. As a member of the Church, sir, I feel that responsibility with especial weight. God has given to those of his ministers who are magistrates the task of tempering justice with clemency. That task I discharge to the best of my poor ability, and I think it has been so discharged now. Your insinuations to the contrary are offensive to me. I do not think you have the least idea what you are talking about.'

'These savage laws,' Ross said, controlling his temper with the greatest difficulty, 'these savage laws which you interpret without charity send a man to prison for feeding his children when they are hungry, for finding food where he can when it's denied him to earn it. The book from which you take your teaching, Dr Halse, says that man shall not live by bread alone. These days you're asking men to live without even bread.'

A low murmur of approval at the back of the court grew in volume.

Mr Warleggan rapped angrily with his hammer.

'The case is closed, Mr Poldark. You will kindly step down.'

'Otherwise,' said Dr Halse, 'we will have you committed for contempt of court.'

Ross bowed slightly. 'I can only assure you, sir, that such a committal would be a reading of my inmost thoughts.'

He left the box and pushed his way out of court amid much noise and the shouts of the usher for silence. In the narrow street outside he took a breath of the warm summer air. The deep gutter here was choked with refuse and the smell was unsavoury, but it seemed agreeable after the smell of the court. He took out a kerchief and mopped his forehead. His hand was not quite steady from the anger he was trying to control. He felt sick with disgust and disappointment.

A long mule train was coming down the street with the heavy panniers of tin slung on each side of the animals and with a number of travel-stained miners plodding solidly along by their side. They had walked miles since dawn from some outlying district with this tin for the coinage hall, and would ride home on the backs of the weary mules.

He waited until they were past and then was about to cross the narrow street. A hand touched his arm.

It was Jinny, with her father, Zacky Martin, in the rear. There were little pink flushes in her cheeks, showing up against the pale freckled skin.

'I want to thank ee, sur, for what you said. Twas more'n good of you to try so 'ard for Jim. We'll always remember of it. Always. And what you said——'

'It did no good,' Ross said. 'Take her home, Zacky. She'll be best with you.'

'Yes, sur.'

He left them abruptly and strode off up Coinagehall Street. To be thanked for his failure was the last straw. His disgust was partly levelled at himself for having lost his temper. Be as independent as you liked when it was your own freedom you were bartering; but at least have a greater restraint when it was someone else's. His whole attitude, he told himself, had been wrong. A good beginning, and then it had gone awry. He was the last person to make a success of such a job. He should have been obsequious, flattering to the bench. He should have upheld and praised their authority, as he had begun by doing, and at the same time have brought it home to them that a lenient sentence might be passed out of the benevolence of their hearts.

Deep down he wondered if even the golden voice of Sheridan would have charmed them from their prey. An even better approach, he thought now, would have been to see the magistrates before the court opened and have pointed out to them how inconvenient it would be for him to be deprived of his manservant. That was the way to get a man off, not by the testimony of doctors or sentimental appeals for clemency.

He was in Prince's Street by this time, and he turned down into the Fighting Cock's Inn. There he ordered a half bottle of brandy and set about drinking it.

Chapter five

IN THE HOT sunshine of the early summer afternoon Demelza and Prudie were thinning out the young turnips which had been sown in the lower half of the Long Field.

Prudie was not slow in her complaints, but if Demelza heard she did not pay any attention. She thrust and dragged rhythmically with her hoe, breaking the young weeds at the same time as she cleared spaces for the growth of the plants. Now and then she paused, hands on hips, to stare out over Hendrawna Beach. The sea was very quiet under the hot sun. Faint airs moved across from time to time, brushing dark gentle shadows over it as over the down of a bird's wing. Where the water was shallow its surface was an ever-shifting pattern of mauve and bottle-green wrinkles.

Sometimes too she hummed a tune, for she loved warmth of any kind, especially the warmth of the sun. Much to Prudie's disapproval, she had taken off her blue bonnet and worked now in one of her blue print frocks with sleeves rolled up and bare legs and hard wooden-soled shoes.

With a groan and a pressing of hands, as if this were a movement not often to be made, Prudie straightened her back and stood upright. With one dirty finger she lifted her bonnet and tucked away a strand of black hair.

'I'll be that stiff in the morning. There's no more I can do to-day. My hips! I'll 'ave no easement all the night.' She plucked at the heel of one slipper, which was tucked under and was letting in a trickle of soil. 'You'd best finish too. There's calves to be meated and I can't do all—— Now who be this?'

Demelza turned and frowned into the sun.

'Why, it's—— What can *he* be wanting, I wonder?'

She dropped her hoe and ran across the field towards the house.

'Father!' she called.

Tom Carne saw her and stopped. She ran up to him. Since his last visit when he had announced his coming marriage her feelings for him had changed. The memory of his ill treatment was faded, and now that there was no point as issue between them she was willing to let bygones be bygones and to offer him affection.

He stood there with his round hat on the back of his head, feet planted stolidly apart, and allowed Demelza to kiss the prickles of his black beard. She noticed at once that his eyes were less bloodshot and that he was dressed in respectable clothes: a jacket of coarse grey cloth, a grey waistcoat, with tick trousers turned up some inches at the bottoms, showing brown worsted stockings and heavy shoes with bright brass clasps. She had forgotten that the Widow Chegwidden had a long purse.

'Well, dattur,' he said; 'so you be still 'ere.'

She nodded. 'And happy too. Hope you're the same.'

He pursed his lips. 'That's as may be. Is there any place we can talk, maid?'

'There's no one can hear us here,' she answered. ' 'Cept the crows and they're not interested.'

At this he frowned and stared across at the house, lying close and warm in the sun.

'I don't know as tis any place for a dattur o' mine,' he said harshly. 'I don't know 'tall. I bin much troubled about ee.'

She laughed. 'What's to do wi' a dattur of yourn?' She was lapsing into the broader speech she had begun to lose. 'And how's Luke and Samuel and William and John and Bobbie and Drake?'

'Brave enough. Tis not o' they I'm thinking.' Tom Carne shifted his position and took up an even firmer one. The gentle breeze just stirred his whiskers. 'Now look ee here, Demelza. I've walked all this way to see ee, an' I've come to ask ee to come home. I've come to see Cap'n Poldark to explain why.'

As he spoke she had a feeling as if something was freezing inside her. The new-found daughterly affection would be among the first things to go if all this had to be thrashed out again. Surely it wouldn't have to be. But this was a new and more reasonable father than she had known before. He was not blustering or shouting or even ordinarily drunk. She shifted to leeward of him to see if she could catch any smell of spirits. He would be more dangerous if one could not so easily put him in the wrong.

'Cap'n Poldark's in to Truro. But I've told ee afore. I want to stay here. And what about . . . how is she . . . the Wid . . . your——'

'Well-a-fine. Tis she in part do feel you be betterer wi' we than 'ere in this house exposed to all the temptations o' the world, the flesh, and the devil. You're but sixteen yet——'

'Seventeen.'

'No matter. You're too young to be wi'out guidance.' Carne thrust out his bottom lip. 'Do ee ever go to church or meetin' house?'

'Not so often.'

'Mebbe if you comed back to us you'd be saved. Baptized in the Holy Ghost.'

Demelza's eyes widened. 'What's to do? What's the change in ee, Father?'

Tom Carne met his daughter's eyes defiantly.

'When you left me I was in the darkness and the shadow o' death. I was the servant o' the devil and was iniquitous and a drunkard. Last year I was convinced o' sin under Mr Dimmick. Now I am a noo man altogether.'

'Oh,' said Demelza. So the Widow Chegwidden had been successful after all. She had underrated the Widow Chegwidden. But perhaps indeed it was more than the widow. It would need Something Awful to have changed the man she knew . . .

'The Lord,' said Tom Carne, 'hath brought me out of a horrible pit of mire an' clay, and set my feet 'pon a rock and hath put a new song in my mouth. There's no more drinkings and living in sin, Dattur. We d' live a good life an' we'd be willing to welcome ee back. Tis your natural place in the world.'

Demelza stared a moment at her father's flushed face, then looked down bleakly at her shoes.

Tom Carne waited. 'Well, maid?'

'It's mortal kind of you, Fathur. I'm that glad there's been a change. But I been here so long now that this is my home. It would seem like leaving home to come back wi' you. I learned all 'bout farming here and everything. I'm part of the house. They'd not be able to get along without me. *They* need me, not you. One day I'll walk over and see ee . . . you an' the boys and all. But you don't need me. You got she to look after you. There's nought I can do 'cept eat your food.'

'Oh yes there is.' Carne stared over the horizon. 'The Lord has blessed our union. Nellie is six months forward an' will be delivered in August month. Tis your proper place and your bounden duty to come 'ome and look after us.'

Demelza began to feel that she was caught in a trap which was only just beginning to show its teeth.

There was silence. A curlew had come down in the field and was taking its little run forward, crested head down, and uttering its sad 'pee-wit' sound. She looked across at Prudie, who had gathered up her tools and was ambling untidily towards the house. She stared at the fields of turnips, half thinned out, the other half to do. Her eyes went across the sand and the sand hills to the cliff where two huts were being built and men moved like ants on the summer skyline. Wheal Leisure.

She couldn't leave this. Not for anything. She had come to look upon it all, quick and dead, all things alike, as owned by it and owning. She was fiercely attached to it. And of course to Ross. If this were anything for him she was being asked to do it would be different; but instead she was expected to desert him. Not until she came here had she lived at all. Though she did not consciously reason so, all the early part of her life was like a dark prenatal nightmare, thought and imagined and feared rather than suffered.

'Where's Cap'n Poldark?' Tom Carne said, his voice having hardened again at her silence. 'I come to see him. I got to explain and then 'e'll understand. There'll be no call for wrastling this time.'

That was true. Ross would not stop her going. He might even expect it of her.

''He's from home,' she said bluntly. ''E'll not be back till dark.'

Carne moved round to meet her gaze, as in the old days he had sidled round to grip an opponent.

'You can't do nothing 'bout un. You got to come.'

She looked at him. She saw for the first time how coarse and common he really was. His cheeks sagged and his nose was crossed with tiny red veins. But then all the gentlemen were not like the one she served.

'You can't expect me to say "yes" just like that and come away, after all these years. I got to see Cap'n Ross. He engaged me by the year. I'll see what he says and leave you know.' That was it. Get him off the farm before Ross came back, get him away and allow herself time to think.

Tom Carne was eyeing his daughter in return, keenly, with a tinge of suspicion. Only now did he take in the full change in her, the way she had advanced, matured, grown to a woman's shape. He was not a man to mince matters.

'Is there any sin twixt you and Poldark?' he demanded in a low sharp voice, in the old voice of the old Tom Carne.

'Sin?' said Demelza.

'Aye. Don't look so innocent.'

Her mouth tightened. The instinct of an outgrown fear saved him from a reply he would not quite have expected from a daughter's lips – even though they were words she had learned from him.

'There's nought twixt us except what should be between master and servant. But you did ought to know I'm hired by the year. I can't walk out without so much as by-your-leave.'

'There's talk about you,' he said. 'Talk that comes so far as Illuggan. Whether tis all lies or no, tedn't right for a young girl to be mixed up in such talk.'

'It's nothing to do wi' me what folks say.'

'That's as may be. But I don't want for a dattur o' mine to be mingled up in such talk. When will he be home?'

'Not till nightfall, I say. He's gone to Truro.'

'Well, tis a long way for me to walk 'ere again. Tell un what I've telled you and then come you over to Illuggan. If you're not back by the end of the week I'll come over again. If tis Cap'n Poldark putting obstacles I'll talk un over with 'im.'

Tom Carne hitched up his trousers and fingered the buckle of his belt. Demelza turned and walked slowly towards the house, and he followed.

'After all,' he said on a more palliative note, 'I'm not asking more'n any dattur would do.'

'No,' she said. (Buckle end of a strap when it suited him; sores on her back, ribs you could count, dirt and crawlers; not more than any daughter would do!)

As they reached the house Jud Paynter came out with a bucket of water. He raised his bald eyebrows at sight of the other man.

Tom Carne said: 'Where's your master?'

Jud stopped and set down his bucket and eyed Carne and spat. 'Over to Truro.'

'What time will 'e be home?'

Demelza held her breath. Jud shook his head. 'To-night mebbe. Or to-morrow.'

Carne grunted and walked on. At the front of the house he sat on the seat and took off his boot. Complaining of his corns, he began to press the boot into a more comfortable shape. Demelza could have screamed at him. Jud had told the truth as far as he knew it. But Ross had told her he expected to be back for supper at six. It was now after five.

Tom Carne began to tell her about her brothers. The five eldest were all at work in mines – or had been until two were put off when Wheal Virgin closed. The youngest, Drake, was starting as forge boy at a wheelwright's next week. John and Bobbie were both saved and had joined the society, and even Drake nearly always went to the meetings, although he was too young to be admitted. Only Samuel was erring. His conviction had worn away and the Lord had not seen fit to send him mercy. It was to be hoped that when she, Demelza, came back among them she would soon lay hold of the blessing.

At another time she would have found quiet fun in his new talk, which for all its glibness fitted him as ill as a Sunday suit. She took in the news of her brothers, of whom she was as fond as they had allowed her to be. But above all was the need to see him gone. She could have kicked him to move his great slow body, fallen upon him with her nails and drawn red scratches across his coarse complacent face. Even when he left she didn't know what was to be done. But at least she would have time to think. She would have time. But if he stayed here talking to-day until Ross came home, then Ross would hear of it to-night and that would be the end. Ross would invite her father to sleep here and bundle them off together in the morning.

She stood quivering and watched him while he bent to pull on his boot, angrily offered to buckle it, jerked upright and stood again silently watching while he picked up his stick and made ready to go.

She walked with him, two paces ahead of him to the bridge, and then he stopped again.

'You've nought much to say,' he observed, eyeing her again. 'Tedn't like ee to be so silent. Have you still enmity and uncharitableness in your heart?'

'No, Father,' she said quickly. 'No, Father. No.'

He swallowed and sniffed again. Perhaps he too felt a strangeness in talking this flowery language to the child he had been wont to order and bully around. In the old days a grunt and a curse had been enough.

He said slowly and with an effort: 'I forgive ee fully and altogether for leavin' me when you did, and I ask forgiveness, God's forgiveness, fur any wrong I did ee with the strap in my drink. There'll be no more o' that, Dattur. We'll welcome you among us like the lost sheep back to the fold. Nellie too. Nellie'll be a mother to ee – what you've lacked this pretty many year. She's been a mother to my flock, and now God's giving her her own.'

He turned and stumped off across the bridge. Standing on one leg and then the other, she watched him go up slowly into the young green of the valley and prayed urgently and angrily – was it to the same God? – that he should not meet Ross on the way.

II

'They calves want feeding,' said Prudie. 'An' my poor feet is tryin' me something bitter. Sometimes I'd like to saw off me toes one by one. Saw 'em off I would, wi' that old garden saw.'

'Here,' said Demelza.

'What's that?'

'The carving knife. Chop 'em off and then you'll be settled. Where's the meal porridge?'

'Well to jest,' said Prudie, wiping her nose on her hand. 'Iggerance always jests. You wouldn't jest when the knife were gratin' on the bone. *And* I'd do it if twere not for considering what Jud would do without un. In bed he says my feet are as good as a warmin' pan; nay, betterer, for they don't cool down as the night go on.'

If she went, Demelza thought, there was no need to go so soon. August, he had said. To-morrow was the last day of May. She need not stay more than a month; then she could come back here to her old duties.

She shook her head. Things would not turn out like that. Once home she stayed home. And whether the ruling force was the leather strap or religious zeal she had a feeling that her job would be the same. She tried to remember what the Widow Chegwidden had looked like behind the counter of her little shop. Dark and small and fat, with fluffy hair under a lace cap. Like one of those little black hens with red combs that would never lay their eggs in the box, but always hid them away and then before you knew where you were they were sitting on a dozen and had gone broody. She had made Tom Carne a good wife; would she make a good stepmother? Plenty worse, maybe.

Demelza didn't want a stepmother, nor a father, nor even a spawn of brothers back. She was not afraid of work, but there she would be working in a home where no kindness had ever been shown her. Here, for all her

ties, she was free; and she worked with people she had grown to like and
for a man she adored. Her way of seeing things had changed; there were
happinesses in her life she had not understood until they were on her. Her
soul had blossomed under them. The abilities to reason and think and talk
were new to her – or they had grown in a way that amounted to newness,
from the gropings of a little animal concerned only for its food and safety
and a few first needs. All that would be stopped. All these new lights would
go out; snuffers would be put on the candles and she would see no more.

Not heeding Prudie, she slopped the meal porridge into a bucket and
went out with it for the six calves. They greeted her noisily, pushing at her
legs with their soft damp noses. She stood there and watched them eat.

Her father, by asking if there was any sin between herself and Ross,
meant of course exactly the same as those women at Grambler and Sawle
who sometimes would turn and stare after her with greedy curious eyes.
They were all thinking that Ross . . .

Red-faced, she gave a little half-scornful titter in the shadows. People
were always thinking things; it was a pity they couldn't think up something
more likely. It was as impossible as turning copper to gold. Did they think
that if she . . . that if Ross . . . would she then be living and breathing as an
ordinary servant? No. She would be so filled with pride that everyone
would know the truth without having to whisper and peer and pry.

Copper into gold. Ross Poldark lying with the child he had befriended
and swilled under the pump and scolded and taught and joked with over
the pilchards in Sawle! He was a man, and maybe he wanted his pleasures
like any other man, and maybe he took them on his visits to town. But she
would be the last person he would turn to, she whom he knew so well, who
had no strangeness, no pretty dresses, no paint and powder, no shy secrets
to hide from him. *Fools* people were with their double-damned, soft-silly
imaginings.

The six calves were fussing round her, rubbing their heads against her
body, sucking at her arms and frock with their wet mealy mouths. She
pushed them away and they came back again. They were like thoughts,
other people's and her own, pressing upon her, worrying her all at one
time, sly and impossible and suggestive, importunate and friendly and
hopeful.

What a fool her father was! With the sudden adultness of a growing
wisdom she saw that for the first time. If there was *anything* between herself
and Ross, like he suggested, would she even for an instant have listened to
him asking her to go back? She would have said: 'Back? I'm not coming
back! This is where I belong!'

Perhaps it was. Perhaps Ross would refuse to let her go. But there was
no proper feeling for her on his part, not beyond a kindly interest. He
would as soon become used to her not being in the parlour as he had to her
being there. That was not enough, not near enough . . .

One of the calves trampled on the bucket and sent it rolling to the back of the stall. She went after it, picked it up, and in the darkness of the shed, in the corner right away from the light, she came up against the most terrible thought of her life. It startled her so much that she dropped the bucket again. The bucket clattered and rolled and was still. For several minutes she stood there holding to the partition, her mind cold and frightened.

Madness. He would think her drunk and turn her out of the house, as he had threatened after that fight with Jud.

But then she must go; by any reckoning she must go . . . There would be no loss. But she would have to take his contempt with her. A big price to pay. Even if she succeeded, she might still earn his contempt. But *she would not go*. She picked up the bucket again and gripped it with whitening knuckles.

The calves came again, pushing at her frock and hands. . . . Her mood wilted. It was not the right or the wrong that troubled her. It was the fear of his contempt. The Idea was bad. Put it away. Lose it. Bury it.

She pushed the calves impatiently aside, let herself out and walked across the cobbles to the kitchen. Prudie was still there rubbing her flat bunioned feet on a dirty towel.

The kitchen smelt of feet. She was still grumbling, might never have noticed that Demelza had been away.

'One o' these days I shall go off like a snip o' the finger. *Then* folk'll be sorry for driving of me. Then folk'll be sorry. But what good will that do me, an? What good do it do to shed bitter tears over a cold corpse? Tis a little more kindness I want now while the breathing's still in me.' She glanced up. 'Now don't tell me you've caught a fever. Don't tell me that.'

'There's nothing wrong wi' me.'

'There must be. You're sweating awful.'

'It's *hot*,' said Demelza.

'An' what're ee doing bringing that bucket sloppering in 'ere?'

'Oh,' she said. 'I forgot. I'll leave it outside.'

Chapter six

HE WAS NOT back. She could not make up her mind whether to wish for his coming. The clock showed eight. Very soon both Jud and Prudie would be in bed and asleep. It would be right for her to stay up and see to his supper. But if he did not come soon he would be staying in Truro overnight. Zacky and Jinny were back. Jack Cobbledick had seen them and the news was about. Poor Jim. Everyone was sorry for him, and feeling ran high against Nick Vigus. Everyone was sorry for Jinny and the two children. No man was the same when he came out of prison.

Demelza looked at the frock and bit her lip and looked at it again. Then she hastily threw bed linen over it as she heard Prudie flip-flopping laboriously up the stairs.

'I'm going to bed, dear,' said Prudie, a bottle of gin in her hand. 'Ef I don't I shall come over faint. Many's the time when I was a girl I used to swoon off without a breath o' warning. If me mother knowed what I 'ave to bear now she'd stand up in 'er grave. She'd walk. Many's the time I've expected of her to walk. You can see for his supper, an?'

'I'll see for it.'

'Not that he's like to be home to-night. I said so much to Jud, but the ole mule says, no, 'e'll wait five and twenty minutes more, so wait 'e will.'

'Good night,' said Demelza.

'*Good* night? It will be a shock if I get so much as a wink.'

Demelza watched her through to her room, then turned back the linen to stare again at the frock. After some moments she covered it and went downstairs.

In the kitchen there was a savoury smell of pie. Jud was sitting before the fire whittling a piece of hard driftwood into a new poker for raking out the burnt furze from the clay oven. As he whittled he quietly muttered his song:

> '*There was an old couple and they was poor,*
> *Tweedle, tweedle, go twee.*'

'It's been a handsome day, Jud,' she said.

He looked at her suspiciously.

'Too 'ot. All wrong for the time o' year. There'll be rain soon. Swallows is flying low.'

'You shouldn't sit so near the oven.'

'What did Fathur say?'

'He wanted for me to go stay with them for a few weeks.'

Jud grunted. 'An 'oo's to do your work?'

'I said I couldn't go.'

'Should think as not. Start o' the summer too.' He lifted his knife. 'That a horse? Reckon it's Mr Ross, just when I'd given un up.'

Demelza's heart gave a lurch. Jud set down the stick and went out to take Darkie to the stables. After a few seconds Demelza walked after him through the hall.

Ross had just dismounted and was untying from behind the saddle the parcels and goods he had bought. His clothes were thick with dust. He looked very tired, and his face was flushed as if he had been drinking. He glanced up as she came to the door and smiled briefly but without interest. The sun had just set over the western ridge of the valley and the sky line was lit with a vivid orange glow. All round the house the birds were singing.

'. . . extra feed,' he was saying. 'The meal they gave her was skinny. Wugh, there's no air to-night.' He took off his hat.

'Will you be wanting me again?' Jud asked.

'No. Go to bed when you wish.' He walked slowly to the door and Demelza drew aside to let him pass. 'You also. Serve my supper and then you can go.'

Yes, he had had drink; she could tell that. But she could not tell how much.

He went into the parlour where the table was set for his meal. She heard him struggling to pull off his boots and silently entered with his slippers and helped him to be rid of the boots. He looked up and nodded his thanks.

'Not an old man yet, you know.'

She flushed and went out to take the pie from the oven. When she returned he was pouring himself a drink. She set the pie on the table, cut him a piece, put it on his plate, cut him some bread, waited without speaking while he sat down and began the meal. All the windows were open. The furnace glow over the hill had faded. High in the sky a ruffle of cloud was saffron and pink. Colours in the house and in the valley were flaunting themselves.

'Shall I light the candles?'

He looked up as if he had forgotten her.

'No, there's time enough. I'll do them later.'

'I'll be back and light 'em,' she said. 'I'm not goin' to bed yet.'

She slipped out of the room, went through the low square hall into the kitchen. So the way was open that she might return. She didn't now know what to do. She wanted to pray for something that she knew the Widow Chegwidden's God disapproved of. She knelt and stroked Tabitha Bethia and went to the window and stared across at the stables. She chopped up some odds and ends for Garrick and by that means lured him into an outhouse and locked him up. She returned and raked out the fire. She picked up Jud's wooden poker and slipped a shaving off it with his knife. Her knees were weak and her hands ice cold. She took a bucket to the pump and drew fresh water. One of the calves was crying. A group of sea gulls were winging their way slowly out to sea.

This time Jud followed her back into the kitchen, whistling between his two big teeth. Darkie was fed and watered. He put away the knife and the stick.

'You'll not be astir in the morning.'

She knew very well who was not likely to be astir in the morning, but for once did not answer him. He went out and she heard him climbing the stairs. She followed. In her room she stared again at the dress. She would have given anything for a glass of brandy, but that was barred. If he smelt anything on her breath that would end it. There was nothing for it but a cold hard face, or else to run like a badger to her hole. The bed looked fine. She had only to shed the decision with her clothes and drop into it. But to-morrow would come. To-morrow offered nothing to hope for.

She took out her broken bit of comb and went to the square of mirror she had found in the library, and began to tug at her hair.

II

The frock was one she had found at the very bottom of the second tin trunk, and from the outset it had enticed her as the apple did Eve. It was made of pale blue satin, the bodice cut low and square. Below the tight waist the gown billowed out at the back like a beautiful blue cabbage. She thought it an evening gown, but really it was one Grace Poldark had bought for a formal afternoon. It was the right length for Demelza, and other alterations she had contrived on wet afternoons. There was a thrill in trying it on, even though no one would ever see her wear it. But now . . .

She peered at herself in the half light and tried to see. Her hair she had combed up and parted at the side and drawn away from the ears to pile it on top of her head. At any other time she would have been pleased with her looks and preened herself, walking up and down peacock fashion to hear the *rough-rough* of the silk. But now she stared and wondered and stared. She had no powder, as a real lady would have; no rouge, no scent. She bit at her lips to redden them. And this bodice. Ross's mother might have been made different, or perhaps she had worn a muslin fichu. She knew that if the Widow Chegwidden saw her she would open her tight little mouth and scream the word 'Babylon!'

She wondered what Ross would say.

She stiffened. She had set to go. There was no more to do, no drawing back.

The flint and steel were clumsy in her hands, and she was hard put to it to light the candle. At last a flame flickered, and the rich blueness of the gown showed up more vividly. She rustled as she moved to the door, then slowly, candlestick in hand, went down the stairs.

At the door of the parlour she paused, swallowed something foreign in her throat, licked her lips, went in.

He had finished his meal and was seated in the half darkness in front of the empty fire grate. His hands were in his pockets and his head was down. He moved slightly at her entry but did not look up.

'I've brought the light,' she said, speaking in a voice unlike her own, but he didn't notice.

Slowly she walked round, conscious of the noise her skirt was making, lit the two candle sconces. With each candle she lit the room grew a shade lighter, the squares of the windows a shade darker. All the sky over the hill was an ice blue, bright and clear and empty as a frozen pool.

He stirred again and sat more upright in his chair. His voice came as a shock to her ears. 'You heard that Jim Carter has gone to prison for two years?'

She lit the last candle. 'Yes.'

'I doubt if he'll survive it.'

'You did all you could.'

'I wonder.' He spoke as if he were talking to himself rather than to her.

She began to draw the curtains over the open windows.

'What else could you've done?'

'I'm not a good pleader,' he said; 'being too infernal conscious of my own dignity. The dignified fool, Demelza, gets nowhere beside the suave flattering rogue. Gentle obsequious compliments were the order of the day, and instead I tried to teach them their business. A lesson in tactics. But Jim Carter may pay the bill with his life.'

She pulled the last curtain. A moth came fluttering in, wings beating the green figured damask.

'No one else'd 've done what you did,' she said. 'No other squire. It was none of your fault that he went poaching and was caught.'

Ross grunted. 'To be frank, I don't think my interference greatly altered the situation. But that is no matter for . . .' He stopped. He stared. This was the moment now.

'I haven't brought the other candles,' she got out. 'We was short and you said you'd get some to-day.'

'Have you been drinking again?'

She said desperately: 'I've never touched nothing since you told me. Honest. I swear to God.'

'Where did you get that dress?'

'. . . From the library . . .' Her ready lies were forgotten.

'So now you wear my mother's clothes!'

She stammered: 'You never told me that. You told me that I mustn't drink, an' I've never touched nothing since. You never told me not to touch the clo'es!'

'I tell you now. Go and take those things off.'

It couldn't have been worse. But in the depths of horror and despair one comes to a new steadiness. There is no farther to fall. She moved a foot or two into the yellow gleam of the candlelight.

'Well, don't you like it?'

He stared at her again. 'I've told you what I think.'

She came to the end of the table, and the moth fluttered past the candles and across the blue of her dress and pattered its reckless wings against the cupboard by the wall.

'Can I not . . . sit and talk for a while?'

Astounding the change. The hair combed up gave her face an altered, a more oval shape. Her youthful features were clean-cut and wholesome, her look was adult. He felt like someone who had adopted a tiger cub without knowing what it would grow into. The imp of a sturdy disrespect for his own position tempted him to laugh.

But the incident wasn't funny. If it had been he would have laughed with a clear mind. He didn't know why it wasn't funny.

He said in a withdrawn voice: 'You came here as a maid and have been a good one. For that you've been allowed certain liberties. But the liberty of dressing yourself in those things is not one of them.'

The chair on which he had been sitting at the table was still half out, and she subsided on the edge of it. She smiled nervously, but with more brilliance than she thought.

'Please, Ross, can't I stay? No one'll ever know. Please . . .' Words bubbled to her lips, overflowed in a whisper. 'I aren't doing no 'arm. Tis no more'n I've done many and many an evening before. I didn't mean no 'arm putting on these clothes. They was rotting away in the old tin box. It d' seem a shame to leave all they pretty things there rotting away. I only meant it to please you. I thought you'd maybe like it. If I stay 'ere now till tis time to go——'

He said: 'Get off to bed at once and we'll say no more of it.'

'I'm seventeen,' she said mutinously. 'I been seventeen for weeks. Are ee always going to treat me like a child? I'll *not* be treated like a child! I'm a woman now. Can I not please myself when I d' go to bed?'

'You can't please yourself how you behave.'

'I thought you liked me.'

'So I do. But not to let you rule the house.'

'I don't want to rule the house, Ross. I only want to sit here and talk to you. I've only old clo'es to work in. This is so – to have somethin' like this on——'

'Do as I say, or you'll go home to your father in the morning.'

From the first desperately shy beginning she had succeeded in working up a feeling of grievance against him; for the moment she really believed that the issue was whether she should be given certain privileges.

'Well then,' she said, 'turn me out! Turn me out to-night. I don't care. Hit me if you want to. Like Father used to. I'll get drunk an' shout the house down, an' then you'll have good reason!'

She turned and picked up his glass from the table. She poured out some brandy and took a gulp of it. Then she waited to see what effect it would have on him.

He quickly leaned forward and picked up the wooden poker and rapped her sharply across the knuckles with it, so that the glass broke and spilled its contents down the disputed frock.

For a moment she looked more surprised than hurt, then she put her knuckles into her mouth. The mature and defiant seventeen became a desolate and unfairly rebuked child. She stared down at the frock where the brandy was soaking through the skirt. Tears came into her eyes, beading upon her thick dark lashes till she blinked them away, beading again and trembling at the rim without falling. Her attempt at coquetry had been a painful failure, but nature was coming to her help.

'I shouldn't have done that,' he said.

He didn't know why he had spoken or why he should apologize for a just and necessary rebuke. Quicksands had moved under his feet.

'The frock,' she said. 'You shouldn't 've spoiled the frock. It was that pretty. I'll go to-morrow. I'll go as soon as the light comes.'

She got up from the chair, tried to say something more, then suddenly was kneeling by his chair, her head on his knees, sobbing.

He looked down at her, at the head with its tumble of dark hair beginning to come awry, at the gleam of her neck. He touched her hair with its light and dark shadows.

'You little——' he said. 'Stay on if you want to.'

She tried to dry her eyes but they kept filling up again. For the first time then he put his hands on her, lifted her up. Yesterday the contact would have meant nothing. Without direct intention she came to be sitting on his knee.

'Here.' He took out his handkerchief and wiped her eyes. Then he kissed her on the cheek and patted her arm, trying to feel the act as a paternal one. His authority was gone. That didn't matter.

'I like that,' she said.

'Maybe. Now go you off and forget this ever happened.'

She sighed and swallowed ruefully. 'My legs are wet.' She pulled up the front of the pink petticoat and began to wipe her knee.

He said angrily: 'You know what people say of you, Demelza?'

She shook her head. 'What?'

'If you act like this, what they say of you will become true.'

She looked at him, candidly this time, without coquetry and without fear. 'I live only for you, Ross.'

A breeze lifted the curtain at one of the open windows. The birds outside were quiet at last and it was dark. He kissed her again, this time on the mouth. She smiled unsteadily through the remnants of her tears, and the candlelight lent a cream-gold charm to her skin.

Then by some mischance she put up a hand to push back her hair and the gesture reminded him of his mother.

. . . He got up, lifting her to her feet so sharply that she almost fell, went to the window, stood with his back to her.

It was not the gesture but the frock. Perhaps the smell of it: something that brought up to him the taste, the flavours of yesterday. His mother had lived and breathed in that frock, in this room, in that chair. Her spirit moved and quickened between them.

Ghosts and phantoms of another life.

'What's to do?' she asked.

He turned. She was standing at the table, holding to it, the broken glass at her feet. He tried to remember her as a thin little urchin trailing across the fields with Garrick behind her. But that was no use at all. The urchin was gone for ever. It was not beauty she had grown overnight but the appeal of youth, which was beauty in its own right.

'Demelza,' he said, and even her name was strange. 'I didn't take you from your father – for – to——'

'What do it matter what you took me for?'

'You don't understand,' he said. 'Get out. Get out.'

He felt the need to soften what he had said, the need to explain.

But the slightest movement on his part would throw restraint away.

He stared at her and she did not speak. Perhaps she was silently admitting defeat, but he didn't know, he couldn't read her. Her eyes were the eyes of a stranger who had usurped familiar ground. They stared at him with a challenge grown faintly hostile and hurt.

He said: 'I am going to bed now. You also go to bed and try to understand.'

He picked up one of the candles, blew out the others in that sconce. He glanced at her briefly, forced a half smile.

'Good night, my dear.'

Still she did not speak or move. When the door closed behind him, then at last in the silent room with only the frustrate moth for company she turned and picked up a candle for herself and one by one began to blow out the others he had left.

III

In his bedroom he was beset by a wave of cynicism of quite surprising violence. What sort of a monk and anchorite was he becoming? Shades of his own father seemed to rise and whisper, 'Young prude!'

Heaven! he said to himself. What moral code had he drawn for himself that he had to obey these nice distinctions? You could fritter away a whole youth tracing the petty differences between one moral obligation and another. Slender refined Elizabeth, gaunt lascivious Margaret, Demelza with her flowering maidenhood. A passionate child rolling in the dust with her ugly dog; a girl driving oxen; a woman . . . Did anything else matter? He owed no one anything; certainly not Elizabeth. She was nothing any longer to him. This was no blind seeking after sensation in order to drown a hurt, as it had been on the night of the ball. God, he had never been so drunk on so little brandy before. That old stiff silk dress, part of an older love . . .

He sat on the bed uncertainly and tried to think. He tried to think over the incidents of the day. The beginning was frustration and the end was frustration. 'Frankly, Mr Poldark, I am inclined to agree with my friend, Dr Halse. It is no doubt very unfortunate that the prisoner is suffering from this disability . . .' Who but a dolt would have expected the magistrates to do anything but agree with each other. 'Must back each other up, *esprit de corps*, good of the community, good of the class.' That was what he had ignored. One did not stand up in a witness box and argue against one's own class in public, let alone harangue them in front of a crowd of court idlers. It wasn't done. Well, he had his own standards of behaviour, though no one gave him credit for them. It was nothing out-of-the-way for the younger gentry of the neighbourhood to tumble their kitchenmaids. They didn't kidnap them when they were under age, that was all. Well, she was of age now, age enough to know her own mind and sense enough to read his before he knew it himself. What was the matter with him? No sense of humour to leaven life? Must every act be dead serious, a weight upon his head and hands? Loving was a recreation; all the poets sang of its lightness, its levity; only the dull clod raised barriers of creed or conscience.

There was no air to-night. The temperature didn't often keep up after dusk.

At least he had in some way earned the increased gratitude of Jinny. These years would seem even longer for her than for Jim. Would he see them through? 'Quite the sentimental fool, egad. Quite the renegade. Mixing with the Indians and fighting against the whites. Traitor to one's own station in life . . .' – 'Then come kiss me, sweet and twenty . . .' – 'Beauty is but a flower Which wrinkles will devour . . .' – 'Upsetting himself about some farm labourer with a bad cough. Rather unbalanced, one supposes. After all, one has to accept the rough with the smooth. Last year when my prize mare took the blood poisoning . . .' – 'Every wise man's son doth know.'

He got up and went to the north window to see if it was open. The sophistries of the poets. To-night he could see nothing straight. Were sweet singers the best counsellors? Yes, the window was wide open. He pulled back the curtain and stared out. In twenty-seven years he had worked out some sort of a philosophy of behaviour; did one throw it over at the first test? There was a tap on the door.

'Come in,' he said.

He turned. It was Demelza, carrying a candle. She did not speak. The door swung to behind her. She hadn't changed and her dark eyes were like lamps.

'What is it?' he said.

'This frock.'

'Well?'

'The bodice unfastens down the back.'

'Well?'

'I . . . can't reach the hooks.'

He frowned at her a moment.

She came slowly up to him, turned, set the candle clumsily upon a table. 'I'm sorry.'

He began to undo the dress. She felt his breath on her neck.

There was still one scar of those he had seen on the way home from Redruth Fair.

His hands touched the cool skin of her back. Abruptly they slipped inside her frock and closed about her waist. She leaned her head back against his shoulder and he kissed her until the room went dark before her eyes.

But now at this last moment when all was won she had to confess her deceit. She couldn't die unshriven.

'I lied,' she whispered, crying again. 'I lied about the hooks. Oh, Ross, don't take me if you h-hate me. I lied . . . I lied . . .'

He said nothing, for now nothing counted, not lies nor poets nor principles nor any reservations of mind or heart.

He released her and lit another candle.

Chapter seven

SHE WOKE AT dawn. She stretched her arms and yawned, at first not aware of the change. Then she saw that the rafters overhead ran a different way . . .

The pipe and the silver snuffbox on the mantelshelf, the oval mildewed mirror above it. His bedroom. She turned and stared unbelieving at the man's head with its copper-dark hair on the pillow.

She lay quite still with closed eyes while her mind went over all that had happened in this room, and only her breathing coming quick and painful showed she was not asleep.

The birds were waking. Another warm still day. Under the eaves the finches made liquid sounds like water dripping in a pool.

She slid quietly to the edge of the bed and slipped out, afraid of waking him. At the window she stared across the outhouses to the sea. Tide nearly full. Mist lay in a grey scarf along the line of the cliffs. The incoming waves scrawled dark furrows in the silver-grey sea.

Her frock – that frock – lay in a heap on the floor. She snatched it up and wrapped it round her, as if by so doing she hid from herself. On tiptoe across to her own bedroom. She dressed while the square of the window slowly lightened.

No stirrings in the house. She was always the first abroad, had often been to the end of the valley for flowers before Jud and Prudie grumblingly saw the light. To-day she must be out of the house first.

Barefoot down the short shallow stairs and across the hall. She opened the front door. Behind the house might be the old grey sea; but in the valley was all the warmth and fragrance which the land had stored up during the short summer night. She stepped out and the warm air met her. She filled her lungs with it. In odd parts of the sky clouds lay thin and streaky, motionless and abandoned as by the sweeping of a careless broom.

The damp grass was not cold to her bare feet. She walked across the garden to the stream, sat on the wooden footbridge with her back to the rail and dipped her toes in the trickle of water. The hawthorn trees growing along its banks were in bloom, but the blossom had lost its whiteness, was turning pink and falling, so that the stream was full of drifting tiny petals like the remnants of a wedding. Where she sat the sweet smell of the

Maybloom scented every breath.

In her loins and in her back there was pain; but the frightening recollections of the night were fading before the remembrance of its triumphs. She had no twinges of conscience as to the way she had gained that end, for to live and fulfil the purpose of life seemed to absolve all. Yesterday it couldn't happen. To-day it had happened. Nothing could touch that; nothing.

In a few minutes the sun would be up, lighting the ridge of the valley behind which a few short hours ago it had set. She drew up her legs, sat a moment on the bridge, then knelt, scooped up the water in her hands and bathed her face and neck. Then she stood up and in a sudden excess of feeling hopped and skipped across to the apple trees. A thrush and a blackbird were competing from neighbouring branches. Under the trees some leaves touched her hair, sprinkling her ear and neck with dew. She knelt and began to pick a few of the bluebells which made a hazy carpet under the trees. But she had taken no more than a dozen when she gave it up and sat against a lichened trunk, her head back, the thin juicy stems of the bluebells clutched to her breast.

She sat so still, her neck curved in lassitude, her skirts drawn up, her bare legs in sensuous contact with the grass and the leaves, that a chaffinch hopped down and began its 'pink-pink' cry beside her hand. Her throat ached to join in, but she knew she would only croak.

A big fly came down also and settled on a leaf close to her face; he had two round brown knobs on his head and at this range looked enormous, a prehistoric animal which had roamed the jungles of a forgotten world. First he stood on four front legs and rubbed the two back ones with sinuous ease up and down his wings; then he stood on the four back and rubbed the two front ones like an obsequious shopkeeper. 'Buzz, buzz!' said Demelza. He went with a sudden hum but was back again in the same position almost at once, this time rubbing his head as if over a wash tub.

A spider's web was outlined in fine beads of moisture above her head. The blackbird which was singing stopped his song, balanced a moment with a tail like a lady's fan, flew away. Two last petals of pink-brown apple blossom, disturbed by the movement, floated indolently to earth. The finch began to peck at one of them.

She put out her hand and made an encouraging sound, but he wouldn't be deceived and fluttered sidelong to a safer distance. In the fields a cow lowed. There was still that about the early hour which set it apart from men. At the back of all the chatter of the birds was the quietness of a world not yet awake.

A rook flew low overhead, his shabby plumage gilded, his wings making a creaky sound as they beat the air. The sun rose and flooded into the valley, casting dewy silent shadows and shafts of long pale light among the trees.

Chapter eight

ROSS WOKE LATE. It was seven before he was stirring.

When he got up he had a nasty taste in his mouth. It had been poor stuff at the Fighting Cock's Inn.

Demelza . . . Stiff old silk of the dress . . . The hooks. What had got into her? He had been drunk, but was it with liquor? The expense of spirit in a waste of shame is lust in action . . . past reason hated – how did it go? He had not thought of *that* sonnet last night. The poets had played him false. A strange affair.

At least there had been an expense of spirit . . .

And the whispering shrews of three villages had only anticipated the truth. Not that that mattered. What mattered was Demelza and himself. What would he find her this morning: the friendly drudge of daylight or the silk-mouthed stranger he had imagined through the summer night?

She had had her way and at the last had seemed to fear it.

The acme of futility was to regret a pleasure that was past, and he had no intention of doing so. The thing was done. It would change the very pith of their personal ways; it would intrude on their growing friendship, distorting every act and image and introducing false values.

His rejection of her in the parlour had been the only sane course. Prudish if you liked, but how far were prudery and restraint confused in the mind of the cynic?

His reasoning was all questions and no answers this morning.

Whichever way one looked at it, a recollection of last night held something distasteful: not Demelza's fault, not his, but arising out of the history of their association. Was this nonsense? What would his father have said? 'Highflown claptrap to explain a thick head.'

He struggled into his clothes. For a time he allowed his mind to slur over the outcome. He went down and swilled himself under the pump, glancing from time to time at the distant cliff line where Wheal Leisure could be seen.

He dressed again and had breakfast, waited on by a back-bent muttering Prudie. She was like a fisherman angling for sympathy. She got no bites this morning. When he had finished he sent for Jud.

'Where is Demelza?'

'Dunno. She belong to be somewhere about. I seed en pass through the 'ouse an hour gone.'

'Are the Martin children here?'

'In the turmut field.'

'Well, Prudie and Demelza can join them when she is ready. I shall not be going to the mine this morning. I'll help you and Jack with the hay. Time it was begun.'

Jud grunted and ambled out. After sitting a few minutes Ross went out to the library and did half an hour's work on the business of the mine. Then he took a scythe from the farmshed and set about giving it a keener edge on the grindstone. Work as a solvent for the megrims of the night. The expense of spirit in a waste of shame . . . Last night before the final episode he had reflected that the day had begun in frustration and ended in frustration. This morning all the old restraints were rising to persuade him that the judgment still held good. Life seemed to be teaching him that the satisfaction of most appetites carried in them the seeds of frustration, that it was the common delusion of all men to imagine otherwise.

The first principles of that lesson had ten-years-old roots. But then, he was not a sensualist so perhaps he couldn't judge. His father had been a sensualist and a cynic; his father took love at its face value and took it as it came. The difference was surely not so much that *he* was frigid by nature (far from it) but that he expected too much.

The sense of separateness from others, of loneliness, had not often been so strong as this morning. He wondered if in fact there was any true content in life, if all men were as troubled as he with a sense of disillusion. It had not always been so. His childhood had been happy enough in the unthinking way that childhoods are. He had enjoyed in a measure the roughness and dangers of active service. It was since he returned home that the evil eye of discontent had been on him, making empty air of his attempts to find a philosophy of his own, turning to ashes whatever he grasped.

He put the scythe on his shoulder and tramped over to the hayfield, which lay on the northeast side of the valley beyond the apple trees and stretching up to Wheal Grace. A large field unenclosed by walls or hedges, and the hay in it was a good crop, better than last year, yellowed and dried by the last week of sun. He took off his coat and hung it over a stone at the corner of the field. He was bare-headed and could feel the warmth of the climbing sun on his hair and open neck. Natural enough that in the old days men were sun worshippers; especially in England, where the sun was elusive and fitful and always welcome, in a land of mists and cloud and drifting rain.

He began to cut, bent a little forward and using the body as a pivot, swinging in a wide semicircle. The grass toppled reluctantly, long sheaves of it bending over and sinking slowly to the earth. With the grass went patches of purple scabious and moon daisies, chervil and yellow buttercups, flowering illicitly and suffering the common fate.

Jack Cobbledick appeared, climbing the field with his high-stepping stride, and then Jud, and they worked together all through the morning while the sun rose high and beat down on them. Every now and then one or another would stop to sharpen his scythe upon a stone. They spoke little, all preferring to keep their own thoughts tight and tidy and untouched. Two larks remained with them most of the morning, fluttering dots in the high sky, singing and diving and singing.

At noon they stopped and sat in a group amongst the slain grass and took long drinks of buttermilk and ate rabbit pasties and barley cakes, Jack Cobbledick meantime remarking in a voice as slow and drawling as his walk that this here weather made you that dry you wanted to drink down more than you could rightly hold; and he'd heard tell the marrying next month at Mingoose was to be the biggest party for years: all the tip-top folk; and he'd seed old Joe Triggs last forenoon and he'd said it was a mortal shame for Jim Carter to lie in prison while Nick Vigus went scot-free, and there was many folk of the same mind; and it was said as Carter was being sent to Bodmin Gaol, which they did say was one of the best in the West country and fever was not so prevalious there as Launceston or the Plymouth hulks. Was that true, did Cap'n Poldark know? Ross said, yes, that was true.

Jack Cobbledick said it was common belief that if Cap'n Poldark hadn't stood up in court and preached to the magistrates Carter would have been sent for seven years' transportation, and folks said as the justices was fair mad about it.

Jud said he knew a man who was sent to Bodmin Gaol for next to nothing, and the first day he was there he got the fever and the second day he was dead.

Cobbledick said folk were saying that if more of the gentry was like Someone They All Knew there wouldn't be all this distress and closing down of mines and crying out for bread.

Jud said the fever was that bad at Launceston in '83 that the gaoler and his wife was strick down with it the same night and was both cold before the light of day.

Cobbledick said the Greets and the Nanfans were for getting up a crowd of men to drive Nick Vigus out of the district but that Zacky Martin had said they mustn't do nothing of the shape; two wrongs didn't make a right, nor never would.

Jud said it was his firm belief that Jim Carter's third child would be born posthumorously.

Presently they were up and off again. Ross soon forged ahead of his companions, driven on by private necessities of his own. As the sun declined he stopped again for a few minutes and saw that they had nearly done. His forearms and back were aching with the exercise, but he had worked some dissatisfaction out of himself. The regularity of the sweeping scythe, the pivoting movement of the body, the steady advance round the edge of the field, eating into the grass and gradually approaching the centre, had helped to lay the uncomfortable ghosts of his discontent. There was a faint north breeze stirring and the heat of the sun had become a mellow warmth. He took deep breaths and mopped his brow and stared at the other men behind him. Then he glanced at the dwarfed figure of one of the Martin children coming towards him from the house.

It was Maggie Martin, aged six, a cheerful child with the family red hair.

'If ee plaise, sur-r,' she piped in her singsong voice, 'thur be a leddy to see ee.'

He put a forefinger under the child's chin. 'What manner of lady, my dear?'

'Mistress Poldark, sur. Over from Trenwith.'

It was months since Verity had been to see him. This might be the beginning of a resumption of their old friendship. He had never needed it more.

'Thank you, Mag. I'll come at once.'

He fetched his coat, and with this and the scythe slung over his shoulder went down the hill to the house. She had come by horse this time, it seemed.

He put the scythe at the door and, swinging his coat, entered the parlour. A young woman was seated in a chair. His heart gave a lurch.

Elizabeth was in a long dark brown riding habit with silver buttons and fine Ghent lace at the cuffs and throat. She wore small brown riding boots and a three-cornered felt hat trimmed with lace which set off the oval of her face and crowned the bright sheen of her hair.

She extended a hand with a smile that hurt him with a memory of things past. She was a lady and very beautiful.

'Why, Ross, I thought we hadn't seen you for a month, and since I was passing this way——'

'Don't make excuses for your coming,' he said. 'Only for not having come before.'

She flushed slightly and her eyes showed a hint of pleasure. Her frailty and charm had not been altered by her motherhood. At every meeting he was surprised afresh.

'It's a hot day to be riding,' he said. 'Let me get you something to drink.'

'No, thank you, I'm quite cool.' And she looked it. 'First tell me how you are, what you have been doing. We see so little of you.'

Conscious of his damp shirt and ruffled hair, he told what he had been doing. She was a little ill at ease. He saw her glance once or twice round the room as if she sensed some alien presence, or as if she was surprised at the comfortable though shabby nature of the furnishings. Her eyes went to a bowl of wood anemones and hart's tongue ferns on the window seat.

'Verity told me,' she said, 'that you were not able to get your farm boy a lighter sentence. I am sorry.'

Ross nodded. 'A pity, yes. George Warleggan's father was chairman of the bench. We parted in mutual dislike.'

She glanced at him briefly from under her lashes. 'George will be sorry. Perhaps if you had approached him it might have been arranged. Though it is true, isn't it, that the boy was caught red-handed?'

'How is Uncle?' Ross changed the subject, feeling that his views on the Carter episode might offend her.

'He grows no better, Ross. Tom Choake bleeds him regular, but it brings him only a temporary relief. We had all hoped that this fine weather would put him on his feet again.'

'And Geoffrey Charles?'

'Doing splendid, thank you. We feared last month that he had taken the measles after escaping all the epidemic, but it was no more than a teething rash.' Her tone was controlled, but something remained in it to give him a twinge of surprise. He had not heard that muffled possessive inflexion before.

They chatted for some minutes with a sort of anxious agreeableness. Elizabeth asked about the progress of the mine, and Ross went into technical details which he doubted if she understood and was sure she could not be as interested in as she seemed. She spoke of the forthcoming wedding, taking it for granted that he had been invited, and he had not the heart to correct her. Francis wanted her to go to London this autumn, but she thought Geoffrey Charles young for the journey. Francis did not seem to understand that Geoffrey Charles could not be left behind. Francis thought, etc. . . . Francis felt . . . .

Her small composed face clouded at this stage, and she said, pulling at her gloves:

'I wish you could see more of Francis, Ross.'

Ross politely agreed that it was a pity he had not more time to spend in visiting his cousin.

'No, I do not mean quite in the sense of an ordinary visit, Ross. I do wish somehow you could have worked together. Your influence on him——'

'My influence?' he said in surprise.

'It would have steadied him. I think it would help to steady him.' She glanced up painfully, then looked away. 'You will think it strange my speaking in this way. But you see, I have been worried. We are both so friendly with George Warleggan, have stayed in Truro with him and at Cardew. George is very kind. But he is so wealthy, and to him gambling is just a pleasant recreation. Not so to us now, not so to Francis. When one plays for higher stakes than one can afford . . . It seems to have a hold of Francis. It is the breath of life to him. He wins a little and then loses so much. Charles is too ill to stop him and he has control of everything. We really cannot go on as we are doing. Grambler is losing money, as you know.'

'Do not forget,' Ross said, 'that I lost money myself before I went away. My influence might not have been so good as you think.'

'I should not have spoken of it. I hadn't intended to. I have no right to burden you with my troubles.'

'I take it as a true compliment.'

'But when you mentioned Francis . . . And our old friendship . . . You were always one to understand.'

He saw that she was genuinely distressed, and turned towards the window to give her time to recover. He wanted to justify her faith in him; he would have given a lot to have been able to put some suggestion to ease the distress from her face. His resentment of her marriage had quite gone. She had come to him.

'I wondered if I should tell Charles,' she said. 'I'm so afraid it would make him more ill – and that would not help us at all.'

Ross shook his head. 'Not that. Let me see Francis first. God knows, I am not likely to succeed where – where others have failed. What I cannot begin to understand——'

'What?'

But she sensed something of what he left unsaid. 'He is reasonable in so many things, but I cannot influence him in that. He – he seems to take my advice as an interference.'

'So he will certainly take mine the same. But I will try.'

She looked at him a moment. 'You have a strong will, Ross. I knew it once. What a man dislikes to hear from his – his wife he may accept from a cousin. You have a way of making your point. I think you could influence Francis very much if you chose.'

'Then I will choose.'

She rose. 'Forgive me, I hadn't intended to say so much. I can't tell you how I appreciate the way you've welcomed me.'

Ross smiled. 'Perhaps you'll promise to come more often.'

'Gladly. I – should have liked to come before but felt I had not the right to come.'

'Don't feel that again.'

There was a footstep in the hall and Demelza came in carrying a great sheaf of fresh-picked bluebells.

She stopped dead when she saw she was intruding. She was in a plain blue linen dress, homemade, with open neck and a bit of embroidery to ornament the belt. She looked wild and unkempt, for all afternoon, shamefully neglecting Prudie and the turnips, she had been out lying in the grass of another hayfield on the high ground to the west of the house, staring down at Ross and the men working on the hill opposite. She had lain there sniffing at the earth and peering through the grass like a young dog, and finally had turned over and gone to sleep in the sweet warmth of the declining sun. Her dark hair was ruffled and there was grass and burrs on her frock.

She returned Ross's gaze and glanced with wide eyes at Elizabeth. Then she muttered an apology and turned to withdraw.

'This is Demelza of whom you've heard me speak,' Ross said. 'This is Mistress Elizabeth Poldark.' Two women, he thought. Made of the same substance? Earthenware and porcelain.

Elizabeth thought: Oh, God, so there *is* something between them. 'Ross has often mentioned you to me, my dear,' she said.

Demelza thought: She's one day too late, just one day. How beautiful she is; how I hate her. Then she glanced at Ross again, and for the first time like the stab of a treacherous knife it occurred to her that Ross's desire for her last night was a flicker of empty passion. All day she had been too preoccupied with her own feelings to spare time for his. Now she could see so much in his eyes.

'Thank you, ma'am,' she said with horror and hatred in her finger tips. 'Can I get you anything, sur?'

Ross looked at Elizabeth. 'Reconsider your decision and take tea. It would be made in a few minutes.'

'I must go. Thank you all the same. What pretty bluebells you've picked.'

'Would you like them?' said Demelza. 'You can have 'em if you'd like.'

'That is kind of you!' Elizabeth's grey eyes flickered round the room just once more. This is her doing, she thought; those curtains. I thought Prudie wouldn't have the idea to hang them so; and the velvet draping on the settle, Ross would never have thought of that. 'I came by horse, though, and unhappily could not carry them. Keep them yourself, my dear, but thank you for the kind thought.'

'I'll tie en up for you and loop them over the saddle,' Demelza said.

'I'm afraid they would droop. See, they're drooping already. Bluebells are like that.' Elizabeth picked up her gloves and crop. I can't come here again, she thought. After all this time, and now it's too late. Too late for me to come *here*. 'You must call and see Uncle, Ross. He often asks for you. Hardly a day goes by.'

'I'll be over next week,' he said.

They went to the door and Ross helped her to mount her horse, which she did with that peculiar grace of her own. Demelza had not followed them, but watched while seeming not to watch from the window.

She's slenderer than me, she thought, even though she's had a child. Skin like ivory; never done a day's work. She's a lady and Ross is a gentleman, and I am a slut. But not last night, not last night. (The memory of it swelled up in her.) I can't be a slut: I'm Ross's woman. I hope she gets fat. I do hope and dearly pray she gets fat and catches the pox and her nose drips and her teeth fall out.

'Did you mean what you said about Francis?' Elizabeth said to Ross.

'Of course. I'll do anything I can – little as it's likely to be.'

'Come to see Charles. For dinner, that would suit. Any day. Good-bye.'

'Good-bye,' he said.

It was their first complete reconciliation since his return; and they were both aware, while not knowing that the other was aware, that the reconciliation had come just too late to count for what it might.

He watched her ride slowly up the valley. Once he saw the glint of her hair as it caught the light from the slanting sun. In this shadowed valley the birds were breaking out into their evening song, choristers trying out their notes in a great still blue-vaulted cathedral.

He was tired, so tired, and wanted to rest. But his peace of mind, hardly bought during the day, was dissipated with her visit.

He turned on his heel and tramped into the house, through to the kitchen. Prudie was preparing the evening meal. He grunted at some complaint she made and went to the stables.

For some minutes he busied himself with the small tasks of the farm; these done he came back to the house and to the living-room.

Demelza was still there, standing by the window. She held the bluebells in her arms. He did not seem to notice her, but went slowly across to his favourite chair, took off his coat and sat for some time staring with a little frown at the opposite wall. Presently he leaned back.

'I'm tired,' he said.

She turned from the window, and moving quietly, as if he were asleep, she came towards his chair. On the rug at his feet she sat down. She began idly, but half contentedly, to arrange and rearrange the bluebells in heaps upon the floor.

Book three

June–December 1787

Chapter one

ROSS AND DEMELZA were married on the twenty-fourth of June, 1787. The Rev Mr Odgers performed the ceremony, which took place very quietly in the presence only of the necessary number of witnesses. The register shows that the bride gave her age as eighteen, which was an anticipation of fact by three quarters of a year. Ross was twenty-seven.

His decision to marry her was taken within two days of their first sleeping together. It was not that he loved her but that such a course was the obvious way out. If one overlooked her beginnings she was a not unsuitable match for an impoverished farmer squire. She had already proved her worth about the house and farm, none better, and she had grown into his life in a way he had hardly realized.

With his ancient name, he could of course have gone into society and paid violent court to some daughter of the new rich and have settled down to a life of comfortable boredom on the marriage dowry. But he couldn't see such an adventure seriously. He realized with a sense of half bitter amusement that this marriage would finally damn him in the eyes of his own class. For while the man who slept with his kitchenmaid only aroused sly gossip, the man who married her made himself personally unacceptable in their sight.

He did not go to dinner at Trenwith as he had promised. He met Francis by design at Grambler the week before the wedding and told him the news. Francis seemed relieved rather than shocked: perhaps he had always lived with an underlying fear that his cousin would one day cast off the skin of civilization and come and take Elizabeth by force. Ross was a little gratified at this unhostile reception of the news and forgot almost until they were separating his promise to Elizabeth. He did, however, then fulfil it, and they parted in a less friendly manner than they might have done.

Out of his old friendship for Verity, Ross would much have liked her to be at the wedding, but he learned from Francis that the doctor had ordered her a fortnight in bed. So Ross held back his letter of invitation and instead sent her a longer one explaining the circumstances and inviting her to come and stay with them when she was better. Verity knew Demelza by sight, but had not seen her for the better part of two years, and Ross thought she would be unable to imagine what germ of senile decay had got into his brain.

If this were so she did not say as much in her letter of reply.

Dearest Ross,

Thank you for writing me so fully and explaining about your marriage. I am the last one to be able to criticize your attachment. But I should like to be the first to wish you the happiness I pray will be yours. When I am well and Papa is better I will come and see you both.

Love,
Verity

The visit to Sawle Church changed more than the name of the one-time kitchenmaid. Jud and Prudie were inclined to take it badly at first, resenting, so far as they dared show it, the fact that the child who had come here as a waif and stray, infinitely beneath themselves, should now be able to call herself their mistress. They might have quietly sulked for a long time if it had been anybody but Demelza. But in the end she talked them or hypnotized them into the view that she was in part their protégée and so her advancement reflected a certain glory on them. And after all, as Prudie remarked privately to Jud, it was better than having to take orders from some fudgy-faced baggage with drop curls.

Demelza did not see her father again that year. A few days after the banns were called she persuaded Ross to send Jud to Illuggan with a verbal message that they were to be married in a fortnight. Carne was down the mine when Jud arrived, so he was able only to deliver the message to a fat little woman in black. Thereafter silence fell. Demelza was nervous that her father might turn up and create a scene at the wedding, but all passed quietly. Tom Carne had accepted his defeat.

On the tenth of July a man called Jope Ishbel, one of the oldest and foxiest miners in the district, struck a lode of red copper at Wheal Leisure. A great amount of water came with the discovery, and all work was held up while pumping gear was brought. The adit from the cliff face was making fair progress, but some time must pass before it could unwater the workings. All this water was looked on as a good sign by those who professed to know.

When news of the find was brought to Ross he opened an anker of brandy and had big jugs of it carried up to the mine. There was great excitement, and from the mine they could see people climbing the ground behind Mellin Cottages a mile away and staring across to see what the noise was about.

The find could not have been more opportune, for the second meeting of the venturers was due in a week's time, and Ross knew that he must ask for a further fifty pounds from each of them. Jope Ishbel's strike armed him with tangible results, for even from the poor quality of the ore that Ishbel had brought to the surface they could get several pounds a ton more than from ordinary copper ore. The margin of profit was widened. If the lode was a reasonably big one it meant the certainty of a fair return.

He did not fail to point this out when the meeting took place in Mr Pearce's overheated offices in Truro, and the general effect was such that further drafts were voted without demur.

This was the first time Ross had seen Mr Treneglos since the great day at Mingoose when his son married Ruth Teague, and the old man went out of his way to be agreeable and complimentary. Over dinner they sat together, and Ross was afraid that an apology was impending for the breach of manners between old neighbours in his not having been invited to the wedding. He knew the fault did not lie with Treneglos and steered conversation away from the subject.

Mr Renfrew caused an awkward moment by getting above himself in his cups and following up a toast to the happy pair by proposing that they should not forget the bridegroom in their midst.

There was a constrained silence, and then Mr Pearce said:

'Indeed, yes. We must certainly not forget that.' And Dr Choake said: 'That would be most remiss.' And Mr Treneglos, who fortunately had caught the trend of the conversation, immediately got to his feet and said: 'My privilege, gentlemen. My pleasure and privilege. Our good friend, damme; recently embarked upon matrimony himself. I give you the toast: Captain Poldark and his young bride. May they be very happy.'

Everyone rose and drank.

'Twould have looked bad if nobody'd mentioned it,' said Mr Treneglos, not quite to himself as they sat down.

Ross seemed the least embarrassed of them all.

II

She had already grown into his life. That was what he thought. What he meant was that she had grown into the life of the house, seeing to his needs eagerly but without fuss, a good servant and an agreeable companion.

Under the new arrangement this didn't much alter. Legally an equal, she remained in fact his inferior. She did what he said, no less eagerly, no less unquestioningly, and with a radiant good will to illuminate it all. If Ross had not wished to marry her she would not have fretted for something else; but his decision to make the union legal and permanent, his honouring her with his name, was a sort of golden crown to set upon her happiness. Those few bad moments when Elizabeth called were almost forgotten and altogether discarded.

And now she was growing into his life in a different way. There was no going back for him, even if he had wished it, which he found he did not. There was now no mistaking that he found her desirable: events had proved it to be no delusion of a single summer night. But he was not yet at all sure how far it was she personally who was desirable to him, how far it was the natural needs of a man that she as a woman met.

She did not seem to be troubled with any heart searchings of her own. If she had grown and developed quickly before, now her personality flowered overnight.

When a person is as happy as she was that summer it is hard for others to be unaffected, and after a time the atmosphere she created began to have its effect on all in the house.

The additional freedoms of marriage came to her slowly. Her first attempt in this direction was a mild suggestion to Ross that some day it would be a good thing to have the mine office moved from the library, as the men walked across her flower beds in their big boots. No one was more surprised than she when a week later she saw a file of men carrying the mine papers up to one of the wooden sheds on the cliff.

Even then weeks passed before she could bring herself to steal into the library without the old sense of guilt. And it needed all the hardihood in the world to sit there trying to conjure tunes out of the derelict spinet when anyone was within hearing.

But her vitality was so abundant that gradually it overcame the barriers which custom and subservience had set up. She began to strum more openly and to sing low-voiced chants of her own devising. One day she rode in with Ross and brought back a few broadsheets of verse which she learned by heart and then hummed to her own tunes at the spinet, trying to fit in sounds where they sounded right.

As if to collaborate with Demelza's happiness, the summer was the warmest for many years, with long weeks of bright quiet weather and rare full days of rain. After the epidemics of the winter the fine clean weather was welcome to all, and the level at which many families spent the summer seemed like plenty compared with what had gone before.

Work on Wheal Leisure was going slowly but well. With the adit making progress towards the workings, every attempt was made to avoid the heavy cost of a pumping engine. Horse whims where devised one beside another and the water thus raised was ingeniously dammed in a hollow and released down a leat to turn a water wheel, which itself worked a pump to raise more water. Copper was being mined now. Soon there would be enough to send a consignment into Truro for one of the ticketings.

III

. . . She had already grown into his life, he thought.

Often now he wished he could separate the two Demelzas who had become a part of him. There was a matter-of-fact, daytime Demelza with whom he worked and from whom for a year or more he had derived certain definite pleasures of companionship. This one he had grown to like and to trust – to be liked and trusted by her. Half servant, half sister, comradely and obedient, the direct and calculable descendant of last year and the year before. Demelza learning to read, Demelza fetching wood for the fire, Demelza shopping with him and digging the garden and never still about her tasks.

But the second was still a stranger. Although he was husband and master of them both, this one was incalculable with the enigma of her pretty candle-lit face and fresh young body – all for his carnal satisfaction and increasing pleasure. In the first days he had held this one in a certain contempt. But events had moved beyond that. Contempt had long since gone – but the stranger was still left.

Two not-quite-distinct persons, the stranger and the friend. It was unsettling in the day, in moments of routine and casual encounter, to get some sudden reminder of the young woman who could somehow call herself into being at will, whom he took and owned, yet never truly possessed. Still more odd was it in the night to see sometimes peering from the drugged dark eyes of this stranger the friendly untidy girl who had helped him with the horses or cut out his supper. At such times he was perturbed and not quite happy, as if he found himself trampling on something that was good in its own right.

He wished he could separate these two. He felt he would be happier if he could separate them entirely. But as the weeks passed it seemed that the reverse of what he wanted was taking place. The two entities were becoming less distinct.

It was not until the first week of August that a complete fusion of the two occurred.

Chapter two

PILCHARDS HAD COME late to the coast that year. The delay had caused anxiety, for not only did the livelihood of many people depend on the arrival of the fish but virtually in these times their existence. In the Scillies and the extreme south the trade was already in full swing, and there were always wiseacres and pessimists who were ready to predict that the shoals would miss the northern shores of the county this year and go across to Ireland instead.

A sigh of relief greeted the news that a catch had been made at St Ives, but the first shoal was not sighted off Sawle until the afternoon of the sixth of August.

A huer, watching from the cliff, as he had been watching for weeks, spotted the familiar dark red tinge far out at sea, and the cry he let out through his old tin trumpet inspirited the village. The seining boats instantly put out, seven men to each of the leading boats, four to the follower.

Towards evening it was known that both teams had made catches much above the average, and the news spread with great speed. Men working on the harvest at once downed tools and hurried to the village, followed by every free person from Grambler and many of the miners as they came off core.

Jud had been into Grambler that afternoon and came back with the news to Demelza, who told Ross over their evening meal.

I'm that glad,' she said. 'All Sawle've been wearing faces down to their chins. Twill be a rare relief; and I hear it is a handsome catch.'

Ross's eyes followed her as she rose from the table and went to trim the wicks of the candles before they were lighted. He had been at the mine all day and had enjoyed this supper in the shadowy parlour with the evening stealing into and about the room. There was no real difference between now and that evening two months ago when he had come home defeated and it had all begun. Jim Carter was still in prison. There was no real change in the futility of his own life and efforts.

'Demelza,' he said.

'Um?'

'It is low tide at eleven,' he said. 'And the moon's up. What if we rowed round to Sawle and watched them putting down the tuck net.'

Her eyes lit up. 'Ross, that would be lovely!'

'Shall we take Jud to help row us?' This to tease.

'No, no, let us go, just the two of us! Let us go alone. You and I, Ross.' She was almost dancing before his chair. 'I will row. I am as strong as Jud any day. We'll go an' watch, just the two of us alone.'

He laughed. 'You'd think it was a ball I'd invited you to. D'you think I can't row you that far myself?'

'When shall we start?'

'In an hour.'

'Good, good, good. I'll make ready something to eat – an' brandy in a flask, lest it be cold sitting, an' – an' a rug for me, and a basket for some fish.' She fairly ran from the room.

They set off for Nampara Cove shortly after nine. It was a warm still evening with the three-quarter moon already high. In Nampara Cove they dragged their small boat from the cave where it was kept, across the pale firm sand to the sea's edge. Demelza got in and Ross pushed the boat through the fringe of whispering surf and jumped in as it floated.

The sea was very calm to-night and the light craft was quite steady as he pulled towards the open sea. Demelza sat in the stern and watched Ross and looked about her and dipped a hand over the gunnel to feel the water trickling between her fingers. She was wearing a scarlet kerchief about her hair and a warm skin coat which had belonged to Ross as a boy and now just fitted her.

They skirted the high bleak cliffs between Nampara Cove and Sawle Bay, and the jutting rocks stood in sharp silhouette against the moonlit sky. The water sucked and slithered about the base of the cliffs. They passed two inlets which were inaccessible except by boat at any tide, being surrounded by steep cliffs. All this was as familiar to Ross as the shape of his own hand, but Demelza had never seen it. She had only once been out in a boat before. They passed the Queen Rock, where a number of good ships had come to grief, and then rounded a promontory into Sawle Bay and came upon the first fishers.

They had let down the seine net – a fine strong mesh of great length, with corks on the upper side and lead on the lower – some distance past the promontory and about half a mile from the shore. With this great net the seiners had enclosed about two acres of water and, they hoped, many fish. There was always the possibility, of course, that they had been wrongly directed by the man on the cliffs who alone could see the movement of the shoal, or that some flaw on the sea bed should have prevented the net from falling cleanly and so allowed the fish room to slip away. But short of such accidents there was every hope of a good catch. And although in calm weather it might be possible to keep the net in position by means of grapnels for ten days or a fortnight, no one had the least intention of relying on the good weather a minute longer than they had to.

And to-night there was a moon.

As low tide approached, the boat known as the follower and carrying the tuck net was rowed cautiously into the enclosed area marked by the bobbing corks supporting the great stop seine. The boat was rowed round within the area while the tuck net was lowered and secured at various points. This done, they began to haul in the tuck net again.

It was at this crucial stage that Ross and Demelza came closely on the scene. They were not the only spectators. Every boat that would float and every human being that could sit in one had come out from Sawle to watch. And those who had no craft or were too infirm stood on the shelving beach and shouted advice or encouragement. There were lights and lanterns in the cottages of Sawle and all along the shingle bar and moving up and down on the blue-white waters of the cove. The moon lit up the scene with an unreal twilight.

Sea gulls flapped and screamed low overhead. No one took much notice of the new arrivals. One or two called friendly greetings. The arrival of Ross on the scene did not embarrass them as the arrival of others of the gentry might have done.

He rowed his boat close to where the master seiner was standing in his craft giving brief orders to the men who were within the circle hauling in the net. As it became clear that the net was heavy a short silence fell. In a moment or two it would be known whether the catch was a fine or a poor one, whether they had trapped a good part of the shoal or some part with fish too small for salting and export, whether by some mischance they might have caught a shoal of sprats instead, as had happened a couple of years ago. On the result of the next few minutes the prosperity of half the village hung.

The only sound now was the bobble and swish of water against fifty keels and the deep 'Yoy . . . ho! Hoy . . . ho!' chorus of the men straining to haul in the net.

Up and up came the net. The master seiner had forgotten his words of advice and stood there biting his fingers and watching the waters within the tuck net for the first sign of life.

It was not long in coming. First one of the spectators said something, then another exclaimed. Then a murmur spread round the boats and increased to what was more a shout of relief than a cheer.

The water was beginning to bubble, as if in a giant saucepan; it boiled and frothed and eddied, and then suddenly broke and disappeared and became fish. It was the miracle of Galilee enacted over again in the light of a Cornish moon. There was no water any more: only fish, as big as herrings, jumbled together in their thousands, jumping, wriggling, glinting, fighting and twisting to escape.

The net heaved and lurched, the big boats heeled over as the men strained to hold the catch. People talking and shouting, the splash of oars, the excited shouts of the fishers; the earlier noise was nothing to this.

The tuck net was now fast and the fishermen were already dipping baskets into the net and tipping them full of fish into the bottom of the boat. It seemed as if everyone was mindful of the haste necessary to take full advantage of good fortune. It was as if a storm waited just over the summit of the nearest cliff. Two big flat-bottomed boats like barges were ferried alongside and men hanging over the side began to work with fury to fill them. Other small boats quickly surrounded the net to take in the catch.

Sometimes the moonlight seemed to convert the fish into heaps of coins, and to Ross it looked like sixty or eighty dark-faced sub-human pygmies scooping at an inexhaustible bag of silver.

Soon men were up to their ankles in pilchards, soon up to their knees. Boats broke away and were rowed gingerly towards the shore, their gunnels no more than two inches above the lapping water. On shore the activity was no less; lanterns were everywhere while the fish were shovelled into wheelbarrows and hurried towards the salting cellars for picking over and inspection. Still the work round the net went on amongst the springing gleaming fish.

At the other side of the bay another but lesser catch was being hauled in. Ross and Demelza ate their cakes and took a sip of brandy from the same flask and talked in lowered voices of what they saw.

'Home now?' Ross said presently.

'A small bit longer,' Demelza suggested. 'The night is so warm. It is grand to be 'ere.'

He dipped his oars gently and straightened the bows of the boat towards the gentle lift and fall of the sea. They had drifted away from the crowds of boats, and it rather pleased him to get this detached view.

He found, quite to his surprise, that he was happy. Not merely happy in Demelza's happiness but in himself. He couldn't think why. The condition just existed within him.

. . . They waited and watched until the tuck net was almost cleared and the fishermen were going to lower it again. Then they waited to see if the second haul would be as big as the first. Whenever they were about to leave some fresh interest held them. Time passed unnoticed while the moon on its downward path came near the coast line and picked out a silver stitching on the water.

At last Ross slowly exerted his strength on the oars and the boat began to move. As they passed near the others Pally Rogers recognized them and called 'Good night!' Some of the others paused, sweating from their labours and also shouted.

'Good catch, eh, Pally?' Ross said.

''Andsome. More'n a quarter of a million fish, I reckon, afore we're done.'

'I'm very glad. It will make a difference next winter.'

'Night, sur.'

'Good night.'

'Night, sur.'

'Night . . .'

They rowed away, and as they went the sounds of all the voices and human activity slowly faded, into a smaller space, into a little confined murmur in the great night. They rowed out towards the open sea and the sharp cliffs and the black dripping rocks.

'Everyone is happy to-night,' Ross said, half to himself.

Demelza's face gleamed in the stern. 'They like you,' she said in an undertone. 'Everyone d' like you.'

He grunted. 'Little silly.'

'No, tis the truth. I know, because I'm one of 'em. You and your father was different from the others. But mostly you. You're – you're——' She stumbled. 'You're half a gent and half one of them. And then you trying to help Jim Carter and giving food to people——'

'And marrying you.'

They passed into the shadow of the cliffs. 'No, not that,' she said soberly. 'Maybe they don't like that. But they like you all the same.'

'You're too sleepy to talk sense,' he said. 'Cover your head and doze off till we're home.'

She did not obey, but sat watching the dark line where the shadow of the land ended and the glinting water began. She would have preferred to be out there. The shadow had lengthened greatly since they came out, and she would have rather made a wide circuit to keep within the friendly light of the moon. She stared into the deep darkness of one of the deserted coves they were passing. To these places no man ever came. They were desolate and cold. She could picture unholy things living there, spirits of the dead, things come out of the sea. She shivered and turned away.

Ross said: 'Take another nip of brandy.'

'No.' She shook her head. 'No. Not cold, Ross.'

In a few minutes they were turning into Nampara Cove. The boat slipped through the ripples at the edge and grounded in the sand. He got out and as she made to follow caught her about the waist and carried her to dry land. He kissed her before he put her down.

When the boat was drawn up into its cave and the oars hidden where a casual vagrant could not find them he rejoined her where she was waiting just above high-water mark. For a while neither of them made a move and they watched the moon set. As it neared the water it began to grow misshapen and discoloured like an overripe blood orange squeezed between sea and sky. The silver sword across the sea became tarnished and shrank until it was gone and only the old moon remained, bloated and dark, sinking into the mists.

Then without words they turned, walked across the sand and shingle, crossed the stream at the steppingstones and walked together hand in hand the half mile to the house.

She was quite silent. He had never done what he had done to-night. He had never kissed her before except in passion. This was something different. She knew him to be closer to her to-night than he had ever been before. For the very first time they were on a level. It was not Ross Poldark, gentleman farmer, of Nampara, and his maid, whom he had married because it was better than being alone. They were a man and a woman, with no inequality between them. She was older than her years and he younger; and they walked home hand in hand through the slanting shadows of the new darkness.

I am happy, he thought again. Something is happening to me, to us, transmuting our shabby little love affair. Keep this mood, hold on to it. No slipping back.

The only sound all the way home was the bubbling of the stream beside their path. The house greeted them whitely. Moths fluttered away to the stars and the trees stood silent and black.

The front door creaked as they closed it, and they climbed the stairs with the air of conspirators. When they reached their room they were laughing breathlessly at the thought of waking Jud and Prudie with such gentle noises.

She lit the candles and closed the windows to keep the moths out, took off the heavy coat and shook out her hair. Oh yes, she was lovely to-night. He put his arms about her, his face still boyish in its laughter, and she laughed back at him, her mouth and teeth gleaming moist in the candlelight.

At that his smile faded and he kissed her.

'Ross,' she said. 'Dear Ross.'

'I love you,' he said, 'and am your servant. Demelza, look at me. If I've done wrong in the past, give me leave to make amends.'

So he found that what he had half despised was not despicable, that what had been for him the satisfaction of an appetite, a pleasant but commonplace adventure in disappointment, owned wayward and elusive depths he had not known before and carried the knowledge of beauty in its heart.

Chapter three

SEPTEMBER OF THAT year was clouded by the death of Charles.

The old man had grunted miserably on all through the summer, and the doctor had given him up a half-dozen times. Then one day, perversely, he collapsed just after Choake had made his most favourable report of the year, and died before he could be resummoned.

Ross went to the funeral, but neither Elizabeth nor Verity was there, both being ill. The funeral attracted a big attendance both of village and mining people and of the local gentry, for Charles had been looked on as the senior personage of the district and had been generally liked within the limits of his acquaintance.

Cousin William-Alfred took the service and, himself affected by the bereavement, preached a sermon which was widely agreed to be of outstanding quality. Its theme was 'A Man of God.' What did the phrase mean, he asked? It meant to nourish those attributes in which Christ himself had been so conspicuous: truth and honesty, purity of heart, humility, grace and love. How many of us had such qualities? Could we look into our own hearts and see there the qualities necessary to make us men and women of God? A time such as this, when we mourned the passing of a great and good man, was a time for self-inspection and a renewed dedication. It was true to say that in the loss of our dear friend Charles Poldark we marked the passing of a man of God. His way had been upright; he had never spoken an ill word. From him you grew to expect only kindness and the courtesy of the true gentleman who knew no evil and looked for none in others. The steady unselfish leadership of a man whose existence was an example to all.

After William-Alfred had been talking in this vein for five minutes Ross heard a sniff in the pew beside him and saw Mrs Henshawe dabbing unashamedly at her nose. Captain Henshawe too was blinking his blue eyes, and several others were weeping quietly. Yes, it was a 'beautiful' sermon, tugging at the emotions and conjuring up pictures of greatness and peace. But were they talking about the decent peppery ordinary old man he knew, or had the subject strayed to the story of some saint of the past? Or were there two men being buried under the same name? One perhaps had shown himself to such as Ross, while the other had been reserved for the view of men of deep insight like William-Alfred. Ross tried to remember Charles before he was ill, Charles with his love of cockfighting and his hearty appetite, with his perpetual flatulence and passion for gin, with his occasional generosities and meannesses and faults and virtues, like most men. There was some mistake somewhere. Oh well, this was a special occasion . . . But Charles himself would surely have been amused. Or would he have shed a tear with the rest for the manner of man who had passed away?

William-Alfred was drawing to the end.

'My friends, we may fall far short of the example which is thus set before us. But in my Father's house are many mansions, and there shall be room for all that believe. Equality of life, equality of opportunity are not for this world. Blessed are the humble and meek, for they shall see God. And He in His infinite wisdom shall weigh us all. Blessed are the poor, for they shall enter into heaven because of their poverty. Blessed are the rich, for they shall enter into heaven because of their charity. So in the hereafter there shall be one mighty concourse of people, all provided for after their several needs, all rewarded according to their virtues, and all united in the one sublime privilege of praising and glorifying God. Amen.'

There was a scraping of viols as the three musicians by the chancel steps prepared to strike up, the choir cleared their throats, and his son wakened Mr Treneglos.

Ross accepted the invitation to return to Trenwith, hoping he might see Verity, but neither she nor Elizabeth came down. He did not stay longer than to drink a couple of glasses of canary, and then he made his excuses to Francis and walked home.

He was sorry he had not come straight back. The attitude of some of the mourners had a certain pained withdrawnness towards himself. Despite his own thoughts at the time of his marriage, he was unprepared for it, and he could have laughed at himself and at them.

Ruth Treneglos, nee Teague. Mrs Teague. Mrs Chynoweth. Polly Choake. Quacking geese, with their trumpery social distinctions and their sham code of ethics! Even William-Alfred and his wife had been a little constrained. No doubt to them his marriage looked too much like the mere admission of the truth of an old scandal. Of course William-Alfred, in his well-intentioned way, took 'the family' very seriously. Joshua had rightly called him its conscience. He liked to be consulted, no doubt.

Old Mr Warleggan had been very distant, but that was more understandable. The episode of the courtroom rankled. So perhaps did Ross's refusal to put the mine business through their hands. George Warleggan was far too careful of his manners to show what he felt.

Well, well. The whole of their disapproval added together didn't matter an eyewink. Let them stew. As he reached his own land Ross's annoyance began to leave him at the prospect of seeing Demelza again . . .

II

In fact he was disappointed, for when he reached home Demelza had gone to Mellin Cottages, taking some extra food for Jinny and a little coat she had made for her week-old baby. Benjamin Ross, too, had been having trouble with his teeth and last month had had a convulsion. Ross had seen his two-and-a-half year old namesake recently and had been struck by the coincidence that Reuben's knife had left a scar on the child's face roughly similar to his own. He wondered if this would be remarked when the boy grew up.

He decided to walk over to Mellin now in the hope of meeting Demelza on the way back.

He met his wife two hundred yards from the cottages. As always it was a peculiar pleasure to see her face light up, and she came running and hopping to meet him.

'Ross! How nice. I didn't expect ee back yet.'

'It was indifferent entertainment,' he said, linking her arm. 'I'm sure Charles would have been bored.'

'Ssh!' She shook her head at him in reproof. ''Tis poor luck to joke about such things. Who was there? Tell me who was there.'

He told her, pretending to be impatient but really enjoying her interest. 'That's all. It was a sober crew. My wife should have been there to brighten it up.'

'Was – was Elizabeth not there?' she asked.

'No. Nor Verity. They are both unwell. The bereavement, I expect. Francis was left to do the honours alone. And your invalids?'

'My invalids?'

'Jinny and the infant.'

'Oh, they are well. A proper little girl. Jinny is well but very much down. She is listless-like and lacks poor Jim.'

'And little Benjy Ross and his teeth. What is the matter with the boy: do they grow out of his ears?'

'He is much better, my love. I took some oil of valerian and told Jinny – told Jinny—— What is the word?'

'Instructed?'

'No——'

'Prescribed?'

'Yes. I prescribed it for him like an apothecary. So many drops, so many times a day. And Jinny opened her blue eyes and said, yes, ma'am, and no, ma'am, just as if I was really a lady.'

'So you are,' said Ross.

She squeezed his arm. 'So I am. I d' forget, Ross. Anybody you loved you would make a lady.'

'Nonsense,' said Ross. 'The blame's entirely yours. Have they heard of Jim this month?'

'Not this month. You heard what they heard last month.'

'That he was well, yes. For my part, I doubt it; but fine and good if it reassures them.'

'Do ee think you could ask someone to go and see him?'

'I've already done so. But no report yet. It is true that Bodmin is the best of a bad lot, for what consolation that may be.'

'Ross, I been thinking——'

'What?'

'You told me I did ought to have someone else in to help in the house, to give me more time, like. Well, I thought to ask Jinny Carter.'

'What and have three infants crawling about the house?'

'No, no. Mrs Zacky could look after Benjy and Mary; they could play with her own. Jinny could bring her mite and sit 'er in a box in the sun all day. She'd be no trouble.'

'What does Jinny say?'

'I haven't asked her. I thought to see what you said first.'

'Settle it between yourselves, my dear. I have no objection.'

They reached the top of the hill by Wheal Grace, and Demelza broke away from him to pick some blackberries. She put two in her mouth and offered him the choice of a handful. He took one absently.

'I too have been thinking. A good flavour this year. I too have been thinking. Now that Charles is gone, Verity is much in need of a rest. It would give me much pleasure to have her here for a week or two, to recuperate from all her nursing.'

They went down the hill. He waited for her to speak, but she did not. He glanced down at her. The vivacity had gone from her face and some of the colour.

'Well?'

'She wouldn't come——'

'Why do you say that?'

'All your family – they hate me.'

'None of my family hate you. They don't know you. They may disapprove. But Verity is different.'

'How can she be if she's one o' the family?'

'Well, she is. You don't know her.'

There was silence for the rest of the walk home. At the door they parted, but he knew that the discussion was not finished. He knew Demelza well enough now to be sure that nothing but a clear-cut issue was ever satisfactory to her. Sure enough, when he went out to go to the mine she ran after him.

'Ross.'

He stopped. 'Well?'

She said: 'They think – your family think you was mad to marry me. Don't spoil this first summer by asking one of 'em to stay here. You told me just now I was a lady. But I ain't. Not yet. I can't talk proper, and I can't eat proper, and I'm always getting cagged wi' dirt, and when I'm vexed I swear. Maybe I'll learn. If you'll learn me, I'll learn. I'll try all the time. Next year, maybe.'

'Verity isn't like that,' Ross said. 'She sees deeper than that. She and I are much alike.'

'Oh yes,' said Demelza, nearly crying, 'but she's a woman. You think I'm nice because you're a man. Tedn't that I'm suspicious of she. But she'll see all my faults and tell you about them and then you'll never think the same again.'

'Walk with me up here,' Ross said quietly.

She looked up into his eyes, trying to read his expression. After a moment she began to walk beside him and they climbed the field. At the gate he stopped and leaned his arms on it.

'Before I found you,' he said, 'when I came home from America things looked black for me. You know why, because I'd hoped to marry Elizabeth and returned to find her with other plans. That winter it was Verity alone who saved me from. . . . Well, I was a fool to take it so to heart; nothing is really worth that; but I couldn't fight it at the time, and Verity came and kept me going. Three and four times a week all through that winter she came. I can't ever forget that. She gave me something to hold on to; that's hard to repay. For three years now I've neglected her shamefully, perhaps when she most needed me. She has preferred to stay indoors, not to be seen about; I have not had the same need of *her*; Charles was ill and she thought it her first duty to nurse him. But that can't go on, now Charles is dead. Francis tells me she's really ill. She must get away from that house for a change. The least I can do is to ask her here.'

Demelza moodily rustled the dry stubble of barley stalks under her foot.

'But why has she need of *you*? If she is ill she needs a surgeon, that's all. She'll be the better looked after at – at Trenwith.'

'Do you remember when you first came here? A man used to call. Captain Blamey.'

She looked at him with eyes in which the pupils had grown dark. 'No.'

'Verity and he were in love with each other. But Charles and Francis found that he had been married before; there were the strongest objections to his marrying Verity. Communication between him and Verity was forbidden and so they used to meet here secretly. Then one day Charles and Francis found them here and there was a violent quarrel and Captain Blamey went home to Falmouth and Verity has not seen him since.'

'Oh,' said Demelza moodily.

'Her sickness, you see, is one of the spirit. She may be ill other ways too, but can I deny her the help that she gave me? To find a change of company, to get away from brooding, that may be half the battle. You could help her so much if you tried.'

'*I* could?'

'You could. She has so little interest in life, and you're so full of it. You have all the zest for living, and she none. We have to help her together, my dear. And for this I want your willing help, with no grudging.'

On the gate she put her hand over his.

'Sometimes,' she said, 'I feel angry-like, and then I go all small and mean. But of course I'll do it, Ross. Anything you say.'

Chapter four

DEMELZA NIGHTLY PRAYED that Verity would not come.

When a reply was brought and she learned that her cousin-in-law had accepted the invitation and hoped to be well enough by next week-end, her heart turned over and climbed into her throat. She tried to hide her panic from Ross and to accept his amused assurances. During the rest of the week her fears found outlet in a frenzy of summer cleaning, so that not a room was left unscoured and Prudie moaned wild complaints each morning at the sight of her.

No amount of work could stave off Saturday's approach and with it Verity's. She could only hope that Aunt Agatha would have a fit or that she herself should go down with measles just in time.

Verity came shortly after midday, attended by Bartle carrying two valises strapped behind him.

Ross, who had not seen his cousin for some months, was shocked at the change. Her cheeks had sunk and the healthy open-air tan was gone. She looked forty instead of twenty-nine. The gleam of vitality and keen intelligence had gone out of her eyes. Only her voice was the same, and her disobedient hair.

Demelza's knees, which had wanted to give way earlier in the morning, were now as stiff and immovable as her lips. She stood at the door in her plain pink frock, trying not to look like a ramrod, while Ross helped his cousin from her horse and kissed her.

'Ross, how good to see you again! It's so kind of you to have me. And how well you look! The life is agreeing with you.' She turned and smiled at Demelza. 'I do wish I could have been at your wedding, my dear. It was one of my biggest disappointments.'

Demelza let her cold cheek be kissed and stood aside to watch Verity and Ross enter the house. After a few moments she followed them into the parlour. This isn't my room now, she thought; not mine and Ross's; someone else had taken it away from us. In the middle of our bright summer.

Verity was slipping off her cloak. Demelza was interested to notice that she was very plainly dressed underneath. She wasn't beautiful like Elizabeth, but quite elderly and plain. And her mouth was like Ross's, and sometimes the tone of her voice.

'. . . at the end,' Verity was saying, 'I don't think Father minded so much. He was so very tired.' She sighed. 'Had he not gone so sudden we would have summoned you. Oh well, that's over, now I feel only like rest.' She smiled slightly. 'I am afraid I shall not be a sportive guest, but the last thing I want is to put you or Demelza to any trouble. Do just as you have always done and leave me to fit in. That is what I want best.'

Demelza racked her brains for the sentences she had prepared this morning. She twisted her fingers and got out:

'You would like something to drink, now, after your ride?'

'I have been recommended to take milk in the morning and porter at night. And I hate them both! But I had my milk before I left, so thank you, no, I'll stay dry.'

'It's not like you to be ill,' Ross said. 'What ails you but fatigue? What does Choake say?'

'One month he bleeds me and the next he tells me I am suffering from anaemia. Then he gives me potions that make me sick and vomits that don't. I doubt if he knows as much as the old women at the fair.'

'I knew an old woman once——' Demelza began impulsively, and then stopped.

They both waited for her to go on.

'It don't matter,' she said. 'I'll go an' see if your room's ready.'

She wondered if the lameness of the excuse was as plain to them as it was to her. But at least they raised no objection, so she gratefully escaped and went across to Joshua's old bedroom, which was to be Verity's. There she pulled back the coverlet and turned and stared at the two valises as if to see through them into their contents. She wondered how she would ever get through the next week.

II

All that evening and all the following day constraint was heavy on them, like an autumn fog hiding familiar landmarks. Demelza was the culprit but she couldn't help herself. She had become the intruder: two were company and three none. Ross and Verity had a good deal to say to each other, and he stayed in more than he would have done. Whenever Demelza entered the living-room their talk always broke. It was not that they had any secrets from her, but that the topic was outside her sphere and to continue it would be to ignore her.

It was always hard at meals to find a subject which would include Demelza. There was so much that would not: the doings of Elizabeth and Francis, the progress of Geoffrey Charles, news of common friends Demelza had never heard of. Ruth Treneglos was blossoming forth as the chatelaine of Mingoose. Mrs Chynoweth, Elizabeth's mother, was troubled with her eyes and the doctors advised an operation. Cousin William-Alfred's second youngest had died of measles. Henry Fielding's new book was all the rage. These and many other items were pleasant to chat over with Ross but meant nothing to Ross's wife.

Verity, who was as susceptible as anyone, would have made her excuses and left on the third day if she had been sure that Demelza's stiffness was the outcome of dislike or jealousy. But Verity thought it arose from something else, and she hated the idea of leaving now with the knowledge that she could never return. She disliked equally the thought that she was coming between Ross and his young bride, but if she went now her name would be forever linked with this visit and she would never be mentioned between them. She was sorry she had come.

So she stayed on and hoped for an improvement without knowing how to bring it about.

Her first move was to stay in bed in the mornings and not get up until she was sure Ross was out of the house; then she would come on Demelza accidentally and talk to her or help her in the work she was doing. If this could be settled at all, then it must be settled between them while Ross was out of the way. She hoped that she and the other girl would lapse into companionship with nothing said. But after a couple of mornings she found her own casual manner becoming too noticeably deliberate.

Demelza tried to be kind, but she thought and spoke from behind a shield. Advances upon that sense of inferiority could easily be mistaken for patronage.

On the Thursday morning Demelza had been out since dawn. Verity broke her fast in bed and rose at eleven. The day was fine but overcast and a small fire burned in the parlour, attracting as usual the patronage of Tabitha Bethia. Verity perched on the settle and shivered and began to stir the logs to make them blaze. She felt old and tired, and the mirror in her room showed a faint yellow tinge to her skin. It wasn't really that she cared whether she looked old or not these days . . . But she was always so listless, so full of aches, could do no more than half the work of a year ago. She slid farther into the corner of the settle. The pleasantest thing of all was to sit back as she was doing now, head against the velvet cover, to feel the warmth in her feet from the fire, to have nothing at all to do and no one to think of . . .

Having slept all night and been awake no more than three hours, she went off to sleep again, one slippered toe stretched towards the fire, one hand hanging over the wooden arm of the settle, Tabitha curled against her foot, purring lightly.

Demelza came in with an armful of beech leaves and wild rose hips.

Verity sat up.

'Oh, beg pardon,' Demelza said, ready to go.

'Come in,' Verity said in confusion. 'I've no business to be sleeping at this hour. Please talk to me and help me wake.'

Demelza smiled reservedly, put the armful of flowers on a chair. 'Do you feel the draught from this window? You should have shut'n.'

'No, no, please. I don't consider the sea air harmful. Let it be.'

Demelza closed the window and pushed a hand through her ruffled hair. 'Ross'd never forgive me if you caught cold. These mallows is dead; their heads are all droopin'; I'll bury them.' She picked up the jug and carried it from the room, returning with it freshly filled with water. She began to arrange the beech leaves. Verity watched her.

'You were always fond of flowers, weren't you? I remember Ross telling me that once.'

Demelza looked up. 'When did he tell ee that?'

Verity smiled. 'Years ago. Soon after you first came. I admired the flowers in here and he told me you brought in fresh every day.'

Demelza flushed slightly. 'All the same, you got to be careful,' she said in a matter-of-fact voice. 'Tedn't every flower that takes kindly to bein' put in a room. Some of them looks pretty but they fair stink when you pick them.' She thrust in a spray or two of the rose hips. The beech leaves were just turning a delicate yellow and they toned with the yellow-orange-red of the hips. 'I been trespassing to-day, picking these. Over as far as Bodrugan land.' She stood back to look at the effect. 'And sometimes flowers don't take kindly to one another, an' no matter 'ow you try to coax 'em they won't share the same jug.'

Verity stirred in her seat. She must take the risk of a frontal attack. 'I ought to thank you, my dear, for what you've done for Ross.'

The other girl's body tautened a little, like a wire on the first hint of strain.

'What he's done for me, more like.'

'Yes, perhaps you're right,' Verity agreed, some of the old spirit creeping into her voice. 'I know he's – brought you up – all that. But you've – you seem to have made him fall in love with you, and that . . . has changed his whole life . . .'

Their eyes met. Demelza's were defensive and hostile, but also puzzled. She thought there was antagonism behind the words but couldn't make out where it lay.

'I don't know what you d' mean.'

This was the final issue between them.

'You must know,' Verity said, 'that when he came home, he was in love with Elizabeth – my sister-in-law.'

'I know that. You 'aven't any need to tell me that. I know it as well as you.' Demelza turned to leave the room.

Verity got up. For this she had to stand. 'Perhaps I've expressed myself badly since I came here. I want you to understand. . . . Ever since he came back – ever since Ross came back and found Elizabeth promised to my brother I have been afraid that he would not – would not get over it as an ordinary man would get over it. We are strange that way, many of our family. We don't have it in us to make a compromise with events. After all, if part of you is – is wrenched away, then the rest is nothing. The rest is nothing . . .' She regained her voice and after a moment went on, 'I have been afraid he would mope his life away, never find any real happiness, such as he might . . . We have always been closer than cousins. You see, I'm very fond of him.'

Demelza was staring at her.

Verity went on: 'When I heard he had married you I thought it was a makeshift. Something to console him. And I was glad even of that. Even a makeshift is so much better than a life that goes withered and dry. I was consoled to feel that he would have companionship, someone to bear his children and grow old with him. The rest didn't really matter so much.'

Again she stopped, and Demelza was about to speak, but changed her mind. A dead mallow flower lay between them on the floor.

'But since I came here,' Verity said, 'I have seen it's no makeshift at all. It is real. That is what I want to thank you for. You're so lucky. I don't know how you've done it. And he is so lucky. He has lost the biggest thing in his life – and found it again in another person. That's all that matters. The greatest thing is to have someone who loves you and – and to love in return. People who haven't got it – or had it – don't believe that, but it's the truth. So long as life doesn't touch that you're safe against the rest . . .'

Her voice had again lost its tone, and she stopped to clear her throat.

'I've not come here to hate you,' she said. 'Nor to patronize you. There's *such* a change in Ross, and it is your doing. Do you think I care where you came from or what is your breeding or how you can curtsey? That's not all.'

Demelza was staring again at the flowers.

'I've – often wanted to know how to curtsey,' she said in a low voice. 'Often I've wanted to know. I wish you would teach me – Verity.'

Verity sat down again, desperately tired with the effort of what she had said. Near tears, she looked at her slippers.

'My dear, I am poor at it myself,' she replied unsteadily.

'I'll get some more flowers,' Demelza said, and fled from the room.

III

Ross had spent most of the day at the mine, and when he came home for a meal at five Demelza had gone into Sawle with Prudie to buy rushlights and candles, and some fish for dinner to-morrow. She was late coming back on account of watching another catch of pilchards, so Ross and Verity had their meal alone. No reference was made to Demelza. Verity said that Francis still spent three or four nights a week in Truro playing whist and faro. This was bad enough in the winter months, but during the summer it was indefensible.

'I think,' Verity said, 'we are a peculiar family. Francis comes near to having all he desires, and now acts as if he cannot settle to anything but must rush off to the gaming tables and plunge further into debt. What is there in us, Ross, that makes us so uncomfortable to live with?'

'You malign us, my dear. It is only that, like most families, we are never all happy at one time.'

'He is fretful and irritable,' Verity complained. 'Far worse than I. He takes no interference with his aims and is quickly angry. It's not a week since he and Aunt Agatha had a cursing match across the dinner table, and Mrs Tabb listening open-mouthed.'

'Aunt Agatha won?'

'Oh, without question. But it is such a bad example for the servants.'

'And Elizabeth?'

'Sometimes she can persuade him and sometimes not. I don't think they get on very well. Perhaps I shouldn't say so, but that is my impression.'

'Why should that be?'

'I don't know. She is devoted to the child, and he fond of him. Yet in a way—— They say children cement a marriage. Yet it seems to me that they have not got on so well since Geoffrey Charles was born.'

'There are no more coming?' Ross asked.

'None yet. Elizabeth has been ailing these last months.'

There was silence for some time.

'Ross, I have been looking through the old library. In the part that has not been cleared there are bits and pieces of lumber which might be of use to you. And why do you not bring out your mother's spinet? It would go in that corner very nice and would enhance the room.'

'It's out of repair and there is no one here to play it.'

'It could be put *in* repair. And Prudie tells me that Demelza is always strumming on it. Besides, you may have children.'

Ross looked up quickly.

'Yes. Maybe I will think it over.'

Demelza came in at seven, full of the new catch which had been taken.

'The shoal was brought inshore on the tide and folk was going out knee-deep and catching 'em in buckets. Then they came in still farther and were wriggling 'pon the sand. It is not so big a harvest as the last; still, I am sorry there is no moon, for then we might have been enticed to go an' watch them again.'

She seemed, Ross thought, at last less constricted, and he was thankful for the improvement. His discomfort during the last few days had been acute, and twice he had been on the point of saying something before them both, but now he was glad he had not. If they would but settle themselves like two cats in a basket, without outside interference, all might yet be well.

There was one question he intended to ask Demelza, but forgot to do so until they were in bed and Demelza, he thought, asleep. He made a note of it for some other date and was himself dozing off when the girl stirred beside him and sat up. He knew then at once that she had not been asleep.

'Ross,' she said in a low voice, 'tell me about Verity, would you? About Verity and Captain – Captain What's-his-name. What was it that 'appened? Did they quarrel, and why was it the – the others broke en up?'

'I told you,' Ross said. 'Francis and her father disapproved. Go to sleep, child.'

'No, no. Please, Ross. I want to know. I been thinking. You never told me what truly happened.'

Ross put out an arm and pulled her down close beside him. 'It's of no moment. I thought you were not interested in my family.'

'I am in this. This is different. Tell me.'

Ross sighed and yawned. 'It doesn't please me to pander to your whims at this time of night. You are more inconsequent even than most women. It happened this way, love: Francis met Captain Blamey at Truro and invited him to Elizabeth's wedding. There he met Verity and an attachment sprang up . . .'

He did not enjoy resurrecting the dismal story. It was over and buried; nobody showed up well in it, and the retelling evoked memories of all the unhappiness and anger and self-criticism of those days. The episode had never been spoken of since: all that idiotic business of the duel, played out without any proper civilised sanctions in the heat of a common brawl . . . The party he had been going to at Ruth Teague's . . . One thing hung on another; and all that period of unhappiness and misunderstanding hung together. It was his marriage which had cut the strands and seemed to have given him a fresh, clean start.

'. . . so that brought it all to an end,' he said. 'Captain Blamey went off and we've heard nothing of him since.'

There was a long silence, and he thought perhaps she had quietly fallen asleep while he spoke.

But then she stirred. 'Oh, Ross, the very shame on you . . .' This in a low troubled voice.

'Um?' he said, surprised. 'What do you mean?'

She slipped away from his arm and sat up abruptly in the bed.

'Ross, how *could* you!'

'I want no riddles.' he said. 'Are you dreaming or talking sense?'

'You let 'em part like that. Verity goin' home to Trenwith. It would break 'er heart.'

He began to grow angry. 'D'you think I relished the adventure? You know what I feel for Verity. It was no pleasure to see her love affair go to pieces like my own.'

'Nay, but you should've stopped un! You should have sided wi' her instead of wi' them.'

'I sided with nobody! You don't know what you're talking about. Go to sleep.'

'But siding wi' nobody was siding wi' them. Don't you see? You should have stopped the duel and stood up to them, instead of letting 'em ride roughshod over all. If you'd helped Verity then they needn't ever of parted, and – and——'

'No doubt,' said Ross, 'the matter seems simple enough to you. But since you know none of the people and weren't there at the time, your judgment may conceivably be at fault.'

Sarcasm on his part was something she couldn't yet quite cope with. She groped for his hand and found it and put it against her cheek.

'Don't get teasy with me, Ross. I did want to know. And you d' look at it like a man would and I d' look at it like a woman. That's the difference. I can see what Verity would feel. I know what she would feel. To love someone and be loved by someone. And then to be quite alone . . .'

Ross's hand, from being quiescent, began slowly to stroke her face.

'Did I say you were the most inconsequent of women? It was an understatement. When I suggest Verity coming here you almost weep. And for half a week and more since she came you have been as stiff as an old gander. Now you choose this unseasonable hour to take Verity's side in a long-buried contention and to lecture me on my shortcomings. Go to sleep before I box your ears!'

Demelza pressed his hand against her mouth. 'You have never hit me when I deserved it, so I am not scared now when I do not.'

'That is the difference between dealing with a man and dealing with a woman.'

'But a man,' Demelza said, 'even a kind one, can sometimes be cruel wi'out knowing it.'

'And a woman,' Ross said, pulling her down again, 'never knows when a subject must be dropped.'

She lay quiet against him, knowing a last word but not saying it.

Chapter five

VERITY HAD KNOWN that night, from the bowl of freshly picked hazel leaves in her bedroom, that she had, with her halting self-exposure of the morning, at last got past Demelza's defences. But in reaching this tentative view she was underrating Demelza. The girl might lack subtlety, but there was nothing grudging in her decisions when she came to them. Nor did she lack the courage to own herself wrong.

Verity found herself suddenly in demand. Nothing more was said, but stiffness ripened into friendship in a day. Ross, unaware of causes, watched and wondered. Mealtimes, instead of being the chief ordeals of the day, were flowering with talk. The need for finding topics had quite gone. If Verity or Ross spoke of someone Demelza didn't know, she at once overflowed with questions and they told her. If someone very local was mentioned, Demelza, unasked, would explain to Verity. There was, too, more laughter than there had been at Nampara for years: sometimes it seemed not so much at the wit of the conversation as born of a relief common to them all. They laughed at Jud's bald crown and his bloodshot bulldog eyes, at Prudie's red nose and carpet slippers, at Tabitha Bethia's mangy coat and at the clumsy friendliness of the enormous Garrick. They laughed at each other and with each other, and sometimes at nothing at all.

In between times, usually when Ross was not there, Demelza and Verity would discuss improvements in the house or search the library and the unused rooms for odd bits of damask or velveteen to decorate or re-cover pieces of furniture. At first Verity had been chary of putting a strain on their new-grown friendship by offering suggestions, but when she found they were solicited, she entered into the spirit of the thing. At the beginning of the second week Ross came home and found the spinet back in the corner it had occupied in his mother's day, and the two women busy with its inside trying to repair it. Verity looked up, a faint pink flush on her sallow cheeks, and pushing a wisp of hair out of her eye, she explained breathlessly that they had found a nest of young mice under the bass strings.

'We were both too softhearted to kill them, so I brushed them into a pail and Demelza carried them out to the waste land on the other side of the stream.'

'Like what you turn up under the plough,' said Demelza, appearing, more tousled, from behind. 'Little meaders. Bald an' pink an' scraggy and too small to run.'

'Encouraging vermin,' Ross said. 'Who brought this spinet in here?'

'We did,' said Verity. 'Demelza did all the lifting.'

'Dolts that you are,' said Ross. 'Why didn't you send for Jud and Cobbledick?'

'Oh, Jud,' said Demelza. 'He's not so strong as we, is he Verity?'

'Not so strong as you are,' said Verity. 'Your wife is self-willed, Ross.'

'You waste your breath in telling me the obvious,' he replied, but went away content. Verity looked far better than a week ago. Demelza now was doing what he asked in good measure. It was what he had hoped for.

II

That night Ross woke just before dawn and found Demelza sitting up in bed. It was one of the rare wet spells of that splendid summer and autumn, and he could hear the rain splashing and bubbling on the windows.

'What is it?' he asked sleepily. 'Something wrong?'

'I can't sleep,'. she said. 'That's all.'

'You won't sleep sitting up like that. Have you a pain?'

'Me? No. I been thinking.'

'A bad habit. Take a nip of brandy and you'll settle off.'

'I been thinking, Ross. Where is Captain Blamey now, Ross? Is 'e still over to Falmouth?'

'How do I know? I've not seen him these three years. Why must you plague me with these questions in the middle of the night?'

'Ross.' She turned towards him eagerly in the half darkness. 'I want ee to do something for me. I want you to go to Falmouth an' see if he's still there and see if he's still in love with Verity . . .'

He half lifted his head in astonishment.

'Begin all that again? Raise it afresh when she's just beginning to forget. I'd as soon raise the devil!'

'She hasn't forgotten nothing, Ross. She hasn't got over it. Tis there at the back just the same, like a sore place that won't heal.'

'Keep your hands out of that,' he warned soberly. 'It doesn't concern you.'

'It does concern me. I am grown fond of Verity——'

'Then show your fondness by not meddling. You don't understand the needless pain you would cause.'

'Not if it brought them together, Ross.'

'And what of the objections which broke up the attachment before? Have they vanished into thin air?'

'One of 'em has.'

'What do you mean?'

'Verity's father.'

'Well, by God!' Ross relaxed on his pillow and tried not to laugh at her impudence. 'It may have occurred to you that I was not speaking of the objectors.'

'About him drinkin'? I know it's bad. But you said he's given up.'

'For the time. No doubt he has taken to it again. I should not blame him if he had.'

'Then why not go an' see? Please, Ross. To please me.'

'To please nobody,' he said with irritation. 'Verity would be the last person to wish it. The attachment is best broken. How should I feel if they came together through my contrivance and he treated her as he did his first wife?'

'He would not if he loved her. And Verity d' still love him. It would not stop me lovin' you if you had killed somebody.'

'Um? Well, I've killed several as it happens. And as good men as myself, no doubt. But not a woman and in a drunken fit.'

'I should not care if you had, so long as you loved me. An' Verity would take the risk, just as she would've done three years back if people 'adn't interfered. I can't bear, Ross, to feel she's so unhappy, down underneath, when we might do something to help. You wanted to help her. We could find out, Ross, wi'out telling her anything about it. Then we could decide, like.'

'Once and for all,' he said wearily, 'I'll have nothing to do with the idea. You can't play fire-in-my-glove with people's lives. I'm too fond of Verity to wish to bring her all that pain back again.'

She breathed a long breath into the darkness, and there was silence for some moments. 'You can't,' she said, 'be very fond of Verity if you're afraid even to go to Falmouth and ask.'

His anger bubbled over. 'Damn you for an ignorant brat! We'll be arguing here till daylight. Am I to have no peace from your nagging?' He took her by the shoulders and pulled her back upon the pillow. She gave a gasp and was still.

Silence fell. The dripping window squares were just visible. After a while, uneasy at her quietness, he turned and looked at her face in the half dark. It looked pale, and she was biting her bottom lip.

'What's the matter?' he said. 'What is to do now?'

'I believe,' she said, 'after all – I have a little pain.'

He sat up. 'Why didn't you tell me! Instead of sitting there prating. Where is the pain?'

'In – my innerds. I don't rightly know. I feel a small bit queer. Tis nothing to alarm yourself.'

He was out of bed and groping for a bottle of brandy. After a moment he came back with a mug.

'Drink this. Drink it down, right down. It will warm you if nothing more.'

'I'm not cold, Ross,' she said primly. She shuddered. 'Ugh, tis stronger than I d' like it. More water would have made it very palatable, I b'lieve.'

'You talk too much,' he said. 'It is enough to give anyone a pain. Damn me if I don't think it was moving that spinet.' Alarm grew in him. 'Have you no sense in your head?'

'I felt nothin' of it at the time.'

'You will feel something from me if I know you have so much as touched the thing again. Where is the pain? Let me see.'

'No, Ross. Tis nothin', I tell you. Not there, not there. Higher up. Leave me be. Get you back into bed and let us try to go to sleep.'

'It will soon be time to rise,' he said, but slowly doing as she suggested. They lay quiet for a while, watching the slow lightening of the room. Then she moved over into his arms.

'Better?' he asked.

'Yes, better. The brandy has lit a beacon inside me. Soon, mebbe, I shall be drunk and start tormenting you.'

'That would be no change. I wonder if you ate something bad. We cured the bacon ourselves, and the——'

'I think perhaps it was the spinet after all. But I'm well enough now. And sleepy——'

'Not too sleepy to hear what I have to say. I don't expect you to coddle yourself for anyone's satisfaction. But next time you have one of your moods and desire to do some fancy thing, remember that you have a selfish man to consider whose happiness is part of your own.'

'Yes,' she said. 'I'll truly remember, Ross.'

'The promise comes too easy. You'll forget it. Are you listening?'

'Yes, Ross.'

'Well, then, I will promise *you* something. We spoke of chastisements the other night. Out of my love for you, and out of my own pure selfishness, I promise to beat you soundly the next time you do anything so foolish.'

'But I won't do it again. I said I would not.'

'Well, my promise stands too. It may be an added safeguard.' He kissed her.

She opened her dark eyes. '*Do* you want me to go to sleep?'

'Of course. And at once.'

'Very well.'

Silence fell within the room. Rain continued to beat on the knotted glass.

Verity's fortnight came to an end and she was persuaded to remain a third week. She seemed at last to have cast off the duties of Trenwith and to be finding her enjoyment here as he had hoped. Her gain in health was obvious. Mrs Tabb would have to manage for another week. Trenwith could go hang.

During this week Ross was away two days in Truro for the first copper auction at which Wheal Leisure was represented. The copper they had to sell was divided into two lots, and both were bought by an agent for the South Wales Copper Smelting Co. at a total price of seven hundred and ten guineas.

The next day Verity said to him:

'This money, when it is paid, Ross. I am very ignorant, but will some of it be yours? Will you have a little spare money then? Ten or twenty guineas perhaps?'

He stared at her. 'Do you wish to buy lottery tickets?'

'The lottery is your own home,' she said. 'You have done wonders since you came back, with bits from the library, old pieces of cloth and the like, but apart from these curtains, I see very little that you've actually *bought*.'

He stared round the parlour. There was a tactfully disguised shabbiness about it.

'Don't think I'm criticizing,' Verity said. 'I know how short of money you have been. I merely wondered if you could spare a little to renew things now. It would not be badly spent.'

The copper company would pay in their draft at the end of the month; the venturers' meeting would follow; the profit would certainly be shared out: it was the way of such concerns.

'Yes,' he said. 'Personally I have no taste for fancy stuff, but perhaps we could ride in while you are still here and you could advise us on our purchases. That is, if you're well enough to make the distance.'

Verity looked out of the window.

'It had occurred to me, Ross, that Demelza and I could ride in alone. We should not then take up your time.'

'What, ride to Truro unescorted!' he exclaimed. 'I shouldn't be easy for a moment.'

'Oh, Jud could escort us as far as the town, if you could spare him. Then he could wait somewhere and return with us.'

There was a pause. Ross came and stood beside her at the window. The rain of the last few days had freshened up the valley. Some of the trees were turning, but there was hardly a sign of yellow on the elms.

'The garden needs some renewal of stock also,' he said. 'Despite Demelza's efforts.'

'Gardens are always straggly in the autumn,' Verity said. 'But you should order some sweetbriar and tansy. And I'll give you a cutting of herb of grace. It's pleasant to grow.'

Ross put his hand on her shoulder. 'How much do you want for your expedition?'

Chapter six

So ON THE first Wednesday in October Demelza and Verity rode into Truro to do some shopping, escorted, or rather followed – not from etiquette but because the track was too narrow to ride three abreast – by an interested but disgruntled Jud.

He was glad of the day off, but had taken some offence at Ross's threats as to what would happen if the two ladies returned to meet him and found him incapably drunk. It was, he felt, coarse and pointless to threaten the skin on his back for a crime he had no intention whatever of committing.

This was only the fourth time Demelza had been to Truro.

Underneath she was greatly excited, but once the journey was begun she tried to maintain an outward show of calm. Since she had nothing but her working clothes, Verity had lent her a grey riding habit, which suited her well enough. More than anything else it helped her to see herself as a lady and behave with the dignity of one. When they set off she watched Verity and tried to copy her poise in the saddle and the straightness of her back.

It was cattle market day in the town, and as they came down a herd of young bullocks blocked the narrow street and Demelza had difficulty in holding Darkie, whose dislike of steers was deep-set. Jud was too far away to be of use, but Verity edged her horse in front of the other animal. People stood to stare, but presently Darkie quieted and they were past.

'Silly old thing,' Demelza said breathlessly. 'She'll be sending me cat-in-the-pan over her tail one of these days.' They crossed the bridge. 'Oo, what a boilin' of people; tis like a fair. Which way do we go?'

The time for one of the tin coinages was near, and at the end of the main street great piles of blocked tin had been set down ready for the day when the government stamp would be affixed. Weighing up to three hundred-weight each, these great blocks were left untended, and glittered darkly in the sun. People milled around them; beggars stood in the gutter; the open market of Middle Row was doing a thriving trade; men and women stood in groups in the street and discussed the business of the day.

'Where are the stables?' asked Demelza. 'We can't leave the horses here 'mong all these folk.'

'At the back,' said Verity. 'Jud will take them round. We will meet you here at four, Jud.'

The heavy rain of the past few days had dried the dust without leaving too much mud in its place, so that the streets were not unpleasant to walk in, and the little rivulets at the side bubbled youthfully to join their parent streams. Verity stopped to spend one and sixpence on a dozen sweet oranges, and then they entered Kenwyn Street, where the better shops were. This too was crowded with shoppers and street hawkers, though the throng was not so dense as about the markets.

Verity saw one or two people she knew, but to Demelza's relief did not stop to speak. Presently she led the way into a dark little shop, stacked almost to the ceiling with antique furniture and carpets and oil paintings and brassware. From the semidarkness a little pockmarked man with a curled periwig shot out to greet his customers. One of his eyes was malformed by some accident or disease, giving him an odd look of duplicity, as if one part of him was withdrawn from the rest and taken with things the customer could not see. Demelza stared at him, fascinated.

Verity enquired for a small table, and they were led into a back room where a number of new and secondhand ones were stacked. Verity asked Demelza to choose one she liked, and after a good deal of discussion the matter was settled. Other things were bought. The little shopkeeper rushed downstairs for a special Indian screen he had to sell.

'How much has he given us to spend?' Demelza asked in a low voice while they waited.

'Forty guineas.' Verity clinked her purse.

'Forty—— Phoo! We're rich! We're—— Don't forget the carpet.'

'Not here. If we get one that is local made we shall be sure of our values.' Verity stared into a dark corner. 'I cannot understand how you keep the time at Nampara. You need a clock.'

'Oh, we d' go by the sun and the daylight. That never fails us. And Ross has his father's watch – when he recalls to wind it.'

The shopkeeper popped up again.

'You have two agreeable-looking clocks there,' Verity said. 'Light another candle so that we can see them. What are their prices?'

II

Out in the street the two girls blinked a little in the sunshine. It was hard to tell which of them was enjoying this the more.

Verity said: 'Now you need also bed linen, and curtains for two rooms and some new crockery and glassware.'

'I chose that clock,' Demelza said, 'because it was such a jolly one. It ticked solemn enough like the other, but when it struck, I liked the way it struck. Whirr-r-r – bong, bong, bong, like an old friend telling you good morning. Where do they sell linen, Verity?'

Verity eyed her thoughtfully for a moment.

'Before that, I think,' she said, 'we'll get a dress for you. We are only a few paces from my own dressmaker.'

Demelza raised her eyebrows. 'That isn't furniture.'

'It is furnishings. Do you think the house should be decorated without its mistress?'

'Would it be proper to spend his money so wi'out his consent?'

'I think his consent may be taken for granted.'

Demelza passed the tip of a red tongue round her lips but did not speak.

They had reached a door and a bow window four feet square screened with lace.

'This is the place,' said Verity.

The younger girl looked at her uncertainly. 'Would you do the choosin'?'

Inside was a plump little woman with steel spectacles. Why, Mistress Poldark! Such an honour after so long a time. Five years it must be. No, no, not perhaps quite that, but indeed a long time. Verity coloured slightly and mentioned her father's illness. Yes, said the seamstress, she had heard that Mr Poldark was mortal tedious sick. She hoped—— Dear, said the seamstress. No, she hadn't heard; very sad! Well, but it was a pretty sight to see an old customer again.

'I'm not here now on my own account, but on my cousin's, Mistress Poldark of Nampara. On my advice she has come to you for a new outfit or two, and I'm sure you will give her the service you have always given me.'

The shopkeeper blinked and beamed at Demelza, then adjusted her spectacles and curtsied. Demelza resisted the impulse to curtsey back.

'How do you do,' she said.

'What we should like,' Verity said, 'is a view of some of your new materials and then we might discuss a simple morning dress and a riding habit something resembling the one she's now wearing.'

'Indeed, yes. Do please take a seat, ma'am. And you also, ma'am. There, the chair is clean. I'll call my daughter.'

Time passed.

'Yes,' said Verity, 'we'll take four yards of the long lawn for the riding habit shirts.'

'That at two and six a yard, ma'am?'

'No, three and six. Then we shall need a half yard of corded muslin for ruffles. And a pair of the dark habit gloves. Now which hat shall it be, Cousin? The one with the feather?'

'That's too dear,' said Demelza.

'The one with the feather. It is neat and not ostentatious. Now there's stockings to be considered . . .'

Time passed.

'And for an afternoon,' said Verity, 'I thought after this style. It is genteel and not fashionably exaggerated. The hoops must not be large. The dress, I thought, of that pale mauve silk, with the front underskirt and bodice of the flowered apple-green, somewhat ruched. Sleeves, would you say, just over the elbow and flared a little with cream lace. Um – white fichu, of course, and a posy at the breast.'

'Yes, Mistress Poldark, that will be most becoming. And a hat?'

'Oh, I shan't need'n,' said Demelza.

'You are sure to sometime,' said Verity. 'A small black straw, I should say for the hat, with perhaps a touch of scarlet. Can you make us something after that style?'

'Oh, certainly. Just what I should've suggested meself. My daughter'll start right away on this to-morrow. Thank you. Most honoured we are, and 'ope we shall keep your patronage. Good day, ma'am. Good day, ma'am.'

The better part of two hours had passed before they left the shop, both looking rather flushed and guilty as if they had been engaged in some not quite respectable pleasure.

The sun had gone from the narrow street and blazed in red reflection from the first-floor windows opposite. The crowds were no smaller, and a drunken song could be heard from a nearby gin shop.

Verity was a little thoughtful as they picked their way among some rubbish to cross the street.

'It will take us all our time to get the business done before four. And we do not want to be overtaken by darkness on the return. I think we should do well to leave the glass and linen to-day and go direct to buy the carpets.'

Demelza looked at her. 'Have you spent too many of your guineas on me?'

'Not too many, my dear. . . . And besides, Ross will never notice whether the linen is new . . .'

III

They found Jud gloriously drunk.

Some part of Ross's threats had stayed with him through his carouse, and he was not on his back, but within those limits he had done well for himself.

An ostler had got him to the front of the Red Lion Inn. The three horses were tethered waiting, and he was quarrelling amiably with the man who had seen him this far.

When he saw the ladies coming he bowed low in the manner of a Spanish grandee, clinging with one hand to the awning post outside the inn. But the bow was extravagant and his hat fell off and went floating down the rivulet which ran between the cobbles. He swore, unsettling the horses with the tone of his voice, and went after it; but his foot slipped and he sat down heavily in the street. A small boy returned his hat and was lectured for his trouble. The ostler helped the ladies to mount and then went to Jud's aid.

By this time a lot of people had paused to see them off. The ostler managed to get Jud to his feet and covered the tonsure and fringe with the damp hat.

'There, ole dear; stick it on yer 'ead. Ye'll need both 'ands for to hold yer old 'orse, ye will.'

Jud instantly snatched off the hat again, cut to the quick.

'Maybe as you think,' he said, 'because as I've the misfortune of an accidental slip on a cow-flop therefore I has the inability of an unborn babe, which is what you think and no missment, that you think as I be open to be dressed and undressed, hatted and unhatted like a scarecrow in a field o' taties, because I've the misfortune of a slip on a cow-flop. Twould be far superior of you if you was to get down on yer bended knees wi' brush an' pan. Tedn't right to leave the streets before yer own front door befouled wi' cow-flops. Tedn't right. Tedn't tidy. Tedn't fair. Tedn't clean. Tedn't *good enough*.'

'There, there now,' said the ostler.

' 'Is own front door,' said Jud to the crowd. 'Only 'is own front door. If every one of you was to clean before 'is own front door, *all* would be clean of cow-flops. The whole blathering town. Remember what the Good Book do say: "Thou shalt not move thy neighbour's landmark." Think on that, friends. "Thou shalt not move thy neighbour's landmark." Think on that and apply it to the poor dumb beasts. Never——'

' 'Elp you on yer 'orse, shall I?' said the ostler.

'Never in all me days has I been so offensive,' said Jud. 'Hat put on me 'ead as if I was an unborn babe. An' wet at that! Wet wi' the scum of all Powder Street: drippin' on me face. Enough to give me the death. Dripping on me 'ead: a chill you get, and *phit!* ye're gone. Clean yer own doorstep, friends, that's what I do say. Look to yourself, and then you'll never be in the place of this poor rat oo has to assault 'is best customers who is slipped in a cow-flop by danging a blatherin' wet hat on 'is 'ead from off the foul stream that d'run before 'is own doorstep which should never 'appen, should never 'appen, dear friends, remember that.' Jud now had his arm round the ostler's neck.

'Come along, we'll go without him,' Verity said to Demelza, who had a hand up to her mouth and was tittering helplessly.

Another servant came out of the inn, and between them they led Jud to his horse.

'Pore lost soul,' said Jud, stroking the ostler's cheek. 'Pore lost wandering soul. Look at 'im, friends. Do 'e know he's lost? Do 'e know he's for the fires? Do 'e know the flesh'll sweal off of him like fat off of a goose? And for why? I'll tell ee for why. Because he's sold his soul to Old Scratch 'imself. And so've you all. So've you all what don't 'eed what the Good Book do say. 'Eathens! 'Eathens! "Thou shalt not move thy neighbour's landmark. Thou shalt not——" '

At this point the two men put their hands under him and heaved him into the saddle. Then the ostler ran round to the other side as he began to slip off. A timely push and another hoist and he was firmly held, one man on either side. Old blind Ramoth stood it all without a twitch. Then they thrust one of Jud's feet deep in each stirrup and gave Ramoth a slap to tell him he should be going.

Over the bridge and all the way up the dusty hill out of the town Jud stayed in the saddle as if glued to it, haranguing passers-by and telling them to repent before it was too late.

IV

The girls rode home very slowly, drenched in a fiery sunset, with occasional snatches of song or a rolling curse to inform them that Jud had not yet fallen off.

They talked little at first, each woman taken with her own thoughts, and content with the excitements of the day. Their outing had given them a much closer understanding of one another.

As the sun went down behind St Ann's, the whole sky flared into a vivid primrose and orange. Clouds which had moved up were caught in the blaze and twisted out of shape and daubed with wild colours. It was like a promise of the Second Coming, which Jud was just then loudly predicting in the far distance.

'Verity,' Demelza said. 'About those clothes.'

'Yes?'

'One pound, eleven and six seems a wicked lot for a pair of stays.'

'They're of good quality. They will last you some time.'

'I've never had a proper pair of stays before. I was afraid they would want for me to take off my clothes. My inside clothes are *awful*.'

'I will loan you some of mine when you go in to be fitted.'

'You'll come with me?'

'Yes. We can meet somewhere *en route*.'

'Why not stop at Nampara till then? Tis only another two weeks.

'My dear, I'm greatly flattered by your invitation, and thank you for it. But they'll need me at Trenwith. Perhaps I might visit you again in the spring?'

They rode on in silence.

'An' twenty-nine shillings for that riding hat. An' that handsome silk for the green-an'-purple gown. I feel we didn't ought to have spent the money on 'em.'

'Your conscience is very restive.'

'Well, an' for a reason. I should've told you before.'

'Told me what?'

Demelza hesitated. 'That mebbe my measuring won't be the same for long. Then I won't be able to wear 'em and they'll be wasted.'

This took a moment to grasp, for she had spoken quickly. The track here became narrow and uneven, and the horses went into single file. When they were able to ride abreast again Verity said:

'My dear, do you mean——'

'Yes.'

'Oh, I'm indeed glad for you.' Verity stumbled with words. 'How happy you must be.'

'Mind you,' said Demelza, 'I'm not positive certain. But things've stopped that belong to be as regular as clockwork with me; an' last Sunday night I was awake all night and feeling some queer. And then again this morning I was as sick as Garrick when he eats worms.'

Verity laughed. 'And you concern yourself over a few dresses! Ross – Ross will be delighted.'

'Oh, I couldn't tell him yet. He's – strange that way. If he thought I was sickly he'd make me sit still all day and twiddle my toes.'

The brightest light had drained from the sky, leaving the clouds flushed with a rich plum-coloured afterglow. All the sparse countryside stood out in the warm light, the goats pasturing in numbers on the moorland, the scanty ricks of gathered corn, the wooden huts of the mines, the grey slate and cob cottages; the girls' faces under their wide hats were lit with it, the horses' noses gleamed.

The breeze had dropped and the evening was silent except for the sound of their own passing: the clicking of the horses' teeth upon the bits, the creak of saddle leather, the clop, clop of hooves. A bit of a crescent moon hung in the sky, and Demelza bowed to it. Verity turned and looked back. Jud was a quarter of a mile away and Ramoth had stopped to crop a hedge. Jud was singing: '"And for to fetch the summer home, the summer and the May – o."'

They came to Bargus. Here in this corner of the dark and barren heath murderers and suicides were buried. The rope on the gibbet swung empty, and had done for a number of months, but the place was unhallowed and they were both glad to be past it before dusk began to fall.

Now they were on familiar ground the horses wanted to break into a trot, but the girls held them in so that Jud should not be left too far behind.

'I'm a bit afeared,' Demelza said, speaking it seemed half to herself but aloud.

Verity looked at her and knew that it was not of ghosts or footpads she was thinking.

'I quite understand, my dear. But after all it will soon be over and——'

'Oh, not that,' Demelza said. 'Tesn't for me I'm afeared but for Ross. You see, he's not liked me for very long. Now I shall be ugly for months and months. Maybe when he sees me waddlin' about the house like an old duck he'll forget he ever liked me.'

'You needn't be afraid of that. Ross never forgets anything. I think—' Verity stared into the gathering dusk – 'I think it is a characteristic of our family.'

The last three miles were done in silence. The young moon was following the sun down. Soon it disappeared, leaving a ghostly smear of itself in the sky. Demelza watched the small bats hover and flicker in their path.

There was a sense of comfort in passing through the coppice about Wheal Maiden and turning into their own valley. Right and left were the new-built ricks of their own, two of wheat, one of oats; deep gold and pale gold they had been in this morning's sun. At the end of the valley the lights of Nampara were gleaming.

Ross stood on the doorstep waiting to lift them down and welcome them in.

'Where's Jud?' he asked. 'Has he——'

'Up there,' said Demelza. 'Only just up there. He's washing his face in the stream.'

Chapter seven

AUTUMN LINGERED ON as if fond of its own perfection. The November gales did not develop, and leaves of the tall elms were drifting down the stream, yellow and brown and withered crimson, until Christmas. And life at Nampara drifted down the stream with the same undisturbed calm. They lived together, those dissimilar lovers, in harmony and goodwill, working and sleeping and eating, loving and laughing and agreeing, creating about themselves a fine shell of preoccupation which the outside world made no serious attempt to breach. The routine of their lives was part of their daily contentment.

Jinny Carter came to the house with a blue-eyed ginger-haired infant in a carrier over her shoulder. She worked well if silently, and the child was no trouble. They arrived each morning at seven, and at seven in the evening Jinny was to be seen with her bundle walking steadily back over the hill to Mellin. News of Jim was scanty. One day Jinny showed Ross an ill-spelt message she had received, written by someone in the same cell as Jim, telling her Jim was well enough and sending her his love. Ross knew that Jinny was living on her mother and sending her earnings to Jim as often as she could find a means. One never knew how much the gaoler pocketed; and it had taken all Mrs Zacky's persuasion, and the claims of motherhood, to keep Jinny from walking the twenty-five miles to Bodmin, sleeping under a hedge, and walking back the following day.

Ross thought that after Christmas he would make the journey himself.

Demelza, freed of much drudgery but still eternally busy, found more time for her spinet playing. She could by now conjure some pleasant sounds from the instrument, and a few simple tunes that she knew well enough to sing she found she could also play. Ross said next year the spinet should be tuned and she should have lessons.

There was a surprise for the Nampara household on the twenty-first of December, when the boy Bartle arrived with a note from Francis, inviting Ross and Demelza to spend Christmas at Trenwith.

'There will be nobody but ourselves,' Francis wrote; 'that is, our household. Cousin W. A. is in Oxford, and Mr and Mrs Chynoweth are spending Christmas with her cousin, the Dean of Bodmin. I feel it a pity that our two houses should not similarly acknowledge their blood relationship. Also we have heard much from Verity of your wife (our new cousin) and would like to have her acquaintance. Come over in the afternoon of Christmas Eve and stay a few days.'

Ross thought hard over the message before passing it on. The wording of the note was friendly and did not give the impression of having been incited by someone else, whether Verity or Elizabeth. He didn't wish to widen any breach which might still exist, and it seemed a pity to reject a move of friendship which was genuinely made, especially from the man who had been his boyhood friend.

Demelza's views were naturally different. Elizabeth was behind it; Elizabeth had invited them in order to examine her, Demelza, to see how she had developed as Ross's wife, to get Ross into an atmosphere where he would see what a mistake he had made in marrying a low-class girl, and humiliate her by a display of fine manners.

By this time, however, Ross had begun to see real advantages in going. He was not in the least ashamed of Demelza. The Trenwith Poldarks had never been sticklers for the *agréments*, and Demelza had a curious charm that all the tuition in the world could not bring. Knowing Elizabeth better, he had no thought that she would stoop to such a trivial act of enmity, and he wanted her to see that he had been content with no common substitute.

Demelza did not find this reassuring.

'No, Ross.' She shook her head. 'You go if you must. Not me. I aren't their sort. I'll be all right here.'

'Naturally,' said Ross, 'we both stay or we both go. Bartle is still waiting and I must give him a wedding present. While I go upstairs for my purse, make up your mind to be a dutiful cousin.'

Demelza looked mutinous. 'I don't want to be a dutiful cousin.'

'A dutiful wife, then.'

'But it would be something awful, Ross. Here I am Mistress Poldark. I can wind up the clock when I like. I can tease you and pull your hair, and shout and sing if I want, an' play on the old spinet. I share your bed, and in the mornings when I wake I puff out my chest and think big thoughts. But there – they are not all like Verity, you told me so yourself. They would quiz me and say 'dear, dear' and send me out to eat with Bartle and his new wife.'

Ross looked at her sidelong. 'They are so much better than you, you think?'

'No, I did not say so.'

'You think I ought to be ashamed of you?'

In argument Ross always carried guns too big for her. She saw, she felt, but she could not reason it out to prove him wrong.

'Oh, Ross, they are your own kind,' she said. 'I am not.'

'Your mother bore you in the same way as theirs,' Ross said. 'We all have similar motions, appetites, humours. My present humour is to take you to

Trenwith for Christmas. It is little more than six months since you swore a solemn oath to obey me. What have you to say to that?'

'Nothing, Ross. Except that I don't want to go to Trenwith.'

He laughed. Arguments between them usually ended in laughter nowadays; it was a signal grace leavening their companionship.

He went to the table. 'I'll write a short note thanking them and saying we'll reply to-morrow.'

The next day Demelza reluctantly gave way, as she usually did on important matters. Ross wrote to say they would come on Christmas Eve and spend Christmas Day at Trenwith. But unfortunately business at the mine would compel him to return that evening.

The invitation was accepted, so no offence could be taken; but if there had been anything halfhearted about it they would not be outstaying their welcome. Demelza would have a chance of meeting them as an equal, but the strain of best behaviour would not be prolonged.

Demelza had agreed because although Ross's arguments could not convince her, his persuasions she could seldom withstand. But she would much rather have gone to the mine barber and had six teeth pulled.

She was not really afraid of Francis or the old aunt; ever a quick learner, she had been gaining confidence all through the autumn. The bogy was Elizabeth. Elizabeth, Elizabeth, Elizabeth. On the eve of Christmas their footsteps beat out the name as they cut up across the fields behind the house and took the path along the cliffs.

Demelza glanced sidelong at her husband, who walked beside her with his long easy stride from which the last suggestion of a limp had now gone. She never really knew his thoughts; his deeper reflections were masked behind that strange unquiet face with its faint pale scar on one cheek like the brand mark of a spiritual injury he had suffered. She only knew that at present he was happy and that she was the condition of his happiness. She knew they were happy together, but she did not know how long such content could last; and she felt it in her heart that to consort with the woman he had once loved so deeply was flying in the face of fate.

The awful thought was that so much might depend on *her* behaviour during the next two days.

It was a bright day with a strong cold wind off the land. The sea was flat and green with a heavy ground swell. The long even ridge of a wave would move slowly in, and then as it met the stiff south-easterly breeze its long top would begin to ruffle like the short feathers of an eider duck, growing more and more ruffled until the whole long ridge toppled slowly over and the wintry sun made a dozen rainbows in the mist flying up from its breaking.

All the way to Sawle Cove they were delayed by Garrick, who thought that Demelza could not be going out without him and was convinced that if he persisted long enough her better nature would come to see the matter as he did. Every few yards a sharp word of command would send his big lumpy body to the earth, where he would lie in complete and submissive collapse and only one reproachful bloodshot eye to prove that life still lingered; but a few more dozen paces would show that he was up and following them with slinking ungainly tread. Fortunately they met Mark Daniel, who was returning by the path they had come. Mark Daniel was standing no nonsense and was last seen marching in the direction of Nampara holding Garrick by one lopsided ear.

. . . They crossed the sand and shingle of Sawle Cove, meeting one or two people who wished them an affable good day, and climbed the cliff hill at the other side. Before striking inland they paused for breath and to watch a flight of gannets diving for fish just off the shore. The gannets manoeuvred beyond the surf, their great stretch of white wings, brown-tipped, balancing them against the press of the wind; then they would dive plummet fashion, disappearing with a splash, to come up once in ten or twenty times with a small lance struggling in their long curved beaks.

'If I was a sand eel,' said Demelza, 'I should fair hate the sight of a gannet. See 'em fold their wings as they go in. When they come up without anything, don't they look innocent, as if they hadn't really meant it.'

'We could do with some rain now,' Ross said, staring at the sky. 'The springs are low.'

'Someday before I die, Ross, I should dearly like to go a journey on a ship. To France and Cherbourg and Madrid, and perhaps to America. I expect there are all sorts of funny birds out in the sea bigger than gannets. Why do you never talk about America, Ross?'

'The past is no good to anyone. It is only the present and the future that matter.'

'Father knew a man who'd been to America. But he never talked of nothing else. Twas half a fairy story, I b'lieve.'

'Francis was lucky,' Ross said. 'He spent a whole summer travelling Italy and the Continent. I thought I should like to travel. Then the war came and I went to America. When I returned I wanted only my own corner of England. It's strange.'

'Someday I should like to visit France.'

'We could pay a visit to Roscoff or Cherbourg any time in one of the St Ann's cutters. I have done it as a boy.'

'I should rather go in a big ship,' Demelza said. 'An' not with the fear of being fired on by the revenue men.'

They went on their way.

Verity was at the door of Trenwith House waiting to greet them. She ran forward to kiss Ross and then Demelza. Demelza held her tight for a moment, then took a deep breath and went in.

II

The first few minutes were trying for them all, but the trial passed. Happily both Demelza and the Trenwith household were on their best behaviour. Francis had a natural charm when he chose to exercise it, and Aunt Agatha, warmed by a tot of Jamaica rum and crowned with her second best wig, was affable and coy. Elizabeth was smiling, her flowerlike face more lovely for its delicate flush. Geoffrey Charles, aged three, came stumping forward in his velvet suit, to stand finger in mouth staring at the strangers.

Aunt Agatha caused some extra trouble at the outset by denying that she had ever been told of Ross's marriage and by demanding a full explanation. Then she wanted to know Demelza's maiden name.

'What?' she said. 'Carkeek? Cardew? Carne? Carne, did you say? Where does she come from? Where do you come from, child?'

'Illuggan,' said Demelza.

'Where? Oh, that's near the Bassetts' place, is it not? You'll know Sir Francis. Intelligent young fellow, they say, but overconcerned with social problems.' Aunt Agatha stroked the whiskers on her chin. 'Come here, bud. I don't bite. How old are you?'

Demelza allowed her hand to be taken. 'Eighteen.' She glanced at Ross.

'Hm. Nice age. Nice and sweet at that age.' Aunt Agatha also glanced at Ross, her small eyes wicked among their sheaf of wrinkles. 'Know you how old I am?'

Demelza shook her head.

'I'm ninety-one. Last Thursday sennight.'

'I didn't know you were as old as that,' Francis said.

'It's not everything you know, my boy. Ninety-one last Thursday sennight. What d'you say to that, Ross?'

'Sweet at any age,' Ross said in her ear.

Aunt Agatha grinned with pleasure. 'You was always a bad boy. Like your father. Five generations of Poldarks I've seen. Nay, six. There was old Grannie Trenwith. I remember her well. She was a Rowe. Great Presbyterians they was. Her father, Owen, was a friend of Cromwell's: they say he was one of the fifty-nine that signed King Charles's death paper. They lost all their land at the Restoration. I remember her well. She died when I was ten. She used to tell me stories of the Plague. Not as she was ever in it.'

'We had the Plague at Illuggan once, ma'am,' Demelza said.

'Then there was Anna-Maria, my mother, who became a Poldark. She was an only child. I was old when she died. Charles Vivian Poldark she married. He was a roamer. An invalid out of the Navy from the battle of La Hogue before ever he met Mama, and he but five and twenty. That's his portrait, bud. The one with the little beard.'

Demelza gazed.

'Then there was Claude Henry, my brother, who married Matilda Ellen Peter of Treviles. He died ten years before his mama. Vomiting and looseness was his trouble. That was your grandfather, Ross. You and Francis makes five, and little Geoffrey makes six. Six generations, and I've scarce been alive any time yet.'

Demelza was at last allowed her hand back, and passed on to greet the staring child. Geoffrey Charles was a plump little boy, his face so smooth that one could not imagine it ever having creased into a thoroughgoing smile. A handsome child, as might be expected with such parents.

Ross's own sight of Elizabeth after six months had not been quite as casual or as unemotional as he had hoped and expected. He had hoped to find himself immune, as if his marriage and love for Demelza were the inoculation against some fever of the blood and this a deliberate contact on his part to prove the cure. But Demelza, he found, was not an inoculation, though she might be a separate fever. He wondered, just at that first greeting, whether after all Demelza's impulse to refuse the invitation had not perhaps been wiser than his own.

Their meeting, Elizabeth's and Demelza's, left him with a sense of dissatisfaction: their manner towards each other was so outwardly friendly and so inwardly wary. He did not know if their greeting deceived anyone else but it certainly didn't deceive him. Naturalness just was not in it.

But Demelza and Verity had taken days to get on friendly terms. Women were like that: however charming taken singly, a first meeting with one of their own kind was an intuitive testing and searching.

Elizabeth had given them one of the best bedrooms, looking southwest towards the woods.

'Tis a handsome house,' said Demelza, dropping her cloak from her shoulders. With the first ordeal over she felt better. 'Never have I seen the like. Tis like a church, that hall. And this bedroom. Look at the birds on the curtains; like missel thrushes, only the specks are the wrong colour. But, Ross, all those pictures hanging downstairs. I should be afeared of them in the dark. Are they all of your family, Ross?'

'I have been told so.'

'It is more than I can understand that people should wish to have so many dead 'uns about them. When I am dead, Ross, I don't want to be hung up to dry like last week's bed linen. I don't want to stare down for ever upon a lot of people I've never known at all, great grandchildren and great-great-great grandchildren. I'd much sooner be put away and forgot.'

'This is the second time to-day you've spoken of dying,' Ross said. 'Do you feel unwell?'

'No, no; I am brave enough.'

'Then oblige me by keeping to some more agreeable subject. What's this box?'

'That?' said Demelza. 'Oh, that is something. I asked Jud to bring it over with our night rails.'

'What is in it?'

'A dress.'

'For you?'

'Yes, Ross.'

'The riding habit you bought in Truro?'

'No, Ross, another. You would not like me to be shabby in front of all your great-grandmothers, would you?'

He laughed. 'Is it a dress from the library you have adapted?'

'No . . . Verity and me bought this also in Truro at the same time.'

'Did she pay for it?'

'No, Ross. It came out of the money you give us for furnishings.'

'Deceit, bud. And you looking so innocent and guileless.'

'You are stealin' Aunt Agatha's name for me.'

'I think I like it. But I am just finding the worm in the bud. Deceit and duplicity. Still, I'm glad Verity did not pay. Let me see it.'

'No, Ross. *No*, Ross! *No, Ross!*' Her voice rose to a shriek as she tried to prevent him from reaching the box. He got one hand to it, but she put her arms round his neck and hugged him to stop any further move. He lifted her up by the elbows and kissed her, then he smacked her twice on the seat and put her down.

'Where's your good behaviour, bud? They'll think I'm beating you.'

'Which is the truth. Which is the truth.' She slipped away from him and danced back with the box held behind her.

'Go down now, please, Ross! You was not to know anything about it! Maybe I'll not wear it, but I want to try it on and dinner is in an hour. Go down and talk to Aunt Agatha and count the whiskers on her chin.'

'We're not attending a ball,' he said. 'This is just a family party; no need to flig yourself up for it.'

'It is Christmas Eve. I asked Verity. She said it was right to change my clo'es.'

'Oh, have it as you please. But mind you're ready by five. And,' he added as an afterthought, 'don't lace your stays too tight or you'll be incommoded. They feed you well, and I know your appetite.'

With this he went out, and she was left to make her preparations alone.

She did not feel that she need heed Ross's final warning to-night at any rate. All day she had had recurring bouts of nausea. The Trenwith dinner was safe from her greed: all that was unsafe was the little she might force down. It would be too bad if she made a show of herself this evening. It would be tragic. She wondered if she had to get up from the table in a hurry where the nearest close-stool was.

She pulled her dress over her head, stepped out of her underskirt and stood for a moment in the smallclothes Verity had lent her, staring at her reflection in the lovely clear mirror of the dressing table. She had never before in her life seen herself so clearly and so entirely. This reflection was not too shameful, but she wondered how she had had the brazenness to move about and dress with Ross in the room when she was wearing the underclothes of her own and Prudie's devising. She would never wear them again.

She had heard it whispered that many good class town women wore white stockings and no drawers. What with hooped skirts it was disgusting, and they deserved to catch their death.

She shivered. But soon she would be unsightly, however dressed. At least, she expected so. It was a surprise to her that so far there had been no change. Every morning she took a piece of string with a knot tied in it and measured herself. But, unbelievably enough, she seemed so far to have lost half an inch. Perhaps the knot had slipped.

A village upbringing had left little out in teaching her the ordinary facts of getting and begetting; yet when it came to herself she found gaps in her knowledge. Her mother had borne six other children, but she remembered so little of what had happened before she was eight.

She must ask Verity. This was now the usual resort for all problems which baffled her. She must ask Verity. It didn't occur to her that there were questions on which Verity might know less than herself.

Chapter eight

DOWNSTAIRS IN THE large parlour Ross found only Elizabeth and Geoffrey Charles. They were sitting in front of the fire, Geoffrey Charles on his mother's knee, and Elizabeth was reading him a story.

Ross listened to the cool, cultured voice; there was pleasure for him in that. But she looked up, saw who it was and stopped.

''Gain, Mummie. Tell it again.'

'In a little while, darling. I must have a rest. Here is your Uncle Ross, come to tell me a story for a change.'

'I know no stories except true ones,' Ross said. 'And they are all sad.'

'Not all, surely,' said Elizabeth. 'Your own must now be happy with so charming a wife.'

Ross hesitated, uncertain whether he wished to discuss Demelza even with Elizabeth.

'I'm very glad that you like her.'

'She's greatly changed since I saw her last, and that's not seven months ago, and I think she will change more yet. You must take her into society and bring her out.'

'And risk the snubs of women like Mrs Teague? Thank you, I'm well enough as I am.'

'You're too sensitive. Besides, she may want to go out herself. Women have the courage for that sort of thing, and she is yet so young.'

'It was with the greatest difficulty that I persuaded her to come here.'

Elizabeth smiled down on her son's curly head. 'That's understandable.'

'Why?'

'Oh . . . it was meeting the family, wasn't it? And she is a little *gauche* yet. She would perhaps expect to find antagonisms.'

'Mummie, 'gain. 'Gain, Mummie.'

'Not yet. In a while.'

'Man's got a mark on his face, Mummie.'

'Hush, dear. You must not say such things.'

'But he has. He *has*, Mummie!'

'And I've washed it and washed it and it won't come off,' Ross assured him.

Thus addressed, Geoffrey Charles fell utterly silent.

'Verity has become very fond of her,' Elizabeth said. 'We must see more of you now, Ross, now that the ice is broken.'

'What of your own affairs?' Ross said. 'Baby Geoffrey is thriving, I see that.'

Elizabeth put out her small slippered feet and allowed her son to slide from her lap to the floor. There he stood a second as if about to run off, but seeing Ross's eyes still on him was overcome with his new shyness and buried his face in his mother's skirt.

'Come, darling, don't be foolish. This is Uncle Ross; like Uncle Warleggan only more so. He is your true and only uncle and you mustn't be coy. Up, up, and say how d'you do.'

But Geoffrey Charles would not move his head.

She said: 'I haven't been too well in health, but we are all worried about my poor mother. She's greatly troubled with her eyes. Park the surgeon from Exeter is coming to examine her in the New Year. Dr Choake and Dr Pryce take a grave view of the disease.'

'I'm sorry.'

'They say it's a recurrent distemper of the eye. The treatment is most painful. They tie a silk kerchief about her throat and tighten it until she is nearly strangled and all the blood is forced into her head. Then they bleed her behind the ears. She has gone now to rest with her cousin at Bodmin. I am very worried.'

Ross made a face. 'My father had no trust in physicians. I hope you'll have good news.'

There was silence. Elizabeth bent and whispered in Geoffrey's ear. There was no response for a moment, then with a sudden, peculiarly sly glance at Ross, he turned and ran from the room.

Elizabeth's eyes followed him. 'Geoffrey is at an awkward age,' she said. 'He must be cured of his little whimsies.' But she spoke in an indulgent voice.

'And Francis?'

An expression he had never seen before flitted across her face.

'Francis? Oh, we get along, thank you, Ross.'

'The summer has gone so quick and I have intended to come and see you. Francis may have told you I spoke to him once.'

'You have your own concerns to tend now.'

'Not to the exclusion of all others.'

'Well, we have kept our head above water through the summer.' She said this in a tone that went with her expression. The personal pronoun might have referred to the finances of the house or to the fastnesses of her own spirit.

'I can't understand him,' Ross said.

'We are as we are born. Francis was born a gambler, it seems. If he's not careful he'll have gamed away all that has come to him and die a pauper.'

Every family, thought Ross, had its rakes and its spendthrifts; their blood was passed on with the rest, strange taints of impulse and perversity. It was the only explanation. Yet Joshua, even Joshua, who had been eccentric enough and roving in his eye for women, had had the sense to settle down when he got the woman he wanted and to remain so settled until nature took her from him.

'Where does he spend most of his time?'

'At the Warleggans' still. We used to have great fun until the stakes became too high. I have only been twice since Geoffrey was born. Now I'm not invited.'

'But surely——'

'Oh yes, of course, if I asked Francis to take me. But he tells me that they're becoming more exclusively male. I would not enjoy them, he says.'

She was staring down at the folds of her blue dress. This was a new Elizabeth who spoke so straightly, in such objective tones, as if painful experience had taught her the lesson of keeping life at a distance.

'Ross.'

'Yes?'

'I think there is one way in which you might help me if you would——'

'Go on.'

'There are stories concerning Francis. I have no means of knowing what truth there is in them. I could ask George Warleggan, but for a special reason don't wish to. I have no claim on you, you know that; but I should esteem it so highly if you were able to discover the truth.'

Ross stared at her. He had been unwise to come here. He could not sit in calm intimacy with this woman without the return of old sensations.

'I'll do anything I can. I shall be pleased to do it. Unfortunately I don't move in the same set as Francis. My interests——'

'It could be arranged.'

Ross looked at her quickly. 'How?'

'I could get George Warleggan to invite you to one of his parties. George likes you.'

'What's the extent of the rumours?'

'They say Francis is going with another woman. I don't know what truth there is in it, but it's plain I cannot suddenly choose to go to the parties myself. I cannot – *spy* on him.'

Ross hesitated. Did she realize all she asked? She was of course reluctant to spy herself, but that would be his task in fact if not in name. And to what end? How could his intervention serve to underpin a marriage if the foundations of the marriage were already gone?

'Don't decide now, Ross,' she said in a low voice. 'Leave it. Think it over. I know I'm asking a great deal.'

Her tone made him glance round, and Francis came in. Sitting in this big pleasant parlour, Ross thought, one would soon come to recognize the footstep of everyone in the house as it approached the door.

'A *tête-à-tête?*' Francis said, raising an eyebrow. 'And not drinking, Ross? This is a poor hospitality we offer. Let me mix you an eggy-hot to keep away the chills of winter.'

'Ross was telling me how well his mine is doing, Francis,' Elizabeth said.

'Lord save us; such talk on Christmas Eve.' Francis busied himself. 'Come over in January – or maybe February – and tell us about it, Ross. But not now, I implore you. It would be dull to spend this evening comparing notes on copper assays.'

Ross saw that he had been drinking, though the signs were very slight.

Elizabeth rose. 'When cousins have been so long separated,' she said pleasantly, 'it's hard to find something to talk of. It would do us no harm, Francis, if we thought of Grambler a little more. I must see Geoffrey to bed.' She left them.

Francis came across with the drink. He was wearing a dark green suit and the lace at the cuffs was soiled. Unusual in the immaculate Francis. No other sign of the rake's progress. Hair as carefully brushed, stock as neatly tied, manners of a greater elegance. There was an extra fullness of the face, which made him look older, and something superficial in his glance.

'Elizabeth makes life a mortal serious business,' he remarked. 'Aarf! as my old father would say.'

'Elegance of expression is something I have always admired in you,' said Ross.

Francis looked up and grinned. 'No offence intended. We have been estranged too long. What's the good of choler in this world? If we took account of every grievance we should only make more bad blood for the leeches. Drink about.'

Ross drank about. 'I have no grievances. The past is past and I'm content enough.'

'So should you be,' Francis said over the rim of his tankard. 'I like your wife. From Verity's account I thought I should. She walks like a mettlesome colt. And after all, so long as her spirit be good, what does it matter whether she comes from Windsor Castle or Stippy-Stappy Lane?'

'You and I have much in common,' Ross said.

'I used to think so.' Francis stopped. 'In sentiment or in circumstance, do you mean?'

'In sentiment I meant. Clearly in circumstance you have the advantage of me. The house and interests of our common ancestors; the wife, shall I put it, of our common choice; money to splash at the card table and the cockpit; a son and heir——'

'Stop,' said Francis, 'or you'll make me weep with envy at my own good fortune.'

'I'd never thought it a conspicuous danger in your case, Francis.'

Francis's forehead puckered in a frown. He set his tankard down.

'No, nor in any other case neither. It's the custom of mankind to judge others in ignorance. They take it——'

'Then correct my ignorance.'

Francis looked at him for a moment or two.

'Pour out my distempers on the eve of Christmas? God forbid. You would find it all so tedious, I assure you. Like Aunt Agatha talking of her kidneys. Finish your drink, man, and have another.'

'Thanks,' said Ross. 'In truth, Francis——'

'In truth, Ross,' Francis mocked from the shadows of the sideboard. 'It is all as you say, is it not? A lovely wife, fair as an angel – indeed, perhaps more of an angel than a wife – the home of our ancestors, hung with their curious visages – oh yes, I saw Demelza admiring them open-mouthed – a handsome son brought up in the way he ought to go: honour thy father and be worshipped by thy mother that thy days may be long in the land which the Lord thy God giveth thee. And finally money to splash at the card table and the cockpit. Splash. I like the word. It has a pleasantly expansive sound. One is put in mind of the Prince of Wales dropping a couple of thousand guineas at White's.'

'It's a relative word,' Ross said evenly. 'Like many others. If one is a country squire and lives in the western wilds one may splash just as effectively with fifty guineas as George with two thousand.'

Francis laughed as he came back. 'You speak from experience. I'd forgotten. You have been the staid farmer so long I'd quite forgotten.'

'Indeed,' said Ross, 'I should say that ours was far the greater hazard, not only in proportion but because we have no benevolent parliament to vote £160,000 to pay our debts or £10,000 a year to squander on the mistress of the moment.'

'You're well informed on the business of the court.'

'All news flies fast, whether it concerns a prince or a local squire.'

Francis flushed. 'What do you mean by that?'

Ross raised his mug. 'That this drink's very warming to the vitals.'

'It may disappoint you to know,' said Francis, 'that I'm not interested in what a set of braggarty pockmarked old grannies are whispering over their turf fires. I go my own way and leave them to fetch up what poisonous gases they choose. We are none of us immune from their clackings. Look to your own house, Ross.'

'You misunderstand me,' said Ross. 'I'm not concerned with gossip or the tales of idle women. But the interior of a debtors' prison is damp and smelly. No one would be the worse for your bearing that in mind before it is too late.'

Francis lit up his long pipe and smoked for some seconds before saying anything more. He dropped a piece of smouldering wood back in the fire and put down the tongs.

'Elizabeth must have been pitching you a pretty story.'

'I don't need her confidences for a pretty story which is known all over the district.'

'The district knows my own affairs better than I do myself. Perhaps you'd advise me to a solution. Should I join the Methodies and be saved?'

'My dear man,' Ross said, 'I like you and have an interest in your welfare. But for all it will affect me you may find your way to the devil by the shortest route. Fortune can provide lands and family but it can't provide good sense. If you wish to throw away what you have, then throw it away and be damned.'

Francis eyed him cynically for a moment, then put down his pipe and clapped a hand on his shoulder.

'Spoken like a Poldark. We have never been an agreeable family. Let us curse and quarrel in amity. Then we can get drunk in company. You and I together, and to hell with the creditors!'

Ross picked up his empty mug and regarded the bottom gravely. Francis's good temper under the quizzing struck a responsive chord. Disappointment, from whatever quarter it had come, had toughened his cousin: it had not changed the essential individual he had known and liked.

At that moment Bartle came in carrying two branching candlesticks. The yellow flames flickered in the draught, and it was as if the firelight had suddenly grown to fill the room. Elizabeth's spinning wheel stood out in the corner, its bobbins shining. A linen doll lay on its back beside the sofa with stuffing hanging from its stomach. On a chair was a wicker basket with needlework and a frame with a half-finished sampler. The light of the candles was warm and friendly; with the curtains drawn there was a sense of cosiness and quiet affluence.

In the room were all the signs of feminine occupancy, and there had been about these few minutes of conversation an underlying maleness which drew the two men together by the bond of their larger, wider, more tolerant understanding. Between them was the freemasonry of their sex, a unity of blood, and the memory of old friendships.

It occurred to Ross in this moment that half of Elizabeth's worry might be the eternal feminine bogy of insecurity. Francis drank. Francis gambled and lost money. Francis had been seen about with another woman. Not an amiable story. But not an uncommon one. Inconceivable to Ross in this case, and for Elizabeth it had the proportions of a tragedy. But it was unwise to lose one's sense of perspective. Other men drank and gambled. Debts were fashionable. Other men found eyes to admire the beauty which was not theirs by right of marriage and to overlook the familiar beauty that was. It did not follow that Francis was taking the shortest route to perdition.

Anyway this was Christmas, and the day was intended to mark a family reunion, not to begin a new estrangement.

One could go no further. Let it rest. Ross thought of Demelza upstairs putting on her best and full of youth and good spirits. He hoped she was not going to overdo it. Fortunate that Verity had had the ordering. The thought of Demelza warmed his mind and lit it up, as the arrival of the candles had lit the room.

To the devil with vicarious worries. Christmas was no time for them. In January they could be revived, if they still had the power to vex and disturb.

Chapter nine

DINNER BEGAN AT five and went on until seven-forty. It was a meal worthy of the age, the house, and the season. Pea soup to begin, followed by a roast swan with sweet sauce; giblets, mutton steaks, a partridge pie and four snipe. The second course was a plum pudding with brandy sauce, tarts, mince pies, apple pies, custards and cakes; all washed down with port wine and claret and madeira and home-brewed ale.

Ross felt that there was only one thing missing: Charles. The great paunch, the more or less subdued belches, the heavy good humour; at this moment the corporeal remains of that massive, mediocre, but not unkindly soul were rotting away and becoming one with the soil that had given it life and sustenance; the organic humours of which it was composed would soon be helping to feed the rank couch grass which overran the churchyard. But in this house from which he had spent few nights away in the course of his sixty-eight years, in this house remained some unspent aura of his presence more noticeable to Ross than the aura of all the portraits of forty-six ancestors.

One did not so much feel sorrow at his absence as a sense of the unfitness of his not being here.

For such a small party the dining hall was too gaunt and draughty: they used the winter parlour, which faced west and was panelled to the ceiling and was convenient for the kitchens. Chance stage-managed Demelza's arrival. Verity had come to the large parlour to tell them that dinner was ready. Elizabeth was there and the four of them left the room smiling and chattering together. As they did so Demelza came down the stairs.

She was wearing the dress that had been made up from Verity's choice, the very pale mauve silk with the half-length sleeves, slightly hooped and pulled apart like a letter A at the front to show the flowered apple-green bodice and underskirt.

What Ross could not quite understand was her appearance, her manner. Natural that he should be pleased with her; she had never looked so charming before. In her own queer way this evening she rivalled Elizabeth, who started any such competition with advantages of feature and colouring over almost all women. Some challenge born in the situation had brought out the best of Demelza's good looks, her fine dark eyes, her hair neatly dressed and tied, her very pale olive skin with the warm glow under it. Verity was openly proud of her.

At dinner she didn't burst her stays. In Ross's opinion she overdid her good behaviour by pecking at many things and always leaving the larger portion on her plate. She out-vied Elizabeth, who was always so small an eater; a suspicious person might have thought her to be mocking her hostess. Ross was amused. To-night she was on her mettle.

A talkative girl at meals, full of questions and speculations, she took little part in the conversation at this meal, refused the burnt claret which the others drank and herself drank only the home-brewed ale. But she didn't look bored and her manner was always one of intelligent interest while Elizabeth spoke of people she did not know or gave some anecdote of Geoffrey Charles. When she was drawn in she answered pleasantly and naturally and without affectation. Aunt Agatha's occasional broadsides didn't seem to disconcert her: she would look at Ross, who sat next to the old lady, and he would shout an answer. This put the onus on him of finding the right one.

Talk turned on whether there was truth in the rumour of another attempt on the King's life. The last such rumour had certainly been true, when Margaret Nicholson tried to stab him at a levée; Francis made some cynical comments on the good cloth used in the royal waistcoat. Elizabeth said she had been told the King's household servants had not been paid for twelve months.

They talked of France and the magnificence of the court there. Francis said he was surprised someone had not tried to sharpen a knife on Louis, who was far more deserving of one than Farmer George. The French Queen was trying to find a cure for all her ills in animal magnetism.

Verity said she thought she would try that for her catarrh, for she had been told to drink half a pint of sea water daily and she found she could not stomach it. Dr Choake blamed all colds on the malignancy of the air: raw meat put on a pole turned bad in forty minutes, while similar meat kept in salt water remained fresh for a long time. Ross remarked that Choake was an old woman. Francis said perhaps there was literal truth in that statement, since Polly was so unfruitful. Elizabeth turned the conversation to her mother's eye trouble.

Francis drank ten glasses of port over the meal but showed little change. A difference, Ross thought, from the old days when he was always the first under the table. 'Boy's no head for liquor,' Charles would grumble. Ross glanced at Elizabeth, but her look was serene.

At fifteen minutes before eight the ladies rose and left the two men to drink brandy and smoke their pipes at the littered and derelict table. Between themselves they talked business; but the conversation had not been in progress many minutes when Mrs Tabb appeared at the door.

'If you please, sir, visitors has just come.'

'What?'

'Mr George Warleggan and Mr and Mrs John Treneglos, sir.'

Ross felt a spasm of annoyance at having this surprise sprung on him. He had no wish to meet the all-successful George to-night. And he felt sure Ruth would not have come had she known he and Demelza were here.

But Francis's surprise was genuine.

'Cock's life, so they come visiting on Christmas Eve, eh? What have you done with them, Emily?'

'They're in the big parlour, sir. Mistress Elizabeth said would you come soon and help entertain them, and they do not intend to stop long.'

'Surely. We will go right away.' Francis waved his glass. 'Right away.'

When Mrs Tabb left he lit his pipe. 'Imagine old George coming to-night. I thought he was spending Christmas at Cardew. A coincidence, what? And John and Ruth. You remember when we used to fight John and Richard, Ross?'

Ross did.

'George Warleggan,' said Francis. 'Great man. He'll own half Cornwall before he's done. He and his cousin own more than half of me already.' He laughed. 'The other half he wants but can't have. Some things just won't go on the table.'

'His cousin?'

'Cary Warleggan, the banker.'

'A pretty name. I've heard him called a moneylender.'

'Tut! Would you insult the family?'

'The family grows too intrusive for my taste. I prefer a community run on simpler lines.'

'They're the people of the future, Ross. Not the worn-out families like the Chynoweths and the Poldarks.'

'It's not their vigour I query but their use of it. If a man has vitality let him increase his own soul, not set about owning other people's.'

'That may be true of Cousin Cary, but it's a small matter hard on George.'

'Finish your drink and we'll go,' Ross said, thinking of Demelza with these new people to face.

'It is more than a little strange,' said Francis. 'Philosophers would no doubt hang some doxy name on it. But to me it seems just a plain perversity of life.'

'What does?'

'Oh . . .' The other hesitated. 'I don't know. We envy some other person for something he has got and we have not, although in truth it may be that he really hasn't it. Do I make myself clear? No, I thought not. Let's go and see George.'

They rose from the ruins of the feast and walked through into the hall. As they crossed it they heard shouts of laughter from the large parlour.

'Making a carnival of my house,' said Francis. 'Can this be George the elegant?'

'Long odds,' said Ross 'on its being John the Master of Hounds.'

They entered and found his guess a good one. John Treneglos was sitting at Elizabeth's hand spinning wheel. He was trying to work it. It seemed a simple enough action but in fact needed practice, which John Treneglos lacked. He would get the wheel going nicely for some moments, but then his foot pressure on the treadle would be not quite even and the cranked arm would suddenly reverse itself and stop. While it was working right there was silence in the room, broken only by an interplay between Treneglos and Warleggan. But every time John went off his stroke there was a roar of laughter.

Treneglos was a powerful, clumsy man of thirty, with sandy hair, deep-set eyes and freckled features. He was known as a fine horseman, a first-class shot, the best amateur wrestler in two counties, a dunce at any game needing mental effort, and something of a bully. This evening, though on a social call, he wore an old brown velvet riding coat and strong corduroy breeches. It was his boast that he never wore anything but riding breeches, even in bed.

Ross was surprised to see that Demelza was not in the room.

'You lose,' said George Warleggan. 'You lose. Five guineas are mine. Ho, Francis.'

'One more try, damme. The first was a trial try. I'll not be beat by a comical contraption of this sort.'

'Where is Demelza?' said Ross to Verity, who was standing by the door.

'Upstairs. She wished to be left alone for a few moments so I came down.'

'You'll break it, John,' said Elizabeth, half smiling. 'You're too heavy-footed.'

'John!' said his wife. 'Get up at once!'

But John had been merrying himself with good brandy and took no notice. Once more he got the wheel going, and it seemed that this time he had done the trick. But at the wrong moment he tried to increase the speed, and the cranked arm reversed and everything came to a jerking standstill. George uttered a cry of triumph and John Treneglos rose in disgust.

'Three more times and I should have mastered the pesty thing. You must give me a lesson, Elizabeth. Here, man, take your money. It's ill gotten and will stick in your crop.'

'John is so excitable,' said his wife. 'I feared for your wheel. I think we are all a little foxed, and the Christmas spirit has done the rest.'

If John Treneglos set no store by fashion, the same could not be said of the new Mrs Treneglos. Ruth Teague, the drab little girl of the Easter Charity Ball, had shot ahead. An instinct in Ross had sensed at the ball that there was more in her than met the eye. She wore a blossom-coloured hoopless dress of Spitalfields silk with silver spangles at the waist and shoulders. An unsuitable dress for travelling the countryside, but no doubt her wardrobe was well stocked. John would have other calls on his pocket now besides his hunters. And John would not have things all his own way.

'Well, well, Captain Poldark,' said Treneglos ironically. 'We're neighbours, but this is how we meet. For all we see of you you might be Robinson Crusoe.'

'Oh, but he has his Man Friday, dear,' said Ruth gently.

'Who? Oh, you mean Jud,' said Treneglos, blunting the edge of his wife's remark. 'A hairless ape, that. He cheeked me once. Had he not been your servant I'd have give him a beating. And what of the mine? Old Father is cock-a-hoop and speaks of shovelling in the copper.'

'Nothing ambitious,' Ross said, 'but gratifying so far as it goes.'

'Egad,' said George. 'Must we talk business? Elizabeth, bring out your harp. Let us have a song.'

'I have no voice,' said Elizabeth, with her lovely slow smile. 'If you have a mind to accompany me——'

'We'll all accompany you.' George was deferential. 'It would suit the night admirable.'

Not for George the self-confident uncouthness of John Treneglos, who traced his ancestry back to Robert, Count of Mortain. It was hardly credible that a single generation divided a tough, gnarled old man who sat in a cottage in his shirt sleeves and chewed tobacco and could barely write his name from this cultured young man in a new-fashioned tight-cut pink coat with buff lapels, a pink waistcoat with gold buttons, and buff nankeen trousers. Only something of the blacksmith's grandson showed in the size of his features, in the full, tight, possessive lips, in the short neck above the heavy shoulders.

'Is Demelza coming down?' Ross asked Verity quietly. 'She has not been overawed by these people?'

'No, I don't think she knows they're here.'

'Let's have a hand of faro,' said Francis. 'I was damned unlucky on Saturday. Fortune cannot always be sulky.'

But he was shouted down. Elizabeth must play the harp. They had come specially to hear Elizabeth play. Already George was moving the instrument out of its corner and John was bringing forward the chair she used. Elizabeth, protesting and smiling, was being persuaded. At that moment Demelza came in.

Demelza was feeling better. She had just lost the dinner she had eaten and the ale she had drunk. The occurrence itself had not been pleasant, but, like the old Roman senators, she was feeling the better for it. The demon nausea had gone with the food and all was well.

There was a moment's silence after she entered. It was noticeable then that the guests had been making most of the noise. Then Elizabeth said:

'This is our new cousin, Demelza. Ross's wife.'

Demelza was surprised at this influx of people whom she must now meet. She remembered Ruth Teague from seeing her once on a visit to Ross, and she had seen her husband twice out hunting: Squire Treneglos's eldest son, one of the big men of the neighbourhood. When she last saw them both she had been a long-legged untidy kitchen wench for whom neither of them would have spared a second glance. Or Ruth would not. By them and by George Warleggan, who from his dress she felt must be at least the son of a lord, she was overawed. But she was learning fast that people, even well-bred people like these, had a surprising tendency to take you at your own valuation.

'Damn it, Ross,' Treneglos said. 'Where have you been hiding this little blossom? It was ungrateful of you to be so close about it. Your servant, ma'am.'

Since to reply 'your servant, sir,' was clearly wrong, besides being too near the truth, Demelza contented herself with a pleasant smile. She allowed herself to be introduced to the other two, then accepted a glass of port from Verity and gulped half of it down while they were looking the other way.

'So this is your wife, Ross,' said Ruth sweetly. 'Come and sit by me, my dear. Tell me all about yourself. All the county was talking of you in June.'

'Yes,' said Demelza. 'People dearly love a gossip, don't they, ma'am.'

Ruth flushed, but John roared and slapped his thigh.

'Quite right, mistress. Let's drink a toast: a merry Christmas to us all round and damnation to the gossips!'

'You're drunk, John,' said Ruth severely. 'You will not be able to sit your horse if we don't leave at once.'

'First we must hear Elizabeth play,' said George, who had been exchanging some close confidence with Elizabeth.

'Do you sing, Mistress Poldark?' asked John.

'Me?' said Demelza in surprise. 'No, only when I'm happy.'

'Damn it, are we not all happy now?' asked John. 'Christmastide. You must sing for us, ma'am.'

'Does she sing, Ross?' Francis enquired.

Ross looked at Demelza, who shook her head vigorously.

'No,' said Ross.

This denial seemed to carry no weight. Somebody must sing to them, and it looked as if it was going to be Demelza.

The girl emptied her wineglass hurriedly, and someone refilled it.

'I only sing by myself,' she said. 'I mean I don't rightly know proper tunes. Mistr – er – Elizabeth must play first. Later, mebbe . . .'

Elizabeth was very gently running her fingers up and down the harp.

The faint rippling sound was a liquid accompaniment to the chatter.

'If you sing me a few bars,' she said, 'I think I could pick it up.'

'No, no,' said Demelza, backing away. 'You first. You play first.'

So presently Elizabeth played, and at once the company fell silent, even the tipsy John and the well-soaked Francis. They were all Cornish, and music meant something to them.

She played first a piece by Handel and then a short sonatina by Krumpholz. The plucked vibrating tones filled the room, and the only other sound was the murmur of burning wood from the fire. The candleglow fell on Elizabeth's fine young head and on her slim hands moving over the strings. The light made a halo of her hair. Behind her stood George Warleggan, stocky and polite and ruthless, his hands behind his back, his large wide-set brown eyes fixed unwinkingly on the player.

Verity had subsided on a stool, a tray with glasses on the floor beside her. Against a background of blue moreen curtains, she sat with hands clasped about knees, her head up and showing the line of her throat above its lace fichu. Her face in its repose reminded one of the younger Verity of four years ago. Next to her Francis lolled in a chair, his eyes half closed, but listening; and beside him Aunt Agatha chewed meditatively, a dribble of saliva at the corner of her mouth, listening too but hearing nothing. In her finery sharply different from the old lady, but having something strangely in common with her in the vitality of her manner, was Ruth Treneglos. One felt that she might be no beauty but that she too would take some killing off when the time came.

Next to her was Demelza, who had just finished her third glass of port and was feeling better every minute; and beyond her Ross stood, a little withdrawn, glancing now and then from one to another of the company with his blue-grey unquiet eyes. John Treneglos was half listening to the music, half goggling at Demelza, who seemed to have a peculiar fascination for him.

The music came to a stop, and Elizabeth leaned back, smiling at Ross. Applause was on a quieter note than could have been expected ten minutes ago. The harp music had touched at something more fundamental than their high spirits. It had spoken not of Christmas jollity and fun but of love and sorrow, of human life, its strange beginning and its inevitable end.

'Superb!' declared George. 'We were more than repaid for a ride twenty times as long. Elizabeth, you pluck at my heartstrings.'

'Bravo!' said John, and the others joined in.

'Elizabeth,' said Verity. 'Play me that *canzonetta* as an encore, please. I love it.'

'It is not good unless it is sung.'

'Yes, yes, it is. Play it as you played it last Sunday night.'

Silence fell again. Elizabeth played something very short by Mozart and then a Canzonetta by Haydn.

There was silence when this was over before anyone spoke.

'It is my favourite,' said Verity. 'I cannot hear it often enough.'

'They're all my favourites,' said George. 'And played like an angel. One more, I beg you.'

'No,' said Elizabeth, smiling. 'It is Demelza's turn. She will sing for us now.'

'After that I could not,' said Demelza, whom the last piece and the strong wine had much affected. 'I was praying to God you had forgotten me.'

Everyone laughed.

'We must hear this and go,' said Ruth with an eye on her husband. 'Please, Mistress Poldark, overcome your modesty and satisfy us as to your attainments. We are all agog.'

Demelza's eyes met those of the other girl and seemed to see in them a challenge. She rose to it. The port had given her Dutch courage.

'Well . . .'

With mixed feelings Ross saw her walk across to the harp and sit down at the seat Elizabeth had left. She could not play a note on the instrument, but the instinct was sound which persuaded her to take up this position: the others were grouped round it to listen and she was saved the awkwardness of standing with nothing to do with her hands. But ten minutes ago was the time when she should have sung, when everyone was jolly and prepared to join in. Elizabeth's cultured, delicate playing had changed the atmosphere. The anticlimax would be certain.

Demelza settled herself comfortably, straightening her back, and plucked at a string with her finger. The note it gave out was pleasing and reassuring. Contrast with Elizabeth: gone was the halo and in its place the dark crown of humanity.

She looked at Ross; in her eyes was a demon of mischief. She began to sing.

Her slightly husky voice, almost contralto, an imperceptible fraction off the note, and sweet-toned, made no effort to impress by volume, rather it seemed to confide as a personal message what it had to say.

> '*I d' pluck a fair rose for my love;*
> *I d' pluck a red rose blowing.*
> *Love's in my heart a-trying so to prove*
> *What your heart's knowing.*

> '*I d' pluck a finger on a thorn,*
> *I d' pluck a finger bleeding.*
> *Red is my heart a-wounded and forlorn*
> *And your heart needing.*

'*I d' hold a finger to my tongue,*
I d' hold a finger waiting.
My heart is sore until it joins in song
Wi' your heart mating.'

There was a moment's pause, and Demelza coughed to show that she had done. There came murmurs of praise, some of it merely polite but some of it spontaneous.

'Very charming,' said Francis, through half-closed lids.

'Egad,' said John Treneglos with a sigh. 'I liked that.'

'Egad,' said Demelza, sparkling at him. 'I was afeared you might not.'

'A sharp answer, ma'am,' said Treneglos. He was just beginning to realize why Ross had committed the solecism of marrying his kitchenmaid. 'Have you any more of the same?'

'Songs or answers, sir?' asked Demelza.

'I have not heard that piece before,' said Elizabeth. 'I am much taken with it.'

'Songs, I meant, chit,' said Treneglos, putting his feet up. 'I know you have the answers.'

'John,' said his wife. 'It is time we were going.'

'I am comfortable here. Thank you, Verity. A good body this port has, Francis. When did you get it?'

Francis roused himself to take a glass. 'Trencrom's firm. Their stuff has been less good of late. I must make a change.'

'I bought some passable port the other day,' said George. 'Regrettably tax had been paid and it ran me in for near on three guineas for thirteen quart bottles.'

Francis raised an ironical eyebrow. George was a good friend and an indulgent creditor, but he could not refrain from bringing into a conversation the price he had paid for things. It was almost the only sign left of his origins.

'How do you contrive for servants now, Elizabeth?' Ruth asked, her voice carrying. 'I have the utmost difficulty. Mama was saying this morning that there was really no satisfying 'em. The young generation, she was saying, have such *ideas*, always wishing to rise above their station.'

'One more song, Demelza, please,' Verity interposed. 'What was that you were wont to play when I stayed with you? You remember, the seiner's song.'

'I like them all,' said John. 'Damme, I had no idea we was in such gifted company.'

Demelza drained her newly filled glass. Her fingers went over the strings of the harp and made a surprising sound.

'I have another,' she said gently. She looked at Ross a moment, then at Treneglos from under her lashes. The wine she had drunk had lit up her eyes. Half the devils from a Cornish moor had got into them.

She began to sing, very low but very clear.

> '*I suspicioned she was pretty*
> *I suspicioned she was wed,*
> *My father telled me twas against the law.*
> *I saw that she was coxy,*
> *No loving here by proxy,*
> *As pretty a piece of mischief as never I saw.*
>
> '*With no intentions meaning*
> *I called at candleteening:*
> *All's fair they say in love as well as war.*
> *My good intentions dropped me,*
> *No father's warning stopped me,*
> *As pretty a piece of mischief as never I saw.*'

Here she paused, then opened her eyes for a second at John Treneglos before she sang the last verse.

> '*The nest was warm around us,*
> *No spouse came home and found us,*
> *Our youth it was as sweet as it was raw.*
> *And now the cuckoo's homing*
> *A-tired of his roaming.*
> *As pretty a piece of mischief as never I saw.*'

John Treneglos roared and slapped his thighs. Even the sophisticated Francis was laughing. Demelza helped herself to another glass of port.

'Bravo!' said George. 'I like that song. It has a pleasant tripping sound. Well sung indeed!'

Ruth rose. 'Come, John. It will be to-morrow before we reach home.'

'Nonsense, my dear.' John tugged at the fob attached to his chronometer, but the watch would not come out of its deep pocket. 'Has anyone the time? It cannot be ten yet.'

'You did not like my song, ma'am?' Demelza asked, addressing Ruth.

Ruth's lips moved a fraction. 'Indeed, yes. I found it most enlightening.'

'It is the half after nine,' said Warleggan.

'Indeed, ma'am,' said Demelza, 'I am surprised you d' need enlightening on such a matter.'

Ruth went white at the nostrils. It is to be doubted whether Demelza understood the full flavour of her remark. But with five large glasses of port inside her she was not given to weighing the pros and cons of a retort before she made it. She felt Ross come up behind her; his hand touch her arm.

'It was not of the matter I was speaking.' Ruth's gaze went past her. 'May I congratulate you, Ross, on a wife so very skilled in all the arts of entertainment.'

'Not skilled,' said Ross, squeezing Demelza's arm, 'but a very quick learner.'

'The choice of tutor means so much, does it not.'

'Oh yes,' agreed Demelza. 'Ross is so kind he could charm the sourest of us into a show o' manners.'

Ruth patted her arm. She had the opening she wanted. 'I don't think you are quite the best judge of that yet, my dear.'

Demelza looked at her and nodded. 'No. Mebbe I should have said all but the sourest.'

Before the exchange became still more deadly Verity interposed. The visitors were moving off. Even John was at last levered from his chair. They all drifted out into the hall.

Amid much laughter and last-minute talk cloaks were put on and Ruth changed her delicate slippers for buckle riding shoes. Her new-fashioned riding cloak had to be admired. A full half hour passed while affectionate good-byes and seasonal wishes were given and received, jokes made and replied to. At last, to the clop and clatter of hooves, the party moved off down the drive, and the big door banged. The Poldarks were alone again.

Chapter ten

ALL THINGS REVIEWED, it had been Demelza's evening. She had come through a searching test with quite remarkable success. The fact that the success was due partly to nausea at the dinner table and partly to five glasses of port at a crucial stage of the evening was known only to her, and she kept it to herself.

As they said good night to their relatives two hours later and mounted the broad portrait-hung stairs, Ross was conscious of this new side of her nature which his wife had shown. All through the evening surprise had mingled with his inner amusement. Demelza's charm, almost beauty, in her new and fashionable dress; the impression she had created; her quiet unassuming dignity over the dinner, when he had expected her to be nervous and stiff or boisterous and hungry. Demelza among the unexpected arrivals, giving as good as she got without compromising her dignity, singing those saucy songs in her low husky voice with its soft native burr. Demelza flirting with John Treneglos under Ruth's very nose – under Ross's own too for that matter.

Demelza being kept with difficulty and tact away from the port when the visitors had gone. (While they were at limited loo, which the girl could not play, he had watched her edge round the room and pour herself out a couple of glasses on the sly.) Demelza now mounting the broad stairs sedately beside him, erect and unruffled in her mauve and apple-green silk, from which emerged her strong slender neck and white shoulders like the white inner heart of a flower.

Demelza more detached from him than he had ever known her. To-night he had withdrawn from her, had seen her with a new eye. Here against the background which was strange to her but which for him had the most definite of associations and standards, she had proved herself and was not found wanting. He was not sorry now that he had come. He remembered Elizabeth's words: 'You must take her into society and bring her out.' Even that might not be impossible if she wished it. A new life might be opening for them both. He felt pleased and stimulated and proud of the developing character of his young wife.

His young wife hiccupped slightly as they reached their bedroom. She too was feeling different from what she had ever felt before. She felt like a jug of fermenting cider, full of bubbles and air, lightheaded, bilious, and as uninterested in sleep as Ross. She gazed round the handsome room with its cream-and-pink flock paper and its brocaded curtains.

'Ross,' she said. 'I wish those birds was not so spotty. Missel thrushes was never so spotty as they. If they wish to paint spots on birds on curtains, why don't they paint the spots the right colour? No bird ever had pink spots. Nor no bird was ever as spotty as they.'

She leaned against Ross, who leaned back against the door he had just closed and patted her cheek.

'You're tipsy, child.'

'Indeed I'm not.' She regained her balance and walked with cool dignity across the room. She sat rather heavily in a chair before the fire and kicked off her shoes. Ross lit the rest of the candles from the one he carried and after an interval they burned up, lighting the whole room.

Demelza sat there, her arms behind her head, her toes stretched towards the fire, while Ross slowly undressed. They exchanged a casual word from time to time, laughed together over Ross's account of Treneglos's antics with the spinning wheel; Demelza questioned him about Ruth, about the Teagues, about George Warleggan. Their voices were low and warm and confidential. This was the intimacy of pure companionship.

The house had fallen quiet about them. Although they were not sleepy, the pleasant warmth and comfort turned their senses imperceptibly towards sleep. Ross had a moment of unspoiled satisfaction. He received love and gave it in equal and generous measure. Their relationship at that moment had no flaw.

In Francis's dressing gown he sat down on the stool beside her chair and stretched his hands towards the glow of the fire.

There was silence.

Presently out of the fount of Demelza's content sprang an old resolve.

'Did I behave myself to-night, Ross?' she asked. 'Did I behave as Mrs Poldark should behave?'

'You misbehaved monstrously,' he said, 'and were a triumph.'

'Don't tease. You think I have been a good wife?'

'Moderately good. Quite moderately good.'

'Did I sing nice?'

'You were inspired.'

Silence fell again.

'Ross.'

'Yes, bud?'

'Bud again,' she said. 'To-night I have been called both Bud and Blossom. I hope in a few years' time they will not start calling me Pod.'

He laughed, silently but long.

'Ross,' she said again, when he had at last done.

'Yes?'

'If I have been a good wife, then you must promise me somethin'.'

'Very well,' he said.

'You must promise me that sometime before – before Easter you will ride to Falmouth and seek Captain Blamey out and see if he still loves Verity.'

There was a moment's pause.

'How am I to tell whom he loves?' Ross asked ironically. He was far too contented to argue with her.

'Ask him. You was his friend. He will not lie about a thing like that.'

'And then?'

'If he still loves her we can arrange for them to meet.'

'And then?'

'Then we shan't need to do any more.'

'You're very persistent, are you not.'

'Only because you're that stubborn.'

'We cannot arrange other people's lives for them.'

Demelza hiccupped.

'You have no heart,' she said. 'That's what I can't fathom. You love me but you have no heart.'

'I'm deeply fond of Verity, but——'

'Ah, your buts! You've no faith, Ross. You men don't understand. You don't know the teeniest thing about Verity! That you don't.'

'Do you?'

'I don't need to. I know myself.'

'Conceive the fact that there may be women unlike you.'

'Pom-ti-pom!' said Demelza. 'You don't scare me wi' your big words. I know Verity was not born to be an old maid, dryin' up and shrivellin' while she looks to someone else's house an' children. She'd rather take the risk of being wed to a man who couldn't contain his liquor.' She bent forward and began to pull off her stockings.

He watched her. 'You seem to have developed a whole philosophy since you married me, child.'

'No I ain't – haven't,' said Demelza. 'But I know what love is.'

The remark seemed to put the discussion on a different plane.

'Yes,' he agreed soberly. 'So do I.'

A longer silence fell.

'If you love someone,' said Demelza, 'tesn't a few bruises on the back that are going to count. It's whether that other one loves you in return. If he do, then he can only hurt your body. He can't hurt your heart.'

She rolled her stockings into a ball and leaned back in the chair again, wiggling her toes towards the fire. Ross picked up the poker and turned over the ash and embers until they broke into a blaze.

'So you'll go to Falmouth an' see?' she asked.

'I'll consider it,' said Ross. 'I'll consider it.'

Having come this far, she was too wise to press further. Another and less elevated lesson she had learned in married life was that if she wheedled long enough and discreetly enough she quite often got her own way in the end.

With ears grown more sharp to the smaller sounds, it seemed to them that the silence of the house was less complete than it had been awhile ago. It had become the faint stirring silence of old timber and slate, old in the history of Poldarks and Trenwiths, people whose forgotten faces hung in the deserted hall, whose forgotten loves and hopes had drawn breath and flourished here. Jeffrey Trenwith, building this house in fire and faith; Claude, deeply involved in the Prayer Book Rebellion; Humphrey in his Elizabethan ruff; Charles Vivian Poldark, wounded and home from the sea; red-haired Anna-Maria; Presbyterian Joan; mixed policies and creeds; generations of children, instant with the joy of life, growing and learning and fading. The full silence of the old house was more potent than the empty silence of its youth. Panels still felt the brush of mouldered silk, boards still creaked under the pressure of the forgotten foot. For a time something stepped between the man and the girl sitting at the fire. They felt it and it left them apart from each other and alone with their thoughts.

But even the strength of the past could not just then break their companionship for long. Somehow, and because of the nature of their being, the old peculiar silence ceased to be a barrier and became a medium. For a moment they had been overawed by time. Then time again became their friend.

'Are you asleep?' Ross said.

'No,' said Demelza.

Then she moved and put her finger on his arm.

He rose slowly and bent over her, took her face in his hands and kissed her on the eyes, the mouth, and the forehead. With a queer tigerish limpness she allowed him to do what he wanted.

And presently the white inner heart of the bud was free of its petals.

Only then did she put up her hands to his face and kiss him in return.

Chapter eleven

THEY WENT HOME the following day after an early dinner, walking as they had come, by way of the cliff path and Sawle Village and Nampara Cove. They had said good-bye to their relatives, and were again alone, striding off together over the heather-covered moor.

For a time they talked as they had talked last night, desultorily, confidentially, laughing together and silent. There had been rain this morning, heavy and windless, but it had stopped while they were at dinner and the sky had cleared. Now clouds had gathered again. There was a heavy ground swell.

Demelza was so glad that her ordeal was over, and decently even triumphantly over, that she took his arm and began to sing. She took big masculine strides to keep up with his, but every now and then would have to give a little skip to make good lost ground. She fitted these in with her song so that her voice gave an upward skip at the same time as her feet.

> 'As I sat on a sunny bank
> On Christmas (hop) Day
> On Christmas (hop) Day,
> As I sat on a sunny bank
> On Christmas Day in the morning.
>
> 'I saw three ships come sailing (hop) in
> On Christmas Day
> On Christmas Day.
> I saw three ships come sailing (hop) in
> On Christmas Day in the morning.'

Before the sun set the black day broke on the horizon and sea and land were flooded with light. At the sudden warmth under the lowering clouds all the waves became disordered and ran in ragged confusion with heads tossing and glinting in the sun.

Demelza thought: I am nearer sure of him than I have ever been before. How ignorant I was that first June morning thinking everything was sure.

Even that August night after the pilchards came, even then there had been nothing to compare me with. All last summer I told myself it was as certain as anything could be. I felt sure. But last night was different. After a whole seven hours in Elizabeth's company he still wanted me at the end. After a talk all to themselves with her making eyes at him like a she-cat, he still came to me. Perhaps she isn't so bad. Perhaps she isn't such a cat. Perhaps I feel sorry for her. Why does Francis look so bored? Perhaps I feel sorry for her after all. Dear Verity helped. I hope my baby doesn't have codfish eyes like Geoffrey Charles. I believe I'm going thinner, not fatter. I hope nothing's wrong. I wish I didn't feel so sick. Ruth Treneglos is worse than Elizabeth. She didn't like me making up to her hare-and-hounds husband. As if I cared for him. Though I shouldn't like to meet him in a dark lane with nobody near. I think she was jealous of me in another way. Perhaps she wanted Ross to marry her. Anyway, I'm going home to *my* home, to bald Jud and fat Prudie and red-haired Jinny and long-legged Cobbledick, going home to get fat and ugly myself. And I don't care. Verity was right. He'll stick to me. Not because he ought to but because he wants to. Mustn't forget Verity. I'll scheme like a serpent. I would dearly love to go to one of George Warleggan's card parties. I wonder if I ever shall. I wonder if Prudie's remembered to meat the calves. I wonder if she burned the heavy cake. I wonder if it's going to rain. Dear life, I wonder if I'm going to be sick.

They reached Sawle, crossed the shingle bar and climbed the hill at the other side.

'Are you tired?' Ross asked, as she seemed to lag.

'No, no.' It was the first time he had ever asked that.

The sun had gone down now, and the brows of the sky were dark. After their brief carnival the waves had reassembled and rode in showing long green caverns as they curved to break.

And Ross again knew himself to be happy – in a new and less ephemeral way than before. He was filled with a queer sense of enlightenment. It seemed to him that all life had moved to this pinpoint of time down the scattered threads of twenty years; from his own childhood running thoughtless and barefoot in the sun on Hendrawna sands, from Demelza's birth in the squalor of a mining cottage, from the plains of Virginia and the trampled fairgrounds of Redruth, from the complex impulses which had governed Elizabeth's choice of Francis and from the simple philosophies of Demelza's own faith, all had been animated to a common end – and that end a moment of enlightenment and understanding and completion. Someone – a Latin poet – had defined eternity as no more than this: to hold and possess the whole fulness of life in one moment, here and now, past and present and to come.

He thought: if we could only *stop* life for a while I would stop here. Not when I get home, not leaving Trenwith, but here, here reaching the top of the hill out of Sawle, dusk wiping out the edges of the land and Demelza walking and humming at my side.

He knew of things plucking at his attention. All existence was a cycle of difficulties to be met and obstacles to be surmounted. But at this evening hour of Christmas Day, 1787, he was not concerned with the future, only with the present. He thought: I am not hungry or thirsty or lustful or envious; I am not perplexed or weary or ambitious or remorseful. Just ahead, in the immediate future, there is waiting an open door and a warm house, comfortable chairs and quietness and companionship. Let me hold it.

In the slow dusk they skirted Nampara Cove and began the last short climb beside the brook towards the house.

Demelza began to sing, mischievously and in a deep voice:

> *'There was an old couple and they was poor,*
> *Tweedle, tweedle, go twee.'*

DEMELZA

A Novel of Cornwall 1788–1790

Book one

Chapter one

THERE COULD HAVE been prophecy in the storm that blew up at the time of Julia's birth.

May month was not a time for heavy gales, but the climate of Cornwall is capricious as any child ever born. It had been a kindly enough spring, as kindly as the summer and winter that had gone before it; mild, soft, comfortable weather; and the land was already heavy with green things. Then May broke rainy and gusty, and the blossom suffered here and there and the hay leaned about looking for support.

On the night of the fifteenth Demelza felt her first pains. Even then for a while she gripped the bedpost and thought the matter all round before she said anything. All along she had viewed the coming ordeal with a calm and philosophical mind and had never troubled Ross with false alarms. She did not want to begin so late. Last evening she had been out in her beloved garden, digging round the young plants; then as it was going dark she had found a disgruntled hedgehog and had played with him, trying to persuade him to take some bread and milk, and had only come in reluctantly as the sky clouded and it went cold.

This now – this thing in the middle of the night – might yet be only the result of getting overtired.

But when it began to feel as if someone was kneeling on her backbone and trying to break it, she knew it was not. She touched Ross's arm and he woke instantly.

'Well?'

'I think,' she said, 'I think you will have to fetch Prudie.'

He sat up. 'Why? What is it?'

'I have a pain.'

'Where? Do you mean . . .'

'I have a pain,' she said primly. 'I think twould be as well to fetch Prudie.'

He climbed quickly out of bed, and she listened to the scratch of flint and steel. After a moment the tinder caught and he lit a candle. The room flickered into view: heavy teak beams, the curtain over the door moving gently in the breeze, the low window seat hung with pink grogram, her shoes as she had kicked them off, one wooden sole upmost, Joshua's spyglass, Ross's pipe, Ross's book and a fly crawling.

He looked at her and at once knew the truth. She smiled a pallid apology. He went across to the table by the door and poured her a glass of brandy.

'Drink this. I will send Jud for Dr Choake.' He began to pull on his clothes, anyhow.

'No, no, Ross; do not send yet. It is the middle of the night. He will be asleep.'

Whether Thomas Choake should be called in to her had been a dissension between them for some weeks. Demelza could not forget that twelve months ago she had been a maidservant and that Choake, though only a physician, owned a small estate which, even if it had been bought with his wife's money, put him on a level from which the likes of her would be seen as unimportant chattels. That was until Ross married her. Since then she had grown to her position. She could put on a show of refinement and good manners, and not at all a bad show at that; but a doctor was different. A doctor caught one at a disadvantage. If the pain was bad she would almost certainly swear in the old way she had learned from her father, not a few genteel 'damn mes' and 'by Gods,' as anyone might excuse from a lady in trouble. To have a baby and be forced to act genteel at the same time was more than Demelza could look forward to.

Besides, she didn't want a man about. It wasn't decent. Her cousin-in-law, Elizabeth, had had him, but Elizabeth was an aristocrat born and bred, and they looked at things different. *She* would far rather have had old Aunt Betsy Triggs from Mellin, who sold pilchards and was a rare strong hand when it came to babies.

But Ross was the more determined and he had had his way. She was not unprepared for his curt, 'Then he shall be woke,' as he left the room.

'*Ross!*' She called him back. For the moment the pain had gone.

'Yes?' His strong, scarred, introspective face was half lit by the candle; the upgrowing dark hair was ruffled and hardly showed its hint of copper; his shirt was open at the throat. This man . . . aristocrat of them all, she thought . . . this man, so reserved and reserving, with whom she had shared rare intimacy . . .

'Would you?' she said. 'Before you go . . .'

He came back to the bed. The emergency had come on him so quickly in sleep that he had had no time yet to feel anything but alarm that her time was here and relief that it might soon be over. As he kissed her he saw the moisture on her face and a worm of fear and compassion moved in him. He took her face in his hands, pushed back the black hair and stared a moment into the dark eyes of his young wife. They were not dancing and mischievous as they so often were, but there was no fear in them.

'I'll be back. In a moment I'll be back.'

She made a gesture of dissent. 'Don't come back, Ross. Go and tell

Prudie, that's all. I'd rather – you didn't see me like this.'

'And what of Verity? You specially wanted Verity here.'

'Tell her in the morning. Tisn't fair to bring her out in the night air. Send for her in the morning.'

He kissed her again.

'Tell me that you love me, Ross,' she said.

He looked at her in surprise.

'You know I do!'

'And say you don't love Elizabeth.'

'And I don't love Elizabeth.' What else was he to say when he did not know the truth himself? He was not a man who spoke his inmost feelings easily, but now he saw himself powerless to help her, and only words of his and not actions would give her aid. 'Nothing else matters but you,' he said. 'Remember that. All my relatives and friends – and Elizabeth, and this house and the mine . . . I'd throw them in the dust and you know it – and you know it. If you don't know it, then all these months I've failed and no words I can give you now will make it otherwise. I love you, Demelza, and we've had such happiness. And we're going to have it again. Take hold of that, my sweet. Hold it and keep it, for no one else can.'

'I'll hold it, Ross,' she said, content because the words had come.

He kissed her again and turned and lit more candles; took up one and went quickly out of the room, the hot grease running over his hand. The wind had dropped since yesterday; there was only a breeze. He did not know the time, but it felt about two.

He pushed open the door on the other side of the landing and went across to the bedroom where Jud and Prudie slept. The ill-fitting bedroom door opened with a long squeak which merged into Prudie's slow rasping snore. He grunted in disgust, for the hot close sweaty smell offended his nose. The night air might be dangerous, but they could surely open the window during the day and let this stink out.

He went across and parted the curtains and shook Jud by the shoulder. Jud's two great teeth showed like gravestones. He shook again, violently. Jud's nightcap came off and a spot of the candle grease fell on his bald patch. Jud woke. He began to curse; then he saw who it was and sat up rubbing his head.

'What's amiss?'

'Demelza is ill.' How call her anything but Demelza to a man who had been here when she came as a tattered waif of thirteen? 'I want you to go for Dr Choake at once. And wake Prudie. She will be wanted too.'

'What's amiss with her?'

'Her pains have begun.'

'Oh, that. I thought ee said she were ill.' Jud frowned at the piece of cooling tallow he had found on his head. 'Prudie and me could manage that. Prudie d'know all that sort of panjandle. Tedn a 'ard thing to learn.

Why, there's always such a dido about en I never can conceit. Tedn easy, mind, but once you've gotten the knack——'

'Get up.'

Jud came out of bed, knowing the tone, and they woke Prudie. Her great shiny face peered through its tangle of greasy black hair as she wiped her nose on a corner of her night rail.

'Aw, my dear, I'll see to the mite. Poor maid.' She began to fasten a pair of filthy stays over her shift. 'I d'know how twas with my mother. She telled me how twas when I was on the brew. Shifted I 'ad. Moved I 'ad. Twas a cruel chronic thing, they said. A weak, ailing little mouse, an' nobody believed I'd see the christening pot. . . .'

'Go to her as soon as you can,' Ross said. 'I'll get Darkie from the stables. You won't want her saddled.'

'Mebbe I can ride bare-ridged that far,' Jud said grudgingly. 'Though if once you d'make a slip in the dark, like as not you're pitched off on yer 'ead, and then snap goes yer neck and where are you?'

Ross ran down the stairs. On his way out he looked in at the new clock they had bought for the parlour. It wanted ten minutes to three. Dawn would not be long. Things were so much worse by candlelight.

In the stable he delayed to saddle Darkie, telling his fumbling fingers that every woman went through this: it became a commonplace of their existence, pregnancies following each other like the summer seasons. But he would see Jud safely off; if the fool slipped he might be hours. He would have gone himself if he could have trusted the Paynters alone with Demelza.

At the front of the house Jud was fastening his breeches under the lilac tree.

'Don't know as I shall rightly see me way,' he said. 'Dark as a blathering sack, tis. By rights I should 'ave a lantern on a pole. A long pole as I could 'old out——'

'Get up or you'll have the pole across your head.'

Jud mounted. 'What's to say as he won't come?'

'Bring him,' said Ross, and gave Darkie a slap across the haunches.

When Jud turned in at the gates of Fernmore, the house of Thomas Choake, he observed disdainfully that the building was little more than a farmhouse, though they put on airs as if it was Blenheim. He got down and rat-tatted at the door. The house was surrounded by big pine trees, and the rooks and jackdaws were already awake, flying round in circles and being noisy. Jud raised his head and sniffed. All yesterday they'd been unsettled at Nampara.

At the seventh knock a window screeched above the door, and a nightcap appeared like a cuckoo out of a clock.

'Well, man, well, man! What is it? What's the damnation noise?'

Jud knew by the voice and eyebrows that he had flushed the right bird.

'Cap'n Poldark sent me for to fetch ee,' he said, mumbling. 'Dem – um – Mistress Poldark's took bad and they d'need you.'

'What Mistress Poldark, man? What Mistress Poldark?'

'Mistress Demelza Poldark. Over to Nampara. 'Er that be going to have 'er first.'

'Well, what's wrong? Didn't they say what was to do?'

'Ais. Tes her time.'

'Nonsense, fellow. I saw her last week and I told Captain Poldark that there would be nothing until June. Go tell them I stand by that opinion.'

The window slammed.

Jud Paynter was a man much interested in the malign indifference of man and providence to his own needs, and interested in not much else; but sometimes an accident roused him for other ends. This was one of the accidents. From feeling disgruntled at the simpering softness of Demelza and the misplaced harshness of Ross in turning him out on a bitter May morning without so much as a tot of rum, he came to reflect that Ross was his master and Demelza one of his own kind.

Three minutes later Dr Choake put out his head again.

'What is it, man? You'll have the door down!'

'I was told to fetch you.'

'You insolent fellow! I'll have you thrashed for this!'

'Where's yer 'orse? I'll 'ave him out while you put yer drawers on.'

The surgeon withdrew. Polly Choake's lisping voice could be heard in the background, and once her fluffy head passed the window. They were in consultation. Then Choake called down coldly:

'You must wait, fellow. We shall be with you in ten minutes.'

Jud was sufficiently alive to the surgeon's peculiarities to know that by this Choake meant only himself.

Twenty-one minutes later, in icy silence, they set off. The rooks were still flying in circles and cawing, and at Sawle Church there was a great noise. Day was breaking. Streaks of watered green showed in the north-east, and the sky where the sun would rise was a bold pale orange behind the black ribs of the night. A wild sunrise and a strangely quiet one. After the winds of the last days the calm was profound. As they passed Grambler Mine they overtook a party of bal-maidens singing as they walked to work, their shrill fresh voices as sweet and young as the morning. Jud noticed that Will Nanfan's sheep were all gathered together in the most sheltered corner of the field.

Reflection on the quiet ride salved some of Dr Choake's annoyance, for when they reached Nampara he did not complain, but greeted Ross stiffly and lumbered upstairs. There he found that the alarm was not a false one. He sat with Demelza for half an hour telling her to be brave and that there was nothing to be frightened of. Then, because she seemed constrained and was sweating a lot, he suspected a touch of fever and bled her to be on the safe side. This made her feel very ill, a result which pleased him for it proved, he said, that a toxic condition had existed and his treatment had brought on a normal and desirable intermission of the fever. If she took an infusion of bark once an hour it would prevent a renewal. Then he went home to breakfast.

Ross had been swilling himself under the pump trying to wash away the megrims of the night, and when he came through the house and saw a thickset figure riding up the valley he called sharply to Jinny Carter, who came every day to work in the house and had just arrived.

'Is that Dr Choake?'

Jinny bent over her own child, which she brought on her back and kept in a basket in the kitchen. 'Yes, sur. He d'say the baby won't be afore dinner at the early side, and he say he'll be back by nine or ten.'

Ross turned away to hide his annoyance. Jinny looked at him with devoted eyes.

'Who helped you with your babies, Jinny?' he asked.

'Mother, sur.'

'Will you go and get her, Jinny? I think I would trust your mother before that old fool.'

She blushed with pleasure. 'Yes, sur. I'll go right off. She'll be that glad to come.' She started as if to go and then looked at her own baby.

'I'll see she comes to no harm,' Ross said.

She glanced at him a moment in pleased embarrassment and then snatched up her white bonnet and left the kitchen.

Ross walked into the low hall, stood at the foot of the stairs, disliked the silence, went into the parlour and poured himself a glass of brandy, watched Jinny's brisk figure dwindling towards Mellin, returned to the kitchen. Little Kate had not moved, but lay on her back kicking and crowing and laughing at him. This mite was nine months old and had never seen its father, who was serving a two-year sentence in Bodmin Gaol for poaching. Unlike the two eldest, who took after their father, little Kate was a true Martin: sandy hair, blue eyes, tiny freckles already mottling the bridge of her button nose.

The fire had not been lighted this morning, and there was no sign of breakfast. Ross raked the ashes but they were dead; he picked up some kindling wood and set about lighting it, wondering irritably where Jud had gone. There must be hot water, he knew, and towels and basins; nothing was being prepared down here. Damn Choake for his impertinence, not even waiting to see him before he left.

Relations between the two men had been cool for some time. Ross disliked his inane wife, who had gossiped and whispered about Demelza; and when Ross disliked someone he found it hard to hide the fact. Now he fumed that he should be at the mercy of this obstinate stiff-necked unprogressive old fool who was the only physician within miles.

As the fire began to take Jud came in, and wind came with him and rushed round the kitchen.

'Thur's something blowing up,' he said, eyeing Ross out of bloodshot eyes. 'Seen the long black swell, 'ave ee?'

Ross nodded impatiently. There had been a heavy ground sea since afternoon yesterday.

'Well, tes breaking all ways. Scarcely ever did I see the like. It might be as someone was lashin' of un with a whip. The swell's nigh gone and the sea's all licky–white like Joe Trigg's beard.'

'Keep your eye on Kate, Jud,' Ross said. 'Make some breakfast in the meantime. I am going upstairs.'

At the back of his mind Ross was aware of the sound of wind rushing about in the distance. Once when he glanced out of the bedroom window his eyes confirmed that the swell had in fact quite broken up and the sea was stippled with white-lipped waves which crossed and recrossed each other in confusion, running heedlessly, colliding and breaking up into wisps of futile spray. The wind was as yet only gusty on the land, but here and there eddies rushed over the water, little winds, vicious and lost.

While he was there Demelza made a big effort to be normal, but he saw that she wished him gone. He could not help her.

Disconsolate, he went down again and was in time to greet Mrs Zacky Martin, Jinny's mother. Flat-faced, competent, bespectacled and sneezing, she came into the kitchen with a brood of five small children dragging at her heels, talking to them, chiding them, explaining to Ross that she had no one to trust them with – Jinny's two eldest and her three youngest – greeting Jud and asking after Prudie, commenting on the smell of frying pork, enquiring about the patient, saying she had a touch of ague herself but had taken a posset before leaving, rolling up her sleeves, telling Jinny to put the colewort and the motherwort on to brew, they being better than any doctor's nostrums for easing of the maid, and disappearing up the stairs before anyone else could speak.

There seemed to be a child on every chair in the kitchen. They sat like timid ninepins at a fair, waiting to be knocked off. Jud scratched his head and spat in the fire and swore.

Ross went back to the parlour. On the table was a bundle of crochet work that Demelza had been doing last night. A fashion paper which Verity had lent her lay beside it – something new and novel come to them from London; there had never been anything like it before. The room was a little dusty and unkempt.

It was fifteen minutes after six.

No birds singing this morning. A moment ago a ray of sunlight had fallen across the grass, but had been quickly put out. He stared at the elm trees, which were waving backwards and forwards as if with an earth tremor. The apple trees, more sheltered, were bending and turning up their leaves. The sky was heavy with racing clouds.

He picked up a book. His eyes scanned the page but took nothing in. The wind was beginning to roar down the valley. Mrs Zacky came in.

'Well?'

'She'm doing brave, Cap'n Ross. Prudie and me'll manage, don't ee worry an inch. Twill all be over long before ole Dr Tommie d'come back.'

Ross put down the book. 'Are you sure?

'Well, I've had eleven o' my own and there's three of Jinny's. And I helped wi' two of Betty Nanfan's twins and four of Sue Vigus's, the first three out of wedlock.' Mrs Zacky hadn't fingers enough to count. 'This won't be easy, not like Jinny's was, but we'll do a proper job, never you fear. Now I'll go get the brandy an' give the maid a tot o' that t'ease her up.'

The house suddenly shuddered under a gust of wind. Ross stood staring out at the wild day, anger with Choake rising in him and seeking outlet like a part of the storm. Common sense told him that Demelza would be all right, but that she should be denied the best attention was intolerable. It was Demelza who suffered there, with only two clumsy old women to help her.

He went out to the stables, hardly aware of the storm that was rising about them.

At the stable door he glanced over Hendrawna and saw that clouds of spray had begun to lift off the sea and drift away like sand before a sandstorm. Here and there the cliffs were smoking.

He had just got the stable door open when the wind took it out of his hand, slammed it shut and pushed him against the wall. He looked up and saw that it would not be possible to ride a horse in the gale.

He set off to walk. It was only a matter of two miles.

A hail of leaves and grass and dirt and small twigs met him as he turned the corner of the house. Behind him the wind was tearing off mouthfuls of sea and flinging them to join the clouds. At another time he would have been upset at the damage to his crops, but now that seemed a small matter. It was not so much a gale as a sudden storm, as if the forces of a gathering anger had been bottled up for a month and must be spent in an hour. The branch of an elm came down across the stream. He stumbled past it, wondering if he could make the brow of the hill.

In the ruined buildings of Wheal Maiden he sat and gasped and groped for breath and rubbed his bruised hand, and the wind blew bits of masonry from the gaunt old granite walls and screamed like a harlot through every slit and hole.

Once through the pine trees, he met the full force of the storm coming in across Grambler Plain, bringing with it a bombardment of rain and dirt and gravel. Here it seemed that all the loose soil was being ploughed up and all the fresh young leaves and all the other small substances of the earth were being blown right away. The clouds were low over his head, brown and racing, all the rain emptied out of them and lying like torn rags before the frown of God.

Down in Fernmore, Dr Choake was beginning his breakfast.

He had finished the grilled kidneys and the roast ham and was wondering whether to take a little of the smoked cod before it was carried away to be kept warm for his wife, who would breakfast in bed later. The early ride had made him very hungry, and he had set up a great commotion because breakfast was not waiting when he returned. Choake believed servants should not be allowed to get fat and lazy.

The loud knocking on the front door was hardly to be heard above the thunder of the wind.

'If that is anyone for me, Nancy,' he said testily, lowering his eyebrows, 'I am from home.'

'Yes, sir.'

He decided after a sniff to take some of the cod, and was irritated that it was necessary to help himself. This done, he settled his stomach against the table and had swallowed the first knifeful when there was an apologetic cough behind him.

'Begging your pardon, sir. Captain Poldark——'

'Tell him——' Dr Choake looked up and saw in the mirror a tall dripping figure behind his harassed maid.

Ross came into the room. He had lost his hat and torn the lace on the sleeve of his coat; water followed him in a trail across Dr Choake's best Turkey carpet.

But there was something in his eyes which prevented Choake from noticing this. The Poldarks had been Cornish gentlemen for two hundred years, and Choake, for all his airs, came from dubious stock.

He got up.

'I disturb your breakfast,' said Ross.

'We – er – hm . . . Is something wrong?'

'You'll remember,' said Ross, 'that I engaged you to be with my wife in her lying-in.'

'Well! She is going on well. I made a thorough examination. The child will be born this afternoon.'

'I engaged you as a surgeon to be in the house, not as a travelling pedlar.'

Choake went white round the lips. He turned on the gaping Nancy.

'Get Captain Poldark some port.'

Nancy fled.

'What's your complaint?' Choake made an effort to outstare his visitor; the fellow had no money and was still a mere youngster. 'We have attended your father, your uncle, your cousin and his wife, your cousin Verity. They have never found reason to call my treatment in question.'

'What they do is their own affair. Where is your cloak?'

'Man, I can't ride out in this gale of wind. Look at yourself! It would be impossible to sit a horse.'

'You should have thought of that when you left Nampara.'

The door opened and Polly Choake came in with her hair in pins and wearing a flowing cerise morning gown. She gave a squeal when she saw Ross.

'Oh, Captain Poldark. I'd no idea. Weally, to see one like this! But the wind upstairs, faith, it upthets one to hear it! I fear for the woof, Tom, that I do, an' if it came in on my head I should be a pwetty thight!'

'You're not a pretty sight peeping round the door,' snapped her husband irritably. 'Come in or go out as you please, but have the goodness to decide.'

Polly pouted and came in, and looked at Ross sidelong and patted her hair. The door slammed behind her.

'I never get used to your old Cornish winds, and thith ith a fair demon. Jenkin says there is five thlates off of the butterwy, and I doubt there'll not be more. How ith your wife, Captain Poldark?'

Choake slipped off his skullcap and put on his wig.

'That will not stand in the wind,' said Ross.

'You're not going out, Tom? But you could not wide and scarthely walk. An' think of the danger of falling twees!'

'Captain Poldark is nervous for his wife,' Choake said whitely.

'But thurely ith it that urgent tho thoon again? I wemember my mother said I was eight and forty hours a-coming.'

'Then your husband will be eight and forty hours a-waiting,' said Ross. 'It is a whim I have, Mrs Choake.'

Pettishly the surgeon flung off his purple-spotted morning gown and pulled on his tail coat. Then he stumped out to get his bag and his riding cloak, nearly upsetting Nancy, who was coming in with the port.

The wind was a little abeam of them on the return. Choake lost his wig and his hat, but Ross caught the wig and stuffed it under his coat. By the time they climbed the rise near Wheal Maiden they were both gasping and drenched. As they reached the trees they saw a slight figure in a grey cloak ahead of them.

'Verity,' said Ross as they overtook her leaning against a tree. 'You have no business out to-day.'

She gave him her wide-mouthed generous smile. 'You should know it can't be kept a secret. Mrs Zacky's Betty saw Jud and Dr Choake on her way to the mine, and she told Bartle's wife.' Verity leaned her wet face against the tree. 'Our cow shed is down and we have the two cows in the brewhouse. The headgear of Digory's mine has collapsed, but I think no one is hurt. How is she, Ross?'

'Well enough, I trust.' Ross linked his arm in Verity's and they began to walk after the stumbling, cloak-blown figure of the physician. He had often thought that if a man were allowed a second wife he would have asked his cousin, for her kindness and generosity and for the soothing effect she always had on him. Already he was beginning to feel shame-faced at his own anger. Tom Choake had his good points and naturally knew his job better than Mrs Zacky Martin.

They caught up with Choake as he was climbing over the fallen elm branch. Two of the apple trees were down, and Ross wondered what Demelza would say when she saw the remnants of her spring flowers.

When she did . . .

He quickened his pace. Some of his irritation returned at the thought of all the women milling about in the house and his beloved Demelza helpless and in pain. And Choake going off without a word.

As they entered they saw Jinny pattering up the stairs with a basin of steaming water, slopping some of it into the hall in her haste. She never even looked at them.

Dr Choake was so distressed that he went into the parlour and sat on the first chair and tried to get his breath. He glared at Ross and said:

'I'll thank you for my wig.'

Ross poured out three glasses of brandy. He took the first to Verity, who had collapsed in a chair, her fluffy dark hair contrasting with the wet streaks where the hood had not covered it. She smiled at Ross and said:

'I will go upstairs when Dr Choake is ready. Then if all goes well I will get you something to eat.'

Choake gulped down his brandy and passed his glass for more. Ross, knowing that liquor made him a better doctor, gave it him.

'We will breakfast together,' Choake said, more cheerful at the thought of food. 'We will just go up and set everyone's mind at rest; then we will breakfast. What have you for breakfast?'

Verity got up. Her cloak fell away and showed the plain grey dimity frock, the bottom eight inches embroidered with mud and rain. But it was at her face that Ross looked. She wore a full, uplifted, startled expression, as if she had seen a vision.

'What is it?'

'Ross, I thought I heard . . .'

They all listened.

'Oh,' said Ross harshly, 'there are children in the kitchen. There are children in the still-room and children for all I know in the clothes closet. Every age and size.'

Verity said: 'Ssh!'

Choake fumbled for his bag. All his movements were clumsy and he made a great deal of noise.

'That is not a grown child!' Verity said suddenly. 'That is not a grown child!'

They listened again.

'We must go to our patient,' said Choake, suddenly ill at ease and faintly sly. 'We shall be ready for breakfast when we come down.'

He opened the door. The others followed him, but at the foot of the stairs they all stopped.

Prudie was on the top step. She was still wearing her night shift, with a coat over it, and her great figure bulged like an overfull sack. She bent to look at them, her long pink face bulbous and shining.

'We've done it!' she shouted in her organ voice. 'Tes a gurl. We've gotten a gurl for ee. 'Andsomest little mite ever I saw. We've knocked her face about a small bit, but her's as lusty as a little nebby colt. Hear 'er screeching!'

After a moment's silence Choake cleared his throat portentously and put his foot on the bottom step. But Ross pushed him aside and went up the stairs first.

Chapter two

HAD JULIA KNOWN the difference she would have thought it a strange countryside into which she had been born.

For hours a blight had stalked across it. So much salt was in the terrible wind that nothing escaped. The young green leaves of the trees turned black and withered, and when a breeze moved them they rattled like dry biscuits. Even the dandelions and the nettles went black. The hay was damaged and the potato crop, and the young peas and beans shrivelled and died. The rosebuds never opened, and the stream was choked with the debris of a murdered spring.

But inside Nampara, in the little world made up of four walls and bright curtains and whispering voices, life was triumphant.

Having taken a good look at her baby, Demelza decided that the infant was complete and wonderful to behold, once her poor bruised little face righted itself. No one seemed to know how long this would take – Ross thought privately that there might be lasting marks – but Demelza, of a more sanguine temperament, looked at the bruises and then looked out at the ravaged landscape and decided that nature in her own good time would work wonders on both. They should postpone the christening until the end of July.

She had ideas about the christening. Elizabeth had had a party for Geoffrey Charles's christening. Demelza had not been there, for that was four years ago come November, when she was less than nothing in the eyes of the Poldark family; but she had never forgotten Prudie's tales of the fine people invited, the great bunches of flowers brought from Truro, the feast spread, the wine and the speeches. Now that she had made her own debut, however modestly, into such society, there was no reason why they should not give a party for *their* child, as good or even better.

She decided to have two parties if Ross could be talked into it.

She put this to him four weeks after Julia was born, as they were taking tea together on the lawn before the front door of Nampara, while Julia slept soundly in the shade of the lilac tree.

Ross looked at her with his quizzing, teasing glance.

'Two parties? We've not had twins.'

Demelza's dark eyes met his for a moment, then stared into the dregs of her cup.

'No, but there's your people and there's my people, Ross. The gentlefolk and the other folk. It wouldn't do to mix 'em, no more than you can't mix cream and – and onions. But they're both nice enough by themselves.'

'I'm partial to onions,' Ross said, 'but cream cloys. Let us have a party for the country people: the Zacky Martins, the Nanfans, the Daniels. They're worth far more than the overfed squires and their genteel ladies.'

Demelza threw a piece of bread to the ungainly dog squatting near.

'Garrick's no better looking for his fight wi' Mr Treneglos's bull,' she said. 'I'm certain sure he's got some teeth left, but he d'swallow his food like a sea gull and expect his stomach to do the chewing.'

Garrick wagged his two-inch stump at this notice.

'Here,' said Demelza, 'let me see.'

'We could gather a very nice picking of the country folk,' said Ross. 'Verity would come too. She is just as fond of them as we are – or would be if she were let. You could even ask your father if it pleased you. No doubt he's forgiven me for throwing him in the stream.'

'I thought twould be nice to ask father and brothers as well,' Demelza said, 'on the second day. I thought we could have that on the twenty-third of July, Sawle Feast, so that the miners would have the day off anyhow.'

Ross smiled to himself. It was pleasant sitting here in the sun, and he did not mind her wheedling. Indeed he took an objective interest in what would be her next move.

'Yes, he's teeth enough to make a show,' she said. 'It is plain laziness, naught else. Would all your fine friends be too fine to be asked to dinner with a miner's daughter?'

'If you open his mouth much wider,' said Ross, 'You'll fall in.'

'No, I shan't; I'm too fat; I'm getting a rare fudgy face; my new stays will scarcely lace. John Treneglos, I reckon, wouldn't say no to an invitation. And even maybe his slant-eyed wife would come if you was here for bait. And George Warleggan – you d'say his grandfather was a smith, so he's no call to be proud even if he is so rich. And Francis . . . I like Cousin Francis. And Aunt Agatha wi' her white whiskers and her bettermost wig. And Elizabeth and little Geoffrey Charles. We should be a rare boiling. And then,' said Demelza slyly, 'maybe you could ask some of your friends you go visiting at George Warleggan's.'

A cool breeze stirred between them. It lifted a frill of Demelza's dress, flapped it idly and let it fall.

'Gamblers all,' said Ross. 'You would not want gamblers at a christening. And twice meeting at a card table is not a close acquaintance.'

She loosed Garrick's slavering jaws and moved her hands to wipe them down the side of her dress. Then she remembered and bent to rub them on the grass. Garrick licked her cheek and a dark curl fell over one eye. The trouble with arguing with women, Ross thought, was that one was diverted from the point by their beauty. Demelza was not less lovely for being temporarily more matronly. He remembered how his first love Elizabeth had looked after Geoffrey Charles was born, like an exquisite camellia, delicate and spotless and slightly flushed.

'You can have your two christenings if you want them,' he said.

For a moment, absurdly, Demelza looked a little troubled. Used to her sudden changes of mood, he watched her quizzically, and then she said in a small voice:

'Oh, Ross. You're that good to me.'

He laughed. 'Don't weep for it.'

'No, but you are; you are.' She got up and kissed him. 'Sometimes,' she said slowly, 'I think I'm a grand lady, and then I remember I'm really only . . .'

'You're Demelza,' he said, kissing her in return. 'God broke the mould.'

'No, he didn't. There's another one in the cot.' She looked at him keenly. 'Did you really mean all those pretty things you said before Julia was born? Did you, Ross?'

'I've forgotten what I said.'

She broke away from him and went skipping across the lawn in her smart dress. Presently she was back. 'Ross, let's go and bathe.'

'What nonsense. And you but a week out of bed.'

'Then let me put my feet in the water. We can go to the beach and walk in the surf. It is quiet to-day.'

He gave her a pat. 'Julia would suffer for your cold feet.'

'. . . I hadn't thought of that.' She subsided in her chair.

'But,' he said, 'there is dry sand enough to walk on.'

She was up in a moment. 'I will go'n tell Jinny to keep an eye on Julia.'

When she came back they walked to the edge of the garden where the soil was already half sand. They crossed a patch of wasteland, threading between thistles and tree mallows, and he lifted her over the crumbling stone wall. They ploughed through soft sand and were on Hendrawna Beach.

It was a soft summery day with white regiments of cloud mustered on the horizon. The sea was quiet, and the small wavelets turning their heads near the edge left behind them on the green surface a delicate arabesque of white.

They walked arm in arm, and he thought how quickly they had refound their old companionship.

Out in the sea were two or three herring boats from Padstow and one from Sawle. They thought it Pally Rogers's boat and waved, but he took no notice, being more concerned with fish than friendship.

She said: 'I think it would be a good thing if Verity came to both our parties. She needs the change and new notions to interest her.'

'I hope you don't intend to have the child held over the font two days together.'

'No, no, that would be the first day. The high folk would see that. The low folk will not mind if they are given plenty t'eat. An' they can finish up what's left from the day before.'

'Why do we not also have a children's party,' said Ross, 'to finish up on the third day what has been left on the second?'

She looked at him and broke out laughing. 'You mock me, Ross. Always you d'mock me.'

'It's an inverted form of reverence. Didn't you know that?'

'But quite serious, do you not think it would be a good genteel notion to have such a gathering?'

'Quite serious,' he said, 'I'm disposed to gratify your whims. Isn't that enough?'

'Then I wish you would gratify me in another. I'm that worried over Verity.'

'What is wrong with her?'

'Ross, she was not meant to be an old maid. She has so much in her warm-like and fond. *You* know that. Well, it isn't the life for her, tending Trenwith, looking to the farm and the house and caring for Elizabeth and Francis and Elizabeth's baby and old Aunt Agatha, and caring for the servants and ordering the supplies and teaching the old choir at Sawle Church and busying about helping the mine folk. That isn't what she did ought to be doing.'

'It is precisely what she enjoys doing.'

'Yes, if it was on her own, like, yes. If she was wed and with a home of her own it would make all the difference. Last September month when she was here wi' us at Nampara she looked betterer in no time, but now she's yellow as a saddle and that thin. How old is she, Ross?'

'Twenty-nine.'

'Well, it is high time something was done.'

Ross paused and threw a stone at two quarrelling sea gulls. Not far ahead, on the cliff top, were the buildings of Wheal Leisure, open now as a result of years of contriving on his part, open and employing fifty-six men and showing a profit.

'You have walked far enough,' he said. 'Back now.'

Obediently she turned. The tide was coming in, eating quietly away at the sand. Every so often a wave would make a larger encroachment and then retreat, leaving a thin fringe of soapy scum to mark its limits.

He said amusedly: 'Nine months ago you would not have Verity at any price. You thought her an ogre. When I wanted you to meet, you went as stiff as a pit prop. But since you met you have never ceased to pester me to find her a husband. Short of going to one of the old witches of

Summercourt Fair and buying her a love potion, I know of no way of satisfying you!'

'There's still Captain Blamey,' said Demelza.

He made a gesture of irritation.

'That too I've heard. And am growing a little tired of. Leave well alone, my dear.'

'I shall never be wise, Ross,' she said after a moment. 'I don't even think I wish to be wise.'

'I don't want you to be,' he said, as he lifted her over the wall.

The following day Verity came. She had caught a bad chill from her wetting of a month ago, but now was well again. She cooed over the baby, said she was like them both and like neither of them, heard of Demelza's schemes for the christening and endorsed them without hesitation, tried valiantly to answer one or two questions Demelza had been afraid to ask Dr Choake, and brought out a fine lace christening gown she had made for the child.

Demelza kissed her and thanked her, and then sat looking at her with such dark serious eyes that Verity broke into one of her rare laughs and asked what was to do.

'Oh, nothing. Will you take some tea?'

'If it is time.'

Demelza pulled at the tassel by the fireplace. 'I do naught but drink all day long since Julia came. And I reckon tea's better than gin.'

The red-haired, fair-skinned Jinny came in.

'Oh, Jinny,' Demelza said awkwardly. 'Would you make us a dish of tea. Nice an' strong. An' make the water to boil before you put it on the leaves.'

'Yes, ma'am.'

'I can't believe that's me,' said Demelza when she had gone.

Verity smiled. 'Now tell me what's troubling you.'

'You are, Verity.'

'I? Dear, dear. Say at once how I have offended.'

'Not offended. But if . . . Oh, it is me that will give the offence. . . .'

'Until I know the subject I can't advise you on that.'

'Verity,' Demelza said. 'Ross told me once, after I'd been plaguing him for hours, told me about that you'd once been fond of somebody.'

Verity did not move but the smile on her face became less soft, its curves slightly changed.

'I'm sorry that should trouble you,' she said after a moment.

Demelza was now too far on to mind her words.

'What's testing me is whether it was right that you should've been kept apart, like.'

A faint colour was moving in Verity's sallow cheeks. She's gone old-maidish and drawn-in, Demelza thought, just like when I first saw her; such a difference, like two people living in the same body.

'My dear, I don't think we can measure the behaviour of others by our own judgments. This is what the world is always at. My . . . father and brother have strong and considered principles and they acted on them. Whether it was right or wrong to do so is hardly for us to say. But what is done cannot be undone, and anyway, it is long since buried and almost forgot.'

'Did you never hear of him again?'

Verity got up.

'No.'

Demelza went and stood beside her.

'I *hate* it. I *hate* it,' she said.

Verity patted her arm, as if Demelza had been the injured one.

'Will you not tell me about it?' said Demelza.

'No,' said Verity.

'Sometimes telling helps – makes it easier, and that.'

'Not now,' said Verity. 'Speaking of it now would be . . . digging an old grave.'

She gave a little shiver of emotion (or distaste) as Jinny brought in the tea.

That evening Demelza found Jud in the kitchen alone. No one could have told from their behaviour whether these two liked each other or held to an armed neutrality. Jud had never been won over by Demelza quite as his wife had been. For long he had felt a grudge that this foundling who had once run at his bidding should now be in a position to order him; but then Jud was sure Fate was cruel to him in many ways. Given the choice, he would have preferred Demelza to some coxy-faced madam used to luxury and being waited on all ends.

'Jud,' said Demelza, taking down the baking board and the flour and the yeast. 'Jud, do you recollect a Captain Blamey who used to come here to see Miss Verity?'

'Do I just,' said Jud.

'I must ha' been here then,' said the girl, 'but I don't recall nothing – anything about it.'

'You was a little small tiddler o' thirteen,' Jud said gloomily, 'an' kep' in the kitchen where ye belonged to be. That's what.'

'I don't suspect you remember much about it now,' said the girl.

'No, I don't know, not I, when I was thur through un all, what next.'

She began to knead the dough.

'What happened, Jud?'

He took up a piece of wood and began to whittle it with his knife, blowing a little between his two teeth. His shiny head with its fringe of hair gave him the look of a dissident monk.

'He'd killed his first wife by accident, like, hadn't he?' she asked.

'I see ee d'knaw all about un.'

'No, not all. Some, not all, Jud. What happened here?'

'Oh, this Captain Blamey fellow, he was tinkering after Miss Verity for a rare time. Cap'n Ross put'n to meet here when they'd been foiled to meet else, an' one day Mister Francis and is fathur – 'im they berred Septemby last – come over and found un in the parlour. Mister Francis called 'im to meet'n outside, and out they stamped wi' them duelling pistols that's hung by the window. Me they broft in to see fair play, as you'd only expect, as you'd be right to expect; and afore the day was five minutes olderer Mister Francis'd shot Captain Blamey and Blamey'd shot Francis. As tidy a bit of work as never you saw.'

'Were they hurt?'

'Not as you'd say 'urted. Blamey'd taken a snick in the hand, and the other ball fetched in Francis's neck. Twas straight and fair doin', and Cap'n Blamey up on his 'orse and rid away.'

'Have you ever heard tell of him since then, Jud?'

'Not a whisper.'

'Don't he live at Falmouth?'

'When he's not to sea.'

'Jud,' she said, 'I want for you to do something for me.'

'Eh?'

'The next time Captain Ross rides to see Jim Carter I want you to do something.'

Jud looked at her with his bloodshot bulldog eyes, old and wary.

'How so?'

'I want for you to ride to Falmouth and ask after Captain Blamey and see if he's there still and see what he's doing.'

There was silence while Jud got up and spat emphatically in the fire. When it had finished sizzling he said:

'Go on with yer mooling, Mrs. Tedn for we to be setting the world in step. Tedn sense, tedn natural, tedn right, tedn *safe*. I'd as lief bait a bull.'

He picked up his stick and his knife and walked out.

Demelza gazed after him. She was disappointed but not surprised. And as she looked at the dough, turning it slowly with floured fingers, there was a dark glint in the depths of her glance which suggested she was not discouraged.

Chapter three

THE DAY OF the christening broke fine, and inside Sawle Church the ceremony passed off well before thirty guests, Julia squinting self-consciously when her second cousin, the Rev. William-Alfred Johns, dripped water on her forehead. Afterwards everyone began to trek back to Nampara, some on horseback, others walking in twos and threes, chatting and enjoying the sun; a colourful procession straggling across the scarred countryside and gazed at with curiosity and some awe by the tinners and cottagers as they passed. They were indeed visitors from another world.

The parlour, large and accommodating as it was, was none too spacious for feeding a company of thirty, some of them with big hoop skirts and none of them used to being overcrowded.

Elizabeth and Francis had both come, and with them Geoffrey Charles, three and a half years old. Aunt Agatha, who had not been outside Trenwith grounds for ten years and not on a horse for twenty-six, had come over looking disgusted on a very old and docile mare. She'd never ridden sidesaddle before in forty-seven years of hunting and she thought it an indignity to begin. Ross got her settled in a comfortable chair and brought her a charcoal foot warmer; then he put some rum in her tea, and she soon brightened up and started looking for omens.

George Warleggan had come, chiefly because Elizabeth had persuaded him. Mrs Teague and three of her unmarried daughters were here to see what was to be seen, and Patience Teague, the fourth, because she hoped to meet George Warleggan. John Treneglos and Ruth and old Horace Treneglos were here, variously out of interest in Demelza, spite, and neighbourliness.

They had also asked Joan Pascoe, daughter of the banker, and with her was a young man called Dwight Enys, who spoke little but looked earnest and likeable.

Ross watched his young wife doing the honours. He could not but compare Demelza with Elizabeth, who was now twenty-four and certainly no less lovely than she had ever been. At Christmas she had been a little piqued by the young Demelza's success, and to-day she had taken pains to see if she could rebuild her ascendancy over Ross, a matter that was becoming more important to her than it had once been. She was wearing a brocaded dress of crimson velvet, with broad ribbons round the waist and tiers of lace on the sleeves. To anyone with a sense of colour the rich crimson made her fairness mesmeric.

Hers was the loveliness of gracious, aristocratic womanhood, used to leisure and bred to refinement. She came from uncounted generations of small landed gentlefolk. There had been a Chynoweth before Edward the Confessor, and, as well as the grace and breeding, she seemed to have in her a susceptibility to fatigue, as if the fine pure blood was flowing a little thin. Against her Demelza was the upstart: bred in drunkenness and filth, a waif in a parlour, an urchin climbing on the shoulders of chance to peer into the drawing-rooms of her betters: lusty, crude, unsubtle, all her actions and feelings a stage nearer nature. But each of them had something the other lacked.

The Rev. Clarence Odgers, curate of Sawle-with-Grambler, was present in his horsehair wig; Mrs Odgers, a tiny anxious woman who had somehow found room for ten children and spread not an inch in the doing, was at talk humbly over the boiled pike on parish problems with William-Alfred's wife, Dorothy Johns. A group of the younger people at the far end of the table were laughing together at Francis's account of how John Treneglos for a bet had last week ridden his horse up the steps of Werry House and had fallen off into Lady Bodrugan's lap, all among the dogs.

'It is a lie,' said John Treneglos robustly above the laughter, and glancing at Demelza to see if she had some attention for the story. 'A brave and wicked lie. True I came unseated for a moment and Connie Bodrugan was there to offer me accommodation, but I was back on the nag in half a minute and was off down the steps before she'd time to finish her swearing.'

'And a round cursing you'd get, if I know her ladyship,' said George Warleggan, fingering his beautiful stock, which failed to hide the shortness of his neck. 'I'd not be astonished if you heard some new ones.'

'Really, my dear,' said Patience Teague, pretending to be shocked, and looking up at George slantwise through her lashes. 'Isn't Lady Bodrugan rather an indelicate subject for such a pretty party?'

There was laughter again, and Ruth Treneglos, from farther along the table, eyed her elder sister keenly. Patience was coming out, breaking away as *she* had done from the dreary autocracy of their mother. Faith and Hope, the two eldest, were hopeless old maids now, echoing Mrs Teague like a Greek chorus; Joan, the middle sister, was going the same way.

'Don't some of our young people dress extravagant these days,' said Dorothy Johns in an undertone, breaking off her more substantial conversation to look at Ruth. 'I'm sure young Mrs Treneglos must cost her husband a handsome penny in silks. Fortunate that he is able to gratify her taste.'

'Yes, ma'am, I entirely agree, ma'am,' Mrs Odgers breathed anxiously, fingering her borrowed necklace. Mrs Odgers spent all her time agreeing with someone. It was her mission in life. 'And not as if she had been accustomed to such luxury at home, like. It seems no time at all since my husband christened her. My first came just after.'

'She's grown quite fat since I saw her last,' whispered Mrs Teague to Faith Teague, while Prudie clattered the gooseberry pies behind her. 'And I don't like her dress, do you? Unbecoming for one so recently – um – a matron. Worn with an eye for the men. You can see it.'

'One can understand, of course,' said Faith Teague to Hope Teague, passing the ball obediently a step downtable, 'how she appeals to a certain type. She has that sort of full bloom that soon fades. Though I must say I'm quite surprised at Captain Poldark. But no doubt they were thrown together . . .'

'What did Faith say?' said Joan Teague to Hope Teague, waiting her turn.

'Well, she's a fine little monkey,' said Aunt Agatha, who was near the head, to Demelza. 'Let me hold her, bud. Ye're not afraid I'll drop her, are you? I've held and dandled many that's dead and gone afore ever you was thought of. Chibby, chibby, chibby! There now, she's smiling at me. Unless it's wind. Reg'lar little Poldark she is. The very daps of her father.'

'Mind,' said Demelza, 'she may dribble on your fine gown.'

'It will be a good omen if she do. Here, I have something for you, bud. Hold the brat a moment. Ah! I've got the screws to-day, and the damned jolting that old nag gave me didn't help. . . . There. That's for the child.'

'What is it?' Demelza asked after a moment.

'Dried rowanberries. Hang 'em on the cradle. Keep the fairies away. . . .'

'He hasn't had the smallpox yet,' said Elizabeth to Dwight Enys, rubbing her hand gently over the curls of her small son, who was sitting so quietly on his chair beside her. 'I have often wondered whether there is anything in this inoculation, whether it is injurious to a young child.'

'No; not if it is carefully done,' said Enys, who had been put beside Elizabeth and was taking in little except her beauty. 'But don't employ a farmer to give the cowpox. Some reliable apothecary.'

'Oh, we are fortunate to have a good one in the district. He's not here to-day,' Elizabeth said.

The meal came to an end at last, and since the day was so fine people strolled into the garden. As the company spread out Demelza edged her way towards Joan Pascoe.

'Did you say you came from Falmouth, did I hear you say that, Miss Pascoe?'

'Well, I was brought up there, Mrs Poldark. But I live in Truro now.'

Demelza moved her eyes to see if anyone was within hearing.

'Do you chance to know a Captain Andrew Blamey, Miss Pascoe?'

Joan Pascoe cooed to the baby.

'I know *of* him, Mrs Poldark. I have seen him once or twice.'

'Is he still in Falmouth, I wonder?'

'I believe he puts in there from time to time. He's a seafaring man, you know.'

'I've often thought I'd dearly like to go to Falmouth on a visit,' Demelza said dreamily. 'It's a handsome place they say. I wonder when is a good time to see all the ships in the harbour.'

'Oh, after a gale, that is the best, when the vessels have run in for shelter. There is room enough for all to ride out the greatest storm.'

'Yes, but I s'pose the packet service runs regular, in and out, just like clockwork. The Lisbon packet they say goes every Tuesday.'

'Oh, no, I think you're misinformed, ma'am. The Lisbon packet leaves from St Just's Pool every Friday evening in the winter and every Saturday morning in the summer months. The week's end is the best time to see the regular services.'

'Chibby, chibby, chibby,' said Demelza to Julia, copying Aunt Agatha and watching the effect. 'Thank you, Miss Pascoe, for the information.'

'My dear,' said Ruth Treneglos to her sister Patience, 'who is this coming down the valley? Can it be a funeral procession? Old Agatha will certainly smell a bad omen here.'

One or two of the others now noticed that fresh visitors were on the way. Headed by a middle-aged man in a shiny black coat, the newcomers threaded their way through the trees on the other side of the stream.

'My blessed parliament!' said Prudie, from the second parlour window. 'It's the maid's father. 'E's come on the wrong day. Didn ee tell him Wednesday, you black worm?'

Jud looked startled and swallowed a big piece of currant tart. He coughed in annoyance. 'Wednesday? O' course I says Wednesday. What for should I tell Tuesday when I was told to tell Wednesday? Tedn my doing. Tedn me you can blame. Shake yer broom 'andle in yer own face!'

With a sick sensation in the pit of her stomach Demelza too had recognized the new arrivals. Her brain and her tongue froze. She could see disaster and could do nothing to meet it. Even Ross was not beside her at this moment but was tending to Great-aunt Agatha's comfort, opening the french windows for her to sit and view the scene.

But Ross had not missed the procession.

They had come in force: Tom Carne himself, big and profoundly solid in his new-found respectability; Aunt Chegwidden Carne, his second wife, bonneted and small-mouthed like a little black hen, and behind them four tall gangling youths, a selection from among Demelza's brothers.

A silence had fallen on the company. Only the stream bubbled and a bullfinch chirped. The cavalcade reached the plank bridge and came across it with a clomp of hobnailed boots.

Verity guessed the identity of the new arrivals and she left old Mr

Treneglos and moved to Demelza's side. She did not know how she could help Demelza unless it was merely by being there, but in so far as she could give a lead to Francis and Elizabeth that she meant to do.

Ross came quickly out of the house, and without appearing to hurry reached the bridge as Tom Carne came over.

'How d'you do, Mr Carne,' he said, holding out his hand. 'I am grateful you were able to come.'

Carne eyed him for a second. It was more than four years since they had met, and then they had smashed up a room before one of them ended in the stream. Two years of reformation had changed the older man; his eyes were clearer and his clothing good and respectable. But he still had the same intolerant stare. Ross too had changed in the interval, grown away from his disappointment; the content and happiness he had found with Demelza had softened his intolerance, had cloaked his restless spirit in a new restraint.

Carne, finding no sarcasm, let his hand be taken. Aunt Chegwidden Carne, not in the least overawed, came next, shook his hand, moved on to greet Demelza. As Carne made no attempt to introduce the four gangling youths, Ross bowed gravely to them and they, taking their cue from the eldest, touched their forelocks in response. He found a strange comfort in the fact that none of them was the least like Demelza.

'We been waiting at the church, maid,' Carne said grimly to his daughter. 'Ye said four o'clock and we was there by then. Ye'd no manner of right to do it afore. We was besting whether to go 'ome again.'

'I said *to-morrow* at four,' Demelza answered him sharply.

'Aye. So yer man said. But twas our right to be 'ere the day of the baptizing, an' he said the baptizing was for to-day. Yer own flesh an' blood 'as more call to be beside you at a baptizing than all these 'ere dandical folk.'

A terrific bitterness welled up in Demelza's heart. This man, who had beaten all affection out of her in the old days, to whom she had sent a forgiving invitation, had deliberately come on another day and was going to shatter her party. All her efforts were in vain, and Ross would be the laughing stock of the district. Already, without looking, she could see the laughter on the faces of Ruth Treneglos and Mrs Teague. She could have torn tufts from his thick black beard (showing streaks of grey now beneath the nose and under the curve of the bottom lip); she could have clawed at his sober, too-respectable jacket or plastered his thick red-veined nose with earth from her flower beds. With a fixed smile hiding the desolation of her heart she greeted her stepmother and her four brothers: Luke, Samuel, William and Bobby: names and faces she had loved in that far-off nightmare life that no longer belonged to her.

And they, at any rate, were overawed, not least by their sister, whom they remembered a managing drudge and found a well-dressed young woman with a new way of looking and speaking. They grouped round her at a respectful distance, answering gruffly her metallic little questions, while Ross, with all that grace and dignity of which he was capable when he chose, was escorting Tom Carne and Aunt Chegwidden round the garden, inexorably introducing them to the others. There was a steely politeness in his manner which bolted down the reactions of those who were not used to exchanging compliments with the vulgar classes.

As they went Tom Carne's eyes grew no more respectful at the show of fashion but harder and more wrathful at the levity these people seemed to consider suitable for a solemn day; and Aunt Chegwidden's mouth pinched itself in like a darned buttonhole as she took in Elizabeth's flamboyant crimson, Ruth Treneglos's tight low-cut bodice and Mrs Teague's rows of pearls and richly frizzled wig.

At last it was over and talk broke out again, though on a subdued note. A tiny wind was getting up, moving among the guests and lifting a ribbon here and a tail coat there.

Ross motioned to Jinny to carry round port and brandy. The more everyone drank the more they would talk, and the more they talked the less of a fiasco it would all be.

Carne waved away the tray.

'I have no truck wi' such things,' he said. 'Woe unto them that rise up early in the morning that they follow strong drink, that continue until night till wine do inflame them! I've finished wi' wickedness and bottledom and set my feet 'pon a rock of righteousness and salvation. Let me see the child, dattur.'

Stiffly, grimly, Demelza held Julia out for inspection.

'My first was bigger than this,' said Mrs Chegwidden Carne, breathing hard over the baby. 'Warn't he, Tom? Twelve month old he'll be August month. A 'andsome little fellow he be, though tis my own.'

'What's amiss wi' er forehead?' Carne asked. 'Have ee dropped 'ur?'

'It was in the birth,' Demelza said angrily.

Julia began to cry.

Carne rasped his chin. 'I trust ye picked her godparents safe and sure. Twas my notion to be one myself.'

Near the stream the Teague girls tittered among themselves, but Mrs Teague was on her dignity, drawing down her eyelids in their side-slant shutter fashion.

'A calculated insult,' she said, 'to bring in a man and a woman of that type and to *introduce* them. It is an affront set upon us by Ross and his kitchen slut. It was against my judgment that I ever came!'

But her youngest daughter knew better. This was no part of any plan but was a mischance she might put to good use. She took a glass from Jinny's tray and sidled behind her sister's back up to George Warleggan.

'Do you not think,' she whispered, 'that we are remiss in straying so far from our host and hostess? I have been to few christenings so I do not know the etiquette, but common manners would suggest . . .'

George glanced a moment into the slightly oriental green eyes. He had always held the Teagues in private contempt, an exaggerated form of the mixed respect and patronage he felt for the Poldarks and the Chynoweths and all those gentlefolk whose talent for commerce was in inverse rate to the length of their pedigrees. They might affect to despise him but he knew that some of them in their hearts already feared him. The Teagues were almost beneath his notice, maleless, twittering, living on three per cents and a few acres of land. But since her marriage Ruth had developed so rapidly that he knew he must reassess her. She, like Ross among the Poldarks, was of harder metal.

'Such modesty is to be expected in one so charming, ma'am,' he said, 'but I know no more of christenings than you. Do you not think it safest to consult one's own interests and follow where they lead?'

A burst of laughter behind them greeted the end of an anecdote Francis had been telling John Treneglos and Patience Teague.

Ruth said in an exaggerated whisper: 'I think you should behave more seemly, Francis, if we are not to have a reprimand. The old man is looking our way.'

Francis said: 'We are safe yet. The wild boar always raises its hackles before it comes to the charge.' There was another laugh. 'You, girl,' he said to Jinny as she passed near, 'is that more of the canary you have? I will take another glass. You're a nice little thing; where did Captain Poldark find *you*?'

The stress was almost unconscious, but Ruth's laugh left no doubt of the way she took it. Jinny flushed up to the roots of her hair.

'I'm Jinny Carter, sur. Jinny Martin that was.'

'Yes, yes.' Francis's expression changed slightly. 'I remember now. You worked at Grambler for a time. How is your husband?'

Jinny's face cleared. 'Nicely, sur, thank you, so far as – so far as . . .'

'So far as you know. I trust the time will pass quickly for you both.'

'Thank you, sur.' Jinny curtsied, still red, and moved on.

'You are taking small interest in your goddaughter, Francis,' Ruth said, anxious to turn him away from his squireish mood. 'The infant is getting well quizzed in your absence. I'm sure she would appreciate a sup of canary.'

'They say all the vulgars are brought up on gin,' said Patience Teague. 'And look no worse for it. I was reading but the other day how many, I forget how many, million gallons of gin was drunk last year.'

'Not all by babies, Sister,' said Treneglos.

'Well, no doubt they will sometimes take ale for a change,' said Patience.

This had all been watched though not heard by Tom Carne. He turned his sharp obstinate eyes upon Mrs Carne.

'Thur's ungodliness 'ere, Wife,' he said through his beard. 'Tis no proper place for a cheeil. Tis no fitty company to attend on a baptizing. I suspicioned no less. Women wi' their wanton clothes and young princocks strutting between 'em, drinkin' and jesting. Tis worse'n ye d'see in Truro.'

His wife hunched up her shoulders. Her conviction was of longer standing and was by nature less belligerent. 'We must pray for 'em, Tom. Pray for 'em all, and your own darter among 'em. Maybe there'll come a day when they'll see the light.'

Julia would not be quieted so Demelza seized the excuse to take her indoors. She was in a despairing mood.

She knew that however the day might turn now it was a black failure to her. Full-flavoured meat for the gossips. Well, let it come. There was nothing more she could do. She had tried to be one of them and failed. She would never try again. Let them all go home, ride off at once, so that she might have done with everything. Only that she might be left alone.

A few moments after she had gone Ruth succeeded in edging her friends within earshot of Tom Carne.

'For my part,' she said, 'I have no care for liquor unless it be brandy or port; I like a good heavy drink, soft to the taste and no bite until it is well down. Don't you agree, Francis?'

'You remind me of Aunt Agatha,' he said. 'The conceits of a woman of discretion.'

There was another laugh, against Ruth this time.

They were passing by Tom Carne and he stepped forward, playing exactly into Ruth's hands.

'One of ye be the cheeil's godfather?'

Francis bowed slightly. Viewed from behind there seemed a hint of satire in the way the rising wind twisted his coattails.

'I am.'

Tom Carne stared at him.

'By what right?'

'Eh?'

'By what right do ye stand for the cheeil at the seat of righteousness?'

Francis had won heavily at the faro tables last night and he felt indulgent.

'Because I was so invited.'

'Invited?' said Carne. 'Aye, mebbe you were invited. But are ee saved?'

'Saved?'

'Aye, saved.'

'Saved from what?'

'From the Devil and damnation.'

'I haven't had any communication on the point.'

John Treneglos guffawed.

'Well, that's where ye're at fault, mister,' said Carne. 'Them as has paid no heed to God's call has no doubt hearkened to the Devil's. Tes one or the other for all of we. There's no betwixt an' between. Tes Heaven an' all the angels or hell-fire an' the brimstone pit!'

'We have a preacher among us,' said George Warleggan.

Mrs Carne pulled at her husband's sleeve. Although she professed to despise the gentry she had not Carne's genuine contempt for them. She knew that outside the small circle of their own meetinghouse people like this ruled the material world. 'Come away, Tom,' she said. 'Leave 'em be. They're in the valley o' the shadow, and nought will move 'em.'

Ross, who had gone with Demelza into the house to try to encourage her to face it out, came again to the front door. The wind was gusty. He saw the argument and at once moved towards it.

Carne had thrown off his wife's arm.

'Four years ago,' he was proclaiming in a voice which carried all over the garden, 'I was a sinner against God and served the Devil in fornication an' drunkenness. Nay, there was the smell of sulphur 'pon me an' I was nigh to Hell. But the Lord showed me a great light and turned me to salvation, an' joy an' glory. But them as has not laid hold o' the blessing and is living in wickedness an' unrighteousness has no call or sanction to stand before the Lord to answer for a puking cheeil.'

'I hope you find yourself rebuked, Francis,' said Ruth.

Francis refused to be provoked.

'For my part,' he said, eyeing Carne, 'I am a little perplexed at this sharp division of the sheep and the goats, though I know it is often done by people of your complexion. What is the hallmark of the change? Are we of different flesh, you and I, that death should bring you a golden crown and me a seat in Hell's cockpit? Who's to say that you are a better keeper of the brat's religion than I? I ask you that in genuine inquiry. You say you are saved. *You* say it. But what's to prove it? What is to hinder me from saying that *I* am Grand Vizier and Keeper of the Seven Seals? What is to prevent me from running round and announcing *I* am saved, mine is the Kingdom and yours the damnation: *I'm* going to Heaven, *you* go to Hell!'

John Treneglos broke into a huge gust of laughter. Carne's fleshy dogmatic face was purpled up and spotty with anger.

'Leave un be,' said Mrs Carne sharply, dragging at him again. ''Tis the Devil himself temptin' of ee to vain argument.'

The christening guests, as if under the pull of a magnet, had all drawn in towards this noisy focal point.

Ross came up behind the group.

'The wind is rising,' he said. 'The ladies would be better indoors. Perhaps you would help Aunt Agatha, Francis?' He made a gesture towards the old lady who, with an ancient instinct for trouble, had left her window seat and was tottering unaided across the lawn.

'Nay,' said Carne. 'I'll not be under the same roof wi' such evil thoughts.' He stared sharply at Ruth. 'Cover yer breast, woman, tis shameful an' sinful. Women ha' been whipped in the streets for less.'

There was an awful pause.

'Damn your insolence!' Ruth snapped back, flushing. 'If – if there's whipping to be done it's you that'll get it. John! Did you hear what he said!'

Her husband, whose mind was not agile and, being set to see the funny side, had at first seen no further, now swallowed a guffaw.

'You impudent splatty old pig!' he said. 'D'you know who you're speaking to? Make an apology to Mrs Treneglos at once, or, damme, I'll have your coat off your back!'

Carne spat on the grass. 'If the truth do offend then it edn the truth that's at fault. Woman's place is to be clothed modest an' decent, not putting out lures for men, shameless an' brazen. If she was my wife, by Jakes ——'

Ross stepped sharply between them and caught Treneglos's arm. For a moment he stared into the flushed angry face of his neighbour.

'My dear John. A common brawl! With all these ladies present!'

'Look to your own business, Ross! The fellow is insufferable ——'

'Leave him come,' said Carne. 'Tes two year since I was in the ring, but I've a mind to show 'im a trick or two. If the Lord ——'

'Come away, Tom,' said Mrs Carne. 'Come away, Tom.'

'But it is my business, John,' said Ross, still staring at Treneglos. 'You are both my guests, never forget. And I couldn't permit you to strike my father-in-law.'

There was a moment's stunned silence, as if, although they knew the truth, the mere statement of it had shocked and quieted them all.

John tried to wrench his arm out of Ross's grip. He didn't succeed. His face got still pinker.

'Naturally,' said Ruth, 'Ross would wish to support one who has connived at all his schemes all along.'

'Naturally,' said Ross, releasing the arm, 'I would wish to be on agreeable terms with my neighbours, but not at the price of allowing a brawl before my front door. The ladies don't like torn shirts and bloody noses.' He looked at Ruth and at the little pink spots showing through her make-up. 'At least, some of 'em do not.'

Ruth said: 'It is quite strange, Ross, how you look upon things since you married. I don't think you were lacking in all courtesy before. I hesitate to think what influence can have been at work to turn you out so boorish.'

'I want an apology,' Treneglos shouted. 'My wife was grossly insulted by that man, father-in-law or no. Damme, if he was of my own status, I'd call him out for what he said! Would you swallow such impudence, Ross? Lord save us, you'd be the last! Rot an' perish me if I'll be content ——'

'The truth's the truth!' Carne snapped. 'An' blasphemy don't aid un to be anything other ——'

'Hold your tongue, man.' Ross turned on him. 'If we want your opinions we'll invite 'em at a proper time.' While Carne was speechless, he turned back to Treneglos. 'Modes and manners vary with the breed, John; those with the same code can speak the same language. Will you allow me as host to apologize for such offence as this may have given you or your wife?'

Hesitating, a little mollified, John flexed his arm and grunted and glanced at the girl at his side. 'Well, Ross, you spit it out well enough. I have no wish to go against that. If Ruth feels ——'

Outmanœuvred, Ruth said: 'I confess I should have taken it better at an earlier stage. Naturally if Ross wishes to protect his new relative . . . Some allowance must be made for those who know no better by those who do.'

A sudden wail from near by caused them all to turn. Aunt Agatha, neglected in the quarrel, had made fair speed across the grass, but just when she was nearing her quarry a mischievous gust had caught her. They saw a barely recognizable old lady crowned with a scum of grey hair, while a purple bonnet and a wig bowled along towards the stream. Francis and one or two of the others at once went in pursuit. Following them, floating down the wind, came a stream of curses from a Carolinian world none of the others had known. Even the Dowager Lady Bodrugan could not have done better.

An hour later Ross went upstairs to find Demelza lying in a sort of dry-eyed grief on the bed. All the guests had amiably gone, by foot or on horseback, clinging to hats; skirts and coattails flying in the wind.

Demelza had helped to see them off, smiling with fixed politeness until the last had turned his back. Then she had muttered an excuse and fled.

Ross said: 'Prudie is looking for you. We didn't know where you were. She wants to know what is to be done with some of the foodstuffs.'

She did not answer.

'Demelza.'

'Oh, Ross,' she said, 'I am in a sore state.'

He sat on the edge of the bed. 'Never worry about it, my dear.'

'It will be the talk of the district. Ruth Treneglos an' all the other Teagues will see to that.'

'What is there to fret about? Tittle tattle. If they have nothing better to do than prate . . .'

'I am that grieved. I thought I would show 'em that I was a fit wife for you, that I could wear fine clothes and behave genteel an' not disgrace you. An' instead they will all ride home snickering behind their hands. "Have you not heard about Cap'n Poldark's wife, the kitchen wench . . ." Oh, I could die!'

'Which would displease us all much more than a brush with John Treneglos.' He put his hand on her ankle. 'This is but the first fence, child.

We have had a check. Well, we can try again. Only a faint heart would give up the race so soon.'

'So you think I am a faint heart.' Demelza withdrew her foot, feeling irrationally irritated with him. She knew that, of all the people this afternoon, Ross had come out best. She faintly resented it because she felt that no one who cared could have been so unruffled; and because of this she faintly resented his manner now, seeing in it more patronage than sympathy, disliking for the first time his use of the word 'child,' as if it spoke more of condescension than love.

And at the back of everything was Elizabeth. Elizabeth had scored to-day. She had looked so beautiful, so poised and graceful, standing in the background, taking no part in the squabble. She had been content to be there. Her existence was enough, just her as a contrast, as an example of all Ross's wife was not. All the time he was sitting here, patting her foot and idly consoling her, he would be thinking of Elizabeth.

'The old man's Methodism,' said Ross, 'was grafted on a well-established tree. Moderation is not in him. I wonder what Wesley would say.'

'Jud was at fault for ever telling 'em there was to be two parties,' Demelza cried. 'I could kill 'im for that!'

'My dear, in a week it will all be forgot and no one the worse. And to-morrow we have the Martins and the Daniels and Joe and Betsy Triggs and Will Nanfan and all the others. They will need no prompting to enjoy themselves and will jig on the lawns; and do not forget the travelling players are coming to give a play.'

Demelza turned over on her face.

'I cannot go on, Ross,' she said, her voice remote and muffled. 'Send 'em all back word. I have done my most, and that is not enough. Maybe it's my own fault for takin' pride in pretending to be what I never can be. Well, it's over now. I cannot face any more. I ha'n't the heart.'

Chapter four

THREE DAYS BEFORE the christening there had been a stormy meeting of the Wheal Leisure venturers at which Ross and Dr Choake had again got at loggerheads, Ross being all for development – Choake called it gambling – and Choake for consolidation – Ross called it obstruction – and the argument had ended by Ross's offering to purchase Choake's share of the mine for three times what he had put in. With great dignity Choake had accepted, so the morning after the christening Ross rode in to Truro to see his banker about raising the money.

Harris Pascoe, a little ageless man with steel spectacles and a stammer, confirmed the view that the mortgage on Nampara could be raised to cover it, but thought the purchase fantastically unbusinesslike at the price. Copper was at seventy-one now, and no one knew where it would end. There was a good deal of bitterness felt for the smelting companies, but what could you expect when often the metal had to lie idle for months before a buyer could be found? Ross liked Harris Pascoe and saw no point in arguing his own side of the case.

On his way out of the house he passed a young man whose face was known to him. He raised his hat and would have passed on, but the man stopped.

'How d'you do, Captain Poldark. It was kind of you to have me yesterday. I'm a stranger in these parts and appreciated your welcome.'

Dwight Enys, whom Joan Pascoe had brought to the party. He had a good head and face; a look of courage strengthened the boyish turn of his cheek and jaw. Ross had never quite passed through this stage. He had gone to America a lanky youth and come back a war veteran.

'Your name suggests a local connection.'

'I have second cousins here, sir, but one does not always wish to presume on relationship. My father came from Penzance, and I have been in London studying medicine.'

'Is it your intention to go in for the profession?'

'I graduated as a physician early this year. But living in London is expensive. I thought to settle in this neighbourhood for a time to go on with my studies and to keep myself by taking a few patients.'

'If your interest is in undernourishment or miners' complaints you will have subjects for your study.'

Enys looked surprised. 'Has someone told you?'

'No one has told me anything.'

'It is the lungs really. It seemed to me that if one was to practise at the same time the proper place was among a mining community where consumption of the lungs is widespread.'

The young man was losing his shyness.

'In the matter of fever too. There is so very much to be learned and experimented on. . . . But no doubt I bore you, sir. I am inclined to run on. . . .'

Ross said: 'The surgeons I know are much more prone to talk of their successes in the hunting field. We must speak of it again.'

After going a few paces he stopped and called Enys back.

'Where do you intend to live?'

'I am staying with the Pascoes for a month. I shall try to take a small house somewhere between here and Chacewater. There is no other medical man in that vicinity.'

Ross said: 'You know, perhaps, that I am interested in a mine which you may have seen from my house yesterday?'

'I did notice something. But no, I hadn't heard. . . .'

'The post of mine surgeon is at present vacant. I think I could get it for you if you were interested. It is very small of course; about eighty men at present, but it would bring you in some fourteen shillings a week and you would gain the experience.'

Dwight Enys's face flushed with pleasure and embarrassment.

'I hope you did not think . . .'

'If I thought that I should not have suggested it.'

'It would be a great help to me. That kind of work is what I wish. But . . . the distance would be considerable.'

'I take it you have not settled on a house. There is scope in our neighbourhood.'

'Is there not a surgeon of some repute?'

'Choake? Oh, there's room enough. He has private means and doesn't overwork. But think of it and let me know what you decide.'

'Thank you, sir. You're very kind.'

And if he's any good, Ross thought as he turned out into the street, I'll see if he can do something for Jim when he comes out, for Choake could not have done less. Carter had been in prison over a year now, and since he had somehow survived in spite of his morbid lung there seemed a hope that he would live through the next ten months and be restored to Jinny and his family. Ross had seen him in January and found him thin and weak; but, for prison life, conditions in Bodmin were supportable. Jinny and her father, Zacky Martin, had seen him twice, walking in one day and back the next;

but twenty-six miles each way was too much for a girl who was still nursing her baby. He thought he would take her in himself sometime.

The quarrel with Choake would leave him irritatingly short of money just when he had begun to see his way clear to spend more on the luxuries of life. The necessities too, for he badly needed another horse. And the birth of Julia had involved him in fresh expense which he could not avoid and did not want to avoid.

He was annoyed with himself for having been so reckless.

He turned in at the Red Lion Inn, which was crowded, and chose a seat in the recess by the door. But his entry had not been unnoticed and after the potboy had been with his order a discreet footstep sounded near by.

'Captain Poldark? Good day to you. We do not often see you in town.'

Ross looked up, a not very welcoming expression in his eyes. It was a man called Blewett, manager and part shareholder in Wheal Maid, one of the copper mines of the Idless Valley.

'No, I have no time to spare except for business visits.'

'May I sit with you? The wool merchants in the parlour have no interest for me. Thank you. I see the price of copper has fallen again.'

'So I have just learned.'

'It must stop soon or we shall all be in bankruptcy.'

'No one deplores that more than I,' said Ross, reluctantly finding common cause with this man whom he disliked only for breaking into his private thoughts.

'One hopes for almost anything to stop the downward trend,' Blewett said, setting down his glass and moving restlessly. 'We have lost eight hundred pounds in trading this year. It is a big sum for people like ourselves.'

Ross glanced up again. He saw that Blewett was really worried; there were dark pouches under his eyes, and his mouth sagged. Before him – and not far away – was the debtors' prison and starvation for his family. It was that which had made him risk the rebuff of a man who had a reputation for being unapproachable. Perhaps he had just come from a meeting with his fellow venturers and felt he must talk or suffocate.

'I don't think conditions can remain long as they are,' Ross said. 'There is an increasing use of copper in engines of all kinds. As the towns use more the price will recover.'

'On a long view you may be right, but unhappily we are all committed to a short-term payment of loan interest. We have to sell the ore attle cheap to exist at all. If the copper and smelting companies were honestly run we might eke out this bad period. But what chance have we to-day?'

'I don't think it can be to the interest of the smelters to keep the prices down,' Ross said.

'Not the market price, no, sir, but the price they pay us. It's all a ring, Captain Poldark, and we know it,' Blewett said. 'What chance have we of getting fair returns where the companies do not bid one against another!'

Ross nodded and stared at the people moving in and out of the inn. A blind man was feeling his way towards the bar.

'There are two ways to combat the evil.'

Blewett grasped at the implication of hope. 'What do you suggest?'

'I'd suggest what is not possible. The copper companies never hurt themselves by competitive bidding. Well, if the mines were in similar unity they could withhold supplies until the copper companies were prepared to pay more. After all, they cannot live without us; we are the producers.'

'Yes, yes. I see what you mean. Go on.'

At that moment a man passed the low window of the inn and turned in at the door. Ross's thoughts were on what he had been saying, and for some moments the familiar stocky figure and slightly wide-legged walk made no mark in his mind. Then he was jerked into attention. The last time he had seen the man was years ago riding up the valley out of Nampara after his fight with Francis, whilst Verity stood and watched him go.

Ross lowered his head and stared at the table.

Between his eyes and the table top – as if he had been staring at the sun – was the visual image of what he had just seen. Fine blue coat, neat black cravat, lace at sleeves; stocky and rather impressive – the face was different, though; the lines deeper about the mouth, the mouth itself was tighter as if for ever held in, and the eyes full of self-assertion.

He did not look either way but went straight through into one of the parlours. A fortunate escape.

'What we need, Captain Poldark, is a leader,' said Blewett eagerly. A man of position who is upright and confident and can act for us all. A man, if I may say so, such as yourself.'

'Eh?' said Ross.

'I trust you will pardon the suggestion. But in the mining world it is everyone for himself and Devil take your neighbour. We need a leader who can bind men together and help them to fight as a body. Competition is very well when the industry is booming, but we cannot afford it at times like these. The copper companies are rapacious – there is no other word. Look at the waste allowance they demand. If we could get a leader, Captain Poldark . . .'

Ross listened with fitful attention.

'What is your other suggestion?' Blewett asked.

'My suggestion?'

'You said there were two ways of combating the evil of our present conditions. . . .'

'The other solution would be for the mines to form a copper company of their own – one which would purchase the ore, build a smelting works close at hand and refine and sell their own products.'

Blewett tapped his fingers nervously on the table.

'You mean – to – to . . .'

'To create a company which would bid independently and keep its profits for the men who run the mines. At present what profits there are go to South Wales or into the hands of merchants like the Warleggans, who have a finger in every pie.'

Blewett shook his head. 'It would take a large amount of capital. I wish it had been possible ——'

'Not more capital than there was, than perhaps there is; but far more unity of purpose.'

'It would be a splendid thing to do,' said Blewett. 'Captain Poldark, you have, if I may say so, the character to lead and to create unity. The companies would fight to squeeze the newcomer out, but it – it would be a hope and an encouragement for many who see nothing but ruin staring them in the face.'

Desperation had given Harry Blewett a touch of eloquence. Ross listened half in scepticism, half seriously. His own suggestions had become more clearly defined as he made them. But he certainly did not see himself in the role of leader of the Cornish mining interests. Knowing his men, their independence, their obstinate resistance to all new ideas, he could see what a tremendous effort would be needed to get anything started at all.

They sipped brandy over it for some time, Blewett seeming to find some comfort in the idle talk. His fears were the less for having been aired. Ross listened with an ear and an eye for Andrew Blamey.

It was nearly time to leave, Demelza, sorely stricken, having been persuaded overnight to go on with her second party. Blewett brought another man to the table, William Aukett, manager of a mine in the Ponsanooth Valley. Eagerly Blewett explained the idea to him. Aukett, a canny man with a cast in one eye, said there was no question but that it might save the industry – but where was the capital coming from except through the banks, which were tied up with the copper companies?

Ross, driven a little to defend his own idea, said well, there were influential people outside the copper companies. But of course this was no seeking venture that could be floated for five or six hundred. Thirty thousand pounds might be nearer the figure before it was ended – with huge profits or a complete loss as the outcome. One had to see it on the right scale before one could begin to see it at all.

These comments, far from depressing Blewett, seemed to increase his eagerness; but just as he had taken out a sheet of soiled paper and was going to call for pen and ink a crash shook the pewter on the walls of the room and stilled the murmur of voices throughout the inn.

Out of the silence came the sound of someone scrambling on the floor in the next parlour. There was a scurry of feet and the flash of a red waistcoat as the innkeeper went quickly into the room.

'This is no place for brawling, sir. There's always trouble when you come in. I'll have no more of it. I'll . . . I'll . . .'

The voice gave out. Another's took its place, Andrew Blamey's, in anger.

He came out, ploughing his way through those who had crowded to the door. He was not drunk. Ross wondered if drink ever had been his real trouble. Blamey knew a stronger master: his own temper.

Francis and Charles and his own early judgment had been right after all. To give the generous softhearted Verity to such a man . . .

Demelza must be told of this. It would put a stop to her pestering.

'I know him,' Aukett said. 'He's master of the *Caroline*, a brig on Falmouth–Lisbon packet service. He drives his men; they say too he murdered his wife and children, though in that case how it comes that he is at large I do not know.'

'He quarrelled with his wife and knocked her down when she was with child,' Ross said. 'She died. His two children were not concerned in it, so far as I am informed.'

They stared at him a moment.

'It's said he has quarrelled with everyone in Falmouth,' Aukett observed. 'For my part I avoid the man. I think he has a tormented look.'

Ross went to get his mare, which he had left to-day at the Fighting Cocks Inn. He saw nothing more of Blamey, but his way took him past the Warleggans' town house and he was held up for a moment by the sight of the Warleggan carriage drawing up outside their door. It was a magnificent vehicle made of rich polished wood with green and white wheels and drawn by four fine grey horses. There was a postillion, a driver and a footman, all in green and white livery, smarter than any owned by a Boscawen or a de Dunstanville.

The footman leapt down to open the door. Out of the carriage stepped George's mother, fat and middle-aged, wreathed in lace and silks but personally overshadowed by all the finery. The door of the big house came open and more footmen stood there to welcome her in. Passers-by stopped to stare. The house swallowed her. The magnificent carriage drove on.

Ross was not a man who would have gone in for display had he been able to afford it; but the contrast struck him to-day with special irony. It was not so much that the Warleggans could afford a carriage with four horses while he could not buy a second horse for the necessary business of life, but that these merchant bankers and ironmasters, sprung from illiteracy in two generations, could maintain their full prosperity in the middle of a slump, while worthy men like Blewett and Aukett – and hundreds of others – faced ruin.

Chapter five

THE SECOND CHRISTENING party went off without a hitch. The miners and small holders and their wives had no mental reserves about enjoying themselves. It was Sawle Feast anyway, and if they had not been invited here most of them would have spent the afternoon in Sawle dancing or playing games or sitting in one of the kiddleys getting drunk.

The first half-hour at Nampara was a little constrained while the guests still remembered they were in superior company; but very soon the shyness wore off.

This was a summer feast in the old style, with no newfangled dainties to embarrass anyone. Demelza and Verity and Prudie had been working on it from early morning. Huge beef pies had been made: repeated layers of pastry and beef laid on top of each other in great dishes with cream poured over. Four green geese and twelve fine capons had been roasted; cakes made as big as millstones. There was bee wine and home-brewed ale and cider and port. Ross had reckoned on five quarts of cider for each man and three for each woman, and he thought that this would just be enough.

After the meal everyone went out on the lawn, where there were races for the women, a Maypole for the children and various games, drop the handkerchief, hunt the slipper, blind man's buff, and a wrestling competition for the men. After some bouts, the final match was between the two Daniel brothers, Mark and Paul, and Mark won, as was expected of him. Demelza presented him with a bright red kerchief. Then, having worked off some of their dinner, they were all invited in again to drink tea and eat heavy cake and saffron cake and gingerbreads.

The event of the evening was the visit of the travelling players. In Redruth the week before Ross had seen a tattered handbill nailed on a door, announcing that the Aaron Otway Players would visit the town that week to give a fine repertory of musical and sensational plays both ancient and modern.

He had found the leader of the company in the larger of the two shabby caravans in which they travelled and had engaged him to do a play in the library at Nampara on the following Wednesday. The lumber in the library had been moved to one end, the half-derelict room brushed out and planks put across boxes for the audience to sit on. The stage was defined by a few pieces of curtain cord tied together and stretched across the end of the room.

They performed *Elfrida* or *The Lost Wife*, a tragedy, by Johnson Hill, and afterwards a comic play called *The Slaughter House.* Jud Paynter stood at one side and came forward to snuff the candles when they grew too smoky.

To the country people it had all the thrill and glamour of Drury Lane. There were seven in the company; a mixed bag of semigipsies, ham actors and travelling singers. Aaron Otway, the leader, a fat sharp-nosed man with a glass eye, had all the showmanship of a huckster, and spoke the prologue and the *entr'acte* through his nose with tremendous gusto; he also acted the crippled father and the murderer, for which last part he wore a black cape, an eyeshade and a heavy black periwig. His time, like his cup later in the evening, was well filled. The heroine's part was played by a blonde woman of forty-five with a goitrous neck and large bejewelled hands; but the best actress of the company was a dark pretty slant-eyed girl of about nineteen, who acted the daughter with an unconvincing demureness and a woman of the streets with notable success.

Ross thought that with proper training she would go far. The chances were that neither opportunity nor training would come her way and that she would end up as a drab lurking at street corners or hang from a gibbet for stealing a gentleman's watch.

But other notions flickered through the head of a man sitting near. The gaunt Mark Daniel, tall and long-backed and powerful, was thirty, and never in his life had he seen anything to compare with this girl. She was so slender, so sleek, so glistening, so dainty, the way she stood on her toes, the way she bent her neck, her soft sibilant singing, the ochreous candle-reflecting glint of her dark eyes. To him there was nothing facile in her demureness. The smoky light showed up the soft young curve of her cheeks, the cheap gaudy costumes were exotic and unreal. She looked different from all other women, as if she came from a purer finer breed. He sat there unspeaking through the play and the singing which followed, his black Celtic eyes never leaving her when she was to be seen and staring vacantly at the back cloth when she had gone behind it.

After the play was over and drinks had gone all round, Will Nanfan got out his fiddle, Nick Vigus his flute and Pally Rogers his serpent. The benches were pushed back to the walls and dancing begun. These were not graceful restrained minuets but the full-blooded dances of the English countryside. They danced 'Cuckolds All Awry,' 'All in a Garden Green' and 'An Old Man's a Bedful of Bones.' Then someone proposed 'The Cushion Dance.' A young man began by dancing round the room with a cushion, until after a while he stopped and sang 'This dance I will no farther go,' to which the three musicians replied in chorus, 'I pray ee, good sir, why say so?' Then the dancer sang, 'Because Betty Prowse will not come to,' and the musicians shouted back, 'She must come to whether she will or no.' Then the man laid his cushion before the girl, she knelt on his cushion and he kissed her. After that they had to circle the room hand in hand singing, 'Prinkum, prankum, is a fine dance, an' shall us go dance it over again.' Then it was the girl's turn.

All went well and fun was fast until the old people were drawn in. Then Zacky Martin, intent on mischief, called out Aunt Betsy Triggs. Aunt Betsy, known for a comic when she got going, danced round with Zacky with a great flutter of skirts as if she was sixteen, not sixty-five. When it came to her turn to go alone she made a war dance of it, and at length she stopped at the end of the room. There was a great roar of laughter, for only one man was sitting there.

'This dance I will no farther go,' she screeched.

'I pray ee, good ma'am, why say so?' shouted everybody in reply.

'Because Jud Paynter will not come to!' said Aunt Betsy.

Another roar and then everybody chorused:

'He *must* come to, whether he will or no!'

There was a sudden scuffle and shouts of laughter as several men pounced on Jud just as he was going to sneak away. Protesting and struggling he was brought to the cushion; he would not kneel so they sat him on it. Then Aunt Betsy flung her arms round his neck and kissed him lavishly – so lavishly that he overbalanced and they both went rolling on the floor together, boots and skirts flying. After more uproar they got to their feet and circled the room together, Jud sheepishly joining in the rest, his bloodshot bulldog eyes half peevish, half wily. It was now his choice. Even with Prudie watching it was still his choice, and she could do nothing, it being only a game.

When he was left alone he plodded slowly round, trying to remember what he had to sing. At last he stopped.

'Here I stays!' he said.

There was more laughter, so much that people could hardly answer him.

'I pr-pray ee, good sir, why say so?'

'Cos I wants Char Nanfan, that's why, see?' Jud glared round as if expecting opposition, showing his two great teeth.

Will Nanfan's second wife was one of the comeliest women in the room, with her great fair plaits bound about her head. Everyone looked to see how she would take it, but she pulled a face and laughed and meekly went forward and knelt on the cushion. Jud viewed the prospect with pleasure for a moment, then wiped his mouth slowly along the back of his sleeve.

He kissed her with great relish, while all the young men in the room gave out a groan.

Jud lingered on, but there suddenly came a great shout from Prudie, who could bear it no longer.

'Leave go, yer great ox! No call to make a meal of 'er!'

Jud hastily straightened up amid more shouts of laughter, and it was noticed that when he fell out of the ring he went back to his corner, which was a long way from his wife.

After a bit the game finished and the dancing began again. From all this Mark Daniel had held aloof. He had always looked down on such prancing as effeminate (his was a silent, gaunt uncompromising maleness, unimpressionable and self-sufficient), but now he noticed that two or three of the actors, having finished their supper, were joining in.

He could hold back no longer and risked an eight-handed reel, which needed no delicacy of step. Then, rubbing his chin and wishing he had shaved more carefully, he joined in a country dance. At the other end of the long line of people he saw the girl. Keren Smith they said her name was. He could not keep his eyes off her, and danced almost as if he did not see the people opposite him.

And in some way the girl knew of his gaze. She never once looked at him, but there was something in her expression which told him she knew, a little self-conscious pursing of her young red lips, the way once or twice she pushed back her hair and tossed her head. Then he saw that for a second or two they would have to dance together. He stumbled and felt the sweat start. The moment was near, the next couple were dancing back to their places: he was off down the line, and she coming to meet him. They met, he grasped her hands, they danced round, her hair flying, she looked up once straight into his eyes; the look was blinding, dazzling; then they separated, he back to his place, she to hers. Her hands had been cool, but the palms of his were tingling as if they had met ice, met fire, been shocked by the touch.

The dance was over. He walked solidly back to his corner. Other people about him were talking and laughing and did not notice any change. He sat down, wiped the sweat off his forehead and calloused hands, which were twice the size of hers and could have crushed them to pulp. He watched her covertly, hoping for another glance but not getting it. But women, he knew, could look without looking.

He joined in nearly all the rest hoping that he might come near her again, but it did not happen. Nanfan's son, Joe Nanfan, who ought to have known better, had somehow got talking to her, and he and a wizened little man from the troop took her attention.

Then the party began to break up. Before any grownups left, Zacky Martin, 'scholar' of the neighbourhood and father of Jinny, got up and said a little piece, about what a brave time they had had, one and all, and how they'd all eaten enough to last 'em a week and drunk enough to last 'em a fortnight and danced enough to last 'em a month. And how twas only fitty here and now to say thank you kindly for a handsome day and all the generosity, to Captain Poldark and Mistress Poldark, and Miss Verity Poldark, and to wish long life and prosperity to them and theirs, not forgetting Miss Julia, and might she grow up a pride to her father and mother as he was sure she would, and that was all he had to say except thank you kindly again and good night.

Ross had them all served with a stiff glass of brandy and treacle. When they had drunk it he said, 'Your good wishes are of great value to me. I want Julia to grow up in this countryside as a daughter of mine and as a friend of yours. I want the land to be a part of her inheritance and friendship her earning from it. I give you our good wishes for the health and happiness of all *your* children, and may we all see a prosperous county and better times together.'

There was a rapturous cheer at this.

The Martins stayed behind – Mrs Zacky to help her daughter with the clearing up – so the Daniels went home alone.

Leading the way Grannie Daniel and Mrs Paul supported Mark's elder brother between them; then just behind, like frigates behind ships of the line, came Paul's three young children. A little to the left, heads close together in whispered talk, were Mark's two sisters, Mary and Ena; at the rear Old Man Daniel hobbled and grunted, and the long silent figure of Mark made up the convoy.

It was a pleasant July night with the western sky still luminous, as from the reflection of a lighted window. Now and then a cockchafer would drone past their ears and a bat lift fluttering wings in the dusk.

Once they had left the stream behind, the only babble was that of Grannie Daniel, a hearty fierce old woman in the late seventies.

The convoy, shadowy uneven figures in the shadowy half dark, breasted the rise of the hill, bobbed and stumbled on the sky line for a few seconds and then plunged down towards the cluster of cottages at Mellin. The valley swallowed them up and left only the quiet stars and the night glow of summer over the sea.

In his bed Mark Daniel lay very quiet listening. Their cottage, set between the Martins and the Viguses, had only two bedrooms. The smaller of these was used by Old Man Daniel and his mother and the eldest of Paul's three children. The other one Paul and his wife Beth and their two younger children took, while Mary and Ena slept in a lean-to at the back of the cottage. Mark slept on a straw mattress in the kitchen.

Everyone was a long time settling off, but at last when the house was quiet he stood up and drew on his breeches and coat again. He did not put on his boots until he was safe outside.

The silence of the night was full of tiny noises after the enclosed silence of the cottage. He set off in the direction of Nampara.

He did not know what he was going to do, but he could not lie and sleep with this thing inside him.

This time there was no silhouette on the sky line, but for a moment the trunk of a tree thickened and then a shadow moved beside the ruined engine house of Wheal Grace.

Nampara was not yet in darkness. Candles gleamed behind the curtains of Captain Poldark's bedroom and there was a light flickering about downstairs. But it was not for these that he looked. Some way up the valley beside the stream were the two caravans which housed the strolling players. He went towards them.

He saw as he drew nearer that there were lights here too, though they had been screened by the hawthorn and wild nut trees. For a man of his size he moved quietly, and he came close to the larger caravan without raising an alarm.

No one was asleep here or thought of it. Candles burned and the players were sitting about a long table. There was much talk and laughter and the chink of money. Mark crept near, keeping open a wary eye for a possible dog.

The windows of the caravan were some distance from the ground, but with his great height he could see in. They were all here: the fat man with the glass eye, the blowsy leading woman, a thin fair man who had played the hero, the shrivelled little comedian . . . and the girl. They were playing some card game, with thick greasy cards. The girl was just dealing, and as she laid a card each time opposite the thin fair man she said something that made them all laugh. She was wearing a kind of Chinese smock and her black hair was ruffled as if she had been running her hands through it; she sat now holding her cards, one bare elbow on the table and a frown of impatience growing.

But there is a stage when even the slightly imperfect is an added lure; somehow Mark was grateful for this falling short from divinity: he stood there looking in, one great hand holding back a prickly hawthorn bough, the uncertain light from the window setting shadows and mock expressions on his face.

There was a sudden roar of laughter, and in a moment the comedian was gathering in all the pennies on the board. The girl was angry, for she flung away her cards and stood up. The fair man leered at her and asked a question. She shrugged and tossed her head; then her mood changed, and with incredible swift grace she slid, pliant as a sapling, round the table to bend and kiss the comedian's bald head, at the same time drawing two pennies away from under his lifted fingers.

Too late, he saw through it and snatched at her hand, but she danced away, showing her fine teeth in glee, and took shelter behind the fair man, who fended off the angry comedian. Almost before Mark could realize it, she was out of the caravan, banging the door and giggling with triumph. Too occupied to notice him in the dark, she ran towards her own caravan fifty yards up the valley.

Mark sank back into the shadows as the comedian came to the door and shouted and swore after her. But he did not follow, for the blowsy woman squeezed past.

'Leave her go,' she said. 'You ought to know she's still a child, Tupper. She can't bear to lose at a game of cards.'

'Child or not, she stole the price of a glass of gin! I've seen folk ducked and whipped for less! Who do she think she is; Queen o' Sheba, with her airs? Dang and rot all women! I'll have her in the morning. D'you 'ear, Kerenhappuch! I'll 'ave you in the morning, you sneavy little dumdolly!'

The answer was the slamming of a door. The leader of the troop elbowed his way past the woman.

'Stop this noise! Don't forget we're still on Poldark land, friends, an' though he's treated us good, you wouldn't get soft smoothing if you found yourself on the wrong side of him! Leave the little neap alone, Tupper.'

The others, grumbling and talking, went in, the woman walking across to the other caravan.

Mark stayed where he was, crouching in the bushes. There was nothing more he could do or see, but he would wait until all was quiet. He would not sleep if he went home, and he was due at Grambler Mine at six.

There was a light now in the other caravan. He straightened up and moved in a semicircle towards it. As he did so the door of the caravan opened and someone came out. There was the clatter of a bucket, and he saw a figure coming towards him. He ducked down into the bushes.

It was Keren.

She passed close to him and went on her way whistling some song softly between her teeth. The clank, clank of the wooden bucket went with her, blatant among the softer noises of the copse.

He followed. She was making for the stream.

He came up with her as she knelt to scoop up a bucketful. They were some distance from the caravan, and he watched a moment and heard her swear impatiently, for the stream was shallow and she never had the bucket more than a third full.

He stepped out of the bushes.

'You rightly d'need a pot or a pan to ——'

She turned and half screamed.

'Leave me alone you . . .' Then she saw it was not the comedian and screamed louder.

'I mean no 'arm,' said Mark, his voice quiet and sounding firm. 'Hush, or you'll rouse the valley.'

She stopped as quickly as she had begun and stared up at him.

'Oh . . . it's you . . .'

Half pleased to be known, half doubtful, he looked down at the delicate oval of her face.

'Yes.' It was lighter here away from the overhanging trees. He could see the moist gleam of her bottom lip.

'What d'you want?'

'I thought to aid you,' he said.

He picked up the bucket and went out into the middle of the stream where there was a narrow channel. Here he was able to fill the bucket and brought it to her side.

'What're you doin' sneakin' around here so late at night?' she asked sharply.

He said: 'I reckon I liked that, what you did to-night. I . . . liked that play.'

'Do you live . . . at the house?'

'No. Over there.'

'Where?'

'Down in Mellin Hollow.'

'What d'you do?'

'Me? I'm a miner.'

She moved her shoulders distastefully. 'That's not a pretty job, is it?'

'I . . . liked the play acting,' he said.

She looked at him obliquely, taking in the size of him, the set of his shoulders. She could see no expression on the shadowy face turned to her.

'Was it you that won the wrestling?'

He nodded, not showing his pleasure. 'But you wasn't ——'

'Oh, I wasn't there. But I heard.'

'That play,' he began.

'Oh, that.' She pouted her lips, turning her profile against the lighter sky. 'Did you like me in it?'

'. . . Yes.'

'I thought you did,' she said calmly. 'I'm pretty, aren't I?'

'. . . Yes,' he answered, forcing out the word.

'You'd best be going now,' she advised.

He hesitated, fumbling with his hands. 'Won't you stay and talk for a while?'

She laughed softly. 'What for? I got better ways of passing my time. Besides, I'm surprised at you. It's very late.'

'Yes,' he said, 'I know.'

'You'd best be off before they come lookin' for me.'

'Shall you be at Grambler to-morrow night?'

'Oh, yes. I expect.'

'I'll be there,' he said.

She turned and picked up the bucket.

'I'll carry that,' he said.

'What? Back to the camp? No, indeed.'

'I'll look for ee to-morrow,' he said.

'I'll look for you too,' she answered back over her shoulder, carelessly. 'You will?'

'Yes . . . maybe.' The words floated to him, for she had gone, the clank of the bucket dulled and sibilant now as it receded.

He stood a moment. 'All right, then!' he called.

He turned and walked home under the quiet stars, his long powerful stride longer than ever and his slow steady careful mind moving in uncharted seas.

Chapter six

DEMELZA A FEW mornings later was eating a silent breakfast and scheming. Ross should have known by now that silence at a mealtime was an ominous symptom. For a few days after the christening catastrophe she had been subdued, but that had been gone some time now. Although she had fully intended to brood her nature had defeated her.

'When was it you was thinking to ride in an' see Jim?' she asked.

'Jim?' he said, coming down from thoughts of copper companies and their misdeeds.

'Jim Carter. You said you was minded to take Jinny in with you next time.'

'So I am. I thought next week. That's if you can spare her and have no objections.'

Demelza glanced at him.

'It is all one to me,' she said awkwardly. 'Shall you be one night away?'

'The gossips have minds like a jericho, and there are some who will whisper over my riding off in the company of a serving maid. Er . . .' He paused.

'Of *another* serving maid?'

'Well, if you put it so. Jinny is not uncomely and they will have no regard for my good name.'

Demelza put up two fingers to push away a curl.

'What's your own mind, Ross?'

He smiled slightly. 'They may whisper till their tongues swell, and have done before to-day.'

'Then go,' she said. 'I'm not afeared of Jinny Carter, or the old women.'

Once the day had been fixed, the next thing was to get a message over to Verity. On the Monday morning, Ross being busy at the mine, she walked the three miles to Trenwith House.

She had only been to the house of her superior cousins-by-marriage once before; and when she came in sight of its mullioned windows and mellow Elizabethan stone she modestly made a circuit to come upon it again from the rear.

She found Verity in the still-room.

Demelza said: 'No, thank ee. We're brave an' well. I came to ask you for the loan of a horse, Verity dear. It is rather a secret, I didn't wish for Ross to know; he's going, next Thursday he's going to Bodmin to see Jim Carter that's in prison an' takin' Jinny Carter with him, so that there's no horse for me to go to Truro, as I wanted to go while Ross is away.'

Their eyes met. Demelza, though slightly breathless, looked empty of guile.

'I'll lend you Random if you wish. Is this to be a secret from me also?'

'No, indeed,' Demelza said. 'For I couldn't borrow a horse if it was a secret from you, could I?'   .

Verity smiled. 'Very well, my dear, I'll not press you. But you cannot go to Truro alone. We have a pony we can loan you for Jud.'

'There's no tellin' what time Ross'll be gone on Thursday, so we'll walk over for the horses if it is all the same to you, Verity. Maybe you'll leave us come in this way, then Francis and – and Elizabeth wouldn't know.'

'It is all very mysterious, I assure you. I trust I'm not conniving at some misadventure.'

'No, no, indeed. It is just . . . something I have had a mind to do for a long time.'

'Very well, my dear.'

Verity smoothed down the front of her blue dimity frock. She looked plain and prim this morning. One of her old-maidish days. Demelza's heart almost failed her at the enormity of her intention.

Ross looked about him with an appreciative eye as he rode up the valley early on Thursday morning with Jinny Carter silent beside him on old near-blind Ramoth. This land of shallow soil soon exhausted itself, and one had to give the ground ample time to recover from a cereal crop; but the fields he had chosen for this year were bearing well. They were all colours from pea green to a biscuit brown. A good harvest would be some compensation for the storm damage in the spring.

As he disappeared over the hill Demelza turned and went indoors. All the day was before her now, all to-day and part of to-morrow if necessary; but Julia put a shorter time limit on her actions. If she was fed at seven she would do well enough with some sugar and water at noon, which Prudie could give her, and then she would last out till five.

Ten hours. There was much to do in the time. 'Jud!'

'Ais?'

'Are you ready?'

'Well, pick me liver, I only seen Mr Ross out of the 'ouse two minutes.'

'We've precious little time to waste. If I ain't – if I'm not back before five little Julia'll be cryin' out, and me perhaps miles away.'

'A danged misthought notion from last to first,' said Jud, putting his bald fringed head round the door. 'There's them as'd say I'd no leave to lend meself to such fancy skims. Tedn sensible. Tedn right. Tedn' *uman*. . . .'

'Tedn for you to argue all morning,' said Prudie, appearing behind him. 'Ef she say go, go and begone. Ef there's a dido with Mr Ross that's for she to suffer.'

'I aren't so sartin,' said Jud. 'I don't know, not I. There's no saying wi' womenfolk 'ow they'll jump when the screw's on 'em. Cuzzle as a cartload o' monkeys. Well, I'm warning ye. If I take the fault for this, may I be 'anged for a fool.' He went off grumbling to get his best coat.

They left soon after seven and picked up the horse and pony at Trenwith House. Demelza had dressed herself carefully to-day in her new close-fitting blue riding habit cut after a masculine style, with a pale blue bodice to give it a touch of something different and a three-cornered small brimmed hat. She kissed Verity and thanked her very affectionately, as if she thought the warmth of her hug would make up for all the deceit.

Jud's presence was useful, for he knew the way to Falmouth across country by narrow lane and mule track, and they touched no town or village where they might be recognized.

Nothing in these hamlets passed unnoticed or unremarked. Every tinner and farm worker stopped in his work, hand on hips, to look over the ill-assorted couple, Jud ugly and whistling on his little shaggy pony, she young and handsome on her tall grey horse. Every cottage had its peering face.

They had no watch between them, but two or three hours before midday they caught a gleam of blue and silver water, and she knew she must be near.

They lost the river among the trees and began sharply to pick their way down a dusty hill with cart ruts, and found themselves among cottages. Beyond the cottages was a great landlocked harbour and the masts of ships. Now her heart began to beat. The hazard of the day began. All her private imaginings in the quiet of the night were to come up against the hard and difficult truth. Her own view of Verity's lover, a soft-spoken, handsome middle-aged sailor, and the picture that Ross had raised by his description of the scene in Truro; these had to be reconciled and confronted with the truth before anything else was begun.

After a few minutes they reached a cobbled square, and the water glittered like a silver plate between some houses of larger size. There were plenty of people in the streets who seemed in no hurry to move aside for a couple of riders. Jud pushed his way through shouting and swearing.

At the other side they looked upon a quay pyramided with merchandise which was being unloaded from a longboat. Demelza stared about her, faintly mesmerized. A group of blue-coated sailors with pigtails stared up at the girl on the horse. A big Negress went by; and two dogs were quarrelling over a crust. Someone leaned out from an upper window and threw more refuse in the road.

'Wot now?' said Jud, taking off his hat and scratching his head.

'Ask someone,' she said. 'That's the proper way.'

'Thur's no one t'ask,' said Jud, staring round at the crowded square. Three important-looking sailors with gold braid on their uniforms were past before Demelza could decide. Jud sucked his two great teeth. She edged her horse past some urchins playing in the gutter and closed up to four men who were talking together on the steps of one of the large houses. Prosperous merchants, fat-stomached and bewigged.

She knew that Jud should have done the asking but could not trust his manners. At that moment Random chose to side-step, and the clatter of his hooves on the cobbles took their attention.

'I beg your pardon for the interference,' Demelza said in her best voice, 'But could you please to direct me to the house of Captain Andrew Blamey.'

They all pulled off their hats. Nothing quite like that had ever happened to Demelza before. They took her for a lady and it made her blush.

One said: 'Pardon me, ma'am, I didn't catch the name.'

'Captain Andrew Blamey of the Lisbon packets.'

She caught an exchanged glance.

'He lives at the end of the town, ma'am. Down this street, ma'am. Perhaps one third of a mile. But the packet agent would direct you, if you called on him. He could also inform you if Captain Blamey is home or at sea.'

'He's home,' said another. 'The *Caroline*'s due to sail on Saturday forenoon.'

'I'm greatly obliged to ye,' said Demelza. 'Down this street, you said? Thank you. Good day.'

They bowed again; she touched her horse and went off. Jud, who had been listening with his mouth open, followed slowly, muttering about fine feathers.

They trekked up a long narrow lane, mainly squalid huts and courtyards with here and there a house or a tiny shop, the land climbing steeply away among trees and scrub to the right. The harbour held two or three dozen ships in an almost closed hand: she had seen nothing like it in her life, accustomed as she was to the sight of an occasional brig or cutter beating away from the land on the dangerous north coast.

They were directed to one of the better houses with a room built out over the front door to form a pillared porch. This was more imposing than she had expected.

She got down stiffly and told Jud to hold her horse. Her habit was thick with dust, but she knew of no place to go and tidy herself.

'I'll not be long,' she said. 'Don't go away an' don't get drunk or I'll ride home wi'out you.'

'Drunk,' said Jud, wiping his head. 'No one 'as the call to leave that at my door. Many's the week as passes an' never a drop of liquor. Many's the time I ain't gotten the spittle for a fair good spit. That dry. An' you says drunk. *You* says drunk. Why, I mind the time when you was tiddley on account of findin' a bottle o' grog, an' twas ——'

'Stay here,' said Demelza, turning her back. 'I'll not be gone long.'

She pulled at the bell. Jud was a spectre of old times. Forget him. Face this. What would Ross say if he could see her now? And Verity. Base treason. She wished she had never come. She wished . . .

The door opened and Jud's grumblings died away.

'I wish to see Captain Blamey, please.'

'He bain't in, ma'am. He did say he'd be back afore noon. Would ye wait?'

'Yes,' said Demelza, swallowing and going in.

She was shown conversationally into a pleasant square room on the first floor. It was panelled with cream-painted wood and there was a model ship among the littered papers on the desk.

'What name sh'll I tell him?' asked the old woman, coming to the end of her chatter.

At the last moment Demelza withheld the vital word. 'I'd better prefer to tell him that myself. Just say a – er – someone . . .'

'Very well, ma'am.'

The door closed. Demelza's heart was thumping in her breast. She listened to the woman's self-important footsteps receding down the stairs. The documents on the desk took her curiosity, but she was afraid to go over and peer at them and her reading was still so slow.

A miniature by the window. Not Verity. His first wife whom he had knocked down to die? Little framed silhouettes of two children. She had forgotten his children. A painting of another ship, it looked like a man-of-war. From here she found she could see the lane outside.

She edged nearer the window. Jud's shiny head. A woman selling oranges. He was swearing at her. Now she was swearing back. Jud seemed scandalized that anyone could match his own bad words. 'Captain Blamey,' she would say, 'I have come to see ee – to see you about my cousin.' No, first she'd best make sure he was not married again to someone else. 'Captain Blamey,' she would begin. 'Are you married again?' Well, she couldn't say that. What did she hope to do? 'Leave it alone,' Ross had warned. 'It's dangerous to tamper with other people's lives.' That was what she was doing, against all orders, all advice.

There was a map on the desk. Lines were traced across it in red ink. She was about to go and look when another noise in the street drew her notice again.

Under a tree a hundred yards back were a group of seamen. A rough lot, bearded and pigtailed and ragged, but in the middle of them was a man in a cocked hat talking to them in some annoyance. They pressed around him, angry and gesticulating, and for a moment he seemed to disappear among them. Then his hat showed again. The men stepped back to let him through, but several still shouted and shook their fists. The group closed up behind and they stood together staring after him. One picked up a stone but another grasped his arm and stopped him from throwing it. The man in the cocked hat walked on without glancing behind.

As he came nearer the house Demelza felt as if the lining of her stomach was giving way. She knew by instinct that this was the person she had plotted and schemed and ridden twenty miles to see.

But for all Ross's warnings she had not imagined he would be like this. Did he never do anything but quarrel with people, and was this the man for loss of whom Verity was sere and yellow before her time? In a flash Demelza saw the other side of the picture, which up till now had evaded her, that Francis and Old Charles and Ross might be right and Verity's instinct at fault, not theirs.

In panic she looked at the door to gauge her chance of escape; but the outer door slammed and she knew it was too late. There was no drawing back now.

She stood rigidly by the windows and listened to the voices below in the hall. Then she heard a tread on the stairs.

He came in, his face still set in hard lines from his quarrel with the seamen. Her first thought was that he was old. He had taken off his cocked hat and wore his own hair: it was grey at the temples and specked with grey on the crown. He must be over forty. His eyes were blue and fierce and the skin was drawn up around them from peering into the sun. They were the eyes of a man who might have been holding himself always ready for the first leap forward of a race.

He came across to the desk and put his hat on it, looked directly at his visitor.

'My name is Blamey, ma'am,' he said in a hard clear voice. 'Can I be of service to you?'

All Demelza's prepared openings were forgotten. She was overawed by his manner and his authority.

She moistened her lips and said: 'My name is Poldark.'

It was as if some key had turned in the inner mechanism of this hard man, locking away before it could escape any show of surprise or sentiment.

He bowed slightly. 'I haven't the honour of your acquaintance.'

'No, sir,' said Demelza. 'No. You d'know my husband, Captain Ross Poldark.'

There was something ship-like about his face, jutting and aggressive and square, weathered but unbeaten.

'A few years ago I had occasion to meet him.'

She could not shape the next sentence. With her hand she felt the chair behind her, and sat in it.

'I've rid twenty miles to see you.'

'I am honoured.'

'Ross don't know I've come,' she said. 'Nobody knows I've come.'

His unflinching eyes for a moment left her face and travelled over her dusty dress.

'I can offer you some refreshment?'

'No. . . . No. . . . I must leave again in a few minutes.' Perhaps that was a mistake, for tea or anything would have given her ease and time.

There was a strained pause. Under the window the quarrel with the orange woman broke out afresh.

'Was that your servant at the door?'

'Yes.'

'I thought I recognized him. I should have known.'

His voice left no doubt of his feelings.

She tried once again. 'I – mebbe I shouldn't ought to have come, but I felt I must. I wanted to see you.'

'Well?'

'It is about Verity.'

Just for a moment his expression grew embarrassed; that name could no longer be mentioned. Then he abruptly glanced at the clock. 'I can spare you three minutes.'

Something in the glance quenched the last of Demelza's hopes. 'I been wrong to come,' she said. 'I think there's nothing to say to you. I made a mistake, that's all.'

'Well, what is it you made a mistake in? Since you are here you'd best say it.'

'Nothing. Nothing will be any use saying to the likes of you.'

He gave her a furious look. 'I ask you, tell me.'

She glanced at him again.

'It is about Verity. Ross married me last year. I knew nothing about Verity till then. An' she never told me a thing. I persuaded it out of Ross. About you, I mean. I love Verity. I'd give anything to see 'er happy. An' she isn't happy. She's never got over it. She's not the sort to get over it. Ross said it was dangerous to meddle. He said I must leave it alone. But I couldn't leave it alone till I'd seen you. I – I thought Verity was right an' they was wrong. I – I had to be sure they was right before I could let it drop.'

Her voice seemed to go on and on, into an arid empty space. She said: 'Are you married again?'

'No.'

'I schemed to-day. Ross has gone Bodmin. I borrowed the horses and came over with Jud. I'd best be getting back, for I've a young baby at home.'

She got up and slowly made for the door.

He caught her arm as she went past him.

'Is Verity ill?'

'No,' Demelza said angrily. 'Ailing but not ill. She looks ten years olderer than her age.'

His eyes were suddenly fierce with pain.

'D'you not know the whole story? They cannot fail to have told you the whole story.'

'Yes, about your first wife. But if I was Verity ——'

'You're not Verity. How can you know what she feels?'

'I don't, but I ——'

'She never once sent me any word. . . .'

'Nor you never sent her any word neither.'

'Has she ever said anything?'

'No.'

'Then it's pitiable. . . . This attempt on your part . . . this – this intrusion . . .'

'I know,' said Demelza, nearly crying. 'I know now. I thought to help Verity, but I wisht now I'd never tried. You see, I don't understand. If folk in our way love one another it is more than enough to bring 'em together, drink or no. If the father's against it then that's some reason, but now the father's dead an' Verity's too proud to make any move. And you – and you . . . But I thought you were different. I thought ——'

'You thought I was likely to sit moping my time away. No doubt the rest of your family has long since written me off as a failure and a drunkard, drooling in taprooms and lurching home of a night. No doubt Miss Verity has long since agreed with her weakling brother that it was better for all that Captain Blamey was sent about his business. What for ——'

'How dare you say that of Verity!' Demelza cried out, standing up to him. 'How dare you! An' to think I've rid myself sore to hear it! To think I've schemed and plotted and lied and borrowed the horses and one thing and the next. An' to say such of Verity when she's ill for pining of you! Judas God! Leave me get out of here!'

He barred her way. 'Wait.'

His epaulettes and gold braid no longer counted.

'Wait for what? For more insults? Let me past or I shall call Jud!'

He took her arm again. 'It is no reflection on you, girl. I grant you did it all from the best of motives. I grant you your good will ——'

She was trembling, but with great self-control did not try to wrench her arm free.

For a moment he did not go on, but peered at her closely as if trying to see all that she had not said. His own anger was suddenly in ashes. He said:

'We've all moved on since those days, grown, changed. It's – you see, it's all forgotten, behind us – but it has left us bitter. There were times when I ranted and railed – if you understood – if you'd known it all you'd see that. When you stir up old things best forgotten you're bound to stir up some of the mud that's settled round 'em.'

'Leave go my arm,' she said.

He made a brief awkward gesture and turned away. She went stiffly to the door and grasped the handle.

She glanced back. He was staring out towards the harbour. She hesitated a second longer and there came a knock at the door.

No one answered it. Demelza stepped aside as the handle turned. It was the woman who looked after him.

'Beg pardon. Did you want something, sir?'

'No,' said Blamey.

'Your dinner's ready.'

Blamey turned and glanced at Demelza.

'Will you stay and take a meal with me, ma'am?'

'No,' said Demelza. 'Thank you. I'd best be getting back.'

'Then perhaps you will first show Mistress Poldark to the door.'

The woman bobbed. 'Yes, surely, sir.'

Conversationally she led Demelza downstairs again. She warned her to mind the step for the light was none too good, the curtain being drawn to keep the carpet from fading as this window looked due south. She said the day was warm and there might be thunder, it being a bad sign that St Anthony's Head was so clear. Still talking, she opened the front door and wished her visitor good day.

Outside in the street Jud was sitting blinking on a stone wall beside her pony. He was sucking an orange he had filched from the orange woman's cart.

'Finished already, Mrs?' he said. 'Reckoned 'e'd soon do for ee. Well, all's for the best, I reckon, as leaves well alone.'

Demelza did not reply. Captain Blamey was still watching her from the upper room.

Chapter seven

JULIA HAD WIND and was thoroughly cross; Demelza had sore buttocks and was thoroughly disheartened. They made a mopish pair, while Jud took the two animals back to Trenwith and Prudie grumbled over the evening meal.

Julia, fed and changed, went into a fitful sleep but Demelza, feeding by herself for the first time in the parlour, swallowed her food anyhow and in lumps, hating the thought of her own defeat but knowing that the defeat was final. Ross had been right. Even Francis had been right. There would never have been hope for a happy marriage for Verity. And yet . . .

Oh, well . . .

There broke upon her deep reflections, levering a way like a swollen female Caliban into her absent mind, the amorphous figure of Prudie. It stood there beside the boiled beef talking at her, making growling and discordant claims on her attention, until at last she was forced to give it.

'Eh?' she said.

Prudie stared back at her, seeing that she had been wasting her breath.

'Got the mullygrubs, 'ave ee, an?'

'No, Prudie, but I'm feeling tired an' cross. And I'm that sore I can scarce sit down. I can't reckon how it is but everytime I touch a bone I go "Oohh!"'

'There's naught t'wonder at in that, maid. . . . 'Osses, I always d'say, is not for ridin' whether saddled or bare-ridged, side-sat or ascrode. Have 'em hitched to a cart an' that's different. But then a ox do do as well, an' twice as peaceable. Only onct 'ave I bin on a 'oss an' that were when Jud brought me from Bedruthan nigh on sixteen year ago. Twere an irkish kind of a journey, up 'ill an' down dell, wi' no rest neither for flesh nor bone. That night I smeared axle grease all over me what's-it, an' none too soon for taking care, else the skin would've bursten, I bla'. I tell ee what I'll do for ee. When you've took yer clothes off I'll come rub ee over them parts wi' some balsam I got at Marasanvose Fair, an?'

'I'll be well enough,' said Demelza. 'Leave me be. I'll sleep on my face to-night.'

'Well, that's as you d'please. I came to tell ee that Mark Daniel's outside by the kitchen door besting whether to come in and see you or no.'

Demelza sat up and winced. 'Mark Daniel? What does he want with me?'

'Nothin' by rights. He come first at noon. They're from home, I says, an'll not be back, she afore supper, I says, an' he afore cockshut to-morrow, I says. Oh, he says, an' goes off an' comes back and says what time time did ye say Mistress Poldark would be back, he says, an' I says supper to-night, I says, an' off he d'go wi' his long legs stalking.'

'Has he asked for me to-night?'

'Aye, and I told him you was suppin' an' not to be disturbed by the likes of he. Gracious knows, there's enough fuss one way and the next without all the bal-men in district callin' round to pass the time o' day.'

'He must want more than that,' Demelza said, and yawned. She straightened her frock and patted her hair. 'You'd best show him in.'

She felt lonely and important to-night. The last time Ross had ridden to Bodmin she had had Verity to stay.

Mark came in twisting his cap. In the parlour he looked enormous.

'Oh, Mark,' she said, 'did you want to see Ross? He's from home and is lying to-night at Bodmin. Was it important or shall you wait until to-morrow?'

He looked younger too in the evening light and without his cap, his head bent for fear of the ceiling beams.

'I wish twas easier to explain, Mistress Poldark. I did ought to have called in to Cap'n Ross yesterday, but twasn't quite decided then, an' I didn't fancy to tell my chickens afore they was bealed. An' now – an' now there's the need to hurry, because . . .'

Demelza rose, careful to avoid grimaces, and went to the window. It would not be dark yet for an hour, but the sun was winking out behind the western rim of the valley and shadows were deepening among the trees. She knew that Mark was a special friend of Ross's, second only to Zacky Martin in his confidences, and she was a little flustered at his call.

He was waiting for her to speak and watching her.

'Why don't you sit down, Mark, an' tell me what it is that's troubling you?'

Presently she looked round and saw that he was still standing.

'Well, what is it?' she said.

His long dark face twitched once. 'Mistress Poldark, I have the thought to be married.'

She gave a little relieved smile.

'Well, I'm glad, Mark. But why should that be worrying you?' As he did not speak she went on: 'Who have you the mind for?'

'Keren Smith,' he said.

'Keren Smith?'

'The maid that came wi' the travelling players, mistress. The dark one wi' the – wi' the long hair and the smooth skin.'

Demelza's mind went back. 'Oh,' she said. 'I know.' She did not like to sound unpleased. 'But what do she say to it? Are they still hereabouts?'

They were still hereabouts. Standing by the door, grim and quiet, Mark told his story. And much that he did not say could be guessed. Almost every night since their first meeting he had followed the players round, watching Keren, meeting her afterwards, trying to persuade her of his sincerity and his love. At first she had laughed at him, but something in his great size and the money he pressed on her at last won her interest. Almost as a joke she had accepted his advances and then suddenly found that what he had to offer was no light thing after all. She had never had a home and had never had a suitor like this.

Mark had seen Keren last night at Ladock. By Sunday of this week they would be at St Dennis on the edge of the moor. She had promised to marry him, promised faithfully on one condition. He must find somewhere for them to live; she would not share his father's house, crowded already, for a single day. Let him only find somewhere just for her alone before Sunday and she would run away with him. But if the company once travelled beyond St Dennis she would not, she said, have the heart to come back. From there they would begin the long trek to Bodmin and not even if Mark took a pit pony for her would she face the moors a second time. It was a flight from St Dennis or nothing. And it was up to him.

'And what do you think to do, Mark?' Demelza asked.

The Cobbledicks had moved into the Clemmows' old cottage; so there was no place empty at all. What Mark had in mind was to build himself a cottage before Sunday. His friends were ready to help. They had picked a possible spot, a piece of rough wasteland looking over on to Treneglos property though still on Poldark land. But with Captain Ross away . . .

It was strange to think of the feelings of love stirring in this tough, short-spoken, gaunt man; stranger still to think of the wayward pretty May fly who had wakened them.

'What d'you want for me to do?' she asked.

He told her. He needed leave to build. He thought he might rent the land. But if he waited until to-morrow it meant missing a whole day.

'Isn't it too late already?' she asked. 'You can't ever build a cottage by Sunday.'

'I reckon we can just do un,' he said. 'There's clay to hand and, private like, thinkin' it might come, I been gathering stuff of nights. Ned Bottrell over to Sawle has got thatchin' straw. We can make do, if only tis a four walls and roof to 'er head.'

Words were on Demelza's tongue to say that any woman who made such conditions ought to be left where she belonged; but she saw from Mark's look that it wouldn't do.

'What land is it you want, Mark?'

'Over the brow beyond Mellin. There's a piece of old scrub an' furse, an' some attle from an old mine ditch. By the bed o' the leat as dried up years ago.'

'I know it . . .' Her mind went over the issue. 'Well, it is not really in my hand to give it to you. What you must do is think to yourself: I'm an old friend, wouldn't Captain Ross let me have this bit o' scrubland to build my cottage?'

Mark Daniel looked at her a moment, then slowly shook his head.

'Tis not for me to decide, Mistress Poldark. Friends in a manner of saying we been all our lives; grown up head by head. We've sailed together, running rum and gin, we've fished together on Hendrawna Beach, we've wrastled together when we was tackers. But when all's done he belong up here and I belong down there, and – and I'd no more think to take what was his wi'out a by-your-leave than he'd think to take mine.'

All the garden was in shadow now. The bright sky seemed to have no link with the gathering dusk of the valley, the land had fallen away into this abyss of evening while the day still blazed overhead. A thrush had caught a snail and the only sound outside was the *tap-tap-tap* as he swung it against a stone.

'If tis not in your power to do it,' said Mark, 'then I must see for a piece o' land elsewhere.'

Demelza knew what chance he had of that. She found when she turned from staring at the sky that she could only see his eyes and the firm parenthesis of his cheekbones. She went across and picked up flint and steel. Presently her hands were lit up, her face, her hair, as the first candle sputtered and glowed.

'Take an acre measuring from the bed o' the dry stream, Mark,' she said. 'I can't say more'n that. How you shall hire it I've no notion, for I'm not learned in figures an' things. That's for you an' Ross to make out. But I promise you you shall not be moved.'

The man at the door was silent while two more candles were lit from the first. She heard him stir and shuffle one foot.

'I can't thank you right, mistress,' he said suddenly, 'but if there's service to be done for you or yours leave me know.'

She lifted her head, and smiled across at him.

'I know that, Mark,' she said.

Then he was gone and she was left alone with the candles lifting their heads in the lightening room.

Chapter eight

SOME GROUND HAZE gathered with the dark, and that night the moon came up like a bald old redskin peering over a hill. In the hollow of Mellin and the barren declivity of Reath beyond, it looked down upon a string of black figures, active and as seeming aimless as ants in the sudden light of a lantern, moving backwards and forwards over the hummock of moorland beyond Joe Trigg's cottage and down towards a path of rubble-scarred ground sloping indeterminately east.

The building was on.

There were nine to help him at the start: Paul, his brother and Ena Daniel, Zacky Martin and his two eldest boys, Ned Bottrell, who was a cousin from Sawle, Jack Cobbledick and Will Nanfan.

First there was the site to be marked; and this must be level enough to support the four walls. They found a patch and cleared it of stones, about a hundred yards from Reath Ditch. Then they roughly marked it into a rectangle and began. The walls were to be made of clay, beaten hard and mixed with straw and small stones. When Ross killed a bullock at the time of the christening Zacky had helped him and had been given a bag of bullock hair off the hide. This was used now, being stirred in with the clay and the stones and the straw to make a binding mixture. Four great boulders were used for the corners of the house, and from one to another of these a rough trough was built of wood about two feet wide and two deep. Into this the clay and stones and all the rest were shovelled and stamped down and left to set while more was mixed.

At eleven the three youngsters, being on the early core, were sent home to sleep, and at midnight Cobbledick turned his long high stepping stride towards bed. Zacky Martin and Will Nanfan stayed until three, Paul Daniel until five, when he had just time to get home and have a plate of barley bread and potatoes before going on to the mine. Ned Bottrell, who ran his own little tin stamp, left at eight. Mark went steadily on until Beth Daniel came over with a bowl of watery soup and a pilchard on a chunk of bread. Having worked without a break for nearly fourteen hours, he sat down to have his food and stared at the result. The foundations were in and the walls just begun. The area of the cottage was slightly larger than intended, but that would be all to the good; there would be time for partitioning off when She was in it. To get her in it: that was his obsession.

This morning early the little children had been round before they went off to the fields; then later three or four of their mothers, staying an hour to help and talk or looking in on their way to work. Everyone had taken his cause to heart and no one had any doubt that he would have his house before Sunday. They might have been critical of the marriage since no one wanted a stranger, but Mark Daniel being who he was and popular, people were willing to swallow their prejudices.

At seven that evening Zacky Martin, Will Nanfan and Paul Daniel, having had a few hours' sleep, arrived back, and later they were joined by Ned Bottrell and Jack Cobbledick. At ten another figure came out of the cloud-shadowed moonlight behind them, and Mark saw by his height that it was Ross. He stepped down the ladder and went to meet him.

As they neared each other likeness might have been remarked between these men. They were of an age, ran to bone rather than flesh, were dark and long-legged and indocile. But at close quarters difference was more noticeable than sameness. Daniel, darker-skinned but sallow with underground work, had a stiffness that the other lacked, was broader in the jaw and narrower at the temples, his hair straight and close-cropped and black without the copper. They might have been distant relatives branching far from a common line.

'Well, Mark,' said Ross as he came up. 'So this is your house?'

'Yes, Cap'n.' Mark turned and stared at the four walls now nearly roof-high, at the gaping sockets where the windows should go. 'So far as it is made.'

'What have you for floor joists?'

'There's wreck timber enough, I reckon. And these pit props. The planchin' will have to wait till later.'

'For an upper room?'

'Ais. I thought it could be builded in the thatch; twill save the wall-building, for I've no more straw to spare – nor time.'

'You've time for nothing. What of the windows and door?'

'Father will loan us his door till I can make another. An' he's hammering up some shutters for us over home. Tis all he can do with his rheumatics. They'll pass for the time.'

'I suppose,' Ross said, 'you're making no error, Mark. In choosing this girl', I mean. D'you think she will settle down here after roaming the countryside?'

'She's never had no home, not since she can mind anything. That is the more reason why she should want one now.'

'When are you to be married?'

'Monday first thing ef all d'go well.'

'But can you?'

'Yes, I reckon. A fortnight gone she promised she'd wed me and I asked parson to call the banns. Then she changed her mind. This Sunday will be the third time. I'll take her over to Parson Odgers Monday so soon as we're back.'

Behind his words lay the shadow of a fortnight's struggle. The prize had one minute looked close within his hand and the next as remote as ever.

'Mistress Poldark'll 'ave told you,' Mark went on.

'She told me.'

'Did I do right in askin' her?'

'Of course. Take more of this bottom if you wish to reclaim it, Mark.'

Mark inclined his head. '*Thank ye*, sir.'

'I'll have the deed drawn up to-morrow.' Ross stared at the shapeless yellow mound. 'It is possible I can find you a door.'

They were not acting at St Dennis but were resting before the long trek to Bodmin to-morrow. This week they had gradually left the civilized west of Cornwall behind and had moved off towards the northern wilderness. For Keren each day had been worse than the last; the weather was too hot or too wet, the barns they played in impossible to manage, leaky and rat-infested or too small to move in. They had made barely enough to keep hunger away, and Aaron Otway, who had been consoling himself as he always did when times were bad, was sometimes almost too drunk to stand.

As if to set her decision on firm lines last night at St Michael was the worst fiasco of all. The persistent rain had kept away all but seven adults and two children, and the players had had to act on wet and smelly straw, with constant drippings on their heads. Tupper had found a fever and had lost the ability (or desire) to make people laugh, and the audience just sat and gaped through it all.

They were to have spent the end of Sunday cleaning up the two caravans ready for a triumphal entry into Bodmin, Otway's idea for attracting an audience on Monday night; but he had been drunk all day and the others were too out-of-sorts or listless to make any move, once they had found a field and turned their animals out to grass. If a wheel fell off to-morrow or an axle broke for lack of grease, well let it.

She had her things packed in a basket, and at what she thought to be midnight she carefully slipped out of her bunk and made for the door. Outside it was fine, and with a shawl about her head she crouched by the wheel of the wagon waiting for Mark.

It was slow waiting, and she was not a patient girl, but to-night she was so set on leaving her present company that she stayed on and on, cursing the summer chill of night and wishing he'd make haste. Minutes passed that seemed like days, and hours that might have been months. Crouching there with her head against the hub of the wheel, she fell asleep.

When she woke she was stiff and chilled through, and behind the church on the hill was a lightening of the sky, the dawn.

She came to her feet. So he'd let her down! All this time he'd been playing with her, making promises he had no intention to keep. Tears of fury and disappointment started into her eyes. Careless of noise she turned to go in, and as she touched the handle she saw a tall figure hurrying across the field.

He came at a shambling half run. She did not move at all until he came up with her and stood seeking his breath and leaning against the caravan.

'Keren . . .'

'Where've you been?' she said wildly. 'All night! All this night I've been waiting! Where've you been?'

He looked up at the window of the caravan. 'You got your clo'es? Come.'

His tone was so strange, short of its usual respect, that she began to move with him across the field without arguing. He walked straight enough now but stiffly, as if he could not bend. They reached the lane.

At the church she said angrily: 'Where've you been, Mark? I'm chilled to the marrow! Waiting all the night through.'

He turned to her. 'Eh?'

She said it again. 'What's amiss with you? What's kept you?'

'I was late startin', Keren. Late. Twas no easy job building a house. . . . At the last. . . . there was last things to do. . . . Didn't start till ten. Thought I should make up by running all the way. . . . But I mistook the road, Keren. I ran wrong . . . kept on the main coach road instead o' turning for St Dennis. . . . I went miles. . . . That's why I came on ee from be'ind . . . Lord save us, I never thought to find ye in time!'

He spoke so slow that at last she realized he was dead-tired, almost out on his feet. Surprise and disappointment made her snap at him, for she had always been pleased at his strength. This was a letdown; surely this great moment of his life should have been enough to liven him up all over again.

They walked on quietly until full day, when a fresh breeze blowing in from the sea seemed to give him a new lease, and from then on he steadily came round. She had put aside some dough cakes from last night's supper, and these they shared at the side of the road. Before they made St Michael he was the stronger of the two.

They stopped at a tollhouse and bargained for some breakfast and rested. The sight of Mark's clinking purse put Keren in a good humour again, and they set off brightly enough on the next lap with her arm linked in his. Only another eight or nine miles to go and they would be there well before noon. She was quite excited now, for novelty always appealed to her; and though she had never in her darkest dreams thought of marrying a miner there was something romantic in the idea of running away and in going to church and making solemn vows and going back with him to a house specially built for her, for them. It was like one of the plays she acted in.

After a time came the discomfort of sore heels, and she went lame. They rested again and she bathed her feet in a stream. They went on, but not very far, and at length he picked her up and began to carry her.

She enjoyed this for a time, it was so much easier than walking and she liked to have his great arms about her and to feel his lungs breathing in the air. People stared, but she did not mind this until they came to a hamlet and walked down the winding muddy lane between the cottages, followed by a trickle of half-naked jeering urchins. She was indignant and wanted him to lay about him, but he walked stolidly on without a glimmer of a change of expression.

After that he carried her in the open country and set her down when a cluster of cottages came in sight. So they made progress but it was slow, and the sun, peering through a rift of cloud, was high as they reached the gates of Mingoose.

A mile and a half to Mellin; then two miles to Sawle Church. If they were not there before noon the wedding would have to wait until to-morrow.

He hastened his steps and at last set her down on the Marasanvose track, with Mellin just over the next rise. They had no time to go and see his cottage. She washed her face in a little pool and he did the same. Then she combed her hair with a property comb she had 'borrowed,' and they limped down into Mellin.

Little Maggie Martin saw them first and went screaming in to her mother that they were here at last. When they reached the first cottage everyone had turned out to meet them. Most of the able-bodied were asleep or at work; but the very old and the very young and one or two of the women did their best to make it a hearty welcome. There was no time to waste in talk, and Mark Daniel and his bride-to-be set off at once for Sawle. But now they were the head of a comet with a tenuous tail, made up of Grannie Daniel and Aunt Betsy Triggs and Mrs Zacky and Sue Vigus and a sputter of excited toddlers.

They hurried, Mark with his great strides nearly outdistancing Keren in the last stages; but it was twenty minutes to noon when they reached Sawle Church. Then they could not find Mr Odgers. Mrs Odgers, confronted by a dark, gaunt, hollow-eyed unshaven man with a desperate and ungenteel manner, confessed timidly that Mr Odgers had given them up and she had last seen him going out into the garden. It was Aunt Betsy who flushed him from behind a black-currant bush, and by then it was ten minutes to twelve. He began to raise objections as to legality and haste, until Mrs Zacky, flat-faced and spectacled and persuasive, took him by one thin arm and led him respectfully into church.

So the spiritual bond was sealed, with the clock in the vestry striking twelve as Mark put a brass ring on Keren's long slender hand.

After the usual formalities (Mark Daniel, his mark; Kerenhappuch Smith, proudly written) they had to call in at Ned Bottrell's cottage near the church and have their health drunk in cider and ale; and it was some time before they could begin the walk back to Mellin. Then the walk became a triumphal procession, for it was the end of the morning core. Something in 'bachelor' Mark's dogged courtship and his house-building had caught the imagination of the miners and bal girls, and a whole group of them joined on and escorted the newlyweds back to Mellin.

Keren was not quite sure how to take all this, how far she should unbend towards these people she was coming to live among. She took a dislike to old Grannie Daniel, and she thought Beth Daniel, Paul's wife, a plain drudge who couldn't open her mouth because of jealousy. But some of the men seemed nice enough and ready to be friendly in a rough but respectful way. She looked up at them out of the corners of her eyes and let them see that they were more acceptable than their womenfolk.

As a special treat they had a big dish of tea and rabbit pasties with leeks and baked barley crusts, and it all passed off pretty well. There were bursts of conversation and as sudden silences, when everyone seemed to be watching everyone else; but this was the first time any of them except Mark had met her and it was bound to be strange.

By the time it was all over the day was done. At Mark's request there was to be no joking or following them to the new house. He'd earned his quiet now.

The evening sun was warm on their backs as they climbed the rise out of Mellin, and it had lit up all the west with a gold light. The contrast of colour was vivid where the bright sky met the cobalt sea.

They went down towards their cottage. Presently she stopped.

'Is that it?'

'Yes.'

He waited.

'Oh,' she said, and went on.

They came near to the door. He thought how commonplace and rough it was, seeing the house he had built behind the figure of the girl he had married. Everything was so crude, made with loving hands maybe; but crude and rough. Loving hands were not enough, you had to have skill and time.

They went in, and he saw that someone had lit a big fire in the open chimney he had made. It burned and crackled and roared and made the rough room cheerful and warm.

'That's Beth's doing,' he said gratefully.

'What is?'

'The fire. She slipped out; I wondered why. She's a rare good one.'

'She doesn't like me,' said Keren, rustling the clean straw underfoot.

'Yes, she do, Keren. Tedn that but only that she's Methody and don't hold wi' playgoing an' such like.'

'Oh, she doesn't,' said Keren ominously. 'What does she know about it, I'd like to know.'

Mark stared round.

'It's . . . awful rough for you, Keren. But it has all been builded in four days and twill take weeks to make it just so as we shall want it.'

He looked at her expectantly.

'Oh, it's nice,' said Keren. 'I think it's a nice house. Fifty times better than those old cottages over the hill.'

His dark face lighted up. 'We'll make it betterer as we go along. There's – there's much to be done. Twas only giving you a roof that I was about.'

He put his arm round her tentatively, and when she put up her face he kissed her. It was like kissing a butterfly, soft and frail and elusive.

She turned her head. 'What's in there?'

'That's where we'll sleep,' he said. 'I'd intended for a room upstairs, but tedn near finished yet. So I made this for the time.'

She went into the next room and her feet again felt straw underfoot. It was like living in a cattle shed. Oh, well, as he said, it could be changed.

He went across and pushed open the shutter to let the light in. There was a big wooden shelf across one corner of the room, raised about a foot from the floor. On it was a sack mattress stuffed with straw and two thin blankets.

'You should have built the house facing west,' she said, 'then we'd have had the evening sun.'

'I didn't think o' that,' he said, crestfallen.

It was hers. Hers alone to do with as she chose, that was something.

'D'you mean you made all this house since I saw you last?' she said.

'Yes.'

'Lord sakes,' she said, 'I can scarcely credit it.'

This delighted him and he kissed her again. Presently she wriggled out of his arms.

'Go leave me now, Mark. Go sit by the fire an' I'll join you presently. I'll give you a surprise.'

He went out, bending his great height in the door.

She stood for a time staring out of the window, at the barren prospect of the gully with the dried-up stream and the mining rubble all around. Up the other side of the valley the ground was better; there was the turret of a house and trees. Why hadn't he built up there?

She went across and put her fingers on the bed. Well, the straw was dry. It wasn't so very long since she'd slept on wet straw. And it could be made so much better still. After the first disappointment her spirits rose. No more wrangling with Tupper or smelling Otway's drunken breath. No more hunger or dismal treks across moors and bogs. No more playing to empty pigsties and half-wit yokels. This was home.

She moved to the window again and closed one of the shutters. A group of sea gulls flying high looked gold and pink in the sunlight against the cloudy eastern sky. The light was failing in this shallow rift in the moor.

especially in the house – always it would be dark early in this house with all the windows facing the wrong way.

She knew he would be waiting for her. She did not shirk her part of the bargain but looked towards it with a faint sensuous lassitude. She slowly undressed, and when she had taken everything off she shivered a little and closed the other shutter. In the semidarkness of the new room she passed her hands caressingly down her smooth flanks, stretched and yawned, then put on her black and pink faded smock and fluffed out her hair. This would do. He'd be overcome as it was. This would do.

Bare feet rustling in the straw, she passed through to the kitchen and thought for a moment he had gone out. Then she saw him sitting in the shadows on the floor, his head against the wooden bench. He was asleep.

She was angry in a moment.

'Mark!' she said.

He did not reply. She went over and knelt beside him and stared into his dark face. He had shaved at Mellin, but already his strong beard was beginning to sprout again. His face was hollow and shadowed with fatigue, his mouth half open. She thought how ugly he was.

'Mark!' she said again, loudly.

His breathing went on.

'Mark!' She grasped the collar of his jacket and roughly shook him. His head tapped against the bench and his breathing halted, but he showed no signs of waking.

She got up and stared down at him. Anger began to give way to contempt. He was as bad as Tupper, lying there so limp and so foolish. What had she married, a man who fell dead-asleep on his wedding night, who hadn't the spark to be excited, who went to *sleep*? It was an insult to *her*. A great insult.

Well, it was as he chose. She was not all that particular. If he wanted to snore away there like a great black dog, well . . . It was his loss, not hers. She'd not defaulted. Let him be. She gave a short laugh, and then began to giggle as she saw the funny side of it. She giggled and giggled as she moved slowly away from him towards the other room. But her laughter was softer now so that she should not wake him.

Chapter nine

ON HIS DAYLIGHT visit to the cottage at Reath, Ross had also noted the turret among the trees on the farther slope. It was one of the gatehouses of Mingoose and was now in a bad state, but there were a number of usable rooms still and Ross had an idea.

He took it to Mr Horace Treneglos, who tramped across regularly to inspect their mine now that it was showing a return.

'Who is this Dwight Enys, what?' Mr Treneglos shouted. 'Think you he's worth encouraging? Think you he's experienced at his profession?'

'Enys is eager, sharp and keen. It is good to encourage youth, and Choake has no intention of serving us since I quarrelled with him.'

'I wisht we'd found a quieter place for our lode,' said Mr Treneglos, clutching at his hat. 'It is always so demmed windy up here. For my part, as you know, I've no great fancy for these physical people, young or old. But I'm out to please you, and if the Gatehouse would satisfy the stripling he may have it at some nominal rent for the repairing.'

A fortnight later there was a ticketing at Truro, to which Wheal Leisure Mine was sending two parcels of ore; so Ross rode in early and called on the Pascoes before the auction began. Dwight Enys was away, but he wrote him a note and left.

Samples of the ore to be marketed had already been examined and tested and whispered over by agents of the copper companies; and at these ticketings it was left only for the various companies to put in a bid for the ore. Not for them the vulgar excitement of a common auction, where one buyer ran another up higher than he wanted to go. Instead each company put in a bid in writing, the chairman opened these offering tickets and the consignments of copper went to the company which had put in the highest bid.

To-day the bidding was even poorer than of late, and some parcels of ore went for less than half their real value. It was the custom of the companies when they did not want a particular parcel to put in a very low bid nevertheless, and if, as not infrequently happened, every other company did the same, one of these low bids made the sale. This meant a heavy loss for the mine concerned, and in the present state of trade no mine could afford it.

A great dinner at the inn always followed the ticketing, given by the mines, at which buyers and sellers – the lions and the lambs, as a wry humorist called them – sat down together; but to-day there was a noticeable lack of good spirits among the feasters. Ross had been surprised to see Francis at the sale – usually the manager of Grambler came – and he knew it to be a sign that his cousin was making a last bid to keep Grambler Mine on its great unwieldy feet.

To-day for all his poise he looked harassed and inept, and as if threatened by spectres which existed in half-ignored corners of his mind.

On his left Ross had Richard Tonkin, the manager and one of the shareholders in United Mines, the largest tin- and copper-producing combine in the county; and halfway through the meal Tonkin whispered in Ross's ear:

'I trust you have made some progress with your scheme.'

Ross looked at him.

'You mean the extension at Wheal Leisure?'

Tonkin smiled. 'No, sir. The project for forming a copper smelting company to promote the interests of the mines.'

Ross's look became a stare. 'I have no such project in hand, Mr Tonkin.'

The other man was a little incredulous. 'I hope you are joking. Mr Blewett told me . . . and Mr Aukett . . . that there was some prospect of such a scheme. I should have been very happy to lend my aid.'

'Mr Blewett and Mr Aukett,' said Ross, 'made much of a chance discussion. I have not given it another thought.'

'That comes as a very great disappointment to me. I was in hope – others too were in hope – that something would arise from it. There can surely be little doubt that we have need of such a company.'

The dinner broke up with men going off in twos and threes to find their horses and ride home before dusk, some staying at the table to sup a last glass of port or nod tipsily over a snuffbox, others talking in groups on the way downstairs or at the door of the inn.

Ross stayed behind to talk with Francis. Though there was now no ill will between them they saw little of each other. Ross had heard that Grambler Mine had been reprieved for the time being, but he kept the conversation to family topics, being afraid of treading on Francis's sensitive corns.

Chatting amiably, they went downstairs, when the innkeeper touched Ross on the arm.

'Beg your pardon, sir, but would you oblige a man by steppin' this way, just for a small matter of a moment or two? An' you too, sir, if tis agreeable an' convenient.'

Ross stared at him and went down two steps into his private parlour. It was a gloomy little room, for the window looked out upon a high wall, but occupying this room in varying positions of comfort were fourteen men.

Francis, following him in, stumbled over the house cat, swore and raised
his foot to kick away the obstruction, then saw what it was and picked the
animal up by its scruff, coming into the room close behind Ross and
elbowing him farther in.

'God's my life,' he said, looking round.

It was not until Ross recognized Tonkin and Blewett and Aukett among
the men that he smelt what was in the wind.

'Sit down, Captain Poldark,' said Harry Blewett, vacating a chair by the
window. 'Glad we was able to catch you before you took your leave.'

'Thanks,' said Ross, 'I'll stand.'

'Damme,' said Francis, 'it looks like a pesky Bible meeting. Here, beast,
yon shall be chairman, and mind you call us to order.' He leaned forward
and dropped the cat on the empty seat.

'Captain Poldark,' Tonkin said, 'it was fortunate that you were late in
coming down, for we have had the chance of talking together here in
private; those of us you see around you; and no doubt you have an idea
what our subject has been.'

'I have an idea,' said Ross.

'Sink me if I can say the same,' remarked Francis.

'We would like your word, sir,' a big man called Johnson leaned across
and said to Francis, 'that anything that passes here is in the strictest
confidence.'

'Very well.'

'We may take it that you find no satisfaction in the business done to-
day?' Richard Tonkin asked.

Grambler had been one of the worst sufferers. 'You may take that,' said
Francis, 'and pin it where you will.'

'No, well, there's many of us here feels quite the same. And we've met
here and now to say what's to be done by it.'

Francis said: 'Then we're here to set the world to rights. It will be a long
session.'

'Not so long as might be,' Tonkin said quietly. 'For we have a plan in
mind, Mr Poldark, which is to form a copper company of our own, one
which will exist outside the ring, will give fair prices for the ore, will smelt
the copper in this county, and will market the refined product direct. All of
us here, more than a dozen, are willing to join together, and between us we
stand for a fair share of the mines in this area; and between us, even in
these hard times, we can lay our hands on a measure of cash. But this is a
small beginning, Mr Poldark, to what will surely come to us when the
project gets about – if it can be done privately and in the right way. And
there's some of the richest mines not here to-day. In good times unfair
prices can be borne because there is a margin for all; but in bad times like
the present there's only one way out short of bankruptcy for half of us
here!'

There was a deep murmur of assent from the men in the room. Ross saw that most of the principal sellers of to-day were present. He realized that something was in motion now that could not be stopped. Tonkin was the eloquent one: he put into words what the others felt.

'Well, it all rings very agreeable, I believe you,' said Francis. 'But you'll be biting off no small mouthful of trouble, one way with another. The copper companies want no cutthroat competition and the banks will be behind 'em. Certain people ——'

'Well, trouble's better'n starvation,' Blewett said.

'Aye, we're not afraid of trouble!'

Francis raised his eyebrows slightly. 'I would not disagree with you, gentlemen.'

'Mind you,' said Tonkin, 'all this is but a beginning. I know – we all know – there's things to be faced. What's right and just isn't always easy to come by. But while we were all here together was a convenient time to see the wheels set in motion. And before we begin, we wish to know who's for us in the venture. For who is not for us ——'

'Is against you?' Francis shook his head. 'Far from it. For who is not instantly for you may have obligations of his own to consider. It does not follow that he may not wish you well.' Francis turned an eye on Ross. 'What is my cousin's view of the matter?'

Tonkin said: 'It was your cousin who first suggested it.'

Francis looked surprised. 'Well, Ross, I had no idea. Nor should I ever have guessed, for as your own mine . . .'

Ross said nothing and his face showed nothing.

'There are disadvantages, we know,' said Tonkin, 'but if it becomes a working reality we shall do away with many of the present anomalies. Look, sir, we cannot go on as we are to-day. Unless there is some change, in a year we shall all be gone. I say for my part, let us undertake this venture with all speed and courage. I would rather fail fighting than lying down and waiting for the end!'

'Well,' said Francis, and adjusted the lace on his cuff, 'I don't doubt you'll give the copper companies a run for their money. And I wish you all good fortune, for God knows we have had none of late. For my part I would prefer to consider the proposal further before making a move. But I wish you well, gentlemen, I wish you well. By the way, who is to take the initiative in your venture. There must be a leader, must there not? Is it to be you, Mr Tonkin?'

Tonkin shook his head. 'No, sir. I couldn't do it. I'm not at all the right man. But we are all agreed who is the right man if he will undertake it, are we not, gentlemen?'

Chapter ten

DEMELZA HAD BEEN expecting Ross since five. At six she prepared supper, making it lighter than usual, for she knew he came back from these ticketings satiated with food and drink and grumbling at the waste of time.

Towards seven she had her supper and thought she would walk up the valley to see if she could meet Ross. Julia was fed; her garden was not crying for attention; she had practised on the spinet just before dinner; her mind was at ease. Very nice. She would walk.

The joys of leisure, rarely indulged, had not yet lost a grain of their newness. This of all things was what made her happiest in the life of a lady. In her childhood she had always worked until there was nothing but a sleep of exhaustion left, and slept until a boot or a shout roused her. As a servant at Nampara she had had her quieter times, but the best of these had been stolen, furtive; nervous alertness woven in with her pleasure. Now if she chose, if she felt like it, she could idle with all the world to see. The very energy of her ordinary ways made these times all the sweeter. She was a lady, wife of Ross Poldark, whose ancestry in these parts went back hundreds of years. The children of her body, Julia first, would be called Poldark, with a good home, money enough, a root, upbringing, a legacy of culture. Sometimes her heart swelled at the thought.

She walked up the valley listening to the first crickets making themselves heard in the undergrowth, and stopping now and then to watch the young birds squabbling in the branches of the elms or an occasional frog hop and slither by the edge of the stream. At the top, by the ruins of Wheal Maiden, she sat down on a block of stone and hummed a little tune and screwed up her eyes for the sight of a familiar figure. Beyond the smoke of Grambler you could see the tower of Sawle Church. From here it looked to be leaning towards the south-west, as a man will in a gale. All the trees leaned the other way.

'Mistress Poldark,' said a voice behind her.

She leapt up.

Andrew Blamey had called.

'I hope you'll accept my excuses, ma'am. I hadn't any thought of scaring you.'

He was standing beside her, thinking that the shock had brought her near to fainting. But it would have taken far more than that to send Demelza over. He kept a hand at her elbow until she was again sitting on the wall. Out of the corner of her eye she thought there was no arrogance in his expression.

She had sworn aloud at the shock, forgetting her manners and annoyed with herself the moment after.

'It is a bad beginning,' he said, 'to have come here with an apology to make and to need another at the outset.'

'I had not thought to see you in these parts.'

'Nor I to see myself, ma'am. Ever again.'

'Then what brings you here, Captain Blamey?'

'Your visit to me. For after it I have had no peace of mind.'

He kept moistening his lips and frowning a little, as if with turns of pain.

She said: 'How did you – Have you walked from Falmouth?'

'I came on foot from Grambler, hoping to be less conspicuous if you should have company. I was in Truro this forenoon and saw both your husband and – and Francis Poldark. Knowing they would be away, the need was too strong.'

'I am expecting Ross back any moment.'

'Then I'd best say what can be said while there is time. No doubt you took a very bad opinion of me from our first meeting, Mrs Poldark.'

Demelza stared at her feet. 'I was a small matter put out.'

'Your visit was sprung on me. It was something I had put away. . . . Its – its sudden outcropping brought with it all the bitterness.' He put his hat down on the wall. 'I am, I grant, a man of strong temper. To control it has been the work of a lifetime. Sometimes still there are moments when the struggle returns. But God forbid that I should quarrel with those who wish me well.'

'Not even your own sailors?' said Demelza, faintly malicious for once.

He was silent.

'Please go on,' she said.

'The sailors quarrel with all their captains just now. For years they have eked out their poor wages by smuggling goods into the ports on each voyage. But it has come to such a pass that we are held to blame. Captain Clarke in the *Swan of Flushing* was detained in Jamaica under prosecution, and others will fare the same. So we have reached an agreement on the belongings that each sailor shall carry. It's not surprising they dislike it, but this is no personal quarrel between my crew and myself: it is a commotion throughout the packet service.'

'I beg pardon,' she said.

'I met you that day already angry from a disturbance. When you spoke it seemed at first an interference. Only later I came to count the exertion you had been to. Then I wished it was possible to have you back to thank you for what you had done and said.'

'Oh, it was nothin'. It was not *that* I wanted, if you understand — —'

'Since then,' he said, 'there has been no peace of mind. To Lisbon and back I carried what you said of Verity. You were allowed time to say little enough, maybe. But . . . Verity had never got over it. You said that, didn't you? And that she was ten years older than her age. How often I've thought of what it means. Ailing but not ill, you said. Because of me. Ailing but not ill. Ten years older than her age. You know, I never knew what Verity's age was. All the time I had her love. We didn't think of such things. I am forty-one, ma'am. She didn't look old when I knew her. Is that what her brother and father have saved her for? There's no more rest until I've seen her. That much you've done, Mistress Poldark, whatever the outcome. The move is with you again. That's what I came to say.'

His eyes had been on her the whole time he was speaking, and she had not felt able to break from his gaze. At last her glance moved to the plain of Grambler; she got up.

'He's coming, Captain Blamey. You'd best not be seen here.'

Blamey stared down with puckered eyes. 'Is *he* against me now? He wasn't at the time.'

'Not *against* you. He was against me stirring up what he thought should be left alone. He'd be angry with me if he knew.'

He looked at her. 'Verity has a good friend in you, ma'am. You take risks for your friends.'

'I have a good friend in Verity,' she said. 'But don't stand there or he'll see you. Let us move behind the wall.'

'What is the best way back?'

'Those fir trees. Wait there until we have gone down.'

'When can I see you again? What arrangements can be made?'

She wracked her brain for a quick decision. 'I can't say now. It depends – on Verity. . . . If ——'

'Shall you tell her?' he said eagerly.

'I don't think so. Not at the start. I – hadn't thought more because I'd give up hope of ever anything being done – since I came to Falmouth. It will depend how I can arrange . . .'

'Write me,' he said. 'Care of the packet offices. I'll come.'

She bit her lip, for she could hardly form her letters. 'All right,' she promised. 'I'll leave you know. What if you're away?'

'I sail on Saturday, there's no choice for that. Set a time for the third week of next month if possible. It will be safer that way. If ——'

'Look,' said Demelza urgently. ''Twill be in Truro; that's safest. I'll send you word, just a place and a time. I can't do more'n that. It will be up to you then.'

'Bless you, ma'am,' he said, and bent and kissed her hand. 'I'll not fail you.'

She watched him leave the shelter of the mine building and run quickly to the trees. At her first meeting in Falmouth she could not imagine what Verity had seen in him to take his loss so to heart. After this she was more able to understand.

The sun had set before Ross reached her. Over the land the smoke from Grambler was rising and blowing across the cottages and drifting towards Sawle. Here in the ruins the crickets were very busy, sawing away among the grass and the stones.

He jumped off Darkie when he saw her and his preoccupied face broke into a smile.

'Well, my love, this is an honour. I hope you've not been waiting long.'

'Four hours behindhand,' she said. 'I should be grown to the stone if I had come here at five.'

'But as you didn't your attachment is so much the less.' He laughed and then looked at her. 'What's wrong?'

She put her hand up and fondled the mare's soft nose.

'Nothing. Except that I been picturing you thrown off by poor Darkie here, or set upon by rogues and robbers.'

'But your eyes are shining. In the distance I thought they were glow beetles.'

She patted his arm but kept her glance on Darkie. 'Don't tease, Ross, I was glad to see you back, that's all.'

'Flattered but unconvinced,' he commented. 'Something has excited you. Kiss me.'

She kissed him.

'Now I know it is not rum,' he added.

'Oh! Judas!' She wiped her mouth distastefully. 'What insult next! If that is all you kiss me for, to pry and spy into my liquors . . .'

'It's a sure way.'

'Then next time you suspect him I hope you'll try it on Jud. "Aye, Mester Ross," he'll say. "Gladly," with a belch, he'll say. An' round your neck his arms'll go like a linseed poultice. Or Prudie, why don't you try your chance on Prudie? She has no beard and a comfortable soft sort of reception. She didn't have a chance at our party, and no doubt you'll not mind her fondness for onions. . . .'

He picked her up and set her sideways on the saddle of his horse, where she had to clutch his arm for fear of falling backwards. In the process her dark eyes looked into his grey ones.

'I think tis you that's excited,' Demelza said, seizing the attack before he could. 'You've been in mischief this day, I'll lay a curse. Have you thrown Dr Choake in a pool or robbed George Warleggan at his bank?'

He turned and began to lead his horse down the valley, one hand firmly and pleasurably on Demelza's knee.

'I have some news,' he said, 'but it is dusty stuff and will not move you. Tell me first how you've spent the day.'

'Tell me your news.'

'You first.'

'Oh . . . In the forenoon I went to call on Keren Daniel and renew our acquaintance. . . .'

'Did she please you?'

'Well . . . She has a small pretty waist. And small pretty ears. . . .'

'And a small pretty mind?'

'It is hard to say. She thinks well of herself. She wants to get on. I believe she d'think that if only she'd seen you first I'd never've stood a chance.'

Ross laughed.

'An' would I?' said Demelza, curious.

He said: 'Insults I have grown accustomed to bear. But, imbecility is something I cannot cope with.'

'What long words you d'use, grandpa,' Demelza said, impressed.

They went on down the valley. A few birds were still chattering in the coloured close of the evening. On Hendrawna Beach the sea had gone a pale opal green against the warm brown of cliff and sand.

'And your news?' she said presently.

'There is a scheme afoot to rival the copper companies by forming a company of our own. I am to lead it.'

She glanced at him. 'What does that mean, Ross?'

He explained, and they crossed the stream and reached the house. Jud came ambling out to take Darkie, and they went into the parlour, where supper was still laid for him. She was about to light the candles but he stopped her. So she sat on the rug and leaned her back against his knees, and he stroked her face and hair and went on talking while the light faded right away.

'Francis was not willing to enter with us at the start,' he said. 'And I don't blame him, for the very continuance of Grambler hangs on Warleggan good will. That will be the trouble for many. They are so deeply involved with mortgages and things that they dare not risk offending those who hold them. But a compromise was suggested and our enterprise is to be a secret one.'

'Secret?' said Demelza.

'If the company is formed it shall be formed by a few people who will act for those who do not wish their names known. I think it will work.'

'Shall you be secret, then?'

His long fingers moved down the line of her chin.

'No. I have nothing at stake. They can't touch me.'

'But doesn't Wheal Leisure owe some money to the bank?'

'To Pascoe's Bank, yes. But they are not connected with the copper companies, so that is safe enough.'

'Why should you have to take all the risks and let other men shelter behind you?'

'No, no. There are others that will help openly; a man called Richard Tonkin. One called Johnson. Many of them.'

She moved a moment restlessly. 'And how far will it touch us?'

'I – may be more from home. It's hard to say.'

She stirred again. 'I'm not at all sure I like it, Ross.'

'Nor I, that part of it. But there was no other they would choose for leader. I tried. . . .'

'We should be pleased at that.'

'It's a compliment to be chosen. Though no doubt before this is done I shall curse my weakness in taking it. There is the need of this enterprise, Demelza. I didn't want the advancing of it, but I found I couldn't refuse.'

'Then you must do what you think best to do,' she said quietly.

There was silence for some time. Her face was quiescent between his hands. The electricity had gone out of her now, that tautness of mind, the elfish vitality of spirit which he could always sense when she had something special on or was in one of her 'moods.' His news had deflated her, for she did not want him more gone from her than now. She longed to have more in common with him, not less.

He bent and put his face against her hair. Vibrantly alive, like herself, it curled about his face. It smelled faintly of the sea. He was struck by the mystery of personality, that this hair and the head and person of the young woman below it was his by right of marriage and by the vehemently free choice of the woman herself, that this dark curling hair and head meant more to him than any other because it made up in some mysterious way just that key which unlocked his attention and desire and love. Closely, personally attached in thought and sympathy, interacting upon each other at every turn, they were yet separate beings irrevocably personal and apart, and must remain so for all efforts to bridge the gulf. Any move beyond a point fell into the void. He did not know at this moment what she was thinking, what she was feeling. Only the outward symbols he had come to understand told him that she had been excited and nervously alert and now was not. Her mind instead was exploring this new thing he had told her, trying to foresee what even he could not foresee who knew and understood so much more.

'A letter came for you this afternoon,' she said. 'I don't know who twas from.'

'Oh, from George Warleggan. I met him this morning. He said he had written to invite me to another of his parties and I should find the invitation at home.'

She was silent. Somewhere in the depths of the house Jud and Prudie were arguing; you could hear the deep growl of Prudie's complaint and the lighter growl of Jud's answer, like two dogs snarling at each other, the mastiff bitch and the crossbred bulldog.

'This will make enmity between you an' George Warleggan, won't it?'

'Very likely.'

'I don't know that that's good. He's very rich, isn't he?'

'Rich enough. But there are older and stronger interests in Cornwall, if they can be roused.'

There was a clash of pans from the kitchen.

'Now tell me,' Ross said, 'what was exciting you when I met you at Wheal Maiden?'

Demelza got up. 'Those two old crows'll wake Julia. I must go and separate them.'

Chapter eleven

DWIGHT ENYS, VERY gratified, rode over on the following day. Together they went to see the Gatehouse in the clump of trees beyond Reath Cottage, and Keren Daniel stood at a window and watched them ride past and thought her own strange thoughts. Demelza had been nearer divining her mind than Keren ever imagined.

Ross was surprised to find that Enys too had an invitation to the Warleggan party; and when he arrived there on the day he soon located him standing rather defensively against the wall in the reception-room.

There was a sprinkling of ladies among the guests and Ross kept his eyes and ears open. All society whispered of some woman Francis was paying attention to, but so far he had never seen her. Uncle Cary Warleggan was here to-night. Cary was not quite on the same respectable level as brother Nicholas and nephew George, and though he was one of the trio which was stretching its financial fingers all over west Cornwall, he generally kept in the background. He was tall and thin and bloodless, with a long nose, which he spoke through, and a wide tight crease of a mouth. Also present was a miller called Sanson with fat hands and a sharp sly look half masked by a habitual blink.

Ross strolled about with Dwight for a while, through the reception-rooms and then out upon the lawns, which ran down to the river at the back of the house. He mentioned Jim Carter and his imprisonment in Bodmin, and Enys said he would gladly go and see the young man any time.

When they returned to the lighted house Ross saw a tall young woman with shining black hair standing beside Francis at the hazard table. His deferential attitude left no doubt.

'A twelve as I'm alive! You nick,' said the lady, her voice slow and deep with a not-unattractive burr. 'And a bad dream to you, Francis. Always you was lucky at this game.'

She turned her head to glance round the room, and Ross felt as if he had touched hot metal.

Years ago when he had left the Assembly Rooms sick at heart and desperate and had gone to the Bear Inn and tried to drink his misery away, there had come to him a tall, gaunt young harlot, distinctive and unusual but down-and-out, importuning him with her wide bold eyes and drawling tongue. And he had gone with her to her derelict hut and tried to drown his love for Elizabeth in a tawdry counterfeit passion.

He had never known her name except that it was Margaret. He had never known anything about her. Not in any wild dream had he thought to find this.

All evidence of poverty gone. She was powdered and scented and so hung with bracelets and rings that at every move she rustled and clinked.

At that moment George Warleggan came into the room. Beautifully dressed and thick-necked and bland, he came over at once to the two gentlemen by the door. Margaret's eyes followed her host and they reached Ross. Seen from this side with the scar, he was unmistakable. Her eyes widened. Then she gave way to a hearty burst of laughter.

'What is it, my love?' Francis asked. 'I see nothing comical in a four and a three when you need a ten for a chance.'

'Mrs Cartland,' said George, 'May I introduce Captain Poldark, Francis's cousin. Mrs Margaret Cartland.'

Ross said: 'Your servant, ma'am.'

Margaret gave him the hand in which she held the dice shaker. How well now he remembered the strong white teeth, the broad shoulders, the feline, lustful dark eyes. 'Me lord,' she said, boldly using her old name for him, 'I've looked for this introduction for years. I've heard such *tales* about you!'

'My lady,' he said, 'believe only the most circumstantial – or those that are witty.'

She said: 'Could any of them fail to be, that concerned you?'

His eyes travelled over her face. 'Or any not seem to be, ma'am, with you to recount them.'

She laughed. 'Nay, it is the stories that *can't* be told that I find most diverting.'

He bowed. 'The essence of a good joke is that only two should share it,'

'I thought that was the essence of a good bed,' said Francis, and everybody laughed.

Later Ross played whist, but towards the end of the evening he came upon the lady alone at the foot of the stairs.

She dropped him a rather sarcastic curtsy, with a rustle of silk and a clink of bracelets. 'Captain Poldark, how fortunately met.'

'How surprisingly met.'

'Not so polite out of company, I see.'

'Oh, I intend no impoliteness to an old friend.'

'Friend? Wouldn't you put it higher than that?'

He saw that her eyes, which he had always thought quite black, were really a very deep blue.

'Higher or lower as you count the matter,' he said. 'I'm not one for splitting hairs.'

'No, you was always a willing man. And now you're married, eh?'

He agreed that he was.

'How monstrous dull.' There was sarcastic laughter in her voice which provoked him.

'Should you despise marriage who appear to have followed it?'

'Oh, Cartland,' she said. 'He's wed and dead.'

'Did you put that on his stone?'

She laughed with feline good humour.

'It was the colic put him away, but not before his time, he was forty. Ah, well. May he rest quieter for knowing I've spent his money.'

George Warleggan came down the stairs. 'You find our new guest entertaining, Margaret?'

She yawned. 'To tell the truth when I have eaten so well almost anything will entertain me.'

'And I have not yet eaten,' said Ross. 'No doubt, ma'am, that explains our difference in sentiment.'

George glanced sharply from one to the other but he made no comment.

It was midnight before Ross left, but Francis stayed on. He had lost heavily at faro and was still playing, the number having been reduced to four: Cary Warleggan, who had also lost, Sanson, who was banker and had won all evening, and George, who had come in late to the game. Margaret was there watching the play, her hand resting lightly on Francis's shoulder. She did not look up as Ross left.

Dwight Enys moved to his half-ruined Gatehouse and took up his duties as bal-surgeon to Wheal Leisure; and Keren Daniel settled with a smothered discontent into her life as a miner's wife; and Demelza, taken apparently with a sudden mood, practised her letters with fanatic zeal; and Ross was much away in the company of the talented and persuasive Richard Tonkin, interviewing, discussing, contriving, estimating – working to bring a pipe dream down to the shape of reality.

Life moved on and Julia grew and her mother began to feel her gums for signs of teeth; the price of copper dropped to sixty-seven pounds and two more mines closed; there were riots in Paris and starvation in the provinces; Geoffrey Charles Poldark had the measles at last; and the physicians attending the King found it hard to follow his mathematics on the subject of flies.

It came to the time for Demelza to write her letter, and she did so with great care and many false starts.

DEAR CAP BLAMY,

HAVE THE GOODNESS TO MET US AT MISTRESS TRELASKS SILK MERCER SHOP IN KENWEN STREET TWENTY OCTOBER IN THE FORENOON VERYTY

WILL NOT GO SO I BEG OF YOU TO TAKE US BY CHENSE.

SIR, I AM, WITH DUE RESPECT,

YOUR FRIEND AND SERVANT,

DEMELZA POLDARK.

She was not sure about the last part, but she had taken it from a book on correspondence Verity had lent her, so it must be all right.

Lobb, the man who acted as postman, was due on the morrow, so after her fiftieth reading she sealed the letter and addressed it in her boldest writing to: CAPTEN BLAMY, PACKUT OFFICES, FALMOUTH.

There was still a week to go, with all the possible chances of mishap. She had Verity's promise on the excuse that she wanted advice on the buying of a cloak for the winter.

As she walked back down the valley with the *Mercury* tucked under one arm and with Garrick making rude munching sounds at her heels she saw Keren Daniel moving across the valley almost to cut across her path.

This was all land belonging to Ross. It was not an enclosed estate, Joshua having been content to set a few stone posts to mark the limits of his land; but Nampara Combe was generally acknowledged as being within a special sphere of privacy on which the thirty or forty cottagers did not intrude unless invited.

It was clear that Keren did not know this.

This morning she was hatless, with her crisp curling black hair blowing in the wind and wore a brilliant scarlet dress of some cheap flimsy material she had filched from the property box. The wind blew it about the curves of her figure, and it was caught provocatively round her waist with a tight green girdle. It was the sort of dress which would make the men look and the women whisper.

'Good morning,' said Demelza.

'Good morning,' said Keren, eyeing her covertly for unfavourable comparisons. 'What a wind! I mislike wind greatly. D'you never have nothing but wind in these districts?'

'Seldom,' said Demelza. 'For my part, now, I like a suggestion of breeze. It stirs up the smells and keeps 'em circulated and makes everyone more interesting. A place without wind'd be like bread without yeast, nothing to keep it light. Have you been shopping?'

Keren looked at her keenly a moment to make sure what was intended. Failing, she glanced at her basket and said:

'To Sawle. It is a miserable small place, isn't it? I suppose you do all your shopping in Truro.'

'Oh, I like to buy from Aunt Mary Rogers whenever it is feasible. She's a brave kind soul for all her fat. I could tell you things about Aunt Mary Rogers . . .'

Keren looked uninterested.

'And then there's pilchards,' said Demelza. 'Sawle pilchards are the best in England. Mind you, it has been a rare bad season for 'em, but last year was wonderful. It set 'em up for the winter. What they'll do this year is beyond imagining.'

'Mistress Poldark,' Keren said, 'don't *you* think Mark is worth something better than being a common ordinary miner? Don't you?'

Surprised, Demelza stared at the sudden question. She said: 'Yes. Maybe. I hadn't thought to look at it that way.'

'Nobody does. But look at him: he's strong as an ox; he's sharp enough; he's keen; he's a worker. But Grambler Mine is a dead end like. What can he do but work an' work, day in day out for a starvation wage till he's too old an' crippled like his father. An' then what's to become of us?'

'I didn't know twas so near starvation,' Demelza said. 'I thought he made a fair wage. He's on tribute, isn't he?'

'It keeps us. No more.'

Demelza saw a horseman come over the hill.

'My father was a miner,' she said. 'Tributer like Mark. Still is. He made a fair wage. Up an' down of course, an' nothing startling at the best. But we should have managed if he hadn't swilled it all away at the gin shops. Mark don't drink, do he?'

Keren moved a stone about with her foot.

'I wondered if it was ever possible Captain Poldark ever had a vacancy in his mine, you see; a vacancy for something better. I only wondered. I thought it might be. Those on tribute there are doing well, they say; and I thought maybe there might be something better sometime.'

'I've nought to do with it,' Demelza said. 'But I'll mention it.' It was not Ross on the horse.

'Mind,' said Keren, tossing her hair back, 'we're nice and comfortable and all that. It isn't that one *needs* to ask favours, so to say. But Mark is so behindhand in that. I said to him one day, "Why don't you go ask Captain Ross; you're a friend of his; he couldn't bite you; maybe he's never thought of you in that way; nothing venture, nothing have." But he just shook his head and wouldn't answer. I always get angry when he won't answer.'

'Yes,' said Demelza.

The horseman was coming through the trees now, and Keren heard him and looked over her shoulder. Her face was slightly flushed and slightly resentful, as if someone had been asking a favour of *her*. It was Dwight Enys.

'Oh, Mrs Poldark. I have just been to Truro and thought to call in on the way back. Is Captain Poldark at home?'

'No, he's in to Redruth, I b'lieve.'

Dwight dismounted, handsome and young. Keren glanced quickly from one to the other.

'I have a letter here, that's all. Mr Harris Pascoe asked me to deliver it.

May I presume to leave it with you?'

'Thank you.' Demelza took the letter. 'This is Mistress Keren Daniel, Mark Daniel's wife. This is Dr Enys.'

Dwight bowed. 'Your servant, ma'am.' He was not sure from the girl's dress to what class she belonged, and he had forgotten who Mark Daniel was.

Under his gaze Keren's expression changed like a flower when the sun comes out. While she spoke she kept her eyes down, her long black lashes on the dusky peach bloom of her cheeks. She knew the young man, having seen him two or three times from her window after that first glimpse of him with Ross. She knew that he had come to live in that turreted house half hidden in a clump of trees just up the other side of the valley from her own cottage. She knew that he had never seen her before. She knew the value of first impressions.

They walked down together towards Nampara House, Keren determined that she should not leave the other two until she was forced. At the house Demelza invited them in for a glass of wine, but to Keren's great disappointment he refused. Keren, quickly deciding that a few minutes of Dr Enys's company was worth more than the interest of seeing the inside of Nampara House, refused also; and they left together, Dwight leading his horse and walking beside Keren.

The twentieth of October was a windy day with dust and dead leaves blowing and the promise of rain. Demelza was on edge, as if she had a long-distance coach to catch; and Verity was amused by her wish to get into Truro by eleven at the latest. Demelza said that it wasn't nervousness for herself but that Julia had been restless in the night and she suspected she was a bit feverish.

At that Verity suggested they might postpone the visit: they could very easily ride in another day when it was more convenient. It would have suited her, for the date had come round for the quarterly meeting of the Grambler shareholders. But Demelza now seemed more than ever keen to go. . . .

This time they had Bartle for company, for Jud was growing ever more wayward.

Halfway there it began to rain, a thin damp drizzle moving across the country like a mesh of fine silk, slower than the low bags of cloud which spun it. About three miles from Truro they saw a crowd of people stretching across the road. It was so unusual to see many people about in the middle of the day that they reined in.

'I think tis a pile o' miners, ma'am,' said Bartle. 'Mebbe tis a feast day we've forgot.'

Verity went forward a little doubtfully. These people did not look as if they were celebrating.

A man was standing on a cart talking to a compact group gathered around him. He was some distance away, but it was clear that he was giving expression to a grievance. Other groups of people sat on the ground or talked among themselves. There were as many women as men among them, all poorly dressed and some with young children. They looked angry and cold and desperate. A good many were actually in the lane, which here ran between clearly defined hedges, and hostile looks met the two well-dressed women on horseback with their well-fed groom.

Verity put a bold front on it and led the way slowly through: and silently they were watched and sullenly

Presently the last were left behind.

'*Phhh!*' said Demelza. 'Who were they, Bartle?'

'Miners from Idless an' Chacewater, I bla'. These are poor times, ma'am.'

Demelza edged her horse up to Verity's. 'Were you scairt?'

'A little. I thought they might upset us.'

Demelza was silent for some moments. 'I mind once when we were short of corn in Illugan. We had potatoes an' water for a week – and mortal few potatoes.'

For the moment her attention had been diverted from the plot on hand, but as they reached Truro she forgot the miners and only thought of Andrew Blamey and what she had engineered.

Chapter twelve

TRURO WORE ITS usual Thursday-morning appearance, a little untidier than most days because of the cattle market of the afternoon before. They left Bartle in the centre of the town and made their way on foot, picking a fastidious path over the cobbles and through the mud and refuse.

There was no sign of a stocky figure in a blue-laced coat, and they went into the little dress shop. Demelza was unusually fussy this morning; but at length Verity persuaded her to pick a dark bottle-green cloth which would not clash with any of the clothes she already had and which greatly suited the colour of her skin.

When it was all over Demelza asked the time. The seamstress went to see, and it was just noon. Well . . . she'd done her part. She could do no more. No doubt the date was wrong and he was still at sea.

The little bell in the shop pinged noisily and her heart leapt, but it was only a Negro page boy to ask whether the Hon Maria Agar's bonnet was finished.

Demelza lingered over some silk ribbons, but Verity was anxious to get her own shopping done. They had arranged to take a meal at Joan Pascoe's, an ordeal Demelza was not looking forward to, and there would be little time for shopping after that.

There were more people in the narrow street when they left the shop. A cart drawn by oxen was delivering ale at a near-by gin shop. Ten or twelve urchins, undersized, barefoot and scabby, and wearing men's discarded coats cut down and tied with string, were rioting among a pile of garbage. At the end of the street by the West Bridge a sober merchant had come to grief in the slippery mud and was being helped to his feet by two beggars. A dozen shopping women were out, most of them in clogs and with loops to their wrists to keep their skirts out of the dirt.

'Miss Verity,' said a voice behind them.

Oh, God, thought Demelza, it has come at last.

Verity turned. Riding and shopping brought a delicate flush to her cheeks which they normally lacked. But as she looked into Andrew Blamey's eyes the colour drained away: from her forehead, her lips, her neck, and only her eyes showed their blue greyness in a dead-white face.

Demelza took her arm.

'Miss Verity, ma'am.' Blamey glanced for a second at Demelza. His own eyes were a deeper blue, as if the ice had melted. 'For years I dared to hope, but no chance came my way. Lately I had begun to lose the belief that someday . . .'

'Captain Blamey,' said Verity in a voice that was miles away, 'may I introduce you to my cousin, Mistress Demelza Poldark, Ross's wife.'

'I'm honoured, ma'am.'

'And I, sir.'

'You are shopping?' Blamey said. 'Have you engagements for an hour? It would give me more pleasure than I can express . . .'

Demelza saw the life slowly creeping back into Verity's face. And with it came all the reservations of the later years.

'I don't think,' she said, 'that any good can come of our meeting, Captain Blamey. There is no ill thought for you in my heart . . . But after all this time we are better to renew nothing, to assume nothing, to – to seek nothing. . . .'

'That,' said Andrew, 'is what I passionately challenge. This meeting is most happy. It brings me the hope of – at least a friendship where hope had – gone out. If you will ——'

Verity shook her head. 'It's over, Andrew. We faced that years ago. Forgive me, but there is much we have to do this morning. We will wish you good day.'

She moved to go on, but Demelza did not stir. 'Pray don't consider me, Cousin. I can do the shopping on my own, truly I can. If – if your friend want a word with you, it is only polite to grant it.'

'No, you must come too, mistress,' said the seaman, 'or it would be talked of. Verity, I have a private room as it happens at an inn. We could go there, take coffee or a cordial. For old times' sake. . . .'

Verity wrenched her arm away from Demelza. 'No,' she said hysterically. 'No! I say no.'

She turned and began to walk quickly down the street towards the West Bridge. Demelza glanced frantically at Blamey, then followed. She was furious with Verity, but as she caught up with her and again took her arm, slowing her footsteps, she realized that Andrew Blamey had been prepared for this meeting while Verity had not. Verity's feelings were just the same as Blamey's had been that morning she went to Falmouth, a shying away from an old wound, a sharp-reared hostility to prevent more hurt. She blamed herself for not warning Verity. But how could she have done that when Verity ——

Coming to her ears were all sorts of noises and shouts, and in her present upset and confused state she came to link them with Blamey.

'You've left him far behind,' she said. 'There's no hurry now. Oh, Verity, it would ha' been fine if you'd given him a hearing. Really it would.'

Verity kept her face averted. She felt stifled with tears, they were in

her throat, everywhere but her eyes, which were quite dry. She had
almost reached the West Bridge and tried to push her way towards it, but
found herself blocked by a great number of people who seemed to be talking
and staring up the way she had come. Demelza too was holding her
back.

It was the miners, Demelza saw now. By the West Bridge there was a
centre block of ancient houses with narrow streets like a collar about them,
and in this roundabout the miners who had come down River Street were
milling, jostling each other, packed tight together, shouting and shaking
their weapons. They had lost direction, being set for the Coinagehall, but
this junction of streets and alleys had confused them. Half a dozen of their
number and several ordinary people had been pushed into the stream by
the pressure from behind, and others were fighting in the mud to avoid
following; the old stone bridge was packed with people struggling to get
across it. Demelza and Verity were on the very edge of the maelstrom,
twigs circling the outer currents and likely at any time to be drawn in. Then
Demelza glanced behind her and saw people, miners, grey and dusty and
angry, coming in a mass down Kenwyn Street.

They were caught between two floods.

'Verity, look!'

'In here,' said a voice, and her arm was grasped. Andrew Blamey pulled
them across the street to the porch of a house. It was tiny, it would just hold
the three of them, but they might be safe.

Verity, half resisting, went with them. Andrew put Demelza behind him
and Verity by his side, protecting her with his arm across the door.

The first wave of the flood went past them, shouting and shaking fists. It
went past them at speed. Then came the impact of the crowd at the bridge;
the speed slackened as rushing water will slacken and fill up a narrow
channel once there is no further escape. The miners became eight, ten,
fifteen, twenty abreast in the narrow street and some of the women began
to scream. They filled the whole of Kenwyn Street, a grey and haggard
horde as far as you could see. Men were being pressed against the walls of
the houses as if they would burst them open; glass cracked in the windows.
Blamey used all his strength to ease the pressure in the doorway.

No one could tell what was happening, but the earliest comers must have
found their direction, and this began to ease the congestion beyond the
bridge. The flood began to move turgidly away across the neck of the
bridge. Pressure eased, the crowd ebbed, at first slowly, then more quickly
towards the centre of the town.

Soon they were stumbling past in ragged columns and the three in the
porch were safe.

Andrew lowered his arm. 'Verity, I beg of you to reconsider . . .' He
caught sight of her face. 'Oh, my dear, please. . . .'

She pushed past him and plunged into the crowd.

The movement was so swift and reckless that neither of the others was quick enough to follow.

Then Blamey went shouting, 'Verity! Verity!' over the heads of the people who separated them, and Demelza followed.

But even that second was enough to set people between them, and he with his greater strength, fighting ahead to catch Verity, soon widened the gap until Demelza lost sight of him.

Demelza was above average height, but they were all tall men ahead of her and she pushed and turned and craned her head to no purpose. Then as they neared the bottleneck of the bridge she had no room or strength to look for the others; she could only fight for herself to avoid being diverted and pushed into the river. Men and women were squeezed upon her from all sides, elbows and staves poking and pressing and jerking; the great crowd animal seized her breath and gave her nothing in return. For moments they were stationary, shouting and sweating and cursing; then, suddenly silent, they would surge one way or another. Several times she lost her foothold altogether and went along without using her legs, at others she stumbled and had to clutch at her neighbours to save herself from going under. Quite near her a woman fell and was trampled on by the crowd. Then another fainted, but she was picked up and dragged along by a man beside her. Beyond her sight there were splashings and screamings and the clash of staves.

Even past the bridge the very narrow street gave no good outlet.

Near its objective, the crowd was getting angrier, and its anger took more of the air, consuming it in great waves of heat and violence. Lights and spots danced before Demelza's eyes, and she fought with the others for room to live. At last they were out of the worst press and bearing down Coinagehall Street. The crowd was making for the big corn warehouses which stood beside the creek.

Captain Blamey was away to her right – she saw him suddenly – and as she began to recover she tried to fight towards him.

The press grew again, bore her forward and slowly brought her to a standstill, surrounded by angry sweating miners and their women. Her good clothes were too conspicuous.

Before the big doors of the first warehouse citizens and burghers of the town were gathered to defend the rights of property. A fat, soberly clad man, the Citizen Magistrate, was standing on a wall, and he began to shout soundlessly into the great growling noise of the mob. Beside him was the corn factor who owned the warehouse, a fat man with a habit of blinking, and two or three constables of the town. There were no soldiers about; the justices had been taken by surprise.

As Demelza pushed her way towards the corner, where Blamey was, she saw Verity. He had found her. They were standing together against a stable door, unable to move farther for the crowd of people about them.

The magistrate had turned from reason to threat. While all that could be done would be done, that did not mean that those who broke the law would not be punished according to the law. He'd remind them of the trouble at Redruth last month when one of the rioters had been sentenced to death and many thrown into prison.

There were cries of 'Shame!' and 'Cruel an' wicked!'

'But we want no more'n what's right. We want corn to live by like the beasts o' the field. Well, then, sell us corn at a fair an' proper price an' we'll go home wi' it peaceable. Name us a price, mister, a fair an' proper price for starving men.'

The magistrate turned and spoke to the corn factor beside him.

Demelza pushed her way between two miners, who glared at her angrily for the disturbance. She had thought to cry out to catch Verity's notice, but changed her mind.

The justice said: 'Mr Sanson will sell you the corn at fifteen shillings a bushel as a concession to your poor and needy families. Come, it is a generous offer.'

There was a growl of anger and dissent, but before he replied the little miner bent to consult with those around him.

At last Demelza got within speaking distance of her friends, but they were separated from her by a handcart and a group of women sitting on the handcart, and she did not see how she could get nearer. Neither Andrew nor Verity saw her, for their gaze was towards the parley at the doors of the warehouse, although it might never have been happening for all they took in.

'Eight shillings. We'll pay ye eight shillings a bushel. Tis the very top we can afford, an' that'll mean hardship an' short commons for all.'

The corn merchant made an expressive gesture with his hands before even the magistrate turned to him. There was a roar of hostility from the crowd, and then suddenly in the silence which followed Demelza heard Andrew's voice speaking low and quick.

'. . . to live, my dear. Have I expiated nothing, learned nothing in these empty years? If there's blood between us, then it's old and long dry. Francis is changed, that I can see, though I've not spoken to him. But you have not changed, in heart you have not . . .'

There was another roar.

'Eight shillings or nothing,' shouted a miner. 'Speak now, mister, if it's to be peace, for we can 'old back no longer.'

Verity put up a gloved hand to her eyes.

'Oh, Andrew, what can I say? Are we to have all this again . . . the meeting, the parting, the heartache?'

'No, my dear, I *swear*. Never the parting. . . .'

Then it was all lost in the roar that greeted Sanson's obstinate refusal. The little miner went from his perch as if a hand had plucked him, and there was a great surge forward. The men on the steps of the granary put up a show of resistance, but they were leaves before a wind. In a few minutes tinners were hacking with their staves at the padlock on the door of the warehouse, and then quickly the doors were open and they surged in.

Demelza clung to the handcart to stop herself being carried towards the warehouse, but then men seized the handcart to load it up with grain, and she had to give way and press herself against the stable door.

'Demelza!' Verity had seen her. 'Andrew, help her. They will knock her down.'

Verity clung to Demelza's arm as if Demelza were the one who had forsaken it. The tears had dried on her face, leaving it streaky and uncomely. Her black fine hair was awry and her skirt torn. She looked unhappy – and painfully alive.

Those inside the warehouse were passing out sacks of grain to those who were waiting for them, and mules, which had been held in the background, were already coming down the street to be laden with the booty. The warehouse, drawing all towards it as a gutter will draw water, was thinning out the people near Demelza and Verity.

'This way,' said Blamey, 'there is a good chance now. Better than later, for maybe they will start drinking when the corn's away.'

He led them back to Coinagehall Street, which was clear of the tinners. But the townsfolk were out in their numbers, talking nervously together and discussing how best to prevent the looting from becoming widespread. The miners had come into town on a fair grievance, but appetite feeds an appetite and they might stay.

'Where are your horses?' asked Blamey.

'We were to have eaten with the Pascoes.'

'I'd advise you to defer it to a later day.'

'Why?' said Demelza. 'Could you not dine there too?'

Blamey glanced at her as they walked round Middle Row.

'No, ma'am, I could not, and though no doubt their bank building is strong and you would be safe inside it, you would later face the problem of leaving it to ride home, and the streets may not be safe by then. If you dine with the Pascoes, then be prepared to stay the night.'

'Oh, I could not do that!' said Demelza. 'Julia would need me, an' Prudie is so wooden.'

'Andrew,' said Verity, her steps slowing, 'won't you leave us here. If Bartle sees you the news of this meeting may reach Francis, and it may seem to him like a deliberate, a – a . . .'

'Let it,' said the seaman. 'There may be other rioters about. I have no intention of leaving you until you are safe out of this area.'

Bartle was in the stables, and while the horses were being saddled they sent a messenger to the Pascoes. Then they were up and away.

There were no rioters in Pydar Street, but people had come out of their houses and were gazing apprehensively down the hill. Some carried sticks themselves.

At the top of the hill the way was too narrow to ride three abreast in comfort, so Demelza, taking things into her own hands, first told Bartle to go a little ahead to see if there were any pickets or rioters and then spurred her own horse forward to join him.

Thus they rode home in silence, two by two, under the lowering sky. Demelza tried to find a little conversation with Bartle, while at the same time straining her ears for sound of talk behind. She did not catch it, but a little took place, a few low words now and then, the first signs of green in a desert after rain.

Chapter thirteen

JUD HAD BEEN fairly behaved for so long that Prudie overlooked the signs of a change. The settled domestic life of Nampara – so unlike old Joshua's regime – had had a pacifying effect on her own impulses and she had come to think that the same was true of him. Ross left early in the morning – he was away three and four days a week now – and when Demelza was out of sight Prudie settled herself in the kitchen to brew a dish of tea and talk over the week's scandal with Jinny Carter, overlooking the fact that an hour ago she had caught Jud taking a sup of gin while he milked the cows.

Jinny, in an odd way, had come to fulfil for Prudie much the same function that Demelza had done; in short, she now did most of the rough work of the house and left Prudie to potter and to brew her tea and gossip and complain of her feet. When Demelza was about it wasn't quite as easy as that, but when she went out things settled into a very comfortable groove.

To-day for once Jinny had been talking of Jim, of how thin and ill he had looked, of how she nightly prayed that the next eight months would slip away so that he might be free to come home. Prudie was glad to hear that she had no thought of leaving her work at Nampara. There was to be no more going down the mine for Jim, Jinny said. She had made him promise he would come back and work on the farm. He had never been so well as when he worked here and they never so happy. It wasn't mining wages, but what did that matter? If she worked they could make do.

Prudie said oh, there was no tellin', things was upsy down and it might be that them as worked on a farm would soon be earning more than them as went below, if half she'd heard tell of copper and tin was true. Look at Cap'n Ross, galloping about the countryside as if Old Scratch was at his coattails, and what was the use? What was the good of trying to puff life into a cold corpse? Better if he saved his smith's fees and looked to his own taties.

During this Jinny was in and out the kitchen three or four times, and on her last return wore an anxious look on her thin young face.

'There's someone in the cellar, Prudie. Truly. Just now as I were passing the door . . .'

'Nay,' said the other woman, wiggling her toes. 'You're mistook. Twas a rat maybe. Or wur it little Julia a-stirring in 'er cot, an? Go see, will ee, and save my poor feet.'

'Couldn' be that,' said Jinny. 'It were a man's voice – grumble, grumble, grumble, like an old cart wheel – coming up from the cellar steps.'

Prudie was about to contradict her again, but then with a thoughtful look she pulled on her slippers and rose like the side of a mountain creakily out of her chair. She flapped out into the hall and peered through the cellar door, which opened in the angle made by the stairs.

For a few seconds the murmur was too indistinct to catch any words, but after a while she heard:

'There was an old couple an' they was – was poor.
Tw – tw – tweedle, go tweedle, go twee.'

'Tes Jud,' she said grimly to the anxious Jinny. 'Drownin' his guts in Cap'n Ross's best gin. 'Ere, stay a breath, I'll root en out.'

She flapped back to the kitchen. 'Where's that there broom 'andle?'

'In the stable,' said Jinny. 'I seen it there this morning.'

Prudie went out to get it, Jinny with her; but when they came back the song in the cellar had stopped. They lighted a candle from the kitchen fire and Prudie went down the stairs. There were several broken bottles about but no signs of Jud.

Prudie came up. 'The knock-kneed 'ound's wriggled out while we was away.'

'Hold a minute,' said Jinny.

They listened.

Someone was singing gently in the parlour.

Jud was in Ross's best chair, with his boots on the mantelpiece. On his head, hiding the fringe and the tonsure, was one of Ross's hats, a black riding hat turned up at the brim. In one hand was a bottle of gin and in the other a riding crop, with which he gently stirred the cradle in which Julia slept.

'Jud!' said Prudie. 'Get out o' that chair!'

Jud turned his head.

'Ah,' he said, in a ridiculous voice. 'C-come in, good women all, good women all, g-good women. Your servant, ma'am. Damme, tis handsome of ee to make this visit. Tedn what I'd of expected in a couple o' bitches. But there, one 'as to take the rough wi' the rough; an' a fine couple of bitches ye be. Pedigree stock, sir. Never have I seen the likes. Judgin' only by the quarters, tis more'n a fair guess to say there's good blood in ee, an' no miss-ment.' He gave the cradle a prod with his riding crop to keep it rocking.

Prudie grasped her broom.

''Ere, dear,' she said to Jinny, 'you go finish yer work. I'll deal with this.'

'Can you manage him?' Jinny asked anxiously.

'Manage 'im. I'll *mince* 'im. Only tis a question of the cradle. We don't want the little mite upset.'

When Jinny had gone, Jud said: 'What, no more'n one lef'? What a cunning crack ye are, Mishtress Paynter, gettin' quit o' she so's there'll be less to share the gin.' His little eyes were bloodshot with drink and bleary with cunning. 'Come us in, my dear, an' lift your legs up. I'm the owner 'ere; Jud Paynter, eskewer, of Nampara, mashter of hounds, mashter of cemeteries, Justice of the Peace. 'Ave a sup!'

'Pah!' said Prudie. 'Ye'll laugh on the other side of yer head if Cap'n Ross catches ee wi' yer breeches glued to 'is bettermost chair. Ah . . . ye dirty glut!'

He had upended his bottle of gin and was drinking it in great gulps, so that bubbles leapt up the side of the bottle.

'Nay, don't ee get scratchy, for I've two more by the chair. Ye've overfanged notions o' the importance of Ross an' his kitchen girl in the scum o' things. 'Ere, 'ave a spur.'

Jud leaned over and put a half-empty bottle on the table behind him. Prudie stared at it.

'Look!' she said. 'Out o' that chair or I'll cleave open yer 'ead with this broom. An' leave the cheeil alone!' The last words came in a screech, for he had given the cradle another poke.

Jud turned and looked at her assessingly; through the blear of his gaze he tried to see how far his head was in danger. But Ross's hat gave him confidence.

'Gis along, you. 'Ere, there's brandy in the cupboard. Fetch it down an' I'll mix ye a Sampson.'

This had once been Prudie's favourite drink: brandy and cider and sugar. She stared at Jud as if he were the Devil tempting her to sell her soul.

She said: 'If I d'want drink I'll get it and not akse you, nor no other else.' She went to the cupboard and genteelly mixed herself a Sampson. With greedy glassy eyes Jud watched her.

'Now,' said Prudie fiercely, 'out o' that chair!'

Jud wiped a hand across his face. 'Dear life, it d'make me weep to see ee. Drink un up first. An' mix me one too. Mix me a Sampson wi' his hair on. There, there, be a good wife now.'

A 'Sampson with his hair on' was the same drink but with double the brandy. Prudie took no notice and drank her own. Then, gloomily, she mixed herself another.

'Tend on yerself,' she said. 'I never was yer wife, and well you d'know it. Never in church proper like a good maid should. Never no passon to breathe 'is blessing. Never no music. Never no wedden feast. Just *took*, I was. I wonder you d'sleep of nights.'

'Well, a fine load ye was,' said Jud. 'An' more's been added. Half enough to fill a tin ship now. And you didn want no wedden. Gis along, you old suss. Twas all I could do to get ee 'ere decent. Ave a drink.'

Prudie reached for the half-empty bottle.

'Me old mother wouldn have liked it,' she said. 'Tes fair to say she was happier dead. The only one she reared, I was. One out of twelve. Tes hard to think on after all these year.'

'One in twelve's a fair portion,' said Jud, giving the cot another push. 'The world's too full as tis, and some should be drownded. Ef I 'ad me way, which mebbe I never shall an' more's the pity, for there's precious few has got the head on 'em that Jud Paynter have got, though there's jealous folk as pretend to think other, and one o' these days they'll 'ave the shock of their lives, for Jud Paynter'll up and tell 'em down-souse that tes jealous thoughts an' no more d'keep away a recognition which, if he 'ad un, would be no more than any man's due who's got the head on 'im, where was I?'

'Killin' off me little brothers and sisters,' said Prudie.

'Ais,' said Jud. 'One in twelve. That's what I d'say, one in twelve. Not swarming like the Martins an' the Viguses and the Daniels. Not swarming like this house'll be before long. Put 'em in the tub I would, like they was chets.'

Prudie's great nose was beginning to light up.

'I'll have no sich talk in my kitchen,' she declared.

'We bain't in your kitchen now, so hold yer tongue, you fat cow.'

'Cow yerself, and more,' said Prudie. 'Dirty old gale. Dirty old ox. Dirty old wort. Pass me that bottle. This one's dry.'

In the kitchen Jinny waited for the crash and commotion of Jud's punishment. It did not come. She went on with her work. Since her youngest, Kate, had begun to get her fingers in things she had given up bringing her to work and had left her in the care of her mother, to grow up along with the other two and with the younger ones of Mrs Zacky's brood. So she was all alone in the kitchen.

Presently she finished her work and looked about for something else. The windows could do with a wash. She took out a bucket to get water from the pump and saw her eldest, Bengy Ross, coming trotting over the fields from Mellin.

She knew at once what it was. Zacky had promised to let his daughter know.

She went to meet the child, wiping her hands on her apron.

Bengy was now three and a half, a big boy for his age, showing no hurt for his ordeal except the thin white scar on his cheek. She met him at the edge of the garden by the first apple trees.

'Well, dear?' she said. 'What did Gramfer say?'

Bengy looked at her brightly. 'Gramfer d'say mine be to close next month, Mam.'

Jinny stopped wiping her hands. 'What . . . all of it?'

'Ais. Gramfer say tis all to close down next month. Mam, can I 'ave an apple?'

This was worse than she had expected. She had thought that they might let half of it go and keep the richer lode. She had hoped no worse. If all Grambler was to close it meant the end of everything. A few lucky ones might have savings to last the winter. The rest would find other work or starve. There was no other work about unless a few got on at Wheal Leisure. Some might try the lead mines of Wales or the coal mines of the Midlands, leaving their families here to see for themselves. It would be a breakup of lives, of homes.

Now there would be no choice for Jim when he came out. He would be lucky even to be taken on at the farm. She had lived all her life in the shadow of Grambler. It was no light-seeking venture, easy begun and easy done. There had been ups and downs, she knew, but never a closure. She did not know how many years it had been going, but long before her mother was born. There had been no village of Grambler there before the mine: the mine *was* the village. It was the centre point of the district, the industry, a household name, an institution.

She went in and picked out a ripe apple from among the 'resters' in the still-room, gave it to Bengy.

She must tell Jud and Prudie – at least tell Prudie, if Jud was not yet in his senses.

Bengy trailing at her heels, she went into the parlour.

Ross heard the news as he was riding home from his meeting with Richard Tonkin, Ray Penvenen and Sir John Trevaunance. An elderly miner, Fred Pendarves, shouted it to him as he was passing the gibbet at the Bargus crossroads. Ross rode on thinking there would be no mines left to profit by their scheme if things went on like this much longer. He had come away from Place House, Trevaunance, in an encouraged mood, for Sir John had promised them his influence and his money, provided they built the copper smelting works on his land; but the news of Grambler's closure set this optimism back.

He rode slowly down Nampara Combe and reached his house, but he did not at once take Darkie to her stable. He had the half thought of going to see Francis.

In the hall he paused and listened to the raised voices in the parlour. Was Demelza entertaining company? He was not in the mood for company.

But that was Jud's voice. And Jinny Carter's raised too. Jinny *shouting*! He went to the door, which was an inch open.

'It is a lie!' Jinny was in tears. 'A wicked filthy lie, Jud Paynter, and you did ought to be whipped, sittin' there in your master's chair drinking his brandy and uttering such falseness. You did ought to be scourged wi' scorpions like they say in the Bible. You horrible nasty beast you ——'

'Hearear,' said Prudie. 'Thash ri', dearie. Give un a clunk on the head. 'Ave my stick.'

'You bide in yer own sty,' said Jud. 'Cabby ole mare. I'm not saying nothin' but what's said by others. Look for yerself. Look at the lad's scar, there on 'is face. Poor lil brat, tedn his fault. But is it wonder folk d'say twas put there as a mark by Beelzebub himself to mark 'is true father for all to see. Folks d'say – and who can blame 'em – who ever see two scars more alike? Like father like son, they d'say: Ross and Bengy Ross. An' then, they d'say: Look he was riding off again wi' she last month but one all the way to Bodmin, and lay there *the night*. Tedn my talking, but tedn surprising there's talk. An' all the weepin' an' shoutin' in Gristledom won't stay it.'

'I'll hear no more,' cried Jinny. 'I comed in here to tell you about Grambler, an' you turn on me like a horrible drunk old dog! An' you, Prudie, I should never have believed it if I hadn't seen it with my own eyes!'

'Ushush! Don't take on so, maid. I'm jush sitting here quiet-like to see Jud gets up to no mishchief. After all's done an' said ——'

'An' as for that poor lil brat thur,' said Jud, 'tedn reasonable to blame he. Tedn smart. Tedn proper. Tedn just. Tedn fitty ——'

'I wish Jim was here! Bengy, come away from the beast. . . .'

She burst out of the parlour with a wild look and her face streaked with tears. She clutched her eldest child by one hand. Ross had drawn back but she saw him. She instantly went very white, the red patches on her face showing up like blotches. Her eyes met his in fright and hostility. Then she ran into the kitchen.

Demelza reached home soon after, having walked across the cliff way from Trenwith. She found Julia still asleep through all the noise and Prudie with her head in her apron weeping loudly beside the cradle. The parlour reeked, and there were two broken bottles on the floor. Chairs were overturned and Demelza began to suspect the truth.

But she could get no sense out of Prudie, who only wailed the louder when she was touched and said they'd both seen the last of Jud.

Demelza fled into the kitchen. No sign of Jinny.

Noises in the yard.

Ross stood by the pump working it with one hand while in the other he held a horsewhip. Jud was under the pump.

Every time he tried to get away from the water he took a crack from the horsewhip, so he had given it up and was now drowning patiently.

'Ross, Ross! What is it! What has he done, Ross?'

He looked at her.

'Next time you take the day for shopping,' he said, 'we will see that better arrangements are come to for the care of our child.'

The seeming injustice of this took her breath away.

'Ross!' she said. 'I don't understand. What has happened? Julia seems all right.'

Ross cracked his whip. 'Get under there! Learn to swim! Learn to swim! Let's see if we can wash some of the nasty humours out of you.'

'Humours' might have been 'rumours', but Demelza did not know that. She turned suddenly and ran back into the house.

Verity got right home without hearing anything of the decision. They had parted from Captain Blamey at the St Ann's Fork, and then Demelza had dismounted at the gates of Trenwith and Verity and Bartle went up the drive alone.

Elizabeth was the only one who looked up at Verity's coming in, for Aunt Agatha did not hear it and Francis did not heed it.

Elizabeth smiled painfully. 'Did the Pascoes let you leave so soon?'

'We didn't go,' said Verity, pulling off her gloves. 'There were miners rioting in the town and – and we thought it wise to leave before the disorder grew worse.'

'Ha!' said Francis from the window. 'Rioting indeed. There'll be rioting in other parts soon.'

'For that reason, I had not the time to get you the brooch, Elizabeth. I am so sorry, but perhaps I shall be able to go in next week ——'

'All these years,' said Aunt Agatha. 'Damn me, twas old afore I was born. I mind well old Grannie Trenwith telling me that her grandpa-by-marriage, John Trenwith, cut the first goffin the year afore he died.'

'What year was that?' Francis said moodily.

'But if you was to ask me how long ago that was, I shouldn't know. I'd say ye'd best look in the Bible. But it was when Elizabeth was an old queen.'

Quite slowly the import of the whole scene came to Verity. The meeting of this morning had gone from her mind. She had ridden away from Trenwith obsessed by the decisions that were to be taken in her absence. She had ridden back and not given it a thought.

'You don't mean ——'

'Then the first underground shaft was put in by the other John seventy or eighty year later. That was the one Grannie Trenwith married. All those years an' never closed. It isn't long since we drew thousands a year out of it. It don't seem right to let it all go.'

With a sudden subtlety unnatural in her, Verity played up to their assumption.

'From what I heard,' she said, 'I wasn't quite sure . . . Does it mean the whole mine? Everything?'

'How could it be otherwise?' Francis turned from the window. 'We can't keep one part drained without the other.'

'Why, when I was growing up,' said Aunt Agatha, 'there was money to play with. Papa died when I was eight, and I mind how Mama spent money on the memorial in Sawle Church. 'Spare no expense,' I heard her say. I can hear her now. 'Spare no cost. He died as surely of his wounds as if he'd fallen in battle. He shall have a worthy stone.' Ah, Verity, so you're back, eh? You're flushed. Why're you so flushed? Tis nothing to warm the blood, this news. It be the downfall of the Poldarks, I can tell ye.'

'What will this mean, Francis?' Verity asked. 'How will it affect us? Shall we be able to go on as before?'

'As shareholders, it will affect us not at all except to destroy the hope of a recovery and to stop us throwing good money after bad. We have drawn no dividend for five years. For mineral rights we have been taking upwards of eight hundred pounds a year, which will now cease. That's the difference.'

Verity said: 'We can hardly then continue ——'

'It will depend on our other commitments,' Francis said irritably. 'We have the farm to work. We own all Grambler village and half Sawle, for what the rents will be worth after this. But if our creditors will be indulgent, there will be a minimum incoming which will make life supportable even if hardly worth supporting.'

Elizabeth got up, sliding Geoffrey Charles quietly to the floor.

'We shall manage,' she said quietly. 'There are others worse than we. There are ways we can save. This cannot last for ever. It is just a question of keeping our heads above water for the time.'

Francis glanced at her in slight surprise. Perhaps he had half expected her to take a different line, complaining and blaming him. But she always turned up trumps in a crisis.

'Now,' said Geoffrey Charles, glancing angrily at his father, 'can I make a noise now, Mama? Can I make a noise now?'

'Not just yet, dear,' said Elizabeth.

Verity muttered an excuse and left them.

Slowly she climbed the broad spacious stairs and glanced with new eyes about her as she did so. She walked down the square low passage with its fine Tudor Gothic windows looking out on the small green central square, with its climbing roses, its fountain that never played and its solidly paved path. Everything about the house was solid, well shaped, built to please and built to last. She prayed it would never have to go.

In her own room she avoided looking at herself in the mirror lest she should see there what had been noticeable to Aunt Agatha's sharp old eyes.

This window looked out on the yew hedge and the herb garden. In the bitterness of four years ago she had looked this way. She had found some comfort here in all the big crises of her life.

She did not know if this was a big crisis or not. Perhaps, looking back, it would not seem so. Grambler was closing, that alone meant a wholesale change in the life of the district. Grambler was closing.

But why not be honest? That was not her crisis. It touched her money, but living the sort of life she did, money had always been remote from her.

It touched her people then. Yes, acutely; it concerned all the people she knew and liked, not only in this house but in the district. It would affect the choir she taught and make ten times harder her work to help the poor. This morning, this morning, they had been her people. What, then, had changed?

Why wasn't she more upset for them? Why was she not as miserable as she ought to be? Why not? Why not?

The answer was plain if she had the courage to own it.

She pressed her hot face against the glass of the window and listened to the beating of her heart.

Chapter fourteen

JUD AND PRUDIE had to leave. On that Ross was adamant. In many ways an easygoing man, he would have tolerated much for the sake of loyalty. Jud's drunkenness he had long been used to, but Jud's disloyal slander could not be swallowed at any price. Besides, there was the child to be thought of. They could never be trusted with her again.

He had them before him next morning and gave them a week to get out. Prudie looked tearful, Jud sullen. Jud thought he had talked Ross round before and in a week could talk him round again. In this he was mistaken. It was only when he discovered it that he became really alarmed. Two days before they were due to go Demelza, taking pity on Prudie, suggested that she might be able to persuade Ross to keep *her*, if she would separate from Jud; but at the last Prudie was faithful and chose to go.

So in due time they left, burdened up with all sorts of lumber and belongings. They had found a tumble-down shack, half cottage, half shed, which was the first house in Grambler at this end of the straggling village. It was dismal and derelict, but the rent was practically nothing and it was next to a gin shop, which would be very convenient.

Their leaving was a tremendous upheaval, and when they had gone Nampara seemed a strange house; one was constantly listening for the flop of Prudie's slippers or the harsh tenor of Jud's grievances. They had been sloppy, idle incompetent servants but they had grown into the marrow of life, and everyone felt the loss. Demelza was glad they had not gone far, for her friendship with Prudie was of too long a standing to break in a few days.

In their place Ross took a married pair called John and Jane Gimlett, a plump couple in the early forties. Five or six years ago they had come to Grambler from north Cornwall to find work in the then still-prosperous west and he had set up as a journeyman shoemaker. But it had not gone well and they had both been working at a tin stamp for over a year. They seemed tremendously eager, willing, competent, clean, good-tempered and respectful – all things the opposite of Jud and Prudie. Only time would show how this would last.

Two days after the drunken fracas Ross had some further trouble with his small staff.

'Where's Jinny this morning?'

'She's left,' answered Demelza moodily.

'Left?'

'Last night. I intended to have telled you but you were so late back. I can't make head or tail of it.'

'What did she say?'

'She said she'd be happier looking after her three children. It was no good me saying all her mother's family would soon be out of work, for she just closed her lips tight and said she wanted to leave.'

'Oh,' said Ross, stirring his coffee.

'It is all to do with that trouble on Thursday afternoon,' said Demelza. 'Maybe if I knew what it was about I could do something. I mean, *she* wasn't drunk. Why should *she* leave?'

'I have a notion,' said Ross.

'I don't see why I should be the only one left in the dark, Ross. If you know, then you did ought to tell me.'

Ross said: 'You remember when I took Jinny to Bodmin I said there'd be talk?'

'Yes.'

'Well, there *is* talk, and Jud was repeating it when I got home. And there are all sorts of poisonous brews being added from the past. That is another reason why Jud must go – apart from Julia.'

'Oh,' said Demelza, 'I see.'

After a moment Ross said: 'Perhaps Jinny does not know Jud is leaving. When ——'

'Yes, she does. Prudie told her yesterday.'

'Well, I will go and see Zacky, that's if you want her back.'

'Of course I want her back. I like her.'

'I have to see Zacky anyway. I have something to offer him.'

'Well, that'll cheer up Mrs Zacky. I've never seen her downcast before. What's it to be?'

'In our venture in copper buying we want an agent, a man unknown in the trade who will act for us and take the limelight. I think I can get Zacky the appointment. He's no ordinary miner, you know.'

'What of Mark Daniel?'

'What about him?'

'You remember I said Keren had asked me if you'd anything good for him?'

'Ye–es. But this would not do, Demelza. We need a man who can read and write and can handle sums of money in a civilized fashion. And one who has a certain knowledge of the world. Zacky's is the minimum that could be acceptable. Besides, we need a man we can trust completely. We must have absolute secrecy. Anything less might be fatal. Of course I would trust Mark with my life . . . but he is not quite the free agent that he was. I feel that, however steady a man is, if he has an unstable wife to whom he is devoted, then there is a corrosion at work on his own foundations.'

Demelza said: 'I don't know what Keren would say if she heard that. Twould never occur to her that she might be a *drag* on Mark.'

'Well, she'll not hear it, so set your mind at rest.'

Keren at the moment was up a ladder. For two days it had rained, and the weather had found its way through Mark's thatching. It had come into the kitchen and then into the bedroom, and last night there had been drips of water falling on their feet.

Keren was furious. Of course Mark had spent the best part of his leisure up this ladder in the rain, but it was her view that in the two months of their married life he should have spent much more time making the house weatherproof. Instead, every wet day he had worked on the inside of the house and every fine day he had been in the garden.

He had done wonders there, had carried away many tons of stone and with them had built a wall surrounding the plot of land. The wall stretched right round now, a monument to one man's tireless energy, and inside the wall the land was being dug and raked and weeded and made ready for next season's crops. And in a corner by the house Mark had built a lean-to shed leading into a small walled compound where later he hoped to keep pigs.

Marriage was a disappointment. Mark's love-making, though sincere, was rough and unromantic and devoid of finesse, and Mark's conversation when he was not making love scarcely existed. Then there were the long hours he was away at the mine, and the weekly change of cores, so that one week he was up getting his breakfast at five, and another week he was coming home to sleep at six-thirty, waking her up but refusing to be wakened when she got up herself. Even this core when he went down at two in the afternoon left her with the whole evening alone. It had been the most exciting one in the early days, for he used to come home just before eleven and strip and wash himself and shave and then they'd get into bed together. But the novelty of that had worn off and usually she found an excuse to avoid his clumsy caresses. It was all so different from the part she had played in *The Miller's Bride*.

He had just gone now, hurrying away to be there in time, and she was left with nine hours to kill. He had had no time to move the ladder so she thought she would try to mend the thatch herself. She was of the opinion that adaptability was enough to solve all problems. She found where he had been working, and picked her way across the damp thatch. It was fine this morning, but there was the promise of more rain. She would like to see his face if he came home in a drenching downpour to-night and found the house quite dry within.

From where she sat now she had a clear view of Dr Enys's turreted house, and she was sorry that the trees about it did not lose their leaves in winter. Three times since that meeting at Nampara she had caught glimpses of him, but they had not exchanged a word. She sometimes thought she would lose the use of her tongue, for few of the neighbours from Mellin came over, and when they did they were not encouraged by their reception. The only person Keren had made a friend of was little Charlie Baragwanath, who usually called in on his way back from work.

For some time now Keren had been having doubts of her own wisdom in leaving the travelling company for this buried-alive existence. She tried sometimes to remember the hardships and discouragements of that life, just to reassure herself; but distance was blurring the view. Even the money she had hoped to find here was not all it seemed. Mark had some money and was generous with it in a way; but the habits of a lifetime could not change in a week. He would give her money to spend as a lump sum, but he did not like to see money spent as a regular thing, to see it frittered. He had had made it plain to Keren that his purse had a limit, and once his purse was empty only the severest pinching and saving would fill it again.

Not perhaps even that now that Grambler was going.

She leaned out to tuck in a piece of thatch and bind it, and as she did so her foothold grew uncertain. Quite gently she began to slide down the roof.

'Well,' said Zacky, rubbing his bristle, 'it is more'n kind of you. I'll not pretend but that I'd like to try it. Mother'll be fair delighted to think there will be money coming in without a break. But I couldn't take that much money, not to start. Give me what I been earning from my pitch, that's fair and proper.'

'As an employee of the company,' Ross said, 'you'll take what you're given. I'll see you have good notice when you'll be wanted. It may mean a few absences from your pitch during the last week or so.'

'That's no matter. The zest is out of it anyway. I don't know what half o' them will do this winter.'

'And now,' said Ross, 'I should like a word with Jinny.'

Zacky looked a trifle constrained. 'She's inside with Mother. I don't know what's got her, but she seem set in her own way. We can't reason with her same as we belonged to when she was a maid. Jinny! Jinny! Come out for a breath. There's a gentleman to see you.'

A long pause followed. Finally the door of the cottage opened and Jinny stood there but did not come out.

Ross went over to her. Zacky did not follow but scraped his chin with the ball of his thumb and watched them.

'Captain Poldark,' Jinny said, dropping him a slight curtsy but not raising her eyes.

He did not beat about the bush. 'I know why you have left us, Jinny, and sympathize with your feelings. But to give way to them is to conform to rules set down by the evil-minded. Through Jud Paynter and his drunkenness they were able to leave a nasty smear across my house and across your reputation. For that he has been got rid of. It would be a mistake for you to give life to the story by taking notice of it. I should like you to come as usual to-morrow.'

She looked up and met his glance.

'Twill be better not, sur. If such stories be about, gracious knows where they'll end.'

'They'll end where they began, in the gutters.'

She was so terribly embarrassed that he was sorry for her. He left her there and returned to Zacky, who had been joined by his wife.

'Leave 'er be for a while, sur,' said Mrs Martin. 'She'll come round. I'll not be long, Zacky. I just be going over to Reath Cottage. Bobbie's been in to say Keren Mark Daniel's met with a accident.'

'What has she done?'

'Slided off the roof. Breaked her arm an' what not. I thought I'd just go'n see if I can be of 'elp. Not as I've a great taking for the maid, but it is only neighbourly to make sartin, as Mark's down the bal.'

'Is she alone?' Ross asked. 'I'll come with you if she needs any attention.'

'No, sur; Bobbie says Dr Enys is there.'

He had been there twenty minutes. By great good fortune he had heard her shouting and had been the first on the scene.

After the first shock of the fall she had half fainted for some minutes, and when she came round she had nearly fainted again each time she moved her arm.

So she had sat there for an eternity, her head throbbing and her mouth dry with sickness. And then he had heard her cries and climbed across the ditch and come over to her.

After that, although there was pain and distress there was also comfort and happiness. He had carried her inside and put her on the bed, and his quick professional hands exploring her body were to her like the hands of a lover new-welcomed and at home.

He said: 'You've fractured the bone. Your ankle will be well enough with rest. Now I must set your arm. It will hurt, but I'll be as quick as possible.'

'Go on,' she said, looking at him.

He had a roll of bandage in his pocket and found two splints among Mark's carpenterings. Then he gave her a drink of brandy and set her arm. She bit her teeth together and never made a sound. Tears came into her eyes, and when he had finished they rolled down her cheeks and she brushed them away.

'That was very brave of you,' he said. 'Take another drink of this.'

She took it because it was in his flask, and began to feel better. Footsteps sent him to the door and he told Bobbie Martin to go for his mother. It had taken less than a month to teach him that if anyone in the district needed a good turn they sent for Mrs Zacky, whose twelve children never impeded her instinct for mothering the neighbourhood.

Then he sat on the bed and bathed her other elbow and bathed her ankle and tied it up. This was sheer bliss to her and her eyes would have let him see it if he had not kept his own on the business in hand. All this done, he talked to her in a tone that had become steadily more dry and professional in the last ten minutes, suggesting that she should call her husband out of the mine.

But she was set against this, and when Mrs Zacky's flat face and spectacles showed in the doorway she greeted her so sweetly that Mrs Zacky thought the district had summed up Mark's wife too quick and too drastic.

Dwight Enys stayed a little longer, his handsome face sober but youthful, telling Mrs Zacky what to do. Then he took Keren's hand and said he would call again in the morning.

Keren said in a soft contralto: 'Thank you, Dr Enys. I didn't know anyone could be so kind.'

He flushed slightly. 'Cruel to be kind. But you took it all well. The arm will give you pain to-night. Do, please, stay in bed. If you get up you may raise a temperature, and then it will be perhaps a long job.'

'I'm *sure* I shall be all right,' Keren said. 'I'll do *anything* you say.'

'Very well. Good day to you. Good day, Mrs Martin.'

Chapter fifteen

GRAMBLER WAS TO close on the twelfth of November, and the day came still and misty with a humid air and a threat of rain. Unhealthy weather, Dr Choake said, which raised up all the putrid vapours. They had run the engine this long to finish the coal in stock.

There were three pumps to the mine. Two engines – both modernized but both left hopelessly out of date by Watt's invention of the separate condenser – and a great water wheel of thirty feet diameter, worked by the Mellingey Stream.

At noon a small party of men gathered in the big central engine house. Present were Francis Poldark, Captain Henshawe, the 'grass' captain, Dunstan, Dr Choake, the two chief enginemen, Brown and Trewinnard, the purser and a few other officials. They stood there and coughed and avoided each other's eyes, and Francis took out his watch.

Up and down went the great bob, to the rattle of the chains, the roar of the furnace and the suck and splash of water with its dull inrush through the leather valves. From the house the mine spread away like a great beast, unsightly, unordered; wooden sheds, stone huts, thatched air shafts, water wheels, washing floors, horse whims, mounds of refuse and stone and cinders, the accumulations, additions and wastages of years. And here and there, running away down little valleys like tributaries of the mine, were the cottages of Grambler village.

Francis looked at his watch.

'Well, gentlemen,' he said, raising his voice, 'the time has come for the closure of our mine. We have worked together many years, but the times have beaten us. Someday perhaps this mine will be restarted and we shall all meet here again. And if we have not that good fortune our sons may enjoy it in our stead. It is now twelve noon.'

He reached up to the lever which controlled the steam in its passage from the giant boiler of the engine, and pulled it down. The great engine bob paused in its stroke, hesitated, lumbered to a stop. Meanwhile the engineman had moved round and opened a valve, and there was a sigh of escaping steam as it rose white in the still, misty air, hovered and seemed reluctant to disperse.

A silence fell on the company. It was not that the engine had never stopped before: it was halted monthly for the boilers to be cleaned; and there had been any number of breakdowns. But this silence was heavy with the knowledge of what it brought.

With an impulse foreign to himself Francis took up a piece of chalk and on the side of the boiler chalked the word RESURGAM.

Then they filed out of the house.

Over at the Sawle end of the mine the smaller engine 'Kitty' was still chattering and thumping. Captain Henshawe raised his hand. The signal was seen, and Kitty thumped and muttered herself into silence.

Now all that was left was the water pump; but this used no fuel and needed little attention, so it was allowed to go on.

The last shift of the tut-workers had been told to come up at twelve, and as the group of men walked slowly towards the offices the miners were appearing in twos and threes at the mouth of the engine shaft, carrying up their picks and shovels and drills for the last time.

A mixed company, they formed a long slow caterpillar to file past the purser and take their last wages. Bearded or clean-shaven, young or middle-aged, mostly small and pallid, wiry and uncouth, sweat-stained and mineral-stained, grave-eyed and silent, they took their shillings and made their 'marks' of receipt in the cost book.

Francis stood there behind the purser, exchanging a word with one or another of the men, until they were all paid. Then he shook hands with Captain Henshawe and walked home alone to Trenwith.

The engineers had gone back to their engines to go over them and decide what could be dismantled and sold for scrap; the purser was adding up his books, the manager and the grass captain began a wide tour of the buildings to take final account of what stock was left. Henshawe changed into old clothes and a miner's hat and went down to make a last inspection.

With easy familiarity he climbed down the shaft to the forty-fathom level, and there stepped off into the tunnel in the direction of the richer of the two bearing lodes, the 'sixty' level.

After walking about a quarter of a mile, he began to drop with the tunnel, picking his way past mounds of dead ground and climbing down ladders and across slippery slopes through mazes of timber used to shore up the roof and sides. He ploughed through water and at length heard the steady pick, pick and bang, bang, bang of men still at work.

There were about twenty tributers left. If they could mine a few more shillings' worth it would all add up on their accounts sheet with the company and would help in the struggle with poverty which would soon begin.

Zacky Martin was there, and Paul Daniel and Jacka Carter, Jim's young brother, and Pally Rogers. They were all stripped to the waist and sweating, for the temperature here was hotter than the hottest summer's day.

'Well, boys,' said Henshawe, 'I thought I'd come tell you that Big Bill and Kitty have stopped.'

Pally Rogers looked up and wiped an arm across his great black beard. 'We reckoned twas about time.'

'I thought I'd tell you,' Henshawe said, 'just to leave you know.'

Zacky said: 'We should have a few days. There's been no weight of rain.'

'I shouldn't bank on too much. She's always been a wet mine. And how will you get the stuff up?'

'By the east shaft. The Curnow brothers are keeping the horse whim going. We'll have to haul it as best we can to there.'

Henshawe left them and went on as far as he could until he reached the flooded eighty-fathom level. Then he turned and went back, found his way through more water to the poorer west lode and made sure that nothing of value had been left. A few rusty tools, a clay pipe, a broken barrow.

It was two o'clock by the time he came up. The unnatural silence greeted him all round. Kitty still steamed a little in the quiet. A few men were pottering about the sheds, and about twenty women were out washing clothes in the hot water from the engine.

Henshawe walked into the changing-shed to put on his own clothes, and saw a half dozen men gathering at the shaft head. He thought of shouting, and then realized that it was the relieving men going down to take over work from their partners. He shrugged his shoulders and turned away. Tributers were a hardy breed.

By eight the following evening the water had risen a good deal but the lode was still untouched. Mark Daniel sent one of the others up to tell those who would come down and relieve them.

Up above it was a ghostly night, dark and gossamer-damp, marking the silence and emptiness of the mine buildings. Usually there were dozens in the changing-sheds, lights in the engine houses, the engineers to pass a word with, all the reassurance of companionship. Now there was no heat, no talk except the exchange of a muttered word among themselves, no light except from two lanterns.

They blew these out after lighting their candles and stolidly took to the ladders: Nick Vigus and Fred Martin and John and Joe Nanfan and Ed Bartle and sixteen others.

By four in the morning some of the lode was covered. They were working in water, and there were deep lakes in low-lying parts of the plot behind them. There was, however, a ledge round; and at a push they could still get away by the east shaft. Nick Vigus went up ahead to tell the newcomers the situation. There was a consultation, and Zacky Martin and the others decided to go down, for there was a chance of a few hours more.

At seven a fall of stone and rubble into one of the pools brought them to a halt. They spent another hour tugging away a few last buckets of ore up the side of the tunnel until they could attach it to a rope and get it pulled along the back of an exhausted lode to the east shaft. Then they climbed up a few feet and sat and watched the water lapping round the long black cavern which had been their working home for months past.

One by one they picked their way out, through the old workings and out of the mine.

Zacky Martin was the last to leave. He sat on the edge of the underground shaft and lit his pipe and stared down at the water, which rose so quietly that it hardly seemed to rise at all. He sat there nearly an hour, smoking and rubbing his chin and occasionally spitting, his eyes under their candle thoughtful and steady.

It might be weeks yet before there was a full house of water, but already the 'sixty' was gone. And that was the best.

He came to his feet, sighed and began to pick his path in the wake of the others, past deserted windlasses, broken ladders, pieces of timber and piles of rubble. It was a honeycomb this upper part, a crazy twisting and turning with tunnels going off in every direction, most of them blind, where earlier miners had driven in search of fresh ore. There were underground shafts to trap the unwary and great hollow caves with dripping roofs.

Eventually he came out at the main shaft at the 'thirty' level. Pick and shovel over one shoulder, he began to climb up it for the last time, taking it in slow steady stages from platform to platform, as became an old-timer. Now the quietude struck him again.

He reached the surface and found that the November day, hardly breaking when he went down, had fallen into a wet mist. It covered the countryside in a blanket, and only near things were clear.

Everybody had gone home. The Curnow brothers had stopped the water pump, and the ore they had raised these two days was dumped in heaps beside the east shaft. It would have to be accounted later, but nobody had the heart to begin it to-day. Even the fat familiar figure of the purser was not to be seen.

After resting a minute or two Zacky picked up his shovel and pick again and turned to go home. As he did so he saw Paul Daniel waiting by the engine house.

'I thought I'd make sartin you was out,' Paul said, rather apologetic as Zacky reached him. 'You was a long time after the rest of us.'

'Yes,' said Zacky. 'Just had a last look round.'

They walked off together towards Mellin.

And then the mine was quite deserted and alone in the mist. And the silence of its inactivity and the silence of the windless misty day was like a pall on the countryside. No rough boot jarred upon the old paved way between the office and the changing-shed. No voice called from the engine house or shouted a joke across the shaft. No women clustered to-day about the engine to get hot water for their clothes. No bal-maidens or spallers talked and chattered on the washing floors. All was in place but nothing stirred. Grambler existed but no longer lived. And in its vitals the water was very slowly filling up the holes and the burrowings of two hundred years.

The mine was still and the day was still and no man moved. Only somewhere up in the mist a sea gull was abroad, and crying, crying, crying.

Book two

Chapter one

On Friday April the third 1789 a ticketing took place in the upstairs dining-room of the Red Lion Inn. The low panelled room was already set out for the customary dinner that was to follow.

There were about thirty men, grouped in chairs round an oblong table raised on a wooden dais by the window. Eight of the men represented eight copper companies. The others were managers or pursers of the mines offering the ore. As was the custom the chair was taken by the manager of the mine which had the largest parcel to offer, and to-day this fell upon Richard Tonkin.

He sat at the middle of the table, with the ticket offers in heaps before him and flanked by a representative of the miners and the smelters. The faces of the men were grave and there was little of the good-humoured raillery of prosperous times. Copper – the refined product – was now fetching fifty-seven pounds a ton.

As the clock struck one, Tonkin got up and cleared his throat.

'The auction is open, gentlemen. There are no further offerings? Very good. I have first to dispose of a dole of ore from Wheal Busy.'

With the two men beside him to supervise he opened the first lot of tickets and entered the bids in a ledger. One or two men shuffled their feet and the purser of Wheal Busy took out his notebook expectantly.

After a few moments Tonkin looked up.

'Wheal Busy ore is sold to the Carnmore Copper Company for six pounds seventeen shillings and sixpence a ton.'

There was a moment's silence. One or two men looked around. Ross saw an agent frown and another whisper.

Tonkin went on. 'Tresavean. Sixty tons.'

He opened the second box. There was another consultation as the figures were written in the ledger.

Tonkin cleared his throat. 'Tresavean ore is sold to the Carnmore Copper Company for six pounds seven shillings a ton.'

Mr Blight of the South Wales Copper Smelting Company got up.

'What name did you say, Mr Tonkin?'

'Tresavean.'

'No. The name of the buyers.'

'Carnmore Copper Company.'

'Oh,' said Blight, hesitated, sat down.

Tonkin picked up his list again, and for a few minutes the auction went on as before.

'Wheal Leisure,' Tonkin said. 'Parcel of red copper. Forty-five tons.'

The man on Tonkin's right leaned across to look at the bids.

'Wheal Leisure ore is sold to the Carnmore Copper Company for eight pounds two shillings a ton.'

Several men looked at Ross. Ross looked at the end of his riding crop and smoothed down a piece of frayed leather. Outside in the yard they could hear an ostler swearing at a horse.

There was some talk at the table before Tonkin read out the next name. But he had his way and went on:

'United Mines. Three doles of ore. Fifty tons in each.'

Entries in the ledger.

'United Mines,' said Tonkin. 'First parcel to Carnmore at seven pounds one shilling a ton. Second parcel to Carnmore at six pounds nineteen shillings and sixpence. Third parcel to the South Wales Smelting Company at five pounds nine shillings and ninepence.'

Blight was on his feet again, his raddled little face sharp under its wig, like a terrier that has been shown the bait once too often.

'Sir, I dislike to intervene. But may I say that I do not know of the existence of any such smelting company as the Carnmore?'

'Oh,' said Tonkin. 'I am assured it exists.'

'How long has it existed?' asked another man.

'That I could not say.'

'What proof have you of its *bona fides*?'

'That,' said Tonkin, 'will very soon be put to the proof.'

'Not until next month when payment is due,' said Blight. 'Then you may find yourselves with all these parcels of ore still on your hands.'

'Aye! Or collected unpaid for.'

Tonkin stood up again. 'I think, gentlemen, we may ignore the last danger. Personally I do not see that as mining agents we can afford to offend a newcomer among our clients by – by casting doubts on his good faith. There have been newcomers in the field before. We have always taken them on their merits and have not been disappointed. It is not five years since we first welcomed the South Wales Copper Smelting Company among us, and that firm has become one of our largest buyers.'

'At starvation prices,' said someone *sotto voce*.

Blight was on his feet again. 'We came into the field, I may remind Mr Tonkin, vouched for by two other companies and with a guarantee from Warleggan's Bank. Who is standing guarantee here?'

There was no answer.

'Who is their agent?' demanded Blight. 'You must have had contact with someone. If he is here, let him declare himself.'

There was silence.

'Ah,' said Blight, 'as I thought. If ——'

'I'm the agent,' said someone behind him.

He turned and stared at a small, roughly dressed man in the corner by the window. He had blue-grey eyes, freckles across the bridge of a large intelligent nose, a humorous mouth and chin. He wore his own hair, which was reddish-gone-grey and cut short after the fashion of a working man.

Blight looked him up and down. He saw that he had to deal with a person in an inferior class.

'What is your name, my man?'

'Martin.'

'And your business here?'

'Agent for the Carnmore Copper Company.'

'I have never heard of it.'

'Well, that's a surprise to me. Chairman up there's been talking of nothing else since one o'clock.'

One of the copper agents beside Tonkin rose.

'What is your purpose, sir, in bidding for this great quantity of copper?'

'Same as yours, sir,' said Zacky respectfully. 'To smelt it and sell it in the open market.'

'I take it you are the agent for a – a newly formed company.'

'That's so.'

'Who are your employers? Who finances you?'

'The Carnmore Copper Company.'

'Yes, but that's a name,' interrupted Blight. 'Who are the men who make up and control this company? Then we shall know where we stand.'

Zacky Martin fingered his cap. 'I think tis for they to choose whether to give out their names or no. I'm but their agent – same as you – making bids on their behalf – same as you – buying copper for 'em to smelt – same as you.'

Harry Blewett could sit by no longer. 'Do we yet know the names of the shareholders of the South Wales Smelting Company, Blight?'

Blight blinked at him a moment. 'Are you behind this scheme, Blewett?'

'No, answer your own question first!' shouted another manager.

Blight turned on him. 'You know well that we came in fully vouched for by friends. Tisn't our reputation that's in question, and ——'

'Nor neither is it theirs! Let 'em default, and then you can talk!'

Tonkin rapped on the table. 'Gentlemen, gentlemen. This is no way to behave. . . .'

Blight said: 'When was the samples taken, Tonkin? Not when all the other agents went round. There must be collusion in this. There was no stranger among us when any of the sampling was done.'

'I mistook the day,' Zacky said. 'I comed around the day after and was kindly allowed the opportunity to sample them by myself. Twas no benefit to the mines.'

'That's not fair doing, Mr Tonkin. There's some sort of collusion in this ——'

'Fair enough,' said Aukett, squinting horribly in his excitement. 'What's there amiss in it? No collusion such as might be set at the door of certain interests I could mention ——'

'Who are you ——'

'Now look ee here,' said Zacky Martin, in a quiet voice that gradually made itself heard because everyone wanted to listen. 'Look ee here, Mister Blight. And you other gentlemen too that seem a shade set about by me and my doings. I've no mind to be awkward or to put a stave in anyone's wheel, see? I want everything amiable and above-ground. Me and my friends is thinkin' of starting a little smelting works of our own, see, and we did think to buy up some o' the copper to-day just to lay in a little store handy-like.'

'Smelting works? Where?'

'But we didn't think to lay the other companies by the ears – far from it. That's not our way. And if so be as we've bought more'n our share to-day – well, I reckon I'll take it on myself to sell back a parcel or two to any of you other companies that are disposed to buy. In a friendly fashion as the saying goes; no bones broke or harm meant. At the price I give to-day. No profit wanted. I'll be at the next ticketing and buy more then.'

Ross saw Blight's expression change. One of the other brokers began to speak, but Blight interrupted him.

'So that's the game, eh? More than ever this stinks of arrangement. A pretty scheme, eh, to hoist the prices and put the legitimate dealers in a false box. No, my man, you and your friends – and I doubt not there's some here to-day – will have to think of another contrivance to catch us old hands. Keep your ore and take it to your new smelting works and *pay for it* at the end of the month, else you'll have all the mine managers whining to you before ten o'clock of the following day!'

Johnson got up, nearly cracking his big head on the beam above him. 'There's no call for abuse, Blight. And if so be as the money does not forthcome, we'll not come whining to you!'

Richard Tonkin rapped the table again.

'Let us complete the auction.'

This time he had his way, and quietness reigned until all the ore was sold. About two thirds of the total – all the best quality stuff – was bought by the Carnmore Company. It was a transaction which amounted to some five thousand pounds.

Then everyone sat down to dinner together.

It was the first real clash there had been between the two sides of the industry. Most of the grumbling had been done in private corners. After all the copper companies were the customers, and one did not in common sense seek out quarrels with such folk.

Zacky Martin sat some distance from Ross. They caught each other's eye once, but no gleam of recognition showed.

There was less talk than usual; men spoke together in lowered tones and with some constraint. But the wine had its effect, and the quarrel (and the deep rift of bitterness lying under the quarrel) was temporarily put away. To-day there was little said of affairs outside the county. Their own shadows loomed too large. The countryside was emerging from the worst winter in living memory – worst for conditions of life and one of the severest for weather. During January and February all Europe had lain under an icy hand, and even in Cornwall there had been weeks of frost and black east winds. Now that April was here and the worst over, men's minds turned to more hopeful things, not only to the summer ahead but to the chance of a kinder working life. Search where you would, there were no signs of a betterment, but at least the spring was here.

The agent of one of the older copper companies, a bluff rugged man called Voigt, told of the riots there had been in Bodmin last week.

'It were only a chance I was there,' he said. 'Just passing through in the coach. A mercy I'm alive, I assure you. They stopped the coach afore it reached the inn because they'd heard there was a corn factor within. Happily he'd not travelled; but we suffered who had. Out we was dragged with no ceremony and small comfort, and smash! went the coach, over on its side; glass and woodwork breaking, horses kicking in the road. Then some rascals put hammers to the wheels, and they were in pieces in no time. A good fortune for me I had not the opulence to be mistook for him they wanted; but a merchant from Helston was upended and rough-handled before they knew their mistake. I was relieved when they left us go.'

'Was there much damage in the town?'

'Oh, yes, of a light nature. There was looting too and some who tried to stop 'em was ill-used. Even when the military came they showed fight and had to be drove off like in a pitched battle.'

'There'll be hangings for that,' said Blight. 'Some example must be made.'

'They took half a hundred of them into custody,' said Voigt. 'The gaol's filled to overflowing.'

Ross's eyes met Zacky's for the second time that day. They were both thinking of Jim Carter, whose time of discharge was drawing near. The gaol had been full enough before.

Ross did not look at Zacky again. Neither did he speak to Richard Tonkin or Blewett or Aukett or Johnson after the dinner. Curious eyes would be watching.

He left the inn and walked round to see Harris Pascoe. The banker rose to greet Ross and diffidently enquired how the purpose of the day had gone.

Ross said: 'You will have drafts of about four thousand eight hundred pounds to pay on the Carnmore account next month.'

Pascoe pursed his lips. 'You b—bought more than you expected?'

'We bought all we could while the price was low. Once they realize we are in earnest they will likely try to outbid us. But with that stock we shall be safe for some months.'

'Was there any inquiry?'

Ross told him. Pascoe fumbled rather nervously with the snuff-stained cambric of his stock. He was in this scheme as their banker, but he had no stomach for conflict. He was in all his dealings a man of peace, using his own money for principled ends, but not caring to defeat the *un*-principled. He liked to look on money in an academic way: figures to be squared with other figures, balances to be brought to an equilibrium; it was the mathematics of his business which appealed to him most of all. Therefore while applauding the intention of this group of men, he was a little nervous lest they should become a worry and a disturbance to his peace of mind.

'Well,' he said at length, 'there you have the first responses of the agents and other small fry. I fancy that the men behind them will express their disapproval more subtly. The next ticketing will be the testing time. I doubt if you'll ever provoke an overt protest again.'

'The essential thing is to keep them mystified,' Ross said. 'Some of the facts will leak out quick enough with Zacky Martin living on my land and the smelting works being built on Trevaunance property.'

'It is surprising that the smelting works has been kept a secret so long.'

'Well, all the components were shipped direct and housed around the disused pilchard cellars. Sir John put out the story that it was a new engine for his mine.'

Pascoe drew towards him a sheet of paper and made two more brief entries on it with his scratchy quill. This was the first printed billhead of the Carnmore Copper Company, and on it in watery ink the banker had entered all the particulars of the company. He had begun with the chief shareholders.

Lord Devoran,
Sir John Michael Trevaunance, Bart.,
Alfred Barbary, Esq.,
Ray Penvenen, Esq.,
Ross Vennor Poldark, Esq.,
Peter St Aubyn Tresize, Esq.,
Richard Paul Cowdray Tonkin,
Henry Blewett,
William Trencrom,
Thomas Johnson.

An imposing list. The company was floated with a capital of twenty thousand pounds, of which twelve thousand pounds was paid up and the rest on call. They were also going into business as merchants, to supply the mines with all the stuff of their trade. It would give them a small steady basis of business to rely on outside the main object of the company.

Pascoe knew that there were men who would be very interested to see this sheet of paper. It would be better locked up. He rose and went to his safe in the corner of the room.

'You'll take t–tea with us, Captain Poldark? My wife and daughter are expecting you.'

Ross thanked him but said no. 'Forgive me, but to get home in good time from one of these days is a treat I look forward to. It has been all riding this winter. My wife complains she has none of my company.'

Pascoe smiled gently as he turned the key in the safe. 'The complaint from a wife has a novelty you do well to consider. A p–pity your cousin Francis could not join the shareholders of the company.'

'He is much too closely committed with the Warleggans. Privately we have his good will.'

The banker sneezed. 'Verity was in to stay the night early this week. She is looking in improved health, don't you think?'

'They have all stood up to the closing of Grambler better than I expected.'

Pascoe walked with him to the door. 'You have heard, I imagine, that there are r–rumours again attaching to Miss Verity's name.'

Ross stopped. 'I have heard nothing.'

'Perhaps I should not have m–mentioned it, but I thought you should know. You and she have always been so close to one another.'

'Well, what is the rumour?' Ross spoke with impatience. Pascoe did not know the cause of Ross's bitter hostility to the word.

'Oh, well, it is to do with that Blamey fellow. Word has c–come from several sources that they have been seen meeting again.'

'Verity and Blamey? What are your sources?'

'If you prefer to disregard it, pray forget I spoke. I have no wish to pass on irresponsible gossip.'

Ross said: 'Thank you for the information that it is abroad. I'll take steps to smoke it out.'

Chapter two

As HE RODE home his thoughts were not stable for a moment. Eighteen months ago he had known himself happy and with prevision had tried to hold the mood as long as it would stay. He was not now discontented, but he was too restless, too preoccupied. Each day led so relentlessly to the next, linked by cause and effect, anticipation and result, preparation and achievement. The chance suggestion made to Blewett nine months ago had led him into a web of new things.

Verity and Blamey? The arrogant man he had seen on the day after Julia's christening had lost everything he had ever had in common with the gentle self-restrained Verity. It could not be. Some evil-minded old crone had hatched it from her own brooding. There was as much truth in it as the slander he had heard on Jud's lips.

There had been no reconciliation between himself and the Paynters. Demelza visited Prudie sometimes, but that was all. Jud was working irregularly for Trencrom, who could always use a man with sailing experience and no scruples. In between times he went the round of the kiddleys and lectured men on their shortcomings.

As for the Gimletts, they had fulfilled all their earlier promise. With plump bounding good humour they trotted about the house and the farm, often working from pleasure when need was satisfied. Jinny had been back at Nampara since Christmas. In the end she had asked to return, common sense and lack of money prevailing over her shyness.

Ross had not seen Jim again, though all winter he had thought of riding to Bodmin and taking Dwight Enys with him. The copper company had taken all his attention. Many a time he had wished he could resign. He was short of the tact and patience to gain the interest of the men of substance, to support their interest when gained and to make all sorts of little adjustments to placate their self-esteem. For that Richard Tonkin was invaluable. Without Richard Tonkin they would have been lost.

But without Ross too they would have been lost, although he did not realize it. He was the stiffening, the unyielding element and a large part of the driving power. Men accepted his integrity where with another they would have asked: 'What has he to gain?'

Well, the company was on its feet now, alive and ready to begin the struggle. And the winter was over, and men and women had come through it (most of them); and the children had whimpered and survived (some of them). The law made it difficult for men to move out of their own district – lest they become a burden upon another parish – but a few had trekked to the waterfronts of Falmouth and Plymouth or to seek a pittance in the inland towns. The rapid-growing population of the mining districts had been checked in a single year.

And the King had gone mad and fought with his gaolers and been ill-treated by them and had torn up his curtains; and young Pitt, his patron locked away, had been preparing for retirement from public life, bowing to the whims of Fate and considering a career at the Bar; and the Prince of Wales, with Mrs FitzHerbert to restrain his worst blatancies, had come back from Brighton to accept a regency, which young Pitt had the insolence to oppose.

And the King had recovered just in time to put his son's hopes out of joint; so all was back where it began, except that George's dislike for Whigs was only less than his dislike for his own family.

And Hastings had come to trial at last. And a clergyman called Cartwright had brought out an extraordinary thing for weaving, which was a power loom worked by a steam engine.

In America the Union was complete; a new nation was born, said the *Sherborne Mercury*, of four million people – one quarter black – which might someday be counted of importance. Prussia had spent the winter putting down the freedom of the press and signing an alliance with Poland to guard her back door if she attacked France. France had done nothing. A palsy had fallen on the splendid court while men died of hunger in the streets.

And Wheal Leisure had moderately prospered all through the winter, though the money Ross made had gone quickly enough, most into the Carnmore Company. A little went to buy a horse for Demelza, and a small nest egg of two hundred pounds he was keeping by for emergency.

As he neared Grambler he saw Verity coming towards him from the direction of the village.

'Why, Ross, imagine meeting you,' she said. 'I have been over to see Demelza. She complains that you neglect her. We have had a long talk, which would have lasted until sundown if Garrick had not upset the tea tray with his tail and wakened Julia from her afternoon nap. We have chattered away like two old fish jousters waiting for the nets to come in.'

Ross glanced at his cousin with new eyes. There was something in her gaze, her manner was lively. He got down in alarm.

'What have you been hatching in my house this afternoon?'

The question was so well directed that Verity coloured.

'I went over to see if the Sherborne man had brought you an invitation as he had us. Curiosity, my dear. Women are never satisfied unless they know their neighbours' business.'

'And has he?'

'Yes.'

'An invitation to what?'

Verity tucked in a wisp of hair. 'Well, cousin, it is waiting you at home. I hadn't thought to mention it but you surprised it out of me.'

'Then let me surprise the rest, so that I may know all the news at once.'

Verity met his eyes and smiled. 'Have patience, my dear. It is Demelza's secret now.'

Ross grunted. 'I have not seen Francis or Elizabeth. Are they prospering?'

'Prospering is not the word, my dear. Francis is so heavy in debt that it looks as if we shall never struggle clear. But at least he has had the courage to withdraw from the Warleggan circle. Elizabeth – well, Elizabeth is very patient with him. I think she is glad to have him more at home; but I wish – perhaps her patience would be more fruitful if it had a little more understanding in it. One can be kind without being sympathetic. I——— Perhaps that is unjust.' Verity looked suddenly distressed. 'I don't take Francis's part because he is my brother. Really it is all his fault . . . or – or seems to be. . . . He threw away his money when he had it. If the money he squandered had been available there would have been more to finance the mine at the last. . . .'

Ross knew why Francis stayed away from the Warleggans and drank at home: Margaret Cartland, finding his money gone, had thrown him over.

'Demelza will blame me for keeping you, Ross. Be on your way, my dear; you must be tired.'

He put his hand on her shoulder a moment and looked at her. Then he got on his horse. 'Tired of hearing men talk of their mines and the price of copper. Your conversation has more variety, and you never give me the opportunity of tiring of it. Now you keep your secrets for Demelza and run away before I come home.'

'Indeed not, Ross,' Verity said, blushing again. 'If I call when you are away it is because I think Demelza may be lonely; and if I go before you come it is because I think you want your hours at home with her. You offend me.'

He laughed. 'Bless you. I know I do not.'

He rode on. Yes, there was a change. Twice he had been on the point of mentioning Blamey's name, twice he had baulked at the fence. Now he was glad. If there was anything there, let it be hidden from him. He had borne the responsibility of knowing once.

As he passed Grambler Mine he glanced over it. One or two windows of the office had been blown in and sprays of weeds grew here and there between the stones of the paved path. Wherever was metal was brown rust. The grass round the mine was an unusual vivid green, and in some corners heaps of blown sand had gathered. Some children had made a rough swing out of a piece of old rope and had hung it across a beam of the washing floors. A dozen sheep had wandered up to the engine house and were grazing peacefully in the afternoon silence.

He moved on and reached his own land and rode down into the valley; and from far off could hear Demelza playing the spinet. The sound came up to him in a sweet vibration, plaintive and distant. The trees were green-tipped and the catkins were out and a few primroses bloomed in the wet grass. The music was a thread of silver woven into the spring.

A fancy took him to surprise her, and he stopped Darkie and tethered her at the bridge. Then he walked to the house and came into the hall unnoticed. The parlour door was open.

She was there at the spinet in her white muslin frock, the peculiar expression on her face which she always took on when reading music, as if she were just going to bite an apple. All the winter she had been taking lessons from the old woman who had been nurse to the five Teague girls. Mrs Kemp came once a week, and Demelza had shot ahead.

Ross slid into the room. She was playing the music from one of Arne's operas. He listened for some minutes, glad of the scene, glad of the music and the bordering quiet. This was what he came home for.

He stepped silently across the room and kissed the back of her neck.

She squeaked, and the spinet stopped on a discord.

'A slip o' the finger and *phit*, yer dead,' said Ross in Jud's voice.

'Judas! you give me a fright, Ross. Always I'm getting frights of some sort. No wonder I'm a bag of nerves. This is a new device, creepin' in like a tomcat.'

He took her by the ear. 'Who has had Garrick in here where he does not belong, breaking our new Wedgwood? A dog – if he can be called that – no smaller than a cow. . . .'

'You have seen Verity, then? Did she tell you of our – of our . . .'

He looked into her eager, expectant face. 'Of our what?'

'Our invitation.'

'No. What is that?'

'Ha!' Pleased, she wriggled free from him and danced away to the window. 'That's telling. I'll tell you to-morrow. Or maybe next day. Will that do?'

His keen eyes went round the room and instantly, irritatingly noticed the slip of paper folded under the spice jar on the table.

'Is this it?'

'No, Ross! You mustn't look! Leave it be!' She ran across and they both reached it together, struggled, laughed, her fingers having somehow got inside his. The parchment tore down the middle, and they separated, each holding a piece.

'Oh,' said Demelza, 'now we've spoiled it!'

He was reading. "'On the occasion of the day of national Majesty the King and the mayor will hold ——'"

'Stop! stop!' she said. 'My part comes in between. Begin again.'

"'On the occasion of the day of national——'"

"'Thanksgiving,'" she put in, "'set aside to celebrate the recovery to health of His——' Now it's your turn.'

"'Majesty the King, namely April the twenty-third next, the Lord——'"

"'Lieutenant of Cornwall, the High Sheriff, the Burgesses——'"

"'And the Mayor of Truro will hold a Grand Assembly and Ball at the Assembly Rooms——'"

"'Commencing at eight o'clock of that day, preceded by——'"

"'Bonfires and general rejoicings.'" He looked at his paper again. "'Captain Poldark are invited.'"

"'And Mrs,'" she cried, "'to attend." "Captain and Mrs Poldark are invited to attend.'"

'It says nothing about that on my invitation,' he objected.

'There! there!' She came up to him and fitted the torn paper with his own piece. "'And Mrs." See, we shall both go this time.'

'Do we each walk in with our own piece?' he asked. 'They would not admit you just as "Mrs". It's altogether too vague.'

'I do not wonder,' she said, 'that they put you to drive the copper companies; for you would drive anyone into bad thoughts.'

'Well, anyway the invitation is useless now,' he said, making a move to drop his half in the fire.

'No, Ross! No!' She caught at his hand and tried to stop him. After a moment or two his mood changed; he gave up the struggle and caught her to him and kissed her.

And as suddenly she was quiet, breathing quickly like an animal which knows it has been caught.

'Ross, you shouldn't do that,' she said. 'Not in the day.'

'How much of our crockery did Garrick break?'

'Oh . . . but two saucers.'

'And how many cups?'

'One, I think. . . . Ross, we shall go to this Assembly?'

'And who let him in here?'

'I think, I believe he just sort of sneaked in. You d'know what he is like. Will never have no for an answer. One minute he was outside and the next he was in.' She wriggled in his grip but this time he had her fast. Her flushed cheek was close to his and he put his nose against it, liking the smell. 'And what of Verity? What news had she?'

'Am I a dandelion?' she said, 'to be snuffed over. Or a carrot to be hung before a – a . . .'

'A donkey's nose?' He laughed. Then she laughed, and their laughter infected each other.

They sat down on the settle and giggled together.

'I shall wear my apple green and mauve,' she said presently; 'the one I wore at Trenwith the Christmas before last. I don't think I am any fatter now.'

Ross said: 'I shall wear a secondhand wig with curls on the forehead, and scarlet stockings and a coat of green silk embroidered with field mice.'

She giggled again. 'Do you think we should be allowed in as Mrs and Miss Poldark?'

'Or two ends of a donkey,' he suggested. 'We would throw lots who was to be the tail.'

A few minutes later Jane Gimlett put her plump, tidy little head round the door; and they sat there together on the settle and laughed at her.

'Oh, I beg pardon,' she said hastily. 'I didn't know you was back, sur. I thought something was amiss.'

Ross said: 'We have an invitation to a ball and by mischance have torn it up. One piece is here and one piece is there. So we were considering what was the best to do.'

'Oh, sur,' said Jane, 'I should stick the twin halves together with a mix of flour paste. Put 'em on a piece o' newsprint to hold 'em firm. No one would be able to make head nor tail of it as it is.'

At that they looked at each other and laughed again – as if Jane Gimlett had told them a very funny joke.

That night before they went to sleep Ross said:

'Now that we are in our right minds again, tell me: Has Verity mentioned Captain Blamey to you of late?'

The question came as a shock to Demelza. She had a sharp struggle with her conscience.

'Why do you ask?'

'There is a rumour that she is meeting him.'

'Oh?' said Demelza.

'Well?' he said, after a wait.

'I wouldn't like to say, Ross. I wouldn't like to say that she hadn't, and then again I wouldn't like to say that she had.'

'In shorter words, you wouldn't like to say anything at all.'

'Well, Ross, what's given in confidence it isn't fair to repeat even to you.'

Ross thought this over.

'I wonder how she met him again. It was most unfortunate.'

Demelza said nothing, but crossed her fingers in the dark.

'There can't be anything serious meant now,' Ross said uneasily. 'That moody bully. Verity would be mad to go on with it, whatever the chances were before. All that bitterness will begin again if Francis gets to know.'

Demelza said nothing, but crossed her legs as well.

'When I heard it I discounted it,' he went on. 'I could not believe that Verity would be so foolish. You are very silent.'

'I was thinkin',' said Demelza quietly, 'that if the – if they still feel the same after all these years, it must never *really* have broke at all.'

'Well,' he said after a pause, 'if you can't tell me what is happening you can't. I won't pretend I'm not disturbed, but I am only glad *I* didn't bring them together. I am more than sorry for Verity.'

'Yes, Ross,' she said. 'I see just how you feel. I'm awful sleepy. Can I go to sleep now?'

Chapter three

IT RAINED ALL night, but by eight the day was clearing and a fresh soft wind blew from the south-west. Mark Daniel had spent his whole morning in the garden, but at half an hour after noon he came in to eat his dinner and get ready for the mine. Keren had made a herb pie out of things she had been able to gather and had flavoured it with two rabbit legs she had bought from Mrs Vigus.

For a time they ate without speaking. In Mark silence was usual, but in Keren it meant either a new grievance or sulks over an old. He glanced at her several times as they sat there.

To test her mood he tried to think of something to say.

'Things is coming up too fast to be safe; it is as if the spring is two months on. I hope there'll be no frost or bitter wind like last year.'

Keren yawned. 'Well, we ought to have something after that January and February. I've never known such months, not anywhere.'

(She blamed him for the weather now, as if the Cornish climate were a part of the general fraud practised on her by marriage.)

'The thrushes in the May tree will be hatching out any time now,' he said. 'Reckon they're so early they'll be sitting a second time.'

There was another silence.

'Peas an' beans'll be a month early too,' said Mark. 'We owe thanks to Captain Poldark for they, for giving us the seeds.'

'It would have looked better for him to have found you better work instead.' She had no good to say of the Poldarks.

'Why, I have a pitch at Wheal Leisure. More he couldn't do.'

'And a poor pitch it is. Brings you in not half what the Grambler one used to.'

'All the best pitches was taken, Keren. Some would say it was my own fault to have took it, for he offered me contract work. Paul was saying but yesterday forenoon we was lucky to have work at all.'

'Oh, Paul . . .' said Keren contemptuously. 'What's Zacky Martin doing, I should like to know? He's working for Captain Poldark, isn't he? I'll wager he's not working miner's hours for a few shillings a week. Why, the Martins've never been better set in their lives. Zacky's been away here and away there – pony provided and all. Why couldn't they give you a job like that?'

'Zacky's more eddicated than me,' said Mark. ''Is father rented a few acres an' sent him to school till he were nine. Everyone round here d'know that Zacky's a cut above we.'

'Speak for yourself,' Keren said, getting up. 'Reading and writing's easy to learn. Anyone can learn it if they've the mind to. Zacky only seems clever because all you folks are slothful and ignorant.'

'Aye, I speak for myself,' Mark said quietly. 'I well know you're different too, Keren. You're cleverer than Zacky or any. An' maybe it's sloth that folk don't learn more an' maybe it ain't. You'll acknowledge it is easier-like to get your letters as a tacker at school than when you're more growed, and one by one, all by yourself wi' no one to learn you. I went as a buddle boy when I were six. I'd no care for letters when I come home from that. Since then I been working wi'out a break except for feast days. Maybe I should ha' learned instead of wrestling, but that's the way of things. An' you can't say I'm idle about the house here and now.'

Keren wrinkled her nose.

'Nobody said you was idle, Mark; but you get little enough for all your sweat. Why, even the Viguses are better off than us – and him without work at all.'

'Nick Vigus is a slippery rogue, an' twas he got young Jim Carter into trouble. You wouldn't want for me to spend all my time poaching or mixing cheap poisons to sell as gin?'

'I'd want you to make some money,' said the girl, but she spoke in a softer voice. She had gone to the open door and was staring across the valley.

Mark finished his meal. 'You've eaten little or nothing,' he said. 'You'll keep no strength in you that way.'

'My strength's all right,' Keren said absently.

'Besides, it is wrong to waste food.'

'Oh, eat it yourself,' she said.

Mark hesitated, and then slowly scooped the piece of pie she had left back into the tin dish.

'Twill stand till to-morrow.'

She glanced away impatiently to the north. Several figures were moving over the hill.

'It's time you were off.'

She stood at the door watching him while he put on his heavy boots and pulled on his coarse drill coat. Then he came to the door and she went out to let him pass.

He looked at her, with the sun striking lights in her curly hair and her dark elfish eyes turned away.

'Don't ee take on about we, Keren,' he said gently. 'We'll come through all right, never fear. This bad time won't last for ever an' we'll soon be on our feet again.'

He bent his great body and kissed her on the neck. Then he moved off a little stiffly in the direction of the mine.

She watched him go. We'll come through all right, she thought; through to what? This cottage and children and middle age? We'll soon be on our feet again. For what? For him to keep on going down the mine, making a bit more money or a bit less for ever and ever until he is too old and crippled like the old men over the hill. Then he'll be here about the house all day long, as they are; while I bring up the last of the children and do menial jobs for the Poldarks to eke out.

That was the best she could look for. She'd been a fool to think she could change him. He didn't *want* to change. Born and bred a miner, he had no horizon but digging for copper and tin. And although he was a great worker and a craftsman he hadn't the learning or the initiative to be able to rise even in the mine. She saw it all clear enough. He was a goat tethered to the peg of his own character and could only consume the riches of the earth which came within his range. And she had bound herself to stay in his circle for the rest of her life. . . .

Tears came to her eyes and she turned back into the cottage. Mark had done much to better the inside during the winter months, but she saw none of it. Instead she swept through into their bedroom and changed her plain dimity frock for the challenging one of flimsy scarlet with the green cord girdle. Then she began to comb her hair.

In ten minutes with her face sponged and powdered, her rich hair glossy and crisp, theatrical sandals on her bare feet, she was ready.

She slipped out of the house and ran quickly down the hill to the bed of the dried-up stream, climbed across it, and ran up the other side towards the wood. Very soon, her breath coming in swift gasps, she was standing before the door of the Gatehouse.

Dwight Enys himself opened it.

Against his better judgment something kindled in his eyes when he saw her standing there with her hands behind her back and the wind ruffling her hair.

'Keren. What brings you here at this time of the day?'

She glanced over her shoulder. 'May I come in before all the old women see me and begin to whisper?'

He hesitated and then opened the door wider. 'Bone is out.'

'I know. I saw him go early.'

'Keren. Your reputation will be worth nothing.'

She walked ahead of him down the dark corridor and waited for him to open the door into his living-room.

'It gets more cosier every time I see it,' she said.

The room was built long and narrow with three slender Gothic windows looking over the hill towards Mingoose. The manner was less medieval than in the other rooms, and he had chosen it as his parlour and furnished it with a good Turkey carpet and some comfortable old chairs and a bookcase or two. It was also the only room with a good fireplace; and a bright fire burned there now, for Enys had cooked his meal on it.

'What time will Bone be back?'

'Oh, not yet; he has gone to see his father, who has had an accident. But how did you see him go?'

'I just watched,' she said.

He looked at her kneeling there. She had interrupted his reading. It was not the first time now nor even the fifth, though her arm was long since better. One side of him was displeased, indignant; the other, not. His eyes took in the gracious curve of her back, like a bow slightly bent, ready at any moment to quiver and straighten. He looked at the faint obverse curve of her throat, at the flamboyant colour of the dress. He liked her in that best. (He thought she knew it.) But to come here to-day, and deliberately.

'This must stop, Keren,' he said. 'This coming ——'

The bow straightened and she looked up as she interrupted him. 'How *can* I, Dwight? How *can* I? I so look forward to coming here. What does it matter if I am seen? What does it matter? There's no harm in it. There's nothing else I care about.'

He was surprised by her vehemence and a little touched. He came over to the fire and stood with a hand on the mantelpiece looking down on her.

'Your husband will get to know. He could not like your coming here.'

'Why not?' she said fiercely. 'It is the only little change and – and company I get. A change from the sort of common folk who live around here. There's not one of 'em been further than a couple of miles from where they were born. They're so narrow and small. All they think to do is work and eat and sleep like – like animals on a farm. They just don't see farther than the top of St Ann's Beacon. They aren't more than half alive.'

He wondered what she expected in marrying a miner.

'I think,' he said gently, 'that if you look deeper you will find all sorts of good things in your neighbours – and in Mark too, if you're dissatisfied with him. Narrow, I grant you, but deep. They have no charity outside the range of their understanding, but within it they are loyal and kind and honest and God-fearing and brave. I have found that in the short time I have been here. Forgive me if I seem to preach, Keren, but in meeting them try to meet them on *their* ground for a change. Try to see life as they see it. . . .'

'And become one of them.'

'Not at all. Use your imagination. In order to understand it's not necessary to *become*. You are criticizing their lack of imagination. Show that you are different, that you do not lack it. I think in the main they are a fine people and I get on well with them. Of course, I know I have the advantage of being a surgeon ——'

'And a man.' She didn't add, 'And a very handsome one.' 'That's very well, Dwight, but you haven't married one of 'em. And they accept you because you're far enough above them. I'm betwixt and between. I'm one of them but I'm a stranger and always will be. If I couldn't read nor write and'd never seen the world they might forgive me in time, but they never will now. They'll be narrow and mean to the end of their days.' She blew out a little sigh from between pursed lips. 'I'm that unhappy.'

He frowned at his books. 'Well, I am not that much beset with company that ——'

She got up eagerly. 'I may come then? I may stay a little? You find it none too bad to talk to me? I promise I'll not bore you with my grief. Tell me what you are doing now, what you are studying, eh?'

He smiled. 'There's nothing in that would interest you. I——'

'Anything would interest me, Dwight. Really it would. Can I stay a few hours to-day? Mark has just gone below. I'll promise not to talk. I'll not be in your way. I can cook you a meal and help you.'

He smiled again, a little ruefully. He knew of old what this offer meant; an enthusiastic approach to his interests, a wide-open, wide-eyed receptiveness on her part, which changed by curious subtle feminine gradations until *his* interest became centred on *her*. It had happened before. It would happen again to-day. He did not care. In fact there was a part of him that looked forward to it.

Two hours had passed, and the expected had not quite happened.

When she came in he had been preparing for record a table of the lung cases treated since his arrival, the type of disease so far as he was able to place it, the treatment given and the results yielded. And for once her interest had held. She had written down the details as he read them out; and as a result he had done the work of three hours in half the time.

She wrote a big unformed hand clearly and well. She seemed to grasp quickly what he said, even when the terms bordered on the medical.

When it was done he said: 'You've been a real help to-day, Keren. I'm grateful for that. It's good of you to have spent this time and patience on my dull records.'

Again for the first time she did not bridle and respond to his praise. She was reading part of what she had written and her pretty petulant little face was serious and intent.

'This cold water,' she said. 'What does it mean, Dwight? Look here: for this man Kempthorne you order nothing but cold water and goat's milk. How will that aid him? It is hard on the fellow to be given nothing at all.'

'Oh, I made him up some pills,' Dwight said. 'Just so that he would feel better, but they were only made of meal, baked hard.'

'Well, why did you not treat him then? Had he done you a bad turn?'

Enys smiled and came over to her.

'Both lungs are affected at the top, but not too serious yet. I have put him on a strict regime if he will follow it: four miles' walking a day, drinking goat's milk with his meals when he can get it, sleeping in the open when it is fine. I have odd notions about things, Keren; but he is one of the best cases so far and is on the mend. I am sure he is better than if I had given him the leeches and antimony and the rest.'

Her hair was brushing his cheek. She turned her head and looked up at him, her full red lips slightly parted to show the gleam of her teeth. 'Oh, Dwight,' she said.

He put his hand on hers on the table. His was a little unsteady.

'Why do you come here?' he said sharply, averting his eyes as if ashamed.

She turned towards him without moving her hand.

'Oh, Dwight, I'm sorry.'

'You're not. You know you're not.'

'No,' she said. 'I'm not. Nor never could be.'

'Then why say it?'

'I'm only sorry if you dislike me.'

Staring at her as if he had not heard, he said: 'No . . . not that.'

He put his hands on her shoulders and bent his head and kissed her. She leaned a little against him and he kissed her again.

He drew back.

She watched him walk over to the windows. It had been a boy's kiss, gentle and sincere. What a mixture he was, she thought. A graduate in the physical profession, learned, and full of new ideas; he could go round these homes, speak with authority, operate, mend broken arms, treat fevers, attend women in childbed. But in his very own life, where close things like love were touched, he was inexpert and shy.

The thought pleased her more than the kiss had done – the implications of the kiss more than either.

She hesitated, looking at his back, uncertain what to do now. Neither of them had spoken. Everything was new between them from this moment: there were no signposts to follow, no tracks or beaten ways.

Everything was new and everything was changed. But a wrong word or act might set it back again, farther back than ever before. This moment might lead to tremendous things. Or it might lead to the blind alley of a broken friendship. Every normal impulse urged her to go on, to snatch at this thing which might not come again for months, perhaps never at all. Normally Bone was close at hand, whistling or making a noise. She thought that now in the isolation, in the emotion, there was no brake.

But with a queer view into his mind she saw that if she did that, if everything happened on the leaping tide of the moment, he might come to regret it almost at once, might come to hate her or despise her as a common woman who had led him to this; whereas if he had time to think it over, to come to the desire slowly and on his own, then he would be unable to put the act on her. It would sit squarely on his own shoulders and he might never even wish to throw it off.

Besides, that way, anything might happen.

She went slowly up to him and stood by him at the window. His face was tense as if he was by no means sure of himself.

She touched his hand. 'You make me very proud,' she whispered, remembering a line out of *Elfrida*; and turned and went out of the room and left the house.

Chapter four

THAT WEEK ANOTHER invitation reached the Poldarks. George Warleggan had decided to hold a party on the day of the celebrations. His guests would sup at Warleggan House, then go on to the Assembly Rooms for the evening, returning to Warleggan House to sleep. He would be glad if Ross and his wife would be of that number.

Ross wanted to refuse. With a rupture certain between himself and George he had no wish to be beholden to him. But for Demelza it was the last step of ambition to see the Warleggans at home, and though she trembled and hesitated after the fiasco of the christening, she would have been desperately disappointed to miss it.

So Ross chose to give way and, once the acceptance had gone, he quietly looked forward to the day, as he always looked forward to taking Demelza out. When Mrs Kemp came she was not allowed to go near the spinet but instead was pressed into teaching Demelza the steps of the more popular dances and giving her lessons in deportment.

Since Demelza's good humours were so pervasive as to give a lead to the whole house, the mood at Nampara became one of pleasurable anticipation. Julia, kicking in her cot, crowed and laughed and joined in the fun.

On the sixteenth of April, Ross had gone up to the mine and Demelza and Jinny and Jane were brewing mead. They were enjoying themselves. They had stirred six pounds of honey into a couple of gallons of warm water and added some dried elder flowers and ginger. This was on the fire to boil in a large pan, and Jane was skimming it with a spoon whenever a frothy scum formed on the surface.

Upon this domestic scene fell the shadow of Zacky Martin aslant in the afternoon sun. As soon as she saw him Demelza knew something was wrong. No, Captain Poldark was not here, he would be up at the mine. Zacky thanked her stolidly enough and moved off.

Jinny ran to the door as he went. 'Father. What's amiss? Is it to do wi' Jim?'

'No, there's no call for you to worry,' said Zacky. 'It was just that I wanted for to see Cap'n Ross on a point or two.'

'Well, I thought ——' said Jinny, half reassured. 'I thought as . . .'

'You'll need to get used to me in and about the house now, Jinny. I'm workin' for Cap'n Ross, you did ought to know that.'

She watched him move away and then returned to the kitchen with a troubled face.

Zacky found Ross talking to Captain Henshawe among the mine buildings on Leisure Cliff. He gave Zacky an enquiring glance.

'Well, sir, it is about Jim. You mind what that man said at the ticketing about Bodmin Gaol being crowded with the rioters who'd be there till next sessions?'

Ross nodded.

'Well, this morning, getting about more, y'understand on business, as I do now, I heard tell that many of the old prisoners had been moved to other gaols to make room.'

'Was the word reliable, d'you judge?'

''S, I reckon. Joe Trelask's brother has been moved; an' Peter Mawes said as how all our Jim's cell was to go to Launceston.'

'Launceston.' Ross whistled slightly.

'They say it's bad there?'

'It has a poor name.' No point in alarming Zacky further. 'But this moving of a man about due for release is monstrous. Who ordered it? I wonder if it is true.'

'Peter Mawes was straight from Bodmin. I thought I should tell you. I thought ye'd wish to know.'

'I'll think over it, Zacky. There may be some way of coming at the truth quickly.'

'I thought you should wish to know.' Zacky turned to go. 'I'll be out in the morning, sur, to see ee over the wet and waste deduction.'

Ross went back to Henshawe; but he could not bring his mind to what they had been discussing. He had always been perversely attached to Jim, and the thought that he might have been moved twenty miles farther from home to the worst prison in the west – possibly on the decision of some puffed-up jack-in-office – irritated and concerned him.

For the rest of the afternoon he was busy at the mine, but when he had finished he walked across to see Dwight Enys.

As he came to the Gatehouse he noticed the improvements Enys had made; but passing the window of Dwight's own living-room, the windows being open, he heard someone singing. To his surprise it was a girl's voice, not very loud but quite distinct.

He did not pause in his stride but as he walked round to the front door the words followed him:

'My love is all Madness and Folly,
Alone I lye,
Toss, tumble and cry,
What a happy creature is Polly!

Was e'er such a Wretch as I!
With rage I redden like Scarlet. . . .'

He knocked with the light stick he carried.

The singing ceased. He turned and stood with his back to the door watching a robin searching among the stones for moss for his nest.

Then the door opened. Dwight's face, already slightly flushed, coloured deeper when he saw who it was.

'Why, Captain Poldark, this is a surprise! Will you step inside, please.'

'Thank you.' Ross followed him into the living-room, from which three minutes before the song had come. There was no one there.

But perhaps because of his knowledge he seemed to detect a subtle arrangement of the room which spoke of a visitor just gone.

Ross stated his business, the news of Jim Carter, and that he proposed to take the coach to-morrow and discover the truth. He wondered if Enys would be interested to go with him.

Dwight at once accepted, his eagerness showing through his embarrassment, and they made an arrangement to meet early and ride into Truro.

Ross walked home wondering where he had heard the woman's voice before.

To keep Jinny from worrying she was not told; but Demelza was prepared to worry over her own man. She never liked Ross going into the confined atmosphere of a prison, which was poisonous at the best; and a journey as far as Launceston across the dangerous wastes of the Bodmin moors seemed set with every kind of hazard.

They left after an early breakfast and when they reached Truro, Ross did some shopping.

Mistress Trelask, just taking the sheets off her stock, was fluttered by the arrival of a tall serious-looking man who introduced himself and said he understood Mistress Trelask had been patronized by his wife and knew her measurements. This being so, he had a mind to buy a new evening gown' for his wife to be made and delivered for the celebration ball.

Mistress Trelask, like a hen caught in a small shed, fluttered and flapped noisily, bringing down in hasty confusion new silk satins and brocades and tonquedelles and velours, before the sting in the end of her visitor's sentence made her qualify the sale by the grave doubt of her ability to make anything in the time, so much being already on hand. Her visitor, who had shown interest in an expensive silver brocade silk, thereupon took up his hat and wished her good morning.

Mistress Trelask immediately flapped a great deal more, and called up her daughter; they chirped together and made little notes and played with pins, while the shopper tapped his boot. Then they said they would see what they could do.

'It is a condition of sale, you understand.'

'Yes,' said Miss Trelask, wiping away a tear, 'I take it so, sir.'

'Very well, then; let us have the business in hand. But you must aid me in it, for I have no knowledge of women's things and want the latest and best.'

'We'll see you get everything after the most fashionable rate,' said Mrs Trelask. 'When could Mrs Poldark call for a fitting?'

'There will be no fitting unless it is on the day of the Assembly,' Ross said. 'I want this as a surprise. If it is not quite right my wife can call in in the afternoon.'

At this there were more flutterings, but the floodgates of concession were already open and they presently agreed.

Later Ross made for a tiny shop with a creaking sign which read: *S. Solomon. Goldsmith and Pewterer.*

'I want to see something for a lady,' he said. 'Something to wear in her hair or round her neck. I have not the time to examine many pieces.'

The tall old man bent his head to lead Ross into the dark room at the back and brought out a tray with a half dozen necklaces, three cameo brooches, a few pearl bracelets for the wrist, eight rings. There was nothing that attracted him. The largest of the pearl necklaces was priced at thirty pounds, which seemed more than its value.

'Pearls are so fashionable, sir. We cannot get them. All the smaller ones are used for decorating gowns and hats.'

'Have you nothing else?'

'It does not pay me to have better things, sir. Perhaps I could get you something made?'

'I wanted it for next week.'

The shopkeeper said: 'I have one little thing I bought from a seaman. Could that interest you?'

He took out a gold filigree brooch set with a single good ruby and a circlet of small pearls. It was foreign, probably Venetian or Florentine. The man watched Ross's eyes as he picked it up.

'What is the price?'

'It is worth at least a hundred and twenty pounds, but I might wait long for a sale and I do not fancy to risk it by mail to Plymouth. I will take a hundred guineas.'

'I'll not pretend to bargain,' Ross said, 'but ninety pounds was the amount I had set aside to spend.'

The shopkeeper bowed slightly. 'I do not bargain myself. Do you, pardon me, intend to pay cash?'

'By draft on Pascoe's Bank. I will pay to-day and call for the brooch this day week.'

'Very good, sir. I will take ninety – ninety guineas.'

Ross rejoined Dwight in time to take the coach, and they were in Bodmin early in the afternoon. There the coach stayed long enough for

people to eat a meal and for Ross to discover that the rumour he had come
to sound was no rumour at all. Jim had gone.

They missed their meal but caught the coach on its last stage. As it set
out for the long lonely trek across the Bodmin moors among the barren
hills and the woodless valleys Ross noticed that the driver and his
companion each carried a musket on the box beside them.

But to-day the crossing was uneventful and they had leisure to admire
the changing colours of the land under a play of blue sky and cloud. They
reached Launceston soon after seven and took rooms at the White Hart.

The gaol was on the hill within the grounds of the old ruined Norman
castle, and they made their way towards it through a narrow tangle of
streets and across a rising path between laurels and bramble until they
came to the outer wall of what once had been the castle keep. A padlocked
iron gateway led through an arch, but no one answered their knocking or
shouting. A thrush twittered on a stunted tree and far overhead in the
evening a lark sang.

Dwight was admiring the view. On this high ground you could see the
moors stretching away on all sides, north towards the sea, which gleamed
like a bared knife in the setting sun, and east and south across the Tamar
into Devon and the wild purples of Dartmoor. No wonder the Conqueror
had chosen the place to build his castle to dominate all the approaches
from the west. Robert, his half brother, had lived here and gazed out over
all this foreign territory, which had now come to him and must be settled
and pacified.

Dwight said: 'There's a cowherd by that fallen fence. I'll ask him.'

While Ross made the gate echo, Dwight went across and spoke to a
dark-faced man in the canvas hat and smock of a farm labourer. He was
soon back.

'At first I could make no sense of him. They speak quite different in
these parts. He says everyone in the prison is ill of fever. It lies over there
on the green, just to the right of our gate. He does not think we shall get in
to-night.'

Ross stared through the bars. 'And the gaoler?'

'Lives distant. I have his address. Behind Southgate Street.'

Ross frowned up at the wall. 'This could be climbed, Dwight. The
spikes are rusty and would pull out of the wall.'

'Yes, but we could do no good if the gaol itself were locked.'

'Well, there's no time to waste, for it will be dark in an hour.'

They turned and went down the hill again.

It took them time to find where the gaoler lived and minutes hammering
on the door of the cottage before it came open a few inches and a ragged,
spotty, bearded man blinked out. His anger wavered a little when he saw
the dress of his visitors.

'You are the gaoler of the prison?' Ross said.

'Iss.'

'Have you a man in your custody named Carter, new moved from Bodmin?'

The gaoler blinked. 'Mebbe.'

'We wish to see Carter at once.'

'It bain't time for visiting.'

Ross put his foot quickly in the jamb of the door. 'Get your keys or I'll have you dismissed for neglecting your duty.'

'Nay,' said the gaoler. 'It be sundown now. There's the fever abroad. It bain't safe to go near ——'

Ross had thrust open the door again with his shoulder. A strong smell of cheap spirits was in the air. Dwight followed into the room. An ancient woman, misshapen and tattered, crouched over the hearth.

'The keys,' said Ross. 'Come with us or we'll go ourselves.'

The gaoler wiped his arm across his nose. 'Where's your authority? Ye must have authority ——'

Ross took him by the collar. 'We have authority. Get the keys.'

In about ten minutes a procession started through the cobbled alleys towards the summit of the hill, the ragged gaoler in the lead carrying four great keys on a ring. Faces watched them go.

As they climbed above the town the sunset flared and the sun dipped and was gone.

The cowherd had driven in his cows and the ruin looked shadowy and silent. They reached the iron gate and passed through it under the stone arch, the gaoler leading the way with slowing steps towards a moderate-sized square building in the centre of the green.

The man's lagging footsteps came to a stop. 'It be overlate to enter in. Ye maun show me the authority. There's fever in plenty. Yesterday one of 'em died. I'm not sure which twas. My mate ——'

'How long since you were here yourself?'

'Nay, but the day before. I would ha' been over to-day, but for me mother an' 'er bein' ill. I sent over the food. Ye maun show yer authority ——'

There was a sudden burst of cries, growing in tone and number, animal not human, barks and moans and grunts, not words. The prisoners had heard them.

'There,' said the gaoler, as Ross drew back. 'Ye see. Twould be unfit fur self-respectin' gents to go nearer. There be fever ——'

But Ross had moved back to look for a window and now saw one set high in the wall on his right. The building was two-storied, and the window was to provide some light and ventilation for the dungeons on the ground floor. It was not three feet long and less than eighteen inches high, being set with thick bars. The cries and shouts came from here but echoed hollow, and it was clear that the window was out of reach of the inmates.

'Open the door, man,' Ross said. 'Here, give me the keys!'

'Not that way!' said the gaoler. 'It ain't been opened that way since they was put in. Come you up to the chapel above and I'll open the trap door where the food d'go down. Tes a danger for fever, even that, I tell ee. If ye've a mind ——'

Dwight said: 'It will be dark in ten minutes. We have no time to lose if we wish to see him to-day.'

'See here,' said Ross to the gaoler. 'This gentleman is a surgeon and wishes to see Carter at once. Open this door or I'll crack your head and do it myself.'

The gaoler cringed. 'It be as much as me job's worth, damme – 'Ere, I'll open of it. . . . Mind, I take no blame, fever or no. . . .'

The great door was unlocked and opened against their pressure, groaning on rusty hinges. Inside it was quite dark, and as they entered a terrible stench hit them. Ross was a man of his age and had travelled in rough places; Dwight was a doctor and had not neglected his duties; but this was new to them both. The gaoler went outside again and hawked and spat and hawked and spat. Ross caught him by the scruff and pulled him back.

'Is there a lantern here?'

'Iss, I reckon. Be'ind the door.'

Trembling, he groped among the refuse and found the lantern. Then he scratched at his tinderbox to get a spark for the candle.

Inside the prison, after all the noise, silence had fallen. No doubt they thought more felons were to be added to their number.

As his eyes grew used to the dark, Ross saw they were in a passage. On one side the window let in the faint glimmer of the afterglow. On the other were the cells or cages. There were only three or four, and all of them small. As the tinder rag at last caught and the candle was lit, he saw that the largest of the cages was not more than three yards square. In each of them there were about a dozen convicts. All down the cages terrible faces peered between the bars.

'A pest spot,' said Dwight, walking down with his handkerchief to his nose. 'God, what an offence to human dignity! Are there sewers, man? Or any medical attention? Or even a chimney?'

'Look ee,' said the gaoler by the door, 'there's sickness an' fever. We'll all be down ourselves afore long. Let us go out an' come again to-morrow.'

'In which cell is Carter?'

'Save us, I dunno. I dunno one from t'other, s'elp me. Ye'd best find him yourself.'

Pushing the gaoler with his quavering lantern before him, Ross followed Dwight. In the last and smallest cage were a half dozen women. The cell was barely big enough for them to lie down. Filthy, emaciated, in rags, like strange devils they screeched and skirled – those of them who could stand – asking for money and bread.

Sick and horrified, Ross went back to the men.

'Quiet!' he shouted to the clamour that was growing again.

Slowly it died.

'Is Jim Carter among you?' he shouted. 'Jim, are you there?'

No answer.

Then there was a rattle of chains and a voice said: 'He is here. But in no fit state to speak for himself.'

Ross went to the middle cage. 'Where?'

'Here.' The demons of the pit moved away from the bars, and the gaoler's lantern showed up two or three figures lying on the floor.

'Is he – dead?'

'No, but t'other one is. Carter is with the fever bad. And his arm . . .'

'Bring him to the bars.'

They did so, and Ross gazed on a man he would not have recognized. The face, wasted and with a long straggling black beard, was covered with a blotchy red rash. Every now and then Jim stirred and muttered and spoke to himself in his delirium.

'It is the petechial type,' Enys muttered. 'It looks to be past its height. How long has he been ill?'

'I don't know,' said the other convict. 'We lose count of days, as you will understand. Perhaps a week.'

'What is wrong with his arm?' Enys said sharply.

'We tried to check the fever by letting blood,' said the convict. 'Unhappily the arm has festered.'

Dwight looked at the delirious man a long moment, then stared at the speaker.

'What are you in this place for?'

'Oh,' said the other, 'I do not think my case can interest you, though at a happier meeting I might entertain you for an idle hour. When one has not the benefit of a patrimony one is sometimes forced to eke out one's livelihood by means which your profession, sir, prefers to keep in its own ranks. Natural that ——'

Ross had stood up. 'Open this door.'

'What?' said the gaoler. 'What for?'

'I am taking this man away. He needs medical attention.'

'Aye, but he be servin' a sentence, an' nothing ——'

'Damn you!' Ross's mounting anger had bubbled over. 'Open this door!'

The gaoler backed against the cage, looked round for a way of escape, found none, and his eyes again met those of the man confronting him. He turned quickly, fumbled with the great keys, unlocked the door in haste, stood back sweating.

'Bring him out,' said Ross.

Dwight and the gaoler went in, their feet slipping over ordure on the damp earth floor. Happily Jim was not one of those chained to another prisoner. They picked him up and carried him out of the cage and out of the prison, Ross following. On the sweet grass outside they laid him down, and the gaoler went stumbling back to lock the doors.

Dwight mopped his forehead.

'What now?'

Ross stared down at the wreck of a human being stirring in the half-dark at their feet. He took great breaths of the beautiful fresh evening air, which was blowing like the bounty of God over from the sea.

'What chance is there for him, Dwight?'

Dwight spat and spat. 'He should survive the fever. But that meddling fool in there . . . though he did it for the best. This arm is mortifying.'

'We must get him somewhere, under cover. He can't survive the night out here.'

'Well, they will not have him at the White Hart. As well ask them to house a leper.'

The gaoler had locked up his prison again and was standing by the door watching them with an envenomed gaze. But he was coming no nearer.

'There must be a shed somewhere, Dwight. Or a room. All men are not inhuman.'

'They tend to be where fever is concerned. It is self-preservation. Our only resort, I should say, is a stable somewhere. A little from the prison would be better, lest the gaoler makes an early report on our doings.'

'There may be a hospital in the town.'

'None that would take such a patient.'

'I'll be all right, Jinny. They won't catch me,' came in a husky voice from the figure at their feet.

Ross bent down. 'Give me a hand. We must get him somewhere, and at once.'

'Avoid his breath,' said Dwight. 'It will be deadly at this stage.'

Chapter five

JIM WAS LAUGHING while they undressed him. It was a peculiar cross-grained broken sound. Now and again he would begin to talk, but it was senseless stuff, now in conversation with a prisoner, now with Nick Vigus, now with Jinny.

They had found a store-barn – some relic, from its architecture, of the early history of the town – and had taken possession, turning out the chickens and the bullock cart and the two mules before informing the farmer who owned it. Then a mixture of bribery and threats had withstood his anger. They had bought two blankets from him and two cups and some milk and some brandy. They had lit a fire at the end of the barn – the farmer had come back to shout about this but, being terrified of the fever, had done nothing more.

So now Dwight made his examination by the light of two candles and the smoky glimmer of the fire. Ross had taken the last of Jim's clothes and flung them outside, and he came back to find Enys gingerly touching the boy's poisoned arm. He lifted one of the candles and looked at it himself. Then he straightened up. He had seen too many cases like it in the fighting in America.

'Well?' he said.

'Well, I must take that arm off if he is to stand a chance, Ross.'

'Yes,' said Ross. 'And what chance is there then?'

'Somewhat less than an even one, I should say.'

'There is not much to commend it. He loses his arm and the poison begins again.'

'Not of necessity.'

Ross went to the door and looked out into the darkness. 'Oh, God,' he said. 'He is in too poor a shape, Dwight. Let him die in peace.'

Dwight was silent a moment, watching the delirious man. He gave him brandy and Jim swallowed it.

'He would feel little, I believe. I am not happy to let him go without a chance.'

'Have you done it before?'

'No, but it is a straightforward thing. Merely a matter of common anatomy and common precaution.'

'What precautions can you take here? And what have you here to do it with?'

'Oh, I could get something. The precautions are to prevent loss of blood or further poisoning. Well, a tourniquet is simple and . . . we have a fire and plenty of water.'

'And the fever?'

'Is on the wane. His pulse is slowing.'

Ross came back and stared at the emaciated bearded figure.

'He had a year or two of happiness with Jinny. They had that together before one thing after another went wrong. He never had health in the best of times. He will be a cripple now, even if he survives. Yet I suppose we must give him the chance. I would like to wring someone's neck for this.'

Dwight got up. 'Notice how our own clothes stink. We should do better to burn them after this.' He looked at Ross. 'You can help me with the operation?'

'Oh, I can help you. I am not likely to faint at blood. My queasiness is at this waste of a young life. I could vomit over that; and would quick enough if the magistrates were here who sent him to gaol. . . . When has it to be?'

'As soon as we can assemble ourselves. I will go and find a barber surgeon in the town and borrow some things of him. I will also call at the White Hart and bring my own bag here.'

Dwight picked up his hat and went out.

Ross sat down beside Carter and filled up the cup with brandy. He intended to get as much down the sick man as possible, and he would take some himself from the other cup. The nearer they all were to being drunk the better. Enys was right. Everything stank from that visit to the prison: the boots on his feet, his gloves, his stock, even his purse. Perhaps his nostrils were wrong. Celebrations for the King's recovery indeed! All those preparations of yesterday and last week seemed cut off from to-night by the gulf of Launceston Gaol.

''Ere, steady on,' said Jim, and coughed loosely. 'I can 'old me own, I can, and well enough.'

Jim could hold his own. The tattered scarecrow lying on the blanket with fever in his veins and poison creeping up his arm, that bearded derelict of a young man could hold his own. No doubt, so far as he had conscious will, he would try for Jinny's sake as he had done in the past. As he had done in the past. This was the crucial test.

Great shadows stirred and moved on the wall behind them. In the flickering firelight, sitting among the straw and the chaff and the feathers, Ross bent and gave the boy another drink of brandy.

On the morning of the twenty-second Ross was still away and Demelza had spent a sleepless night. At least she thought it sleepless, although she had in fact spent the time in a succession of dozes and sudden wakenings, fancying she heard the beat of Darkie's hooves outside her bedroom window. Julia had been fretful too, as if aware of her mother's unease; though with her it was no more than a sore gum.

Demelza wished she could have a sore gum in place of her own gnawing anxiety. As soon as light came she was up, and chose to revert to her old custom of going out with the dawn. But to-day, instead of making up the valley for flowers, she walked along Hendrawna Beach with Garrick at her heels.

There was a good deal of driftwood left by the tide, and she paused here and there to turn something over with her foot to see if it was of special value. She still sometimes had to remember that what would have been well worth the salving a few years ago now was beneath her station to bother with.

As the light grew she saw that they were changing cores at Wheal Leisure, and a few minutes later several figures came on the beach, miners who had finished their eight hours and were doing a bit of beachcombing to see what could be carried home to breakfast. The sea had not been generous of late, and every tide the beach was picked clean by the searchers. Nothing was too small or too useless. Demelza knew that this winter even the snails in the fields and lanes had been gathered to make broth.

Two or three small wiry men passed her, touching their caps as they went; then she saw that the next was Mark Daniel; and he did not seem interested in the harvest of the tide.

Tall and stiff, with a mining pick over his shoulder, he ploughed his way across the soft sand. Their paths crossed, and he looked up as if he had not noticed her.

She said: 'Well, Mark, how are you going along? Are you comfortable-like in your new house?'

He stopped and glanced at her and then looked stolidly out over the sea.

'Oh, aye, ma'am. Well-a-fine. Thank ye, ma'am, for the asking.'

She had seen very little of him since the day he had come to beg the land. He was thinner, gaunter – that was not surprising, for so was almost everyone – but some new darkness moved at the back of his black eyes.

She said: 'The tide has left us nothing this morning, I b'lieve.'

'Eh? No, ma'am. There are them as say we could do with a profitable wreck. Not as I'd be wishing hurt to anyone. . . .'

'How is Keren, Mark? I have not seen her this month; but to tell truth there is so much distress in Grambler village that makes us seem well placed. I have been helping Miss Verity with her people there.'

'Keren's brave 'nough, ma'am.' A sombre gleam showed. 'Is Cap'n Poldark back yet, if ye please?'

'No, he's been away some days, Mark.'

'Oh. . . . It was to see he I was comin' this way. I thought as he was back. John told me . . .'

'Is it something special?'

'It can bide.' He turned as if to go.

She said: 'I'll tell him, Mark.'

He said hesitatingly: 'You was a help to me last August, and I ain't forgot, mistress. But this – this is something better only spoke of between men. . . .'

'I expect he'll be here before morning. We have an invitation in Truro for to-morrow. . . .'

They separated, and she walked slowly on along the beach. She ought to be getting back. Jinny would be at Nampara now, and Julia was still restless.

Some seaweed crunched behind her, and she turned to find that Mark had followed.

His black eyes met hers. 'Mistress Poldark, there's bad things being spoke of Keren.' He said it as if it were a challenge.

'Was that what you wanted to say?'

'There's tales bein' spread.'

'What tales?'

'That she be going with another man.'

'There are always tales in these parts, Mark. You know that the grannies have nothing else to do but whisper over their fires.'

'Aye,' said Mark. 'But I'm not easy of mind.'

No, thought Demelza, neither should I be, not with Keren. 'How can Ross help you?'

'I thought to have 'is view on what was best. I thought he'd know betterer than me.'

'But is – is there any man specially spoken of?'

'Aye,' said Mark.

'Have you said anything to Keren? Have you mentioned it to her?'

'No. I ha'n't the heart. Mistress, I ha'n't the heart. We've only been wed eight months. I builded the cottage for she. I can't put myself to believe it.'

'Then don't believe it,' Demelza said. 'If you've not the mind to ask her straight, leave it be and do no more. There's always evil tongues in this district, and like serpents they are. Maybe you know the things that used to be whispered about me. . . .'

'No,' said Mark, looking up. 'I never took no heed of such talk . . . not – not before . . .'

'Then why take heed of it now? Do you know, Mark, that there's whispers about that Captain Poldark is the father of Jinny Carter's first child, all on account of them having scars similar placed?'

'No,' said Mark. He spat. 'Beg pardon, ma'am, but tis a cabby lie. I know that; an' so do any other right-minded man. A wicked lie.'

'Well, but if I chose to think there was truth in it I might be just as miserable as you, mightn't I, Mark?'

The big man looked at her, an uncertain but noticeable reassurance on his face. Then he looked down at his hands.

'I near strangled the man who told me. Maybe I was overhasty. I've scarce done a stroke at the mine these two days.'

'I know how you must have felt.'

Suddenly he sought justification and, finding it, found suspicion again.

'You see – you see, she's that pretty an' dainty, mistress. She's far above the likes of me. Maybe I did wrong in plaguing her to wed me; but – but I wanted her for wife. She's too good for a miner's wife, and when I know that, I d'feel anxious. I get hard and overhasty. I get suspecting. And then when there's whispers, and a man who belongs to call himself friend takes me aside and says – and says . . . It is easy to slip, Mistress Poldark, and feel there's truth in what may be lies.' He considered the sea. 'Dirty lies. If they bain't . . . I couldn't stand by. So 'elp me, I couldn't. Not and see 'er go to another. No. . . .' The muscles of his throat worked a moment. 'Thank ye again, ma'am. I'm more in your debt. I'll forget and start anew. Maybe I'll come and see Cap'n Poldark when he is home; but maybe what you've said'll put things straight in my mind. Good day to ye.'

'Good day,' said Demelza, and stood watching his great figure striding east towards the sand hills and his home. She began to walk back the way she had come, towards Nampara. Who is Keren carrying on with? she thought, instinctively believing what she had sought to discredit. Who *is* there that she could carry on with? Keren, who affected to look down on all the cottage folk.

When Ross came back she would mention it to him, see what he said. It looked as if someone ought to warn not Mark but Keren. She would be very sorry for Keren – and the man – if Mark found them out. Keren should be told that her husband was suspicious. It might just frighten her off someone and perhaps save a tragedy. She would remember to tell Ross when he came home.

Then as she climbed the wall from the beach she saw Ross dismount at the door of Nampara and go into the house; and she ran quickly up the slope calling him. Mark Daniel and Keren were forgotten, and would stay forgotten for a long time.

Chapter six

SHE FOUND HIM in the parlour taking off his gloves.

'Ross!' she said. 'I thought you was never coming home. I thought ——'

He turned.

'Oh, Ross,' she said. 'What's to do?'

'Is Jinny here yet?'

'I don't know. I don't think she can be.'

He sat down. 'I saw Zacky early. Perhaps he was able to tell her before she left.'

'What is it?' she asked.

He looked up at her. 'Jim is dead.'

She faltered and looked at him, then dropped her eyes. She came over and took his hand.

'Oh, my dear . . . I'm that sorry. Oh, poor Jinny. Ross, dear . . .'

'You should not come near me,' he said. 'I have been in infection.'

For answer she pulled up a chair beside him, stared again at his face.

'What happened?' she said. 'Did you see him?'

'Have you brandy?'

She got up and brought him some. She could tell he had drunk a good deal already.

'He had been taken to Launceston,' he said. 'We found him in gaol with the fever. The place should be burned down. It is worse than an ancient pest house. Well, he was ill and we took him out. . . .'

'You took him out?'

'We were stronger than the gaoler. We carried him to a barn and Dwight did what he could. But a quack doctor had let blood while he was in the gaol, and his arm had festered and gone poor. There was only one hope, which was to have it off before the poison spread.'

'His – his arm?'

Ross finished the brandy at a gulp.

'The King and his ministers should have been there – Pitt and Addison and Fox; and Wilberforce, who weeps over the black slaves while forgetting the people at his own door, and the fat Prince with his corsets and his mistresses. . . . Or perhaps they would have been entertained by the spectacle, they and their powdered and painted women; Heaven knows, I have lost hope of understanding men. Well, Dwight did his best and spared no effort. Jim lived until the early morning; but the shock was too great. At the end I think he knew me. He smiled and seemed to want to speak but he had not the strength. So he went: and we saw him buried in Lawhitton Church and so came home.'

There was silence. His vehemence and bitterness frightened her. Upstairs, as from a homely world, was the sound of Julia grizzling. Abruptly he rose and went to the window, stared out over his well-ordered estate.

'Was Dr Enys with you in all this?' she asked.

'We were so tired yesterday that we lay last night in Truro. That is why we are here so early to-day. I – saw Zacky on the way home. He was riding on company business but turned back.'

'It were better that you had not gone, Ross. I ——'

'It is bad that I did not go a fortnight sooner. Then there would have been hope.'

'What will the magistrates and the constables say? That you broke into the gaol and helped a prisoner to escape, Ross. Will there not be trouble over that?'

'Trouble, yes. The bees will hum if I do not plaster them with honey.'

'Then . . .'

'Yes, let them hum, Demelza. I wish them good fortune. I should be almost induced to go among 'em as arranged at to-morrow's celebrations if I thought they might catch the fever from me.'

She came urgently up to him. 'Don't talk so, Ross. Do you not feel well? Do you feel you have caught it?'

After a moment he put his hand on her arm, looking at her and seeing her for the first time since he came home.

'No, love. I am well enough. I should be well, for Dwight took strange precautions which seemed to please him: washing our clothes and hanging them over a burning pitch barrel to get out the stink of the gaol. But do not expect me to dance and play with these people to-morrow when their handiwork is still fresh in my mind.'

Demelza was silent. Between the thankfulness that Ross was home – perhaps safe but at least home – and the sorrow for Jim and Jinny, a desolation was beginning to appear, a knowledge that all her own plans were in ruin. She might have argued but she had neither the tongue nor the lack of loyalty to do so.

For it did seem to her just then a matter of loyalty. He must do as he chose and she, at whatever disappointment, must accept it.

He was not at all himself that day. She, who had known Jim little enough, wondered at the bitterness of his loss. For it was bitterness as well as sorrow. He had known Jim's loyalty to himself and had given a greater loyalty in return. Always it seemed to him he had striven to help the young man and always his efforts had come too late. Well, this was the last effort and the failure was final. At five he went to see Jinny. He hated the thought of meeting her but there was no one else to do it.

He was gone an hour. When he came back she had a meal ready for him, but at first he would not touch anything. Later, coaxingly, like tempting a child, she got him to taste first one thing and then another. It was a new experience for her. At seven Jane cleared the table and he sat back in his chair by the fire, stretching his legs, not appeased in mind but quieter in body and just beginning to relax.

And then the frock came.

Demelza frowned at the great box and carried it in to Ross, only just getting through the parlour door.

'Bartle has just brought this,' she said. 'Over from Trenwith. They sent into Truro to-day for provisions, and Mistress Trelask asked would they deliver this. What can it be?'

'Is Bartle still there? Give him sixpence, will you.'

Ross stared at the box bleakly until Demelza came back. Then she too stared at it, between glances at him.

'I thought it was a mistake. I thought Bartle must have brought it wrong. Have you been buying something at Mistress Trelask's, Ross?'

'Yes,' he said. 'It seems like a year ago. On my way to Launceston I called in to order you a frock.'

'Oh,' said Demelza, her dark eyes widening.

'For the celebrations to-morrow. That was when I still thought we should go.'

'Oh, Ross. You're that kind. Could I see it?'

'If you've the interest,' he said. 'It will do for sometime in the future.'

She fell on the box and began to pull at the cord. She at last wriggled it free and lifted the lid. She pulled out some sheets of paper and loose cloth packing and stopped. She put in her fingers and began to lift out the gown. It shimmered silver and scarlet.

'Oh, Ross, I never thought . . .'

Then she put it back and sat on her heels and began to cry.

'It will do for some other time,' he said again. 'Come, you do not dislike it?'

She did not answer but put her hands to her face, and the tears trickled through her fingers.

He reached for the brandy bottle but found it empty.

'We could not enter with any enjoyment into the visit to-morrow, not now, with this fresh in our minds. *Could* you?'

She shook her head.

He watched her for some moments. His mind was fumed with brandy but he could not see her crying like this without discomfort.

'There is something else in there if you will look. At least, I asked that a cloak should be sent.'

But she would not look. And then John showed Verity in.

Demelza got quickly up and went to the window. Without handkerchief, she stared hard at the garden and wiped her cheeks with her hands and with the lace cuffs of her frock.

'I am *de trop*,' Verity said. 'Well, it's no good to withdraw now. I knew I should not have come to-night. Oh, my dear, I am so sorry about Jim.'

Demelza turned and kissed her but did not meet her eyes.

'We – we have been a little upset, Verity. It is tragical about Jim, is it not. . . .' She went from the room.

Verity looked at Ross. 'Forgive me for being so intruding. I had intended coming over yesterday but have been busy getting Elizabeth off.'

'Off?'

'With Francis. They are sleeping for two nights at the Warleggans. I stayed behind and thought you might allow me to ride in with you to-morrow.'

'Oh,' said Ross. 'Yes, if we were going.'

'But I thought it was settled long since. You mean . . .' Verity sat down. '. . . because of Jim.'

Sombrely he reached out and kicked at the log on the fire. 'Verity, I have a strong stomach, but the sight of a powdered head would turn it.'

Verity's glance had several times strayed to the open box.

'This is what Bartle brought? It looks something like a frock.'

In a few words Ross told her. Verity pulled at her gloves and thought what a strange man Ross was, at once a cynic and a sentimentalist, a strange blend of his father and his mother and a personal x equation belonging to neither. Abstemious enough by the standards of the day, he was now drinking himself into an ugly stupor over the death of this boy, who had not even been employed by him for a year or more before his imprisonment. An ordinary man in his station would have passed over the loss with a grunt of regret and not have ventured within two miles of a gaol to prevent it. And this gesture of the frock . . . No wonder Demelza wept.

They were all sentimentalists at heart, the Poldarks, Verity thought, and she realized suddenly for the first time that it was a dangerous trait, far more dangerous than any cynicism. She herself at this moment, happy among all the distress and discontent; life was full for her again, and she had no right to let it be on the strength of a *mésalliance* which might any time end in disaster, which was a deliberate closing of the eyes to one side of life, a forgetting of the past and a planning for an unrealizable future. Sometimes in the night she woke up cold at the thought. But in the day she went on and was happy.

Francis too. Half his ailments came from the same source. He expected too much of life, of himself, of Elizabeth. Especially of Elizabeth. When

they failed him he resorted to gambling and to drink. He wouldn't come to
terms. None of them would come to terms.

'Ross,' she said at last, after the silence, 'I do not think you are wise to
stay away to-morrow.'

'Why?'

'Well, you would disappoint Demelza desperately, for she has been
building on this ever since the word came, and however much she may
grieve for Jim and Jinny she will bitterly regret it if she does not go. And
this frock you have rashly and beautifully bought will heap coals of fire on
her disappointment. Then you would disappoint me, who would now have
to ride in alone. But most important you should go for your own sake. You
can't help poor Jim now. You have done your most, and can't reproach
yourself for that. It will do real harm to sit and mope here. And your move
in forcing the gaol will not be popular. Your presence among people to-
morrow will emphasize that you are one of their class, and if they
contemplate any move it will, I think, give them pause.'

Ross got up and stood a moment leaning against the mantelpiece.

'Your arguments fill me with disgust, Verity.'

'Everything at the moment, my dear, no doubt seems disgusting. I know
the mood too well. But being in that mood, Ross, is like being out in the
frost. If we do not keep on the move we shall perish.'

He went over to the cupboard and looked for another bottle of brandy.
There was none there.

He said suddenly, confusedly: 'I cannot think straight to-night. Demelza
said she did not wish it.'

'Well, she would say that.'

He hesitated. 'I'll think it over, Verity, and send you word in the
morning.'

Chapter seven

WHEN IN THE end, without consulting anyone further, Ross decided to go to the celebrations after all, and when, after an uneventful ride in, Demelza found herself shown up into one of the bedrooms of the Great House, the town house of the Warleggans, there were several worms of discomfort within her to spoil the first flush of excitement.

First there was compassion for Jinny, who last night had tried to hang herself from a beam in her own kitchen; second there was anxiety about Ross, who had not yet been entirely sober since his return and carried his drink like a gunpowder keg which any chance spark might set off; third there was unease over Julia, who had been left in the care of Mrs Tabb at Trenwith.

But all these reservations, vital though they were, could not quite destroy the pleasure of the adventure.

Some inherent good taste told her that this house had nothing to equal the Elizabethan charm of Trenwith, but she was overwhelmed by its bright furnishings, its soft carpets, its glittering chandeliers, its many servants. She was overwhelmed by the large number of guests and the easy familiarity with which they greeted each other, their expensive clothes, their powdered hair and patched faces and their gold snuffboxes and glittering rings.

They were all here; George Warleggan had seen to that; it was like a preliminary regal reception before the public entertainment of the ball. Or all were here who would come. The Lord Lieutenant and his family had politely declined; so had the Bassetts, the Boscawens and the St Aubyns, not yet ready to put themselves on a level with these wealthy upstarts. But their absence was unremarked except by the perceptive or the malicious. Demelza had a confused recollection of meeting Sir John This and the Hon Someone Else, and had passed in a dazed fashion in the wake of a servant up the stairs to her bedroom. Now she was waiting for the arrival of a maid, who was coming to help her put on her new gown and to dress her hair. She was in a panic about it and her hands were cold; but this was the price of adventure. She knew herself far better able to cope with John Treneglos, who traced his ancestry back to a Norman count, than to face the prying eyes of a saucy servant girl who if she didn't know what Demelza had been would soon be ready to guess.

Demelza sat down at the dressing table and saw her flushed face in the mirror. Well, she was really here. Ross had not come up yet. Dwight Enys was here, young and handsome. Old Mr Nicholas Warleggan, George's father, big and pompous and hard. There was a clergyman called Halse, thin and dried-up but vigorous-looking and moving among the aristocracy like one of them, not cringing for a bone like Mr Odgers of Sawle-with-Grambler. Dr Halse and old Mr Warleggan, Demelza knew, had been among the magistrates who had sentenced Jim. She was afraid for what might happen.

A knock came at the door and she checked an impulse to start up as a maid entered. 'This has come, ma'am. I was telled to bring it up to you. Thank you, ma'am. A dressing maid'll be along in just a few minutes.'

Demelza stared at the packet. On the outside was written: Rs. Poldark, Esquire,' and over that Ross had just scrawled in ink not yet dry: 'For delivery to Mrs Demelza Poldark.'

She pulled at the wrapping, took out a small box, parted some cotton packing, gasped. After a moment, gingerly, as if afraid of burning herself, she put in a finger and thumb and drew out the brooch.

'Oh,' she said.

She lifted it and held it to her breast so that she could see the effect in the mirror. The ruby glowed and winked at her. This gesture of Ross's was tremendous. It melted her. Her eyes, black and liquid with emotion, glowed back at herself above the ruby. This gift, if anything, would give her confidence. With a new dress and *this* no one surely could look down on her. Even the maids could hardly do so.

Another knock at the door and another maid entered. Demelza blinked and hastily crumpled up the packing in which the brooch had come. She was glad to see they had sent an elderly maid.

Well, she was in it. It wasn't decent, she was sure of that, but the maid didn't seem to think anything was amiss. Of course other women wore this sort of thing; it was all the fashion; but other women might be used to this sort of gown; she was not.

It was the same general shape as the afternoon gown Verity had bought her, only more so. The afternoon dress was cut away from her neck and the tops of her shoulders, but this one was so much lower. It was amazingly ruched at the sides, and there was a lot of beautiful lace hanging over her hands, where she didn't need it. How Ross had bought it she could not conceive. It had cost a pretty penny, that was clear. He spent money on her as if it was chaff. Dear, dear Ross! Unbelievably dear. If only poor Jim's death had not come between these presents and their wearing, how happy to-night would be!

The maid had just finished her hair, piling it up and up. Since Julia's birth she had not kept it clipped but had let it grow, and the sudden luxuriance of her surroundings as Ross's wife had seemed to give great richness to it so that its darkness fairly gleamed with colour. The maid had brought her powder box, but she instantly concurred in Demelza's refusal; such hair was not to be whitened. She did not however agree with Demelza's hesitant refusal of make-up, and she was now attending to my lady's face. Demelza's restiveness under her hands had the result of keeping her dresser's enthusiasm within bounds, and she came out of it with her dark eyebrows slightly lengthened, only a moderate amount of powder to harden the soft glow of her skin and an excusable amount of rouge on her lips.

'One patch or two, ma'am?' said the maid.

'Oh, none, thank ee. I have no liking for 'em.'

'But ma'am would not be finished without one. May I suggest one just below the left eye?'

'Oh, well,' said Demelza. 'If you think so.'

Five minutes later, the jewel on her breast, she said:

'Can you tell me which is Miss Verity Poldark's room?'

'The second down the passage, ma'am. On the right-hand side.'

Sir Hugh Bodrugan tapped his snuffbox with hairy fingers.

'Damme, who's that filly just come in the room, Nick? The one wi' the dark hair and the pretty neck. With one of the Poldarks, ain't she?'

'I've never put eyes on her before. She's a pridey morsel to look at.'

'Reminds me of my mare Sheba,' said Sir Hugh. 'Same look in her eyes. She'd take some bridling, I'll lay a curse. Damme, I'd not refuse the chance.'

'Enys, you know the Poldarks. Who's that handsome creature Miss Verity has just led in?'

'Captain Poldark's wife, sir. They have been married about two years.'

Sir Hugh brought his thick eyebrows together in an effort of remembrance. Thinking was not his favourite pastime.

'Aye, but was there not some story that he'd married below him; a farm wench or some such?'

'I could not say,' Dwight answered woodenly. 'I was not here at the time.'

'Well, maybe that is she,' said Nick.

'Lord's my life, I'll not believe it. Farm wenches just don't come that way. Or not on my estate. I only wish they did. I only wish they did. Nay, she's no vulgar: her flanks are too long. Here, Enys, you know the lady. Grant me the favour.'

She had come down thinking she would find Ross, but in this crowd it would be all but impossible. A footman stood beside her, and she and Verity took a glass of port. Somebody called Miss Robartes monopolized

Verity, and before she knew it they were separated. People began talking to her, and she answered them absently. As always port helped her, and she thought how wrong Ross had been to deny it her at the christening. It was specially needed to-night to give her confidence about her frock. Then she saw Dwight Enys bearing down on her and she greeted him with relief. With him was a beetle-browed, stocky elderly man with a hairy nose, and Dwight introduced him as Sir Hugh Bodrugan. Demelza looked at him with quickened interest and met a gaze that surprised her. She'd seen that look in a man's eyes twice before: once from John Treneglos at the Christmas party the year before last, once to-night from a stranger as she came down the stairs.

She breathed it in for a moment before curtsying.

'Your servant, ma'am.'

'Sir.'

'Cod, ma'am, Dr Enys tells me you are Mrs Poldark from Nampara. We've been neighbours two years and not met before. I hurry to repair the omission.' Sir Hugh snapped his fingers to a footman. 'Wine for this lady, man, her glass is empty.'

Demelza sipped another glass. 'I have heard of you often, sir,' she answered.

'Indeed,' Sir Hugh puffed out his cheeks. 'And I trust that the report was not disfavourable, eh?'

'No, sir, not at all. I hear that you keep plump pheasants which are a trouble to the poor poachers when they come to steal 'em.'

Sir Hugh laughed. 'I have a heart too, and no one has ever stole that yet neither.'

'Perhaps like the pheasants you keep it too well guarded.'

She noticed Dwight looking at her in surprise.

'Nay, ma'am,' said Sir Hugh, making eyes at her downright, 'it is not guarded at all for them as knows how and when.'

'Good God, Hughie,' said his stepmother, coming on them suddenly. 'I thought you'd gone without me, you wicked old devil. Seen about the carriage, have you? I can't tramp across in all this falallery.' The Dowager Lady Bodrugan, who was twenty years younger than her stepson, hitched up her fine satin cloak in a disgusted fashion and stared Demelza up and down. 'Who is this? I haven't the pleasure, miss.'

'This is Captain Ross's wife. From Nampara. Damme, I was saying we've been lax in our manners not asking 'em over to an evening of whist. . . .'

'D'you hunt, mistress?' demanded Constance Bodrugan.

'No, ma'am.' Demelza finished her port. 'I have some sympathy for the foxes.'

Lady Bodrugan stared. 'Pah, a Methody or some such! I smelt it. Let's see, weren't you a miner's daughter?'

Inwardly Demelza trembled with sudden unruly anger. 'Yes, ma'am. Father hung at Bargus for the crows to pick; an' Mother was a highwaywoman an' fell over a cliff.'

Sir Hugh roared with laughter. 'Serves you right, Connie, for your quizzing, Take no account of my stepmother, Mrs Poldark. She barks like her hounds, but there's little vice in it.'

'Damn you, Hugh! Keep your apologies for your own behaviour. Just because you feel ——'

'Why, there!' John Treneglos pushed his clumsy way into the circle. For once he was dressed up, and his freckled sandy face was already flushed with drink. 'Hugh and Connie, tagging at each other as usual. I might have known! And Mistress Demelza,' he added with assumed surprise. 'Well, now, here's a good meet. Tallyho! Mistress Demelza, I want you to promise me the first country dance.'

'Well, that you can't have, John,' said Sir Hugh. 'For she's promised it to me. Haven't you, ma'am. Eh?' He winked.

Demelza sipped another glass which someone had put into her hand. It was the first time she had seen John Treneglos since his quarrel with her father, but he seemed to have ignored or forgotten that. Out of the corner of her eye she saw Ruth Treneglos edging her way through the crowd towards her husband.

'I thought that was the second, Sir Hugh,' she said.

She saw 'the look' come strongly into John Treneglos's eyes as he bowed. 'Thank ee. I'll be waiting to claim the first.'

'Here's Captain Poldark,' said Dwight, almost with a note of relief in his voice.

Demelza turned and saw Ross and Francis and Elizabeth entering the room together. Dear life, she thought, what do these men think they are? There isn't one of 'em I'd glance at twice with Ross in the room. The strong bones of his face stood out hard and severe to-night, the scar hardly showing at all. He wasn't looking for her. Beside him Francis was slight. By the colour and shape of their eyes they might have been brothers.

They might have been brothers entering a hostile room and preparing to fight. Demelza wondered if others read their expression the same, for the noise and chatter in the room grew less.

Then George Warleggan came smiling suavely up and began to move among the guests, remarking that it wanted ten minutes to eight.

The night was fine, and Demelza persuaded Ross to walk to the Assembly Rooms. The distance was nothing, and if they picked their way they would get there clean. There were already a lot of people in the streets, many of them drunk, and Demelza had the wish to see how her own kind were enjoying the night.

Two great bonfires roared, one in the cockpit overlooking the town, the other in High Cross opposite the Assembly Rooms. It was rumoured that there were to be fireworks at Falmouth, but this sophistication was not for Truro. In places lanterns had been hung on poles in the narrow streets, and the quarter moon had not yet set, so there was a fair amount of light.

Demelza wanted too to rebuild her contact with Ross. The sudden admiration of those men had surprised and elated her, but they really didn't mean anything at all. She wanted to be with Ross, to keep his company, to encourage his enjoyment, to have his admiration. But she couldn't break down the wall that his anger and resentment had set up. It was not resentment against her, but it kept her outside. Even his concern for the success of the copper company – overriding this winter – had been forgotten. She had tried to thank him for his wonderful gift but he hadn't seemed to respond.

Just for a moment his eyes had changed, warmed when he saw her in the frock, but she had not been able to keep his interest, to keep him away from his thoughts.

They reached the steps of the Assembly Rooms and paused to look back. The bonfire was roaring and crackling in the centre of the little square. Round it the figures were moving and dancing, yellow and black in the flickering flame-light. Beyond and to the right the bow windows of the houses were dotted with faces, old people and children watching the fun. To the left the light wavered through the quiet trees and set white among the gravestones. Then a carriage and a sedan chair drew up at the door of the Rooms, and Ross and Demelza turned and went up the stairs.

Chapter eight

A GATHERING AT which the Lord Lieutenant of the County was present was a gathering of importance. For the Lord Lieutenant was the King's Man, and from him came all things great and small. Or, to be explicit, what came from him were appointments to be Justice of the Peace, and to be a J.P. meant to be the possessor of undisputed local power. For good or ill the J.P.s ruled, unchecked by Privy Council or the public purse. So the Lord Lieutenant was a man to be sought after, flattered and fawned on.

To-night there was to be cardplaying, toasts, dancing and a wide range of refreshments. The room had been hung with red, white and blue streamers, and behind the dais, where the band played, a big painting of King George was set up.

Almost as soon as she got there Demelza saw Andrew Blamey. He had taken up a quiet place where he could see the door, and she knew he was watching for Verity. Her heart began to thump for an extra reason, for Verity was coming with Francis and that might mean trouble.

Being at the Warleggans had given her some idea what to expect, and the arrival of the people she had moved among there gave her time to take a grip. It was extraordinarily pleasing and reassuring too to see and be greeted by other people she had met before. Joan Pascoe spoke to her and introduced a young man called Paul Carruthers, who was an ensign in the Navy. Dr and Mrs Choake were there, but they kept their distance. Patience Teague unexpectedly attached herself; Demelza was very flattered until she began to suspect it was because she was in the party of George Warleggan. Then a fat pale man called Sanson (whom she remembered at the food riots) pushed his way in, blinking all the time, and took Ross in conversation. It was something about some gaming loss he had had. Before she knew it they were separated.

She was surrounded with people she did not know or knew slightly. Sir Hugh was here again and John Treneglos and a man called St John Peter, better-looking than the others and young. Several of them were talking to her and she was answering them absent-mindedly, keeping her attention for the other things. Which was the Lord Lieutenant, how did they ever get so many candles burning so even, could she get back to Ross, had Andrew Blamey moved from his corner, what sort of flowers were they in the tall vases, was her frock holding up, would she ever be able to dance with her hair so high? Several times the people about her laughed, and she wondered anxiously if one of the others had said something witty or she had somehow made a fool of herself.

She needed a drink, that was certain. The three ports at the Warleggans had made her feel well and confident, but the confidence was wearing off. More courage was needed out of a glass.

Suddenly there was a whirring noise from the band and all the noise ceased as if you had rubbed it off a slate and people stood up stiff and she realized they were playing 'God Save the King.' Very soon everyone joined in, and they sang it to the roof. When it was over the noise broke and rippled over the floor again. Then someone had found her a seat between Patience Teague and Joan Pascoe, and she was trying to fan herself with the fan Verity had loaned her.

Dwight Enys arrived with another young man, and she thought she saw the colour of Verity's dress.

Someone at the far end of the hall was speaking, but she could not see without standing up and she only heard words here and there, about 'our Gracious Majesty' and 'Divine Providence,' and 'all his people' and 'thankful hearts.' Then the voice stopped and there was a ripple of applause. Faintly could be heard the scrape of bass viols tuning up. Several men came about her. They.wanted her to dance the first minuet. Where was Ross? She looked up at the faces and inclined her head slightly at St John Peter. Then a man called Whitworth, good-looking but dressed in an absurdity of fashion, pressed her for the second. She accepted but refused any for the third. Ross would come back.

The band struck up and no one went on the centre of the floor at all except two quite old people, very grand, who led off all by themselves. Then after a minute or two the band paused and everyone applauded again and began forming up.

She went out with St John Peter, who noticed that his partner's expression had changed, from that rather absent, ready-for-flight look which her talk proved so takingly deceptive, to a faint frown of serious thought. He wondered at her lack of response to his sallies. He didn't realize that she needed all her care to remember what Mrs Kemp had taught her.

Presently she found she could do well enough, and as the dance came to an end and they waited for the repeat she knew she had nothing to fear.

Near by Joan Pascoe said: 'We never see you now, Dwight. Do you never ride in to Truro?'

'I am very occupied,' said Dwight, flushing at the hint of reproach in her voice. 'The work of the mine takes much of my time, and there are so many interesting cases in the district.'

'Well, you can always pass a night or take a meal with us when you come in for your drugs. Mama and Papa will be pleased to see you.'

'Thank you,' he said a little stiffly. 'Thank you, Joan. I'll surely keep it in mind.'

They separated and bowed and the figure re-formed.

'. . . George is very popular to-night,' St John Peter said, inclining his head towards the painting at the end of the hall. 'I remember well how he was abused over the American war.'

'How old is he?' Demelza asked.

'Who?'

'The King.'

'Oh, about fifty, I should say.'

'I wonder what a mad king thinks he is,' she said. 'Twould be queer if he mistook himself for the King of England.'

St John Peter laughed. 'You know we are cousins, ma'am?'

'Who? You and the King?'

'No. You and I. Ross's grandmother and my grandfather were brother and sister.'

'But Ross's grandmother wasn't my grandmother.'

'No. Cousins-in-law. That makes it more refreshing, don't you think?'

'Quite refreshing,' said Demelza absently. 'Faith, I am most refreshed.'

Peter laughed again as they moved apart.

'. . . You should not have come to-night, Andrew,' Verity said. 'People have seen us already. In a day or two the whole district will know.'

'It is what I wished. No good can come of secrecy, my love. Let's face it out together.'

'But I'm afraid for Francis. If he sees you to-night he may cause trouble. He is in the wrong mood.'

'Have we to wait for ever to get him in the right one? He can't stop us. He may even not object strongly now. He has grown up, is not the young hothead. We can't go on with these secret meetings. There's nothing underhand in our love. Why should there be? Why should it be warped and distorted by my old sin, which I've paid for again and again? I intend to see him to-night.'

'No, not to-night, Andrew. Not to-night. I have a feeling . . . A foreboding.'

The flute, the hautboy and the strings were playing an old Italian minuetto, graceful and refined. The strains of the music, thin and unforced though they were, reached every corner of the dance-room and penetrated through to where the refreshments were being served, to the rest-room, to the card-room. . . .

. . . Sanson had said when they met at the door: 'I have been looking to the opportunity to play you again, Captain Poldark. The good cardplayer is very rare and it is a pleasure to sit with such an expert one.'

'Thank you, I've no taste for gaming to-night,' Ross had said.

'I find that most disappointing, Captain Poldark. Last time you were very successful at my expense, and I had looked forward to the opportunity of levelling our scores. Most disappointing.' He said this in a deliberate voice.

'I'm here to escort my wife. That being so, it wouldn't fill my purpose to spend the evening in the card-room.'

'Which is your wife? I would like the pleasure.'

Ross looked about, but Demelza had been surrounded.

'Over there.'

'She seems well attended, if I may say so. Might I suggest a short game, just while the evening is warming up?'

Ross caught sight of Mrs Teague in an astonishing dress of light green and gold gauze, with green foil leaves and gold spangles. With her was Elizabeth's mother, Mrs Chynoweth, whom he detested. At that moment George Warleggan arrived with Francis and Elizabeth.

'Ah, Sanson,' he said, 'there'll be no pleasure dancing in this crush. Have you got a table?'

'I have seats saved. But they will be gone if we don't hurry. I was prevailing on Captain Poldark to join us.'

'Come along,' said George. 'With Francis we can make a foursome.'

'Captain Poldark has not the taste for it to-night,' Sanson said. 'I am sixty guineas out, and had hoped to recoup myself ——'

'Or go sixty guineas outer?' suggested George. 'Come, Ross, you can't refuse the dear fellow his fair revenge. Francis is eager to start. Don't spoil the game.'

There were too many people here, people of the kind who had sent Jim to prison. Painted and powdered up, dressed to the eyes, high-heeled, fan-flicking, snuffbox-clicking, people with titles, people wanting titles, place holders, place seekers, squires, squireens, clergymen with two or three rich livings, brewers, millers, iron, tin and copper merchants, ship owners, bankers. People of his own class. People he despised.

He turned. 'What do you want? What do you wish to play?'

'. . . Where is Francis?' Mrs Chynoweth asked peevishly a few minutes later. 'The dancing has begun and you are not dancing, Elizabeth. It's not good enough, really it is not! He might be here at least to commence with his wife, if nothing more. It will make more talk. Go and see where he is, Jonathan.'

'Yes, my pet.'

'Do sit down, Father,' Elizabeth said. 'Francis is in the gaming-room with Ross and George; I saw them enter. He will not come back for you. Leave him for a little.'

'It's not good enough. Really it's not good enough. And if Francis was not coming, why did you refuse that Dr Enys and those other gentlemen? You are too young to spend your evening sitting by the wall. The first gathering you have permitted yourself in so many years, and then to squander the time.' Mrs Chynoweth fanned herself vigorously to show her frustrations. The last years had changed her cruelly. At Elizabeth's wedding she had been a beautiful woman, but her illness and the doctors' treatment had distorted the eye of which she had lost the sight, and her face was swollen and drawn. She was a deeply disappointed woman too, for Elizabeth's marriage, of which she had hoped so much, had gone just the same way as her own – or even worse, for Jonathan had never dared to get his name linked with another woman; he had only lost money irritatingly and steadily for twenty-six years.

'Elizabeth,' said George Warleggan, coming on them suddenly, 'grant me the favour of the second dance.'

She looked up and smiled at him. 'I promised you the first, but you were busy with your gaming.'

'No, I was seeing the others settled. I had no thought but to be in time. Mrs Chynoweth' – he hunched his big shoulders and bowed – 'how charming you look to-night. You only do wrong to sit beside Elizabeth, whose beauty has no match. I swear her seat will be occupied the moment I take her away.'

Mrs Chynoweth bridled like a girl at her first compliment, and when people began forming up and Elizabeth had left them she sighed.

'A shame, a wicked shame, Jonathan!'

'What, my pet?'

'That Elizabeth should have thrown herself away on one of the Poldarks. We were too hasty. What a supremely good match she would have made with George.'

'A bit of an upstart, what?' said Jonathan, stroking his silky beard. 'No class about him, you know.'

'Blood is overrated,' said his wife impatiently. She was tempted to say she had made the mistake of marrying it. 'It takes but a generation to make class, Jonathan. Times have changed. Wealth is what counts.'

The dance began.

Demelza was recovering her confidence, but her throat was parched.

'A clergyman?' she said in a puzzled voice, looking at her partner's double-breasted cutaway coat, canary embroidered waistcoat, brown silk breeches and striped stockings. 'No, I would not have guessed it.'

The newly ordained vicar of St Trudy and St Wren squeezed her hand. 'Why not, eh, why not?'

'The one I know at Grambler wears a patched suit an' a straw wig.'

'Oh, pooh, no doubt some poor little clerk doing duty for his master.'

'What are you?' she asked. 'A bishop?'

Whitworth bowed low. 'No, mem, not yet. But with your encouragement, mem, I soon would be.'

'I didn't know clergymen danced,' she said.

'It is an accomplishment some of us have, mem.'

'Like bears?' she suggested, looking at him.

Whitworth broke into a low laugh. 'Yes, mem, and we can hug too.'

'Oh, I'm that frightened.' She bowed to him with a little pretended shiver.

The young man's eyes kindled. He could hardly wait until they came together again to continue.

. . . George and Elizabeth had been dancing in well-mannered silence. Then George said:

'Elizabeth, you ravish me in that gown. I sigh to be a poet or a painter. There's such purity of colour, such beauty of line. . . .'

She smiled up at him more warmly than she had ever done before. She had been thinking of Geoffrey Charles at home at Trenwith without her protective care; but George's words recalled her.

'Really, George, you're too kind. But I should take your compliments more seriously if you were less free of them.'

'Free? My dear, I am never free with my compliments. With whom have I ever been free except with you, whom I admire and reverence?'

'Sincere, then,' she said. 'Is it sincere to praise my poor mother?'

He glanced at the couple by the wall. No one had come to occupy Elizabeth's seat.

'No, I confess it is not. But I have the respect for her that I would naturally have for your mother, and I sympathize with her in her misfortune. She has been a beauty, remember, or a near beauty, used to the praises of men. How must she feel now, never to know a second glance except perhaps in compassion?'

Elizabeth looked quickly up at her partner. It was the most sensitive thing she had ever heard him say.

'You're *very* kind, George,' she said quietly. 'You always are. I'm afraid you have little reward for your – for your attendance on me. I'm a dull creature these days.'

'My reward is in your friendship and confidence. As for your being a dull creature, how can what is treasured be dull? You are lonely, agreed. You spend too much of your time at Trenwith. Your child is grown now; you should come more often to Truro. Bring Francis if you ——'

'Bring Francis to the gaming tables again? It is the only reward for the end of Grambler, that he sees less of the green cloths and more of his family.'

George was silent a moment. He had gone wrong there.

'Is Francis good company now that he stays at home?'

Elizabeth bit her lip. 'I have my house and my child. Geoffrey Charles is not yet five. He's delicate and still needs watching.'

'Well, promise at least that this is not an isolated occasion. Come again to stay with me in town or at Cardew. I in turn will promise not to encourage Francis at the cards. In fact I'll undertake never to play with him if that would please you.'

'He is playing now, George.'

'I know, my dear. It was unfortunate but there was no stopping him.'

Chapter nine

IN THE CARD-ROOM there was the prospect of mischief.

Four tables were occupied, one of faro, one of basset and two of whist. Francis always played faro if he could, but the first person he saw on entering was Margaret Cartland sitting at the faro table with her new friend, a man called Vosper. She turned and waved with ironical good humour, but Francis bowed and at once moved to an empty whist table, ignoring the four seats Sanson had kept for them. Ross, not caring either way or about anything, followed him. They sat down opposite each other, and Sanson took one of the other chairs. George Warleggan, however, was talking with a man in black by the door, and presently he came across and said that as several gentlemen were here before him, he was standing down in favour of one of them. Of course, they all knew Dr Halse.

At the Warleggans, Ross had avoided the man. Since he was there as a guest he did not seek trouble, but with the horror of Launceston fresh in his mind the sight of this cleric-cum-scholar-cum-magistrate, who more than anyone on the bench at the time had been responsible for Jim's sentence, was a goad in a raw place.

When Dr Halse saw who was at the table he hesitated a moment, then came forward and took his seat opposite the miller. Ross did not speak.

'Well,' said Francis impatiently, 'now we are set, what are the stakes?'

'A guinea,' suggested Sanson. 'Otherwise the exchange of money is slow. Do you agree, sir?'

'It is more than my customary stake,' said Dr Halse, sniffing at his handkerchief. 'So heavy a hazard makes the game overserious. We do not do well to put this burden on our pleasures.'

'Perhaps you would prefer to wait for another table,' said Ross.

It was the wrong tone for the hardy doctor. 'No,' he said through his nose; 'I do not think I shall. I was here first and intend to remain.'

'Oh, don't let us begin with an argument,' said Francis. 'Let it be half a guinea and have done.'

Polly Choake peered into the gaming-room and withdrew.

'What ith the matter with the Poldark couthins?' she whispered to Mrs Teague. 'They came to the Athembly like they wath two tigers thtalking after pwey. Never tho much as glanthing left or right, in they go and settle to cards afore ever the Lord Lieutenant has made hith thpeech. And there they thit glowering away and playing as if the Devil wath in 'em both.'

Mrs Teague's creased eyelids came down knowingly at the sides. 'But didn't you hear about Francis, dear? That woman has thrown him over. After the way he's frittered money on her too. And as for Ross, well, what else could you expect; no doubt he's bitterly regretting having married that cheap hussy who's showing herself up so bad to-night. I shouldn't be a bit surprised if he took to drink serious.'

Polly Choake glanced across the room. She had not noticed that Demelza was showing herself up, but she welcomed the opinion and instantly concurred in it.

'I think it wicked the way thome mawwied women behave their selves. Thwowing theirselves about the woom. An' of course the men encourage it. I'm thankful the doctor ith above thuch behaviour.'

'. . . Who is that young person dancing with your son, Lady Whitworth?' asked the Hon Mrs Maria Agar, lowering her lorgnette.

'I am not sure. I have not yet had the favour of an introduction.'

'She is quite beautiful, don't you think? A small matter – how shall I put it – different. I wonder if she is from London?'

'It is very possible. William has many friends there.'

'I have noticed she dances rather different too; more – how shall I put it – more lilt in the body. I wonder if that is the new style.'

'No doubt. They say that at Bath one has to be continually taking lessons to be up with the new steps.'

'I wonder who she is with, which party she came with.'

'I have no idea,' said Lady Whitworth, knowing well enough it was the Warleggans but holding her fire until she was on firmer ground.

The second dance came to an end. Demelza looked about for Ross but saw only other men. So many men seemed to want the third dance that she thought there must be a great shortage of women. Inclination getting the better of good manners, she said she was a little thirsty, and almost at once an embarrassing number of drinks were brought. A trifle primly she chose port and promised the third dance to one William Hick. Not till the band struck up did she realize it was the first country dance, and John Treneglos, sandy and rough, came over to claim it. There was a sharp exchange between him and William Hick, and Treneglos looked as if he was going to throw Hick off the floor.

'Dear, dear,' said Demelza, as she was led away by John, 'how you do growl at the smallest thing. I never knew there was so many fierce men about.'

'Young princock,' said Treneglos. 'Young upstart.'

'Who, me?' she asked.

'No, bud. Of course not you, bud. Young Hick, I mean. These town dandies think they can bluster their way in anywhere. He's found he is mistook. And will find it more if he prances in my stable again.'

'Dear life. I don't like the ring of that. Must we all be put in stables even at a ball? Why not kennels, an' then you can call women what you really think them.'

Treneglos lost his ill humour and guffawed aloud with laughter, so that many people looked. Ruth Treneglos, dancing near with Dr Choake, shot them a venomous glance.

'No, chit, I'd make exceptions even to that rule, though I'll confess there's many it would be convenient for.'

'An' where d'you put the buds and the chits?' she asked. 'D'you grow them in your garden or pin 'em on sheets of paper like butterflies?'

'I cherish 'em and nourish 'em. To my bosom, dear girl. To my bosom.'

She sighed. The port was just going down. 'How uncomfortable for the chits.'

'None of them have complained so. You know the old saying: "Them as tries never flies."' He laughed again.

'I thought,' she said, 'it was: "Them as never tries never cries."'

'It may be over Illugan way, but at Mingoose we're bolder.'

'I don't live at either. I live at Nampara, where we have our own modes and customs.'

'And what are they, pray?'

'Oh,' she said, 'they can only be learned by experience.'

'Ha,' he said. 'Well, I crave that experience. Will you learn me?'

She raised her eyebrows at him. 'I wouldn't really dare. I'm told you're so good at games.'

Verity and Blamey had sat out this dance together in the refreshment-room.

Andrew said: 'There's nothing in our way. A few people will not forget, they hold to the old memories. But that is unimportant beside the many who have forgotten or never knew. There's no cause ever again for bitterness between us. You have only to take this step. I have a good lodging – half a house – in the centre of Falmouth, very convenient and comfortable. We can settle there until a better is found. Five years ago perhaps not, but now I can afford the luxuries you need and desire ——'

'I need no luxuries, Andrew. I would have married you before and gladly and worked and lived in any small cottage. It never has been that. I should be happy and proud to share your life. I – I had always thought I could make a home for you . . . in a way that you did not have before. I still want to. . . .'

'My dear, that's what I wished to hear.'

'Yes, but hear me out. It is not luxuries – or popularity if that is short. It is a quiet mind. Our attachment broke last time on my family's opposition. My father and Francis. Perhaps you can excuse them; perhaps not. Well, Father is dead. It isn't pleasant to feel I should be going against his strongest opinions – that I should be disobeying his most express wishes. But I would – I feel I could reconcile that. I feel that . . . he'll understand now and forgive me. Not so Francis.'

'That's why I want to see him.'

'Well not to-night, Andrew. My dear, I know how you feel. But try to be patient. Francis is two years younger than I am. I – I remember him since he could just walk. Mother died when I was fourteen and he twelve. In a way I have been more than an ordinary sister to him. He has been spoilt all his life. His moods anger me often, but I love him – even for his faults. He's so headstrong and rash and impulsive and – and lovable with it. I know so well his wry sense of humour when he can almost always laugh at himself, his generosity when he can give away money that he greatly needs, his courage when it's most required. He's so much like my mother in all those things. I've noticed it and watched it all these years. That's why, if you can understand, I want to get his willing consent to our marriage. I don't want to quarrel with him and leave a bitter break between us. Especially now, when he is hard hit from other things. Trust me a little longer. I want to pick just the right time to speak to him, when we're alone and will not be interrupted. I think I can do it then.'

The seaman had been watching the expressions come and go in her eyes. He stirred restlessly.

'I'll trust you; of course I'll trust you. That goes without question. But . . . things can't be put off indefinite. Events have to move on. Once they're put in train there's no stopping them. We've met several times now, and our meeting has not gone unremarked. Perhaps it was unwise of me to stop it. Do you know that one of my brother captains in Falmouth knew I was meeting a woman in Truro? That's how far it has gone, and that was one reason why I came here to-night. It is not fair to expose you to sly glances and whispering tongues. If you do not tell Francis someone else will.'

'I wish you would go, Andrew,' she muttered. 'I have a feeling that things would go wrong if you met here.'

. . . In the card-room Ross and Francis had won five guineas of their opponents' money.

'You did not return my trump lead, Doctor,' said Sanson, taking snuff. 'Had you done so we should have saved the game and the rubber for a breathing spell.'

'I had only two trumps,' said Halse, austere. 'And no suit to establish if they were cleared.'

'But I had five,' said Sanson, 'and a good suit of spades. It is an elementary principle to return one's partner's lead, sir.'

'Thank you,' said Halse; 'I am acquainted with the elementary principles.'

'No one can question,' Ross said to Sanson, 'that your partner has all his principles at his finger tips. It is a general misfortune that he does not make use of them.'

Dr Halse took out his purse. 'The same might well be said of your manners, Poldark. Ignorance, which is the only excuse, can hardly be your plea. Several times you have been gratuitously offensive. One can only speculate on the bad humours which come of an ill-spent life.'

'Offensive?' Ross said. 'And to a Justice of the Peace, who compounds all the virtues of magistracy, except perhaps peace and justice, in his person. No, you do me wrong.'

The doctor had gone very pinched about the nostrils. He counted out five gold coins and stood up. 'I may tell you, Poldark, that this insulting attitude will do your case no good. No doubt the common people you mix with have blunted your faculties as to what may and may not be said in refined society. In such circumstances one is inclined to pity rather than to condemn.'

'I agree,' Ross said, 'that it alters one's perspective. You should try such mixing, man, you should try. It would enlarge your outlook. I find the experience even enlarges one's sense of smell.'

Other people were listening now. Francis grunted as he pocketed the money. 'You're drastic to-night, Ross. Sit down, Halse. What's the point in life except to gamble. Come about, and cut for another rubber.'

'I have no intention of cutting at this table again,' said the clergyman.

Ross was watching him. 'Have you ever been in a gaol, Dr Halse? It is surprising the variety and fullness of stench that thirty or forty of God's creatures – I suppose they are God's creatures, though I defer to an expert view – can give off if confined for weeks in a small stone building without drains, water or attention. It becomes not so much a smell as a food. For the soul, you understand.'

'The matter of your behaviour at Launceston has not gone unremarked,' Dr Halse said fiercely, like a dry, brittle, angry dog. 'Nor will it escape our full attention very shortly. There will be a meeting of the justices concerned, of whom I may say I am one, to decide ——'

'Give them this message,' said Ross, 'that I have shown greater forbearance sitting at table with one of their number and not breaking his head than they if they opened all the crawling fever gaols in Cornwall and let the prisoners free.'

'You may be sure they shall have a full account of your grossness and vulgarity,' the doctor snapped. All the room was attending. 'And you may understand that if it were not for my cloth I would call you out for what you have said to me.'

Ross got slowly to his feet, uncoiling himself from the low table.

'Tell your fellows when you see them that it would give me pleasure to meet any of them who can spare the time from their high offices and have not the impedimenta of holy living to maintain. Especially those responsible for the upkeep of Launceston Gaol. But let the invitation be catholic, for I feel catholic towards them.'

'You offensive young drunkard!' The clergyman turned sharply on his heel and left the card-room.

A moment's silence fell on the people he had left. Then Margaret Cartland broke into a peal of her infectious laughter.

'Well done, His Lordship! Let the church keep to its own offices and leave the rest to us. Never have I heard a prettier squabble over a mere game of trumps. What did he do, let you down with a revoke?'

Ross took a seat opposite her at the faro table. His glance at her was so disquieting that even she was checked.

Ross said: 'Get on with the game, Banker.'

Margaret's bold impertinent eyes travelled round the room.

'Come, Mr Francis, follow your cousin's lead! Lay a stake on the spade queen; she is poorly backed and we should be patriotic to-night.'

'Thank you.' Francis met her gaze. 'I have learned never to stake on women. It is close in here; I will take a breath of air.'

There had been another minuet; and in the refreshment-room Verity at last persuaded Andrew to leave. She had done so on the undertaking that she should talk to Francis within the week. A little incautiously, perhaps feeling the need to prove her sincerity to him, she walked with him round the edge of the floor, carefully avoiding the card-room, until they reached the main doors of the hall. A footman opened them and they went out. Coming up the stairs from the street below was Francis.

Chapter ten

DEMELZA WAS BEGINNING to feel like a lion tamer who has been putting his pets through their paces and finds them getting out of hand. She didn't know whether to brazen it out or run for safety. The smaller lions she could manage very well: men like Whitworth, William Hick and St John Peter. But the big beasts, like John Treneglos, and the old lions, like Sir Hugh Bodrugan, were a different matter. Relays of port had added courage to natural wit; but there was a limit to her resource and she was thankful it was all happening in a public room, where they couldn't snarl over her more openly. If she had been the perspiring sort she would have perspired a lot.

Recently Ensign Carruthers, whom Joan Pascoe had introduced, had come to swell the numbers. A young man called Robert Bodrugan had also put in an appearance but had quickly been sent off by his hairy uncle. The ball of conversation kept flying at her and she would toss it back at someone indiscriminately. They laughed at almost everything she said, as if she were a wit. In a way it was all very enjoyable, but she would have liked it in smaller measure to begin. And every now and then she stretched her neck to peer over someone's shoulder in search of Ross.

It was in doing this that she caught sight of Verity re-entering the ballroom from the outer door. She knew instantly by her eyes that something was seriously wrong.

After a moment Verity slowed her steps and was lost to view by the dancers forming up for a gavotte. Demelza rose to her feet also.

'No, no,' she said to several men and moved to pass through them. They parted deferentially and she found herself free. She looked about.

'Come, miss,' said Sir Hugh at her shoulder, but she moved on without answering him. Verity had turned, was walking quickly away from her towards the ladies' withdrawing-room. Demelza followed, walking round the floor by herself with her unusual long-legged stride and with a confidence she would not have known an hour ago.

Near her quarry, she found her way barred by Patience Teague and her sister Ruth Treneglos and two other ladies.

'Mistress Demelza,' said Patience, 'permit me to introduce two of my friends who are anxious to meet you. Lady Whitworth and the Hon Mrs

Maria Agar. This is Mistress Poldark.'

'How d'you do,' said Demelza, sparing a moment to eye Ruth warily, and curtsying to the ladies in the way Mrs Kemp had taught her. She instantly disliked the tall Lady Whitworth and liked the short Mrs Agar.

'My dear child,' said Lady Whitworth, 'we have been admiring your dress ever since the Assembly began. Quite remarkable. We thought it had come from London until Mrs Treneglos assured us to the contrary.'

'Tisn't the dress,' said Mrs Agar. ''Tis the way it's worn.'

'Oh, thank you, ma'am,' Demelza said warmly. 'Thank you ma'am. I'm that gratified to have your praise. You're all too kind. Much too kind. And now, if you'll forgive me I am this moment hurryin' to find my cousin. If you'll ——'

'By the way, dear, how is your father?' Ruth asked, and tittered. 'We have not seen him since the christening.'

'No, ma'am,' Demelza said. 'I'm very sorry, ma'am, but father is overparticular who he meets.'

She bowed to the ladies and swept past them. Then she entered the withdrawing-room.

There were two maids in the little stuffy room, and three ladies and piles of cloaks and wraps. Verity was standing before a mirror, not looking into it but looking down at the table in front of her, doing something with her hands.

Demelza went straight across to her. Verity was pulling her lace handkerchief to shreds. 'Verity. What is it? What is it?'

Verity shook her head and could not speak. Demelza glanced round. The other women had not noticed anything. She began to talk, about anything that came into her head, watching Verity's lips tremble and straighten and tremble again. One lady went out. Then the other. Demelza pushed a chair up behind Verity and forced her to sit down.

'Now,' she whispered, 'tell me. What is it? Did they meet? I was afeared they might.'

Verity shook her head again. Her hair, as hard to confine as dark thistledown, was coming undone in her distress. As three more women came chattering in Demelza stood up quickly behind Verity's chair and said:

'Let me tidy your hair. It is all this dancin' has loosed the pins. Sit quite still an' I'll have it right in a jiffy. How warm it is in there! My hand is quite exhausted wi' working my fan.'

She went on talking, taking out pins and putting them in again, and once or twice when Verity's head began to tremble she put her fingers, cool and firm for all the port, on Verity's forehead, resting them there until the spasm passed.

'I can't go through it all again,' Verity said suddenly in an undertone. 'Not all that again. I knew it might come, but now I can't face it. I – I can't face it.'

'Why should you?' Demelza said. 'Tell me what happened.'

'They – they met as he was going. At the top of the stairs. I knew it would be wrong to-night. I have been waiting an opportunity, but Francis has been cross-grained for weeks. They had another terrible quarrel. Andrew tried to be conciliatory, but there was no arguing with him. He struck Andrew. I thought Andrew was going to kill him. Instead of that he just looked at Francis – I felt somehow that his contempt was for me as well . . .'

'Oh, nonsense. . . .'

'Yes,' said Verity. 'I did. Because I wanted the best of both worlds. Because I had wanted to keep Francis's affection as well as Andrew's and had been afraid to tell Francis. If I'd told him before, this would never have happened – not like this. I've been afraid to come out into the open. I've been – timid. I think it's the one weakness Andrew cannot countenance ——'

'You're wrong, Verity. Nothing matters if you feel for each other like you do. . . .'

'– So he went. Without a glance or a word for me. That was worse than last time. I know now I shan't ever see him again. . .'

In the card-room Ross had lost thirty guineas in as many minutes and Francis nearly as much in half the time. Francis had come back to the room after his airing with a face grey with anger.

He had sat down at the faro table without speaking and no one had addressed him; but the expressions of the two cousins were casting a blight over the game. Even the banker, a man named Page, seemed ill at ease; and presently Margaret Cartland yawned and got up, slipping a few pieces of gold back into her purse.

'Come, Luke, we've been in the saddle too long. Let's take a little stroll round the ballroom before the reels begin.'

Her new lover rose obediently; he glanced uneasily at Francis but Francis ignored them as they went out.

At the door, her hand possessively on Vosper's arm, she surveyed the scene of the dance. It came to an end as she watched, the formal arrangements broke up into knots which themselves gradually dispersed as people moved off towards the refreshment-room or to corners under the ferns.

'These dainty dances bore me excessively,' she said. 'All that posturing with no result.'

'You prefer your posturings to have some result,' said Vosper. 'I'm glad to learn it.'

'Oh, tut, naughty,' she said. 'Remember where we are. Oh, damn, I believe it is the interval.'

'Well, no matter; I can use my elbows as well as the next, sweet.'

Margaret continued to survey the floor. There was one knot which refused to break up. It was largely men, but she saw a woman or women somewhere in the middle. Presently the knot, like a swarm of bees, began to move towards a few vacant chairs, occupied them; and then a section of the drones moved off in search of food and drink. Now she was able to see that there were two women concerned, a pleasant-faced, sad-looking person of about thirty and a striking girl with a mass of dark hair and very clear-cut shoulders above a shimmering frock with crimson ornaments.

'Sit in the card-room, my sweet,' said Vosper. 'I'll bring you something there.'

'No, let 'em fight. Tell me, who's that young woman over there? The one in silver with her chin tilted. Is she from this district?'

Vosper raised his quizzing-glass. 'No idea. She has a pretty figure. Hm, quite the belle. Well, I'll go get you some jellies and heart cakes.'

When he had gone Margaret stopped a man she knew and found out who the two women were. A little surprised smile played round her lips at the news. Ross's wife. He playing faro with a bitter and angry face while she flirted with a half dozen men and paid him no attention. Margaret turned and looked at Ross as he staked money on a card. This side you could not see the scar.

She wasn't sorry this marriage was a failure. She wondered if he had any money. He had all the aristocrat's contempt for small amounts, she knew that; but it was the income that counted, not the small change. She remembered him five years ago in that hut by the river and wondered if she had any chance of offering him consolation again.

Luke Vosper came back but she refused to go in, preferring to stand at the door and watch the scene. Some ten minutes later the banker drew out the last two cards of a deal and this time Ross saw he had won. As he gathered in his winnings he found Margaret Cartland stooping beside him.

'Me lord, have you forgot you have a wife, eh?'

Ross looked up at her.

Her big eyes were wide. 'No joke, I assure you. She's quite the sensation. If you don't believe me, come and see.'

'What do you mean?'

'No more than I say. Take it or leave it.'

Ross got to his feet and went to the door. If he had thought of Demelza at all during this last hour he had thought of her in Verity's safekeeping. (It never occurred to him to think of Verity in Demelza's.)

The first dance after the interval was to begin shortly. The band was back on its platform tuning up. After the quiet of the card-room the talk and laughter met him. He looked about, aware that both Margaret and Vosper were watching him.

'Over there, me lord,' said Margaret. 'Over there with all those men. At least, I was told it was your wife, but perhaps I was misinformed. Eh?'

It was to be another gavotte, less stately and sedate than the minuet and popular enough to get most people on the floor. Competition for

Demelza was still strong. During the interval and fortified by some French claret for a change, she had put forward all her talents in conversation to take notice from Verity, who was sitting mute beside her.

It was really her own fault that at this stage the snarling grew worse; for, what with thinking of Verity and her anxiety for Ross, she had been careless what she said, and no less than three men thought she had promised the dance. John Treneglos had been dragged away for a time by his furious wife; but Sir Hugh Bodrugan was one of the three, trying by weight and seniority, she thought, to carry her off from Whitworth, who was relying on his cloth to support him in the face of Sir Hugh's scowls; the third was Ensign Carruthers, who was sweating a lot but was sticking to the Navy's tradition and not striking his flag.

First they argued with her, then they argued with each other, and then they appealed to her again, while William Hick made it worse by putting in remarks. Demelza, a little overwrought, waved her glass and said they should toss a coin for her. This struck Carruthers as eminently fair, only he preferred dice; but Sir Hugh grew angry and said he had no intention of gaming on a ballroom floor for any woman. All the same, he was not willing to give up the woman. Demelza suggested he should take Verity. Verity said, 'Oh, Demelza,' and Sir Hugh bowed to Verity and said, thank you, a later dance, certainly.

At that moment a tall man showed at the back of the others and Demelza wondered with a sinking feeling if this was a fourth claimant. Then she raised her head and saw it was indeed.

'Forgive me, sir,' said Ross, pushing a way in. 'You'll pardon me, sir. You'll pardon me, sir.' He arrived on the edge of the ring and bowed slightly, rather coldly to Demelza. 'I come to see if you were in need of anything, my dear.'

Demelza got up. 'I knew I'd promised this dance to someone,' she said.

There was a general laugh, in which Sir Hugh did not join. He had been drinking all evening and did not at first recognize Ross, whom he saw seldom.

'Nay, sir. Nay, ma'am; this is unfair, by Heavens! It was promised to me. I tell you it was promised to me. I tell you it was promised. I'll not have it! I'm not accustomed to have my word called in question!'

Ross looked at him, at the silk ruffles of his shirt stained with splashes of wine, at his broad heavy face, hair growing in tufts in the nostrils and the ears, at the curled black wig worn low over the brow, at his dark purple coat, red silk embroidered waistcoat and silk knee breeches. He looked him up and down, for Sir Hugh, no less than the others, had had his hand in Jim's death. The fact that he had been dancing with Demelza was an affront.

'Have you promised this dance?' Ross said to Demelza.

Demelza looked up into his cold eyes, sought there for understanding and found none. Her heart turned bitter.

'Yes,' she said. 'Maybe I did promise this to Sir Hugh. Come along, Sir Hugh. I hardly know quite how to dance the gavotte, not properly like, but you can show me. You showed me splendid in that last country dance, Sir Hugh.'

She turned and would have gone out with the baronet to join the others who were now all formed up. But Ross suddenly caught her hand.

'Nevertheless, I take this by right, so you must disappoint all your friends.'

Sir Hugh had recognized him now. He opened his mouth to protest. 'Damn it! it's late in the evening to show a lively interest ——'

But Ross had gone, and Demelza, furious and desperately hurt, went with him.

They bowed to each other as the music began. They didn't dance at all well together.

'Perhaps,' said Demelza, trembling all over, 'perhaps I'd ought to have asked for an introduction seeing it's so long since we met.'

'I don't doubt you have been well consoled in my absence,' said Ross.

'You were not concerned to come and see whether I was or no.'

'It seems that I was unwelcome when I did.'

'Well, everyone wasn't so ill-mannered and neglectful as you.'

'It is always possible at these places to collect a few hangers-on. There are always some such about looking for those who will give them encouragement.'

Demelza said with triumphant bitterness: 'No, Ross, you do me wrong! And them too! One is a baronet an' lives at Werry House. He has asked me to tea and cards. One is a clergyman who has travelled all over the continent. One is an officer in the Navy. One even is a relative of yours. Oh, no, Ross, you can't say that!'

'I can and do.' He was as furious as she was. 'One is a lecherous old roué whose name stinks in decent circles. One is a simpering posturing fop who will bring the church more disrepute. One is a young sailor out for a lark with any moll. They come for what they can get, they and their kind. I wonder you're not sick with their compliments.'

I'll not cry, said Demelza to herself, I'll not cry. I'll not cry. I'll not cry.

They bowed to each other again.

'I detest them all,' Ross said on a slightly less personal note. 'These people and their stupidity. Look at their fat bellies and gouty noses, and wagging dewlaps and pouchy eyes: overfed and overclothed and overwined and overpainted. I don't understand that you find pleasure in mixing with them. No wonder Swift wrote of 'em as he did. If these are my people, then I'm ashamed to belong to them!'

They separated, and as they came together again Demelza suddenly fired back.

'Well, if you think all the stupids an' all the fat and ugly ones are in your class you're just as wrong as anyone! Because Jim had ill luck and died, an' because Jim and Jinny were good nice people you seem to think that all poor folk are as good and nice as they. Well, you're mortal wrong there, and I can tell you because I know. I've lived with 'em, which is more'n you'll ever do! There's good an' bad in all sorts and conditions, an' you'll not put the world to rights by thinking all these people here are to blame for Jim's death ——'

'Yes, they are, by their selfishness and their sloth ——'

'And you'll not put the world to rights neither by drinking brandy all evening an' gambling in the gambling-room and leaving me to see for myself at my first ball and then coming halfway through an' being rude to them that have tried to look after me ——'

'If you behave like this you'll not come to another ball.'

She faced him. 'If you behave like this I'll not want to!'

They found they had both stopped dancing. They were holding up people.

He passed a hand across his face.

'Demelza,' he said, 'we have both drunk too much.'

'Would you kindly move off the floor, sir,' said a voice behind him.

'I don't want to quarrel,' Demelza said with a full throat. 'I have never, you know that. You can't expect me to feel the same about Jim as you do, Ross. I didn't know him hardly at all, and I didn't go to Launceston. Maybe this is commonplace for you, but it is the first time I ever been to anything. I'd be that happy if you could be happy.'

'Damn the rejoicings,' he said. 'We should never have come.'

'Please move aside, sir,' said another exasperated voice. 'If you wish to hold conversation do it elsewhere.'

'I talk where I please,' said Ross, and gave the man a look. The fellow wilted and backed away with his partner.

Demelza said in a soft voice: 'Come, Ross. Dance. Show me. A step this way, isn't it, an' then a step that. I've never properly danced the gavotte, but it is nice and lively. Come, my dear, we're not dead yet, an' there's always to-morrow. Let us dance together nicely before we fall out worse.'

Chapter eleven

THE BALL WAS over but not the night. At midnight they had joined in singing patriotic songs and 'God Save the King,' and those belonging to Warleggan's party had left after that.

But when they reached the Warleggans' house there was little sign of anyone ready for bed. Food and drink were waiting for them: hot pasties, cakes and jellies, syllabubs and fruits, punch and wines, tea and coffee. People quickly settled down to play whist and backgammon and faro; and Sanson pestered Ross into joining him at a table of french ruff.

Demelza anxiously watched him go. The whole of the assembly had passed off without his knocking anybody down or insulting the Lord Lieutenant; but he was still in a peculiar mood.

It had been a hectic evening. The excitement had been faintly unhealthy. Oh, yes, she had enjoyed it, but her pleasure had never been free.

Nor, though the numbers were down, was she without followers here. Sir Hugh had got over his umbrage, John Treneglos had escaped from his wife and Carruthers had stuck to his guns. Verity disappeared upstairs, but when Ross left Demelza she was not allowed to do the same. Protesting, she was persuaded towards the faro table, a chair found for her, money put in her lap, advice and instruction breathed in each ear. That she knew nothing about the game carried no weight: anyone could play faro, they said; you just put money on one of the cards on the table, the banker turned up two cards of his own, and if your card when it came went on one pile, you won, and if it went on the other, you lost.

This seemed easy enough, and after wriggling in her seat to make sure that Sir Hugh didn't put his hand back on her bare shoulder, she settled meekly to lose the money she had been lent.

But instead of losing she won. Not briskly but steadily. She refused to be reckless. She would not stake more than a guinea on any card; but each time she staked she found others following her, and when the card turned up to win there were growls of triumph behind her. William Hick had popped up from somewhere, and a tall, handsome, rather loud-voiced woman called Margaret, whom Francis didn't seem to like. In the next room someone was playing a piece by Handel on the spinet.

They had lent her twenty pounds, she had taken careful note of that; and she thought if she ever got to seventy, leaving fifty for herself, she would get up with her winnings and all the kind men in the world wouldn't stop her. She had reached sixty-one when she heard William Hick say to someone in an undertone:

'Poldark is losing heavily.'

'Is he? But I thought the banker had just had to pay him.'

'No, I mean the other Poldark. The one playing with Sanson.'

Something turned cold inside her.

She staked and lost, staked again and lost, staked hurriedly with five guineas and lost.

She got up.

'Oh, no,' they protested, trying to persuade her to stay; but she would have no argument, for this time it was not personal choice but an urgent panic need to find Ross. She just had the wit to count out the thirty-four sovereigns belonging to her, and then she pushed her way through and looked about.

In the corner of the second room a crowd was round a small table, and at it were Ross and Sanson, the fat miller. She drew near them and, careless of danger to her frock, squeezed in until she could see the cards.

French ruff was played with thirty-two cards, each of the players being dealt five, and the play being as at whist except that the ace was the lowest court card. The hazard and lure of the game lay in the fact that before playing either player could discard and take up from the pack as many new cards as he chose and do this as many times as he chose, at the discretion of the nondealer.

Demelza watched for some time trying to understand the play, which was difficult for her. They played quickly and besides exchanging money at the end of each rubber they bet in the middle of nearly every hand. Ross's long lean face with its prominent jawbones showed nothing of all his drink, but there was a peculiar deep-cleft frown between his brows.

Ross had first played the game with a high French officer in a hospital in New York. They had played it for weeks on end, and he knew it inside out. He had never lost much at it, but in Sanson he had met his match. Sanson must have played it all his life and in his sleep. And he had astonishing luck to-night. Whenever Ross assembled a good hand the miller had a better. Time after time Ross thought he was safe and time after time the freak draw beat him. His luck was out and it stayed out.

When he had given drafts for two hundred pounds, which was about as much as Harris Pascoe would honour and which was all the ready money he had in the world, he stopped and sent a footman for another drink.

'I'm finished, Sanson,' he said. 'I do not think the luck could have stayed so much longer.' Someone tittered.

'It is hard to predict,' said Sanson, blinking rapidly and rubbing his white hands together. 'Give me some surety if you want to continue. It is not late yet.'

Ross offered his gold watch, which had belonged to his father and which he seldom wore.

Sanson took it. 'Fifty guineas?'

'As you please.'

Ross's deal. He turned up diamonds as trumps, and picked up the nine, ten, ace of diamonds, the knave, ten of spades.

'I propose,' said Sanson.

'How many?'

'The book.'

'I'll take two,' said Ross. Sanson changed all his cards for five new ones, Ross threw his spades and picked up the king of hearts and the eight of spades.

'Propose,' said Sanson.

Ross nodded, and they again threw, Sanson two and Ross one. He picked up the king of spades.

Sanson indicated that he was satisfied. 'I'll lay for ten guineas.'

'Twenty,' said Ross.

'I'll take it.'

They played the hand. Sanson had the king, queen, seven, eight of trumps and a small club and made four tricks to Ross's one.

'The luck of Old Nick,' someone whispered near Demelza.

In a few minutes the fifty guineas was gone.

Sanson sat back and wiped a little sweat from round his fat face. He blinked rapidly at the watch.

'Well, it is a good piece,' he said to a friend. 'A little high-priced. I trust it keeps good time.' There was a laugh.

The manservant came back with the drinks.

'Bring me a new pack of cards,' Ross said.

'Yes, sir.'

'What do you intend to play with?' Sanson asked, a trifle sarcastically.

'Assets I can realize,' said Ross.

But Demelza knew that he meant the Wheal Leisure shares. She had been edging nearer to him, and now she abruptly leaned forward and put her thirty-four sovereigns on the table.

'I have a little loose money, Ross.'

He glanced up in surprise, for he had not known she was there. First his eyes looked through her, then they looked at her, but this time they were not unfriendly. He frowned at the money.

'To please me, Ross.'

The footman came with the new pack. Hearts were trumps and Sanson dealt Ross the queen, knave, seven of hearts and nine, seven of clubs.

'I propose,' said Ross.

'No,' said Sanson, refusing the discard. 'Ten guineas again?'

He clearly had a good hand, but his refusal of the exchange meant that Ross's winnings would be doubled. It was a fair hand he had, and he nodded. It turned out that Sanson had the king, ace, ten of trumps, the king of diamonds and the king of spades. Sanson ruffed Ross's first club lead with a trump and led his king. Ross dropped his queen on it.

It was a bluff, and the bluff succeeded. Sanson thought he was void and led his ace of trumps, which Ross took with his knave. Then he made his seven of trumps and his seven of clubs.

Everyone seemed pleased, with the exception of Sanson.

For a time the luck changed, and presently Ross had nearly a hundred pounds before him. Demelza didn't speak. Then the luck veered back and Sanson picked up hand after hand which was cast-iron. The money went down and disappeared. The watchers began to thin. Somewhere in the distance a clock was striking two. For some time Ross had not been drinking. The brandy he had ordered was untouched.

Sanson wiped his hands and blinked at Ross.

'Confess you are beat,' he said. 'Or have you other jewellery to sell?'

'I have shares.'

'No, Ross; no, Ross,' whispered Demelza. 'Come away! The cock will be crowing soon.'

'How much are they worth?'

'Six hundred pounds.'

'It will take me a little while to win all that. Would you not prefer to resume in the morning?'

'I am fresh enough.'

'Ross.'

'Please.' He looked up at her.

She was silent. Then she saw Sanson's eyes on the ruby brooch Ross had bought her. She drew back an inch or two and instinctively put up a hand to cover it.

Ross was already dealing again.

Suddenly she put the brooch on the table beside him.

'Play for this if you must play.'

Ross turned and looked at her, and Sanson stared at the brooch.

'Is it real?' he asked.

'Stay out of this, Demelza,' Ross said.

'You mustn't lose the other things,' she whispered. 'Play with this; I give it you freely – if you must go on.'

'What is it worth?' Sanson asked. 'I am no judge of stones.'

'About a hundred pounds,' Ross said.

'Very well. I accept that. But it is late. . . .'

'Your deal.'

They played, and Ross began to win. Those who had stayed to watch did not leave now. The whist players had gone to bed and the faro table at length broke up. Some of those who had been playing came over to watch. At three o'clock Ross had won back enough to cover his watch. At a quarter after three Demelza's winnings were back on his side of the table.

George Warleggan intervened. 'Come, come, this won't do. Ecod, Ross, you must have a little pity on us all. Put a closure after this hand, and then you may begin all over again to-morrow if you choose.'

Ross looked up as he took a very small sip of brandy.

'I'm sorry, George. Go to bed if you want, but the outcome of this game is still too far undecided. Send your servants to bed; we can find our own way.'

Sanson wiped his forehead and his hands. 'Well, to tell the truth, I am overtired myself. I have enjoyed the play, but I did not challenge you to an all-night sitting. Drop it before the luck turns again.'

Ross did not budge. 'Play for another hour and then I will rest.'

Sanson blinked. 'I think our host has the first claim ——'

Ross said: 'And let us double all stakes bid. That should expedite a result.'

Sanson said: 'I think our host ——'

'I am *not* content to leave this game where it stands,' Ross said.

They stared at each other a moment, then Sanson shrugged his fat shoulders.

'Very well. One hour more. It is your deal.'

It seemed that Sanson's advice had been good, for from that moment the luck changed again in his favour. By half-past three Ross had sixty pounds left. At a quarter to four it was gone. Sanson was sweating a good deal. Demelza felt as if she was going to be sick. There were seven watchers only now.

With half an hour to go they began to bargain for the shares in Wheal Leisure. Sanson put all sorts of obstacles in the way of accepting them as a stake. It might have been he who was losing.

Five minutes had gone in arguing, and four o'clock struck with the position unchanged. At five past four Ross picked up the king, ten, ace of trumps and two useless cards. At the first discard he picked up two kings. He bet fifty pounds on it, which meant the actual stake was a hundred. When they played it turned out that Sanson had the five remaining trumps and made the odd trick.

Demelza looked round for a chair but saw none near enough. She took a firmer grip of Ross's chair and tried to see through the mist that was in her eyes.

Ross dealt himself the seven, eight, nine of diamonds and the nine, ten of spades. With hearts trumps it was a hopeless hand.

'Propose,' said the miller.

'How many?'

'One.'

'I'll take the book,' Ross said, and threw away all five. And then it seemed that he forgot Sanson had to draw first, for he stretched out his hand to draw at the same time. Their hands somehow got mixed up with each other, and instead of drawing more cards Ross's hand had caught Sanson's wrist. Sanson gave a grunt as Ross slowly turned his hand up. In the palm of the hand was the king of trumps.

There was a moment's silence.

Ross said: 'I wonder if you will explain how you came to have a card in your hand before you drew one from the pack.'

Sanson looked as if he was going to faint. 'Nonsense,' he said. 'I had already drawn the card when you caught it.'

'I rather think that was so, Ross,' said George Warleggan. 'If ——'

'Oh, no, he had not!' Hick and Vosper broke in together.

Ross suddenly released the fat man's wrist and instead caught him by the ruffles of his shirt, pulling him out of his seat and half across the table.

'Let me see if there are any more tricks inside you.'

In a moment the quiet scene had broken into confusion. The table was upset and sovereigns and guineas were rolling across the floor. Sanson was struggling on his back while Ross ripped open his shirt and pulled his coat off.

There were two playing cards in the inner pocket of his coat. That was all.

Ross got up and began to examine the coat, taking out his own bills and putting them on a chair. Sanson stood there mutely and then made a sudden rush to retrieve his coat. Ross held him off, then dropped the coat and thrust him sharply away. The man half sat in a chair, choked, got up again. Ross twisted him round and took him by the back of his shirt and the seat of his silk breeches.

'Open the window, Francis,' he said.

'Listen, Ross' – George interposed his heavy figure – 'we don't want any horseplay ——'

But Ross stepped aside and carried the struggling miller to the french window. They went out and down the four steps. Some of the others followed but George Warleggan did not go farther than the top step.

The river was out. Under the late stars it looked like a black pit with sloping sides. As he got near the bank Sanson began to struggle harder and tried to kick himself free. They neared the edge. On the very brink he began to shout for help. Ross shook him till he stopped. Then he tensed his muscles, lifted the man off his feet, swung back and away. The effort nearly took him over the brink himself. Sanson's shouts, thin and childlike, ended in a heavy *plop*.

Ross recovered his balance and stared down. He could see nothing. He turned away and went back to the house, not looking at any of the people he met. Near the steps George caught his arm.

'Has he gone in the river?'

'He has gone where the river should be. It was not at home.'

'Man, he'll suffocate in that mud!'

Ross looked at him. Their eyes met together with a peculiar glint, like the memory of an old strife.

'I am sorry for assaulting your guest and causing this commotion,' Ross said. 'But if you will give such fellows the protection of your roof you should arrange for a more convenient way of disposal.' He went in.

Demelza had been in the bedroom ten minutes when Ross came up. She had undressed, hanging up her lovely frock in the massive mahogany wardrobe, and taken down her hair and combed it and put on her nightdress with the frill of lace under her chin. She looked about sixteen, sitting up in bed and watching him with a wary expression.

For though she understood Ross's mood she did not know how to manage it. He was beyond her to-night.

He shut the door and glanced at her, eyes so light-coloured, as they always were when he was angry. He looked at her sitting there and then looked down at something in his hand.

'I have brought your brooch,' he said. He was dead-sober now, might not have touched a glass all day.

'Oh, thank you.'

'You left it on the chair.'

'I didn't rightly like to touch it, Ross.'

He moved over and put it on the dressing table. 'Thank you for the loan of it.'

'Well, I – I – I didn't like to think of Wheal Leisure . . . all your planning and scheming . . . Have you got it all back?'

'What?'

'All you lost to-night.'

'Oh, yes.' He began to undress.

'When did you first think he was cheating, Ross?'

'I don't know. . . . When you came. No, later than that, but I wasn't sure.'

'Was that why you wouldn't let up?'

'At times he didn't cheat and then I began to win. I knew if I kept on long enough he'd have to start cheating again. His hands kept getting sticky with sweat; it was my chief hope.'

'What happened to him, Ross? He wasn't . . . suffocated?'

'George got two servants.'

'I'm glad. Not for his sake but . . .' She began to slip out of bed.

'Where are you going?'

'To put the brooch away safe. I couldn't sleep with it lying there.'

'You'll have to sleep with it lying somewhere.'

'Then let it be under my pillow.'

She looked tall and very young and slender in her long white cotton nightgown. She did not look like the mother of Julia.

Ross caught her elbow as she came back.

'Demelza,' he said.

She stopped and looked up into his strained face, still uncertain.

'It has not been a good night for your debut into society.'

'No,' she said, lowering her head.

His hands went round the back of her neck and buried themselves in the mass of her hair where it curled over her shoulders. He pulled on it gently until she was again meeting his gaze.

'Those things I said to you in the dance-room.'

'Yes?'

'They were not well said.'

'About?'

'You had a right to the attentions of those men since I was so neglectful.'

'Oh . . . but I knew why you were. It wasn't for want of knowing – or sympathizing. I was worried. They came round like a swarm o' bees. I didn't have time to think. And then when you came . . .'

She climbed back into the big curtained bed, and he sat on the edge on her side, his feet on the step. She nursed her knees and looked at him.

'And then there was Verity.'

'Verity?'

She told him.

A long silence followed, one of those communicative, friendly silences which frequently fell between them.

'Oh, God,' he said, 'it is a wry world.' He leaned back against her knees. 'All this week I've wanted to strike at the air, for there was nothing more substantial to strike at. As you know. But I believe I am too tired to hate any more just at present, Demelza.'

'I'm glad,' she said.

After a few minutes he got into bed beside her and lay quiet, staring up at the canopy of the bed. Then he leaned across and blew out the candle.

She put her arms about him and drew his head on to her shoulder.

'This,' he said, 'is the first time I have been sober for four days.'

It was the first time they had ever lain like this, but she did not say so.

Chapter twelve

THERE WAS NO doubt next morning that the Warleggans looked with disfavour on the end of the gaming quarrel. Constraint and stiffness was marked. Ross wondered if they expected their guests to sit down and be ruined in silence.

But he had not much time for considering the matter just then, for he had to see Harris Pascoe before they left for home.

All during these days the copper company had almost been forgotten; but there was much business now to do and much to discuss. After a while the banker said nervously:

'I hear you have been in Launceston for a few days.'

'So you've heard.'

'It is a curious thing, you know, that I hardly ever stir from my house except now and then to walk up the hill for the good of my health – and yet all the n-news of the world comes to me. I trust you're no worse for the adventure?'

'No worse if you mean in body. Of course there is another few days for the fever to come out.'

Pascoe winced slightly. 'I – er – gather that your action in breaking open the gaol has not been a popular one.'

'I did not expect it to be.'

'Quite so. The young man died? Yes. . . . Mind you, I don't think very much will come of it in that case. The question of whether the prison was in fact fit for human habitation would naturally come up at any inquiry on your behaviour, and it would not be in the interests of the magistrates concerned to have too much publicity given to the incident. Really, you know, almost all of them are well-meaning gentry with apathy as their worse crime. Many of them rule with admirable public spirit. And they have regard enough for what the country thinks not to wish to show up badly. I think they will decide to close their ranks and ignore your part in it. That's my personal opinion for what it's worth.'

Ross tapped his riding boot.

'It is p-perhaps a little unfortunate,' Pascoe said, looking out of the window, 'that several of your fellow shareholders on the Carnmore Copper Company should be, so to say, on the other side of the fence.'

Ross looked up. 'What do you mean?'

'Well, they are magistrates, are they not, and as such likely to see the matter in their own light: St Aubyn Tresize and Alfred Barbary and the others. However that may not at all eventuate.'

Ross grunted and rose. 'What they don't seem to see is that we shall have plenty to fight without fighting among ourselves.'

Pascoe fixed his spectacles and dusted some snuff off his coat. 'I was not at the ball last night, but I am told the Assembly altogether was most enjoyable. Your wife, I understand, was quite the success of the evening.'

Ross looked up sharply. Pascoe was not normally a man of sarcasm. 'In what way?'

The banker met his gaze in slight surprise. 'In the pleasantest way, I imagine. If there is an unpleasant way of being a success I have yet to learn it.'

'Oh,' said Ross. 'Yes. I was very much out of sorts last night. I took little notice.'

'I hope it isn't any symptoms of the fever?'

'Oh, no. . . . You were saying?'

'About what?'

'About my wife.'

'Oh, I was merely repeating what came my way. Several ladies remarked on her beauty. And I believe the Lord Lieutenant asked who she was.'

'Oh,' said Ross, trying not to show his surprise. 'That is very gratifying.'

Harris Pascoe went with him to the door. 'You're staying with the Warleggans?'

'We could hardly refuse. I don't think we are likely to be asked again, for the news of my being concerned in the copper company can't be long in leaking out.'

'No-o. And the trouble last night between yourself and Matthew Sanson will be a further strain on good feeling.'

'You're certainly well informed.'

Pascoe smiled. 'A man called Vosper told me. But that s-sort of quarrel is soon about the town.'

'There's no reason why it should be a reflection on the Warleggans. They were not even playing at the time.'

'No, but he's a cousin, you know.'

Ross halted. 'Of the Warleggans? I didn't know.'

'The old man, the grandfather – you knew he was a blacksmith? Yes, well he had three children. The daughter married a good-for-nothing fellow called Sanson, father of Matthew Sanson. The eldest child of the old man is Nicholas, George's father, and the younger son is Cary.'

'Oh,' said Ross, thinking it over. There was a lot to think over. 'He's a miller by trade, isn't he?'

'S-so they call him,' said Harris Pascoe with a peculiar expression.

They took leave of the Warleggans at one, George magnanimously coming down the steps to see them off. No word more of the fracas of the night, and Sanson was as if he had never been. They separated with laughter and thanks and various insincere promises to meet again very soon, and the five Poldarks turned their horses up Princes Street. As she was about to mount, an ostler from the Seven Stars Tavern came across to Demelza and gave her a sealed letter; but with so many people about she had only time to thrust it into the pocket of her riding coat and hope that the others hadn't noticed.

They did not leave constraint behind, for Francis had not spoken a word to his sister since last night, and while they rode bunched together no one seemed inclined to talk. But when they reached the open moors Ross and Francis rode ahead and the three girls followed in line abreast, with the two Trenwith servants and the baggage on ponies behind. So it happened that Ross and Francis had the last friendly talk they were to have for many a day; and behind them, since Verity had nothing to say, Elizabeth and Demelza spoke together as equals for the first time in their lives.

Ross and Francis, carefully avoiding the subject of Captain Blamey, talked of Matthew Sanson. Francis had not known of his relationship with the Warleggans.

'Damn me,' said Francis, 'what troubles me is that I have played with the skunk for the last three years. There's no question but that he has been the greatest gainer. He used to lose sometimes, but seldom to me. It gives me to wonder how much I've been cheated.'

'Of most of it, I should guess. Look, Francis, I don't think this should stay as it is. I've no more to gain by pursuing it, but you have. And so must others have. I don't think you can afford to consider the Warleggans.'

'We might try to squeeze some of his back winnings out of him?'

'Why not? He's a miller and swimming in money. Why should he not be made to pay?'

'I wish I had thought of it before we left; I could have sounded some of those I know will be feeling sore. I've an uncomfortable feeling that before we can do anything he will clear out of the district.'

'Well, there are his mills. He can't abandon them.'

'No-o.'

Ross saw that Demelza and Elizabeth were talking, and the sound of their voices on the wind gave him pleasure. It would be strange and gratifying if those two women made up a friendship. He had always wanted that.

When they reached Trenwith they had to go in and take tea. And Geoffrey Charles had to be inspected as well as Julia, so it was late before Ross, carrying the crowing baby in his arms, and Demelza, edging up her horse to peer at his bundle, began the last three miles to Nampara.

'Verity has taken it bad again,' Ross said. 'Sitting there through tea scarcely speaking. Her expression made me uneasy. Thank God, at least, that we had no part in it.'

'No, Ross,' said Demelza, the letter burning in her pocket. (She had looked at it a moment at Trenwith.

MISTRESS DEMELZA [it began],

Since you brought us together this second time, I turn to you for further help at this crisis in our affairs. Francis is quite impossible; there can never be any reconciliation. Therefore Verity must choose, and choose quickly between us. I do not fear her choice but only lack the means to communicate with her and make final arrangements. It is in this that I ask your help. . . .)

'No, Ross,' Demelza said.

As they reached the coppice, turning into their valley, the sun came out, and they stopped a moment to look down. He said suddenly: 'I dislike coming back to-day, to our house and to our land, because it's to the thought of Jinny's misery and to my failure.'

She put her hand on his. '*No*, Ross, it can't be. We're coming back to our happiness and to our success. I'm sad for Jinny too, shall always be; but we can't let other people's misery spoil our lives. We *can't*, for else there'd be no happiness for anyone ever again. We can't be all tied up one with another like that, or why did God make us separate? While we've got our happiness we must enjoy it, for who knows how long it will last?'

He looked at her.

'That's all ours,' she said, 'and we must cherish it, Ross. Tis no good crying for the moon and wanting everyone to be so lucky as we are. I'm content an' I want you to be the same. You were once, not so long ago. Have I failed you?'

'No,' he said. 'You have not failed me.'

She took a deep breath. 'How lovely it is to see the sea after being away for more than a day.'

He laughed a little – the first time since he had come home.

The wind had been blowing from the south-east for a fortnight. Sometimes the sea had been flat and green and at others full of spumy feathery breakers. But to-day a great swell had developed. They could see the long lines of breakers parading slowly in, the sun-green tops breaking far out and spreading the whole bay with white valleys of glinting foam.

As they dipped among the trees Garrick came bounding towards them, froth on his mouth and his red tongue lolling with excitement. Darkie knew him and ignored the show, but Caerhays, Demelza's new horse, did not like it a bit and there was some side-stepping and head-shaking before it all quieted down. As they restarted they saw a girl's figure running across towards the rising ground on the side. Her long black hair blew out, and she carried a bag, which she swung as she ran.

'That's Keren Daniel again,' said Demelza. 'Whenever she go to Sawle for anything she takes a short cut back across my garden.'

'No one has told her different, I suppose. By the way, I was asked this morning if Dwight Enys was going with a woman in the neighbourhood. Have you heard any such rumour?'

'No,' said Demelza, and then everything slipped into place. 'Oh.'

'What is it?'

'Nothing.'

They reached the bridge and crossed it. Ross had the sudden impulse to meet Demelza's desire for happiness, to atone to her for what had been unpleasant in last night. Why not? Strange sometimes how easy bitter words came, how hard the kind ones.

'You've heard me speak of Harris Pascoe?'

'Your bank person?'

'Yes. He appears to be the best-informed man in the county. He had not even been to the Assembly last night yet he knew all about your success there.'

'My success?' Demelza said, looking for sarcasm just as Ross had done.

'Yes; about how the ladies had said how beautiful you were and how the Lord Lieutenant had wished to know your name.'

'Judas!' said Demelza, going very hot. 'You're joking.'

'I'm not at all.'

'Whoever told him that?'

'Oh, it would be on good authority.'

'Judas,' said Demelza again. 'I never even knew which the Lord Lieutenant was.'

'So you see others were in good mood to appreciate you, even if I was not.'

'Oh, Ross, I can't believe it,' said Demelza, with a funny little lift in her voice. 'No one could notice anything in such a crush. He was saying it to please you.'

'Far from it, I assure you.'

They reached the door of their house. It was open but no one was there to greet them.

'I'm . . . It seem queer to think of,' she said. 'It must have been your lovely dress.'

'A nice frame doesn't make a nice picture.'

'Phoo. . . . It's made me feel queer. I never thought to think . . .'

John Gimlett came trotting round the house, apologizing for not being there to greet them; his shining round face was good-tempered and friendly and made them feel they were welcome home. Ross was going to hand him the baby but Demelza protested and was helped down first.

She took the kicking baby from Ross and stood for a moment gathering her more comfortably into her arms. Julia at once knew who was holding her, and a grin of welcome spread across her chubby face. She crowed and put up a clenched fist. Demelza kissed the fist and examined the child's face for signs of change. Julia looked vaguely less comely than she had done thirty-six hours before. Demelza came to the view that at that age no child was tidy for long without its mother. (The ladies had said how beautiful, and the Lord Lieutenant had asked . . . 'Your lovely dress it was, Ross'; but, 'A nice frame doesn't make a nice picture,' he had said.) Demelza had known that when Julia grew up she would be proud of her father; it had not occurred to her that she might also be proud of her mother. A splendid thought, shining like that sun on the sea. She would do all she could. Learn to be a lady, learn to grow old with grace and charm. She was only young yet, so there was still a chance to learn.

She raised her head and looked across at Ross just dismounting. Last night and the night before she had feared for him. But to-day he had got back his balance. If she could persuade him to stay at home for a little now, she thought he would gain back his content. It was up to her really to see that he did.

Julia wriggled and crowed. 'Na-na-na,' she said. 'Do-do-buff-war-na-na,' and laughed at her own absurdity.

Demelza sighed, with a sense of the complexity of life but of its personal goodness to her, and turned and carried her baby into the house.

Chapter thirteen

KEREN HAD BEEN hurrying for a very good reason. She had Mark's supper, two salted pilchards for which she had paid twopence, in her bag, and she did not want to be late in cooking it. She reached home, running most of the way, burst into the cottage, began gathering sticks for lighting a fire. Mark had been doing a turn of work for Will Nanfan on his small holding to earn more money. All this week while he had been on the night core his routine had been: down the mine from ten until six in the morning, sleep from seven to twelve, hoe his own garden for an hour, then a mile's walk to Nanfan's, where he worked from two till seven. He had been getting home about half past seven, when he would turn in for another hour or so before it was time for supper and tramping off to the mine again. Hard going but necessary, for Keren was not a good manager. She always wanted to be buying something to eat instead of contriving something. It was an attitude of mind quite foreign to her neighbours.

Down in Sawle she had stayed watching two men fight over a disputed net. Now she found she was home in good time and need not have hurried. But she did not swear at herself or inwardly rail at Mark for keeping her so tied to time – and that for another very good reason. Dwight was home to-day.

She had not seen him for nearly a week. And he was home to-day.

She cooked the supper and woke Mark and watched him eat it, pecking at things herself like a bird. She was unstable in this as in all things, choosing to half starve herself when the food did not appeal, then when something tasty came along she would eat until she could hardly move.

She sat there watching Mark get ready for the mine, with a curious hidden tenseness in her body as she had done many times before, and always with the same reason. He had been more morose of late, less pliable to her moods; sometimes she thought he was watching her. But it did not worry her, for she was confident of always being able to outwit him and she was careful not to do anything suspicious when he was about. Only on these night cores of Mark's was she really free, and up to now she had been afraid to make use of them – not afraid of discovery but afraid of Dwight's opinion of her.

The sun had gone down behind a mass of night cloud, and its setting was only to be noticed by a last flush in the sky before dark. In this room the shadows were already heavy. Keren lit a candle.

'You'd be best to save your light till tis full dark,' Mark said. 'What wi' candles at ninepence a pound an' one thing and another.'

He was always complaining about the price of things. Did he expect her to live in the dark?

'If you'd built the house the other way round it would have kept a lot lighter in the evening,' she said.

She was always complaining about the way the house faced. Did she expect him to pick it up and set it down again just as she fancied?

'Mind you bolt the door while I'm away,' he said.

'But that means I've got to get up to let you in.'

'Never you mind. You do as I say. I don't fancy you sleeping here alone and unwatched like you was this morning. I wonder you fancy to sleep that way yourself.'

She shrugged. 'None of the local folk'd dare venture here. And a beggar or a tramp wouldn't know you were away.'

He got up. 'Well, see you bolt it to-night.'

'All right.'

He picked up his things and went to the door. Before he went he glanced back at her sitting there in the light of the single candle. The light shone on her pale skin, on her pale eyelids, on her dark eyelashes, on her dark hair. Her lips were pursed and she did not look up. He was suddenly visited by a terrible spasm of love and suspicion and jealousy. There she sat, delectable, like a choice fruit. He had married her, yet the thought had been growing in him for weeks that she was really not for him.

'Keren!'

'Yes?'

'And see you don't open it to no one afore I git back.'

She met his gaze: 'No, Mark. I'll not open it for no one.'

He went out wondering why she had taken his words so calmly, as if the thought held no surprise.

After he left she sat quite still for a long time. Then she blew out the candle and went to the door and opened it so that she could hear the bell at the mine ringing the change of core. When this came she shut the door and bolted it and lit the candle again, carrying it into her bedroom. She lay down on the bed, but there was no danger of falling asleep. Her mind was crammed with thoughts and her nerves and body atingle.

At length she sat up, combed her hair, scraped round the box to find the last of the powder, put on a shabby black cloak and tied up her hair with the scarlet kerchief Mark had won. Then she left the house. As she went she hunched her shoulders up and walked with a careful hobble, to deceive anyone who might see her.

There was a light in the Gatehouse as she had expected, in the window of his living-room. There was also a glimmer in one of the turreted windows. Bone was going to bed.

She did not knock at the door but tiptoed round among the brambles until she reached the lighted window facing up the hill. There she stopped to take off her scarf and shake out her hair. Then she tapped.

She had some time to wait, but did not knock again for she knew how good his hearing was. Suddenly the curtains were drawn back and a hand unlatched the window. She found herself looking into his face.

'Keren! What is it? Are you well?'

'Yes,' she said. 'I – I wanted to see you, Dwight.'

He said: 'Go round to the front. I'll let you in.'

'No, I can manage here if you'll help.'

He stretched out a hand; she grasped it and climbed nimbly into the room; he hastily shut the windows and pulled the curtains across.

A fire crackled in the grate. Two candelabras burned on the table, on which papers were spread. He was in a shabby morning gown and his hair was ruffled. He looked very young and handsome.

'Forgive me, Dwight. I – I couldn't come at any other time. Mark is on night core. I was so anxious . . .'

'Anxious?'

'Yes. For you. They told me you'd been with the fever.'

His face cleared. 'Oh, that. . . .'

'I knew you were home Tuesday but I couldn't get across and you didn't send me any word.'

'How could I?'

'Well, you might have tried somehow before you left for Truro again.'

'I did not know what work Mark was on. I don't think there was any reason to worry about me, my dear. We disinfected ourselves very thoroughly before we came home. Do you know that even my pocket-book stank after being in that gaol and had to be burned?'

'And then you say there was no danger!'

He looked at her. 'Well, you are good to have worried so. Thank you. But it was dangerous to come here at this time of night.'

'Why?' She met his gaze through her eyelashes. 'Mark is down the mine for eight hours. And your servant is in bed.'

He smiled slightly, with a hint of constraint. All the way into Truro yesterday and at times in the middle of the Assembly, Keren Daniel had been before him. He saw plain enough where their way was leading, and he was torn between two desires, to halt and to follow. Sometimes he had almost decided to take her, as he saw she wanted him to, but he knew that once begun no man on earth could predict where it would end. The thought was bulking between him and his work.

He had been grateful for the ball last night and the sudden refreshing contact with people of his own class. It was helpful to meet Elizabeth

Poldark again, whom he thought the most beautiful woman he had ever seen. It had been helpful to meet Joan Pascoe and to contrast her poised, clear-skinned, clean-thoughted maidenhood with the memory of this wayward, impulsive little creature. He had come back to-day sure that this fantastic playing with fire must stop.

But faced with Keren, the choice was not so easy. Joan and the other girls were 'at a distance'; they were remote, they were young ladies, they were people who made up the world. Keren was *reality*. Already he knew the taste of her lips, the melting touch of her body.

'Well,' she said, as if reading his thoughts, 'aren't you going to kiss me?'

'Yes,' he said. 'And then you must go, Keren.'

She slipped her cloak on quickly and stood up to him with her hands behind her back, her attitude one of odd urgent demureness. She put up her face and half closed her eyes.

'Now,' she said. 'Just one.'

He put his arms about her and kissed her cool lips, and she made no attempt to return his kiss. And while he was kissing her the knowledge came that he had missed this during the last week, missed it more than anything in life.

'Or a thousand,' she said under her breath.

'What?' he asked.

She glanced sidelong away. 'The fire's nice. Why should I go?'

Dwight knew then he was lost. And she knew too. There was nothing he could do about it. He would follow now. He would follow.

'What did you say?' he asked.

'Or a thousand. Or twenty thousand. Or a million. They're yours for the asking.'

He put his hands up to her face, pressed it between his hands. There was a sudden tender vehemence in his touch.

'If I take there'll be no asking.'

'Then take,' she said. 'Then take.'

Chapter fourteen

ON SATURDAY THE second of May in the morning, in one of the upper rooms of the Great House, there was a meeting of the three chief business members of the Warleggan family. Mr Nicholas Warleggan, large and deliberate and hard, sat with his back to the window in a fine Sheraton armchair; Mr George Warleggan lounged by the fireplace, tapping every now and then with his stick at the plaster ornamentations; Mr Cary Warleggan occupied the table, looking over some papers and breathing through his nose.

Cary said: 'There's little from Trevaunance. There was no official ceremony, according to Smith. At noon Sir John Trevaunance and Captain Poldark and Mr Tonkin went down to the works, Sir John said a few words and the workmen lit up the furnaces. Then the three gentlemen went into one of the tin huts which have been set up, and drank each other's health and went home.'

Mr Warleggan said: 'How is it situated, this works?'

'Very convenient. At high tide a brig can come into Trevaunance Cove and edge right alongside the quay, and the coal is unloaded beside the furnaces.'

George lowered his stick. 'What are they doing for rolling and cutting?'

'At present they've come to an agreement with the venturers of Wheal Radiant for the use of their rolling and battery mill. That is about three miles away.'

'Wheal Radiant,' said George thoughtfully. 'Wheal Radiant.'

'And what of the ticketing?' asked Mr Warleggan.

Cary rustled his papers.

'Blight tells me the meeting was very crowded. That was to be expected, for the news has got around. Things went much as planned and the Carnmore Company got no copper at all. The high prices of course pleased the mines. It all passed off very quiet.'

George said: 'They bought enough last time to keep them going three months. It is when they begin to run short that we shall have the fireworks.'

'After the ticketing,' Cary said, 'Tremail discreetly sounded Martin on his loyalty to the company. However, Martin became very unpleasant and the conversation had to be broke off.'

Mr Nicholas Warleggan got up. 'I don't know if you are party to this, George, but if so it is not a departure that I view with any pleasure. I have been in business now for forty years, and much if not all you have been able to do has been built on the foundations laid by me. Well, our bank, our foundry, our mills have been raised on principles of sound business and honest trading. We have that reputation and I am proud of it. By all means fight the Carnmore Copper Company with the legitimate means to hand. I have every intention of putting them out of business. But I do not think we need descend to such measures to gain our end.'

Having said so much, Mr Warleggan turned his back and stared out over the lawns and the river. Cary sorted his papers. George traced the mouldings with the point of his stick.

Cary said: 'This absurd secrecy is no better than a sharp practice, contrived to mislead and confuse.'

'I do not think we can hold that against them,' Mr Warleggan said ponderously. 'They have as much right as we have to use agents and figureheads.'

Cary breathed through his nose. 'What does George say?'

George took out his lace handkerchief and flicked away a little plaster which had floated down upon his knee. 'I was thinking. Isn't Jonathan Tresidder the chief shareholder in Wheal Radiant?'

'I believe so. What of it?'

'Well, does he not bank with us?'

'Yes.'

'And has some money on loan. I think it could be made clear to him that he should choose which side of the fence he wishes to come down on. If he helps the Carnmore with his mill let him go elsewhere for his credit. We can't be expected to subsidize our competitors.'

Cary said rather sarcastically: 'And what does Nicholas think of that?'

The old man by the window clasped his hands but did not turn. 'I think if it was gone about straightforwardly it could be considered a legitimate business move.'

'It's certainly no worse than the way you treated the owners of the paper mills at Penryn,' Cary said.

Mr Warleggan frowned. 'They were holding up all our projects. Expediency will often justify severity.'

George coughed. 'For my part,' he said, 'although I don't condemn these manœuvres of Cary's – they're too unimportant to concern us much – yet I'm inclined to agree with you, Father, that we're too big to stoop to them. Let's defeat this company by fair means.'

'Fair means,' said Cary.

'Well, business means. We'll have all the smelters and merchants backing us. There should be no difficulty in squeezing these interlopers out once we know who they are ——'

'Exactly,' said Cary.

'And we shall know, never fear. Don't tell me a secret can be kept for very long in these parts. Someone will begin to whisper to someone else. It is just a question of not being too impatient and of knowing enough not to go too far.'

Cary got up. 'You mean you wish these enquiries stopped?'

Mr Warleggan did not speak, but George said:

'Well, kept within the limits of dignity. After all we shall not be ruined even if the company establishes itself.'

'You seem to forget,' Cary said pallidly, 'that the man directing this company is the man responsible for Matthew's disgrace.'

'Matthew got nothing more than he deserved,' said Nicholas. 'I was shocked and horrified at the whole thing.'

George rose also, stretching his bullneck and picking up his stick. He ignored his father's last remark.

'I have forgot nothing, Cary,' he said.

Book three

Chapter one

'READ ME THE story of the Lost Miner, Aunt Verity,' Geoffrey Charles said.

'I have read it you once already.'

'Well, again, please. Just like you read it last time.'

Verity picked up the book and absently ruffled Geoffrey Charles's curly head. Then a pang went through her that at this time to-morrow she would not be there to read to him.

The windows of the big parlour were open, and the July sun lay across the room. Elizabeth sat embroidering a waistcoat, with dusty sun bars touching colour in her beige silk frock. Aunt Agatha, having no truck with fresh air, crouched before the small fire she insisted on their keeping and drowsed like a tired old cat, the Bible, this being Sunday, open loosely in her lap. She did not move at all, but every now and then her eyes would open sharply as if she had heard a mouse in the wainscot. Geoffrey Charles, in a velvet suit and long velvet trousers, was a weight on Verity's knees where she sat by the window in the half shadow of a lace curtain. Francis was somewhere about the farm. In the two topped beech trees across the lawn pigeons were cooing.

Verity finished the story and slid Geoffrey Charles gently to the floor.

'There is mining in his blood, Elizabeth,' she said. 'No other story will suit.'

Elizabeth smiled without looking up.

'When he grows up conditions may have changed.' Verity rose. 'I do not think I will go to Evensong. I have a headache.'

'It will be with sitting in the sun. You sit too much in the sun, Verity.'

'I must go now and see about the wine. You can never trust Mary to look at it, for she falls into a daydream when she should not.'

'I'll come with you,' said Geoffrey Charles. 'Let me help you, eh?'

While she was busy in the kitchen Francis came in. This summer he had been trying to help about the farm. The work somehow did not suit him; it sat bleakly on his nature. Geoffrey Charles ran towards him but, seeing the expression on his father's face, changed his mind and ran back to Verity.

Francis said: 'Tabb is the only man left with any farming in him. Ellery is worse than useless. He was told to rebuild the hedge in the sheep field, and it has broke in a week. It has taken us best part of an hour to get the flock back. I'll turn the fellow off.'

'Ellery has been a miner since he was nine.'

'That's the whole trouble,' Francis said wryly. He looked at his hands, which were caked with dirt. 'We do our best for these local people, but how can you expect miners to become hedgers and ditchers overnight?'

'Are the oats undamaged?'

'Yes, thanks be. By a mercy the first sheep turned down the lane instead of up.'

The oats were to be cut next week. She would not be here for it. She could hardly believe that.

'I shall not come to church this evening, Francis. I have a headache. I think it's the warm weather.'

'I'm much of a mind to stay away myself,' he said.

'Oh, you can't do that.' She tried to hide her alarm. 'They're expecting you.'

'Elizabeth can go by herself. She will stand for the family well enough.'

Verity bent over the boiling wine and skimmed it. 'Mr Odgers would be heartbroken. He was telling me only last week that he always chooses the shortest psalms and preaches a special sermon for Evensong to please you.'

Francis went out without replying, and Verity found that her hands were trembling. Geoffrey Charles's chatter, which had broken out again when his father went, was a tinkling noise that came to her from a distance. She had chosen Sunday at four as the only time of the week when she could be sure of Francis's being out. His movements these last months had been unpredictable; to this conventional habit he had been faithful. . . .

'Auntie Verity!' cried the boy. 'Auntie Verity! Why don't you?'

'I can't listen to you now, sweetheart,' she said abruptly. 'Please leave me alone.' She tried to take hold of herself, went into the next kitchen, where Mary Bartle was sitting and spoke to her for a few minutes.

'Auntie Verity. Auntie Verity. Why aren't any of you going to church this afternoon?'

'I am not. Your father and mother will be going.'

'But Father just said he was not.'

'Never mind. You stay and help Mary with the wine. Be careful you don't get in her way.'

'But if ——'

She turned quickly from the kitchen and, instead of walking through the house, went quickly across the courtyard with its disused fountain and came in at the big hall. She ran up the stairs. It might be the last time she would see Geoffrey Charles, but there was no chance of saying good-bye.

In her bedroom she went quickly to the window. From this corner of it, by pressing her face against the glass, she could just see the drive by which Francis and Elizabeth would walk to church – if they were going.

Very faintly in the distance the bells had begun to ring. Number three was slightly cracked and Francis always said it set his teeth on edge. Francis would take ten minutes or a quarter of an hour to put on clean linen. She expected that at this moment he and Elizabeth were debating whether he should go or not. Elizabeth would want him to go. Elizabeth must make him go.

She sat there stilly on the window seat, a curious chill creeping into her body from the touch of the glass. She couldn't for a second take her eyes from that corner of the drive.

She knew exactly how the bell ringers would look, sweating there in the enclosed space of the tower. She knew how each one of the choir would look, fumbling in the pews for their psalters, exchanging whispers, talking more openly when she did not come. Mr Odgers would be bustling about in his surplice, poor, thin, harassed little fellow. They would all miss her, not merely to-night but in the future. And surely all the people whom she visited, the sick and the crippled, and the women struggling, overburdened with their families. . . .

She felt the same about her own family. Had times been good she would have left with a much freer heart. Elizabeth was not strong, and it would mean another woman to help Mrs Tabb. More expense when every shilling counted. And no one could do just what she had done, holding all the strings of the house economically together, keeping a tight but friendly hold.

Well, what other way was open? She couldn't expect Andrew to wait longer. She had not seen him in the three months since the ball, all word having gone through Demelza. She had already put off her flight once because of Geoffrey Charles's illness. It was almost as bad now, but leave she must or stay for ever.

Her heart gave a leap. Elizabeth was walking down the drive, tall and slender and so graceful in her silk frock and straw hat and cream parasol. Surely she could not be going alone. . . .

Francis came into view. . . .

She got up from the window. Her cheek had stuck to the glass and it tingled sharply with returning blood. She looked unsteadily round the room. She knelt and from under the bed drew out her bag. Geoffrey Charles would still be running about, but she knew how to avoid him.

With the bag she came to the door, stared back round the room. The sun was shining aslant the tall old window. She slipped quickly out and leaned back against the door trying to get her breath. Then she set off towards the back stairs.

Having given way to Elizabeth and made the effort to go to church, Francis felt a slow change of mood. This country farmer-squire life he led left him bored and frustrated almost to death. He longed for the days he had lost.

But now and then, since all things are relative, his boredom waned and he forgot his frustration. It was the more strange to-day since he had been so angry over the sheep; but the afternoon was so perfect that it left no room in a man's soul for discontent. Walking here with the sun-warmed air on his face he had come up against the fact that it was good just to be alive.

There was perhaps a certain pleasure in finding most of the congregation waiting outside for them, ready to bob or touch their hats as they came by. After grubbing about the farm all week one was curiously grateful for this buttress to one's self-esteem.

Even the informal sight of Jud Paynter sitting on one of the distant gravestones drinking a mug of ale was not to be cavilled at.

The church was warm but did not smell so strongly as usual of mildew and worm and stale breath. The thin little curate bobbing about like an earwig was not an active irritation; and Joe Permewan, rasping away at the bass viol as if it were a tree trunk, was worth liking as well as laughing at. Joe, they all knew, was no angel and got drunk Saturday nights, but he always sawed his way back to salvation on a Sunday morning.

They had said the psalms and read the lessons and echoed the prayers, and Francis had been gently dozing off to sleep when the sudden bang of the church door roused him. A new worshipper had come in.

Jud had been to France for a couple of nights and had been merrying himself on the share-out. Sobriety never turned him to his Maker, but as always when the drink was in him he felt the urge to reform. And to reform not only himself but all men. He felt the fraternal pull. This afternoon he had wandered from the kiddleys and was in fresh fields.

As Mr Odgers gave out the psalm he came slowly down the aisle, fingering his cap and blinking in the dark. He took a seat and dropped his cap, then he bent to pick it up and knocked over the stick of old Mrs Carkeek sitting next to him. After the clatter had died he pulled out a large red rag and began to mop his fringe.

'Some hot,' he said to Mrs Carkeek, thinking to be polite.

She took no notice but stood up and began to sing.

Everyone in fact was singing, and the people in the gallery by the chancel steps were making the most noise of all and playing instruments just like a party. Jud sat where he was, mopping himself and staring round the church. All this was very new to him. He looked on it in a detached and wavering light.

Presently the psalm was done and everybody sat down. Jud was still staring at the choir.

'What're all they women doin' up there?' he muttered, leaning over and breathing liquorously on Mrs Carkeek.

'Sh-sh. Tis the choir,' she whispered back.

'What, they, the choir? Be they nearer Heaven than we folk?'

Jud brooded a minute. He was feeling kindly but not as kindly as all that. 'Mary Ann Tregaskis. What she done to be nearer Heaven than we?'

'Ssh! Ssh!' said several people around him.

He had not noticed that Mr Odgers had come to be standing in the pulpit.

Jud blew his nose and put the rag away in his pocket. He turned his attention to Mrs Carkeek, who was sitting primly fingering her cotton gloves.

'Ow's your old cow?' he whispered. 'Calved yet, have she?'

Mrs Carkeek seemed to find a flaw in one of the gloves and gave it all her attention.

'Reckon 'er's going to be one of the awkward ones. Reckon ye did no good by yerself, buyin' of 'er from old Uncle Ben. Slippery ole twitch, he be, and in the choir at that. . . .'

Suddenly a voice spoke loudly, as it were just above his head. It quite startled him, seeing that everyone else seemed afraid of speaking a word.

'My text is from Proverbs Twenty-three, verse Thirty-one. "Look not thou upon the wine when it is red. At the last it stingeth like an adder and biteth like a serpent."'

Jud raised his head and saw Mr Odgers in a sort of wooden box with a sheaf of papers in his hands and an old pair of spectacles on his nose.

'My friends,' said Mr Odgers, looking round, 'I have chosen the text for this week after due thought and anxious prayer. My reason for so doing is that on Thursday next we celebrate Sawle Feast. As you all know, this holiday has long been the occasion not merely for harmless healthy jollification but for excessive indulgence in drink. . . .'

'Earear,' said Jud, not quite to himself.

Mr Odgers broke off and looked down severely at the bald old man sitting just below him. After staring for a moment and hearing nothing more he went on:

'For excessive indulgence in drink. It is my plea this evening to the members of the congregation that on Thursday next they should set a shining example in the parish. We have to remember, dear friends, that this feast day is no time for drunkenness and debauchery; for it was instituted to commemorate the landing of our patron saint, St Sawle, from Ireland, who came to convert the heathens of west Cornwall. It was in the fourth century that he floated over from Ireland on a millstone and ——'

'On a what?' Jud asked.

'On a millstone,' Mr Odgers said, forgetting himself. 'It is a historical fact that he landed ——'

'Well, I only axed!' whispered Jud in irritation to the man behind, who had tapped him on the shoulder.

'*Sanctus Sawlus*,' said Mr Odgers, 'that is the motto of our church, and it should be a motto and a precept for our daily lives. One which we bear with us as St Sawle brought it to our shores ——'

'On a millstone,' muttered Jud to Mrs Carkeek. 'Who ever 'eard of a man floating on a millstone. Giss along! Tedn sense, tedn reasonable, tedn right, tedn proper, tedn true!'

'You will see that we have with us to-day,' said Mr Odgers, rashly accepting the challenge, 'one who habitually looks upon the wine when it is red. So the Devil enters into him and leads him into a house of God to flaunt his wickedness in our faces ——'

''Ere,' said Jud unsteadily. 'I aren't no different not from them up there. What you got in the choir, eh? Naught but drunkers and whores' birds! Look at old Uncle Ben Tregeagle with 'is ringlets settin' up there all righteous. And he'd do down a poor old widow woman by sellin' 'er a cow what he know is going to misfire.'

The man behind grasped his arm. 'Here, you come on out.'

Jud thrust him back in his seat with the flat of his hand.

'I aren't doing no harm! Tes that little owl up there as be doing the harm. 'Im an' his whores' birds. Tellin' a wicked ole yarn about a man *floating* on a millstone. . . .'

'Come along, Paynter,' said Francis, who had been urged by Elizabeth. 'Air your grievances outside. If you come disturbing us in church you are likely to end up in gaol.'

Jud's bloodshot eyes travelled over Francis. Injured, he said: 'What for d'ye turn me out, eh? I'm a fisherman now, not nobody's servant, an' I know millstones no more float than fly.'

Francis took his arm. 'Come along, man.'

Jud detached his arm. 'I'll go,' he said with dignity. He added loudly: 'Tes a poor murky way ye take to repentance by followin' the likes of he. Ye'll go to the furnace, sure as me name's Jud Paynter. The flesh'll sweal off of yer bones. A fine lot of dripping ye'll make. Especially old Mrs Grubb, there, 'oo's takin' up two seats wi' her fat! And Char Nanfan in the choir expectin' of 'er third!'

Two large men began to lead him up the aisle.

''Ullo, Mrs Metz, buried any more husbands, 'ave ee? Why and there's Johnnie Kimber as stole a pig. And little Betty Coad. Well, well. Not wed yet, Betty? Tes 'igh time . . .'

They got him to the door. Then he shook himself free and sent out a last blast.

'Twon't always be the same as this, friends. There's doings in France, friends. There's riots and bloody murder! They've broke open the prison an' the Governor's 'ead they've stuck on a pole! There'll be bonfires for some folk here afore ever they die! I tell ee ——'

The door slammed behind him and only distant shouting could be heard as he was led to the lych gate.

People slowly began to settle down again. Francis, half annoyed, half amused, picked up a couple of prayer books and returned to his pew.

'Well,' said Mr Odgers, mopping his brow, 'as I was saying, quite apart from the – er – legend or – er – miracle of St Sawle . . .'

Chapter two

THEY WALKED HOME with Mr and Mrs Odgers. Francis admitted the arguments of his womenfolk that, with ten children to feed, this was probably the only square meal the Odgers got in a week (and this not so immensely square as it had once been); but it did not make them any better company. He would not have minded so much if they had been less agreeable. Sometimes he twisted his own opinions just to take a contrary view and found amusement in watching Odgers's acrobatics in following. One thing the Odgers were obstinately determined not to do and that was fall out with the Poldarks.

They walked home in twos, the ladies on ahead, the gentlemen pacing behind. Oh, Lord, thought Francis, if only the man could play hazard and had money to lose.

'That fellow Paynter is going to the dogs,' he said. 'I wonder why my cousin got rid of him? He stood enough ill behaviour from him in the past.'

'It was some scandal he spoke, so I heard. The man is a thorough-going scoundrel, sir. He deserves to be put in the stocks. I do not think the congregation ever settled down proper after he left.'

Francis suppressed a smile. 'I wonder what he had to say of France. Was he making it all up, I wonder?'

'There has been some story about, Mr Poldark. My wife in the course of her parish duties had occasion to visit Mrs Janet Trencrom – you know, the niece-by-marriage of *the* Mr Trencrom. Mrs Trencrom said —— Now what were her words? Maria! What was it Mrs Trencrom told you?'

'Oh, well, Mrs Trencrom said they were full of it in Cherbourg, but of course it will have been magnified. She said that French prison – what is it called? – was overthrown by rioters about Tuesday or Wednesday last and the Governor and many of his men slaughtered.'

'I query the truth of it,' Francis said, after a moment.

'I trust there is *no* truth in it,' Mr Odgers said vehemently. 'Mob law is always to be deplored. That man, Paynter, for instance, is a dangerous type. He would have the houses about our ears if we gave him half a chance.'

Francis said: 'When there are riots in this country they are not led or incited by tipsy old men. There, Odgers, look at that field of oats. If the weather holds we shall begin to cut to-morrow.'

At Trenwith Francis led the little curate out into the garden while the ladies tidied themselves. When they went into the winter parlour for supper and Mrs Odgers's small, anxious grey eyes were glistening at the sight of all the food, Francis said:

'Where's Verity?'

'I went to her bedroom as soon as I came back, but she was not there,' Elizabeth said.

Francis put his mouth against Aunt Agatha's long pointed ear.

'Have you seen Verity?'

'What? Eh?' Aunt Agatha rested on her sticks. 'Verity? Out, I believe.'

'Out? Why should she go out at this time?'

'Leastwise, I fancy she be. She came and kissed me an hour gone and she had on her cloak and things. I didn't gather what she said; folk mumble so. If they was learned to talk out like they was learned in my young days there'd be less trouble in the world. No mines working. I tell ye, Francis, tis a poor world for the old and aged. There's some that would go to the wall. Nay, Odgers, I tell you myself, there's little comfort in ——'

'Did she say where she was going?'

'What? Verity? I tell you I could catch nothin' she said. But she left some sort of letter for you both.'

'A letter?' said Elizabeth, jumping at the truth far before Francis. 'Where is it?'

'Well, aren't you goin' to ask to see it? Damme, no curiosity these days. I wonder what I did with it. It was just here in my shawl.' She hobbled to the table and sat down, her wrinkled old hands fumbling in the laces and folds of her clothes. Mr Odgers waited impatiently until he too could sit down and begin on the cold fowl and the gooseberry pies.

A couple of lice were all she disturbed at first, but presently one claw came trembling out with a sealed paper between finger and thumb.

'I thought it smelt somewhat of an insult puttin' wax on a letter I was to carry,' said the old lady. 'Eh? What d'you say? As if I cared for Miss Verity's secrets. . . . I bring to mind well the day she was born. The winter o' fifty-nine. Twas just after the rejoicings on the takin' of Quebec, and me and your father had rid over to a bearbaiting at St Ann's. We'd scarce got home and inside the house when ——'

'Read this,' said Francis, thrusting the open letter towards Elizabeth. His small features were pinched with a sudden uncontrollable anger.

Her eyes glanced swiftly over it.

I have known and loved you all my life, dear Francis [it ran], and you Elizabeth more than seven years, so I pray you will both understand the grief and loss I feel that this should be our Parting. For three months and more I have been torn two ways by loyalties and effections which lived and grew in me with equal Strength, and which in happier circumstances could have existed without conflict. That of the two I have chosen to tear up the deeper rooted and follow after a Life and destiny of my own with a man whom you distrust may seem to you the height of folly, but I pray you will not look on it as a desertion. I am to live in Falmouth now. Oh, my dears, I should have been so happy if only distance were to separate us. . . .

'Francis!' Elizabeth said. 'Where are you going?'

'To see how she went – if there is time to bring her back!' He left the room with a sudden swing.

'What's to do?' asked Agatha. 'What's got him? What does the note say?'

'Forgive me.' Elizabeth turned to the gaping Odgers. 'There is —— I am afraid there has been some misunderstanding. Do please sit down and have your supper. Don't wait for us. I am afraid we shall be a little time.' She followed Francis.

The four remaining house servants were in the big kitchen. The Tabbs, just back from church, were telling the Bartles about Jud Paynter. The laughter stopped suddenly when they saw Francis.

'At what time did Miss Verity leave this house?'

'Oh, an hour and a half gone, sur,' said Bartle, glancing curiously at his master's face. 'Just after you'd gone church, sur.'

'What horse did she take?'

'Her own, sur. Ellery went with her.'

'Ellery. . . . Was she carrying anything?'

'I dunno, sur. He's back in the stables now, just giving the 'orses their fodder.'

'Back . . . ?' Francis checked himself, and went swiftly out to the stables. The horses were all there. 'Ellery!' he shouted. The man's startled face appeared round the door.

'Sur?'

'I understand you have been riding with Miss Verity. Is she back with you?'

'No, sur. She changed 'orses at Bargus Cross. A gentleman was waiting for her there with a spare 'orse, and she changed over to 'is and sent me back.'

'What sort of gentleman?'

'Seafaring I should guess, sur. Leastwise, by his clothes . . .'

An hour and a half. They would already be beyond Truro. And they could take two or three different routes. So she had come to this. She had made up her mind to mate herself with this wife-kicking drunkard, and nothing should stop her. Blamey had the Devil's power over her. No matter what his record or his ways, he had but to whistle and she would run.

When Francis got back to the kitchen Elizabeth was there.

'No, mistress,' Mary Bartle was saying. 'I don't know nothing about that, mistress.'

'Ellery is back without her,' Francis said. 'Now, Tabb; and you, Bartle; and you women; I want to hear the truth. Has Miss Verity been receiving letters through your hands?'

'No, sur. Oh, no, sur,' they chorused.

'Come, let's talk it over quietly,' Elizabeth suggested. 'There is little we can do at present.'

But Francis was bitterly careless of appearances. He knew it must all come out in a day or two. He would be the butt of the district: the man who tried to stop his sister's courting, and she calmly eloping one afternoon while he was at church.

'There must have been some contact unknown to us,' he said sharply to Elizabeth. 'Have any of you seen a seafaring man hanging about the grounds?'

No, they had seen nothing.

'She has been out and about visiting poor people in Sawle and Grambler, you know,' Elizabeth said.

'Has anyone been calling here unknown to us?' Francis demanded. 'Someone who saw Miss Verity and might have carried a message?'

No, they had seen no one.

'Mistress Poldark from Nampara has been over often enough,' said Mary Bartle. 'By the kitchen way ———'

Mrs Tabb trod on her toe, but it was too late. Francis stared at Mary Bartle for a moment or two, then went out, slamming the door behind him.

Elizabeth found him in the large parlour standing, hands behind back, at the window, looking over the garden.

She closed the door to let him know she was there, but he did not speak.

'We must accept the fact of her going, Francis,' she said. 'It is her choice. She is grown-up and a free agent. In the last resort we could never have stopped her if she had chosen to go. I could only have wished she had done it openly if she was to do it at all.'

'Damn Ross!' Francis said between his teeth. 'This is his doing, his and that impudent brat he married. Don't you see . . . he – he has stored this up all these years. Five years ago, knowing we disapproved, he gave them leave to meet at his house. He encouraged Verity in the teeth of all we said. He has never got over his defeat. He never liked to be the loser in anything. I wondered how Verity met this fellow again; no doubt it was at Ross's contrivance. And for these last months after my quarrel with Blamey, knowing I had broken the link again, he has been acting as agent for Blamey, keeping the skunk's interests warm and using Demelza as a postman and go-between!'

'I think you're a little hasty,' Elizabeth said. 'So far we don't even know that Demelza is concerned in it, let alone Ross.'

'Of course,' he said passionately, still not turning from the window, 'you will always stand up for Ross in all things. You never imagine that Ross could do anything to our disadvantage.'

'I am not standing up for anyone,' Elizabeth said, a spark of anger in her voice. 'But it is the merest justice not to condemn people unheard.'

'The facts shout aloud for anyone with half an ear. There's no other way Blamey could have arranged her flight. She has had no post. I've seen to that. Demelza alone could not have done it, for she never knew Blamey in the old days. Ross has been riding about all over the countryside on his damned copper concerns. What more easy than to call in at Falmouth from time to time and bear a message both ways.'

'Well there's nothing we can do about it now. She is gone. I don't know what we shall do without her. The busiest season of the year; and Geoffrey Charles will miss her terribly.'

'We'll get along. Be sure of that.'

'We should go back to the Odgers,' Elizabeth said. 'They'll think us very rude. There's nothing to do to-night, Francis.'

'I want no supper just yet. They'll not mind my absence so long as they're fed themselves.'

'What must I tell them?'

'The truth. It will be all over the district in a day or two anyway. Ross should be pleased.'

There was a tap on the door before Elizabeth could open it.

'If you please, sir,' said Mary Bartle, 'Mr Warleggan has called.'

'Who?' said Francis. 'Devil take it! I wonder if he has some news.'

George came in, well groomed, polite, heavy in the shoulders and formidable. A rare visitor these days.

'Ah, well, I'm glad to find you have finished supper. Elizabeth, that simple dress suits you to ——'

'Good God, we haven't yet begun it!' Francis said. 'Have you brought news of Verity?'

'Is she away?'

'Two hours since. She has gone to that skunk Blamey!'

George glanced quickly from one to the other, sizing up their moods, not pleased by his brusque greeting. 'I'm sorry. Is there anything I can do?'

'No, it's hopeless,' Elizabeth said. 'I have told Francis we must swallow it. He has been quite raving since. We have the Odgers here and they'll think we have all gone crazy. Forgive me, George, I must go and see if they have begun supper.'

She swept past George, whose admiring glance flickered after her. Then be said: 'You should know, Francis, that women can't be reasoned with. They are a headstrong sex. Let her have her bit, dear boy. If she falls at a fence it will be none of your doing.'

Francis pulled at the bell. 'I can't face those two agreeable sheep for supper. Your arrival on a Sunday evening was so unexpected that for a moment I hoped . . . How I hate the thought of that fellow getting his way with her after all!'

'I have spent the day at the Teagues and was feeling monstrous tired of the lady's chatter, so I thought of an agreeable duty to perform at Trenwith. Poor Patience. There she sits on the hook, waiting for me to bite; a nice enough girl in an oncoming sort of way, but no true breeding about her. I'll swear her legs are on the short side. The woman I marry must not only have the right blood but show it.'

'Well, you have come to a household that'll offer you no graces to-night, George. Oh, Mrs Tabb, serve supper in here. Bring half of one of the boiled fowls if the Odgers have not yet picked 'em clean, and some cold ham and a pie. I tell you, George, there is that in this flight which makes me more than commonly angry.'

George patted down the front of his silk flowered waistcoat. 'No doubt, dear boy. I see I could not have called on a more untimely night. But since we have you so seldom in Truro these days I'm compelled to wait on you and mix duty with pleasure.'

It reached Francis's taut and preoccupied mind that George was leading up to something. As his chief creditor George was in a dangerously powerful position; and feeling had not been too good between them since the gambling affray in April.

'An *agreeable* duty?'

'Well, it may be considered so. It has to do with Sanson and the matter you raised some time since.'

So far neither Francis nor anyone else had got anything out of the miller. He had left Truro the day following Ross's exposure and was believed to be in London. His mills, it turned out, belonged to a company and that company to other companies.

George took out his gold-mounted snuffbox and tapped it.

'We have talked this over several times, my father and I. While there's no obligation in it, Sanson's conduct is a stain we feel rather deeply. As you know, we have no ancestors to bring us repute; we must make our own.'

'Yes, yes, you are clear enough,' Francis said briefly. It was seldom that George mentioned his humble beginnings.

'Well, as I told you in May, many of your bills given to Matthew Sanson have found their way into Cary's hands. He has always been somewhat the treasurer of the family, as Matthew was the black sheep, and your bills were accepted by Cary in exchange for cash advances made to Matthew.'

Francis grunted. 'I take that as no advantage.'

'Well, yes, it is. We have decided between us as a family to cancel one half of all the drafts which came into Cary's hands from Matthew. It will not be a crushing matter, but it will be a token of our will to undo what wrong has been done. As I say, not a big thing. About twelve hundred pounds.'

Francis flushed. 'I can't take your charity, George.'

'Charity be hanged. You may have lost the money unfairly in the first place. From our viewpoint we wish it, to re-establish our integrity. It is really nothing at all to do with you.'

Mrs Tabb came in with the supper. She set up a table by the window, put her tray on it and two chairs beside it. Francis watched her. Half his mind was still battling with the desertion of Verity, the perfidy of Ross – the other half facing this princely gesture from a man he had begun to distrust. It *was* a princely gesture and one that no stubborn pricky pride must force him to refuse.

When Mrs Tabb had gone he said: 'You mean – the money would be put to reducing my debt to you?'

'That's for you to decide. But I'd suggest one half of it should go to reducing the debt and the other half should be a cash payment.'

Francis's flush deepened. 'It is very handsome of you. I don't know quite what to say.'

'Say nothing more about it. It's not a comfortable subject between friends, but I had to explain.'

Francis dropped into his chair. 'Take some supper, George. I'll open a bottle of my father's brandy after in honour of the occasion. No doubt it will loosen up my anger over Verity and make me a more easy companion. You'll stay the night?'

'Thank you,' said George.

They supped.

In the winter parlour Elizabeth had just excused herself and left again. Mr Odgers was finishing up the raspberry syllabub and Mrs Odgers the almond cake. With only the old lady's eyes on them their manners had eased up.

'I wonder if he means to do the honest thing by her,' Mrs Odgers said. 'They could not get married to-night, and you never can tell with these sailors. He may well have a Portugee wife for all she knows. What do you think, Clarence?'

'Um?' said Mr Odgers, with his mouth full.

'Little Verity,' said Aunt Agatha. 'Little Verity. Imagine little Verity going off like that.'

'I wonder what the feeling will be in Falmouth,' said Mrs Odgers. 'Of course in a port morals are always more lax. And they may go through some marriage ceremony just to pull the wool over people's eyes. Anyway, men who kill their first wives should be forbidden ever to marry again. Don't you agree, Clarence?'

'Um,' said Mr Odgers.

'Little Verity,' said Aunt Agatha. 'She was always obstinate like her mother. I bring to mind when she was six or seven, the year we held the masquerade ball . . .'

In the large parlour the brandy had come.

'I can't bear these sneaking underhand dealings,' Francis said bitterly. 'If he had had the guts to come here and face me out maybe I should not have liked that, but I shouldn't have held him in such dead contempt.' After his estrangement from George the reaction was carrying him back beyond the old intimacy. As good as in his pocket was six hundred pounds he had never thought to see again – and the same amount cut from his debts. Never could it have been more welcome than to-day. During the coming months it might just make all the difference. It meant an easing of their life and the strain of bitter economy. A grand gesture which deserved the grand recognition. Adversity showed up one's friends.

'But all along,' he continued, 'that has been his way. At the outset he went sneaking behind our backs and meeting the girl at Nampara – with Ross's connivance. All the time it has been this sneaking, sneaking. I've half a mind to ride to Falmouth to-morrow and flush them from their love nest.'

'And no doubt you'd find he had just left for Lisbon and she with him.' George tasted the brandy on his lips. 'No, Francis, leave them be. It is no good putting yourself in the wrong by trying to force her to return. The harm is done. Maybe she'll soon be crying to come back.'

Francis got up and began to light the candles. 'Well, she shall not come back here, not if she cries for a year! Let her go to Nampara, where they have fathered this thing. Damn them, George.' Francis turned, the taper showing up his angry face. 'If there is one thing in this that cuts me to the root it is Ross's cursed underhand interference. Damn it, I might have expected a greater loyalty and friendship from my only cousin! What have I ever done to him that he should go behind my back in this fashion!'

'Well,' said George, 'I suppose you married the girl he wanted, didn't you?'

Francis stopped again and stared at him. 'Oh, yes. Oh, yes . . . But that's long ago.' He blew out the taper. 'That was patched up long since. He is happily married himself; more happily than . . . There would be no point in feeling a grudge on that score.'

George looked out on the darkening garden. The candles threw his blurred hunched shadow on the wall.

'You know Ross better than I, Francis, so I can't guide you. But many people – many people we accept on their face value have strange depths. I've found it so. It may be that Ross is one such. I can't judge, but I do know that all my own overtures towards him have met with rebuffs.'

Francis came back to the table. 'Aren't you on friendly terms? No, I suppose not. How have you offended him?'

'That's something I can't guess. But I do know when his mine was opened all the other venturers were for the business being put through our bank, yet he fought tooth and nail until he got them to accept Pascoe's. Then sometimes remarks he has made have been repeated to me; they were the words of a man with a secret resentment. Finally there is this wildcat scheme he has launched of some copper-smelting company which privately is directed at us.'

'Oh, I don't think exactly at you,' Francis said. 'Its aim is to get fairer prices for the.mines.'

George glanced covertly at him. 'I'm not at all upset about it, for the scheme will fail through lack of money. Still, it shows an enmity towards me which I don't feel I deserve – any more than you deserve to have had this betrayal of the best interests of your family.'

Francis stared down at the other man, and there was a long silence. The clock in the corner struck seven.

'I don't think the scheme need necessarily fail through lack of money,' Francis said whitely. 'There are a good many important interests behind it. . . .'

Chapter three

IT WAS AN easterly sky, and as they reached Falmouth the sun was setting like a Chinese lantern, swollen and crimson and monstrous and decorated with ridges of curly cloud. The town was a grey smudge climbing the edge of the bay.

As they went down the hill Andrew said: 'Your last letter left all to me, my dear; so I trust what I have done you'll find to your liking.'

'I'm willing to do whatever you say.'

'The wedding is set for eleven to-morrow – at the Church of King Charles the Martyr. I took a licence from Parson Freakes yesterday morning. Just my old landlady and Captain Brigg will be there as witnesses. It will be as quiet as ever possible.'

'Thank you.'

'As for to-night' – Andrew cleared his throat – 'I had thought at first the best would be to take a room at one of the inns. But as I went round they all seemed too shoddy to house you.'

'I shall not mind.'

'I misliked the thought of you being there alone with perhaps noisy and drunken men about.' His blue eyes met hers. 'It wasn't right.'

She flushed slightly. 'It wouldn't have mattered.'

'So instead I'd like you to go to your new home, where Mrs Stevens will be there to see to your needs. I'll sleep in my ship.'

She said: 'Forgive me if I seem dull . . . It isn't that at all. It's only the wrench of leaving the things I've loved so long.'

'My dear, I know how you must feel. But we have a week before I need sail. I believe it will all seem different to you before I go.'

Another silence fell. 'Francis is unpredictable,' she said suddenly. 'In some ways, though I shall miss them so much, I wish we were further than a score of miles. It is within too-easy riding distance of some quarrelsome impulse.'

'If he comes I will soon cool it for him.'

'I know, Andrew. But that is above all what I don't want.'

He smiled slightly. 'I was very patient at the Assembly. At need I can be patient again.'

Sea gulls were flying and crying. The smell of the sea was different from home, tanged with salt and seaweed and fish. The sun set before they reached the narrow main street, and the harbour was brimming with the limpid colours of the afterglow.

People, she thought, stared at them. No doubt he was a well-known figure in the town. Would the prejudice be very strong against him? If any remained, then it was her task to break it down. There could clearly be none against her.

She glanced sidelong at him for a moment, and the thought came into her head that they had met not three dozen times in all their lives. Had she things to face that she knew nothing of yet? Well, if they loved each other there was no other consideration big enough to stand beside it.

They stopped and he helped her down and they went into the porticoed house. Mrs Stevens was at the door and greeted Verity pleasantly enough, though not without a trace of speculation and jealousy.

Verity was shown the dining-room and kitchen on the ground floor, the graceful parlour and bedroom on the first floor, the two attic bedrooms above, which were for the children when they were home, these children she had never seen. Esther, sixteen, was being educated by relatives; James, fifteen, a midshipman in the Navy. Verity had had so much opposition to face at home that she had hardly yet had time to consider the opposition she might find here.

Back in the parlour Andrew was standing looking out across the glimmering colours of the harbour. He turned as she came and stood beside him at the window. He took her hand. The gesture brought comfort.

'Which is your ship, Andrew?'

'She's well back from here, in St Just's Pool. The tallest of the three. I doubt if you can make her out in this light.'

'Oh, yes, she looks beautiful. Can I see over her sometime?'

'To-morrow if you wish.' She suddenly felt his happiness. 'Verity, I'll go now. I have asked Mrs Stevens to serve your supper as soon as she can. You'll be tired from your ride and will not mind being quiet.'

'Can you not stay to supper?'

He hesitated. 'If you wish it.'

'Please. What a lovely harbour this is! I shall be able to sit here and see all the shipping go in and out and watch for your coming home.'

In a few minutes they went down into the little dining-room and ate boiled neck of mutton with capers, and raspberries and cream. An hour ago they had been very adult, making a rash gesture with strange caution, as if unable quite to free themselves of the restraints and hesitations grown with the years. But the candlelight loosed thoughts, softened doubts and discovered pride in their adventure.

They had never had a meal together before.

Net curtains were drawn across the windows, and figures crossed and recrossed them in the street outside. In the room they were a little below the level of the cobbles, and when a cart rumbled past the wheels showed up more than the driver.

They began to talk about his ship, and he told her of Lisbon, its chiming bells, the endless blazing sunlight, the unbelievable filth of the streets, the orange trees, the olive groves. Sometime she must go with him. Was she a good sailor?

She nodded eagerly, never having been to sea.

They laughed together, and a clock in the town began to strike ten. He got up.

'This is disgraceful, love. Compromising in the eyes of Mrs Stevens, I'm sure. She'll expect us to have eaten all her cakes.'

'I'm so glad you stayed,' she said. 'If you had gone before I should have felt very strange here alone.'

His self-disciplined face was very much unguarded just then. 'Last night I closed a book on my old life, Verity. To-morrow we'll open a new one. We must write it together.'

'That's what I want,' she said. 'I'm not at all afraid.'

He walked to the door, and then glanced at her still sitting at the table. He came back.

'Good night.'

He bent to kiss her cheek, but she offered him her lips. They stayed so a moment; and his hand on the table came up and lay on her shoulder.

'If ill comes to you, Verity, it will not be my doing. I swear it. Good night, love.'

'Good night, Andrew, my love, good night.'

He broke away and left her. She heard him run upstairs for his hat and then come down again and go out. She saw him pass the window. She stayed there for a very long time, her eyes half closed and her head resting back against the high-backed chair.

Chapter four

AT ABOUT THE time Verity was climbing the stairs with a candle to sleep in her new bed, Mark Daniel was taking up his pitch in Wheal Leisure Mine.

With him was one of the younger Martin boys, Matthew Mark, who was there to help him by carrying away the 'dead' ground as he picked it and dumping it in a pit in the near-by cave. The air was so bad in here that their hempen candles would not burn properly; so that they worked in more than half darkness. The walls of the tunnel streamed with moisture and there was water and slush underfoot. But Matthew Mark thought himself lucky to work for so experienced a man for sixpence a day – or night – and he was learning fast. In another few years he would be bidding for a pitch of his own.

Mark never had much to say when he was working, but to-night he had not spoken a word. The boy did not know what was wrong and was afraid to ask. Being only just nine, he might not have understood quite what was gnawing at his companion even if he had been told.

For days now Mark had given up trying to believe there was nothing wrong. For weeks he had known in his heart but had said no to himself. The little signs had piled up, the hints from those who knew and did not dare, the sly glances; small by themselves, they had grown like snowflakes on a roof, weight to weight, until the roof crashed in.

He knew now, and he knew who.

She had been clever. He had always looked for signs of a man in the cottage but had never found any. He had tried to catch her out, but always she thought ahead of him. Her wits moved quick. The snow leopard was sharper than the black bear.

But in the wet weather of last week she had not been so clever. The ground had been so soft that even though she kept to the stony places there were marks here and there of her feet.

He dreaded this week of nightwork because it would bring him to some climax. The fear he felt in breaking out was because he could not shake his anger free from the clinging strands of his love. They still bound him; he struggled in a mesh with his grief.

The powder for blasting was needed now. He could go no farther with the pick. He said as much to Matthew and picked up his great hammer and the steel borer. With ease come from long practice he chose his place in the hard rock, drilled a deep hole in the face of the work, pulled out the borer and cleaned and dried the hole. Then he took up his case of powder and dropped powder in. Through the powder he pushed a tapering rod like an iron nail and filled up the mouth of the hole with clay, ramming it hard with his boring bar. This done, he pulled out the nail and into the thin hole threaded a hollow reed filled with powder, for a fuse.

He took off his hat, gently blew the smoky candle until it flickered into a flame and lit the reed. Then they both backed away round the first corner.

Mark counted twenty. Nothing. He counted another twenty. He counted fifty. Then he picked up his can and swore. In the darkness he had planted it against the wall and water had got into it.

'A misfire,' he said.

'Have a care, Mr Daniel,' Matthew said. Blasting was the part of mining he did not like. 'Give it a while.'

But Mark had grunted and was already walking up to the charge. The boy followed.

As Mark drew out the reed there was a flash and a rumble and the rocks flew in his face. He put up hands to his eyes and fell back. The wall gave way.

The boy lost his head and turned and ran away, going for help. Then he checked himself and pushed his way through the choking black fumes to where Mark was trying to climb out from among the rocks.

He caught at his arm. 'Mr Daniel! Mr Daniel!'

'Get back, boy! There's only a part gone.'

But Matthew would not leave him and they groped their way to the bend in the tunnel.

Matthew blew on his candle, and in the flickering light stared at Mark. His gaunt face was black and striped with blood, his front hair and eyebrows singed.

'Your eyes, Mr Daniel. Are they all right?'

Mark stared at the candle. 'Aye; I can see.' There was another roar in the tunnel as the rest of the charge went off. Black smoke billowed out and around them. 'Take heed, boy, an' a warning that you always d'use the powder wi' a greaterer care.

'Your face. Thur's blood.'

Mark stared down at his hands. 'Tes these.' His left hand was bleeding from the palm and fingers. The dampness of the powder had caused the accident but it had saved his life. He took out a dirty rag and wrapped it round his head.

'We'll wait till the fumes clear, an' then we'll see what it's brought down.'

Matthew sat back on his heels and looked at the blood-streaked figure. 'You did ought to see surgeon. He's proper with wounds an' things.'

Mark got up sharply. 'Nay. I'd not go to him if I was dying.' He turned into the smoke.

They worked on for a time, but he found it hard to use his injured hand, which would not stop bleeding. His face was stinging and sore.

After an hour he said: 'Reckon I'll go up to grass for a bit. You'd best come too, boy. There's no good breathin' this black air if you've no need.'

Matthew followed him gladly enough. The nightwork tired him more than he would admit.

They reached the main shaft and climbed up it; the distance was nothing to Grambler and they were soon sniffing the fresh night air and hearing the rumble of the sea. There was a lovely biting sweetness in filling your lungs as you came up to grass. One or two men were about, and they clustered round Mark giving him advice.

He had come up to have a proper bandage put on and go below again. But as he stood there talking with the others and let his fingers be tied up, all the old trouble came back and he knew with angry panic that this was the moment for the test.

For a while he resisted, feeling it sprung on him too soon, that he had need to be prepared. Then he turned to Matthew and said:

'Run along home, boy. Twill be better for me not to go b'low again to-night.'

When Matthew Mark was out and working he never let himself think of sleep – it didn't do – but now he was overwhelmed. It was little after midnight. A whole six extra hours in bed! He waited respectfully for a moment to walk part way home with Mark, but another gruff word sent him off in the direction of Mellin Cottages.

Mark saw him out of sight, then briefly bade good night to the other men and followed. He had told them he didn't know whether to bother Dr Enys; but in fact his mind was quite made up. He knew just what he was going to do.

He walked quietly home. As the cottage showed up in the starlight he felt his chest grow tight. He would have prayed if he had been a praying man, for his own mistake, for Keren's trueness, for a new life of trust. He came to the door, reached out for the latch, grasped it, pressed.

The door opened.

Breathe hard now and clumsily go in; he couldn't hold his breath, it panted away as if he'd been running for his life. No stop to make a light but pass through into the bedroom. Shutters were closed, and in the dark with unhurt hand grope a way round the walls of the cottage – his cottage – to the bed. The corner, the rough blanket. Sit on the edge and hand move over bed for Keren – his Keren. She was not there.

With a deep grunt of pain he sat there knowing this was the end. His breath was in sobs. He sat and panted and sobbed. Then he got up.

Out in the night again a pause to rub fingers over his eyes, to look right and left, to sniff, to set off for Mingoose.

The Gatehouse looked in darkness. He made a circle, sizing it up. A chink of light in an upper window.

Stop and stare and try to fight down the pain. It was in his blood, beating through him. The door of the house.

And there he stopped. To hammer to be let in would give warning. Time to think before they opened. She might slip out another way. They both thought so much quicker. They'd brazen it out. This time he must have proof.

I'll wait, he thought.

He crept slowly away, his long back bent, until he was just right to watch the front door or the back.

I'll crouch here and wait.

The stars moved up the sky, climbing and turning on their endless roundabout. A gentle wind stirred and sighed among the bracken and the brake, stirred and moved and then lay down again to sleep. A cricket began to saw among the gorse, and somewhere overhead a night-hawk cried: a ghostly sound, the spirit of a long-dead miner walking sightless over his old land. Small animals stirred in the undergrowth. An owl settled on the roof top and harshly cried.

I'll wait.

Then in the east a faint yellow light showed, and there crept up into the sky the wasted slip of an old moon. It hung there sere and dry, climbed a little, and then began to set.

The door of the Gatehouse opened a few inches and Keren slipped out.

For once she was happy. Happy that this was only the first night of Mark's night core. Their way – hers and Dwight's – was still strange, touched with things which had never been in her first thoughts. Possessive and a little jealous, she found herself forced to allow a division of his loyalty. His work was his first love. She had reached him by taking an interest in his work. She held him by maintaining it.

Not that she really minded. In a way she enjoyed playing the role of sober helpmeet. Something like her old part in *Hilary Tempest*. She sometimes dreamed of herself as his wife – Mark out of the way – wholly charming in a workmanlike but feminine dress, helping Dwight in some serious strait. Her hands, she knew, would be cool and capable, her manner superbly helpful; he would be full of admiration for her afterwards; and not only he but all the gentry of the countryside. She would be talked of everywhere. She had heard all about Mistress Poldark having been a great success at the celebration ball, and quite a number of people had been riding over to see her since then. Keren could not think why.

It had gone to her head, for she'd thought fit last month to come the lady and drop a hint to Keren about being careful what she did; and Keren had resented it. Well, if she were so successful in society, Keren, as a doctor's wife, would go much further. She might not even stay a doctor's wife all her life. There was no limit to what might happen. A big, hairy elderly man, who had been over to the Poldarks one day, had met her as she crossed Nampara Combe, and he had given her more than a moment's look. When she knew he was a baronet and unmarried she'd been thankful for wearing that flimsy frock.

She ploughed through the rough undergrowth on her way back to the cottage. It had been the half after three by Dwight's clock, so there was nice time. As well not to run it too close. A mist had settled on the low ground between the two houses. She plunged into it as into a stream. Things were hung heavy with moisture; the damp touched her face and glistened on her hair. Some moonflowers showed among the scrub, and she picked one as she passed. She groped across the gully, climbed again and came out into the crystal-cool air.

So to-night as she lay naked in Dwight's arms she had encouraged him to talk: about the work of the day, about the little boy who had died of the malignant sore throat over at Marasanvose, about the results of his treatment on a woman in bed with an abscess, about his thoughts for the future. All this was like a cement to their passion. It had to be with him. She did not really mind.

The moon was setting as she reached the cottage, and dawn was blueing the east. Back the way she had come the gully was as if filled with a stream of milk. Everywhere else was clear.

She went in and turned to close the door. But as she did so a hand from outside came to press it open. 'Keren.'

Her heart stopped; and then it began to bang. It banged till it mounted to her head and seemed to split.

'Mark!' she whispered. 'You're home early. Is anything wrong?'

'Keren . . .'

'How dare you come startling me like this! I nearly died!'

Already she was thinking ahead of him, moving to attack and defeat his attack. But this time he had more than words to go on.

'Where've you been, Keren?'

'I?' she said. 'I couldn't sleep. I have had a pain. Oh, Mark, I had such a terrible pain. I cried for you. I thought perhaps you could have made me something warm to send it better. But I was all alone. I didn't know what to do. So I thought maybe a walk would help. If I'd known you was coming home early I'd have come to the mine to meet you.' In the half-dark her sharp eyes caught sight of the bandage on his hand. 'Oh, Mark, you're hurt! There's been an accident. Let me see!'

She moved to him, and he struck her in the mouth with his burnt hand, knocked her back across the room. She fell in a small injured heap.

'Ye dirty liar! Ye dirty liar!' His breath was coming in sobs again.

She wept with her hurt. A strange, kittenish, girlish weeping, so far from his own.

He moved over to her. 'Ye've been wi' Enys,' he said in a terrible voice.

She raised her head. 'Dirty yourself! Dirty coward! Striking a woman. Filthy beast! Get away from me! Leave me alone. I'll have you sent to prison, you! Get out!'

A faint light was coming in from the glimmering dawn; it fell on his singed and blackened face. Through the screen of her hands and hair she saw him, and at the sight she began to cry out.

'You've been wi' Enys, lying wi' Enys!' His voice climbed in great strides.

'I've not! I've not!' she screamed. 'Liar yourself! I went to see him about my pain. He's a doctor, ain't he? You filthy brute. I was in such pain.'

Even now the quick-thoughted lie gave him pause. Above all things he had always wanted to be fair, to do the right thing by her.

'How long was you there?'

'Oh . . . over an hour. He gave me something to take an' then had to wait an ——'

He said: 'I waited more'n three.'

She knew then that she must go and go quickly.

'Mark,' she said desperately, 'it isn't what you think. I swear before God it isn't. If you see him he'll explain. Let's go to him. Mark, he wouldn't leave me alone. He was always pestering me. Always and all the time. And then when once I yielded he threatened he'd tell you if I didn't go on. I swear it before God and my mother's memory. I hate him, Mark! I love only you! Go kill him if you want. He deserves it, Mark! I swear before God he took the advantage of me!'

She went on, babbling at him, throwing words at him, any words, pebbles at a giant, her only defence. She sprayed words, keeping his great anger away from her, twisting her brain this way and that. Then when she saw that it was going to avail no longer she sprang like a cat under his arm, leapt for the door.

He thrust out one great hand and caught her by the hair, hauled her screaming back into his arms.

She fought with all strength in her power, kicking, biting, scratching. He pushed her nails away from his eyes, accepting her bites as if they were no part of him. He pulled the cloth away from her throat, gripped it.

Her screaming stopped. Her eyes started tears, died, grew big. She knew there was death; but life called her, sweet life, all the sweet of youth, not yet gone. Dwight, the baronet, years of triumph, crying, dying.

She twisted and upset him and they fell against the shutter, whose flimsy catch gave way. They leaned together out of the window, she beneath him.

A summer morning. The glazing eyes of the girl he loved, the woman he hated; her face swollen now. Sickened, mad, his tears dropped on her face.

Loose his hold, but her beautiful face still stared. Cover it with a great hand, push it away, back.

Under his hand, coming from under his hand, a faint gentle click.

He fell back upon the floor of the cottage, groping, moaning upon the floor.

But she did not move.

There was no cloud in the sky. There was no wind. Birds were chirping and chattering. Of the second brood of young thrushes which Mark had watched hatch out in the stunted hawthorn tree only a timid one stayed; the others were out fluttering their feathers, shaking their heads, sharp with incentive, eyeing this strange new world.

The ribbon of milky mist still lay in the gully. It stretched down to the sea, and there were patches across the sand hills like steam from a kettle.

When light came full the sea was calm, and there seemed nothing to explain the roar in the night. The water was a pigeon's-egg blue with a dull terra-cotta haze above the horizon and a few pale carmine tips where the rising sun caught the ripples at the sand's edge.

The ugly shacks of Wheal Leisure were clear-cut, and a few men moving about among them in their drab clothes looked pink and handsome in the early light.

The mist stirred before the sun's rays, quickened with the warmth and melted and moved off to the low cliffs, where it crouched in the shade for a while before being thrust up and away.

A robin that Keren and Mark had tamed fluttered down to the open door, puffed out his little chest and hopped inside. But although the cottage was silent he did not like the silence, and after pecking here and there for a moment he hopped out. Then he saw one of his friends leaning out of the window, but she made no welcoming sound and he flew away.

The sun fell in at the cottage, strayed across the sanded floor, which was pitted and scraped with marks of feet. A tinderbox lay among the sand, and the stump of a candle, a miner's hat beside an upturned chair.

The moonflower Keren had picked lay on the threshold. Its head had been broken in the struggle but the petals were still white and damp with a freshness that would soon begin to fade.

Chapter five

ROSS HAD BEEN dreaming that he was arguing about the smelting works with Sir John Trevaunance and the other shareholders. It was not an uncommon dream or one which went by contraries. Half his waking life was made up of defending the Carnmore Copper Company from inward fission or outside attack. For the battle was fully joined, and no one could tell which way it would go.

Nothing much was barred in this struggle. Pressure had been brought to bear on United Mines, and Richard Tonkin had been forced out of the managership. Sir John Trevaunance had a lawsuit dragging on in Swansea over his coal ships.

Ross dreamed there was a meeting at Trevaunance's home, as there was to be in a few days, and that everyone was quarrelling at once. He pounded the table again and again trying to gain a hearing. But no one would listen and the more he pounded the more they talked, until suddenly everyone fell silent and abruptly he found himself awake in the silent room and listening to the knocking on the front door.

It was quite light and the sun was falling across the half-curtained windows. The Gimletts should be up soon. He reached for his watch but as usual had forgotten to wind it. Demelza's dark hair clouded the pillow beside him, and her breathing came in a faint *tic-tic*. She was always a good sleeper; if Julia woke she would be out and about and asleep again in five minutes.

Hasty footsteps went downstairs and the knocking stopped. He slid out of bed and Demelza sat up, as usual wide-awake, as if she had never been asleep at all.

'What is it?'

'I don't know, my dear.'

There was a knock on the door and Ross opened it. Somehow in such emergencies he still expected to see Jud standing there.

'If you please, sur,' said Gimlett, 'a boy wants to see you. Charlie Baragwanath, who's gardener's boy over to Mingoose. He's terrible upset.'

'I'll be down.'

Demelza breathed a quiet sigh into the bedclothes. She had thought it something about Verity. All yesterday, lovely yesterday, of which they had spent a good part on the beach in the sun paddling their feet in the sun-warmed water, all the time she had thought of Verity. It had been Verity's day of release, for which she, Demelza, had plotted and schemed for more than a year. She had wondered and waited.

With only her eyes showing over the rim of the bedclothes she watched Ross dress and go down. She wished people would leave them alone. All she wanted was to be left alone with Ross and Julia. But people came more, especially her suitors, as Ross satirically called them. Sir Hugh Bodrugan had been several times to tea.

Ross came back. She could tell at once that something was wrong.

'What is it?'

'Hard to get sense out of the boy. I believe it is something at the mine.'

She sat up. 'An accident?'

'No. Go to sleep for a little. It is not much after five.'

He went down again and joined the undersized boy, whose teeth were chattering as if with cold. He gave him a sip or two of brandy and they set off through the apple trees over the hill.

'Were you first there?' Ross asked.

'Aye, sur . . . I – I b'long to call that way on my way over. Not as they're always about not at this time o' year when I'm s'early; but I always b'long to go that way. I thought they was all out. An' then I seen 'er . . . an' then I seen 'er. . . .'

He covered his face with his hands.

'Honest, sur, I near fainted away. I near fell away on the spot.'

As they neared the cottage they saw three men standing outside. Paul Daniel and Zacky Martin and Nick Vigus.

Ross said: 'Is it as the boy says?'

Zacky nodded.

'Is anyone . . . inside?'

'No, sur.'

'Does anyone know where Mark is?'

'No, sur.'

'Have you sent for Dr Enys?'

'Just sent, sur.'

'Aye, we've sent fur he, sure 'nough,' said Paul Daniel bitterly. Ross glanced at him.

'Will you come in with me, Zacky,' he said.

They went to the open door together, then Ross stooped his head and went in.

She was lying on the floor covered with a blanket. The sun from the window streamed across the blanket in a golden flood.

'The boy said . . .'

'Yes . . . We moved 'er. It didn't seem decent to leave the poor creature.'

Ross knelt and lifted back the blanket. She was wearing the scarlet kerchief Mark had won at the wrestling match twenty months before. He put back the blanket, rose, wiped his hands.

'Zacky, where was Mark when this happened?' He said it in an undertone, as if not to be overheard.

'He should have been down the mine, Cap'n Ross, should by rights have been coming up now. But he had an accident early on his core. Matthew Mark was home to bed before one. Nobody has seen Mark Daniel since then.'

'Have you any idea where he is?'

That I couldn't say.

'Have you sent for the parish constable?'

'Who? Old Vage? Did we oughter have done?'

'No, this is Jenkins's business. This is Mingoose Parish.'

A shadow fell across the room. It was Dwight Enys. The only colour in his face was in the eyes, which seemed suffused, as in a fever. 'I . . .' He glanced at Ross, then at the figure on the floor. 'I came . . .'

'A damned nasty business, Dwight.' Friendship made Ross turn away from the young man towards Paul Daniel, who had followed him in. 'Come, we should leave Dr Enys alone while he makes his examination.'

Paul seemed ready to challenge this; but Ross had just too much authority to be set aside, and presently they were all out in the sun. Ross glanced back and saw Dwight stoop to move the cloth. His hand was trembling and he looked as if he might fall across the body in a faint.

All that day there was no word of Mark Daniel. Blackened and hurt, he had come up from the mine at midnight, and in the early hours of Monday morning had put his stamp upon unfaithfulness and deceit. Then the warm day had taken him.

So much everyone knew. For like the quiet movement of wind among grass, the whisper of Keren's deceit had spread through villages and hamlets round, and no one doubted that this had brought her death. And curiously, no one seemed to doubt the justice of the end. It was the Biblical punishment. From the moment she came here she had flaunted her body at other men. One other man, and they knew Who, had fallen into her lure. Any woman with half an eye would have known that Mark Daniel was not to be cuckolded lightly. She had known the risk and had taken it, matching her sharp wits against his slow strength. For a time she had gone on and then she had made a slip and that had been the end. It might not be law but it was justice.

And the Man in the case might thank his stars he too wasn't laid across the floor with a broken neck. He might yet find himself that way if he didn't watch out. If they were in his shoes they'd get on a horse and ride twenty miles and stay away while Mark Daniel was at large. For all his scholaring he was not much more than a slip of a boy, and Daniel could snap him as easy as a twig.

There wasn't much feeling against him, as there might well have been. In the months he had been here they had grown to like him, to respect him, where they all disliked Keren. They might have risen against him as a breaker of homes; but instead they saw Keren as the temptress who had led him away. Many a wife had seen Keren look at *her* man. It wasn't the surgeon's fault, they said. But all the same they wouldn't be in *his* shoes. He'd had to go in and examine the body, and it was said that when he came out the sweat was pouring off his face.

At six that evening Ross went to see Dwight.

At first Bone would not admit him; Doctor had said in no circumstances was he to be disturbed. But Ross brushed him aside.

Dwight was sitting at a table with a pile of papers before him and a look of hopeless despair on his face. He hadn't changed his clothes since this morning and he hadn't shaved. He glanced at Ross and got up.

'Is it something important?'

'There's no news. That's what is important, Dwight. If I were you I should not stay here until nightfall. Go and spend a few days with the Pascoes.'

'What for?' he asked stupidly.

'Because Mark Daniel is a dangerous man. D'you think if he chose to seek you out Bone or a few locked doors would stop him?'

Dwight put his hands to his face. 'So the truth is known everywhere.'

'Enough to go on. One can do nothing in private in a country district. For the time being ——'

He said: 'I'll never forget her face! Two hours before I'd been kissing it!'

Ross went across and poured him a glass of brandy.

'Drink this. You're lucky to be alive and we must keep you so.'

'I fail to see any good reason.'

Ross checked himself. 'Listen, boy,' he said more gently, 'you must take a good hold on yourself. This thing is done and can't be undone. What I wish above all is to prevent more mischief. I'm not here to judge you.'

'I know,' said the young man. 'I know, Ross. I only judge myself.'

'And that, no doubt, too harshly. Anyone sees that this tragedy has been of the girl's making. I don't know how much you came to feel for her.'

Dwight broke down. 'I don't know myself, Ross. I don't know. When I saw her lying there, I – I thought I had loved her.'

Ross poured himself a drink. When he came back Dwight had partly recovered.

'The great thing is to get away for a time. Just for a week or so. The magistrates have issued a warrant for Mark's arrest, and the constables are out. That is all that can be done for the moment and it may be enough. But if Mark wants to evade capture I'm sure it will not be enough, because although every villager is bound by law to help in his capture, I don't believe one of them will raise a hand.'

'They take his side, and rightly so.'

'But not against you, Dwight. However, in a day or two other measures may be taken, and in a week Mark should be put away and it should be safe for you to return.'

Dwight got up, rocking his half-empty glass.

'No, Ross! What d'you take me for! To skulk away in a safe place while the man is tracked down and then to come slinking back! I'd sooner meet him at once and take the outcome.' He began to walk up and down the room. Then he came to a stop. 'See it my way. On all counts I've let these people down. I came among them a stranger and a physician. I have met with nothing worse than suspicion and much that's been better than kindness. Eggs that could be ill spared pressed on me in return for some fancied favour. Little gestures of good will even from people who are Choake's people. Confidence and trust. In return I have helped to break up the life of one of their number. If I went now I should go for good, a cheat and a failure.'

Ross said nothing.

'But the other way and the harder way is to see this thing out and to take my chance. Look, Ross, there is another case of sore throat at Marasanvose. There is a woman with child at Grambler who nearly died last time with the ill management of a midwife. There are four cases of miner's consumption which are improving under treatment. There are people here and there trusting on me. Well, I've betrayed them; but it would be a greater betrayal to leave now – to leave them to Thomas Choake's farmyard methods.'

'I was not saying you should.'

Dwight shook his head. 'The other's impossible.'

'Then spend a few days with us. We have a room. Bring your man.'

'No. Thank you for your kindness. From to-morrow morning I go about as usual.'

Ross stared at him grimly. 'Then your blood be on your own head.'

Dwight put his hand up to his eyes. 'Keren's blood is already there.'

From the Gatehouse, Ross went direct to the Daniels. They were all sitting round in the half gloom of the cottage doing nothing. They were like mourners at a wake. All the adult family was present except Beth, Paul's wife, who was sharing Keren's lonely vigil in the cottage over the hill. Despised by Keren in life, Beth could yet not bear the thought of allowing her to lie untended all through the summer evening.

Old Man Daniel was sucking his clay pipe and talking, talking. Nobody seemed to listen; the old man didn't seem to care. He was trying to talk his grief and anxiety out of himself.

'I well call to mind when I was on Lake Superior in 'sixty-nine thur were a case not mislike this'n. On Lake Superior in 'sixty-nine – or were it 'seventy? – a man runned off wi' the storekeeper's woman. I well call it to mind. But twur through no fault ——'

They greeted Ross respectfully, Grannie Daniel hopping tearfully off her shaky stool and inviting him to sit down. Ross was always very polite to Grannie Daniel, and she always tried to return it in kind. He thanked her and refused, saying he wanted a word in private with Paul.

'Twur through no fault of 'is. A man runned off wi' the storekeeper's woman, an' he plucked out a spade an' went arter 'em. Just wi' a spade. Nought else but a spade.'

Paul straightened up his back and quietly followed Ross out into the sun. Then he closed the door and stood a little defensively with his back against it. There were other people about, standing at the doors of their cottages and talking, but they were out of earshot. 'No news of Mark?'

'No, sur.'

'Have you an idea where he could be?'

'No, sur.'

'I suppose Jenkins has questioned you?'

'Yes, sur. And others in Mellin. But we don't know nothing.'

'Nor would you tell anything if you did know, eh?'

Paul looked at his feet. 'That's as may be.'

'This is a different crime from petty theft, Paul. If Mark had been caught stealing something from a shop he might be transported for it; but if he hid for a time it might be forgotten. Not so with murder.'

'How do we know he done it, sur?'

'If he did not, why has he fled?'

Paul shrugged his big shoulders and narrowed his eyes at the declining sun.

'Perhaps I should tell you what is likely to happen, Paul. The magistrates have issued a warrant and sent out the constable. Old blacksmith Jenkins from Marasanvose will do his best and Vage from Sawle will help too. I don't think they'll be successful.'

'Maybe not.'

'The magistrates will then organize a search. A man hunt is a very ugly thing. It should be avoided.'

Paul Daniel shifted but did not speak.

Ross said: 'I have known Mark since I was a boy, Paul. I should be unhappy to think of him hunted down perhaps with dogs and later swinging on a gibbet.'

''E'll swing on a gibbet if he give his self up,' Paul said.

'Do you know where he is?'

'I don't know nothing. But I can 'ave me own ideas.'

'Yes, indeed.' Ross had found out what he wanted. 'Listen, Paul. You know Nampara Cove? Of course. There are two caves. In one cave is a boat.'

The other man looked up sharply. 'Yes?'

'It is a small boat. One I use for fishing just around the coast. The oars I keep on a shelf at the back of the cave. The rowlocks are at home so that she shall not be used without my sanction.'

Paul licked his lips. 'Aye?'

'Aye. Also at home is a detachable mast and a pair of sails which can turn the boat into a cutter. She's a weatherly little craft, I know from experience. Not fit for ocean going when the seas are steep; but a resolute man could fare a lot worse in summer time. Now Mark is finished so far as England is concerned. But up in the north there's Ireland. And down in the south is France, where there's trouble at present. He has acquaintances in Brittany and he's made the crossing before.'

'Aye?' said Paul, beginning to sweat.

'Aye,' said Ross.

'An' what of the sails and the rullocks?'

'They might find their way down to the cave after dark. And a few bits of food to keep a man alive. It was just an idea.'

Paul rubbed his forearm over his forehead. 'Be thanked for the idea. Why, if ——'

'I make one condition,' Ross said, tapping him on the chest with a long forefinger. 'This is a secret between two or three. Being accessory to murder is not a pretty thing. I will not have the Viguses privy to it, for Nick has a slippery way of letting things escape him when they are to the detriment of others. There are those in authority who would find a greater relish in their meals if I ran my neck into a noose. Well, I don't intend to do that, not for you nor your brother nor all the broken hearts in Mellin. So you must go careful. Zacky Martin would help you if you needed another outside your own family.'

'Nay, I'll keep it to myself, sur. There's no need for others to be in on it. Twould kill the old man to see Mark swing – an' mebbe old Grannie too, though there's no guessing what she'll survive, like. But tes the disgrace of it. If so be ——'

'Do you know where he is now?'

'I know where I can leave un a note; we used to play so as lads. But I reckon twill be to-morrow night 'fore anything can be done. First I've to fix a meetin', and then I've to persuade'n as tis best for all that he go. They d'say he's fair broke up with it all.'

'Some have seen him then?'

Paul glanced quickly at the other man. 'Aye.'

'I don't think he will refuse to go if you mention his father. But make it urgent. It must be not later than to-morrow.'

'Aye. I'll do that. If so be as it can be fixed for to-night I'll leave ee know.

An' *thank* ee, sur. Them as don't know can't ever thank ee, but they would, fairly they would!'

Ross turned to walk back. Paul re-entered the cottage. Inside Old Man Daniel was going on just as if he had never stopped in his quavering, rusty voice, talking round and round to stop the silence from falling.

Chapter six

THOUGHTFULLY ROSS WALKED back to Nampara. He found John Gimlett cleaning the windows of the library, for which Mrs Gimlett had been making needlework curtains. The industry of the Gimletts, contrasting with the sloth of the Paynters, always surprised him afresh. The garden prospered. Last year Demelza had bought some hollyhock seeds, and in the windless summer they had coloured the walls of the house with their stately purples and crimsons. Julia lay in her cot in the shade of the trees and, seeing her awake, he walked across and picked her up. She crowed and laughed and clutched at his hair.

Demelza had been gardening, and Ross ran with Julia on his shoulder to meet her. She was in her white muslin dress and it gave him a queer twist of pleasure to see that she was wearing gloves. Gradually, without pretentiousness or haste, she was moving towards little refinements of habit.

She had matured this summer. The essential impish vitality of her would never alter, but it was more under her control. She had also grown to accept the startling fact that men found her worth pursuing.

Julia crowed with joy and Demelza took her from him.

'There is another tooth, Ross. See here. Put your finger just here. Is your finger clean? Yes, it will do. Now.'

'Yes, indeed. She'll soon be able to bite like Garrick.'

'Is there any news of Mark?'

In an undertone Ross told her.

Demelza glanced at Gimlett. 'Will it not be a great risk?'

'Not if it is done quick. I fancy Paul knows more than he has told me, and that Mark will come to-night.'

'I am afraid for you. I should be afraid to tell anyone.'

'I only hope Dwight will keep indoors until he is safe away.'

'Oh, there is a letter for you from Elizabeth,' Demelza said, as if she had just remembered.

She felt in her apron pocket and brought out the letter. Ross broke the seal.

DEAR ROSS [it ran],
As you may know Verity left us last night for Captain Blamey. She left

while we were at Evensong and has gone with him to Falmouth. They are to be married to-day.

ELIZABETH.

Ross said: 'Well, so she has done it at last! I greatly feared she might.' Demelza read the letter.

'Why should they not be happy together? It is what I have always said, it is better to take a risk than mope away all your life in dull comfort and secureness.'

'Why "As you may know"? Why should she think I would know?'

'Perhaps it is already about.'

Ross pushed back the hair Julia had ruffled. It was an action which made him suddenly boyish. Yet his expression was not so.

'I do not fancy her life with Blamey. Yet you may be right in thinking she'll be happy with him. I pray she will.' He released his other hand from Julia's clinging grasp. 'It never rains but it pours. This means I must go to Trenwith and see them. The letter is abrupt in tone. I expect they are upset.'

So it has all come, Demelza thought, and Verity by now is married to him, and I too pray they will be happy together, for if they are not I shall not be easy in my bed.

'It is less than an hour to sunset,' Ross said. 'I shall have to make haste.' He looked at her. 'I suppose you would not go and see them in my place?'

'Elizabeth and Francis? Judas, no! Oh, no, Ross. I would do a lot for you, but not that.'

'I don't see that you need feel such alarm. But of course I must go. I wonder what at last brought Verity to the plunge – after all these years. I think also she might have left some letter for me.'

When Ross had gone Demelza set Julia on her feet and allowed her to walk about the garden on her leading strings. She toddled here and there, crowing with delight and trying hard to get at the flowers. In the meantime Gimlett finished the windows and picked up his pail and went in, and Demelza thought her thoughts and watched the sun go down. It was not the sort of sunset one would have expected to follow the day; the sky was streaked and watery and the light faded quickly.

As the dew began to fall she picked up the child and carried her in. Gimlett had already taken in the cot and Mrs Gimlett was lighting the candles. The Paynters' going had helped Demelza in her quest for ladyship.

She fed Julia on a bowl of bread and broth and saw her safely to sleep, and it was not till then that she realized Ross had been gone too long.

She went down the stairs and to the open front door. The fall of night had drawn a cloud across the sky, and a light cool wind moved among the trees. The weather was on the change. Over in the distance she caught the queer lap-dog bark of a moor hen.

Then she saw Ross coming through the trees.

Darkie neighed when she saw her at the door. Ross jumped off and looped the reins over the lilac tree.

'Has anyone been?'

'No. You've been a long time.'

'I've seen Jenkins – also Will Nanfan, who always knows everything. Two other constables are to help Jenkins. Bring a candle, will you; I'd like to get those sails down at once.'

She went with him into the library.

'The wind is rising. He must go to-night if it's at all possible. To-morrow may be too late for another reason.'

'What's that, Ross?'

'Sir Hugh is one of the magistrates concerned, and he's pressing for calling in the military. Apparently she – Keren – apparently Sir Hugh had noticed her, seen her about, thought her attractive, you know what a lecherous old roué he is ——'

'Yes, Ross. . . .'

'So he's taking a personal interest. Which is bad for Mark. He has another reason too.'

'How is that?'

'You remember at St Ann's last week when the Revenue man was mishandled. The authorities have sent out a troop of dragoons to-day to St Ann's. They are to be stationed there for a time as a cautionary measure, and may make a search during their stay. Sir Hugh, as you know, is a friend of Mr Trencrom and buys all his spirits there. It would not be unnatural to take attention from the smugglers for a day by asking help in a search for a murderer.'

'. . . Shall I come down to the cave with you?'

'No, I shall not be more than half an hour.'

'And – Verity . . . ?'

Ross paused at the door of the library with the mast on his shoulder.

'Oh . . . Verity is gone sure enough. And I have had a fantastic quarrel with Francis.'

'A quarrel?' She had sensed there was something else.

'In good measure. He taxed me with having arranged this elopement and even refused to believe me when I said not. I've never been so taken aback in my life. I gave him credit for some degree of – of intelligence.'

Demelza moved suddenly, as if trying to shift the cold feeling that had settled on her.

'But, my dear . . . why you?'

'Oh, they thought I had been using you as a go-between; picking up his letters somewhere and getting you to deliver them to Verity. I could have knocked him down. Anyway, we have broken for a long time. There will not be any easy patching up after what has been said.'

'Oh, Ross, I'm . . . that sorry . . . I . . .'

To hide his own discomfort he said lightly: 'Now stay about somewhere while I'm gone. And tell Gimlett I'm back. It will occupy him to tend on Darkie.'

So in a few minutes more she was alone again. She had walked a little way along the stream with him and had watched his figure move into the dark. From this point you could hear the waves breaking in the cove.

Before she had been uneasy, a little nervy and anxious, for it was not pleasant to be helping a murderer to escape. But now her unhappiness was a different thing, solid and personal and settled firm, as if it would never move, for it touched the all-important matter of her relations with Ross. For a year she had worked untiringly for Verity's happiness, worked open-eyed, knowing that what she was doing would be condemned by Ross and doubly condemned by Francis and Elizabeth. But she had never imagined that it would cause a break between Ross and his cousin. That was something outside all sensible counting. She was desperately troubled.

So deep was she in this that she did not notice the figure coming across the lawn towards the door. She had turned in and was closing the door when a voice spoke. She stepped back behind the door so that the lantern in the hall shone out.

'Dr Enys!'

'I hadn't thought to startle you, Mistress Poldark. . . . Is your husband in?'

Having begun to thump, Demelza's heart was not quieting yet. There was another kind of danger here.

'Not at the moment.'

Her eyes took in his dishevelled look, so changed from the neat, comely, black-coated young man of ordinary times. He might have been without sleep for a week. He stood there indecisive, conscious that he had not been asked in, knowing something guarded in her attitude but mistaking the causes.

'Do you imagine he'll be long?'

'About half an hour.'

He part turned away as if leaving. But there he stopped. 'Perhaps you'll forgive me for intruding on you . . . ?'

'Of course.'

She led the way into the parlour. There might be danger or there might not: she could not avoid it.

He stood there very stiffly. 'Don't let me interfere with anything you may be doing. I don't at all wish to interrupt you.'

'No,' she said in a soft voice, 'I was doing nothing.' She went across and drew the curtains, careful to leave no nicks. 'As you'll see we are late with supper, but Ross has been busy. Would you take a glass of port?'

'Thank you, I won't. I . . .' As she turned from the window he said impulsively: 'You condemn me for my part in this morning's tragedy?'

She coloured a little. 'How can I condemn anyone when I know such a small bit about it?'

'I shouldn't have mentioned it. But I have been thinking – thinking all to-day and speaking to no one. To-night I felt I must come out, go out somewhere. And this house was the only one . . .'

She said: 'It might be dangerous to be out to-night.'

'I think highly of your opinion,' he said. 'Yours and Ross's. It was his confidence that brought me here; if I felt I had forfeited it, it would be better to cut and go.'

'I don't think you've forfeited it. But I don't think he will be pleased by you coming here to-night.'

'Why?'

'I should rather not explain that.'

'Do you mean you want me to go?'

'I b'lieve it would be better.' She picked up a plate from the table and set it in another place.

He looked at her. 'I must have some assurance of your friendship – in spite of all. Alone in the Gatehouse this evening I have come near to – near to . . .' He did not finish.

She met his eyes.

'Stay then, Dwight,' she said. 'Sit down and don't bother 'bout me.'

He slumped in a chair, passed his hands across his face. While Demelza pottered about and went in and out of the room he talked in snatches, explaining, arguing. Two things were absent, self-pity and self-apology. He seemed to be trying to make out a case for Keren. It was as if he felt she was being harshly judged and could offer no defence. He must speak for Keren.

Then the third time she went from the room and came back he did not go on. She glanced at him and saw him sitting tense.

'What is it?'

'I thought I heard someone tapping at the window.'

Demelza's heart stopped beating altogether; then she gulped it into motion again. 'Oh, I know what that is. Don't you get up. I will see for it myself.'

Before he could argue she went out into the hall, shutting the parlour door behind her. So it had come. As she had feared. Now of all times. Pray Ross would not be long. Just for the moment she had to handle the crisis alone.

She went to the hall door and peered out. The dim lantern light showed an empty lawn. Something moved by the lilac bush.

'Beg pardon, ma'am,' said Paul Daniel.

Her glance met his; strayed beyond him.

'Captain Ross has just gone down to the cove. Is . . . anyone with you?'

He hesitated. 'You know about un?'

'I know.'

He gave a low whistle. A dim figure broke from the side of the house. Paul leaned behind Demelza and pulled the hall door half shut so that the light should not shine out.

Mark stood before them. His face was in the shadow but she could see the caverns of his eyes.

'Cap'n Ross is down in the cove,' said Paul. 'We'd best go down to 'im.'

Demelza said: 'Sometimes Bob Baragwanath and Bob Nanfan go fishing there at high tide.'

'We'll wait by yonder apple trees,' said Paul. 'We'll be well able to see 'im from thur.'

And well able to see anyone leave the house. 'You'll be safer indoors. You'll – be safer in the library.'

She pushed open the door and moved into the hall, but they drew back and whispered together. Paul said:

'Mark don't want to tie you folk up wi' this more'n he can. He'd better prefer to wait outside.'

'No, Mark. It don't matter to us. Come in at once!'

Paul entered the hall and after him Mark, bending his head to get in the doorway. Demelza had just time to take in the blisters on his forehead, the stone grey of his face, the bandaged hand, before she opened the door of the bedroom which led to the library. Then as she picked up the lantern to go in there was a movement at the other side of the hall. Their eyes flickered across to Dwight Enys standing in the threshold of the parlour.

Chapter seven

SILENCE SWELLED IN the hall, and burst.

Paul Daniel had slammed the outer door.

He stood with his back to it. Mark, gaunt and monstrous, stood quite still, the veins growing thick and knotted in his neck and hands.

She moved then, turned on them both.

'Dwight, go back into the parlour. Go back at once! Mark, d'you hear me! Mark!' Her voice didn't sound like her own.

'So tes a bloody trap,' said Mark.

She stood before him, slight and seeming small. 'How dare you say that! Paul, have you no sense? Take him. This way, at once.'

'You bastard, you,' said Mark, looking over her head.

'You should have thought of that before,' said Dwight. 'Before you killed her.'

'Damned slimy adulterer. Tradin' on your work. Foulin' the nests o' those you pertend to help.'

'You should have come for me,' Dwight said, 'not broken a girl who couldn't defend herself.'

'Yes, by God ——'

Demelza moved between them as Mark stepped forward. Blindly he tried to brush her away, but instead of that she stood her ground and hammered him on the chest with her clenched fists. His eyes flickered, lingered, came down.

'D'you realize what this means to us?' she said, breathless, her eyes blazing. 'We've done nothing. We're trying to help. Help you both. You'd fight and kill each other in *our* house, on *our* land. Have you no loyalty and – and friendship that stands for anything at all! What's brought you here to-night, Mark? Mebbe not the thought to save your own skin, but to save the disgrace for your father an' his family. Twould kill him. Well, which is most important to you, your father's life or this man's? Dwight, go back into the parlour *at once!*'

Dwight said: 'I can't. If Daniel wants me I must stay.'

'What's 'e doing 'ere?' said Paul to the girl.

Dwight said: 'Mistress Poldark tried to drive me away.'

'You bastard,' said Mark again.

Demelza caught him by the arm as he was about to raise it. 'In here. Else we shall have the servants coming and there'll be no secret at all.'

He did not move an inch under her pressure. 'There'll be no secret wi' him in the know. Come outside, Enys. I'll finish you there.'

'Nay.' Paul had been useless so far, but now he took a hand. 'There's no sense in that, Mark. I think bad of the skunk, same as you, but twill finish everything if you fight him.'

'Everything's finished already.'

It *isn't*!' cried Demelza. 'It *isn't*, I tell you. Don't you see! Dr Enys can't betray you without betraying us.'

Dwight hesitated, every sort of different impulse clamouring. 'I won't betray anyone,' he said.

Mark spat out a harsh breath. 'I'd as lief trust a snake.'

Paul came up to him. 'It is an ill meetin', Mark; but we can't do nothin' about en. Come, old dear, we must do what Mistress Poldark say.'

Dwight put his hands up to his head. 'I'll not betray you, Daniel. Three wrongs don't make a right any more than two. What you did to Keren is with your conscience, as – as my ill-doing is with mine.'

Paul pushed Mark slowly towards the bedroom door. Abruptly Mark shook off his arm and stopped again. His gaunt terrible face worked for a moment.

'Mebbe this ain't the time for a reckoning, Enys. But it will come, never fear.'

Dwight did not raise his head.

Mark looked down at Demelza, who was still standing like a guardian angel between him and his wrath. 'Nay, ma'am, I'll not stain your floor with more blood. I'd not wish hurt to this 'ouse. . . . Where d'you want for me to go?'

. . . When Ross came back Dwight was in the parlour, his head buried in his hands. Mark and Paul were in the library, Mark every now and then shaking with a spasm of anger. In the hall, between them, Demelza stood sentinel. When she saw Ross she sat down in the nearest chair and burst into tears.

'What the Devil . . . ?' said Ross.

She spoke a few disjointed words.

He put the sail down in the corner of the hall.

'My dear . . . Where are they now? And you . . .'

She shook her head and pointed.

He came over to her. 'And there's been no bloodletting? My God, I'll swear it has never been nearer . . . .'

'You may swear it in truth,' Demelza said.

He put his arm about her. 'Did you stop it, love? Tell me, how did you stop it?'

'Why have you brought the sail back?' she asked.

'Because there'll be no sailing yet. The swell has got up with the tide. It would overturn the boat before we ever could get her launched.'

An hour before dawn they went down to the cove, following the bubble of the stream and the descending combe, with a glowworm here and there green-lit like a jewel in the dark. The tide had gone out but the swell was still heavy, rushing in and roaring at them whenever they got too near. That was the trouble with the north coast: a sea could get up without warning and then you were done.

In the first glimmerings of daybreak, with the deathly moon merging its last candlelight in the blueing east, they walked slowly back. Twenty-four hours ago there had been a terrible anger in Mark's soul, bitter and blighting and hot; now all feeling was dead. His black eyes had sunk deep into the frame of his face.

As they neared the house he said: 'I'll be gettin' on my way.'

Ross said: 'We'll house you here till to-morrow.'

'No. I'll not have ye into it more.'

Ross stopped. 'Listen, man. The country folk are on your side, but you'll bring trouble on them if you shelter among 'em. You'll be safe in the library. To-night may be calm enough, for no wind is up.'

'That man may tell about you,' said Paul Daniel.

'Who? Enys? No, you do him an injustice there.'

They went on again.

'Look, mister,' said Mark, 'I don't concern whether I hang or fly. Nothing don't matter a snap to me now. But one thing I'm danged sure on is that I'll not skulk where I bring trouble to them as friends me. An' that's for sartin. Ef the soldiers d'come, well, let em come.'

They reached the house in silence.

'You always were a stubborn mule,' Ross said.

Paul said: 'Now look ee here, Mark. I've the thought ——'

Someone came out of the house.

'Oh, Demelza,' Ross said in half irritation, 'I told you to go to bed. There's no need to worry yourself, my dear.'

'I've brewed a dish of tea. I thought you'd all be back about now.'

They went into the parlour. By the light of a single candle Demelza poured them hot tea from a great pewter pot. The three men stood round drinking it awkwardly, the steam rising before their faces, two avoiding each other's eyes, the third staring blindly at the opposite wall. Paul warmed his hands on the cup.

Demelza said: 'You can hear the roar upstairs. I thought it was no use.'

'It were roarin' last night,' Mark said suddenly, 'when I come up from the mine. God forgive me, twas roarin' then. . . .'

There was a grim silence.

'You'll stay here to-day?' said Demelza.

Ross said: 'I have already asked him but he'll not hear of it.'

Demelza glanced at Mark and said no more. He was not to be argued with.

Mark lowered his cup. 'I was reckoning to go down Grambler.'

There was another silence. Demelza shivered.

Paul hunched his shoulders uncomfortably. 'The air may be foul. You know what Grambler always was for foul air. There's easier berths than that.'

'I was reckoning,' said Mark, 'to go down Grambler.'

Ross glanced at the sky. 'You'll not be there before it is light.'

Demelza too glanced out of the window, at the ruin on the sky line. 'What of Wheal Grace? Is there still a ladder for that?'

Ross glanced at Mark. 'The ladder was sound enough six years ago. You could use a rope to be sure.'

Mark said: 'I was reckoning to go down Grambler.'

'Oh, nonsense, man. No one could blame me for your hiding in Grace. Don't you agree, Paul?'

''S I reckon he'd be safe there. What do ee say, old dear? The light's growing fast. No military man would follow down there.'

Mark said: 'I don't like it. Tes too close to this 'ouse. Folk might suspect.'

'I'll go and get you some food,' Demelza said.

An hour later the day broke. It was an unhappy day for Demelza, and she had lost her good spirits.

At nine o'clock the burly Sam Jenkins mounted a pony outside his forge and rode over to Mingoose, stopping in to see Dr Enys on the way. At fifteen minutes to ten Sir Hugh Bodrugan also arrived at Mingoose; the Rev Mr Faber, rector of St Minver Church, followed. The conference lasted until eleven, then a messenger was sent to fetch Dr Enys. At noon the meeting broke up, Sir Hugh Bodrugan riding over to Trenwith to see Mr Francis Poldark and then going on to St Ann's, where he met Mr Trencrom, and they went together to see the captain of the dragoons. It was a somewhat stormy meeting, for the captain was no fool, and Sir Hugh rode home to dinner with the fine rain to cool his heated whiskery face. Thereafter some hours went by in expectant calm. At four Ross walked down to look at the sea. The gentle rain had quieted it, but there was still an ugly swell. Both low tides would be in daylight, but any time after midnight might do on the falling tide. At five word came through that the soldiers, instead of being set to the man hunt, had been searching the St Ann's houses all afternoon and had uncovered a fine store of contraband. Ross laughed.

At six three dragoons and a civilian rode down the narrow track of Nampara Combe. Nothing like it had ever been seen before.

Demelza was the first in the house to sight them and she flew into the parlour, where Ross was sitting thinking over his quarrel with Francis.

He said: 'No doubt they are making a social call.'

'But why come here, Ross, why come here? D'you think someone has told on us?'

He smiled. 'Go change your dress, my dear, and prepare to be the lady.'

She fled out, seeing through the half-open front door that the civilian was Constable Jenkins. Upstairs she hurriedly changed to the sound of clopping hooves and the distant rattle of accoutrements. She heard them knock and be shown in; then the faint murmur of voices. Anxiously she waited, knowing how gentle Ross could be or how much the opposite. But there was no uproar.

She turned her hair here and there with a comb and patted it into place. Then she peeped behind the curtain of the window, to see that only one of the soldiers had entered. The other two, in all the splendour of black and white busbies and red coats, waited with the horses.

As she went down and reached the door there was a sudden tremendous burst of laughter. Heartened, she went in.

'Oh, my dear, this is Captain McNeil of the Scots Greys. This is my wife.'

Captain McNeil looked enormous in his red and gold coat, dark gold-braided trousers and spurred shiny boots. On the table stood a huge busby and beside it a pair of yellow gauntlet gloves. He was a youngish man, plump, well groomed, with a great sandy moustache. He set down the glass he was holding and bowed over her hand military fashion. As he straightened up his keen brown eyes seemed to say: 'These outlandish country squires do themselves well with their womenfolk.'

'You know Constable Jenkins, I think.'

They waited until Demelza had taken a chair and then sat down again.

'Captain McNeil has been describing the amenities of our inns,' said Ross. 'He thinks the Cornish bugs have the liveliest appetite.'

The soldier gave a softer echo of his tremendous laugh.

'Nay, I wouldn't say so much as that. Perhaps it is only that there are more of 'em.'

'I have offered that he should come and stay with us,' said Ross. 'We are not rich in comfort but neither are we rich in crawlers.' (Demelza blushed slightly at Ross's use of her old word.)

'Thank ye. Thank ye kindly.' Captain McNeil twisted one end of his moustache as if it was a screw that must be fastened to his face. 'And for old times' sake I should be uncommon pleased to do so. It terrns out, mistress, that Captain Poldark and I were both in a summary affray on the James River in 'eighty-one. Old campaigners together as ye might say. But though here I would be near the scene of the merrder, I'm much too far from the contraband we picked up this noon, and contraband was what I was sent into this part to find, ye see.' He chuckled.

'Indeed,' said Demelza. (She wondered what it would feel like to be kissed by a man with a moustache like that.)

'Hrr – hmm,' said Constable Jenkins diffidently. 'About this murder . . .'

'Och, yes. We mustn't forget ——'

'Let me fill your glass,' Ross said.

'Thank ye. . . . As I was explaining to your husband, mistress, this is but a routine inquiry, as I understand he was one of the airly finders of the body. Also it is said the wanted man has been seen in this neighbourhood. . . .'

'Really,' said Demelza. 'I had not heard it.'

'Well, so the constable says.'

'It was rumoured so, ma'am,' Jenkins said hastily. 'We don't know where it come from.'

'So I made this call to see if ye could advise me. Captain Poldark has known the man since boyhood and I thought perhaps he would have some notion of where he might be lairking.'

'You might search for a year,' said Ross, 'and not exhaust all the rabbit holes. All the same I do not imagine Daniel will linger. I think he will make for Plymouth and join the Navy.'

Captain McNeil was watching him. 'Is he a good sailor?'

'I have no idea. Every man here has some of the sea in his blood.'

'Now tell me, Captain Poldark: are there overmany places on this coast where a boat may be launched?'

'What, a naval boat?'

'No, no, just a small boat which would be handled by one or two men.'

'In a flat sea there are half a hundred. In a steep sea there isn't one between Padstow and St Ann's.'

'And what would ye call the present?'

'To-day it is moderate, dropping a little, I fancy. It may be feasible to launch a boat from Sawle by to-morrow evening. Why do you ask?'

Captain McNeil screwed up his moustache. 'Are there overmany suitable boats about whereby a man could make his escape, d'you imagine?'

'Oh, I see your point. No, not that one man could handle.'

'Do ye know anyone with a suitable boat at all?'

'There are a few. I have one myself. It is kept in a cave in Nampara Cove.'

'Where d'you keep the oars, sur?' ventured Constable Jenkins.

Ross got up. 'Can I persuade you to stay to supper, gentlemen? I will give the order now.'

The blacksmith was a little nervous at this favour, but Captain McNeil rose and declined. 'One day I'll call again and we'll have a lively crack over old times. But I should appreciate the favour of being shown the cove and cliffs if ye can spare the time now. I have a notion that it would help me one way or another. If ye can shoot at two birds with the one ball as ye might say . . .'

'Well, there is no hurry,' said Ross. 'Try this brandy first. I trust you will be able to tell from the flavour whether or not duty has been paid on it.'

The soldier broke into his great good-humoured laugh.

They chatted a while longer and then the captain took his leave of Demelza. He clicked his heels and bowed low over her hand, so that the soft whiskers of his moustache tickled her fingers. For a second he looked at her with bold admiration in his brown eyes. Then he picked up his gloves and his great busby and clanked out.

When Ross came back from showing him the cove and cliffs Demelza said:

'Phew, I'm that glad it turned out that way. And you were so good. No one would have dreamed you knew anything. What a nice man. I should not mind so much being arrested by him.'

'Don't underrate him,' Ross said. 'He's a Scotsman.'

Chapter eight

HEAVY WINDLESS RAIN set in as night fell.

At ten, when the tide was nearly full, Ross went down to the cove and saw that the swell had dropped. There could not have been a more favourable night; the darkness was like extra eyelids squeezing away the thought of sight.

At midnight two men waited inside the roofless engine house of Wheal Grace. Paul Daniel, with an old felt hat, and a sack over his shoulder, Ross in a long black cloak that came to his ankles and made him look like a bat. Presently in the depths of the pit there flickered a light.

With the ceaseless drum of the rain in their ears, falling on their hats and bodies and on the long wet grass, they waited and watched.

As he neared the top the light went out. He head and shoulders showed above the rim on the shaft and he clambered out and sat a moment on his haunches. The rain drummed on the grass.

'I thought twas near morning,' he said. 'What of the tide?'

'It will do.'

They set off down the valley to the house.

'There's money in that mine,' said Mark. 'To keep from going off my head – I went all over.'

'Someday perhaps,' said Ross.

'Copper . . . I've never seen a more keenly lode. An' silver lead.'

'Where?'

'On the east face. Twill be underwater most times. . . .'

The parlour light showed brightly, but Ross made a detour and came up against the library wall. Then he groped for the door and they were inside in the darkness. There was some scraping and then a candle burned in the far corner – in the corner where Keren had acted and danced.

A meal was set on a table.

Mark said: 'Tes dangering you needless.' But he ate rapidly while the other two kept watch.

With the lighted parlour as a decoy, Demelza was sitting in the darkness of the bedroom above keeping watch up the valley. After the visit of the soldier Ross was taking no chances.

Very soon Mark was done. He looked terrible to-night, for his strong beard was half an inch long and the heavy rain had washed streaks down the dirt of his face.

'There's this,' said Ross, putting forward a parcel of food, 'and this.' An old coat. 'It is the best we can do. You will need all your efforts to be out of sight of the land by morning, for there's no breeze to help you.'

Mark said: 'If thanks would bring things for ee . . . But listen . . .'

'Tell me on the way down.'

'I been thinking of my house, Reath Cottage, that I builded for she. You won't – you won't let it fall down?'

'No, Mark.'

'There's stuff in the garden. That's for you, Paul. It has yielded well.'

'I'll see for it,' said Paul.

'And,' said Mark, turning his eyes on Ross, 'and there's one thing else. It's . . . You'll see she's buried proper? Not in a pauper's grave. . . . She was above that. . . .'

'I'll see to it,' Ross told him.

'There's money under the bed in the cottage. It'll be enough to pay. . . . I'd like a stone. . . .'

'Yes, Mark. We'll see it's done right.'

Mark picked up his things, the food, the coat.

'Keren on the stone,' he said indistinctly. 'She never liked Kerenhappuch. Keren Daniel. Just Keren Daniel. . . .'

They set off for the cove. The rain had not put out the lights of the glowworms. The sea was quieter to-night, grumbling and hissing under the steady downpour. It was not quite so black here; the white fringe of surf was faintly phosphorescent, easing the night's dark weight. They left the stream and moved across the soft sand. They were within a few yards of the cove when Ross stopped. He put out a hand behind and drew Paul level.

'What is that?' he breathed.

Paul put down the mast and stared. He had very sharp eyes, well used to dark places. He bent a little and then straightened.

'A man.'

'A soldier,' said Ross. 'I heard the creak of his belt.'

They squatted.

'I'd best go,' said Mark.

'Nay, I'll quiet him,' said Paul. 'They're soft enough under their tall hats.'

'No killing,' said Ross. 'I will do it. . . .' But the elder Daniel had gone.

Ross crouched in the sand, pulling the mast towards him. Mark began to mutter under his breath. He would have given himself up. Ross thought: McNeil has strung his men out all along the cliffs. Shooting at two birds. This way he may either pull in the murderer or some free traders. But if he's watching all points between here and St Ann's his men will be widely spaced.

Creep forward.

A sudden sharp challenge. They rushed forward. The musket exploded, flat and loud, in the mouth of the cave. A figure sank on to the sand.

'All right,' said Paul, short of breath. 'But a damnation noise.'

'Quick, the boat!'

Into the cave; Ross flung in the mast and the sail; Mark groped for the oars.

'I'll get them; you launch her!'

The brothers began to slide the boat through the soft sand. Twice it stuck. Then they had to drag the stirring figure of the soldier aside. Ross came with the oars, thrust them in, put his weight to the boat and it went sliding down towards the sea.

The sound of boots striking rock somewhere, and shouts. Men were coming.

'This way!' shouted a voice. 'By the cave!'

Reached the sea. The fringe of surf might show them up.

'Get in!' Ross said through his teeth.

'Rullocks!' said Mark.

Ross took them from his pocket, passed them to Mark; one fell in the sand. They groped: found it: Mark was in: pushed off. A wave broke among them and swung the boat; nearly capsized; back in shallow water. Mark got the oars out.

'Now!'

The noise they were making. Men were running towards them. A musket was fired. Straighten up; waves were malevolent; shove again together! The boat suddenly came to life, floated off into the blackness. Paul fell on hands and knees in the surf, Ross caught his shoulders, hauled him to his feet. A figure came up and grasped his cloak. Ross ducked as a musket exploded in his ear. He knocked the soldier flat upon the sand. They ran along the beach. Figures were after them as they turned in towards the stream. Ross stopped short and hit at a figure running past him. The man rolled into the stream. Then he changed his course and began to climb up among the bracken that stood four feet high along the side of the combe. They could seek him all night here. Unless they could light a torch they were helpless.

He lay flat on his face for a few minutes gaining his breath, listening to men shouting and searching. Was Paul safe? He moved again. Another danger existed and must be met.

This way it was farther to Nampara. You climbed through the bracken until it gave way to open ground and patches of gorse, then you struck the west corner of the long field and, keeping in the ditch at the side of it, made your way down the hill to the back of the house.

This he did. The Gimletts had been in bed hours, so he slipped in through the kitchen, peeped into the parlour and blew the candles out, quickly mounted the stairs to his bedroom.

Demelza was by the north window but was across the room as soon as his footsteps creaked at the door.

'Are you safe?'

'Ssh! Don't wake Julia.' While he told her what had happened he was pulling off his long cloak, dragging his stock from his neck.

'Soldiers! Their . . .'

He sat down suddenly. 'Help me, my dear. They may call on us.'

She fell on her knees and began to unlace the tall boots in the dark.

'I wonder who gave you away, Ross? *Could* it have been Dwight Enys?'

'Heavens, no! Sound reasoning on the part of the – charming McNeil.'

'Oh, Ross, your hands!'

Ross stared closely at them. 'I must have cut the knuckles when I hit someone.' Then his fingers closed over Demelza's. 'You're trembling, child.'

'So would you be,' she said. 'I've been sitting up here alone in the dark; and then those shots . . .'

Her voice died as a knock came at the front door.

'Now gently, my love, gently. Take your time. That knock is not very peremptory, is it? They are not sure of themselves. We'll wait for another knock before making a light.'

He stood up, gathered together the clothes he had taken off and moved to the cupboard.

'No,' Demelza said, 'under the cot. If you can lift it carefully I'll slip them under.'

While they were doing this the knock came again, and louder.

'That should wake Gimlett,' said Ross, making a light himself. 'He'll think he is always being roused in the middle of the night.'

There was water in the room and Demelza hurriedly poured some in a bowl. As the light of the candle grew she took up a flannel and bathed his face and hands. When Gimlett came to the door Ross was just putting on his gown.

'What is it now?'

'If you please, sur, there's a sergeant o' the soldiery askin' to see you downstairs.'

'Confound it, this is a time to call! Ask him in the parlour, John. I'll be down very soon.'

Chapter nine

MR ODGERS MIGHT have thought his pleas effective, for Sawle Feast passed barely marked. But in fact conditions preached the surest sermon.

And the soldiers still lay like a blight on the land. Everyone had been hoping for their going, but instead a contingent moved to Sawle and showed no signs of feeling themselves unwanted. They bivouacked in an open field just behind Dr Choake's house, and to everyone's disappointment the weather cleared again and no wind blew to strip them in sleep.

Ross had spent an uncomfortable few days. Apart from the chance of trouble over Mark Daniel, there was his breach with Francis. They had never quarrelled in this way before. Even during the ups and downs of these last years Francis and he had always held each other in mutual respect. Ross was not upset at being suspected of helping Verity to elope but at being disbelieved when he denied it. It would never have occurred to him to doubt Francis's word. But it had seemed as if Francis didn't *want* to believe the denial, almost as if he was afraid to believe it. It was all inexplicable and left a nasty taste.

On the Friday, Ross had to go to Trevaunance. Richard Tonkin was to be there, and they were to go into the general accounts before the general meeting that evening. Ever since the opening of the smelting works opposition to the working of the company had been fierce. Mines had been induced to boycott them, attempts made to squeeze them from the available markets for the refined product; they had been overbid again and again at the ticketings.

But so far they had ridden the storm.

This was the first time Ross had been out since Tuesday evening, and when he reached Grambler he was not overpleased to see a tall cavalry officer coming the other way.

'Why, Captain Poldark.' McNeil reined in his horse and bowed slightly. 'I was on my way to see ye. Can ye spare the time to turn back for a half-hour?'

'A pleasure I have been looking forward to,' Ross said, 'but I have a business appointment at Trevaunance. Can you ride with me that far?'

McNeil turned his horse. 'Aye, mebbe we can talk a wee bit as we go. I had intended calling on you airlier but I've been more than a little busy what with one thing and another.'

'Oh, yes,' said Ross, 'the smugglers.'

'Not only the smugglers. Ye'll remember there was the small matter of that mairderer's escape.'

'D'you think he has escaped?'

Captain McNeil screwed his moustache. 'Has he not! And from your cove, Captain, and in your boat!'

'Oh, that. I thought it was a brush with the free traders you'd had. The sergeant ——'

'I think Sergeant Drummond left ye in no doubt as to his views.'

'I judged him mistaken.'

'May I ask why?'

'Well, I understand there were several men concerned. Murderers do not hunt in packs.'

'No, but he had the sympathy of the neighbourhood.'

They jogged along in silence.

'Well, it was a pity you did not catch one of the rascals. Were any of your troopers hurt?'

'Not as ye would say hurrt. Except in a small matter of dignity. It might have gone ill with one of the lawbreakers if he had been caught.'

'Ah,' said Ross. And, 'Do you know much of churches, Captain? Sawle Church reminds me of one I saw in Connecticut except that it is so badly preserved.'

'And then,' said the officer, 'there was the matter of the rowlocks. How do ye suppose they were got?'

'I should say Daniel – if it was he – stole a pair somewhere. Every man here is a fisherman in his spare time. There are always rowlocks about.'

'Ye do not seem very upset at the loss of your boat, Captain Poldark.'

'I am becoming philosophical,' Ross said. 'As one nears thirty I think it is a state of mind to be sought after. It is a protection, because one becomes more conscious of loss – loss of time, of dignity, of one's first ideals. I'm not happy to lose a good boat but sighing will not bring it back any more than yesterday's youth.'

'Your attitude does you credit,' McNeil said dryly. 'Might I, as a man a year or so your senior offer ye a word of advice?'

'Of course.'

'Be careful of the law, Captain. It is a cranky, twisty old thing and you may flout it a half dozen times. But let it once come to grips with ye, and ye will find it as hard to be loose from as a black squid. Mind you, I have a sympathy with your point of view. There's something about arrmy life that makes a man impatient of the Justice and the parish constable; I've felt it so myself; indeed I have. . . .' He gave a brief, sudden chuckle. 'But that ——' He stopped.

Ross said: 'See those children, McNeil. It is the only beech copse round here, and they are gathering the leaves and will take them home to be cooked. It is not a very nourishing dish and makes their stomachs swell.'

'Yes,' said the captain grimly. 'I see them well.'

'I confess I sometimes feel impatient of a lot of things,' Ross said. 'Including the parish constable and the local magistrates. But I think it dates from earlier in my life than you imagine. I joined the Fifty-second Foot to escape them.'

'That's as may be. Once a rebel, always a rebel, you may say. But there are degrees of rebellion, Captain, just as there are degrees of misdemeanour, and when the parish constable comes to be supported by a troop of His Majesty's cavalry ——'

'And a crack regiment at that.'

'And a crack regiment, as ye say; then recklessness becomes folly and is likely to lead to bad consequences. A military man out of uniform may be no respecter of perrsons. A military man in uniform will be still less so.'

They left Sawle Church behind and took the track past Trenwith.

Ross said: 'I feel we have a good deal in common, Captain McNeil.'

'That's one way of putting it.'

'Well, I have been in and out of scrapes a good part of my life, and I imagine you have been the same.'

The captain laughed, and a flock of birds rose from a neighbouring field.

'I think perhaps you will agree,' Ross said, 'that though we may revere the law in abstract, in practice there are considerations which take a higher place.'

'Such as?'

'Friendship.'

They rode on in silence.

'The law would not admit that.'

'Oh, I do not expect the law to admit it. I was asking you to admit it.'

The Scotsman screwed in his moustache. 'No, no, Captain Poldark. Oh, dear, no. You are out of uniform but I'm still in it. I'll not be manœuvred into a corrner by such moral arguments.'

'But moral argument is the most potent force in the world, Captain. It was that more than force of arms which defeated us in America.'

'Well, next time you must try it on my troopers. They will appreciate the change.' McNeil reined in his horse. 'I think we have gone far enough, Captain.'

'It is another mile to Trevaunance yet.'

'But farther I doubt before we reach agreement. It's time we parted. I should have appreciated an assurance that ye had taken good heed of my warning ——'

'Oh, I have done that, I do assure you.'

'Then there's no more need be said – this time. It may be that we shall meet again – in different circumstances I should hope.'

'I shall look forward to it,' Ross said. 'If you are ever in these parts again consider my house at your disposal.'

'Thank you.' McNeil extended his hand.

Ross took off his glove and they shook hands.

'Have ye hurt your hand somewhere?' McNeil said, glancing down at the scarred knuckles.

'Yes,' said Ross, 'I caught it in a rabbit trap.'

They saluted and separated, Ross going on his way, McNeil turning back towards Sawle. As the soldier rode away he twisted his moustache vigorously and now and again a subdued laugh shook his big frame.

The smelting works now straggled up the side of Trevaunance Quay.

A long way off it was possible to see the immense volumes of smoke from the furnaces, and on this still day it hung in the valley shutting out the sun. Here was industry with a vengeance, with great piles of coal and heaps of ashes and an unending stream of mules and men busy about the copper house and the quay.

He dismounted first beside the works to look them over.

Several reverberatory furnaces had been built, some for roasting and some for fusing the ore. The copper was roasted and then melted, whilst at intervals the waste was removed, until after twelve hours it was turned out in a molten state into a trough of water. This sudden cooling brought it to a mass of small grains, which were roasted for another twenty-four hours and again turned out, until eventually the coarse copper was run off into sand moulds to cool. This melting and refining had to take place several times before it reached a proper state of purity. The whole process averaged a fortnight. Small wonder, Ross thought, that it took three times as much coal to smelt a ton of copper as a ton of tin. And coal at fifty shillings a wey.

Although the place had been open only three months he noticed already how ill and wan many of the men were who worked there. The great heat and the fumes were too much for any but the strongest, and there was a higher sickness rate here than in the mines. A factor he had not foreseen. He had laboured long hours to bring this thing to pass, believing it meant prosperity for the district and perhaps salvation for the mines; but there did not seem much prosperity for the poor devils who worked here.

The fumes were blighting the vegetation in this pretty cove. The bracken was brown a month in advance of its time and the leaves of the trees were twisted and discoloured. Thoughtfully he rode up to Place House, which stood on the other side of the valley.

When he was shown in Sir John Trevaunance was still at breakfast and reading the *Spectator*.

'Ah, Poldark, take a seat. You're early. But then I'm late, what? I do not expect Tonkin for half an hour.' He flipped the paper. 'This is a confoundedly disturbing business, what?'

'You mean the riots in Paris?' said Ross. 'A little extravagant.'

Sir John put in a last mouthful of beef. 'But for the King to give way to them! Ecod he must be a lily! A round or two of grapeshot is what they wanted. It says the Comte d'Artois and several others have left France. To bolt at the first grumble of thunder!'

'Well, I fancy it should keep the French occupied with their own affairs,' Ross said. 'England should take the hint and put her own house in order.'

Sir John munched and read in silence for a while. Then he crumpled up the paper and threw it impatiently to the floor. The great boarhound by the fireplace rose and sniffed at the paper and then walked off, disliking the smell.

'That man Fox!' said the baronet. 'Damme, he's a fool if ever there was one! Going out of his way to praise a rabble such as that. One would think the gates of Heaven had opened!'

Ross got up and walked over to the window. Trevaunance stared after him.

'Come, man, don't tell me you're a Whig! Your family never was, not any of 'em.'

'I'm neither Whig nor Tory,' Ross said.

'Well, drot it, you must be something. Who d'you vote for?'

Ross was silent again for some time and bent and patted the hound. He seldom thought these things out.

'I'm not a Whig,' he said, 'nor ever could belong to a party that was for ever running down its own country and praising up the virtues of some other. The very thought of it sticks in my crop.'

'Hear, hear!' said Sir John, picking his teeth.

'But neither could I belong to a party which looks with complacency on the state of England as it is. So you'll see the difficulty I'm in.'

'Oh, I don't think ——'

'And you must not forget,' Ross said, 'that it is but a few months since I stormed a gaol of my own. And one which held considerably more than the six prisoners of the Bastille. It is true I didn't parade the streets of Launceston with the gaoler's head stuck on a pole, but that was not for lack of feeling like it.'

'Hm!' said Sir John uncomfortably. 'Hrrrm! Well, if you will excuse me, Poldark, I'll change my gown to be ready for Tonkin.'

He left the room hastily and Ross continued to pat the head of the boarhound.

Chapter ten

DEMELZA HAD BEEN wrestling with her conscience ever since Monday evening, and when Ross left on the Friday she knew she would have no peace unless she gave way.

So after he had gone she walked over to Trenwith. She was almost as nervous as she had ever been in her life, but there was no escape. She had hoped for a letter from Verity yesterday with the *Mercury*, but none had come.

Making the mistake of most early risers, she was surprised to find that Trenwith House had an unawakened look, and when she plucked at the doorbell Mary Bartle told her that Mrs Poldark was still in bed and that Mr Poldark was breakfasting alone in the winter parlour.

This might suit better than she had hoped and she said:

'Could I see him, if you please?'

'I'll go and ask, ma'am, if you'll wait here.'

Demelza wandered round the splendid hall, staring up at the pictures, able to take a longer view of them than she had ever done before. A strange crew, more than half of them Trenwiths, Ross said. She fancied she could detect the Poldark strain coming in, the stronger facial bones, the blue, heavy-lidded eyes, the wide mouth. Those early Trenwiths were the men with the looks, soft curling dark beards and sensitive faces, and the red-haired girl in a velvet gown of the style of William and Mary – but perhaps the Poldarks had given a new vigour. Was it they too who had brought the wild strain? Elizabeth had not been painted yet. That was a pity, in fairness Demelza had to admit it.

The house was very quiet, seemed to lack something. She suddenly realized that what it was lacking was Verity. She stood quite still and saw for the first time that she had robbed this household of its most vital personality. She had been the instrument of a theft, perpetrated on Francis and Elizabeth.

She had never looked on it that way before. All the time she had seen Verity's life as incomplete. She had looked at it from Andrew Blamey's point of view but not from Elizabeth's or Francis's. If she had thought of them at all she had considered them as clinging to Verity from selfish motives, because she was so useful to them. It hadn't occurred to her that everyone in this household might in fact love Verity and feel her personal loss – not until she stood in this hall, which seemed so large and so empty to-day. She wondered how she had had the impertinence to come.

'Mr Poldark will see ee right away,' said Mary Bartle behind her.

So while Sir John Trevaunance was entertaining Ross at his breakfast table, Francis was entertaining Demelza.

He got up when she went in. Unlike Sir John he was fully dressed, in a buff-coloured morning coat with velvet lapels, a silk shirt and brown breeches. His look was not friendly.

'I'm sorry,' he said shortly, 'Elizabeth is not down. She breakfasts upstairs these days.'

'I didn't come to see Elizabeth,' Demelza answered, flushing. 'I came to see you.'

'Oh. In that case, please sit down.'

'I don't want for you to interrupt your meal.'

'It is finished.'

'Oh.' She sat down, but he stood, a hand on the back of his chair. 'Well?'

'I have come to you to tell you something,' she said. 'I b'lieve you had a quarrel with Ross over Verity leaving the way she did. You thought he was at fault.'

'Has he sent you here this morning?'

'No, Francis; you know he would not do that. But I – I have to clear this up, even if you hate me for it ever after. Ross had nothing to do with Verity's elopement. I know that for certain.'

Francis's angry eyes met hers. 'Why should I believe you when I have disbelieved him?'

'Because I can tell you who did help.'

He laughed shortly. 'I wonder.'

'Yes, I can. For I was the one who helped, Francis, not Ross. He knew nothing about it. He didn't approve of her going any more than you did.'

Francis stared at her, frowned at her, turned sharply away as if shaking her confession aside, went to the window.

'I believed it was . . . I believe it was for Verity's happiness,' she stumbled on. She had intended to tell him the whole truth but her courage failed her. 'After the Assembly I offered to act as – as a go-between. Captain Blamey wrote to me an' I passed the letters to Verity. She gave letters to me and I gave them to the *Mercury* man. Ross didn't know nothing at all about it.'

There was silence. A clock in the room was ticking. Francis took a deep breath, then blew it out slowly on the window.

'You damned interfering . . .' He stopped.

She got up.

'Tisn't pleasant to come here and confess this. I know how you feel for me now. But I couldn't let this quarrel betwixt you and Ross go on from my fault. I didn't wish to hurt you or Elizabeth, please know that. You're right: I was interfering; but if I did wrong twas out of love for Verity, not to hurt you ——'

'Get out!' he said.

She began to feel sick. She had not thought the interview would be nearly as bad as this. She had tried to repair a mistake, but it did not seem that she had done any good at all. Was his feeling for Ross any different?

'What I came for,' she said, 'was to take the blame. If you hate me, that's maybe what I deserve, but please don't let this be a quarrel between you and Ross. I should feel ——'

He put up his hand to the catch of the window as if to open it. She saw that his hand was trembling. What was the matter with him?

'Will you go,' he said, 'and never enter this house again. Understand, so – so long as I live I never want you to come near Trenwith again. And Ross can stay out as well. If he will marry an ignorant trull such as you then he must take the consequences.'

He had controlled his voice so hard that she could only just hear what he said. She turned and left him, went out into the hall, picked up her cloak, passed through the open doorway into the sun. There was a seat beside the wall of the house and she sat on it. She felt faint, and the ground was unsteady.

After a few minutes the breeze began to revive her. She got up and began to walk back to Nampara.

Lord Devoran was not present, being kept away by an attack of tissick. Mr Trencrom was away also, being still privily occupied with the claims of his suffering employees – those who had had the misfortune to be found with contraband goods in their cellars and lofts.

From the beginning Ross felt there was something wrong. This was a general meeting of the shareholders and as such was not held until after dark. No general meeting had ever yet been held in daylight, since there might always be a spy about watching comings and goings.

A score had turned up. Chief item for discussion was Ray Penvenen's proposal that a rolling and cutting mill should be built at the top of the hill where his land joined Sir John's, he personally to pay half the cost, the company the other half. The project was urgent, for the venturers of Wheal Radiant had suddenly refused to renew the lease on their battery mill. Unless the company put up its own mill at once it would be forced to sell the copper solely in block ingots.

The only debatable point was the selection of site. Nevertheless Ross was for making the concession to Penvenen's *amour-propre*, for Penvenen had what was at a premium, free money. What Ross expected was opposition from Alfred Barbary. And he got it. The dreary old argument was dragged up about the north-coast shareholders' getting all the plums.

Ross listened to the wrangle but noted again that the cross-eyed Aukett sat silent, plucking at his bottom lip. A carpet manufacturer called Fox might have been turned to stone. Presently Tonkin, who made the perfect chairman, said: 'I should like the opinion of some of the other shareholders.'

After the usual sort of hesitation some views were given, mainly in favour of the mill near the works. Then Aukett said: 'It's all very well, gentlemen, but where's our half of the money coming from, eh; that's what I'd like to know?'

Tonkin said: 'Well, it was understood by the leading shareholders that additional calls might be expected and we all accepted that. The need is great. If we can't roll and beat the copper we miss nearly all our small markets. And the small markets may just turn the scale. We can't force the Government to buy our copper for the Mint, but we can expect our own friends to buy their requirements from us.'

There was a murmur of agreement.

'Well, that's very well,' said Aukett, squinting worse than usual in his excitement, 'but I'm afraid our mine will be unable to meet any such call. Indeed, it looks as if someone will have to take over the shares I hold.'

Tonkin looked at him sharply. 'Whether you sell the shares is your own concern, but so long as you retain them you're in honour bound to accept the responsibilities we all jointly incurred.'

'And so we'd like to,' said Aukett. 'But you can't get blood out of a stone. Whether we like it or not we shall have to contract out of the undertaking.'

'You mean default?'

'No, there's no question of defaulting. The shares are paid up. And our good will you'll retain, but ——'

'What's wrong?' said Blewett. 'You told me on Tuesday that the higher prices at the last ticketing had put the Wheal Mexico venturers in better heart than they'd been for years.'

'Yes,' Aukett nodded. 'But yesterday I had a letter from Warleggan's Bank telling me they could no longer support our loan and would we make arrangements to get it transferred elsewhere. That means ——'

'You had that?' said Fox.

'That means ruin unless Pascoe's will take it over, and I have my doubts, for Pascoe's was always on the cautious side and want more security. I'm calling in at Warleggan's on my way home to see if I can persuade them to reconsider it. It's unheard of suddenly to withdraw one's credit like this ——'

'Did they give any reason?' Ross asked.

'I had a very similar letter,' Fox interrupted. 'As you know I have been extending my business in several directions and I have drawn heavily during the last year. I went to see Mr Nicholas Warleggan last evening and explained that a withdrawal of their facilities would mean the failure of these schemes. He was not very amenable. I believe he knew all about my interest in Carnmore and resented it. I really believe that was at the bottom of it.'

'It was.' Everyone looked at St. Aubyn Tresize. 'My private business is not for discussion at this table, gentlemen. But money has been advanced to me during the last few years from Warleggan's Bank. They have the finest security in the world: land; but it is a security I don't propose to forfeit. If they foreclose at this stage I shall fight them – and they'll not get the land. But they will get most of my assets – including my shares in the Carnmore Copper Company.'

'How the Devil have they come to know all this?' Blewett demanded nervously. 'More than half of us here have some indebtedness that can be assailed.'

'Someone has been talking,' said a voice at the bottom.

Richard Tonkin tapped the table. 'Has anyone else here had word from the Warleggans?'

There was silence.

'Not yet,' said Johnson.

'Well, drot it,' said Trevaunance. 'You should all bank with Pascoe, as I do; then you'd not get into this mess. Get Pascoe's to take over your accounts.'

'Easier said than done,' Fox snapped. 'Aukett's right. Pascoe's want a better security. I was with them and could not get enough free money and I changed to Warleggan's. So there's small hope of me being able to change back.'

Ray Penvenen grunted impatiently. 'Well, that's a matter personal to you. We can't all start confessing our private difficulties or it will smack of a Methody revival. Let's get back to this question of the mill.'

At length it was agreed that the mill should be put up as a separate venture by Penvenen on the site of his own choosing. The Carnmore Company should hold only thirty per cent of the shares. Unreality had come to sit among them. Very well for Penvenen with his upcountry interests, to dismiss the matter as of no moment. Mines worked on credit, and these were not times for facing its withdrawal. Ross saw the same look on many faces. Someone has let us down. And if three names are known, why not all?

The meeting closed early. Decisions were taken, proposals went through; the name of Warleggan was no more spoken. Ross wondered how many of the decisions would be put into effect. He wondered if there was any danger of their stiff fight becoming a debacle.

When it was over he shook hands all round and was one of the first to leave. He wanted to think. He wanted to consider where the leak might have occurred. It was not until he was riding home that a very uncomfortable and disturbing thought came to him.

Chapter eleven

DEMELZA WAS IN bed but not asleep. When she spoke he gave up the attempt to undress in the dark.

'You're roosting early,' he said. 'I hope this is a sign of a reformed life.'

Her eyes glittered unnaturally in the growing yellow light of the candle.

'Have you any news of Mark?'

'No; it's early.'

'There are all sorts of rumours about France.'

'Yes, I know.'

'How did your meeting go?'

He told her.

She was silent after he had finished. 'D'you mean it may make more difficulties for you?'

'It may.'

She lay quiet then while he finished undressing. her hair coiled on the pillow. One tress of it lay on his pillow as he came to get into bed. He picked it up and squeezed it in his fingers a moment before putting it with the rest.

'Don't put out the light,' she said. 'I've something to tell you.'

'Can't you talk in the dark?'

'Not this. The darkness is so heavy sometimes. . . . Ross, I b'lieve we should sleep sweeter without the bed hangings these warm nights.'

'As you please.' He put the candle beside the bed where it flung yellow fancies on the curtains at their feet.

'Have you heard anything more of Verity?' she asked.

'I've not stirred from Trevaunance Cove all day.'

'Oh, Ross,' she said.

'What is the matter?'

'I . . . I have been to Trenwith to-day to see Francis.'

'The Devil you have! You'd get no welcome there. And certainly no news of Verity.'

'It wasn't for news of Verity I went. I went to tell him he was mistaken in thinking you'd encouraged Verity to elope.'

'What good would that do?'

'I didn't want that blame laid to me, that I'd caused a quarrel between you. I told him the truth: that I'd helped Verity unbeknown to you.'

She lay very still and waited.

Annoyance was somewhere within him but it would not come to a head: it ran away again into channels of fatigue.

'Oh, Heavens,' he said at length, wearily. 'What does it matter?'

She did not move or speak. The news sank further into his understanding, set off fresh conduits of thought and feeling.

'What did he say?'

'He – he turned me out. He – he told me to get out and . . . He was so angry. I never thought . . .'

Ross said: 'If he vents his ill-humour on you again . . . I could not understand his attitude to me on Monday. It seemed just as wild and unreasonable as you say ——'

'No, Ross, no, Ross,' she whispered urgently. 'That's not right. It isn't him you should be angry with, it is me. I am in the fault. Even then I didn't tell him all.'

'What did you tell him?'

'I – that I had passed on letters from Andrew Blamey and sent him letters from Verity ever since the Assembly in April.'

'And what didn't you tell him?'

There was silence.

She said: 'I think you will hit me, Ross.'

'Indeed.'

'I did as I did because I loved Verity and hated her to be unhappy.'

'Well?'

She told him everything. Her secret visit to Falmouth while he was away, how she had contrived a meeting and how it had all happened.

He did not interrupt her once. She went right through to the end, faltering but determined. He listened with a curious sense of incredulity. And all the time that other suspicion was beating away. This thing was a part of it. Francis must have realized that Verity and Blamey had been deliberately brought together. Francis had suspected *him*. Francis knew all about the Carnmore Copper Company. . . .

The candle flame shivered and the light broke its pattern on the bed.

It all came round to Demelza. The thing welled up in him.

'I can't believe you did it,' he said at last. 'If – if anyone had told me I should have named him a liar. I'd *never* have believed it. I thought you were trustworthy and loyal.'

She did not say anything.

The anger came easily now; it could not be stemmed.

'To go behind my back. *That* is what I can't stomach or – or even quite believe yet. The deceit ——'

'I tried to do it openly. But you wouldn't let me.'

She had betrayed him and was the cause of the greater betrayal. It all fitted into place.

'So you did it underhand, eh? Nothing mattered, no loyalty or trust, so long as you got your own way.'

'It wasn't for myself. It was for Verity.'

'The deceit and the lies,' he said with tremendous contempt. 'The continual lying for more than twelve months. We have been married no long time but I prided myself that this, this association of ours, was the one constant in my life. The one thing that would be changeless and untouchable. I should have said there was absolute trust and confidence between us. I should have staked my life on it. Demelza was true to the grain. There wasn't a flaw in her —— In this damned world ——'

'Oh, Ross,' she said with a sudden great sob, 'you'll break my heart.'

'You expect me to hit you?' he said. 'That's what you can understand. A good beating and then over. But you're not a dog or a horse to be thrashed into the right ways. You're a woman, with subtler instincts of right and wrong. Loyalty is not a thing to be bought: it is freely given or withheld. Well, by God, you have chosen to withhold it . . . !'

She began to climb out of bed, blindly; was out and clung sobbing to the curtains, released them and groped round the bed. Her whole body shook as she wept.

As she reached the door he sat up. His anger would not subside.

'Demelza, come here!'

She had gone and had shut the door behind her.

He got out of bed, took up the candle and opened the door again. She was not on the stairs. He went down shedding grease, reached the parlour. She was trying to close the door but he flung it open with a crash.

She fled from him towards the farther door, but he put down the candle and caught her by the fireplace and pulled her back. She struggled in his arms, feebly, as if grief had taken her strength. He caught her hair and pulled her head back. She shook it.

'Let me go, Ross. Let me go.'

He held her while the tears ran down her cheeks. Then he let her hair go and she stood quiet, crying against him.

She deserves all this and more, he thought. More, more! Let her suffer! He could well have struck her, taken a belt to her. Drunken hind and common drudge. What a foul mixture and mess!

Damn her for an impudent brat! Verity married to Blamey and all, *all* this trouble through her meddling. He could have shaken her till her teeth chattered.

But already his sense of fairness was fighting to gain a word. It was her fault in part, but not her blame. At least not the consequences. Verity married to Blamey might be the least of them. Damn Francis. Incredible betrayal! (Did he run too fast and too far? No, for it surely all fitted.)

'Come, you'll get cold,' he said roughly.

She took no notice.

She had already had the quarrel with Francis. That too must have upset her, for she had been very low when he got home. Curious that that should have upset her so much.

His anger was slowly subsiding, not disappearing but finding its true level. She could not stand his tongue. What had he said? Or *how* had he said it? The Poldarks were an unpleasant lot when they were crossed. Damn Francis, for all this trouble really lay at his door: the first break between Verity and Blamey, his later obstinate refusal to reconsider his dislike. Demelza no doubt had acted for the best. The road to Hell being so paved.

But she had no right to act so, for best or worst. She had no right. She had interfered and lied to him; and although now she was desperately upset, in a day or two she would be happy and smiling again. And all the consequences would go on and on and on, echoing in this man's life and that.

She had stopped now and she broke away from him.

'I'll be all right,' she said.

'Well, do not stay down here all night.'

'You go on. I'll come in a little.'

He left her the candle and went back to the bedroom. He lit another candle and walked over to the cot. Julia had kicked off all the bedclothes. She was lying like a Muslim worshipper, her head down and her seat in the air. He was about to cover her when Demelza came in.

'Look,' he said.

She came over and gave a little gulping 'Oh,' when she saw the child. She swallowed and turned her over. Julia's curly brown hair was like a halo for the innocent cherubic face. Demelza went quietly away.

Ross stayed staring down at the child, and when he turned Demelza was already in bed. She was sitting well back among the curtains, and he could only see the pyramid of her knees.

Presently he got in beside her and blew out the candle and lay down. She did not move to settle for a long time. Extravagant and contrary in all things, he thought: her loyalties, her griefs. She betrays me, deceives me without a flicker out of love for Verity. Am I to blame her, who know so much about conflicting and divided loyalties?

She causes this breach between Francis and me. The enormity of it, bringing perhaps failure and ruin.

'Ross,' she said suddenly, 'is it as bad as all that, what I've done?'

'No more talk now.'

'No, but I must know that. It didn't seem so wrong to me at the time. I knew it was deceiving you, but I thought I was doing what was best for Verity. Truly I did. Maybe it's because I don't know any better, but that's what I thought.'

'I know you did,' he said. 'But it isn't just that. Other things have come into it.'

'What other things?'

'Nothing I can tell you yet.'

'I'm that sorry,' she said. 'I never dreamed to make trouble between you and Francis. I never *dreamed*, Ross. I'd never ha' done it if I thought that.'

He sighed. 'You have married into a peculiar family. You must never expect the Poldarks to behave in the most rational manner. I have long since given up expecting it. We are hasty – quite incredibly hasty, it seems – and sharp-tempered; strong in our likes and dislikes and unreasonable in them – more unreasonable than I ever guessed. Perhaps, so far as the first goes, yours is the common-sense view. If two people are fond of each other let 'em marry and work out their own salvation, ignoring the past and damning the consequences. . . .'

There was another long silence.

'But I – I still don't understand,' she said. 'You seem to be talking in riddles, Ross. An' I feel such a cheat and – and so horrible. . . .'

'I can't explain more now. It is impossible until I am sure. But as for what I said . . . I spoke in heat. So forget it if you can and go to sleep.'

She slid an inch farther down the bed.

She blew out a long breath. 'I wish – I shall not be very happy if this quarrel between you and Francis does not quickly heal.'

'Then I am afraid you will be unhappy for a long time.'

Silence fell and this time was not broken. But neither of them went to sleep. She was on edge after the quarrel, desperately unsatisfied and not much relieved by her tears. She felt insecure and much in the dark. She had been told of other reasons for his anger but could not guess them. She bitterly hated anything to be incomplete, especially to leave a trouble unresolved. Yet she knew she could go no further to-night. He was restless and overtired and uneasy. Thoughts ran through his head in endless procession. After a time she closed her eyes and tried to go to sleep. But he did not even try.

Book four

Chapter one

ON CHRISTMAS EVE Demelza opened a letter from Verity which ran as follows:

MY DEAR COUSIN DEMELZA,

Your welcome letter reached me yesterday morning and I am replying – prompt for me! – to say how pleased I am to learn all are well, with all this sickness abroad. In this Town it is very bad, two or three things rage and who has not got one takes another. However, thanks to God, we too escape, at Church on Sunday the Pews were but half filled owing to it, and afterward we called on Mrs Daubuz the mayor's wife to condole with her on the loss of her baby son. We found her very sad but resigned, she is a fine woman.

I am glad that you have at last had news that Mark Daniel is safe in France – that is if anyone can be safe there at this present. It was a horrible thing to happen and I wish it had never been, I can sympathize with Mark but not condone his act.

We have been very busy here for a week past. The East India Fleet consisting of three fine ships and a frigate, with two Fleets from the West Indies as well as one from Oporto bound home are all come into our port except a few from the Leeward Islands, which are gone up Channel. The Harbour is a fine sight with above 200 sail of Vessels in view from our House. The Fleets are very valuable and the Town is full of Passengers from them.

Well my dear I am very happy in my new life. I think age is much how you feel, as a spinster of nearly thirty-one I felt old and sere but as a married woman I do not at all seem the same. I have put on weight since I came and get no more Catarr, perhaps it is the softer Climate which suits me, but I think that is not it. Andrew too is happy and is always whistling in the house. It is strange because no one at Trenwith ever whistled. Some things I miss terrible, some of my old work, and often I long to see the old faces, especially when Andrew is away, but so far my dear you can claim that your faith in us has not gone Awry. Bless you for all you did.

I could have wished that this Christmas time could have seen a reconsiling of us all, a real gathering of just the six of us, with of course

Julia and Geoffrey Charles. That would have been good, alas I'm afraid Francis will never soften. But I know Ross will, and in the Spring when the weather improves and Ross is less busy I want you both to come over and spend a week with me. We have quite a number of friends and no one dislikes Andrew who knows him well.

My dear I am so sorry that all Ross's work seems to be coming to nought, it is too bad and such a Pity, for the industry needs all the help it can get, there are distressed tinners round here and some entered the Town last week and made a disturbance. So far it has been a terrible winter and I hope and pray with so many near starving that nothing will happen here like what has happened across the water. Try not to let Ross take this to heart as sometimes he is inclined to do, feeling that any failure is *his* failure. If the very worst comes and the smelting works closes it may be only a setback for a few years, and happier times will see a reopening. Captain Millett one of the Frigate Captains said yesterday that what we need is another war. A terrible solution, but there were others in the room to agree with him. Better Poverty than that, I say.

My only regret is that Andrew is away so much. He leaves this evening and will be gone all Christmas and into the New Year. I have thought often to go with him but he says wait until the summer when the Bay of Biscay will not be so Steep. He loves the sea devotedly but is known throughout the Service as a 'driver.' Always when he comes home he seems strained, as if the voyage has tried his nerves, he is easier to cross and a trifle moody. I think too he drinks a little during his time at sea, no wonder, for he needs something to sustane him, but never touches a drop while ashore. It takes me one day of his precious time at home to make him quite content, then soon he has to be up and away.

I have not met my two 'children' yet. That is something of an Ordeal which may be mine about Easter, when *The Thunderer* with James Blamey on board as a cadet, is expected home. Esther Blamey, Andrew's daughter, is at boarding school and lives with his Sister near Plymouth. It may be that she will come and visit us too in the Spring. Pray for me then! I do so wish to make a home for them here and to make them welcome, if only our relationship will allow. I sometimes think I am such a poor mixer and wish I had an Easy manner, which some people have.

Our housekeeper, Mrs Stevens was taken so ill with pains in the stomach last night that we sent for Dr Silvey, but he said it was cramp and gave her a piece of roll Brimstone sewed in fine linen to hold near the affected part when she felt the pain. This has been a wonderful cure, but for my part I do not think she takes enough rhubarb.

I shall think of you this Christmas. I am very, very glad you gave me the courage to make my own life.

God bless and keep you both
VERITY.

Chapter two

Ten o'clock had struck before Ross returned that night. It was a fine night and an hour before Sawle Church choir had been up to the door singing carols. Demelza had never had much to do with religion but she still said the prayers her mother taught her, adding a postscript of her own to keep them abreast of the times; and at Christmas she had always felt an inward impulse to go to church. Something in the ancient wisdom of the story and the fey beauty of the carols tugged at her emotions; and with a suitable invitation she would have been willing to join the choir. She specially wanted to help them this evening hearing their depleted voices struggling through 'Remember, O thou Man.' But even her enjoyment of the two carols was a little spoiled by anxiety as to how she had best behave when they knocked on the door. She sent Jane Gimlett for the cakes she had made that afternoon and took down a couple of bottles of canary wine from Ross's cupboard.

They came in, a sheepish, blinking, uncertain lot, headed by Uncle Ben Tregeagle; ill-clad and undernourished every one, and only eight in all, for two of the choir were ill with the ulcerous sore throat and three were sick with influenza and Sue Baker had her fits. So Uncle Ben said, looking sly and foreign with his hooked nose and his long greasy black hair curling in little ringlets on his shoulders.

Demelza nervously gave them all a drink and took one herself; she would almost sooner have entertained Sir Hugh Bodrugan than these humble choristers; at least she knew where she was with him. She pressed cakes on them and refilled their glasses and when they rose to go she gave them a handful of silver – about nine shillings in all – and they crowded out into the misty moonlit night, flushed and merry and opulent. There they gathered round the lantern and gave her one more carol for luck before filing off up the valley towards Grambler.

Laughing now at her own absurdity and her success in spite of it, she went back into the parlour and began to pick out on the spinet the simple tune of 'In Dulce Jubilo.' Then she sat down and filled in with the other hand. She was getting good at this, though Mrs Kemp frowned on it and said it wasn't music at all.

While she was so playing she heard Ross return. She met him at the door and at once saw how everything was.

'I've saved some pie for you,' she said. 'Or there's cold chicken if you want. And some nice fresh cakes and tarts.'

He sat down in his chair and she helped him off with his boots.

'I had supper with Tonkin. Not a feast but enough to satisfy. A glass of rum will do and a bite or two of your cake. Have we had visitors?'

Demelza explained. 'There's a letter here from Verity. It came this morning.'

Ross read it slowly, puckering his eyes as if they too were tired. She put her hand on his shoulder, reading it again with him, and he put his fingers over hers.

The quarrel between them on that July evening had long been ignored but never forgotten. It had been ignored, and for that reason was still felt more by her than by him, it being her temperament to dislike anything not clear and downright. Also he had been fighting other things all these months and away more than at home. That he suspected Francis of betrayal had come to her gradually, and with it all the rest of his reasoning; so that she sometimes felt not only responsible for his quarrel with his cousin but also for the mounting difficulties of the copper company. It was not a pleasant thought and had lain heavy on her, far heavier than he knew. It was the first real shadow on their relationship and it had spoiled her happiness all this autumn. But outwardly there was no change.

'So your experiment prospers more than mine,' he said. 'Perhaps your instinct was the surer.'

'Is there no better news for you?'

'Johnson and Tonkin and I have gone through the books item by item. Sir John has come to the view, which I think will be general among those who are left, that it is better to cut our losses than to refuse to admit defeat. There will be a final meeting after the ticketing on Monday. If the decision goes against us I will spend Tuesday helping to wind up our affairs.'

'Who are for going on, do you know?'

'Tonkin of course, and Blewett and Johnson. All men of good will and no financial standing. Lord Devoran is for going on so long as he is asked for no more money. Penvenen is already considering converting his mill to other uses.'

Demelza sat down beside him. 'You'll have till Monday free?'

'Yes – to make merry over Christmas.'

'Ross, don't get bitter. You see what Verity says.'

He sighed, and the sigh turned to a yawn.

'. . . She says you feel everything too deep and that is the trouble, I b'lieve What difference will it make to our money, Ross?'

'I may have to sell some of the Wheal Leisure shares.'

'Oh, no!'

'Perhaps only half – those I bought from Choake.'

'But they are paying a – a dividend, d'you call it – it would be such a shame! Is Harris Pascoe not a friend of yours?'

'He's a banker, my dear. His first obligation is to his depositors.'

'But he must have a pile of money heaped up in the vaults. It would be no use to him! He knows he will be safe with your promise to pay. Why, you will be able to pay him in a few years out of the div – what I said – if he will only give you time.'

Ross smiled. 'Well, that will all be thrashed out. I shall have to be in Truro for two days, and Pascoe has invited me to stay with him. It will be difficult for him to be too hard on a guest.'

Demelza sat in gloomy silence, nursing her knees.

'I don't like it,' she said at length. 'It isn't fair, Ross! It is wicked an' inhuman. Have bankers got no Christian bowels? Don't they ever think, "How should I feel if I was in debt?"'

'Come, my dear; don't you too get despondent or we shall be a pretty pair to wish each other a happy Christmas.'

'Ross, could we not raise a mortgage on this house?'

'It's already raised.'

'Or sell the horses and the oxen. I don't mind walking about my business or going short of some foodstuffs – it is only what I was always used to. Then there is my best silver frock and my ruby brooch. You said that was worth a hundred pounds.'

He shook his head. 'All told these things wouldn't discharge the debt, nor half of it. We must accept the position if it has to be.'

'*Is* there a chance of going on?'

'Something will depend on the ticketing on Monday. And there is a movement on to drop the smelting but prevent the failure by becoming merchants pure and simple. I dislike face-saving.'

Demelza looked at him. She wondered if she was very selfish to feel glad that in the coming year there might be fewer calls on his time. If the failure of the company meant a return to old ways then there was some recompense even in failure.

Christmas passed quietly inside Nampara and out – the calm before the storm. He had had scarcely so much leisure since the project took shape. They had worked shorthanded on the farm all through the summer to cut down expense. He had scraped to put everything into Carnmore, and now it seemed he might just as well have thrown it over the cliff.

A bitter reflection but one that had to be faced. Ever since that meeting of the company in July, Ross and his fellow shareholders had been fighting a losing battle. St Aubyn Tresize, Aukett and Fox had all as good as resigned that day, and since then almost every week had seen a fresh casualty. Those the Warleggans could not touch directly they worked round to affect indirectly. Miners found their credit suddenly withdrawn or their coal supplies held up. Sir John was still fighting his case in Swansea. Alfred Barbary's title to some of the wharves he used in Truro and Falmouth was called in question, and litigation was pending here until he contracted out of the Carnmore. Even Ray Penvenen was not immune.

Of course it was not all the Warleggans, but it was the result of forces put in motion by them. If their grip had been complete the company could not have survived a month, but there were gaps in all their schemes. Only one third of the other copper companies were directly controlled by them, the rest were in friendly co-operation with the same ends in view.

On Boxing Day, the only windy day of the week, Ross and Demelza rode over to Werry House to visit Sir Hugh Bodrugan. Ross disliked the man but he knew Demelza had been secretly hankering to go ever since her first invitation nine months ago and he felt it right to humour her. They found Sir Hugh bottling gin, but he gave up with a good grace and ushered them into the great parlour, where Constance, Lady Bodrugan, was busy among her puppies.

She was not so rude as Ross remembered her, and received them without blasphemy. She had got used to the strange idea of her elderly stepson's having this liking for Ross Poldark's underbred wife. They took tea at a respectful distance from the greatest log fire Demelza had ever seen, and surrounded by spaniels, boarhound puppies and other breeds, whom Constance fed with cakes from the table and who made polite conversation a tenuous affair punctuated by the snaps and snarls of the disputing feeders. Every now and then a great gust of smoke would billow out from the fireplace, but the room was so high that the fog made a canopy over them and drifted away through the cracks in the ceiling. In this peculiar atmosphere Demelza sipped strong tea and tried to hear what Constance was saying about her treatment for dog's distemper; Ross, looking very tall and rather out of place on a chair too small for him, nodded his lean intelligent head and threw the ball of conversation back at Sir Hugh, who was just then leaning back scratching his ruffles and wondering what sort of a bedfellow Demelza would really make.

After tea Sir Hugh insisted on showing them the house and the stables, although by then darkness was near. They walked down draughty passages, led and followed by a groom with a horn lantern, up staircases to a great room on the first floor once elaborately decorated but now damp and mildewed, with creaking boards and cracked windows. Here the Dowager Lady kept her yellow rabbits in great boxes along one wall and bred her puppies in boxes opposite. The smell was overpowering. In the next room was a family of owls, some dormice, a sick monkey and a pair of racoons. Downstairs they went again, to a passage full of cages with thrushes, goldfinches, canary birds and Virginia nightingales. Sir Hugh squeezed her arm so often that Demelza began to wonder if this show was all a pretext for being with her in dark and draughty places. In one room, where the wind was so high that they might have been out of doors, the rear lantern went out and Sir Hugh put his short thick arm round her waist. But she slipped away with a faint rustle of silk and moved quickly up to Ross.

The stables were the best-kept part of the house, with many fine hunters and a pack of hounds, but inspection was abandoned halfway, Lady Bodrugan not being concerned for the comfort of her guests but thinking the horses would be needlessly disturbed.

So back they went to the great parlour, in which the fog had thickened since they left. Demelza had not yet learned to play whist, so they had a hand of quadrille for an hour, at which she won five shillings. Then Ross got up and said they must go before the wind grew worse. Sir Hugh, perhaps with vague hopes of further intimacies, suggested they should stay the night, but they thanked him and refused.

On the way home Demelza was rather silent, more silent than the gusty night dictated. When they got into the shelter of their own combe she said:

'It isn't always the people with the biggest house who are the most comfortable, is it, Ross?'

'Nor the best-bred who are the cleanest.'

She laughed. 'I did not fancy staying there the night. The wind was everywhere. And I should have dreamed of finding that old sick monkey in my bed.'

'Oh, I don't think Sir Hugh is sick.'

Her laughter bubbled up again, overflowed and ran with the wind.

'Serious, though,' she said breathlessly, 'what is the use of a big house if you cannot keep it nice? Are they short of money?'

'Not desperate. But old Sir Bob squandered most of what was not entailed.'

'It must be strange to have a stepson old enough to be your father.' Little eddies of laughter still bubbled inside her. 'Serious, though, Ross, would he have money to loan you to tide you over just for the present?'

'Thank you, I would rather the company was put away decently.'

'Is there no one else? Would old Mr Treneglos help? He has done well out of the mine you started for him. How much do you need to carry on a while longer?'

'A minimum of three thousand pounds.'

She pursed her lips together as if to whistle. Then she said:

'But for yourself, Ross, so as not to have to sell the Wheal Leisure shares. That's what I care about most of all.'

'I shall be more sure when I've talked of it with Pascoe,' Ross said evasively. 'In any event I would not be willing to borrow from friends.'

Chapter three

HE WOULD NOT be willing to borrow from friends.

He said that to himself as he left for Truro on the Monday morning. At heart he would have agreed with Demelza, that his own happiness lay with her and little Julia and having leisure to labour on his own land and to see it grow. That was what he had thought at the beginning and nothing could alter it. He might even look back on this year as a nightmare well over and best forgotten. Yet nothing would remove the stigma of the failure, nothing would remove the sting of the Warleggan triumph.

And nothing would solve the bitter disappointment of having to part with the whole of his holdings in Wheal Leisure, which he knew was coming, though he had hidden it from Demelza. To lose that was the worst blow of all.

At the clump of firs Zacky Martin was waiting.

The pony and the horse fell naturally into step, having now made many journeys together. Ross tried to forget the business on hand and asked after Zacky's family. The Martins were a tenacious stock. Mrs Zacky made them all drink pilchard oil during the winter and although it was foul and stank it seemed to be to their good. Jinny's three were brave, thanking you, Zacky said; and Jinny herself more better in spirits. There was a miner at Leisure called Scoble, a widow man in the thirties, lived beyond Marasanvose, no doubt Captain Poldark knew him.

'You mean Whitehead?'

'That's of him. They call him that on account of his hair. Well, he's taking an interest in Jinny, and she won't have nothing to do with him. Tisn't as she dislike him, she say, but that no one could do for Jim's place. That's well enough and as it should be, her mother say, but you've three young children to think of, and he's a nice steady feller with a little cottage, still some years to run and no children of his own. Mebbe in a year or so, Jinny say, I could consider it, but not yet for a while, twouldn't be possible. That's well enough, her mother say, but he's lonely and you're lonely, and men don't always wait and wait, for there's other girls'd be glad of the chance and they single and no family.'

Ross said: 'There is a lot in what Mrs Zacky says. And no need to fear appearances. I know a clergyman in Truro called Halse who married his second wife within two months of losing his first. It is nothing unusual in the upper classes.'

'I'll tell her that. It may help her to see it right. It is no good to marry a man if you dislike him; but I don't think she do; and I b'lieve it would do her good once the ice was broke.'

When they reached the fork near Sawle Church they saw Dwight Enys, and Ross waved a hand and would have branched off towards the Bargus crossroads, but Dwight signalled him to stop. Zacky rode on a few paces to be out of earshot.

As Dwight came up Ross noticed how his good looks had come to have a cadaverous threat.

His place in the countryside was secure enough now; his work during the epidemics of the autumn had made sure of that. All remembered and a few still whispered behind his back, but none wished him gone. They liked him, they respected his work, they depended on him. Since the closing of Grambler many of Choake's former patients had come to Enys. Not that such work showed much return, but no one ever asked in vain. He was working off the disgrace within himself. But when not working he liked to be alone.

'You look in need of a holiday,' Ross said. 'I am lying to-night with the Pascoes and they would be pleased to see you.'

Dwight shook his head. 'It is out of the question, Ross. There is a mountain of work. If I was absent for three days I should never catch up in three months.'

'You should leave Choake more to do. It is not a fair distribution, for you do a hundred poor cases and he does ten rich.'

Dwight said: 'I am getting along. Old Mr Treneglos called me in last week for his gout, and you know how he distrusts our profession.' The smile faded. 'But what I had to tell you is not good news. It is about Mr Francis Poldark. Had you heard? They say he is ill, also their little son.'

'Oh . . . ? No. Have you seen them?'

'Dr Choake is of course in charge. It is rumoured it is the sore throat. *Morbus strangulatorius.*'

Ross stared at him. This disease had been hanging round the district for nearly nine months. It had never been quite epidemic in the way the familiar diseases were epidemic; but it struck here and there with great rapidity and terrible results. Sometimes a whole family of children was swept off. It flared up in this village or that and then went underground again.

'Only last week,' Dwight said, frowning, and as if following his thoughts, 'I looked up what records there were on the matter. There was a bad outbreak in 'forty-eight. In Cornwall, that was. But since then we have been tolerably immune.'

'What is the cause?'

'No one knows. Some put it down to a mephitic quality of the air, especially when near water. All our views are much in the melting pot since Cavendish proved there was both dephlogisticated and inflammable air.'

'I wish you could get to see them, Dwight.' Ross was thinking of Elizabeth.

The younger man shook his head. 'Unless I am called in . . . Besides, I lay no claim to a cure. The results are always unpredictable. Sometimes the strong will go and the weak survive. Choake knows as much as I do.'

'Don't belittle yourself.' Ross hesitated, wondering whether he should obey his impulse to ride at once and see Elizabeth. It was the Christian thing to do, to forget all the old bitterness. Almost impossible with the copper company dying before his eyes. And the ticketing would not wait. He had only just time to get there.

As he was hesitating, Dr Choake himself topped the hill out of Sawle riding towards them. . . .

'You'll pardon me,' Dwight said. 'This man has tried to make every sort of trouble for me. I don't wish to meet him now.' He took off his hat and moved away.

Ross stood his ground until Choake was fairly up with him. The physician would have ridden by without a word if he could have got past.

'Good day to you, Dr Choake.'

Choake looked at him from under his eye-thatches.

'We'll trouble you to move aside, Mister Poldark. We are on urgent business.'

'I'll not detain you. But I hear that my cousin is gravely ill.'

'Gravely ill?' Choake bent his eyebrows after the departing figure of his rival. 'Dear me, I should not be inclined to lend an ear to every story if I were you.'

Ross said curtly: 'Is it true that Francis has the malignant sore throat?'

'I isolated the symptoms yesterday. But he is on the mend.'

'So soon?'

'The fever was checked in time. I emptied the stomach with fever powder and gave him strong doses of Peruvian bark. It is all a question of competent treatment. You are fully at liberty to enquire at the house.' Choake moved to edge his horse past. Darkie blew through her nostrils and stamped.

'And Geoffrey Charles?'

'Not the throat at all. A mild attack of quartan fever. And the other cases in the house are the ulcerous throat, which is quite a different thing. And now good day to you, sir.'

When Choake was past Ross sat a moment gazing after him. Then he turned and followed Zacky.

The ticketing was over and the feast about to begin.

Everything had gone according to plan, someone else's plan. The usual care had been taken to see that the Carnmore Copper Company did not get any of the copper. The mines did well out of it – so long as the Carnmore was in existence as a threat. As soon as Zacky ceased to put in his bids the prices would drop into the ruck again.

Ross wondered if the mines – the remaining mines – were really as powerless as the Warleggans had shown them up to be. They had not been able to stay together so they had fallen by the way. It was a dismal, sordid, disheartening business.

Ross sat down at the long dinner table with Zacky on his one hand and Captain Henshawe, representing Wheal Leisure, on his other. It wasn't until he was served that he noticed George Warleggan.

Ross had never seen him before at a ticketing dinner. He had no plain business there, for although he owned the controlling interest in a number of ventures he always acted through an agent or a manager. Strange that he had condescended, for as George grew more powerful he grew more exclusive. A brief silence had fallen on the men gathered there. They knew all about Mr Warleggan. They knew he could make or break a good many if he chose. Then George Warleggan looked up and caught Ross's eye. He smiled briefly and raised a well-groomed hand in salute.

It was a sign for the dinner to begin.

Ross had arranged to meet Richard Tonkin at the Seven Stars Tavern before the others arrived. As he came out of the Red Lion Inn he found George Warleggan beside him. He fell into step.

'Well, Ross,' he said in a friendly fashion, as if nothing had happened between them, 'we see little of you in Truro these days. Margaret Vosper was saying only last night that you had not been to our little gaming parties recently.'

'Margaret Vosper?'

'Did you not know? The Cartland has been Margaret Vosper these four months, and already poor Luke is beginning to fade. I do not know what there is fatal about her, but her husbands seem unable to stand the pace. She is climbing the ladder and will marry a title before she's done.'

'There is nothing fatal in her,' Ross said, 'except a greed for life. Greed is always a dangerous thing.'

'So she sucks the life out of her lovers, eh? Well, you should know. She told me she'd once had the fancy to marry you. It would have been an interesting experiment, ecod! I imagine she would have found you a hard nut.'

Ross glanced at his companion as they crossed the street. They had not met for eight months; and George, Ross thought, was becoming more and more a 'figure.' In his early days he had striven to hide his peculiarities, tried to become polished and bland and impersonal, aping the conventional

aristocrat. Now with success and power firmly held, he was finding a new
pleasure in allowing those characteristics their freedom. He had always
tried to disguise his bullneck in elaborate neck-cloths; now he seemed to
accentuate it slightly, walking with his head thrust forward and carrying a
long stick. Once he had raised his naturally deep voice: now he was letting
it go, so that the refinements of speech he had learned and clung to seemed
to take on a bizarre quality. Everything about his face was big, the heavy
nose, the pursed mouth, the wide eyes. Having as much money as he
wanted, he lived now for power. He loved to see himself pointed out. He
delighted that men should fear him.

'How is your wife?' George asked. 'You do not bring her out enough.
She was much remarked on at the celebration ball, and has not been seen
since.'

'We have no time for a social round,' Ross said. 'And I don't imagine we
should be the more wholesome for it.'

George refused to be ruffled. 'Of course you will be busy. This copper-
smelting project takes a good portion of your time.' A pretty answer.

'That and Wheal Leisure.'

'At Wheal Leisure you are fortunate in the grade of your ore and the
easy drainage. One of the few mines which still offer prospects for the
investor. I believe some of the shares are shortly coming on the market.'

'Indeed. Whose are they?'

'I understood,' said George delicately, 'that they were your own.'

They had just reached the door of the Seven Stars, and Ross stopped
and faced the other man. These two had been inimical since their school
days but had never come to an outright clash. Seeds of enmity had been
sown time and again but never reached fruit. It seemed that the whole
weight of years was coming to bear at once.

Then George said in a cool voice but quickly: 'Forgive me if I am
misinformed. There was some talk of it.'

The remark just turned away the edge of the response that was coming.
George was not physically afraid of a rough and tumble but he could not
afford the loss to his dignity. Besides, when quarrelling with a gentleman it
might not end in fisticuffs even in these civilized days.

'You have been misinformed,' Ross said, looking at him with his bleak
pale eyes.

George humped his shoulders over his stick. 'Disappointing; I am always
out for a good speculation, you know. If you ever do hear of any coming on
the market, let me know. I'll pay thirteen pound fifteen a share for 'em,
which is more than you – more than anyone would get at present in the
open market.' He glanced spitefully up at the taller man.

Ross said: 'I have no control over my partners. You had best approach
one of them. For my part I would sooner burn the shares.'

George stared across the street. 'There is only one trouble with the

Poldarks,' he said after a moment. 'They cannot take a beating.'

'And only one trouble with the Warleggans,' said Ross. 'They never know when they are not wanted.'

George's colour deepened. 'But they can appreciate and remember an insult.'

'Well, I trust you will remember this one.' Ross turned his back and went down the steps into the tavern.

Chapter four

IT WAS AFTERNOON before Demelza heard the bad news of Trenwith. All three of the younger Poldarks had it, said Betty Prowse, with only Aunt Agatha well, and three out of the four servants had taken it. Geoffrey Charles was near to death, they said, and no one knew which way to turn. Demelza asked for particulars, but Betty knew nothing more. Demelza went on with her baking.

But not for long. She picked up Julia, who was crawling about on the floor under her feet and carried her into the parlour. There she sat on the rug and played with the child before the fire while she wrestled with her torment.

She owed them nothing. Francis had told her never to come near the house again. Francis had betrayed them to the Warleggans. A despicable, horrible thing to do.

They would have called in others to help, perhaps some of the Teague family or one of the Tremenheere cousins from farther west. Dr Choake would have seen to that for them. They were well able to look after themselves.

She threw the linen ball back to Julia who, having rolled on it to stop it, now forgot her mother and began to try to pull the ball apart.

There was no reason for her to call. It would look as if she were trying to curry favour and patch up the quarrel. Why should she patch it up, when Elizabeth was her rival. Elizabeth had not appeared so much in that light this last year; but she was always a danger. Once Ross saw that fair fragile loveliness . . . She was the unknown, the unattainable, the mysterious. His wife he knew would be here always, like a faithful sheep dog, no mystery, no remoteness, they slept in the same bed every night. They gained in intimacy, lost in excitement. Or that was how she felt it must be with him. No; leave well alone. She had done enough interfering.

'Ah-ah!' Demelza said. 'Naughty girl. Don't tear it abroad. Throw it back to Mummy. Go to! Push with your hand. Push!'

But it was her interference which put her in an obligation deep down. If she had not contrived Verity's marriage, Verity would have been there to take charge. And if she had not so contrived Francis would never have quarrelled with Ross or betrayed them. Was it really all her fault?

Sometimes she thought Ross thought so. In the night – when she woke up in the night – she felt that sense of guilt. She glanced out of the window. Two hours of daylight. The ticketing would be over. He would not be home to-night, so she could not have his advice. But she did not want his advice. She knew what she knew.

Julia was crowing on the rug as she went to the bell. But she did not pull it. She could never get used to having servants at call.

She went through to the kitchen. 'Jane, I am going out for a while. I expect to be back before dark. If not, could you see to put Julia to bed? See the milk be boiled an' see she takes all her food.'

'Yes, ma'am.'

Demelza went upstairs for her hood and cloak.

The company had assembled in the private room of the Seven Stars. They were a depleted and a subdued party. Lord Devoran was in the chair. He was a fat dusty man dressed in snuff brown, and he had a cold in the head from leaving off his wig.

'Well, gentlemen,' he said stuffily, 'you have heard Mr Johnson's statement of accounts. It is all very disappointing I aver, for the company was started in such high hopes not fourteen months ago. It has cost me a pretty penny and I suspicion most of us are a good degree poorer for our interest. But the truth is we bit off more'n we could chew, and we've got to face the fact. Some of us I know feel sore about the tactics of those who have fought us; and I can't say myself that I'm any too satisfied. But it has all been legal, so there's no redress. We just haven't the resources to carry on.' Devoran paused and took a pinch of snuff.

Tonkin said: 'You can form a company like this with fair enough prospects and find many people willing to invest a little. But it is altogether a different matter to find people willing to buttress up a shaky concern or to buy shares suddenly flung on the market. They see that the company is in difficulty and aren't agreeable to risk their money then.'

Sir John Trevaunance said: 'The company would have stood twice the chance if we had restricted it to people with unassailable credit.'

Tonkin said: 'You can't hold an inquiry into people's finances when they wish you well. And of course it was not thought that the exact composition of the company should ever become publicly known.'

'Oh, you know what it is in these parts,' Sir John remarked. 'No man can keep a secret for five minutes. I do believe it is something in the air, it is moist and humid and breeds confidences.'

'Well, somebody's confidences have cost us dear,' said Tonkin. 'I have lost my position and best part of my life's savings.'

'And I am for bankruptcy,' said Harry Blewett. 'Wheal Maid must close this month. It is doubtful if I will stay out of prison.'

'Where is Penvenen to-night?' Ross asked.

There was silence.

Sir John said: 'Well, don't look at me. I am not his keeper.'

'He has lost interest in the sinking ship,' Tonkin said rather bitterly.

'He is more interested in his rolling mill than in the copper company,' Johnson said.

'As for a *sinking* ship,' Sir John said, 'I think in truth the ship may be considered sunk. There is no question of desertion. When one is left struggling in the water it is but natural to make what provision one can to reach dry land.'

Ross had been watching the faces of his companions. There was the barest touch of complacency about Sir John that he had not noticed before Christmas. In this venture Sir John stood to lose the most – though not proportionately the most. The great smelting furnaces stood on his land. During the company's brief life he had been the only one to receive a return for his larger investment – in the shape of port dues, increased profit from his coal ships, ground rent and other items. This change was therefore surprising. Had he during Christmas caught sight of some dry land not visible to the others?

All the time Ross had been striving to sense the mood of the other men. He had been hoping for signs of a greater resilience in some of them. But even Tonkin was resigned. Yet he was determined to make a last effort to bring them round.

'I don't altogether agree that the ship is yet sunk,' he said. 'I have one suggestion to make. It might just see us through the difficult months until the spring. . . .'

Trenwith House looked chill and grey. Perhaps it was only her imagination harking back to the last visit. Or perhaps it was knowing what the house now held.

She pulled at the front doorbell and fancied she heard it jangling somewhere away in the kitchens right across the inner court. The garden here was overgrown, and the lawn falling away to the stream and the pond was green and unkempt. Two curlews ran across it, dipping their tufted heads and sheering away as they saw her.

She pulled the bell again. Silence.

She tried the door. The big ring handle lifted the latch easily and the heavy door swung back with a creak.

There was nobody in the big hall. Although the tall mullioned window faced south the shadows of the winter afternoon were already heavy in the house. The rows of family pictures at the end and going up the stairs were all dark except for one. A shaft of pale light from the window fell on the portrait of the red-haired Anna-Maria Trenwith, who had been born, said Aunt Agatha, when Old Rowley was on the throne, whoever he might be.

Her oval face and the fixed blue eyes stared out through the window and over the lawn.

Demelza shivered. Her finger touching the long table came away dusty. There was a herby smell. She would have done better to follow her old custom and go round the back. At that moment a door banged somewhere upstairs.

She went across to the big parlour and tapped. The door was ajar and she pushed it open. The room was empty and cold and the furniture was hung in dust sheets.

So this was the part they were not using. Only two years ago she had come to this house for the first time, when Julia was on the way, had been sick and drunk five glasses of port and sung to a lot of ladies and gentlemen she had never seen before. John Treneglos had been there, merry with wine, and Ruth his spiteful wife, and George Warleggan; and dear Verity. This house had been glittering and candlelit then, enormous and as impressive to her as a palace in a fairy tale. Since then she had seen the Warleggans' town house, the Assembly Rooms, Werry House. She was experienced, adult and grown-up now. But she had been happier then.

She heard a footstep on the stairs and slipped back quickly into the hall.

In the half-light an old woman was tottering down them clutching anxiously at the banister. She was in faded black satin and wore a white shawl over her wig.

Demelza went quickly forward.

Aunt Agatha's ancient tremblings came to a stop. She peered at the girl, her eyes interred before their time in a mass of folds and wrinkles.

'What – eh . . . ? Is it you, Verity? Come back, have ye? And about time too ——'.

'No, it's Demelza.' She raised her voice. 'Demelza, Ross's wife. I came to enquire.'

'You what? Oh, yes, tis Ross's little bud. Well, this be no time for calling. They're all sick, every last jack of them. All except me and Mary Bartle. And she be so busy attending on them that she's no time to bother with a old woman. Let me starve! I b'lieve she would! Lord damme, don't an old body need just so much attention as a young?' She clung precariously to the banister and a tear tried to trickle down her cheek, but got diverted by a wrinkle. 'Tis all bad managing, and that's a fact. Everything has gone amiss since Verity left. She never ought to have left, d'you hear. Twas selfish in her to go running after that man. Her duty was to stay. Her father always said so. She'd take no notice of me. Always headstrong, she was. I bring to mind when she was but five ——'

Demelza slipped past her and ran up the stairs.

She knew where the main bedrooms were, and as she turned the corner of the corridor an elderly black-haired woman came out of one of the rooms carrying a bowl of water. Demelza recognized her as Aunt Sarah

Tregeagle, Uncle Ben's putative wife. She dipped a brief curtsy when she saw Demelza.

'Are they in here?'

'Yes, ma'am.'

'Are you – seeing after them?'

'Well, Dr Tommy calls me in, ma'am. But tis midwifing that belongs to be my proper work, as ye d'know. I come 'cos there was no one else. But my proper work be lying-in – or laying-out, when need be.'

Her hand on the door, Demelza stared after the woman, who was slopping water on the floor in her carelessness. Everyone knew Aunt Sarah. Not the nurse for these gentlefolk. But of course there was no choice. The smell of herbs was much stronger here.

She opened the door gently and slipped in.

After the meeting of the shareholders Ross did not go straight back to the Pascoes. They did not sup till eight, and he did not want to spend an hour making polite conversation with the ladies in the parlour.

So he strolled through the back streets of the little town. Deliberately he turned his mind away from all the things which had just finished. Instead he thought about himself and his family, about his rake of a father, who had been in and out of trouble all his life, making love to one woman after another, fighting with this husband and that parent, cynical and disillusioned and sturdy to the end. He thought of Demelza and of how his estrangement from Francis sometimes seemed to come between her and him. It had no business to but it did – a sort of reservation, a bar sinister on their clear intimacy. He thought of Garrick her dog, of Julia, laughing and self-absorbed and untroubled with the perplexities of the world. He thought of Mark Daniel away in a foreign land, and wondered if he would ever bring himself to settle down there, or whether one day homesickness would lure him back into the shadow of the gibbet. He thought of the sickness at Trenwith and of Verity.

The drift of his steps had taken him out of the town and towards the river, which was full to-night and gleamed here and there with the lights of ships and the lanterns moving about the docks. There were three vessels moored alongside the wharves: two small schooners and a ship of some size for this creek, a brigantine Ross saw when he got near enough to make out the yards on her foremast. She was a nice new ship, recently painted, with brass glistening on the poop. She would draw so much water, he thought, as to make it unsafe to put in and out of here except at the high tides. That was the reason for all the bustle to-night.

He strolled on towards the trees growing low to the riverbank and then turned to come back. From here, although there was no moon, you could make out the wide gleam of the flood tide with the masts like lattices in the foreground and the winking pins of light in the black rim of the town.

As he came near the brigantine again he saw several men going aboard. Two sailors held lanterns at the top of the gangway, and as one of the men reached the deck the lantern light fell clear on his face. Ross made a half movement and then checked himself. There was nothing he could do to this man.

He walked thoughtfully on. He turned back to look once, but the men had gone below. A sailor passed.

'Are you for the *Queen Charlotte?*' Ross asked on impulse.

The sailor stopped and peered suspiciously. 'Me, sur? No, sur. *Fairy Vale*. Cap'n Hodges.'

'She's a fine ship, the *Queen Charlotte*,' Ross said. 'Is she new to these parts?'

'Oh, she's been in three or four times this year, I b'la.'

'Who is her master?'

'Cap'n Bray, sur. She's just off, I reckon.'

'What is her cargo, do you know?'

'Grain for the most part; an' pilchards.' The sailor moved on.

Ross stared at the ship a moment longer and then turned and walked back into the town.

The heavy smell of incense came from a little brazier of disinfectant herbs burning smokily in the centre of the bedroom. Demelza had found them all in the one room. Francis lay in the great mahogany bed. Geoffrey Charles was in his own small bed in the alcove. Elizabeth sat beside him.

Any resentment she might once have felt for Demelza was as nothing before relief at her coming now.

'Oh Demelza, how kind of you! I have been in – in despair. We are in – terrible straits. How kind of you. My poor little boy. . . .'

Demelza stared at the child. Geoffrey Charles was struggling for breath, every intake sounded raw and hoarse and painful. His face was flushed and strained and his eyes only half open. There were red spots behind his ears and on the nape of his neck. One hand kept opening and shutting as he breathed.

'He – he has these paroxysms,' Elizabeth muttered. 'And then he spits up or vomits; there is relief then; but only for – for a time before it begins all over again.'

Her voice was broken and despairing. Demelza looked at her flushed face, at the piled fair hair, at the great glistening grey eyes.

'You're ill yourself, Elizabeth. You did ought to be in bed.'

'A slight fever. But not this. I can manage to keep up. Oh, my poor boy. I have prayed – and prayed . . .'

'And Francis?'

Elizabeth coughed and swallowed with difficulty. 'Is . . . a little . . . on the mend. There – there my poor dear . . . if only I could help him. We paint his throat with this Melrose; but there seems small relief . . . . '

'Who is it?' said Francis from the bed. His voice was almost unrecognizable.

'It is Demelza. She has come to help us.'

There was silence.

Then Francis said slowly: 'It is good of her to overlook past quarrels. . . .'

Demelza breathed out a slow breath.

'If . . . the servants had not been ill too,' Elizabeth went on, 'we could have made a better shift. . . . But only Mary Bartle . . . Tom Choake has persuaded Aunt Sarah . . . It is not a pretty task . . . He could find no one else.'

'Don't talk any more,' Demelza said. 'You should be abed. Look, Elizabeth, I – I didn't know if I came to stay for a long time, for I didn't know how you was fixed ——'

'But ——'

'But since you need me I'll stay – so long as ever I can. But first – soon – soon I must slip home and tell Jane Gimlett and give her word for looking after Julia. Then I'll be back.'

'Thank you. If only for to-night. It is such a relief to have someone to rely on. Thank you again. Do you hear, Francis, Demelza is going to see us through to-night.'

The door opened and Aunt Sarah Tregeagle hobbled in with a bowl full of clean water.

'Aunt Sarah,' said Demelza, 'will you help me with Mrs Poldark. She must be put to bed.'

After supper at the Pascoes, when the ladies had left them and they were settling to the port, Harris Pascoe said:

'Well; and what is your news to-day?'

Ross stared at the dark wine in his glass. 'We are finished. The company will be wound up to-morrow.'

The banker nodded his head.

'I made a last effort to persuade them otherwise,' Ross said. 'For the first time in years copper has moved up instead of down. I put that to them and suggested we should try to keep together for another six months. I suggested that the furnace workers should be invited to work on a profit-sharing basis. Every mine does the same thing when it strikes bargains with tributers. I suggested we should make one last effort. A few were willing but the influential men would have none of it.'

'Especially S-Sir John Trevaunance,' said the banker.

'Yes. How did you know?'

'You are right about the price of copper. I had news to-day, it has risen another three pounds.'

'That is six pounds in six weeks.'

'But, mind you, years may pass before the metal reaches an economic level.'

'How did you know Sir John would be opposed to my suggestion?'

Harris Pascoe licked his lips and looked diffident.

'Not so much opposed to your suggestion in p-particular as to a continuance in general. And then I was rather going on hearsay.'

'Which is?'

'Which is that – er – Sir John, after battling against the wind for twelve months, is now preparing to sail with it. He has lost a tidy sum over this project and is anxious to recoup himself. He does not wish to see the smelting works lying idle permanently.'

Ross thought of Sir John's voice that evening; he remembered Ray Penvenen's absence.

He got up. 'Do you mean he is selling out to the Warleggans?'

The little banker reached for his wine.

'I think he is willing to come to some accommodation with them. Beyond that I know nothing.'

'He and Penvenen are going to make a deal to cover their own losses while the rest of us go to the wall!'

'I imagine it likely,' said Pascoe, 'that some sort of a caretaker company will be formed, and that the Warleggans will have a representative on it.'

Ross was silent, staring at the books in the cabinet.

'Tell me,' he said, 'this evening I thought I saw Matthew Sanson boarding a ship in the docks. Could that be possible?'

'Yes, he has been back in Truro for several months.'

'He is allowed to come back here and trade as if nothing had happened? Are the Warleggans complete masters of the district?'

'No one cares sufficiently about Sanson to make a fuss. There are only four or five people whom he cheated, and they are not influential.'

'And the ship he sails in?'

'Yes, that is the property of a company controlled by the Warleggans. There's the *Queen Charlotte* and the *Lady Lyson*. No doubt they're a profitable side line.'

Ross said: 'If I were in your shoes I should tremble for my soul. Is there anyone besides you in the town they don't own from head to toe?'

Pascoe coloured. 'I like them little more than you. But you're t-taking an extreme view now. The average man in the district only knows them as rich and influential people. You know them as something more because you chose to challenge them on their own ground. I am only sorry – profoundly sorry – that you have not been more successful. If g-good will would have sufficed you would have triumphed without a doubt.'

'Whereas good will did not suffice,' Ross said. 'What we needed was good gold.'

'It was not my project,' said the banker, after a moment. 'I did what I could and will be the poorer for it.'

'I know,' Ross said. 'Failure puts an edge on one's tongue.' He sat down again. 'Well, now comes the reckoning. Let's get it over. The company will almost clear itself; so that leaves only our personal ends to be settled. What is my indebtedness to you?'

Harris Pascoe straightened his steel spectacles. 'Not a big sum – about n-nine hundred pounds or a little less. That is over and above the mortgage on your property.'

Ross said: 'The sale of my Wheal Leisure shares will meet most of that – together with the dividend we have just declared.'

'It will rather more than meet it. By chance I heard of someone enquiring for shares of Wheal Leisure only yesterday. They offered eight hundred and twenty-five pounds for sixty shares.'

'There is one other small matter,' Ross said. 'Harry Blewett of Wheal Maid is worse hit than I am. He fears going to prison and I don't wonder. The shares and the dividend will come to nearly a thousand and I want the extra to go to him. It's possible that with it he'll be able to keep his head up.'

'Then you wish me to sell the shares at that price?'

'If it's the best you can get.'

'It is better than you would receive if they were thrown on the open market. Thirteen pounds fifteen shillings a share is a good price for these days.'

'Thirteen pounds . . .' The wineglass suddenly snapped in Ross's fingers and the red wine splashed over his hand.

Pascoe was standing beside him. 'What is wrong? Are you ill?'

'No,' said Ross. 'Not at all ill. Your glass has a delicate stem. I hope it was not an heirloom.'

'No. But something . . .'

Ross said: 'I have decided different. I do not sell the shares.'

'It was a m-man called Coke who approached me . . .'

Ross took out a handkerchief and wiped his hand. 'It was a man called Warleggan.'

'Oh, no, I assure you. What makes you ——'

'I don't care what nominee they chose. It is their money and they shall not have the shares.'

Pascoe looked a little put out as he handed Ross another glass. 'I had no idea. I s-sympathize with your feeling. But it is a good offer.'

'It will not be taken,' Ross said. 'Not if I have to sell the house and the land. I'm sorry, Harris; you'll wait for your money whether you like it or not. You cannot force me for another month or so. Well, I'll get it before then – somehow. In the meantime, I'll keep my own mine smelling sweet if I go to gaol for it.'

Chapter five

MR NOTARY PEARCE was at home playing cribbage with his daughter when Ross was announced. Miss Pearce, a comely young woman of twenty-five who never made enough of her good looks, rose at once and excused herself, and Mr Pearce, pushing aside the table, poked at the huge fire with his curtain rod and invited Ross to sit down.

'Well, Captain Poldark; I declare this is quite an event. Can you stay for a hand of cribbage? Playing with Grace is always a little dull, for she will not hazard a penny on the outcome.'

Ross moved his chair farther from the fire.

'I need your advice and help.'

'Well, my dear sir, you may have them if they are mine to give.'

'I want a loan of a thousand pounds without security.'

Mr Pearce's eyebrows went up. Like the other shareholders of Wheal Leisure, he had stood aloof from the battle of the copper companies. But he knew very well which way it had gone.

'Hrr-hm. That is rather a severe proposition. *Without* security, you said? Yes, I thought so. Dear, dear.'

Ross said: 'I should be willing to pay a high rate of interest.'

Mr Pearce scratched himself. '*Without* security. Have you tried Cary Warleggan?'

'No,' said Ross. 'Nor do I intend to.'

'Just so. Just so. But it will be very difficult. If you have no security, what can you offer?'

'My word.'

'Yes, yes. Yes, yes. But that would really amount to a friendly accommodation. Have you approached any of your friends?'

'No. I want it to be a business arrangement. I will pay for the privilege.'

'You will pay? You mean in interest? Yes . . . But the lender might be chiefly concerned for his capital. Why do you not sell your shares in Wheal Leisure if you need the money so badly?'

'Because that is what I am trying to avoid.'

'Ah, yes.' Mr Pearce's plum-coloured face was not encouraging. 'And your property?'

'Is already mortgaged.'

'For how much?'

Ross told him.

Mr Pearce took a pinch of snuff. 'I think the Warleggans would raise that figure if you transferred the mortgage to them.'

'Several times in recent years,' Ross said, 'the Warleggans have tried to interest themselves in my affairs. I mean to keep them out.'

It was on Mr Pearce's tongue to say that beggars could not be choosers, but he changed his mind.

'Have you thought of a second mortgage on the property? There are people – I know one or two who might be willing for the speculative risk.'

'Would that bring in sufficient?'

'It might. But naturally such a risk would be a short-term one, say for twelve or twenty-four months ——'

'That would be agreeable.'

'– and would carry a very high interest rate. In the nature of forty per cent.'

For a loan of a thousand pounds now he would have to find fourteen hundred by this time next year, in addition to his other commitments. A hopeless proposition – unless the price of copper continued to rise and Wheal Leisure struck another lode as rich as the present.

'Could you arrange such a loan?''

'I could try. It is a bad time for such things. There is no cheap money about.'

'That is not cheap money.'

'No, no. I quite agree. Well, I could let you know in a day or two.'

'I should want to know to-morrow.'

Mr Pearce struggled out of his chair. 'Dear, dear, how stiff one gets. I have been better but there is still some gouty humour lurking in my constitution. I could let you know to-morrow possibly, though it might take a week or so to get the money.'

'That will do,' Ross said. 'I'll take that.'

On Tuesday he delayed leaving the town until five in the afternoon.

He and Johnson and Tonkin and Blewett wound up the Carnmore Copper Company before dinner. Ross did not pass on Harris Pascoe's hint of yesterday. There was nothing any of them could do now to prevent Sir John's entering into some agreement with the Warleggans if he chose to. There was nothing to prevent the smelting works from coming into the hands of the Warleggans or a new company being formed to exploit their own hard work. But the company would be one of the circle, and he would see that it did not force up prices for the benefit of the mines.

Although Tonkin was not ruined, Ross felt most sorry for him, for he liked him the best and knew the quite tireless work he had put in, arguing, persuading, contriving. Fifteen months of fanatical energy had gone into it, and he looked worn out. Harry Blewett, who had been the instigator and first supporter of the idea, had pledged his last penny, and to-day was the end of everything for him. The big, dour, hard-headed Johnson stood the failure more confidently than the others; he was a better loser because he had lost less.

After it was over Ross went to see Mr Pearce again, and learned that the money was forthcoming. He wondered if Mr Pearce himself had advanced it. The notary was an astute man and fast becoming a warm one.

Then Ross went back to the Pascoes. The banker shook his head at the news. Such improvident borrowing was utterly against his principles. Better by far to cut your losses and start again than to plunge so deep in that there might be no getting out – merely to put off the evil day.

While he was there Ross wrote to Blewett saying he had placed two hundred and fifty pounds to his name at Pascoe's Bank. This was to be considered a five-year loan at four per cent interest. He hoped it would tide him over.

The journey home in the dark took Ross about two hours. On the way down the dark combe, just before the lights of Nampara came in sight, he overtook a cloaked figure hurrying on ahead of him.

He had been feeling bitter and depressed, but at sight of Demelza he mustered up his spirits.

'Well, my dear. You are out late. Have you been visiting again?'

'Oh, Ross,' she said, 'I'm that glad you're not home before me. I was afraid you would have been.'

'Is anything wrong?'

'No, no. I'll tell you when we're home.'

'Come. Up beside me. It will save a half mile.'

She put her foot on his and he lifted her up. Darkie gave a lurch. Demelza settled down in front of him with a sudden sigh of contentment.

'You should have someone with you if you intend to be abroad after dark.'

'Oh . . . it is safe enough near home.'

'Don't be too sure. There is too much poverty to breed all honest men.'

'Have you saved anything, Ross? Is it to go on?'

He told her.

'Oh, my dear, I'm that sorry. Sorry for you. I don't belong to know how it has all happened. . . .'

'Never mind. The fever is over. Now we must settle down.'

'What fever?' she asked in a startled voice.

He patted her arm. 'It was a figure of speech. Have you heard that there is illness at Trenwith, by the way? I had intended to call to-day but I was so late.'

'Yes. I heard . . . yesterday.'

'Did you hear how they were?'

'Yes. They are a small bit better to-day – though not yet out of danger.'

The house loomed ahead of them as they crossed the stream. At the door he got down and lifted her down. Affectionately he bent his head to kiss her, but in the dark she had moved her face slightly so that his lips found only her cheek.

She turned and opened the door. 'John!' she called. 'We're back!'

Supper was a quiet meal. Ross was going over the events of the last few days; Demelza was unusually silent. He had told her that he had saved his holding in Wheal Leisure, but not how. That would come when repayment was nearer. Sufficient unto the day.

He wished now he had kicked George Warleggan into the gutter while there was the opportunity: George was the type that was usually careful to avoid giving an excuse. And to have the impertinence to bring Cousin Sanson back. He wondered what Francis would have to say. Francis.

'Did you say Geoffrey Charles was better also?' he asked. 'The sore throat is usually hard on children.'

Demelza started and went on with her supper.

'I b'lieve the worst is over.'

'Well, that is some satisfaction. I shall never have room for Francis again after the trick he served us; but I would not wish that complaint on my worst enemy.'

There was a long silence.

'Ross,' she said, 'after July I swore I would never keep a secret from you again, so you had best hear this now before it can be thought I have deceived you.'

'Oh,' he said, 'what? Have you been to see Verity in my absence?'

'No. To Trenwith.'

She watched his expression. It did not change.

'To call, you mean?'

'No . . . I went to help.'

A candle was smoking but neither of them moved to snuff it.

'And did they turn you away?'

'No. I stayed all last night.'

He looked across the table at her. 'Why?'

'Ross, I had to. I went but to enquire, but they were in desperate straits. Francis – the fever had left him but he was prostrate. Geoffrey Charles was fit to die at any moment. Elizabeth had it too, though she would not admit it. There was three servants ill, and only Mary Bartle and Aunt Sarah Tregeagle to do anything. I helped to get Elizabeth to bed and stayed with Geoffrey Charles all night. I thought once or twice he was gone; but he brought round again and this morning was better. I came home then an' went again this afternoon. Dr Choake says the crisis is past. Elizabeth, he says, has not took it so bad. I – I stayed so long as ever I could, but I told them I could not stay to-night. But Tabb is up again and can see to the others. They will be able to manage to-night.'

He looked at her a moment. He was not a petty man, and the things that came to his lips were the things he could not say.

And, though at first he struggled to deny it, he could not in the end fail to acknowledge that the feeling moving in her had moved him no differently in the matter of Jim Carter. Could he blame her for the sort of impulse on which he had acted himself?

He could not subdue his thoughts, but honesty and the finer bonds of his affection kept him mute.

So the meal went on in silence.

At length she said: 'I couldn't do any other, Ross.'

'No,' he said, 'it was a kind and generous act. Perhaps in a fortnight I shall be in a mood to appreciate it.'

They both knew what he meant but neither of them put it more clearly into words.

Chapter six

A SOUTH-WESTERLY gale broke during the night and blew for twenty hours. There was a brief quiet spell and then the wind got up again from the north, bitterly cold, and whipping rain and sleet and snow flurries before it. New Year's Day 1790, which was a Friday, dawned at the height of the gale.

They had gone to bed early as Demelza was tired. She had had a broken night the night before, Julia being fretful with teeth.

All night the wind thundered and screamed – with that thin, cold whistling scream which was a sure sign of the 'norther.' All night rain and hail thrashed on the windows facing the sea, and there were cloths laid along the window bottoms to catch the rain that was beaten in. It was cold even in bed with the curtains drawn, and Ross had made up a great fire in the parlour below to give a little extra heat. It was useless to light a fire in the bedroom grate, for all the smoke blew down the chimney.

Ross woke to the sound of Julia's crying. It reached very thinly to him for the wind was rampant, and he decided, as Demelza had not heard, to slip out himself and see if he could quiet the child. He sat up slowly; and then knew that Demelza was not beside him.

He parted the curtains, and the cold draught of the wind wafted upon his face. Demelza was sitting by the cot. A candle dripped and guttered on the table near. He made a little hissing sound to attract her attention, and she turned her head.

'What is it?' he asked.

'I don't rightly know, Ross. The teeth, I b'lieve.'

'You will catch a consumption sitting there. Put on your gown.'

'No, I am not cold.'

'*She* is cold. Bring her into this bed.'

Her answer was drowned by a sudden storm of hail on the window. It stopped all talk. He got out of bed, struggled into his gown and took up hers. He went over to her and put it about her shoulders. They peered down at the child.

Julia was awake but her plump little face was flushed, and when she cried her whimper seemed to end in a sudden dry cough.

'She has a fever,' Ross shouted.

'I think it is a teething fever. I think . . .'

The hail stopped as suddenly as it had begun and the scream of the wind seemed like silence after it.

'It will be as well to have her with us to-night,' Demelza said. She bent forward, it seemed rather clumsily to him, and picked up the child. Her dressing gown slipped off and lay on the floor.

He followed her back to the bed and they put Julia in it.

'I will just get a drink of water,' she said.

He watched her go over to the jug and pour some out. She drank a little slowly, and took some more. Her shadow lurched and eddied on the wall. Suddenly he was up beside her.

'What is the matter?'

She looked at him. 'I think I have caught a cold.'

He put a hand on hers. Although the icy breeze was in the room her hand was hot and sweaty.

'How long have you been like this?'

'All night. I felt it coming last evening.'

He stared at her. In the shadowed light he could see her face. He caught at the high frilly collar of her nightdress and pulled it back.

'Your neck is swollen,' he said.

She stepped back from him and buried her face in her hands.

'My head,' she whispered, 'is that bad.'

He had roused the Gimletts. He had carried the child and Demelza down into the parlour and wrapped them in blankets before the drowsy fire. Gimlett he had sent for Dwight. Mrs Gimlett was making up the bed in Joshua's old room. There there was a fire grate which would not smoke, and the only window faced south; a more habitable sick-room in such a gale.

He found time to be grateful for having changed the Paynters for the Gimletts. No grudging grumbling service, no self-pitying lamentation on their own ill luck.

While he sat there talking in the parlour, talking softly to Demelza and telling her that Julia was a sturdy child and would come through quick enough, his mind was full of bitter thoughts. They flooded over him in waves, threatening to drown common sense and cool reason. He could have torn at himself in his distress. Demelza had run her head recklessly into the noose. The obligations of relationship . . .'

No, not that. Although he could not see through to the source of her generous impulses, he knew it was much more than that. All these things were tied together in her heart: her share in Verity's flight, his quarrel with Francis, his quarrel with her, the failure of the copper company, her visit to the sick house of Trenwith. They could not be seen separately, and in a queer way the responsibility for her illness now seemed not only hers but his.

But he had not shown his anxiety or resentment three days ago; he could not possibly show it now. Instead he wiped her forehead and joked with her and watched over Julia, who slept now after a bout of crying.

Presently he went out to help Jane Gimlett. A fire was burning already in the downstairs bedroom, and he saw that Jane had stripped the bed upstairs to make up this one so that there should be no risk of damp. While he was helping Demelza to bed the whole house echoed and drummed, carpets flapped and pictures rattled. Then the front door was shut again and Dwight Enys was taking off his wet cloak in the hall.

He came through and Ross held a candle while he examined Demelza's throat; he timed her heart with his pulse watch, asked one or two questions, turned to the child. Demelza lay quiet in the great box bed and watched him. After a few minutes he went out into the hall for his bag, and Ross followed him.

'Well?' said Ross.

'They both have it.'

'You mean the malignant sore throat?'

'The symptoms are unmistakable. Your wife's are further advanced than the baby's. Even to the pink finger ends.'

Dwight would have avoided his eyes and gone back into the room but Ross stopped him.

'How bad is this going to be?'

'I don't know, Ross. Some get past the acute stage quick, but recovery is always a long job, three to six weeks.'

'Oh, the length of recovery is nothing,' Ross said.

Dwight patted his arm. 'I know that. I know.'

'The treatment?'

'There is little we can do: so much hangs on the patient. I have had some success with milk – boiled, always boiled, and allowed to cool until it is tepid. It sustains the patient. No solids. Keep them very flat, and no exertion or excitement. The heart should have the least possible work. Perhaps some spirits of sea salt painted on the throat. I do not believe in bloodletting.'

'Does the crisis come soon?'

'No, no. A day or two. In the meantime be patient and have a good heart. They stand so much better a chance than the cottage people, who are half starved and usually without fire and light.'

'Yes,' said Ross, remembering Dwight's words two mornings before. 'The results are always unpredictable,' he had said. 'Sometimes the strong will go and the weak survive.'

Chapter seven

THE NORTHERLY GALE blew for three days more.

In the late part of New Year's Day snow began to blow in flurries before the wind, and by next morning there were drifts of it against all the hedges and walls, though the gale-swept ground was free. The pump in the yard was hung with tattered icicles like a beggar woman, and the water in the pail was frozen. The clouds were livid and low.

In the middle of the day the hail began again. It seemed hardly to fall at all but to blow flatly across the land. One felt that no glass would withstand it. Then it would rap, rap, rap a dozen times and suddenly stop and one could hear the wind like a roaring mighty beast rolling away in the distance.

To Demelza all the noise and fury was a true part of her nightmare. For two days her fever was high, and something in being in old Joshua's big box bed threw her errant mind back to the first night she had ever spent at Nampara. The years slipped off and she was a child of thirteen again, ragged, ill fed, ignorant, half cheeky, half terrified. She had been stripped and swilled under the pump and draped in a lavender-smelling shirt and put to sleep in this great bed. The weals of her father's latest thrashing were still sore on her back, her ribs ached from the kicks of the urchins of Redruth Fair. The candle smoked and guttered on the bedside table and the painted statuette of the Virgin nodded down at her from the mantelpiece. To make things worse she could not swallow, for someone had tied a cord about her throat; and there was Someone waiting behind the library door until she fell asleep and the candle went out, when they would creep in in the dark and tighten the knot.

So she must stay awake, at all costs she must stay awake. Very soon Garrick would come scratching at the window, and then she must go to open it and let him in. He would be a comfort and a protection through the night.

Sometimes people moved about the room, and often she saw Ross and Jane Gimlett and young Dr Enys. They were there, but they were not real. Not even the child in the cot, her child, was real. They were the imagination, the dream, something to do with an impossible future, something she hoped for but had never had. They *now* lay in the guttering candle and the nodding statuette and the aching ribs and the cord round her throat and the Someone waiting behind the library door.

'Ye've slocked my dattur!' shouted Tom Carne, while she trembled in the cupboard. 'What right ha' you to be seein' her back! I'll have the law on you!'

'That statuette seems to be worrying her,' Ross said. 'I wonder if it would be wise to move it.'

She looked over the edge of the bed, out of the cupboard, down, down, to two tiny figures fighting on the floor far below her. Ross had thrown her father into the fireplace but he was getting up again. He was going to put something round her throat.

'Are ye saved?' he whispered. 'Are ye saved? Sin an' fornication an' drunkenness. The Lord hath brought me out of a horrible pit of mire an' clay an' set my feet 'pon a rock. There's no more drinkings an' living in sin.'

'Saved?' said Francis. 'Saved from what?' And everyone tittered. They weren't laughing at Francis but at her, for trying to put on airs and pretending to be one of them when she was really only a kitchen wench dragged up in a lice-ridden cottage. Kitchen wench. Kitchen wench. . . .

'Oh,' she said with a great sigh, and threw her life and her memories away, out over the edge of the bed into the sea. They fell, twirling, twisting away, growing ever smaller, smaller. Let them drown. Let them perish and die, if she could but have peace.

'Let him drown in the mud,' Ross said. 'Cheating at cards – let him drown.'

'No, Ross, no, Ross, no!' She grasped his arm. 'Save him. Else they'll say tis murder. What does it matter so long as we've got back what we lost. So long as we haven't lost Wheal Leisure. We'll be together again. That is all that counts.'

She shrank from the touch of something cool on her forehead.

'It's unusual for the fever to persist so long,' said Dwight. 'I confess I am at a loss to know what to do.'

Of course Mark had killed Keren this way. The men had not told her, but word had gone round. Against the window somehow, and then he had choked the life out of her. They were trying to do that now to her. She had been dozing and Someone had come in from the library and was just tightening the cord.

'Garrick!' she whispered. 'Garrick! Here, boy! Help me now!'

'Drink this, my darling.' Ross's voice came from a long way away, from the other room, from the room that was not hers, echoing out of her dreams.

'It is useless,' said Dwight. 'She can't swallow anything at present. In a few hours perhaps, if . . .'

Garrick was already scratching, eagerly scratching.

'Open the window!' she urged. 'Open quick, afore tis . . . too . . . late.'

Something large and black and shaggy bounded across the room to her, and with a gasp of joy she knew that they had done as she said. Her face and hands were licked by his rough tongue. She wept for sheer relief. But suddenly to her horror she found that the dog had somehow made a horrible mistake. Instead of knowing it was his mistress he thought she was an enemy and fastened his teeth in her throat. She struggled and fought to explain, but her voice and her breath were gone, were gone. . . .

The candle had blown out and it was cold. She shivered in the dark. Julia was crying with her teeth again, and she must get up and give her a drink of water. If only the wind was not so cold. Where was Ross? Had he not come back? He takes things so much to heart, Verity said, he takes things to heart. Well, then, I must not disappoint him this time. Deceived him once. Deceived him. I must not let him down. Clear, clear, but how might it happen? If you don't know you can't be sure.

Something with Julia and herself. But of course, Julia was sick. She had been watching by her bed all night. Francis was sick too, and Elizabeth was sick if she would only admit it. There was a horrible taste of copper in her mouth. It was those herbs they were burning. Aunt Sarah Tregeagle had come straight from carol singing to tend on them all. But where was . . .'

'Ross!' she called. 'Ross!'

'He's gone to sleep in his chair in the parlour, ma'am,' said a woman's voice. It was not Prudie. 'Do you want for me to call him? He's been without sleep these three nights.'

It would not do for any of them to be asleep if her father came. He would bring all the Illuggan miners and they would set fire to the house. But he had reformed. He was a new man altogether. He had married Aunt Mary Chegwidden. How would he come this time, then? Perhaps with a choir of Methodists and they would sing outside the window. It seemed funny, and she tried to laugh but choked. And then she knew it was *not* funny, for *there* they were outside the window, there as she looked down on them, a great sea of faces. And she knew that they were hungry and wanted bread.

They were in a huge crowd stretching right up the valley and shouting. 'Our rights be bread t'eat an' corn to buy at a fair an' proper price. We want corn to live by, an' corn we'll have, whether or no!'

And she realized that the only bread she could give them was her own child. . . .

Beside her was Sanson, the miller; and Verity and Andrew Blamey were talking in the corner, but they were too lost in each other to notice her. She wept in an agony of fear. For the miners were crazy for bread. In a minute they would set fire to the house.

She turned to look for Ross, and when she turned back to the window the massed, staring tiny faces were already fading behind dense columns of white smoke.

'Look,' said Jane Gimlett, 'it is snowing again.'

'Snowing!' she tried to say. 'Don't you see, it is not snow but smoke. The house is on fire and we shall be smothered to death!' She saw Sanson fall and then felt the smoke getting into her own breath.

Choking, she put up a hand to her throat and found that someone else's hand was already there.

On the morning of January the fourth the wind broke and it began to snow in earnest. By midday, when the fall ceased, the fields and the trees were thick and heavy with it. Branches bowed and thick floes drifted down the stream. John Gimlett splitting wood in the yard had to tug at the logs to get them apart, for the cold had bound them tight. Gimlett's nine ducks padding laboriously towards the water looked dirty and jaundiced in this purity. On Hendrawna Beach the tide was out and the great waves leaped and roared in the distance. The ice and foam and yellow scum which had covered the beach for a week was itself overlaid by the cloth of snow. Sand hills were mountain ranges, and in the distance the dark cliffs brooded over the scene, wearing their new dress like a shroud.

The hush everywhere was profound. After the fanatic ravings of the gale it was as if a blanket had fallen on the world. Nothing stirred and a dog's bark echoed round the valley. The roar of the sea was there but had somehow become lost in the silence and could only be heard by an effort of thought.

Then at two the clouds broke up and the sun came out dazzlingly brilliant, forcing a brief thaw. Branches and bushes dripped, and small avalanches of snow, already part thawed from within, began to slip down the roof. Dark stains showed on one or two of the fields, and a robin, sitting among the feathery snow of an apple branch, began to sing to the sun.

But the break had come late in the day, and soon the valley was streaked with shadow and the frost had set in again.

About four o'clock, as it was getting dark, Demelza opened her eyes and looked up at the wooden ceiling of the bed. She felt different from before, calmer and quite separate. She was no longer the child of nightmare. There was only the one reality and that was of this moment of waking to the long smooth shadows in the room, to the livid glimmering paleness of the ceiling, to the curtains drawn back from the latticed windows, to Jane Gimlett nodding sleepily in the glow of an old peat fire.

She wondered what day it was, what time of day, what kind of weather. Some noise had stopped; was it in her head or out in the world? Everything was very peaceful and unemphatic, as if she looked at it from a distance, no longer belonged to it. All life and energy was spent. Was she too spent? Where was Ross? And Julia? Had they all been ill? She was not clear on that. She would have liked to speak but somehow was afraid to try. In speaking she either broke the shell of quiet in which she lay, or stayed within it for ever. That was at the very heart of the choice. She did not know and was afraid to try. And Jud and Prudie, and her father and Verity and Francis . . . No, no, stop; that way, down that turning lay the nightmare.

Just then some of the peat fell in and caused a sharp glow and heat to fall on Jane Gimlett's face. She woke, sighed and yawned, put on more fuel. Presently she got up from her seat and came over to the bed to glance at the patient. What she saw there made her leave the room in search of Ross.

She found him slumped in his chair in the parlour staring into the fire.

They came back together and Ross went over alone to the bed.

Demelza's eyes were closed, but after a moment she seemed to feel the shadow across her face. She looked up and saw Ross. Jane Gimlett came to the bed with a candle and put it on the bedside table.

'Well, my love,' said Ross.

Demelza tried to smile, and after a moment's frightened hesitancy took the risk of trying her voice.

'Well, Ross . . .'

The shell was broken. He had heard. Somehow she knew then she was going to get better.

She said something that he did not catch; he bent to hear it and again could not.

Then she said quite clearly: 'Julia . . .'

'All right, my darling,' he said. 'But not now. To-morrow. When you're stronger. You shall see her then.' He bent and kissed her forehead. 'You must sleep now.

'Day?' she said.

'You've been ill a day or two,' he said. 'It has been snowing and is cold. Go to sleep now. Dwight is coming to see you again this evening and we want you to show improvement. Go to sleep, Demelza.'

'Julia,' she said.

'To-morrow. See her then, my love. Go to sleep.'

Obedient, she closed her eyes and presently began to breathe more deeply and more slowly than he had seen her do for five days. He went over and stood by the window, wondering if he had done right to lie to her.

For Julia had died the night before.

Chapter eight

THEY BURIED THE child two days later. The weather had stayed quiet and cold and heaps of snow lay in sheltered corners about the fields and lanes. A great number of people turned out for the funeral. Six young girls dressed in white – two Martins, Paul Daniel's daughters, and two of Jim Carter's younger sisters – carried the small coffin the whole of the mile and a half to Sawle Church, and all the way along the route were people who stood silently by and then quietly fell in behind the other followers to the church. Sawle choir, uninvited, met the procession halfway, and each time the six girls stopped to rest they sang a psalm, in which the mourners joined.

Dwight Enys walked with Ross, and behind them were John Treneglos and Sir Hugh Bodrugan. Harry Blewett and Richard Tonkin had come, and Harris Pascoe had sent his eldest son. Captain and Mrs Henshawe followed Joan Teague with one of the cousins Tremenheer. Behind them were Jud and Prudie Paynter, all the rest of the Martins and Daniels and Carters, the Viguses and the Nanfans, and then followed a great mass of ragged miners and their wives, small farmers and farm labourers, spallers, wheelwrights, fishermen. The sound of all these people singing psalms in the still, frosty air was very impressive. When they finished and before the shuffling movement of the procession began again, there was each time a brief hush when everyone heard the distant roar of the sea. In the end Mr Odgers found he had to read the burial service before more than three hundred and fifty people, overflowing the church and standing silent in the churchyard.

It was this unexpected tribute that broke Ross up. He had hardened himself to all the rest. Not being a religious man, he had no resources to meet the loss of the child except his own resentful will. Inwardly he railed against Heaven and circumstance, but the very cruelty of the blow touched his character at its toughest and most obstinate.

That Demelza was likely to live did not in this early stage strike him as cause for thankfulness. The one loss had shocked and shaken him too much. When his mother had taken him to church as a child he had repeated a psalm which said: 'To-day if ye will hear His voice, harden not your hearts.' But when his mother died, even while he was crying, something within him had risen up; a barrier to shield off his weakness and tenderness and frailty. He had thought: All right, then, I've lost her and I'm alone. All right then. To-day the adult impulse followed the childish.

But the curious silent testimony of respect and affection given to-day by all these ordinary working or half-starving neighbours of his, turning out from field and farm and mine, had somehow slipped through his defences.

That night the gale blew up again from the north, and all the evening he sat with Demelza. After a collapse when they broke the news to her yesterday she was slowly regaining the lost ground. It was as if nature, bent on its own survival, had not allowed her tired brain strength to dwell on her loss. The one thing it was concerned with was preserving her body. When the serious illness was really over, when the convalescence began, then would be the testing time.

About nine Dwight came again and after he had seen Demelza they sat in the parlour for a time.

Ross was brooding, inattentive, did not seem to follow the simplest remark. He kept on repeating how sorry he was he had not asked the mourners in for food and wine after the funeral. It was the custom in this part of the world, he explained, as if Dwight did not know, to give people food to eat and wine to drink and plenty of it at a funeral. The whole countryside had turned out to-day, he couldn't get over that; he had not expected it at all and hoped they would see that with Demelza still so ill, things couldn't be done as they should have been.

Dwight thought he had been drinking. In fact he was wrong. Since the third day of their illness Ross had lost the taste. The only physical thing wrong with him was lack of sleep.

There was something mentally wrong with him, but Dwight could do nothing for that. Only time or chance or Ross himself could set things to rights there. He could find no submission in defeat. If he was to regain his balance there must be some recoil of the spring of his nature, which had been pressed back within itself unbearably.

Dwight said: 'Ross, I have not said this before, but I feel I must say it sometime. It is how acutely I feel that I was not able to save – her.'

Ross said: 'I had not expected to see Sir Hugh to-day. He has more compassion in him than I thought.'

'I feel I should have tried something else – anything. You brought me into this district. You have been a good friend all through. If I could have repaid that . . .'

'There was none from Trenwith at the funeral,' said Ross. 'I expect they are all still unwell.'

'Oh, if they have had this they will not be out for weeks. I have seen so much of this during last summer and autumn. I wish so much . . . Choake will no doubt say it was due to some neglect on my part. He will say that he saved Geoffrey Charles ——'

'Demelza saved Geoffrey Charles,' Ross said, 'and gave Julia in his place.'

The gale buffeted tremendously against the house.

Dwight got up. 'You must feel that. I'm sorry.'

'God, how this wind blows!' Ross said savagely.

'Would you like me to stay to-night?'

'No. You need the sleep also and need your strength for to-morrow. I can spend all this year at recovery. Take a hot drink and then go.'

Ross put a kettle on the fire and had soon mixed a jug of grog, which they drank together.

Ross said: 'They were a poor lot at the funeral, Dwight. I wish I could have fed and wined them after. They needed it.'

'You could not be expected to victual the better part of three villages,' Dwight said patiently.

There was a tap on the door.

'Beg pardon, sir,' said Jane Gimlett, 'but Mistress is asking for you to come and see her.'

'Is anything wrong?'

'No, sur.'

When Dwight had gone Ross went into the bedroom. Demelza looked very slight and pale in the big bed. She stretched out her hand and he took it and sat on the chair beside her.

Two candles flickered on the table, and the fire smouldered and glowed in the grate. Ross tried to find something to say.

'We had a letter from Verity this forenoon. I don't know what has become of it.'

'Is – she – well?'

'Seems so, yes. I will read it you when it comes to light, She was enquiring for Francis and family. She had only just heard that there was some sort of sickness in the house.'

'And us?'

'. . . She had not heard about us.'

'You – must write, Ross. An' tell her.'

'I will.'

'How are they . . . Ross? Elizabeth and . . .'

'Ill, but improving.' He nearly added: 'Even Geoffrey Charles,' but killed his bitterness. Above all, there must never be any of that. He leaned his head against the wooden side of the bed and tried to forget all that had passed in these last weeks, all the frustration and the pain, tried to think himself back to the happy days of a year ago. So they sat for a long time. The wind was backing a little, would probably blow itself out in the north-west. The fire sank lower, and now and then the candles ducked and trembled.

He moved his hand a little, and at once she caught it more firmly in hers.

'I was not leaving you,' he said, 'except to stir the fire.'

'Let it stay, Ross. Don't go just now. Don't leave me.'

'What is it?' he asked.

'I was . . . only thinking.'

'What?'

'That Julia – will be lonely. She always so hated the wind.'

Ross stayed beside the bed all night. He did not sleep much but dozed fitfully off and on, while the wind buffeted and screamed. Awake and asleep the same thoughts lived in his brain. Frustration and bereavement. Jim Carter and the Warleggans and Julia. Failure and loss. His father dying untended in this same room. His own return from America, his disappointment over Elizabeth and happiness with Demelza. Was all that last joy gone? Perhaps not, but it would have changed its tone, and would be edged with memories. And his own life; what did it add up to? A frenzied futile struggle ending in failure and near bankruptcy. He would be thirty in a few weeks' time. No great age, but a part of his life was ended, a phase, an epoch, a turning, and he could not see himself starting again along the same track. What had ended with this phase? Was it his youth?

How would he feel to-night if everything had happened different, if he had triumphed over the prison authorities and the Warleggans and disease and was not bereaved and beaten, lightheaded and tired to death? He would have been asleep and safe from these thoughts. Yet would the phase have ended just the same? He did not know and was too down to care. It did not seem just then that success in anything had ever been possible or that anything would ever be possible again. Failure was the end of life, all effort was dust, necessary and complete. All roads led to the bleak parapet of death.

In the cold gale of the early morning he fetched more wood, piled the fire high and then drank several glasses of neat brandy to keep out the chill. When he sat down again beside the bed the spirit seemed to set fire to his brain and he fell asleep.

He dreamed fantastic things, in which stress and conflict and the will to fight were all that meant anything: he lived over again in a few moments a concentrate of all the trouble of the last months and climbed back to wakefulness slowly, to find a grey daylight filtering through the curtains and John Gimlett bending before the fire.

'What time is it?' Ross asked in a whisper.

John turned. 'About fifteen minutes before eight, sur, and there's a ship drifting in on the beach.'

Ross turned and looked at Demelza. She was sleeping peacefully, her tumbled curls about the pillow; but he wished she did not look so white.

'Tes 'ardly light enough to see him proper yet, sur,' whispered Gimlett.

'I did but notice him when I went for the wood. I do not think any other has spied him so far.'

'Eh?'

'The ship, sur. He looks a tidy size.'

Ross reached for the brandy bottle and drank another glass. He was stiff and cold and his mouth was dry.

'Where away?'

'Just b'low Damsel Point. He cleared the point but he'll never get out o' the bay in this wind an' sea.'

Ross's brain was still working slowly but the new brandy was having effect. There would be pickings for the miners and their families. Good luck to them.

'I b'lieve ye could see him from an upstairs window by now.'

Ross got up and stretched. Then he went out of the room and listlessly climbed the stairs. The north window of their old bedroom was so thick with salt that he could see nothing at all, but when he had got it open he soon made out what Gimlett meant. A two-masted ship of fair size. She was dipping and lurching in the trough of the waves. All her sails were gone except a few strips flying in the wind, but some sort of a jury rig had been put up forward and they were trying to keep way on her. Unless she grew wings she would be on the beach soon. It was low water.

Losing interest, he was about to turn away, when something took his attention again and he stared at the ship. Then he went for his father's spyglass and steadied it against the frame of the window. It was a good glass, which his father had had in some bargain from a drunken frigate captain at Plymouth. As he peered the billowing curtains blew and flapped about his head. The wind was dropping at last.

Then he lowered the glass. The ship was the *Queen Charlotte*.

He went down. In the parlour he poured out a drink.

'John!' he called, as Gimlett went past.

'Please?'

'Get Darkie saddled.'

Gimlett glanced up at his master's face. In his eyes was a light as if he had seen a vision. But not a holy one.

'Are you feeling slight, sur?'

Ross drained another glass. 'Those people at the funeral, John. They should have been entertained and fed. We must see that they are this morning.'

Gimlett looked at him in alarm. 'Sit you down, sur. There's no need for taking on any more.'

'Get Darkie at once, John.'

'But ——'

Ross met his glance, and Gimlett went quickly away.

In the bedroom Demelza was still quietly sleeping. He put on his cloak and hat and mounted the horse as it came to the door. Darkie had been confined and was mettlesome, could hardly be contained. In a moment they were flying off up the valley.

The first cottage of Grambler village was dark and unstirring when Ross slithered up to it. Jud and Prudie had had smuggled gin in the house and, finding no free drink outcoming from the funeral, had returned, complaining bitterly, to make a night of it on their own.

Knocking brought no response so he put his shoulders to the door and snapped the flimsy bolt. In the dark and the stink he shook someone's shoulder, recognized it as Prudie's, tried again and scored a hit.

'Gor damme,' shouted Jud, quivering with self-pity, 'a man's not king of his own blathering 'ouse but what folks burst in ——'

'Jud,' said Ross quietly, 'there's a wreck.'

'Eh?' Jud sat up, suddenly quiet. 'Where's she struck?'

'Hendrawna Beach. Any moment now. Go rouse Grambler people and send word to Mellin and Marasanvose. I am on to Sawle.'

Jud squinted in the half-light, the bald top of his head looking like another face. 'Why for bring all they? They'll be thur soon enough. Now ef ——'

'She's a sizeable ship,' Ross said. 'Carrying food. There'll be pickings for all.'

'Aye, but ——'

'Do as I say, or I'll bolt you in here from the outside and do the job myself.'

'I'll do en, Cap'n. Twas only as you might say a passing thought, like. What is she?'

Ross went out, slamming the door behind him so that the whole crazy cottage shook. A piece of dried mud fell from the roof upon Prudie's face.

'What's amiss wi' you!' She hit Jud across the head and sat up.

Jud sat there scratching inside his shirt.

'Twas some queer, that,' he said. 'Twas some queer, I tell ee.'

'What? What's took you, wakin' at this time?'

'I was dreamin' of old Joshua,' said Jud. 'Thur he was as clear as spit, just like I seen un in 'seventy-seven, when he went after that little giglet at St. Ives. An' damme, ef I didn't wake up an' *thur* he was standin' beside the bed, plain as plain.'

'Who?'

'Old Joshua.'

'You big soft ape, he's been cold in 'is grave these six year an' more!'

'Aye, twas Cap'n Ross, really.'

'Then load me, why don't ee say so!'

'Because,' said Jud, 'I've never seen 'im look so much like old Joshua before.'

Chapter nine

By superb seamanship Captain Bray kept her off the beach for over an hour.

In this he was helped by the sudden lull in the storm, and once there even seemed a chance that he would fight his way clear.

But then the tide began to flow strongly and all was lost. Ross was home again just in time to see her come in.

He remembered the scene years after. Although the tide was out the sand was wet and foam-covered right up to the sand hills and the shingle. In places the cliffs were grey to the top with foam; and suds whirled in flocks between the cliffs like gulls wheeling. Along the edge of the sea proper a block rim of thirty or forty people were already come at his summons for the harvest. Riding in quickly, stern foremost, racked and tossed and half smothered by the sea, was the *Queen Charlotte*. As Ross climbed the wall the sun sprang up out of the broken black clouds fleeing to the east. A sickly unearthly yellow lit the sky, and the mountainous waves were tarnished with flecks of gold light. Then the sun was swallowed up in a tattered curtain of cloud and the light died.

She struck stern first as her captain aimed to do, but did not run in firm enough and a side wash lurching in a great pyramid across the tide broke over her and slewed her round broadside. In a few seconds she had heeled over, her decks facing the shore and the waves spouting.

Ross ran across the beach, drunkenly in the gusts; she had come ashore midway up, just this side of Leisure Cliff.

There was no chance of reaching her yet, but she was quickly being washed in. The waves had a tremendous run on them, would flood in halfway to the sand hills and then go out, leaving great glassy areas of water a half inch deep.

The men on board were trying to launch a boat. This was the worst thing, but on an incoming tide they stood no better chance by staying in the ship.

They lowered her from the well deck and set her in the water without mishap, and then, with only three or four in, a flood of water swirled round the lee side of the brigantine and swept the small boat away. The men rowed frantically to keep within the shelter, but they were as in a tide race and were borne quite clear. A wave rushed on them, and smothered in water, they were carried inshore. Then they were left behind in the trough, and the next wave turned the boat upside down and broke it to pieces.

The men on shore had given way before the tide, but as the biggest waves passed, Ross and a few others stood staring out at the wreck while the retreating water rushed past their knees trying to carry them along.

'We'll not get to un this morning,' said Vigus, rubbing his hands and shivering with cold. 'Tide'll break un to bits, an' we shall have the pickings on the ebb. Might just so well go home.'

'I can't see one o' they men,' said Zacky Martin. 'I expect they've been sucked under and'll be spewed out farther downcoast.'

'She'll not stand in this sea even for one tide,' Ross said. 'There'll be pickings soon enough.'

Zacky glanced at him. There was a savagery in Ross this morning.

'Look fur yourself!' someone shouted.

An immense wave had hit the wreck and in a second a straight stiff column of spray stood two hundred feet in the air, to collapse slowly and disintegrate before the wind. Two men grasped Ross and dragged him back.

'She's going over!' he shouted.

They tried to run but could not. The wave caught them waist-high, swept them before it like straws; they were carried part way up the beach and left behind struggling in two feet of water, while the wave rushed on to spend its strength. There was just time to gain a foothold and brace themselves against the sudden rush back again. Ross wiped the water out of his eyes.

The *Queen Charlotte* could not last now. The great weight of the wave had not only carried her in; it had almost turned her bottom up, snapping off both masts and washing away all but one or two of the crew. Spars and tangles of wreckage, barrels and masts, coils of rope and sacks of corn were bobbing in the surf.

People streaming down to the scene carried axes and baskets and empty sacks. They were a spur to those who were before them and soon the shallow surf was black with people struggling to reach what they could. The tide washed in everything it could strip away. One of the crew had come ashore alive, three dead, the rest had gone.

As the morning grew and the day cleared more people came, with mules, ponies, dogs to carry away the stuff. But only a small part of the cargo was yet ashore, and there was not enough to go round. Ross made the people divide the spoils. If a barrel of pilchards came in it was broken open and doled out, a basketful to everyone who came. He was everywhere, ordering, advising, encouraging.

At ten three kegs of rum and one of brandy came in together and were at once opened. With hot spirit inside them men grew reckless and some even fought and struggled together in the water. As the tide rose, some fell back into the sand hills and lit bonfires from the wreckage and began a carouse. Newcomers plunged into the surf. Sometimes men and women were caught in the outrun of a wave and went tobogganing back into the sea. One was drowned.

At noon they were driven off most of the beach and watched the pounding of the hulk from a distance. Ross went back to Nampara, had something to eat, drank a great deal and was out again. He was gentle in reply to Demelza's questings but unmoved.

A part of the deck had given way and more sacks of corn were coming in. Frantic that these should be taken before all the corn was spoiled, many had rushed down again, and as he followed them Ross passed the successful ones coming away. A great dripping sack of flour staggered slowly up the hill and under it, sweating and red-faced, was Mrs Zacky. Aunt Betsy Triggs led a half-starved mule, laden with baskets of pilchards and a sack of corn. Old Man Daniel helped Beth Daniel with a table and two chairs. Jope Ishbel and Whitehead Scoble dragged a dead pig. Others carried firewood, one a basket of dripping coal.

On the beach Ross found men trying to loop a rope over a piece of hatchway which the sea was carrying out again. Restless, unsatisfied, trying to forget his own hurt, he went down to join them.

By two-thirty the tide had been ebbing an hour and nearly five hundred people waited. Another hundred danced and sang around the fires on the sand hills or lay drinking above high water. Not a piece of driftwood or a broken spar lay anywhere. Rumour had whispered that the Illuggan and St Ann's miners were coming to claim a share. This lent urgency where none was needed.

At three Ross waded out into the surf. He had been wet on and off all day, and the stinging cold of the water did not strike him now.

It was bad going out – unless the sea malevolently chose to take you – but when he judged himself far enough he dived into a wave and swam underwater. He came up to face one that nearly choked him, but after a while began to make headway. Once in the lee of the wreck he swam up and grasped the splintered spar which had once been the main mast and now stuck out towards the shore. He hauled himself up; men on shore shouted and waved soundlessly.

Not safe yet to climb to the high side of the deck. He untied the rope about his waist and hitched it to the root of the mast. A raised hand was a signal to the shore, and the rope quivered and tautened. In a few minutes there would be a score of others aboard with axes and saws.

Still astride the mast, he glanced about the ship. No sign of life. All the forecastle had given way and it was from here that the cargo had come. There would be pickings astern. He glanced to the poop. A different sight now from Truro Creek. All this week of gales and blizzard she must have been beating about in the channel and off Land's End. For once the Warleggans had met their match.

He stepped off the mast and, leaning flat on the deck, edged his way towards the poop. The door of the cabin faced him askew. It was an inch or two ajar but jammed. A trickle of water still ran from a corner of it as from the mouth of a sick old man.

He found a spar and thrust it into the door, tried to force it open. The spar splintered but the gap widened. As he got his shoulder into the opening the ship rocked with another great wave. Water flung itself into the air, high, high; as it fell the rest of the wave swirled round the ship, rising to his shoulders; he clung tight, it swirled, dragged, sucked, gave way at last. Water poured from the cabin, deluged him long after the rest had gone. He waited until this too had fallen to his waist before he forced his way in.

Something was tapping gently at his leg. Curious green gloom as if underwater. The three larboard portholes were buried deep, the starboard ones, glass smashed, looked at the sky. A table floating, a periwig, a news sheet. On the upper wall a map still hung. He looked down. The thing tapping his leg was a man's hand. The man floated face downwards, gently, submissively; the water draining out by the door had brought him over to greet Ross. For a second it gave the illusion of life.

Ross caught him by the collar and lifted his head. It was Matthew Sanson.

With a grunt Ross dropped the head back in the water and squeezed his way out into the air.

As the tide went out hundreds waded out and fell on the ship. With axes they burst open the hatches and dragged out the rest of the cargo. A quantity of mixed goods in the rear hatch was undamaged, and more kegs of rum were found. The deck planks were torn up, the wheel and binnacle carried off, the clothing and bits of furniture in the bunks and cabins. Jud, well gone in liquor, was saved from drowning in two feet of water, his arms clasped round the gilt figurehead. He had either mistaken her for a real woman or the gilt for real gold.

As dusk began to fall another bonfire was set up near the ship to light the scavengers on their way. The rising wind blew whorls of smoke flatly across the wet beach where it joined the fires on the sand hills.

Ross left the ship and walked home. He changed his clothes, which were stiff with half-dried salt, had a brief meal and then sat with Demelza. But the restless devil inside himself was not appeased; the pain and the fury were not gone. He went out again in the gathering windy dark.

By the light of a lantern a few of the more sober citizens were burying seven corpses at the foot of the sand hills. Ross stopped to tell them to go deep. He did not want the next spring tide uncovering them. He asked

Zacky how many had been saved and was told that two had been taken to Mellin.

He climbed a little and stared down at the crowd round a bonfire. Nick Vigus had brought his flute and people were jigging to his tune. Many were drunk and lay about, too weak to walk home. The wind was bitter, and there would be illness even in this bounty.

A hand caught his arm. It was John Gimlett.

'Beg pardon, sur.'

'What is it?'

'The miners, sur. From Illuggan an' St Ann's. The first ones are comin' down the valley. I thought ——'

'Are there many?'

'In their 'undreds, Bob Nanfan d'say.'

'Well, get you back into the house, man, and bolt the doors. They're only coming to loot the ship.'

'Aye, sur, but there's little left to loot – on the ship.'

Ross rubbed his chin. 'I know. But there's little left to drink either. We shall manage them.'

He went down to the beach. He hoped the Illuggan miners had not spent all the daylight hours drinking by the way.

On the beach things were quieter. The bonfire sent a constant shower of sparks chasing across the sand. Just beyond the wreck the surf piled up, a pale mountainous reef in the half-dark.

Then his arm was caught a second time. Pally Rogers from Sawle.

'Look ee! What's that, sur? Isn't it a light?'

Ross stared out to sea.

'Ef that be another ship she's coming ashore too!' said Rogers. 'She's too close in to do else. The Lord God ha' mercy on their souls!'

Ross suddenly caught the glint of a light beyond the surf. Then he saw a second light close beside. He began to run towards the edge of the sea.

As he neared it the foam came to meet him, detaching itself from the mass and scudding and bowling across the sand in hundreds of flakes of all sizes. He splashed into a few inches of water and stopped, peering, trying to get his breath in the wind. Rogers caught him up.

'Over thur, sur!'

Although the gale had grown again a few stars were out, and you could see well enough. A big ship, bigger than the brigantine, was coming in fast. A light forward and one amidships but no stern light. One minute she seemed right out of the water, and the next only her masts showed. There was no question of manœuvring to beach her; she was coming in anyhow as the waves threw her about.

Someone aboard had seen how near the end was, for a flare was lit – rags soaked in oil – and it flickered and flared in the wind. Dozens on the beach saw it.

She came in nearer the house than the *Queen Charlotte* and seemed to strike with scarcely a jar. Only her foremast toppling slowly showed the impact.

At the same moment the vanguard of the St Ann's and Illuggan miners streamed on to the beach.

Chapter ten

Pride of Madras, an East Indiaman homeward bound with a full cargo of silks, tea, and spices, had suddenly appeared, a flying wraith in the fog of the storm, off Sennen in the forenoon of that day.

She had seemed certain to strike Gurnard's Head but the lull in the gale had just given her sea room. Then she had been seen off Godrevy, and a little later the miners of Illuggan and St Ann's, with news of the *Queen Charlotte* wreck in their ears, had heard that a finer prize was due any minute at Gwithian or Basset's Cove.

So they had been pulled two ways, and instead of marching for Nampara had flocked into the gin shops and kiddleys of St Ann's while scouts kept watch on the cliffs.

She had slipped right under St Ann's Beacon unseen in the mist, and it was not until just before dusk that she had been picked up again ducking across the mouth of Sawle Cove. She must come ashore within a few miles, and the miners had followed along the cliffs and down the lanes, so that their leaders reached Hendrawna Beach at the same time as the ship.

What followed would not have been pretty in the sun of a summer afternoon. Happening as it did through a winter's night, starlit in a gale, it was full of the shadowed horror and shrill cadences of another world.

She came in so swiftly that only half a dozen of the locals knew of her until she lit the flare. Then when she struck, everyone began to run towards her. They and the newcomers converged together. Rivalry flared up in a second.

To begin they could not get near her; but the tide had still another two hours to ebb and very soon the venturesome, reckless with rum and gin, plunged through the surf. There was still one light on the ship though the waves were breaking right over her, and two sailors were able to swim ashore, one with a rope. But they could get no one interested enough to hold it, and a third sailor, washed ashore half conscious, was set upon and stripped of his shirt and breeches and left groaning naked on the sand.

Great numbers of miners were now coming, and soon the grey of the sands was black in a huge semicircle before the ship. Ross played no part in it now, either in wreck or rescue. He had edged a little away to watch, but those who saw his face saw no disapproval on it. It was as if the goad of the pain in him would leave him no respite for judgment and sanity.

Others of the crew had got ashore, but now it was the common thing to seize anything they carried, and those who resisted were stripped and roughly handled and left to crawl away as best they could. Two who drew knives were knocked unconscious.

By seven the ship was dry, and by then there were three thousand people on the beach. Barrels in which the pilchards had come ashore were set alight, and these, thick with oil, flared and smoked like giant torches. The ship was a carcase on which a myriad ants crawled. Men were everywhere, hacking with knives and axes, dragging out from the bowels of the ship the riches of the Indies. Dozens lay about the beach, drunk or senseless from a fight. The crew and eight passengers – saved at the last by Zacky Martin and Pally Rogers and a few others – broke up into two parties, the larger, led by the mate, going off into the country in search of help, the rest huddling in a group some distance from the ship, while the captain stood guard over them with a drawn sword.

With rich goods seized and fine brandy drunk, fights broke out everywhere. Smouldering feuds between one hamlet and another, one mine and the next, had come to flame. Empty bellies and empty pockets reacted alike to the temptations of the night. To the shipwrecked people it seemed that they had been cast upon the shore of a wild and savage foreign land where thousands of dark-faced men and women talking an uncouth tongue were waiting to tear them to pieces for the clothes they wore.

As the tide began to creep round the ship again Ross went aboard, swarming up by a rope that hung from her bows. He found an orgy of destruction. Men lay drunk about the deck, others fought for a roll of cloth or curtains or cases of tea, often tearing or spilling what they quarrelled over. But the saner men, aware like Ross that time was short, were labouring to clear the ship while she was still intact. Like *Queen Charlotte*, *Pride of Madras* lay beam on, and another tide might break her up. Lanterns were in the hold, and dozens of men were below passing up goods in a chain to the deck, where they were carried to the side and thrown or lowered to others waiting on the sand. These were all St Ann's men, and farther forward the Illuggan men were doing the same.

Aft he found some from Grambler and Sawle tearing out the panelling in the captain's cabin. Among all the hammering and the shrill squeaks of wood, Paul Daniel slept peacefully in a corner. Ross hauled him to his feet by the collar of his jacket, but Paul only smiled and sank down again.

Jack Cobbledick nodded. 'Tes all right, sur. We'll see to 'e when we d'leave.'

'Another half-hour is all you can take.'

Ross went on deck again. The high wind was pure and cold. He took a deep breath. Above and behind all the shouts, the laughter, the distant singing, the hammering, the scuffles and the groans, was another sound, that of the surf, coming in. It made a noise to-night like hundreds of carts rumbling over wooden bridges.

He avoided two men fighting in the scuppers, went forward and tried to rouse some of the drunks. He spoke of the tide to some of those who were working, had bare nods in exchange.

He stared over the beach. The funnels of fire and smoke from the barrels were still scattering sparks over the sand. Sections of the crowd were lit in umber and orange. Milling faces and black smoke round a dozen funeral pyres. A pagan rite. Back in the sand hills the volcanoes spumed

He slid over the side, hand by hand down the rope. In water up to his knees.

He pushed his way through the crowd. It seemed as if normal feelings were coming to him. Circulation to a dead limb.

He looked about for the survivors. They were still huddled together just beyond the thickest of the crowd.

As he came near, two of the sailors drew knives and the captain half lifted his sword.

'Keep your distance, man! Keep clear! We'll fight.'

Ross eyed them over. A score of shivering exhausted wretches; if they had no attention several might die before morning.

'I was about to offer you shelter,' he said.

At the sound of his more cultured voice the captain lowered his sword. 'Who are you? What do you want?'

'My name is Poldark. I have a house near here.'

There was a whispered consultation. 'And you offer us shelter?'

'Such as I have. A fire. Blankets. Something hot to drink.'

Even now there was hesitation: they had been so used that they were afraid of treachery. And the captain had some idea of staying here the night to be able to bear his full witness to the courts. But the eight passengers overruled him.

'Very well, sir,' said the captain, keeping his sword unsheathed, 'if you will lead the way.'

Ross inclined his head and moved off slowly across the beach. The captain fell into step beside him, the two armed sailors followed close behind and the rest straggled after.

They passed several dozen people dancing round a fire and drinking fresh-brewed tea (ex *Pride of Madras*) laced with brandy (ex *Pride of Madras*). They overtook six mules laden so heavy with rolls of cloth that their feet sank inches in the sand at every step. They skirted forty or fifty men fighting in a pack for four gold ingots.

The captain said in a voice trembling with indignation:

'Have you any control over these – these savages?'

'None whatever,' Ross said.

'Is there no law in this land?'

'None which will stand before a thousand miners.'

'It – it is a disgrace. A crying disgrace. Two years ago I was shipwrecked off Patagonia – and treated less barbarously.'

'Perhaps the natives were better fed than we in this district.'

'Fed? Food – oh, if it were food we carried and these men were starving ——,'

'Many have been near it for months.'

'– then there might be some excuse. But it is not food. To pillage the ship, and we ourselves barely escaped with our lives! I never thought such a day could be! It is monstrous!'

'There is much in this world which is monstrous,' Ross said. 'Let us be thankful they were content with your shirts.'

The captain glanced at him. A passing lantern showed up the taut, lean, overstrained face, the pale scar, the half-lidded eyes. The captain said no more.

As they climbed the wall at the end of the beach they saw a group of men coming towards them from Nampara House. Ross stopped and stared. Then he caught the creak of leather.

'Here is the law you were invoking.'

The men came up. A dozen dismounted troopers in the charge of a sergeant. Captain McNeil and his men had been moved some months before, and these were strangers. They had marched out from Truro on hearing of the wreck of the *Queen Charlotte*.

This much the sergeant was explaining when the captain burst in with an angry flood of complaint, and soon he was surrounded bv the passengers and crew, demanding summary justice. The sergeant plucked at his lip and stared across at the beach, which stirred and quickened with a wild and sinister life of its own.

'You go down there at your own risk, Sergeant,' Ross said.

There was a sudden silence, followed by another babel of threat and complaint from the shipwrecked people.

'All right,' said the sergeant. 'Go easy. Go easy now, we'll put a stop to the looting, never you fear. We'll see no more is carried away. We'll put a stop to it.'

'You would be advised to delay until daylight,' Ross said. 'The night will have cooled tempers. Remember the two customs officers who were killed at Gwithian last year.'

'I have me orders, sir.' The sergeant glanced uneasily at his small band and then again at the struggling smoky mass on the beach. 'We'll see all this is put a stop to.' He patted his musket.

'I warn you,' Ross said, 'half of them are in drink and many fighting among themselves. If you interfere they'll stop their quarrelling and turn on you. And so far it has been fists and a few sticks. But if you fire into them not half of you will come out of it alive.'

The sergeant hesitated again. 'Ye'd advise me to wait until first light?'

'It is your only hope.'

The captain burst out again, but some of the passengers, shivering and half dead from exposure, cut him short and pleaded to be led to shelter.

Ross went on to the house, leaving the troopers still hesitant on the edge of the maelstrom. At the door of the house he stopped again.

'You'll pardon me, gentlemen, but may I ask you for quietness. My wife is just recovering from a grave illness and I do not wish to disturb her.'

The chattering and muttering slowly died away to silence.

He led the way in.

Chapter eleven

ROSS WOKE AT the first light. He had slept heavily for seven hours. The inescapable pain was still there but some emotional purging of the night had deadened its old power. It was the first time for a week he had undressed, the first full sleep he had had. He had gone up to his old room, for Demelza had seemed better last night, and Jane Gimlett had said she would sleep in the chair before the fire.

He dressed quickly, stiffly, but was quiet about it. Below him in the parlour and in the next two rooms twenty-two men were sleeping. Let them lie. All the strain of last night had brought the stiffness of the French musket wound back, and it was with a sharp limp that he went to the window. The wind was still high and the glass as thick with salt. He opened the window and stared out on Hendrawna Beach.

Dawn had just broken, and in a clear sky seven black clouds were following each other across the lightening east like seven ill-begotten sons of the storm. The tide was nearly out and both wrecks were dry. The *Queen Charlotte*, lying almost deserted, might have been an old whale cast up by the sea. Around and about the *Pride of Madras* people still milled and crawled. The sands were patchy with people, and at first he thought Leisure Cliff and those east of it had been decorated by some whim of the revellers. Then he saw that the wind had been the only reveller, and costly silks had been blown from the wreck and hung in inaccessible places all along the beach and cliffs. Goods and stores were still scattered on the sand hills and just above high-water mark, but a large part was already gone.

There had been bloodshed in the night.

Jack Cobbledick, calling in just before midnight, had told him that the troopers had gone down to the beach and tried to stand guard over the wreck. But the tide had driven them off and the wreckers had gone on with salvaging their prizes as if the soldiers had not existed. The sergeant, trying to get his way by peaceful measures, was roughly handled; and some of the soldiers fired into the air to scare the crowd. Then they had been forced off the beach step by step with about a thousand angry men following them.

A little later an Illuggan miner had been caught molesting a St Ann's woman, and a huge fight had developed which had only been broken by the inrush of the sea threatening to carry off the booty, and not before a hundred or more men were stretched out on the beach.

Ross did not know whether the troopers had again tried to take over the wreck when the tide went back, but he thought not. It was more likely that they still kept discreet watch in the sand hills while the sergeant sent for reinforcements.

But in another six hours the ships would be nothing but hulks, every plank and stick carried away, the bones picked clean.

He closed the window, and as the rimed glass shut out the view the pang of his own personal loss returned. He had planned so much for Julia, had watched her grow from a scarcely separable entity, seen her nature unfold, the very beginning of traits and characteristics make their quaint showing. It was hardly believable that now they would never develop, that all that potential sweetness should dry up at its fount and turn to dust. Hardly believable and hardly bearable.

He slowly put on his coat and waistcoat and limped downstairs.

In the bedroom Jane Gimlett slept soundly before a fire that had gone out. Demelza was awake.

He sat beside the bed and she slipped her hand into his. It was thin and weak, but there was a returning firmness underneath.

'How are you?'

'Much, much better. I slept all the night through. Oh, Ross. Oh, my dear, I can feel the strength returning to me. In a few days more I shall be up.'

'Not yet awhile.'

'And did you sleep?'

'Like the ——' He changed his simile. 'Like one drugged.'

She squeezed his hand. 'An' all the folk from the ship?'

'I have not been to see.'

She said: 'I have never seen a real shipwreck, not in daytime. Not a proper one.'

'Soon I'll carry you up to our old bedroom and you can see it all through the spyglass.'

'This morning?'

'Not this morning.'

'I wish it was not this time o' year,' she said. 'I seem to be tired for the summer.'

'It will come.'

There was a pause.

'I believe to-morrow will be too late to see the best of the wreck.'

'Hush, or you'll wake Jane.'

'Well, you could wrap me in blankets an' I should come to no harm.'

He sighed and put her hand against his cheek. It was not a disconsolate sigh, for her returning life was a tonic to his soul. Whatever she suffered, whatever loss came to her, she would throw it off, for it was not in her nature to go under. Although she was the woman and he a fierce and sometimes arrogant man, hers was the stronger nature because the more pliant. That did not mean she did not feel Julia's death as deeply and as bitterly, but he saw that she would recover first. It might be because he had had all the other failures and disappointments. But chiefly it was because some element had put it in her nature to be happy. She was born so and could not change. He thanked God for it. Wherever she went and however long she lived she would be the same, lavishing interest on the things she loved and contriving for their betterment, working for and bringing up her children. . . .

Ah, there was the rub.

He found she was looking at him. He smiled.

'Have you heard of them at Trenwith?' she asked.

'Not since I told you before.' He looked at her and saw that despite her loss there was no trace of bitterness in her thoughts of Elizabeth and Francis. It made him ashamed of his own.

'Did they say there was any loss among those who were in the *Pride of Madras*?'

'None of the passengers. Some of the crew.'

She sighed. 'Ross, I b'lieve the miners, the Illuggan and St Ann's miners, have made a rare mess of the garden. I heard 'em tramping over it all last evening, and Jane said they had mules and donkeys with them.'

'If anything is damaged it can be put to rights,' Ross said.

'Was Father amongst them, did you see?'

'I saw nothing of him.'

'Maybe he is reformed in that way too. Though I doubt there must have been many Methodies among those who came. I wonder what – what he will say about this. . . .'

Ross knew she was not referring to the wreck.

'Nothing that can make any difference, my dear. Nothing could have made any difference.'

She nodded. 'I know. Sometimes I wonder if she ever really stood any chance.'

'Why?'

'I don't know, Ross. She seemed to have it so bad from the start. And she was so young. . . .'

There was a long silence.

At length Ross got up and pulled the curtain back. Even this did not wake Jane Gimlett. The sun had risen and was gilding the waving treetops in the valley.

As he came back to the bed Demelza wiped her eyes.

'I think, I believe I like you with a beard, Ross.'

He put his hand up. 'Well, I do not like myself. It will come off sometime to-day.'

'Is it going to be a fine day, do you think?'

'Fine enough.'

'I wish I could see the sun. That is the drawback to this room, there is no sun until afternoon.'

'Well, so soon as you are well you shall go upstairs again.'

'Ross, I should like to see our room again. Take me up, just for a few minutes, please. I believe I could walk up if I tried.'

On an emotional impulse he said: 'Very well: if you wish it.'

He lifted her out of the bed, wrapped a blanket round her legs, two round her shoulders, picked her up. She had lost a lot of weight, but somehow the feel of her arm about his neck, the living companionable substance of her, was like a balm. Still quiet to avoid rousing Jane, he slipped out of the room, mounted the creaking stair. He carried her into their bedroom, set her down on the bed. Then he went to the window and opened one to clean a circle in the salt of the other. He shut the window and went back to the bed. Tears were streaming down her face.

'What is wrong?'

'The cot,' she said. 'I had forgotten the cot.'

He put his arm about her and they sat quiet for a minute or two. Then he picked her up again and took her to the window and sat her in a chair.

She stared out on the scene, and with his cheek pressed against hers he stared with her. She took up a corner of the blanket and tried to stop the tears.

She said: 'How pretty the cliffs look with all those streamers on 'em.'

'Yes.'

'Redruth Fair,' she said. 'The beach puts me in mind of that, the day after it is over.'

'It will take some clearing, but the sea is a good scavenger.'

'Ross,' she said, 'I should like you to make it up with Francis sometime. It would be better all round.'

'Sometime.'

'Sometime soon.'

'Sometime soon.' He had no heart to argue with her to-day.

The sun shone full upon her face, showing the thin cheeks and the pallid skin.

'When something happens,' she said, 'like what has just happened to us, it makes all our quarrels seem small and mean, as if we were quarrelling when we hadn't the right. Didn't we ought to find all the friendship we can?'

'If friendship is to be found.'

'Yes. But didn't we ought to seek it? Can't all our quarrels be buried and forgot, so that Verity can come to visit us and we go to Trenwith and we can – can live in friendship and not hatred while there's time.'

Ross was silent. 'I believe yours is the only wisdom, Demelza,' he said at length.

They watched the scene on the beach.

'I shan't have to finish that frock for Julia now,' she said. 'It was that dainty too.'

'Come,' he said. 'You will be catching cold.'

'No. I am quite warm, Ross. Let me stay a little longer in the sun.'

JEREMY POLDARK

A Novel of Cornwall 1790–1791

Book one

Chapter one

In August 1790 three men rode along the mule track past Grambler Mine and made towards the straggling cottages at the end of the village. It was evening and the sun had just set; clouds had been driven up the sky by a westerly breeze and were beginning to flush with the afterglow. Even the mine chimneys, from which no smoke had issued for best part of two years, took on a matured mellow colour in the evening light. In a hole in the taller of the two pigeons were nesting, and their flapping wings beat against the wider silence as the men passed. A half dozen ragged children were playing with a homemade swing suspended between two of the sheds, and some women standing at the doors of cottages, hands on elbows, watched the horsemen ride by.

They were soberly dressed, respectable riders in a clerkish black, and they sat their horses with an air of importance; not many such were seen nowadays in this half-derelict, half–deserted village which had come into being and had existed solely to serve the mine and which, now that the mine was dead, was itself perishing of a slower decay. It seemed that the men were going to pass right through – as might have been expected – but at the last one nodded his head and they reined in their horses at a more dejected-looking shack than anything they had yet seen. It was a one-storey cob hut with an old iron pipe for a chimney and a roof patched and repatched with sacking and driftwood; and at its open door on an upturned box sat a bowlegged man sharpening a piece of wood. He was under the average height, strongly built, but getting up in years. He wore old riding boots bound with string, yellow pigskin breeches, a dirty grey flannel shirt which had lost one sleeve at the elbow, and a stiff black leather waistcoat, whose pockets bulged with worthless odds and ends. He was whistling almost soundlessly, but when the men got down from their horses he un-pursed his lips and looked at them with wary bloodshot eyes; his knife hung over the stick while he sized them up.

The leader, a tall emaciated man with eyes so close together as to suggest a cast, said:

'Good day. Is your name Paynter?'

The knife slowly lowered itself. The bowlegged man put up a dirty thumbnail and scratched the shiniest spot on his bald head.

'Mebbe.'

The other made a gesture of impatience. 'Come, man. You're either Paynter or you're not. It's not a subject on which there can be two opinions.'

'Well, I aren't so sure 'bout that. Folk is too free with other folks' names. Mebbe there can be two opinions. Mebbe there can be three. It all depend what you d'want me for.'

'It *is* Paynter,' said one of the men behind. 'Where's your wife, Paynter?'

'Gone Marasanvose. Now if you be wanting she . . .'

'My name is Tankard,' said the first man sharply. 'I'm an attorney acting for the Crown in the coming case of Rex versus Poldark. We want to ask you a few questions, Paynter. This is Blencowe, my clerk, and Garth, an interested party. Will you lead the way inside?'

Jud Paynter's wrinkled teak-coloured face took on a look of injured innocence, but under this conventional defence there was a glint of genuine alarm.

'What are ee coming troubling me for? I said all I had to say afore magistrates, an' that were nothing. 'Ere I am, living a Christian life like St Peter himself, sitting before his own front door interfering with no one. Leave me be.'

'The law must take its course,' said Tankard, and waited for Jud to get up.

After a minute, glancing suspiciously from one face to the other, Jud led the way inside. They seated themselves in the shadowy hut, Tankard staring distastefully about and lifting his coattails to avoid the litter as he sat down. None of the visitors had delicate noses, but Blencowe, a pasty, stooping little man, looked back wistfully at the sweet evening outside.

Jud said: 'I don't know nothing about'n. You're barking up the wrong door.'

'We have reason to believe,' said Tankard, 'that your deposition before the examining justice was false in every particular. If——'

'You'll pardon me,' said Garth in an undertone. 'Perhaps you'd be letting me speak to Paynter for a minute or two, Mr Tankard. You remember I said, afore we came in, that there's more ways . . .'

Tankard folded his thin arms. 'Oh, very well.'

Jud turned his bulldog eyes upon his new adversary. He thought he had seen Garth before, riding through the village or some such. Snooping perhaps.

Garth said in a conversational, friendly tone: 'I understand you were Captain Poldark's servant at one time, you and your wife, for a great many years and for his father afore him?'

'Mebbe.'

'And after working faithful for him all those years you were suddenly put off, turned from the house without a word of warning.'

'Ais. Tweren't right or proper, I'll say that.'

'It is said, mind you, this is but hearsay, y'understand, that he treated you shameful afore you left – for some fancied misdeed – used his horsewhip and near drowned you under the pump. Would that be so?'

Jud spat on the floor and showed his two great teeth.

'That's against the law,' interposed Tankard, squinting down his long thin nose. 'Offences against the person: common assault and battery. You could have proceeded, Paynter.'

'And it can't have been the first time, I'll wager,' said Garth.

'No, nor it wasn't neither,' Jud said after a minute, sucking at his teeth.

'People who ill-treat faithful servants don't deserve them these days,' said Garth. 'There's a new spirit abroad. Every man is as good as his neighbour. Look what be happening in France.'

'Ais. I d'know all about that,' said Jud, and then stopped. It wouldn't do to let these prying busybodies into the secret of his visits to Roscoff. All the time this Poldark stuff might be a blind to trap him into other admissions.

'Blencowe,' said Tankard. 'Have you the brandy? We could all do with a tot, and no doubt Paynter will join us.'

. . . The afterglow faded, and the shadows in the littered hut grew darker.

'Take it from me,' said Garth, 'the aristocracy is finished. Their day is over. Common men will be coming into their rights. And one of their rights is not to be treated worse than dogs, not to be used like slaves. D'you understand the law, Mr Paynter?'

'The Englishman's house is his castle,' said Jud. 'An' habeas corpse, and thou shalt not move thy neighbour's landmark.'

'When there's trouble at law,' said Garth, 'like what there was here in January, it's often hard for the law to act like it should. So it acts as best it may. And where there's riot and wrecking and robbery and suchlike, it says nothing about those who follow if so be as it can lay hold on those who lead. Now in this case the ringleader is plain to be seen.'

'Mebbe.'

'No mebbe about it. But reliable evidence is hard to come by. Evidence of responsible men like yourself. . . . And, mind you, if the law sees it cannot prove a case against the ringleader, then it will look further and smoke out the lesser men. That's the truth of it, Mr Paynter, as sure as I'm sitting here; so it's best for all that the right man should stand in the assizes.'

Jud picked up his glass and set it down again, it being empty; Blencowe hastily proffered the brandy bottle. There was a comfortable bobbling sound as Jud upended it.

'I don't see why for you d'come to me, when I wasn't there at all,' he said, caution still uppermost. 'A man can't see farther'n he can blaw.'

'Listen, Paynter,' said Tankard, ignoring Garth's warning sign. 'We know a great deal more than you think. These inquiries have been in train for near on seven months. It would be better for you if you made a clean breast of it all.'

'Clean breast indeed——'

'We know that you actively co-operated with Poldark on the morning of the wreck. We know you were on the beach all through the rioting of that day and the following night. We know you played a leading part in resisting the officers of the Crown when one was seriously injured, and in many ways you are as culpable as your master——'

'I never 'eard sich loitch in all me life! Me? I was never nearer the wreck nor what I am now——'

'But as Garth explained, we're willing to overlook this if you will turn King's evidence. We've a weight of testimony against this man Poldark, but wish to make it stronger. It's plain you owe him no loyalty. Why, on your own showing he's treated you shamefully! Come, man, it's common sense to tell us the truth, as well as your common duty.'

With some dignity Jud got to his feet.

'Also,' said Garth, 'we'd make it worth your while.'

Jud pivoted thoughtfully on his heel and slowly sat down again. 'Eh?'

'Not official, of course. It wouldn't do to come official. But there's other ways.'

Jud stretched his head to peer out through the door. There was no sign of Prudie. It was always the same when she went to see her cousin. He looked sidelong at each of the men in the hut, as if he might weigh up their intentions unnoticed.

'What other ways?'

Garth took out his pouch and rattled it. 'The Crown's out for a conviction. The Crown's willing to pay for the right information, like. Strictly on the quiet, of course. Strictly between friends. Like offering a reward for an arrest, as you might say. Isn't it, Mr Tankard? Nothing different from that.'

Tankard did not speak. Jud got his glass and sucked up the rest of the brandy.

Almost under his breath he said: 'First threatenings an' now bribery. Bribery as I'm alive! Money for Judas, I reckon they'm thinking. Stand up in a court o' law agin an old friend. Worse'n Judas, for he did it on the quiet like. An' for what? Thirty bits o' silver. An' I'm reckoning they wouldn't offer me that much. They'd want for me to do un for twenty or ten. Tedn reasonable, tedn proper, tedn Christian, tedn *right*.'

There was a short pause.

'Ten guineas down and ten guineas after the trial,' said Garth.

'Ha!' said Jud. 'Just what I thought.'

'It's possible it could be raised to fifteen.'

Jud got up, but slowly this time, sucked his teeth and tried to whistle, but his lips were dry. He hitched up his breeches and two fingers went into a waistcoat pocket for a pinch of snuff.

'Tesn't fair to come on a man like this,' he grumbled. 'Me head's goin' round like a trool. Come again in a month.'

'The assizes are fixed for early September.'

Tankard also got up. 'We shouldn't require a long deposition,' he said. 'Just a few sentences covering the main facts as you know them – and an undertaking to repeat them at the appropriate time.'

'An' what would I say?' asked Jud.

'The truth, of course, as you can swear to it.'

Garth interrupted hastily: 'The truth, of course, but maybe we could guide you as to what we most want, like. It is the assault upon the soldiers that we're wishing to have witness of. That was on the night of the seventh-eighth of January. You were on the beach at the time, weren't you, Mr Paynter? No doubt you saw the whole incident.'

Jud looked old and wary. 'Naw . . . Don't remember nothing 'bout that, now.'

'It might be worth twenty guineas if so be as your memory came round to it.'

'Twenty now and twenty after?'

'. . . Yes.'

'Tes worth all o' that for such a stramming big story.'

'It's the truth we want, man,' said Tankard impatiently. 'Were you or were you not a witness of the assault?'

Garth put his pouch upon a rickety old three-legged table which had once belonged to Joshua Poldark. He began to count out twenty gold coins.

'What,' said Jud, staring at the money, 'when that there soldier got his head cleaved open, an' all the rest of 'em was pushed off of Hendrawna Beach fasterer than what they came on. I laffed at that. Didn I laff! Was that what you was meaning?'

'Of course. And Captain Poldark's part in it.'

Shadows were filling the hut with the approach of night. The clink of coins had a liquid sound, and it seemed for a moment as if all the light that was left lingered over the dull gold island of the guineas.

'Why,' said Jud, swallowing, 'I reckon I mind that well enough. Though I took no part in it myself, see. I was – thereabouts all the time.' He hesitated and spat. 'Why didn't you tell me you was meaning that all along?'

The following day a young woman on a horse went through Grambler in the other direction, passed Sawle Church, skirted Trenwith and presently began to go down the steep track into Trevaunance Cove. She was a dark young woman, a little above average in height, dressed in a close-fitting blue riding habit, a pale blue bodice and a small tricorn hat. Connoisseurs would have disagreed as to whether she was beautiful, but few men would have passed her without a second glance.

Leaving the smelting works, whose ochreous fumes had lighted the vegetation of the cove, she rode up the other side to where Place House, squat and solid against wind and storm, brooded over the sea. As she got down it was plain that the young woman was nervous. Her gloved fingers fumbled with the bridle of her horse, and when a groom came out to hold him she stumbled over what she had to say.

'Sir John Trevaunance, ma'am? I'll ask if he be in. What name shall I say?'

'Mistress Poldark.'

'Mistress Poldark. Er–yes, ma'am.' Did she imagine the slight glance of added interest? 'Will you come this way, please.'

She was shown into a warm little morning room from which a conservatory led off, and after sitting pulling at the fingers of her gloves for a few minutes she heard footsteps returning, and a manservant came to say Sir John was in and would see her.

He was in a long room like a study, overlooking the sea. She was relieved to find him alone except for a great boar hound that crouched at his feet. She found him, too, less imposing than she'd feared, being of a figure not much taller than herself, and ruddy-complexioned and rather jovial about the eyes and jowl.

He said: 'Your servant, ma'am. Will you take a seat.'

He waited until she had chosen the edge of a chair and then sat at his desk again. For a minute she kept her eyes down, knowing he was looking her over and accepting the scrutiny as part of the necessary ordeal.

He said warily: 'I haven't had the pleasure before.'

'No. . . . You know my husband well. . . .'

'Of course. We've been associated in business until . . . recently.'

'Ross was very grieved to give up the association. He was always that proud of it.'

'Hrrrm! Circumstances were too much for us, ma'am. Nobody's fault. We all lost money in the transaction.'

She looked up, and saw that his scrutiny had gratified him. It was one of the few comforting factors in Demelza's excursions into society, this faculty she had of pleasing men. She did not see it yet as power, only as a buttress to faltering courage. She knew that her visit here was irregular by any standards of etiquette – and he must know it as well.

From where they were sitting they could both see the smoke drifting across the bay from the smelting works, and after a moment he said rather stiffly:

'As you – hrrm – no doubt know, the company has been reformed – under new management. It was a blow for us all when the concern failed, but y'understand how I was placed. The buildings were on my land – indeed under my very nose – I'd sunk more capital than anyone in the concern, and it would've been crazy to let 'em rot away in idleness. The opportunity came to obtain fresh capital and it was only common sense to take it. I trust Captain Poldark understands how it was.'

'I'm sure he does,' said Demelza. 'I'm sure he'd only wish you well with any new venture – even if he wasn't able to partake in it himself.'

Sir John's eyes flickered. 'Kind of you to say so. As yet we barely meet expenses, but I think that will improve. Can I offer you some refreshment? A glass of canary, perhaps?'

'No, thank you . . .' She hesitated. 'But p'raps I should like a glass of port if twouldn't be putting you out.'

With an ironical eyebrow Sir John rose, and pulled the bell. Wine was brought and polite conversation made while it was drunk. They talked of mines and cows and carriages and the broken summer. Demelza grew easier in manner and Sir John less wary.

'To tell the truth,' said Demelza, 'I think it is the caudly weather that's making trouble with all the animals. We have a fine cow called Emma; two weeks ago she was yielding rich, but now the milk's gone into her horn. Same with another, though that was not so surprising——'

'I've a fine Hereford, worth a mint of money,' Sir John said. 'Calved only for the second time two days ago and now sick and ill with a paraplegia. Had the cow doctor, Phillips, over five times. It will break my heart if I have to lose her.'

'Is the calf safe?'

'Oh yes, but it was a bad time. And afterwards Minta not able to stand. Something is amiss with her teeth too – loose in the jaw – and a sort of separation to the joints of her tail. Phillips is completely defeated, and my own man no better.'

'I mind when I lived at Illuggan,' said Demelza, 'there was a case like that there. The parson's cow was taken ill with just that sort of complaint. And after calving too.'

'Did he find the cure?'

'Yes sir, he found the cure.'

'What was it?'

'Well, it wouldn't be for me to say whether the parson did right, would it? He wasn't above calling in an old woman, called Meggy Dawes – she lived just over the stream, I remember. A rare hand at curing warts and the King's Evil. Once, a boy went to her with a kenning on the eye. It was a bad one, but no sooner did she——'

'But about the cow, ma'am.'

'Oh yes. Is she to be seen, Sir John? I'd dearly like to see her to be sure if it is just the same complaint as in the parson's cow.'

'I'll take you to her myself, if you'll be so good. Another glass of port to sustain you?'

A few minutes later they made their way across the cobbled yard at the back of the house and into the shippon where the cow lay. Demelza noticed the massive stonework of the outhouses and wished they were hers. The cow lay upon her side, her soft brown eyes mournful but uncomplaining. A man rose from a wooden seat and stood respectfully by the door.

Demelza bent to examine the cow – with a professionalism of manner that came from her seven years at Nampara, not at all from her Illuggan childhood. The animal's legs were paralysed – and her tail had a curious disjointed appearance about halfway along its length.

Demelza said: 'Yes. It is exactly the same. Meggy Dawes called it Tail-Shot.'

'And the cure?'

'It is her cure, mind you, not mine.'

'Yes, yes, I follow that.'

Demelza passed the tip of her tongue over her lips. 'She said to slit open the tail here, about a foot from the end, where the joint has slipped, and put in a well-salted onion – then bind it in place with some coarse tape – keep it there about a week, then leave off the tape. Only a little food once a day, and a cordial made of equal parts of rosemary, juniper berries and cardamon seeds without their hulks. I remember well. That's what she said.'

Demelza glanced experimentally at the baronet. Sir John was chewing his bottom lip.

'Well,' he said, 'I've never heard of the cure, but then the disease is rare too. You are the first person who seems to have encountered it before. Damme, I've a mind to try it. What do you say, Lyson?'

''Tis better'n seeing the animal suffer, sir.'

'Exactly what I feel. I have heard that these old women are wonders when it comes to the lesser-known distempers. Could you repeat the instruction to my man, Mrs Poldark?'

'With pleasure.' After a minute or two they walked back across the yard and into the house.

Sir John said: 'I trust Captain Poldark is keeping in good heart over his coming trial.'

As soon as he spoke he regretted having been so incautious. One felt that she had deliberately avoided this subject, so putting on him the onus of mentioning it. But she did not take up the case as passionately as he had feared.

'Well, of course we're very unhappy about it. I think I worry more than he does.'

'It will soon be here and over now, and a good chance of acquittal, I think.'

'D'you really think so, Sir John? That comforts me greatly. You'll be in Bodmin yourself during the assizes?'

'Um? Um? Well, that I don't know. Why do you ask?'

'I have heard tell there is to be an election during September, and with the assizes on the sixth I thought you might by chance be there.'

'You mean to help my brother? Oh, he's well able to look after his seat.' The baronet glanced without trust at her composed face as they re-entered the big room he used as an office. It wasn't easy to guess what she was thinking. 'Even if I was in the town I should have too much in hand to attend the court. Besides, with respect, ma'am, I shouldn't wish to see an old friend in distress. Shall wish him well, of course – but no one wants to seek entertainment in the spectacle.'

'We've heard tell there are to be two judges,' she said.

'Oh, not two to the case. Two will share the assize between 'em, I expect. Wentworth Lister is not an ill fellow, though it's years since we met. You'll have a fair trial, be sure of that. British justice will see to it.' The boar hound had come across, and he took a sweet biscuit from a drawer and gave it to the dog.

'It is fair puzzling to me,' said Demelza, 'how a man – a judge – can come down all the way from upcountry and listen to a case and get the hang of the rights and ways of it all in a few hours. It don't seem possible to me. Does he not ever ask for the truth in private before the case begins?'

Sir John smiled. 'You'll be surprised how quickly a trained brain can sum up the true facts. And remember, it will not depend upon the judge but upon the jury, and they are Cornish folk like ourselves, so there's good cause to look on the bright side. Another sip of port?'

Demelza refused. 'It's a little heady, I suspicion. But very taking in flavour. When all this is over we'd like for you to come and see us one day, sir. Ross asked me to say that.'

Sir John said he'd be charmed, and the dog dropped crumbs from his biscuit all over the floor. Demelza rose to go.

He added: 'I shall pray for good results from your treatment for Minta.'

So did Demelza, but she didn't show her doubts. 'Perhaps I might have news of her?'

'Of course. I'll send word over. And in the meantime . . . should you be passing this way again – only too pleased.'

'Thank you, Sir John. I sometimes ride the coast for my health. It is uneven for a good horse, but I like the views and the bracing air.

Sir John went with her to the door and helped her to mount, admiring her slim figure and straight back. As she rode out of the gates a man on a grey horse came in.

'Who was that?' said Unwin Trevaunance, dropping his grey riding gloves on top of a pile of tin cheques. Sir John's younger brother did everything deliberately, giving consequence to actions which hadn't any. Thirty-six or -seven, tall, lion-faced and masterful, he was a much more impressive personality than the baronet. Yet Sir John made money and Unwin did not.

'Ross Poldark's wife. Attractive young woman. Hadn't met her before.'

'What did she want?'

'That I don't yet know,' said Sir John. 'She did not appear to want anything.'

Unwin had a cleft between his eyes, which deepened when he frowned. 'Wasn't she his scullery maid or some such?'

'Others have risen before her, and with fewer talents, I'd swear. She has a certain elegance already. In a few years it will be hard to tell her from a woman of breeding.'

'And she came for nothing? I doubt it. To me she looks a dangerous woman.'

'Dangerous?'

'We exchanged a glance as she left. I'm not unskilled in summing people up, John.'

'Well, neither am I, Unwin, and I think I'll take the risk.' Sir John gave another biscuit to the hound. 'She has a ready cure to offer for Minta, though rot me if I think it'll work. . . . Did you find Ray?'

'Yes. Oh yes. I told him Caroline wanted to break the journey down here to be in Bodmin during the election; but Caroline has written him also, so it was no news. Like her to ask me to ask her uncle and then to write herself!'

'She's only a girl. Be patient with her, Unwin. You'll *need* patience. She's temperamental and wayward. And there are others will think her a good catch beside yourself.'

Unwin bit at the top of his riding crop. 'The old man's an ingrained miser. There he was this morning, turning over the accounts with his scabby hands, and the house – no mansion at the best of times – nearly falling down for want of repair. It's really no fit place for Caroline to spend half her life.'

'You'll be able to alter all that.'

'Aye. Someday. But Ray's no more than fifty-three or -four. He might live ten year yet.' Unwin went to the window and stared out across the sea, which was quiet this morning. The low cloud over the craggy cliffs had darkened the colour of the water to a deep veined green. Some sea gulls had perched on the wall of the house and were throatily crying. To the tall man, accustomed now to London life, the scene was melancholy. 'Penvenen's got some uncommon views altogether. He was giving it as his opinion this morning that Cornwall is over-represented in Parliament. Says the seats should be redistributed among the new towns in the midlands. Stuff and nonsense.'

'Take no notice of his little foibles. He often says these things to annoy. It is a way he has.'

Unwin turned. 'Well, I hope we have no more elections for another seven years. It will cost me upwards of two thousand pounds just for the pleasure of being returned – and you know that doesn't end it – or begin it for that matter.'

Sir John's eyes took on a cautious bloodless look, as they always did when money was mentioned. 'Your profession's of your own choosing, my boy. And there's others worse off. Carter of Grampound was telling me he would have to pay as much as three hundred guineas a vote when the time came.' He got up and pulled the bell. 'Mistress Poldark was asking me if I should be in Bodmin for the hustings. I wonder what her purpose was in that?'

Chapter two

THE MORNING WAS well gone when Demelza turned Caerhays towards dinner and home. As she skirted the grounds of Trenwith House she wished she could have dropped in for a few minutes' friendly chat with Verity. It was something she greatly missed and could never get used to. But Verity was in Falmouth, if not further afloat – happily married, it seemed, in spite of all foreboding; and she, Demelza, had been the active conniver in the change, so she could not complain. Indeed it was Verity's elopement which had caused a sharper breach between the families, and, in spite of Demelza's self-sacrifice of last Christmas, the breach was not properly closed. The responsibility was not now Francis's. Since the illnesses of last Christmas and little Julia's death he seemed most anxious to show his gratitude for what Demelza had done. But Ross would have none of it. The failure of the Carnmore Copper Company lay insuperably between them. And if what Ross suspected about that failure was right, then Demelza could not blame him. But she would have been much happier with it otherwise. Her nature always preferred the straightforward settlement to the lingering bitter suspicion.

Just before she lost sight of the house she saw Dwight Enys coming along the track in her wake, so reined in her horse to wait for him. The young surgeon took off his hat as he came up.

'A fine morning, ma'am. I'm glad to see you enjoying the air.'

'With a purpose,' she said, smiling. 'Everything I d'do these days is with some purpose or another. Very moral, I suppose, if you look at it that way.'

He answered her smile – it was difficult not to – and allowed his horse to walk along beside hers. The track was just wide enough for them to go abreast. He noticed professionally how slight she had stayed since her illness of January.

'I suppose it depends whether the purpose was moral or not.'

She pushed in a curl that the wind had dislodged. 'Ah, that I don't know. We should have to ask the preacher. I have been to Place House doctoring Sir John's cattle.'

Dwight looked surprised. 'I didn't know you were expert in that.'

'Nor am I. I only pray to God his Hereford cow takes a turn for the better. If it dies I shall have advanced nothing.'

'And if it lives?'

She glanced at him. 'Where are you bound, Dwight?'

'To see some of the folk of Sawle. I am increasingly popular with the patients who can afford to pay nothing. Choake gets ever lazier.'

'And more unfriendly, like. What is at back of all this – this trying to get Ross convicted?'

The doctor looked uncomfortable. He flicked the loose loop of the reins against the sleeve of his black velvet coat. 'The law, I suppose . . .'

'Oh yes, the law. But something else. Since when has the law been so fussy about strippin' a wreck or rough-handling a few excise men – even suppose Ross had any part in that, and we know he did not. It is only what's been going on since I was born and for hundreds of years before that.'

'I'm not sure that that's true – not altogether. I'd do anything to help Ross – and will do, you know that . . .'

'Yes, I know that.'

'But I don't think it's any good blinking that you can ignore the law ten times, but the eleventh – if it gets you – it will hold on like a leech, and no letting go till the thing's thrashed out. That's the truth. Of course, in this case one wonders if, now the law *has* moved, there may not be other influences at work also——'

'There's men been round asking questions even of the Gimletts, our own servants. There can scarcely be a cottage in the district that hasn't had its caller, all trying to pin the blame on Ross! It's the law, no doubt, but the law wi' plenty of money to spend and time to waste – for there's none of his own folk will give him away, and they might know it. Ross has his enemies but they're not among the miners who helped him at the wreck!'

Sawle Church, its tower leaning like Pisa, was reached, and Dwight halted at the head of Sawle Combe. On the hill some women were cutting a sloping field of corn; it was stacked round the edge but as yet uncut in the middle, and looked like an embroidered kerchief.

'You will not come down this way?'

'No, Ross will be expecting me back.'

'In so far,' said Dwight, 'in so far as there is any influence at work beyond the law, I should not put it down to pompous nobodies like Surgeon Choake who have neither the money nor the venom to do serious harm.'

'Nor do I, Dwight. Nor do we.'

'No . . .'

Demelza gripped her riding crop tighter but did not speak.

He said: 'For your information, I have not visited the Warleggans for twelve months.'

She said: 'I have only met George properly. What are the others like?'

'I know them very little. Nicholas, George's father, is a big hard domineering man, but he has a reputation for honesty that is not lightly to be had. George's uncle, Cary, is the one who keeps in the background, and if there is anything shady to be done I should guess he does it. But I confess they have always been gracious enough to me.'

Demelza stared across at the silver-blue triangle of sea blocking up the end of the valley. 'Sanson, who lost his life in the wreck, was a cousin of theirs. And there are other things between Ross and George – even before the smelting company. It is a good time to pay off old scores.'

'I should not worry overmuch about that. The law will only take account of the truth.'

'I'm not so sure,' she said.

On Hendrawna Beach the scene was quite different from Trevaunance Cove. Although there was little ebb and flow about the rocks, on the flat sandy beach the sea roared, and a low mist hung over it in the still mild air. Coming back from his usual morning walk as far as the Dark Cliffs, Ross glanced across at the cliffs where the shacks of Wheal Leisure were built, and could hardly see them through the haze. It was like walking in a vapour bath.

Since the loss of Julia and the opening of the prosecution against him, he had forced himself to make this walk daily. Or if the mood took him and the weather was favourable he would go out in the new dinghy and sail as far as St Ann's. Such activity didn't lift the cloud from his mind, but it helped to set it in proportion for the rest of the day's tasks. His daughter was dead, his cousin had betrayed him, his much-laboured-over smelting scheme was in ashes, he faced charges in the criminal court for which he might well be sentenced to death or life transportation; and if by some chance he survived that, it would be only a matter of months before bankruptcy and imprisonment for debt followed. But in the meantime fields had to be sown and reaped, copper had to be raised and marketed, Demelza had to be clothed and fed and cherished – so far as it was in his scope to cherish anyone at this stage.

It was Julia's death which still hit him hardest. Demelza had grieved no less than he, but hers was a more pliant nature, responding involuntarily to stimuli that meant little to him. A celandine flowering out of season, a litter of kittens found unexpectedly in a loft, warm sunshine after a cold spell, the smell of the first swathe of hay: these were always temporary reliefs for her, and so sorrow had less power to injure her. Although he didn't realise it, much of the cherishing this year had been on her side.

After the storms of Christmas it had been a quiet winter; but there was no ease in the district, Ross thought, any more than there was ease in himself. Copper prices had risen only enough to bring a slight increase of profit in the mines now open, nothing to justify the starting of new ventures or the reopening of old. Life was very close to survival level.

As he left the beach and climbed over the broken wall he saw Demelza coming down the valley, and she saw him at the same time and waved, and he waved back. They reached the house almost at the same time, and he helped her down and gave the horse to Gimlett, who had come hurrying round.

'You've dressed up for your morning ride today,' he said.

'I thought twas bad to get slovenly and be seen about as if I didn't care for being Mrs Poldark.'

'There are some who might feel that way just at present.'

She linked his arm and put pressure on it to get him to walk round the garden with her.

'My hollyhocks are not so well this year,' she said. 'Too much rain. All the crops are late too. We need a rare hot September.'

'It would make it stuffy in the court.'

'We shall not be in court all the month. Only one day. Then you'll be free.'

'Who says so? Have you been consulting your witches?'

She paused to pick a snail from under an old primrose leaf. She held it distastefully between gloved finger and thumb. 'I never know what's best to do with 'em.'

'Drop it on that stone.'

She did so and turned away while he crushed it. 'Poor little bull-horn. But they're so greedy; I shouldn't mind if they were content with a leaf or two. . . . Talking of witches, Ross, have you ever heard of a cow illness called Tail-Shot?'

'No.'

'The back legs are paralysed and the cow's teeth come loose.'

'A cow's teeth are always loose,' Ross said.

'And the tail has a queer unjointed look – as if it were broken. That gives it its name. D'you think twould cure the disease to open up the tail and put in a boiled onion?'

Ross said: 'No.'

'But it would do no harm if the cow was going to get better anyhow, would it?'

'What have you been up to this morning?'

She looked into his distinguished bony face.

'I met Dwight on the way home. He is going to be at assize.'

'I don't see what need there'll be of him. Half Sawle and Grambler will be there, it appears to me. It will make quite a Roman holiday.'

They walked round in silence. The garden was motionless under the lowering clouds, leaf and flower taking on the warmer, firmer substance of permanent things. Ross thought, there are no permanent things, only fleeting moments of warmth and companionship, precious stationary seconds in a flicker of troubled days.

The clouds broke in a shower and drove them in, and they stood a minute in the window of the parlour watching the big drops pattering on the leaves of the lilac tree, staining them dark. When rain came suddenly

Demelza still had the instinct to go and see if Julia were sleeping outside. She thought of saying this to Ross but checked herself. The child's name was hardly ever mentioned. Sometimes she suspected that Julia was a bar between them, that though he tried his utmost not to, the memory of her courting infection to help at Trenwith still rankled.

She said: 'Is it not time you went to see Mr Notary Pearce again?'

He grunted. 'The man frets me. The less I see of him the better.'

She said quietly: 'It is my life, you know, as well as yours that's at hazard.'

He put his arm round her. 'Tut, tut. If anything happens to me you will have much still to live for. This house and land will be yours. You will become principal shareholder in Wheal Leisure Mine. You will have a duty – to people and to the countryside . . .'

She stopped him. 'Nay, Ross, I shall have nothing. I shall be a beggar again. I shall be an unfledged miner's wench——'

'You'll be a handsome young woman in your first twenties with a small estate and a load of debts. The best of your life will be ahead of you——'

'I live only through you. You made me what I am. You *think* me into being handsome, you *think* me into being a squire's wife——'

'Stuff. You'd surely marry again. If I were gone there'd be men humming round here from all over the county. It isn't flattery but the sober truth. You could take your pick of a dozen——'

'I should *never* marry again. Never!'

His hand tightened on her. 'How thin you are still.'

'I'm not. You ought to know I'm not.'

'Well, slim then. Your waist used to have a more comfortable feel.'

'Only after Julia was born. That was . . . different then.' There, the name was out now.

'Yes,' he said.

There was silence for a minute or two. His blue eyes were lidded and she could not read his expression.

She said: 'Ross.'

'Yes?'

'Perhaps in time it will seem different. Perhaps we shall have other children.'

He moved away from her. 'I do not think any child would be grateful for having a gallows bird for a father. . . . I wonder if dinner is ready.'

When Dwight parted from Demelza he rode down the steep narrow track to Sawle village, into the bubble of the stream and the clatter of the tin stamps. It was a short enough time since he had come to this district, a callow young physician with radical ideas about medicine; but it seemed a decade in his life. In that time he had earned the confidence and affection of the people he worked among, had inexcusably broken his Hippocratic oath, and since then had painfully re-established himself – entirely in the eyes of the countryside, who laid the blame on the girl, very partially in his own, which at all times were self-critical and self-exacting.

He had learned a great deal: that humanity was infinitely variable and infinitely contradictory, so that all treatment consisted of patient experiment and trial and error; that the surgeon and the physician were often mere onlookers at battles fought under their eyes; that no outward aid was one quarter as powerful as the ordinary recuperative power of the body, and that drugs and potions were sometimes as likely to hinder as to help.

If he had been a self-satisfied man he might have found some comfort in having come this far, for many of the surgeons and apothecaries he met had learned nothing like this in a lifetime and were never likely to. He avoided members of his own profession, for he found himself constantly at loggerheads with them. His only comfort was that they were often as much at variance among themselves, having only one element in common, an absolute and unquestioning confidence that their own method was infallible – a confidence that seemed in no way shaken when one of their patients died. If a sick man collapsed under treatment that was the fault of the sick man, not of the method.

What Dr Thomas Choake believed Dwight was not sure. Since their early quarrel they had seen little of each other; but as they practised over much the same territory they were bound to have occasional contacts. Choake always had an instant remedy to hand – sometimes he seemed even to have decided on a remedy before he saw the patient. But whether these remedies sprang from a fixed theory of medicine or merely from the impulses of his own brain Dwight was never able to tell.

This noon Dwight had several patients to visit, the first a call on Charlie Kempthorne. Two years ago Kempthorne had had a consumption of both lungs, the top only of each affected, but enough to spell a death sentence. Now he was apparently well, and had been all this year, was free of cough, had put on weight and was working again, not as a miner but as a sailmaker. He was at home, as Dwight had expected, and sitting at the door of his cottage busy with a coarse needle and thread. He grinned all over his lean over-brown face when he saw the physician, and got up to greet him.

'Come inside, sur. Tis a pleasure to see you. I bin saving some eggs till you passed by.'

'I'm not here to stay,' said Enys pleasantly. 'Just a visit to see you're following instructions. Thank you all the same.'

'Tis no 'ardship to go on with the treatment. Here I sit in the dryth, day in day out, stitching away – and makin' more money than I did as a sumpman!'

'And Lottie and May?' Kempthorne had two scrawny little daughters, of five and seven. He had lost his wife in a drowning accident three years ago.

'They'm down to Mrs Coad's. Though what they d'learn I'm vexed to think.' Kempthorne wet the thread in his mouth and paused with it between finger and thumb to look at the other man slyly. 'I suppose you d'know there's more fever abroad. Aunt Sarah Tregeagle asked for me to tell you.'

Dwight did not comment, having a distaste for discussing diseases in general terms with his patients.

'The Curnows have it, and Betty Coad and the Ishbels, she asked for me to tell you. Of course, tis no more'n you've reason to expect in August month.'

'A fine big sail, that.'

Charlie grinned. 'Aye, sur. For the *One and All* of St Ann's. She need all her canvas.'

'Would you make sails for the revenue boats as well?'

'Only if so be as I could stitch in a flaw so that they ripped up when giving chase.'

From here to the open square at the foot of the hill it was not safe to ride a horse, and Dwight walked thoughtfully down the steep rutted track of Stippy-Stappy Lane. These cottages, the better ones of the village, occupied one side of the lane; on the other, beyond the overgrown Cornish wall, the valley fell steeply into a gully where a part of the Mellingey River ran away to the sea and worked the tin stamps. Each house was about six feet below its neighbour, and at the last of them Dwight tethered his horse. As he knocked at the door a shaft of brassy sunlight fell through the clouds upon the clustered cottages below, giving their roofs a wet gleam, anticipating the rain.

Here lived Jacka Hoblyn, who had his own tin stamp, Polly his wife, their daughter Rosina, a semi-cripple, and their younger daughter Parthesia, a lively little creature of eleven, who opened the door. There were two small rooms downstairs, with lime-ash floors, in one of which Rosina carried on her work as a sempstress and patten maker. Parthesia said her mother was in bed and hopped ahead of him up the outside stone staircase to the raftered loft where they all slept. Having seen him in, she skipped off again in search of Father, who she said was sick too.

Polly Hoblyn, who was forty and looked fifty-eight, greeted him brightly; and Dwight smiled back, taking in all the usual symptoms of an attack of the tertian ague: the muscle tremors, the pinched pale face, the dead white fingers. It was an unusually bad attack. The encouraging circumstance was that he had been called in – however tentatively and apologetically – to deal with it. Two years ago people with the ordinary complaints bought stuff, if they could afford it, from Irby, the druggist at St Ann's, or from one of the old women of the neighbourhood; certainly they never dared call in Dr Choake unless they had broken a limb or were *in extremis*. That Dr Enys did not mind administering to folk who could pay only in kind, or not even that way, they were slowly coming to appreciate. Of course there were those who said he experimented on the poor people; but there are always uncharitable tongues.

He mixed the woman a dose of Peruvian bark; then, having watched it go down between the clenching teeth, he put out two fever powders to be taken later and a dose of sal polychrest and rhubarb for tonight. At this point the light in the door darkened as Jacka Hoblyn appeared in the doorway.

'Good day to ee, Surgeon. Thesia, bring us a nackan from down b'low. I'm sweaten like a bull. Well, what's amiss with Polly?'

'The intermittent fever. She should stay in bed two days at least. And you? I think you have the same. Come over here to the light, will you.'

As he got near, Dwight caught the strong whiff of gin. So it was one of Jacka's times. Parthesia came dancing up with a square of red cloth, and the man mopped his heavy brow with it. His pulse was small, hard and quick. The fever was at a later stage, and would cause an overmastering thirst.

'I got a touch. But moving around is best for it, not loustering tween the blankets. Fasterer you move, fasterer he go.'

'Now look, Hoblyn, I'd like you to take this now, and this powder in water before you go to bed tonight. Understand?'

Jacka ran a hand through his upstanding hair and glowered at him. 'I don't 'old with doctor's traade.'

'Nevertheless, you should take this. You'll be far better for it.'

They stared at each other, but Dwight's prestige was just too much for the streamer, and with some satisfaction he watched the strong dose of soluble tartar disappear. The night powder, if Hoblyn was sufficiently alert to drink it, contained ten grains of jalap, but that didn't so much matter. Dwight felt a greater concern for the health of the three women than for the man.

As he was leaving he saw Rosina limping up the hill with a jug of milk. She was seventeen, and her fine eyes had not yet been spoiled by endless hours of close sewing in a bad light. She smiled and curtsied as they met.

'Your family should be improved tomorrow. See your mother takes her powder.'

'I will surely. Thank you, sur.'

'Your father gets – troublesome when he is in liquor?'

She blushed. 'It make him ill-tempered, sur; hard to get along with, as you might say.'

'And – violent?'

'Oh no, sur – or but seldom. And then he d'make it up to we afterwards.'

Dwight slid past the little bow window of Aunt Mary Rogers's shop and reached the huddle of broken-down cottages at the foot of the hill known as the Guernseys. Here the worst squalor began. Windows stuffed with boards and rags, doors propped beside the openings they had been designed to fill, open cesspools, with rat runs from one to another, broken roofs and lean-to shacks where half-naked children crawled and played. Coming here, Dwight always felt conscious of his own decent clothes: they were phenomena from another world. He knocked at the first cottage, surprised to see both halves of the door closed, for the room within depended for its light on what came through the door. A week ago he had delivered Betty Carkeek of her first-born son when two fishwife-midwives had done their worst and failed.

He heard the baby crying inside and after another minute Betty came to the door, opening the top half a suspicious inch.

'Oh, tis you, sur. Do you come in.' Betty Carkeek, née Coad, was not the sort who faded away, given half a chance, but he had been relieved when the fourth and fifth days were past without any sign of childbed fever. She should do well enough now. He followed her into the stone hut – it was hardly more – stooping his head on the threshold, and saw Ted Carkeek sitting over a small fire stirring some sort of an herb brew. Ted and Betty had only been married a month, but staying home when there was work to do, and work so hard to get, seemed a poor way of showing your devotion.

He nodded to the young man and went to look at the baby. Ted got up and moved to go out, but Betty stopped him, and he grunted and went back to watching his brew. The child was snuffly with a cold and its breathing rapid; Dwight wondered what the inexperienced girl had done; one was always struggling against ignorance and neglect.

'Your mother not here, Betty?'

'No, sur. Mother's some slight.'

Of course. Kempthorne had mentioned the Coads. 'The ague?'

'Yes, I reckon.'

The stuff on the stove began to bubble and the fire spat as beads of moisture fell upon it. Smoke curled away from the open chimney and wove itself about the blackened rafters.

'And yourself?'

'Proper, thank you. But Ted's not so smart——'

'Hold your clack,' said Ted from the fireplace.

Dwight took no notice. 'You're up too soon,' he said to the girl. 'If Ted is home he can look after you.'

'Tis I been tending on he, more like.'

Ted made another impatient movement, but she went on: 'Let Surgeon see ee, Ted. There's nought to be gained by sceedling there by the fire. He's no telltale, we did ought to know that.'

After a minute Ted grumpily rose and came into the light of the door. 'I sprit open my shoulder, that's all. Physic won't do him no good.'

Dwight pulled back the sack the boy had over his shoulder. A musket ball had glanced off the bone and come out, leaving in the first place a clean enough wound. But there was a good deal of inflammation now, not improved by the poultice of boiled yarrow leaves.

'Have you clean water here? What's that you're brewing on the fire?' Dwight went about dressing the wound, making no comment on the circumstances.

And because he didn't ask, the explanation came, though not until the dressing was done and he had bled the man and was ready to leave. Ted Carkeek was partner with four others in a cockleshell of a boat with which in quiet weather they would venture the long and hazardous voyage to France to pick up spirits and bring them back for sale. Theirs was no large-scale business like Mr Trencrom's; but by means of four or five runs a year they were able to make enough to help things along. They had left last Saturday and returned Wednesday, putting in to Vaughan's Cove, a strip of beach connecting at times with Sawle Cove, to find Vercoe and two other excise men waiting ready to lay hands on them. There had been a scuffle, their boat had sunk, drifting on the rocks in the confusion, and Ted Carkeek had been shot in the shoulder. A disagreeable affair, and one which might have repercussions.

'Twasn't as if we was doin' wrong,' Ted said indignantly. ''Tis only turning a penny like other folk – and now we've to start again from nought, if so be as we're left be. Like as not we'll have soldiers in searching the houses, like what they did in St Ann's!'

Betty said: 'What we all d'want to know is, how the gaugers knowed where they was going to land. Tisn't natural. Someone's been talking.'

Dwight fastened the clasps of his leather bag, giving a last uneasy glance in the direction of the child. There was little he could do for so young a baby; in any case Mrs Coad would certainly make her daughter disobey him and give it some witch's brew of her own. The child would survive or not according to its constitution. He said: 'The excise men have long ears. You'll need to rest that shoulder, Ted. No work for a week at the least.'

'It edn the first time that's happened,' said Ted. 'Old man Pendarves and Foster Pendarves was caught in April. Red-handed. It's not natural, I'll lay.'

'Did many in the village know of your trip?'

'Oh . . . yes, I s'pose. Tis hard for 'em not to guess when you're gone half the week. But not where we was going to bring the stuff in. That were knowed by only six or seven. If I could lay me hands on the one that couldn't make to hold his tongue – or, still more, give us away on purpose . . .'

It was dark and stuffy in the room, and Dwight had a sudden urge to put his hands up to the slanting beams and push them away. These people might as well live in a cave, shut off from light and sun.

'Are others of your family ill, Betty?'

'Well, not ill as you'd say. Joan and Nancy has fever too, but they're sweating nicely and on the mend.'

'Have they been nursing your baby?'

Betty stared at him, more anxious to say the right thing than the truthful. 'No, sur,' she got out at last.

Dwight picked up his bag. 'Well, I should not let them.' He turned to leave. 'Don't be too free with your suspicions, Ted. I know it is easy to advise, but once you get suspecting people it's hard to know where to stop.'

As he left the cottage and crossed the square towards the fish cellars where several families eked out an existence, he was frowning at the problems the outbreak of fever had brought him. All this summer he had been troubled by a new virulence in this seasonal complaint – not merely by the virulence of taking it bad the way Mrs Hoblyn had done, but by the emergency of new symptoms when people should have been on the mend. Discolourations of the skin developed, and swellings and then a new loss of strength. Two children had recently died – apparently from this – and several adults were much more ill than they ought to have been. Even the children who got better were feeble and yellow, with tumid bellies and weak legs. If measles came they would go off like flies. He had tried all his favourite weapons but none of them seemed to do any good. Dwight sometimes wondered if he ought to invent a new complaint called privation disease to cover the ills that he found.

Chapter three

Ross RODE IN to Truro on the following Monday. Demelza would have gone with him had she not sensed that he preferred the journey alone. He was like that at present.

When he got in he called at once on Mr Nathaniel Pearce.

Last February, when the law had so suddenly and unexpectedly moved in the matter, Ross had still been feeling the worst effects of his bereavement and his several failures, and he had endured the justice's examination in an angry and resentful mood. It had early been clear that he must employ some lawyer to act for him – and who more natural than his own and his father's, Mr Notary Pearce, who also was his co-partner in Wheal Leisure and his creditor to the sum of fourteen hundred pounds?

But several times during the months of waiting Ross had wished himself sufficiently of one mind to make a change before it was too late. Pearce was a good negotiator, adept in conveyances, a sharp and adroit enough man where money was concerned; but there were younger and keener men to prepare briefs for the assizes. Also in this bitter cleavage which had broken out between two factions in the district during the last few years, Pearce was one of the few men with a foot still in each camp. He was a friend of Ross's and a friend of the Warleggans. A shareholder in Wheal Leisure, he nevertheless banked with the Warleggans – although he sometimes did legal business for Pascoe's. He was a personal friend of Dr Choake's, but had loaned money to Dwight Enys. In principle it was all very good; detachment and impartiality were to be admired. But lately, with ruin and broken homes following in the wake of the last struggle, it just wasn't wholesome any more.

Ross found him in better spirits than usual. The chronic gout that was settling on him had eased, and he was using his new mobility in a furious attack upon boxfuls of ancient legal papers that filled the room. A clerk and an apprentice were helping in the orgy, carrying boxes to his desk and then bearing away the crackling yellow parchments which Mr Pearce weeded out and flung upon the floor.

When he saw Ross he said: 'There now, Captain Poldark; what a pleasant surprise; do take a chair, if there is one – Noakes, clear a chair for Captain Poldark – I am just sorting a little of the older stuff; nothing modern, you follow, selecting a little of the older stuff for disposal. You're keeping well, I hope; this uncertain weather suits some people.' He scattered a dozen mothy letters on the floor and set his bob wig straight. 'My daughter was saying only yesterday – Noakes, take these boxes with you: all this Basset and Tresize stuff has to remain *intacta*. . . . A little joke there, Captain Poldark, if one knows the subject of the 1705 files. . . . The older families naturally expect their lawyer to preserve all correspondence relating; but space is the obstacle; one needs cellars. My daughter was saying wet summers are healthy summers, do you agree?'

'I'll not keep you long,' said Ross.

Pearce glanced at him and set down the bundle of papers he had grasped. 'No. Quite so. But I have a free morning. There are one or two things. Noakes – and you, Biddle – you can leave us. Never mind the boxes. Dear, dear, not in front of the desk. That's right. . . . Now, Captain Poldark. We're quite cosy. One minute, just to poke the fire. . . .'

So they settled to be cosy in the hot, paper-littered room, and Mr Pearce scratched himself and informed Ross what arrangements had so far been made for his downfall. The assizes would be formally opened on Saturday the fourth, prox., though no business would be transacted until the Monday. Ross would be required to present himself to the Governor of the Prison not later than Thursday the second. The Hon. Mr Wentworth Lister and the Hon. Mr H. C. Thornton, two of His Majesty's judges out of the Court of Common Pleas, were to hold the commission. Probably H. C. Thornton would deal with the *nisi prius* side, and Wentworth Lister would handle the Crown cases. The lists were very crowded because when the winter assizes had been due to take place there had been so much fever in Launceston that the lawyers had refused to come down, and nearly all the cases had been postponed until the summer. It was likely, however, that Ross's trial, being considered an important one, would be put forward to the Tuesday or the Wednesday.

'Who is leading for the Crown?'

'Henry Bull, I believe. I could have wished for someone different – though, mind you, I've never seen him, don't know him, except by repute; and by repute he's a trifle hard-hitting, shall we say. No great lawyer, one understands, but keen to get his verdict. Still, that's as may be. You've a great deal of good will, Captain Poldark; it all helps; dear me, it's of high importance where a jury is concerned.' Pearce reached forward with his curtain rod and jabbed at the fire again.

'Good will and ill will,' said Ross, watching the other's face.

'Indeed, one doesn't hear of it. Naturally, there may be some; we all have enemies; it's hard to come through life without them. But not many, I'm thinking, being committed in a magistrate's court as you were, can have had their bail money paid in by two of the magistrates on the bench. And after the things you said it was, I declare, a considerable tribute. You were a thought – hrr – hrr – reckless, to say the least, as I've suggested before.'

'I only said what I thought.'

'Oh, I've not doubt of that; indeed not. But if one may venture the suggestion – it doesn't always do, Captain Poldark, to say exactly what one thinks without regard to one's circumstances – that's if one wishes to – er—— In this case, with Lord Devoran and Mr Boscoigne sympathetic towards you, some – some formula might have been found if you had not committed yourself so willingly. I hope, when the opportunity comes for you to speak in court, you will have greater regard for your safety. In my view – humble as it is – a lot will hang on your attitude then.'

'Hang is the word.' Ross got up and made his way among the papers to the window.

'Let us hope not. Dear me, no. But, remember, you will have a jury to consider – always very susceptible to good and bad impressions. You can do a great deal for yourself, believe me. Of course, counsel will advise you when you see him – and I do trust you'll accept his advice.'

Ross watched a spider crawling up into its web in a corner of the windowpane. 'Look, Pearce, there is one thing I have not done and must do – that is, make a will. Can you have it done – drawn up now so that it may be signed before I leave?'

'Why, yes, it's not impossible so long as the testamentary conditions are not involved. Noakes can be got in when you please.'

'It should not be involved at all. A simple straightforward statement that I leave all my debts to my wife.'

Pearce picked up a book and allowed a fat finger to travel experimentally along its edge for dust. 'Not so bad as that, surely, ha, ha! Things are somewhat tight for the moment, but no doubt they'll ease.'

'They'll ease if they're allowed to ease. If things go wrong at Bodmin, you'll barely see your money back. So it's self-interest as well as common justice to get me my freedom.' There was a faint ironical spark in Ross's eyes.

'Just so. just so. We shall all work for it, believe me. A great deal depends on the jury. I confess I should feel a small matter more settled if there had not been so much trouble in France. We have to face it. That disturbance in Redruth in the autumn; ten years ago it would have been a case for the petty sessions – now one hanged and two transported . . .' Mr Pearce scratched under his wig. 'Shall I call in Noakes again now?'

'Please do.'

The lawyer levered himself out of his chair and pulled the bell. 'We still have the defence statement to complete. It's *essential* if you're to plead not guilty that . . .'

Ross turned from the window. 'Leave it today. I don't think I'm in the mood. When the gaol is waiting I may bring my mind to a better grip of the affair. . . .'

He had a standing invitation to dinner with the Pascoes, and when he left Mr Pearce's office, as it was by then two o'clock, he walked at a leisurely pace towards the bank, which was in Pydar street. Another bad day; August was refusing to relent. A cold northwest wind was bringing heavy showers, and the hot sun that broke between had no time to dry the streets before the clouds blew up again for the next storm. In this town where little rivulets ran down the side of the streets even in the dryest of summers, and half-hidden streams bubbled in every side alley, a town that one could not leave except by bridge or ford, one got a sense of saturation. In low-lying places the muddy pools were slowly submerging the cobbles and joining to become lakes.

To avoid one stretching half across Powder Street, Ross turned up the slit of Church Lane, and the wind, suddenly finding new venom, blew at his coattails and tried to snatch his hat. Another man behind him was not so lucky, and a black felt with a wide brim came hobbling along the wet cobbles to finish up at Ross's feet. He picked it up. As its owner came along he saw that it was Francis. So much had happened in their relationship since the angry scene of last August that they met like strangers, remembering the old emotions but no longer feeling them.

'God's my life,' said Francis. 'What a pesky wind. One is blown down this alley like a pea down a pipe.' He accepted the hat but did not put it back on his head. His hair continued to blow about. 'Thank you, Cousin.'

Ross nodded briefly and moved to pass on.

'Ross . . .'

He turned. Francis was thinner, he noticed. The threat of stoutness had gone; but he looked no better for it. 'Well?'

'We meet irregularly, and that no doubt's too often for you. It's not a view I'd criticise; but there's a thing or two I want to say in case another year passes before the opportunity occurs again.'

'Well?' Ross's unquiet eyes stared past the other man.

Francis hunched up the high velvet collar of his coat. 'Talking in this funnel's trying on the temper. I'll walk with you a few paces.'

They fell into step. Francis did not speak until they reached St Mary's Church and turned along beside the railings of the churchyard.

'Two things, I think, in the main. You cannot want my good wishes or be in a mood to appreciate them, but when you go to Bodmin next month you may know that you have them just the same.'

'Thanks.'

'The second is that should my help be of any use you may have that also.'

'I don't think it can be.'

'Nor I, in the main concern, or I'd proffer it with greater eagerness. But in one eventuality . . .'

He hesitated and stopped, both in speech and in motion. Ross waited. Francis was rapping at the railings with his stick.

'Gravestones are a good place for confidences, no doubt. Supposing things should go wrong with you next month, how is Demelza fixed?'

Ross raised his head as if conscious of some challenge – not from Francis, but from this circumstance which was rearing itself in other people's minds as well as his own. 'She'll survive. What is it to you?'

'Only that help may be offered in a variety of ways. I'm no doubt as nearly bankrupt as you, or nearer; but if after next month you are in prison and I out, she can turn to me if she needs help or advice. I have a name still in the county and happen to have a little hard money put by. She may have that if she needs it, or anything else I own.'

It was Ross's impulse to say, What, turn to a traitor and a sneak thief like you, who betrayed and ruined a dozen good men and a fine project for the sake of petty spite; but he had no proof, and anyway it was over and gone. Resentment and bitterness and old grudges were dead things which rotted the hands that grasped them. Something Demelza said last winter just after Julia's death: 'All our quarrels seem small and petty. Oughtn't we to find all the friendship we can – while there's still time?'

He said: 'Is that Elizabeth's view too?'

'I haven't consulted her. But I'm sure it would be.'

The sun had gone in for the next shower. The light was hard and metallic, the street still and colourless as in a steel engraving.

'Thank you. I hope the offer will not be necessary.'

'That's my hope too, of course.'

The thought welled up suddenly in Ross that but for this man *none* of the rest might have happened. The copper company on its feet, his child alive. No stopping it this time. Yet here he was, soberly talking as if nothing had happened. A blow in the face.

He said in a changed voice: 'I have just made my will. Pearce has it. No doubt he'll be capable of discharging his duties if the worst comes to the worst.' He raised his crop in a half salute, not meeting his cousin's eyes, and turned on his heel to continue to the Pascoes'.

Harris Pascoe was behind the counter when he went in; but the banker at once beckoned him to come to the side, and they entered the private room together. Over a glass of brandy Pascoe said:

'We have young Enys to dinner – the first time for several months. Joan is pleased, but I am a little doubtful of the attachment. It has run on so long that I don't think it will come to anything. Especially after Dwight's affair with that w-woman last year.'

'The girl threw herself at him,' Ross said. '. . . I hope I shall not be the skeleton at the feast today.'

'No indeed. Your visits are as rare as Enys's. Come along in. I can join you in a minute.'

'There was business in my visit as well,' said Ross. 'To do with my approaching assize call.'

He found a certain detached interest in watching the responses of various people when he mentioned his coming trial. In some people's eyes a morbid speculative gleam would betray itself behind the show of sympathy; others would shy away as if they had been told you were going to have your leg off. Harris Pascoe wrinkled his mouth in distaste and made a show of fixing his spectacles more firmly behind his ears.

'We hope for a happy outcome of that.'

'But in the meantime a prudent man puts his affairs in order.'

'There's very little more to do at present, I think.'

'Except become solvent.'

'Ye-es. Q-quite so. Quite so. Would you like to look at your account while you are here?'

They went into the bank, and Pascoe opened one of the great black books, dusted a little stale snuff off a page and coughed.

'The position in a nutshell is this. You have a credit balance of a little over a hundred and eighty pounds. You have a permanent mortgage on your property with the bank of two thousand three hundred pounds, bearing seven per cent interest. You have a further indebtedness outside, I understand, of – of one thousand pounds, is it? – b-bearing interest at forty p-per cent – repayable when?'

'This December or next.'

'This December or next. And your income – in round figures, as it were?'

'Not more than three hundred a year net.'

Harris winced again. 'Er – yes. That's after living expenses are paid, I suppose?'

'Ordinary expenses of food, yes.'

'Well, it just won't go, will it? You'll remember when you c-contemplated taking out that second bill I advised you instead to sell the mine shares. However, I'm not here to say I told you so. Any other substantial debts?'

'No.'

A bluebottle had entered through an open window and was exploring the room with great vigour. The banker pushed the ledger along the desk, and Ross signed his name against the last entry in his account.

'I am concerned,' he said, 'to see some sort of security for my wife. I try not to take a pessimistic view of this trial, but no good comes of being an ostrich.' He raised his deceptively sleepy eyes, and there was a touch of irony in them again. 'There are various ways in which the law can deprive her of my support – so if she comes to widowhood or grass widowhood before her time I should take some comfort in knowing she would not be without a home.'

'I think you can be assured of that,' the banker said quietly. 'Your liquid assets will meet the second mortgage. If they do not quite I will make up the difference.'

They walked back into the private room. 'You have the disadvantage of being my friend,' Ross said.

'Not all d-disadvantage.'

'I've a long memory – if the law will allow me to keep it.'

'I'm sure it will.' In some embarrassment, since the conversation seemed to be becoming emotionally charged, he went on in a different tone. 'There is one thing I should t-tell you, Poldark, though it's not yet public property. I am enlarging the scope of my business and taking partners into it.'

Ross had his glass filled. It was not good news to him, who at the moment felt himself dependent on the personal good will of the banker, but he could not show that.

'A considerable step, but naturally you wouldn't take it without reason.'

'No. I think I have good reason. Of course, when my father began his tin discounting it was a d-different matter. Business was simple and straightforward thirty years ago, and we did not issue bank notes until I was married. We have always held a high r-reputation, and so long as such a trust existed there was no need for complicated systems of finance. But things have changed and we must move with the times. Nowadays a bank is subject to all k-kinds of new responsibilities and stresses – and they are more, I think, than one man – or one family – should shoulder.'

'Who are to be your new partners?'

'St Aubyn Tresize, whom you know. He has money and prestige and wide interests. The second is Annery, the solicitor. A warm man. The third is Spry.'

'I don't know him.'

'From Come-to-Good. A quaker. I shall be managing partner and we shall be known as P-pascoe, Tresize, Annery & Spry. I think the meal will be ready now. A drop more brandy just to top up your glass?'

'Thank you.'

As they moved towards the stairs which led up to the living rooms of the house, Pascoe added:

'In fact it was our experience of last autumn which finally decided me to take this action.'

'You mean the failure of the Carnmore Copper Company?'

'Yes. . . . No doubt, fighting it out as you fought it out – in the arena all the time – you could feel the pressure of the hostile interests, the other copper companies and the banks concerned, plainly enough. But sitting here – you know I hardly ever go out – sitting here in this quiet bank one was aware of s-subtle stresses too.'

'Also hostile.'

'Also hostile. I was not, as you know, directly interested in the copper venture. It is not my business as a custodian of other people's money to take speculative risks. But I was aware that if I had been so concerned I should not have been strong enough to stand the strains that could have been put on me. Credit is an unpredictable thing – as unstable as quicksilver. One cannot box it up. One can only give it away – and once given it is elastic up to the very point of breakage. Last autumn I realised that the days of the one-man bank are over. It – disturbed me – shook me out of a comfortable rut in wh-which I had been for many years. All this year I have been feeling my way towards some broader organisation.'

They went up the stairs to dinner.

Chapter four

WHEN FRANCIS GOT home it was just after six. He had had to ride into the teeth of the wind all the way, and there had been a half dozen torrential showers, some of them with more than a suggestion of hail, to stream off his horse's head and his cape and to strike at his face under the insecure hat, to trickle down his neck and soak his riding breeches above the leather leggings. Twice too he had nearly come off when his horse slipped in mud-filled ruts more than a foot deep. So he was not in a good temper.

Tabb, last of the two remaining house servants, came to take his horse and began to say something; but a gust of wind and another flurry of rain bore it away and Francis went into the house.

It was a silent house these days; and already it showed signs of poverty and neglect: wild weather and salt air is hard on man's work, and there were damp stains on the ceiling of this fine hall and a smell of mildew. Portraits of the Poldarks and the Trenwiths stared coldly across the unfrequented room.

Francis tramped to the stairs, intending to go up and change, but the door of the winter parlour flew open and Geoffrey Charles came galloping down the hall.

'Daddy! Daddy! Uncle George is here and has brought me a toy horse! A *lovely* one! With brown eyes and brown hair and stirrups I can put my feet in!'

Francis saw Elizabeth had come to the door of the winter parlour; so now there was no escape from greeting an unexpected visitor.

As Francis went in George Warleggan was standing by the fireplace. He was wearing a snuff-coloured coat, silk waistcoat and black cravat, with fawn breeches and new brown riding boots. Elizabeth looked a little flushed, as if the surprise call had pleased her. George came seldom these days, being not too sure of his welcome here. Francis had queer moods and resented his indebtedness.

Elizabeth said: 'George has been here an hour. We were hoping you would be back before he had to leave.'

'Quite an honour these days.' Francis bent to satisfy Geoffrey Charles with admiration for his new toy. 'Now I am here you'd best stay till this shower is over. I've been anointed many times on the way home.'

George said evenly: 'You've lost weight, Francis. So have I. We shall all look like sans-culottes before the century is out.'

Francis's eyes travelled over George's broad frame. 'I notice no change for the better.'

The cream curtains in this room were inches farther across the windows than Francis liked them; they diffused the light, giving it a tactful and opaque quality which irritated him. He went across and pulled them sharply back. When he turned he saw that Elizabeth had flushed at his last remark as if it was her responsibility.

'We ordinary people,' George said, 'are affected by the vagaries of fortune. Our faces, our figures are marked and warped by all the storms that blow. But your wife, my dear Francis, has a beauty which is untouched by ill luck or indifferent health and only grows more radiant when the tide turns.'

Francis threw off his coat. 'I think we all need drink. We can still afford drink, George. Some of the old instincts remain.'

'I have been pressing him to sup with us,' Elizabeth said. 'But he will not.'

'Cannot,' said George. 'I must be back at Cardew before dark. I had been as far as St Ann's this afternoon on mining business and could not resist calling on you when so near. You come so little to town these days.'

George was right, Francis thought cynically as his wife took a wineglass from him, Elizabeth's beauty was too pure to be affected by everyday circumstance. George still envied him one thing.

'And how's mining?' he asked. 'One advantage of being out of it is that one can take a purely academic interest in its vagaries. Are you thinking of closing Wheal Plenty?'

'Far from it.' George poked the carpet with his long malacca stick and then stopped because just there the pattern of the carpet was wearing thin. 'Tin and copper are both rising. If it goes on we may be able to restart Grambler one day.'

'If that was possible!' said Elizabeth.

'Which it is not.' Francis drained his glass at a draught. 'George is romancing for your benefit. Copper would have to double its price to justify a new outlay on Grambler now it is closed and derelict. Had it been saved from closing there might have been another story. It will not reopen in our lifetime. I am fully resigned to spending the rest of my days as an impoverished farmer.'

George humped his shoulders. 'I'm sure you are making a mistake. You're both making a mistake remaining shut up here. There is plenty to be had of life even in these depressed days. Poldark is still a good name, Francis, and if you moved in society more opportunity would come of bettering yourself. There are patronages to be had, if nothing better, paid offices which carry no obligation and no loss of prestige: indeed, the reverse. I could become a burgess any day if it pleased me, but at present it pleases me to keep out of the political field. As for you . . .'

'As for me,' said Francis, 'I am a gentleman and want no patronage – either from gentlemen or others.'

He said it without emphasis, but the sting was there. George smiled, but it was not the sort of observation he would be likely to forget. Few people had the courage to make such remarks to him nowadays.

Elizabeth made an impatient movement. 'It's surely not reasonable to quarrel when there is friendship – when there are friendships to be had. Pride can go too far.'

'Talking of the Poldarks,' Francis went on, taking no notice of her. 'I saw that other representative of the name in Truro today. He didn't seem unduly depressed by his forthcoming trial, though he was not anxious to discuss it with me. One can hardly blame him.'

Francis bent again to speak to his son and the others were silent.

George eventually said: 'I wish him an acquittal at his trial, of course. But I don't think the outcome will affect your good name, Francis. Am I my brother's keeper? Still less so, then, of a cousin.'

Elizabeth said: 'What chance is there of an acquittal, do you think?'

'A lovely horse,' said Francis gently to Geoffrey Charles. 'A lovely horse.'

'I don't see how there can be a clear acquittal,' George said, dabbing his lips with a lace handkerchief and watching Elizabeth's expression. 'Ross was a free agent at the time of the wrecks. No one coerced him into doing what he did.'

'If one believes he did it!'

'Naturally. That will be for the court to find. But the fact that he has – has rather treated the law with contempt on a number of previous occasions will be inclined to weigh to his detriment.'

'What previous occasions? I know of no others.'

'Nor is the court supposed to,' Francis said, straightening up. 'But it will not be left in ignorance. I came upon this pretty little sheet in Truro today. There are sure to be others in Bodmin before next week.'

He took a crumpled paper out of his pocket, straightened it, and, avoiding Geoffrey Charles's outstretched fingers, passed it to Elizabeth.

'I thought of showing it to Ross,' Francis added, 'but decided it was discreeter to leave him in ignorance.'

Elizabeth stared at the paper. It was a typical broadsheet, run off a cheap press, the ink blurred and unevenly spread.

True and Sensational Facts in the life of Captain R-s- P–d–k, bold adventurer, seducer and suspected murderer, shortly to stand his trial on Criminal Charges at B–m–n Assizes next. Price One Penny. Written by an Intimate Friend.

After a minute she put the paper down, and looked at Francis. Francis looked steadily, interestedly, back at her. The thing was written in the form of a biography, and none of the salacious rumours of the last two years was missing – all set out as if the facts were beyond dispute.

Francis offered it to George, but he waved it away. 'I have seen them about. One of our coachmen was caught reading a similar thing yesterday. They are not important.'

'Not important,' said Francis gently, 'except to Ross.'

'Come here, boy,' George said to his godson, 'you have the reins entangled with the saddle. Look, this is the way it goes.'

Elizabeth said: 'But if all this is believed it will prejudice the jury, will prejudice everyone! They talk of a fair trial . . .'

'Don't distress yourself, my dear Elizabeth,' George said. 'These scurrilous broadsheets are always going about regarding someone or other. No one takes account of 'em. Why, only last month there was some sheet issued purporting to show in the most lurid and circumstantial detail that feeble-mindedness and insanity runs all through the Royal Family and that the King's father, Frederick, was a pervert and a degenerate beyond recall.'

'And isn't it so?' Francis asked.

George shrugged. 'I suppose there is some sludge of truth in the basest slander.'

His meaning was obvious.

'It states,' said Elizabeth, 'that Ross served in the American war only to escape charges of this sort being brought against him before. But he was only a boy at the time – there was some boyish escapade, I know, but nothing serious. And this – about Demelza. . . . And this——'

Francis read: ' "*Furthermore, there are numerous brats scattered throughout the countryside whose parentage might be in doubt did there not exist the strange Circumstance of the scar wherewith the Devil hath cursed all the Captain's offspring – this scar being so like unto his own that the same branding iron might have been Employed. Here in good earnest we find——*" '

'What does that mean?' Elizabeth asked.

'Jinny Carter's child has a scar,' said Francis. 'Jinny Scoble, as she now is. The pamphleteer has been to some trouble to scrape up all the – er – what did you call it? – all the sludge. 'By an Intimate Friend.' I wonder who it could be. Not you, George, I suppose?'

George smiled. 'I earn my bread in a more orthodox manner. Only a bankrupt would sell his services that way.'

'Money is not always the strongest inducement,' said Francis, his gibe turned against him.

George bent his head to rest his chin on the knob of his stick. 'No, perhaps spite could play its part. . . . Anyway, the matter is unimportant, isn't it? If the stories are all untrue they can be refuted.'

But he had touched Francis on a raw spot and his characteristic turning of the point when he had made it did not quite come off. It had long been George's practice to swallow insults and to pay them back at leisure. Francis had been brought up to no such self-control. It was fortunate that just then Geoffrey Charles fell off his horse and pulled the animal over on top of him, for when the clamour had subsided the worst moment was past. For two reasons Elizabeth exerted herself to prevent a recurrence of it. First, George almost owned the things they stood in. Second, on personal grounds, she did not want to lose his friendship. Admiration such as he brought was rare enough in the life she led. She knew it was her due, and the knowledge made it all the harder to be without.

Chapter five

BODMIN AT THE time of the summer assizes of 1790 was a town with three thousand inhabitants and twenty-nine public houses.

A historian passing through two centuries before had noted the unhealthiness of the situation, the houses in the mile-long main street being, he pointed out, so shut off from sun by the hill behind that no light could have entrance to their stairs nor open air in their rooms. When it rained, he added, all the filth of the outbuildings and stables was washed down through these houses into the street; and, further, the main water supply ran openly through the churchyard, which was the ordinary place of burial for town and parish.

The intervening years had not changed the situation, but there was nothing so far as Ross could see in the hard-bitten look of the inhabitants to suggest they suffered any unusual apprehensions from sickness or pestilence. Indeed in the previous summer, while cholera raged in the districts around, the town had escaped.

He presented himself at the gaol on Thursday the second of September, and Demelza followed on the Saturday. He had been opposed to her being at the trial at all, but she had insisted so vehemently that for once he gave way. He reserved a room for her at the George and Crown, and a place for her on the midday coach, but unknown to him she had been making extra arrangements of her own. Bailey's Flyer began its long run from the west country at Falmouth, and when she met it at Truro at eleven forty-five Verity was travelling in it.

They greeted each other like old lovers, kissing with a depth of affection that trouble brought to the surface, each aware of the other's love for Ross and of a uniting purpose.

'Verity! Oh, I'm that glad to see you; it's been an age – and no one to talk knew they had a quarter of an hour's wait, so steered her cousin-in-law into the inn. They sat in a corner by the door and talked in earnest confidential tones. Verity thought Demelza looked years older than at their last meeting, and thinner and paler, but somehow it all suited her dark hair and brows and wayward eyes.

'I *wish* I could write like you,' Demelza said. 'Letters that tell something.

I can't write, no more'n Prudie Paynter, and never shall. It is there, there in my mind, but when I pick up the quill it all puffs away like steam out of the spout of a kettle.'

Verity said: 'But tell me now, who is to be for Ross's defence, and what witnesses will be called in his favour? I am so *ignorant* of these things. How is the jury chosen? Is it of freemen and will they look on such a crime indulgently? And the judge . . .'

Demelza tried to satisfy her from the information she had. She was surprised to find Verity as unlearned in the law as herself. They struggled with its complexities together.

Verity said: 'Andrew would have come, but he is at sea. I should have been happier with him to lean on. But perhaps it's for the best. . . . You don't know, I suppose, if Francis will be at the assizes?'

'No. . . . No, I don't think so. But there will be a great many there. We're lucky, so they say, to have accommodation, because there's an election this coming week – between Unwin Trevaunance and Michael Chenhalls on the Basset side, and Sir Henry Corrant and Hugh Dagge on the Boscoigne. There'll be a big fuss about that.'

'You're well informed. Is that Unwin Trevaunance, Sir John's brother?'

'Yes. We – I – have got to know Sir John a slight bit. Of course Ross have known him for years – but I . . . He happened to have a sick cow – and I cured her – or she got better of her own – and so I've been over there once or twice and have details of the election.'

'A sick cow?'

Demelza coloured a little. 'It was nothing important. Verity, I don't want for you to mind if I act strange this week end. It is only a track of my own I'm following, like, and maybe it will lead somewhere and maybe it will lead to a dead end. But it is just the way I feel about things, and I hope you'll understand. Are you really happy with Andrew?'

'I'm very happy, thank you – thanks to you, my dear. But what is it you intend to do this week end?'

'Maybe nothing at all. It is only just a warning. And have you met your stepchildren yet?'

Verity opened her new velvet bag, took out a handkerchief, then drew the strings of the bag together again. She frowned at the handkerchief.

'No . . . not yet. I haven't met them yet because – James is away still and – but I'll tell you about it later . . . I think we should take our seats now.'

They went out to the waiting coach, with its fresh horses stirring restlessly in the traces and the postboys to hand them up. They were the first in the vehicle, but a moment later three more entered, and several climbed on top. It was to be a crowded journey.

The clash of election and assize had given the soberer citizens of Bodmin some anxious thought: the coincidence was maladroit, to say the least; inns would be packed to suffocating one week and empty the next; the solemn process of the law might be disconcerted by the no less important but noisier processes of an election contest in which some bad blood was already being shown. Everyone knew that there were two mayors in the town, each representing a rival patron; but no one yet knew which would prevail during this all-important week.

The election of the members of Parliament, in more cordial circumstances, might have been put through in a couple of hours and no one the worse, since there were only thirty-six electors, members of a Common Council under the mayor. Unfortunately the dispute as to the mayoral office raised questions about the validity of the Council, each mayor having his own version of the electoral roll. Mr Lawson, one mayor, had among his common councillors his brother, his wife's brother, a cousin, a nephew, and four sons, and this was a situation which Mr Michell, the other mayor, passionately challenged.

As to the law, the lists were crowded with cases from the deferred spring assizes, the gaol crowded with felons, and the inns crowded with litigants and witnesses. On the Friday Ross had his first interview with his counsel, Mr Jeffery Clymer, K.C., a burly man of forty with a possessive nose and one of those chins which no razor's edge will whiten. All considered, Ross thought it a good thing the barrister came in his robes or the turnkey might have been reluctant to let him out again.

Mr Clymer thought the case of the Crown v. R. V. Poldark would not come on before Wednesday morning. In the meantime he thumbed through Mr Pearce's brief, shot questions at his client, tutted over the answers and sniffed at a handkerchief soaked in vinegar. When he left he said he would be round on Monday with a list of witnesses who had been subpoenaed to appear and a draft of the line of defence he would advise his client to pursue. The one tentatively sketched out by Mr Pearce was quite useless – it admitted altogether too much. When Ross said that was the defence Mr Pearce had prepared on his instructions, Clymer said fiddlesticks, it wasn't for a client to issue instructions of that sort; a client must be guided by his legal advisers or what was the good of having them. You couldn't plead not guilty and say in the next breath, I did it after all. It was an infernal pity Captain Poldark had made such admissions and offered such expressions of opinion to the examining justice. Asking for trouble, that's what you'd call it. Whole purpose of the defence now must be to remove that impression, not emphasize it. Ignoring Ross's look, he said it would profit them both if Captain Poldark would spend the week end thinking this over, and also in casting back in his memory for any new recollection that would help. After all, he said, rubbing his blue chin, no one but the prisoner could know *all* the facts.

One condition of Ross's consent to Demelza's presence in the town was that she should make no attempt whatever to see him in gaol. In fact she was not altogether loth, for she would not then have to account for her movements. Only to Verity need she make excuses, and at the worst Verity had no control over her.

As soon as they got to the inn there was trouble, for the landlord had put up another double bed in their room and claimed the right to let two other women share it. Only a long and painful argument and some extra money from Verity won them their privacy. They had a meal together and listened to the slamming of doors, the cries of ostlers, the hurrying feet of the maids and the singsong of some drunken wayfarers under the window.

'I think we shall have to plug our ears to sleep,' said Verity, taking the pins out of her hair. 'If it's like this at seven what will it be in another three hours?'

'Never worry,' said Demelza, 'they'll all be drunk insensible.' She stretched herself, arching her back like a cat. 'Oh, that old coach: joggle, joggle, bump. Three times I thought we were going to upset or spend the night in the mud.'

'It has given me a sick headache,' Verity said. 'I shall take a draught and lie down early.'

'In another hour I believe I should have felt the same. What were you going to tell me about your stepchildren, Verity?'

Verity shook out her hair and it fell in a cloud about her shoulders. The action was like some new and secret blossoming of her personality. She did not look eleven years older than Demelza now. Happiness had brought the keen intelligence and vitality back into her eyes, and an extra roundness to her cheeks made the wide generous mouth less unproportionate.

'It's nothing,' she said. 'Nothing beside what is happening to Ross.'

'I want to hear,' said Demelza. 'Have you not even seen them once yet?'

'. . . It is the only flaw at present. Andrew is very fond of his children, and I hate to feel they will not come because I am there.'

'Why should you feel that? It is naught to do with you.'

'It should not be. But . . .' She split one side of her hair into three parts and began to plait them. 'It is a very peculiar position, with Andrew's first wife dying as she did and the children being left so young – with that scar: their mother dead, their father in prison; brought up by relatives. Their father has always been at a disadvantage with them. They have come to see him occasionally, but never since we married. Of course James could not, for he is with the fleet and depends on the movements of his ship; but he has never once written. And Esther is only at Plymouth. . . . Andrew hardly mentions them now, but I know he thinks about them. I know he would be very happy if we could come together. I have wondered sometimes whether to go to Saltash to meet Esther – not telling Andrew, while he is away.'

'No,' said Demelza. 'I wouldn't do that. She should come to you.'

Verity stared at her reflection in the mirror, then at Demelza, who was changing her stockings. 'But suppose she never comes.'

'Get Andrew to invite her.'

'He has already done that, but she has made excuses.'

'You must use a bait, then.'

'A bait?'

Demelza wriggled her toes, and her eyes considered expressively the three pairs of shoes she had to choose from.

'Is she fond of her brother?'

'I believe so.'

'Then get him to Falmouth first. Perhaps it is only shyness with them both, and he might be easier to entice in the first place.'

'I should like to think you're right, for he must be home soon. He was expected back at Easter, but his ship was diverted to Gibraltar . . . What is that?'

Above the noises of the inn and street a man was shouting. He had a loud voice and a bell.

'The town crier,' said Verity.

Demelza had just taken off her riding habit, but she went to the window, which was at floor level, and knelt and peered through the lace curtains.

'I can't hear what he's saying.'

'No . . . it is to do with the election.'

Through the mirror Verity looked at Demelza's crouched figure which had some of the alertness of a young animal – the cream satin underskirt, the little décolleté bodice of Ghent lace. Three years ago she had lent Demelza her first dainty underclothes. Demelza was a quick learner. Verity's lips moved in an affectionate smile.

The crier was not coming their way, but in a temporary lull in the local noises they caught some disconnected words. 'Oyez! Oyez! Hear ye, hear ye . . . by the sheriff's precept . . . Notice of election . . . The mayor and aldermen of the borough of Bodmin . . . Speaker of the House of Commons, does command, issue and proclaim on Tuesday, the seventh day of September, in the year of our Lord . . .'

'Does that mean the election is to be Tuesday? I thought it was Thursday,' Demelza said.

'The notices will be posted now. We can see them tomorrow.'

'Verity . . .'

'Yes?'

'You are tired tonight?'

'I shall be well enough in the morning.'

'You will not mind if I go out by myself for a little?'

'Tonight? Oh no, my dear. It would be the height of folly. You'd never get along the pavements. You'd be in grave danger.'

Demelza went across to the things she had unpacked, considered them in the failing light. 'I'm not scared. I should keep to the main streets.'

'You don't realise what it is like! In Falmouth, even on a normal

Saturday night, it's impossible to venture without escort. *Here*, when there is free drinking, and the town's crowded with sightseers . . .'

'I am no lent-lily to snap off at the first touch.'

'No, my dear, but it would be madness, I assure you. You don't realise . . .' Verity watched the other girl's face. 'If you're resolved, then I must come with you.'

'That you cannot. . . . You've helped me so often, Verity, but in this you cannot help me. It is – just something . . . between Ross and me. . . .'

'Between . . . Did Ross ask you to do this?'

Demelza wrestled with her conscience. She knew the mischief which had come from her white lies before. But also the good!

'Yes,' she said.

'In that case . . . But are you sure he meant you to go out alone? I can scarcely believe that he could ever have agreed to . . .'

'I am a miner's daughter,' Demelza said. 'I was not brought up gentle. Gentleness – is that the right word? – came upon me when I was half grown. I have Ross to thank for that. And you. But it don't alter me underneath. I still have two marks on my back where Father used the belt. There's naught a few drunks could do but what I couldn't give them back. Tis all a matter of being in the mood.'

Verity watched her cousin's face a minute longer. There was a strength of line belying the soft feminine expression of mouth and eye.

'Very well, my dear.' Verity made a gesture of resignation. 'I am not happy about it, but you are your own mistress now.'

Chapter six

THERE WAS NO moon to light the town that night, but every shop, tavern and house contributed its share to the yellow flicker of the streets. In accordance with custom both parties in the election were offering free drink to their supporters, and there were already numbers of people stumbling as they walked, or sitting in a lazy stupor in alcoves or against a handy wall.

When Demelza came out she turned down the hill and in a few minutes was in the main thoroughfare, which this afternoon she had thought the narrowest and most crowded in the world. The shops and inns and houses, tight squeezed, had along their frontages a succession of slated porticoes reaching into the road-way on stone posts and forming an unbroken way down both sides of the street. The space left for traffic was little more than wide enough for one coach, and, since in the case of shops the porticoes were often used for the display of goods, pedestrians found themselves out in the road much of the time. Such an arrangement might have served for the normal life of the town; it was inadequate now.

The street was crammed with people, milling about, pushing up one side and down the other, rough but good-tempered so far. A few yards from the Queen's Head she came to a stop, unable to go farther because of the press. Something was going on at the hotel, but at first she could only see the scarlet and orange banners which hung from the upper windows. People were shouting and laughing. Near the portico against which she was standing a blind man was whining and trying to find his way through; a woman quarrelled with a brass worker over the price of a bell; a man, half drunk, was sitting on a stone step used for mounting horses, stroking the cheek of a vacant-faced full-bosomed young country girl on the step below. Two ragged urchins in cut-down coats came suddenly to blows and rolled over, scratching and biting, in the dried mud. A half dozen people laughed and formed a ring, hiding them from view.

There was a sudden shout and a rush towards the Queen's Head, and the press here was eased. A window of the upper room of the inn had been opened and people were cheering and shouting at the figures in the window. Others were rolling and fighting in the road just below. Another great cheer and a rush. The people above were throwing things down, scattering them in the road. An urchin came doubling and ducking through the crowd, holding his hands under his armpits, his face contorted but triumphant. Three men were fighting and Demelza had to duck under the portico to avoid them. One crashed into the stall of the brass worker, who came out with a flood of shouts and curses to drive them off.

'What's to do?' Demelza asked him. 'What are they about?'

The man eyed her up and down.

'Scattering red-hot coins, they be. From a frying pan. Tis the custom.'

'Red-hot coins?'

''S. Tis the custom, I tell ee.' He went in.

She worked her way nearer and could see the cook at the window in his tall hat, and two men with huge red and gold favours in their buttonholes. There was a great scream and a rush as more money was flung down. The human beings milling together in the flame and shadow had lost some part of their individuality and moved with a mass impulse not quite their own, not quite the sum of all the separate souls. She felt if she was not careful she might become a part of the mob in the yellow dark, be caught up in it, and lose her individual purpose and volition, being sucked towards the window with each wave that broke. She found herself beside the blind man.

'You'll not get through by yourself, old man,' she said. 'Where do you want to go?'

'Guildhall, Mrs,' he said, showing broken teeth. 'Tes up along, no more'n a short way.'

'Take my arm. I'll help you.' She waited for the next rush, and then thrust her way forward, finding comfort in being able to join with somebody, be of use to somebody, against the rest.

The blind man breathed gin over her. 'Tes rare an' kind of ee t'elp a poor old man. I'll do the same for ee one day.' He cackled as they got through the worst of the press. 'Tis a rare dring tonight, you; an' worse to follow, I misdoubt.'

'Where is the Basset headquarters?' she asked, peering up the street. 'I thought this afternoon it was up here?'

The blind man squeezed her arm. 'Well, tes no more'n a few paces now. But 'ow would it be if ye came along of me – up Arnold's Passage. I can give ee a nice little drop o' dripshan. Warm ee up, twould.'

She tried to get her arm free, but his fingers were tight and playing a little tune on her arm.

'Leave me go,' she said.

'No offence, Mrs. No 'arm meant. I thought you was a docy little maid. I can see naught, ye follow – so tes all a question of feel wi' me, and ye feel young and friendly. Young and friendly.'

Two riders came down the street, picking a slow way among the people, trying to quiet their horses which were nervous and restive, often unable to go forward at all. She steered the blind man past them and then wrenched her arm free. He tried to catch her fingers but failed, and she pushed her way ahead, her heart beating quickly.

As she got opposite the Guildhall another great press of people came down the street from the west, shouting and singing and carrying someone precariously on a chair. She was just able to slip into the arched entrance of the Crown. They seemed about to go right past, but some stopped, and a man stood on another's shoulders to try to reach the blue and gold flag just above them. He had caught at a corner, when a dozen or more men rushed past Demelza out of the hotel, sent the climber flying off the other man's shoulders and in a minute a fight was in progress. Someone threw a brick, and Demelza retreated farther into the yard and tried to tidy herself. Then she went in.

How to dress for her purpose had been a difficult decision and unsatisfying when made. She wanted to look her best, but could not have faced the streets in evening things. So the result was a compromise which sapped some of her dearly needed confidence.

'Yes'm?' An impudent page boy was standing before her. She saw by his eyes that he had not quite placed her in the social scale.

'Is Sir John Trevaunance staying here?'

'Not's I know, mum.'

'I think he's here now. He told me he'd be here this evening.' A rash claim.

'I can't say, mum. They're dining. There's guests.'

'Still dining?'

'Should be over soon'm. They started in at five.'

'I'll wait,' she said. 'Do you leave me know so soon as they're finished.'

She sat down in the lobby of the hotel, trying to appear unconcerned and at ease. Outside the noise was worse, and she wondered how she would get back. She tried not to be nervous. Waiters were scurrying backwards and forwards from a room on her left. She did not want to be found sitting here like a beggar waiting for alms. She beckoned one of the waiters.

'. . . Is there a withdrawing room where I may wait for Sir John Trevaunance in greater comfort than here?'

'Er – yes, madam. Top o' the stairs. Can I get you a refreshment while you wait?'

A brilliant idea. 'Thank you,' she said. 'Would you bring me some port.'

This was not the election dinner, which would be on Monday, but a preliminary gallop, as Sir Hugh Bodrugan called it. And, since there were a few women present, the evening was on a discreeter level than Monday's would be. A few of the weaker brethren were tipsy; but most carried it off in good style.

At the head of the table were Sir John Trevaunance and his brother

Unwin. Between them was Caroline Penvenen, and on Sir John's left was Mrs Gilbert Daniell, with whom the other three were staying. Beyond her was Michael Chenhalls, the other candidate, and next came Miss Treffry, the mayor – *their* mayor – Humphrey Michell, and Sir Hugh Bodrugan. Among the other guests were notables of the town and district, wool merchants and civic officials.

When the ladies left them the men sat over their port for half an hour before pulling in their sprawling legs and standing about in yawning, chatting groups amid the debris of the meal. The noise at the front of the hotel was not noticeable in the long dining room, but when they got upstairs the shouts and the cheers and the scuffling and the laughter were plain enough. As Unwin mounted the stairs beside his elder brother, Caroline Penvenen came towards him carrying her tiny dog. Her face was a study in charming petulance.

'Horace is upset by the noise,' she said, drawing her long fingers over the silky head and ears. 'He is of a nervous disposition and inclined to fret when frightened.'

'Horace is a very lucky dog to have so much affection centred on him,' said Unwin.

'I shouldn't have brought him, only felt he would be lonely with old Mr Daniell for company. I feel sure he would have found it quite desolate to sit in that dismal drawing room all the evening, with a draught whistling under the door and an old man *snoring* probably in the best chair. . .'

'I would point out, my dear,' said Sir John in a lowered voice, 'that we are Mr Daniell's guests – and that Mrs Daniell is just behind you.'

Caroline smiled brilliantly at the younger man. 'Sir John does not approve of me, Unwin. Did you know that? Sir John is convinced I shall disgrace him yet. Sir John thinks that woman's place is in the home, and not being obtrusive and a responsibility at election times. Sir John does not look with favour on any woman until she is at least thirty and past mischief; and even then . . .'

It was while the two men were politely trying to convince her otherwise that Demelza came out of a side room and saw her quarry close at hand. She came towards them with less hesitancy than she would have done half an hour ago, wondering all the same who the tall striking girl was with the red hair and the fiery grey-green eyes.

When Sir John saw her he looked surprised.

'Why, Mrs Poldark; this is a pleasure. Are you staying here?'

'For the time, yes,' said Demelza. 'There is a big commotion outside. I wonder if it is to do with this election?'

Sir John laughed. 'It's my belief so. . . . May I introduce . . . I don't think you will have met Miss Caroline Penvenen – although she is a neighbour of yours for part of each year, at Killewarren. Mrs Demelza Poldark, from Nampara.'

The ladies expressed themselves charmed at the acquaintance, though Caroline was summing up Demelza's dress and Demelza knew it. 'I stay with my uncle,' said Caroline, 'Mr Ray Penvenen, whom you may know. I have no parents and he reluctantly takes the responsibility of an orphan niece, as monks take a hair shirt. So at times I remove the penance by removing myself; and others wear the shirt for him. I was but then condoling with Sir John in the matter.'

'Believe me,' said Unwin, who did not look very pleased at Demelza's arrival, 'you do yourself less than justice. If responsibility you are, which I doubt, there are many who would have it. You have but to say the word for half the men in the county to be at your side. And if——'

'Men?' said Caroline. 'Must it only be men? What's wrong with women? Don't you agree, Mrs Poldark, that men put a false estimate on their own importance?'

'I'm not sure as to that,' said Demelza. 'For, you see, I'm married and am on the wrong side of the fence, like.'

'And is your husband all that important? Faith, I shouldn't admit it if it were the truth. But, Unwin, were you not telling me there was a Poldark to be tried at the assizes this year? Is it any relation to this lady?'

'That's my husband, ma'am,' said Demelza, 'so perhaps twill be understood why I hold him in some extra worth just now.'

For a second or two Caroline looked confused. She patted her dog's snub nose. 'And did he do wrong? What is he charged with?'

Gruffly Sir John told her, and she said: 'Oh, la; if I were the judge, then I'd sentence him forthwith to be returned to his wife. I thought excise men were not classed as human beings these days.'

'I wish you were judge, then,' said Demelza.

'I'd like to be, ma'am, but since I'm not I wish your husband well, and hope he'll come home again to domestic bliss.'

The conversation was broken by Michael Chenhalls, who said:

'They're shouting for us, Unwin. I suggest we go out on the balcony before they try to break into the hotel.'

'As you please.'

'I'll come with you,' said Caroline. 'I like to hear a mob when it is baying.'

'Baying for me?' said Unwin.

'No . . . just baying.'

'You as well may get a brick thrown as a bouquet.'

'That's as it should be. Spice in the pudding.'

They moved off towards the room with the balcony, and Demelza was alone with her quarry at last. She didn't think she would be left so for long.

'A taking young lady, Sir John.'

Sir John dryly agreed. 'She's but eighteen, you'll understand, and a thought high-mettled. She'll settle down.'

'I am not many years older.'

He looked at her with a quizzing interest. This was the fourth time they had met, and there were few women he had so quickly come to friendly terms with.

'Marriage has a maturing effect. . . .' He chuckled. 'Though drat it, take the ring off and you'd *look* little older.'

Demelza met his gaze very frankly. 'I don't want to take it off, Sir John.'

He shrugged uncomfortably. 'No, no. Naturally not. No one'd wish it. Naturally not. Have no fear, ma'am, your husband'll get a fair trial. Perhaps more than fair. And Wentworth Lister's a very able man. No prejudices. I can vouch for that.'

Demelza glanced around. Well, she must plunge in now.

'That,' she said, 'was what I wanted to see you about. . . .'

On the balcony the candidates had been greeted with an immense roar, as if a lion had opened its mouth.

When she could make herself heard Caroline said: 'They look like a field of turnips – only not so neatly set. What a rabble, dear Unwin. What is to be gained from pandering to them like this?'

'A custom,' said Unwin, bowing his fine head towards the mob. 'It's only for five or six days, and then they can be forgotten for as many years. I hope you're looking gracious, for it all helps.'

'Could I ever look anything else? You know, I should make you a very fine wife . . .' Unwin turned. '. . . *If* I decided to marry you. What could be more tactful than my behaviour tonight: criticising Mrs Daniell's house within Mrs Daniell's hearing; mentioning the Poldark case before Poldark's wife. What a triumph I should be among your parliamentary friends!'

Unwin didn't reply, but bowed and waved to the people below. Down the street towards the Queen's Head the maelstrom was beginning to move.

Caroline pulled her beautiful embroidered shawl about her shoulders. 'I hope Horace isn't biting the footman. His teeth are singularly sharp, and he has a knack for choosing the painful places. What a pretty woman that Mrs Poldark is. It's her eyes and skin that make it all. Pity she doesn't know how to dress.'

'We can go in now,' said Unwin, the cleft deepening between his brows. 'The novelty of seeing us is wearing off and if we stay longer they'll start expecting something else.'

'D'you know,' said Caroline, 'I should like to go to the assize for a day. I've never seen the way it all works, and I believe it would be very diverting.'

They turned to go in. 'Diverting if you got fever.'

'Oh, then I should be in bed for a few days and you should visit me. Does that appeal? Come, you promised me. What is the use of having influence if you don't use it?'

. . . In the lobby behind them Sir John pushed his wig back to mop his forehead.

'My dear madam, I have no influence of that sort! You don't know what you're asking. I tell you, it would prejudice your husband's case, not help it.'

'Not if it was put in the right way, surely.'

'Yes, if it was put any way. His Majesty's judges are not to be suborned by this sort of approach when a case is sub judice.'

Demelza felt her heart growing cold with disappointment and despair. She allowed her eyes to travel interestedly over Sir John's face. 'It is only that if you was to tell him all the truth about it before the case began he would know what to expect. What's amiss with that? Isn't it the truth they want? Is it real justice they want to give – or is it some other sort: law justice, made up of what lies the witnesses tell in the box?'

Sir John gave her a look more of sorrow than of anger. It was rather plain where her friendship and charm had all this time been leading.

'My dear ma'am, it's a little late to explain, but I can only assure you I'm advising you right. For one thing, Wentworth Lister wouldn't listen to me. It would be more than my friendship was worth. Ecod, I should be out of favour with every legal man in the country!'

Sir Hugh Bodrugan had seen her now. In a minute he would be over.

She said: 'It was not as if it was money you was offering him – but only truth. Is that so much to be despised?'

'That may be how you look at it. But how would he know it was the truth?'

'Just now – when I was sitting here before you came up – I heard a man say your brother had paid two thousand pounds for this seat in Parliament. Is that so, Sir John?'

'What's that to do with you?'

At his cold tone she gave in. 'I'm sorry. I meant no 'arm – no harm coming here tonight. I – don't understand, that's all. I don't see why it is right to pay electors for voting one way and so mortal hard to *ask* a favour of a judge. Perhaps twould be better if we did offer to pay him.'

'Then you *would* be sent to gaol. No, ma'am; be assured it's best to leave it all alone.' At her change of tone his had grown more sympathetic. 'Damme, don't think I do not sympathise. I hope and believe Poldark will be a free man by the end of the week. The surest way of attaining the opposite – the *opposite*, ma'am – would be to try to influence his lordship in any way. It is one of the peculiarities of life in England. I cannot explain why it should be so, but the law has always been above corruption. . . .'

He was looking towards the door where Caroline and Unwin and the Chenhalls were re-entering. So he did not catch the expression that flickered in Demelza's eyes. It was only there for a second, like a flag of defiance over a part-surrendered fort.

Chapter seven

ON SUNDAY MORNING there was a procession to church, headed by the legal fraternity in the town. It came down St Nicholas Street right past their inn, and Demelza and Verity knelt and watched it go. Demelza's knees came over weak at the sight of the two judges in the full regalia of their office – scarlet robes and heavy wigs: one of them tall and rawboned, the other of middle size and stout. She hoped that Wentworth Lister was the stout one. The enormity of her proposition to Sir John was brought home to her at sight of the material he had to work on. In the afternoon, rallying, she called at the hotel again and took tea with Sir Hugh Bodrugan, as invited. It was a respectable genteel occasion, and for once, with him, she was successful in keeping the conversation decent. But he wouldn't be an easy man to hold at arm's length for long.

On Monday morning Mr Jeffery Clymer had his final interview with Ross. He read rapidly through the new notes Ross had made, drawing his black eyebrows together until they were a continuous irregular portico above his eyes, like the porticoes of Fore Street.

Then he said: 'It won't do, Captain Poldark. Just won't do.'

'What's wrong with it?'

'What I told you on Friday. Got to realize, my dear man, criminal court is not a pitched battle, it's a field of manœuvre. You may speak the truth, the whole truth and nothing but the truth; but it all depends *how* you speak it! Got to be tactful, persuasive, throw yourself on the mercy and indulgence of the law. Be humble and innocent, not stiff-backed and defiant. Say what you like after the verdict; before that have a care. Weigh every word. Look: this is the sort of case you must put forward.'

Ross took the parchment from the plump hairy hands of the barrister and tried to concentrate above the clatter of the cells. After a minute or two he put it down.

'There are limits even if one's neck is at stake.'

Clymer looked his client over, summing him up professionally, the long strong frame, the bony well-bred face, high-strung under its reticence, the scar and the hair and the blue-grey eyes. He shrugged. 'If I could speak for you, that's what I'd say.'

'If you could speak for me, I might let you say it.'

'Well, then, what's the difference? Of course, it's your own life to do with as you please, your own freedom – if that's what you call it. Got a wife? Got a family? Don't you think it's worth making this concession for them? Mind, I make no promises *with* this line. But with yours you would as well do without me and save your guineas.'

In another cell some men were brawling, and at the back of this one two thieves were dicing for a neckerchief another had left behind. Got a wife? Got a family? Don't you think it's worth making concessions? Would it really be for Demelza's sake or for his own? The thought of captivity was stifling to one of his restless nature. In these few days he had seen enough. Was he justified in changing his defence at the last moment in an attempt to save his own skin?

He said shortly: 'Have you the list of witnesses for the Crown?'

Clymer handed him another sheet and wafted a handkerchief before his nose while Ross read it.

Vigus, Clemmow, Anderson, Oliver, Fiddick . . . 'No one can say the law has been slipshod in making up its case.'

'It never is, once it's *got* a case. Persevering – that's what you'd call it. Where a couple of hundred people are involved in a crime it usually fastens on one or two men – the most likely, perhaps the most culpable, though not always – it fastens on one or two and tries to force the others to turn King's evidence. Makes one or two the scapegoats, as it were. You're the scapegoat, Captain. Unfortunate. These men your friends?'

'Some of them.'

'Doesn't follow of course. Friend will turn nastier than an enemy to save his own skin. Bad thing about human nature – got a yellow streak. Came from Cain. Never know when it's going to show. We've all got it somewhere and fear brings it out.'

'I suppose,' Ross said, hardly listening, 'these men have no choice but to appear if the law subpoenas them . . . Paynter! I didn't expect him.'

'Who's that? Something fresh?'

'A man who was my servant for years.'

'Was he in this?'

'Oh yes. I woke him first and sent him to rouse Sawle.'

'Sawle a man?'

'No, a village.'

Mr Clymer wafted vigorously. 'Terrible smell in here, terrible smell. Was this Paynter on the beach when the excise men turned up?'

'On the beach but too drunk to know anything.'

'Trouble with some people – when they don't remember, they invent. That's often the defence's opportunity. Sharp-witted man?'

'I wouldn't say so.'

'Ah. No doubt you could shake him. Though some of these dullards are wickedly obstinate in the box. Bullheaded, that's what you'd call 'em.'

Ross handed the list back. 'Wednesday morning, do you think?'

'Wednesday morning.' Clymer stood up and folded his gown about him. 'Don't know why I'm troubling. If you want to hang it's your own affair.' The gaoler had come forward but he waved him away. 'Remember seeing a man strung up at Tyburn once. They cut him down for dead but he grimaced and twitched for quite five minutes after.'

'I've seen that happen when a man's head was shot off by a cannon ball,' Ross said. 'It's a still more peculiar sight when the head and the body are some paces apart.'

Clymer stared. 'Yes? . . .'

'Yes.'

'Ha, well . . . I'll leave this draft defence with you. Think it over. But don't regret you didn't use it *after* the verdict. There's nothing to be done then. The prosecution will have plenty of harsh things to say about you without your helping 'em in any way out of a mistaken sense of pride. Pride's all right in its place. Got plenty myself. Couldn't get along without it. But a court of law's not the place for a display of it.'

Dwight Enys put up at a little inn in Honey Street. A sudden illness in Mellin Cottages had delayed him so that he did not reach Bodmin until Monday afternoon. At the assize court he saw that Ross's name was not on the list for Tuesday; then he called at the George and Crown, but found only Verity there.

He left soon and dined quietly at the inn. Having hurried, he now found himself with one day to kill. In the morning he thought he would visit the lazar house he had passed a mile or so out of the town. He had never seen a leper and it might add to his knowledge to observe them.

The tiny dining room of this inn was separated from the tap-room only by half-height swing doors, and as he was finishing the cold pigeon pie there was some little commotion and he heard the word 'surgeon' mentioned. It was not, however, his business and he helped himself to the apricot jellies and the cream. After a minute the owner of the inn pushed through the door and, seeing Dwight, came perspiring over to him.

'Begging your pardon, sur, but be you a surgeon or an apothecary or some such like?'

'I am.'

'Well, sur, a footman has this minute run over from the Priory House to say there's someone taken tedious sick, and was there a physician to be had? Tis urgent, so I'm told. Twould be obliging to the Daniells and a keenly act as you might say. . . .'

In the taproom was a liveried footman looking breathless and a shade anxious. A Miss Penvenen was the lady who was took ill, a Miss Caroline Penvenen; a guest staying in the house. No, he hadn't seen her himself and didn't know what was amiss except that it was urgent and their own apothecary lived at the far end of the town.

'Very well. I'll be with you in a minute.' Dwight ran up the stairs and picked up the small bag of medicines and surgical instruments he seldom travelled without.

It was a fine night and only a few yards to the Church Square and up the hill at the other side. They turned in at a gate and came to a big square gentleman's residence overlooking a small park. Water glimmered through the ornamental trees.

The footman led the way into a square hall lit by six massive candles which flickered and bobbed like servant girls as they went by. Through a half-opened door Dwight saw a table set for supper, gleaming knives, polished fruit, flowers. A man's voice talking in a measured even tone; used to being listened to. Up the stairs. Good wrought-iron work and plenty of white paint. Two Opies and a Zoffany.

Along a red-carpeted passage and a turn. The footman knocked at a door.

'Come in.'

Dwight was ushered in and the footman withdrew. Sitting on a low couch was a tall, slender, strikingly handsome girl in a richly patterned dressing gown of white lawn.

'Oh, are you an apothecary?' she demanded.

'A physician, ma'am. Can I be of help to you?'

'Yes. That's if you know the use of drugs the way an apothecary does.'

'Of course. What is the matter?'

'You attend on the Daniells regular?'

'No. I'm a stranger to the town. Your footman came to the inn where I was staying and said you were urgently ill.'

'Yes, I see. I only wanted to be sure.' She got up. '*I* am not ill, though. It's my little dog, Horace. Look. He has had two fits and now's half awake only, as if faint. I'm greatly concerned about him. Will you attend to him at once, please.'

Dwight saw that beside her on the sofa was a small black pug curled on a silk cushion. He looked at the pug and then he looked at the girl.

'Your *dog*, ma'am?'

'Yes,' she said impatiently. 'I've been worried out of my life for half an hour. He'll not drink and scarcely knows me. It's all this commotion and excitement there's been, I'll swear. I shouldn't have brought him; I have only myself to blame.'

It was a beautiful room, decorated in scarlet and gold. Candles on the dressing table reflected in endless multiples through double mirrors. No doubt the chief guest room. A lady of consequence. He said gently: 'Your footman made a mistake. It would be a farrier you really sent him for.'

He caught the flicker in her eyes before she bent her head. 'It's not my custom to employ a horse doctor for Horace.'

'Oh, some of them are skilful enough.'

'That may be. I don't choose to employ them.'

He didn't move.

She said sharply: 'I want the best advice. I'll pay for it. I'll pay your ordinary fee. Come, what is it? You can have it in advance.'

'That can wait until I have the honour of attending you.'

Their glances clashed again. Something in her attitude had irritated him even more than the nature of the call.

'Well,' she said, 'are you going to treat the dog, or do you not know your trade well enough? If you're a beginner, perhaps you had better go and we'll call someone else.'

'It was what I was about to suggest,' he said.

As he reached the door she said: 'Wait.'

He turned. He noticed that there were faint freckles across the bridge of her nose.

She said: 'Have you never had a dog of your own?' The tone of her voice was different.

'. . . Yes, I had once.'

'Would you have let him die on a point of – of formality?'

'No . . .'

'Then will you let mine?'

'I imagine it's not as serious as that.'

'I hope not myself.'

There was a moment's hesitation. He came back into the room. 'How old is he?'

'Twelve months.'

'Fits are not uncommon at that age. An aunt of mine had a spaniel . . .'

He bent to examine Horace. There didn't seem much wrong with the animal except that its breathing was stertorous. Pulse was fairly steady and there was no sign of fever. At the best of times, he thought, it would be a miserable little beast. For one thing it was much too fat and pampered. Dwight was aware that its graceful arrogant young mistress was closely watching him.

He looked up. 'I see no cause for anxiety. There's an excess of some the vital humours, and I'd advise you to follow a lowering system of treatment. Keep him very short of sweetmeats and pastries. And let one of the servants give him regular exercise each day. Real exercise. Running and jumping. He's got to get rid of the poisons causing these convulsions. In the meantime I'll write you a prescription that you can get a druggist to make up.'

'Thank you.'

He took out his notebook; she meekly fetched him a pen and ink and he wrote out a prescription for a paregoric of black cherry water and Theban opium.

'Thank you,' she said, taking the slip. 'You were saying?'

'What?'

'About your aunt.'

His mind had moved on beyond that. He suddenly smiled, the last anger going. 'Oh, my aunt had a spaniel, but that was many years ago. He used to have fits when she played the spinet. One hesitates to say whether he was musical or the opposite.'

Caroline's smooth young face, which had been so taut a few minutes ago, flashed its own answering smile, though there was still a glint of disappearing hostility at its edge.

'What is your name?' she said.

Tuesday dawned with heavy showers which made the dry mud into wet mud but didn't affect the spirits of those who were determined to make the most of election day. Dwight went first to the assize building, but there was no notice yet of the following day's list so he felt entitled to introduce himself to Mr Jeffery Clymer to find out.

Mr Clymer was at breakfast, his mauve chin paler for the morning's shave, and in a great confusion and hurry; but he allowed Dwight a seat at the table and a glimpse of Wednesday's case list. The cases which were to come before the Hon. Mr Justice Lister were briefly stated.

R. v. Smith for misdemeanour

R. v. Boynton for larceny

R. v. Polkinghorne and Norton for vagrancy

R. v. Poldark for riot and assault

R. v. Inhabitants of the township of Liskeard for non-repair of highway

R. v. Corydon for receiving stolen goods

R. v. Inhabitants of the Parish of St Erth for obstruction of estuary

Dwight put the paper back on the table. 'How can all those be possibly got through tomorrow?'

'Have to be, my dear man,' said Clymer, chewing. 'Crowded list. Don't want to be here all month. Due in Exeter the sixteenth. But don't worry; they'll be run through all right. A lot of 'em are simple cases.'

'Including that of Rex v. Poldark?'

'Oh no, hum . . .' Mr Clymer paused to pick his teeth with his little finger. 'Far from it. But we shall get through. Could only wish for a different attitude on the part of my client. Stiff-necked, that's what you'd call it. Doesn't understand the law. And still unrelenting. Perhaps the look of the judge will make him change his tune. Wentworth Lister's no milksop. Well, well, I must be off. Got a case at eleven. Old woman accused of poisoning her grandson with ground glass. She's seventy-two and not a penny piece. Better all round if she was hanged to make an easy passing, but we must see what the judge says.'

As Dwight got up to go a servant tapped at the door.

'If you please, sir, a Mr Francis Poldark to see you.'

Mr Clymer gulped at his coffee. 'Another Poldark? What does this mean? Do you know him, sir?' When Dwight had briefly answered, 'Another witness, d'ye think? This fellow Pearce doesn't know his business if he allows people to come in with their stories five minutes before the trial. No mention of him in the brief at all!'

'He was ill at the time of the wrecks. But he may have called to make general enquiries about his cousin.'

Mr Clymer irritably unbuttoned his morning gown. 'Not Captain Poldark's wet nurse, y'know. Have other businesses to attend to. Foster!'

'Sir?' The clerk put his head round the door.

'Bring me R. v. Penrose and R. v. Tredinnick.'

'Yes, sir.'

'All this election farce. Most untimely and unsettling. Place overcrowded with drunken rogues and pickpockets. No service in the hotels. Bedbugs. Disgraceful: that's what you'd call it.' The barrister turned to the gaping servant. 'Well, show him up if you must. Show Mr Poldark up!'

'I'll take my leave before he comes,' Dwight said. 'That will be one less in your way. We shall meet tomorrow.'

'Be there by ten. The early cases may be run through very quick.'

On the way down the stairs Dwight met Francis coming up. Francis said:

'I came in great haste, but hear the case isn't until tomorrow.' He was dusty and unkempt.

'That's true.'

'Do you know where I can get a room for tonight? The town is fermenting with people.'

'I think you may have to go some distance out.'

'Which inn is Ross's wife staying at?'

'The George and Dragon. But your sister was saying they were crowded too.'

Francis looked up quickly. 'My sister?'

'They're staying together.' Dwight's professional eye could not help registering that Francis looked pallid and out of condition. The stamina had gone with the flesh he had lost. 'Your wife isn't with you?'

'. . . The court is no place for a woman. What are all these damned flags and banners waving in the breeze?' Dwight explained. 'Oh, of course, I had forgot. Cornwall abounds in rotten boroughs and suitable people to fill 'em. Think you this man upstairs has any forensic ability? So many of them are braggarty, potbellied old roués, caring only for their fees and a handy wench when it's over.'

Dwight smiled. 'I found him irritable but alert. I shall judge better tomorrow.' They passed on, and then Dwight turned again. 'If you should be out of a place to sleep tonight and nothing at all in view, you may share my room, though there's only one bed in it. The London Inn, near the church.'

'You may be held to that. If there's floor space I can use a rug and lie easy enough. Thank you.'

Dwight left the hotel and turned up the street. It was fine now and a walk would do him good. Just out of the town a handsome carriage drawn by four grey horses, with a driver and a postilion in green and white livery, passed him on the way in. As it lurched along, going slowly because of the appalling state of the road, Dwight saw George Warleggan alone inside.

When Dwight got back from his visit to the lazar house – where he had found only seven resident lepers, most of them drunk, and the building nearly falling down for want of elementary repair – he was only just in time to squeeze into the Guildhall to watch the election.

The platform at the end was filled with the town's notables, and Dwight was surprised to see the tall red-haired girl as the only woman among them. Outside was a good deal of noise, for the hundreds of people who could not get in were jammed in the street shouting rival slogans. Proceedings began with the usual sheriff's precept; then a fat man called Fox, who was a county magistrate, got up to administer the oath to the returning officer. Here was the crux of the matter. The two mayors, Michell from one end of the platform, and Lawson from the other, jumped forward and claimed their right to be that man. A long legal argument followed. Both sides had brought barristers to put their claim, but neither convinced the other, and tempers grew frayed. People in the hall began to shout and stamp their feet, and the floor shook.

Dwight stared over the bobbing heads and wondered how Horace was faring. He glanced at the people crushed around him, some in wigs, some with their own hair tied in bows at the back, others, labourers and workingmen, with lank uncut hair falling to their shoulders. Two near him had got skin diseases and a third was far gone in consumption and spat blood into the straw underfoot. In the corner was a woman who had lost her nose with the French disease.

Suddenly a compromise – of sorts – was struck on the platform, though it was come to more because of the noise of the mob outside than from any will to make concessions. The mayors were to be joint returning officers and would be jointly sworn in as such. Anyone could see that this would lead to further trouble when the election proper began, but at least it allowed progress of a sort.

Growing tired of it all, Dwight edged a step or two nearer the door, though he did not see much prospect of getting out until it was all over. Silence fell on the people round him and he saw that the first voter had stepped up. This was Alderman Harris, a man with a stomach equal to his great reputation, and he recorded his vote – for Trevaunance and

Chenhalls – amid a burst of cheering and only a few catcalls. Then came Roberts, a Whig Quaker, who was also allowed to pass unchallenged. Another Whig followed and, acting as warily as his rival, Michell passed him without comment. A third Whig, however, was too much to swallow. The barrister acting for the Basset interests objected on the grounds that Joseph Lander had long been invalidated from membership of the corporation on the grounds of insanity and that he had been three times put in the stocks for indecent behaviour.

This caused an uproar, and two men near Dwight started fighting. One of them shoved Dwight against the woman who had lost her nose, and she opened a mouth like a door and screamed as if she was being murdered. When she was at last quieted Dwight saw that a doctor was standing up giving evidence that Joseph Lander's mother and father were incestuously related and both had died insane – but before he could follow the argument the two men were fighting again; and when one of them was hauled insensible from under the other's feet Joseph Lander had passed from the scene.

The young physician began to wish he hadn't come. Every other man who came up to vote was challenged, and the arguments lasted interminably. One man, obviously at death's door, was carried up on a stretcher and put on the floor while they quarrelled over him like sea gulls over a strip of offal. Sir Hugh Bodrugan, stocky and hairy and authoritative, was allowed to pass unchallenged, just because, Dwight thought, no one dared face him out. What he was doing on the corporation was a mystery; but there were several like him, men who lived miles away and had no connection whatever with the town.

The girl was looking hot and bored; and suddenly she leaned towards Unwin Trevaunance and began to whisper in his ear. Trevaunance in some obvious irritation argued with her, but she rose and slipped out of a side door. On the impulse of the moment Dwight began to fight his own way out.

It was a long struggle, much resented and resisted, but he got there in the end and found himself hot and bruised and breathless in the passage. This passage was choked with people, and the stairs leading to the street were worse. He turned towards the back, knowing that Caroline Penvenen could not have gone out by the front door.

At the end of the passage the crowd thinned a bit, and two special constables were guarding the door which led to the platform. They stared at him with suspicion as he came up.

'Which way did Miss Penvenen go?'

One of them nodded. 'Down thur, sur.'

Dwight saw a door in the opposite wall, and pushed his way through to it. It led into the back room of the shop next door and thence to the main street. When he came out he thought she had gone, for the crowds were shouting and dancing about the ale-houses opposite, and the porticoes made it hard to get a view down the street. Then he turned and saw her standing against the wall beside the shop door, watching him.

She was hatless, evidently caring nothing for convention; her rich auburn hair, rather coarse in texture, curled to her shoulders. The pearls about her neck were worth any footpad's risk.

'Dr Enys,' she said as he bowed. 'Why are you following me?'

Again he felt that prick of irritation. 'I saw you leave and thought you might need my help.'

'Should I be likely to?'

'Election day is not the quietest of times.'

'I found it all very dull.'

'Naturally. But there are those who do not.'

The shop door burst open and a servant came out. He stopped at sight of them and touched his forelock.

'Oh, Mistress Penvenen, ma'am, the master asked me to see ee home safe. He couldn't leave hisself, not just now. Tis——'

'I needed no foster mother to escort me home,' she said impatiently. 'Go back to Mr Unwin and look after him. He'll need it maybe. Go on! Go on!' she added as the man hesitated. 'I don't want you.'

A section of the crowd was chanting the marching song again, but others were booing derisively. Someone aimed a brick at the Guildhall window, but it missed and broke to pieces on the wall, scattering a shower of smaller stones upon the people underneath.

'Rabble,' said Caroline. 'Like the shirtless beggars and thieves who pretend to hold France. England would be happier for a few thousand less of them.'

The shopkeeper behind them was busy putting up his shutters. There was a clatter of heels as someone clambered across his portico, and he pushed his way out into the street and began swearing and shouting at him to come down.

'In a mass,' said Dwight, 'a rabble, yes. And a drunken rabble's a dangerous thing; I wouldn't trust its behaviour a yard. But take each man to himself and he's likeable enough. A weak creature, as we all are, liable to jealousies and petty spites, as we all are, selfish and afraid, as we all are. But often generous and kind and peaceable and hard-working and good to his family. At least as much all those things as the average gentleman.'

Caroline looked at him. 'Are you a Jacobin, like your friend Ross Poldark?'

So she had been making enquiries about him. 'It's clear you don't know Ross Poldark.'

'No. I expect to see him tomorrow – and hope for better entertainment than I've had today.'

Dwight said sharply: 'No doubt you're the sort of woman who takes a window at Tyburn – for the pleasure of seeing someone choked to death.'

'Is it any business of yours if I am?'

'No. I'm thankful not.'

'I find you a little impertinent for one of your station, Dr Enys.'

'I don't suppose my station to be that of a lackey, ma'am.'

'You might establish your claim with some show of gentility then.'

His flush didn't fade. 'This is a rough county, Miss Penvenen. As you'll see if you look around you. . . . Not that I've noticed any strict attention to the conventions on your part.'

She lifted her head. 'There are limits, don't you think? And it seems only necessary for me to mention Poldark's name for you to fly into a rage and overstep them. Is he your hero, Dr Enys? Shall you be able to make a rabid speech tomorrow in his defence? Be careful that you don't forget your manners then, or the judge will not give you a hearing.'

'The judge is not a woman, ma'am.'

'And what do you mean by that?'

'I mean he's not likely to be swayed by prejudice.'

'Not even by an odious conceit such as some men suffer from?'

'Oh, conceit. I shouldn't put that as the special property of one sex. . . .'

As he spoke his attention was taken by an extra commotion across the road. Two men were fighting or struggling, it seemed for the possession of some papers.

'It's very gracious of you to instruct me,' Caroline said. 'I wonder you're so solicitous for one you so greatly despise.'

'You quite misunderstand what I . . .' He broke off.

'Naturally.'

There were cries and shouts and laughter from across the street, and some papers flew high in the air and scattered over the crowd. Other men had joined in the struggle now. Dwight muttered his excuses to Caroline and ran across the road. He tried to force his way through the ring of spectators.

It was hard going, for no one would move an inch for another, but at last he got through and found Francis struggling with three men who were apparently trying to restrain his violence towards a fourth who cringed among a heap of papers in the gutter.

'Mangy moulting carrion crow,' Francis was saying, in quite a quiet voice considering his struggles. 'Let me pluck a few more feathers. You wanted to distribute 'em, did you not, and I'll do it for you. This way . . .' He half broke free, but they grabbed him again.

'Hold hard, sur,' said one. 'Ye've plucked 'im near to the bone, I bla'.'

There was a laugh. Francis had had a good deal to drink. The man in the gutter, a tattered black-coated fellow, was holding his head and groaning, but with an eye on the sympathy of the crowd. Scattered about in the mud were dozens of broadsheets, and Dwight picked up one which lay at his feet. The leaflet was entitled *True and Sensational Facts in the life of Captain R-s- P-d-k.*

'Things that grow in dunghills breed pestilence,' said Francis. 'They should be trod back before they move from their middens. Let me go, fellow. Take your scabby hands off me.'

'Mr Poldark . . . are these men annoying you? What has gone wrong?'

Francis raised an eyebrow. 'Dr Enys. Well, it would be a mistake to imagine that by clinging to me like blowflies they're amusing me at all.' He wrenched himself free, the men having slightly relaxed their grasp at the sight of Dwight's sober bearing. 'God damn it, there's no respect for quality in this town. One cannot squash – ah, there he goes!'

Seeing his attacker free again, the tattered man in the gutter had turned, like one of the worms Francis had compared him to, and wriggled his way between the legs of the spectators. Francis threw his stick after him, but it only caught a fat man on the shins.

'And now he goes free, to lay his eggs elsewhere. Well, I fancy these he has left are well addled.' Francis ground the papers in the mud. Then he pulled his cravat round to the front and tried to adjust it. 'Go on, go on!' he said to the gaping crowd. 'There's no more entertainment for you. Back to your spawning.'

Dwight said: 'These scurrilous sheets. But it won't help to take the law into one's own hands.'

'What are they doing but taking the law into their own hands trying to poison the public's mind before the trial? It's a monstrous encroachment on individual rights. I'll wreck every one of 'em I come across.'

Dwight made a noncommittal reply and turned to go.

'As for you,' said Francis to the man who had held him, 'when the constables of this flea-ridden town want your help no doubt they'll enlist it. Until then restrain your interfering humours or they may lead you into trouble.' He ran a hand through his hair. 'Come and drink with me, Enys.'

'I'm sorry . . . I was engaged when I heard the commotion and – broke off a conversation.' Dwight peered back over the crowding people but could see no sign of Caroline.

'Conversation,' said Francis, 'is what I require. Intelligent conversation. I have spent the day in the company of rogues and thieves and bawds, beginning with the biggest blackguard of them all. Now I crave an hour's respectability. Suitably primed, I think you could dispense it.'

Dwight smiled. 'Another time I'd be honoured. But at the moment, if you'll excuse me . . .'

He pushed his way back to the Guildhall and looked every way. But she was not to be seen. Evidently she had no fear at all and had gone off on her own.

Unnoticed by him, a sudden silence had fallen on the crowds. Now he heard someone speaking, and knew it was the announcement of the election result. But he was too late to catch what was being said. All he heard was the roar of the crowd at the end – and that was a roar of frustration and annoyance.

Whatever the result, rivalry hadn't been appeased by it.

Chapter eight

VERITY SAT ON the low window seat watching the forty or fifty horses being driven by the hotel grooms down from the grazing fields above the town. Every evening about this time they came clattering and snorting past, forcing a dangerous way along the narrow street. Every morning they were driven up.

She had spent much of her time at this window since she came, peering down on the heads of passers-by, just as in Falmouth when Andrew was away she would sit in the window above the porch working at her embroidery and gazing out over the harbour. There was no such view here, just a narrow hilly street and an endless movement of people to and fro.

She had heard the result of the election an hour ago, a fiasco which would inevitably lead to more petitions and counterpetitions before Parliament and endless quarrels within the town. The two returning officers had shown different results. Mr Lawson had returned a Whig and a Tory, Mr Michell two Tories. The town was in a ferment.

By now Andrew would be in Lisbon. Tomorrow, while Ross was standing his trial, he would be setting sail for home. His son James, at Gibraltar, was no great distance from him, but could as well be in another hemisphere. Sometimes she doubted whether she would ever meet his two children; in her heart, in spite of what she had told Demelza, she had grown to fear it more than desire it. James and Esther were the standing evidence of Andrew's first tragic marriage. Perhaps they felt that themselves and so would not come. Perhaps they merely felt that the new wife had pushed them out. In any event Andrew Blamey's second marriage so far was an unqualified success, and Verity was terrified that his children might endanger it.

There was a knock at the door, and Joanna, the untidy serving maid, stood there, hair awry under a mobcap, and a streak of dirt across her cheek.

'If ee plaise, ma'am, a gent to see ee. Name of Mr Francis Poldark.'

Verity's heart lurched. 'Mr – *Francis* Poldark? . . .'

'Iss, I bla. He say you d'know he. Perhaps tis the other leddy——'

'It is this lady,' said Francis, entering. 'I am her brother, wench, so there's no bawdy tattle for you when you go below. Get down to your taps and leave us be. And wipe your snotty nose.'

Joanna, gaping, slid out, and brother and sister faced each other for the first time for fourteen months, since the day when, abetted by Demelza and in the face of his bitterest opposition, Verity had run away and married Andrew Blamey.

Her heart sinking, she saw at once that he was drunk. And she knew how much that meant. Six or seven years ago their father had been known to complain that Francis would never have a head on him and slid under the table after the first bottle like any common clerk. But time and patience had cured all that. It needed real perseverance these days.

'You alone?' he said.

'Yes . . . I – didn't know you were in the town, Francis.'

'Everyone's in the town. Apothecary, ploughboy, poor man, thief . . . I thought you were staying with Demelza.'

'She's gone out this evening. We've been together all day.'

He frowned at her as if trying to see her with the unprejudiced eyes of a stranger. His shirt was torn at the neck and his coat stained with mud. Only she knew how passionately he had resented her marriage. Since they grew up his love for her had been selfish, possessive – a little more than brotherly. His distrust of Blamey's bad record had been the centripetal force round which the other little resentments clung.

'Mrs *Blamey*,' he said contemptuously. 'How does it feel to be called that?'

'When you came . . . I hoped . . .'

'What? That I was come for a reconcil – conciliation?' He looked round for a seat and moved across the room to find one, sat carefully in it, putting his hat on the floor beside the chair and stretching out one muddy riding boot. His movements were too deliberately steady. 'Who knows? But not with Mrs Blamey. My sister – that's different. A treacherous slut.' But he said it without conviction or venom.

She said: 'I've so wished to come back and see you all – I've been asking Demelza. All your sickness over Christmas – and Demelza's loss. In Falmouth we've had our share, but . . . How is Elizabeth? Not with you, I suppose?'

'And how is Blamey?' said Francis. 'Not with you, I suppose? Tell me, Verity, d'you find married life less of a snare than the rest of us? We plunge into it, poor deluded devils, convinced there is something within that we're missing and must not miss. But it is a gin, is it not, with iron teeth – and once it fastens on us . . . How is Blamey; lashing his sailors, I conceit, in Biscay or the Baltic. You've got stouter, you was always such a thin kipes of a girl. Have you brandy or rum in the room?'

'No . . . only port.'

'Of course, Demelza's drink. How she loves it. She should take care or she'll become a tippler. I saw Ross in Truro, two weeks gone; he seemed very little put about by all the legal fuss and the lying scabby rumours. Like Ross, that. He's a hard nut and they'll not crack him with a mere assize, however much they count on it.' He stared at her with a pursed, angry face, but looking through rather than at her. 'I wish I were Ross and going to stand before my judges tomorrow; I'd tell them a thing or two, I'd shock them. Francis Poldark, of Trenwith, Esquire.'

One more effort. 'I'm glad you've come, Francis. I should be so relieved to feel all the heartburning was over. It has been my one unhappiness since I left.'

He ripped a bit of torn lace off the edge of his cuff, idly rolled it between finger and thumb, and flipped it across the room in the direction of the fireplace. 'Happiness – unhappiness: tags to tie upon the same mood! Pretty ribbons that mean no more than the flags of this cursed election. *Aarf!* as Father used to say. This morning I quarrelled violently with George Warleggan.'

She got up. 'I'll order you some refreshment, my dear.' When she had pulled the bell: 'We're all praying for an acquittal tomorrow. They say it's by no means hopeless. Demelza has been about some business of her own all week end. It is something to do with the trial, but I don't know what. She can't rest.'

'Acquittal! Nor would I in her shoes. This morning I went round to the counsel who's defending Ross and said to him: "Tell me the truth now, I want no cuckoo-spit, but the truth: what are his chances for tomorrow?" And he said: "As for the third charge, there's a very fair chance; but I see no getting out of the first two – on his own admission and on his pigheaded attitude now. There is still time to change and make a fight of it, but he will not do so, so it is a lost cause to begin."'

The serving maid came to the door again, but for a moment they were both too preoccupied to heed her. At length Francis sent her scurrying off for gin.

He said: 'I met George at the Garland Ox just after. He looked so damned opulent and self-satisfied that I couldn't stomach him. My gorge rose and I vomited a good deal of spleen. It did me a world of good.'

They were silent for a long time. She had never seen him like this before. She didn't know if the change had come in twelve months or only in tonight. Two things struggled in her mind, concern for him and concern for what he had said about Ross.

'Was it wise to quarrel with George? Don't you still owe him money?'

'I greeted him by saying: "What, are the carrion gathering before the buck's killed?" When he showed signs of swallowing that outwardly but resenting it inwardly I thought it time to place my opinion of him beyond a doubt. His damned suaveness didn't avail him. With a politeness to match his own, I dwelt on his looks, his clothes, his morals, his parentage and his earlier ancestry. We quarrelled with a becoming vigour. The position between us had needed clearing up for some time.'

'Clearing up,' said Verity restlessly. 'It will be a very happy clearing up if he forecloses on you. He has been an old friend, I know, but I wouldn't consider it beyond him to pay you out for an insult in whatever way he can.'

Joanna came back with the gin. Francis tipped her and watched her go. He slopped some of the spirit into a glass and drank it. 'Oh, no doubt he thinks he'll take it out of me tomorrow. But he may be defrauded.' Francis stared with a peculiar expression at his empty glass. He might have been staring at the bitter procession of his life, ever dwindling in thought and achievement down a vista of days till it came to this desolate moment, when the dregs were all that remained. It was a moment when lunacy and unreason became part of the wider comity.

'Tomorrow is still remote,' he said. 'It may never happen.'

'The whole procedure was cursed irregular,' said Sir John Trevaunance, dusting snuff off his sleeve. 'Ecod, if I'd been there it would never have been allowed to happen.'

'Easy to talk,' said Unwin, like a sulky giant. 'Neither would give way, and the crowd was howling outside. We had to give 'em some result or they would have wrecked the place. As it was, when Michell and Lawson went to the window together I thought they would be stoned.'

'Michell's returns were sent straight off?'

'Yes, by post rider. But so were Lawson's.'

'It's important which the sheriff has in his hands first. There's no reason in it, but a greater regard is usually taken of the first in.'

They were at the reception following the election dinner. It had been decided after hurried consultation to go ahead as if there had been a full-scale Tory victory. The Boscoigne faction was doing the same and at the Guildhall reception which followed the dinners there was an intermingling of the rival parties. Both judges were present and several people of rank in the county who had not been concerned in the election.

'There'll be pressure on me to stand aside,' said Unwin viciously. 'There's a smell of it already. Without me Chenhalls and Corrant can occupy the seats comfortably. If I have to go, Basset will hear of it.'

'There's no question of your stepping aside.' Sir John chewed his bottom lip. 'In fact, since you're second in both polls, you're really the only one who's fully elected.'

A set dance was in progress, and Unwin watched Caroline's tall graceful movements as she danced in a square with Chenhalls and some cousins of the Robartes. 'Well, we are three members for two seats. That will not pass.'

'It's only a question of time,' said Sir John, staring at a dark young woman talking to one of His Majesty's judges. 'When the plea is heard before the Chancery Court Lawson's mayoralty will be declared illegal, there's no doubt. That will automatically make his election figures invalid. Anyway, they smack of fraud. Whoever heard of a Whig mayor returning one candidate of the other colour when there are two of his own?'

'It suggests impartiality.'

'Nonsense, it suggests fraud. But in any case, if this should not be thrashed out before Parliament reassembles, don't hesitate to claim your seat. There have been similar occurrences in recent years at Helston and Saltash. Daniell reminds me that at Saltash two rival electoral bodies have existed for a very long time, and different committees of appeal have held first one body to be legal and then the other. More than that, Unwin. In an election to fill a single seat four or five years ago, the rival electoral bodies each elected a member – and *both* have taken their places in the Commons.'

'Yes, I heard something of it in the House.'

'Well, that was in '85 or '86. And Daniell assures me that in spite of petitions and counterpetitions both elected members continue to sit. If that can happen, there's no reason to be despondent about the present result. I believe it to be most important that you regard yourself as re-elected and act accordingly.'

The dance came to an end and was politely applauded. Without looking towards the Trevaunances, Caroline drifted off with Chenhalls in the direction of the supper room. Relations between the lovers had not been of the sweetest today. She had insisted on attending the hustings – much against all his advice. Then, suddenly bored, she had slipped out in the most obvious way when Unwin couldn't possibly leave to accompany her, and had sent his servant scuttling back when he told him to follow. After all that she'd arrived back in the hall just as the results were given, and had snapped his head off when he asked the cause. When I am your husband, he thought, looking towards her, as she stood in the doorway . . . Her shoulders gleamed whitely even in this subdued light. *If* I am your husband; and that was a disturbing thought. This election had been more expensive than ever. Doubts as to the results made his position much more unstable – whatever John said. And there were mounting debts in London. He started towards her, but Sir John clutched his arm.

He looked at his brother impatiently, expecting more sage but unwelcome advice. But Sir John was staring the other way.

'Tell me . . . who's that with Wentworth Lister? That woman – talking to him.'

Unwin frowned his cleft frown. 'Demelza Poldark, it looks like.'

'God, well . . .' Sir John swallowed. 'I thought so. So she wouldn't take no for an answer.'

'What d'you mean?'

The other said expressively: 'How the devil has she got in here? Who could have introduced her? And now she's talking to Longshanks Lister –

just as she intended. God's my life, she'll hang her husband if she's not careful – and go to prison for contempt of court herself! She's playing with fire.'

'I've seen her about with Hugh Bodrugan.'

Sir John took out a handkerchief and mopped his face. 'Well, I had no hand in it, that's one thing. Hugh always was a lecherous fool; she'll have had to pay her forfeits there. Well, I wish her luck of the encounter. She'll need it.'

Unwin said: 'I told you the first time I set eyes on her that she was a dangerous woman.'

Demelza was well aware that she was playing with fire. As soon as she saw the tall cadaverous judge at close quarters she knew this was going to be the hardest meeting of her career.

She had put on her pale mauve silk with the half-length sleeves and the flowered apple-green bodice and underskirt. It was the one Verity had chosen for her three years ago.

Sir Hugh Bodrugan did not know Lister, but had got Mr Coldrennick, the M.P. for Launceston, to introduce them. Then, grunting and hairy, he had gone off with Coldrennick and left Demelza with her quarry, as promised.

The Hon. Mr Justice Lister was about sixty years of age, six feet tall, with long tapering legs, slightly bowed, and an austere lined face stamped by forty years of courtrooms. He was not enjoying himself in this reception because he was a shy man when away from his work, and had no interest in the powder and patch of fashionable assemblies. He had come because the accommodation in the judges' lodgings was so cheerless that he had dined out every night – and now could not refuse the organisers, who had been his hosts.

When he met this young woman he fully expected her to ask him a few inane questions and simper at him and move on, as other young women had done. He had no interest in women, except that they appeared as the motive power behind a good many of the felonies which came under his scrutinizing eye. He was a bachelor and a pessimist.

But this young woman had lingered longer than most. At the moment she had asked him a question and he had not caught it. He lowered his head.

'What did you say?'

'Does your lordship dance?'

He shook his head. 'But don't let me deter you. No doubt you have partners enough waiting to claim the privilege.'

'Oh no, my lord. I should better prefer to watch. I believe it is the on-looker who most enjoys the dance.'

He put out his bottom lip. 'I am of an age, madam, when the spectacle of others in effort is more rewarding than the effort itself. I should not have imagined you were.'

'But what has age to do with it?' Demelza asked. 'Isn't it wise to – to keep out of the crush sometimes so as we may see what we look like when we're in it?'

He glanced at her a little more keenly. 'If you observe that rule in matters of more serious import you will make a good deal of your life.'

'In matters of more serious import,' Demelza said 'life don't always give you the choosing.'

'Every subject's soul is his own,' said Lister. 'How he uses it is no one else's responsibility.'

'Oh yes, my lord, I believe you truly. But sometimes tis like a bird in a cage. It can sing never so sweet but being dropped down a well will not put an end to it.'

He smiled dryly. 'You argue with a ready wit, ma'am.'

'Your lordship's too kind. Of course it is a pre-presumption on my part. I am really so ignorant about all these things. You know so much.'

'We know what we are allowed to know,' said Lister. 'Conscience is nearer judgment than knowledge.'

'I wonder,' she said, 'if that ever worries you?'

'What?'

'Judgment. I mean,' she went on hastily at his look, 'isn't it hard to judge to perfection unless you d'*know* to perfection? Forgive me if I don't understand.'

'My dear madam, there is room for improvement wherever we look. Infallibility exists in divine creation, not elsewhere.'

. . . In the refreshment room Unwin said: 'In what way have I offended?'

'In no way, my dear,' said Caroline, her fingers travelling over her hair. 'Why should you have?'

'That I don't know. I lay myself out to please you all ends, incurring the disapproval of my party to get you to the hustings – but tonight you ignore me for Chenhalls or any other middle-aged beau who comes along. I'm surprised you've not danced with Bodrugan yet.'

'Thank you, dear, I prefer bearbaiting out of doors.' Caroline's sweet voice had a touch of ice. 'But why should I not dance with the middle-aged beaux if they give me pleasure? I'm not yet tied to your apron strings – and thankful too, for they would be gloomy tiresome sulky depressing apron strings tonight, and hardly to be borne.'

Unwin took a grip on himself and smiled. 'I'm sorry, Caroline. It is this accursed election – pray forgive me. As soon as the situation is cleared up I shall be better company, I promise. I should be now, given half a chance.'

'Always it was "when the election is over." Now apparently it is not over. Oh, John! John!'

'Yes?' said the elder Trevaunance acidly. He disliked being called by his

Christian name by this wand of a girl. He bore it only for his brother's sake.

'Do you know a physician who lives in or around Sawle by the name of Enys? Dwight Enys, I believe.'

'M'yes. Lives on Poldark land or just on the Treneglos estate. Young feller. Know nothing about him much. Why?'

'He is in the town, I believe to give evidence at tomorrow's assize. Has he private money, I wonder?'

'Why? Have you met him?' Unwin asked suspiciously.

'By chance he was the man we called in to see Horace. I told you about him. And very stiff-necked at being summoned to attend a pet dog.'

'Infernal impudence. Had I been there I should have told him so.'

'Oh, *I* told him so. But impudence is not so grave a sin, Unwin. Do you think? It shows a certain resilience and spirit. . . .'

. . . In the ballroom conversation had shifted a little away from the dangerous subject. Wentworth Lister was staring at the dark girl with narrowed eyes. 'Modesty, a Greek philosopher once said, is the citadel of beauty and of virtue; the first of virtues is guilelessness, the second the sense of shame. It is a precept which has helped me in my estimate of women over many years.'

'And your estimate of men?' said Demelza.

'Yes, and in that too.' The dance came to an end and the judge glanced slowly round the room. It was warm in here, and he was sorry he had put on his third pair of stockings.

'Pray do not let me detain you longer,' he said rather resentfully. 'I'm sure you must have other and more pleasant claims upon your time.'

Demelza moistened her lips. 'Judas; I was thinking I was trespassing on yours.'

To this he had to give a polite denial, and she in turn glanced quickly about. Though there were plenty of people moving around them, none just at that moment seemed bent on disturbing the tête-à-tête. The judge was not an attractive figure.

'I wish they would play something softer next time,' she said. 'It is hard to be heard. They make too much use of the flute and the pipes.'

He said: 'You play yourself, perhaps?'

'Only a very little.' She smiled at him with sudden brilliance. 'And sing – when I'm alone, like.'

'I agree with you in a preference for the violins and the viols. As for singing, there is none worth hearing today.'

Something in his tone caught her animal-sharp ears. It was a single breath of feeling among the dry rushes of his character.

'The Cornish do a rare lot of singing.'

His lips smiled. 'They put their voices together. No doubt that is what you mean. The church choir on Sunday.'

'Of course – it is not maybe like what you get in London.'

'There is little in London either. Little that is uncontaminated by modern tendencies. Frivolous and insipid glees. Italianate pasticcios and simpering artificiality. To catch the pure stream one must go back two hundred years – or more.'

Lister closed his mouth sharply and took a pinch of snuff. Having dusted away the powder with a lace handkerchief, he clasped his hands behind his back and stared across the room as if determined not to be lured into further expressions of opinion.

Demelza said desperately: 'What's wrong with the church music, my lord? I don't rightly follow you.'

'Ha!' said Lister.

The Trevaunances had reappeared out of the supper room. Caroline's flame-coloured head just topped Sir John's, and was little below Unwin's.

Demelza said: 'It is the first church I have heard with one of those organ pieces. There is one in to Truro, but I never heard it. It is a grand sound, but I rather prefer the older way when it is well done.'

The judge sniffed and dabbed. 'You are fortunate that your ear is not entirely ruined by modern tendencies. No doubt you have never heard of singing in organum?'

'No, my lord. It is not singing with the organ?'

'It is certainly *not* with the organ. . . .'

. . . Sir Hugh Bodrugan had talked out the implications of the electoral position with Mr Coldrennick and wanted something more to drink. He was sick and tired of Bodmin and would be glad to get home tomorrow to his dogs and his horses and Connie with her curses, and room in his great ramshackle house to stretch and sprawl and belch. This was all too confined for him. Only bright thing in his visit was meeting Demelza Poldark, who was always sharp-witted enough to keep him awake and freshen things up. He stared across at her where she was still talking to the tall spindly judge. She was damned elusive, that was the trouble. A bit of angling was all part of the fun, he knew that; he didn't want his fish landed too easy; but so far he'd only kissed her twice – but once on the mouth – and squeezed her a couple of times in interesting places. A damned tantalizing long-legged minx. It was time he was getting back to her.

He said just the last part to Mr Coldrennick, breaking in on some dull observations about burgage tenures.

'Yes,' said Mr Coldrennick. 'I suppose so. Must confess I've seldom known the learned judge so conversational. Young Mrs Poldark has a way with her.'

'Oh, she's a way with her,' said Bodrugan grimly. 'Damme, yes. It's the will that's lacking.'

As they got near they could hear the judge's voice. 'My dear young lady, no harmony, even of the most primitive kind, existed in the church until the tenth or or eleventh centuries. Plainsong was begun then by higher and lower voices singing at a distance of a fourth or a fifth instead of in unison. It was no doubt years before it was found that thirds and sixths, instead of being more were less discordant and infinitely more melodious and variable in effect. There is a Scottish hymn – ah – to St Magnus . . .'

'Hrrm-hm!' said Sir Hugh Bodrugan.

The Hon. Mr Justice Lister raised his head and gave the interrupter a look he usually reserved for malefactors. At sight of it Coldrennick would have sheered away, but Bodrugan was not to be intimidated by anything.

'Ha, there, it's time for a bite of something more to eat, m'dear. There's such a shindy of people that I need you to steer me across in the right direction. Your lordship'll pardon us, no doubt.'

'I'm not at all hungry, Sir Hugh,' Demelza protested. 'Perhaps twould be possible to wait awhile. His lordship was talking about church music, an' it is a rare instruction I should like to go on with.'

'Nay, it will wait until another occasion, won't it, my lord. Church music, ecod! That's a subject for election night.'

'A subject for any night,' said Lister, 'if you have the disposition to grasp it. There are those, plainly, who have not.' He was going to add something more from between his tight-held lips, but two ladies came up from the direction of the supper room, and there were others approaching. He said to Demelza: 'There is also certain Elizabethan music, madam. Byrd and Tallis are names to remember. And – in a lighter and different fashion – Thomas Morley.'

'I'll remember them,' she said, and thanked him in her most careful style. Bodrugan was waiting to move away, and the other women now spoke to the judge. But after a moment he turned again to Demelza. There was a faint glimmer of approval in his deep-set eyes as he looked her up and down.

'I don't recall your name, madam, or whom I've had the pleasure of addressing.'

'Poldark,' she said, and swallowed. 'Mrs Ross Poldark.'

'I am obliged to you,' he said, and inclined his head. The name clearly meant nothing to him – yet.

Chapter nine

AFTER DARK THE streets reached their peak of noise and drunkenness, and Dwight's first intention was not to go out again. Caroline no doubt would be at the ball, but he had no invitation, and in any case no evening clothes. After supper he sat for a while in his bedroom reading a medical book, but the wilful Miss Penvenen and her doings kept intervening. She existed at the corner of his eye, in the depths of his ear, in the back of his mind. He remembered the rustle of her silk dress like something new and heard for the first time, he saw the tip of her tongue once when she licked her lips, he heard her voice, cool and irritating but as unforgettable as a line of music. Eventually he threw the book on the bed and went down to the taproom for a couple of drinks, but it was noisy and overcrowded, so, for lack of something better to do, he decided to stroll up the hill to the tiny hospital, which was under the charge of a Dr Halliwell. Bodmin was one of the few towns progressive enough to have such an accommodation – mostly, if you were injured, you died in the street or in your own bed – and he thought it might be interesting to compare this tiny provincial establishment with the great institutions which flourished in London.

So he just missed Francis, who turned into the inn after he had left.

Francis asked for him and, on being told he was out, said that he had been promised a share of his room for the night. The inn-keeper eyed him doubtfully, trying to size him up, impressed by his gentlemanly speech and bearing which weighed against his muddy tattered clothes, suspecting he was drunk yet not quite reconciling that with his fine-drawn expression and resolute speech.

'I'm sorry, sur, but twouldn't be for the likes of me to let one gent into another gent's chamber wi'out a by-your-leave. Twouldn't be playing fair, like.'

'Nonsense. Dr Enys invited me. What time will he be back?'

'I dunno, sur. He didn't say.'

Francis put down his saddlebag. 'It is a common custom in times of need to ask two gentlemen to share the same chamber. And you know it. And we are not strangers but friends. Come, tell me what Dr Enys is paying and I'll give you the same.'

'That and gladly when Dr Enys comes in.'

'I am not prepared to wait all the night for it.' Francis took out a purse and from it some gold coins. 'I'll pay you my rent now, so that you can't be the loser.'

The landlord's eyes boggled. 'It's but a small chamber, your honour, and but a single bed.'

'I have no care for the size of the bed.'

The landlord stared again and then turned to the potboy. 'Here, Charlie, take this gent up to number six.'

Francis paid his dues and followed the boy up the creaking stairs. Once in the room and rid of the boy he shut the door and turned the key. A low narrow chamber with a plain deal table before the empty fireplace, a single bed by the half-shuttered window, two candles flickering, lifting the shadows beside the bed. He leaned against the door for a minute, taking in the room, then picked up one of the candles and carried it to the table. Then he undid his bag, took out a clean shirt, washed himself, put on the shirt and a clean neckcloth. He sat down at the table, took some sheets of paper from his bag, and after some thought began to write. All this was undertaken with deliberation but it was not quite the deliberation of drunkenness. He had passed through drunkenness to a deadly sobriety beyond.

For five minutes the room was possessed by a new quiet made explicit by the single scratching whisper of the pen. Occasionally there were noises outside, or a burst of laughter would drift up through the squat walls from the taproom like echoes of a remote world. Just now and then one of the candle flames would tremble and a flicker of smoke come into being and detach itself and drift away. He wrote with a concentration which came from both outward and inner urgency: he was not only writing against the clock but against some imperative mechanism within himself which told him that the thing he had to do could wait no longer.

At length he signed his name, got up, went to his bag again, took out a pistol. It was a single-barrel duelling weapon of the flintlock type employing a heavy bullet and a light charge of powder. He primed it and set it on the table beside him. Then he looked round. All was ready. The silence of the room had become oppressive, it beat in his ears; it echoed the terror of the final initiative, the last compulsion of mind and muscle to which all this had been proceeding as a river hurries to the annihilation of the sea.

He raised the pistol to his head.

The hospital, Dwight found, consisted of a few rooms on the first floor of a squat building near the assize court. Beneath it was the Reading Society; you visited the ground floor to gain a book, the first floor to lose a leg. He was not fortunate enough to find Dr Halliwell, who had not yet returned from a day's shooting, but a stout dropsical woman, after a brief suspicious argument at the door, showed him round the two wards.

The beds were arranged much on the London principle, built into the walls, with wooden sides, rather like great drawers pulled out of a cabinet, each ward being lit by a single lantern in which a squat candle steadily burned. The crowds and events of the week end had brought their crop of accidents and illnesses, so the hospital was fairly full. There was the usual close and horrid smell. The patients were four in a bed, lying head to feet; and there did not seem to have been much attempt to sort them out according to their various infirmities. Under the lantern a woman who had had her hand amputated shared a bed with another in the first stages of labour, and the third in their company, to any trained eye, was plainly dying. She had a flushed, feverish face, and pale violet blotches on her hands, and her breathing was halting and strained.

'A doxy found in the streets,' said the stout woman, hitching up her stomach. 'Give birth to twin boys a week past. She'll be gone afore morning, if you ask me. . . . This other one's been in labour no more than an hour yet. Tis her father's child, they say, though *she'll* say naught. We put 'em in together for company like. . . . This here be the men's ward.'

Dwight did not stay long. He did not know Dr Halliwell, and one could never be sure that his visit might not be unwelcome. When he got out into the street again he took some grateful breaths of the night air. It had been raining heavily while he was inside, and more was blowing up from the west; but it had not at all damped the spirits of the revellers, and there were dozens still roistering in the streets. He saw two of the more respectable merchants being pushed home in wheelbarrows.

The innkeeper met him with the news of the unexpected visitor. Dwight had forgotten all about his morning invitation to Francis, and their encounter this afternoon made him wish he'd never issued it. He went up the stairs expecting to find his guest sprawling asleep on the bed, and his irritation was increased when he found the door locked. He thumped on it impatiently, hoping his guest was not too drunk to hear. There was no reply. It was too bad, for there might be no means of waking the man before morning. The landlord probably would not have another key, even supposing this one was not blocking the keyhole on the other side.

Dwight thumped again with all his strength. The dark narrow passage was cobwebbed in every corner, and there were cracks along the walls where they bulged as if some superior weight was leaning on them from the other side. A claustrophobe would have shrunk and hurried through before they collapsed together and trapped him. From one of the wider cracks near the door a black beetle showed up for a moment as if disturbed and resenting the noise. Suddenly Dwight heard a movement inside the room and the key turn.

With relief he lifted the latch and went in and was surprised to see the bed empty and unused and Francis walking slowly back to the table on which the two candles burned.

His irritation going, Dwight laughed a little awkwardly.

'You'll excuse the noise. I thought you might be asleep.'

Francis did not reply but sat down at the table and stared at two sheets of paper in front of him. He didn't look as drunk as when they last met. With mounting surprise Dwight noticed the clean shirt, the neat neckcloth – and the completely bloodless face.

After a minute he said: 'The landlord told me you'd come. I thought you might have difficulty. The town is fairly seething.'

'Yes,' said Francis.

Aware of some deeper tension within the room than he had yet penetrated to, Dwight slowly unbuttoned his coat and threw it off, stood for a moment in his shirt sleeves, uncomfortable, hesitating. The other man's silence forced him to go on.

'I was sorry for leaving so sharply this afternoon, but, as I explained, I had to rejoin a friend. You've supped, I suppose?'

'What? Oh yes.'

'If you're writing a letter go on with it.'

'No.'

Silence fell. Dwight stared at the other more closely.

'What's wrong?'

'Are you a fatalist, Enys?' Francis brought his brows together in a sudden grimace of nervous resentment. It broke over his frozen face like a storm. 'D'you believe we are masters of ourselves or merely dance like puppets on strings, having the illusion of independence? I don't know.'

'I'm afraid I'm a little tired for a philosophical discussion. Have you some personal problem before you that puts the question more conveniently?'

'Only this.' Francis swept the papers impatiently aside and picked up the pistol they had covered. 'Five minutes ago I tried to shoot myself; but the thing misfired. Since then I have been debating whether I should try again.'

A glance showed Dwight that the other man was not joking. He stared at Francis, trying to find something to say.

'You're a little shocked,' Francis said, and pointed the pistol at his face and squinted down the barrel, his finger on the trigger. 'Of course it wouldn't have been in the best of taste – to have made use of the hospitality of your chamber for such a purpose – but none of my own was to be had, and to do it in some dark corner a street is faintly vulgar. I'm sorry. Anyway, the thing's not done yet, so you have a talkative companion for a few moments instead of a silent one.'

Dwight stared at him, resisting the impulse to say or do the obvious things. A wrong move might be fatal. After a long minute he forced himself to relax, to move across to the ewer and basin by the window so that his back was towards the other. He began to wash his hands, and found they were not quite steady. He felt that Francis was closely watching him.

'I don't understand you,' he said at length. 'I don't understand why you could possibly wish to destroy yourself – and, if you did, why you should ride twenty-five miles to a strange town to do it.'

There was a rustle of papers as if Francis were putting them together.

'The deceased behaved irrationally before he died. Is that it? But who behaves rationally even when wanting to stay alive? If we were thinking brains suspended in fluid . . . But we're not. We have viscera, my dear Enys, as you should know; and nerves and blood and things called emotions. One can develop a quite unreasoning prejudice against spilling one's blood on one's own doorstep. Impulses are hard to put under a slide rule.'

'If this was an impulse, then I hope it's past.'

'No, it is not. But now you are here give me your opinion. What happens to a resolve when you put the barrel to your head and pull the trigger and the hammer clicks and nothing takes place? Do you accept the jibe, not having had the foresight to buy fresh powder or the intelligence to realize that powder kept for long in this damned Cornish atmosphere gets damp? Or is it the last humiliation to shirk another try?'

Dwight began to dry his hands. 'It's the only sensible course. But you didn't quite answer my question. Why suicide? If I may say so, you're young, propertied, respected, have a wife and son, safely got through serious illness, are under no cloud——'

'Stop,' said Francis, 'or I shall weep for joy.'

Dwight half turned, and out of the corner of his eye saw that the pistol now lay on the table again, a hand resting lightly on it. 'Well, if you were your cousin, I might see a greater reason for all this. He has lost his only child, is likely to have some sentence tomorrow, failed last year in an enterprise he put all his heart to . . .'

Francis got up, pushing the table aside with a squeak, stalked across the room. 'God damn you, be quiet. . .'

Dwight set down the towel. 'No doubt Ross still has his self-respect. Which you perhaps have lost. . . .'

Francis turned. At close quarters his face was streaky with dried sweat. 'What makes you feel that?'

The pistol was a long way away. Dwight felt a little more confident of being able to deal with this situation. Francis looked ill as well as angry.

'I think there must be a loss of self-respect before suicide can be even thought of.'

'You do, eh?'

'Yes, I do.'

Francis made the facial movements of a laughter which was more bitter for its silence. 'There are times when it may be the only means of restoring one's self-respect. Can you conceive that, or is it outside your scope?'

'It's not outside my scope to imagine such a situation. But I'm not able to imagine why you should feel yourself in it.'

'Let's see, what were those gracious words you used: young, propertied, respected? But young by what standards? And propertied, did you say? The question is, who owns property in these bankrupt days? Usually some upstart sneering moneylender with a smooth voice and the ethical code of a cuttlefish. . . . And respect?' Francis said the word savagely. 'Respected by whom? We are back at the same old gate, respect of oneself, which is the impasse. Drink loosens the disillusion but sharpens the paradox. A pistol ball has no morning after.'

Dwight went across and lit another couple of candles on the mantelpiece. The shadows at the end of the room lifted, showing the faded flock paper, the dusty antlers of the stag. The light was like a creeping sanity, moving over the dark places of the mind. 'A pistol ball is very – dramatic,' he said slowly.

'Sudden solutions usually are. You ought to know that – in your profession. But you can't rule them out because they offend your sense of propriety.'

'Oh, I don't. All the same, I prefer things on a more homely level. Let's have a drink and talk it over. What's the hurry? We've all night before us.'

'Dear God . . .' Francis let out a slow breath and turned away. 'My tongue's like burnt paper. . . .'

In the street outside someone was laughing inanely. Dwight went to the cupboard.

'I've brandy here. We can sample that.' He heard Francis folding the papers and stuffing them into a pocket. When he turned Francis had picked up the pistol again, but was taking out the bullet. Half done, he hesitated and the glitter came back into his eyes.

'Drink this,' said Dwight quickly. 'Cheap gin will poison you and bring up all sorts of unhealthy thoughts.'

'The thoughts were there without the gin.'

'Well, you can tell me about them if it pleases you. I don't mind.'

'Thank you, but I'll keep my sorrows to myself.' He accepted the glass and looked at it. 'Well, here's to the devil. I don't know whose side he has been on tonight.'

Dwight drank without comment. The emotional storm was blowing itself out. Chance had prevented Francis from making his gesture. In exhaustion he would now wish to talk of anything but tonight's motives. But that was just why it was important that he should do so. Only by getting him to talk it out of himself could one make reasonably sure that the crisis should not happen again.

Chapter ten

BEFORE THE REFORMATION the Franciscans had been a power in the town, owning much of the property at its heart; and although the monks no longer walked the streets in their grey habits or cared for the sick and poor, the property remained as their monument, turned to secular use but unmistakably ecclesiastical in design. Of such was the Refectory of the Grey Friars, where the assizes were held.

Its Great Hall, a hundred and fifty-odd feet long and sixty in height, with its east window of stained glass, was an impressive chamber; but it bore its age – a matter of five hundred years – with increasing uncertainty, and there were other drawbacks to its use as a court of justice.

The weather turned from warm to sultry overnight, and when dawn broke a thick mist had fallen over the town. It did not clear much as the sun gained power, and when the judges walked across from their lodgings in their wigs and ermine the fog drifted about them like wet smoke.

Demelza had had a terrible night, dozing to find nightmares round every corner and starting into a wakeful reality which was no escape. She felt that she had failed utterly last evening, that the outcome of all her efforts had been a futile conversation without issue and without point, that she had failed Ross in every way.

It was not until last night that she had realized how much she had been privately and foolishly building on her own efforts; all these weeks of waiting she had fed on the hope of being able to give crucial help. Yet it was some native good sense which had prevented her from pressing her overtures with the judge when they at last met. She bitterly blamed herself now for not casting herself and her story on his mercy; but if she had been confronted with the opportunity again she would have done just the same. Ill judgment might have conceived the meeting, but good judgment had saved it from the worst disaster.

Verity had been nearly as upset as she when she returned. Francis had called, in a strange drunken mood, and had departed in a stranger which left her in a state of increasing anxiety. Worried almost equally for both the Poldarks, she too had hardly slept, and when she saw Francis ahead of her going into the assize courts she felt sudden relief, as if she had not expected to see him safe and well today. But the other care remained, and when she got inside, the anxiety was doubled by what she saw of the earlier cases that came on.

Places had been saved for them near the front of the hall, which was already crowded when they took their seats. Guards and turnkeys, jurors and witnesses, barristers and notaries filled the front of the hall, and behind were the public places. The few front rows here had been saved for people of note, and many who were in town for the elections had come to see the fun. Verity saw Unwin Trevaunance with a red-haired girl, and Sir Hugh Bodrugan and several ladies and gentlemen of quality with fans and snuffboxes. In a corner by himself, holding a long malacca stick, was George Warleggan. Behind these rows were the rabble.

The hall, though high, was ill ventilated and stuffy, and one could tell that it would soon grow hot with the press. There were men at the door and inside selling hot pasties and chestnuts and lemonade, but they were driven out just before ten o'clock. Then the clerk of the court rapped with his hammer and everyone stood up, and the Hon. Mr Justice Lister, connoisseur of church music, came in, bowed solemnly to the court, and sat down with the sheriffs and aldermen. He pulled the great bunch of aromatic herbs nearer to him and put a vinegar-soaked handkerchief on the top of his papers. Another heavy day was begun.

The first case was soon disposed of. Demelza could not follow the matter at all. The counsel speaking had such a plummy voice that she only caught one word in three, but she gathered it was something to do with what were called the prisoner's recognisances. These being discharged, the man was marched out of the dock again. Then there was a hum of interest as three men and two women were ushered in together. One of the men was Ross Poldark. His dark coppery hair was well combed, the scar, as always at times of stress, noticeable on his cheek. He looked paler from his week's imprisonment. She remembered Jim Carter's fate.

They were swearing in a jury, but she heard nothing of it. She was thinking of Ross as she had seen him for the first time, that day years ago at Redruth Fair. To her it seemed a century – yet though she had grown older, changed beyond recognition or imagining, he had become curiously younger to her while remaining in essence the same. He was a man of moods, yet he was her constant, something unchanging, infinitely reliable, the pivot of her life. There could never be anyone else. Without him she would not be more than half alive.

Mr Justice Lister looked hollow-eyed and inhuman this morning, capable of any enormity. The jury were sworn in and there were no objections. Now, to Demelza's surprise, all but one of the prisoners were led out again, Ross among them. The trial of the Crown versus Boynton, F.R., for larceny had begun.

She didn't listen to it. It passed over her head in a sickly haze which would be remembered more vividly than it was experienced. Only some time later she heard the jury find the prisoner guilty of stealing a pair of knit-thread lady's stockings, value two shillings and sixpence, and a packet containing half a thousand pins, value sixpence, from a haberdasher's shop. She heard Mr Justice Lister take into account that this was a first offence and sentence him to be burnt in the hand and discharged. Hardly had he been led away than the two women came in and the next case was on. She realized with a dreadful sinking apprehension that Ross was next.

The two women were vagrants. They had been caught flagrantly begging. They had no visible means of support. It was a plain case and the jury speedily found them guilty. But this was a crime on which the Hon. Mr Justice Lister felt rather strongly and he delivered a long and damning homily on the evils of such a life. Looking at him, Demelza realized there was no mercy here. His diction was beautiful, his phrases as elegantly rounded as if they had been written out the night before. But the substance was to condemn. Abruptly, without any raising of the voice or change of expression, he sentenced the two women to be whipped and the case was over.

At this there was a good deal of stirring in the court, for some of the men wanted to push their way out to see the women stripped and flogged in the church square, and others were as anxious to take the vacant places; so it was in the midst of this confusion that Ross was led in. This time as he passed to the dock he glanced a moment aside and his eyes caught Demelza. A faint encouraging smile flickered across his face and was gone.

'Quiet,' said Verity. 'Quiet, my dear. We must try to keep calm.' She put her arm round Demelza and held her tight.

It was clear now that this was the important case of the day. More barristers-at-law came in, and the bench on which they sat was full. Demelza tried to see some change in the judge's expression, some flicker of interest, but there was none. He might never have met Mrs Ross Poldark the night before. Mr Jeffery Clymer sat just below the dock, where he could maintain contact with his client. Henry Bull, K.C., leading counsel for the Crown, had left the preceding cases to his junior, but this one he was handling himself. A dark man and handsome in a coarse way, with skin so olive and eyes so amber brown as to suggest a touch of the tar brush. It had been to his disadvantage all his life; he had had to struggle hard against the whispering voices of his colleagues and rivals – and the struggle had left its mark.

The clerk of arraigns began proceedings by saying:

'Ross Vennor Poldark, hold up thy hand. Gentlemen of the jury, look upon the prisoner. He stands indicted by the name of Ross Vennor Poldark, of Nampara, of the County of Cornwall, Esquire, who, on the seventh of January in the year of our Lord seventeen hundred and ninety, not having the fear of God before his eyes but being moved and seduced by the instigation of the devil, did incite divers peaceable citizens to riot, and

furthermore did commit riot contrary to the laws of the land. And
furthermore that the said Ross Vennor Poldark feloniously, wilfully and
with malice aforethought, with force and arms, did plunder, steal, destroy
and take away divers goods belonging to two ships in distress. And
furthermore . . .'

The voice went on, it seemed to Demelza for hours, saying the same
things over and over again in different words. She felt really faint now, but
tried to hide it. Eventually the voice stopped. Then Ross said: 'Not guilty,'
and the clerk said: 'Culprit, how will thou be tried?' and Ross said: 'By God
and my country.' Then the dark foreign man got up and began to say it all
over again.

But here was a difference. The clerk had droned his words – legal
phrases dry and brittle as seed husks which didn't seem to have any life in
them. Mr Henry Bull, K.C., breathed on them and brought them to life
with a vengeance. He was telling a simple story to the jury – no official stuff
in this – just a simple story which anyone could follow.

It seemed that in the great gale of January last, which they would all no
doubt remember, a ship – a Cornish-owned ship, mark you – got into
distress and was driven ashore on Hendrawna Beach, just below the house
of the prisoner, a man comfortably circumstanced, a mine owner and a
landowner with an ancient name. The jury might have expected that such a
man's first thought – he being the first to see the ship – would have been
for the safety of those on board. Instead, as evidence would be brought to
prove, his only concern had been to rouse the lawless spirits of the
neighbourhood in great numbers, so that when the wreck came in it should
be plundered with the utmost despatch. And that it was plundered, in a
matter of a few hours, and without a thought for the safety of the crew or
any attempt to help them ashore, witnesses would be called to show. The
man who stood in the dock had personally swum out to the wreck before
anyone else and personally directed operations for the dismemberment of
the ship. At this time there had been one passenger still left on board. No
one knew whether prompt help could have saved him. It was only known
that no such help was given and that the man lost his life.

Counsel further suggested that the prisoner had had watchers posted all
along the cliffs keeping a lookout for further prey, for when yet another
ship, the *Pride of Madras*, was driven ashore a few hours later, all the
dissident and lawless sweepings from five parishes were waiting to welcome
her in – and it was doubtful if, even supposing the crew could have got her
off again with the flood tide, she could not have been held ashore by sheer
weight of numbers. All this at the instigation of the prisoner, who must
bear the perfidy of the acts of his followers. Some of the crew of this ship
had been severely beaten as they struggled ashore and robbed even of their
clothes. They had been left insensible and naked in the freezing cold, and
it was virtually certain that among those who lost their lives there were

several who should be alive today had they received the Christian treatment
any distressed sailor was entitled to expect. Their ship had been torn to
pieces in a single tide. The ship's master, Captain A. V. Clark, would be
called to testify that he had not been so barbarously used when cast ashore
among the savages of Patagonia two years earlier.

Even this was not all – by no means the worst of it – and Henry Bull
wagged a long brown forefinger. When His Majesty's excise men,
supported by a small contingent of dismounted dragoons, had come upon
the scene the prisoner had come before them and warned them not to
interfere, at peril of their lives – had threatened them in the most direct
and offensive manner. When they disregarded this and went down upon
the beach they were set upon by the prisoner and others, and a serious fight
had developed and one of the excise men, John Coppard, had received
very serious injuries. There were, in fact, two deaths on the beach that
night among the rioters, and many injured. Reliable witnesses put the
numbers of the wreckers at two thousand.

The voice went on, welling sometimes in Demelza's ears, at others
growing faint and far away. Indiscriminately it piled up the calumny, the
truth, the lies and the half-truths, until she felt she must scream. It was
very hot in the hall; the windows were steaming up and the walls running
with moisture. She wished now she had never come – anything better than
listening to this. She tried to stop her ears, but that was no use. If the worst
was to be heard she had to listen.

At last Bull came to the close of his speech. It was not within his present
scope to call the jury's attention, he said, to the previous acts of
lawlessness which had disfigured the prisoner's character. But . . .

Here Mr Jeffery Clymer, who had been drawing circles and squares with
his pen, leapt to his feet and vehemently protested – a protest which was
upheld by the judge, and Mr Bull was forced to withdraw. This he did
willingly, having planted what he wanted in the jury's mind. It was not
permissible to say *anything* about the prisoner's previous character, he went
on; *but* – and here was the big but – it was admissible and very relevant to
draw deductions from certain statements prisoner had made to the
examining justice – statements which attempted to *justify* his actions,
statements which branded him as an obvious Jacobin and an admirer of the
bloodshed and tyranny across the water. Such men, Bull went on to imply,
were doubly dangerous at times like these. Each member of the jury must
be possessed of some property. If he wished to keep that property intact,
men like the prisoner must be made an example of. The flame of sedition
and unrest must be stamped upon at its very outset. A sometime soldier and
gentleman had a special responsibility. For him to side with the rogues and
riffraff of the towns, encouraging them and instructing them in acts of
violence they would not by themselves have the wit or intelligence to
conceive, was an outrage on society. Such a man deserved to be put away.

Hanging was barely good enough. Justice must be done, and he demanded no less than justice.

When he sat down there was a visible stirring in the court; and then after a minute junior counsel for the Crown got up and added a further speech of his own, it being the custom in serious cases to allow two speeches for the prosecution and none for the defence. At last it was over and the first witness was called. This was Nicholas Vigus.

He came into the courtroom blinking, hesitating, a cherub surprised in some nefarious practice. In an age when wigs were so much worn, the smooth fresh tight skin of his head seemed in faintly indecent contrast with the pockmarks in his face. In his thin sly voice, growing more confident as he went on, he testified that on the morning in question he had been wakened soon after dawn by the prisoner thunderously knocking on the next-door cottage and calling 'Zacky! Zacky! Good pickings for all! There's a wreck coming ashore and we'll strip her to the last plank!' Later he deposed to seeing the prisoner on the shore leading operations and generally directing the crowds, also that the accused had been the first to swim to the ship and board her. Also he had directed operations against the second ship and been generally active all through the day. Witness had seen accused go up to excise officers when they arrived and have high words with them but had not been near enough to hear what passed. Later he had gone away and not been present at the fight. That concluded his evidence. Everyone looked at Ross.

Ross cleared his throat. The beginning for him; till now he had been unable to disrelate himself from a spectator's part, critical, unstirred, noting the colour of Mr Henry Bull's fingernails more than his invective, judging the ages and occupations of the jury without much thought to the fact that they were judging him. Now he must stir himself to fight, must feel this thing personally and passionately if he was to survive. The conflict between Clymer's advice and his own inclinations was still unresolved. But sight of Demelza had made him feel that he must fight.

'Was there a very strong gale blowing that morning, Nick?'

Vigus blinked slyly at Ross, the confidence ebbing again. ''S, I reckon.'

'It's true, isn't it, that the Martin cottage is not next door to yours but next but one.'

''S, I reckon. Daniel's is between.'

'You must have had good hearing to have been sure of what I said so far away.'

'Oh, tisn't so far away. I 'eard what you said sure 'nough.'

'Have you always resented it that I didn't wake *you*?'

There was a little cackle of laughter at the back of the court.

'Made no diff'rence to me,' said Vigus sullenly. 'I wasn't consarned with a wreck.'

'But you were on the beach all through the day?'

'Off and on, like. I went down to see what was to do.'

'Did you not play any part in salvaging things that were being washed ashore?'

'No. I aren't one of those sort.'

'Not ever?'

'No.'

'D'you mean you live near the beach and yet never pick up things that are washed ashore from wrecks?'

'Oh . . . sometimes. But not this time. Not when tis a proper wreck with men drowning, and the like.'

'Did you help the men who were drowning?'

'No-o.'

'Why not?'

'I didn't happen to see any.'

'Did you see me swim out to the first wreck?'

'. . . Yes.'

'Didn't I carry a line with me?'

'Mebbe. I don't recall.'

'What does that suggest?'

'Don't know. It don't suggest nothing to me.'

Ross glanced at Mr Clymer, who instantly shook his wigged head. Nick Vigus was allowed to go. Three more witnesses were brought in to testify to certain aspects of the story and to confirm what Nick Vigus said. Then the usher spoke again.

'Call Jud Paynter.'

Demelza stared at their onetime servant as he sidled slowly to the witness box, walking rather as if he hoped he wouldn't be noticed getting there. It was quite unbelievable to her that he should be in this company – prepared to testify against Ross, barefaced, in a court of law. Verity put a restraining hand on her arm again as she seemed about to stand up. Jud mumbled through the oath, then looked round for somewhere to spit, but thought better of it and glanced at Mr Henry Bull who was waiting for him.

'Your name is Jud Paynter and you live with your wife in Grambler village?'

'Ais.'

'Tell us what happened on the morning of the seventh January last.'

'Well . . .' Jud cleared his throat. 'Me and the old woman was asleep – that's Prudie, see . . .'

'You mean your wife?'

'Well . . . yes, sur, in a manner o' speaking . . .' Jud smiled apologetically. 'Prudie and me was asleep when along come Cap'n Ross makin' a rare to-do, and afore I can spring up and unclitch the door 'e bursts it off its hapses and rushes in and says there's a ship ashore down to Hendrawna Beach. "Do ee bestir yourself good an' fine," he says. We was always the best of friends, Cap'n Ross and me. Many's the time when 'e was a little tacker no biggerer'n pot high——'

'Yes, yes. Keep to the point. What then?'

Jud's bloodshot eyes roamed round the court, carefully avoiding contact with all comers.

'Yes, what then?'

'Then he says to me he says, "Do ee go run and roust all the men ye can – for like as not thur's women and childer on the ship, he says, 'and they must be saved from a watery grave. . . ." '

There was a moment's irritable consultation between the law officers.

'Come, my man, recollect yourself,' said Henry Bull. 'Think again.'

Jud stared up at the Gothic roof for inspiration. Then he licked his gums.

'Well?'

'Well, that's what 'e said, sur. Sure 'nough.'

'And I tell you to think again. What you say is not in accordance with your sworn statement.'

'What?'

'You did not say this when giving testimony before the Crown's attorney and his clerk.'

'Eh?'

'Tell us what you originally said.'

'That's what I said: no more'n no less.'

'Nonsense, man. Have I your lordship's permission? What you said was – let me read it to you – "When Captain Poldark came to my hut he told me to hurry down and rouse my friends because there was a wreck, and the sooner it was stripped the better, before the preventive men turned up." That was what you said.'

Jud squeezed up his face for a second, and then let it set into a look of hurt reproach.

'Nay, *nay*, sur, I never heard such words out of me mouth! Yer worship, I never thought upon no such thing. Tedn fair, tedn just, tedn *right*.'

'This statement, I would remind you, Paynter, was made before witnesses and signed with your mark. It was read over to you before you signed.'

'Well, I'm 'ard of hearing,' said Jud, staring barefaced at the counsel. 'Tes more'n likely they mistook what I did say an' I mistook what they did say. Tes more'n likely, that's for certain.'

Mr Bull angrily swung his gown behind him and bent over his brief. He proceeded to lead Jud through the story of the day, but very soon there was another disagreement and another angry argument. Upon it came Mr Justice Lister's cold quiet voice.

'Do you know, witness, what the punishment is for perjury?',

'Perjury?' said Jud. 'I ain't never done nothing like it, yer worship. I can't even write me own nàme, leave alone other folk's. And I was never near the wrecks but once and then twas to lend a 'elping 'and wi' the folk struggling in the waves. Nobody'd do less'n lend a 'elping 'and.'

The judge gazed at Paynter for a long steady moment, then said: 'I don't think this witness is going to assist your case, Mr Bull.'

Mr Clymer got up in a very fatigued manner. 'May I draw your lordship's attention to the fact that in the first instance, when called before an examining justice, Paynter gave no such evidence as he is alleged to have done at a later date. He seems to have denied knowledge of the events we are dealing with.'

There was some angry argument and rustling of papers. But Henry Bull was not giving up. 'There is some very important evidence at a later stage, your lordship. If I might put that to the witness . . .'

'Very well.'

'Now, Paynter,' said Bull, fixing him with an eye, 'turn your mind to the events on the night of the seventh. You were present when the excise men and the soldiers came upon the beach. In your statement you say that the prisoner, Captain Poldark, was the leader of the men who attacked the excise officers and that you saw him strike John Coppard, who fell to the ground seriously injured. That is a true statement, is it not? Remember his lordship's warning: you are on oath. You can be sent to prison yourself!'

Jud sucked his two teeth and hesitated. 'Nay!' he said suddenly, almost under his breath. 'I don't know nothin' 'bout'n.'

'What? What's that?' said the judge.

''Tes all a new story to me, your worship. I never heard such words out o' me mouth. Tedn true. Tedn nothin'!'

Henry Bull took a deep breath. He turned sharply to the judge. 'My lord, I ask your permission to call Mr Tankard and Mr Blencowe.'

Mr Justice Lister moved the aromatic herbs before his nose.

'I would remind you, Mr Bull, of the case of Nairn and Ogilvie – which cannot be unfamiliar to you – when the court remained in session without a break for forty-three hours. I do not intend that to happen here – and you have a lot of witnesses yet to call.'

Bull flapped his gown irritably. 'M'lord, this is a matter of the gravest importance. This man has just made a very serious charge against two junior officers of the Crown. It seems to me vital——'

'I should have thought, Mr Bull,' said his lordship wearily, 'that the situation was plain to the meanest intelligence. This witness has clearly committed perjury at some period of the proceedings. Whether he committed it at an earlier stage or is committing it now is not surely of great importance to your case, since the evidence of a perjured witness can hardly bear much weight. Whether the Crown wishes to charge him on that account is a matter for the appropriate officers to decide. I should certainly not oppose it. But it must also be perfectly clear that this man is of such low intelligence and limited mental capacity that it would in any case be difficult to draw a distinction between wilful and natural stupidity. If you will accept my advice you will turn him out of the box and get on with your case.'

'Of course it is as your lordship pleases,' said Bull sulkily, and Jud was ushered unceremoniously from the court.

Chapter eleven

WHILE THE NEXT witnesses were making their procession to and from the box Verity watched the jury. They were decently dressed, sober-looking men, mostly of middle age: small gentry and tradesmen. In Cornwall as a whole there would be a certain lack of condemnation for the things Ross had done or was accused of doing. Wrecks were looked on as legitimate spoil. Excise men were the most hated and despised of people. But Henry Bull had been cunning in his final appeal. Among propertied people there was now an almost universal dread of a miners' insurrection. Jacobin clubs which had opened in England to lend the French revolutionaries support, the wild scenes in Redruth last autumn, the recurring bread riots, and the seething discontent of which they were a symptom, all tended to a feeling of horrid insecurity. One saved one's twenty pounds a year, one built a new linhay or bought a new farm cart with a sense of uncertainty about the future. It was very unsettling, and if a riot such as this they were hearing about was allowed to pass without heavy punishment for the ring-leader . . .

Captain Clark was in the box, and described the scenes on the beach that night as a Dante's Inferno, with great bonfires blazing, hundreds of drunken men and women capering and fighting, mules laden to breaking point with spoils from his ship, assaults upon his poor shipwrecked crew, how he and two other men stood guard over the passengers with knives and a drawn sword to save them from being torn to pieces.

When it was done there was an unaccustomed silence in the court. The sailor had brought the scene vividly to life, and it seemed that the people in the court were picturing it, some of them shocked that their countryfolk should have gone so far. Eventually Ross said: 'Captain Clark, do you recall my coming to you on the beach and offering you and your crew shelter for the night in my house?'

Clark said: 'I do indeed, sir. It was the first act of common charity shown us on that dreadful night.'

'Did you avail yourself of it?'

'Yes, most certainly. Nineteen of us in all spent the night in your home.'

'You were well treated there?'

'Most kindly treated.'

'Did you, while you were on the beach, hear me or see me encouraging anyone to wreck your ship?'

'No, sir. . . . I may say it was dark except for the bonfires. But I hadn't set eyes on you until you came forward and offered us shelter.'

'Thank you.' Ross leaned over and had a whispered consultation with Mr Clymer. 'Captain Clark, did you see the meeting between myself and the sergeant of dragoons?'

'Yes.'

'Was there any quarrel between us?'

'As far as I remember, you warned him not to go down to the beach and he accepted your warning.'

'Would you consider it a friendly warning that I offered, meant to avoid bloodshed?'

'It could have been. Yes, I think it's fair to say so.'

'There was no fight between us?'

'Not when I was there, certainly not.'

'Did I accompany you into the house?'

'You did.'

'Thank you.'

'One moment, Captain,' said Henry Bull, whisking up as the sailor was about to leave the box. 'How long did the accused stay with you when you entered the house?'

'Oh, about ten minutes.'

'And when did you see him next?'

'About an hour later.'

'Were there any excise men in the party when you met the troopers?'

'Not that I saw or noticed.'

'There was nothing, so far as you know, to prevent the accused leaving the house again as soon as you were settled, and having a further argument with the soldiers?'

'No sir.'

'Thank you. Call Captain Ephraim Trevail.'

A short thin man came to the stand, and stated that he had witnessed the fight between the excise men and the soldiers, and verified that he had seen Ross as the ringleader and identified him as the man who had struck John Coppard down. So far as Ross knew he had never seen him before, but he could not shake his evidence. Mr Jeffery Clymer passed up a note telling him not to press a hostile witness. Then Eli Clemmow was called and told exactly the same story. It was more than three years since Ross had seen this man. He felt his anger rise.

When it was his turn to speak he said: 'Where do you live, Clemmow?'

The man's lips slipped back to expose his prominent teeth. They were like a special malice which had been kept hidden until now. 'Truro.'

'How was it that you were at Hendrawna, nine miles away, when the wreck came in?'

'I wasn't. I 'eard tell about the first wreck and walked over to see the fun.'

'At one time you lived on my land, didn't you?'

'S'right.'

'But I turned you off, d'you remember, because you were a constant worry and disturbance to the neighbourhood.'

'You mean you turned *brother* out of house and home – for doin' nothing 't all!'

'You hate me for it, don't you?'

Eli checked. 'Nay . . . nay. I care naught for ee.'

Mr Clymer passed Ross a note which read: 'Can you shake him as to detail?'

Ross said slowly: 'Tell me, Clemmow, which of the two wrecks came in closest to my house?'

The lips sucked but there was no reply. After a time Ross said: 'Did you hear my question?'

''Twas dark when I got there.'

'Which was the bigger of the two ships?'

After a long pause: '*Pride o' Madras*.'

'How many masts had she?'

'. . . two or three.'

'How did you know which she was?'

'I –'eard tell.'

'Was the bigger one nearest my house or farthest away?'

Another pause.

Ross said: 'I suppose you saw the bonfire on Damsel Point?'

'. . . Yes.'

'There was *no* bonfire on Damsel Point or near it. You were never on Hendrawna Beach that night, were you? You never left Truro.'

'Yes, I were! You're only tryin' to trick me!' Eli Clemmow's face was white and tight. He went on to explain; but Mr Henry Bull, rising again, cut him short.

'Have you ever been to sea, Mr Clemmow?'

'Well – er – no, not so's you could say "to sea". But——'

'So that if there were two shipwrecks on a beach in the dark, some distance from each other, you might find it hard, having no expert knowledge, to say which was the larger?'

'Yes, that's true 'nough!'

'Much harder, no doubt, than if you had helped actively to wreck the ships and assault the crews?'

Eli nodded gratefully.

'Did you notice where the bonfires were particularly?'

'No. They was about – just 'ere and thur.'

'How far were you from the struggle which developed between the prisoner and the excise men?'

'Which it is *alleged* developed,' said Mr Jeffery Clymer, getting up and sitting down again all in one movement.

'Which it is alleged developed?'

'Oh . . . close as you are to me.'

'And the story you have told on oath – that is a true eyewitness account of what took place?'

'Yes, true as I'm standing here!'

Demelza's faintness kept coming in waves. It would lean over her and then at the last moment move away again, leaving her shaken and sick. The excise man, Coppard, had been called, had confirmed the general story, but, to give him credit, had been vague as to whether he had been attacked by the accused or even whether the accused man had been there at all. The sergeant of dragoons had come and gone. The afternoon was half spent, and so far there had been no break for refreshments. Two street sellers had got in through the half-closed doors and were doing brisk if illicit business in the back rows. The heat and the smell were stifling.

The last witness for the prosecution was Hick, the justice who had taken all the depositions, including Ross's own. Some difficulty had arisen on the Truro bench when it became known that the law expected them to proceed with this case. Some of the magistrates were so favourably disposed towards the accused man that it would have been plainly unfair for them to have taken charge. Others, such as the Rev Dr Halse, were equally prejudiced against him. In the end the nonentity, Ephraim Hick, had been chosen to preside. Hick's main interest was the brandy bottle – but the depositions had come through with a fair enough degree of impartiality.

Hick now had to put in this testimony and this testimony was dangerous in the extreme.

From the answers the prisoner had made at his interrogation it appeared that he fully admitted the charge of having roused the neighbourhood when the first wreck came in. To the question, 'What purpose had you in mind?' he had answered, 'There were families in the district who were starving.' Question, 'Did you lead these people to the wreck?' Answer, 'They needed no leading. They knew the district as well as I did.' Question, 'Did you incite them to attack the crew of the *Queen Charlotte*?' Answer, 'None of the crew of the *Queen Charlotte* was attacked.' 'Were you the first to board her, and, if so, what was your purpose in so doing?' 'My purpose was to see what cargo she carried.' 'Was any of the crew left on board when you reached her?' 'No, only one passenger, and he was dead.' 'Was he dead when you reached the ship?' 'Of course. Are you accusing me of murdering him?' 'Did you help your friends to board the ship by means of a line?' 'Yes.' 'Did you make any effort to get the body of the dead man ashore?' 'None whatever.' 'Did you help to wreck the ship and carry away its cargo?' 'No.' 'Were you present while this was being done?' 'Yes.' 'Did you make any attempt to stop it?' 'None at all. I am not a magistrate.' 'But you were the only gentleman present, the only person with sufficient authority to stop this plundering in its early stages?' 'You exaggerate my influence.'

Later on the interrogation went on: 'Were you among the first persons to see the second shipwreck?' 'I believe so.' 'Did you encourage your friends to attack the crew of the *Pride of Madras?*' 'Certainly not.' 'Did you stand by and let them be assaulted without protest?' 'They were not assaulted by any men known to me. By this time great numbers of miners were on the beach from farther afield.' 'That doesn't answer my question.' 'It is all the answer I can give you. I was not able to be in every place at the same time.' 'But you went aboard the *Pride of Madras?*' 'I did.' 'Long before offering the shipwrecked sailors any help?' 'Some time before.' 'Did you approve of this riot which had started?' 'I did not consider it a riot.' 'Do you approve of it now?' 'Do you approve of whole families being without enough food to keep them alive?'

At the end the accused had denied all knowledge of the attack upon the soldiers and excise men.

This concluded the Crown's case.

There were only five witnesses for the defence. First were John and Jane Gimlett, who were called to testify that the prisoner had not left the house again after entering it with the shipwrecked crew. The first hour, while they were serving hot drinks to the castaways, he had spent by the bedside of his sleeping wife, who was seriously ill. Henry Bull did much to intimidate them but nothing at all to shake them. If the prisoner had left the house again it could not have been until very much later – until well after the time of the assault. Then came Zacky Martin and 'Whitehead' Scoble, who testified to Ross's seemly behaviour at an earlier stage. Last witness was Dwight Enys.

He did not know how the case had gone up to this time. The sun was out now, and beat down through the tall windows. Among the spectators he caught sight of a vivid auburn head. So she was here as she had said.

It was a strange position to be confronted by Ross and asked to give his testimony. After speaking for a moment or two he turned more directly to the judge.

'My lord, I am the physician who attended on Captain Poldark's wife and child during their attack of malignant sore throat (*mobus strangulatorius*). During this attack I was very constantly in the house, and I know that Captain Poldark had had no sleep for almost a week. His only child died, and she was buried the day before the wreck. His wife was still dangerously ill. I attended him professionally the night before the wreck, and formed the opinion that he was on the verge of a mental breakdown. That breakdown,

I consider, did take place – and any strangeness in his actions during the next two days is almost wholly to be attributed to that condition.'

There was silence. Everyone was listening intently now. Henry Bull glanced at Ross, whisked his gown and got up. This witness's testimony was dangerous to the prosecution's case.

'You are an apothecary, Dr Enys?'

'No. A physician.'

'I understand that is a distinction without a difference – at least in the provinces.'

'I don't know all the provinces. In fact there's a very great difference.'

'Cannot almost any man set himself up as a physician if he wants to?'

'He has no right to.'

'What right have you?'

'I am a licentiate of the London College of Physicians.'

Mr Bull stared out of the window. He had not expected that reply.

'You have travelled a long way to practise, Dr Enys.'

'I am a Cornishman by birth.'

'How old are you, may I ask?'

'Twenty-six.'

'And have you been qualified long?'

'Nearly three years.'

'Three years. . . . And under whom did you study in London?'

'I studied the theory and practice of physic under Dr Fordyce in Essex Street, midwifery under Dr Leake in Craven Street – and some surgery with Mr Percival Pott at St. Bartholomew's Hospital.'

'Oh, surgery too! Very interesting. And under whom did you study mental afflictions?'

'Under no one in particular. . . .'

'Then your views on the subject can hardly be expected to carry much weight, can they?'

Dwight stared at the King's attorney. 'You must know, sir, that no practical medical instruction is available on this subject. It is one of which knowledge can only be gained by clinical experience——'

'Which no doubt you must have had in great measure.'

'. . . I have had some experience. I couldn't say in great measure.'

'You'll have visited and studied at Bedlam, of course.'

'No, I have not.'

'Not? You haven't even been there?'

'No.'

'Indeed, then——'

'I'm not suggesting that Captain Poldark was *insane*. I am saying, that in my view he was temporarily – not himself, through grief and lack of sleep.'

'Would you excuse him on those grounds?'

'Certainly. Yes.'

'Do you think that everyone who loses a child in infancy is justified in creating a riot throughout three parishes with great loss of property and considerable loss of life?'

'I do not believe that Captain Poldark created the riot. But if he acted strangely in certain ways I believe he did so because of a temporary unsettlement of his reason. He's not a man normally given to lawless acts.'

'That is a matter which will come out after the verdict,' said Bull silkily. 'At present I suggest you do not bring his character into it.'

'I can only give you my opinion as his physician.'

'We have already heard that. Thank you, Dr Enys.'

Dwight hesitated. 'It is an opinion I would stake my reputation on.'

'We do not know what your reputation is, Dr Enys. But thank you just the same.'

'One moment.' It was the Hon. Mr Justice Lister. Dwight stopped. 'You say you formed this opinion of the prisoner the night before. On what did you base your opinion?'

'On . . . on his general behaviour, my lord. He was not entirely coherent in his remarks. When his daughter died a great many people came for the funeral. All classes came, from the highest to the lowest. He's held in very great respect, you see. But because his wife was ill, it was impossible to give them any sort of refreshment – as is customary, my lord, at funerals in Cornwall. The fact weighed heavy on Captain Poldark's mind. He went on and on repeating his regret that he hadn't been able to feed them. He wasn't drunk – he drank very little at that time. It was, in my view, solely a mental condition.'

'Thank you,' said the judge, and Dwight left the stand.

There was another stirring in the court. People got up and stretched their legs and spat and rustled papers. But no one moved to go out, and those pressing to enter were unable to. It was the prisoner's last chance now, to sway the court and the jury if he might by his eloquence – or, if that were lacking, as it usually was, to read the defence he had prepared with the help of his counsel and trust that that would serve.

Chapter twelve

It was now or never. His own defence, stating what he had felt and done, briefly and bluntly. . . . Or Clymer's mock humility, denying everything, even putting new interpretations on what he'd said in the magistrate's court. . . . Or a compromise, using the more temperate part of his own and the less disingenuous of Clymer's. If he attempted that he would stumble and falter.

They were waiting. . . .

'My lord,' Ross said, 'this case has taken much of your time already. I'll try to take as little more as may be necessary to ask your clemency – and the jury's understanding. The worst that can be said of me has been said by the counsel for the Crown. Witnesses have been called in support of his case, and I have called witnesses to disprove it – or certain parts of it. The best that can be said of me has been said by them. You have heard both sides and can form your own conclusions.

'It's true that on January the seventh last there were two wrecks upon Hendrawna Beach, just below my house, that my servant informed me of the first one when it was just coming light, and that I took a horse and told several people of the neighbourhood. If you ask me my motive, I cannot remember. At least, I did it, and in due course a great number of people came upon the beach and the ships were stripped bare. I was there most of the day – but although my house was afterwards searched no goods from the ships were found there. In fact I took none. Rather strange, don't you think, for the ringleader of a lawless mob to take none of the spoils for himself?

'Now as to this lawless mob. In his speech the counsel spoke of there being more than two thousand people on the beach. That is true. But later be spoke of these people as being the – if I remember rightly – the dissident and lawless sweepings of five parishes. I wondered if he knows how sparsely the countryside is populated in this district. The whole population of five parishes would not be above six thousand, including women and children. Does he suggest that every able-bodied man in those parishes is a dissident and lawless scoundrel? I don't feel that, as reasonable people, you will agree with such an estimate.'

Ross turned back to the judge, warming a little to his theme because for the moment it was not so directly concerning himself.

'No, my lord, of the two thousand on the beach not fifty came with any intent to break the law, not ten but would be loyal and faithful subjects of the King when given chance to be so. All the rest came – as people will come whatever their class – to witness a sensational happening, whether it is a fire, or a wreck – or an assize – or an execution. They needed no invitation from me. They would have quickly been there without it. Perhaps half a hundred were there more quickly because of my summons. That was all. There is a mine on the cliffs almost overlooking the beach. When someone at the workings caught sight of the wreck – as they must have done soon – do you not think his action would have been the same as mine: to rouse his friends – without searching into his heart for this or that motive, but just to rouse his friends?'

As Ross paused to collect his thoughts, someone sniggered loudly at the back of the court. He knew at once who it was. Eli Clemmow had done just the same thing three years ago at the petty sessions when Ross had been speaking on Jim Carter's behalf. Then it had had the effect of breaking the continuity of his reasoning and diverting the attention of the justices. It must not happen that way again.

'Gentlemen of the jury,' he said, 'as to what happened when those people got on the beach and saw the ships wrecked, I must ask you to think for a moment of the traditions of our county. That attempts are made or have ever been made to lure ships upon the rocks by means of false lights is a calumny which has been spread only by the prejudiced or the ignorant. But that people search the beaches for flotsam and look upon the leavings of the tides as their own especial property is too commonly known to need emphasis. The law says such flotsam belongs to the Crown – or perhaps to this or that lord of the manor – but in fact when the stuff is of little value no attempt is made to reclaim it from the people who found it. In times of dire want these little pickings have often been the means of keeping people – honest decent people – alive. So a habit – a tradition is formed. What happens, then, when a whole ship comes in? People flood to the beach to see the wreck, and to help in the rescue work – there are two widows in my parish who would not be widows if their husbands had not tried to save shipwrecked sailors. But when the rescue work is done, are they to stand idly by and wait for the arrival of the excise men? The law says yes. The law, of course, is right. But when men have seen their children without a crust for their bellies or a rag for their backs, it's hard for them to reason as they should.'

He had got the attention of the court again.

'The counsel has suggested that these people are revolutionaries – that I am a revolutionary – branded with the desire to overthrow authority. I answer, quite simply, that nothing could be further from the truth. We are not. As for the assaults upon the crew of the second ship – this was a disgraceful episode which I will not attempt to excuse. But it was done by men in drink and by men from far afield who had come – certainly not at my invitation – when news of the first wreck had travelled to them.

'Finally, as to the attack on the excise men. No defence or excuse is needed because I was not there. I never saw the excise men. They never saw me. I warned the sergeant of dragoons not to go on the beach at that juncture because everyone was by then very excited, and I wished to avoid bloodshed. By the time these men arrived there was very little they could do.'

Ross looked through Clymer's notes again, but found nothing more he could, even in this new mood, bring himself to add.

'So that is all I have to say. I pray I am equal to whatever fortune is in store for me, and put myself upon the candour, the justice and the humanity of your lordship, and upon yours, my countrymen, gentlemen of the jury.'

He bowed and sat down in the back of the dock, and as he did so there was a little grumble of approval at the rear of the court.

Verity whispered: 'I don't think we could get out now if we wanted to. The doorway and benches are so crammed.'

'No. We must stay. I shall be all right.'

'Here, try these smelling salts again.'

'No, no. Listen.'

'There are three charges,' said the Hon. Mr Justice Lister coldly, 'on which this man stands before you. He is charged with riot, with wrecking and with assault upon an officer of the Crown. You have heard the evidence, and it is your duty to bring in a verdict in accordance with that evidence. You may find him guilty on all three charges – or on any one of them.

'Now as to the third charge – namely assaulting and injuring an excise officer – there is some conflict of evidence. Two witnesses have sworn to his being the man, two have given testimony that he could not possibly have been there. The excise officer himself is doubtful on the point of identity, and none of his colleagues has been called to assist the prosecution. It was a dark and windswept night and it is possible that there has been a confusion of identity. It is a matter for you to decide whether you prefer to accept the testimony of his two servants who swear that he never left the house again or the testimony of Trevail and Clemmow, who declare that they saw him strike the officer down. But where there is a reasonable element of doubt, let me remind you, it is an axiom of English law that an accused man should receive the benefit of it.'

To Demelza's fevered imagination it seemed that he glanced towards her as he spoke.

'As to the first two charges, these are very differently based. The prisoner admits that he summoned people to the wreck, but claims – appears to claim, that his aim was as much to succour the shipwrecked as to pillage the vessel, and that the riot inadvertently developed without his encouragement or desire. That, if I interpret him correctly, is his defence now – and it is the crux of the matter; yet certain of his statements and certain of his actions at the time lay themselves open to a different interpretation. If, for instance, he was *really* concerned to save the passengers and crews, why was he not more active in doing so? How was it that, between swimming out to the first ship and a belated offer of shelter to the people of the second ship – many hours later – he apparently made no efforts on their behalf? They did not see him. He says he did not see them. But he admits to being on the beach. What was he doing there all those hours?'

Mr Justice Lister was speaking without notes. In fact he had taken none during the trial.

'The prisoner's physician has been called to testify to Captain Poldark's distressed condition at the time of the wrecks – suggesting virtually that he was not responsible for his actions at the time. Whether you consider such testimony sufficiently weighty to be of vital importance is for you to decide. I would only point out that such a condition, if it ever did exist, can hardly have prevailed at the time of the justice's examination – which took place *six weeks later*. You have heard the statements made by the accused at that examination carefully read to you, and I have no doubt they are present in your minds. You will remember he was asked: "What purpose had you in leading your friends to the wreck?" To which his reply was: "There were people in the district who were starving." Later he was asked: "Did you approve of this riot which had started?" And he answered: "I did not consider it a riot." What then, you may wonder, did he consider it? Did he look upon it as a justifiable act of robbery and pillage?

'Now you may say, "But if the third charge is unproven, it is difficult to prove an illegal act against the prisoner in person on the other counts. Where is the testimony providing concrete evidence of his guilt? For instance, did anyone see him carry off one stick or stone from either of the ships?" The answer is, no. But in law, if you are satisfied that a riot took place, it is only necessary to be further satisfied that the prisoner was sufficiently involved in the affair as to be guilty as a principal. A common intent to commit a felony makes the act of one the act of all – and it is not necessary even to be present at the actual commission of the felony for a man to be held guilty. For instance a man could be out of sight of a murder, but if he was keeping watch for the murderers and cognisant of their intent he would be held guilty.'

The court was very silent now. Demelza's heart was going colder and colder.

'Further, in law, where several people join together to commit an act which is itself unlawful, and a worse crime comes from anything done in the prosecution of that unlawful design – then one and all are guilty of the worse crime, however abhorrent it may personally be to some of them, and however little they may have had intent to commit it. It remains therefore for you only to decide on the evidence you have heard: first, whether in fact the prisoner was upon the beach at the time of the wreck; second, whether he was there with others with the intent to strip the wreck; third, whether such a pillaging and riot and assault took place.'

His extraordinary memory had absorbed it all like a sponge: now at a squeeze it all came out again – sometimes seeming to be a little in the prisoner's favour, but mainly against him. One could not suspect Mr Justice Lister of any prejudice: he was not loading the scales but merely assessing their respective weights and finding one side heavier than the other. He was performing the duty for which he had received his commission from the King, and by reason of which he held his elevated position in society.

'The prisoner,' he ended, 'has attempted to find mitigating circum-stances for the crimes of riot and wrecking in the distress generally prevailing among poor people at this time. This is an irrelevance which you are in duty bound to ignore. He has devoted a part of his final plea to a defence of his own countryfolk, who are, in any case, not on trial at this assize at all. You may consider this a not unadmirable sentiment on his part, but you would be failing in your obligations to society if you allowed sympathy or a narrow emotional patriotism to influence you in any decision you deemed to be right. I will ask you now to discharge the duty which you have undertaken by your oaths, regardless of the consequences and regardless of everything except your desire to do justice between the Crown and the accused. Will you now consider your verdict.'

In the general buzz that broke out Verity saw the judge glance at the clock. It was almost four and there were several cases yet to come. The jury put their heads together, whispering self-consciously, aware of everyone's eyes upon them. Several times Verity had thought Demelza was going to faint, but thankfully she had seen her gain a greater control of herself this last ten minutes. It was as if the worst had already happened and now she was reacting against the blow.

'You may retire if you wish,' said the judge to the foreman.

The foreman nervously thanked him and again consulted with his fellows. Then he leaned over to the usher and the usher went to the judge. The clerk of the court rapped with the hammer and the judge stood up, bowed and went out. The jury had decided to retire.

It's all over, thought Ross, and so much better if I'd stuck to my guns and made the speech I wanted. Hedging at the last moment. Cowardice and compromising. Pretending to myself that it was for Demelza. My own weakness and cowardice and Clymer's damned overbearing manner. And it will avail absolutely nothing at all. Even if I had gone the whole hog and crawled on my belly the way he wanted. As it is, two stools. Not even the satisfaction of feeling that I told them exactly what I thought – about the trial, about the distress, about the wreck. Dirt in my mouth.

The judge with his thin sour face. A human machine for administering the law. If I go to prison I really shall come out a revolutionary – climb up and slit his throat one night as he snores in bed. Far safer to hang me.

And Demelza? Difficult to see her without turning one's head. Just see the colour of her skirt out of the corner of my eye, and her hands on her lap. They can't keep still, can they, darling? Perhaps I should have crawled, really crawled, for her sake. Mercy, mercy. The quality of mercy is not strained, it droppeth as the gentle rain from heaven upon the place beneath. What the devil are the jury arguing about? It must be perfectly plain to them, just as plain as to the judge, who practically directed them.

Surprise to see Verity here. Must write to her and ask her to look after Demelza. Should have thought of that before. Demelza will take advice from her. Perhaps it was as well Julia died: wouldn't have been nice to grow up knowing . . . But perhaps if she hadn't died none of this would have happened. Perhaps Dwight wasn't too far off the truth. Nonsense, I was in my right mind, sane as could be. Must write and thank him nevertheless. Sober young fellow. Pity he got in that mess.

Suppose I shall get a few minutes with Demelza when it's over. But what to say . . . Meetings like that are robbed of their sense by being so limited. What *were* the jury doing? Tis mightiest in the mightiest, it becomes the thronèd monarch better than his crown. His sceptre shows the force of temporal power. . . . Temporal power. The Hon. Mr Justice Lister. Temporal power . . . The jury were coming back.

It had only been ten minutes, but, as Zacky said at the back of the court, it seemed like a month. They filed slowly in, the twelve good men and true, looking as self-conscious as when they went out, and the foreman had a guilty look, as if he thought himself liable to be charged with a lesser felony and brought before the court for judgment. Everyone stood while Mr Justice Lister came back, and silence settled suddenly on the court as he sat down.

The clerk rose and said: 'Gentlemen of the jury, have you agreed upon a verdict?'

'We have,' said the foreman, swallowing nervously.

'Do you find the prisoner guilty or not guilty?'

'We find him . . .' The foreman stopped and started again. 'We find him not guilty upon all three charges.'

For a last moment the silence hung like a wave, and then broke. Someone at the back of the court started to cheer, and others took it up. It was answered almost at once by boos and cries of 'Shame!' Then it stopped, and a backwash in tiny rivulets of conversation lapped about the court. The clerk's gavel hammered them out of existence.

'If there is any further disturbance,' said his lordship, 'the courtroom will be cleared and proceedings taken against offenders.'

Ross remained where he was, not quite knowing whether to believe the verdict or whether there was some further malevolence the law might be capable of. After a moment his own self-contained blue eyes met the judge's.

'Prisoner at the bar,' said Mr Justice Lister. 'You have been tried on three charges by a jury of your fellow countrymen and found not guilty. It only remains for me, therefore, to order your discharge. But before you go I wish to offer you a word or two of advice. It would not be proper for me to comment upon the verdict brought in by this jury – except that you should feel in your heart a gratitude towards God for a deliverance which owes much to mercy and little to logic. In a few moments you will be leaving this court a free man – free to rejoin your deserving wife, and to begin a new life with her. Your able defence – and your reputation in other fields – marks you as a man of talent and capacity. I urge you in your own interests to subdue those instincts to lawlessness which may from time to time come upon you. Take warning from today. May it bear fruit in your heart and in your life.'

Tears were beginning to fall on Demelza's hands.

Chapter thirteen

THEY WENT HOME that same evening. He had a morbid distaste for the interest his presence aroused in the town, and his whole concern was to get away from staring eyes. There was no coach, so they hired horses and left at half past six.

Demelza had wanted Verity to go with them and to stay for a few days at Nampara before returning to Falmouth, but she obdurately refused; instinct told her that at this stage they should be by themselves. Dwight, too, was to have ridden with them, but he was in involved at the last moment in helping some injured man. The rest of them – Jud Paynter and Zacky Martin and Whitehead Scoble and the Gimletts – were coming on by stage wagon tomorrow and walking from St Michael.

So they left Bodmin quite alone; left the buzzing town, from which the crowds drawn by the election were already beginning to dribble away. By next week, when the judges and the counsel were posting on to Exeter, Bodmin would be back to normal.

It was dusk before they passed Lanivet and dark by the time they were half across the moors. Mist had blown up again and once or twice they thought they had missed the way. They talked scarcely at all, and discussion as to the right road was a welcome topic when other words would not come. At Fraddon they rested for a while, but soon were in the saddle again. They reached Treneglos land about nine-thirty and later made a detour to avoid Mellin Cottages. This was another inducement to return early, to be home before the news spread so that there were no cheering cottagers to welcome them. The uncomplex Demelza would not have minded in the least – a triumphal procession was what the occasion deserved – but she knew how Ross would hate it.

So they came upon their own property at last: the stone posts where the gate had once hung, the descending valley among the wild nut trees. As always fog made the land secretive and strange; it was not the familiar friendly countryside they knew and owned, it reverted to an earlier and less personal allegiance. Ross was reminded of that night seven years ago when he had come home from Winchester and America to find his house derelict and the Paynters drunk in bed. It had been raining then, but otherwise just such a night. There had only been the dogs and the chickens and the drip of moisture from the trees. He had been numb with the blow of Elizabeth's engagement to Francis, angry and resentful of a hurt only half realized, desperately alone.

Tonight he was coming back to a house yet more empty because Julia was not there, but riding beside him was the woman whose love and companionship meant more than all the rest; and he was returning free of the cloud which had shadowed his life for six months. He should feel happy and free. During his time in prison he had thought of all the things he should have said to Demelza and would never have the opportunity of saying. Now with unexpected reprieve came the old cursed constriction on his tongue, blocking up emotional expression.

The mist was less thick in the valley, and presently they saw the black shape of their house and crossed the stream and reined in at the front door beside the big lilac tree.

Ross said: 'I'll take the horses round if you'll get down here.'

Demelza said: 'It seems funny without even Garrick to give a friendly bark. I wonder how he is, over to Mrs Zacky's.'

'Likely to scent your return at any moment, I should think. A half mile is nothing to him.'

She slipped down and stood a moment listening to the clatter and clop as the horses were led round to the stable. Then she opened the front door with its familiar friendly squeak and went in. The smell of home.

She groped into the kitchen, found the tinderbox and scraped it. By the time Ross came in she had a fire flickering and a kettle perched precariously on the sticks. She had lit the candles in the parlour and was reaching up to draw the curtains.

As he saw the stretch of her young body, the dark hair lank with the clammy night, the olive colour in her cheeks, an impulse of warmth and gratitude towards her came to him. She had never for a moment expected him to rejoice at his deliverance. She might not understand the causes, but some instinct told her that spiritually he was still – at the most – a convalescent. It would take time, perhaps a long time.

She looked round, met his gaze and smiled. 'There was some water left in the pitcher. I thought we could brew a dish of tea.'

He took off his hat, flung it in a corner and ran a hand through his hair. 'You must be tired,' he said.

'No. . . . Glad to be home.'

He stretched and wandered slowly round the room, glancing at things he had virtually said good-bye to a week ago – now renewing their acquaintance as if after many years. The house was isolated and empty in a dark, still world. The pulse of living had died while they were away.

'Shall I light up a fire in here?' she asked.

'No. . . . It must be late. My watch has stopped – and I see the clock has stopped. Did you forget to wind it?'

'Could you expect me to remember that?'

'I suppose not.' He smiled rather absently, went across to the clock Verity and Demelza had bought three years before. 'What do you think the time is?'

'About eleven.'

He set the hands and began to wind up the weights. 'I should have thought later than that.'

'We'll ask Jack Cobbledick in the morning.'

'How will he know?'

'By the cows.'

Ross said: 'Couldn't we ask them tonight?'

She laughed, but with a slight break in her voice. 'I'll go'n see if the kettle's singing.'

While she was gone he sat in a chair and tried to arrange his thoughts, to sort them out so that he knew what his own feelings were. But relief and relaxation were still so entangled with the old tensions that nothing clear would come. When she returned with cups and a steaming teapot he was wandering round the room again, as if after his week's captivity even these confining walls were irksome.

She said nothing but poured out the tea. 'P'raps Jack half suspicioned someone would be back tonight, for he left a jug of milk. Come and sit down, Ross.'

He sat in the chair opposite her, accepted a cup, sipped it, his lean introspective face showing the strain more now than at any time. This side she could not see the scar. The tea was warm and grateful, soothed one's stretched nerves, hinted at the old companionship.

'So we're to start life afresh,' he said at length.

'Yes . . .'

'Clymer said I was amazing lucky – that a Cornish jury was the most pigheaded in the world. He charged me thirty guineas; I thought it not unreasonable.'

'I thought he did nothing at all.'

'Oh yes. . . . Again and again it was his guidance. And the speech I made – was partly his.' Ross's face twitched. 'God, how I disliked that!'

'Why? It was a handsome speech, I thought. I was so proud of you.'

'Proud . . . Heaven forbid,'

'And others thought the same. Dwight told me he'd heard that was what got you off.'

'Which is worse. To have to go crawling for one's freedom.'

'Oh *no*, Ross! There was no crawling in that. Why should you not defend yourself – explain what you did?'

'But it was not *true*! At least . . . if it was not false it was an evasion of the truth. I had no thought of saving life when I roused the neighbourhood. It was the Warleggans' ship. That was all I cared about. When I found

Sanson dead in the cabin I was glad! That was what I should have told the jury this afternoon – and would have but for Clymer and his counsels of expedience!'

'And now to-night you would not be free, but perhaps sentenced to transportation. Do you think, Ross, that that would have been a good exchange – just for stretching a story so's to put it in the best light? And if you'd said what you wanted, would it have been more than half the truth, *more* the truth than what you did say? Dwight was right, an' you know it! You were crazed with grief – and the jury's verdict was the only fair one.'

Ross got up. 'Whitewashing my neighbours too. We know they were all on the beach for what they could get, and with little thought to the shipwrecked sailors. Who would blame them?'

'Right enough. Who would blame them – or you?'

Ross made an angry, disquieted movement. 'Let's talk of other things.'

But instead they talked of nothing, and silence fell. The house seemed to hold itself together about them. She tried to bring up the election, but it didn't make sense. Eventually he sat down again and she refilled his cup.

'I'd dearly love to go on doing this forever,' she said.

'Drinking tea? You'd find it incommoding after a while. . . . But why?'

'It is the *homely* thing,' she said.

One of the candles began to sputter, and she got up and snuffed it. The smoke it had made drifted upwards in a dark spreading curl.

'It's you and me,' she said, 'in our own house; nothing between us – no interruption. Maybe it's because I'm just of common stock, but I want the home about me: candles burning, curtains drawn, warmth, tea, friendship, love. Those are what d'matter to me. This morning – even a few hours ago – I thought it was all gone for ever.'

'Common stock? Don't believe it.' After a minute he added: 'Nor was Julia of common stock, and she was like you.'

'That is the other thing I want,' she said, taking the opening.

'What?'

'A fire – and perhaps a cat by the hearth . . . but mostly a child in the cot.'

His jaw muscles tightened, but he didn't speak.

'What is it?' she asked.

'Nothing. It's time for bed. Tomorrow I am to become a farmer again – eh?'

'No, tell me, Ross.'

He stared at her. 'Was not the last experience enough for you? I want no more fodder for the epidemics.'

She stared back at him, horrified. 'Not ever?'

He shrugged, uncomfortable and a little surprised at her expression. He had thought she felt the same as himself.

'Oh, it may be they will come in due course. We cannot help that. But not yet, pray heaven. And they can never take Julia's place. I should not want them to. I should not want them at all yet.'

She was about to say something more but checked herself. She had known in court to-day that she was with child again, and since the moment of his acquittal had been keeping the knowledge to herself like some secret to be betrayed in due time, when it would perhaps help him in the struggle back to normal life again, give a new interest, a renewed purpose. Now the gold had suddenly peeled off and revealed something tawdry and inferior – and unwanted. She went round snuffing the other candles, getting the smoke in her eyes, thankful that he was staring into the fire. The triumph of the day had gone. She was as desolate as he.

Just then there came a tentative knock on the front door. At first they thought they had mistaken it, but it came again. In surprise Ross went out and across the hall and flung it open. The flickering light of a horn lantern showed up half a dozen people standing in the mist. There was Paul Daniel and Jack Cobbledick, and Mrs Zacky Martin and Beth Daniel and Jinny Scoble and Prudie Paynter.

'We seen the light,' said Mrs Zacky. 'We thought to come'n see if twas you back, my son.'

'Praise the Lord,' said Beth Daniel.

'Es it all right?' asked Paul Daniel. 'Are ee free and it all over?'

'You're early for carols,' said Ross, 'but come in and take a glass of wine.'

'Aw, no, we'd no thought t'intrude, my dear. Twas only wanting to know, and seeing the window alight . . .'

'Of course you must come in,' said Ross. 'Aren't you all my good friends?'

Chapter fourteen

LATER THAT NIGHT a coach drew up outside the largest of the town houses in Princes Street, Truro, and a chilled and yawning postilion got down to open the carriage door for George Warleggan. George got out, ignoring his servants, and walked slowly up the steps. Finding the door bolted, he pulled irritably at the bell. Another sleepy footman let him in, took his hat and cloak and stared after him as he mounted the handsome staircase. There was no look of sleep in George's eyes.

At the top of the first flight he hesitated, saw a light under his uncle's door, and went across. Cary was in a shabby old dressing gown and a nightcap but was working over his accounts by the light of two candles. When he saw who had come in he took off his steel spectacles and put down his pen. Then he blew out one of the candles, since less light would be needed for talking.

'We expected you yesterday. Did you have to lie there the night?'

'The trial did not come on until today – and was not over until four. Then one had to eat.'

Cary breathed through his nose and eyed George. 'I should have stayed another night. A wonder you did not break your axles in the dark or flounder in a bog.'

'We did once, but came out with some effort. I was not prepared to spend another night in a dirty noisy inn, with indifferent service and no curtains to the bed.' George went over to a decanter on the table and poured himself a drink. He sipped it, aware that Cary was still watching him.

'Well,' said Cary, 'I assume you are not here at this time of night for the pleasure of my company?'

'He got off,' George said; 'the accursed ignorant jury disregarded all the evidence and found him not guilty – because they liked the colour of his eyes.'

'On all counts?'

'On all counts. So the judge gave him a lecture, telling him to be a good boy in future, and then he was discharged.'

Cary sat perfectly still. His little brown bright eyes were fixed on the single unwavering candle flame. 'Was it not even suggested that he had murdered Matthew? I tell you, *that* should have been the charge.'

'And I tell you, my dear uncle, it would not have held for a moment. Matthew was found drowned. There was not an atom of proof and we could not have manufactured it. As it was, the evidence we tried to strengthen in our own way was of little value. Some of it, even, was of advantage to the other side. That man Paynter. I must see Garth in the morning. . . .'

'And what of the other things?' said Cary. 'His misdeeds in the past. It is little more than twelve months since he broke in Launceston gaol and took out a prisoner – and nothing done about it. And then soon after he was helping that murderer Daniel to escape. Does all that count for nothing?'

George took his glass over to a chair and sat down. He studied the colour of the wine. 'The law, as you should know, deals in one thing at a time. It also deals only in past convictions, not past suspicions. The judge had the facts before him, but he had no chance of using them. We are thwarted, dear Cary, and must accept our defeat.' It was as if George was salving his own frustration by taunting the other man.

There was a rap at the door and Nicholas Warleggan came in. He was more properly ready for the night, in a flowing gown and a black skullcap.

'Well, Father,' said George in ironical surprise, 'I thought you were at Cardew.'

'Your mother went alone. I heard the carriage stop. Well, what was the result?'

'He was acquitted of all charges and now no doubt is back at Nampara sleeping the sleep of a free man.'

'The man responsible for Matthew's disgrace,' Cary said, 'and later for his death.'

Nicholas Warleggan glanced sharply at his brother. 'There is always the danger of a suspicion becoming an obsession.' To George he said: 'So your efforts have been useless. I have been most uncomfortable about it all through.'

George still twirled his glass round by its stem. 'Your conscience gets ever more restive on our account. My dear uncle, why do you buy cheap wine? I call that economy very unsuitable.'

'It is perfectly palatable to me,' said Cary. 'If you do not like it you need not drink it.'

George glanced at his father. 'What have we done but exert pressure which would assist the law? Of course we shall drop it, for there is nothing more to do. Is there, Cary?'

'I shall not relax my efforts in any way,' said Cary, scarcely opening his mouth. 'Poldark is in deep water financially. We can yet see him in prison or drive him out of the county.'

'In other words,' said George, 'there are more ways than one of killing a cat. You cannot blame us, Father, if we take an interest in his mine.'

'I have no objection whatever to any proper business move,' said

Nicholas, padding across the room. 'I have no love for any of the Poldarks – arrogant, overbred, indolent squireens. If you can purchase the outside shares in his mine, by all means do so: it is one of the most profitable for its size in the county. But retain a sense of proportion. In a few years, George, with my prestige and your ability we shall be in a position where the Poldarks will not be worth our notice – they are not in fact even now. It's not becoming to our position or dignity – this feud——'

'You have no thought for Matthew,' said Cary sharply.

'No, in that respect I have not. He was morally at fault and brought his troubles on himself.'

'Did you see Pearce yesterday?' asked George.

Cary sniffed. 'Yes. He says Mrs Jacqueline Trenwith is not prepared at present to dispose of the shares. I don't like Pearce. He quibbles. He thinks he can run with the hare and hunt with the hounds.'

'We can cure him of that. His convictions wear away very easily. Sit down, Father; you walk about as if the house were on fire.'

'No, I'll go to bed,' said Nicholas. 'I must rise early in the morning.'

'While I was in Bodmin,' George said, 'I also had a brush with Francis Poldark. We chanced to meet, and he being then sober but anxious to amend the condition, I invited him to an inn where we drank together. But once in the inn he grew offensive and tried to pick a quarrel with me.'

'What did he say?'

'He accused me quite openly of being behind this charge against his cousin, of trying to ruin his family in any underhand way I could, of behaving in the ill-bred manner he would expect of the grandson of a blacksmith – who still lived in a hovel near St Day because the family of Warleggan was ashamed to own him.'

There was silence in the room except for Cary's breathing. Nicholas Warleggan's neck had gone a dull red.

Cary said: 'And you sat there and allowed *that* to pass?'

George looked at his hands. 'With these I could have broken his back. But I've had better things to do with my life than learning to be a pistol shot, and I had no intention of allowing a weakling like Francis to dictate my behaviour.'

'Quite right,' muttered Nicholas. 'It was the only way to act. But I'm perplexed that he should have done this. Only last year he was at bitter loggerheads with his cousin . . .'

'That, I think, is what troubles him,' George said pleasantly. 'It doesn't lie easy on his conscience.'

'And how did you leave him?' said Cary.

'In polite enmity.'

Cary made an angry gesture, shutting one of his account books with a snap. 'All his finances are in our hands. We can break him tomorrow – financially, which is the better way. . . .'

George hunched his shoulders. 'No. . . . We can't do that. At least not so obviously. For the moment I intend to make no move at all.'

'Why not? You care nothing now for his good will.'

'Not *his* good will,' said George, getting up. 'But there is another person to consider.'

Book two

Chapter one

As THE AUTUMN lengthened and winter came in Ross made a determined effort to set aside the troubles and anxieties that were past and accept in earnest the life of a small farmer squire with a mining interest – the life he had abandoned with regret only two years ago. But although he had left the happy routine with reluctance, he couldn't recapture the pleasure by simple means of a return to it.

Also some chill had come upon his relationship with Demelza. Her thoughts were not as open to him. Dating strangely from his acquittal, the laughter had gone, and the instant understanding. He tried more than once to break down this new reserve but failed, and the failure left its mark on his own responses.

Although he was thankful enough to be free of the menace of the assizes, the lesser but still serious danger of his own approaching bankruptcy kept him company most days. Even a sale of all his shares in Wheal Leisure would not balance his debt. A proud man, he hated indebtedness of any sort. He still hated the memory of the trial. Although he had probably gone free as a result of his change of front at the last moment, he constantly despised himself for having made it.

A few weeks after the trial Verity wrote:

My dear Cousin Ross,

I am writing you this time instead of Demelza because what I have to say is perhaps a little more to you than to her, though of course you may let her read this if you wish.

First may I say again, thank God for your deliverance – and in that prayer Andrew truly and sincerely joins. I know how wicked it was that the charge was ever brought against you, and in that respect acquittal was no more than your right. Yet there is the deepest cause for thankfulness in each one of your friends that there was no miscarriage of Justice – and the true hope that any embitterment which the arrest caused in you has been salved by this happy Outcome.

While I was in Bodmin I saw Francis twice. The first time he called at the inn and, although he was somewhat the worse for drink, I felt that he had come to see me in the intention of making up the Quarrel between us;

but when it came to the Point he had not the words and so went away unsatisfied. Therefore after the trial I sought him out and spoke to him again.

This second meeting confirmed the other opinion formed at the first: that something is gravely wrong with him. He is frighteningly bitter – in the way you are sometimes, Ross. Yet not like you, because I think he is more likely to do a mischief to himself than to others.

I know you and Francis have quarrelled, but have very strongly the Feeling that he wishes to be reconsiled. I don't know what was the full cause of the quarrel except that of course it began as a result of my elopement with Andrew – so I feel doubly concerned for the outcome. If he makes some further approach to you I beg you to be accommodating – if not for his sake then for mine, who still love him in spite of all his faults. It may be that you could help him back to a proper balance.

I don't like developments in France. It is unwholesome for a King to be led into Paris as if he were a prisoner, and there is much Feeling here about it. Try not to speak too openly in favour of liberty and freedom, Ross, for one can be so misunderstood. One is snapped up at the first mention of such things – by people who only twelve months ago were all in favour of reform. You will think this letter is quite a Lecture.

We went to Gwennap yesterday at the invitation of one of Andrew's friends. A dreadful place and bleak as a desert with hillocks of cinders and large engines creaking and groaning. All the whims are worked by mules, and poor impish, half-starved children hang over them flogging them round without respite. Steam and vapour hung over the scene like a pall. One wonders how Wesley dared to go there. Being even half-way home gave me a decided twinge.

I hear my stepson may be back in England *this* summer – a mere twelve months after his ship was due. I hope to meet him then.

> My dearest love to you both,
> Verity

In December Demelza was making rushlights with Mrs Gimlett, an employment that needed some practice and skill. The rushes had been cut in October and put in water so as to prevent drying or shrinkage. After they were stripped they had been laid out on the grass to whiten and 'take the dew' for a week, and then dried in the sun. The last treatment was to dip the rushes in scalding fat so that when withdrawn it congealed about the stem. Last year she had bought six pounds of grease from Aunt Mary Rogers for two shillings, but this year, in the desperate need for the smallest economy, she had saved her own fat, even the scummings of her bacon pot, and was hoping it would do as well.

These small economies were the only way she could make some contribution to the general need. Sometimes, too, in this quiet December she had got Ross's dinghy out and rowed twenty or thirty yards offshore where she had been able to catch mackerel and skate enough for the whole household. Ross did not know of this, and Gimlett was impressed to help her and sworn to secrecy. Today the kitchen was full of the sputterings of the grease, and some of the smoke and steam of the process, when there came a ran-tan on the front door which she knew to be the knock of a stranger.

Jane Gimlett went to the door and reappeared after a minute hastily wiping her greasy hands.

'If you please, mistress, it is Sir Hugh Bodrugan. I asked him into the parlour. I hope twas the right thing to do.'

Sir Hugh had been calling irregularly for the last eighteen months but she had not seen him since the trial. The thought came to her that if she went in to him like this with spots of grease on her face it might cure him of his interest. But vanity and a sense of her own low beginnings were too strong. She flew upstairs and made quick repairs.

When she went in he was sprawling in Ross's best chair examining the silver duelling pistols which he had taken down from the wall; he was wearing a red hunting coat and brown corduroy breeches and, since she had last seen him, a new wig. He got up and bowed over her hand.

'Y'r servant, ma'am. Thought I'd call and refresh our friendship. Pleasant time we had in Bodmin, but a shade inconclusive.' The bawdy twinkling black eyes met her own as he straightened up. They were almost on a level, she slightly the taller.

'Maybe you looked on it different from me, Sir Hugh. I found it exhausting.'

He laughed. 'Well, ye've a husband no one expected you to have. I trust he appreciates the escape. And I trust he appreciates you.'

'Oh, we appreciate each other, Sir Hugh. We are very happy, I assure you.'

A shadow of discontent passed across his face. 'But not above helping a neighbour in distress, eh?'

'In distress,' she said, looking away from his bold glance. 'I didn't know baronets was ever in distress.'

'Oh yes,' he said with a thick chuckle. 'They are mortal like other men. Liable to all the ills and disappointments – and all the temptations, as you must know.'

She went to the table at the side. 'Can I offer you port, sir, or is brandy more to your fancy?'

'Brandy, please. It lies easier on the stomach.'

As she poured out the drink she knew he was watching her and was sorry that her frock was a cheap one, though she knew well enough that he was not really interested in her frock.

He came over for the glass and took it with his left hand, putting his arm round her waist as he did so. After a moment they were seated again, he gulping at his glass, she on the edge of a chair at a discreet distance and gently sipping.

'Tis not that sort of distress, I trust?' she said gravely.

'It well could be, ma'am, it well could be.'

'Then I fear I have no cure for you.'

'You have it, miss, but withhold it, being hard of heart. However at this instant that's not the distress I seek your aid for. It's my mare Sheba.'

She stared at him over the rim of her glass, the dark wine making some added glimmer in the dark of her eyes. 'Sheba? What is wrong and what can I do for you?'

'She's sick, with some infernal fever that she can't throw off. Her eyelids are swollen and she has a racking cough. She can barely walk, and her knee joints crack at every movement as if they were dry sticks.'

'I'm sorry to hear it,' she said, putting out one slipper and then, as he glanced down, withdrawing it. 'But why do you come to me?'

Sir Hugh blew through his lips. 'Why do I come to you? Because I was consulting Trevaunance on the problem this morning, and he says you cured a pedigree cow of his when all the farriers had failed! That's why. Is that not a good reason?'

Demelza blushed and finished her port. As she did so she heard a horse outside and Ross dismounted at the door. Gimlett ran past the window to lead Darkie to the stables.

'It was mostly a matter of good fortune, Sir Hugh. It so happened——'

'All cures are good fortune one way or another, but everyone hasn't the honesty to acknowledge it. Trevaunance was telling me that you're learned on herbs and gypsy lore. If you——'

'Oh no,' Demelza began. At that juncture Ross came in.

He looked surprised and not too pleased to see the thickset hairy baronet sprawling in his chair and talking to Demelza in such a familiar manner. He had never quarrelled with Sir Hugh, but had never liked him. Also, as a result of his visit to Truro, he had his own affairs very much on his mind, and he had only half his attention to spare for an unexpected visitor.

'Sir Hugh has called——' Demelza began.

'My mare Sheba is ill, Poldark, and I've called to solicit your wife's good offices. She's been ailing for more than two weeks – Sheba, I mean – and Connie's in the greatest of a passion over it; she swears it is the groom's fault. Anyway, it ain't natural for the mare to be ill so long and she but six years old. Treneglos was saying one of his had it and died of it! We can't *afford* to lose her. It ain't natural at all.'

Ross dropped his riding gloves on a chair and poured himself some brandy. 'How can Demelza help you?'

'Well, I hear she's a rare hand with herbs and spells and suchlike. Trevaunance only told me this morning, or I should have been over before.

Damn it, the farriers have no more idea than the man in the moon!'

'The farriers——' Ross began.

'I was just saying to Sir Hugh,' Demelza said hastily, 'that Sir John was putting too much store on a little advice I gave him back in August month. It was no more'n a word I dropped about his sick cow, and she grew better by accident.'

'Well, come over and drop a word about my sick mare, and see if *she* gets better by accident. Cod, it will do no harm surely.'

Demelza hesitated, opened her mouth to speak.

'After all,' said Sir Hugh, 'it is no more than repaying one good turn with another. We're neighbours and should do what we can to be neighbourly: that's what I thought at Bodmin. Come yourself, Poldark, if you've the mind. Connie'll victual you well enough, I'll say that for her. We dine at three. I shall expect you tomorrow, what?'

'I'm sorry,' Ross said. 'I have business which will keep me at the mine all day. Perhaps we can arrange one day next week.'

Demelza got up to refill Sir Hugh's glass. 'Maybe I could go, Ross?' she said gently. 'Not to dine, but just for half an hour to see the mare. I can do naught, of course, but if Sir Hugh really wants it and nothing less will satisfy him . . .'

Bodrugan took the drink. 'That suits me fine. I'll expect you any time after eleven. And anything you want – medicines, plasters, clysters, herbs – just say the word. I'll have a groom ready to ride to Truro.'

After a few more sentences Ross went upstairs, but Sir Hugh was not hurrying. He finished his brandy and took a third, while Demelza wondered how Jane was managing the rushlights. At length he left, stocky, authoritative and vigorous – squeezed Demelza's hand lengthily, climbed on his big horse and cantered across the bridge and up the valley.

She went into the kitchen and found Jane had finished the job and was cleaning up the mess. After about ten minutes she heard Ross come down again, and she followed him back into the parlour.

'Did you eat in Truro? We've some pie left.'

'I ate in Truro.'

She glanced at him, took in his bleak expression, thought it a criticism of her attitude towards Sir Hugh.

'We're neighbours, Ross. You couldn't expect for me not to receive him.'

'Who? Oh, Bodrugan.' Ross lifted an eyebrow. 'I suppose you will not go tomorrow.'

'Of course I'll go,' she said, a faint edge on her voice. 'I promised, didn't I?'

He said with irony: 'D'you really suppose he wants you to cure his mare? I had a greater regard for your intelligence than that.'

'You mean you've no regard for my intelligence at all.'

'I've a great respect for it – sometimes. But you must realize what Bodrugan is after. He makes it very plain.'

Because it was three-quarters true she resented it the more. 'I think I ought to be able to judge that for myself.'

'No doubt you think so. But be careful that his title doesn't dazzle your eyes. It has that effect with some people.'

'Especially,' she said, 'a common miner's daughter who doesn't know any better.'

He looked at her a moment. 'That's for you to demonstrate.'

He turned to go, but she was at the door first.

'You're detestable – saying things like that!'

'I'm sure I didn't start this argument.'

'No, you never do start arguments, do you, with your cold looks an' your bitter tongue! You just freeze everyone up an' – an' despise everything that isn't up to your standard. It's – it's unfair and horrible! Perhaps that's what you want me always to feel. Perhaps you're sorry you ever bothered to marry me!'

She turned and was out of the door, slamming it behind her, and he heard her running up the stairs.

. . . Supper was late that evening.

Mrs Gimlett said her mistress had a headache and would not be down, so Ross ate the meal alone. It was a dish of boiled rabbits with savoury garnishings, but he imagined that it had not quite the flavour as when Demelza cooked it. Afterwards there was apple tart and cream and hot scones. When he had finished he put some tart and cream in a dish and a couple of the scones and took it upstairs.

He found her in their room lying on the bed. It was her favourite retreat in her rare moments of despair. She had her face in the pillow, and she didn't move when he came in or when he sat on the bed.

'Demelza.'

She might have been dead for all the response this produced.

'Demelza. I've brought you some tart.'

'I don't want nothing to eat,' she said in a muffled voice.

'All the same, a mouthful or two can be put away somewhere. I want to talk to you.'

'Not now, Ross,' she said.

'Yes, now.'

'Not now.'

He stared at her tangle of dark hair, at her figure's tantalizing twisted grace.

'You've got a hole in your stocking,' he said.

She wriggled and after a moment sat up. Her face was streaked and she wiped it with a corner of lace, hating him but not wanting to be unsightly in his eyes.

'Eat this, my dear.'

She shook her head.

He put the dish down. 'Look, Demelza, if there have to be quarrels I like them to have a good substantial basis with a nice groundwork of grievance on both sides to work upon. But I don't see a basis for this in a fat hairy old man who comes here pestering you for favours. In your heart I think you know Bodrugan just as well as I do. So perhaps there is some other irritant at work. Do you know what it is?'

She made a little gesture which did not convey much.

'You speak of my cold looks and bitter tongue,' he said. 'But after living in this house six or seven years and being married to me for over three, my peculiarities can't be any surprise to you. I admit them, but they've not grown on me overnight like Billy Thomson's beard. You've suffered under them and thrived under them for long enough. So I can't help but feel there is an underlying cause which makes them no longer bearable. I've noticed a falling off in the hours we spend together and in the sort of satisfaction they bring. Haven't you?'

She said indistinctly: 'It is not of my seeking.'

'Perhaps,' he said, 'we expect too much if we expect the early glow to last. We had fifteen or eighteen months that were as near perfect as any man or woman could wish for; but now at the beginning of this second stage we're disappointed that absolute happiness has gone and each is inclined to blame the other. So minor irritations magnify and we come to a quarrel. That's the plain truth, is it not?'

'If that's how you see it,' she said, keeping her head away.

'Isn't that how you see it? Well, not yet, but perhaps you will come to see it that way.'

Not only does he not want our child but he no longer wants me, she thought.

'In the meantime,' he went on gently enough, 'let's strive for tolerance in our irritations. I'll do my most to avoid condescension towards you – which is the last thing I feel. And if you find my company cold as well as dull, try to excuse it, because I've subjects enough to engage me, and a passing sourness of expression is much more likely to be concerned with a passing thought than being a sign of any dissatisfaction with you.'

After saying that, he leaned forward and kissed her on the cheek and left her again, having only succeeded in considerably deepening the misunderstanding between them.

A good deal later that night she came downstairs and found him at the table in the parlour with all his books around him. In the old days she would have sat on the arm of his chair and tried to make out how he came by the balance; but that would not do now. A half-full brandy bottle was at his elbow, and she wondered if it had been new to begin the evening. He glanced up with a brief smile when she came in, but soon was working again.

She went across and poked the fire, threw on another couple of billets of wood and sat quiet watching the blue tentative flames.

She could hear the steam hissing, and an owl screeched sometimes in the dark. A quiet night. All December so far had been the same, a time of early dews and wet leaves underfoot and darkness lingering in the day as if it were the earth's natural element. It was gentle weather – but gentle with the atmosphere of decay. There seemed nothing new or young in the world.

Suddenly she looked up from biting her finger and saw that Ross was watching her. To cover her thoughts she said:

'Do you still not get paid for being head purser of the mine, Ross?'

'It saves money and I draw a greater profit.'

'And so does everyone else. Where Father used to work they paid the head purser forty shillings a month. We are so poor now that it would help.'

'But not enough.' He began to fill his long pipe. 'These are not all cost books. Some are for my own accountings. I shall not be able to meet my obligations in three weeks' time.'

'Did you see your moneylender today then?' She tried to say it casually, though she knew all it meant to them both.

'Pearce would be flattered by your name. Yes, I saw him. He has agreed to extend the loan for another year.'

'Then . . .'

'Pascoe has also agreed to add interest to mortgage with his bank – while cautioning me that, now he has partners to consider, he may not be able to do it for a further year. But he's unlikely to have the need, for I can't find the four hundred pounds interest for Pearce, nor near it, without selling out of the mine; and without that we shall not drag on a very long time.'

She felt suddenly ashamed of herself for having picked this day to quarrel with him.

'How much are you lacking?'

'A little over two hundred pounds.'

'Could you not . . .'

'Oh yes, I could perhaps borrow the money – that much – from some friend, but what's the use? I should only get in even deeper. It would have been better, as Pascoe advised, to sell a year ago to the Warleggans and have done with them and started free of the worst debt.'

'It's not like you to be down in the mouth, Ross. But even borrowing from a friend wasn't quite what I meant. We have – some things, a few things, which did ought to bring us in money.'

'Such as?'

'Well . . . there's my ruby brooch. You said that was worth a hundred pounds.'

'The brooch is yours.'

'You gave it me. I can give it back if I want to. And there's Caerhays. I can manage well without a horse. I scarcely ever go beyond what I can comfortably walk. I always *did* walk. An' the frock would fetch something – and this clock, and the new carpet in our room.'

'I couldn't consider it. If I went to prison you would have to live on those things and what they brought. I'm not just going to empty them into the bottomless pit.'

'Then there's some of the farm stock,' said Demelza, more happy now she had something definite to consider. 'All rare good stock but more than we properly need. It seems simple enough to me. If you pay off this interest debt you can make more money somehow. But if we sell the mine shares these other things'll be no manner of use to anyone. *They* won't bring us in money to live on. Wheal Leisure does. Besides . . . it wouldn't be like you to give in to the Warleggans.'

She had touched the raw spot. He got up, thrusting back his chair, and stood while he lit his pipe from a piece of twisted paper.

'You always did argue like a lawyer. You always will.'

That pleased her. The light flickered about her face.

'You'll do that, won't you, Ross?'

'I don't know.'

'We could raise two hundred pounds,' she said. 'I'm sure we could.'

Chapter two

THE FOLLOWING DAY Demelza rode a little defiantly off to meet the Bodrugans at Werry House. She was in a reckless mood, and for the moment it didn't seem so much to matter that she knew nothing whatever about horses. When she saw the sick mare she had a rush of misgivings, but it was plain that Sir Hugh expected her to prescribe some vile-smelling nostrum and that he put down as false modesty her expressed wish not to interfere. She'd cured Sir John's Minta and could at least make an attempt to do the same here.

She stared at the mare for some time and then glanced up to meet a look of curiosity and challenge on Constance Bodrugan's face. Well, if that was the way they felt . . . If the mare died they could well afford the loss, and it might ease Sir Hugh's attentions once and for all. . . . If she had to commit a crime she might as well do it with a flourish. . . .

She ordered all the blisters, clysters, ointments, salves, pills and poultices of the professional horse doctors to be thrown away. That cleared the air quite a bit. Then she told them to go out and gather nine leaves of heart-fever grass and nine flowers of the scarlet pimpernel and tie them in a silk bag round the mare's neck. When these were eventually brought she recited a poem over the animal.

'Herb Pimpernel, I have thee found
Growing upon Christ Jesu's ground.
The same gift the Lord Jesus bare thee
When His blood He shed to spare thee;
Herb and grass this evil pass
And God bless all who wear thee – Amen.'

It was a doggerel she had heard old Meggy Dawes of Illuggan recite: she rather thought Meggy had used it as a cure for warts, but anyhow it couldn't do any hurt.

Then she prescribed the same cordial of rosemary, juniper and cardamon which she had recommended for the pedigree Hereford. After that they all went back to the house and she took two glasses of port and a biscuit and watched a litter of puppies chewing the rug at her feet. The port just in time helped to kill off the growth of self-criticism. She refused an invitation to lunch and left before one, her virtue unimpaired, followed by the blustering good wishes of Sir Hugh and the speculative glances of Constance Lady Bodrugan. She could guess what Constance would say if the mare died.

Ross didn't mention the visit over dinner, but at supper he said:

'What was the matter with Bodrugan's blood mare? Influenza, d'you think?'

So he had taken it for granted that she had gone in spite of his disapproval. 'I don't know at all, Ross. It might well be. She's awful bad, with a quivery feel to the muscles like Ramoth before he died.'

'What did you do for her?'

Uneasily she told him.

He laughed. 'You'll have every veterinarian in the county up in arms. You're stealing their fire.'

'I don't care for that. But she's a rare lovely animal. I hope she comes round. I expect twould be quite a loss if she died.'

'She must be worth upwards of three hundred guineas.'

Demelza dropped her knife and went pale. 'You're joking, Ross!'

'I may be wrong, of course. But King David was her sire. And he——'

'Judas!' Demelza got up. 'Why didn't you tell me before?'

'I thought you knew. Anyway, I'm sure you'll have done her no harm.'

Demelza went to the side table. 'It was *mean* of you not to tell me, Ross.'

'I thought you knew! Bodrugan is always boasting of it, and you have had his acquaintance for more than a year. But perhaps when you meet you don't talk of horses.'

She did not take him up on that quip, but moved the dishes restlessly about, her wilfulness turned against her. After a minute she came back to the table and sat down again.

'By the way,' he said, 'what did happen in Bodmin? How was it you came to meet Sir Hugh while you were there? And why does he seem to think you're under some obligation to him?'

She said: 'I don't know how they dared send for me.'

At much the same time that Demelza was rashly making her second essay in animal medicine, Dwight Enys, applying all his conscience and skill to the less valuable human animals of Sawle, was making discoveries about his own shortcomings. Doctoring, he found, was not only a constant fight against other people's ignorance but also against one's own.

It was Parthesia Hoblyn's gums which gave him the clue to the disease which had been spreading through the village all autumn. If any excuse could be found for his own incompetence it lay in the paludal fever which had so constantly masked the more serious complaint. In this case, as in most of the others, the girl had taken the fever, had recovered, had taken it again, and after the second attack all the life had gone out of her and she had been breathless and exhausted with the least effort. Discoloration of her arms like bruises had made him suspect, first, her father and then, when he proved blameless, the disease known as purpura. He had given her an occasional fever powder to clear the blood, and had ordered her to sit out on mild days and drink cold water – a course that Jacka Hoblyn strongly disapproved of. (Busy about the house, he said; that was what she should be; it would work off the bad humours far better than sitting at the door breathing in all the moisture and the steams.)

And then Dwight met Ted Carkeek (whose shoulder wound was long since healed and almost forgotten) and Ted by chance mentioned that his father had died at sea; and going from him Dwight came straight into Vercoe, the bearded excise officer from St Ann's – an ex-naval man – who stopped to ask him about his wife with an abscess under her tooth and went on talking about life aboard ship; and straight afterwards Dwight called on the Hoblyns and saw Parthesia's gums – and everything then was suddenly plain and he was abusing himself for having been so criminally blind. These listless blotchy ailing people of Sawle, with their nose bleedings and their sallow skins, were the victims of an outbreak of scorbutus. Choake, presuming he now came into the village at all, had not spotted it; and *he* had not spotted it; so people went on suffering and being wrongly treated.

'Parthesia, I'm going to change your medicine. I think you need a change, do you not? I haven't the ingredients here,' he said to Rosina, who was standing by the chair, 'but I think a sulphur medicine might help. In the meantime, have you any source of fresh vegetables in or around the village?'

'Vegetables? No, sur. We don't belong to have vegetables – not above a few potatoes – before April or May.'

'Or fruit – lemons in particular, or lemonades . . . no, of course you haven't. I have green things sometimes myself. Can you not get them in Truro?'

'They're too dear for the likes of we. Those things d'run away with the money in no time.'

He looked thoughtfully into Rosina's beautiful eyes. 'Ye-es. . . . Still I must urge you to afford them. It's vital. They'll do Thesia far more good than all my draughts or all your mother's home doctoring.'

Rosina blushed. 'I'll ask Father. Maybe we could perhaps send in for some when the next mule train go in.'

He went away thinking it over. Counsels of perfection which the Hoblyns, being people just above the privation level, might possibly be able to follow. But what of the rest? They could no more get fresh vegetables or fruit than if they were becalmed in the Pacific Ocean. Yet what good would his sulphur potions or diaphuretic salts be to them without it? At the best palliatives. Probably not that. It was infuriating. Amid all the doubts and disappointments of medicine there existed for this disease a certain cure – and the cure was unobtainable.

Nor could he himself afford to feed a village, or some chosen families, on green stuffs of his own buying.

Trenwith House was still the province of Thomas Choake; but Dwight, by roundabout and unsought ways, had come to have an interest below stairs in Mrs Tabb who, having fallen and badly cut her arm a few days before, would have no one but Dr Enys to dress it. She had walked to his house but had gone queer when she got there, so he had said he would call next time and save her the seven-mile walk. He found the wound not suppurating much, and applied a blister of spanish fly to help it. Having left an ointment for later use, he walked down the stairs escorted by Tabb – and saw Elizabeth Poldark in the hall.

'Dr Enys. We don't often see you in our house.'

'No, ma'am.' He smiled. 'I try not to poach on a colleague.'

She said slowly: 'The game is only preserved on professional visits.'

'Thank you. I'll remember that. I've not seen your husband since we met in Bodmin.'

'Francis told me of your kindness. We were all most relieved at the outcome of the trial. . . . Will you take a glass of wine?'

They turned towards the winter parlour. 'If refinement of taste is enough, then our married life has been an idyll,' Francis had said on that long night in Bodmin. Refinement of taste? Was that all this woman had to offer? Her young withdrawn loveliness always caught at Dwight's heart. Oh, he knew he was impressionable, but . . .

In the parlour Aunt Agatha crouched over a smoky fire. The old lady's hands trembled and fumbled unceasingly about in her lap, like wrinkled grey moles searching for something they could never find; but her spirit was as determined as ever, and the sharp old eyes looked Dwight over as he was reintroduced. Of course she remembered him at Ross's baby's christening party, she said, it being her habit nowadays never to admit she could forget anything. She could always tell an attorney's face. They seldom – what? what? Yes, that's what she'd said. And what was doctoring like in Truro these days? In her young days there'd been a Dr Seabright with a big following. Used to prescribe fresh horse dung as a cure for the pleurisy. Lived over what was now Pearce's Hotel. Very popular, but he caught farcy cutting up a horse and was dead within the month.

'Aunt Agatha will not hear us; she's very deaf,' Elizabeth said, and turned the conversation to commonplaces of the countryside. Dwight expanded as he always did in sympathetic female company, and only now and then did the memories of that night come to disturb him. They blew across his brain like phantasms of a not quite real experience. The unwinking candles; Francis's disembodied face, bitter and drawn; the harsh confidences, originally sought, but when given half turned away from; through it all ran Elizabeth, Elizabeth, the loved but the unloving, the Galatea who never woke.

Perhaps some shadow crossed Dwight's face, for Elizabeth broke off what she had been talking about.

'Dr Enys, may I ask you a question? . . . From something he said I've come to suspect that my husband – that Francis tried to commit suicide when he was in Bodmin. Do you know if it is true?'

That was a poser. In embarrassment Dwight glanced at the old lady, who was still watching him as if she could hear every word.

'Your husband and I shared a room in Bodmin, as you know. The atmosphere of the town was very excitable at that time and Mr Poldark was – susceptible to the general feeling of recklessness and hard drinking. We – talked a long time together, well into the night, and I think his having someone to talk to helped him over a difficult period. I don't think you need worry about it.'

Aunt Agatha said: 'Shingles I had, I recollect, and he gave me blood from a cat mixed with cow milk to put on the sore place mornings and evenings. And treacle water at nights. He was a skirt little fellow, I mind, but as bright as a bee.'

'You haven't answered my question, Dr Enys,' Elizabeth said.

'That's the only answer I can give. . . . I've known nowhere worse than this district for wild rumours, and I should advise you to ignore them.'

There was a glint in Elizabeth's eyes as she turned. 'Perhaps you don't realize how cut off we are here from the general social world, Dr Enys.'

'No . . . I hadn't realized it.'

'Our cousins from Nampara don't come, we can no longer afford to entertain, and Francis is seldom in a mood for polite visiting. So perhaps it will explain to you why I am put to this strait in begging information from a – stranger.'

There was a slight tremor in her voice. Dwight said: 'I should be sorry if you looked on me as that. I shall be only too happy if I can be of help or value to you – and I hope you'll call on me in any way you think fit.'

'In those days,' said Aunt Agatha, chewing at her gums, 'no gentleman never went out without his sword. Didn't *dare*. I mind seeing a highwayman hanged at Bargus. Pretty-looking man, he was, in a crimson suit o' clothes and a gold-laced hat. Went off very well, too, bold as brass to the last kick. You wouldn't have dared rode from Truro like that, young man, dressed as if you was going to a burying.'

'I live between Nampara and Mingoose,' said Dwight in a raised voice.

'Yes, I know tis easy enough now. Here to Truro they say's as safe as your own backlet. All the spirit's gone out of the world.'

Elizabeth said: 'Francis will have told you of the estrangement between ourselves and our cousins?'

'I know of it, yes.'

'Do you think Ross is settled down after all his trouble?'

'I always feel', Dwight said, 'that Ross is like a volcano. He may be quiet forever – or erupt tomorrow.'

He caught a look in her eyes which seemed to show agreement. He went on: 'Demelza I've seen less of than before.' (Which was true enough. Sometimes indeed it might have been that Demelza was trying to avoid him, though he could think of no reason.)

'Where's Geoffrey Charles?' said Aunt Agatha. 'Where's the boy . . . ?'

'Would you think,' Elizabeth said, 'that they were happy together?'

'. . . He's going to be a tartar,' said the old lady. 'Not seven yet and up to all manner o' saucy tricks. I'd give him a good nooling. No cheeil's right without a stick to his back once in a while.'

Dwight said: 'Perhaps I should answer that if I knew the answer.'

'She was good to us last year,' Elizabeth said. 'Without her one or more of us might have died. Would you take her a message from me? Tell her – would you say that we once spent a happy Christmas together at Trenwith and say that we should like them to come again this year. Impress it on her, would you, that we really want them, need them? D'you mind doing this for me?'

'Of course I will.'

'Perhaps you'd join us yourself. We shall have no special attraction to offer you, but——'

He thanked her, said he would be delighted, and took his leave. On his way out he saw Francis coming in, walking up the drive from the direction of the main gate. They didn't directly pass each other, but Francis raised an ironical finger to his forehead. He was roughly dressed and his boots were caked in mud, but he looked better than when last Dwight had seen him.

The short day was closing, and it would be dusk before he reached Grambler. The sullen sea was already blurred where it could be glimpsed between the declivities of the land. The damp mild pall of clouds drifted across from the coast in infinite deepening layers of brown like forerunners of the long night.

As he came out upon the main track above Grambler he saw a squat bowlegged figure tramping ahead. It was Jud Paynter, and in a hurry. He glanced behind nervously at the sound of a horseman, but his aggrieved face cleared when he saw who it was.

'Evening, Paynter.' Dwight was riding past when Jud raised his hand.

'Handsome weather we're 'aving, Mester Enys. Proper job for the time o' year. Twill pass the winter away.'

Dwight replied conventionally, then he slackened his reins to move on again.

'Mester Enys.'

'Yes.'

'I s'pose tes axing more'n you could do to keep aside of me till we get to Grambler.'

'Not if there's some good reason. It's only half a mile.'

''Alf a mile can be a cant of a way. Aye, an' thur's reason, sure 'nough. Thur's a couple o' great men inching up behind me, and I aren't taking to the notion at all. No, not me. Not Jud Paynter. I aren't aiming to be churched just yet. See any sign of 'em, did ee?'

'What d'you mean?'

'What I d'say, that's what. Just in St Ann's I am, about me ordinary, proper, reasonable, human, respectable, decent, fair an' honest business when first I seen the two of 'em eyeing me as if I was a green goose ready for the Christmas pot. Ullo, I says. Footpaths, I says, Or some such, I says. I'd best be off home, else they'll likely slit me throat when I aren't looking. Tes a crying shame,' Jud went on, 'what the country's coming to. Can't stir outside your own front door wi'out blackguards lying in wait. Tedn right. Tedn proper. Tedn *fair*.'

Dwight looked at the bald old rascal beside him. 'Do they know you to be carrying money?'

'Me?' said Jud, startled. 'I aren't carrying money. Not more'n a few pence to buy an honest glass o' rum.'

'Why should anyone try to rob you, then? Why not me? My horse alone would be the better prize.'

Jud shrugged. 'There you are. Tes the way of things. Maybe they think there'd be more of a dido if you was ditched. Nay. Tes the widows an' orphans, that's what the bad men d'go for.'

'Which are you?' Dwight asked.

'Who, me?' said Jud. 'Why, I been a orphan ever since me mother and father died.'

They made slow progress, Dwight having difficulty in keeping his horse in check, Jud panting along grumbling behind. Dwight had a pot of ointment to deliver in the village, so he left that and was just overtaking Jud again when he reached his shack. Prudie was at the door.

'So there ye are, you splatty old pig,' she said, and then she recognized the horseman. 'Avnoon, Dr Dwight,' she added sheepishly.

'Good day to you, Prudie. You must be glad to see your husband safely home.'

'Home, an? I ain't 'ad sight or sound of him these pretty many days. Reckon he b'long to think he can go off an' come back just when he d'take the fancy. Dirty old gale.'

'You know where I been,' said Jud. 'Know it fine an' well. Earning money, I been, to keep ee in lazy idleness. And Doctor d'know just so well as you, though he may pretend elsewise.'

Dwight said: 'A good run?'

''Twas none so poor.'

'Was that why the men were following you?'

'What men?' demanded Prudie, wiping her swollen red nose on her sleeve.

Jud looked uneasy while Dwight explained.

'Tes naught to do wi' the trade,' he said. 'Tes just as I told ee. Footpaths looking for some poor 'elpless old man to rob. I tell ee tes a bad business when law and order d'go for naught. I——'

'Well,' said Prudie, 'I can't suppose what's amiss with 'im. Ever since he come 'ome from that trial he's been like this – scared to go abroad after dark, 'e is. Scared of 'is own shadow oft times, I reckon. Say "bo" to him an' he'll run like a meader.'

'Tedn true! Tedn right! I aren't afraid of nothing except what tis natural to be afraid of. An' I aren't no meader, see, so there.'

'Be as it will, tis somethin' to do wi' that trial,' said Prudie. 'Dear know what tis, but you was there, Dr Dwight, my son, an' mebbe *you* can guess. Like as not Jud was tiddly when he went in the stand, an' tis a mystery to me how he wasn't locked away there and then!'

'But what has that to do with his being afraid now?'

'That's what I been saying till I'm swelled out wi' saying it,' Jud stated violently. 'What you got t'eat, wife? I'm leary enough without all this slack-jaw. Ef ye paid more heed to yer cooking and less to yer talkin' the world'd be a sight betterer place. There's no peace, not in the home nor out of it!'

Dwight took the hint and began to move on. Prudie's voice followed him like an organ with all the stops pulled out.

'Law or no, tis on account o' something to do wi' that there trial. You can't fox me, ole man. All the time, soon as it go dark, you're hoppin' and dodging like a flea on a hot plate. Thur's somethin' behind it, an' I'll get to the root of un yet!'

Dwight's last view was of Jud going grumpily into the cottage, and Prudie's threats and warnings blew after him through the wide dusk.

Chapter three

THE BROOCH FETCHED seventy pounds. The pawnbroker said prices had come down since they bought it; also there was not the sale for expensive jewellery in Cornwall. Ross said it was as much as they could reasonably expect. Demelza's horse, Caerhays, fetched thirty-five guineas, and the carpet ten. Ross said the frock was *not* to be sold. Very well, he should go to prison and she would never wear it again and the moths would get at it and it would go out of fashion, and it was too big already about the waist because she had lost weight and he should go to prison; but the frock was not to be sold. Demelza took a warmth and comfort from that.

Then they started on the farm stock. They sold their two-year-old colt, Sikh, for ten guineas, and their two best cows for fourteen guineas apiece. It was not a good time of year for disposing of farm stock. Ross sold with the bitter consciousness that the people who bought his animals would be able to dispose of them in three months' time at a profit. They got two pounds, twelve shillings and sixpence each for two month-old heifer calves. Without oxen, ploughing would be almost impossible, so there could be no economy there. They sold their pigs and almost all their poultry. Jane Gimlett was in tears, and Jack Cobbledick only just avoided them. With some twenty-five pounds still to be got Ross went round his farm. Of all his livestock, built up carefully over seven years, he now had one cow, due to calf in April, one horse, his team of oxen, a half dozen chickens and a few ducks. It was while they were on this tour that Dwight arrived with Elizabeth's invitation.

'Tell them . . .' said Ross, and stopped, the anger swelling, 'that we are so busy savouring the sweets of——'

'Tell them,' said Demelza hastily. 'But it isn't for Dwight to be our messenger, is it? Shall you accept for yourself, Dwight?'

'I think so. Christmas isn't a great deal of pleasure spent alone.'

'There are worse alternatives,' said Ross.

After a minute Dwight added: 'Of course I should enjoy it better at Trenwith if you were there. . . .'

'Complimentary but inaccurate.'

'I'll take the chance.'

'There's no chance to take.'

The awkward silence was broken by Garrick, who suddenly appeared and came bounding across the yard like a monstrous French poodle, wagging his stump and showing a lolling red tongue. As usual he had no respect for the decencies; Dwight had to duck out of the way, and Ross came off with a couple of muddy paw marks on the front of his shirt.

'The trouble with Demelza,' Ross said, brushing himself, 'is that she adopts strange animals and then doesn't sufficiently tame them. We had Sir Hugh Bodrugan over the other day.'

Dwight laughed. 'Sir Hugh has never shown any special ambition to lick my face.'

'Not yours perhaps.'

'Oh, Ross,' Demelza said, 'why could we not go to Trenwith?'

Ross looked at his empty yard. 'D'you seriously ask that?'

'I know I should not; but . . . it is a pity to think too much in the past.'

How fail when it so much influenced the present? 'Tell them that we will come when Verity and Blamey are invited and not before.'

'I don't think it will be very long before that happens,' said Demelza. 'Verity and Francis were reconciled at Bodmin.'

'We can all be reconciled together, then.'

After a minute Demelza said: 'That's what I should like too. But if we were to make the first move . . .'

Ross thought, Oh, God, what if my bankruptcy *is* Francis's fault (and the chances are it would have happened in any case), perhaps Demelza is right. She often is. Reconciliation is what Verity wants. And Demelza wants it. And Elizabeth. The last thought wakened in him a desire, almost a need, to see Elizabeth again. He'd never quite got over his attachment, it was something fundamental, a weakness if you liked, overlooked but still there.

'Well,' he said, 'we'll think it over. At this present moment twenty or thirty pounds is more important than all the Christmas reunions. Perhaps you'd like to take out a mortgage on my property, Dwight. It would have to be a third mortgage and bear interest at a hundred per cent. There's nothing like moneylending for bringing in a fair return.'

'You may have ten pounds, which is all I own. It could go to no better cause.'

'Nor is it yet a lost cause, though we have moments of doubt. D'you remember Tregeagle, who had to drain out Dozmare Pool with a sea shell? Mine's the opposite task.'

They moved on. Dwight began to talk about his discovery of scurvy in Sawle, and this occupied them until they returned to the house, where John Gimlett was working on a library window, repairing the rusty hinge of a shutter.

'If you're short of turf we can let you have some,' Ross said. 'There's enough stacked for two winters almost.'

Garrick, having shown his overflowing affection, had galloped off again, but at this stage he was seen returning carrying something in his mouth. It proved to be the hindquarters of a rabbit which he laid at Demelza's feet.

'Go away!' said Demelza in disgust. 'Horrid dog! Take it away!'

Ross picked up the corpse and heaved it across the stream, the dog bounding in hot pursuit.

'I wonder what Garrick would be worth in the open market,' he said. 'One overgrown mongrel. Carnivorous. Fights bulls and guards babies. Trained to sit on seedlings and scratch up flowers. Good crockery breaker. Suffers sometimes from bad breath. Results guaranteed.'

Dwight laughed. As they went into the house he said: 'Shall you be able to keep the Gimletts?'

'They won't leave. We can feed them, and that's all they want for the time. And I can't work the farm without Cobbledick.'

'Seriously,' Dwight said, 'my ten pounds is yours if it's any use.'

'Seriously,' said Ross, 'it will have to be the clock, Demelza, and a few bits of furniture. Then there's my father's pistols and the old telescope.'

So it has all come round like in a circle, thought Demelza. Three years since we spent Christmas at Trenwith. And just such another day, cloudy and quiet. Then I was that frightened I hardly knew what I was saying. Scullerymaid going to visit the gentry. Now it's all changed. Nervous in a way, but not that way. *They're* poor. Just as poor as we – and Francis is working on his own land, and Elizabeth . . . Elizabeth has lost her terrors, and is full of gratitude to me for what took place last Christmas. Dear Verity isn't there. But I've no fear of doing the wrong thing or making a fool of myself. Yet I'm not near so happy as then. And the queer thing is I'm expecting another child, and again hiding it from Ross, though for a different reason – and it's just about four months forward, the same as last time.

'D'you remember,' she said, 'when we were walking this way before? Garrick kept following on and laying down when we spoke to him, just as if for once he was going to do as he was told.'

'Yes,' said Ross.

'And you remember we met Mark Daniel and he took Garrick by the ear and marched him home. . . . D'you ever hear anything of Mark now, Ross?'

'I don't know how he's faring with all this upset, but Paul saw him last in Roscoff.'

'Don't you think it would he safe enough for him to come home?'

'No. If things get too bad in France he should go to Ireland or America; but there'd be no peace of mind for him here, even under an assumed name.'

Last time there had been Verity at the door to greet them. Today Demelza noticed the weeds growing in the drive, the grass rank under the trees, the patched-up window and the unpainted gate leading to the orchard. Tabb let them in, and the old faded Trenwiths, in their dresses and cloaks of crimson and amber, stared coldly over the ringing empty hall. As they took off their cloaks Elizabeth came out of the winter parlour.

Demelza was surprised to see her wearing the frock of startling crimson velvet with the cascades of fine lace which she had worn at Julia's christening. There had been no suggestion that this was to be a party, and Demelza, feeling that any display in the present circumstances would be looked on as bad form by these well-bred people, had come in her newest afternoon dress.

So she's still interested in Ross, thought Demelza, with a sharp twinge, and any gratefulness to me won't make the least difference. I might have *known*. Nevertheless she went forward with a smile on her face and was graciously welcomed. Too graciously, she at once thought. It didn't ring true, like the sick Elizabeth of twelve months ago. What a fool I've been.

Francis was not there to welcome them, but when they had taken off their cloaks he came out of the big parlour. He was a little hesitant at this first proper meeting, and there was a glass in his hand. The two men eyed each other for a second.

Francis said: 'Well, Ross . . . so you came.'

'I came.'

'It's – a good thing, I think. *I'm* glad, anyway.'

He put out his hand rather tentatively. Ross took it, but the clasp was not a long one.

Francis said: 'We were always good friends in the past.'

'The best way,' Ross said, 'is to forget the past.'

'I'm very willing. It's a bitter subject.'

That said, the reconciliation formally made, there seemed nothing to add to it, and so the constraint grew up again.

'Did you walk here?'

'Yes.' A sore point, with Caerhays sold. 'I see Odgers is getting some repairs done to Sawle Church at last.'

'To the roof only. It has rained in so persistently these last few months that often the choir have had to sing with water dripping down their necks. I wish the damned steeple would fall down. It always persuades me I'm drunk when I get to the northwest of it.'

'Someday perhaps, when a Poldark is rich again, we shall be able to do something about it.'

'I think the church will have fallen down naturally before then.'

'My dear,' said Elizabeth, linking Demelza's arm, 'I was afraid you would never bring him. If he makes up his mind there's seldom much prospect of changing it. But perhaps you are clever enough to know how to set about it.'

'I'm not clever,' said Demelza. Indeed I'm not, she thought. Can I hold my own this week end, like I did three years ago? This time I haven't the heart. I'm too miserable and sick in mind to want to fight for him if he doesn't want me.

'My father and mother will be here for dinner,' said Elizabeth. 'Also Dwight Enys. I'm afraid we shall have no visitors after. You remember last time, George Warleggan and the Trenegloses turned up and you sang those enchanting songs.'

'I haven't seen the Trenegloses for ages,' said Demelza, as they went into the big parlour.

'Ruth is expecting her first child next month. There'll be great excitement if it is a boy. They say old Mr Horace Treneglos is already planning for his first grandson. There's not a lot of money about these days but when a family has been in existence more than six hundred years . . . Of course, ours is older.'

'What, the Poldarks?'

Elizabeth smiled. 'No. I'm sorry. I meant my own family. We have records back to 971. Ross, it's like old times to see you in this room.'

'It's like old times to be here,' said Ross enigmatically.

'And old times,' said Francis, bringing a wineglass across, 'is precisely what we are doing our best to forget. Here's to new times, I say. If there are any, then they can be no worse than what's gone, and good riddance.' He smiled into Demelza's eyes.

Demelza slowly shook her head, smiling back. 'Old times were good to me,' she said.

It wasn't the sort of meal they'd had before, either, though it was the best put on for two years. They had ham and fowls and a leg of mutton, boiled, with caper sauce, and afterwards batter pudding and currant jelly and damson tarts, and black caps in custard, and blancmange.

Demelza had never met Elizabeth's father and mother, and she was astonished at them. If keeping records since 971 made you look like that, then she'd rather have an ancestry that was decently forgot. Mr Chynoweth was thin and wry, with little pompous mannerisms that surprised because they claimed too much. Mrs Chynoweth was a dreadful sight, corpulent, with one eye discoloured and a swollen neck. Not having seen her before her illness, Demelza couldn't imagine where Elizabeth had got her ravishing looks. It didn't take long either to discover that they were people with a grievance. Something had gone wrong with their lives and they resented it as a personal affront. Demelza preferred old Aunt Agatha any day, for all her whiskers and her dribbling chin. You couldn't answer her back, but her conversation had vitality and point. It was a pity someone didn't write down her flow of memories before she died and they were all gone, lost forever in yesterday's dust.

After dinner, to Demelza's horror, though she should have remembered this was the routine, the women went off on their own, leaving the men over the port; and in any nightmare Demelza could not have chosen three more fearful companions than Elizabeth – in her present mood – Aunt Agatha and Mrs Chynoweth. They all walked upstairs and into Elizabeth's bedroom and chattered round the mirror and tidied their hair and in turn visited the noisome apartment down the passage which Demelza thought so much worse than the outdoor arrangements of Nampara; and Elizabeth adjusted Aunt Agatha's lace cap, and Mrs Chynoweth said she'd heard the new fashions at London and Bath were verging on the indecent; and Aunt Agatha said she still had some recipes somewhere for the face: pomatums and suchlike, and lip salves, white pots and water of talk: she'd find 'em for Demelza before she left. And Elizabeth said Demelza was very quiet, was she quite well? And Demelza said, Oh *yes*, fine and well; and Mrs Chynoweth gave her a casual glance up and down that seemed to strip her secret bare, and said the new fashion was for the waist to be right up under the arms and for the whole dress to fall quite like a candle sconce to the floor and the less worn under, the better. Demelza sat on the rosewood bed with its pink quilted satin hangings, and adjusted her garters and thought, Ross was right, we should never have come back here till Verity came; *she* makes all the difference, she's my mascot, my luck; I'm dull tonight and even port won't help; so Elizabeth'll score all round with her lovely sheeny hair and sapling waist and big grey eyes and her educated voice and her grace and poise. How is the rest of this evening and tomorrow to be got through?

Downstairs the port had circulated twice, and Jonathan Chynoweth, who had a humiliatingly weak head, was looking drowsy and talking with a slurred speech. Dwight, who had never had the money to drink regularly, was aware of his own deficiencies and kept sipping a drop and adding a drop when the bottle came round. The cousins, of course, were hardly aware that they had yet begun.

Francis said to Ross: 'These are the last three bottles of the '83 port. Did you lay in much of it at the time?'

'I hadn't the money then – just back from America and the place in a ruin. I've nothing earlier than last year's. When that's done we shall have to resort to cheap gin.'

Francis grunted. 'Money. The lack of it is poisoning both our lives. Sometimes I could rob a bank – would if it were Warleggan's and I could escape the gallows.'

Ross glanced idly at him. 'What made you quarrel with 'em?'

It was the first question which touched on the fundamentals between them. Francis instantly realized its importance and the impossibility of giving a full answer here. Yet he must not seem to evade it. 'A realization that your estimate of them was the right one.'

There was a pause while the clock struck. The metallic vibrations trembled round the room long after it had finished, seeming to seek a way out.

Francis drew three straight lines down the tablecloth with a fork's prongs. 'These things – soak in slowly. They're hardly noticed, until suddenly you wake up one day *knowing* that the man who has been your friend for years is a – blackguard and . . .' he waved his hand, '. . . that's all!'

'Have you moved your affairs?'

'No. I'll say that for them. I was offensive enough to George to blow his hat off, but he's done nothing about it.'

'I should move them.'

'Impossible. No one else would take the debt.'

'Look,' said Dwight uncomfortably, 'I've had what drink I want, and if you'd like to discuss private money matters . . .'

'Ecod, there's nothing private in debts,' said Francis. 'They're everybody's property. It's the one consolation. . . . Anyway – I've nothing private from *you*.'

The bottle was passed round.

'By the way,' said Francis, 'what has Demelza been doing with Bodrugan's mare?'

'Doing with it?' Ross said cautiously.

'Yes. I met him this morning, and he was all cock-a-hoop because his beloved Sheba was on the mend. I didn't even know the beast had been ill. He said it was Demelza's doing. The recovery, I mean, not the sickness.'

The bottle came to Ross. 'Demelza has some skill with animals,' he said hardily. 'Bodrugan came over and seemed anxious for her advice.'

'Well, she's in his good graces now. He was fairly slapping his boots about it.'

'What was wrong with the animal?' Dwight enquired.

'You must ask Demelza,' Ross said. 'No doubt she will explain.'

'Quarrelling with the War-Warleggans,' said Mr Chynoweth. 'A bad business. Very influ-influential. Tentacles.'

'How eloquently you express yourself these days, Father-in-law,' said Francis.

'Eh?'

'Let me fill your glass just this once more and then you can go to sleep comfortable.'

'For twelve months,' Ross said, 'they've been trying to buy a share in Wheal Leisure.'

'I don't doubt it. They'd be interested in any paying concern, and any belonging to you in particular.'

'Wheal Leisure doesn't belong to me. I wish it did.'

'Well, you're the largest shareholder. Have you had any success in linking up with the old Trevorgie workings?'

'No. We abandoned it for some of the wet months and then took it up again. I don't think the others will sanction the expense much longer.'

'There's good work there somewhere.'

'I know. But the men's wages mount up when you see them in the cost book.'

'You remember when we went down the old workings together, Ross. It doesn't seem so long ago. There's money in Trevorgie and Wheal Grace. I could smell it that day.'

'You need to put money in before you can take money out. It's one of the imperatives of mining.'

'Both copper and tin have gone up again,' said Dwight. He accepted the bottle and let it cool his fingers for a moment. 'D'you think there's any chance of restarting Grambler?'

'Not a dog's chance,' said Francis. 'Here, drain up your glass, you're not keeping pace at all.' He stared at Ross, whose lean restless face as yet showed no flush. 'You know old Fred Pendarves. For a month now I've had him prospecting over my land. And Ellery helping him. I don't think if he lived to be eighty you'd make a farmer out of Ellery or get him to tell the front of a cow from the tail; but he's been bred to mining like a terrier's bred to ratting, and between 'em I'm hoping for some sort of a workable venture. At heart I'm just the same as Ellery: there's copper in my blood, and if I have to go on living then I've got to start mining again, not rooting up stroil or driving pigs to market.'

A gentle snore came from Jonathan Chynoweth, whose head was resting gently back against his chair.

'Driving pigs to market indeed,' said Francis.

Ever since he came back from America, Ross thought, he and Francis had had something or other to quarrel about; but almost always when he met Francis he wondered if the quarrel was worth while. Francis had a way with him, always had had: a wry dry humour that carried one along, made one forget the bitterness and the possible betrayals. Perhaps the attraction was still mutual, for Francis had brightened up a lot since he came.

'Don't let me damp you,' he said, 'but even a hole in the ground costs money. Unless one can pick copper out of the subsoil as they did in Anglesea. . . .'

'I – have *some* ready money,' said Francis. 'A few hundred. It might see me through. Anyway, that's how it shall be spent.'

When Francis had offered to help Demelza with money if things went wrong at Bodmin, Ross had dismissed it as a rhetorical flourish. But here it was again. Ready money in a near-bankrupt.

'Well, and have they found anything yet?'

'Oh, traces enough. There's mineral everywhere, as you know. But I can't afford to take chances. I want a reasonable venture. What d'you think of this *Virgula Divinitoria*? It's supposed to be a sure test of where there is metal underground.'

'The name's impressive. Do you know the English for it, Dwight?'

Mr Chynoweth twitched and woke up. 'Where am I?'

'In bed with your wife, old man,' said Francis, 'so have a care lest we take advantage of you.'

Mr Chynoweth blinked at him, but was too stupefied to be insulted. He reached for his glass, but before he grasped it his head was nodding again.

'I gather it's only a sort of divining rod,' said Dwight. 'Even supposing it worked, I think it would be disappointing to sink a shaft expecting copper and find only lead.'

Ross said: 'Or even a tin kettle left by one of the old men.'

Francis said: 'Of course you're lucky with both Wheal Grace and Wheal Maiden on your land. We never did nothing here except for Grambler. It took all our attention and all our money.'

'Two derelict mines,' said Ross, and remembered what Mark Daniel had said about Grace: 'There's money in that mine. Copper. . . . I've never seen a more keenly lode.' 'More expensive to restart than to begin a new working,' he added.

Francis sighed. 'Well, I suppose all your interest is in Wheal Leisure now.'

'All my money is.'

'And that's the same thing, eh? And I shall have to recourse to *Virgula Divinitoria* or the wisdom of old Fred Pendarves. Pass the port, Enys; you're making no good use of it.'

There was a tap on the door and Tabb came in.

'If you please, sur, there's a man asking for Dr Enys.'

'What man?'

'He's from Killewarren, sur. I think he wants for Dr Enys to go to someone who's ill.'

'Oh tell 'em to be ill on a more convenient night.'

Dwight pushed back his chair. 'If you'll excuse me . . .'

'Nonsense,' said Francis, pouring his port so quickly that the froth circled to the centre. 'If you must see the fellow ask him in here; see what he wants.'

Tabb glanced at Dwight and then went out, to bring back a small clerkly man in black. They hadn't heard it begin to rain, but his cloak dripped water on the rug.

'Oh, it's Myners,' said Francis. 'What's amiss at Killewarren?'

The little man looked at Dwight. 'Are you Dr Enys, sir? I went to your house but was told you was here. Beg pardon for disturbing you. It is Miss Penvenen wanted to see you, and she sent me over to fetch you.'

'Miss *Caroline* Penvenen?'

'Yes, sir.'

So she was still in Cornwall – and no doubt her dog was having fits again.

'Has she not her own doctor?'

'Yes, sir, but she said for to fetch you. She's been ill for near on three days. It's her throat, sir, that is giving her grave trouble.'

A silence fell on the table. The casual good-fellowship of Francis, Dwight's first impatience, were not proof against this. The malignant sore throat, which had struck both families last year, had hardly been heard of this. If it came in the district again . . .'

'What symptoms?' Dwight said.

'I don't rightly know, sir. I'm only the bailiff. But Mr Ray Penvenen said she was mortal sick and I must fetch you.'

Dwight got up. 'I'll come at once. Wait and show me the way.'

Chapter four

PENVENEN LAND STRETCHED up almost to the back of Grambler village, but the house, Killewarren, had its main entrance near Goon Prince and was about three miles from the gates of Trenwith.

They had not heard the rain indoors because it was coming in a fine silent slag from the southwest, moving with a tired wind. But it was more wetting than straight rain, and the night was dark with a close inner blackness more proper to a confined space than out of doors; even Myners had some difficulty in keeping to the grass-grown track that led home.

They did not talk much, because the way was often too narrow to ride abreast and the going so uneven that an incautious step might throw you. Dwight, too, had mixed feelings at the prospect of meeting the tall girl again; anxiety and a slight apprehension that was not entirely to do with her illness. More than ever he was glad he had not been free with the port.

He had never been to her home – or her uncle's home – and when they turned in at the gates he rather expected to see such another gracious Tudor residence as Trenwith, or a small but solid Palladian house like Sir John Trevaunance's; so it was a surprise to find an ill-lit, rather shabby, rambling building which seemed to be little more than an extensive farmhouse. They went in through a porch and hall, up some stairs and along a narrow passage to a big untidy living room at the end of it, where a man with spectacles was turning the pages of a book. He took off his spectacles when Dwight was shown in – a sandy, stocky man in a coat sizes too big for him. As he came nearer Dwight saw that his red eyelids were almost lashless and that his hands were covered with warts. Ray Penvenen, bachelor, a onetime 'catch' of the county who had never been caught.

He said in a thin, rather musical voice: 'Are you Dr Enys?'

'Yes.'

'My niece is ill. Dr Choake has been attending her for two days, but she is worse and she insisted on sending for you.'

As Penvenen fumbled to put his spectacles away Dwight wondered how he managed to keep his hands clean.

'Does Dr Choake know I am being called?'

'No. We've not seen him since this morning.'

Dwight said: 'Of course, you know, it makes it very difficult——'

'I'm well aware of the usual etiquette, Dr Enys, and I'm not responsible for the breach of it. It is my niece who has sent for you. But in fact I am not satisfied. She's in great pain to-night – and the throat can be so dangerous.'

Dwight saw that Penvenen was more worried than he appeared.

'Did Dr Choake diagnose the complaint?'

'Yes. A quinzy.'

'Is there any fever?'

'That we don't know. But she can hardly swallow at all.'

They set off again, back down the passage and up a half dozen steps, and turned towards the south end of the house. Penvenen came to a door and stopped and knocked.

It was a big timbered room with an open fireplace in which a turf fire was flickering; wind down the chimney was fanning the smoke, and the blue damask untasselled curtains at the windows stirred furtively as the air was sucked through the door. A serving girl got up as they came in and Dwight went over to the bed.

Her tawny hair was loose and over her shoulders, and her fiery grey-green eyes a little dulled with pain, but she smiled at him with a faint sardonic twist to her lips. Then with an accompanying gesture she lifted the sheet and disclosed Horace asleep on a blue cushion beside her.

Dwight smiled back at her and took the seat the servant girl had left. He felt Caroline's pulse. It was quick but not sufficiently so to indicate a serious fever. He asked her one or two questions, which she answered by shakes or nods of her head. He saw her throat muscles quivering and then the effort she made to swallow.

'Will you open your mouth, Miss Penvenen.'

She did so and he peered at her throat.

'Would you get me a spoon, please,' he said to the maid. 'A tablespoon if you have one.' When she had gone he said to Penvenen: 'What treatment has Dr Choake prescribed?'

'. . . Two bleedings; that's so, isn't it, Caroline? A strong purge; and some sort of a draught, here. That's the lot, isn't it?'

Caroline pointed to the back of her neck.

'Oh, and a large blister. That's it. He said it was simply a question of getting the poisons to disperse.'

Dwight smelled the mixture. It was probably syrup of gill and Gascoigne's powder with a few other things in cinnamon water. The maid came back and Dwight took the spoon and sat on the bed.

The left side of the throat was much inflamed and there was no sign of suppuration yet. The uvula, the soft palate and the pharynx were all involved. At least there was nothing to suggest the disease they all feared. It seemed in fact a fairly clear case of quinzy and there was not a great deal he could do to improve on Choake's treatment. Her hands and forehead were quite cool, that was the only unusual sign. She was in a lot of pain.

'Mr Penvenen,' he said, 'would you kindly bring that candle over and hold it *quite* still. Just here. Here. That's it. Thank you.' He pressed the tongue down with the spoon again.

Penvenen's breathing was heavy and rather stale, his nodular hand only just steady enough. Little blisters of grease followed each other down the side of the candle and congealed upon the silver stick.

After a time Dwight released her and stood up. He had seen something, and a twist of excitement went through him. Penvenen also straightened, glad of the change of position, hitching the shoulders of his coat. They were all watching Dwight, but he was only aware of the green-eyed girl in the bed.

He turned his back on them and walked slowly to the fire. On the mantelshelf were things of hers. A velvet purse, embroidered and shutting with a spring; a gold repeating watch, probably French; a lace handkerchief with her initial in the corner; a pair of oiled dogskin gloves. He felt in his pocket and took out the etui that he always had with him. In it were the few small instruments that he found it useful to carry. A tooth forcer, a pair of tweezers, a fleam, tiny incision shears. He slid out the tweezers. Too short. Yet it would take an hour and a half to get the thing he really wanted. *Might* do. He had long fingers. And in another hour or so the swelling might have got so bad that what he wanted to do would not be possible at all.

He went back to the bed. 'Would you hold the candle for me again, Mr Penvenen? Miss Penvenen, sit up a little more, your head against the wood of the bed instead of against the pillow. Thank you.' For a minute his eyes met hers steadily. He seemed to see into the depths of them as into the far reaches of a pool, where the springs began. 'I can help you if you'll keep quite still. You mustn't jerk or jump. It may hurt a little, but I'll be as quick as I can.'

'What is it?' asked Penvenen. 'What are you going to do?'

'He's – going to lance my throat,' she said in a whisper.

'No, I'm not. I want you to keep still. Will you do that?'

She nodded. 'Of course.'

Penvenen could not hold the candle steady now. It flickered and bobbed; and the bed curtains got in the way; Dwight had the impulse to tear them all down. Eventually he got the light where he wanted and pressed her tongue down with the spoon. He inserted the tweezers. He could tell she had complete confidence in him; she opened her mouth wide and didn't flinch away.

It really wasn't too difficult after all. The tweezers reached quite well, and at the third attempt he got them firmly fixed on the bit of foreign matter. He tried not to tear the swollen tonsil, and after a minute the thing came out, followed by a little spurt of blood.

He stood up, nearly knocking Penvenen's candle over. 'Rinse your mouth now.' He drew back and motioned to the maid to come forward, then went over to the fire to examine his prize. Warm and comforting to feel the triumph. Supreme satisfaction. But it would be unworthy to show it.

He turned back. Some blood had come from the throat and the usual suppurative matter. She met his eyes again.

'Is that better?' he said, a little flushed in spite of himself. She nodded.

'It will get easier now. I have nothing here, but if your man cares to come with me I can make him up something to wash the throat. Or any apothecary will give you a melrose mixture tomorrow.'

'What,' said Penvenen, and cleared his voice, 'what did you take away?'

Dwight said: 'When did you last eat fish, Miss Penvenen?'

'I . . .' She wrinkled her nose. 'On Wednesday.'

'You must be more careful.' He showed her the tiny piece of sharp fishbone he had taken from her throat. 'It has caused you inconvenience and might have been serious if it had been left longer.'

At Trenwith they spent a quiet evening, cosy but a little isolated. The rain had kept even the usual carol singers away. They played quadrille for a time to the sound of Mr Chynoweth's snores and when Dwight got back he changed into a pair of Francis's breeches and joined in the games and won all the money. He was quiet about his visit to Killewarren, but Demelza could see he was inwardly excited or pleased. When waiting for his cards his fingers would be drumming the chair, and there was an unusual flush on his face.

All through the evening Francis went out of his way to be nice to Demelza; and when he chose to exert himself, which was not often these days, there were few men who could be more agreeable company. It was as if he was trying to efface in her memory the day when he had turned her out of the house. Demelza met him, as she would have met most people, with forgiveness and good will. Nevertheless she was a little uneasy for Ross, who naturally had more time with Elizabeth.

If Dwight had had leisure from his own thoughts to observe them he might have felt this regrouping strangely apt. Demelza's impish wit had an echo in Francis's wry sense of humour; socially they were well suited. And Ross and Elizabeth had much in common; all those interests and tastes which had helped to make them boy and girl sweethearts.

Just before eleven Mrs Chynoweth helped her yawning husband to bed, and Aunt Agatha went soon after, but the others stayed till midnight had struck. Then they counted up their sixpences and drank a glass of hot punch before going off desultorily up the broad stairs. Demelza was feeling tired and overfed and got undressed and between the sheets quickly, trying not to think too sentimentally of the last time they had slept in this house. Ross sat on the bed for a minute or two talking over the evening, and then remembered his pipe which he had left in the winter parlour where they had dined. He took a candle and went back through the darkened house, his light flirting with the ancient shadows. There was a gleam under the door of the winter parlour; and when he went in he found Elizabeth clearing away the remains of the evening meal.

He explained what he had come for. 'I thought everyone was upstairs,' he said.

'Emily Tabb has a bad arm, and Tabb has been unwell. We can't expect them to do everything.'

'Then you should press your guests. They have good will but no knowledge of how the house is run.' He began to move some of the plates.

'No,' she said, 'I don't want you to bother. It will only take me half an hour.'

'A quarter, then, if you're helped. Don't worry; I know the way to the kitchen.'

She smiled, but obliquely, privately, as she turned away. Her looks had been troubling him all evening. Rich crimson flared about the unsubdued whiteness of her arms and throat; her eyes had new lights in them. She had made no provocative move at all, but in her cool cultured way her manner was not without challenge.

He followed her into the large kitchen.

'What did the Bartles do when they left you?'

'Mary is in service in Truro. Bartle was trying for work in the brewery, but I haven't heard if he got it.'

'The Poldarks have fallen low,' he said. 'You must be sorry you married into the family.'

She picked up an empty tray. 'Do you think I should answer that?'

'Perhaps you think I shouldn't have asked it.'

'Oh. . . . You're free to say what you like, Ross. If anyone has the right, you have. I don't take offence so easily these days.'

They went back into the dining room and began to fill the tray together.

He said: 'I'm surprised to hear Francis has a little money put by. I wonder it hasn't been spent on eking out your ordinary life.'

'He doesn't want to spend it that way. It's a special sum – six hundred pounds.'

'Do the Warleggans know of it?'

'They gave it him.'

'What?'

'It was a token payment for all the money he'd lost at the gaming tables to Sanson. They felt Sanson's disgrace was a reflection on their family and offered him this. But he won't spend it at present. He hasn't spent a penny.'

Ross put a hand through his hair. 'That's very strange.'

They went on with the clearing.

When the last dishes were in the kitchen Elizabeth said:

'Thank you for your help, Ross. You're very kind – and forgiving, perhaps. Somehow I hadn't thought . . .'

'Forgiving?'

She avoided what she had meant to say. 'But of course there has long since been nothing to forgive, has there? Your marriage with Demelza has been so happy.'

He realized she had turned the conversation. He leaned back on the table behind him and watched as she stacked the plates. 'I like that dress.'

Her lips moved in a half-smile.

'You've grown up a little since we first met,' he said.

'A little? I feel old . . . old.'

'I doubt the truth of that remark.'

'Why?'

'You have your mirror. My reassurance can't add anything to it.'

'Oh.' she said, 'your reassurance isn't unwelcome.' And she turned to carry a dish into the kitchen beyond.

He waited until she came back. 'Demelza would have helped you willingly if you had asked her.'

'Demelza . . . Of course. Yes, she would, wouldn't she.'

Elizabeth began to put some unused cutlery away in a drawer. Then she reached up to the cupboard above and tried to open it, but the door had stuck.

'Let me,' Ross said, and came up behind her. He put his hand on the knob and jerked the cupboard open, and she stepped back against him. Just for a moment they were together and her hair brushed his face. He put his arm round her, his hand closing against the velvet of her other arm. Time briefly ceased to have progression and became an intimate perception of a single emotion breathed by them both – then he stepped away.

'Thank you,' she said, and picked up the jar and put it in the cupboard. 'It's all the rain and damp weather – makes the wood swell.'

'Have you finished now? It must be nearly one o'clock.'

'Almost. You go on, Ross. I don't need you any more.'

'Not any more?'

She laughed slightly, but with a catch in her voice. 'Well, not that way.' She had still not turned to face him.

When he got upstairs Demelza was sitting up in bed darning a torn ruffle on one of his shirts. He was faintly and unreasonably irritated because she was not asleep or trying to get off, for then she would not have noticed how long he had been.

In fact she noticed more than that, some change in his face, on which she instantly put the right interpretation and a wrong emphasis.

He went across and put his pipe on the table, began to unbutton his coat.

She said: 'This weather'll hold up the start of ploughing. The land'll get so soggy and sad.'

'Oh, we may have some fine days next month.' Because she had not asked, he forced himself to say: 'Elizabeth was in the dining room clearing the remains of the feast. I helped her with a few things.'

'She should've told me. I didn't like to offer.'

'That's what I said.'

Did you, Ross? Did you? And what else? 'When I saw Elizabeth I was sorry not to have my better frock. I didn't know we were to dress up.'

'You looked very nice as you were.'

But she looked nicer. 'Well . . . I'm glad there's peace in the family again. But I'll not be satisfied really till Verity and Andrew come as well.'

'Nor I.' He undressed quickly and got into bed beside her. She went on stitching.

I suppose, she thought, this had got to come someday. Elizabeth had Ross fast even though she married Francis. Then I came along and took him from her. But always there were some ties, some ropes left that wouldn't break; and when his interest in me began to slacken it was as sure as life he'd turn again to her. And now she's no longer in love with Francis. She's heart-free, though still bound in marriage. What will happen? He's hers again for the beckoning. He doesn't want me or my child. I think I want to die.

'Would you like me to blow out the light?' she asked.

'No . . . I don't mind. When you're ready.'

'There's just this end to do. You must have caught it somewhere.'

'All my shirts are wearing out.'

He thought: Were beauty under twenty locks kept fast . . . if she went to London or Bath she'd have half the aristocracy at her feet. Instead she's immured here, in an ancient house and with a bankrupt husband, doing half her own work. It must be galling to her to feel her life's slipping away. She was twenty-six last birthday. Perhaps that's the reason for the change. But it's a change towards *me*.

'What are you thinking of, Ross?'

'Um? Oh, about the rain. The Mellingey will be in flood very soon.'

What would have happened, he thought, if she'd married me? Would events have been very different? Would the results have been different? We're the slaves of our characters: would I have been happier, or she? Perhaps there are elements in her nature and mine which would have made our life together difficult.

Demelza said: 'I was that thankful to know it was not the morbid sore throat at Killewarren. Always now I shall be frightened out of my life of it.'

'So shall we all.'

'I met Miss Penvenen at Bodmin. She's a handsome girl.'

'Did you, now? Where did you see her?'

'She was – we were just introduced one day . . . Dwight was a small matter unsettled when he came back. I think he may feel a taking for her.'

'Isn't she promised to Unwin Trevaunance?'

'I don't know. Twould be a pity if Dwight got into something again – I mean, made a second bad choice.'

'Yes. . . .'

And what of this young woman beside him, whom he had loved devotedly for four years – and still did love? She had given him more than perhaps Elizabeth ever could: months of unflawed relationship, unquestioning trust (which he was now betraying in thought). Oh, nonsense. What man did not at some time or another glance elsewhere; and who could complain if it remained as a glance? (Chance was a fine thing.) And if there had been a cooling between him and Demelza, hers had been the first move, not his.

He said: 'What *did* you do with your time while you were in Bodmin? You've never told me.'

Demelza hesitated, but felt this the worst moment for confessions. 'I was so worried I can't hardly remember. . . . I don't know what I should've done if it hadn't been for Verity, that I don't.'

'No,' said Ross dryly. So she was hiding something. Queer if she too had met someone. But who? In that seething jumble almost anyone in Cornwall. One of the Trevaunances? She had been visiting there before the trial on some strange business of her own. It would explain her interest now in Caroline Penvenen, her shying away from where they had met. Oh, it was impossible. The Trevaunances were not her sort, nor they hers. . . . He stirred restlessly.

'I've just finished,' said Demelza, and put the shirt on the table and blew out the light.

They lay quiet, listening now to the purr of the rain on the glass. Demelza put her hands behind her head, but the movement was uncomfortable and she lowered them. How much longer shall I be able to hide it? she thought. There's no sign yet – I think, but Mrs Chynoweth's one good eye seemed to see everything. Ross is not observant that way; but if Mrs C. suspects, she'll tell Elizabeth, who'll tell Francis, who may say something to Ross. Anyway, he will have to know sometime. Put it off, put it off.

Count your blessings. He's safe from the worst things, from the debtor prison for another year, from the hangman or transportation – if he behaves – forever. He can't hardly go off with Elizabeth. Even if he's unfaithful – should that matter? In a few months or years he may tire of her. She may get old and withered, or fat and ugly. But that's much more likely to happen to me.

'Are you asleep?' he said.

'No.'

He leaned over and kissed her forehead. 'Good night, my love.'

'Good night, Ross,' she said.

After that the silence fell again and was not broken. She thought, trying to forget the heartache, if my child's a boy, perhaps it will make a difference, alter his feelings. We'll call him Jan, or Humphrey – or even Ross.

But if it's a girl . . . then we shall have no ready name.

Chapter five

ON THE LAST day of the old year Myners brought a message to the Gatehouse where Dwight was experimenting with certain poisons to see if in small doses they had any medicinal values.

The letter, on green note paper, had been sealed with a heraldic ring and read as follows:

Dear Dr Enys,

Having saved my life on Christmas Eve, you appear to have no further interest in my recovery. Perhaps you will be interested to know that it is now complete. My uncle and I would nevertheless esteem it a favour if you would call on us in the near future to assure yourself of this and to receive Payment and our thanks for your skill of a week ago.

I am, sir,
Yours, etc.,
Caroline Penvenen

Dwight stared at the letter and then, after a struggle with himself, went to his escritoire and wrote his reply while the bailiff waited.

My dear Miss Penvenen,

I am happy to hear of, and offer my felicitations on, your recovery. I did not, in fact, anticipate any other outcome once the fishbone had been removed. Nevertheless I should certainly have called, and ask your Pardon if my not doing so has seemed lacking in courtesy; but, as you will understand, you are my colleague Dr Choake's patient, and it would be a breach of etiquette on my part if I continued to attend you without his knowledge or consent. In these circumstances I have regretfully had no alternative but to assume an indifference to your health which I did not feel.

As to Payment, I am amply recompensed for the small service I performed by the knowledge of your gratitude.

I am, madam,
Your obedient servant,
Dwight Enys

When Myners had gone back with this message Dwight turned again to his mixtures, but the experiments had lost their savour. In any case he had only his own stomach to experiment on, and he was already feeling very unwell from the last draught he had taken, so he went for a walk round the garden to see if the air would help the attack to pass off.

After an hour, when he was feeling better, Myners arrived back with another message. It ran:

Dear Dr Enys,

To you, no doubt, the saving of my life may seem a very small Service indeed. To me, as I am sure you will understand, the matter assumes a slightly greater importance. Naturally I should not expect you to change your opinion on this point; but I should inform you that when Dr Choake called on the following day my uncle sent him about his Business, and I have therefore been without medical attention since.

I should be obliged if you would call today; and enclose a guinea, which is the smallest value, little as I esteem myself, that I can put upon your visit of Christmas Eve.

I am, sir,

Yours, etc.,

Caroline Penvenen

Dwight went to the escritoire and sat tapping his pen in agitation. Why not admit the truth? He was in love with the girl – desperately so. And the train of incident, although the women were so vastly different, was disturbingly close to events in his love for Keren. One of Choake's patients – himself called in suddenly in an emergency – some sudden attraction – Choake turned away the following day and Dr Enys chosen as a permanent medical man. This far the same. Of course Keren was married; but everyone knew that Caroline was promised to the younger Trevaunance. In a sense this situation was more explosive, for although he had eventually fallen in love with Keren, the infatuation had been mainly hers. Not so this time. Indeed he might be going much too fast: the infatuation might be wholly his. But the potential danger was obvious. He did not deceive himself. Despite his good breeding, Caroline was as much above him as Keren had been below him. Ray Penvenen weighed money and rank in the same scale. What was lacking in one must be made up by the other, and rumour was about that Unwin Trevaunance, despite his being a member of Parliament and brother of a childless baronet, might only just make the grade. Hence the delay in marriage.

Was he to intrude into this situation, already aware of his own feelings and half afraid, half hoping that it involved hers?

Yet how to get out of it without seeming an obvious boor? A voice within him said, Well, perhaps it would mean only this one visit; she looked a healthy young woman not given to physical ill humours. It would be pleasant to see her again, to receive her thanks. And, finding as he did so many of the big houses closed against him by this doctor or that – and not having the reputation or experience to be called in as a consultant – wouldn't it be the plainest common sense to set his feelings aside and take this opportunity of establishing himself with the richest family in the district? What other physician in his place would hesitate?

Nor would even he have hesitated if it had not been for the memory of the tragedy of Keren. That had brought home to him his own weaknesses, and it would be reckless to disregard them.

He picked up the pen again.

My dear Miss Penvenen [he wrote],

I am obliged to you for your further letter. In the first place I would assure you that it is far from likely that I saved your life. Medically one would have expected the Swelling eventually to burst and expel the foreign matter, though this not without considerable further pain and inconvenience to Yourself. In the second place I would assure you that I meant not to put any estimate upon the importance of the complaint in its relation to yourself but only to the trifling inconvenience I was put to in attending upon you.

Further, the value of your life or health is so plainly beyond computation that to express it in terms of money would seem an Impertinence, and I am therefore taking the liberty of returning the guinea you so kindly enclosed.

I will wait upon you tomorrow, Saturday, in the forenoon.

I am, madam,
Your obedient servant,
Dwight Enys

Seventeen ninety-one came in without change of weather or other outward sign to mark the beginning of a new year. Saturday was indistinguishable from Friday, grey and fine but with rain always heavy on the wind. For Dwight, however, Friday was the day he had given way to a reckless impulse; Saturday the day he must implement it. He rode over to Killewarren with the conflict still rife in his mind.

The house was no less shabby in the light of day. However much better circumstanced Ray Penvenen might be than his neighbours, he had no intention of outshining them in renewal and repair.

Caroline was waiting in the big upstairs living room with its heavy crimson plush velvet curtains and its warm turkey rugs. She looked as tall as a sunflower in a low-cut frock drawn tight at the waist and a wide green skirt. Horace came yapping at him, but she silenced him, and Dwight went across to the window where she was standing. He touched her hand.

'Dr Enys,' she said, 'how kind of you to come at last. I haven't been waiting above two hours, and the time has passed quickly looking over the garden. A happy New Year!'

'Thank you. . . . And to you, Miss Penvenen.' As usual he had flushed. 'I'm – sorry if you've been waiting. One or two other calls took me longer than I expected. And I said the forenoon. It's only just after eleven o'clock.'

'The other calls, of course, were more important than mine,' she said sweetly.

'Only in that the people were more gravely ill.'

'Were you so certain I was not?'

'Your letter said not.'

'I might have been bravely hiding a serious disease. Did that never occur to you? Oh, faith, you can't be as good a doctor as I thought.'

'I am not a good doctor. There are few such if any about. . . .'

'You think I should have kept Dr Choake?'

'I'd prefer not to discuss it.'

'Very well then, discuss me. Perhaps you would like to examine my throat again?'

'Yes . . .'

He moved nearer to her and she opened her mouth. Their faces were on a level; she was at least five feet nine, he thought. He turned her face a little more to the light. He noticed again the slight freckles on her nose. Her skin was warm and firm under his fingers.

'Say *"Ah!"'*

'*Ah* . . .' said Caroline.

'Yes, very satisfactory. You'll have no more trouble there.' He withdrew his hands, still embarrassed, and she closed her mouth.

She laughed.

'What is it?' he said.

'Nothing.' She shrugged her bare shoulders, half turning away. 'How different you are sometimes from others. Today I might be a sword's edge, you flinch away at a touch. The other night it was not so. It was: "Turn this way," and "turn that." "Keep your head still! Open your mouth and keep it open! Bring me a spoon! Hold the candle steady! Now!"'

He half smiled through his flush. 'You were ill then.'

'So one needs to be ill to call forth the physician, eh? Shall I swoon now or have a fit of the vapours?'

Something was shuffling and stamping in the room underneath.

'D'you so much prefer the doctor to the ordinary man?'

She looked out of doors, her grey-green eyes narrowed. 'I have to confess a liking for a man who knows his own mind.'

Dwight's heart began to thump.

'A man may know his own mind – and at the same time his own place.'

Her eyes did not flicker. 'That's a complaint I shouldn't have thought you *ever* suffered from.'

'Well, now that you've discovered that I do, what would you suggest to remedy it?'

Caroline turned from the window. 'Why, refreshment, of course. Refreshment is the remedy for all manner of embarrassments. And pray don't be frightened by the noises below. This room is over the stables and our horses are restive for lack of exercise.'

He watched her while she poured two glasses of wine. He was grateful for this opportunity to collect his thoughts.

When she came back she said: 'I should think your hero, Mr Ross Poldark, must be a man who very clearly knows his own mind every instant of the day. *And*, having come to his decisions, I imagine he puts them through with the utmost ruthlessness and determination. Canary?'

'You're quite right.' He took the glass. 'Thank you. At least you're quite right as to the determination. But I shouldn't put his wife behind him at all in that respect.'

'I've met her.' Caroline sighed. 'A handsome enough creature in a sort of way. But not with the "stick at nothing" look of her husband. You must bring him over sometime. I think he would divert me.'

'I'm afraid that would be difficult.'

'He's not on call like a lackey – or a doctor? Is that what you were going to say? Well, I did not suppose he would be. But perhaps we can arrange it. A biscuit?'

'No, thank you.'

The horses were shuffling again. She bent her head. 'That's Firefly. I know his stamp. Are you fond of riding, Dr Enys? For pleasure, I mean.'

'I'm in the saddle so much about my business that I get little time——'

'We must ride together one of these days.' She put a hand up to her tawny hair. 'I'll let you know. I may even venture to summon you here from a sick bedside – from some really important case, not merely a fishbone or a triviality of that nature.'

'I'm sure you'll appreciate,' he said impatiently, 'that there are in fact serious cases about that make demands on one's time – and one's compassion. Scrofula among the undernourished children, phthisis among their fathers; the tertian fever has been everywhere this year, and scorbutus is spreading in Sawle. Thomas Choake is more interested in his hunting and those of his fashionable patients who can pay him. I deal with what I can and the rest go to ignorant rascally druggists or old women who brew rats' tails and sell them as elixirs. It's hard sometimes to maintain a sense of proportion that everyone can appreciate.'

'Yes,' she said after a minute, quizzically, 'I think I do like you after all.'

'It is very gratifying: I'm sensible of the honour. Now, I'm afraid I must be going as there are several more in this district I must see. Will you give my kind respects to your uncle . . .'

'Wait. Don't be so stiff. I should prefer five minutes more of your attention. What are all these diseases with their Latin names? They interest me. What are you doing for them? Can you cure them? I think I should like to have been a physician or a barber surgeon – I have never had the least aversion for blood.'

'I can do next to nothing for the scroftulus conditions. Once the poisonous humour betrays itself the sufferer is likely to face a lingering death. For phthisis there are two cures for every forty failures. Few people die of the tertian ague but many fall a prey to other things from its weakening effects. For scorbutus I can do everything and nothing. A doctor's drugs are useless, but certain foods can bring about an almost immediate cure. However, those foods are unprocurable by the people of Sawle, so they must bleed and die.'

'What foods? Breadfruit from the South Seas?'

'No, the ordinary staples of life. Green vegetables, fruit, fresh meat. Any one of those three in sufficient quantity.'

'Why do they not buy them then? I suppose they're too poor. But scorbutus is only scurvy, isn't it? Thousands of our sailors suffer from it and are no worse when they get home.'

'It depends on the length of the voyage. Many die.'

'But *they* cannot get the foods anyhow. Why don't the people of Sawle spend less on gin? Drunkenness is no less for all their poverty. Or why do they not run oranges instead of brandy when they sail to France?'

He said: 'Oranges, when they can be had at all, are selling at twopence-halfpenny or threepence each. Meat is prohibitive. Gin costs them sixpence a quart or less. They're only human after all. And, even so, many of them are as sober as you or I.'

She inclined her head. 'Thank you. I'm very much complimented by the association. In fact I have quite a taste for brandy when given the opportunity. . . . But there, Dr Enys, shall you do any good by attempting to preserve all these people? They will multiply and multiply and so there'll be ever more mouths to feed. Admitted it is sad to see them die, but it keeps the numbers in check and preserves a balance. If there's more food than people then the people grow in numbers until there's more people than food. When that happens some die off until the food is equal to maintain the others. Is it for us to interfere? Ah, I see I've shocked you.'

'Only by assuming that you yourself are different from the rest and not to be included in this stocktaking.'

She smiled sweetly. 'Well, of course I'm different from the rest It's no virtue but a happy chance. I was born a Penvenen, and so am rich and educated. If I had been born poor and weakly I should no doubt die of one of your nasty diseases, but don't expect me to weep about it now!'

'It's a comfortable reasoning,' Dwight said, 'but dangerous. Isn't it the sort of philosophy which has caused all this trouble in France?'

Before she could reply the door opened and Ray Penvenen came in. He greeted the young doctor cordially enough, though not with the freedom his niece permitted herself. After a few minutes Dwight left, glad to escape and to sort out his impressions. The unfamiliar scent of her clung about him all the day, perhaps in his memory more than in his nostrils. Even the taste of the wine was foreign, quickening to the pulse. That philosophy, he thought; the perfect one for the middle-aged bachelor with money dulling his heart. But not for the girl of nineteen or twenty. Monstrous. And so was she; but against judgment he was deeper in than ever. There was no escape – except to hope that she would quickly become an M.P.'s wife and move up to London to keep house there. Out of sight would not be out of mind, but it would at least be out of danger.

Ray Penvenen hitched his coat to set it more firmly on his shoulders. 'I hear Unwin is coming down tomorrow.'

'Yes,' said Caroline. 'For about a fortnight.'

'You did not tell me.'

'I thought Sir John would this morning.'

'Unwin will expect some definite word from you while he is down.'

'Did Sir John say as much?'

'Not as much. But he let it be understood.'

Caroline moodily picked up her skirts and perched on the window seat. 'The petition has not even been heard yet. He can hardly expect me to marry a member of Parliament who doesn't know whether he really is one. That's demanding a good deal.'

Ray said dryly: 'My dear, you're not overtly marrying Unwin for the prestige and the position. One is supposed to marry because one loves a man.'

'Oh, love, yes, I've heard of it. But is Unwin marrying me because he loves me or because he covets the twenty thousand pounds you and Uncle William have settled on me? Ask him that.'

'My dear, it is for you to ask him – if you choose.' Penvenen glanced at his niece and then, remembering her capabilities, added hastily: 'Or perhaps you'd better not. I was only warning you that the question of a date for your marriage may be broached during his stay, and it's as well to ponder what your response will be.'

'Dear, dear, it all sounds very pompous. . . . Uncle, I'm an heiress but have little money to handle. Now I rather like the feel of money, the jangle it gives, the weight in one's purse, the tawny yellow colour of the gold. Suppose you gave me some. Um? What do you say?'

Penvenen's face always looked different when this subject was mentioned. 'I have no objection to advancing you something – though there's little you could find to spend it on. You're admirably clothed, well fed and housed, have three hunters and a personal maid. I should not have thought . . . How much do you want?'

'Oh . . . fifty pounds, perhaps.'

A glass clattered as Penvenen locked the canary away.

'You can't be serious.'

'Oh yes, indeed. Why not? It's a round comfortable sum and will last me some time. After all, what is the use of being rich if one can't have a little flutter now and then?'

'I can't possibly give you so much. For gambling of some sort it would be a sheer waste. You know I disapprove of the gaming tables – and two or three tickets is all one needs in a lottery. One is just as likely to draw a prize with few as with many.'

Caroline smiled at her hands. 'Oh, this is a new kind of gaming, Uncle. It appeals to me, and I have a fancy to indulge the whim.'

Chapter six

THE FOLLOWING WEEK, one of the quarterly meetings of the Wheal Leisure venturers was due, and it was Mr Treneglos's turn to entertain the others at Mingoose. A distribution which was equal to a fifteen per cent return on their investment meant sixty per cent for the year and was something to be well satisfied with. Three years ago the mine had employed fifty-six men. Now it took just over the hundred and was a spot of prosperity in a depressed countryside.

Ross was not, however, altogether surprised when Mr Renfrew again proposed that the exploratory tunnel being driven towards the ancient Trevorgie workings should be stopped and the labour turned to more productive purposes. There had been such propositions before, put mainly by Mr Pearce, but they had been defeated. Ross had been aware for some time that some of his colleagues had been coming round to Mr Pearce's view, so now he waited and did not speak as it was his impulse to. Mr Pearce also was silent, and it was as if both were waiting for the neutral voters to declare themselves.

Presently Henshawe said: 'I think we should persevere a month or two more. We've gone so far that it's a pity to abandon it now.'

'I b'lieve we've come right past the workings,' said Renfrew. 'Missed them. We might go on for years more and never connect.'

'Not according to that old map,' shouted Mr Treneglos, trying to make himself heard above the noises in his head. 'Remember that old map showed the Trevorgie workings as turning and branching towards Marasanvose, and we're not at the branch yet. All the same, I'm disappointed. I never thought twould be such a long job. It's a drain on our profits all the time.'

Ross said: 'It was the means of our finding the second lode. That's not wholly unprofitable.'

'No,' said Mr Pearce, entering the lists also. 'But the best mass was found in the other direction. We should do better, I declare, to strike out farther to the northeast where the going is easier and the quality promises better.' He scratched himself.

Mr Treneglos undid the top button of his trousers. 'Well, tis as the majority says. There's no doubt we can afford it, what? We've a handsome profit to show, and a better in prospect. But damme, I'm coming round to the contrary view from what I've held all along. Twas not as if we was driving an adit which would help to unwater the mine. We've tunnelled under the valley and now we're tunnelling under the hill. What did you say, Pearce? What?'

Pearce shook his wigged head, disclaiming speech.

Ross said: 'I have talked the company into continuing twice; but I don't want to again if the feeling's against it. I still think we should do well to persevere; but the proposition was mine in the first place, and when you add up the men's wages over the months it totals to a sum in the end. So I'll say no more and leave it to the vote.'

The vote was taken. Ninety parts (Ross's and Henshawe's) were for continuing, one hundred and fifty against.

Ross said: 'One thing I should have brought up. I take it the men on the work will not be set off – that they'll be put to other employment.'

Mr Renfrew screwed up his eyes, 'I should like to see a widening of the main shaft. The air is still bad, and we could profitably use 'em that way.'

The venturers discussed this for some minutes, the matter was settled and the meeting seemed about to break up.

Then Mr Pearce coughed and said, smiling apologetically: 'There's one other matter I should have brought up earlier. Awaiting the right opportunity, as it were. That is to say, that one of the adventurers – that is one I act for, if you understand – Mr Benjamin Aukett, has disposed of his holding in the mine to a Mr Henry Coke. I am not sure yet whether Mr Coke will wish to attend the meetings, but I rather – hm – gather he will wish me to represent his interest as I did Mr Aukett's. In any case the sale has only just taken place, and I shall be able to report more fully in April.'

He went on talking, hitching up his stomach from time to time and carefully avoiding Ross's eyes.

'Who?' shouted Mr Treneglos. 'Who? Never heard of him. A Whig, I suppose. Where's he live? What's his profession? Oh. Gentleman. Well, that's a good sign. Hope he's as docile as Aukett. Bring him along sometime if he cares to come. We've nothing to conceal. That's the feeling of the meeting, I take it?'

The others agreed.

Captain Henshawe said: 'I wonder if you know what his share changed hands at?'

'No, my dear sir,' said the lawyer. 'Not an idea in the world.'

Renfrew said: 'I was offered four hundred and fifty pound for my share last month. That is fifteen pounds for a five-pound part. It shows a tempting profit. An' it shows just how hard people is looking for an investment these days.'

'What was the name of the man who approached you?' said Ross.

'Name of Garth. Never heard of him. A civil-spoken fellow, but not what you'd call a gentleman.'

'I take it you're not intending to sell?'

'No,' said Renfrew, observing Ross's expression with some surprise. 'It pays me better to stay in, apart from all the tackle an' gear I supply.'

The meeting ended soon after, and, as was their custom, Captain Henshawe and Ross walked home together, in the gathering misty afternoon.

'Well,' said Henshawe, trying to be hearty, 'it's near on three years since you paid four-fifty for Surgeon Choake's share. At the time you'll mind me telling you I thought it a deal more than it was worth. But your belief's been justified. It's my way of thinking old Aukett got upwards of five hundred for his share to make him willing for the sale.'

'That's my belief too.'

Henshawe never liked it as much when the scarred side of Ross's face was towards him. The scar was more than half hidden by the long side hair, but all the same the tail of it down his cheek was a token of wildness and intractability, qualities which Henshawe deplored since he was a peace-loving and an easygoing man.

'I do not suppose,' he said, 'that twill make any difference to the running of the mine; in fact it cannot, for Mr What's-it will have to tag along with the majority. Anyway, there's little anyone could cavil at while the profits are so good.'

'No,' said Ross.

'It's a pity the work towards Trevorgie has come to naught, but maybe we shall be able to start again in a few months.'

'Maybe,' said Ross.

They walked along in silence. Ross said:

'I wonder if Mrs Trenwith will stand firm?'

'Mrs Trenwith? You mean hold on to her share? I haven't a doubt. She's got too strong a nose for a profit, I reckon, to part with it easy.'

'There are two kinds of profit.'

'Yes, well, if she did, it would not be serious, would it? Interests in other mines change hands every day – when there's anyone these days to buy 'em. I agree we're very comfortable as we are, but I don't suppose a new adventurer or two will upset our applecart.'

'No,' said Ross.

They came to the parting of the ways.

'You'll drink with me before you go on?'

'No, thank you, sur. I'm full to the brim as it is. I'll be getting home along while the light holds.'

Ross turned down through the apple trees towards his house. As he came in sight of the front door he saw that there was a strange horse waiting.

Jane Gimlett met him in the hall. 'If you please, sur, there's a gent to see you. Bin here a half-hour he has. Name of Trencrom. You asked me always to tell you so as you'd know whether to go in or no.'

'. . . Where is Mrs Poldark?'

'In with Mr Trencrom, sur.'

Ross took off his hat and smoothed back his hair. Mr Trencrom's presence explained the large horse outside; but what explained Mr Trencrom? He was in no mood for company. Demelza alone, perhaps. No one else. He went in.

His wife, in one of her white muslin frocks, had her back to him and was pouring tea. The visitor faced him from the largest armchair.

Mr Trencrom was one of those peculiar people who have an iron in every fire. Like the Warleggans, he had the talent for turning his interests into money, but unlike them he had no ambition to social advancement. He had been born the son of a wool stapler and that was what he would always remain. He had part shares in seines, part shares in tucking mills, part shares in tin stamps, part shares in little shops in little towns. And everywhere the money added up and brought in more. His investment in the Carnmore Copper Company had been almost the only substantial loss of his career, and Ross had not seen him since the venture failed. Of course everyone, certainly all the magistrates, knew what his chief business was.

In appearance he was very stout. He had only two enemies in the world: the gaugers and his own bronchial tubes.

'Well, Captain Poldark,' he said breathlessly. 'Excuse me rising. Been very ill this winter. Damp air does me no good. Your charming wife. I said I took no liquor. She made tea. Delicious. How are you? My dear sir.'

'I find the climate trying,' Ross said.

Demelza glanced at him and saw at once that there was trouble.

'You'll take something too, Ross?'

'Something stronger,' he said. 'You've ridden far on a dull afternoon, Mr Trencrom.'

'Yes, as you say. It's some years since I was in this part. What distressing news from France, Captain Poldark. They say Mirabeau is gravely ill again and nearly blind. If he should die.'

'I haven't followed their politics very closely of late.'

'Nor I from choice. But when one is – in constant contact. If Mirabeau goes there'll be a landslide – I'm told. The King's position. Very dangerous. England can't stand by and watch.'

'I don't think it can be our affair what happens to Louis.'

'Well, up to a point – that's true. But there are limits.'

'Limits on both sides. For we are without an army or a navy.'

'Yes, yes, of course you're right. All the same – I have grave fears for the future.'

Ross sat in a chair and put his elbows on the arms.

There was silence.

'However,' said Mr Trencrom, 'I have not called merely to discuss the foreign situation. As you will have guessed. No doubt.' He coughed. It was an extraordinary sound for so large a man; his mountainous body quivered, and a small thin wheezy noise was eventually produced as if deep inside him a very small dog was dying of asphyxiation. Then he wiped his mouth and continued. 'Purpose one. To renew our acquaintance. That is done. Purpose two. To enquire after your affairs. If they prosper. Purpose three. To speak of mine. Now if——'

'Suppose,' Ross said, 'that we spoke of yours first. By doing so we might come at a quicker understanding and be able to treat of mine in an incidental way.'

Mr Trencrom smiled at Demelza. 'He was always one for coming to the point. I like directness. Of course. But it somewhat depends – whether his affairs prosper – as to whether he is interested in mine. However . . .'

'Half the countryside is interested in yours, Mr Trencrom,' said Ross.

The fat man's smile became a chuckle, which ended in his tiny wrung-out cough.

'It might well be – that they have reason to be anxious for my welfare, Captain Poldark. Things are none too satisfactory in the trade. I do not know – how long I shall be able to carry on to the present extent.'

'I should have thought business was never more prosperous.'

'Ah. Business is far from prosperous. Let me explain.'

Mr Trencrom went on to explain in his breathless voice as if he were all the time climbing a steep hill. With some horrid premonition of his direction, Demelza poured Ross a cup of tea and, forgetting his own demand, Ross drank it. Business, said Mr Trencrom, was brisk enough so far as consumption went. People were drinking as much as ever and, although money was scarce, there was always a market for cheap good-quality liquor. Mind you, he was being frank with them as he would not be with everyone. He spoke in confidence and knew they would respect it.

Light faded in the room, but no one seemed to notice its going. At the back of the house somewhere Gimlett was chopping sticks; each series of sounds began with a tentative tap-tap growing firmer and heavier and slower until the screech of splitting wood. Through the window the cloudy fading sky was grey as iron.

The one great difficulty of the trade, Mr Trencrom explained, was the tiresome business of the landing of the goods. Vercoe, the customhouse officer at St Ann's, and his assistant Coppard were hard men, ever on the alert and ever ready to pounce. Attempts had been made to soften them, to bring them to a more reasonable frame of mind, but their only answer was to apply for extra help. And there was a rumour they might be getting it. How much easier, Mr Trencrom said, if they had only been sensible like the gaugers at Newquay and Falmouth, where the officers were given a percentage of the profit on the smuggled goods and no more said.

Mr Trencrom finished his tea and smiled an acquiescence when Demelza rose for his cup. This much, he said, was bad enough; but this had been the case ever since Vercoe came to the district four years ago. What was making it worse now was the presence of an informer or informers among the village people themselves. It had begun at St Ann's last year, so they had brought in their cargoes at Sawle, where landing was so much more difficult. In the last six months, however, the same thing had happened at Sawle; and business was almost at a standstill. Now this, said Mr Trencrom, would be bad enough in the south, where there were numbers of navigable harbours and creeks. But on this north coast it meant ruin and perhaps more. Only last month, in that sudden bad weather which had blown up, his cutter the *One and All* had had to be warned off from landing because the gaugers were there on the spot, and she'd been driven back towards Land's End with not a creek or a cove or a harbour under her lee but meant destruction. They had made the Scillies and come in the following night; but she might have been lost with all hands and a valuable cargo. One couldn't *risk* that sort of thing.

'You have my sympathy,' said Ross. 'But what's the moral to the story?'

'The moral, Captain Poldark. Is that we must find another navigable inlet. And you possess the only one for miles.'

Demelza paused with the cup in her hands, her eyes going from face to face.

'I think,' Ross said quietly, 'that you overestimate the advantages of Nampara Cove. There is no great depth of water and several dangerous rocks at the entrance.'

Don't I know it, thought Demelza, since I nearly went aground on one yesterday.

Mr Trencrom strangled his small dog again. 'I don't overestimate nothing, Captain Poldark. It's not ideal. But we could land very comfortable there on quiet nights. It's not too far from where we distribute. And tis not overlooked, like. It could all be quite private.'

'Until the informer got wind of the change.'

'Well, we should introduce – a closer system of secrecy. And only come in here twice or thrice a year. As for yourself you'd need to know nothing of it.'

Ross got up and walked to the window. Demelza had not moved with her cup.

'As for myself,' Ross said, 'it would be plain that I knew everything of it. But leave that for the moment. What inducement do you suggest would make me responsive to this scheme?'

'Ross,' Demelza said, but he didn't look at her.

'Oh,' said Mr Trencrom, 'that would be arranged amicable, I'm sure. A percentage on the profit. Or a lump sum for each landing. We've been in business together before. We'd not quarrel over that.'

There was a light in Ross's eyes as he looked out over the garden, but he was careful not to let it be seen by his visitor. 'I'm afraid,' he said, 'I should like some proposal. One could only consider the suggestion by weighing the risks against the benefits. At present we know only the risks. . . .'

'Hm – ah. Well . . .' Mr Trencrom stretched out a fat hand for the tea Demelza was still holding. 'Thank you, ma'am. Delightful. It's very difficult betwixt friends. One wishes to be fair. But things are not what they was. Everything is more trying than it used to be. What had you in mind yourself? Would five per cent of the profits seem fair?'

'Can you suggest a lump sum per cargo?'

'Well . . . fifty pounds, say?'

'I thought,' said Ross, 'that you had come here to talk business, Mr Trencrom.'

The fat man wheezed over his tea, and his breath made bubbles on the surface.

'Is that a very poor offer? I don't think so. Fifty pounds is a big sum of money. What do you suggest – yourself?'

'Two hundred and fifty pounds per cargo.'

'My dear sir! Impossible! You don't understand.' Mr Trencrom's feelings were hurt. 'It would make the voyage virtually without——'

Ross said: 'I'm not without experience of the trade myself. Fifteen years ago when I was a boy, my father and I would make the trip to Guernsey twice or so a year. We could fill our tiny cutter with brandy, gin and tea for a hundred pounds. If we had chosen to – as we did sometimes – we could have sold the cargo as soon as we landed it for double the money. Your cutter, the *One and All*, will carry a cargo of ten times that size – and of greater value, for prices have risen. It's not hard to work out the profit.'

Mr Trencrom slightly pouted. 'Oh, these small private runs. They always show – the big profits. Give quite a false impression. No overheads. No organization to maintain. Quite different as a commercial undertaking. I have the cutter to maintain. Wages to pay – usually a portion of the cargo. Palms to grease. Deliveries to arrange. Travellers who go round for orders. Storage. Mules. Ropes. Nets. Tackle. A very different thing, my dear sir. Do you know how much I pay my riders merely – for carrying away the goods from the shore? Half a guinea per night, plus all their expenses of food and drink! Plus half a bag of tea weighing forty pounds – or the equivalent, which they can resell if they wish for twenty-five shillings. Or more! All off the profits. I couldn't possibly afford to pay you more than a hundred pounds a run. After all, you would do nothing. You would sit quiet in your home here. Behind drawn curtains. Others would do it all. Merely for the privilege of using your cove.'

Ross shook his head. 'I'm sorry. I shouldn't be willing to do it for that.'

'Don't do it at all, Ross,' said Demelza.

'But why?' said Mr Trencrom, turning to her. 'I'm sure you agree it's not a wicked trade to be concerned in. Man-made laws. Not by God. Quite unreasonable that taxes should be paid on these necessaries of life. You'd make two or three hundred pounds a year. Very welcome, surely.'

'Nampara Cove is my land,' Ross said. 'If you run a cargo at St Ann's or Sawle or on Hendrawna Beach no one is accountable but the people who run it. If you run one here and are surprised it will go hard with me to put on a look of innocence, with mules tramping almost under my windows. I have already been at the assizes once. I don't wish to appear there again. The inducement would have to be big to make me take that risk. I've suggested to you what that inducement would be.'

'No, Ross,' said Demelza. 'No!'

Ross turned his eyes on her. 'I'll not hide from Mr Trencrom that the money would be specially useful just now. Otherwise I should not consider it. It's really up to him to choose.'

About half an hour later a big brown horse carrying a fat man in a big brown cloak rode up the valley away from the house. Darkness had fallen, but a moon behind the clouds made it possible to see the track. It would be a lonely ride to St Ann's and there were nervous people who would not have fancied it; but Mr Trencrom was not as delicate as he made himself out. Also he carried a brace of pistols. There was a dejected, defeated set to his shoulders as he made his way through the trees.

When he had disappeared from view Ross shut the door and stood a moment in indecision in the hall, then returned to the parlour.

Demelza's back as she lit the candles had a taut look. Ross went to the cupboard and poured himself a drink.

'The Warleggans,' he said, 'have at last got a foot in Wheal Leisure. Pearce came today with the news that Benjamin Aukett had sold out. Their nominee is a man called Coke.'

Demelza did not reply.

'I suspected it would be only a matter of time,' he said. 'When there are seven shareholders, one or another will sooner or later give way to the temptation of a large profit. I shouldn't be surprised if Pearce sells his share any time. So now we shall have George at our board.'

She said: 'What does it matter?'

'Um?' He stared at her back broodingly.

'What does it matter? Oh, I dislike the Warleggans just so much as you; but if they come to have a share in your mine we can do naught about it. An' they can't steal *your* share. That's all that matters. It is none of it any excuse for having the tub carriers on our land!'

He said sharply: 'Two hundred pounds is excuse enough for that. I want no other.'

'It'll not buy you out of prison.'

'I shall not be in there, thank you.'

'You'll have small choice if the landing is surprised.'

'Nonsense. It's a risk, I know – but not as big as I made out to Trencrom. It would be possible in fact to claim ignorance. We might not be believed, but there would be no proof to the contrary.'

She put her hand on the mantelshelf. 'I can't *stand* it all again! All the worrying anxious time of the trial – and before; not sleeping, like a cloud all day. Picturing this an' that. Transported, hanged, rotting in gaol. The days in Bodmin – all I did – or tried to do. It isn't fair. Not again, so soon. It isn't fair to yourself . . . or to anyone!'

He looked at her again and perceived that she was very upset. He said more gently: 'Now you're seeing bogles in the dark. There's nothing to be scared of in a little free-trading. I was only afraid lest I had set my price too high. That's why I came down fifty. Today, on top of this news of the Warleggans, if he but knew it, Mr Trencrom was an angel in disguise.'

'The devil!' she said vehemently. 'No less.'

'Perhaps I should lie meek under this latest of George's encroachments, but it's not in me to do so. Besides . . . you may have forgotten it, but we have recently sold *all* our stock, your brooch and horse, the clock and the newer furnishings of the house. Not, mark you, to cancel our debts but to postpone them for a mere twelve months. We're not out of the wood if we sit together in bucolic bliss and weave daisy chains. I'm more likely to go to prison that way than any other.'

She said: 'I can't help it. I want your child to be free from fear.'

Ross put down his glass. '*What?*'

There was a tap at the door and Jane Gimlett came in.

'Please, will you be wanting supper at the usual time? I put the pie on to hot up just in case, like.'

'The usual time,' said Demelza.

'And the ham? There's a fair cutting on it yet, though tis largely fat.'

'Put it on,' said Demelza.

'The scones has come out nice, 'm. I thought I'd leave you know.' She went out.

One missed the ticking of the clock in here. A new piece of wood, not quite dry, was hissing on the fire. Little bubbles of moisture were forming at one end of it, trying to escape the flames.

Ross said: 'When did you know?'

'September.'

He made a gesture. 'Good *God* . . . *!* Not to tell me . . . !'

'You didn't want it.'

'What?'

'You said you didn't want another child – after Julia.'

'Nor did I – nor do I——' He picked up his glass, set it down again without drinking. After a minute he added: 'To grow into our hearts, and then to die. But if one is coming – that's different.'

'How different?'

'Well . . . it's different.'

'I wish I could believe that.

'Why should you not? It's the truth.' He turned. 'I don't know what to say – how to say it . . . I just don't understand you. You've been closer about it even than last time. When do you expect – the birth?'

'May.'

He frowned, trying to shut out his memories.

'I know tis the same month,' she said desperately. 'I could've wished for any other. But that's the way things are. I shouldn't be amazed if it's born the same day, three years after. It's been the same so far – the visit to Trenwith and all. But all history don't repeat itself. I don't believe it can. Anyway, I'm sorry.'

'Sorry? What for?'

'That it's happened. That it has got to come. That you'll have this extra burden which you don't want.'

He came and stood beside her at the fireplace. 'Now stop crying and be sensible.'

'I'm *not* crying.'

'Well, wanting to, then. Is this what's been on your back all winter?'

'Not on my *back*,' she said.

'As you like. Ever since September you've been withdrawn from me – poking up your head now and then like a sheep from behind a fence. I couldn't reach you. Is this child the cause of all of it?'

'If I have, then it may be.'

'Because you thought I didn't want it?'

'Tis only what you said.'

He said in exasperation: 'God damn it, you should know I'm not used to dealing with women! You search the earth to find some special secret feminine grievance to *gnaw* over for months on end, and then produce it coolly on the mat to explain all the irrational hedging and dodging of an entire winter——'

'I didn't search the earth for it!'

'Well, I thought you could distinguish between a theoretical case and a practical one – evidently that isn't so.'

'I wasn't well educated——'

'No more was I. Look.' He thumped the flat of his hand on the mantelshelf. 'Look. If you ask me, do I want more children, I'll say, no. We're nearly paupers, the world's awry, and we've lost Julia. Correct? That's a theoretical case. But if you say you're having another child, do I dislike the prospect, I'd say, yes, for all these reasons I still dislike the prospect; but a prospect is not a child, and a child can be *welcomed* for all that. D'you understand what I mean?'

'No,' she said indistinctly.

He stared at his tobacco jar on the shelf, his first protest exhausted, his mind leaping forward to what this news entailed. And all the memories of Julia it revived. The storm at her birth, the two christening parties, the drunken Paynters that day Demelza was out, the high hopes, the love – and the storm at her death, It had come in a cycle, had conformed to a pattern, like a Greek tragedy prepared by a cynic. It was to happen again. History had to repeat itself in the early stages whatever the later might bring.

He glanced down at her. What did it mean for her? Weeks of discomfort, agony at the end, then months of unremitting care. All that had gone to Julia and much more; yet it had all been lost. What right had he to claim a monopoly of grief? . . . He'd never done that, and yet . . .

He said more gently: 'I've noticed no stoutness so far.'

She said: 'By April I shall look like Mr Trencrom.'

It was the first time they had laughed together for a long time; but her laughter was still dangerously near tears, his a not quite voluntary surrender of his irritation.

He put his hand on her shoulder, trying to express something that he couldn't yet say. Strange, the meaning of contacts! His firm clasp of this arm was entirely permissible, familiar, pleasurable, the touch of a known and loved person, however exasperating. His clasp of another arm at Christmas had had electricity in the touch. Was it because he loved Elizabeth more – or because he knew her less?

Demelza said: 'If you – still care what is going to happen to us . . . then you must have more care in what you undertake.'

'I shall have care in everything I undertake – believe me. I've every possible intention of keeping on the right side of the law.' He released her shoulder. 'Or at any rate the blind side. . . . Thank God at least that we have a capable physician in the neighbourhood.'

'I'd still rather have Mrs Zacky,' said Demelza.

Chapter seven

THE NEXT DAY Ross was up before dawn and spent the morning at the mine, arranging with Zacky Martin about the redeployment of the men who had been tunnelling towards Wheal Trevorgie. He spent longer than he need have done at the workings and went down to see how things were below grass. He felt as if the acquisitive hand of the Warleggans was already over Wheal Leisure. He had not slept well during the night, his brain being active with all the developments of yesterday.

As to Demelza's news, he could not yet evaluate his own feelings, but reflection didn't dissipate the sense of insult that he had been kept in the dark so long. To him it looked like a wilful misunderstanding of his views – or at least a painful lack of trust in his good sense. Soon after noon he walked back with Zacky, who was slipping home for a snack before returning for the change of cores. At last there was some sign of a lift in the weather; the vast burden of cloud which had hung about so long was thinning, splitting up, and drifting away before a northeasterly breeze. The contours of the land were unequivocal, demarcating the colder lighter sky.

'Tis a pity we've stopped that working,' said Zacky. 'I feel we was driving towards rich stuff. But maybe it is no more'n an old wives' dream.'

'Where d'you estimate we had got to?'

Zacky stopped and rasped his chin. 'Twouldn't be hard to take proper measurings, but it is hard to be sure without, sur. Just to be guessing, I'd say near on that clump of trees.'

Ross scanned the distance from where the buildings of Wheal Leisure littered one skyline to where the broken wall and chimney of Wheal Grace stood upon the rising ground near Mellin.

'About halfway?'

'I reckon. There's no map, I b'lieve, of the old Trevorgie workings.'

'No accurate one. But I went down with my cousin seven years ago and they were pretty extensive in this direction. That air adit is the only sign, but I believe several were filled up. My father worked the newer, Wheal Grace, part towards the southwest. You were never in Wheal Grace?'

'I wasn't in these here parts till I was twenty, and then I went straight on Grambler. Of course, I've often thought twould injure no one to have a closer look at Trevorgie from that end. That's if you could get by with the foul air.'

'It was none too bad when we went down. But we didn't go far. What we saw was all exhausted tin ground, and poor at that. Of course, Mark Daniel . . .'

'Mark Daniel?' said Zacky cautiously.

They went on. They were only a few hundred yards from the house Mark had built. In one part the roof had already fallen in. It seemed tactless to mention his name just here – so close to where he had killed his little faithless moonflower wife.

'I don't know if Paul ever told you,' Ross said, 'but the day before Mark escaped to France he hid down Grace. Before he left I – happened to see him and he told me there was a lot of rich stuff in the mine.'

'. . . Paul never told me. But I can add two an' two, like. Did he say where the ore was to?'

'No. . . . At least, I fancy he mentioned the east face.'

'That's Trevorgie. That's sense – for your father'd never have abandoned a rich lode. Anything might've happened when Trevorgie was worked.'

'Yes,' said Ross, staring at the chimney of Wheal Grace. They separated just beyond Reath Cottage and Ross went up to the old mine building. There was very little left. Abandoned for twenty years, the bits of machinery had long since been carried away, and nature had licked over the scars. Ross sat down and put his chin in his hand.

It was pleasant enough sitting here among the whispering grass, and he scarcely moved for half an hour. There was some community of spirit between the man and the scene. Strange ideas were milling in his head, at least two of them having taken shape from his conversation with Mr Trencrom. All of them derived from the events of yesterday and all of them were moving him to one end. At length he got up and walked slowly, half aimlessly, back to Reath Cottage, pushed open the door and went in. It was dark, as it always would be except in the mornings; Mark had built it facing the wrong way. People wouldn't pass the place after dusk; they said Keren still hung there sometimes with her broken little face out of the window. The earth floor was covered with brambles and gorse, and rank white grass, predatory and unhealthy, sprouted among the stones. An old stool stood in the corner, some faggots lay by the fireplace. He went out into the open again, deriding himself for being glad to go.

From here you looked straight across the declivity to the Gatehouse. Every time Dwight Enys rode out on his doctoring this derelict cottage would stare and watch him leave. No wonder Enys still showed the scars of that time; he could not very well forget it. Ross began to walk over towards the Gatehouse. As he got near he saw Dwight at the door, and his horse was standing ready saddled. Dwight saw him and smiled and came to meet him.

'Hope this is not a professional visit? No? You come so seldom that I was a little anxious.'

Ross said: 'The courtesies can only be squeezed out of me like drops from a reluctant lemon. But now and then it's convenient to be agreeable for a change.'

Dwight laughed. 'Be careful you don't overpraise yourself. I suppose you're not responsible for my astonishing windfall, are you? Mention of the lemon came very easy to your lips.'

'Just at the moment I'm praying for windfalls, not bestowing 'em. What has come your way?'

'Those sacks. They're full of oranges. They came this morning, twelve in all, delivered on three mules by a surly fellow who would scarcely open his mouth – all the way from Falmouth. I'm astonished.'

'So should I be.'

'Oh, they're not for me. They're for sick people in Sawle; I guess that much. I've been trying to remember how many I have mentioned this need to. You were one of them.'

'Sorry. You must look among your *rich* friends, Dwight.'

'I didn't know I had any,' Dwight replied, knowing all the time he had one. 'There must be close on a hundred dozen oranges here. Enough at least to check the scurvy if intelligently used. I have sent Bone off to borrow two old mine mules from the Nanfans. I'm waiting for him to return before I set off on my round. We must distribute some of the fruit this afternoon.'

Ross glanced at his animated face. It was easy to see how Enys felt about this: to be fighting an enemy unarmed and then suddenly to find the weapons put into one's hands . . .

He said: 'I came to ask you if by chance you receive any periodicals from London? The *Sherborne Mercury* is a little restricted in its news.'

'Nothing – except *Medical Facts and Observations* edited by Dr Simmons. That's sent to me monthly. I have seen a London paper sometimes at the Pascoes'.'

'With the trial over my head for six months and then the business of settling back into normal life, I've had little attention for general events. What do you think of developments in Europe?'

Dwight found the query a little surprising, for he usually regarded Ross as much better informed than himself. 'In France, do you mean? Have you read *Reflections on the French Revolution*?'

'No.'

'Nor I. But it has had an immense sale – as of course you know. I understand Burke argues that the revolutionaries are really the enemies of liberty while doing everything in its name.'

'It's not unlikely. There's strong feeling over here about the whole business; but for myself, while going into no extravagant praise of the revolutionaries, I can't help but nurse some sympathy for their original aims.'

Dwight looked at Ross. 'I know. There were many such to begin, but they have been steadily forfeiting such sympathy.'

Bone came in sight. They waited till he reached them. Will Nanfan could lend them the mules and would send them over early in the afternoon. Ross turned to walk back. He had not told Dwight one of the things he had come to speak of, but the impulse had died when he got to the Gatehouse. Dwight would guess soon enough and he wouldn't be wanted until May.

The sun was shining brilliantly by the time Dwight turned in at the gates of Killewarren, and the wind was rattling the withered leaves on the young oak trees. The gravel in front of the house was strewn with fir twigs which had been nibbled off by the squirrels in the upper branches. He knocked at the door and asked if Miss Penvenen were at home, and was admitted to a small room off the hall. Presently the maid came back and said Miss Penvenen would see him.

She was in the usual living room but was in a black riding habit over the shoulders of which her tawny hair fell to its full length like an escaping flame. She was standing by the fireplace when he came in, eating from a plate of sandwiches, and there was a wineglass on the mantelshelf. She laughed when she saw him.

'Good day, Mr Apothecary. Whom have you come to blood? My uncle's in Redruth and is not expected home till four.'

Dwight said: 'My call's on you, Miss Penvenen. I'm sorry if it's inconvenient, but I'll not keep you long.'

She glanced at the clock. 'I can give you five minutes, or as long as it takes to eat these sandwiches. This good east wind won't last forever, and I've had a merry morning. Up at dawn and we picked up a fox on his drag. He was a beauty and ran straight as a die to beyond Ponsanooth. I was second at the kill, and it was lively country. Around twelve we drew Killevreth Wood and found another, but my horse went lame just as he went away; so I'm back here for a brief refreshment while they saddle Thresher. D'you ever hunt, Mr Sober Face?'

Dwight said: 'Did you arrange for a consignment of oranges to be delivered to my house today?'

She looked at him widely.

'Oranges? You did say oranges? If I made you a present at all it would be of a better instrument for removing fishbones. You hurt my lips with your fingers, d'you remember?'

'Yes,' he said, 'I remember.'

They stared at each other then. He was just near enough to detect that faint unfamiliar scent she used; the mannish clothes made her look more womanly.

'So it was you,' he said. 'I thought it could be no one else.'

'Indeed?'

'I'm – very grateful. They'll be – life-giving.'

'You don't suppose I am interested in the fate of a few fishwives, do you? Heavens, what nonsense!'

'Then why did you do it?'

She looked him over, seemed about to deny it, then suddenly changed her mind. 'Just to make a *mock* of you.'

He flushed. 'An expensive form of mockery, isn't it?'

She finished her wine. 'I don't like to be under an obligation – especially to a man – especially to you. You wouldn't take my money – threw it back in my face.'

'I don't want your money——'

'So I reasoned your conscience wouldn't let you be too proud to accept a present for your poor starving fisherfolk. Nor has it. It's you who are under the obligation now.'

'I'm very obliged – for the condescension.'

'You amuse me very much,' she said.

'I like you very much too.'

For the first time he saw a faint flush on her cheeks.

'Don't be impertinent.'

'Wasn't it impertinence you said you admired? I forget.'

'You forget a great deal.'

'I shall not forget this generous gift, however hard you try to disguise it——'

She turned away from him as the door opened and Unwin Trevaunance came in.

'Oh, *there* you are. Lord, I looked everywhere. You could at least . . .' He stopped short when he saw Dwight.

'Did you get him?' she asked.

'No. . . . He ran short and the scent was confused. What was the matter?'

'Firefly went lame. It's his pastern again, so I came home. I shall be ready for off in half a minute.'

'I've had nothing to eat since breakfast. I'm ravenous.'

'Put something in your pocket. If we dally about we may lose the hunt. Oh. . . . Do you know Dr Enys?'

Unwin inclined his lion's head. He didn't look too pleased to have been deserted in the field, and to come all the way home to find Caroline in earnest conversation with a flushed but good-looking young man, who might be only a country physician of some sort but had an air of his own.

'I don't think I've had that pleasure.'

'Pleasure is quite the word,' said Caroline, buttoning her coat. 'He's most skilful in curing dogs of distressing convulsions. Horace has not been troubled near so bad since he took that mixture you prescribed, Dr Enys. He has a little spot on his ear now, which you might look to after we've gone.'

Dwight refused to be provoked. 'For twelve bags of oranges he shall have the best attention I can give him, ma'am.'

Unwin looked irritated. He began to take some things from the table and Caroline wrapped them in a napkin for him.

'You'd better attend to him this morning then,' said Caroline, indicating Horace, who was snuffling round and round in his basket to find the most comfortable spot. 'Next week we shall be gone.'

'Gone?' said Unwin, looking at her. 'Gone where?'

'Oh, didn't I tell you? Dear Unwin; I'm so sorry. Uncle William said I should go back there in February. After all, I've been in these parts since September, and the hunting's so much better in Oxfordshire.'

'You certainly did not. I——' Unwin stared at Dwight, plainly wishing him in Hades.

'Do you intend to be away long, Miss Penvenen?' Dwight asked.

'It will depend what entertainment there is. Usually there's plenty. But don't worry: I've ordered more oranges for you next week also.'

'Oranges, oranges?' Trevaunance said impatiently. 'Is this some "entertainment" I'm not privy to? Come, Caroline, I hope I can persuade you to a delayed departure – but in the meantime we should make the most of this lovely day while it's here.' He went to the door and opened it for her.

'No, no, you cannot come, my sweet,' said Caroline in a honeyed voice to Horace, who had slipped out of his basket like lightning. 'You would be frightened by all the bigger doggies. You shall stay at home with the nice doctor who'll cure your ear and your fits and maybe take away any bones you swallow. There, there.' She put the dog into Dwight's arms and smiled at him. Their eyes were on a level, and, out of perversity and knowing herself doubly safe in Unwin's presence, she allowed the full challenge of her interest in him to show. There were tiny specks of amber on the pupils; the long lashes, so often narrowed, were for one second wide to show the grey-green depths.

Then she laughed. 'Good-bye, Dwight. May I call you Dwight? It's a quaint name. One thinks of someone shy and a little unprogressive. Your mother must have thought of something different, mustn't she? Who was right? I don't at all know. Perhaps we shall meet again someday.'

'I shall look forward to it,' said Dwight.

She went out, leaving him with the struggling dog. Unwin glanced at him with an unfriendly assessing eye as he followed. Dwight heard them going down the passage, heard him speaking and her laughter before their footsteps died away.

Chapter eight

ROSS'S IDEA WOULD not let him alone. For a long time he did not speak of it to anyone, not even Demelza, whose eager brain might have been useful in helping him to a decision. But the consequence would be such that he felt he could not decently expect anyone else to take a share of the responsibility. Besides, Demelza, for all her acuteness, was a woman and would probably be swayed by considerations that hadn't any business to be brought in.

He spent a great deal more time than hitherto reading the *Sherborne Mercury* and other news sheets which he borrowed and bought where he could. He also read Pryce's book, *Mineralogia Cornubiensis*, and several other treatises on the history and practice of mining, before making any overt move.

Henshawe was the first man to approach – straight, canny, the best judge in the district, and as close as a clam.

One day in early March, after an hour's talk in the barren library of Nampara, during which old samples were thumbed and old maps pored over, Henshawe and Ross, with candles in their hats and some tackle over their shoulders, walked casually up the hill to the weather-beaten stone chimney of Wheal Grace; and no more was seen of them for three hours. When they returned to the house, muddy and tired, Demelza, who had been anxious for the last ninety minutes, restrained an impulse to scold them and gave them tea laced with brandy, scanning their faces for unspoken comment. It was queer, she thought, that people should find Ross hard to read. She couldn't tell what he was thinking – any more than you could tell what a lot of those smiling-faced people were really thinking behind their smiles – but she could usually tell what he was *feeling*; and she knew now that he was not displeased with the outcome of the afternoon's business.

When Henshawe had gone he was more cheerful than he had been for a long time, much more like his old self. She realized more clearly than she had ever done before the need that Ross had for some continuing activity of mind and body. He was essentially a person who wanted to be planning and moving ahead, and however agreeable he might find the life of a country gentleman under its most favourable conditions, in poverty and frustration the life was intolerable. Further, the unseen but oppressive influence of the Warleggans was something which sooner or later must produce an explosion. If this business that was now afoot provided some sort of a safety valve, she was thankful for it.

There were more hours spent in the draughty old library the next day and the next. One evening Zacky Martin was called in, and after that he seemed to be there most of the time. Later Ross and Henshawe rode to Camborne, and another time to Redruth, to discuss certain problems with certain people. But no strangers called at Nampara. On the twenty-third of March, which was a Wednesday, Ross rode into Truro and called on Harris Pascoe to tell him he had decided to sell half his holding in Wheal Leisure.

The banker took off his spectacles and looked at him cautiously before commenting.

'I think it a wise move. There is a stage at which one has to f-face facts and cut one's losses. Of course, in a sense, it is not a loss but a sizeable profit; and that's satisfactory. All the same, you have my sincerest sympathy; I know how much this venture has meant to you. I suppose you want to repay half the debt you contracted with Pearce. Very sensible indeed.'

Ross frowned at the brand-new clock above the counter. 'That's the only new face I see about. Is that Mr Tresize or Mr Spry?'

Pascoe smiled. 'The change isn't yet quite complete. But I'm sure you'll like my new partners when you meet them. Now t-tell me: what do you want for your shares in Wheal Leisure?'

'Twenty pounds a share.'

The banker whistled. 'Will anyone *pay* that? It's a very high price. And you know how cautious people are about investing these days.'

'Not in a profitable concern.'

'No. . . . Perhaps you're right. Well, I can let it be known they're in the market.' Harris Pascoe looked up at his client again, remembering an incident not so long ago. 'I s-suppose you have no objections who the shares go to?'

Ross picked up a pen and ran his fingers slowly along the feather. 'Beggars can't be choosers, can they?'

'No-o.'

'Except as to price. Naturally I don't want it known that I'm eager to sell or someone may start making lower offers.'

'It's a change of front for you, Captain Poldark. But I think you're wise.'

Soon afterwards the first 'run' was made into Nampara Cove.

In the late afternoon of a quiet damp day Jud Paynter, of all people, came rolling down the combe on his bowlegs with a letter from Mr Trencrom, touching his fringe to Ross in the old way, whistling almost noiselessly between his front teeth and glancing in an inquisitive hangdog fashion about the house where he had spent many years of his life.

Ross read the note and said: 'That's convenient. Does Mr Trencrom expect a reply?'

'Not bi word o' pen. I'll tell 'im tes all fitty. 'E depend 'pon me do Mr Trencrom these days. His right-arm man, I reckon. Couldn' do without me. Proper job I got now.'

'You've the knack with a cutter,' Ross agreed. 'But then, you were always one for sailing near the wind, weren't you, Jud.'

'Wind or no, it d'make no difference,' said Jud, blinking. He was never quite comfortable in Ross's presence, faintly defiant, faintly resentful, wanting to be cocky and familiar but never gathering the courage. As long as he lived he would never forgive Ross for turning him out of the house; but his resentment was always nearer indignation than spite.

Some such thought as this crossed Ross's mind, and he said: 'I haven't thanked you for your peculiar testimony at the assize court. I don't know what you intended to say when you first went into the box, but in the end no one knew whether you were for me or against me, and even the judge was arguing. It's no mean feat to confuse the law.'

Nature had not designed Jud's face for the expression of pleasure, but the way he wiped his nose on the back of his hand suggested he was gratified.

'Aw . . . I always d'say to Prudie, when a man's in trouble, then he d'know his neighbours. I won't disknowledge twas a tryin' time to be stood up afore this judge just like as if *I'd* been the 'ardened lawbreaker. But I've mind of you since you was a little tacker no biggerer than pot high, so what was there to do else?'

'What puzzles me is how you came in that position. There's rumour about that you were paid money to swear against me. That isn't true, of course?'

'Never no word of it! Tedn true, tedn right, tedn proper! There's nasty lying tongues about tryin' to make grief betwixt us. Don't ee believe a word of un. If the truth be told . . .'

Jud paused, sucking his teeth. 'If the truth be told,' Ross prompted.

'If the truth be told, tes all on account o' my good nature. Don't like to say no, see. People d'come an' asks me one thing an' I say ais and naw just to be easy, like. They get very friendly along of you, an' a drop o' gin; an' afore you can spit they've congled up some notions you never thought 'pon, not in your wildest dreams. That's how tis, as sure as me mother was married. Then when tes time for the court o' law, what's to do? Only to act like you was put in wi' the bread an' took out with the cakes, like. That's the truth if I go around land tomorrer.'

Ross looked down at the shifty bulldog face. He didn't believe a word of it, but he laughed.

'Go tell your new master that I'm ready to draw my curtains.'

In fact on this first run, because of Demelza's anxiety and because of her condition, Ross observed all the prohibitions, though it went against the grain to do so. As dusk was falling he had the candles lighted and the curtains drawn, and they sat reading together until they heard the first clink of horses' hooves by the stream. Then Demelza got up and played on the spinet, and hummed and sang a little. Later they had supper, and presently the horses began to pass again, though this time it seemed their hooves were heavier on the ground. Occasionally a gruff voice could be heard and a footstep or the chink of metal.

In spite of all the precautions Demelza's heart thumped alarmingly; and as soon as supper was over she went back to the spinet and drowned the noises outside. The Gimletts had been given sufficient information to guess the rest, so they sat quietly in the kitchen and did not stir from the house. Once or twice Ross lifted his head from his book and glanced at Demelza. Once or twice his thoughts wandered to the informers, and he asked himself if the whole operation would go through without mishap. Mr Trencrom had assured him that every effort would be made to keep the landing secret and that only twenty riders would be used as against a larger number usually. Watchers would be posted all along the cliffs and valley so that decent warning might be given of any gaugers about. But many must know of the run. If there was an informer, he must know that the cutter had been gone some days and was due back. Did he know where?

At ten the sounds began to taper off, and by eleven all was peace again. At midnight they went to bed, but both slept restlessly, imagining from time to time they heard noises around the house. No caller, however, came to disturb them, and just before dawn Ross got up and went down to the cove.

A restless white fog moved over the land, and he thought it lucky it had not come down to impede progress last night. Great care had been taken to remove any signs of the operations. Above high-water mark the sand had been rolled or scraped with flat boards so that no one could tell the amount of disturbance there had been. Horse tracks all the way down to the cove in the soft ground could not be so easily hid, but a day's rain would wash them away. It smelt like rain. The undergrowth had been crushed down in places. A curlew was crying in the colourless dawn light.

He walked across to the cave where the dinghy was kept. It was a buoyant little craft he had bought in St Ann's just before last year's collapse to replace the one in which Mark Daniel had made his escape. As he bent over it a footstep sounded on the dry seaweed behind him, and he turned swiftly to find that Demelza had followed him. Her face looked small, detached, like a sculpture, framed in its dark hair on the pedestal of her dark cloak.

He said: 'You shouldn't have come out so soon. The air is chill.'

'I like it. I feel I've been behind those drawn curtains for a week.'

'Our visitors have been very careful. Nothing scarcely to show. I think they have moved this boat – they or someone else. When I left it on Thursday it was farther up the cave.'

'Was it, Ross?' Why do I not tell him that I was out in it myself yesterday, that for the first time I managed without Gimlett and caught eight mackerel and a dab? Because I know he would stop me and I don't want to be stopped. Ross could not have been more thoughtful for her, but sometimes all the restrictions and prohibitions oppressed her and made her feel caged and constricted. The Gimletts were faithful watchdogs; too faithful. Oh, she was comforted and warmed by Ross's consideration – yet he had not altogether convinced her. It seemed to her that on the night of their return home after the trial he had spoken from his heart. Since knowing there was actually a child on the way he had spoken out of a confusion of feeling and a kindness of disposition. It might be she was wrong, but that was how it seemed to her.

'It's good to feel last night is over,' she said.

'It's good to feel we're that much better off.'

'I'm still afraid. Promise you'll not go on with it a minute longer than we really need.'

'Well, I've no real fancy for commercializing our little cove. Are you well or ill this morning that you're up so early?'

'Well if other things are well. The brume is lifting, look.'

The shallow fog was smoking in the widening light, as if someone had lit a bonfire for a mile or so upon the sea. Out of the darker mist the sun already threw premonitory beams; and across the swept-clean upper sky a single smear of cloud was lit a brilliant cadmium yellow. They watched the fog grow luminous along its higher reaches; then familiar landmarks began to jut out with startling clearness, like stage scenery unveiled. The sea licked quietly at the sand, uncommunicative, saying nothing of the night.

Ross stirred. 'Did you know Ruth Treneglos was safely delivered of a baby daughter early yesterday?'

'No! At last. Are they well?'

'Well except in temper. I hear they're monstrously disappointed it's a girl after all this delay. They say old Horace is so furious at not having a grandson that he's refused to speak to John since.'

'Poor Ruth!'

'I should save your pity for the baby, who may deserve it.'

Demelza glanced up at him. 'Who told you, Ross?'

'Dwight. He was not there, of course, but is almost on their doorstep.'

Full dawn had crept round them hardly noticed so that suddenly, instead of being unobserved figures discussing the night, they had become the observed, focused by the absence of darkness, conspicuous under the rose-flushed sky. With a common instinct they drew back into the mouth of the cave.

Ross said: 'I've been talking to Dwight about Francis.'

'Oh?'

'Dwight tells me that Francis's quarrel with George Warleggan was over me.'

'How does he know?'

'They shared a bedroom in Bodmin. Francis wanted to do away with himself. It all bears out what Verity wrote in her letter – and much more besides.'

She said: 'I'm glad we made it up at Christmas.'

'So am I – now.'

As they turned to plough across the sand she said: 'I'd like to put my feet in the water.'

'It would freeze your vitals at this hour.'

'My vitals feel peculiar enough,' said Demelza. 'Perhaps I'd better leave them be.'

That day Ross went to Truro and heard that the shares had sold. They had been bought by Mr Coke, and had fetched their price. The newcomer, the unknown Mr Coke, was now the largest shareholder in the mine. It was a wrench at the last, hearing they had irrevocably gone. On his way home he made a detour to call at Trenwith.

He found Francis beside the lake, sawing up a tree. The occupation came strangely to him. Fate would never make Francis anything but what he had been born.

'I always dislike the burning of ash,' Ross said as he dismounted. 'One feels it has grown for better things.'

'Perhaps that's why it resents the saw,' said Francis, whose face had coloured more at sight of Ross than from the exertion. There was no ease between them yet. 'Elizabeth's indoors, I think, and will be glad of a visitor. I'll follow in two or three minutes.'

'No, it's you I want to see. We can talk here.'

'Any excuse to stop.' Francis wiped his hands. 'How is Demelza?'

'Well enough, thank you. Better than last time.'

'What can I do for you, Ross?'

Ross tethered Darkie to a sapling and sat on a piece of the fallen tree. He picked up a thin branch and began to trace thoughtful squares and circles in the sandy gravel of the path. 'Have Ellery and Pendarves found you buried treasure yet?'

'. . . Hardly so much as that. There's a likely place where my land abuts on the head of Sawle Combe. But it would be right on Choake's front door, and he would squeak at that. Also the signs are for tin and I've still a special attachment for copper.'

'I'm opening Wheal Grace,' Ross said.

'What? You don't mean it? That's cheerful news! What made you change your mind?'

'Circumstances. We hope to start in three months. It's a gamble, of course.'

Francis put on his coat. 'You're going to follow the Trevorgie workings?'

'Henshawe and I have been down several times. God knows who did all that work but the place is honeycombed. It's mostly shallow but even so the lower level is flooded and we haven't been able to explore it. So we expect to put up an engine. We reckon there's enough ore in the shallow levels to make the venture worth while.'

'Who is investing the money?'

'I am. I've sold half my shares in Wheal Leisure and can realize six hundred pounds.'

Ross began to pull off his gloves. They had both been carefully mended by Demelza, and for a moment he looked at them with distaste at the thought of the necessity for darning.

'D'you see anything of George these days?' he asked.

'I haven't seen him since September. Our quarrel was not the sort that is likely to be made up.'

'Not ever?'

Francis looked at him. 'I can't answer for what may happen in heaven.'

'This feud,' Ross said carefully, 'between George and *me* is one which it can be to nobody's advantage to join. It would be particularly to your detriment to take up more than – say – a neutral attitude. Although he's made no move against you up to now he could do so any time.'

'My dear Ross, my attitude has gone far beyond the neutral. You may not welcome me as a fellow standard-bearer, but I'm afraid there's no choice.'

Darkie stamped her foot and whinnied.

'You've told me more than once,' Ross said, 'about this money you're saving to invest in a mine. How much was it: six hundred pounds or thereabouts?'

There was a sharp silence.

'Thereabouts.'

'With twelve hundred pounds we could do a great deal.'

'Yes?'

'It could be.'

'You're suggesting – we should go into partnership?'

'Yes.'

'There's nothing at all I'd like better. But – it's rather taken my breath away. Are you sure you want that?'

'If I'd not wanted it I shouldn't have suggested it.'

'No. . . . God, it's a strange world.' Francis wiped his forehead again, put the handkerchief away, wriggled the saw out of the half-sawn log.

'It may be a fight,' said Ross. 'You would do better to keep out. George has a long arm.'

'To the devil with George.'

'If this prospers, then I want no outsiders who can dispose of their shares just as and when they please. But you may well lose your money.'

'I like a gamble. . . . But if anyone had told me six months ago that you and I . . .'

'One can gamble on a man as well as on a mine.'

Francis stirred the shavings with his foot. 'I can't guarantee the *mine.* . . .'

'If you feel like that, that's all that matters.'

'I feel like that. . . . And – thanks.'

'Forget the past,' Ross said. 'Take this proposition or leave it on its merits.'

'I take it, of course. Come up to the house and we'll seal the contract in a glass of good brandy.'

As they walked along they did not speak at all. Ross's proposal had astonished Francis and excited him; but he was not easy in his mind. Two or three times he glanced at his cousin, and almost at the door of the house be stopped.

'Look, Ross, I . . .'

'What?'

'Don't think I don't want this. It – could mean a lot to me. But before we – go any further there's something it's necessary to tell you. If it were not for your offering this – this thing it wouldn't be in me to blurt it out. But now . . . The proposition shouldn't go forward until you know . . .'

Ross stared at his embarrassed face.

'Is it something that is past?'

'Oh, God, yes. But all the same——'

'If it's past, then forget it. I don't think I want to hear what you may be going to tell me.'

Francis flushed. 'If that's the case, I don't think I want to hear it myself.'

They stared at each other.

Francis said: 'The Poldarks, then.'

Ross nodded slowly. He felt he had not misjudged his man this time. 'The Poldarks.'

Chapter nine

WIDOW TREGOTHNAN'S KIDDLEY in Sawle was crammed to the doors.

Two unmistakable signs that a cargo had been successfully run in the neighbourhood were a relaxation in the tension of day-to-day living and an increase in drunkenness. Money was temporarily easier, and gin and rum were cheap. The little subwave of prosperity ran right through the villages, beginning among the men concerned in the run and losing its height and momentum the further it spread from them.

Sally Tregothnan – a loud, laughing woman of forty-odd – was herself behind the counter that served as a bar, and giving as good as she got. The four public houses in the village were enjoying their fair share of trade, but Widow Tregothnan's was the meeting place of the choicer spirits. The widow was often known as Sally Chill-Off. She was not supposed to sell anything stronger than beer, but there had never been a moment in the village's history when she had not been prepared to add a little something to her ale 'to take the chill off,' even when her customers were on their beam ends. So prosperity brought her a roaring trade. Among those present tonight were Ned Bottrell, Jud Paynter, Charlie Kempthorne, Paul Daniel, Jacka Hoblyn and Ted Carkeek. Men like Pally Rogers and Will Nanfan, though they were ringleaders in the trade, frowned on drink for themselves as contrary to their Methodist principles.

Jud Paynter was at his happiest. He had gin at his elbow, gin in his stomach and an audience.

'Now then,' he said, 'now then, if you d'want to know what tis like to stand up in a court o' law an' speak the words o' truth an' have the judge an' jury an' all the lawyers listening openmouthed, I'll tell ee. There they was, jury row on row like sparrows on a branch, lawyers in their black nightshirts like they was ready to leap into bed, fancy doxies wi' parasols, the whole darned, danged, blathering boiling of 'em, mured together cheek to cheek. Twas some handsome sight, I tell ee.'

'Go on,' said Sally Tregothnan. 'Go on.'

'Tes true. Without a word of a lie. When first I stood up there and looked around, I was sweatin' like dung. But when I got goin' I give 'em a fair proper talking to, as if I was the shepherd and they was the sheep. Damme, twould've done ye all a power o' good to have 'eard'n.'

'Reckon you did oughter have been a preacher,' said Charlie Kempthorne, winking at Ned Bottrell.

Jacka Hoblyn drained his glass and looked at Jud from under his heavy brows. 'I'm sick and tired of hearing all this spudder. Tis over and done with these pretty many months and there's no more to it. Who knows what you was like in the court when there's nobody but you to tell us?'

'I'm *tellin'* ee,' Jud said, showing his two teeth indignantly. 'If ye've got ears to hear, I'm telling ee. Here was I, say this pot, and there was Judge, say Paul Daniel, but not grinning like a ram's cat; and there was Ross Poldark in the dock, say Jacka Hoblyn, but not squattin' down like a hen wi' the cluck; and Judge says to me, "Mester Paynter," he says, says he, "did this man do wrong or no?" an' I says to him I says, "Judge," I says, "this man once done wrong by me but I aren't one to carry a grudge where it don't belong to be carried, for who d'know betterer'n Jud Paynter what the Good Book d'say, which is if the Lord do strike thee upon one eye turn thou the other and let'n 'ave a good clunk at that too. So tis fair to say that I'm speakin' the honest truth an' no word of a lie when I d'tell ee this man Jacka Hoblyn, Ross Poldark I d'mean, is as innocent as a new-dropped babe in its first wettels. Grudge," I says, "I've no judge against ee or any man living or dead. I b'lieve in all as tes written for all to read. Thou shalt not move thy neighbour's landmark. Nor shalt thou covet thy neighbour's wife, nor his mate, nor his hoss, nor his axe, nor anythink that is his." '

'Here, mind where you're sweeping wi' your great hands!' said Sally Tregothnan.

'So I goes on till nigh every soul to be seen has melted into hot tears, hardened sinners and doxies alike. Then the grudge turns to the court an' opens up his arms like a huer that's seen the pilchards an' 'e says, "My friends, my friends, my friends, my friends, my friends, my friends . . ."' Jud paused and groped for his glass, found it, and carried it along a winding lane to his lips.

"Stuff an' nonsense," said Jacka Hoblyn in a disagreeable voice. 'No judge never said nothing of the sort.'

''Old hard, me dear,' whispered Paul Daniel. 'Give 'im a bit more rope an' who knows but what he'll 'ang hisself.'

But Jud had lost track of his remarks. He tried hard to put his glass down until at length Sally took it from him. He mopped his forehead with his coat sleeve and looked round with a glassy eye. He began to sing in a broken quavering tenor.

'There was an old couple an' they was poor. Tweedle, tweedle, go-twee. They lived in a sheep shed without any door. By the side of an elmin tree.'

'Dear Jakes, it is more than I can stomach,' said Hoblyn. 'Sitting up there like an Aunt Sally at a Christmas fair.'

Charlie Kempthorne coughed as he moved surreptitiously nearer to Jacka. Smoke and drink still tickled up his chest at times. 'I seen Rosina out this morning,' he said confidentially. 'She's growing away into a 'andsome girl.'

'Eh?' said Jacka, staring at him suspiciously.

'She'll be wedding soon, I suppose? Though maybe there'll be some as is put off like wi' that leg, on account of 'er walking lipsy.'

Jacka granted and finished his drink. Charlie blinked and glanced at the other man's heavy brow.

'Twouldn't do for 'er to live an' die a maid just on account of being clecky in one leg.'

'She's but seventeen,' said Jacka, filling his pipe. 'There's many a young rip'll be coming after she afore long.'

'Maybe an olderer sort of person would be more fitty like,' said Kempthorne, licking his lips.

'An' this old couple,' sang Jud, ' 'ad got no gold. Tweedle, tweedle, go-twee. So they was feelin' fair bedoled. In the lewth of the elmin tree.'

'Now me,' said Kempthorne, 'just for instance, as you might say. I aren't doin' so dusty out o' my sailmaking an' suchlike. Gettin' a little nest egg together. Mind, I got two childer, one of——'

'Aye,' said Jacka, 'poor little brats.'

'There's naught amiss with them that growin' up won't cure. What they need more'n aught else is a woman's care. I've had a thought for Mary Ann Tregaskis; but——'

'If she'd 'ave you.' When he was in his first drink was not the time for Jacka Hoblyn's nature to show at its most agreeable.

'Well, that's as may be. I 'aven't asked her. But there's many as would jump at the chance. I got a bit o' ground back of Andrewartha's for swedes, an' I shall be havin' a litter of veers next month. An' sailmaking's maybe not all I shall do with the needle afore I'm through. I got me ten yards o' black velveteen in to Redruth last week, cheap, at two shillings the yard, and I've a mind to cut it out and make it up as breeches in a genteel way; twould sell to folk aiming to be gentry if not to the gentry themselves. And there's other things I got, picked up here an' there, that'd maybe surprise you.'

'Yes?' said Jacka, pouring another drink.

'Yes. An' I 'ad the thought twould fit in very well for a girl as is 'andy with a needle to fix up with a man who's 'andy the same way, like. I 'ad that thought.'

'You 'ad, eh?' said Jacka, and stared appraisingly at Kempthorne. He brooded for a minute. 'How old are you, Charlie? Nearly as old as me, I reckon.'

'I'm only thirty-nine,' said Charlie.

'And d'you spit blood still?'

'Nay, I've not done that for near on two year. Look, Jacka, I tell ee, I'm getting on in the world, and there's many a maid could do worse . . .'

'Maybe the maid would have somethin' to say 'bout that herself.'

'Nay, Rosina's an easy-natured sort o' girl – takes after her mother. An' you, Jacka, o' course. An' you. She'd do what her dad thought right, I'm sure of it.'

'Aye,' growled Jacka, 'maybe she would. Maybe that's the way she's been brought up. But I aren't one for doing things in haste – except when there's need for haste. And there'd better not be now.'

'No haste at all! Just think around it in your leisure, like. And maybe I'll drop in an' see Rosina now and then, if tis all the same to you, just to see how the land lays. . . .'

'Now this old couple,' sang Jud, 'was poddlin' around. Tweedle, tweedle, go-twee; when they seen a long-cripple come out o' the ground. From under the elmin tr-tree. . . .'

Later that night Jud made his stumbling way home towards Grambler under the hasty light of a half-moon rushing through high white clouds. The air had turned keen, and if April had not been well advanced one might have expected frost. Jud was still in a jovial mood, though not untinged with forebodings about the eternal damnation of the world. Now and then he forgot it and went on with his interminable song, for which there always seemed to be a new verse; now and then he stumbled over a rut or a stone and consigned the world to the hell-fire and brimstone from which he'd long been trying to save it.

But it was after one of his rarer quiet periods that he heard the footsteps behind.

Time had partly lulled the fears of autumn and Christmas, and tonight the drink had warmed him and given him courage; all the same he turned quickly, his hackles up and reaching for his knife. It was the lonely stretch just before you reached the first cottage of Grambler; gorse bushes and heather and a few wind-contorted trees.

There were two men, and in the half-darkness he realized with a sinking feeling that they were strangers; one was tall, wore an old hat pulled low over his eyes.

'Mister Paynter,' said the short man, and Jud thought he had heard that voice somewhere before.

'What d'ye want?'

'Nothing partic'lar. Just a little talk.'

'I don't want no talk. Keep yer distance or I'll slit you wi' this knife.'

'Oh, indeed. Quite a warrior now, eh? More of a warrior than you were last September.'

'I don't know what yer mean,' Jud said anxiously, backing away. 'Tes all foreign to me.'

'What, don't remember getting some money on the cheap, like, eh? Just thought you could tell as many lies as you liked and get away with it, eh? Clever, aren't you? Smart. All right, Joe, let 'im 'ave it.'

The little man sprang forward and Jud's knife flashed in the moonlight, but before he could turn, the tall man lifted a heavy bar he carried and crashed it down with great violence upon Jud's head. There was a rush of moonlight and then his knees gave way and he fell forward into the enduring dark.

When Prudie heard that her husband had been murdered she gave a piercing scream and rushed out in the early morning light to greet the cortege that wormed through the village towards her. Two old scavengers, Ezekiel Scawen and Sid Bunt, had found the body in the ditch beside the road, and some miners had brought a board and were carrying him on his last journey home. Whether the attackers had intended to make it a killing job or whether the savage blow and the night's exposure had together proved too much for a constitution weakened by years of drinking no one would ever know. Robbery was generally believed to be the motive, and two crippled sailors working their way along the coast to St Ives were set on and might have been roughly handled if they had not been able to prove they had spent the whole night in the lowly house of the Rev Clarence Odgers.

Ross wouldn't let Demelza go over, but he went himself and conveyed his sympathy to Prudie. In a queer way Jud had become an institution, not merely in the neighbourhood but in his life. Though they saw little of each other these days, Ross had always been aware of Jud's existence, grumbling, drunken, and self-righteous in his blundering hangdog way. The district wouldn't ever be quite the same without him. He said something of this to Prudie, who sniffed into a red duster that had been Jud's and confessed to Ross her suspicion that Jud's death was a result of something that had happened at Bodmin, because he'd never been easy in his mind since then – always he'd seemed to be expecting something. Now it had come with a vengeance. Ross didn't speak, but stood staring thoughtfully out of the window, considering the possibility. After waiting hopefully for some response, Prudie gave it up and said, Well, dear life, whatever was at the root of it, she didn't know how she'd ever make out now he was gone. And her cousin from Marasanvose, who'd come over for company, sniffed in a corner and wiped her nose on her sleeve.

They had put the body in the lean-to shed that communicated with the single-storey two-roomed shack by way of the back door, and after staring at his old servant for a moment or two, Ross returned to the two sniffing women and said they must tell him if there was any way in which he could help.

'We'm going to teel 'im Thursday,' said Prudie, her hair over her face like a horse's tail, 'an' I want for to give him a rare good berryin'. 'E was always one to like the best, and the best we shall give un, shan't us, Tina.'

'A-a-is,' said Tina.

''E was a proper man, was Jud,' said Prudie. 'Reckon we had our ups and down together, an? Reckon he could be a rare ole ornery monkey upon times, but that didn't count nothin' wi' me. He was my old man, see, and now 'e's dead an' gone, strick down from be'ind in the night. Tis 'orrible, 'orrible to think on!'

'If you'll let me know the time of the funeral, I'll be at the church,' said Ross.

'Ned Bottrell's making a box for'n. I d'want it all done proper, like he was a gent, see. We'm goin' t'ave hymns an' all. Mester Ross . . .'

'Yes?'

'I want for ee to tell me if I'm doin' right. This forenoon when we'd laid 'im out decent I went for to empty out his 'baccy pouch – one 'e carried along with 'im most times everywhere he went, and twas a mercy he didn't take it Tuesday – for when I come to empty of it, damme if golden sov'reigns didn't scatter 'bout all over the floor like mice that's seen a cat. Fifteen of 'em there was, and me never knowed nothin' about'n. Where he come by 'em gracious knows – in the trade, I reckon – but what's plaguing me is whether tis right and fitty to spend the gold on 'is berrying, an?'

Ross stared out through the open door. 'The money is yours now, Prudie, to do with as you will. Everything that was his passes to you; but there's better uses you could put it to than to squander it on a big funeral. Fifteen pounds is a tidy nest egg and would keep you fed and clothed for a long while.'

Prudie scratched herself. 'Jud would've wanted berryin' respectable. Tes a matter o' being *respectable*, Mest' Ross. Load me if it ain't. We must give the ole man a send-off fitty ways. Mustn't us, Tina?'

'A-a-is,' said Tina.

Chapter ten

JUD'S SEND-OFF FITTY ways began at two o'clock the day before the funeral. Prudie had submerged her grief in the preparations, and a long table made of old boxes had been fastened together in the larger of the two rooms. More old boxes outside served as chairs and tables for those who couldn't squeeze in. And there were many such until the heavy rain of nightfall drove them away.

Prudie as chief mourner had managed to gather together enough black clothes to make an impressive display. Her cousin had lent her black stockings, and she'd made a skirt out of a piece of serge bought at Aunt Mary Rogers's shop. An old black blouse of her own was decorated with mourning beads and a bit of ragged lace, and Char Nanfan had actually produced a black veil. Barely recognizable in this array, she sat in a place of honour at the head of the table unmoving throughout the meal and waited on by Cousin Tina, Char Nanfan, Mrs Zacky Martin and a few of the younger end.

The Rev Mr Odgers had been invited to the feast but had discreetly declined; so pride of place next to the bereaved widow was given to Paul Daniel, who was Jud Paynter's oldest friend. On the other side was Constable Vage, who was conducting the inquiry into the murder, and others present were Zacky Martin, Charlie Kempthorne, Whitehead and Jinny Scoble, Ned Bottrell, Uncle Ben and Aunt Sarah Tregeagle, Jack Cobbledick, the Curnow brothers, Aunt Betsy Triggs, and some fifteen or twenty assorted hangers-on.

Soon after two the feast began with a long draught of raw brandy all round, and then everyone set to eating and drinking at a great rate as if there wasn't a minute to be lost. At the outset the splendid widow ate more genteelly than the rest, taking in nourishment under the heavy veil as under a visor. But as the brandy warmed her vitals she threw back the emblem of bereavement and tucked in with the rest.

About five the first part of the feast was over, and by sunset many of the women began to drift off, having families or homes to see to, and the number in the room came down to about a score. This was twice as many as could decently breathe in a cramped space already full of smoke and steam and tobacco fumes. Jugs of brandy, rum and gin were now going round freely, with hot water and sugar to be added to taste. At this point the hymns began. Uncle Ben Tregeagle, as doyen of the church choir, was allowed to lead them, and Joe Permewan scraped an accompaniment like rusty metal on his bass viol. They sang all the hymns and anthems they knew and some they didn't know, and then got on to patriotic songs. They sang 'God Save the King' four times and 'And Shall Trelawney Die' twice, and a few ditties that weren't too savoury if looked at in the most formal light.

But now no one was feeling formal, least of all Prudie, who, her nose shining like a hurricane lamp, allowed herself to be persuaded to get up and sing a song which had the chorus:

> 'An' when he died, he shut his eyes,
> An' never saw money no more.'

Then Aunt Betsy Triggs got up and did her famous dance, ending up sitting in Constable Vage's lap. The roar that greeted this dwindled to a shamefaced silence as everyone came to realize they were overstepping the traces.

Prudie worked her feet into her tattered carpet slippers and slowly got up again.

'My dear, *dear* friends,' she said 'don't take on on account o' me, I beg you. Take no heed of my grief. An' take no heed of the ole man out there that's going to be teeled tomorrer. Tis just a per-personal matter twixt 'im and me. No reason why ye have got to stay quiet as meaders just on account o' that. Eat, drink an' do what you will, for tis no affair of his what I do with his money now 'e's going to his long lie.' She hunched her great shoulders and glowered. 'I-facks, tis more'n I can b'lieve 'ow he did conceal the gold away from me all these many year. Hid it from his own wife, 'e did. Or as near his wife as makes no concern.'

Charlie Kempthorne tittered, but Constable Vage poked him solemnly in the ribs and shook his head; that was not the place to show amusement.

'My blessed life,' said Prudie, and hiccupped. 'He was a whited sepulchre, was my old man, if the truth be known. An old cloamin' tomcat hollow to the toes. As cuzzle as they come. I'd as lief trust a beaver. But there twas, that's how tis, an' no one can deny it. 'E was my old man, see.'

Paul Daniel grunted. After the merriment everyone was feeling sentimental and full of liquor.

'An' he was a talker when the drink was in him. Talk. 'E'd outtalk preacher any day of the week, Sundays including. But I seen him goin' down'ill for months. Twasn't all murdering lyin' thiefs what done for him. Twas semi-decay. Tha's what twas. He'd lived a hard life an' it told in the end.'

She sat down abruptly before she had finished because her knees gave way. Constable Vage got up. At ordinary times he was a wheelwright.

'Brothers and sisters,' he said. 'I aren't one for slack-jaw as ye all well know; but it wouldn't do if we ended this feastin' without a thought or two for our dear brother Jud, newly departed to the flowery fields and green meads o' paradise. Wicked men 'as struck him down, but the law will track them out, never doubt.' He folded his hands over his stomach.

''Ear, 'ear,' said Prudie.

'So we must not forget the vacant chair at this table.' Vage looked round but could not see even an empty packing case. 'The vacant chair,' he repeated. 'And it is only right an' proper that we drink a toast to our dear departed brother.'

'A-a-is,' said Tina.

'To our dear brother,' said Prudie, raising her glass.

The toast was drunk.

'May he rest easy,' said Joe Permewan.

'Amen,' said Uncle Ben Tregeagle, shaking his ringlets.

'Tis a poor life,' said Aunt Sarah. 'From the cradle to the grave in two snaps of the fingers. I see it all. Layin' out and lyin' in. That's me job, but it makes you think.'

'Amen,' said Uncle Ben.

'I'd sooner be a fish jouster any day,' said Betsy.

'There's many I've found worser to lay out than Jud,' said Sarah. ''E stretched out a good deal of a long man, but there warn't so much round the middle as I suspected.'

'Amen,' said Uncle Ben.

''Old hard with your "amens," old man, said Prudie. 'We aren't in church yet. You can say yer prayers tomorrow.'

Charlie Kempthorne began to giggle. He giggled and giggled until everyone hushed him for fear he'd wake the guests already asleep on the floor.

'I aren't partic'ler what I do for the living,' said Betsy. 'But when they ain't living they give me the shrims. Even poor Joe I didn' dare touch – an' him me own brother these fifty year or more.' She began to weep gently.

''Ere, Ned,' said Prudie, 'do ee go'n draw the spigot of that next keg of brandy. I'm as thirsty as a cat wi' nine chets. Tis early yet.'

Bottrell winked at her and went into the other room, which had served as a kitchen today. Prudie sat back, her massive arms folded, surveying the scene with a satisfied expression. Everything had gone off handsome so far. Most of the remaining guests would sleep here the night, and tomorrow, pleasurable thought, it would all begin again. The burying was at noon, so they'd have the coffin out early if it was fine, and placed outside the door on a bench of chairs and packing cases. All the other mourners would be back straight after breakfast, and they'd begin singing hymns. One hymn and then a glass, another hymn and then another glass until about eleven o'clock. Then the bearers would take up the coffin and carry it a hundred yards or so, and Ned Bottrell would follow behind with an anker of brandy and they'd have a hymn and refreshments, another hundred yards and more refreshments, until they got to the church. They should manage that by twelve o'clock, if they managed it at all. Prudie remembered that real bumper funeral of Tommy Job's when the bearers had been stretched out flat with half a mile still to go.

Aunt Sarah Tregeagle said: 'When I first started layin' out, mind, it used to shrim me up too, so I did used to say a little charm over to meself that I'd learned from Grannie Nanpusker, that was a white witch. Afore ever I laid me 'ands on one that'd gone dead I used to say: 'God save us from mystifications, conjurations, toxifications, incantations, fumigations, tarnations, devilations and damnations. Amen. Rosemary, tansy, sweet briar, herb o' grace.' An' I never come to no 'arm at all.'

'My blessed Parliament,' said Prudie.

'Amen,' echoed Uncle Ben sleepily.

But there was nothing sleepy in the way Ned Bottrell burst back into the room. He wasn't carrying any brandy, and his face was white.

'It's gone!' he shouted.

'The brandy!' said Prudie, lurching to her feet. ' 'Ere, who's stolen it? Twas there an hour gone——'

'Not all *three* kegs!' said Constable Vage, instantly alert. 'Why we did oughter have heard them. They couldn't move three kegs without——'

'Nay,' said Ned Bottrell, shouting above the clamour. 'Not the drink, the corpse!'

They got it out of him bit by bit, in a rising clamour of voices. Lured by morbid curiosity and professional pride, he had carried the lantern from the kitchen and taken a peep in the shed, just, as he put it, to see if the ole man was comfortable in his nice new box. And there was the coffin, but the body was gone.

Some of them were as shaken as Ned, but Prudie took the situation firmly in hand. First she said Ned was as full as a can and couldn't see straight and the ole man was still there, she'd lay a guinea. But when Ned invited her to come and see, she said her feet was hurting her and sent Constable Vage instead. When Vage, clearing his throat a good deal and patting his stomach, returned to confirm the story, she drained another glass and stood up.

'Tis they body stealers,' she said in a booming voice. 'You d'know what tis like. I reckon tis those same thievin' lyin' murderers that corpsed him on Monday night. Come us on, my sons.'

With a great show of resolution a dozen of them, led now by the widow, pushed through into the lean-to shed and stared down at Ned Bottrell's box. It looked a good bit of carpentry, and even in this moment of crisis Ned couldn't refrain from giving it an admiring glance. But it was quite empty.

Prudie nearly tipped it up by sitting suddenly on the edge and bursting into tears.

'There, there, now,' said Paul Daniel, who had been wakened from a sound sleep and dragged in here without a full explanation. 'It edn as if he'd been took sudden. We was all prepared for the worst.'

'He's been took sudden, sure 'nough,' said Joe Permewan. ''Tis *where* 'e's been took that's mystifying me.'

'We can't 'ave a funeral without someone to teel,' said Betsy Triggs. 'Twouldn't be decent.'

'There, there, now,' said Paul Daniel, stroking Prudie's lank hair. 'You must be brave, my dear. We've all got to come to it sooner or later. Rich an' poor, gentle an' simple, saint an' sinner. We all must be brave.'

'Brave be *danged!*' shouted Prudie, reacting ungratefully. 'Go hold yer 'ead! I want to know what they done wi' my ole man!'

There was a brief silence.

'We must look,' said Constable Vage. 'Maybe he hasn't been took far.'

This suggestion seemed better than doing nothing, so two more lanterns were lit. When they opened the door it was raining heavily and was pitch-dark, but after some shufflings and hesitation three small search parties were organized, while the women went back to the feast to console Prudie.

Prudie was inconsolable. It was the disgrace, she said. To have a husband an' then not to have a husband, that was how she saw it, and she said she'd never live it down. Betsy Triggs was quite right, you couldn't have a burying without someone to bury. The lying murdering thieves had not only robbed her of her old man, they'd even taken away the pleasure of seeing him planted decent. Everyone was coming back tomorrow for a proper slap-up funeral, and there was three ankers of brandy not touched yet, and all those pies and cakes, and the preacher engaged, and the hole dug, and nothing to put in it. It was more than flesh and blood could stand.

Aunt Sarah Tregeagle thought she'd help the time away with a story of one of her layings out, when a man had died with his knees up; but no one seemed to want to listen, so in the end she tailed off and silence fell. This was nearly as bad, they found, so Uncle Ben, who had been excused the search on account of age, turned to Joe Permewan, who had been excused the search on account of rheumatics, and asked him to play a tune. Joe said, all right, it was just what he'd thought of suggesting himself, and got out his bass viol; but he was so fuddled with drink that when he came to play, the noise he made was even worse than the silence. As Prudie said, it was just as if he was drawing the bow over his own guts.

Ben then suggested a singsong, but nobody had the breath for this, and Prudie began to take offence at Jack Cobbledick's snores from the corner under the window. It was insult on insult, she said. However, no amount of thumping would wake him, so they just went on and on.

Then Betsy Triggs heard footsteps at the door and they all waited eagerly to see what news the returning searchers brought.

Jud Paynter limped in. He was in his best underclothes and was very wet and very cross. The tablecloth he'd borrowed from the kiddley down the lane wasn't much protection from the rain.

''Ere,' he said truculently, 'what's all this? An' where's my pipe?'

Chapter eleven

JUD'S RECOVERY WAS a nine days' wonder and scandal in the district. The doctors and apothecaries who had not bothered with him when he was supposedly dead now rode long distances to see the freak who had recovered. They peered at him and sounded him and took samples and talked in long Latin names about it. They prescribed febrifuges and antimonies and inserted setons and administered glysters, and one of them even wanted to fire off a pistol near his ear to help to disperse any lingering fever. Only Jud's language made it impossible. After the first impetus of his recovery he was very ill again, and he lay in bed with a dirty bandage round his head glowering up at his tormentors.

Ordinary people in the district also flocked to see him, but when he began to get better their presence annoyed him so much that Prudie couldn't let them in any more. Even then they clustered round his window and peeped in through the broken boards, and when he saw them he would shout and swear and aim anything he could lay his hands on, so that Prudie had to hide even her best boots.

Gratitude for his escape didn't stir him deeply; his chief feeling was anger with Prudie.

'Darned old fool,' he said to Ross when Ross called. 'Darned old fool. She spends all me money on me funeral, and I aren't dead. All me money! Drunk away, like it was poured down a drain. She could as lief've throwed it to the crows!'

'How did you first – come round?'

Jud said with dignity that he had been lying quiet in his coffin when the rain coming through the leaky roof had begun to fall on his face, and this had wakened him. He explained that he had been dreaming of gin but the taste was wrong, and when he first sat up he thought he was at sea in the *One and All*. It seemed to be a rough night so he climbed out of his bunk and went on deck, but when he got there it was raining faster than ever and he saw trees and knew he was home after all.

'Then I feels thirsty so I goes down Jake's lane to Jake's kiddley and goes in wanting for a drop o' custom to ease me, like, and damme, what d'you think, they all ups and screams like they was stuck veers and goes scrabbling over each other to get out o' the other door – and leaves me all alone. So I finishes up the drinks they'd left, an' puts the table sheet round me 'ead and goes home to find Prudie.'

'She thought the money was hers,' Ross said. 'Everyone thought you were dead. It was her wish to give you a fine funeral.'

'It was her wish to have a rare old caprouse, that's what twas. Drunk they all was. Drunk as emmets round a jam pot. And on *my* gold. When I was strick down there was fifteen gold sov'reigns. What is there now, eh? Three sov'reigns and two kegs of brandy an' a wooden coffin standing on its end like a grandfather's clock wi' no face! Tedn right, I tell ee!'

In the weeks that followed Jud made a slow recovery. He limped about with a stick, one leg dragging a little, and would speak to no one. Nor did he take kindly to the enquiries of his friends. It was almost impossible to go out for a drink without being asked what Heaven looked like or whether Gabriel hadn't answered his knock, and if there was gin or brandy up-along.

All his life he'd been a disgruntled man, but what made his present grievance almost impossible to bear was that he could tell no one the worst of it. He had risked the reprisal to gain the guineas, and now had suffered the reprisal and lost the guineas as well. If he ever did see Gabriel there would be a fine tale to tell.

On the first Friday in May Ross and Francis rode in to make final arrangements about the opening of the mine. They explained something of their plans to Harris Pascoe in the back room of the bank, and Pascoe eyed the cousins and wondered how long the partnership would last. He had only the outsider's view of their misunderstandings, knowing nothing of the long friendship of their youth, and he was grateful for being spared the necessity of refusing them a loan on their venture.

Francis said 'There is one point on which I already have Ross's agreement. I want my interest in this mine to be vested in my son's name.'

'Your little boy? He's only a child, isn't he?'

'I'm heavily in debt to Warleggan interests and have recently quarrelled with the family. So far, I'll give 'em credit, no pressure has been put on me; but you know how Ross and the Warleggans get on, and if they learn we are in partnership they may try to get at him through me. If this interest belongs to Geoffrey Charles, no one can touch it.'

'We c-can arrange that. There are, of course, a few extra difficulties which may crop up in the possession of this sort of property by a minor. I suppose you would not prefer it in your wife's name?'

Francis looked at his fingers. 'No. I would not.'

'Just so. Very well, then. When do you intend to begin work?'

'The first of June,' Ross said. 'The engine pieces are already well ahead, but of course we shall not need pumping gear right at the outset.'

'I suppose you're having a Boulton and Watt?'

'Well, no. There are two young engineers from Redruth Henshawe speaks highly of, and we think they will build a more efficient one at a smaller cost.'

'Only t-take care not to get involved in litigation over that. Watt has the important patent, and I believe there are some years for it yet to run.'

Soon after, they called on Nat Pearce, who was to draw up the deeds of association; then they had a meal at the Red Lion Inn. Francis had some business of his own to do, so he left Ross talking to Richard Tonkin, who had joined them at the meal. Tonkin had news of many of their former associates, but Ross would have welcomed this at any other time more sincerely than now when he was trying his best to forget all the circumstances of twelve months ago.

Tonkin went on to say he had heard that Margaret Vosper, née Cartland, née nobody knew what, had left her husband and was making up to Sir Hugh Bodrugan. Ross said, Indeed, indeed, thinking, Well and good if it keeps him from sniffing round my home like a mangy old tomcat. They rose from the table and moved to go downstairs. At the top of the stairs they saw George Warleggan coming up.

Tonkin half hesitated, glanced at Ross, saw no change in his expression, and continued down a step behind him. George had seen them now, but he made no effort to avoid them. Indeed avoidance was impossible; they would meet at the bend in the stairs.

Ross would have gone down as if the other man did not exist, but George put his long malacca cane against the banisters waist high, barring his path. It was a dangerous thing to do.

'Well, Ross!' he said. 'This is favourably met. We've not seen each other for some time.'

Ross looked at him.

'As you remark.'

A ruby as big as a pea made oriental gleams in George's extremely expensive neckcloth. Ross, by comparison, was shabby.

George said: 'You're not looking so well as when I last saw you. Can it be the anxieties of the trial?'

'Nor you,' said Ross. 'Can you have had some disappointment?'

'Ecod' – George poked the rail with his stick – 'I know of nothing to cause me disappointment. I am well satisfied with my many enterprises. I hear, by the way, that you're embarking on a new one.'

'As usual you have your ear well to the ground,' said Ross. 'Or should it be to the keyhole?'

The sense of inferiority in the depths of George's consciousness was one that Ross more than any other man could call up. It was altogether the strongest element in his lust for power and far more important as a cause of his hatred for Ross than any of the more obvious reasons.

He withdrew his stick. 'I like a gambler. Especially one who plunges when the luck is running against him.'

'A good gambler,' said Ross, 'always knows before other people when his luck is beginning to turn.'

'And a bad gambler believes it when it isn't true.' George laughed. 'I must confess I found some amusement in your choice of partner. Francis of all people! Have you forgotten what he did for the Carnmore Copper Company?'

Ross was well aware that Richard Tonkin was listening intently.

He said: 'By the way, one of the witnesses at my trial was only three weeks ago set on and nearly died from an attack made by hired bullies of some sort. I shouldn't like to feel that this kind of retaliation was to become a common practice.'

The flicker of surprise in George's eyes looked genuine. He leaned against the wall to let two people pass up the stairs.

'He must be an idle creature who has time to carry on personal vendettas with village riffraff. But why should you suppose it to be anything of the kind?'

'Whoever is behind it would be mistaken if he thought intimidation could remain one-sided. The miners, you know, have their own way of showing their displeasure.'

'We all have,' said George politely. 'Oh, I hear you've been disposing of part of your holding in Wheal Leisure – one of the few really profitable ventures in the county. A grave mistake, I'm sure.'

Ross's eyes were heavy-lidded now. 'Time will show.'

George said: 'Of forty-four engines built in Camborne and Illuggan during the last ten years only four are still working. In Leisure you had a rare combination of good ore and easy drainage. At Grace you have certainly not the drainage. What are you looking for – gold?'

'No,' said Ross, 'freedom to call our souls our own.'

George, flushing, said quickly, spitefully: 'I suppose you know where Francis got the money he's investing in your mine, do you?'

'I've an idea. It was very obliging of you.'

'Yes, we paid it him – the Warleggans – for services rendered. Six hundred pounds . . . or thirty pieces of silver.'

Down in the taproom two men were quarrelling over a mug of beer: their rough growling voices seemed to Tonkin like the reverberation of some worn-out clockwork mechanism which failed to move the arrested figures on the stairs. Then before he could do anything they slipped into motion.

Ross reached out a hand and grasped George by the neckcloth. It had annoyed him from the first moment he saw it. With it he pulled George towards him and shook him. For a second of surprise George did nothing, but choked with the sudden tightened clasp about his throat – then he lifted his cane to hit Ross across the head. Ross grasped the hand at the wrist and twisted it down. George bunched his other fist and hit Ross a swinging blow on the side of the head. They overbalanced and crumpled against the banisters which, being immensely strong, did not give way.

Tonkin stepped forward with an appeal to their common sense, but he was ignored; for a moment they were beyond common sense; a man below had seen them and was calling for the innkeeper.

George, empurpling, swung his great fist again, but he was off balance and the force was half astray. The cane clattered to the floor, and Ross, loosing his grip, hit George in the mouth. Then at last he released the neckcloth and grasped George about the waist. Like two bulls they swung across the stairs, knocking Tonkin out of the way. There was little in it for strength, but Ross had led the harder life. George felt his feet going. Raging angry at this exhibition, he sought Ross's eyes with his thumbs; but it was too late. He was lifted off his feet, was going over the banisters. At the last moment he sought to cling to something, but only tore the front out of Ross's shirt. With a great crash he fell to the floor below, landing on a chair and a small table and smashing them as if they were matchwood.

Ross swayed and gasped and spat, began to come down the stairs. His forehead was bleeding and the blood was trickling along his eyebrow and down one cheek. George was twisting and groaning on the floor. The landlord came rushing out and halted appalled at the sight; then ran to the foot of the stairs.

'Captain Poldark, sir . . . disgraceful! What is the meaning of it, please? . . . Mr Warleggan, what has happened? . . . Are you hurt, sir? Captain Poldark, I want an explanation. . . . Mr Tonkin, pray give me an explanation. One does not expect the gentlemen . . . a table and two good chairs . . . damage perhaps to the banisters. Captain Poldark . . .'

As Ross came down the last step the little innkeeper got in his way; Ross saw the red waistcoat and, in the last flicker of an anger such as he had not felt for years, he shoved it out of his path. He meant it as no more than a gesture but the little man staggered back and sat down abruptly against the wainscot, and a plate came down from the wall and smashed beside him. As Ross walked out of the inn George Warleggan was just getting to his knees.

At Nampara they were cutting hay. The crop was good this year, and John and Jane Gimlett and Jack Cobbledick were at work together with two of the younger Martin children, superintended a little discontentedly by Demelza, who had been forbidden to take a hand in it. She was proscribed so many things these days and didn't like it. She felt fine, and it was a waste loafing about when there was much to do.

It was a bright day with a strong southeast breeze, and after dinner she didn't follow the haymakers up to the field again but fed her small stock of poultry and did a few odd jobs about the house – all this with a restless air, as if mere activity brought no satisfaction in itself. Verity had written last week, saying with some obvious apprehension that her two stepchildren

were coming to visit her *at last* – but most of her space was filled with
loving concern and advice. Demelza thought: Don't overtire myself indeed;
I never get a chance; Ross has set the Gimletts on me like terriers. I should
not be astonished if they do not drop their scythes soon and come scurrying
back to see if all is well.

She went to the front door and looked over her garden. The soft winter
had suited it and the flowers were forward. Strange, she thought, if women
were like that – brought on by the warm weather, retarded by the cold
weather. The wind was fluffing the tulips about; she picked off the heads of
one or two dishevelled ones, then went back through the house to the little
dairy where the cheeses were standing to ripen, lifted the cloths to see that
no mould was forming, moved through the outbuildings. From there it was
a natural progression to the Long Field and the headland beyond.

A considerable swell on the sea today; the waves ran into Hendrawna
Beach like brides to their wedding, a veil of spray blowing round their
heads. Near the rocks the swell moved more sleekly, the veils sank as they
were left behind, white lace first in the shallower green, then misting to a
mottled luminous cloud in the darker depths. Beyond the breakers were
two fishing boats from St Ann's. She turned and clambered down, treading
on the curled fronds of the new bracken, to Nampara Cove.

In the shelter it was quite warm and quiet and the sea rippled invitingly.
She took off her shoes and stockings and let the water lick her feet. Very
pleasant and soothing. After a while she went over to the dinghy and found
that the last time she had used it – with Gimlett a week ago – they had
forgotten to carry the rowlocks up to the house. Ross would have been
cross, since anyone could use or even steal the boat if they could row it
away. In the bottom of the boat was a tin with some bait in it; it would be
smelly by now.

Within the cove the air was still, and, looking out, the bright day
glimmered like a cameo. The waves seemed small enough, and she realized
that, so long as she kept within the protection of the cove, they would be
innocuous. Of course if anyone knew she had taken the boat out there
would be a great to-do; but Ross was miles away, and the others could
whistle if they chose.

She had learned from experience how to drag the light craft over the
sand without straining herself; it was a knack; and, taking special care now
that it was May, she got the boat to the edge without difficulty, Then she
tucked up her skirts and pushed the boat into the water. In a minute she
had climbed over the side and a pull or two at the oars straightened her up
so that there was no danger of being pushed back broadside on.

She rowed out until near the mouth of the cove and dropped her anchor
overboard. It caught almost at once. There was more swell here than she
had expected, but it was a pleasant sensation. In triumph, though with
some distasteful wrinkling of her nose, she began to bait her line.

Chapter twelve

THE SUDDEN BRAWL with George Warleggan had left Ross in a ferment of angry thoughts. He didn't remember in his life having lost his temper in quite that way before. George's face, George's sneers, the oppressive influence of the Warleggans over all his life, had suddenly boiled up into a moment of uncontrollable fury. There had been at least one instant in the past when it might have done so with greater reasonableness; but that was the way things happened. Now the murder was out with a vengeance.

(It was lucky, he realized, that George *hadn't* killed himself, that *he* hadn't killed him. From the way he was getting up from among the ruins of the table it looked as if he was not seriously hurt.) But news of the fight would spread like a fire in dead gorse. In an hour it would be on everyone's lips in Truro; in a day . . . Not that that mattered – except for the subject of the quarrel. There lay the poison.

It was a poison not only on people's lips but in Ross's mind, and a mere brawl wouldn't exorcise it. While he washed himself and bought a new shirt he tried to see the thing reasonably.

That Francis had in some degree let down the copper-smelting venture was a circumstance which Ross had come in an unspecified way to accept. Something had happened which must be overlooked and forgotten. That Francis had suffered in his own conscience because of it was plain to anyone who had met him in the last twelve months. Well, it was over and past. There was no certainty at all that the company would not have crashed just as completely without his help; and if there *had* been a betrayal it had taken place in sudden anger during the quarrel over Verity's elopement. It had never once occurred to Ross that Francis could deliberately have 'sold' them for money. Even now, out of some knowledge of Francis's character, he rejected it; it was the impulse to reject it which had led to the fight; it was because the insinuation couldn't be denied in words that violence had been necessary.

So the fight had been in defence of Francis's character, and yet the defendant was unsure of what he defended. An uneasy stand. The grim little confirmatory details gathered themselves and stuck. The Warleggans had certainly paid Francis the money. Was Elizabeth's explanation – presumably obtained from Francis – a reasonable one? Would the

Warleggans part with six hundred pounds on a point of principle? What other reason, except a revulsion of feeling at his own treachery, could Francis have for being reluctant to spend the money on his own comfort and convenience? Why did the great window at Trenwith lack an elementary repair?

What then if it was true? If it was true, better go across and tell Pearce not to waste his time drawing up a document which never could be implemented. But how be sure? Only by challenging Francis outright. And the very challenge, showing that he considered such a betrayal for money possible, would end their association either way. He understood Francis well enough for that.

There was trivial shopping to be done in spite of all this upset. Ross went about it in an angry daze which made him a tribulation to the shopkeepers. They stared curiously at his bruised forehead and preoccupied face as they laid out their wares. One moment he would think, George is a liar and got his deserts; the next the poisonous doubts would creep back. Was this enormity what Francis had been about to confess at Trenwith last month?

If the cause of the fight got about and people believed what George said, Francis's position would become impossible anyway. Ross had glimpsed Tonkin's expression. If people believed George, Francis would not be able to show his face in Truro.

Thank God at least that Trencrom had paid up and that money at this important time was not quite so tight. Four yards of pink ribbon, four yards of blue ribbon, at sixpence a yard. Seven yards of lace edging cost five shillings. It would most likely be the wrong sort when he got home, but Demelza would make the best of it, as she made the best of everything. More huckaback towelling. These were things Demelza herself would have bought while she was still able to ride, but they had simply not had the money. A pair of blankets. There was a pair at sixteen shillings and one at twelve. In a sudden economy he bought the cheaper, and then squandered the difference on some yards of crimson velvet for a sash for Demelza for use when she was again the shape to wear it.

Her time was likely to be any day now. The sooner the better. A new comb. That was the usual cry. She always broke them pulling them through her hair.

What would she say about this new development? She had always been for reconciliation – but would she urge him to forgive and forget if *this* were true? She might say, why let everything be ruined at this late stage by a wild accusation from George? A quarrel between the cousins was exactly what he desired.

That at least was common sense. And if they quarrelled, who *was* to finance the mine? His own money wouldn't go far enough. Was the planning of the last two months to end in futility without even a gambler's throw? Exactly what George would wish.

As he finished what he had to buy Ross realized he had arranged to meet Francis at the coaching inn. That could not be now. He was sorry he had pushed the little innkeeper over – somehow the damage and the insult should be made up to him – but he couldn't go back there today. (There might be formal repercussions from his fight with George but he rather doubted it: George might wish he had met him with bare fists in a place with more room for manœuvre than a flight of stairs, but it was unlikely that he would risk his skin with weapons against a soldier. All the same, it would be open war in every other way.)

He went to the Seven Stars Tavern and sent a potboy who knew Francis by sight to keep watch for him at the entrance to the Red Lion. Then he sat in a dark corner and ordered brandy and tried to force a decision before they came back. On it, on what he decided now, from his reasoning mind's absolute freedom of choice, would spring the whole pattern of the future. Everything was done or undone, promised or forbidden, fecund or sterile according to the judgment of to-day. To-morrow it would have happened. There were two choices open to him, not three. He could not accept George's word before Francis's. Either he challenged Francis with the story – with the inevitable result – or he trusted his cousin's integrity. Even compromise would be fatal. To ignore everything George had said and yet let it fester in his mind would be worse than a clean break.

The grandfather's clock ticked in the corner. Outside in the narrow street the warm gusty wind stirred the dust in sandy whorls; it lifted the coattails and ruffled the wig of a fat old gentleman with a stick and unsteady legs who made his way laboriously past the inn; it pushed a ball of paper delectably nearer the nose of a watching cat; nine miles away the dinghy dragged its anchor an inch or two and Demelza's hair blew across her face as she pulled in an empty line. In the inn, from the dark corner opposite Ross, a man stood up and came across to him. It was Andrew Blamey, Verity's husband.

Ross stared at him, trying to collect his thoughts, then, more from instinct than conscious will, got up and took the extended hand.

Blamey said gruffly: 'Well, sir, it must be more than two years.'

'I should have said a good deal more.' There was a perceptible hesitation. 'Will you join me?'

'I come seldom to Truro these days, but I brought a schooner up for a friend who is unfamiliar with the river and am waiting now for the five o'clock coach home.'

They talked for some minutes, though not easefully. Andrew Blamey asked with real concern after Demelza's health. It was always a surprise to Ross how Demelza seemed to have the respect of so many of these difficult men. Francis would do anything for her. Sir John Trevaunance had sent over some hothouse peaches last week. These men were not in the Bodrugan-Treneglos class who paid her attentions because she was physically exciting and had a sharp wit.

In return he politely asked about Verity and noticed a little flicker across Andrew's face.

'Does that mean she's not well?'

'No, she was in excellent health when I left this morning.' He cleared his throat. 'There is one small matter – though no doubt to an outsider . . . My two children will be visiting us for the first time tomorrow, and I shall be at sea.'

Ross glanced towards the door. As the other dilemma was shifted from the dead centre of his attention he tried to concentrate on what the sailor said.

'H.M.S. *Thunderer* is due in Falmouth tonight or early tomorrow. James has been away two years – I fully expected to be ashore all this week, so ordered my daughter, who hitherto has refused to come – purely out of shyness, I imagine – to pay us a visit at the same time. But last night *Arwenack* fouled an old wreck as she came into the roads and will need repairs to her bows. So *Caroline* must sail in her place tomorrow.'

Time was getting ever shorter – and he no nearer the crucial choice. Belatedly, with a quickening of eye and thought, a sharp apprehension of the other issues, he realized that another explosive situation was threatening here. Francis and Blamey had never once met except to quarrel violently in seven years. Blamey must be warned now, got away. And yet . . . if *he* was expected to make a gesture of trust and forgiveness and understanding, who else might not be expected to do the same?

He said abruptly, harshly: 'You see something of Europe in your travels. What do you think are the prospects for peace?'

Blamey stopped at this new tack. 'What? Well, I see little of Europe beyond Lisbon. But I hear a good deal. It's a sounding board. There is nervousness about.'

'On account of France?'

'On account of the revolutionary parties. They spring up everywhere, encouraged by the French. I mean the minorities in Germany and Austria and Portugal who really owe allegiance only to Paris, as you might say. That's the danger, for if war breaks out one feels they will side with the French against their own countryfolk.'

'There are such parties in England, but I think they make a noise beyond their size.'

'In England, yes. Elsewhere I'm not so sure.'

'And the temper of the French?'

Blamey shrugged. 'One hears the side of the émigrés, of course. But if conditions inside the country become intolerable, I should be inclined to think——'

He stopped. Francis had come in.

It was dark in the low-roomed inn after the brightness outside, and he only saw Ross. So he came up to the table smiling.

'Well, so I hear you've been in parlour games with George! He has marked you. But they tell me he has a sprained shoulder and can hardly stand. What was the spark that——'

Francis saw Blamey and came to a stop. Blamey got up bristling like a dog ready for a fight.

And quite suddenly the situation crystallized itself for Ross. The disorderly segments of his own problem became formalized by this new situation in which he was hardly more than a spectator. With time for thought it might have seemed an oversimplification, but the time for thought was past. Here was the acid test for Francis. Forgive us our trespasses . . .

Francis said: '*You* . . .'

Ross did not get up. 'Sit down, Francis. I'll order you drink.'

All the old arrogance was back in Francis's face. 'Thank you, I'll not trouble you in this company. . . .'

Ross said: 'This is the last moment to wipe out the past.'

Something in his voice caught Francis's attention. He looked at Ross and Ross was looking at him. He flushed and hesitated.

Uneasily, from under frowning brows, Blamey glanced at Ross too. The special significance of the moment had somehow communicated itself to them both. Neither spoke for a perceptible space while the potboy who had brought Francis hovered near waiting for his tip. Ross gave it him and ordered brandies. The boy went away and the three men were alone again.

Blamey said: 'The quarrel has never been of my seeking.'

Francis dusted his cuff and swallowed something.

'My sister seems to find her new life agreeable,' he said bitterly.

'So she should,' said Ross. 'It's natural for a woman to be married, and we can't forever be scratching over it like cocks on a dunghill.'

'In any case she takes no account of my approval or disapproval. . . .'

'She would be very much happier with a reconciliation,' Blamey said. 'That's why I desire it.'

It was quite handsomely said. Francis stared across the room at the returning boy, thrust his hands in his pockets as if seeking something.

'If that is the case . . .'

The boy put down the drinks and left. Ross glowered up at the other men, the new bruise on his forehead showing red and angry above the white of the scar. He wasn't saying any more. It was up to them now. If they could not find the formula he was done with them both.

Appropriately it was Francis who made the decisive move. He sat on the arm of the settle and picked up his glass.

'The Warleggans'll be raging mad after this brush, Ross. I've come near to laying hands on George myself but never quite found the opportunity.' He glanced at Blamey and seemed to force himself to speak. 'You haven't heard the news perhaps. That Ross and George Warleggan met on the stairs of the Red Lion this afternoon and that Ross took George in as pretty a hug as has been seen in the county for a twelvemonth and threw him from top to bottom. It's all over the town.' He looked at Ross. 'It's true, I suppose?'

'A thought exaggerated, but the substance is correct.'

Blamey had quietly seated himself again. He twisted his glass but did not drink.

'Verity told me of a developing feud. But what was the cause of the quarrel today?'

Ross looked past them at the old grandfather's clock. It was nearly five.

'I took a dislike to his neckcloth.'

Demelza had caught two infant dabs who obviously didn't know any better, but in the main the fish were not biting. She didn't blame them. The bait was too smelly even for mackerel. After a time she decided to call the attempt off; and she threw the fish she had caught back into the water, since their food value wouldn't be worth all the enquiries and concern and the near scolding.

Looking back for the first time for some minutes, she saw that the anchor must have been dragging a bit, for she was almost out of the mouth of the cove and the land looked farther off than usual. It was a pleasant sight, the low-lying black cliffs, the curve of the sand, the pebbles and scraggy vegetation where the Mellingey ran into the sea. You could feel and see the swell of the waves as they moved past the cliffs on their way to Hendrawna Beach.

She went to the end of the boat and pulled in the anchor. Then she scrambled back and took up the oars and set her face to the sea. A few pulls and she would be home.

She wondered how Ross's business in Truro was going. This gamble on Wheal Grace had been taken without her knowledge, and although she would never criticize after the event, it had never quite won her approval. Grace was the shot in the dark, the guess that might go wrong. It was the sort of venture to indulge in when you had a thousand pounds to spare, not when you were living on the precipice of debt.

Out here you could feel the breeze quite strongly, and the dinghy was so light, almost keelless, that it was inclined to be blown off its course. Several times she corrected it after glancing behind her, and the third time she was a little perturbed to see the cliffs no nearer at all. Up to now she had pulled only with her arms and not at all with her body, knowing that she must be careful of that; but now she began to put more weight behind the oars and was comforted to feel the boat respond on the heaving sea.

Sometimes she suspected, while considering it rather disloyal to do so, that Ross in opening a new mine had allowed his judgment to be warped by his detestation of the Warleggans – so that his desire to be free of their interference had led him to overoptimism about Wheal Grace. As for Francis, he, she knew, was a gambler too, but a much less astute gambler than Ross, so that his participation in the scheme was no reassurance at all. It was well enough for the rest of them. Henshawe risked a hundred pounds which he could comfortably spare. The two young engineers from Redruth were to be paid for their engine as they built it. The tutworkers and spallers got their monthly wages; the tributers spent only their time and trouble; it was the Poldarks who risked all the rest.

She had been rowing for two or three minutes, confident she was gaining ground, but when she looked round she saw that her progress had been diagonal and towards the sharp rocks of Damsel Point. They were only fifteen or eighteen feet away and the sea slithered and slapped around them, not making a lot of fuss but rising and falling enough to knock the bottom out of a boat. She veered quickly away and in doing so lost most of the ground she had won. It was while righting her course again that she began to feel queer. At first she thought it was a touch of the seasickness. Then she knew it was not.

On the clifftop, half in the shadow, half in the sun, some jackdaws and some choughs were quarrelling. The sweep of black wing against black wing glinted like jet. The sky was an indefinite pallid blue with faint streaks of sunlit cloud trailing across it from the south. She began to row in earnest, putting all her strength into it, knowing now it was touch and go. In the roots of her dark hair where it grew at the sides of her brow tiny beads of sweat formed. Her bottom lip was caught up and her eyes went cloudy.

She thought, Well, this is my own fault, nobody's but my own. So I get through it myself or go under. This will be a nice homecoming for Ross. Then it seemed for a minute that she must give up rowing, that her life must be sacrificed for two minutes with her head between her knees; but with the horizon blurring and the noise of sea rushing into her head she kept on. A beast, a devil, had seized her and she must give up or die.

Then when it seemed impossible to breathe any more the grip was suddenly relaxed. The beach was perceptibly nearer now. No distance. Like a mirage it danced over her shoulder, luring her with its safe dry sand and its promise of home.

The choughs flew off, quite low over her head, glints of red about their legs; they were defeated; the jackdaws were triumphantly settling into the hollows on the cliff edge. They were farther away. Progress. But the Beast was nearer again, waiting to pounce. She thought, Ross will be home at seven; I shall not be home by then, never home again. But somehow I must get home. He will have no one to tell about the mine. Wheal Grace. Named after his mother. Perhaps it will be lucky. It was lucky once. The house had been built from the proceeds. There'd been money enough in mining in the past. Trenwith built out of Grambler. Tehidy from Dolcoath; half the big houses of Cornwall had come that way. But money enough had been lost too.

The wind contrarily, wickedly, had grown stronger, the ebbing tide pulled at the light boat, out towards the open sea. Perhaps there would be someone about who would see her, someone walking along the cliff. Or if she allowed her dinghy to drift out one of the St Ann's fishing boats would surely catch sight of her. While there was life . . .

Unexpectedly a wave broke under her and she missed her stroke; the boat moved as if an arm six times as strong had used the oar. She turned and saw she was nearly ashore. It was the wrong end of the little cove, by the stream, not so sheltered and the waves were breaking; but it would do. She tried to guide the craft, but a second wave turned her broadside on and almost upset her. Then it burst upon the beach, dropping the dinghy upon the stones before sucking it out again with a rattle and a roar. She climbed over the side and as another wave burst jumped into the sea and clutched the boat, trying instinctively to pull it ashore. The effort wrenched her and she gasped and let go. She had hurt herself. Then she fought her way through the returning surf and found herself on hands and knees on dry land. The Beast had come back, and she crouched there unable to move, in its direst grip.

Three minutes passed. The waves continued to beat out their rhythm; but the sun had gone behind a tiny cloud. Robbed of its colour, the cove looked suddenly shabby and cold and the sea dangerous. Halfway across the cove it deposited the dinghy upside down, its oars lost and a plank staved in.

Demelza stirred and got to her feet. She was soaking wet and could hardly stand. She squeezed out the front of her skirt and blouse and began painfully to limp up the valley to the house.

Chapter thirteen

ON THE FOLLOWING afternoon Verity stood at the window of her house overlooking Falmouth Harbour, listening for the arrival of the Plymouth coach. She would have dreaded this coming meeting even with Andrew at her side. In his absence the situation, in occasional moments of panic, seemed unfaceable. Then she would rally and ask herself what but a little constraint had she to fear from two young people still only in their middle teens?

Although James must have been in the town some hours he had not shown up yet. She glanced at the clock behind her, and as she did so the horn sounded clearly. She could not see the coach from here, but she could picture it turning into the yard of the inn, the lathered horses, the passengers climbing down, the bells ringing, sailors yawning at the door, the man she had sent to meet Esther scanning the faces; Esther herself, the girl, half woman, the face in that miniature but older by five years.

Verity swung round on the small circular mirror, peered at herself. To the girl she would seem old, dowdy, a usurper. Youth was so mercilessly hard in its decisions; it had its own unyielding standards and had not yet learned enough to know that time would prove them arbitrary. She stood there until the doorbell rang; then she took a deep breath and went down. Masters was at the door with a slight, rather tall girl.

'You're Esther? Come in, my dear. I've been looking forward to meeting you. You must be tired. Can you take the box right up, Masters; you know the room? Do come in, my dear.'

Cheek was cold. Face a little broad over the cheekbones, noticeable grey eyes, honest but self-centred, slightly hostile. 'Mrs Stevens is in bed with stomach trouble,' Verity explained. 'She has been ailing on and off for weeks. I have a meal ready for you.'

'Thank you, ma'am. May I first go to my room?'

'Of course. Come down just at your leisure.'

In the upstairs parlour again Verity walked to the window. No warmth. Did her own welcome ring false?

A three-masted packet boat was shaking out her sails as she moved slowly among the other shipping towards the open sea, taking advantage of the first ebb. Captain Buckingham in *Percuil*, bound for the West Indies.

Verity forced herself to sit down, pick up her embroidery. Calm and unstrained friendship. *She* was the adult, must set the temper of the stay.

Esther was a long time, but when she came in she looked older without her bonnet. Verity got up.

'I've set our meal in here, Esther. I always dine here when I'm by myself, for I love to watch the shipping.'

'Yes, ma'am.' Those eyes. So small and *so* direct. Could it be fright, not hostility?

'Your father was greatly disappointed to have to sail. He had looked forward to this moment for a long time.'

'They did not tell me he wouldn't be here, not until I had taken my seat in the coach.'

At supper the girl toyed with her food. A slight smear of pock-marks on her cheeks marred her clear skin.

'You know your brother's in port, Esther?'

'I knew he was coming. I did not know he was here.'

'The *Thunderer* dropped anchor this morning. Your father had a note from him last month when a frigate put in with mails.'

'Yes, I heard too.'

So he wrote to his sister. 'I believe he has been with the East Indies Fleet. . . . Are you happy at your school?'

'Yes, ma'am. I leave at the end of the year.'

They talked awhile but made no progress. She parried questions like a swordsman parrying dangerous thrusts. It was impossible to get near her. With a sinking heart Verity rose and went to the side table to carve the beef. She could see a nightmare week end terminating in complete failure. Esther would go away, and when Andrew came back he would know that she had failed.

'I don't think you're at all like your father, are you, my dear?'

Esther's lack of response had forced it out of her. She could feel the girl's eyes boring into her back.

'No, ma'am. I take after my mother.'

'Oh, I didn't know that. . . . Well, I think you are going to be very attractive.'

'Mother was *very beautiful*,' said Esther. 'I wish I was like her in that.'

Verity looked up and suddenly found that the oval mirror with the convex surface reflected the dining table. The girl was sitting straightly in her chair, white frilled dress cascading from narrow shoulders. Her face wore an extraordinary expression of pride and resentment. Verity's knife wavered, slid across the beef. She looked down.

'Of course,' she said, 'I can never begin to replace your own mother, but I hope you'll always look on me as a loving and well-wishing friend.'

'You know Father killed her, don't you?' Esther said.

There was silence.

Verity turned. 'I know all I want to know.' She put the plate before her stepdaughter. 'That there was a terrible accident, and——'

'He killed her. Ever since then people have been trying to teach me different, but I know! He went to prison for it, didn't he? She hadn't any near relatives. They sent me to his. They've tried to poison her memory, but they'll never do that. I know she was good and a saint. I know!'

Verity brought her own plate and sat down. Unhappiness and resentment put an edge on her voice. 'I know it's not a fit subject for discussion between us. Please finish your meal.'

'So I'm to be forbid to speak of Mother before you too, ma'am.'

'Certainly not. Unless speaking of your mother means speaking against your father.'

'He has plenty to speak for him. She hasn't one but me.'

Verity's heart was thumping. 'It's right and good,' she said, 'that you should think and speak of your mother. But it is neither right nor good to dwell on her death. Remember the happiness she had, not the——'

'She never had any happiness.'

Their glances met.

'How do you *know*?' Verity said angrily. 'I think it's necessary that we should come to an understanding, Esther——'

She broke off and listened to a loud rantan at the street door. I *can't* face the other one tonight, she thought. Between them they'll . . . I can't. I can't.

Esther's eyes were lowered at last. 'That's James,' she said.

In dead silence they sat there together, listened to the front door being opened and feet on the stairs. The feet hesitated for a moment, then there was a rap at the door and it opened and a square-built boy came in. Darker than his sister, smart uniform of a naval midshipman, curly hair, brown eyes.

'Well, I wondered if there was anyone aboard,' he said in an unnecessarily big voice. 'I thought as the door was unhitched there'd most likely be a skeleton crew. Good day to you, Essie. You've grown.' His eyes wandered to the other person. 'I suspicion you'll be . . .'

With a great effort Verity rose. 'Come in, James. I've been looking for you all day.'

He banged the door behind him. 'Are you Miss Verity?'

'Well, I was. Now I am——'

'Ha! I know. May I call you Aunt? Twould split the difference, so to speak. Sorry I missed Father. If I'd known I should ha' spoke to the captain sharp and told him to make haste. He and I are on good speaking terms, though for the most part the speaking is on his side.'

He came across, flung his cap on the window seat, patted Esther on the head, came round the table to Verity, looked her up and down. He was taller than she. 'I've heard a lot about you, Aunt.'

He put his hands on her shoulders and kissed her just below the ear.

Then he gave her a hug that squeezed all the breath out of her.

'You'll pardon the liberty,' he said, speaking as if he was in a high wind, 'but one don't get a new mother every day o' the week. When I had the letter we were in Penang, so I says, "Come, lads, we've a toast to drink, for I've a new mother, an' that's better than a wife any week, being more comfort and less responsibility." I never wrote, not being over-handy with a pen, but drink your health we did with a will.'

'Thank you,' said Verity, feeling suddenly warm. 'That was kind of you.'

'Well' – he glanced round – 'nice to be home again. Though the walls are uncomfortable steady. D'you know, I truly believe that is why sailors get foxed so soon as they come ashore, it is so that the deck shall rock again like they've been used to. Esther dear, do not look so sour at me.'

'You've not changed a bit,' said Esther.

The boy turned and laughed aloud at Verity. 'That, ma'am, is not intended as a compliment. D'you save any supper?'

'Yes, I did!' said Verity. 'Mrs Stevens is in bed, so I'll fetch it.'

'Avast! I'll go below myself. That's if you'll trust me in the galley. Mrs Stevens will not.'

'Go down and bring up anything you want,' said Verity.

They ate in stony silence until he came back.

'You've not been aboard a man-o'-war, ma'am?' said James, stretching his legs in satisfaction. 'I wonder if I could arrange it. I wonder if you'd pass as my real mother. No, you're too young. Still, stepmothers have rights. Ha! I think it could be arranged.'

'Perhaps Esther would like to come.'

'No, thank you, ma'am.'

'Essie doesn't like the sea. More's her misfortune. But I fancy a good sailor has been lost in you.'

'It remains to be seen, for I've never sailed. Do you take sugar, James?'

'Thick wi' sugar. So as the spoon will stand. As for sailing in bad weather, I never knew what rough weather was till we ran into a hurricane off the Nicobar Islands. . . .'

'Sugar, Esther?'

'Thank you.'

'We were out for a cruise after the Malay pirates when the weather blew up. . . .' Firmly launched on his story, James talked and sipped and sipped and talked. Esther had shown no friendliness for her brother, had unbent in no way. Her eyes still had that hurt, hostile look, as if she had just witnessed something shameful, as if the world was against her and she knew it was only waiting its chance to pull her down.

'. . . We squared the boom, saw the boats made fast, lashed the guns afresh, double-breeching the lower deckers, then we got the t'gallant mast down on deck, in fact everything to set up a ship safe and snug. D'you follow my meaning, or do the words confuse you, eh?'

'Very much,' said Verity, 'but go on.'

'Ha! Well, at four bells the hurricane broke, with the sea fairly raging; it was a terrible thing to be in. After an hour or so I thought to turn in but my bunk was full to the brim with water so I decided twould be drier on deck.' James laughed and made the ornaments rattle. It caught at Verity and made her laugh too. 'Comic to look back on, but at the time wi' the waves riding beside us fit to swamp an island and the gale screeching like a thousand hungry parrots there was another face to the picture!'

'I think I will go to bed,' said Esther, 'if I may be excused.'

Verity said: 'You'll be tired after your journey. Would you care to lie on in the morning?'

'Thank you, I always wake early. Good night, James. Good night to you, ma'am.'

Again Verity touched her cold cheek, and then she was gone.

James said: 'Mind if I smoke, ma'am? It is a dirty habit one gets into.'

'No, of course not.'

'Well, just then the captain called me up on the poop, and as I got there I heard him say to the lieutenant: "The ship makes a very good weather of it upon this tack," he says, says he; "but we must wear her. Do you go forward and have the hands stand by." "There's no canvas can stand against this," says the lieutenant. The captain says: "We must take the risk," he says, "for the wind have backed, and we are drawing close upon Sumatra." I should not worry over Essie, ma'am. She is not so hard as she makes out.'

The change of topic was so abrupt that Verity half smiled. But she did not speak.

'Lord bless you, everyone thinks she's unfriendly; but half of it is just her trim. Different people take the same thing different ways, as you might say. You know about Mother, of course. Ha! Well, you'd say it was as bad for one of us as for the other; but you'd be wrong. I was eight when it happened and Essie nine. The year after, when I was nine, I weighed anchor and went to sea; I shook it all off as the littlest frigate will shake off the head of a comber that's flopped aboard when she wasn't looking. But Esther – Esther's been like a craft wi' no canvas. She got waterlogged with the shock and she's been wallowing in the trough ever since. Instead of trying to forget it, she's brooded and brooded and made her mother a saint. Which she wasn't, nor anything near; God forgive me for saying so. And when she meets someone fresh, especially someone new to the family like you, all that side of her comes up and she seems a bad case. I've told Father before now she needs careening; no one can sail sweet with a foul bottom – beg pardon, Aunt, if it sounds indelicate, but it's true. Howsoever, she will improve as the days go by. Mark my words.'

Verity moved her cup, set it down again, stared at her hands.

'Oh, James, I'm so happy that you came. I'm happy to have made one friend so soon. I am so happy that . . .' She stopped and choked.

He laughed, a sudden boyish laugh. 'It looks as if I shall be spending most of my leave looking after you, Aunt.'

There was another knock on the street door.

She said: 'You've no more brothers or sisters, have you.?'

'Not to my knowledge. Though it would be a lively enough lark, wouldn't it? Stay on deck, ma'am. I'll see who it is.'

When he had gone down she walked to the window. The day was nearing its close, and clouds had gathered over the harbour. Three fishing boats, one with copper-coloured sails and two with white, were moving sedately in like swans coming home to rest. She didn't know the man at the door. He had come by horse.

James came up the stairs four at a time.

'It is a man with a letter for you he will hand to no one but you personal. He says his name is Gimlett.'

Gimlett. Ross's servant. Demelza . . . 'Oh,' she said and flew down the stairs.

'Mrs Blamey, ma'am?'

'Yes. You have a message?'

'A letter, ma'am. Captain Poldark asked for me to give it into your hands.'

With excited and apprehensive fingers Verity fumbled with the seal and at last got it open. The letter inside was very short.

Dear Verity,

We have a son. It was yesterday evening, after an anxious time, but both so far are well. His name will be Jeremy. We wanted you to be the first to know.

Ross

Chapter fourteen

IT WAS JUST a small party at Nampara House: Francis and Elizabeth and Andrew Blamey and Verity – and Dwight Enys, who was now almost one of the family. Not a christening party for Jeremy, because it was natural to shrink from repeating anything which had happened in Julia's life; this marked the opening of Wheal Grace – the first men engaged, the first sods broken. Demelza, handicapped by weakness and a delicate baby, had left all the catering to the Gimletts, and they'd done well enough. Boiled cod with oyster sauce, a piece of boiled beef, roast neck of pork, two small turkeys with ham, fried rabbits, a plum pudding, tartlets and pies – with apples and olives and almonds and raisins for dessert. Demelza looked round and thought: This is much more than we can afford, but of course it's quite right not to skimp for such an occasion.

It was nearly a month since she'd reached the house that day, soaked and exhausted – to find no one about, the surveillance she'd disliked gone when it was most needed, the house terrifying in its emptiness, the garden and the trees rustling and the nearest help half a mile away. It seemed a year since she had fought her way from kitchen to parlour, her hands full of paper and shavings to start a fire. Minutes later, Jane Gimlett had found her crouched in a chair, unable to move in a room full of smoke; Cobbledick was sent flying on his long legs for Dr Enys and had the luck to find him home. Ross returned at seven to find Jeremy just born and Dwight despairing of them both.

Well, all that time was over and they had both survived; though Jeremy still did not seem oversecure. Very different from Julia, who from her earliest moments had put forward all the claims she could to be considered a permanency. Perhaps it was an omen, Demelza thought, that this frail one would survive where the lusty one died.

Over the meal the men had been talking of a book called *The Rights of Man* in which an atheist, Tom Paine, advocated a parliament of nations to prevent war, and many other sweeping reforms; but Demelza had only been indifferently attending. She thought: So Francis and Andrew Blamey are sitting at the same table at last; it isn't *complete* reconciliation, but that will follow as they have time in each other's company – in the way Ross's and Francis's has followed. And Verity will no longer be shut off from

Trenwith and there will no longer be the strain of ill feeling.

And Elizabeth . . . Elizabeth blooms like a painting; she has had a better year. By contrast, I'm dowdy and untidy, pale as a sheet from being indoors, no good as a hostess and unattractive to any man. No wonder Ross looks at her with interest. She doesn't love Francis, but she's more content.

And Dwight? He looks happy to be here. A good thing Caroline Penvenen has gone, because there was something between them. He ought to marry Joan Pascoe, who will have lots of money and yet wouldn't consider herself too good for him.

And me . . . ?

They drank a toast to the new mine, and when they sat down again silence fell. On the fortunes of Wheal Grace the financial survival of all the Poldarks would now depend. It was a sobering thought. Well, at least, thought Demelza, we are all together this time. And Jeremy is in the next room waiting for me, already knowing me. And Ross is at least temporarily content in knowing the venture started. Was it time now, she wondered, to lead the way out, leaving the men to their usual talking and drinking? And if so, should she get up and then speak, or speak before she got up?

Forestalling her, Francis rose instead.

'Toasts', he said, 'are a plaguey nuisance at the best of times. But I've a fancy to propose one more now, and I was never one not to indulge a fancy. I want to drink to our hostess, Demelza.'

Taken completely by surprise, Demelza for once in her life blushed up to the roots of her hair. 'Oh no!' she said. 'Twould be most uncalled for.'

In a confusion of voices she heard Andrew Blamey, siding with his old enemy, say, 'It's the very thing,' and the others concur, Elizabeth a second later than the rest. Then they seemed all to be looking at Ross, and Ross looked up and smiled.

'Demelza is wrong; it has been long called for. Thank you, Francis.'

Francis, thus encouraged, fiddled with his glass, and looked across the table at her, embarrassed, but determined. 'I was never one for speechmaking, but there it is. She came to live among us almost while we were unaware of it. But we've all come aware of it in time. There's not one among us – unless it's young Enys here – who has not had some special benefit from her coming. Damme, that's no more than the truth, and there's little more I can say. But if it wasn't for her there'd be none of us gathering here together today – and if there's any merit in being a united family, then the merit's not the family's but *hers*. It isn't where you're born in this world, it's what you do. She is proper that proper doth. So I say we should drink to Demelza – a lady of the first quality. . . .'

It was a lot for Francis to say. Horribly affected, Demelza sat there while they drank the toast. When it was done a silence fell more difficult than the last, because they were all waiting for her to say something.

She blinked the mist out of her eyes and stared at the magenta-coloured wine in her glass. She said in a low voice: 'If I've done anything good for the family – look what you've done for me.'

Outside Garrick was barking, chasing a sea gull off the lawn. It might wake Jeremy. They seemed to be waiting for her to say something more. In desperation a few words of the church service she'd attended in Bodmin came to her mind. She added: 'I've only followed the devices and desires of my own heart.'

Verity patted her hand. 'That's what we love you for.'

When the party broke up Ross went a little way up the valley to see his guests off. Demelza, being convalescent, stayed behind; and when they had crossed the river in the slanting sun she walked back into the house and peered down at the sleeping Jeremy.

A small baby, unlike Julia and dark, active, thin-featured and delicate. Strange the difference. Perhaps in some way he reflected the changed circumstances in which he had been conceived and born. Demelza thought: I am content. Perhaps not the rich happiness of two years ago, because Ross is still an uncertain quality, but content. Could one expect more? They had all come through many hazards. Of course the future was uncertain, full of dangers of its own. The mine might fail, Jeremy might die in a teething convulsion like the last of the Martin children, Ross might go off with Elizabeth, or the next 'run' into Nampara Cove might be surprised by the gaugers. But was any future, anyone's future, unfraught by hazards of some sort? The only security was death. So long as one wanted to go on living one had to accept the risks. Well, she accepted them. . . .

Outside Ross saw the visitors on their way and then walked slowly back alone. The stream bubbled and whispered down the valley beside him, adding its satirical commentary to his evening thoughts.

The gamble was on. The fight was on. They were setting out on this venture in the teeth of unfavourable circumstances and all the opposition the Warleggans could muster. George had been indoors for a week after his fall, and there had been talk of a summons for assault. But nothing had come of it. George had not cut a sufficiently dignified figure to want it all thrashed out in public. Nor was the cause of the quarrel so much common property as Ross had imagined it might become. What he hadn't at first realized was that the Warleggans would show up in a very bad moral light if they accused Francis of any such transaction; and for the sake of their business reputation they wouldn't want that. George, too, had evidently lost his temper that day, had tried to poison the new friendship between the cousins with the most venomous accusation he could call up. (And nearly had succeeded!)

Francis certainly knew nothing as yet of the cause of the brawl – though last week he had complained of a peculiar coldness on the part of several people he had had dealings with in Truro. The evil rumour, once let loose, wouldn't easily die. It would be liable to smoulder underground and flicker up again where least expected. If it ever came to Francis's ears it might yet prove a menace to their new partnership.

Ross glanced across at the first signs of activity around the ruins of Wheal Grace: a few ugly sheds, a heap of stones, a mountain of cut gorse, a cart, a new track across the hillside. Nothing of beauty; in twelve months the whole hill would be disfigured. But the disfigurement would have its own appeal to a man with mining in his blood. The question was, what would a further twelve months show? Another smokeless chimney stack, silent sheds, grass growing in the mule tracks, an engine rusty and derelict? Everything seemed to point to it.

Two things could save them, could save the Poldarks and their houses. The first was rich copper at an easily workable level. The second was that the market price of the ore should not merely show its present upward tendency but should leap thirty or forty pounds a ton. Ross had gambled on both. For the first he relied largely on Mark Daniel's comments on that August night two years ago. Mark could not have been so impressed – and in such circumstances – without good cause.

For the second, Ross had gambled much more dangerously. Across the Channel a neighbouring country was in the grip of a revolutionary fervour. How long would it keep its energy within the confines of its own territory? If war came in Europe England might well stay out. The Channel was the surest wall. But it could not stay out unarmed. A defenceless country was an impotent country. A rearming country needed copper for its arms.

That was the other chance.

The air was hazy, heavy in the evening light. All the smells of the earth were strong; a blackbird twittered endlessly on a fallen stump; and the smoke from a chimney of the house grew like a slow worm, for once unhurried by the wind. In the distance a grey multitude of sea gulls were wheeling and crying over Hendrawna Beach.

That was the other chance.

He came more slowly to the garden in front of the house. At the door he stopped to sniff the lilac which in a day or two would be in full bloom. Human beings were blind, crazy creatures, he thought, forever walking the tightrope of the present, condemned to ever changing shifts and expedients to maintain the balance of existence, not knowing even as far ahead as to-morrow what the actions of to-day would bring. How could one plan a year ahead, how influence the imponderables?

A butterfly settled on the lilac and stayed a moment with poised trembling wings. Not by a hairbreadth would a single external circumstance move to accommodate him and his schemes – he knew that. As well ask, on the butterfly's behalf, for the postponement of sunset or tomorrow's gale. That was as it might be. Within the radius of his own endeavour he accepted the challenge. He might at some later date look back upon this day as marking the beginning of his prosperity or the last move towards his ultimate ruin. The tightrope was there. No one could see beyond the next step.

Within the house there were movements, and from where he stood he saw Demelza come into the parlour carrying some things of Jeremy's which she spread before the fire. Her face was preoccupied, thoughtful, intent, but not on what she was doing. He realized that all the struggle and anxiety of the next few months would not be his alone. She would bear her share of the burden. She was bearing it already.

WARLEGGAN

A Novel of Cornwall 1792–1793

Book one

Chapter one

IN THAT COASTAL triangle of Cornwall lying between Truro, St Ann's, and St Michael, social life did not extend far in the 1790s. There were six big houses – or six inhabited by gentlefolk – but circumstances did not encourage intercourse between them.

Into one of these, Mingoose House, the oldest and most easterly, Ruth Treneglos, *née* Teague, had done her utmost to bring a new social zest; but childbearing had cramped her style of late; her rough-booted husband John was interested only in hunting, and her father-in-law was too deaf and scholarly to care who came and went in his front rooms. In Werry House, the largest and most disreputable Sir Hugh Bodrugan sprawled and belched like a lecherous volcano while Constance Lady Bodrugan, his stepmother, who was young enough to be his daughter, bred dogs and fed dogs and talked dogs most of her waking hours.

On the other and western side of the triangle Place House, an unbecoming Palladian residence put up in the early years of the century, was occupied by Sir John Trevaunance, a widowed and childless baronet; and Killewarren, which was not much more than a glorified farmhouse, by Mr Ray Penvenen, who was richer and even more cautious than his neighbour.

To the two houses in between, one actually on the coast, the other near it, it would have come natural to look for more enterprise, not only because they were where they were but because each was occupied by a young married couple of whom social occasions might have been expected. Unfortunately, neither household had any money.

Between Sawle and St Ann's, on high ground but protected by trees, Trenwith House, Elizabethan and mellow and beautiful, was occupied by Francis Poldark and his wife Elizabeth and their son, who was nearly eight years old, and Francis' great-aunt, Agatha, who was so old that everyone had forgotten to count. Three miles to the east was the sixth and smallest of the houses, Nampara, Georgian and utilitarian and never properly completed but not without a certain individuality and charm, which was characteristic too perhaps of its owners. Ross Poldark lived here and his wife Demelza; and their son Jeremy had just passed his first birthday.

So of the six houses, the first two were preoccupied with dogs and babies; the second two had the means to entertain but not the will; the last two the will only. Therefore some surprise and speculation were caused when, in May 1792, five of the households received an invitation from the owner of the sixth to a supper party on the twenty-fourth of the month. Sir John Trevaunance wrote that he was taking the opportunity while his sister was staying with him and while his brother Unwin, a Member of Parliament for Bodmin, also was down.

This seemed such a poor reason for breaking with the habit of years that everyone cast about for a stronger motive. Demelza Poldark at least had no difficulty in finding one.

When the letter was delivered, Ross was up at the mine, the new mine where he spent nearly all his time nowadays, and Demelza waited impatiently for his return.

As she laid things for the light meal they would have – supper was not until eight – Demelza wondered what the outcome would be of this latest and probably last gamble. Wheal Leisure, the mine on the cliff, which Ross had started in company with six other venturers in '87, continued to prosper; but last year he had sold half his holding in it and had sunk the money in this much more speculative enterprise.

The result so far had been failure. The fine new pumping engine, designed by two young engineers from Redruth, had been set up and all the claims made out for it had been confirmed. But the thirty-fathom level, which was as deep as the old men had gone, offered nothing but worked-out gunnies; and the new forty- and fifty-fathom levels they were driving to strike the lodes again had been most unproductive, yielding poor stuff where there was any yield at all. The engine might work with greatest possible efficiency; it still used coal; and while things stayed as they were, every day brought nearer the day when silence would fall on the valley and the engine begin to rust.

As she glanced up through the window, she saw Ross coming across the garden in company with his cousin and partner Francis. They were talking attentively, but Demelza could see that it was over no sudden discovery. Often she watched Ross's face as he came in.

She picked up Jeremy, who in his efforts to walk was threatening to pull the cloth off the table, and with him in her arms went to the front door to meet them. The wind billowed the skirt of her green-striped dimity frock.

When they were near enough, Francis said:

'Demelza, you never grow up; you look seventeen. I hadn't intended to come today, but damn it, I feel revived for the air; I think tea with you might complete the cure.'

She said: 'Is this your first time out of doors? I hope you haven't been down the mine.'

'My second. And I have not. Ross has been exploring on his own again, with the usual measure of success. Jeremy boasts another tooth, I believe. I fancy there were only three last time I looked.'

'Seven!' said Ross. 'You're on dangerous ground.'

They laughed and went indoors. The early part of tea Jeremy made sure was devoted to him; but presently Mrs Gimlett came in to bear him away, and the adults were allowed some peace. Demelza, a little breathless and with a curl rakishly over one eye, poured herself a second cup of tea.

'And are you truly better, Francis? The fever is quite gone?'

'It was just the influenza,' said Francis. 'We all had it, but I the worst. Choake bled me and gave me Peruvian bark, but I recovered nevertheless.'

Ross stretched himself, easing his long legs. 'Why do you not have Dwight Enys? He's keen and up-to-date and has a knowledge of the latest physical ideas.'

Francis grunted. 'Tom Choake has always looked after us. Personally I think these medical jockeys are much the same. Anyway, our friend Enys is in a little trouble himself over old John Ellery, I understand.'

'What's the matter with him?'

'It seems he had a toothache and Enys took out three teeth but dug for the roots, as is his fashion. Choake contents himself with twisting off the crowns, as you know. But this time something has gone wrong with Dwight's methods and Ellery has not been out of pain since.'

Demelza said: 'I thought Dwight looked a small matter worried when he called yesterday.'

'He takes his failures too much to heart,' said Ross. 'I should think it a great disadvantage in his profession.'

'It is a great disadvantage in any profession,' said Demelza, carefully not looking at him.

Francis raised an ironical eyebrow. In the brief silence that followed, and to cover it, Demelza took down her envelope from the mantelshelf.

'We have an invitation, Ross! Just think of it in these bad times. Have you had one, Francis? I suppose it will be quite a big affair. I wonder if we should dress. What does Elizabeth say of it?'

'From the Trevaunances?' said Francis while Ross read it. 'Yes, we had a note today. The old man has grown extravagant with his grey hairs. I feel there's some motive in his madness, though, knowing Sir John.'

'Ah,' said Demelza, ''twas much the same thought came to me.'

'What motive?' asked Ross, looking up from the letter.

Francis glanced at Demelza, but she was waiting for him. He laughed. 'We're uncharitable, Ross, your wife and I. Ray Penvenen's niece, Caroline, is an heiress in her own right. Unwin Trevaunance has been stalking her for two years. This may well be to announce the kill.'

'I did not know the girl was back again.'

'She returned from Oxfordshire, I believe, last week.'

'But then,' said Demelza, 'should it not be – if it were to announce an

engagement – should it not be Mr Penvenen who give the party? I thought
that was the way. Ross, you promised once to buy me a book on etiquette,
but you never did so.'

'You behave better without it. I like a wife who is natural and not
stiffened up with all manner of artificial observances.'

Francis said: 'Anyway, Ray Penvenen would never give a party even to
celebrate his own engagement, so that need not discourage us from the
speculation.'

'You will go of course?' asked Demelza.

'I think Elizabeth had her visiting look on when I left her this afternoon.'

Ross said: 'I hope if they intend to join up, those two, they'll be sharp
about it. If Caroline Penvenen is to be in the neighbourhood for long, it is
likely to unsettle Dwight. I'd be glad to see her safely tied to Unwin.'

'I heard there was something between her and Enys last time she was
down, but I should think he's wise enough not to get himself entangled
there.'

Demelza said: 'It seems to me no man is wise enough if the woman is not
wise enough.'

Ross glanced up good-humouredly. 'That's an acute remark. D'you
speak it from personal experience?'

She met his eyes. 'Yes, Ross, from personal experience. Think how
foolish Sir Hugh Bodrugan would be over me if I let him.'

Not until he spoke had he seen the latency of what he said, which might
even refer to their own marriage; and he was glad that she had taken it in
the right way. He did not reflect that two years ago he would never have
had any doubts on the point.

At about the time Francis and Ross walked down from the mine to tea,
George Warleggan was dismounting from his horse outside Trenwith
House.

To look at him one would not have thought him the grandson of a
blacksmith, the first generation of his family to be genteelly educated –
unless the clothes he wore told the tale they were intended to disguise. No
country squire would have dressed so well for an afternoon call, even had
he wanted to impress the lady of the house, as George did.

When Mrs Tabb showed him in and, rather in a flurry, went to look for
Mrs Poldark, George strolled about the hall tapping his boot with his crop
and staring up at the ancestral pictures. This was a different poverty from
the poverty he might have seen at Nampara House three miles away.
Francis and Elizabeth might be no better off than their cousins; but you do
not reduce a mellow Elizabethan house to dilapidation in a few years.
George was staring at the magnificent window with its hundreds of small
panes of glass when he heard footsteps and turned to see Elizabeth
skimming down the stairs.

She slowed as soon as she saw him and came down the last steps hesitantly.

'Why, George . . . when Mrs Tabb said – I couldn't quite believe . . .'

'That I had really ventured to come.' He bowed over her hand politely. 'I was passing near, so brought my godson a birthday present. I thought perhaps I might be permitted that much.'

Still uncertain, she took something that he handed her. 'But it isn't Geoffrey Charles's birthday for months.'

'Last year. I'm late, not early.'

'Does Francis . . .'

'Know I'm here? No. But if he does? Surely this rather childish enmity has gone on too long. Really, Elizabeth, it gives me such pleasure to see you again. Such pleasure . . .'

She smiled at him, not flushing as she would have done a few years ago, but warming all the same to his admiration. She did not know how much of George was genuine, but she knew this was. She thought he had grown more stocky since they had last met, so that one saw in his greater bulk the shadow of the middle-aged man he would become. But however he had behaved to Ross – and that she certainly resented – he had never been anything but scrupulously fair with Francis and unfailingly charming to her.

In the winter parlour she unwrapped the small parcel he had brought, and found that it was a gold watch. She tried to return it to him, troubled and feeling him overgenerous, but he would have nothing to do with that.

'Drop it in a drawer for a while if you feel he's too young. The quarrel surely doesn't include him. By the time he's old enough to carry it, perhaps we shall all be friends again.'

She said: 'The quarrel was not of *my* seeking. We are very quiet here nowadays, and I should be glad of all my friends. But you know Francis as well as I do. He is wholehearted in his feelings, and if he were to come in now the – our friendship might come to worse hurt than ever before.'

'In other words he would try to kick me out,' George said pleasantly.

'Well, no doubt you'll think me overdeliberate in all things, but I have posted my manservant on the rising ground near Sawle Church. If he sees Francis coming, he can give me good warning, so you needn't fear a brawl.' He hunched his big shoulders. 'I should have hesitated to do so if I believed there was risk of your thinking me a coward.'

Elizabeth sat down on the window seat and looked out over the herb garden. George watched her carefully, like a business deal to be negotiated.

Elizabeth said: 'Before anything else I want to thank you for your kindness to my mother and father. My mother is still so unwell, and to ask them to your home . . .'

'I told them especially not to tell you.'

'I know; Father said so. But he wrote of it all the same, and of all your kindness while they were there.'

'It's of no moment. I have always admired your mother, and think her so brave in her eye trouble. I wonder they don't sell their house and live with you here.'

'I have – thought of it myself sometimes. But Francis does not believe it would be a good arrangement——' She checked herself.

George sat down and put the silver end of his riding crop against his teeth. 'Elizabeth, I don't expect you to be in any way disloyal to Francis' views of me and this quarrel, but don't you *personally* think it time it was forgot? What good is it doing any of us? Francis is cutting off his own hand. You know as well as I do that, were there any malice on my side, I could bankrupt him tomorrow. To you it's not a pleasant thing to say, but can you doubt it?'

'I don't doubt it,' Elizabeth said, flushing now.

'I only wish it were different. I should like to help to make it different. But while this feud continues . . . I should like you to help me to heal it.'

She unloosed the catch of the window and opened it a few inches to let in a gentle breeze. Her profile was clear-cut like a cameo against the brown of the curtain.

'You say you'll not ask me to be disloyal and then press me to take sides——'

'No. Not at all. To mediate.'

'Do you think my mediation would have so much effect? George, you know Francis' mind just as well as I do. He believes you to have been behind the prosecution of Ross, to have——'

'Oh, Ross . . .'

As soon as he spoke, he saw he had said the wrong thing; but he went on, keeping the resentment out of his voice.

'I know you have a vast affection for Ross, Elizabeth. I wish I could enjoy the favour in your eyes that he does. But let me put this clearly to you. Ross and I have never seen eye to eye since we were at school. It is – something fundamental. We do not like each other overwell. But on my side it is no more than that. On his it is a disease. He plunges headlong from one misfortune to another and blames me for them all as they come upon him!'

Elizabeth had got up. 'I wish you wouldn't say this. It isn't fair to ask me to listen.'

She might have walked away across the room, but he didn't move aside and she found herself at close quarters with him and not quite able to get out of the window bay.

'Don't you hear Ross's side? Why is it unfair to hear mine? Let me tell you of his position and what he has done to extricate himself.'

She said nothing more. Aware that he had overcome the first hurdle, George went on: 'Ross is impulsive, over stiff-necked, rash. You can't blame me for that. It is the fault of being born with money, coming from generations of people who have always had money. But no one need behave as he has behaved. Four years ago he began this ill-conceived plan for smelting copper in Cornwall. He blames me for its failure, but it was doomed to failure from the start. Then, when he was hard set as a result, he was too proud to go to his friends for assistance; and so, added to his other debts, he signed a bill for a thousand pounds at a usurer's rate of interest – it has but now come into my uncle's hands, that is how I know – and he has been paying this interest on it ever since. Nor is he satisfied with this, but he last year sold the half of his interest in a profitable mine and induced Francis to go into partnership with him in this white elephant, Wheal Grace, which his father exhausted twenty years ago! When he ultimately beggars himself and you as well, no doubt he'll blame me for having stolen the copper out of his ground overnight!'

At last she escaped and walked across the room. He was overstating his case, but the truth might lie somewhere midway between his argument and Francis'. Her feeling for Ross had never quite been definable to herself, and there was some grain of perverseness which took pleasure in seeing the other side.

George did not follow her. After a minute he said: 'You know, don't you, that you're one of the loveliest women in England.'

The clock on the mantelshelf began to strike five. When it had finished, she said: 'If what you say were even half true, it would be – kind of you; but I think, with Francis not here, a liberty. As I know——'

'If the truth's a liberty, then I've taken it,' George brushed a hand down his embroidered waistcoat, not perfectly at ease but not at all in retreat, 'because the truth it is. I move in society a great deal and I assure you I am neither flattering you nor presuming. Turn round. Look at yourself in the glass. Or perhaps you know yourself too well to realize. Men realize. Other men besides myself. And there would be many such, of both sexes, if you moved about more freely and were to be seen. Even now I hear people say, "D'you remember Elizabeth Poldark – Chynoweth that was? Now *there* was a beauty for you. I wonder what's come of her."'

'Do you suppose——'

'If,' said George, 'if Francis would let me, I could help him. Let him play with his mine if he wants to, but that need only be a side issue. Once before when I came here I mentioned sinecure positions. Today I could get him nominated for two. There is no disgrace in them. Ask your parson how he gained his church or your major his battalion – by having a friend speak for him at the right time. This – this existence is no existence at all for you. Your poverty is not only undeserved – it's unnecessary!'

Elizabeth was silent. Whatever she thought of George's compliments, it was a sore spot he touched. She was twenty-eight now, and her lease of beauty was not indefinite. She could count on the fingers of one hand the number of her outings since her twenty-fifth birthday.

'Oh, George, you're very kind. Don't think I don't know that. The more so because I realize you have nothing to gain. I——'

'On the contrary,' said George, 'I have everything to gain.'

'I scarcely know quite what to say. You heap favours upon my mother and father, upon my son, and would on Francis if he would allow you. I wish I could see some end to this quarrel, I truly wish I could. But – in suggesting that it's a trivial thing, don't you deceive yourself? None of it's as simple as you make it sound. I wish it were. I should be happy enough to see our friendship restored.'

He came over to the fireplace. 'And will do your part to restore it?'

'If you will do yours.'

'How?'

'Help to convince Ross that you are not his enemy.'

'I am not interested in Ross.'

'No, but Francis is Ross's partner now. You'll not reassure one without the other.'

George stared down at his riding crop. Perhaps the look in his eyes was not for her.

'You credit me with supernatural powers. What do you want me to do?'

'If you'll do what you can,' said Elizabeth, 'I'll do what I can.'

'I hope I may hold you to that bargain.'

'You may.'

He bent over her hand and this time kissed it, with a rather dated formality which yet conveyed what he meant it to convey.

He said: 'Please don't bother to show me out. My horse is at the door.'

He left the room, shutting the door after him, and crossed the great empty hall. The wind was rattling a loose window. As he reached the front door, Aunt Agatha came out of the small drawing room and began tottering across in his direction. He tried to avoid being seen, but – although she was nearly stone-deaf – her eyesight was sharp enough.

'Why, if it isn't George Warleggan, or I'm a dunce! Don't mumble now! People will mumble. 'Tis years since you put foot inside our place, I'll swear. Getting too grand for us, are you?'

George smiled and bowed over the withered hand. 'I salute you, old hag. The worms must be tired of waiting. It's not seemly when people rot while they're still above ground.'

'Getting too grand for us, I b'lieve,' said Agatha, one trembling claw going to join the other on her stick. 'Look at that waistcoat. I remember you when you was a boy, George, not hardly bigger'n Geoffrey Charles. Quite overawed you was, coming here that first time. Different now.'

George smiled and nodded. 'There should be a law to poison off old women, ma'am. Or a pillow pressed over the face would not take long. If you were the last of the Poldarks, I'd do it myself. But never fret, your great-nephews are digging their own graves. It won't be long.'

A slow bead of water escaped from Aunt Agatha's eye and slid diagonally down one of the furrows on her cheek. This was no sign of emotion, it just happened from time to time.

'You was always Francis' friend, I remember, never Ross's. What's that you say? Nervous you was, that first time, and hardly fledged, an' Charles saying, what's the boy brought home from school with him now? Well, times has changed. I mind the years when you couldn't have rid over from Truro in all that falallery without being turned heel over tip by some footpad or needy tinner. Have you seen Francis?'

'I've seen Elizabeth,' said George, bowing again. 'You remind me of forgotten things, old woman. Die soon, won't you, and be forgotten yourself.'

'Good-bye,' said Aunt Agatha. 'Come again and stop to supper. We're uncommon short of company these days.'

Chapter two

FRANCIS REACHED HOME just before six. He found Elizabeth sitting by the window, embroidering a stool cover, and Aunt Agatha crouching over the tiny fire.

'Whoo, it's hot in here.' He went across to one of the windows and opened it. 'Really, old lady, you'd be better in bed than cramping your old bones there.' But he did not say it unkindly.

Aunt Agatha screwed up her eyes at him. 'You've missed our visitor, Francis. Missed him by a skin, I should say. 'Tisn't often we've a visitor these days. You should have asked him to supper, Elizabeth.'

Francis looked at his wife and she flushed, furious that the old lady had forestalled her and furious that she cared.

'George Warleggan came.'

'George?' The way Francis said the word was enough. 'You saw him?'

'Yes. He didn't stay long.'

'So I should think not. What did he want?'

Elizabeth raised her grey eyes, which at times like this could look especially candid and virginal. 'I don't think he wanted anything. He said he thought it unnecessary to go on with this quarrel.'

'This quarrel . . .'

'And very cordial he was too,' said Aunt Agatha. 'Fortune's improved his manners, or I'm a dunce. Quite like old times, 'tis, having a man make a knee to you.'

Francis said: 'I wonder if he knew my back was turned.'

Elizabeth went on with her embroidery. 'He said he and you had been friends since childhood; he did not wish the estrangement to continue as it was. He had, he said, no desire at all to intrude on your private affairs or Ross's, his only wish being to help us to a fuller enjoyment of our lives. . . .'

'You speak as if you have learned the lesson well.'

Elizabeth's fingers flickered uncertainly over her work basket, selecting a new colour. 'That was what he said. You may take it or leave it as you please, Francis.'

Aunt Agatha said: 'I mind it was the year of that Du Barry scandal, or was it the year after, that you first brought him here. Stuggy little boy, he was, and the clothes they sent him in! Velvets and silks, you could see his mother'd no taste; and he staring about like a bull calf that had strayed from its stall.'

'He has an easy, oily tongue,' said Francis, 'and a persuasive damned way of putting things. I know it to my cost. Does he suppose we shall live a fuller life because of the boon of his friendship? I don't think his flatteries can convince you of that.'

'I can form my own judgments,' Elizabeth said. 'Though I couldn't but be aware that if it wasn't for his forbearance in the matter of mortgages we should not be living a life at all!'

Francis bit his thumb thoughtfully. 'I confess I don't understand his forbearance. It's out of character. Now that I'm in partnership with Ross . . . That's why the adventure at Wheal Grace is in Geoffrey Charles's name. But George makes no move.'

'Except towards friendship,' said Elizabeth.

Francis went to the open window and let the cool air waft on his face. 'I can't help but feel that I owe my immunity to you.'

'To me? That's silly. Really, Francis——'

'Silly? Far from it. George has been making sheep's eyes at you for years. I'd never supposed him to be sufficiently human to let any warmer feeling interfere with his business aims, but lacking a better explanation . . .'

Elizabeth got up. 'I hope you'll find a better. I must go and read to Geoffrey Charles.'

As she passed Francis, he caught her arm. The relationship between them had been kinder these last two years, though it was never warm. He said: 'We may disagree, but I think his coming today has a plain enough reason. Whatever you may think he feels for me or I may think he feels for you, we can't doubt what he thinks of Ross. If by befriending us he can put a new division between us and Ross, he will certainly have gained his object. Do you want him to do that?'

Elizabeth was silent for a moment. Then she said: 'No.'

'Nor I.' He released her arm and she went slowly out.

Aunt Agatha said: 'You should have asked him for supper. We've plenty as it happens. But 'tisn't like it was when Charles was alive. I sadly miss your father, boy. He was the last one that knew how to entertain in a proper genteel way.'

On his way home, at Bargus Cross where the gibbet stood, George met Dwight Enys, who was coming from the direction of Goon Prince. Dwight would have saluted and ridden on, but George halted and the two horses closed together.

'Well, Dr Enys, you ride far on your medical duties. Never to Truro, I suppose?'

'Seldom to Truro.'

'And when in Truro you do not venture as far as the Warleggans.'

Dwight made some show of quieting his horse while he thought out his reply. He decided to be frank. 'I've had nothing but friendship from your family, Mr Warleggan, and feel nothing but friendship in return; but the Poldarks of Nampara are my chief friends; I live on the edge of their land, work among their mining folk, sup at their table, and share their confidences. In that event it seems better that I should not attempt to get the best of both worlds.'

George did not move his neck but allowed his eyes to explore Dwight's shabby velvet coat with its gilt buttons.

'Are the two worlds so divided that an independent man cannot pass from one to the other of his own free will?'

'I have taken it so,' Dwight said.

George's face darkened.

'Men's tongues in some things outrun women's. Your own affairs prosper?'

'Well enough, thank you.'

'I was at the Penvenens' place last week, and gather that you are the regular physician there now.'

'Mr Penvenen keeps in very good health. I don't see much of him.'

'They tell me that his niece is back.'

'Indeed.'

'I understand you did some clever operation upon her throat and saved her life.'

'I think men's tongues have outrun the women's in that also.'

George did not greatly appreciate having his own words turned back upon him. He began to feel a growing dislike for young Enys, who spoke so bluntly and hardly bothered to hide his sympathies. George did not spend his time in company which cared nothing for his approval or disapproval.

'For my part,' he said, 'I have no faith in physicians or apothecaries. I think they kill as many as they cure. My family is fortunate in not yet being effete, as so many of the older families are.'

He rode on, followed by his servant. Dwight stared after him, then tugged on his horse's rein and went his way. That he had offended an influential man he knew. In his profession he would have preferred it otherwise, but he had long since chosen his friends. What did concern him was something else. 'They tell me that his niece is back,' George had said. If Caroline Penvenen was really home, it meant the destruction of his peace of mind.

Dwight's business was in Sawle; and as he was leading his horse down the steep slippery lane to the fish sheds at the bottom, he heard a clatter behind him and saw that Rosina Hoblyn had fallen on the stones. She had been carrying a bucket of water, and he looped the reins of his horse over a post and went to help her to her feet. But he could not get her up. Any tentative approaches he had made to the subject of why the nineteen-year-old Rosina walked with a bad limp had been headed off by her family, who seemed to be afraid of the subject. Now her pretty thin face was white with pain, and he had to lift her to her feet.

' 'Tis my knee, sur. 'Twill be all right in a moment. Sometime he go like this and I can't move him at all. Thank you.'

Her younger sister Parthesia came skipping out of the house and retrieved the bucket and curtsied at the doctor and put an arm out to help Rosina.

'No, not yet,' she said, and to Dwight: 'if I wait, 'twill ease off.'

After a few minutes they got her inside. Dwight was glad that Jacka the father was not there, as his moods could go all ways.

With his 'no nonsense' face, Dwight waved away Rosina's and Mrs Hoblyn's protests that it was really all nothing at all, that if she sat on the table and swung her leg it would pass off, and bent to examine the knee, half fearing to find heaven knew what scrofulous condition.

He did not find it. Swollen certainly and a little red, but the skin was not shiny or hot to the touch.

'You say this trouble began eight years ago?'

'Yes, sur, 'bout that.'

'Does it hurt all the time?'

'No, sur, only when it d'go stiff like this.'

'And have you had the same trouble with your hip?'

'No, sur, there's nothing amiss wi' that.'

'Do you ever have a discharge from the knee?'

'No, sur. 'Tis just as if someone turn a key and lock it,' said Rosina, pulling down her skirt.

'Has any other physician seen it?'

He had the feeling that they were exchanging glances behind his back. Rosina said: 'Yes, sur – when it first went wrong in '84. But 'twas Mr Nye, and he's gone dead since then."

'What did he say?'

'Didn't say nothing 'bout it,' Mrs Hoblyn put in hastily. 'Didn't know what 'twas at all.'

The feeling of the house was so obviously discouraging that Dwight told the girl to use a cold compress and said he would see her again next week when the pain had gone. When he came out, dusk was almost falling and he had his most unpleasant call still to make.

At the bottom of the hill was a flat green triangle of grass and weed above the shingle, and on one side of it were fish sheds with cottages and shacks built over them. You crossed a narrow humped bridge to reach them. Dwight stood for a moment staring out to sea. The wind was rising and the further cliffs were hardly visible in the gathering dusk. It was still possible to see the grim jaws of the narrow inlet. An old man fumbled with a net over one of the boats. Sea gulls fought for a fish head behind the inn. A candle glimmered in a window.

Above the rush of the waves Dwight fancied he could hear the whispered voices of the villagers. ' 'Ere, heard about John James Ellery, 'ave ee? Had toothache, that was all – went to the surgeon over to Mingoose – surgeon took three teeth away. John James has been in mortal pain ever since, and like to die! I'd fight shy of 'e, if I was sick!'

Dwight turned impatiently to go, and as he did so a man came quietly from behind the inn and seemed to want to avoid him. But Dwight stopped and the man stopped. It was Charlie Kempthorne, whom Dwight had cured of miner's consumption, and who was laying suit to Rosina Hoblyn, though he was a widower of forty-odd with two children and she only nineteen.

'You're out an' about late, sur, aren't ee? 'Tis no eve to be anywhere but home by the fireside – that's for them as is lucky t'ave a fire to sit by.'

'What I was about to say to you.'

Kempthorne grinned and coughed. 'There's business best done in the half-light, y'understand. When the Customs men don't see ee.'

'If I were a Customs man, I should be at my busiest in the half-light.'

'Ah, but they d'like their firesides, like other sensible folk.' There was a trace of uneasiness in Charlie's expression as he slid past.

Phoebe Ellery opened the door for Dwight and led him upstairs. You climbed to John James Ellery's room by a wooden ladder from the room below where sacks of potatoes and nets and oars and cork floats were stacked. It was impossible to stand upright in the bedroom, and this evening the 'chill' had just been lit to fend off the encroaching night. Most of the glass had gone from the window, and the wind beat through, plucking at the sacking and bringing in a spatter of rain. A great black-and-white cat stalked about the room, scarcely ever still for a moment and making ominous purple shadows of its own. The sick man had his face wrapped in an old cloth and kept muttering: 'Lord, 'ave mercy on me; Lord, 'ave mercy on me.'

Phoebe stood in the doorway watching Dwight with relentless, reproachful eyes. ' 'E'll be better in a while,' she said. 'The pain last for an hour, maybe, and then d'go off for a space, see.'

There was little Dwight could do, but he stayed half an hour and administered laudanum and listened to the noisy waves, and by the time he left the spasm was passing.

It was a wild night and Dwight spent it restlessly, lost in a sense of his own failure and in the futilities of his profession.

Chapter three

ROSS AND DEMELZA were among the last to arrive at the Trevaunances on the evening of the twenty-fourth of May, having been forced to borrow a horse from Francis, who still had three in his stables; and a company of about twenty people were already talking and laughing in the big drawing room as they went upstairs. It took Demelza half an hour to change, and Ross, who had little to do for himself, read the latest copy of the *Sherborne Mercury* which had been obligingly left in the bedroom.

France was at war with Austria. Only three weeks ago the revolutionary pot had at last boiled over. The paper said M. Robespierre had opposed the move and had resigned his post as Public Prosecutor, but the others were mad keen for war and already a great army had invaded Belgium. A clash with the Austrian troops might be expected at any time. What of our own position? It was well for Mr Pitt to forecast fifteen years' peace, as he had done in March; prophecies cost nothing; but when they were accompanied by further cuts in our tiny army and skeleton navy, the danger to our safety and survival was plain.

Ross was so far gone that he did not hear Demelza's first words, and she had to repeat them before he looked up.

As he rose he was conscious that his wife's charm and attraction had not been lessened by three years of trial and worry and near poverty. At times it got itself hidden under the everyday mask of work and the routine of living, but this made its emergence all the more startling. At such moments he recognized with instant attention the quality in her that made her attractive to so many men.

As he went to the door to open it for her, he said: 'D'you ever now have any fears about going into society – as you did in the old days? I never know now whether you're nervous or not.'

'For the first ten minutes my knees knock,' she said. 'But luckily 'tis the part of me best covered.'

He laughed. 'I know what will cure it.'

'What?'

'Port.'

'Yes, quite often, yes. But other things too.'

'Such as?'

She lifted her bare shoulders in a slight movement of doubt. 'Knowing other people have a confidence in me.'

'The other people including me?'

'Chiefly you.'

He bent slowly and kissed her neck in the soft part where neck and shoulder join. 'Might I proffer you that confidence now?'

'Thank you, Ross.'

He kissed her again, and she put up a hand to smooth back his hair by the ear.

'You still have some feeling for me?'

He looked at her in astonishment, staring deeply into her eyes. 'Good God, you should know that!'

'Yes, Ross, but there is feeling and feeling. It is the one and not the other that I am asking about.'

'Would you want to involve me in a philosophical argument with all your beaux waiting to flirt with you downstairs?'

'They are not my beaux. And I do not think it would be a – what you said argument.' She put her hand on the door.

He said: 'Demelza.'

'Yes.'

'If there are two feelings, then I don't think you can put them in separate compartments ever, because one is a part of the other and inseparable. You should know that I love you. What other reassurance do you ask?'

She smiled obliquely but with a new warmth. 'Only that I should be told it.'

'So now you've been told it. Does that make such a difference?'

'Yes, that makes such a difference.'

'I'll keep a note of it for Wednesdays and Saturdays in future.'

'Sundays is a better day. The thing will sound right on a Sunday.'

So they went down in a cheerful enough mood and found all their neighbours there, the younger Trenegloses, the Bodrugans, Dr and Mrs Choake, and of course the Penvenens.

And George Warleggan.

It was a blunder of the first magnitude on the Trevaunances' part to have invited him and Ross to the same party; but now it had happened, it had to be gone through with. Rumour had magnified the fight between them last year into vast and murderous proportions; and their presence here together to-night added a spice to the meal for those who had no particular concern for the outcome.

But George offered no provocation and for a time avoided all contact with the Poldarks. Whatever else being thrown over the stairs did, it gave one a physical respect for one's enemy.

At dinner Ross found himself near the top of the table with Constance

Lady Bodrugan on his right hand, Elizabeth on his left, and Caroline Penvenen directly opposite.

He had heard so much of Caroline that it would have been strange if she had tallied with his expectations. He thought her not so beautiful as Elizabeth nor so charming as Demelza; but her clear-eyed, quick-thoughted vitality instantly took a man's attention. The emeralds about her milky-coloured throat precisely suited her; they changed suddenly like their wearer in different lights, were now cool and unfathomed, now sharp and glinting. He had no difficulty in understanding Unwin Trevaunance's feelings, always supposing him to be susceptible to other influences than gold. One wondered at their relationship, because it seemed strained to-night. Caroline treated him with bare courtesy, and one imagined that after marriage things would be different. A man did not have that leonine head and jutting bottom lip for nothing.

They were hardly seated when Sir John said: 'You have met Miss Penvenen, Ross? Caroline, this is Captain Poldark,' and Ross studied her wide-awake grey-green eyes.

Miss Penvenen inclined her head in acknowledgment. 'We met for the first time this evening, John; though in truth I have seen Captain Poldark before – in somewhat different case.'

'When was that?' asked Ross.

'Oh, you could not be expected to notice me. It was at your trial at Bodmin when you were charged, you will remember, with plundering two ships. I was one of the audience.'

'I remember well enough,' said Ross. 'But audience suggests entertainment, and I can't suppose the entertainment was very good.'

'I have known worse. You see, in a play one knows virtue is going to be triumphant; but in real life one trembles on the brink of iniquity and fears for the outcome.'

'I think you must have been at the wrong trial, Miss Penvenen. There was precious little virtue in my case and no triumph in my acquittal – unless it was a triumph for the wrongheadedness of the jury. Your sympathy should have been with the judge.'

Caroline's eyes flashed. 'Oh, it was, I assure you. I noticed how sad he looked when he could not punish you at all.'

During the first part of the dinner Ross talked to Elizabeth. Her pleasure was no less than his and was plain to Demelza who, near the foot of the table, found herself between Sir Hugh Bodrugan, who always had such a marked and possessive partiality for her company, and Captain McNeil of the Scots Greys. McNeil was that officer who had been in the district once before, some years ago, stationed here with a company of dragoons to watch over the unrest in the mining districts and to put down the smuggling.

Whatever anyone else might feel about the disposition of the table,

Malcolm McNeil had no complaints. He only wished Sir Hugh wouldn't be so monopolistic. Again and again he tried to gain Mrs Poldark's attention, and again and again the hairy baronet grabbed it back. His first real opportunity came when Sir Hugh had to carve another slice off the joint for Mrs Frensham, Sir John's sister, and McNeil at once asked Demelza if he might presently do the same for her.

'Thank you, no,' said Demelza. ''Tis quite surprising seeing you here, Captain McNeil. I thought you was gone back to Scotland and the clans.'

'Oh, I have been back in the meantime,' he assured her, screwing in his great moustache at her admiringly. 'And overseas. And in London and Windsor. But I grew an affection for this piece of country – and some of the people – and when the occasion came to revisit it and them . . .'

'With your dragoons?'

'No dragoons this time.'

'Not one?'

'Only myself, Mrs Poldark. I'm sorry to disappoint ye. I was ill with a fever, and afterwards, meeting Sir John in London, was invited to take my sick leave here.'

Demelza glanced at him amiably. 'You don't look a sick man, Captain McNeil.'

'Nor am I now, ma'am. Let me fill your glass. Is it canary ye have been drinking?'

'I know only three flavours, and it is none of those three.'

'Then canary it must be. And I have found a great amount of plaisure as well as health in admiring your beautiful coast line——'

'Not looking for smugglers?'

'No, no, Mrs Poldark; not this time. Why, are there some still? I thought my last visit had quite put them down.'

'And so it did. We was all downcast after you had gone.'

The Scotsman glanced at her with a twinkle. 'That is a remark capable of two interpretations.'

Demelza looked up the table and saw Ross smiling at Elizabeth. 'I didn't think, Captain McNeil, that you could have supposed me a smuggler.'

McNeil's chuckle, restrained as it was by his standards, was enough to silence the rest of the table for a second or two.

Mrs Frensham said, smiling: 'If that pleasantry will bear repetition, I think you should not keep it to yourselves.'

Demelza said: 'Oh, it was not a jest on my side, ma'am. Captain McNeil was assuring me that he had not come down this time to catch smugglers, and I told him I did not know what else he could expect to catch in these parts.'

Sir Hugh Bodrugan rumbled: 'Damme, I differ as to the jest.'

Mrs Frensham said: 'Captain McNeil has been convalescent. His purposes here, he assures me, are wholly innocent; otherwise we should have put a guard over him and locked him in his room.'

'I truly believe, ma'am, you should do so at once,' said Demelza, at which Sir Hugh and the Captain laughed again.

At the other end of the table Sir John Trevaunance, with a not unobvious purpose in mind, had made a derogatory remark about young Dwight Enys. Ellery had died that morning, and Sir John was of the opinion that the scandal should receive public attention. Ellery, a hale and hearty man of sixty . . . Enys had so probed into the jaw that the wound had never healed. His old friend Dr Choake would bear him out. . . . Ignorance and neglect. But Sir John found the move a mistaken one, because not only did Caroline speak quickly in Dr Enys' defence but she found an ally in Ross Poldark, and the baronet, to his annoyance, and still more to Unwin's, found himself between two fires. Ross had thought Caroline pert on their first introduction; but now for he moment they were in accord, and it was noticeable at the end of the argument that Caroline's eyes travelled over him approvingly.

Elizabeth said in an undertone to Ross: 'She's lovely, isn't she?'

'Very striking. Beauty's a matter of taste.'

'Is it true, do you think, that what the eye doesn't admire the heart doesn't desire?'

'Oh, without doubt. Do you know anything to disprove it? Well, it has been so with me. As you should know.'

'I know very little of you, Ross. How often have we met in five years? A dozen times?'

Ross was silent. 'I was not thinking of the last five years. But perhaps you're right. I am inclined to agree, I know very little of you either. And you've changed so much – inwardly I mean. . . .'

'Have I? Tell me in what way the deterioration is most noticeable.'

'That's asking a reassurance, isn't it? You may have it. It's a different Elizabeth, that's all. The opposite of deterioration. But startling at times. I understand now how young you were when you promised to marry me.'

Elizabeth put her hand out to her wine glass but only fingered the stem. 'I should have been old enough to know my own mind.'

Something in the way she spoke surprised him. The sudden feeling in her voice was like self-contempt. It swung their talk right away from the polite, slightly flirtatious conversation that had been passing between them.

He looked at her, trying to weigh this up, said cautiously to provide her with the normal escape: 'Well, let us agree you were young. . . . And you thought I was dead.'

Elizabeth glanced down the table to where Francis was talking to Ruth Treneglos. The emotion had perhaps caught her unawares too. Or perhaps she decided she had escaped too often. In a perfectly cool, young voice she said: 'I never really believed you were dead. I thought I loved Francis better.'

'You *thought* you loved him. . . .'

She nodded her head. 'And then I discovered my mistake.'

'When?'

'Quite soon.'

His rational mind still refused to accept this sudden conversation at its full value, but somewhere inside him his heart was beating, as if the intelligence reached him through another channel. Twenty-odd people at this table, his own wife talking to the cavalry officer with the big moustache, Sir Hugh at her other hand waiting to break in; George Warleggan, for the most part silent and intent but his gaze every now and then flickering up from his food or from his partners to rest upon Elizabeth's hair or mouth or hands. Incredible that Elizabeth should choose this moment to make such a confession, after nine years. Incredible that it should be true. . . .

'These damned mongrels that roam about,' said Lady Bodrugan feelingly, 'breeding and interbreeding; they make it uncommon hard to keep one's stock pure. You're that much luckier, John, dealing only in cattle. What did you say your dog was, miss?'

'A pug,' said Caroline. 'With beautiful black curly hair and a gold-brown face no bigger than the centre of this plate. Unwin regards him with the *utmost* respect and affection, don't you, dear.'

'Respect, yes,' said Unwin, 'for his teeth are devilish sharp.'

Ross said to Elizabeth: 'This is some pleasant joke you are trying on me?'

Elizabeth smiled with a sudden brittle brilliance. 'Oh, it's a joke indeed. But it is against myself, Ross. Didn't you know? I wonder you never guessed.'

'*Guessed* . . .'

'Well, if you did not guess, it might have been more gallant of you to have met this barefaced confession halfway. Is it such an astonishment that a woman who changed her mind once could change it twice? . . . Well, yes, perhaps it is, for it has always been an astonishment and a humiliation to me. . . .'

After what seemed a long time Ross said: 'That first Easter I came to you after you married – you told me then plain enough that you loved only Francis and had no thoughts for anyone else.'

'Was that when I should have told you? Only a few months after my marriage, and with Geoffrey Charles already alive in me?'

Something was taken away from Ross and another dish put in its place. Whatever the object of the party, Sir John was not sparing his cellar, and talk at the table was louder than it had been. Yet Ross had to struggle with himself not to push his chair back and get away. That Elizabeth should have chosen this moment. . . . Unless it was that only the presence of other people had given her the courage to tell him point-blank what she had long wanted him to know. . . . And where a few minutes ago he had made no sense of what she said, now he saw it as sensible enough. Every second that passed fitted it more inescapably into the pattern of the last nine years.

'And Francis?' he said. 'Does he know?'

'I've said already too much, Ross. My tongue. A sudden impulse – it had best be forgotten. Or if not forgotten, disregarded. What were we talking of before this?'

Three places down the table, Francis. His slightly raffish face, in which the vivid lines of youth were losing themselves in a too early deterioration. . . . As if conscious just then of something toward, he glanced up at Ross, wrinkled one eyebrow and winked.

Francis had known. Ross saw that now. Francis had known so long that his early outbreaks of disillusion and disappointment were far behind him. His own jealousy long spent, and perhaps his love with it, he felt no discomfort at seeing Ross and Elizabeth together. His quarrels in earlier years, the enigmas of his behaviour, were all explained. And now so far as he was concerned it was all past – part of an era best forgotten, in this new time of tolerance and good will.

Perhaps, Ross thought, that was why Elizabeth had now ventured to tell him; because *her* feeling was spent and she believed Ross's to be; she'd offered it as an explanation, an apology of things past, something due to him now that danger no longer existed for any of them in the confession.

Elizabeth had turned to answer some question put by the man on the other side of her, and it was a moment or two before Ross was able to see her face again. Even then she didn't meet his eyes, but he knew instantly by something in her expression – if he had not in fact known all along – that for her the question was not in the very least a dead one and she did not suppose it to be so for him.

After the ladies had left, there was half an hour with the port, and then the sexes were reshuffled for tea and coffee.

Ross had one other meeting with Caroline Penvenen. He was passing a small withdrawing room when he heard angry words and recognized the voice as Unwin Trevaunance's. He had only gone a few more paces when he heard the door bang sharply and quick footsteps caught him up at the door of the main drawing room. He stepped back to let Caroline go in before him. She smiled at him rather breathlessly, her eyes still glinting with a disappearing emotion.

As he seemed about to move away, she said: 'Might I have your company for a moment or two?'

'For as long as you wish it.'

She stood beside him, scanning the people with narrowed eyes. He was aware now how tall she was and how graceful.

'I'm gratified you are loyal to your friends, Captain Poldark.'

'Loyal? I hope so. But do you mean . . .'

'I mean to Dr Enys. Because I must tell you that when I met him first he was most loyal to you.'

'When was that?'

'Before your trial, of course. He was quite hot-blooded in your defence.'

In the general run of life people shied away from mentioning his trial to Ross. His was not a face that encouraged liberties. But this girl seemed to suffer no hesitancies. She spoke either from a complete lack of perception and sensitiveness or else out of her own particular conception of honesty which admitted no taboos. Since she seemed to wish to be friendly, he took the charitable view.

'Must I suppose from that that you gave him reason for defence?'

'Oh, yes, of course. For if you wish to discover a man's true feelings, it is always best to provoke him.'

'Are those the tactics you're applying now, Miss Penvenen?'

She smiled pleasantly. 'It would be presumptuous of me to imagine that I could.'

'Shall you stay with your uncle for the summer?'

'It depends. In October I shall be twenty-one – and then shall be my own mistress. It's a provoking long time coming.'

'Perhaps before then you will be married.'

'Would that not only be exchanging one keeper for another?'

'Always supposing you look on a husband in that light.'

'Never having had one, I cannot tell. But having seen so many of them about, I should not have thought it an unflattering description.'

'At least it's unflattering to your uncle.'

Caroline laughed. 'But why? He has kept me. Isn't that being a keeper? There have been no bars across the windows – at least only invisible bars of conventionalism and disapproval. But I fancy I should like my freedom for a while.'

As they were talking Unwin went past them with a thunderous face, and Caroline kept Ross in conversation while the other man was in the room. Good-humouredly aware that he was being used, Ross reflected that his hope of seeing them quickly married did not seem likely to come off.

It deteriorated further when Unwin disappeared and was seen no more that evening. Cards were played until midnight, but the fact that there had been a tiff between the young couple was underlined by Ray Penvenen's sour face; and all this put a blight on the last part of the evening.

Just when the party was going to break up, George Warleggan found himself temporarily isolated with Francis and immediately took the opportunity of speaking to him.

'Good evening to you. May I say I'm glad to see you again after all this time.'

Francis stared at him. 'I'm sorry I cannot say the same, George.'

'If it's true, then *I'm* sorry. It need not be.'

'That's where we differ. I made my choice long ago. I prefer to keep my hands clean.'

George's face darkened. 'This empty spite. . . . In your cousin I have come to expect no reason——'

'Well, then, if that's reason, expect none in me.'

If George had had serious hope of a *rapprochement*, it did not survive this. He turned away and found himself face to face with Ross.

There was a moment's silence. One or two now watching hopefully expected an immediate battle. They edged nearer to catch the words which would provide the spark.

Ross stared down at the other man. 'Good evening to you, George.'

George's formidable face twitched slightly. 'Well, Ross, imagine our meeting here!'

'We must have supper together sometime.'

'I shall look forward to it. . . . I hope your mine prospers.'

'It will.'

'I wish I had your confidence.'

Ross said: 'Must you be envious even of that?'

George flushed and opened his mouth to say something as Ross moved away. But a word now would undo the restraint of years. Now for the first time he had Ross where he wanted him. Restraint was a virtue. He had only to endure in silence to triumph.

As Ross and Demelza rode home, accompanied for the first part of the way by Francis and Elizabeth, a half-spent moon rose and tinselled the landscape for them, lighting the dew on the fields and the spider webs in the hedgerows. There was not much talk among any of the four. Elizabeth was keyed up with what she had said and nervous as to the result, because you could never predict what Ross would do. Francis was sleepy. And Ross, lost in his thoughts of the past and his speculations for the future, was curiously detached from the scene though inescapably aware of the figure of Elizabeth, cause of it all, riding on ahead of him.

Demelza, with her instinctive, animal perceptions, knew that something quite fresh had cropped up in Ross's life. She felt that Elizabeth must be at the bottom of it, but could not imagine what new thing had suddenly grown out of the old allegiance. 'I hope to be able to wait on you, ma'am,' Captain McNeil had said, a very nice admiration in his look. Of all the men she had ever met, Malcolm McNeil was the only one who could begin to hold a candle to Ross. 'One of these days *I'll* give a party, my dear,' Sir Hugh Bodrugan had said, fingering her arm.

Just before it came time for them to separate, Francis said:

'Is it true the tub-runners have had another successful run?'

'Yes,' said Ross. 'I heard so.'

'Vercoe and his gaugers will be in an ill-humour.'

'I've no doubt.'

'There was a whisper about – I've forgot where I heard it – but there was a whisper about that you were concerning yourself in the Trade.'

Silence fell. Demelza pulled a little more tightly at her horse's reins, and the horse shook his head with a jingle of distaste.

Ross said: 'Where did you hear that?'

'Does it matter so much? It was some time ago and I think concerned that run in March.'

'There has never been a time when some foolish rumour has not been flying round regarding one of us, Francis.'

Another pause. 'Well, I'm glad there's no truth in it anyway.'

'Glad? I did not know you had any special feeling for the Customs men.'

'Nor have I, Ross. But I have some feeling for you nowadays. And I do not like this informer, this sneak, this telltale who is about. Everyone knows of his existence; no one knows who he is. If he was identified, he would soon come to a bad end. But while he is about there is a double danger. Of course if I were Mr Trencrom, with big stakes in the business, connections, and a sizeable cutter to maintain, I should I suppose go on and trust in the Lord. I'd have to. But if I were an ordinary threadbare country gentleman, looking to turn an extra penny, or a miner or a blacksmith, thinking of smuggling as a side-line, this is the last time of day I should want to have any hand in the work.'

It was a long speech for Francis, and as he spoke they had come to the fork in the track. The four riders halted.

Ross said: 'I suppose you'll do your best to quash this story if you should run against it again.'

'I will. Oh, I will. Well, good night to you both.'

Ross said: 'So far as the Trade goes, there are of course degrees of help one may render. Not all kinds entail running the boats ashore or bearing off the goods.'

'All kinds can be dangerous if there is an informer about.'

'If I were a threadbare country gentleman looking to turn an extra penny, I might agree with you. But in some circumstances risk must be weighed against reward.'

'I think I should prefer not to know any more. My wish was to convey friendly warning, not to pry into your secrets.'

'It seems you already know the secret. It will be a good thing if you have the details too. Some time ago Mr Trencrom came to see me, he being in some straits because the informer had made it impossible for him to run in a cargo at any of the usual places. He asked if he might use Nampara Cove. At the time the Warleggans were making themselves obnoxious by getting a foothold in my other mine, Wheal Leisure. I agreed to Trencom's proposition, and he uses my cove and land – but twice only a year and for each landing he pays me £200.'

Francis whistled. 'It's a tidy sum. Enough to tempt any man. If there were not this danger, I should have jumped at it myself.'

'If there were not this danger, I should not have been offered it.'

'No. . . . No, I see. But this money – is it to keep Wheal Grace in operation for longer than we'd planned? If so——'

'I have debts,' said Ross briefly. 'One of them carries an excessive rate of interest. With this money from Trencrom I am able to survive. Without it our mine would never have been started.'

'You should have told me.'

'What?'

'Of these debts. The money we've invested in Wheal Grace might have been better employed.'

'If Wheal Grace fails, it might have been better employed in some other venture. It has never been enough in itself to pay what I owe.'

Francis stared at his cousin's face, which was half lit by the climbing moon. He would have liked to clear up this point between them, but there were too many pitfalls. Their present friendship, their present partnership, meant too much to him to be jeopardized by an ill-considered question now.

As Ross and Demelza rode on alone, Demelza said: 'I wonder who told him.'

'About the Trade? It was bound to get abroad. When twenty or thirty men know. . . .' As if reading her thoughts, he added: 'Oh, I know that's what you've always said. But it's a risk to be fairly taken. So long as no one learns the date of a run, all's well. Gaugers will not spend every night out.'

'I would rather go barefoot.'

'There is no risk of that.'

'There are worse risks.'

'I differ.'

'Don't jest, Ross. It's no jesting matter. You have been in too much trouble these last years.'

By now they were riding down into their own valley. On the other side the new engine of Wheal Grace slithered and sighed as it pumped the water up from the depths of the earth.

To divert her Ross said: 'And did you enjoy the evening? Did it come up to your expectation?'

'Yes, it was all very agreeable. Only we were separated, as you might say, at the very beginning and were almost strangers by the end of it.'

'It is the fashion of modern society. But I noticed Captain McNeil looked after you very well.'

'Yes, he did indeed. He's a very polite, genteel sort of man, Ross, and is going to call on us one day next week.'

'Hm. It is not an uncommon pattern. You only have to crook your little finger and they all come.'

'You have an awful wicked tongue for exaggeration, Ross. I wonder sometimes it does not drop off. And Caroline Penvenen?'

'Caroline?'

'Yes, you saw very much of her. What do you think of her? She kept you in a corner, did she not, and wouldn't let you come forth.'

Ross pondered a minute. 'She kept me in no corner that I did not wish to be kept in,' he said, 'but I certainly think she is the wrong wife for Dwight. She would wipe her feet on him.'

Chapter four

ELLERY'S DEATH MADE a big difference to Dwight. Surgical and physical skill could be exercised in a poor and primitive community only upon a foundation of confidence and trust. Without that foundation you were lucky if you exercised anything at all. In two weeks more than half Dwight's patients disappeared from his doorstep or made excuses when he called.

His visits to St Ann's were at no time frequent, but he had one or two faithful patients there and among them, a paying one too, was Mrs Vercoe, the wife of the Customs Officer, whose youngest child he had pulled through an illness during the winter. On the day following the party to which he'd not been invited, he paid them a visit and was just in time to see Vercoe himself separating at the front door of his whitewashed cottage from a tall fair-haired man with a fine cavalry moustache. Although plainly a gentleman, the stranger had not come by horse, because he strode away across the fields towards the cliff path.

Inside the cottage Clara Vercoe greeted Dwight. Hubert was not so well, she said, had vomited after his latest bottle of physic and she'd given him no more. Hubert, looking papery and wasted, was brought forward into the sunlight falling through the open doorway, and Dwight cast a professional eye over him while pretending to admire his story book. It was a new kind, cheaply printed in Plymouth on sheets of stiff paper with line pictures illustrating *The History of Primrose Prettyface* and bound between covers of thin horn with a wooden handle. The first picture was of an angel, and Hubert had coloured the wings red.

Dwight wondered if this was another echo of the Ellery affair and if his draught was being blamed for some digestive upset. He said he would change the stuff, and poured some of it into a cup to examine and taste.

While he was there Jim Vercoe came back into the cottage for a telescope, and Dwight followed the direction in which it was pointed, towards a sail on the horizon.

You could not but admire a man who persisted in his task in the face of bribes offered, occasional threats, and the social ostracism that came his way. Something of the unpleasantness Vercoe often had to meet showed in his bearded face. Dwight would have admired him the more if there had not been also a trace of that grim satisfaction about him which some men find in getting disliked in the course of their duty.

'The sky's very clear this morning,' Dwight remarked as the Customs Officer lowered his glass.

'Sharp's a knife, surgeon. There'll be more rain afore nightfall.'

'We been watching for the revenue ship all week,' said Mrs Vercoe with a nod. 'Jim's been asking for 'er for long enough.'

''Twill be all over the village soon,' Vercoe said irritably. 'Women's tongues is too slipper in what don't concern 'em.'

'Eh, Dr Enys wouldn't say anything, would you, sir?'

'No more than I should if I saw a man with a cask of brandy.'

Vercoe stared at him resentfully for a moment. A man with the standing of a physician had no right to be that impartial.

''Tis hard to do a proper job when all the gentry are against ee, surgeon, and when there's scarcely a place for an honest boat to find safe harbourage anywhere along this coast. They just won't venture in when the weather's heavy. Even Padstow's no safe refuge if a gale blow up. But ye can't keep a watch from Mount's Bay!'

'I should have thought the disadvantage works both ways. The seas that keep away your revenue cutter will stop men from landing a cargo.'

'Ah, 'tis not so simple as that. The runners will take more risks, and they d'know every rock and eddy like the back of their hands. What I need 'bove all is more men ashore. 'Tis fighting uphill all the way. And the worst thing of all mebbe is knowing that after all if you catch your men, as like as not they'll be brought before the local magistrates and acquitted and set free.'

Dwight said: 'I know it is hard, but I should not say that *all* the gentry are against you. Or even all the people. I understand you have your informers, and they should be worth their weight in – well, gold.'

Vercoe's face coloured with a dark, angry flush. 'That's what you come down to, surgeon, when you're hard set. You're not helped by the honest men, so then you've to use the rats.'

A few minutes later Dwight rode into the main street of the village and dismounted at the little shop where his medicines were made up. He stooped in and waited among the multicoloured bottles and the bundles of coloured straw for making bonnets and the green canisters of mixed tea until Irby, the druggist, squeezed himself out of the dungeon where he mixed his prescriptions. Irby was a little fat man with a stub of a nose and steel spectacles with lenses no bigger than the acquisitive eyes behind them.

Dwight began by asking pleasantly to see the order he had made out and asking Mr Irby to taste the draught and to note the amount of sediment in the bottom of the bottle. Mr Irby was effusive, co-operative, but astonished; there would of course be sediment: the drugs Dwight had ordered would refuse to mix and a precipitate would form. Dwight with deference corrected him. If the drugs were pure, it was quite impossible, etc., etc. At this point the conversation, while still polite, began to carry a sediment of its own. Dwight said he wished he might examine the drugs from which the physic was made up. Mr Irby squinted round the sides of his spectacles and said that he had been practising in St Ann's for twenty years and no surgeon had ever cast a reflection on his competence before. Dwight said that in this respect he did not doubt his competence; it was a plain question of whether the drugs were adulterated. Mr Irby said he had never bought cheap drugs and he did not propose to be accused of that now. Dwight said he was sorry to have to insist, but he had a right by law as a physician to enter and examine the drugs in any druggist's establishment, and this he intended to exercise. Followed by Mr Irby, he went down the steps into the dungeon and peered about him in the uncertain light, at the Glauber's salts, the Dover's powders, the gamboge, the nux vomica, the paregorics, and the vermifuges.

The noise of Mr Irby's annoyance brought Mrs Irby from a deeper dungeon behind the first, but Dwight went carefully on with his examination. He found what he had suspected: that cheap substitutes had been bought and labelled for more expensive drugs, and in two cases the powders had been adulterated with something, ground bone or chalk. All these he tipped into a wooden pail. When it was full, he walked out through the shop with it, followed by the druggist angrily demanding recompense and justice. As he went he saw a tall woman standing in the shop, but it was so dark that he did not take much note of her. He carried the pail round the backs of the houses, found the nearest open cesspool, and tipped the contents in. When he came back he saw that the woman was Caroline Penvenen.

Five minutes later he left the shop, trying to dust the powder from his breeches and boots. Mr Irby followed him to the door calling down the wrath of God, but abruptly disappeared – being lugged in by his wife, who was a powerful woman as well as an astute one and did not wish their neighbours to know more than could be helped.

Dwight glanced at the splendid chestnut held by a mounted groom, but he didn't stop. As he got to his own horse, Caroline came out of the shop.

He took off his hat and the breeze fanned his face.

She said: 'Dr Enys, as I'm alive! How diverting. And with such an expression as if the Last Trump'd blown. I almost mistook you for the vision of Judgment.'

He had been expecting, half dreading this meeting. Now that it had come, it had all the anticipated sense of shock, it brought all the old feelings alive. In the middle of his anger he recognized them, every one. Her brilliant hair blowing in the breeze was a renewed offence; so was the curve of her strong feminine mouth, the laughter in her eyes.

Dwight said: 'There are times, ma'am, when we can't wait for the Last

Trump, but must pass a little judgment by the way.'

She swung up upon her horse, and the animal side-stepped spiritedly on the cobbles. 'And who is next to receive a chastising? May I accompany you for the entertainment?'

'You may accompany me, but I've no entertainment to offer. I'm riding home now.'

She shook her head. 'You underrate yourself, Dr Enys. Your company is fair entertainment for me any day.'

He bowed. 'Thank you, but we differ as to that. I've no ambition to be your court jester. Good day.'

He rode off fairly boiling. She thought him a fool, and no doubt she was right. His life seemed bounded with futilities, and her being on the spot served to point them. He had just left St Ann's when he heard the thump of hooves in the lane and Caroline drew abreast of him. Her groom was left behind.

She said angrily: 'We meet after fifteen months and you haven't even a civil word for me!'

That, he thought, was a trifle cool. 'I'm old-fashioned in these matters, Miss Penvenen. I thought civility should be shown on both sides.'

'I might have known better than to expect any from you.'

'Indeed you might.'

'The truth is that you do not like to be laughed at.'

'That is the truth.'

They were silent for a little way. She turned her whip over and over in her gloved hands and glanced at him. 'I'm sorry.'

He looked at her, startled, and she at once laughed.

'There, Dr Enys, you didn't expect me to say that and it has quite frightened you. You see how dangerous it is to prejudge a person. I should have thought your medical training would have warned you against it.'

'So it should. The symptoms were deceptive.'

'And now that you find yourself undeceived, don't you owe *me* an apology?

'Yes. . . . I'm sorry.'

She inclined her head. 'Do you think that if I show a properly sober frame of mind and promise never to laugh again, we might share this road as far as Trenwith?'

'You're staying with your uncle?'

'Yes.'

'Unwin Trevaunance is down, I hear.'

'He is.'

The groom was not overtaking them but was following just out of earshot.

'And how is the scurvy in Sawle?' she asked.

'Not so bad as last year. The potato crop didn't fail, and I sometimes wonder if even potatoes help to keep it at bay. On the whole——' He stopped and looked at her face; but if she was secretly deriding him, she gave no sign this time.

'Perhaps I'm wrong in calling you Miss Penvenen.'

'Why? Oh. . . . No, I'm not married yet.'

'Is it to be soon?'

She wrinkled her nose. 'Not soon. At least, not to Unwin. He's jilted me.'

'What?'

'Well, I'm not sure which way round it was, but Uncle says it was the other way. Uncle was in the greatest of a passion when he learned of it – said I had been leading Unwin a dance. But really, Dr Enys, there's no harm in a man performing a dance once in a while, is there? Why should I sell myself to Unwin just to become Lady Trevaunance when Sir John dies? I was not meant to be an M.P.'s wife. I should get no pleasure in spending all my money furthering Unwin's career. I'd better prefer to spend it furthering my own!'

Dwight hoped his feelings did not show in his face.

'And what brought you to this sudden decision?'

'Oh. . . .' A glint came into her eyes. 'I think it was my first real meeting with Ross Poldark.'

'Ross Poldark happens to be married.'

'Yes . . . and incidentally last night had no eyes for anyone but his cousin-in-law – that lovely fair-haired woman with the grey eyes. I think that's their relationship, isn't it? But it looked closer.'

'You misunderstood it. Anyway——'

'Anyway, he had no eyes for me, you were going to say. Quite true. I shouldn't object to Poldark as a husband, I believe, but some one spoke him first. No . . . what I mean is that when one sees a ship of the line, one is that much less content with a third-rater. Do you understand me, dear Dr Enys?'

'I understand you,' said Dwight, wondering what his own category was in His Majesty's Navy.

'So you can appreciate it is a very sad story,' said Caroline, 'of a young woman left almost at the church door, and no redress. Can you wonder that at any moment she may fall ill and go into a decline?'

'I can understand,' Dwight said, 'that she will now have more time on her hands.'

There was a long pause. After it Caroline said steadily: 'You dislike me very much, don't you?'

He flushed. 'D'you really think that?'

'Have you ever given me cause to think otherwise?'

They had already passed Trenwith, passed her turning for Killewarren. He said suddenly: 'If what I feel for you is dislike – for coming between me

and my work sometime *every* day in the last fifteen months – if that's dislike . . . If being unable to forget your voice, or the way you turn your neck,
or the lights in your hair – if that's dislike . . . If wanting to hear that you're
married and dreading to hear that you're married . . . If resenting the
condescension that pretends you're not out of my reach . . .' He stopped,
unable to finish his sentences. 'Perhaps you can identify these symptoms
for me.'

They rode on in silence, and then Caroline reined in her horse.

'I must go back. I shall be late for dinner as it is. Tell me, do you ever
ride for pleasure?'

'Seldom.'

'I shall be out on Thursday early. Would you like to meet me at the gates
soon after seven?'

At least she was not laughing now. He could hardly believe that within
ten minutes of their meeting all his good resolutions had been tipped
overboard, with apparently no effort on her part and no resistance on his.
He knew as plainly as if it had been issued by proclamation that, Unwin or
no Unwin, Caroline was not for him. Her uncles would make very sure that
she either married a title or more money. A penniless doctor with a good
name but nothing to it would be better occupied putting straws in his hair.

The groom was coming up with them. She said: 'Or I could be ill if you
preferred it. How long does it take to develop the scurvy?'

'It's an unpleasant disease,' Dwight said, taking off his hat, 'and so bad
for the complexion. I shouldn't advise it.'

A week passed before Malcolm McNeil paid his visit to Nampara. He
walked over one bright summerless afternoon, without prior notice since
he wanted it that way, and on foot since he was keen to harden himself
before returning to duty. As he came down the valley, he noticed the
changes that three years had brought. On the opposite hill was a new mine
with a pumping engine hissing and clanking, and a whole litter of sheds and
piles of refuse, and leets and a smithy and a spalling house. Industry had
advanced at the expense of farming. More fields lay fallow than a rotation
of crops justified, and there were few cattle or sheep or pigs about. A dark-
lashed baby was asleep in a cot near the front door. The servant who let
him in left him in the parlour, which seemed to him to have become
smaller and poorer since his last visit. A kitten came and mewed round his
legs, and he picked it up and gave it his forefinger to bite.

Mrs Poldark was about five minutes, and she looked flushed when she
came in.

'I'm sure this is an ill-chosen time, ma'am.' he said. 'I was passing and
thought to avail myself of your kindness. . . .'

'No, not at all. But Ross, I'm sorry to say, isn't here. He's over to the
mine. I'll send Gimlett to fetch him.'

McNeil vigorously protested, and she allowed herself to be persuaded, knowing that Ross was likely to be deep in some work – probably fathoms deep – and would not want interruption. McNeil sat down and fastened his moustache more firmly in and let the kitten slide on to the shabby rug.

Being a Scotsman and a widely travelled one, he had not been much impressed by the women in these parts on his last visit. But there had been three good-lookers at the party the other evening, and this Mrs Poldark was the one with that little something more than looks which teased his curiosity. He fancied he knew potentialities when he saw them; and a spark was seldom long absent from this young woman's fine eyes. It was like the glint of a soldier's sabre at night.

He said: 'You have heard the latest war news, perhaps?'

'War news? I didn't know we were at war.'

He smiled. 'Nor are we, ma'am I mean the French war with the Austrians. The information has just come through.'

'Is it good or bad?'

'Oh, good. Without question. The French broke into Belgium like a rabble, it's said, expecting no doubt to make men run at the sight of their unshaven faces; but when they met the Austrians, one disciplined charge was enough; the whole French army tairned and ran from the battlefield. And when their own officers – their own generals – tried to stop them, they murdered them, stabbing them with bayonets!'

'And what does that mean? That France is defeated already? Have they other armies?'

'None in the field. . . . So much for your revolutionaries. It's strange how nairvous people have been at the thought of these cutthroats let loose. Folk forget that when a country throws away its discipline it throws away its strength. I trust this will be a lesson to the noisy windbags in Paris.' He paused and stretched a booted leg and twisted his moustache. 'Though for myself . . .'

Demelza waited. 'What for yourself, Captain McNeil?'

'Well, I confess I should not have been discontented to have a tilt at them some way or another. I should not be wishing Britain into war, ye understand, but for a soldier a small bout of fighting now and then restores his self-respect.'

'I shouldn't have thought 'twould be likely *you* would lose that.'

'No. ma'am. But in times of peace one is sent on – one is liable to be called upon for distasteful and rather shabby missions which . . .' McNeil stopped and withdrew his leg and looked at Demelza. Demelza looked at him without a flicker of a change of expression. He swallowed and said: 'I'm sorry. I thought I heard a baby crying.'

She got up and went quickly to the window, peered out. 'No. I can see him. He's still asleep.'

'Perhaps it's your little girl. Though by now I suppose she will be——'

'She died, Captain McNeil. More than two years ago.'

'Oh . . .' He got up. 'Forgive me, ma'am. I'm sorry.'

Demelza came back. 'It's nothing to forgive. You were not to know.' She stood by the table for a moment, fairly close to him.' Pray sit down.'

'It must have been a grievous blow. You will feel a gap in your life. . . .'

'It is hard to explain, for 'tis more than a gap. Or it has been with us. There is a change. Nothing hasn't been the same since. Those who are left are different people trying to live the same lives.'

McNeil stood looking at her. He cursed himself for having got the conversation on the wrong leg. Yet in what she said he detected an alloy of something besides sadness. She did not look in the least a discontented woman, but all clearly was not well between her and life. It might be a circumstance worth exploring.

Ross was not, as Demelza not unreasonably supposed, fathoms deep; he was in conference with Francis and Captain Henshawe in the changing shed near the mine. The two young engineers, Bull and Trevithick, who had built the engine, had been over to correct a minor fault, and Ross had taken the opportunity of sounding them on the potentialities of their child. It seemed plain to him, and they confirmed it, that the engine was capable of a good deal more than was at present demanded; and he proposed that the main shaft should be sunk another twenty fathoms so that two new levels could be begun. This meant engaging more men; but as he pointed out to Henshawe and Francis, the prospect of profit was increased out of proportion to the expense. The great expense was the engine. While it worked, let it do the maximum.

Francis the gambler was all for it, Henshawe more cautious; but inevitably, as the chief partners, the cousins had their way. Henshawe's interest was nominal, and in any case he was not an obstructive man. He knew Ross's overriding need of quick results. Nor did he comment, as he might have done, that in his wide experience of mines in this district he had seldom known the copper lodes to improve with depth, as was often the case further west. Nothing was so unpredictable as a mine – one reason why they were always feminine – and he was not prepared to take the responsibility of standing in the way of Ross's instinct.

After the meeting Ross walked home alone, content that the effort was to be made but content with nothing else.

Elizabeth's confession at the party had had an unexpected effect on him. Behind the strong and sometimes lawless impulses that moved him from time to time was a bitterly clear-minded critic who saw his own acts, usually after he had performed them, with great detachment. Sometimes, though not very often, this critic turned on others. It did so now on Elizabeth. She wasn't at all less attractive to him – much the reverse. But he found himself *liking* her less. Her single mistake had distorted all their lives, pulling them out of their natural pattern. Then, having picked the wrong man, she had let him know it, and he, deprived of her love but not of his need for her, had run the conventional course downhill watched and blamed by Ross who thought he had all he could desire. Their lives had been the tragedy of one woman who couldn't make up her mind.

Far better now if *he* had never known. The knowledge served no purpose but to destroy what was left of his peace of mind. The result of all this, contrariwise, had been a new warmth in his feelings for Demelza. He wouldn't have been able to explain why, unless it was that he felt Demelza incapable of any such behaviour.

When he got to his own front door he heard a man's voice and surprised the coattails of Malcolm McNeil, who was just taking his leave.

Demelza smiled over her visitor's shoulder. 'Oh, Ross, I was afraid you was underground, or I should have sent for you. Captain McNeil has been entertaining me with stories of the American war. I wonder you never speak of it yourself.'

McNeil said: 'Captain Poldark is more modest, I've no doubt. The latest news suggests we shall not need him again just yet.'

'Oh, you've heard it?' said Ross in slight disappointment. 'My cousin has just told me. It may of course be exaggerated.'

'From what I gather, the road to Paris is open. The sooner the city is occupied the better.'

'No doubt you're right. I confess I still have a sneaking sympathy for the republicans – if only they would behave like reasonable men and not like apes. If I were a Parisian, I should not want to open the gates to Francis of Austria.'

McNeil said: 'By the way, did ye hear more of the man who killed his wife when I was last here, and escaped from your cove?'

'Mark Daniel? No. I expect he was drowned. The dinghy he stole from us was barely seaworthy.'

'Indeed, so?' McNeil looked at Ross with an unbelieving eye.

'Well, I'll be on my way. I'm returning to Salisbury in a few days' time, but I doubt I shall be down again before long. It is a fascinating part.'

This last remark he seemed to address to Demelza. She said: 'I hope you'll take back a good report of our behaviour this time.'

McNeil said: 'How could I do otherwise, ma'am?'

Ross watched the Scotsman's broad-shouldered figure walking briskly up the valley.

'He is a thought less impressive out of his soldier's clothes. I hope he did not come here because he suspects us of being concerned in the tub-carrying.'

'Oh no, he invited himself to call when we met last week. He is here only for his health this time. He has no interest in smuggling at all.'

'Did he tell you so?'

'Yes. . . . Yes, he did.'

'Hm,' said Ross.

Demelza's indignation grew with her alarm.' I don't see that there is any reason to suspect him at all!'

'Only that that was his business last time, and Cornwall is a long way to come just for a convalescence.'

'I'm certain sure you're wrong.'

'You were careful what you said, I suppose?'

'Of course! You should know I am more frightened of discovery than you are.'

Ross said musingly: 'I think I shall ride over and see Trencrom tomorrow.'

'Why? He promised there was to be no more landing in our cove until September.'

'No, nor shall there be. I want to locate Mark Daniel.'

'I should not suppose it safe for him to come back.'

'No. But he was in Cherbourg last Christmas. You know why we opened Wheal Grace. It was part on account of the old maps, part on account of what Mark told us when he hid in the old workings before we helped him to escape. Well, we have spent months trying to find what he found. Why should we not get him to help us? In a few more months it will be too late.'

'I'd rather Mark came than you went, Ross. Up till now you've taken no real part in the Trade.'

'Well, the first thing is to see if he can be found.'

'No, Ross, that isn't the first thing.'

'All right, I'll not go if it can be avoided.'

Mr Trencrom lived in an unpretentious six-roomed house tucked away as if not to be seen behind a sharp cleft in the hillside half a mile from the village of St Ann's. Although it was known that he was a very rich man, no evidences of wealth were allowed to appear in his house or in the clothes he wore, and there was plenty of speculation as to where he kept his money and what he did with it. Nothing suggested the miser in the size of his body or the warmth of his welcome when Ross called the next evening; and Ross came straight to the point, explaining the enquiries he would like put in hand.

'Mark Daniel,' said Mr Trencrom, squeezing his small voice out of his large chest. 'Let's see, that was the one that killed his wife, wasn't it? On account of her going with that Dr Enys. Remember well. Quite a fuss. 'Twould be dangerous still, I conceit, for him to come back. To England. Have you asked any of my men?'

'No. I came first to you.'

Mr Trencrom acknowledged the courtesy. 'Might deliver a letter. But Daniel can't read, eh? I'll ask Nanfan or Paynter to enquire. Nanfan's best because he's a relative. I'll do that, Captain Poldark. Nights are too light just at present. Can have too much of a full moon, eh?' He coughed, a weak consumptive paroxysm, as if someone had sat on a rusty spring in his sofa. 'There's trouble about. That man Vercoe. And that military fellow up at the Place. Shall be glad to see the back of him. There's more in it – than meets the eye. And look at France. Chaos. I should not fancy to be Mark Daniel. Living there these days.'

Ross got up to leave. 'I'll call and speak to Nanfan. Does he always go?'

'No. Leave arranging to me. Oh, Captain Poldark, as a favour – just one for another, as you might say. I thought of calling to see you. But it's a long way, and after dark these summer days. Not in my first bloom.'

'Yes?'

'One drawback to your cove. Frequently thought of it. Must be done in a single night. You've always insisted, haven't you, everything must be carried away. Don't blame you. But 'tis awkward. If we could *store* some of the stuff – two, three days. As we used to do in Sawle and places. Ten men do in three nights what thirty do in one. Less chance for the informer. Get the stuff ashore and *hide* it. The main thing.' Mr Trencrom tried to push himself out of his chair. 'See what I mean?'

'You're suggesting we should hide it for you in our own house?'

'Didn't say house. Not necessarily. Though even there – if a cache were carefully dug——'

'I'm sorry. That's putting my neck in a noose. At present I always have the defence that the run is being made without my knowledge. But if one item of your goods is found in my cellar . . .'

Mr Trencrom clasped and unclasped his fat hands. 'You ask a favour of me, sir. What's the difference? Oh, in degree, I suppose, something. But the obligation, the benefit. . . .'

Ross had known Mr Trencrom for some years; it was not the first time he had found him less easygoing than he looked. 'If you prefer it, I can go to Falmouth and take ship to Cherbourg myself.'

'Have reason to believe Mark Daniel has left Cherbourg.'

'Where is he, then?'

Mr Trencrom nearly asphyxiated himself with a cough. Coming up purple and panting, he said: 'Captain Poldark, now. Have no idea. But my men would have a better chance. Your mine is not paying yet. I understand?'

Ross stared at him grimly. 'D'you wish me to confirm that or to acknowledge the blackmail?'

'Oh, please. Between friends. We work together, do we not? Profit of both. Have no wish to offend. But we can't do without each other – just at present. I suggested this – thought you might not object. Would be willing to make some small extra payment for the convenience; small of course; my profits negligible, just as a good-will token. Twenty-five guineas, say. . .'

'For each cargo?'

'Well . . . yes, I suppose.'

Ross reflectively flapped his gloves. His struggle to remain solvent had distorted his views on money, but not to this extent. He was going to refuse again, but Mr Trencrom said:

'Don't decide now, sir. Take a little time. If you think more of it, leave me know. In the meanwhile I will see after your friend Daniel.'

'Thank you. Are you any further forward in tracing how the leakage in your arrangements arises?'

'Nothing substantial. So far we have been able to avoid serious trouble this year. But am not happy about it. As you'll understand. When it began I thought 'twas someone outside our circle. Hard, you know, bringing in goods, using forty or more men – not to let it get about. The *village* knows. The countryside. But last September, as you'll remember, we began to run a cargo in at Strand Cove. Most unusual to be able to. Usually the heavy swell. I issued instructions to our riders where to go only six hours before the run was due to begin. But we'd floated no more than a dozen ankers ashore when Vercoe and his men sprang out of ambush. Six of our best men arrested. Only thanks to his shortage of men the rest escaped. It can't happen again. It mustn't, Captain Poldark. And the *One and All* has been gravely imperilled.'

'Well, only Vercoe knows who is at the bottom of it,' said Ross grimly. 'And Vercoe won't tell.'

Mr Trencrom asphyxiated himself again. 'Perhaps even Vercoe – does not know. I sometimes – wonder. Perhaps he gets messages – under the door. 'Tis a dangerous game for the informer. There is very bad feeling about.'

At the moment Mr Trencrom said this the informer was in the Hoblyns' cottage in Sawle.

Chapter five

DWIGHT HAD HAD a busy week. As well as riding with Caroline, he had had a crop of sudden ailments to face; and it was from the last of these, a case of bilious fever in Sawle, that he was returning when he decided on the impulse of the moment to call in at the Hoblyns' cottage.

The evening was well on, and he found all the Hoblyns indoors and with them Charlie Kempthorne, who had got Rosina in a corner and was making up to her under the lowering gaze of Jacka her father. Not that Jacka particularly disapproved of Charlie, except for his age; it was rather that courting in any shape or form was one of the great number of things he didn't hold with. He couldn't complain that it was happening under his own nose, because he had refused Charlie permission to take Rosina for a walk.

Dwight apologized for the intrusion, said he had come to see Rosina; Rosina said hastily her knee was *quite* better thank you; Dwight ignored this and said would she and Mrs Hoblyn come into the next room. This left the two men alone, for Parthesia was in bed.

Charlie hadn't liked the interruption. He fancied he had been making some progress, and now it was all set back. But perhaps this could be turned to account. After a minute he scratched his short-cropped head and said: 'Reckon Rosina's coming round t'our way of thinking, Jacka. 'Twill soon be a question of naming the day, like.'

'It isn't to my way of thinking,' Jacka said. 'I'm thinkin' nothin' yet awhile.'

'But you're not saying me nay,' said Charlie. 'An' Rosina 'll see that for herself. She's always been a good obeying kind of girl——'

'She better be,' said Jacka.

'An' 'tis plain to she that what with 'er crooked pinbone she'll be lucky to get a good steady man who's maybe a bit olderer than she but all the better for that. *An'* got a tidy nest egg, what's more. And adding on every day. You should mind that, Jacka Hoblyn.'

'I'll mind what I've the wish to mind.'

'Let 'er go get forced put by some farmer's boy, an' what's the end to it? A 'ovel no betterer than a pigsty. I can give 'er a *home*, with cloam cups to drink out of like she was a lady. And I'll tell ee another thing. That field that's to rent from Surgeon Choake's house. Corner of it runs down nigh to the top of the lane, back o' my yard. Next year I thought to take it. 'Tis just what I d'need to——'

'I can't conceit where you get all your money,' said Jacka.

Charlie looked at him keenly for a moment. 'Ah, but that's just it. Money d'add to money all the while. Start with just a little and treat it right, an' it'll go on growing while you're asleep. Mind, it need a steady 'and. But that's what I got. And sail making's different from bal work. There's more profit to it. Reckon my consumptives was a blessing dressed up, else I'd still have been down mine and no better off at forty than thirty!'

Jacka knitted his black brows. 'Wonder what surgeon's about, coming this time of night. 'Tes no concern of his to visit when he's not asked.'

'D'you pay 'im for every time?'

'Nay, give him his due, he's no great one for that.'

Kempthorne spat on the sanded floor. 'Well, I shouldn't like it ef 'twas *my* house. It don't seem right, 'im coming round any hour of the day, fingering a girl's knee. That's 'ow bad things d'start.'

Jacka stared at Charlie. 'I thought you was a friend of his. I thought 'twas he cured you of the miner's cough.'

'So 'twas. I've nought against him. I'm only saying as it 'pears to me. When all's said, he's only a youngster – and you know what happened with Daniel's wife.'

There was a moment's silence. Jacka's eyebrows were like a scar. He stared at Charlie without pleasure and then strode into the next room.

He found Rosina sitting on the end of the bed, and Dwight was putting a bandage round her knee. Mrs Hoblyn glanced up nervously.

Dwight was cheerful, having at last discovered the cause of their reluctance to let him treat Rosina. 'Oh, Hoblyn, glad you came in. Mrs Hoblyn has been explaining about Mr Nye.'

'Ah?' said Jacka.

'Mr Nye said it might be better to amputate the leg. Of course there's no fear of that. A ridiculous suggestion. I want you to keep your knee bound for a week until I come again.' He finished his work and stood up.

'Yes, sur,' said Rosina.

'I don't see as 'tis necessary for you to be calling, surgeon,' said Jacka, not quite confident of himself. 'Rosina d'get along well and fine as she is. She been like it too long now for a cure. When she's sick, that's different like.'

'Rosina gets along,' said Dwight. 'But it isn't a happy or a healthy way to live. I can promise no improvement, but I intend to try.'

'Sometimes more 'arm than good comes of probing at things.'

Dwight flushed. 'Have no fear: she'll not die of it.'

'Well, I believe in leaving well alone.'

'But you have hardly the right to deny your daughter the chance of proper treatment.'

This was treading on Jacka's corns. 'Who's no right?' he shouted. 'I've a right to do what I will with my own. Don't forget that, surgeon.'

'Jacka, please!' said Mrs Hoblyn.

'Hold your clack, woman!'

'I'll *not*!' said Polly, standing up to him for once. 'Dr Enys is doing his best, and takin' pains, and that's more'n have ever been done for my girl before. You ought to be *shamed*, turning on him like this!'

Dwight caught sight of Charlie at the door, and some expression on his face made Dwight feel that the little sailmaker was enjoying the scene. For some reason he didn't want Rosina cured. Was it because his own suit would then be less hopeful?

Dwight was in time to step in front of Jacka as he made a movement towards his wife. It looked as if there might be a scuffle, but Jacka gave way. As usual his anger was short-lived, and suddenly it changed its direction, towards the man who had primed it.

'Get out of the room,' he bawled at Charlie. ' 'Twill be time enough to come in 'ere when you're wed to my daughter and not before!'

Nevertheless, as Dwight took his leave he knew that his next visit would be very much on sufferance, and he would have to produce some result soon or admit failure.

The next Tuesday was the first warm day of the delayed summer. The toe of England, eddying along through cold and cheerless days, had suddenly and at last reached warmer water. Even at seven, which was the hour he had agreed to meet Caroline, the air was gentle and mild.

She always kept him waiting, but this time less long than usual. They cantered away from the gates of Killewarren in the early sun, and she suggested they should turn south, among trees long held in bud but now a sudden full brilliant green. She seemed to know her way.

When they had gone about four miles, she turned up a lane which petered out into a clearing azure with bluebells and she said: 'Let's get down, shall we, Dwight. I want to talk, and it's not easy on a nag.'

He dismounted at once and tried to help her, but she slid off as nimbly as a boy and laughed at him.

'Let's sit over here. It's good to be idle sometimes. Or *I* think so. Perhaps you feel always you should be tending someone.'

'Not always. Not now.'

They sat on a green mound punctured with rabbit holes, and Caroline picked a bluebell and swung it idly to make the bells quiver.

'I'm returning to Oxfordshire, Dwight.'

Something lurched inside him. 'When?'

'On Friday's coach. I shall be in Uncle William's bosom by Monday.'

'What has made you decide to go?'

'Oh, I didn't decide. Uncle Ray is very angry with me about my treatment of Unwin, and he thinks I shall be better banished from this place altogether.'

Dwight looked at her. Her wide eyes were contemplative, narrowed with the sunshine; the bright light brought extra colours to them, greys and flecks of hazel and deeper greens.

'I don't know what to say. I thought – I hoped you'd be staying.'

'I hoped I'd be staying too.'

Overhead a blackbird was chattering. 'When d'you expect to come again?'

'At Uncle Ray's invitation? Oh, that's very doubtful. He no longer approves of me or of my doings. And I suspect that someone has told him of my morning rides with his physician.'

'It's understandable then that he wants to send you away.'

'Why?' she asked provokingly.

'If you lower yourself by being seen about with Dr Enys, and not even a groom in attendance, it will be Mr Penvenen's first duty to come between you and your indiscretion.'

Caroline threw away her bluebell. 'So you agree with Uncle Ray. You think I should better be kept out of harm's way until I am safely married.'

'If I were your uncle . . .'

'But since you're not my uncle?'

Dwight got up. 'What do you expect me to say?'

She leaned back on her elbows. 'I should have expected you to say, no.'

'And so should I like to. You know, Caroline, without the need of words to colour it or make it more explicit, that I – that I . . .'

After a minute Caroline said: 'Sit down, Dwight. We can't talk if you stride about.'

He stopped and sat again, his knees in his hands, a little away from her, frowning, ill at ease, deliberately not looking at her.

She said: 'Tell me, Dwight, I never know; there are two men in you: the strong, confident, impatient one, that so often goes with you in a sick room; and the oh-so-much younger, nervous, susceptible one that often rides with me. Which of them is it, do you suppose, that cares for Caroline Penvenen and grieves when she goes and thinks of her in her absence?'

A rabbit scampered across the greensward and ducked quickly into a hole. Dwight said: 'Questions are always directed at me. Perhaps I'll face yours if you face mine. How much are you concerned for the answer?'

'You ask a great deal.'

'No more than you ask of me.'

'Oh, yes, I think it is.'

Dwight watched her fingers stroking the fold of her skirt. 'Very well, then. I'll answer yours first. There are no two men in me but only one –

and that one thinks of you continuously so that the image of you is never absent. But . . . what you complain of is not to be wondered at. Money was never plentiful for me, and studying took all I had. There was no time for drawing rooms or polite talk. I was not brought up to know the right addresses to pay beautiful women. I hardly ever met women – except as cases. As cases I know them well. So when I have dealings with people now, I differ with the dealings. If you come to me with a sore throat or a bad knee, you are a patient and I know you well. I know what to do and I do it. And you think, that man has confidence. But if I meet you in a drawing room, you're not a patient but a woman, someone whose moods and manners I've never learned to understand. I don't know the right prescription for gallantry: I never had leisure to learn it. I don't know how to flatter you, and if you laugh at me – as you not seldom do – I grow more tongue-tied each minute; and when you sharpen your wits on me, I feel a dullard and a clod. There's the explanation of it all. What I feel for you as a person doesn't waver between strength and weakness; it only wavers between hope and despair!'

She had stopped looking at him and was staring across at the other edge of the glade. The curve of her throat gave him pleasure and pain. As he explained himself he had gained in confidence.

He said at last: 'And you?'

She smiled a little and shrugged. 'You want me to answer your question now?'

'Yes.'

'Perhaps this is our last meeting, so perhaps I can. Poor Dwight, have I laughed at you so often? Have I shown such perfect confidence and poise? You flatter me, you truly do. What elegance I must display! How graciously I've been taught. . . .'

'I wasn't criticizing you.'

'I'm sure you would not dare. But let me explain *my* self. You say you spent all your time learning to be a physician, and so had no time for the formal courtesies. I'm sorry for you. Dear, dear, I am. But do you know what I have spent my time learning to be? Why, an heiress, of course.'

She leaned over on her elbow and looked at him. Her auburn hair, tied with a ribbon at the back, lay on her shoulder.

'An heiress must learn *all* the courtesies. She must learn to draw and paint and play a musical instrument even if she's tone-deaf and only makes horrid noises. She must know French and perhaps a little Latin; she must understand how to carry herself and how to dress and how to ride and how to receive the compliments of her suitors. The one thing she never learns is anything about the successful marriage she is being prepared for. So you see, dear Dr Enys, it would not be surprising if she also gave the impression of being two persons and with some higher justification than you. You say you don't know how to pay compliments to women or how to behave in the best manner. But at heart you must know women very well. How different in my case. I don't know men at all. I'm expected to be in love at the touch of a hand or at a prettily turned compliment. But until I marry – if my dear uncles have their way – I shall know nothing of what a man is really like.' She paused and straightened up. 'From hearsay, I know what happens when people sleep together. It does not sound excessively genteel. One can take a risk in the gavotte and come to no harm. One should be a little more careful, I fancy, before choosing a bed partner for the rest of one's days.'

There was a long silence. The confession had moved Dwight in a new way. It was a new Caroline he suddenly saw – not supremely sure of herself and contemptuous of his efforts to please, but as unsure in her own way as he was, and hiding her unsureness behind a mask of laughter and ridicule. He was suddenly no longer infatuated but deeply in love.

'And Unwin?'

'Unwin was a suitor ready made. He came with all the possible recommendations. And there was no lack of confidence within him, Dwight. He seemed to think I should be flattered at the idea of marrying a seat in Parliament. Sometimes I caught him looking at me, and then I knew that he was interested in my money first, my body second, but myself, for myself, little at all.'

'And I?'

Caroline smiled at him queerly.'It is not very easy to say this to your face, is it? When we first met in Bodmin and quarrelled, I thought, there is a man who . . . And again when you came to examine my throat. It was not that I *liked* you, it was that I felt——' She sat up. 'No, I can't tell you. Let's go.'

'Tell me.'

'I don't know what I feel for you – there that's the truth. Now go away.'

She got to her feet and moved a step towards her horse, but he jumped up and barred her way. 'You must tell me, Caroline.'

She flared at him, but he caught her wrist and held it. She said: 'Well you should *know* without being told. I wondered what it would be like to be kissed by you, whether I should like it or hate it, whether it would feed or kill my interest in you. But I didn't know and I haven't known and I shan't ever know – and now it does not matter, because I'm going away. Oh, there have been other men who've attracted and *plenty* more who will! But I shall not marry the first of them nor the second. In October——'

But she said no more. He put his hands on her elbows and pulled her against him and kissed her on the cheek and then on the mouth. After a moment her hands gripped his shoulders tight, not pulling him closer but slightly pushing him away, as a woman will whose critical mind is aware that she has got only what she asked for. They stood there so long that a chaffinch fluttered down and stayed pecking at the grass until one of the horses shuffled and frightened it off.

At last a flight of rooks cawing and settling in the trees separated them. There was a curious strained silence when they broke. Dwight was out of breath and he thought Caroline was too.

He said: 'And now no doubt you hate me.'

'No doubt I hate you.'

'And will be glad to go, cured of your curiosity.'

'You'd best,' she said, 'you'd best help me on my horse – if we're to get back.'

He moved to bend to make a step for her foot, but at the first contact of her skirt he straightened and she was in his arms again. They reeled against the horse, which shied and whinnied; a tree came up against them, and she leaned her back against it as he kissed her again, more deliberately this time.

Already the sun was higher than it should have been. This time he really helped her to mount, and then he climbed up on to his own horse, and the soft morning breeze wafted on their faces.

Their horses were ready to move off, but neither of the riders made any sign.

'When will you be back?' said Dwight.

'When I choose.'

'You'll write?'

'If you wish me to.'

He made a gesture of hopelessness. Did she want reassurance of *that?* 'If you come back . . .' he began.

'It will be the same over again? But in October there will be one change.'

'What is it?'

'I shall be twenty-one. Uncle Ray can do nothing to prevent me from returning to this district after October the twenty-sixth.'

They moved off slowly out of the glade, and nothing was left but some hoof prints and a few broken bluebells to mark the emotion which had flared there.

Chapter six

THE FINE WEATHER did not last, and June ended wet, to be followed by a wetter July and August. The rain beat upon the crops endlessly, flattened them, and turned them black. High winds swept the county, and the sun drifted pale and lost across the sky among the intermittent storms.

In the cobbled streets of Paris new and strange terrors stalked. The eruption which had cracked the surface of the continental despotisms had suddenly festered and turned in upon itself. Hopelessly menaced from the east, tottering to its fall, it was pulling down upon itself the whole structure of civilized society. In this last phase of *felo-de-se* no infamy was too bad. News of the butchery of three hundred priests was followed by stories of children playing with heads and four days' continuous slaughter of the packed prisons. Men whispered of the Princess Lamballe torn limb from limb, her head stuck on a pike; judgment pronounced by the mob and those found guilty cut obscenely into pieces on the spot among the corpses already piled; the prisons no sooner empty than filled again.

Mr Trencrom, keeping up his illicit traffic in spite of politics and the weather, reported that Mark Daniel was no longer in Cherbourg but had moved farther along the coast; they hoped to get in touch with him on the next trip. At Wheal Grace the excess of outgoings over revenue was enough to depress the most obstinate mind; and every inch of rain that fell added to the cost of fuel.

In August, Caroline Penvenen wrote to Dwight Enys:

Dear Dwight,

I am not a prisoner in a tower guarded by a wolf, but in order to write to you and see it posted before Uncle William's sultry eye falls on it is no mean Achievement. Your last letter I snatched away from under his very hand and in the nick of time; so when you reply to this pray direct it care of Mistress Nancy Aintree at the Black Dog, Abingdon, where I can redeem it at my leisure. Never have I known a month so long as this; its first fifteen days have seemed like thirty; my adolescence dies hard. How is your Ross Poldark, does his mine prosper and his cousin-in-law continue to eye him acquisitively? How are all your patients and especially the pretty one with the bad knee? Is her father still suspicious of you? I don't wonder. Can you recommend me some genteel, not unpleasant Malady which

I may take leisure to develop between now and October the twenty-sixth?

Oxford has many miserable French refugees about its closes: aristocrats with powdered wigs and holes in their stockings. They paint a picture of streets running with gore; I wonder if they overcolour, the more to excite our pity. Uncle William entertains them, but when they have gone he grunts, 'A few more heads and it would have been the easier for us!' You see now where I come by my Sensibility. The Penvenen family has no equal for it.

Dear Dwight, I wonder if you truly miss me, or if I am like a recurrent fever that enters your Veins, creating a hectic flush of excitement and leaving you wasted and tabid after I am gone? I know I should leave you alone, I really do, but I cannot suppose myself strong enough for such Resolution. My first small experience of you, I must confess though it's unmaidenly, was endurable, so that it's not too much to suppose a second would be the same. Between now and October I will try to get into some flirtation here, partly so that when my birthday comes Uncle William will the more readily see me gone, and partly so that when I come down I may have some surer grounds for comparison.

This I think you are unlikely to approve at first thought; yet I know you will not really wish to deprive me of what modest experience I may be able to gain which will help to make me a Woman of discrimination.

Believe me,
Your sincere friend,
Caroline Penvenen

In early September, a small new lode was found at Wheal Grace bearing better results than the old ones. But the discovery could only postpone the evil day, not prevent it. Ross and Francis still spent two days a week in the old upper levels. Lack of air became one of the worst obstacles, for most of the old air shafts had been filled in. In other places the roof had fallen, and one had to choose whether to abandon the search in that direction or to bring out workers to dig or blast a way through.

On the fifteenth of September, Ross and Francis had arranged to meet Zacky Martin and Jope Ishbel and to make some final investigations. They spent the morning blasting and trying to drain the old work, which was out of range of the engine. At noon Zacky went, and an hour later the cousins came up and changed out of their streaming things and walked down to Nampara for dinner. Ross found a letter waiting for him. Usually the man who brought the weekly paper carried the letters, but this had been delivered by a journeyman draper who called to see Demelza in the hope of tempting her to buy. The letter was from his friend and banker, Harris Pascoe.

Dear Captain Poldark,

I have not had the pleasure of seeing you for some months; and I should be glad to receive a call from you to sign your account with us, when it is convenient to you.

This letter, however, is of another matter, of which I have some knowledge though personal to yourself. When the Carnmore Copper Co. failed in '89 and you found events pressing you to discharge certain debts I believe you raised a loan of £1,000 from Mr Notary Pearce at an abnormal rate of interest. This loan, I have always understood from you, was in the form of a second mortgage on your house and land, of which this Banking House holds the first mortgage.

As you know, I rarely stir from my home; but much information comes to me unsought and I have heard recently that this loan was not in fact raised upon a second mortgage but was in the form of a Note of Hand or a Promissory Note. Pray tell me if this is so, because the Bill – if it is yours – is no longer, I am told, in Mr Pearce's hands but has found its way into the possession of Mr Cary Warleggan.

Your relationship with the Warleggans is your own concern, and I should not wish to intrude on it; but if it is what I suppose it to be, then I should not be astonished at your receiving notice at any time that the Bill must be immediately repaid. I do not know how your venture is prospering or whether you have been able to set aside any considerable sum to meet such an emergency, but as your friend I thought it my duty to tell you what I had learned.

Call in when next you are in town: we should be glad to have you dine or sup with us.

Yours etc.,
Harris Pascoe

At dinner Ross had little to say. Demelza sensed that the bad news, whatever it was, involved the Warleggans – Ross had a special face for them – but her pride would not let her ask when Francis was there. When the meal was near its end Ross said: 'I'll not be able to go down with you this afternoon. This letter calls me to Truro.'

'But you were there yesterday,' Francis objected. 'Can't this wait awhile?'

'No. I'm sorry. No.'

'You'll be back tonight?' said Demelza.

His eyes met hers over Francis' head. 'I'll try. But late. Don't wait up.'

She watched him as he left the room to change. She stayed talking with Francis; but when Ross came down, she slid out of the room and stood with him at the front door waiting for Gimlett to bring the mare.

Ross put his hand on her shoulder. 'I don't want to explain now. The letter was from Harris Pascoe – certain things I had overlooked. I'm going to see him, that's all.'

She looked up into his face. 'Bad, Ross?'

'Not good. But I shall know more tonight.'

'You'll not be in trouble today?'

'Should I be likely to be, with Harris Pascoe?'

'Not if you stay closeted with him. But there are others you might chance to meet.'

He smiled grimly. 'The weather is cold enough for November. Go in now and talk to Francis. Have you noticed how fond of our house he is become since the mine opened? He's as much here as at his own home.'

'I've noticed.'

'Go in and give him another glass of port and take one yourself.'

'I dare not before supper or I should tope all day. About this letter——'

But Demelza was interrupted by the arrival of Gimlett leading Darkie. Ross kissed her on the cheek and mounted and rode off up the valley. It seemed to his wife that the clouds were so low he was overtaken by them and half shrouded in them before he was lost to view.

When she went in, Francis had risen from the table and was sitting by the fire she had lighted an hour ago.

'No, don't get up,' she said. 'Ross bade us finish the port, but I can't take it myself, not so early; I'd do no work for the rest of the day else.' She set the decanter with his glass on a table beside him and took a seat opposite, stretching out her scarlet slippers to the warmth. 'In a minute I must go see if Jeremy is happy. He never takes his dinner so kindly from Mrs Gimlett as from me. Did you have no good fortune this morning, Francis?'

'We've chosen the most barren piece of land in the Duchy, I believe.'

'And the lowest levels?'

'A venture of faith without good reason behind them. Perhaps they'll succeed, because reason certainly has failed. . . . Strange, Ross having to go in to Truro again. Can it be something to do with the Warleggans?'

She looked at him in surprise. 'I don't know. But I wondered the same. Always when there is a hint of trouble one wonders if it is the Warleggans at the root of it.'

'Or Francis,' said Francis. 'There was a time when I was at the root of it along with George.'

'Oh, I do not think so,' she said quickly. 'That time has gone anyhow.'

'That time has gone. But I don't forget it. At least I do not forget one thing.'

'I think I will go and see for Jeremy.'

'No.' He hesitated, rubbing his hand on the chair. 'No, I have long wanted to tell you this. It must come sometime. . . . Years ago——'

'This is best not started, Francis.'

'Years ago – it would be August of '89 – when the copper smelting company was fighting for its existence – George came to see me one evening. It was the night Verity had left. I blamed you bitterly for her marriage – for everything. In a sudden impulse of anger I gave off information to George which enabled him to put pressure on the share-holders of the company to withdraw their support. That is the one thing I cannot get over or forgive myself. . . .'

Demelza got up. 'Why d'you insist on saying this to me – now?'

'Because for long enough I have been facing up to it. I cannot go on accepting your friendship, sitting like a stray dog at your fireside, with this not completely cleared up between us. The more our friendship has become of value, the less can it be left as it is. I suspect that Ross already knows the worst – but he won't let me tell him in so many words, he heads me off, and at the last I turn coward and let the matter drop. And so it rests.'

Somewhere at the back Garrick was barking; he had been shut out and resented it. Demelza did not speak. Francis got up, put his hand over hers for a minute, and turned towards the window.

Demelza said in great distress: 'It was such a thing to do to us. Had you no other way of hurting Ross?'

'An angry impulse – and then it's too late. But I don't begin to make excuse. You also knew?'

'Yes – partly. But – but to hear it spoken outright . . .'

Francis looked sick. 'You can't rebuild a friendship by ignoring what has destroyed it. I had to tell you. I'll go now.'

'No, wait. Ross is right, isn't he?'

'Not in this.'

'Yes, in this. For if we break now, we shall injure each other the more. And the copper smelting could never have prospered, Francis, we know that. Even the Warleggans when they took it over could not make it pay. Sir John Trevaunance is selling the machinery.'

'Do you excuse a murder because the victim was dying anyhow?'

'Not excuse it, no. But I'll not condemn to order neither. Does Elizabeth know?'

'Does she know what I did? No. It doesn't concern her at all. Except that she does not understand my worst antagonism for George Warleggan.'

After a long silence she said: 'You – haven't finished your port.'

'No? . . . All I've finished is our friendship – which I prized, though you may doubt it.'

'I don't doubt it, Francis, but I doubt if you have finished with it. One bad thing does not outweigh many good. 'Tis the balance that counts.'

'It did not count with me that night.'

'So ever after you regretted it. Should you wish me to make the same error?'

'Yes.'

'Well, then, I shall not.'

'Not even to please me?' said Francis.

'Not even to please you.'

'I don't wonder,' Francis said, 'that Ross loves you. For I could do so myself.'

She glanced at him quickly, soberly, then bent and put another billet of wood on the fire. 'Do you suppose he still does?'

'Ross? Of course. Why, what did you think?'

'I believe he loves Elizabeth better.'

When she stood up, neither of them spoke for some moments.

He said: 'Well, if this is the day of confidences, may I tell you something about yourself, Demelza?'

'Of course.'

'You have one failing, and that is you don't think enough of yourself.'

'Oh, I think very well of myself, Francis. You would be surprised.'

'I'd be surprised at nothing you think or do except that. You came here as a miner's daughter, married into this ancient derelict family, took its standards as your own. So you mistake your own value, your own vitality, even your value to Ross. There are two qualities in blood, Demelza. There's the quality of family and the quality of freshness. Ross was a wise man when he chose you. If he's as sensible as I think he is, he'll realize it. If you're as sensible as you ought to be, you'll make him.'

Demelza's eyes were warm. 'You're very kind.'

'*Kind*. . . . You see. There you go.'

'Well, are you not? I think so. But Francis, 'tisn't so easy as you think. I have to compare against your wife, who's so lovely – an' has breeding as well. And not only that. She was Ross's first love. How do you compete with perfection?'

'I don't believe Ross is so silly. I think . . .' He stopped. 'I believe that a greater regard for yourself, a greater personal independence on your part . . . Now I sound disloyal to Ross – but it's true. If you look on his feeling for Elizabeth as something unreal, and by opposing to it your own warm blood and your own good sense . . . How can she stand against those?'

'But Elizabeth is – far from lacking in warm blood herself.'

Francis again did not reply for a minute or two. 'It's not my wish to speak against Elizabeth now; but whatever she lacks or has, she lacks perfection. Every human being does. Indeed, knowing you even so little – and noticing the effect you have on other men – I should have thought you quite capable of holding Ross at your side when you want to, if you're so minded.'

She glinted a half smile at him. 'I may not say you're kind, so I'll say thank you.'

'I can't answer for another man – and yet I'm pretty sure. . . . Get rid of the notion that someone has done you a favour by taking you into our family.'

She stood quite still, thoughtful, young, made a wry mouth. 'I will think over it all, Francis. I believe it will make company for me for the rest of the afternoon.'

'Think over the first part too.'

'No. Not that.'

'Yes, that.' He bent and kissed her cheek. 'For we can none of us separate ourselves from the consequences of our behaviour. I have been trying to for long enough.'

It was beginning to rain again as Francis walked back to the mine. The reaction from clearing his unquiet mind to Demelza had left him more at peace with himself than for a long time. He had spoken on impulse, but the impulse had been part of a long-standing desire to tell her, to put himself straight not only with her but with his own conscience. Her reception of the news, its natural healthiness, had made him feel better about it all. Her attitude and Ross's, he felt, excused him nothing, but it made possible a continuance of their friendship with a new honesty on his side.

He went into the changing shed of the mine and picked up a few of his belongings. He had come this far almost without thinking. His horse was in the Nampara stables; he had had no intention of going down the mine again. But the shed was empty; and when he got inside, the thought came to him that the last thing he wanted was to go home.

His own house depressed him; Elizabeth depressed him. He knew that this happier mood would go quick enough; for the moment he could not bear to part with it. He began to slip on the old drill trousers and the woollen coat.

There were few people about in the rain. In the engine house one of the Curnow brothers was tending the great pump as it quietly sucked and slithered. He touched his cap to Francis as he came in, and moved round to meet him, ducking under the great beam as it swung easily down.

'Going b'low by yourself, sur? Thur's Ned Bottrell outside could go along of ee.'

'No, I'm all right. I shall do no more blasting but shall pick over the stuff that has come down.'

A minute later Francis was climbing down the ladder of the main shaft. This shaft had originally been the lode from which the mine had begun; so it did not go straight down but at a sharp inclination as the lode had run and as it had been mined. At the third platform and the two-hundred-and-fortieth rung he stepped off into the thirty-fathom level. All this part of the mine was now deserted. The rest of the workers were below.

On his way to the piece of ground they had been blasting this morning, he squeezed through narrow clefts where there was barely room for his pick, scrambled across heaps of rubble with echoing caverns as high as cathedral transepts, skirted great pits falling away into the depths of the earth, climbed up and up where the old miners had followed a lode on its underlie; finally he reached the underground shaft or little wind as it was called – with the ruins of the old windlass still beside it – and slithered down the shaft, as if down the chimney of a house, to the big narrow slit of a gunnies where they had been this morning.

Francis saw that the water at the bottom had gone down a foot since they left, the result of their blasting, but it was evidently not yet finding its way to the sump of the mine.

The air was close and bad here, and his only light, from the hempen candle in his hat, flickered smokily over the scene. He worked for half an hour cleaning the rocks from the mouth of the tunnel, but no more water seemed to be entering it. Not only the air but the water was warm, and after a while he swung himself up into another excavation about six feet above water level. He found that, instead of being shallow as it appeared from below, it turned sharply and increased in height so that he was able to stand upright.

Interested, he followed it for about a hundred feet, scraping here and there at the slimy walls, moving on until he came to a place where the old men had found the lode again and had left an arch of it to support their tunnel. Here they had worked downwards, in what was known as a winze, and here also it seemed this morning's gunpowder had had some effects, for the rocks were dripping and he could hardly keep his feet as he picked his way round the edge to another tunnel opposite.

This tunnel meandered on for a matter of a hundred yards; but then the air began to get fouler, and he turned back. As he did so, a flicker of his candle found some answering glimmer in the rock. He bent and rubbed with his finger. Here was the coppery green of metal-bearing ground.

The old men had missed it or had passed on. It might well be that their reasons were adequate. There had been other such places. One could not be sure of anything till one had picked away a few pieces, weighed them in the hand, examined in a better light the quality of the ore.

He needed his pick, which he had left in the big gunnies. A quarter of an hour's work here . . . If it looked like ore-bearing rock of any promise, he would carry a half-dozen specimen lumps up to grass.

Luck if after all this time . . . While Ross was away and he down here alone! Silly to speculate, to imagine; it had happened before, the expectation and the disappointment.

He stumbled back as far as the winze and stopped to gain a breath or two of better air and to wipe the sweat off his face. Very hot. If this could be, it would give him not only a fresh entitlement to Ross's friendship but to his own self-respect.

He moved cautiously round the edge of the winze; and as he did so, his boots suddenly slipped on the slimy surface. He twisted sharply to save himself, slithered down the slope, bumping his head and shoulders, trying to clutch, to distribute weight. Then in horror he fell, into water, plunging into it, coughing, choking, smothering in foul water; to breathe, to suffocate; he came up in pitch-darkness, treading water, floundering in search of some rock to save him.

He'd never been a swimmer; his best a dozen strokes. His clothes kept him up, spreading out like a tent; then the water seeped in; they began to clog, to drag. His flailing hands found the wall and he clutched at it.

Although he'd fallen clear, he'd thought to find the wall so sloping that he could crawl out. Not so. He kicked with his toes to get footholds that instantly slipped, clawed with fingernails, barked his knees, hit his face against the rock. He'd slid down the slope into another underground shaft. The fall had been short, but he'd no true idea how far the water was from the top of the shaft.

Cough foul water out. Heavy boots dragging down, drowning in futile darkness, deep in the earth away from the comfort and the voices of men. His fingers found a hold. . . . Slowly, with infinite effort, he pulled his body a few inches out of the water.

While his fingers held, he could think: might be a ladder still in the wall strong enough to bear him. For that, when he'd recovered, he must gather the courage to flounder round the shaft. It was bigger than the other one but could still only be small; enough for a ladder and a bucket they usually said.

What might have been triumph had suddenly become disaster. Two years ago in Bodmin he had put a pistol against his head and pulled the trigger. It had not gone off because the powder was damp. Then he had wanted to die. Death now would be the crowning irony.

He had been trying to kick his boots off; his fingers aching, change hands; one boot off. Lighter, lighter; this old woollen coat. He had stopped coughing; lungs free at least. To shout? As well shout in your coffin with the sexton planting the flowers.

A surprise for you, Ross. Feel this piece. Not just killas, is it? And here's some crushed under the hammer. I thought I'd do it while you were away. At least it's a justification at last of your faith in me. Henshawe can't believe his eyes. . . .

The other boot off. Struggle out of the coat. Hot down here. Like a rat in a bucket. He'd watched one once, but had had to go away before it died. Persistent things, clinging to life. More persistent than he.

This was the moment to try to swim round. Why had he never been confident in the water? As much as he could do to *force* himself to let go.

Round he went, kicking out ineffectually with his legs but keeping just afloat. Quite big, probably seven feet across; perhaps not a shaft but just a plot, used when ore was being mined quicker than it could be got to the surface.

No ladder, and no certainty he could find the fingerhold again. Panic gripped; a great shout that went echoing round and round in the confined space. Noise was comforting, as light would have been comforting.

He missed the fingerhold but instead found a nail. There had been a ladder, but it was gone. Try to find a foothold in some niche below; none. . . . Nor anything to reach above. A rusty six-inch nail was a better fingerhold than the one lost. Could hold on quite long time. And it might *be* a long time.

Trying to keep the fear in hand, to fight away the loneliness and the darkness, begin to work it out. Down about four. The mine worked three cores, the next changing at ten. If it was five now, that might mean nearly *five* more hours before anyone saw his clothes in the changing shed or remarked on them or began to ask. Ross had gone to Truro, could not be back till late. Demelza – what reason would she have? His horse in the Nampara stables. Any time she might notice this herself or later Gimlett would say . . . But hours perhaps before they did anything.

His own home. Elizabeth anxious? Not until seven.

Any reckoning in hours. And even if there was an alarm, the search would take time. His mind travelled back along the twisting dark tunnels to the main shaft – all the way he had come, all the great mass of rock that lay between him and the daylight and the air. The atmosphere in this pit was choking and foul. Hours of patience, hours of strain lay ahead. His fingers would give way, he would *drown* long before help came.

Fear his greatest enemy. Darkness the other traitor. Light had left the world. Nothing shone, no shine, no sleek water, no metal or stone. He'd still little idea how far below the rim of the pit he was; but the grim thought came that if they had not blasted this morning and allowed some of the water to drain, this pit might have been full and left him no harder task than clawing a way back up the greasy winze.

He changed hands for the twentieth time and as he did so the nail moved. Fear grip your throat, begin to shout, at the top of your voice, over and over again. Help, help, help, I am lost in the very deeps of the earth. Not eight feet underground but two hundred; blind already but not deaf, shuddering in the warm water, fingers burning, last grip loosening; one nail, one rusty nail.

He tried to make himself let go, to splash around again in the darkness; he might have missed something last time, some better handhold; but he no longer had the courage to try; he might never find this place again.

Time passed. Try to count. Sixty minutes make one hour. He reckoned three hours had passed. Must be after eight now. Someone must come soon. They would of course come straight to the place where they had been blasting this morning. A drip of water somewhere, and this his ears again and again magnified into rescuing footsteps. To keep his sanity he counted up to two hundred and then shouted and began again. But he was getting lightheaded. And the strain on his arms. Cramp seized him often, his legs were leaden, already swollen and dead. Sometimes he forgot numbers and talked with people who came close to him in the water. His father, gouty and eruptive and purple. 'Francis, Francis. Where are you, boy?' Aunt Agatha, not as she now was but younger and severe, dandling him on her knee. He was running across the sands of Hendrawna with Ross after him, their feet glinting in the sun.

He began to count again; and then suddenly heard a crash of splintering wood and looked up and saw Ross kneeling at the edge of the shaft reaching down a hand to help him out. Ross said sourly: 'My God, why can't you learn to swim!' and Francis reached up a despairing hand to grasp the help. Their fingers seemed to touch, and then a foul swirl of liquid closed over Francis' mouth and nose and he kicked and struggled to get to the surface again: he had lost grip of the nail, had nearly lost life in his dream of salvation, only death had wakened him; only death; in time the automatic responses of the body. So it would be every time, every time until the last.

Try to reassure yourself. This time tomorrow. . . . In a few weeks you will be able to laugh about this experience. Or be dead. . . . This time tomorrow between comfortable sheets, recovering. Or a swollen corpse covered with a sheet in the great hall of Trenwith waiting an early burial.

His breath was going. That was the worst. If he shouted now, he had to suck at the air for half a minute afterward to recover. By now it was well after ten. Somebody must come soon. He could not disappear without trace and cause no comment. Curnow had seen him come down. They would grow anxious. They would think. What were their brains *for!* Henshawe was often at the mine between five and six. Often he joined Ross and Francis to see how the work was going. *Not* today. Not of course today.

Francis let out a higher-pitched shout, much nearer a scream. He stopped, gasping at the air. The nail turned in his painful clutch. Any further movement and it would come out.

'Help, help!' he shouted. 'Help, help!' a dozen times, and a dozen times more. It went on and on and on, until the volume decreased and the breath in was as noisy as the breath out. Tears were running down his cheeks.

There's *reason* for me to live now! Oh, *God*, I don't want to die. . . .

At about this time Elizabeth closed the book in which she had been teaching Geoffrey Charles to read.

'It's time for your supper, my darling. Papa will be home soon, and you know he likes you to be in bed by seven.'

'Just this bit, Mummie.'

'No. You've had more than your share today.'

'Can I go out and play until Papa comes?'

'No, darling. You can play until your supper's ready. Don't be far away when I call you. . . . And put on your cap!'

Geoffrey Charles galloped from the room, and Elizabeth looked up at the clock. It was nearly half past six.

Chapter seven

Ross was back just before eight. He found Demelza upstairs repairing for the fifth time the curtains over the north windows of their bedroom. She hadn't heard him come.

'Why, Ross! You're earlier than I expected. Have you supped?'

'Sufficiently. What are you doing?'

'A little tear that Jeremy made this morning. He dearly likes something to cling to for support.'

'Soon you'll have made new curtains with your stitches.'

'Not quite so bad. What was in your letter?'

He sat in a chair and began to pull at his boots; then as she came over, he let her pull them off instead. It was a relic of their old days which for some reason she liked to preserve. While she was doing it, he told her what the letter said.

'And it was true, about the mortgage, I mean?'

He nodded. 'True enough. When I borrowed the money, my first concern was to get it; I didn't greatly care how. It was Pearce when I went to him who first spoke of a second mortgage. The next day he produced the money and I signed the paper for it. . . . I accepted this as a form of mortgage, though in fact it was a promissory note. I suppose I knew, but I paid no heed to it at the time. Nor should I have needed to if Pearce had kept possession of it, as any friend and honest man would. I went to visit him. D'you think me a bully, Demelza?'

'Were you rough with Mr Pearce?'

'I didn't put a finger on him, but I suppose I was rough in manner; I thumped his table and broke the lid of his snuffbox. He quivered like a jelly, all fat and no backbone; but the damage is done. The bill has been passed on as Pascoe said, and Cary Warleggan now possesses it. So we have to face that.'

'You didn't go to see *him*?'

'I called at his house, but he was away. I think it was the truth, for the blinds were down.'

'And what now, Ross?'

'The Warleggans can do nothing until November. Then they can give me a month to redeem the note. In December I must find fourteen hundred pounds or default.'

She put his boots beside the chair but remained kneeling, her elbows on his knees, looking not at him but into space.

'Can we borrow no money elsewhere?'

'I don't know.'

'What shall you do?'

'There are seven weeks before the notice can be given. I have Pascoe to thank for that. And four more after that before it takes effect.'

She did not much like the look on his face, and she wriggled her knees round and got up.

She said: 'Are you sure Cary will do this, will demand repayment?'

'Would you not if you felt as they do for me?'

'Have I ever seen Cary?'

'At that party. A man of fifty-odd with small eyes and an uncomfortable way of using them. George, though I detest him, has certain principles – at least I think so. Cary has none. He's the moneylender of the family, the scavenger. George is accepted in most circles of society. Soon he will be in all. That will impose some standards on him. Nicholas, his father, of course, is reputable enough. Uncle Cary is the best hated of them all.'

She shivered. 'I wish I could earn money, Ross. I wish I could help you in some way. All I do is – is mend your curtains and bear your child and see after the farm and cook your meals and——'

'I should have thought that one person's work.'

'But there's no *money* in it. Not even a gold piece. One thousand four hundred pounds! I'd steal it if I could, turn highwayman or bank thief! Harris Pascoe would never miss it. Why does he not *lend* it you?'

Ross looked at her gravely, wryly. 'This is a new phase. Always before you've been pressing me to keep within the law——'

He stopped as there was a knock on the door. It was Gimlett to say that Tabb was below and wanted to know if Mr Francis was still here.

'Here? Of course not.' Ross looked at Demelza. 'What time did he leave?'

'About an hour after you. He walked up to the mine. At least——'

'His horse is still here, sur,' said Gimlett. 'I give him his feed, but didn't think to tell mistress as I reckoned she'd know about it.'

Ross pushed past him and went downstairs. Tabb was standing in the hall. Tabb explained that Mrs Poldark had been getting anxious, so she'd sent him over just to make sure Mr Poldark was come to no harm. Usually, now the nights was drawing in, the squire belonged to be home by seven. Ross went round to the stables. Francis' horse was there right enough and looked up expectantly at the sound of footsteps.

Demelza had followed. Ross said: 'Did he not say anything when he left? Perhaps he's walked over to Mingoose House.' To Tabb he said: 'Ride to Mingoose House, will you. In the meantime I'll go to the mine and see how long he stayed there and in what direction he left.'

A new moon was out and the misty rain had cleared. Demelza walked with Ross, hopping now and then to keep up, though her own stride was long. The engine house was lit and there were lights in two of the sheds.

Ross went into the changing shed, where a lantern burned low. On a peg were Francis' ordinary clothes.

Outside, Demelza was thoughtful, waiting.

'I think he may be still here.'

'Here? But, Ross . . .'

They stared at each other for a moment; neither spoke.

Below ground eight hours was the usual core, but tending the engine twelve. This change was made at eight, and the elder Curnow was now in charge. His brother, he said, had told him nothing when he went off. As they were asking, Captain Henshawe came in and Ross explained the situation to him.

'Well, sur, he may be down there still, forgetful of the time; but I should not suppose so. Hold hard a minute, and I'll fetch a couple of men to go down with us.'

Demelza stood in the engine house. The curious slow, regular sucking motion of the great engine was like an animal gasping, a giant sea mammal newly landed, breathing out its life on the wet sand. A strange conviction of fatality had come on her. She had no reason for knowing, yet felt as if she knew.

Other men had come in now, and they watched Ross and Henshawe and Jack Carter and young Joe Nanfan climb into the bucket and lurch bumping out of sight. After they had gone, those that were left clustered in a self-conscious group; and she knew they would have been more at home if she had not been there. She, the miner's daughter become squire's wife, had more than the disadvantage of womanhood.

But she forced herself to go towards them and ask if none had seen Mr Francis this afternoon and if someone would go and knock up Daniel Curnow and find out what he knew.

Then came a long wait. Gimlett had stolen up from the house and stood beside her. 'The wind's cold, ma'am, shall I get ee a coat?' 'No . . . thank you.' It was not the cold of the night that she felt but an inner cold that no coat would cure. Tabb came galloping back. They'd not seen Mr Francis at Mingoose. 'You'd best go tell Mistress Poldark,' said Demelza. 'Very good, ma'am.' 'No, wait. Wait a little while.'

Looking back, Demelza could see the lights in Nampara, the one in their bedroom that she had left. Beyond it and to the right the sea, with a dagger of moonlight in the black heart of the water. 'We can none of us separate ourselves from the consequences of our own behaviour,' Francis had said. 'I have been trying to for long enough.'

One of the men returned from Dan Curnow's cottage. Curnow had seen

Mr Francis go down about four but had not seen him come up. He had not thought of mentioning it to his brother. Peter Curnow spat in disgust.

A few minutes later a miner came running up the ladder. It was Ellery, who was working on the sixty-fathom level. Some of them had been told and were helping with the search. Francis had not been found but his pick had, standing with the handle out of the water near where they had been blasting this morning.

Demelza looked at Tabb. 'I think you had best go fetch your mistress.'

It was Ross, carrying a lantern, who first swung himself up into the tunnel which Francis had followed. Like Francis he was surprised to see that the tunnel went on, and he beckoned Henshawe to follow him.

They were tired of shouting: their voices only beat back against them from the walls of rock or were thrown away in the echoing darkness. They reached the winze and tried to cross it, but Ross's foot slipped on the slimy rock and Henshawe had to catch his arm.

'Thanks. It's a place for——' Ross stopped and crouched on his heels and turned the light of the horn lantern down the winze. Just within sight was water, and floating on the water was a miner's hat. And there was something else there besides the hat.

'Have you your rope?'

'Yes. . .'

'Put it round my waist.'

He went down and found the body floating. Francis had been dead about an hour. In one of his hands, clutched so that they could barely unfasten it, was a rusty nail.

Book two

Chapter one

ON A LATE afternoon in mid-November 1792 a private coach was making its way at a fair pace along the main highway from Truro to the far west. A fine misty rain was falling, as always in that terrible year, and the woods which ran intermittently beside the road were already dark and vaporous. The road was in bad condition, potholed and rutted deep in mud; but the driver, who had not been this way before, kept his whip constantly flicking across his horses because full darkness was not far away and he did not like the look of the country they were passing through. His mistress had told him that they were nearly home, but women were unreliable in their estimates, as today's journey had proved; and in this wild county they would be a fat and easy prize for any highwayman who happened to be lurking near.

They had just emerged from one lowering copse whose branches nearly met overhead when his courage bumped into his boots at the sight of a man standing by a dismounted horse at the roadside. Coming across those wild and boggy moors this morning he had cursed himself for ever having accepted employment under a strongheaded, wrong-headed slip of a woman, and this was the outcome. He rose in his seat and lashed at the horses; but as they lurched forward, the coach splashed into a deep hole and dipped wildly and almost toppled him into the road. By the time they had gained a proper speed again they were past the horseman, who was only sufficiently interested in them to raise his head.

They were past him by a few dozen yards when a loud rapping caused the coachman to lift the hatch, and he heard his mistress telling him to stop.

'It's right enough, ma'am. No 'arm or damage done. The 'orses——'

'Stop, I tell you. That gentleman. I want to speak to him.'

Sulkily the driver brought the coach to a stop. Its back wheels cut and slithered in the mud, and the solitary rider, who had been attending to his own horse, again lifted his head. He was now too far behind to hear any of the conversation, but presently the coachman got down and came splashing gingerly back to him.

'Captain Poldark, sir?'

'Yes?'

'Mistress Penvenen, sir. Would like a word with ee.'

In the coach were two women, one a maid. Ross took off his hat and Caroline extended her green-gloved hand.

'You're late to be on this road, Captain Poldark. My coachman thought you were a highwayman.'

'If I were, I should choose a more opulent highway. One might wait here six nights in seven and not see a private carriage.'

'Oh, sir, I'm very poor,' said Caroline. 'But seriously, I thought you might be in trouble.'

'Thank you, it's nothing. My mare has cast a shoe.'

'Well that can be a trifle more than nothing. What shall you do, walk home? It's a fatiguing long way.'

'I can get her shod in Chasewater. You're just returning to Cornwall, Miss Penvenen?'

'As you see. Too early to be Santa and too late to be Guy. Why don't you share the coach to Killewarren and borrow one of my uncle's horses? We can have yours shod and send her over in the morning.'

Ross hesitated. He was tired and wet and depressed, and the suggestion was not a bad one. But he was a bit chary of this forward young woman.

'Thank you. Perhaps if I might come as far as you go on the Chasewater road. . . .'

'We turn off soon. Baker, will you see that Captain Poldark's mare is securely tied to the coach. And proceed slowly, please; you need have no fear of highwaymen now that we have captured one of our own.'

That this was just raillery the maid, Eleanor, seemed slightly to doubt, for when the coach began to move again she stared open-mouthed at the big man opposite, bent uncomfortably on his occasional seat, with his muddied boots and his pale, lidded eyes and the scarred side of his face towards her.

Caroline, perhaps herself a little surprised at the size of him in a confined space and not as much at ease as she wanted to be, changed her tone.

'I was greatly sorry to hear of your cousin's death. Uncle Ray is not prolific with his letters, but he wrote about that. It was a very tragical occurrence. It seems no time at all since we all met at the Trevaunance table.'

'It *is* no time at all. We miss him very much.'

'I hope it has not brought your mining venture to a stop. I – understand you and he were partners.'

'It goes on. We've been able to continue it.'

'Profitably?'

Ross met her candid gaze. 'Not profitably.'

'As yet, I suppose you would add. Uncle William was saying that if this war spreads it will help the price of metals. Is Francis' widow intending to live on in that big house alone?'

'Eventually, I think, her mother and father will live with her. But she is not alone. There is her son and her aunt and two servants. . . .'

'And how is Dr Enys?'

Well, at least she was not one to beat about the bush. 'As diligent as ever.'

'Only diligent?'

'It was not meant as a derogatory term.'

'Of course I should have known that,' said Caroline. 'The last time we met it was to form a common front on his behalf.'

'I do not think we shall need to be so ready in his defence now. Everyone then was accusing him of killing off old Ellery. Now they're loud in wonderment because he has cured a village girl of her lameness.'

Caroline lifted her face quickly. 'Rosina Hoblyn?'

'Oh, you know her?'

'By name. Dwight mentioned her. She is *cured*?'

'Cured. She walks as straight as you or I, and the villagers think he is a miracle worker just for a change.'

'How very diverting! And how did he come to perform it?'

'He has an explanation, but no one listens to it. Last Saturday he had fourteen lame people waiting outside his house.'

Caroline smiled and pushed away a strand of her hair, which today was tied with deliberate oversimplicity at the nape of her neck. The roof lantern, which had been lighted when Ross got in, swayed with the lurches of the coach, and her expression seemed to change among the changing shadows.

After they had turned off the main road, he said: 'What time is your uncle expecting you?'

'He's not expecting me.'

'Oh. . . . A sudden decision, I suppose——'

'Not a sudden decision on my part, Captain Poldark. One carefully prepared for. This coach, the coachman engaged, my luggage packed. But Uncle Ray has not invited me; and since we have come down probably faster than the post, I don't suspect he will have had any letter from Uncle William to warn him.' Seeing Ross's expression, she laughed. 'It's a way people have when they first become independent. You'll remember we discussed it at the Trevaunance party.'

So, thought Ross, she means to have Dwight if she can. Why did I get into this coach and accept a favour of her? To the devil with all women. And instantly, unbidden, his mind flashed away to that other woman, Elizabeth, frail in her grief and her black clothes, still out of his reach yet dangerously closer to him; his first love, and loving him – so she had said – depending on him now in all things; the contacts increased with the impediments half gone; she now half shareholder in the mine on Geoffrey Charles's, her son's, behalf; he the only near male relative, head of the Poldarks now and executor with Elizabeth of his cousin's will.

Francis' death had left an unexpectedly big gap in the life of the countryside. Duties and responsibilities had been expected of him which now devolved on Ross. Mr Odgers, the curate of Sawle-with-Grambler, came to Ross for everything, even seemed to expect Ross to share the family pew and the weekly victualling of the Odgers family. And another magistrate would have to be found. There had been a Poldark to do the job since the days of William and Mary. Could a man be invited to sit on the bench who before now had expressed his contempt of it? It was all very difficult.

In the coach silence had fallen. To-day Ross felt he had touched rock bottom in his fortunes and in his spirits. Yesterday he had received a formal notice from Cary Warleggan that the accommodations of the bill were to be withdrawn in four weeks' time, and to-day he had been making a last effort to find the money. Credit was tight everywhere, but that was not the main difficulty. The greatest obstacle was Wheal Grace. Everyone who knew anything knew that she was failing. You might loan a thousand pounds to a needy squire and take the risk for the sake of the interest. But no one would lend money to a man whose mine was on the point of foundering. If you did, you visualized your capital going down the common drain. That, no doubt, was one of the reasons Nathaniel Pearce had unloaded the bill, glad to be rid of it when its chances of redemption were small.

Ross would not altogether have blamed him had the thing gone to anyone but the Warleggans. But of course no one but the Warleggans would possibly have taken it. They didn't want the money, they wanted the man.

A week or so after Francis' death a small bunch of good ore had been found in the tunnel he had been exploring at the time, but that had been almost the extent of new discovery since September. Mark Daniel perversely had chosen this time to disappear into the maelstrom of France, and no one so far had traced him. In parts of England the blackened corn still lay in the fields. Miraculously preserved by the sloth of their enemies, the French had found fresh heart and fresh armies and last week had captured Brussels. The shadow of famine and of war on all men's minds.

The coach at last turned in at the gates of Killewarren, and the coachman steered a cautious way up the shrubby drive towards a welcome light above the front door. He had to ring three times before it was opened by a servant girl who said: 'Why, Mistress Caroline, good life, an' we was cleanin' your room only this morning. Why, ma'am, do ee come in. Is the master expecting you?'

Ross followed Caroline into the hall: it was a very ordinary house for so warm a man, shabbily genteel but no more; three candles in glass globes thinly lit the black polished oak cupboards, the marble busts at the foot of the narrow stairs. 'With your consent I'll not intrude on your uncle this afternoon. I know you'll be tired from your journey, and his pleasure at seeing you again . . .'

Caroline smiled at him as she unfastened the strings of her hat.

'Will not be so great as you predict,' she said quietly. 'So it would not be an unkind act if you came up while your saddle's changed. Do not fear you'll be detained overlong, for a glass of wine is all you'll get from him, if that. While I am here, he improves; but I've been gone some months and I expect he will have slipped back into the old ways.'

Demelza sent for Dwight about seven and, being free, he came straight over and examined Jeremy.

'It is the usual thing: a sore throat and a touch of fever. He is prone to this overheating.'

'Too prone,' said Demelza, allowing Jeremy his rather tetchy freedom. 'Every time it happen, I think of Julia and get in a fever myself. Julia never was like this; at least – not till the last time. . . .'

'It's a way some children have and some have not. But I'd like you to call me always, just in case. Ross is out?'

'. . . He went to Truro – on business – and then was to have gone on to Redruth to see Trevithick. Something is not quite right with the engine, though I think 'twould be all the same now if no one bothered.' Demelza swooped quickly to catch Jeremy as he lurched drunkenly across towards her. She looked up sidelong, experimentally, at Dwight, a curl falling across her brow as she did so. 'Do you think I coddle him, Dwight?'

Dwight smiled. 'Yes. But it's natural – and right. In three or four years it will be different——'

'I don't want to be like Elizabeth and Geoffrey Charles.'

'Don't worry on that score. Look at him already – twice the child he was a few months ago——' Dwight stopped. 'Is that Ross now?'

'I think so. He's long overdue.' Demelza went to the window and peered out. 'Yes. But on a strange horse. I hope there's been no mishap.'

For the moment she could not leave Jeremy; and when at last she got him into bed and went down, Ross was already in the parlour and insisting that Dwight should stay to supper. Dwight made several excuses, all of which were ignored; so smilingly he gave it up, and Mrs Gimlett laid a third place.

Ross said: 'We need a visitor, Dwight. We've been pretty much down these last days, and it's as much your duty to see after our moral welfare as our physical. If there's anyone with broken bones to-night, they'll trace you here quick enough; so set your conscience at rest.'

'My conscience is all right. But I'm sorry to hear of your condition.'

'I'll tell you more later. I have been trying to raise money all day, and it's a subject that can only decently be spoken of on a full belly.'

'I hope you've not sold Darkie,' Demelza said, 'for that would spoil my supper before it began.'

'No. . . . She cast a shoe near Stickler's Wood, and I was offered a lift in a private coach to Killewarren and so came home on a loaned horse.'

There was a sudden silence. Demelza raised her dark eyebrows. 'Killewarren? It was Mr Penvenen's private coach?'

'Mr Penvenen doesn't own a private coach,' said Dwight.

'It was Caroline Penvenen,' said Ross. 'She'd driven down from London – or Oxford, is it? Her uncle wasn't expecting her. Were you, Dwight?'

'Yes. . . .'

To fill the succeeding pause Demelza said: 'I expect she wanted to surprise her uncle. When was she last here, was it May or June? It must be strange to have two homes.' When neither man spoke, she leaned forward and snuffed one of the candles. 'Will they send Darkie over to-morrow, Ross?'

Ross said: 'There's no need to discuss it if you choose not, Dwight. But we're old friends, and sometimes it's good to have things out. She asked me how you were and said she hoped to see you before long.'

'How did her uncle receive her?'

'Not graciously. I think she was glad of me as a foil. But she's hard to withstand when she lays herself out to please – as perhaps you know – and he looked to be coming round when I left.'

Dwight's long, slight hands fumbled with his doily napkin. 'You're not merely old friends but my oldest and best. If good would come of discussing this – this between myself and Caroline – I'd gladly discuss it. But I see none. . . . Perhaps I owe you some explanation, and in that case——'

'You owe us nothing,' said Ross. 'But I'd be sorry to see a situation grow half-realized. You know how it is sometimes.'

'You mean, I know how it was last time. The dangers are different here, though, aren't they? Well, I confess I'm in love with Caroline, and we've written; and now she's here again, and for better or for worse, we shall be seeing each other soon. I have no money and she has a great deal, so the attachment . . . Do you dislike her very much?'

This was said to Demelza, and she was taken aback by it. 'No. Dwight. I don't know her except to exchange a few words, and you can't not like a person you don't know. I am not the best one to judge.'

'Nor I,' said Ross. But I believe she's altered my opinion of her to-day – and I'm at a loss to say why. Certainly not for the favour of a lift. . . .'

'There's a hardness to her,' said Dwight slowly. 'I'd be a fool to deny it. It's like a – a brittle shiny armour, and its use has been the same. There is so much else behind it. . . . In any case these things do not go by measure. The alchemy's too subtle to be weighed up.'

'Yes,' said Ross, thinking suddenly of Elizabeth, and, as if there were telepathy between them, Demelza looked at him and knew what he was thinking.

Dwight said: 'The attachment's bad, no doubt; but I can't shake or break myself of it. Perhaps she will be wiser. It's a discreditable situation which could come only to a weak man; a strong one would break the dilemma somehow.'

'The longer I live,' Ross said, pulling his brows together painfully, 'the more I distrust these distinctions between strong men and weak. Events do what they like with us, and such – such temporary freedom as we have only fosters an illusion. Look at Francis. Was there ever a sorrier or more useless end or one less deserved or dictated by himself, or more unfitted to the minimum decencies and dignity of a human being? To drown like a dog in a well, and for nothing – to miss help by the space of an hour – to go out from this room and walk over to the mine and within a short while to slip on a greasy floor and be dead, and for *nothing*.' Ross pushed back his chair in sudden vehemence. 'It is what I have always resented most in life: the wantonness, the useless waste, the sudden ends that make fools of us, that make nonsense of all our striving and contriving. . . . You've been with me in most of the worst of it, Dwight: Julia's death and much else. If you see a difference in result between any strength or weakness that's been shown, I confess you're cleverer than I am.'

Dwight did not speak, but after a minute Demelza said: 'Oh, yes, that's true, Ross. But is it all the truth? I feel that there are some things good which have come to us for our own striving. And though, for the whole, luck has been against us, sometimes it has moved for us and may yet do again. Wheal Grace is failing, but Wheal Leisure has prospered – and, if there was Julia, there is also Jeremy – and there was your acquittal from the trial; and – and much else besides.' She stared into the candle flame for a moment with a curiously blind stare, then blinked and was herself again. 'It may be that if on balance we have been unlucky, Dwight will not be so. There may *be* some happy way for him and Caroline, and a little patience will find it.'

In spite of a matter-of-fact tone, she spoke, Dwight thought, with a curious sense of fatality, as if she knew things had gone wrong for herself and could not now be righted. It was the first time he realized what Francis' death had meant to her, to them both, in terms of their own relationship.

Chapter two

NOVEMBER IS A bad month for secret assignments out of doors; but Caroline had hunted the country too often to be at a loss, and she sent a note to Dwight to meet her at the old mine at the edge of the wood near Bargus. When Dwight got there, his pulse quickened at the sight of a horse already tethered to a tree. He slid off his own horse, looped the reins over a stump, and went quickly into the old stone house. Caroline was crouching beside the open shaft; and as he entered, she threw a stone down and listened to its echoing fall.

She straightened up quite casually. 'No wonder there are so many illegitimate babies in Cornwall; it's so easy to be rid of them. I suspect that these old shafts are kept open for the purpose, Dwight.'

It was very shadowy in here and he could not see her expression, but he came over to her determined not to be put out of countenance, determined this time to play her at her own game.

'Not only babies but women, who spoil one's sleep, who interrupt one's work, who send unprincipled letters, who flirt and have no heart. It's a good and easy way of disposal, and who should be the wiser? Does anyone know where you've come?'

She stood balanced on the edge of the shaft as if challenging him.

'No one knows, Dwight; but I don't tremble with fear. Were my letters unprincipled? Did they spoil your sleep? Were they not a source of pleasure also? Be honest. Confess to me.'

Dwight put his hand on her elbow, drew her away from the edge, turned her towards him. They looked at each other, unfamiliars but friends. She lifted one eyebrow slightly and smiled. He bent forward and kissed her. Then they stood for a while in each other's arms while a gleam of sunshine fell through the ruined doorway and the only sound was the movement of their horses outside. It was a reunion from which obvious passion was absent.

'Your letters were pleasure and pain in equal halves, as no doubt they were meant to be. Do you like to torment those who love you?'

She looked at him closely, searchingly, renewing her own acquaintance. 'No. . . . Perhaps I like to torment myself. I don't know. I can't say. All I know is that I'm back, that my uncles are furious, that I'm my own mistress, that I've made an appointment with you, and that you have come. Just now it's uncomplicated – clear in my mind. Don't expect too much of me, Dwight. Don't press me too hard.'

'I love you,' he said. 'That's uncomplicated too. Whether for you this is just a sample of life to be taken and then conveniently forgotten——'

'No, it is not; and you know it is not. And that was only in a half of my letters or a third, and the nice parts you've wilfully overlooked. Anyway, I'm not used to writing love letters any more than I am used to being made love to. It is——'

'I hope your experiments in Oxfordshire were satisfactory.'

'Yes, *yes*. Delectable. Quite enchanting. So much so that I've hurried down here as soon as the lawyers agreed to release my money. . . .'

They talked on, aware of their temporary isolation and making the most of it, yet both knowing that secret meetings could not be secret for long. Convinced now of all that he needed to be convinced of, Dwight would have liked to face up to their difficulties at this very first encounter; but he sensed that Caroline was still groping her way towards an understanding of her own feelings. Until then one could only live for the day.

As the weather was lifting, they went out of the old ruin and she perched on a stone wall while he stood beside her.

'I met your Captain Poldark again,' she said. 'But of course he told you. The more I see of him the more I like him. I must confess that, if you want me to be honest.'

'You'll not make me jealous of him. I only wish his circumstances were happier.'

'Circumstances? Is it his cousin's widow who is the circumstance, or has he some other trouble?'

'Financial,' said Dwight, and hesitated. He'd no wish to betray a confidence; but some desire to turn her off the scent, to steer her away from asking him about the Elizabeth-Ross relationship, made him say more than he intended.

'I thought he looked a shade down-in-the-mouth when we met. And so you were having supper with his wife when he returned. Perhaps that's cause for jealousy on my part. Tell me, what's the hold she has on men? She's pretty enough, I grant, but so are others who get far less attention. Do you know the secret?'

'It's not a question of knowing a secret. It's just a question of knowing Demelza.'

'Is she the sort of woman that all men desire – except her husband? It so often happens. What an advocacy for married life! Don't you think I should be very ill-advised to marry, Dwight?'

'No, I don't think you would be ill-advised to marry, if you marry the right man.'

'Ah, the right man, of course.' She picked up two stones from the crumbling wall, weighed them in her palm, like subjects for discussion. 'But tell me what you have been doing yourself. I hear you've performed a miracle upon your little fisher girl and that she can now dance the cotillion. Is it really so?'

Remembering her earlier derision, he glanced quickly at her; but her face was serious enough. Then she met his gaze and laughed. 'No, no, I mean it. Tell me. Why should I not be interested?'

'Well, it was all greatly talked up, and I suspect you of pretending a polite attachment for the subject.'

'Then you don't understand me yet, Dwight. When last I was here I had to defend you against some supposed failure. Why shouldn't I be told of your triumphs?'

Perhaps it was something in one of her letters that still left him reluctant. 'The matter was made overmuch of, as I say. The girl had been lame for eight years from some disease of the knee. At least, one assumed disease. After some futile attempts to do good with blisters and the like, I made an effort to study the structure of the knee – first the bone formation, and then in other ways.'

'What other ways?'

'Last month a dead sailor was washed up on Hendrawna Beach and buried in the sand by the miners. I went down in the night and took part of one leg away and so was able to study the ligaments as they are in a living person.'

'You did?' she said, watching him, interested in this new light on his character.

'Yes. Then one day——'

'Did you not find it unpleasant?'

'Well, it wasn't pleasure I was looking for.'

'You may think it unfeminine,' said Caroline, 'but do you know I believe I should be interested to watch such work.'

'Would you?'

'Yes, I would. I see it shocks you. Go on.'

'It does not shock me at all. Then one day at the beginning of this month I was able to put the girl's knee right with my hands. It was nothing more than a displacement. But the years have caused atrophy of the muscles and some local inflammation. At present she is about with a bandage on it, but I think she can discard that when she has the confidence.'

Caroline put her hand over his. 'So now you are a miracle worker and have people waiting outside your house every morning. Bravo. I will tell my uncle. It will irritate him.'

'It irritates me,' said Dwight, 'but I can make use of it.'

'And no doubt your little girl looks on you with the most adoring eyes.'

'No doubt she does,' said Dwight shortly.

'And so she should. There are not many physicians of your accomplishments using all their energies to help the poor. How do you live, Dwight? Tell me that.'

He glanced at her. As always she asked questions frankly, bluntly, with no apparent awareness that she might be on delicate ground. Yet surely she, if anyone, had the right to know.

'I've an income of a few pounds a month, and this is supplemented by about £40 a year from the two mines and by those of my other patients who can afford to pay. Often I get gifts in kind from those who have no money to spare. In the main I keep out of debt. That's all I care for – or it's all I *have* cared for.'

'Will the Hoblyns pay you?'

'In some way. And not all the gentry on my list are as healthy as your uncle. Old Mr Treneglos, who would never have a surgeon near him, regularly calls me in——'

'That's what I mean,' said Caroline. 'Have you not thought of setting up in a town, especially a fashionable town – such as Bath or Oxford – where you would be able to work among people of your own kind? It is nice to help the poor, but charity – some charity – begins at home; and I believe you would be well received anywhere, not just among fisherfolk. Although you may not believe it, your manner at the bedside is an impressive one; and you have qualifications, Captain Poldark says, rarely met with outside of London. . . .'

Although she did not think he noticed, he had seen the glance she gave his clothes when they came out into the daylight. But much that she implied by what she didn't say was salved by its obvious purpose.

He said: 'When I came back to Cornwall, I'd no thought but to open a business in a town; it was Captain Poldark who invited me here. But to help poor people was part of my own purpose – still is. And in a town – even in Bath and Oxford – the poor are in greater need of attention than the well off. I don't want to become a society pet.'

She slipped off the wall and went over to her horse, made some pretence of fumbling with the saddle. The wind stirred her tawny hair, lifting it away from her ear and letting it fall. He was at once angry with himself for sounding pompous, for having irritated her. Yet what he said was the truth! Would she have disguised her own feelings for his benefit?'

He went over to her: 'Caroline, you may think——'

She turned and smiled. 'What should I think, Dwight? That you're the most noble of men? Or does it even matter? The sun has gone in and I'm chilly. That's of the chiefest moment. Let us ride.'

Before he could help her, she had pulled herself into the saddle, and her horse stepped spiritedly across the soft turf. She checked it while he mounted and came up with her.

'It matters everything what you think, Caroline; but because it matters so much, I can't pretend to you to gain an easy favour——'

'I'll race you. As far as Jonas' Mill, eh? You know the way?'

She swung her horse round and headed it for the rough common beyond the ruined mine. To gallop across this stone-strewn ground was asking for a fall; but she set off at a pace which Dwight with his inferior mount couldn't hope to equal.

But if Caroline knew the neighbourhood well, Dwight knew it better. He cantered along the track beside the common until she was safely across and had taken the stone wall at the other side. Then he spurred his horse forward down the track. A minute or two later a hamlet of four cottages was surprised to see the black-coated figure of their surgeon, who normally rode at a discreet trot, flying through as if for his life. Behind him in the settling dust children gathered and stared.

Dwight took the track which came out at Bargus Crosslanes and plunged as recklessly as Caroline could have wished through the rough scrub on the other side. Then he jumped from his horse and slipped and slithered with it down the slope beyond. Jonas' Mill came in sight, and at the same moment Caroline again. Dwight swung into the saddle. The only way of getting to the mill before her was to jump the stream that worked the mill. It was quite narrow, but his horse was not a hunter. As Caroline saw him, he set his horse at the stream. They rose together and the horse landed half in and half out of the water at the other side, floundering and almost falling. Dwight slithered off its back into a foot or so of water and hauled the horse up the sloping bank. By the time Caroline came up he was mounted again and waiting for her, while the miller and the miller's wife peered in astonishment out of windows and a small boy driving a yoke of oxen forgot to call to his team.

Caroline reined in her horse beside him, her eyes glinting. 'That was very – clever of you, Dr Enys. It's obvious that such – accomplishments would be quite – misplaced in city life.'

'I have others,' said Dwight, more out of breath than she was, 'I have others – that would not.'

'But you can't bear the thought of Bath, Dr Enys.'

'And you can't bear the thought of marriage, Miss Penvenen.'

'I see no connection.'

'I am used to dealing with connections which – can be worked up.'

'To a man of such talents anything is possible.'

'Nothing is possible without you, Caroline.'

She sobered a little, meeting his glance. Her face was flushed with the gallop. She no longer looked displeased. John Jonas came out of the mill rubbing his hands on his apron.

'All right, sur, are ee? Did the young lady's horse run away with her, eh?'

'No,' said Dwight. 'No one has run away with her yet.'

Chapter three

SHE WAS IN the winter parlour when Ross called. Black suited her. He hadn't yet overcome the feeling that he had no business at Trenwith without Francis to welcome him. Ever since Francis' death there had been a new constraint between them, coming from her confession months before; a barrier to replace a barrier, because without it . . .

She'd stood the bereavement well, as, considering her fragile look, she stood all strain well – for whether she loved Francis in the ordinary sense or not, he was her husband, the father of Geoffrey Charles, and long-standing ties of affection and habit had been broken.

'I have brought you the last returns of Wheal Grace,' he said. 'I copied them from the cost book last night. They don't make invigorating reading, but I thought you should have them.'

'Why?'

'Why? Because you're a partner, of course. Virtually so, since Geoffrey Charles is too young to look after his own interests.' He put the papers on the table and opened them up.

'Can you not tell me all that matters? I need no proofs in writing.'

'Yet you should have them. It's the business way, and others may think it needful if you do not.' He waited a moment, but she did not come to the table.

'What others are there?'

'Pearce, or your father, or – well, here the figures are for you to look at. What matters is that we shall not be able to go on later than January. I think possibly it would be better to finish at the end of the year.'

Her skin looked cool, as if the clothes she wore did not belong to it, their blackness some part of a world she did not quite inhabit. 'Ross, you know all of my finances, but I don't know yours. I know the end of this venture will hit you hard, but not how hard. From something that Francis said. . . .'

'Yes?'

'I had the impression that Wheal Grace had become as much a gambler's throw for you as for him. Are you gravely in debt?'

'Grave is the word. One foot in and the other shortly following. But that's a risk I took. I can't complain because it has gone wrong. What I do much regret is losing your money also.'

'Well, it was Francis' money. And he also knew the risk he was taking.'

'Then I regret it for Geoffrey Charles's sake.'

On this she was without argument, without subterfuge even to herself. 'More than anything I feel my poverty because of him, Ross. I can't bear the thought of his coming into his inheritance and finding it. . . . When Francis came into this estate, there was money to live – and would have been for our children. This last has been a wise investment compared to much of the rest. At least it was a gamble in a mine and not on the turn of a card!'

It was on Ross's tongue to ask if she realized how much she had contributed to this state of affairs, but his tongue was tied.

'If your father and mother live with you, it will help you and them, I suppose. They may get a good price for Cusgarne from one of the rich merchants; the expenses of living can be pooled.'

'Yes. . . .'

'Isn't that your intention?'

She breathed deeply, gave him a brave and painful smile. 'It was, Ross. But just at the moment it's too soon. I want time to think about these things. Francis' death is – is too close to me.' She came at last to the table, looked down at the papers he had brought, flipping them over in her fingers but not reading them.

Ross said: 'You've seen George again?'

'I had to. He's my chief creditor as you know. So much so that he's almost my only important one. It was a little difficult without you, but he quite understood that you could not meet.'

'What are his views on the debts?'

'Very generous. They always have been.' She raised her eyes again. 'I can't rob him of that credit. He was always generous to Francis too.'

Ross nodded, his face showing neither approval nor disapproval. 'Had he any fresh proposals?'

'Yes. He offered to waive interest on the debts for a period of years. Of course I could not accept that.'

'Why not?'

'Well. . . . There have been enough favours. I don't feel justified in accepting more.'

Ross studied the colour moving under the delicate flush of her skin. 'It depends why, does it not? If you refuse his favours out of loyalty to me, it's a mistaken loyalty. My quarrel with George is not your quarrel. Nor even need Francis' be, now. George has always – admired you – tried to win your approval. If he still wants to do so, I should let him. You may well retain your private opinion of him just the same.'

She did not speak.

'If on the other hand,' said Ross, 'you feel that acceptance of his favours means you must offer him favours in return – such as . . .'

'Such as?'

He frowned at the papers. 'You can imagine them better than I. At the least you might feel that becoming a friend of his would alienate people you like better. That you must decide for yourself – I can't advise you.'

'I already have,' said Elizabeth quietly folding the papers unread.

Ross accepted them back, and they talked for a time desultorily about day-to-day things. But although what they said was unimportant, the saying of it was not. They had never before met like this, each week, confidentially, as friends. Each week tied the invisible strings.

When he left, she walked slowly back to the winter parlour and from the window watched his dwindling figure as he rode down the drive. If she had been given to self-questioning, she would have admitted that she had not been entirely honest with him over the help she was receiving from George – but would have pleaded excuse on the grounds that it was a necessary outcome of her bereavement. She not only wanted to be thought well of by both men, she needed to be. George had proposed that, being Geoffrey Charles's godfather, he should hold himself responsible for the cost of the boy's education up to the time of his finishing at Oxford. She could not refuse this, and Ross would not have expected her to. But she did not want to tell him of it, nor of the several smaller favours. It compromised the position she wished to take up in his mind. Perhaps more than anything else at present she wanted Ross's approval for herself.

But from the moment of Francis' death all her emotions had needed new names. A pattern set and grown in years had dissolved overnight. She wished that circumstances would have permitted her to correct the mistakes of past years. At present she was only groping towards an understanding of them.

When horse and rider had disappeared round a bend in the drive, she rang for Mrs Tabb to fetch Geoffrey Charles from his great-great-aunt's bedroom, where he was playing. Aunt Agatha was in bed today with rheumatism, and her strength, Elizabeth thought, was failing. When the little boy came, his mother kissed him fondly and began to give him his history lesson. These hours she spent with her son were the best of her day; she found mother love uncomplex and wholly satisfying; in such a relationship there were no mental reservations, no attitudes to be sustained, and no conflict.

She had not so far found her widowhood objectionable in the conventional ways; she felt little loneliness as such, she had more time to devote to herself and more for Geoffrey Charles. But she grievously missed a man to take the responsibility of day-to-day living. The making of decisions was always something she had disliked, and in an estate of this character there was no avoiding them. Some in fact could only be dealt with satisfactorily by a man. Tabb did what he could, Tabb did everything he could, but sometimes he traded on his new position and she had to watch that too.

While Geoffrey Charles was reading aloud to her, she walked across and studied herself in the mirror, twisting a strand of hair in among the rest, staring closely at her eyes and skin. There were a few little lines about her eyes which had not been there five years ago. But they were not enough to make any difference yet. When she smiled they disappeared. She must remember not to smile much in private, for that would deepen the lines, but to smile much in public, for that would hide them.

What had George said: one of the most beautiful women in England? His usual exaggeration. But beautiful enough. It was not conceit to know that. Nor did she think it disloyal to Francis to be aware of a growing freedom. She had been in a cage too long, confined within the bars of this house. It remained to be seen whether she had forgotten how to fly.

Demelza never asked what took place on Ross's weekly visit to Elizabeth, and he seldom volunteered the information. But on one thing Demelza was quite resolved. Whatever her inner promptings might be, she would never allow herself to entertain any suspicions of Ross's behaviour or allow him to suppose that she had any. Although she seldom voiced them, she had strong views on what a wife's attitude ought to be in such circumstances.

To-day when he returned she had other news for him.

'There's a message from Mr Trencrom. Jud brought it. He says they'll be over tonight. He wouldn't say what he meant.'

'It's a matter I've intended telling you of. Mr Trencrom wants me to have a cache dug on my land for storing his goods during a run, so that they can be taken away at leisure. Of course he's willing to pay for it.'

'But will that not greatly increase the risk to us?'

'It matters very little. In a month we shall crash anyhow.'

She did not speak but went on brushing out the stable, where he had found her. He could guess by her face something of what she felt.

'That doesn't make sense to me,' she said eventually.

'Well, if I go to prison for debt, this will mean more money coming in. And the quicker the debt is paid, the quicker I shall be out again.'

'That is supposing the goods are not found on our land. You will stay longer in prison if you are convicted for that.'

'I do not think I shall be.'

'Where is this – this thing to be?'

'In the old library. It can all be done in one night, and nothing to show to-morrow.'

She was silent again. She would say no more in criticism, he knew, either to him or to herself; but that did not make her forbearance any easier to accept.

He said casually: 'And how was Jud?'

'Grumbling as usual. John tells me he has joined the Methodies.'

'I should not be astonished: he has always had a fancy for hell fire.

Demelza, I wish you would not do this work; it's not right you should take it on yourself.'

'Gimlett was busy and you were out. But I like it, Ross. It stops me from thinking. About this hole, this cache, how many will know of it?'

'Four to dig it. Six or eight perhaps who use it.'

'Jud Paynter?'

'Possibly.'

'Well, I——'

'Oh, I know he's leaky in his liquor. But he drinks less since his recovery – and I think we underrate him. Look at his behaviour at my trial. Trencrom trusts him, and Trencrom can't afford to make mistakes.'

'Neither can we.'

'As you say.' He stared at her for a moment, disliking himself for comparisons which sometimes now rose uninvited in his brain. 'Demelza, I am not making much of our situation yet; for there's still a few weeks to go, and I may still find the money. If I do not, I have made arrangements with Mr Trencrom so that a sum shall be paid to you monthly for the favours he receives. My remaining shares in Wheal Leisure will go to meet part of the debt, so there will be nothing from that. But Mr Trencrom's dole will keep you comfortably enough, and anything you can save from it can be put aside to wipe off the rest of the debt. In no time——'

'You do not need to fear for me. I was used once to living on nothing, and can do it again. And Jeremy I shall see for. Don't worry about us. What matters is paying off the money you owe.'

He took the broom from her, and after a brief resistance she gave it up. He carried on with the work.

'I had some expectation of Mr Trencrom. I'm a deal more use to him out of prison than in; and if there is a forced sale of this house and land, the new purchasers may not be friendly to his schemes.'

'I thought your Mr Pascoe had promised that the property should not be sold.'

'So he has. Indeed, the property already belongs to him under the mortgage deed; but Trencrom does not know of the promise.'

Demelza pushed back her hair with her wrist. 'You'll soil your best clothes. 'Tisn't sensible to do that now.'

'Well I'd as lief wear 'em out as save them for the moths.'

She said vehemently: 'Why do you not appeal to your friends, Ross – or let me appeal for you? Sir John Trevaunance would be sympathetic, I know. And Sir Hugh Bodrugan, though you may not like him, has good will towards me. And Mr Ray Penvenen, and old Mr Treneglos. They might well join with Mr Trencrom in putting up so much each so's to save you from the bankruptcy. It is not charity, for they know you are honourable and would pay them back. Why not let me try? Do let me try!'

He stopped and leaned on the broom handle, his eyes lidded in thought.

After a few seconds he smiled and shook his head. 'No good, my dear. The sum is too great and so is my pride. And since you've so good an opinion of these friendships, keep it, for they would not stand the strain you suppose. One or two would help, I know, but others would not; and we can save ourselves the disappointment. Anyway, I've never asked favours and will not begin now. We'll get through it as we may, and presently start afresh. When that time comes, I shall keep to farming and leave all mining alone. Even brushing out stables will be a kindly thing to come back to!'

The four to dig it was six, with Jud leaning on his stick to superintend. An overblown moon climbed above the sand hills at nine-thirty, so there was need only of one small lantern within the library. At ten the cores changed at the mine, and by half past the last of the miners had dispersed. From then on, three of the six men were busy wheeling the excavated ground across the valley to the nearest dump. No one would notice that it had grown a little in the night. The six men were Ned Bottrell, Paul Daniel, Ted Carkeek, Will Nanfan, Whitehead Scoble, and Pally Rogers. About eleven there was an alarm, but it was only Charlie Kempthorne with a message for Ned Bottrell that he was a father for the fifth time. This was good excuse for a tot of brandy and some rough-and-ready jokes.

At one Demelza went to bed; but Ross stayed until an hour before dawn, when the work was finished. The seven tired men – Jud, who had done no work, complaining he was the most tired of them all – tramped back up the valley in the light of a moon which had grown smaller and paler as the dark hours passed.

Chapter four

CAROLINE AND HER uncle had never got on so well since her break with Unwin Trevaunance, and her return to Killewarren and attitude since had done little to smooth things out. She spent every fine day riding, often with a groom but sometimes alone, and was silent through her meals or edgy if questioned. She paid few social visits in the neighbourhood and seldom wished to be found at home if called on. Rumours had not been slow to reach him, but he understood her well enough to know that he must move cautiously if they were to be checked or countered.

One night at supper she provoked a discussion by saying: 'Tell me, Uncle, what do you know of Ross Poldark?'

Blinking, cautious, watching her as if he suspected some deeper meaning in the question than he was privy to, he told her what he knew. Ross's father, the best-known libertine in six parishes; Ross's service overseas during the American war; his return after his father's death and his bitter disappointment, so people said, that Francis was to marry the Chynoweth girl; his foolish marriage a year or so later to a girl he had taken from some miner's cottage in Illuggan; his starting of Wheal Leisure and, later, his leadership of the proposal to begin copper smelting in Cornwall; the failure of the scheme; the death of his child; the shipwrecks and the riots which followed; his trial and his acquittal; his——

'Yes, Uncle, thank you, I know from there.' Caroline took a sip of wine, and her eyes looked darker for the reflection from the glass. 'His father, you say, was bad-behaved with the women of the neighbourhood. I should imagine the son has sowed his wild oats also. Or he looks as if he has. You do not mention that.'

Penvenen regarded the girl dryly. 'I was not attempting to spare his reputation – or your delicacy. I do not know if anything specially unsavoury has clung to him in that respect – although it has in many others. Of course this taking a half-starved beggar girl, or whatever she was. . . . I was in London at the time, but I believe it caused trouble among the miners and with her father.'

'But he married her,' said Caroline.

'Yes, he married her.'

She waited while her plate was taken away. Beside her in a basket on another chair was Horace, and she picked him up and set him on her lap.

'Did you lose much in your association with Ross Poldark in the copper company?'

'Enough. Everyone lost money. It was an ill-conceived enterprise at best.'

'I understand you escaped somewhat earlier and somewhat better than the others.'

The candles were between them, but she saw his sharply raised eyes.

'Who told you that?'

She laughed. 'Unwin. He said once that you and Sir John made a deal with the Warleggans and left the ship to sink. That was his phrase.'

'The ship – as you term it – was already on the rocks when we came to an arrangement with the Warleggans. We did so only to preserve capital investments we had made, he in his furnaces, I in the battery mill. No one lost a penny more because of our action. Unwin knew nothing of the situation at first hand.'

She held a piece of meat under the pug's nose, but he only sniffed at it and turned away. 'Is the horrid beef not to your liking, my pet? Very well, you shan't be pressed. Thomas, bring me the sweet biscuits – you know the ones Horace adores.'

'Yes, ma'am.'

'But you shall have to go back in your basket for those, my sweet, or you would crumble them all over my frock. There, is that to your liking? . . . I hear Ross Poldark is on the verge of insolvency now.'

'Indeed.' Her uncle had not appreciated her comments, and his reply was short.

'He has some debts outstanding from that time, and the Warleggans have got hold of them and are pressing him hard.'

'You are well informed.'

Thomas came back with the biscuits, and she thanked him with a smile. For a minute or two she devoted her whole attention to Horace. 'Not so very well informed, Uncle, for I cannot ask him to his face and I do not know the Warleggans well enough to ask them. But it seems a pity that so big a man should be squeezed out for so small a sum, don't you think? If he went out at all, he should go in the grand manner to suit his looks and his style.'

Mr Penvenen said: 'I imagine Dr Enys could enlighten you on any further details you wished to know.'

Horace snuffled over his biscuit in the sudden silence. Caroline said: 'I believe I shall go into Truro tomorrow morning. It is a poor place to shop, but I need some shoes made. In Oxford shoe buckles are quite out of fashion and I myself prefer the string. And do you know there is quite a craze for feathers in the hair. I don't personally favour them, I feel too much like yesterday's fowl.'

'I think,' said Ray Penvenen, 'that although you are now your own mistress, Caroline, you should not allow a natural pleasure in your freedom to obscure the observances of good society in which it has been my privilege and your Uncle William's to enlighten you since your parents died. Although we may seem to be in a rough and isolated part of the country here, it would be a mistake to think that the conventions do not obtain. For instance, to ride far and unattended in the company of a young man of eligible years is to invite comment of an unsavoury nature, whether one is in Cornwall or in Oxfordshire. No doubt this is quite innocently intended, but it can have far-reaching consequences and is neither quite fair to me, who may seem to be countenancing it, nor to the young man, who may derive encouragement from it and ambitions beyond his proper sphere.'

Soft-footed, the manservant closed the door and went out. After a second or so a breath of air imperceptible to the skin reached the candles and their flames trembled like fronds in a still pool.

Caroline said: 'I'd always thought – I've always believed – that a mark of true quality and rank is to behave according to one's personal lights and to pay no attention beyond that to the mesh of artificial conventions with which would-be people of quality surround themselves.'

'That is true to a point. But a person of quality only acts in such a way so far as his behaviour affects himself. When it affects other people, he is no longer a free agent.'

'It was what I was going to say. There are only two people concerned in this beside myself, and that is you and Dr Enys. Your concern is that you might be thought to be approving of my behaviour. Is that it? Well, if I am too much on your conscience, should I not be better advised to leave this house and live elsewhere?'

'Possibly,' he agreed quietly, 'if it were not for the affection that we hold for each other.'

She frowned a moment, looking angry and troubled. Then she covered her feelings by turning to Horace. 'Another biscuit, my love? Uncle Ray is becoming cross with me. There will, I fear, shortly be angry words on both sides. And possibly a scene. And things would be said which we should both later somewhat regret. That is a pity, don't you think? Do you not suppose we should better change the subject?'

Horace made a gruff noise in his throat and contrived to lick her fingers and his own nose at the same time. Ray stared across at his pretty niece in perplexity, partly disarmed but not at all less suspicious. There was a genuine bond between them, and he often blamed himself for weakness in his treatment of her. But he did not know how to continue the attack without provoking the scene she forecast. He did not suppose that what he had said would make any difference to her early-morning rides, but he knew that insistence at this stage might well lead to her carrying out her threat – to the grief and detriment of them both. And such a move would completely defeat his object by taking her right outside his influence. He wondered if he was approaching this problem from the wrong quarter and through the wrong person.

Supper ended in peace. Later, when he was in his study, he summoned his servant and asked if he could find out what arrangements Miss Caroline had made for visiting Truro in the morning. The man came back to say she had ordered her carriage for nine-thirty. Mr Penvenen bit the end of his quill for a few seconds and then wrote a short note.

Dear Dr Enys,

If you are free, I should be obliged if you could call on me tomorrow morning between ten-thirty and eleven. It is some time since you made a routine medical call.

Yours etc.,
R. R. E. Penvenen

About five minutes to eleven Dwight turned his horse in at the gates of Killewarren, not without a quickening of anticipation at the prospect of seeing Caroline again without the necessity of contrivance. But no Caroline was about when he went in, and he was silently shown upstairs into the big untidy drawing room with its antlers and its sporting pictures where he had first met Ray Penvenen.

Mr Penvenen was there to meet him again, or rather was standing with his back to him, staring out at the grey day. His coat as usual was sizes too big for him, and the warts were noticeable on his clasped hands. After a studied pause he turned.

'Ah, Dr Enys, you had my letter?'

'Yes,' said Dwight, knowing now and blaming himself for not having known before. 'I hope I've not kept you waiting.'

'There's time enough. My niece happens to be in Truro, and I thought this would be an opportunity to discuss matters with you.'

'Medical matters?'

'No. I must apologize if my note gave you that impression.'

'Well, yes, it did.'

Ray Penvenen picked up his spectacles from the desk but did not put them on. His lashless eyes were lowered. 'Perhaps you would care to sit down.'

'No, thank you.'

Somewhere near at hand Horace was yapping monotonously. 'Imagine you have some idea why I have sent for you.'

'I don't think it is for me to speculate, Mr Penvenen.'

'I could have wished you showed a similar delicacy in all your dealings, Dr Enys.'

'I'm sorry you should think I have not.'

'Yes . . . well, yes. . . . I think you have not – though I should be happy to learn that you have been offending thoughtlessly and without a full appreciation of what is involved. I refer, of course, to your growing friendship with my niece.'

'I wonder in what way you consider that offensive?'

Penvenen glanced dryly at the young man.

'Come, Dr Enys. You can't be so unaware of the ways of the world. For more than a month, if not longer, you have been paying attentions to my niece. You must know that your first duty was to approach me and ask my permission. The fact that you have not done so shows that you suspect such permission would not be forthcoming. Isn't that so?'

Dwight bit his lip, angry with himself as well as with the man in front of him.

'All you say is true.'

'Ah. . . . Well, then, what explanation have you to offer?'

'None at all. Except that none of it has been so deliberate as you suppose. One's feelings grow unsolicited and unencouraged. There has been no one point when I have said to myself . . . But I now have such feelings for your niece; I won't attempt to deny that.'

'You have not considered how her ill-advised meetings with you reflect on her reputation?'

'No, I have not: I don't suppose——'

'There's no need for us to quarrel, Dr Enys.' Penvenen folded his hands under his coattails and smiled. 'Caroline is a forceful young woman, a thoroughly delightful person but as mettlesome as an unbroken colt. She has never been sufficiently curbed – it would be an ungenerous task, but perhaps I and my brother are to blame for not attempting it. We try to humour her so far as we can. It is nothing uncommon for her to take violent likes and dislikes to people – often she drops them as quickly as she has taken them up. It may be so in your case; it probably will; but even then I should be opposed to these quasi-secret meetings. As for a serious attachment, to a young man in your position. . . . Apart from consideration of money and blood——'

'I don't think blood need enter into it.'

'But I do, my dear sir. There was a Penvenen at Prince Rupert's side at Marston Moor. And we have lived in this district for ninety years——'

'An Enys fitted out and manned a ship to fight the Armada. Ninety years ago one of my ancestors was High Sheriff of Cornwall.'

Mr Penvenen cleared his throat. His careful geniality was not quite proof against this reply. 'And as to money?'

'I admit the obstacle.'

'Caroline is an heiress, Dr Enys. She is my heir and my brother's heir, so she will be – to say the least – rich in her time. She is far too important a person to become entangled with a penniless country doctor. I'm glad you realize it.'

Dwight had controlled his quick temper so far, but everything Mr Penvenen said made things worse. The fact that he was using arguments Dwight had used against himself added to the insult.

'Ultimately, isn't it for Caroline to decide her own life?'

Ray Penvenen took one of his hands out and grasped the velvet lapel of his coat. 'That is where you are in error. Caroline must marry with our consent or she will not inherit any money from us.'

'That again must be for Caroline to choose.'

'And how do you think she will choose when I put the choice before her? She has been brought up in the greatest luxury. Nothing for her comfort has ever been spared. D'you suppose she'll sacrifice all that for what you have to offer? Are you justified in expecting it?'

Dwight stared angrily across the room. The desk was open, with a litter of papers on it. Above the desk was a small water colour of a red-haired child.

'It may be, of course,' said Penvenen, 'that you think my niece has a large private fortune of her own. Let me——'

'I neither know nor care what money she has.'

'Very creditable of you. But hardly practical. Caroline has about six thousand pounds of her own. That is all you could expect to get if you married her, Dr Enys.'

Dwight said: 'Up to now, Mr Penvenen, I've suffered your comments with a due degree of civility. I owed it to you as Caroline's uncle and guardian. But there are limits to what a man may stand. God knows I've never given you reason to imagine me a fortune hunter, and I should have thought that such knowledge as you have of me might have inclined you to a less offensive view. If you suppose that no man who has not an eye on her money can fall in love with your niece, you greatly underrate her charm and insult her as much as you do me——'

'Now there is no need——'

'When I came here today, I was as distracted – I suppose – as any man ever has been, over this matter of Caroline's money. For months I've faced an insoluble problem. At least today you've given me a slender hope for the solution of it.'

The whiter Mr Penvenen's face became, the pinker grew the rims of his eyes. 'You are going a little far, Dr Enys. I suppose you realize that this will mean the end of our professional relationship——'

'You've shown me a way out,' said Dwight, pacing across the room, 'by telling me that Caroline's fortune isn't as great as I thought. One of substance, I admit, but not an insuperable bar. It would be possible for a penniless doctor to marry such a fortune without being eclipsed by it. It would be possible with such a fortune for a wife to maintain herself and yet not entirely dominate the purse strings. Thank you, sir, for that!'

'You will leave this house,' said Ray Penvenen, 'and not come here again. You will have no further communication with my niece. I forbid it and shall take steps to enforce it. Good day to you.'

Dwight stopped in his pacing opposite the little cold man. 'Caroline is of age, Mr Penvenen. Your control can only be exercised within the limits of your property. But perhaps you yourself have pointed the solution to our difficulties.'

'I have nothing further to say to you, Dr Enys!'

'I have this to say to you, sir, in all deference. Just now you asked me if I thought Caroline would give up all you had to offer for what little I have to offer. That's the crux, isn't it? Well, we must leave it to her to decide!'

'I see I have been gravely mistaken in your character, Dr Enys. I very much regret ever having invited you here.'

'Many times in the last months I have very much regretted having come. But at least we understand each other now.'

'We understand each other,' said Ray Penvenen, as Dwight went out.

Harris Pascoe was not busy when Miss Penvenen was announced; but he had the appearance of industry, being occupied at his favourite pastime of juggling with figures. He was not a man of strong passions, and things like credit and debit balances offered to him the cold white peaks of aesthetic pleasure. When Caroline was shown in, he reluctantly closed the last book and stood up.

'Miss Penvenen. I haven't had the p-pleasure. I know your father, of course.'

'My uncle. Yes, it's on account of his speaking of you that I've come to you today. Not of course that he knows I'm here . . . .'

Harris Pascoe rubbed the soft part of his pen along the line of his cheek. Although he found his dearest pleasure in mathematics, he was not insensible to figures of another sort, and he acknowledged to himself that this young woman was worth looking at.

'And can I help you?'

Caroline took off her long green gauntlet gloves, flipping them against her knee. 'It's a peculiar mission I'm on, Mr Pascoe; at least you may think so, and I shouldn't quarrel with you for having that opinion. I want to know if you can help me to help a friend of mine who is in trouble. There, it sounds rather mysterious, doesn't it? And not quite respectable. Would you like me to explain?'

There was a suggestion of mischief in her eyes, so Harris Pascoe was at his most stolid. 'If you please.'

'I have money, Mr Pascoe, and am seeking an investment. I understand that Captain Poldark has a bill out which will shortly come due for redemption. Do I use the right professional words? I understand that the present possessor of the bill is not willing to renew it. I should like to buy that bill. Could you arrange the purchase for me?'

The banker pulled his snuffbox towards him, opened it, and stayed for a moment with finger and thumb poised over the box. Then he closed it unused.

'You are looking for an *investment*, Miss Penvenen?'

She nodded brightly. 'From what I hear it should be a good one. The rate of interest is exceedingly high. Of course if you prefer to call the transaction by some other name, I shall not quibble.'

'Forgive me, you have c-control of your money?'

'Since I was twenty-one.'

'What does your uncle – but you say he does not know of this visit.' Does Captain Poldark?'

Caroline smiled. 'Do you suppose he would let me interfere in his affairs?'

'No. . . .' Pascoe got up and dusted some loose snuff from his waistcoat. 'You are putting me in rather a d-difficulty, Miss Penvenen. Captain Poldark is a client of mine and also a personal friend. It is not my custom to discuss a client's affairs with any third person; but I'll not disguise from you what I think you already well know – that a renewal of this bill would be a matter of the utmost importance t-to him. But also – but also your uncle is a valued client of mine, and I should be doing less than my duty to him if I allowed you to make this rash purchase – even supposing it can be made – without warning you that you could hardly make a more risky investment. Indeed, I don't feel I could proceed as you suggest without consulting your uncle in the matter first.'

Caroline looked down and gently stretched the fingers of her gloves.

'I am an independent person, Mr Pascoe. If you consult my uncle, you'll be disclosing a private conversation to a third party. I thought you never did that. And if you refuse to make this investment for me, I shall have to go elsewhere.'

Harris Pascoe perceived that his visitor was not to be trifled with.

'You're aware that it's not a good risk?'

'I'm aware that most people would not think it a good risk. But we all have our own opinions.'

Pascoe went to the window and stared down into the street. Absently he took note of the smart private coach waiting outside, the man in green livery on the box, the gaping urchins, the citizens too who had stopped to stare. If the girl had plenty of money, why should he exert himself to dissuade her? There'd be difficulties enough. . . .

'There are difficulties in your suggestion which would be not at all of my making, Miss Penvenen. For one thing, I do not think the present owner of the bill would be willing to s-sell it.'

'Why not? He wants the money, doesn't he?'

'There is more than money involved.'

'Oh, yes, the Warleggans, of course; I have heard something of it. But is there not a way round that difficulty?'

'Not by offering to purchase the bill. At the very least they would, I think, demand some extortionate premium on it which would put it quite out of your reach.'

'You don't know my reach, Mr Pascoe.'

'Possibly not. But allow me at least to advise you on the most economical way of going about the business.' He came back to the table and sat down, picked up his pen in some irritation, and made a few figures. 'Obviously, if you are quite set on doing this, the best thing is to lend Captain Poldark the fourteen hundred pounds personally to discharge the bill and have him sign a new bill for this amount.'

For the first time Caroline looked a little confused. 'I'm afraid that's impossible. That's what I haven't told you yet. He mustn't on any account know who has advanced the money.'

Pascoe considered her dryly. 'I see. But I'm afraid it is unavoidable. I don't think there is any other way. I don't think you have the *least* chance of persuading Mr Cary Warleggan to part with the bill, at any price. You have no doubt read *The Merchant of Venice.*'

There was silence for a few moments. Caroline said: 'I don't for a moment think Captain Poldark would accept the money from me.'

'Hm. . . . No, it's possible. You're a friend of his, of course? But a woman. I see your point.'

Caroline got up. She was as tall as the banker, and her slightness made her look taller. She folded her gloves carefully, not looking at him. But something in the shape of her face made him aware of what the look in her eyes was likely to be.

'Well, thank you for seeing me. I shall have to go elsewhere. I can expect you to tell no one of my call?'

'I shall tell no one. But don't be in t-too great a hurry. I think I have a suggestion to make which might help us to overcome this difficulty.'

'Yes?'

'Pray sit down again. Give me a moment or two to work this out.'

Caroline resumed her seat. Through narrow long-lashed eyes she watched Mr Pascoe open his snuffbox. She waited, patient now, for him to make his suggestion.

Chapter five

LOBB THE SHERBORNER had spent the night locally, so a letter was delivered to Ross just as he was leaving the house for the mine. He broke the seal and read what Harris Pascoe had to say, hardly certain that the slanting December sunlight was not in some manner distorting what he read. Having come through it twice with the same interpretation, he moved quickly round to the stables and began to throw a saddle over Darkie. Gimlett heard him and stopped his work and came into the stable.

'Can I help ee, sur?'

'No. . . . I can do it. Oh, Gimlett, where is your mistress?'

'Gone looking for Garrick, who ran off after a stray cat.'

'Tell her I've been called to Truro on business, will you? I hope to be back in time for tea.'

'Yes, sur.'

Before eleven Ross was dismounting outside the banking premises of Messrs. Pascoe, Tresize, Annery, and Spry. He dropped his reins over the post, lifted the latch of the bank door, and went purposefully in. Harris Pascoe was not engaged, nor indeed surprised to see his visitor, though the swift response was several hours earlier than he had expected. He looked up speculatively at Ross's expression as he was shown in.

Ross sat down and crossed his long legs and rubbed a finger carefully across his upper lip.

'Good day to you, Harris.'

'Good day. You're an early caller this morning.'

'Not earlier than I wish to be. This letter. . . .' Ross took it from his pocket.

'Oh, yes. You received it s-safely. I imagine the contents would come as a surprise to you.'

'Surprise is not an overstatement.'

The banker smiled at his ledgers. 'Naturally I was happy to be the sender of such tidings.'

'No happier than I was to receive them. What is the explanation?'

'You already have the explanation in the letter.'

'Not one that satisfies me. After trying desperately to raise the wind for six weeks, I feel a little sceptical that it has suddenly decided to raise itself.

Who is this anonymous person who has suddenly come forward as you say and placed this money at my disposal?'

'I'm not at liberty to give you the name.'

'Is it you?'

Pascoe looked up and met the grey, unquiet eyes. 'No.'

'Is it a friend of mine – someone I know?'

'I can't tell you.'

'If I know no more than this, how can I accept it? On what conditions is it loaned me?'

'You have them in the letter. A new promissory n-note on the same conditions as the old, but at a lower rate of interest.'

'And whom do I promise to pay?'

'It will be left blank. The note won't leave my keeping anyway unless you d-default.'

Ross got up, put his finger tips on the enormous desk. 'It's monstrous, Harris. It really is. Have you been deluding some poor fool into thinking me a better risk than I really am?'

'No.'

'So it is a friend. Damn it, I still suspect you. I can't think——' He stopped and pushed a hand through his hair.

'I'd be glad to take the credit. But in my position as a banker I was not able to lend the money. . . . Had I been able to, I should have advanced it weeks ago and saved you the anxiety.'

'Well, I really can't accept this money blindfold. It's asking too much.'

'Of whom?' said Pascoe politely.

Ross subsided in his chair. It was the chair Caroline had occupied five days ago. He picked up his crop and turned it round in his bony fingers. His finances these last years reminded him often of a man deprived of air, choking, but again and again reprieved at the point of death. But never before had he come so close to the end of things as this December. Even now he felt very little sense of relief. He couldn't at all believe it. He raised his heavy-lidded eyes and stared at the man opposite. Pascoe was about to sneeze, but the sudden stare stopped it and he had to content himself with a sniff.

'It is none of the Warleggans? No swapping of horses without betterment, or accepting some favour from George at Cary's expense?'

'It is none of them.'

'Can they do anything to stop this; I mean can they retain the bill they have?'

'Not this way. With your permission I shall go over tomorrow and redeem the bill. The money is immediately available when you sign this new note.'

Ross stared at the piece of paper as if by doing so he would penetrate the secrets that were being withheld from him. 'Is it Mr Trencrom?'

'I cannot tell you anything more.'

'You can't give me even a hint?'

'I'm afraid not.'

'But you, knowing the person, advise me to accept the offer?'

'I, knowing the person, advise you to accept. You'd be criminally foolish if you did not.'

That was enough. Ross dipped the quill in the pot and slowly signed his name. 'Are you in communication with this bashful gentleman?'

'I may be from time to time.'

'Well, would you convey my compliments to him and tell him I shall not lie easy till I know his name. I'm in his debt literally and figuratively for a greater amount than I have been to anyone else ever in my life. As to the monetary sum, I shall feel as much constrained to pay it as if it were a debt of honour; and for the personal obligation, perhaps the occasion may occur when I may pay that too.'

'I'll t-tell the gentleman,' said Pascoe, fixing his spectacles more firmly on his nose. 'I'm sure your acceptance will make pleasant hearing to him. It's plain that he has your welfare at heart.'

'I have his also.' said Ross.

Garrick chased the cat up a tree, so Demelza tied him securely at a distance and then tried to entice the cat down. This didn't work so she looped up her skirt and climbed the tree herself. It was from the vantage point of the topmost branches, swaying dangerously, that she saw Ross riding up the valley. She coo-eed but he didn't hear, and she retrieved the cat and climbed down in an apprehensive frame of mind. Sudden changes of plan on Ross's part always betokened bad news.

Gimlett's story of a letter confirmed her suspicions; and she spent the day in some foreboding, hiding her worst fears in a flurry of work. In the afternoon, with Jeremy plucking at her skirts and getting into all sorts of trouble, she made butter, putting the scalded cream she had saved into her stone bowl and beating it regularly round with her hand. But today it would not turn, and she began to have fears either that the cow was sick or that this was some sort of omen. Sir Hugh Bodrugan had been over last week, pressing her to see a cow of his that would not calve, convinced beyond all reason that she was capable of white witchery. She had refused. Two lucky coincidences had given her a name, and the only way to retain it was not to tempt fate any more.

Prudie Paynter had had some doggerel she used for making butter turn when she was a servant here, and Demelza tried it over now; but perhaps Ross's scepticism had infected her, for nothing happened. The afternoon was very cold, her hands were very cold, and she found it hard to keep up an even, unhurried motion.

The day had been still, no air moving and quiet except for the roar of the surf. Often the sea was a continual unperceived noise, but on days such as this it overcame the mind's defences and life moved to its beat. It was as if a great army of heavy vehicles was passing near the house, and now and then the air tremored on one's ears. A faint mist drifted inland from the breaking waves, greying the edges of the cliffs and sand dunes. In the garden the birds pecked at the hard ground, and sea gulls circled the upper air.

The Carnbarrow Hunt was to meet at Werry House next week, and Sir Hugh had invited her over. Demelza wondered if her refusal had been right. She knew Ross's views, but she still felt Sir Hugh might be persuaded to help them – at a price. She had coaxed a concession out of him once before and come to no hurt. Surely she might do so again.

The cream began at last to turn, and after a few minutes she went out and drew a pitcher of ice-cold water from the pump to wash away the buttermilk. She had done this and was patting the butter into shape when Ross came.

She didn't stop to carry her board out to the stillroom, but slid through the house, nearly upsetting Jeremy, who lurched suddenly into her path.

Ross was already in, an unusual thing, having left his mare by the door. His expression was hard to read; almost always she knew, but this time it didn't conform to any of the recognized patterns.

'There's going to be a hard frost,' he said. Some of the shallower pools are freezing already.'

'Yes, I thought the same,' she said. 'There's all the signs. That sky. . . . Jeremy, darling, *where* did you get the jam!'

The little boy had come tottering in carrying a large jar from the lip of which a dark crimson streak was already beginning to escape. On the very verge of dropping it he was able to present it to his father before it slipped from his hands. Then he sat down with a crump on the floor and said, 'Gar!'

'Thank you,' said Ross, 'a very friendly gesture . . .' He put the jar on the table. 'He's more forward than Julia was, isn't he? I can't remember at this age. . . .'

'She was fatter and more content to stay in one place. We shall have to watch his legs. . . . Ross, why did you go into Truro?'

'Some extra business to do with Pascoe. A matter of small importance.'

She knew then from some glint in his eye that the news was not bad.

'What is it? What's to do? Tell me if it is something better. I have been thinking all day. . . .'

He sat down and warmed his hands at the fire. Gimlett had come out and was leading Darkie past the windows. 'Pascoe was agreed that there was likely to be a frost.'

'No, Ross.' She went over to him. 'Don't play now! This is too important. Tell me, please.'

He looked up at her eager face.

'Someone – some anonymous person – has chosen very foolishly to take over my debt, my promissory note which the Warleggans hold. It means that – for the time at least – the urgency to find the money is gone. Of course, it will still have to be found some day. But not *this* Christmas.'

Demelza stared at him. 'D'you mean – that you won't have to default – that there's still a chance. . . .'

'There's still a chance. Just that.'

'Oh, my dear.' She sat abruptly in a chair. After a moment Jeremy crawled towards her and she picked him up and covered him with kisses of relief. 'Oh, Ross, I can't hardly believe that. After all this worry it's *beyond* belief. . . .'

'You describe it exactly. It's beyond belief. All the way home I've been telling myself that things are just as black as they ever were before this threat blew up – that we are still poverty-stricken to the last edges of pauperdom – that in a month or so the mine must close – that we have practically nothing to live on. But just at the moment those things don't mean anything at all.'

'And it's *true*! It's true! Oh, thank God!' She suddenly set Jeremy down and ran across and kissed him on the cheek. 'I'm that *glad* for you, Ross! But glad isn't the word! There must be a better. I wish I knew a better! What is anonymous?'

He pulled her down till she was sitting on his knee. 'No name. We don't know our benefactor.'

'Some friend?'

'Some friend. To whom I owe one thousand four hundred pounds. The percentage of interest is also halved, so that after this year I shall only pay him two hundred and eighty pounds each Christmas.'

'God bless him, whoever he is!'

'Amen, I say to that.'

'Have you no idea?'

'Vague speculations on the way home. Each seems more unlikely than the last.'

There was silence for some minutes. He said: 'Where were you when I left?'

'After a stray cat Garrick was chasing. 'Twasn't fair, for the creature had a bad leg and I've told him oftentimes not to touch cats. Might it not mean now that the mine could go on a little longer?'

'Where is the cat now?'

'In the kitchen in a basket.'

'I thought so.' Ross stretched down to a bag at his feet. Demelza, a bit unused to this situation nowadays, made a move to rise but he would not let her. 'I've bought you a pound of Soachong tea. It is better than the stuff we get through Trencrom. I thought you'd like to try it.'

'Thank you, Ross. That's kind of you. . . . *Now* perhaps in a short time we shall not need to do anything for Mr Trencrom. D'you think it possible? Then we should be *really* free, out in the open, able to breathe again!'

'And I brought you a new brush and comb. I thought it a good thing to have one in reserve before you broke the present one.'

Demelza took the articles handed to her, turned them over in her hands. The comb had a twisted handle, like a plait of hair. 'Very – extravagant,' she said indistinctly.

'Very. I also got two pairs of worsted stockings each for the Gimletts. They were not dear: two shillings a pair. They've had little enough of late. And I have here a bonnet for Jeremy and a pair of knitted gloves. I thought he might be jealous if he was left out. I'm not sure as to the size. I suspect they will smother him.'

Demelza got up. The light was going, and over the hill the winter's day was infinitely remote. Everything was still except for the muffled roar behind the house, and this was less dominant for the time because the tide was out. Already the secret spell of frost had been cast over the valley.

'They look a good fit. That's clever to have guessed. And what did you buy yourself?'

Ross said: 'I was in doubt between a silk cloak and a jewelled sword, so I put it off till next time. This was my last purchase.'

He got up too and handed her a pair of women's garters. They were very fancy.

'For me?' said Demelza.

'I notice you've been wearing no stockings often this winter, and can only suppose you were in some straits to keep them up.'

Demelza burst into tears.

'Oh, come, come, I meant no offence. It was just a passing thought. If you'd prefer not to have them——'

'It isn't *that*,' she said. 'You know very *well* it is not that.' She put her hands to her face. 'It is the relief. . . . And then buying all these things.'

'They were none of them extortionate.' He put his arm round her, but her breakdown was checked by a sudden howl from Jeremy, who, unused to seeing his mother in tears, was moved to copy her. Demelza knelt over him and comforted him, wiping his eyes as well as her own. After a few seconds she glanced up at Ross.

'I'm sorry. It was the relief. You see – I love you so much. . . .'

Ross stared down at them both, moved himself and happy. The light from the window glinted on her hair, on the curve of her back, on Jeremy's clutching hands.

'I must put them on,' he said.

Demelza looked up. 'You mean Jeremy's bonnet and gloves?'

'What else,' rejoined Ross, smiling grimly.

With the usual sort of difficulty, Jeremy was invested with his new regalia. It all fitted pretty well, and should have done, since the shop-keeper had tried them on her own child first. Presently he went tottering off, the bonnet at a rakish angle, one glove not properly tied.

She had known that Ross hadn't meant that. She held the garters in her hand, and he took them from her, so she sat down uncertainly. She was wearing stockings tonight, old ones, but they were black and her skin above them glistened like ivory. He put the garters on with a good deal of care. It was months, almost years, since there had been this sort of thing between them, that odd fusion of desire and affection for which there is no substitute. Her eyes in the gathering darkness glowed at him. They stayed for a while hardly moving, he kneeling and she leaning back in the chair. His hands were cool on her legs. Remember this, she thought. In the times of jealousy and neglect, remember this.

He said: 'So you are not to be rid of me, my love.'

'I am not to be rid of you, my love.'

Over in the corner by the door Jeremy thumped down and began methodically to pull off his gloves.

Chapter six

VERITY, FRANCIS' SISTER, had written inviting Ross and Demelza to stay with them over Christmas; but with ruin coming apace, there had been no alternative to a refusal. This sudden reprieve changed the situation, and Ross agreed they should go over on Christmas Eve and stay the night. He did not feel he could leave the mine longer than that. Verity, so closely tied always to Francis, had taken his death hard; and as Demelza pointed out, it was their duty to be with her on this first Christmas after. Elizabeth was going with Geoffrey Charles, so that the family could be all together in this way, yet in a house and a locality with no memories.

At the last moment, to everyone's surprise and to Demelza's private relief, Elizabeth changed her plans. Her mother had been ill again, and she decided she must spend it at Cusgarne, her old home outside Truro. She told Ross of this when he paid her his weekly visit four days before Christmas.

His call was later than usual and he found her at supper, eating by herself in the winter parlour. He sat at the table talking to her, noticing how scanty the food was, refusing some himself. This room, the most used, was the most shabby. She looked tired and ill tonight, her delicacy suddenly fragile. Aunt Agatha was no better and seemed likely to become bedridden. An added strain of carried meals and all the other sickroom attentions. Tabb worked eighteen hours a day in the fields, and Mrs Tabb looked after the few animals they had retained. Ross could estimate the amount Elizabeth would have to do.

Afterwards he went upstairs, treading the dark corridors to Aunt Agatha's room. By the light of two candles Aunt Agatha was interviewed, propped up in bed, her bright beady eyes winking in the candle light, plying him with ceaseless questions whose answers she could not hear, running off into long strings of reminiscence out of a past dead and buried for everyone but herself. She told Ross she was ninety-seven and was determined to live to be a hundred. Whether the age was right or not, he didn't at all put it past her to have a pretty good try. She might be sinking, as Elizabeth thought, but she still had a long way to sink.

So Christmas came, Christmas Day being on a Tuesday and very windy and cold. In the night there had been flakes of snow, but these cleared before the day came. A fateful season, with Pitt calling out the militia, and associations of yeomen and gentry and shopkeepers everywhere being formed. And the French in Antwerp now, glowering across the Scheldt estuary, held in check only by a British guarantee of the Netherlands.

Ross, eating his Christmas dinner with the Blameys – Andrew, Verity's husband, on leave from his ship, and the two children of his first marriage, James a midshipman, boisterous and warmhearted, and Esther as reserved as her brother was open – Ross stared across the grey wind-flecked water of Falmouth Harbour, pondered on the prospects of war and whether he should go to France himself to find Mark Daniel while there was still peace; and who his benefactor was; and how he might discharge his own ethical debt to Elizabeth and to Geoffrey Charles.

And fifteen miles away his benefactor was eating an even quieter meal of roast beef and plum pudding in company with her uncle, her crisp auburn hair subdued into a tight coil, as her nature had been subdued these last weeks. When she came back from Truro, Ray Penvenen had told her of his interview with Dwight. They had quarrelled, uncle and niece, as he had expected that they should; but, rather to his own surprise, she had suddenly capitulated and there had been a semiaffectionate reconciliation. No definite undertaking on her part – he did not expect it – but the outcome was as he desired. For a time he was a trifle suspicious of his victory, and he still kept a watch on her movements through one or another of the servants; but he had slowly come to the conclusion that he had stamped on the attachment just in time. He expected to go to London in early February, and he proposed that Caroline should accompany him. She showed no splendid enthusiasm for the idea, but at least she raised no objection; and Mr Penvenen was privately determined that she should not return. He had a sister in London, married to a rich merchant, with seven children of her own. It would do her no harm in the world to have an eighth for a while.

And Dwight Enys dined alone and later than the rest, having been out and making the most of his time while the daylight lasted. Lottie Kempthorne, Charlie's eldest girl, who was nine, had developed the smallpox and was very ill. An ominous occurrence. This year, except for a high mortality from an outbreak of measles in June, there had been no serious epidemics. A disagreeable way of entering the new year, with one of the worst plagues to combat. While Dwight was in the cottage, he noticed Lottie's younger sister May playing with a new kind of story book. It was called *The History of Primrose Prettyface* and was printed on good stiff paper and bound between covers of horn. As he ate his dinner, he tried to remember where he had seen another such book; but his mind soon turned to thoughts of Caroline.

Among presents which had come to him to-day was one from the Hoblyns: a finely woven scarf. On an old piece of ruled exercise paper was printed: '*From Rosina, with love.*' He wondered who had done this, for he knew none of them could write. Other gifts had come in kind today: eggs; a piece of bacon; two loaves of bread; a cake; six tallow candles; a woven mat – tokens of gratitude from people from whom each gift meant a real sacrifice.

. . . And Elizabeth. Elizabeth did not spend Christmas Day at Cusgarne after all.

She found her mother less ill than she had expected, but did not on that account feel any less obliged to stay with them as planned.

But at noon a message came from George Warleggan saying he had just heard of her being there and inviting them all to the new Warleggan country house, Cardew, where he was entertaining a few close friends over the week end. Mrs Chynoweth, reluctant to venture out, pressed acceptance on Elizabeth with glowing descriptions of its magnificence. Elizabeth struggled with her sense of duty and turned the invitation down. At two George himself arrived, having come to fetch her. So, rather to her own surprise, on this gusty cheerless day with a half-gale blowing itself out, she found herself sharing his carriage, having left Geoffrey Charles in the care of her parents.

Cardew, begun to Nicholas Warleggan's requirements only ten years ago, she found all that it was reputed to be: a house with an enormous Ionic portico, lavishly furnished public rooms with massive fireplaces and moulded ceilings, and thirty-five bedrooms, besides staff quarters, gun rooms, workshops, stillrooms, stables, greenhouses, and walled gardens. In the front of the house the grounds had been laid out to give an uninterrupted view of an artificial lake with a rolling parkland beyond.

The house made Trenwith look like a country cottage and Cusgarne more down-at-heel than ever. And after Cusgarne it was so warm and draughtless. George derived enormous pleasure from showing Elizabeth over it all, a fact not unremarked by the other members of the Warleggan clan. There were about two dozen guests in the house, people carefully chosen by Mr Nicholas Warleggan for their likely value to him in his business or social dealings; and he would have been better pleased if George had not gone off in the middle of the day, to return with this young woman and devote the whole of his attention to her.

Had there been anything 'in it' for George, he would have felt differently. It was high time George was married, and the *right* time. There were three or four young women in their late teens whom Mr Warleggan had picked over, all eligible for one or more reasons but chiefly for title or blood connections – since George could provide the money – and Nicholas would have been pleased to see his son making some recognizable movement towards one of them. This long-standing sentimental infatuation for a delicate uninfluential widow was all wrong – especially for a woman who, even by marriage, bore the name of Poldark.

In any case, even supposing that some sort of a match was made of it – and Nicholas, knowing Elizabeth, thought the chances remote – and supposing one swallowed the disappointment of such a poor match, Elizabeth, with only one child by her former marriage and he eight years old, was unlikely to be fecund; and above all things Nicholas wanted to see several stout grandchildren about the house. He wished that it had been Elizabeth who had fallen down the mine instead of Francis.

Thought of the Poldarks took his eye round to his brother Cary, talking in a corner to the younger Boscoigne. Cary was becoming a responsibility to the more respectable members of the family. Being closely concerned in much of the Warleggan financial structure, he could not be pushed into the background like Grandfather Warleggan, yet in his dress and in his manners he refused to advance with Nicholas and George. He could not be induced to wear a wig or to discard his skullcap or to keep his old coats free from snuff and ink stains. By his presence he brought one down to his level. Tony Boscoigne must be secretly laughing at him now, perhaps taking note of his peculiarities so that he could ape them afterwards to his friends. It was useless having a fine house and all the splendour that money could buy if one had to countenance such relatives.

And Cary's influence on George was constantly a bad one. Neither of them realized as he, Nicholas, did the tremendous importance of personal and commercial probity. Establish that name, that reputation, and within the limitations of ordinary finance you could accomplish anything. Cary's only concern was to gain his end and let the principles go hang.

Nicholas thought of their recent meeting when Harris Pascoe had called upon them with young Poldark's draft in settlement of the promissory note. As it happened they had all been in the building, and Cary had stormed in to him with a face so white he had supposed him ill. There and then, with Harris Pascoe waiting in an outer office, they had had a passionate scene. Cary had fairly ranted, and George, though he controlled himself better, had really felt little different. It had taken all his own personal influence to calm Cary down, to persuade them both that this was nothing more than a normal business setback and should be treated as such. Indeed, no money was lost at all; money was made, for Mr Pearce had parted with the bill at a discount; and it would be beneath their dignity as men of affairs to be put out of countenance over some loss of revenge upon an impoverished and unimportant country squire. They had long been too big for that. It did not become them.

So far as George was concerned, Nicholas was satisfied he had won his point; but with Cary one could never be certain. One supposed he was conforming to an agreed line, and then suddenly he would do something quite heterodox which showed he had never had any intention of acquiescing at all.

Ross nursed his own special problem through Christmas and nearly into the New Year. Then he went to see Harris Pascoe. He wanted first of all, he said, to sell his remaining thirty shares in Wheal Leisure. He had made six hundred pounds out of the last and expected no less from these. Pascoe grunted and shook sand over a document. 'I suppose you have to do it? It's a pity now. War's almost certain. This bringing of the King to trial will inflame tempers on both sides. Copper will be rising in price all the time.'

'I am not compelled to do it, I want to do it. Perhaps you can get more than six hundred for the shares.'

'It's a tidy price. I s-suppose you will use the money in some way to keep your other mine alive?'

'No. I'm reconciled to the loss of that. I want the money for a special purpose. I want to leave it in your hands for the moment. Since you consented to act for an anonymous client once, you can hardly refuse to do so again.'

Pascoe stared at his lean visitor, who at times was coming to have a wolfish look.

'I don't follow you.'

'Francis' widow and his family are in dire poverty. More so now than we are. And she has no man. Two years ago Francis sank his last six hundred pounds in Wheal Grace. I feel a sting of responsibility for the result. I want Elizabeth Poldark to have that six hundred pounds back.'

'And will she accept it?'

Ross brooded for a moment. 'No. Or I think not. That's where I want your help. When my shares in Leisure are sold, I want you to make her an offer for her holding – or her son's holding – in Wheal Grace, on behalf of an anonymous client you represent. She's bound to accept that, and the money can then be transferred to her.'

Ross watched the sleet melting and trickling down the windows. The old year was true to its reputation to the last.

He added: 'It's not an original idea, being cribbed from your friend who used it on my behalf.'

Mr Pascoe blew the sand away and shook his document backwards and forwards to be sure it was dry. 'You mean you are offering £600 for a half share in a mine which is about to close?'

'We are not closed yet, of course. The miracle may always happen.'

'And do you suppose your cousin-in-law will b-believe some stranger is foolish enough to make such an offer?'

'Could I believe anyone was foolish enough to accept a renewal of my promissory note?'

Mr Pascoe coughed. 'No. . . .'

There was another silence. Pascoe's eyes moved to the clock. 'You'll take dinner with us?'

'Thank you.'

They got up. Pascoe said: 'As your banker and your creditor, I must try to dissuade you from making this quixotic move. F-frankly I consider it ill-advised. You can't afford it. Indeed you can't. This is the *only* money you have.'

'I can't afford it,' said Ross. 'And – I have my own wife to keep and my own son to care for. But I'm here to look after them myself. Francis is not. If I do this, I shall order my life with a clearer conscience.'

'Would it not be as satisfactory if you made over your *income* from the Leisure shares, I mean temporarily, until things improve for Mrs Poldark. One never quite knows how circumstances change. It wouldn't be a lot for her, no big lump sum, but it would mean a regular payment every quarter.'

'No,' said Ross. 'It would not be as satisfactory.'

Harris Pascoe went over to a side cupboard beside the window and took a decanter and two glasses from it. 'I did not s-suppose that any advice I chose to give you would be heeded.'

Ross rubbed his chin. 'Your advice is always welcome, Harris. Like your friendship, I know its solid value. But in these matters where blood and sinew come into it and sometimes affection and dislike, we have to behave according to the chemicals in us. This act would give us satisfaction and that would not. So we do things, make moves which can't seem sensible to an onlooker such as yourself. But always it's good to have someone by who points steadily to magnetic north. That's what you do. And we remember it with gratitude, even when we remember it too late.'

Harris Pascoe clinked his glass as he poured out the canary. 'I will, of course, do what I can to help you, Ross. I cannot withhold that, though I withhold my approval. It is a very honourable gesture you are making. I hope you will not come to regret it.'

The Fox and Grapes was a small rather lonely posting inn midway between Killewarren and Redruth. In it, at about this time, two other people were also drinking canary and making plans.

Fifteen minutes before, Caroline Penvenen and her groom had ridden up; and Caroline had said she wanted some refreshment and some shelter from the weather and he must go on ahead of her and assure the Teagues that she would be with them very shortly. The lad looked uncomfortable, hot, and reluctant to go, part betraying his secret instructions from his master; so Caroline impatiently told him to wait outside for her; she would rejoin him when her thirst was quenched.

In the little dark parlour of the inn with its framed needlework pictures, its Indian fern, and its pewter mugs, she peeled off her gloves and stood a moment warming her hands by the fire, uncertain whether the arrangement had worked out as planned. She had seen no horse outside, but it would be a common precaution to tether it out of sight. As the innkeeper's wife came bustling in with the wine, she drew a breath to ask; and then she saw two glasses on the tray and Dwight standing on the threshold of the door.

Very soon they were in each other's arms. A cynic would have noted the sharp advance in their relationship since Mr Penvenen's move. Caroline perhaps would have taken the same course in any event, but without opposition she might have been months longer taking it. Instead at the moment she was making the running, and Dwight was giving her her head – willingly and happily as to destination but doubtfully as to course. Perhaps something of the conflict in his mind showed in his expression, for abruptly she broke away and said:

'Do you not feel as I do? I should be sorry to go too fast and too far.'

'Neither, my darling, for that would be impossible. I – only wonder as to method. By nature I dislike secrecy – as I know you do – if it can be avoided. I should like to go to your uncle now and tell him what we intend. . . .'

'You don't know Uncle Ray. He has a streak of obstinacy common to all the Penvenens. But is there perhaps some special reason for your disliking the idea of an elopement?'

'Why d'you ask?'

'Because I feel there is.'

He came behind her chair, put his hand on her forehead. 'It's such a poor reason that I'm ashamed of it. You've heard of Keren Daniel?'

'The girl who . . .'

'Yes, the girl I fell in love with, though she was a patient of mine – the girl whose husband, Mark Daniel, found her unfaithful . . . and killed her – when he should have come to kill me.'

'Do you know, I heard a different version – that she threw herself at your head, etc. I can always be sure of one thing, Dwight, that your charity, which covers so much, never extends to yourself.'

'One version or the other, the facts are not in dispute. A man of my profession who acts as I acted is entitled to consider himself very low.' Dwight was going to move away, but she caught his hand on her shoulder. 'People were kind – charitable as you call it. The version that you heard has become the accepted one. Sometimes I accept it myself. But there is a stigma still. Therefore – one's future conduct becomes of the greatest moment. . . .'

'And marrying me . . .'

'Marrying you openly would set a seal on my happiness – yes, and on my respectability too – that I don't deserve – but gladly take. Marrying you in secret, running away with you at night – though I willingly, gladly take that too – smacks a little of the fortune hunter, of the morally equivocal person which my affair with Keren suggests I really am. To leave also all my friends and patients without a word hints at desertion too, a desertion vastly different from the affair of Keren but not altogether different in effect. . . .'

He broke off and covered her hand with his other one. It lay quiescent between his, but he did not delude himself that that signified quiescence on Caroline's part. He had said more than he intended.

She said quietly enough: 'Do you liken me to Keren?'

'Good God, no. You're as far apart——'

'Isn't this really, truly, something in yourself, Dwight? Haven't you to overcome it in any case? Nowhere I've been have I heard a word of blame for you in Keren's death. She threw herself at every man. Why should anyone think worse of you for marrying me?'

'Not marrying you, no——'

'Or of running away with me.' She withdrew her hand but not angrily. 'Dwight, you may feel I'm unreasonable in not doing as you want – but I have such a strong instinct that the other way is right. If we – come out into the open before we go – now, with a whole month to wait, there will be all manner of complications, new difficulties to face. It will mean leaving my uncle's house, breaking with him directly; and although I know I can do that, I don't want to. I don't at all want to if it can be avoided. Although I pretend to care nothing what he thinks, my ties are really quite strong. I owe him things which I should not if he were my father. . . . If we leave in secret, run away, he will be furious. He will denounce us both in the strongest possible language. But he will denounce us only to himself, for there will be no one else to say it to. Nothing will be said to us which it would be impossible for his dignity's sake to withdraw. Nor should I say anything definite, final, wounding, as I should if confronting him to his face. This way, with luck, there should be nothing to stop a reconciliation in six or twelve months. He will accept what cannot be undone. But the other way there would be a "if-you-leave-this-house-you-leave-it-for-ever" scene, and his pride would prevent him from retracting.'

Dwight was silent, and was silenced. There was nothing to advance against this. It was true what Caroline said, that his reluctance was something he must personally fight and overcome. In any case, it was manifestly unfair to burden her with the aftereffects of an old love affair – for it was nothing more than that. He liked her better not less well for her loyalty to the old man, which was something she had not betrayed until it came to the point of defying him. Like most of her feelings, she had kept it well hidden.

Dwight still woke up sometimes with a sense of incredulity that this brilliant, vital young woman had consented to marry him at all. She was giving up so much to do so. It would be a measure of his own smallness and ingratitude if he queried her way of doing it.

A week later Elizabeth sent a message that she wanted to see Ross. He rode to Trenwith in the teeth of a northwesterly gale. When he got there, he thought he had never known the old house so empty. The wind howled down the big open chimney in the hall, loose panes in the great window rattled ceaselessly, a worn mat by the door floated and flapped in the air current. Human life and warmth had gone from the place.

Elizabeth was upstairs, and he watched her come down the broad staircase in that swift, light-footed way she had made peculiarly her own. She was wearing a little white masculine jacket over her tight-waisted grey dress. She saw his eyes light up at the sight of her.

'Ross.' She offered him her hand. 'Please come in. I am sorry to have brought you from your work. But I had the strangest letter from Mr Harris Pascoe yesterday, and I want to know what I must do.'

He followed her into the winter parlour, and she took up two letters from beside the spinning wheel. She gave him the first. Although he knew very much what its contents were, he went through it carefully, interested to see just how Pascoe had worded the thing. When he'd finished, he looked up at her.

'Well, isn't it astonishing?' she said. 'That anyone should offer us – at this stage – as much for my share in Wheal Grace as Francis first put into it? Has there been some new discovery of ore?'

'None. I wish there had. It's strange, I agree. Indeed, it's hard to understand. Everyone knows we must finish soon. And Pascoe says he may not disclose who it is. You had this yesterday?'

'Yes.' She hesitated, lashes dark on her cheek. 'My first thought was that it was George Warleggan. You know of his attempts to help me. Indeed I think he tries to make things better for me just as persistently as he tries to make them worse for you. And I thought that by buying these shares he was perhaps seeking both ends at the same time. . . . So I wrote to Mr Pascoe – sent it in by Tabb yesterday. Tabb waited for an answer.'

She offered him the second letter. 'Dear Madam,' Ross read, 'I thank you for your communication delivered to me today. I am able to assure you that, should you and Captain Poldark decide to sell your son's holding in Wheal Grace, the interest will not pass to any member of the Warleggan family nor to anyone representing them. The prospective buyer is an independent gentleman with your son's and your own best interests at heart. There will be no attempt to interfere with the present control of the mine. I have the honour to be, madam, your obedient servant, Harris Pascoe.'

Ross handed the letter back. She was watching him closely, and he had to say something. 'Extraordinary.'

'And what do you advise? I do not know if we should consider it.'

'Consider it? We should accept the offer.'

'That surprises me too. I thought you would fear interference from an outsider.'

'In other circumstances I should. But there is Pascoe's letter. And I have to tell you of a certain good fortune which has come to me recently.' He explained about the anonymous loan to himself. 'I can only suppose the same person is trying to help you. Some eccentric with the Poldark good at heart. . . . He could not have come at a more opportune time.'

'Have you any idea who it might be?'

'None at all. But I trust Pascoe. I know he would not betray us into any false position.'

The tightness of her waist seemed to emphasize the shape of her small breasts as she turned away from him. 'I – this money would of course make all the difference.'

'We should be out of our minds not to take it – for Geoffrey Charles's sake. There's little prospect for the mine unless this newcomer will invest fresh money. He may have some such idea. If so, it can only be to my benefit. I shall hope to meet him.' Ross thought he was coming through the interview rather imaginatively. But not without a curious feeling as if he were cheating Elizabeth instead of helping her at great cost to himself. He had not told Demelza what he'd done, and he hoped it would be a long time before she found out.

Elizabeth said: 'You're sure you feel this is right, Ross – for yourself, I mean? Perhaps you are pretending to like this because you believe it is best for us. I should dislike to think I was being false to our friendship.'

'You're not being false to anything, Elizabeth. I mean what I say. You should sell. It will enormously ease your position. I'm only grateful to you for hesitating, for your loyalty and for your interest all through.'

She smiled across at him with a new brilliance. 'Loyalty's not all on one side, Ross, nor ever has been. Thank you for coming this morning.'

He rode home feeling already well paid for his sacrifice but with the old allegiance grievously reawakened.

Chapter seven

MR COKE, THE Warleggans' nominee, bought the shares, at £22 10s. od. a share.

After paying Pascoe £600 for Elizabeth, Ross had £75 over. This he could put to the reduction of one of his other debts or could set aside for future interest payments. Or he could buy another month's supply of coal and keep Grace going through February.

Henshawe said: 'I think 'twould be a pity to hang on longer than we'd planned. I'm so disappointed as you, except that my loss is a hundred and not six. But there's such a thing as a feel about a mine. She've been awkward from the start. I'd never have believed the poorness of the yield.'

'We shall get little enough for the engine. I shall feel tempted to dismantle it and keep it for the time.'

'There's never been a *sign* of the Trevorgie lode,' said Henshawe, his eyes frowning at the map. 'I do believe 'twas an old wives' tale from first to last. First we drove seeking it from Leisure, and then from Grace. If 'twas there at all, we should have found some sign of it.'

'And Mark Daniel,' said Ross broodingly. 'All our prophets have been false.'

'D'you think he was in his right mind that night you speak of?'

'He may have been deceived by one or two of the false promises that raised our hopes. There was that fine deposit in the northeast end of the thirty level. . . .'

'Copper £103 a ton last week.' Henshawe bit the nail of his little finger. 'When we started Leisure, 'twas only £80. 'Twas a crying pity you had to sell your Leisure shares just now. I reckon we shall make a little fortune out of her before we're done. . . . If there was any *quality* in the stuff we'd raised from Grace . . .' He took his finger out of his mouth and stared at it.

'What were yesterday's assays from the seventy level?'

'Copper, tin, silver lead; some of each; not enough of any. 'Tis as if the lodes have gotten mixed, contaminated like. The copper's *less* both in quality and quantity than it was ten fathom nearer grass.'

Ross lifted a piece of the ore-bearing rock, turned it over and over in his hand. 'I fancy there's more tin than anything in this.'

'Copper lodes often do peter out that way.'

'What happens farther down still? The fault will not disappear, surely. Isn't there a chance of a renewal of copper at increased depth?'

Henshawe shook his head. 'Nobody knows how the earth was made. Some do say that the sea runs far inland and underground and makes the springs, forcing them along and up, like to the blood of a man's veins. So the copper runs too, like to a bone or a sinew, and then stops for reasons we know naught of. . . . She've been a grievous disappointment; but if I was you, I should not throw good money after bad.'

Ross stared out of the half-shuttered window. The pale, grey January light fell on the scar half hidden by the hair growing down in front of his ear. All the old disquiet in his face to-day. The old rebellion against the pressure of inanimate things, the stubborn secret anger. You could never get away from it, Henshawe thought, something inborn.

'How would it be this last month,' Henshawe said, trying to remove the look, 'if we drove down again – not exactly starting an eighty level, but following these poor indications as if they was good and seeing what another ten fathom have to show. I don't give much for the prospect; but 'twould perhaps settle a query in your mind, like.'

'How long *can* we go on, with no fresh capital?'

'If this next parcel of ore fetch what the last did, I'd say three weeks. Of course if we closed the deeper levels, I'd say two or three weeks more than that.'

'Your money's in as well as mine. I can't decide for us both.'

'You've six times my stake, sur. I'll abide by what you say.'

'Yet you're the mining man.'

'There's little or no mining in this now. 'Tis instinct so much as anything, and your instinct's so good as mine.'

'Very well,' said Ross after a moment. 'We'll go down.'

When Henshawe had gone, Ross stayed in the old library for an hour or more, checking entries in the cost book. Presently, it being reckoning day, a file of miners formed outside and came in one by one, made their marks in the book against their names, and received the money due to them. Almost all of them had their own private marks, few being content with the conventional cross. All of them knew that in a matter of weeks they would come here for the last time. Ross had a word for each one, often a joke or a wry comment. They were not his chief friends, most of whom he had engaged at Wheal Leisure when opening it; but they had become his friends during the last year.

When the last had left he still stayed on, though it was well after two. Again and again he weighed up the samples of ore, comparing what had been raised this week with what had been mined last. Several times he took up a hammer and split pieces off. Once he nearly went through the floor in doing so. It was as well that he was not immediately above the cache, which had been made at the far end of the room under the last window. Where the trap door had been cut two big metal trunks stood, hiding the joins in the floor boards.

That reminded him, he must see Mr Trencrom, for Mr Trencrom was not playing fair. The storage place had been made on the strict understanding that goods should be put there for a limited time only – three or four days at the most until they could be carried away. There were things in there now, a roll of fancy lace and ten five-gallon casks of geneva rum which had been left more than three weeks. That wasn't good enough.

At that moment Demelza called him from the front door, and he put his head out and answered her. The house being L-shaped, he let himself out of the end door, slipped its padlock on, and was about to walk across the garden when he saw Will Nanfan coming down the valley.

Will was an old friend. For the time he was comfortably off, with a small holding, five grown children, and a pretty second wife. He was a big fair man in his fifties, still handsome, and played the fiddle.

'Good day, sur, I'm glad to find ee in. I thought 'twould be a good time to call.'

'Come inside, Will. You have news for me?'

'Yes, but I'll not come in if 'tis all the same to you. I just dropped by to tell ee we've found Mark Daniel.'

Ross looked up sharply. 'Found him? At Cherbourg?'

'No, sur, not at Cherbourg. He's in Ireland.'

Ross stared across at the chimney on the hill. It was throwing out black smoke, which meant inefficient firing. He did not speak.

'That's why we couldn't seem to trace 'im. The people he'd been with said he'd left, but they'd no notion where. Nine months ago there was a deal o' trouble in Cherbourg. All this kick an' sprawl over the revolution. There was house burning and what not. Folk began to look askance at Mark, him being a foreigner; so he bested to go to Ireland, and slipped away in one of the Irish ketches that run goods over from time to time. He's living, they d'say, in Galway; or 'twas some such outlandish name.'

'How did you find this out?'

'Got talking with the skipper o' one of the ketches. He's a friend of Mark's, it 'pears. We do business wi' the Irish vessels, upon times. They run into the Scillies same as we do; they've depots to leave goods there same as we 'ave. They haven't the size, y'know, and often come back that far laden to the gunnels.'

Ross said: 'When will you be seeing this man again?'

'O'Higgins? Next week, like as not. The *One and All* will not be sailing till near the end of the month, but I'm takin' the cutter over to the Scillies on Monday if the weather d'lift.'

'Will you give him a message from me?'

'I've already said for him to tell Mark Daniel ye are wanting to see him.'

'Good. I'll send a note to Mark. Someone will read it to him, even if it's the priest. Come in here.' Ross unlocked the door of the library again and went over to the desk.

Demelza, who had been occupying her waiting time giving Jeremy his food, got up and went to the window just as Nanfan left the library. When Ross came across, he looked preoccupied but not displeased. They ate the meal in silence for a time, the sole conversationalist being Jeremy, who was intelligible only to himself.

Ross told her the purpose of Will Nanfan's visit. Demelza said simply: 'I'm glad we shall know.'

'Yes. I'd been afraid perhaps he was dead. It's so long.'

'Shall you get him to come here?'

'I've asked him to meet me in the Scillies. There's less danger for him there, and I'm sure he'll come.'

'And how shall you get there?'

'I may pay a fishing boat to run me out from Penzance. Or I can go when Trencrom makes his next run.'

'You won't be quite so sure, that way, as bringing Mark to the mine. I'm sure he'd be willing to come.'

'He would. But a half-hour's conversation, with a plan of the workings, is all I need. I shall know then just what he was talking about and where it is likely to be found.'

Lottie Kempthorne was a great deal better. As Charlie put it: 'She have very good symptoms upon her now, and the smallpox are coming out kindly.' Dwight watched the other child, but there was as yet no sign. Nor was there another case in the village. It seemed too good to be true. He called in one afternoon and was not at all pleased to find Rosina Hoblyn and her mother there.

Charlie was in high spirits, and after a few moments Dwight learned why. Rosina, with her father's glowering permission, had at last promised to marry Charlie. At this Dwight glanced a little in surprise at Rosina, and she flushed. He had never thought her enamoured of her middle-aged suitor, and he was not convinced now. She was following the line of least resistance, edged by his persuasions down the path he wanted her to follow, her father softened for his part by what Charlie could offer her.

It might well turn out a happy marriage. This cottage, with the improvements Charlie had made, was lighter and much more comfortable than the one she would leave. And apparently she would no longer need to spend her whole day over a needle. Even as she was now, with her lovely face and unhalting walk, the chances were that any other offer she might get would come from some callow boy earning five or six shillings a week with only a tumble-down shed to offer her for a home.

All the same, thought Dwight, there might have been love and youth between them; and even if the glow lasted only a short time, it was not, in this drab world, a thing to be lightly sacrificed. He knew that.

'We reckon,' said Charlie, 't'build on another room next year, so's Lottie an' May can sleep to theirselves. Then Rosina and me, if mebbe we get a family increase, can have things fitty and proper, like.'

Dwight glanced round the room. He was not an observant man in the ordinary way of things, and the slow changes which had taken place inside this cottage during the last eighteen months were suddenly apprehended by him as if they were the work of recent weeks. The new curtains, the good earthenware cups, the matting at the door, the candles in suitable sticks, the glass in the window. He looked at Kempthorne, and Charlie, who by some instinct had been driven to look at him, quickly lowered his eyes.

'I hope you'll be very happy,' Dwight said.

'And we hope you'll come to our wedding,' said Charlie quickly. 'Don't us, Rosina? Why, all we have we owe to surgeon. Rosina's lipsy leg cured. And me with my consumptives. If it edn been for that, I should never be living a decent life and making money from my sail making.'

'And now Lottie on the mend,' said Mrs Hoblyn.

'When do you expect to have your wedding?' Dwight asked.

'Next month, sur. Banns aren't called yet, and 'twill take a little time for to get things ready. Lottie'll be out an' about 'fore then.'

'Oh, yes, she'll be out and about before then.' If the miracle happened and no one else caught it. Charlie was still watching him. Charlie was a mystery: good-natured, friendly as a dog, always working, always smiling, always grateful for what you did. He never allowed anyone to forget, in Dwight's hearing, that he owed his good health to the surgeon. Yet Dwight, more especially of late months, was not quite comfortable in his presence. In a crisis he felt he would sooner trust the slow scowl of Jacka oblyn than the ready show of Charlie Kempthorne's yellow teeth.

On his arrival home he did not see Bone about; and his visitor's horse was tethered round the side of the house, so that he walked into the parlour unsuspecting.

She was standing by the window, tall and straight as a lance, and she turned at once smiling at him.

'Caroline. . . . Is something the matter?'

'Everything is the matter. I have surprised your secret life! *"From Rosina, with love."* Is that how your patients address you?'

She handed him the scarf that Rosina had made for him, to which the printed note was still pinned. He accepted it but put it over the back of a chair, took her hands.

'You should have sent a message, my love. Have you been allowed out without your faithful groom?'

'No, I gave him the slip. I mustn't stay long.'

'It's *more* than good to see you. Let me look at you. Always when you are away from me . . .'

'There is a complication to report, and I came to report it. Uncle Ray has advanced our departure for London by one week. He now proposes to leave Killewarren on the third of February.'

He stared at her. 'We can put forward our own going by a couple of days, then. That's all. It will mean a slight rearrangement, but we can leave on the first.'

'Have you heard again from Paul Hardwicke?'

'Yes. He thinks there will be a clear opening in the town when Dr Marquis retires. Until then it should not be difficult, he says, to find full occupation in temporary work. He counsels against my setting up on my own.'

'No doubt there is a certain cliquishness among the apothecaries. Dwight, I think it would be a good thing if we fixed our going for the second. If I am supposed to be leaving for London on the morning of the third, it will make my packing that much easier. Instead of escaping with a bundle through a top window in the approved fashion, I can get my trunks downstairs and safely stowed in the coach.'

'Do you still very much insist on going in – your own coach?'

'Of course. Why are you so much against it? Because it looks as if *I* am running away with *you*?'

He frowned uncomfortably. 'Not altogether. But I – well I have a feeling for providing the means of travel. It's going to be a moot point with us many times in the future, no doubt; I shall have to accustom myself to having a wife with a will and money of her own——'

'Especially a will.'

' – but in the first instance I should have better preferred us to travel by my arrangement and at my expense. I admit there is no logic to it.' He smiled. 'You have the coach – why shouldn't it be used? But——'

'Why not indeed? Once we have left Cornwall no one is to know it is not your coach. I shall certainly not say any different.'

Bone could be heard outside now, raking the gravel path near the front door. The interview could not last much longer, and they talked on at an accelerated pace. This meeting might be their last before they met to be married, but he would not kiss her.

'I care nothing for poxes, small, large, or cow,' said Caroline. 'But I am bitterly jealous of your Rosina – still Hoblyn by name if no longer hobbling by nature. A nice scarf, if a thought coarse for a gentleman. I chanced to see her only last week when I happened to be in Sawle. Pretty enough, I grant you. I hope you will not jilt me, dear.'

'I think I am a little sensitive to such jokes,' said Dwight, taking the scarf from her again, 'and therefore hope you'll not make them. If there is any jilting, it will be on your side, and you know it. I shall not rest easy until you wear a ring on your finger and I have put it there.'

'So long as it is not a ring through my nose, you may put it there as soon as you can.'

She began to pull on her gloves. He had gone over to a side table, a trifle put out by what she had said although he tried not to be. She followed him with her eyes, which were a little doubting under their mockery.

'You do not regret making this move, Dwight?'

He turned at once. 'Heavens, no! How could I regret it?'

'Often since we decided to go I have noticed a discomfort in you, an unease, call it what you wish.' She threw back her hair to tie her own scarf. 'Is it still against your principles?'

'No, nor ever was. Believe me, please.' He stared at her and then half laughed himself. 'You're incorrigible, Caroline. For a moment I believed you were serious. You must rate me for having so literal a mind.'

'I think,' said Caroline acutely, 'that you would not have taken it seriously if it had not been a serious consideration in your thoughts.'

'Utter nonsense. I could shake you.' He took her by the elbows but only held her firm. 'Caroline, look at me. I love you. Does that mean anything to you? Does it mean *anything* at all?'

'Oh, yes, quite a certain amount, I assure you.'

'That's an admission anyhow. Then perhaps you'll not goad me with these strange doubts which you put into my mind ready-made. It's very mischievous of you – and a little unfair. We are utterly agreed as to the end – how could I have second thoughts as to that? – and as to the method, what doubts I had I voiced long since and have now forgotten.'

She put her gloved fingers up to his stock, patted it, then allowed her hand to travel affectionately down the line of his cheek.

'I'm sorry if I plague you so grievously. It is only that sometimes I wonder when the "end in view" has become a commonplace, sitting at your fireside and sharing your bed and never absent from your table, I wonder whether then you will not perhaps sigh for your Cornish patients and your lost integrity.'

'Can I say more than no? And why should the doubts be all on your side? What of you, throwing away thirty or forty thousand pounds for a down-at-heel physician? When the first excitement's faded and the novelty's over and it means living to an economy you've never been used to . . . not able to keep up with the rich people of Bath, hunting to a restricted purse, dressing and entertaining at the same rate.'

'In the first place, as you know, I do not suppose I am throwing away thirty or forty thousand pounds, not if we arrange to quarrel at a distance and leave loopholes for reconciliation. My uncles bark worse than they bite, and they have no one else to leave their money to except a hatch of nephews and nieces who're already well provided for. But if they do remain estranged and will their money to the Astronomical Society, I shall certainly not complain and shall think the exchange a fair one. I intend to live my life in my own way and shall not be bribed by them into remaining their domestic tabby. It will do me *good*, Dwight, to stand on my own feet, and I want you to help me. . . .'

'I'll help you, my darling,' he said. 'I think perhaps we shall have to help each other.'

Chapter eight

A HALF-HOUR'S CONVERSATION might be all Ross needed with Mark Daniel; but the arrangements for such a conversation, and its venue on one of a group of wind-swept islands well out in the Atlantic in mid-winter, needed a margin on either side to allow for delays. Ross estimated he would be away a week.

A message had arrived from Mark that he was willing to come. Ross had suggested the twenty-ninth of January as an approximate date, because Trencrom had said the *One and All* would leave on the twenty-eighth and they could drop him off at St Mary's the following day and pick him up on their return. Mark had agreed to the twenty-ninth, but, with his own journey in an Irish ketch even more dependent on wind and weather than Ross's, he might well be days early or late.

With such news Ross decided to risk his last £75 in the purchase of coal. What had seemed a useless gesture now looked a fair business risk.

As the month neared its end political crisis again overshadowed the personal worries of men. The long-drawn trial of Louis the Sixteenth had ended in a sentence of death. There was still chance of a reprieve, but few really believed it would come about. The Convention could hardly retract now. Changes took place in England overnight. The noisy Jacobin clubs silently closed their doors. Arguments which had gone on for years in taproom and in coffee shop came to an end. Men waited. Some went home and looked out old fowling pieces and rubbed up relics of earlier wars.

On the twenty-fourth it was known that the execution had been carried out. That settled it. Few people in England had much admiration for Louis beyond the manner of his dying; and it was less than one hundred and fifty years since they had cut off the head of their own king; but sentiment does not derive from logic. Theatres closed, crowds demonstrated outside the Palace. The French ambassador was given his papers. Now it was only a question of time.

It was in this atmosphere that Ross took leave of Demelza on Sunday the twenty-seventh and made his way by easy stages to St Ives, where the *One and All* had been undergoing repairs. Her crew, mainly St Ann's men, had found their own way down the coast in ones and twos; and soon after six on the following morning the seventy-ton cutter slipped out on the flood tide.

A thin layer of powdered frost lay on her decks and did not melt until the sun rose. It seemed to Ross, standing in the bows with the small waves lipping at the yellow gunwales as she went about, that the sun came up directly above where Nampara would be. To feel a deck under his feet again after so long was unfamiliar and exciting.

To Demelza, rising early and knowing that if things went according to plan he would be at sea before dawn, the wintry day was charged with apprehension. No study of the battered old linen map, showing the Scilly Isles far out of reach of the French regicides, was a complete reassurance. As she went about her daily work, she blamed herself for getting into the habit of worrying. It was entirely outside her nature so far as her own safety went, but with Ross the tendency had grown on her. She must check it; she must correct it. One could only wish that he was a man less prone to attract trouble.

Determined to be practical, she hummed and sang at her work all morning, and in the afternoon for the first time for months opened her spinet and played a few airs. Once she had taken lessons from Mrs Kemp, but that was in the happy days of moderate prosperity when Julia was alive. She wished she could find time and interest to take it up again. Just playing a chord sometimes gave her exquisite pleasure; it struck down into her soul, not merely heard but felt, emotion of a new kind. In the middle of this exercise Dwight Enys arrived.

When she opened the door to him he said: 'Was that you playing? I'm sorry, I'd no wish to disturb you. Is Ross in?'

His cloak was flecked with hail, though she had not noticed the shower.

'No, Dwight. He's . . . from home for a day or two. Won't you come in?'

He took off his cloak and hat on the threshold and shook them. Over the hills the sky was as brown as an old blanket with the passing storm.

'Did you walk?' she asked as he followed her into the parlour.

'Yes. I came about five because I thought Ross was usually back then. I should have come days ago but have been putting it off.'

'You'll take tea? It's that cold. I wish 'twould snow and then the cold might come down.'

'Do you know when Ross will be back?'

'By Saturday, I believe. Is it something urgent?'

'Oh . . . no, not urgent. Not in the ordinary sense.' Hesitating, non-plussed, Dwight sat on the edge of a chair. 'Jeremy is well?'

'Yes. Can you hear him? He has Jinny Scoble's two little boys in to play, and Jinny is minding them for me.' She turned to watch the kettle, which was making some preliminary, intermittent noises. 'I'll go fetch the teapot. I forgot to bring it in.'

When she came back, he was staring out of the window. Dusk had come suddenly, as if the sides of the valley had closed in, and the firelight flickered and glowed across the room. She thought, I wonder if he's safely there now; I wonder what the Scillies look like. She pictured them as high barren rocks. Dwight helped her to light the candles.

As the light flickered on her skin, she said: 'I know Ross wouldn't mind you knowing. You have all our other secrets, almost, so another makes small difference. He has gone with Mr Trencrom and is dropping off at the Scilly Islands to meet Mark Daniel, who has been found at last. The *One and All* will pick Ross up again and bring him home about Friday or Saturday, when they will – anchor off our cove.'

Friday was the first of February. Too late for him. 'I hope Daniel has some good news for you.'

The candles had died down to tiny pearls of light, and these now began to melt the tallow and to burn lozenge-shape.

'It seems a century since that night,' said Dwight. 'When you stood between us, you only, and Mark would have killed me. I'd have welcomed death, then, because I'd betrayed all the things I valued most – and the people who trusted me.'

'We were all overwrought that night. I'm glad nothing worse happened.'

In a distant part of the house there was a bump and after a pause a giggle of children's laughter. Demelza, who had expected tears, relaxed again.

Dwight said: 'The last thing I want is to remember that time. Because I came today to see Ross to tell him that I am leaving this district very shortly . . .'

She waited for him to go on. 'Is it to do with Caroline?'

'Yes. We're to be married. But because of her uncle's opposition it must take place in secret. So we're leaving together late on Saturday night.' He went on to explain why any other solution was impossible, why they could not live here, why he owed it to her to start afresh in a town where neither of them was known. Demelza listened in silence, and her silence to his overstrained perceptions was a criticism.

She said: 'Well, I'm glad to hear it for your sake, Dwight; sorry for our own. 'Twill not be only in Sawle and Grambler that you'll be missed. We shall feel – quite lost. And Jeremy.'

'Thank you. . . .'

The kettle now seemed to be bursting with steam and water, and the fire was spitting its protests. She made tea.

'I've been in correspondence with a physician who studied with me in London. He's ill and needs a change, so has agreed to come for six months on trial, with the prospect of staying. It will be far better than leaving no one at all. Wright is a good man, older than I am, but with similar views. I'm sure you will like him.'

'Yes.'

'Of course I know it will not be the same for a time. Without conceit I know that. And it means also something for me – on which I can depend. I shall miss people – and of course chiefly you.' He frowned out of the window to hide his feelings. 'I want you to tell Ross, will you, how much I feel I owe to him, to you both, for your friendship. The whole thing has been a great grief to me.'

After a few moments Demelza brought him a cup of tea. 'Marrying someone you love isn't a time for grief, Dwight. The last thing Ross or I should want – or I'm sure that any of your friends would want. . . . Worry about us and our ailments so much as you like until Saturday. But after Saturday you should forget all that and begin your new life as if Sawle and Grambler had never been. 'Twould not be unfeeling to do that. It would be good sense.'

When Dwight had gone, Demelza cleared away the tea things. Time Jeremy was thinking of bed. Dwight's visit had left her lonelier than ever. The discussion had curiously skirted the character of the girl in the case. Ross had once predicted Caroline would wipe her feet on Dwight, but perhaps he had revised his opinion since then. Demelza knew Bath by repute. That it would suit Caroline was fairly clear. Whether Dwight would settle into the conventional pattern remained to be seen.

Strolling round the small bleak island of St Mary's, Ross waited impatiently for some sign of the Irish ketch bearing Mark Daniel. So far in two days there had been none. The winds had been contrary, veering and backing between northwest and east. An active man, and, with so much at stake in this meeting, he found the time unbearably slow. Three French crabbers put into the sheltered water between St Mary's and Tresco on Tuesday when the weather was bad, but their crews did not come ashore.

Hugh Town was little more than a straggle of thatched cottages and fish cellars clutching the shore of the island where it curved in a natural harbour. Every night the new revolving oil light on St Agnes Island, only installed three years, sent out its warning to wandering ships. Previously the light had come from an oak log fire. Although in the centre of the island and eighty feet above sea level, it had sometimes been put out by the sea. For more than a hundred years now no local man had been permitted to be in charge of it, after one wreck when the fire wasn't kindled until the ship was on the rocks.

Dressed in old clothes, Ross was still conspicuous about the island, and at the tiny inn where he stayed conversation stopped whenever he came into the room. On the Wednesday he was rowed over to St Martin's and spent a couple of hours up the Beacon Tower, watching the horizon for ships. From this vantage point the multiplicity of tiny islands looked like an anchored fleet.

On the Wednesday, Mr Ray Penvenen told his niece that in view of the prospect of war he thought it better to leave for London on the Friday instead of the Sunday. He had certain banking interests, and he would prefer to be in touch with them as soon as possible. But Caroline did not like this at all. Apparently she was not ready to go. Nothing would induce her to leave before Sunday morning. If he wanted to go before, he must leave without her. After argument, in which she seemed needlessly downright, he gave way. She had been so considerate to his views in other respects that he felt he must humour her in this. Nevertheless his mind was not quite easy, and several times that evening she looked up from her reading to find his eyes on her.

On the Thursday, Dwight had to go into Truro to draw some money and to obtain letters of credit for his journey. On coming out of the bank he almost bumped into a tall fair soldier in the uniform of the Scots Greys. Such figures might soon become a commonplace of countryside and town, but this man's great moustache was familiar. Then Dwight remembered where he had seen him before – leaving the cottage of Vercoe the Customs Officer at St Ann's. It was almost twelve months ago: sometime last spring.

On Thursday afternoon a small fishing vessel appeared in Crow Sound and presently nosed her way into the quieter waters of the Road. She was fore-and-aft rigged, but she carried a large square sail on her mainmast. After about half an hour a dinghy brought a man ashore.

Chapter nine

THEY HAD THEIR interview in Ross's private room upstairs. Only in the middle of this room was it possible for either of them to stand upright. A fire burned in the tiny grate, flickering on the yellow stone walls and lighting an old needlework sampler with 'God Save Our Queen' worked in red wool. The rough floor boards were covered with a home-woven rug, and threadbare heavy curtains over door and window kept out some of the draught.

A disastrous change in Mark. Once these two men, of an age and a build, had been superficially alike. Not so now. Mark's hair was white and had worn up at the temples. He was thinner, and the enormous power had gone from his hands and shoulders. He had not been able to live with his memories.

They gripped hands and sat down and passed the ordinary talk of friends who have not met for a long time. Mark was working for a boatbuilder in Galway. He had made few friends, he said, and had not married again. 'I d'feel I still am married,' he said. 'Nought will change that.' Ross brought out a bottle of brandy, but Mark would not touch it. 'I keep guard on my tongue,' he said. 'Night an' day. Night an' day.'

Ross told him what he could of his family, accepted messages for them all. Although the next hour would decide so much, he found he could not rush his fences. They spoke of France and Mark's reasons for leaving it, the crisis now. Mark was more interested in England and the scenes he had left. All this life he was living now was an uneasy dream, something from which he still hoped to wake. Ross realized that he was living only for the possibility of being able to return some day to his own home. It was not an ambition in which Ross felt he could honestly encourage him. Too many people remembered, would remember for another twenty years. If he returned, the magistrates would be forced to move against him.

At length silence fell. Ross looked at the other man, who was twisting his bony knuckles and frowning. 'You know why I wanted you to come here?'

'Yes. You said in your letter, sur. I got it read. Ever since, I been tryin' to think.'

'You don't remember?'

'Oh, I mind what I said well 'nough. And I mind what I saw. But 'tis hard to remember just where I saw it. I was fair crazed that day. I wandered. . . .'

'Would a plan of the workings help?'

'Oh, *yes*. 'Twould, there's no doubt.'

Ross lifted the model schooner off the plush-covered table and unrolled the plan he had brought. It was one he had drawn just before he left, carefully omitting any work which had been done since the mine reopened. A plan of a mine, so essentially a three-dimensional thing, is hard to put on paper; but he had tried to make it easier by using three colours of ink for the three levels which the old men had worked.

He spread the map carefully and pinned it down; then because Mark puckered his eyes he carried the table impatiently to the salt-rimed window, and they bent over it together. Now. Now. This was the moment. The preparation and the waiting. . . . But Mark was still hesitant to begin, unable to get his bearings. Never a quick thinker, the years of exile had slowed him down in every way. He could have been in his sixties instead of his early thirties. Presently, having related the plan to all the familiar landmarks above ground, he began to retrace the steps he had taken on Tuesday the twelfth of August, 1789.

A hard task, fraught with all the obstacles of bitter remembrance, on which his mind for four years had been trying to close the door. And while he struggled, Ross watched, knowing all that it meant for himself and Demelza and Jeremy. Had he been a praying man, he would have prayed now, to some deity, to some patron saint, that what this man said – some magical words he would utter – would change the picture from failure to success, would make all his striving and contriving into a sensible pattern that showed adequate return for work done, a prospect of money to be earned for money spent – no more senseless searching after a hopeless mirage, no more groping and wandering in the dark.

'I went down . . . so far as I could tell there was water; then I walked – 'twould be in the thirty level – I walked – thinkin' to myself. . . . An' then I stopped and sat down. There was hours to spend. I thought to end everything by casting myself. . . . And then I went on, bearing east so far as I recollect. There's a deep gunnies here. . . .'

'That's so,' said Ross.

'I climbed across'n – a plank, 'alf rotten . . .' He stopped. 'Ye've put a stone, sur? There was enough cash for a stone?'

'Yes. We put a stone. With the words you said. "*Keren Daniel. Wife of Mark Daniel. Age 22.*"'

He rubbed a hand across his forehead. 'Twenty-two, that's all she was. I did ought to've known better. She was but a child. . . . That surgeon, Enys, is he still around? I reckon 'twas he I should've killed.'

'Try to remember, Mark. What did you do then?'

Mark turned his tortured eyes back to the map. 'Well 'twas just above the gunnies, bearing right. There was an old pick down there; and to keep myself from thinking I began to cast around, just as if I was looking for a pitch to take. Soon enough, picking at the rock. . . . A fine bit o' ground it looked to me.'

'Where was it?' said Ross, pointing. 'Just here?'

'Yes, I reckon. There on. It ran at a steep inclination. . . .'

'We found it,' said Ross. 'It was good ground while it lasted, but there was no breadth. It was a foot wide where you saw it, but three fathoms down it ran as thin as paper, and above, of course, it had been stoped. Henshawe thinks it was an offshoot from the champion lode.'

There was silence. The wood crackled on the fire, and Mark Daniel breathed through his nose. 'Then I went on again. Climbin' now all the while. . . . An old air shaft——'

'Here,' said Ross, pointing.

' 'Twas filled in. I reckoned I was barely fifteen fathoms from grass. From there ye can turn two ways. I turned east.'

'This way?'

' 'S, I reckon. Sixty or seventy paces on you double back 'pon yourself, and in the turn. . . . There's a cross-course. And about it, 'tis all keenly country; mostly silver lead it 'peared to me, and iron.'

A man came up the street outside carrying a bunch of glimmering fish on the end of a stick. They looked like some exotic fruit he had plucked from the sea bed. His footsteps struck musical echoes along the cobbled street.

'You'd an amazing good eye to see it there,' Ross said grimly.

'Why?' Mark frowned at him. 'Did you . . .'

'We struck it twenty fathoms below. We've stoped all that ground. It's been our best find. The cross-course had thrown the old men out, and we picked up their copper vein forty-odd feet to the south of that turning. . . . But something had gone awry with the lode just the same, for the quality's indifferent. At least it is if you have an engine to run. Perhaps in the old days it might have paid its way. . . .'

Mark stared out to sea. The ketch that had brought him had already left. A week might pass before it came again.

Ross said: 'There's no hurry. We're marooned here. Take your time.'

'Nay. I'll go on now. 'Tis little more I can tell ee, I fear. I sat down an' dozed for a while, then I woke an' thought 'twas dark time already an' I hastened back. But goin' back, at the big gunnies, I took the east level instead of the west. I'd went no more'n two hundred paces when I knew 'twas wrong. But I found my way back by a branch level. See here; here 'tis.'

'Yes. Yes, I see.'

'In this there's two narrow gunnies, an' betwixt them is good ground I'll wager. Ye go down over broken steps where the lode's been worked. But only the bottom's been worked. All the backs is untouched. There's fine quartzy rock, and gossan. 'Twas too high for me to get to'n, but I'd lay there was a mint o' money in that one place alone!'

Ross did not speak for a minute. He stared at the map and then got up as if to stretch his cramped muscles. He took out a handkerchief and wiped the moisture off the palms of his hands.

'And then after that you came up?'

'I waited nigh the main shaft, waited for the dark and for Paul's light to show. I thought the day would never end. . . .'

'Yes,' said Ross. 'It was an anxious time.'

Mark watched him as he moved across the room, stooping to avoid the beams. 'This last place I've telled you of. Is it no betterer? Have ye proven it useless like the others?'

'Let's go for a walk, shall we? The room is close and there's no space to breathe or straighten. Fresh air will help us both.'

Mark stood up somewhat reluctantly as Ross opened the door. 'Aye, whatever you d'say, sur. But I'd be obliged if ye'd answer. . . .'

'What you tell me will bear investigation, Mark, I'm sure of that. There's no doubt a deal of its promise has escaped us. I think you've given me several valuable hints.'

They said more on the way downstairs and out, until Mark seemed partly satisfied. He did not know how much depended on his answers, but he knew what was entailed in the opening of a mine, and he would have been grievously upset to fail his friend. So Ross's first concern was to hide his own feelings, and that at the moment was very hard.

He did not in fact feel that Mark had failed him – only that he himself had failed those who gave him their affection and their trust. By building so much upon the chance utterances of a man crazed with rage and grief, he had brought himself to this present pass. Now, as he walked along with Mark by the side of the sea, and while the cold breeze stung his face and chilled the sweat which had broken out on him during the interview, now it seemed to him that he had known for some time that this last throw would fail. The expectation was too much. At the beginning it could have been true; but experienced miners could hardly explore the old workings for months on end and not find whatever good ground was to be found. In his heart he had feared this; but it was the old story of the drowning man and the straw.

This last discovery Mark spoke of had been the first Ross's men had found. What Mark had seen was one of those complex mixtures which abound in mineral-bearing ground; quartz in this particular case, with schorl and oxide of iron and oxide of tin. Any good miner might have expected results from it.

But the ground had hardly paid for the working.

By Saturday, Dwight had given up hope of seeing Ross again before he left. Demelza had had no word, and no one seemed to know when or where the run was expected. That was as it should be, of course. And even Mr Trencrom was dependent on wind and weather.

What Dwight did not know was that Mr Trencrom had business dealings with the owner of a farm on the windy sand dunes of Gwithian. Farrell, the master of the *One and All*, brought his vessel in close enough to be seen before darkness fell. Then he stood hastily away from the land again, for Hell's Mouth was not far off; and the farmer's son mounted an excellent pony given him by Mr Trencrom for the purpose and rode the fifteen miles to see his benefactor.

So in the early dusk there was unaccustomed movement in a number of cottages and farmhouses of the district, a quiet preparing for a night of strenuous but stealthy work. An emptying of sacks and a saddling of mules, a coiling of ropes and a fetching out of black-tarred lanterns. Here and there, too, a pistol was primed or a flintlock taken down from the wall.

But this was not the whole of the preparations going on. At St. Ann's, about a cottage separated a little from the rest and overlooking the bay, other men were quietly gathering; and inside, in the living room, the three leaders were making final arrangements: Captain McNeil, Customs Officer Vercoe, and his assistant Bell. Vercoe was titular head of this expedition, but McNeil by virtue of his rank was deferred to on all decisions of importance. He also commanded the largest part of the men at their disposal, seven dragoons.

Vercoe said: 'Well, sir, 'twill be safer to be off soon, for it would never do to be seen moving about later on when the tub carriers are round. 'Tis a long cold time, I know.'

'It was a long cold time last night,' said McNeil. 'The colder for being fruitless. Your informer is reliable, I suppose?'

'He has been times before. He said he'd no means of knowing whether the run would be last night, to-night, or to-morrow.'

'With this latest news from London, I see no prospect of keeping my men longer than the end of the week – or of staying myself. So this is really the last chance. It would aggrieve me if this run took place elsewhere while we were watching an empty cove.'

Vercoe grunted and rubbed his beard. ' 'Twould grieve me more. For upwards of thirty months I've been waiting for a chance such as this, to make a big haul. If all goes well to-night or to-morrow, the whole Trade in these parts may be stamped out for a generation. That's what I d'want more than aught else!'

McNeil looked at him interestedly, wondering what inner compulsions drove the man to make a crusade of his daily task. Then he shrugged his shoulders and rose. 'So be it. Bell, ye've impressed on your men that they do not stir till they hear Mr Vercoe's whistle? We do not want the trap to go off half cock.'

'Aye, aye, sir.'

'I'll answer for my own men, of course. And I've impressed upon them there must be no unnecessary bloodshed. Don't forget these smugglers are our own countrymen, and very soon there will be plenty of blood to let in another cause. The same dispositions as last night.'

'Aye, aye, sir.'

'Very well. We had best be starting.'

As the time for his leaving drew near, Dwight grew more and more restless. For the twentieth time he looked at the clock. It was half past nine. He had arranged to be at Killewarren at eleven. Ninety minutes to spend. There would be no possible excuse for starting for another forty-five minutes yet.

He rang for Bone, and when the young man came asked him a half dozen unnecessary questions and then dismissed him, not knowing how often before he had done the same thing. Nerves. Elopement nerves. At this moment what was Caroline doing? Would she suffer in the same way? Not from the goads of a conscience never easy for four years, but perhaps from nerves of another kind. The strong control she had of herself did not delude him into supposing her anything but highly strung.

All to-day Dwight had been unable to get the face of Keren Daniel out of his head. The interview with Demelza, and knowing Ross was meeting Mark, had suddenly brought Keren to the forefront of his mind. This was only a change of position, he realized that now; she had never been far away.

Sixteen minutes to ten. For Caroline he would willingly give up anything. The trouble was he was giving up nothing material; instead he was bettering himself. Self-flagellation. . . . Well, that was all right to a point, but beyond that point neurotic. In two hours he would be in a coach with her. Would any of his friends deny him the right to happiness? He fancied not one. In two hours he must draw a curtain across his past life.

Bone had come into the room again. Had he rung once more in his agitation?

'If you please, sur, there's Parthesia Hoblyn at the door. Says her sister's took queer. She asked for you to go see her, but I said you was busy to-night.'

Dwight glanced at the clock. Lottie Kempthorne quite recovered. No other cases had followed, and that little short of a miracle; even May had escaped. But Rosina. How long ago? Was it possible? He counted. It was still possible. He went through into the hall and found little Parthesia slumped in a chair getting her breath. Three miles from Sawle, and she had probably run all the way in the dark.

'What is wrong with your sister?'

Parthesia got up. 'Oh, sur, 'tis her knee. But an hour gone, sur, she was climbing the cobbles and it went just like it used to go afore ever you cured it, only worse she d'say. Fathur carre'd her indoors, sur, and she was that locked we could scarce bring her to a chair, sur. So Ma says, go ee to surgeon and see if he can right it.'

Four or five minutes to ten. Sixty-odd minutes yet. Sawle on the way, a mile or so out, but that nothing on a horse. Time enough to discharge a last duty – if he wanted to, and if he could. He would greatly have preferred not. In the last week he had made a round of farewell visits, though no one else knew them as such. This call if answered . . .

But this call if *not* answered? Peace of mind on his journey to Bath? The knee locked again. If his cure had been a temporary thing, it might mean . . . But his valise, packed and ready to go. He could not ride into Sawle with it.

'Wait here,' he said to Parthesia, who had been watching him, and called Bone aside.

Bone knew everything that was planned. You could trust your confidences to him.

'I'm going with the girl,' Dwight said. 'But I can't take my bag or it will rouse comment. I want it at the gates of Killewarren by eleven o'clock. Can you do that for me?'

'Aye, sur, I'll see for it.'

'It's some miles. Perhaps you can borrow a horse.'

'Hatchard will lend me a pony if I say 'tis for you. I'll go straight over now.'

'Have a care at Killewarren. Don't let yourself be seen before I come.'

When Bone had gone, Dwight put on his cloak, his hat, stared a moment round the room, taking a last familiar look. Then he went out to join Parthesia. In another way this call was not unwelcome. It would pass the last dragging hour. The waiting was over.

Parthesia rode before him. Her added weight was nothing. A little sprite of a girl, thin of body and small of bone. It was a clear cold night, moonless, with a freckle of stars misted by high herringbone cloud. He wondered if Ross was home yet. The run was expected. Going about his work late this afternoon he had noticed one or two signs which observed in innocence would have meant nothing, but, seen with an informed eye, meant business to-night. Near Sawle they passed two men on horses who drew well off the track to allow them to pass. Dwight wished them good night, but neither replied. Their faces were hidden in thick mufflers. He felt the little girl in front of him shiver as if she was afraid they were robbers. He was a little puzzled.

In the Hoblyns' cottage Jacka was waiting with an anxious scowl. Rosina was sitting on the edge of her chair, her face still white, though she said her leg was easier. In a breath she said she'd told them not to fetch him to-night, that she'd turned her leg on one of the cobbles and it had all gone tight, that she'd thought to send up for Charlie till she recollected Charlie was ill, that Parthesia had gone off unbeknown to her, that it was leaving off the bandages that had done it and she was sure by morning . . .

Dwight put his fingers round her knee, feeling for the displacement he had found before, recognizing it again, but not certain how he had set it right. An experimental pressure had done it, some knack which, had he been able to repeat it in other cases, he would have soon perfected. But it was months now. His success had surprised him almost as much as it had anyone else. He asked her to bend her knee, but at present she could not. The joint or cartilage was right out of place. It might need fomentations and some days of manipulation. But he was leaving to-night. This was the last chance. He pressed hard with his fingers and felt her wince.

'Did you say Charlie was ill?' he asked, talking to distract her attention. 'What is the matter with him?'

'Oh, sur, you d'know that. 'Twas on account of you telling him to stay abed that he's not helping wi' the run tonight. He told me that only this morning.'

Suddenly Dwight's hands got in the right place. It was as if some memory clicked into place in his mind before anything clicked in the knee. Confidence and satisfaction. He moved his fingers, pressed. The girl cried out but, as once before, more from shock than from pain. The displacement was gone.

Dwight released her and straightened up. 'You have the bandage?' he said to Mrs Hoblyn.

'Yes, sur.' She fled, squeezing past Jacka, who was standing in the doorway now.

'You can stand up,' Dwight said.

Rosina flexed her knee carefully. Colour came and went in her face, and for a moment she looked as if she was going to cry.

''Tis all right again, maid?' asked Jacka apprehensively from the doorway.

She stood up. 'Oh, sur, I'm *that* grateful. I was so afeared that 'twas gone for good. I – I can't thank ee enough. 'Tis like a miracle.'

With lessons to be learned. 'I was overconfident,' Dwight said. 'I think you should wear a bandage always. Or for a year to begin, till the tendons knit together.'

Mrs Hoblyn came scurrying back. Dwight bound the knee, telling Mrs Hoblyn to watch carefully. It would not do for this to happen again. He could not come one hundred and fifty miles even for Rosina. Time was getting on. It must be well after ten-thirty. Time to go. They could drive all night if necessary, or stop after putting a comfortable distance between themselves and Killewarren. Dr Dwight Enys and Miss Caroline Penvenen, travelling as friends.

Jacka had brought out a bottle of rum, slopped some into a cup, and was pressing it upon him. Dwight did not want it, but he knew this expressed the height of Jacka's approval, so he sipped a little while they watched Rosina walking gingerly about the room. Dwight occupied his last moment or two telling Mrs Hoblyn what she must do and what she must not do if it ever happened again. Mrs Hoblyn didn't make things any better by saying with shining eyes: 'Why, sur; we should just make 'er sit quiet like till you came!'

Sometimes a remark is like an insect's sting which at first is barely felt but grows uncomfortable as time passes. What Rosina had said about Charlie Kempthorne had at first been barely noticed by Dwight, and his success with the displacement had swamped it. Anxious now to be off, he was at the outer door pursued by their gratitude before the poison began to work.

As Jacka followed him out of the house, Dwight said: 'What is this about Charlie being ill? Did he tell you he was ill? Did he say I told him he must not get up?'

'Ais. Leastways, he told them as wanted him t'elp with the run.'

'I don't understand. What happened?'

Jacka peered at him. ' 'Twasn't Charlie's proper turn t'elp with the tub-carrying. They takes it turn an' turn about, ye know. 'Twas Trencrom's notion, to spread the risk an' to spread the reward. Men'll take a chance once in two months what they'll not take every month. But yesterday eve, Joe Trelask breaks 'is leg at the mill. Falls down the ladder, they d'say——'

'Yes. I know that. Go on.'

'So Charlie Kempthorne were next on the list, an' they sent round last night t'tell him to be ready. Then he says he's some slight. 'Tis the fever, he says, an' surgeon's told him he mustn't stir abroad on account of his lungs.' Jacka Hoblyn's frown was such as to penetrate the darkness. 'Mean to say 'twas all make-believe?'

'So far as my part in it goes.'

'Well, the scaly little cheat! What's he about to tell such a stramming great story; 'tis hard to guess his reasons. . . .'

'When is the wedding to be?'

'Tomorrow two weeks.'

'No doubt it was on account of that, Jacka. He was anxious to avoid the risk, perhaps anxious about his health too. It is a thing any man would do.'

Jacka grunted and ran a thumbnail up and down between his front teeth. 'Not any man by a long sight, surgeon. Not you, I'll wager; not me. He's no right or title to lie about'n. I'll tax him with it first thing in the morning.'

'Let it be,' said Dwight quietly. 'As you say, it is not our concern. Good night, Jacka.'

'Good night, sur. And thank ee.'

Dwight led his horse up the steep hill, Jacka watching him go. Charlie Kempthorne's cottage was at the top of the hill, just out of sight of the Hoblyns. Dwight stopped in front of it, stared up at the window. There was a light in the upper room. Twenty minutes to eleven. He could be at Killewarren comfortably in twenty minutes – if he started now. But he must start at once. Caroline would already be putting on her cloak, perhaps was now sitting waiting in her bedroom ready to snuff out the candle and steal downstairs. Bone would be at the gates with his valise.

But this monstrous suspicion grown in his mind was something which overrode his obligations to himself and to her. If he had not fancied the ride to Bath with the thought of Rosina lame again and unvisited, how much less could he face it with this problem unresolved. Five minutes would not make him late. In five minutes he could be sure.

Chapter ten

RAY PENVENEN'S HABITS were sufficiently set to make his movements predictable at most hours of the day or night; but to-night, his last night here, he was perversely late going to bed. Old-maidish mannerisms had grown on him, and final preparations for going took the form of innumerable scribbled notes to be left with this servant and with that to remind them of their duties. Caroline stood it until half-past ten and then said:

'You are working overlate to-night, Uncle. There's all to-morrow morning to spend before we leave, and it would be the greatest pity if you found no way of spending it. Are you coming to bed?'

He looked first at the clock and then at her over his glasses. 'I have a little more to do, Caroline. An estate in the country is not like a London house, it cannot be locked up and left unoccupied. It must continue to be looked to or it will run into chaos.'

'And are not Garth and the other men you employ capable of doing this? I should have thought so – or you would not employ them.'

'Oh, they know what to do within their limitations. But they lack initiative and, since we shall be away a month, it is necessary to supply it. For instance . . .' He went on to explain some of the decisions which might need to be made. Since she had asked, he supposed her to be interested in the answer; but once or twice he caught her eyes straying, and they were straying in the direction of the clock. 'Why do you enquire?' he ended quite suddenly, breaking off in the middle.

Her eyes came quickly back. 'Why? Shouldn't I be interested? It's not unladylike, I suppose? But I am also interested in your health. I don't think you have been looking so well of late, and it would be a woeful pity to wear yourself out with the effort of making ready to take a holiday.'

He looked at her suspiciously, but his suspicion was only of sarcasm not of deeper motive. When he saw no hint of mockery in her eyes, he patted her hand and said: 'There, there, I shall not be above half an hour more. Go to bed if you are tired, my dear. I am grateful to you for your solicitude.'

She turned away to hide her frustration, and for the next ten minutes pottered about the room on one pretext or another. But still he remained seated, making no move to go. At length she came back to the desk and said:

'Well, if you will not leave I must, for my eyes will not stay open. You'll come now?'

'Almost finished. Good night, Caroline.'

He put up his forehead to be kissed, and she brushed her lips perfunctorily upon it, forgetting in her anxiety that this was her leave-taking of him, certainly for many months, perhaps for ever.

Out on the landing above the hall she remembered, but now it was too late. Her shadow kept her company along the corridor to her bedroom, preceding her like a welcoming innkeeper. In the bedroom she lit a candle and stared at her cloak, her hat, her scarf, her gloves, all waiting. Her bags were downstairs and in the coach, as also was Horace. She pulled the bell twice to show that she wanted her maid Eleanor.

When the girl came, she said: 'My uncle is late to-night. We shall have to delay a little while. Tell Baker, will you. . . . Are the other servants abed?'

'All but Thomas, miss. 'E be waiting for the master, to put out the lights and bar the doors, miss. He be grumbling, Baker say, at being kept abroad so late.'

Caroline bit her lip. 'Tell Baker to make no move until he has gone. It would be a great disaster if Thomas saw the horses being harnessed.'

'Very good, miss. . . . Will that be all?'

'No. Make a move as if you were going to bed. If you can, slip out of the house unnoticed and sit in the coach. Thomas otherwise may wonder why you are hanging about. Also I am afraid Horace will get terrified in the dark. And he yaps loud when frightened. Stay there until I come.'

'Very good, miss. I'll go fetch my bonnet and cloak.'

'But careful! Don't let anyone see you.'

When Eleanor had left, Caroline paced up and down the bedroom a half-dozen times, still biting her lip. Then she abruptly took up her outdoor things, glanced round to see that nothing was left which should not have been left, propped the letter for her uncle more prominently on her dressing table, and snuffed out the candle and left the room.

Her shadow was sulking in its corner. As she moved along the passage, it jumped quickly to follow at her heels. The light was still under the door of the big drawing room. She hesitated and then slipped into the maid's cupboard on the other side of the landing. Just room for her among the brushes and the dusters, but she was afraid to move lest something should topple over.

So she stayed another ten minutes, stiff and cramped, the door sufficiently ajar to see the lighted angle of drawing-room door. It must be close on eleven by now.

Mr Penvenen came out. He was carrying a candle, and a leather case under his arm. The room beyond was now in darkness. He closed the door after him and walked to the candle-lamp in the corner and put it out. Then he came straight across to the cupboard where Caroline was standing.

Hypnotized, like a child caught in a terrible dream, she watched him walk towards her. Then the door slammed shut in her face and she heard his slippers creaking away. . . .

In total darkness she let out a slow breath, began to count, determined not to move too soon. At five hundred she lifted the latch and looked out. The landing was in darkness.

Knowing she might yet bump into Thomas on his rounds, she crept along the corridor to the stairs and stole down them. They had never creaked so much before. Once down, she made for the servants' quarters, which directly adjoined the stables. There was a light in the kitchen and the door was ajar. Baker, her coachman, sat before a low fire in his shirt sleeves and stockinged feet, sharpening a piece of wood. He looked sleepy and ready for bed. If it was assumed, he was acting well.

He got up sharply when she came in. She put a finger to her lips, breathless in spite of herself. These last minutes were minutes of unexpected tension.

'Thomas?'

'Gone up, miss, three minutes since. I doubt 'e'll be down again.'

'Wait another five, then get the horses.'

'Yes, miss.'

'I'll go straight out to the coach. Eleanor is already there. We'll wait for you to come.'

'Very good, miss.'

As she turned to go out of the kitchen she looked up at the clock. It was five minutes after eleven. Dwight would be waiting.

Lottie Kempthorne wakened almost as soon as the cold night air fanned upon her face. She did not move but saw her father quite close to her at the window, peering out.

She heard his low voice. ' 'Tis just a fever and I thought to send for ee, surgeon, but then I thought to wait till cock-light afore I give ee the trouble. Maybe tomorrow if you was passing this way——'

A voice outside said: 'I'll see you tonight.'

'I b'lieve it has been brought to an intermission, an' by tomorrow——'

'Let me in. I want to speak to you.'

When grumbling to himself her father shut the window and began to pull on his breeches, Lottie still did not stir. She had learned that she must take no heed of her father's comings and goings, and a question now would be likely to earn her a growl and a cuff. So she lay comfortable enough on the thin hard bed, listening to May's quiet breathing beside her.

Father went down, taking the candle, and she heard him unbar the door below. (Most people in Sawle never locked their doors day or night, but

Charlie was an exception.) She heard him talking to the man who came in, and presently sat up, scratching herself in the darkness. She wondered what Dr Enys could possibly be wanting calling so very late and speaking in such a strange voice. Dr Enys had been so kind to her and usually he was very gentle. Perhaps something terrible had happened.

Her curiosity would let her rest no longer, and she slid out of bed and crept shivering to the trap door which led down to the room below. She lifted it a couple of inches and peered down.

Her father was being examined; he was in a chair, hedging and protesting while Dr Enys stood over him, his face white and hard. The first words that came up to her were:

'You have no fever, man, as you well know. Nor have you had any. Why did you tell people that story?'

'Maybe 'tis not fever to you, surgeon; but three hours gone I was sweaten like a weed. An' what with Lottie just free of the pox . . . And see now! Feel my 'and. If that edn clammy . . .'

But the face of Dr Enys, kind Dr Enys, did not change. 'This is an excuse, isn't it, Kempthorne, this sham illness – thought up to avoid any part in the tub-carrying tonight? Why did you want to have no part in it?'

Lottie's father, whom Lottie loved, licked his lips and began to button his shirt. 'I was all of a shrim. First it comed on me back like cold water, like ice. Then——'

'For two years or more there's been an informer about, carrying tales for gold. You know that, don't you, Charlie?'

'Course I know. Everyone d'know. Have you caught him?'

'I rather think I have.'

Lottie shifted her cramped feet and lifted the hatch another few inches. Father had got up.

'What, me? Dear life, surgeon; that's a purty notion to get in your head. And not a nice one, I must say. Proper insulting. And all on account of a fever that took me sudden. Why, just afore you came my teeth was rattling——'

'Where did you get these things?' Dr Enys asked, pointing angrily about the room, and Lottie was afraid he might see her. 'How did you pay for them? Curtains, rugs, cups, window glass; all paid for out of sail making? Or out of selling your friends?'

Her father was smiling, but she who knew him knew it was not a friendly smile. 'Out of sail making, surgeon. That's true as my life. An' no one can show different. Now ye can *go*, surgeon, and leave me be, and take your nasty evil suspicion likewise. Coming here in the dark of the night, casting such sneavy untruths——'

'It is you who'll have to go, Charlie; and go quickly if you care for your life. You've informed on your friends to-night, haven't you? What time is the run to take place? Is there still time to warn them?'

'And what shall I say 'bout you, surgeon? That you've coveted Rosina ever since ye laid eyes and hands on her, eh? That ye suspicion me to try and stop the wedding, eh? I know. *I* know all the things ye've done to her, all the fingerin' and fumblin' there's been – on the quiet like, when her mother warn't there. She's telled me, Rosina has. Ye should be grateful that somebody'll still marry her——'

Dr Enys made a swift movement, and her father broke off as if he expected violence; but the surgeon had turned towards a side table where she and May had been playing that evening. She craned her neck to see what he had picked up, and saw with astonishment that it was a picture book of hers called *The History of Primrose Prettyface*.

'Where did you get this, Charlie?'

'I buyed it.'

'Where did you buy it?'

'In to Redruth.'

'You lie. This book first belonged to Hubert Vercoe, the Customs Officer's boy. I saw it first in his house.' The doctor was flipping through the pages.

'Nay, that edn clever at all, surgeon. It proves nought. There's many such books on sale in Redruth. Why——'

'I doubt if there's one. But here is the surest identification, here on the first page. Hubert Vercoe coloured the wings of this angel red. He told me so himself and I saw it in his hands.' Dr Enys shut the book and slipped it into his pocket.

In the silence that followed Lottie could hear May turn over in bed and whimper as if aware that her company and her warmth had gone. Below the two men watched each other like dogs Lottie had seen, bristling and tight-muscled.

'What are ee going to do?'

'You shall know when I've done it.'

The doctor picked up his riding crop and made a move towards the door, but her father was quicker and was there before him. Even Dr Enys couldn't believe that that smile was friendly now. 'Stay, surgeon. What are ee going to do?'

'Get out of my way!'

Neither of them moved.

Dr Enys said: 'What time is the run?'

'Midnight. Ye're late, surgeon. Too late by a long chalk. Go home and go to bed. That's the proper place for ee.'

'What made you do it, Charlie? What made you a traitor to your own folk?'

'Nobody's my folk, surgeon. Who did ought for me? My first wife was drownded before folk's eyes. None of the women made move to save 'er. Not one. They left her drown. And me? Who put forth a hand t'elp me when I was low? Not one. Everyone looks only for theirselves in this life.'

'Not to betray. Not to sell other men for money. Judas was no worse.'

Lottie saw Father's hand close round the wooden stake he used for barring the door. It was behind his back, but she saw it.

'There's naught I care for your fancy names, surgeon. I looks to myself just the same as you. An' ye'll get no admission more'n that. When me and Rosina's wed, we'll clear out of this place——'

'If you did this to gain Rosina, you're likely to lose her by it——'

'I done what I done, surgeon. You cured me of the consumptives, but ye don't order me life. Oh, *no*. . . .'

Lottie cried out as her father jumped at the other man with the wooden bar raised. Dr Enys must have seen it coming, for he jerked his head back and the stick cracked on his shoulder. The pain creased across his face and he fell against the table behind him. Transfigured, unrecognizable, her father leaped after him, swinging the stake again; but the doctor's fall saved him. Crash went the table, Dr Enys rolled into the corner, sat up while her father was picking a way towards him among the legs of the table. The surgeon clutched a stool, raised it, and the stick jarred against it, hurting her father's hand for he almost dropped it. The doctor pulled himself up, caught the stick; they grappled, reeled against the wall.

Lottie swung the trap, let it fall back, went down a few steps into the room, tears trickling unheeded down her pock-marked cheeks. She called to them but they did not hear, these two men who meant more to her than all the rest of life; they were fighting to kill, to maim, you could see it in their eyes. She wanted the courage to come between them, to stop them, to put life back where it had been an hour ago. A terrible nightmare, worse than any of her fever, worse than personal pain.

Father had his hands on the other man's throat, but seemed to lack the strength to do what he wished. She saw his bloodshot eyes, murder still in them but fright also. Crash to the floor again, he under.

Behind her own crying Lottie heard a thin echo. May was awake now. May often cried if she woke in the night, without reason, without good cause. Lottie took two more steps down, nearly tripped over the ragged edge of her night shift, her mother's once.

Father had kicked himself free, was crawling again towards the stick; but the surgeon caught his ankle, pulled him flat. Her father kicked with his free foot, caught the surgeon's face, just grasped the stick. Dr Enys freed him, started forward, leaped at his back; down again. A familiar sound; something Lottie had known all her life; her father coughing. It seemed to affect the doctor at the same time. He released his grip, straightened, a look of concern, something not to do with to-night, out of other nights, other days. Her father was down, stayed down, climbed slowly to his knees, then did not move. For a few seconds both children had stopped crying and the only sound was the familiar rustling cough. Dr Enys pulled himself shakily to his feet. Blood on his face, his neckcloth torn.

Her father looked round. Then he leaped up, clutched a knife lying on the side under the crockery. As he took it up, Dr Enys saw his danger, moved after him. The knife up, but the doctor struck at the same time. The knife clattered. The doctor seemed to measure his distance and hit twice more. Father coughed again just once; he might not have been hurt, but he crumpled up, went on his knees, rolled over, and was really still.

Lottie had her hands to her ears now, helplessly, as if words and sounds would hurt more than sight, the tears beginning to trickle again. Her mouth grimaced to speak, but she could not. She stood and wept bitterly for a lost illusion. A great desolation was in her, a sense of being forsaken as no one had ever been forsaken before.

Chapter eleven

No OFFICIAL WORD had reached Demelza, but she knew. As soon as dark fell she drew the curtains across the windows and lit all the candles to give the house an extra feeling of home and security. He might not come until early morning, but she had no thought of bed. To-night was doubly important. She felt she would know as soon as their eyes met whether he had good news or bad.

She delayed supper until nine before sitting down alone at the table and pecking at the cold leg of mutton and the apple jam tartlets. After, she went into the kitchen, anxious not even to hear the telltale clop of horses' hooves, the jangle of harness, the occasional gruff voice. Jane Gimlett was there alone, John Gimlett being out looking for a lamb which had strayed; and to give colour to her own presence, she began to reiron the ruffs on Ross's shirts. All of them were well worn, well darned, should long since have been cast aside.

Jane Gimlett chattered for a time; but presently, finding her mistress silent, her own talk dropped away. Upstairs Jeremy slept soundly.

Feathers the kitten came and rubbed its head against Demelza's skirts. Then, finding itself unrebuffed, it wriggled under the hem of her skirt and put its forepaws round her ankle. After another minute or so it somehow got its back legs tangled up and began to wriggle and kick. Demelza bent and disentangled it and put it on the table beside her. It arched its back and opened its infant mouth in a silent snarl and then stepped sideways as if blown by the wind and almost fell off the table. She picked it up again and put it in its basket beside the ancient Tabitha Bethia, who was asleep and let out a single mew of protest.

She turned the chicken, which was cooking on a spit in case Ross should be hungry on his return, and thrust forward the potato saucepan on its iron trivet so that it stood over the hot ashes. The tide was right about midnight, and she thought he would be here by then or soon after. She took the piece of bacon out of the smoke chamber over the flue of the fire to see if it was sufficiently cured. Then she returned to the table.

On this came Gimlett, bucket in hand, out of breath, stumbling over the mat as he pushed open the door.

'John!' said his wife. 'What's amiss? Did ee find him?'

'There's a soldier!' said Gimlett, clattering the bucket down. 'By the stile at the turn of the Long Field. I nigh bumped into un! I thought 'twas one of the tub-runners.'

Demelza put her iron down. It was as if a colder iron had moved in her. 'Are you *sure*, John? How are you sure?'

'I snatched a glimpse of his tunic, mistress. And he was carren a musket too! I says to him, "Fine night, my son," and he says "Aye." Just the word "Aye." 'Twas no Cornishman, I knew; and then I catched sight of his musket!'

'Did you see anything of the traders?'

'Yes, mistress, about an hour gone. I seen two moving down to the cove.'

Oh, God, to think, to think, this might be Ross's liberty, even his life. It was what she had feared often before, but then it had not involved Ross except as an accessory. This time of all times, when he was coming home. The room closed on her like a prison. 'John, do you think – do you think you can get out of the house unseen, make your way down to the cove? Go out of the back again, quickly, quick, by way of the cliff. And Jane, how many candles have we? Enough to lighten all the windows d'you suppose?'

'A score, I b'lieve, ma'am. We was to have bought more last week——'

'John, waste no time. Do what you can even if it means——'

Demelza stopped. Gimlett said: 'The sky's clearing. The stars is bright as frost, but I can——'

He had looked at Demelza, and he too stopped. She was staring past him at the door. Captain McNeil was standing there, in uniform this time; and another figure could be seen in the background.

'Good evening to ye, Mrs Poldark. I'm sorry to break in on your privacy. Your man saw one of my troopers, so I shall have to ask you to keep within doors for the next hour or two.'

Demelza picked up one of Ross's shirts; with trembling but controlled fingers she folded it carefully.

'Captain McNeil. . . . This is a surprise. I'm – at a loss. . . .'

'I will explain it to ye, ma'am, if you will give me a moment in privacy. Is Captain Poldark at home?'

'. . . No. He's away. . . .'

A look passed across McNeil's face. 'I see. Then a word with you, if I might have it.'

'Certainly. . . .'

'One moment. How many sairvants have you in the house, ma'am?'

'Two. These two only.'

'Then I'll ask them to stay here in the care of my trooper. Wilkins!'

'Aye, sir.'

With uncertain steps, her heart choking, she led the way into the parlour.

'Please sit down, Captain McNeil. 'Twas quite unthoughtful of you to appear sudden at my kitchen door like – like a pedlar with a tray of rings, when I thought you miles away, in London or – or in Edinburgh. You should have written.'

'I ask your pardon, ma'am. I had no intention of disturbing anyone in this house, but your man blundered into one of our pickets. I——'

'Pickets? It has a very military ring. Do you suppose that there is an enemy about?'

He screwed in his great moustache. 'An enemy of a sort. We have news that smugglers have the intention to use your cove to-night. Vercoe, the Customs Officer, has repeatedly appealed for a reinforcement of his men. To-night I and my troopers are providing it. That's why I asked to see Captain Poldark.'

She had gone to a cupboard and taken out a decanter. He was still on his feet, and in his uniform he looked enormous – and cumbersome beside her slightness.

'You'll take a glass of wine?' she said.

'Thank ye, no. Not while on duty.'

'But why Captain Poldark? What have we to do with it?'

'Nothing I trust – I hope. But it is your land, ma'am. I think you can hardly be so innocent as you look. Where is Captain Poldark?'

She shook her head. 'From home. I told you. He is in St. Ives.'

'When will he return?'

'To-morrow – I b'lieve. Please sit down, Captain McNeil. When you are standing, the room is too small for you.'

He half smiled as he obeyed her, took out his watch, replaced it. 'Believe me, it grieves me, ma'am, to be in this position relative to yourself.'

'So 'twas what some said, that when you were staying with the Trevaunances you were really acting as a spy.'

He said sharply: 'No, *most* untrue. I came as a convalescent. Whilst down here I did nothing but pay a courtesy visit to the Customs authorities, since I had been concerned with them three years before. I ask you to believe, Mrs Poldark, that it is not in my nature to do what is – dishonourable!'

'Then why – now?'

'This is different, quite different. I come as a soldier, ma'am. This Trade, this organized Trade, must be stamped out. I can only obey the orrders I am given!'

She was surprised that the note of contempt in her voice should have pricked him so.

'Yet you wish to lock me in my own house. . . .'

'For the rest of to-night. I cannot leave you or your servants free to run down and warn the smugglers.'

'So you cannot trust me, Captain McNeil?'

'In this I cannot.'

She looked at him through her lashes. 'You ask me to believe in your honour but will not believe in mine.'

'With your husband out of the house and perhaps implicated?' He got up and stood a moment with his hands on the back of the chair. 'Captain Poldark has been a soldier himself. It will grieve me if he is involved – I trust for his sake that he is not. I do not lightly make war on friends. But once before I warned him of the danger of flying in the face of the law. If he has done so now, he must take the consequences. Believe me, ma'am, for the favour of your good will I would pay a very high price. Indeed, almost any pairsonal price that you ask. But not one which involves a – a neglect of duty.'

A gruff voice could be heard in the kitchen. It was on her lips to tell McNeil the truth, to explain the cruel mischance of Ross's involvement, this once alone, and to throw herself and Ross on his understanding and good will. But she stopped in time. Her meetings with McNeil had been few, but already she was coming to have an understanding of his character. In justifying his actions to her, he had revealed both his quality and his limitations. Good-natured, shrewd, susceptible to women, he yet pursued his duty with a single-mindedness which was above weakness. Mercy was as little likely to move him as money or sex.

'What do you wish me to do?'

'Stay in here, ma'am. I can ill spare Wilkins, but he must stay with you since it was his blunder that gave you warning. It should not be many hours.'

'And when you have taken your traders and locked them up – then we shall be free to go to bed and – and forget you?'

He flushed and bowed. 'That is so. And if anyone is taken connected with this house, it will be to my deep regret as well as yours. I trust this is the last time I will be involved in such a mission. From now on we shall have better work to do.'

'What do you mean?'

'Fighting people of a different race, ma'am. And of a different way of belief. France declared war on England yesterday. Had they done so a few weeks ago, we should have been spared this unhappy meeting.'

Dwight got out of the cottage and shut the door and leaned against it. Dark here, but it was the darkness of the frosty night, not that inner dark which had nearly swamped him. Bruised and shaky and in pain, but now no fear he would faint. Air revived him; as he stood there trying to think, it was a tonic – a cold breath penetrating through sweaty clothes, chilling but enlivening.

Walk to your horse, unloop the reins, struggle, pull yourself into the saddle. Already after eleven. Caroline waiting by now. Bone there, might have explained. (But he could not explain what he did not know.) In ten minutes could be there – fifteen anyhow. In half an hour away.

But that was a mere hypothesis which could not be put to the test. There was still more than half an hour to midnight. Even for Caroline. . . .

He pulled on the reins and turned his horse. Unused to carrying up this steep and stony path, the horse stumbled, struck sparks from the loose rock. Good to get away from that cottage into the cold dark. Two children crying, staring at him, who'd been their friend; terrified hostile eyes, while Charlie lay in his own hearth. As he left he heard them move; as soon as the door closed they would come padding down, staring at their father; Lottie would damp a rag, try to revive him, in the end no doubt would succeed. But what was his future? What was their future?

At the top of the hill he spurred his horse away from Killewarren, away – for the moment – from Bath and elopement and his love and his new life. Left shoulder heavily throbbing, though no bones broken; blood from the scratches on his neck drying down the front of his shirt.

Had there been more time he might have gone back for Jacka Hoblyn. *He* would have been quick enough in such an emergency; they might have put out in a boat to warn the cutter. But time would have run out before anything was begun. Even now perhaps too late.

In Grambler two lights, but the same objection: by the time anyone was roused. The full responsibility was on his own shoulders.

The officer he had seen in Truro; the two horsemen who had drawn silently off the track to-night to let him and Parthesia go by. This was no ordinary ambush; he had read as much in Charlie's eyes; the grand betrayal; perhaps Charlie had decided that after his marriage he would give up the dangerous game. Imprisonment or transportation for a dozen men, worse if there was resistance; imprisonment and ruin for Ross.

The night was dark enough to make quick movement dangerous; when he reached the ruins of Wheal Maiden, he slid off his horse, tethered it inside the broken wall. Then he went down the valley, haste and caution warring.

All the way he saw no one. A couple of lights over at the mine. The ground was dry underfoot and hard with frost; impossible to tell how many others might have passed this way before him. A light in the parlour window of Nampara. By now, no doubt, Demelza knew to expect Ross back to-night.

On the way down plans had been forming. The Nampara household could help. When every second counted. . . .

Perhaps the silence of the valley made him suspicious, or the obvious light so late. He went to the front door and lifted a hand to rap, then lowered it and moved round the great lilac bush across the flower bed to the lighted window. Curtains were drawn, but there was a chink. He peered in. On the table a grey busby.

A stiff and curious tableau. The big soldier by the door in his red coat and gold-braided trousers, stolid, glassily staring; John and Jane Gimlett, on chair edge, strained, uncomfortable; and Demelza by the fire. To-night, rather than the beauty in her face, you saw the strong bones underlying it. Normally they were imperceptible. It was as if she had ceased to be man or woman and become something common to both. The knuckles of her hands were white.

Dwight thought he heard a movement behind him, sharply straightened up, but it was only some stirring of the light breeze.

So what he had to do must be done himself. Round the house; a light burning in the kitchen window. He picked a way across the cobbled yard between the stone sheds. The curtains of this window not drawn; the room empty. He tried the latch and the door opened. Warmth and kitchen smells. An iron upended on the table and a cat asleep in a basket before a dying fire. A kitten, lying almost in the cinders, mewed and stretched at sight of him. The solitary candle near its end.

He saw what he wanted just inside the door, a small lantern used for carrying out of doors. As he took it down, Garrick began to bark. In haste, fumble with the shutter which had jammed. He could not leave and do it outside, for then he had no means of lighting the candle. As he pulled at the catch, he thought he heard a movement in the parlour. He stepped quickly behind the door, but there were no footsteps. Garrick stopped barking, and as silence fell the catch moved and the shutter came open. Move to the stub of candle and light the lantern from it. On a trivet on the fire a pan with some potatoes had boiled dry. The kitten was lying on its back near his boot waiting for a friendly hand to bite. He closed the shutter, slid out of the house. The latch of the door clicked.

Greater haste now across the yard, with Garrick barking again, over the stile at the back. Cloak covering the lantern, run towards the Long Field. This field occupied all that was cultivable of the headland which separated Hendrawna Beach from Nampara Cove. It reached up as far as where the outcroppings of rock and the gorse and bracken began.

Over its newly ploughed surface he stumbled, climbing till he could see the sea on both sides. Only a thin surf whispered on the beach to-night; its irregular hem demarcated the sand. The inlet of Nampara could just be seen from here, a rift in the mounting cliffs towards Sawle.

He had gone a few yards more when he saw a man standing beside a boulder, silhouetted against the low stars. Dwight's lantern could not have been entirely hidden, and only that the man was staring out to sea saved him. Back inch by inch, slowly pivoting until the boulder was between them. Exertion or tension had made him sweat again, but now it was welcome, warming his body to the night. Crouching low he skirted the sentry, going round the north side of Damsel Point until he was near the edge of the cliff. There he lowered his lantern behind a low stone wall and peered down into the darkness of the cove.

At first he saw nothing; and then, dawning on his eyes at no definite moment, he knew the ship was there. Something unnatural in the sea, low and black, unlike a rock even if a rock could be there. Straining, he could suddenly detect even the single mast and – for a second only – a glimmer of light aboard.

No light ashore. The cove, the centre of the cove, where sand and shingle met the stream, was empty. In the darker corners there might be men and beasts waiting; but so far as one could tell, nothing breathed or stirred under the frosty sky.

He lugged out his watch and peered at it like a blind man, then knelt beside the lantern to see. Ten minutes after twelve. The run had not yet begun.

In despairing haste he swung round, staring at the land about him. The other side of the wall was as good a place as any.

He wrenched out his pocket knife, opened it, and went back a few yards to the nearest gorse bush. Gorse is a nightmare of prickles but is brittle to the boot or the sharp twist. Part with knife, part with hands he tore a big piece off, dropped it over the wall. Then the next one. He could afford no time to build a stock. The thing must be fed while it was burning.

So he hacked a dozen bushes, dry stuff and highly inflammable. Together a fair pile to begin. Abandoning secrecy, he uncovered the lantern and climbed over the wall. Taking out the single candle, carefully shielding it from the air, he held it under the lowest part of the pile.

For a grievous space he thought the light would blow out; then a flame ran suddenly like quicksilver among the gorse, and in a moment the pile was blazing and crackling.

Chapter twelve

ROSS HAD BORNE the trip home with impatience. The eagerness and anticipation of the outward voyage was all gone, and once he was in sight of Cornwall he wanted to land at once instead of tacking about just over the horizon for twelve hours.

Not that there was anything useful to do when he reached Nampara, nor any good news to impart. The pricked bubble of his hopes had left nothing in its place; all he wanted was to get home, to turn his back on mining for ever, and to forget what he had thrown away.

For the first time in his life he began to feel old. Often these last years he had known himself a failure, but always within him there had been a fundamental conviction that this was a temporary phase, a 'down' which in the nature of events must be followed by an 'up.' At least a part of this conviction had derived from a knowledge of his own youth and vigour. His meeting with Mark Daniel had shaken that belief.

His realization again of the façade of mining expectations he had erected on the chance words of this man, uttered four years ago, shook his confidence in himself and in his own judgment. He bitterly blamed himself for his rash overconfidence, for an enthusiasm which in the light of experience looked wanton and silly. He had thrown away a profitable investment in a mine of his own starting and had poured everything he had, and persuaded Francis to do likewise, into a played-out mine which had failed his father a quarter of a century ago. Not only had he gambled with money, he had gambled with security and the security and happiness of his wife and child.

Mark's appearance had upset him. There had been a close tie between them in the old days; they had played together as boys, fished and wrestled as youths. This ageing man, grey-haired and puckering his eyes at the map. ... Was he, Ross, as untouched by time as he imagined? Was he deluding himself into believing that youth was still on his side? How many other misconceptions had his sanguine brain given room to?

He was not in his most companionable mood, and after a few attempts Farrell and the rest of the crew gave up the effort of engaging him in conversation. After nightfall the cutter edged her way slowly inshore until by eleven-thirty she came to anchor not a cable's length from the mouth of

Nampara Cove. The flat-bottomed longboat was lowered, and Farrell readily agreed with Ross's suggestion that he should go ashore with the first cargo. But Farrell would make no move to have any cargo shifted until the signal came from the shore.

It came at ten minutes to twelve, a single dark-lantern at the sea's edge, shining only seawards, and exposed for half a minute. Farrell gave his orders, and the barrels were lowered into the longboat.

A mixed bag, as Ross had realized when he looked at the cargo on the way home, but an immensely valuable one. No wonder Trencrom did not need to make runs more than a few times a year. Tea and tobacco and five-gallon casks of brandy and geneva; and a good quantity of rich materials: gold and silver brocade, silk gloves, ribbons, and girdles.

The spirits made up the larger amount of the cargo and these were loaded first. It was for the most part white brandy, with a tub of colouring mixture supplied. Its strength was 120° above proof; and in his own time Mr Trencrom would dilute his import before selling it, making three tubs to sell for every one that came ashore. He paid four shillings a gallon in France, and the price in England duty paid was twenty-eight shillings. Even sold at half price, the degree of profit escaped Ross, since there were some four hundred tubs of brandy alone aboard tonight; but he thought he would have less compunction than ever in levying his toll for the use of his land.

The boat was so filled that the gunwale was only an inch or two above the water, and Ross settled in the bows as the six oarsmen began quietly to row ashore.

For a little while there was no sound but the liquid dip of oars and the lap and bobble of water as it ran against the boat. The arms of the cove closed round them and shut out the great sounding emptiness of the sea. Instead, close at hand was the whisper of the surf, for once innocuous and sibilant. Inshore the stars were not as bright as they had been at sea: a faint haze had crept across them too tenuous for cloud. Presently the boat lifted and fell and grated upon sand and two of the men jumped out and held fast to prevent the run back. Out of the darkness around them four figures instantly came, two to help pull the boat more firmly ashore, two to wade into the surf to begin the unloading.

Ross stepped upon the wet sand. A new wave licked his boots as he walked inshore. He recognized Ted Carkeek and Ned Bottrell, and after a moment Paul Daniel loomed out of the darkness.

'All right, sur? Did ee find Brother?'

'Yes, I found him. . . .'

'Was 'e well? Did 'e give a message?'

'There's a message for you and for Beth and for his father. Tomorrow morning I'll come round and see you.'

'And did 'e help? Where was the good country?'

'I'll talk of it tomorrow, Paul.'

Behind them there was scarcely any talk at all, just a rapid business-like unloading of the first barrels. Often it was different from this; often they had to fight the surf and float in the tubs as best they could. Ross moved on, and Will Nanfan came towards him leading a mule. Knowing he would have some of the same questions to answer again, Ross prepared to make an excuse and pass quickly by. But the excuse was never made. Behind him came a sharp exclamation from one of the men. Ross saw someone staring, and at once a reflection of light showed upon the beach. A bonfire was leaping and smoking on Damsel Point.

Events moved more quickly than the mind accepted them. Muttered curses from the men around him, a clear shout from a voice not belonging, and then a shrilling whistle. Suddenly in the flickering light extra figures were climbing down the sides of the cove; then lantern lights, not shaded.

A surprise – gaugers – the long-expected – but this night of all nights. . . . Ross swung round, saw confusion about the longboat. He ran back.

'Quick! Relaunch! Get out there and tip the tubs. . . .' He flung his weight against the side of the boat; two or three others joined him. The boat slithered and grated. Two figures in it began heaving out the tubs together. Figures racing, strangers in flat caps, and some in tall. Nanfan had gone plunging away with his mule. A wave came and swirled around their knees; the boat floated but was being washed farther up the beach. 'Hold her! Steady! Give way!'

One of the men had gone down in the sea, his feet from under him, but two others joined. They held their ground, and as the wave slid back the longboat began to go with it. A musket exploded somewhere. One man jumped on the boat, then another. Ross followed until almost waist-deep. Oars were out, anyhow, but just enough to keep her straight. A man stood in the bows, held out his hand to Ross. Ross made a move to jump, then changed his mind. To be aboard again, isolated, perhaps tacking up and down for a week; he'd take his chance.

He turned, saw the place alive with men – the way up the track blocked with mules – confusion and men fighting, laying about them with sticks. As he ploughed his way out of the water a tall man in a busby: 'Halt, there! In the King's name!' Ross veered sharply. '*Halt* or I fire!' Turned again and ducked. The musket exploded in his ear as he knocked the man flat in the water.

Nothing he could do. Another shot, and then another. He ran left towards the cave where he kept his boat. An easy climb from there. Someone lurched at him out of the shadow – this time evasion came too late. He went down, the other on top. 'Got you, now! Lie still, you bastard, or I'll—— One over here, Bell!' Bearded. Vercoe. Ross doubled and sharply stiffened. Vercoe toppled, still clutching. They rolled, Vercoe under. Running steps. Twice he hit the Customs Officer, wriggled free, rolled over as the footsteps came up. Vercoe shouted: 'Not me, you fool! Over there – he's just gone!'

Ross at the cliff face turned as the newcomer caught him – the hard wooden stick of the gauger. They grappled. The stick clattered. A lucky swing with all his weight. The gauger fell in Vercoe's path.

As he climbed, Ross heard them following. In the cove a small war. Lights dancing. Untended, the gorse fire had waned. Climbing with all the knowledge of childhood, he pulled away. But a musket ball smacked into the rock beside him. Someone on the cliff taking careful aim. He reached the top, breaths gulping, crawled around the gorse, made diagonally for the first wall of his own land. He sucked the blood off his knuckles and spat. The two gaugers reached the top; lovely target if one had a gun. So the trooper must have thought, for the two men suddenly checked and Vercoe's voice bellowed an order across the cliff. It gave time for Ross to leap over the wall and begin to run doubled along the other side.

Demelza's sharp ears had caught the first distant crack of a musket, and she could stand it no longer. She started to her feet and was half-way to the door before the soldier was able to move.

''Ere, no, ma'am, None o' that! You heard what the Captain said.'

'I have a little boy upstairs! He will be frightened. I must bring him down!'

'No, ma'am. Cap'n McNeil said ye was to stay here in this room.'

'Please let me pass!' she said furiously.

'Now calm you down, ma'am. I has my orders and——'

'I'll not calm down! You don't make war on babies, do you? Get out of my way!'

He hesitated, glanced at the Gimletts. 'Is there a baby?'

'Course there is!' John Gimlett snapped.

The trooper turned to the drawn-faced young woman before him: 'I don't hear nothing. Which room is 'e in?'

'The one at the head of the stairs.'

He rubbed his finger along his chin and slowly drew back. 'I'll watch for ye, then. Have a care there's no trickery, ma'am.'

He followed her out into the hall and stood almost in the doorway where he could see into the room and also up the stairs. Demelza flew up the stairs and into their bedroom. Unaware of the dangers that pressed upon his parents, Jeremy slept peacefully.

This room had dormer windows looking both north and south. Demelza ran to the first of these, peered out. At first the night looked quiet and still, but then she detected the flicker of the bonfire on Damsel Point. She opened the casement window. From here the roof sloped sharply to the recently added guttering. But at the end, over the kitchen, it joined to the thatched end of the linhay where the carts were kept.

She wriggled her body through the small window and out on to the roof. Then she crawled along it like a cat to the end and slid off it into the thatch. She followed this to the lowest part, where there was a five-feet drop, and jumped.

She landed on all fours, tearing her skirt and bruising wrist and knee. Then she was on her feet and running towards the Long Field.

Breathless, she had just reached the stile when a figure climbed it. She had no difficulty in recognizing the set of his shoulders, the long lean head. They stared at each other in the dark.

'Demelza!'

'*Ross*! I thought you was killed. . . . Thank *God* you're safe! I thought——'

'Not safe,' he said. 'Followed. Which way is best into the house?'

'Neither. There's a soldier there. I said you was in St. Ives. Are you hurt?'

'Nothing.' While they spoke, they were walking rapidly the way she had come, he behind her in case of a shot. 'I think I was – recognized. Not sure. Is the – upper valley guarded?'

'Don't know. I've been crazed with worry. You could go towards Mellin.'

'They'll send that way——' At the entrance to their yard he stopped, listening. The yard was quiet except for a scratching at a stable door where Garrick was waiting to welcome him. 'They're coming – down the field now. Are you safe here? They offer you no hurt?'

'No, none, of course. But you——'

'Go in then. I'll hide in the library – in the cache. Safe enough there.'

'You can't get . . .'

'Yes – round the side. I have the key.'

'But *is* it safe. . . .'

'Must risk it.'

In a moment he had disappeared from her side. She heard the running footsteps. She hastily slipped back into the house – stumbled through the dark kitchen and into the hall. The soldier swung his musket on her, surprised and then angry.

'Where've ye been? How did ye get down?'

She took a deep breath. 'By the back stairs.'

He said: 'What back stairs? Ye never told me! Why did ye——'

'Well, I'm back! Is that not enough!'

The soldier too heard the running feet on the cobbles and again lifted his musket. Vercoe and his assistant Bell burst in upon them.

'Put your musket down, man!' Vercoe said in a quarter-deck voice. He was blazing with anger. 'One of your kind has took pot shots at us already!' He turned to Demelza. 'Where is Captain Poldark, ma'am?'

'In St Ives, I believe.'

'Then you believe wrong! I was wrestling with him on the beach not ten minutes gone. Has he come in here, trooper?'

'Nay. No one's come in here but you.'

'We last seen him making this way. He'll be somewhere about the house, never doubt!'

'You've no right to come breaking in here!' Demelza protested, finding relief in anger. 'What right have you to trespass on our property? My husband will hear of this! Why, if——'

'He surely will. And soon, I trust——'

'How do you know 'twas him? Is it daylight outside? Did you speak him by name? Of course not! I tell you he's from home and——'

'Look ee, ma'am,' said Vercoe, controlling his anger. ''Twas Captain Poldark I seen on the beach or his brother an' twin. I'll beg your pardon if I've the need to, but I don't suppose it likely. . . . An' what's that blood on your gown?'

'Blood?' she said, looking at the smear. Her stomach twisted. So Ross was hurt. 'It came from my wrist. I grazed it against the wall just now. See——'

Vercoe made an impatient gesture. 'You'll give us permission to search the house?'

'If I did not give it, you would take it.'

'Well, mebbe. The law must be served. Will you please go in the parlour with the servants.'

'No I surely will not! You may force yourself into the house, but you may not order me about. I shall come with you!'

Before Vercoe could argue about it, there was the sound of more footsteps in the kitchen and another trooper appeared. With him, half dragged and half led, was Dwight Enys, a bloodstained rag about his head. The soldier had caught him in the process of feeding the bonfire, and had knocked him out.

In the cove the pitched battle in the dark had died down. Seven of the smugglers had been captured, of whom two were wounded and one killed. A soldier and an excise man had been wounded. But owing to the premature alarm, the others had escaped. What was worse, the cutter had been able to weigh anchor and haul off from the lee of the land before the government cutter, standing rapidly in from the north-east, had been able to head her off. Shots had been exchanged, but the *One and All*, built in Mevagissey especially for the Trade, had run clean away from the government ship.

The smuggler killed was Ted Carkeek. He left a widow of twenty-one and two young children. The soldier wounded was Captain McNeil. Someone had shot him in the shoulder. An inch or so lower, and he would have companioned Ted.

He was almost the last to reach Nampara House, where by orders his men had forgathered with their prisoners. He came into the parlour holding a rough pad to his shoulder. The parlour was already part hospital, with Dwight, paper-coloured from loss of blood, trying to help those who were worse off than himself. As McNeil surveyed the scene and exchanged a word with his corporal, Vercoe and Bell and Demelza came down the stairs.

'Well?'

Vercoe shook his head. 'No, sur. Captain Poldark's not here, though I'll swear he was on the beach.'

'I've still three men posted: they may bring him in. You've tried the cellars?'

'Yes, they're empty.'

'No contraband?'

'None.'

McNeil met the angry flash of Demelza's eyes. 'Ross is in St Ives,' she said 'I've told these men. And I told you.'

'I should be happy to believe you.'

'You're wounded,' she said. 'Your coat – all that blood. . . . I'll get Dr Enys.'

'When my work is done.' He turned to Vercoe. 'We must comb the cottages round. You've examined the outhouses of this place, the stables, the library?'

'The stables. Not the library. 'Twas locked. I left that till you came.'

'We'll go now, then.'

Demelza felt as if this time her face must betray everything.

'The library?' she said, when they turned to her. 'I – have the key somewhere. . . . But your wound, Captain McNeil.'

'Will keep a little while. It is not the first time I have been blooded.'

They went through into Joshua's old bedroom. Vercoe and McNeil, and Bell carrying a lantern. With fumbling fingers Demelza unlocked the door to the library and went in. The long shabby room showed up, never used for its named purpose, full of mining samples and boxes of lumber and two desks and an iron safe. As soon as the lantern followed in, she knew he had come as he said he would. The metal trunks which normally stood above the trap door had been moved.

She stood against the door, not able to trust her legs, while the men went round the room. Vercoe carried a musket belonging to one of the troopers. He looked like a hunter after game. And the game was gone to earth.

First they examined the things in the room itself, opening the desks and the boxes, looking for contraband. After a moment or two she followed them halfway, watching them from the centre of the room. Then quite close to her she saw a spot of blood. It was tiny and already drying. She moved a little and put her foot on it, rubbed it into the boards.

But she might have known it was no use. Something in Vercoe's words or the way he spoke them had forewarned her that this was to be no ordinary search. They began to examine the floor.

So the informer had done his work.

They had come to the metal trunks, and Vercoe had seen the joins in the floor boards. He knelt by them and motioned Bell to bring forward the lantern.

Demelza said: 'I want you——'

Malcolm McNeil straightened up and looked at the girl who had come up behind him. He said: 'I think you would do well to leave us.'

She shook her head, not trusting her voice any more. He gazed at her a second longer, and then made a gesture for the two gaugers to continue.

Vercoe had found a spade and was forcing it into the narrow nick of the floor boards. With a squeal of strained wood they began to come up, for they were being lifted from the wrong side. After a minute he got his hand under the lifted boards, and Bell, putting the lantern down, knelt to help him. The trap door came up and the cache was open. McNeil took a step forward.

From where Demelza stood she could not see in. The room was humming and drumming about her ears. Rectangles of wall and roof began to dissolve into the uncertain geometries of faintness and nausea. All three men were around the hole, like jackals about a fallen beast, like hounds at the kill. For a few seconds they were involved in the general unreason of failing eyesight, of distortion and instability. Then she put out a hand and with a great effort steadied herself against a chair.

She did not know who would speak first, whether it would be Ross or one of his captors; but in fact it was McNeil, and all he said was: 'Well. . . .' and made a gesture to Vercoe. Vercoe grunted.

Then no one spoke again and no one stirred. At last she forced her limbs to move. She looked down.

The cache was empty.

Chapter thirteen

AT THREE O'CLOCK the following afternoon, having been granted his freedom on recognizances of £20, Dwight rode in at the gates of Killewarren. If there had been need for subterfuge before, the time for it was over.

For a while he could get no answer either to his rings or his knocks; but eventually the door was opened by the footman Thomas who had often shown him in before. He raised his eyebrows at sight of Dwight's bandaged head and bruised face.

'I've called to see Miss Caroline Penvenen.'

'She's gone, sir. This forenoon with her uncle.'

'Gone?'

'They've left for London. House be closed, sir, except for the servants. I don't know when they be coming back. A month may be.'

Dwight was unable to think what to say. 'What time did they go?'

'Just after ten. They was both anxious to be off, so they decided to dine on the way.'

'Was any message left, do you know? I had expected one.'

The man stared at him doubtfully. 'Not as I know. But I'll ask the housekeeper if you'll step inside.'

'I'll wait here.'

The man was gone several minutes and then brought back a sealed letter. 'Miss Penvenen gave this to the housekeeper, just as she was leaving. No address. Just Dr Enys. I suppose she knew you'd call, sir.'

Dwight turned away from the house and, ignoring the man's talk, stood by his horse fumbling with the seal.

The letter was dated: '9 A.M. Sunday, the third of February, 1793.'

Dear Dwight,

I am leaving with my uncle for London within the hour, a move which cannot surprise you after the fiasco of last night. Need I tell you of it? Your servant will already have given his account.

I waited. Oh yes, I waited like a dutiful Bride, you will have been gratified to know, for nearly two hours, while my coachman and my maid yawned their heads off – and no doubt snickered behind their hands – and your servant made so many excuses that I wondered at his invention.

But at the beginning he had told me all it was really necessary to know.

It is for the best this way, Dwight. Certainly far better that it should have happened now than later. I have known of your unhappiness for more than a month. Ever since we agreed to elope I have seen the struggle going on, the fight between your infatuation for me and your real love, which is your work in Sawle and Grambler. Well, your real love has won, and won so triumphantly – on the very day when I might most have expected to occupy your mind – that I am quite put to Rout.

Now you need not worry about it any more: you need give up nothing but me, and that you have already done. Perhaps it is for the best in more ways than one. We know so small a part of each other, I of you and you of me. No doubt we should have learned more in Bath, and then it would have been a little late.

So this is good-bye, Dwight. Do not fear I shall come to Cornwall to disturb you again. Not by two hundred miles. Thank you for the lessons you have taught me. They at least will not be forgotten by

> *Your sincere friend,*
> *Caroline Penvenen*

At five o'clock that afternoon, just before the first dusk, six men waited on Charlie Kempthorne in his cottage at the head of Sawle Combe. Their faces were as grim as their mission merited; but they found no one to welcome them. Charlie Kempthorne had gone, taking with him his easy smile and his cough, and a bag of silver he had saved and hidden under the floor. He had also taken his wedding clothes, which he had been making himself, and his Bible and such of his more recent purchases, like the cups and saucers and the mirror, as he could carry.

All he left was Lottie and May crouching terrified in a corner of the room upstairs. When they could be persuaded to speak, they said their father had given them a silver piece each and had gone at daylight, warning them not to stir out of doors for fear of their lives. They did not know where he had gone. Frustrated and angry, some of the men wanted to burn the cottage and beat the children; but moderate views prevailed, and word was sent to St Ann's to the aunt of the little girls to come and claim them quickly.

Charlie also left behind his wife-to-be. Dwight's interference had broken two romances. Rosina, at first incredulous, presently found in her memory small factual proofs. She had never really loved Charlie, but after a while she had responded gratefully to his admiration and attentions. It needed an emotional somersault now to realize and to condemn; for a while it was more than she was capable of and she went about in a daze, knowing hurt but not hate, answering the questions put to her flatly and without interest. Only occasionally a spark of anger showed when someone's question seemed to suggest that her own innocence could not be as complete as it seemed.

The six men who had called on Charlie did not give up their efforts at the sight of an empty cottage. They believed he would not move very fast or be able to travel without leaving a trail. News travels far in country districts, and the informer is the most hated of men. They thought they might catch up with him yet.

At seven o'clock that evening Ross came out of the cache where he had been hiding without food or water for eighteen hours – and in air that no one unused to the bad air of mines would have been able to tolerate for a quarter of the time. He had forced himself to wait until full dark, knowing that other men could be as patient as he. When he climbed up into the library, his eyes – so long accustomed to darkness – were able to pick out the window, the articles of furniture, and the door into the garden. He tried this, expecting it to be locked; but it was not and he stepped into the fresh air. There were lights in the house, but before he would approach it he made a cautious detour of the out-buildings and the surrounding garden and stream. Then he approached the house and looked in at each of the lighted windows. All the troopers had gone.

So at last he went in to Demelza, who for eighteen hours had been wondering what had become of him and had been imagining that the blood from his knuckles had been escaping from some untended artery.

The cache, having been dug to Mr Trencrom's specifications, had a false side moving on a central swivel, with a secondary and larger cache beyond. It was a not uncommon device among the more intelligent of the smuggling fraternity of Cornwall, but it was one that seldom failed to deceive. The men who had done this job, being all miners except for one farmer and one carpenter, had completed the work with exceptional thoroughness and skill. They had made the second cache large enough to conceal a considerable amount of contraband, but Ross had not supposed when he watched it done that it would ever be used to conceal himself.

Book three

Chapter one

DWIGHT'S INTERVENTION, IF it had not done everything that was intended, had saved Mr Trencrom's cargo. The *One and All* put back to the Scillies for two weeks and later landed her goods in three separate lots at different points along the coast. It had also saved Ross, for Mr Trencrom looked after his friends. Those who had been caught on the spot he could do nothing to help, but those who were luckier received his able support. Ross was informed that when the case of Black Saturday came up at the Quarter Sessions at the end of the month, a farmer and his son from Gwithian would be produced who would swear that Captain Poldark had spent the night of the second, February, at their farm.

A week or so after the fight a surgeon called Wright came to stay with Dr Enys and helped him on some of his cases. A few days afterwards Dr Enys left for London.

Later Dwight was sorry that he had been so precipitate, that he had not waited until after the sessions, but at the time he felt he could delay no longer. He had bribed Caroline's London address out of Thomas and had written twice giving her on each occasion – lest one letter should go astray – his full account of the adventures of the night and his reasons for acting as he did. Knowing her to be fundamentally reasonable, he had expected that her letter of farewell – written in understandable heat and haste – would sooner or later be retracted and that they could eventually make new plans. He had hung on day after day and had said each night, I'll wait until tomorrow, and then at last had dropped everything and gone.

So in the event, with a journey of five days each way and the sessions compelling his return, he was left with only one day in London to make his apologies and bring about a reconciliation.

It was enough had Caroline been half willing. They were staying with Mr Penvenen's sister Sarah, and Dwight called twice and twice was refused admittance. Then in the evening, reasoning that her uncle was likely to be behind the refusal, he called a third time, knowing her in, and tipped a footman to take up a private note to her. He waited impatiently until the footman returned with a reply which ran:

Dear Dwight,

Yes, I received your letters. I am glad that the choice you made was of value to Ross Poldark and the other smugglers. But the choice – your choice – was made before ever you knew this man was an informer. So it cannot affect mine. Do you not see that? I am very, very sorry. It is better for us both that it should be so.

Caroline

Early the following morning he made a final effort to see her, but it was useless and so he came home.

While the Quarter Sessions were pending, the coastal district of Sawle and St Ann's had more urgent and imminent things to concern it than the new war with France. The bench of magistrates it was known had been chosen to represent impartiality; but many considered it had been chosen for its partiality for the letter of the law. Its chairman was the Rev Dr Halse, who had always been known for his severity on the bench, and it was not long before the free traders caught were summarily tried and convicted. Four of them received twelve months' imprisonment and two, Ned Bottrell and a man from St Ann's, were sentenced to transportation for ten years. These were savage sentences for Cornwall, where smugglers even when they were convicted usually got off light, and feeling was high by the time Dwight Enys came before the bench.

The case of Dr Enys was a peculiar one. It had not been clearly established how far he was implicated, and the witnesses who were called went no further towards making the position clear. Dwight himself refused to offer any explanation for his movements, and Dr Halse's exasperation became obvious. No man, no educated man, could suddenly appear on the cliff edge and start building a bonfire without certain conclusions being drawn. This much and a lot more Dr Halse said in a long homily which followed his consultation with the other ten members of the bench. It was, he said, a peculiar disgrace that a well-known physician of the neighbourhood should allow himself to become so involved in this reprehensible traffic. A heavy responsibility rested upon all men of reputation to help to stamp out the illegal conduct of their less enlightened neighbours, not to encourage it, not to participate in it, as, failing any other explanation, it must be assumed Dr Enys had been doing. The opinion of the bench was that Dr Enys should be fined £50 or serve three months' imprisonment.

Dwight accepted the censure and the fine unmoved; and when the hearing was over, he refused to accept either sympathy or offers of help from those who had heard the case. All through this month, for a young man normally so kindly and tolerant, he had shown unexpected brusqueness and rancour towards friends and sympathizers. His popularity in Sawle and district had shot up to new heights – except at the house of Vercoe – and there were many who wondered why he would not be befriended. He showed impatience at any friendly move and a blank face to all advice and condolence.

Even Ross and Demelza he had seemed to avoid; and when he and Ross rode home together from the sessions, it was almost the first time they had had a private conversation.

For a while they discussed the outcome of the day. Ross thought that neither Bottrell nor the St Ann's man would serve their sentences. Already the Navy was crying out for men, and the two prisoners, both with experience of the sea, would probably be given the choice of fates. 'Not that one is much better than the other, but there's a matter of self-respect involved. I should suppose Bottrell at least will choose the Navy.'

'I was glad you were not charged, Ross. I thought they might have tried to pin something on you seeing that it was your land and knowing how hard they worked to get you convicted at the Assizes.'

'So they very well would have but for Trencrom. He provided me with witnesses to show that I was far away at the time of the run.'

'A man came to me just as I was leaving the court, said he was from Mr Trencrom and that Mr Trencrom would insist on paying my fine.'

'What did you say?'

'I refused, of course. I did not go to that trouble for Trencrom's sake.'

'No, you did it for mine. Have I told you what I feel about that?'

'You need not bother. Anyone else would have done just the same.'

'Anyone else would not. I'm under an enduring debt.'

'Oh, nonsense.'

They went on for a few minutes. The day was windy but not cold. Sea gulls were wheeling and screaming overhead and a gleam of sun gave sudden brilliance to their wings. Ross was the last person to push enquiries where they were unwelcome, but he was aware that something was very much amiss with this young man.

'I saw your friend Wright the other day. I suppose you still intend to leave the district now that this fuss is over?'

'I've no settled plans at all.'

'Then – your marriage to Caroline?'

'Is off. It was an adolescent folly. Fortunately we discovered it in time.'

Ross stared at his friend. 'As an outcrop of this smuggling affray?'

'No, of course not.'

'Demelza insists that it must be. She says you told her you were leaving late on the Saturday night. How was it affected by your arrest?'

'Not to my detriment, I see now. We should never have made anything of it, Ross. We were – incompatible, in the grip of a foolish passion. It couldn't have lasted and would have led to misery on both sides.'

'What has it led to now?'

'A temporary unhappiness that later we shall be grateful for. If you but realized it, I am in your debt, not you in mine.'

Dwight spoke firmly enough, but Ross saw that it was costing him a good deal. He would have liked more than anything to say something to help, but privately he was of the same opinion as Dwight. The relationship had been foredoomed. Far better the bitter disappointment now than the humiliation and misery of a lifelong *mésalliance*.

After a time Ross, having searched his brain for a new subject, said:

'McNeil the dragoon officer looks none so well from his wound. Is it true he's staying with the Bodrugans?'

'Yes. They'd known him since his first visit and invited him. I still attend him.'

'You? That surprises me.'

Dwight smiled slightly. 'I know. Both sides of the law. But I took out the ball and dressed his wound at your house on the Saturday night, and he seemed grateful that I did not bleed him. Anyway he requested I should see him again, and I've done so.'

'You'll have had some good talk on the ethics of smuggling.'

'We do not discuss it. But I don't think he bears any ill will – except to the man who shot him. He's by no means fit to travel yet and should not have been in court today; he bitterly begrudges every day which prevents him from joining his regiment and fighting the French.'

'I think if he's patient, the opportunities for glory will not all go in the first months.'

'No, possibly not. It's hard to foresee how long it will last.'

'Well, when a nation with less than fifty thousand troops, mostly in foreign parts, engages to fight one with an army of half a million, all at home and striking from central lines. . . . '

'We have allies.'

'Prussia and Austria? They blew hot and cold last year when their opportunities were greater. Holland? I think the Dutch will need more than a few of our gunboats and a regiment of Foot Guards to give them the will to fight.'

Dwight said: 'I have thought these last weeks I should wish to do something myself. It's difficult to know what, but the notion attracts me now – and it would I think help to relieve the – the sense of futility.'

'Well, take your time. Think all round it, for once you're in the pan it's hard to jump out.'

Just before they separated Dwight said: 'And your visit to – to Mark Daniel, was it all to no purpose?'

'It was to some purpose, for it showed me what an oversanguine fool I've been.'

'He had no advice that was of use?'

'None at all.'

'How long shall you go on?'

'Until the coal is done.'

Dwight was silent until he drew rein to turn off.

'How was Daniel, Ross?'

'The thing had left its mark, as you'd suppose.'

'Yes . . . as I would suppose.'

Ross rode down the valley. Another matter of importance to himself came out of the events of Black Saturday. Nampara Cove was now useless to Mr Trencrom. The gaugers could not watch it every night, but the notoriety of the raid and all that had gone with it put the cove out of bounds for a long time to come. There could be no question now of the Poldarks taking the risk, for Mr Trencrom would not take the risk. That was going to make a great difference to Ross's income, just the vital difference he had not counted on. He had gambled again, and again lost. . . .

He had asked Demelza not to come to the Quarter Sessions; and since he was not in danger himself, she had agreed. Now he had it all to tell, and supper was late as a consequence. Afterwards they talked of the mine. The venturers of Wheal Radiant were interested in the headgear; and this morning before the sessions began he had seen a representative of another mine for the sale of the surplus stores.

Demelza said suddenly: 'Ross, I have never mentioned it; but one day at the beginning of the year I went into St Ann's to buy a few things we needed – you remember, I asked for Darkie – and while I was there I met Mr Renfrew the chandler. . . .'

He had picked up the *Sherborne Mercury* to glance through its pages; now to give himself time to think he carefully folded it and took it across to the shelf by the window where the old copies were stacked.

'And Mr Renfrew said it was a poor thing you'd sold the last of your shares in Wheal Leisure. I've never sought to ask you about it because – well, if you did not want to tell me, you did not. Perhaps you thought to save me worry. Or perhaps Mr Renfrew is mistaken and he was speaking of the first shares you had sold.'

Ross came back to the fire and stood beside it. 'No, it is true. I sold them in early January. I made £675 for them, which showed a handsome profit on my investment. Of course we have not the income. . . .'

'Has all that had to go into Wheal Grace?'

Because she made it easy for him to lie to her, he could less than ever do so. 'No. Only £75 of it. The rest I used in discharging a debt of honour. . . .'

After a moment's silence Demelza said: 'Oh, well, I thought he would know, being in the mine himself. Ross, do you think that the beer we brewed last will be right to drink yet? The other is gone, and John I know favours a little with his supper.'

'Tell him to try it. It should be fair enough. Demelza, I have wanted to explain about this for a long time but have not known quite the best way to do it. I was waiting in fact for a good opportunity, waiting for a time when it would no longer matter what I had done with the money. Instead the explanation comes on me when it matters more than ever.'

She looked thoughtfully at him. 'It is your money, Ross. You must do with it as you please.'

'Not entirely. My obligations are various. But one, in this particular, seemed above the others.'

Something in his expression gave her a hint of what was coming. She put down the thing she was sewing.

So he told her what he had done.

'Sometimes,' he ended, 'one feels an obligation in one's mind. Regardless of whether it is so truly or not, it *seems* a matter of conscience and so becomes one. I had induced Francis to sink his money in the mine. Now he's dead and Elizabeth and Geoffrey Charles are penniless and alone. However indifferent a protection I am to you and Jeremy, I am alive and active – constantly doing what I can; I offer some sort of shelter from – from the wind. Elizabeth has none such. With this money they can do a great deal, tide over these first difficult years.'

'Yes. I see that.'

'Before Christmas, of course, I was in no shape to help anyone at all. But my unknown friend gave me the breathing space. And he gave me the idea that I might copy him. It was rash, but I needed – for my soul's sake – to be free of the burden of the sense of obligation. Of course I was then relying on the money from Trencrom continuing for the next few years.'

Demelza did not speak. She broke the cotton and stared at it with narrowed eyes.

'With Trencrom's money all was well,' he said, 'and we could spare this interest and capital. Without it we're in difficulties again – or shall be in time. Fortunately there's nine months of the year still to go. But I repent my generosity, and unhappily so must you also.'

She began to thread her needle again.

'Do you blame me?' he asked.

'Of course not. Not for myself, I don't. I am not so sure for Jeremy. But then 'tis done, and no good will come now of talking of it.' She hesitated, pushing her dark hair away from her forehead as if it was some unwelcome thought. 'Do you think Elizabeth is in so much need?'

'I think she *was*. Why?'

'Well, I have heard that George Warleggan is being very obliging to her.'

'I've no doubt he would be if she would let him. But she will not. Who spoke to you of it?'

'Sir Hugh Bodrugan.'

'Has he been here again?'

'Yes, he came to call one afternoon last week. He was passing, he said.'

'You didn't tell me?'

'I forgot. He wanted for us to go to the Meet at his house last week. I said we had another engagement because I knew you would not go.'

He bent to light his pipe, but the mouthpiece would not draw so he knocked out the tobacco and began to fill it afresh. He was surely the last person now to complain either at someone's fancy for his wife or at her failure to tell him of a passing visit. But perhaps the irritation he felt rose not from Sir Hugh's visit but from what he had said.

'One of George Warleggan's ambitions, long before Francis died, was to drive a wedge between them and me, and the easiest way to attempt it was by befriending them. Once he succeeded, and both Francis and I suffered as a result. . . . In trying to help Elizabeth now, he is only continuing the same tactics. Although that wasn't my aim in arranging for her to get this money, it does have the effect of strengthening her hand against him.'

'Yes,' said Demelza, and went on with her sewing.

On the twelfth of March, which was a Tuesday, Captain Henshawe came to see Ross in the library, where Ross was working. There was a peculiar expression on his face, and he carried a small sack which he put down on the floor while he took off his hat and wiped his forehead.

'You're hot?' said Ross. 'You'll soon cool off here. There's a draught that's been mislaid from January blowing under the door. What's that, the last of our coal?'

Henshawe said: 'Young Ellery's just come up and brought this bag with him. I thought you might like to see what was in it, sur.'

He emptied the bag on the floor. There were about a dozen pieces of quartzose rock, not noticeably different from a thousand others that had been mined and crushed in the last twelve months. Henshawe's eyes travelled curiously over Ross's face as Ross looked at them.

'Pick 'em up,' said Henshawe.

Ross did so, weighed one or two in his hand, put them on his desk, tried a couple more.

'What is it – lead?'

'Tin.'

'What sort of proportion?'

'Goodly. There's a thin streak or two of copper, as you can see, and some siliceous minerals. It's in that main shaft we've been sinking below the sixty fathoms. Plumb light-blue killas. They come on it today.'

'You've been down?'

'Yes. They've been driving through granite and hard black killas, as you know; but they passed out of that yesterday, following the eastward split of the old copper lode, as we decided. There's been tin mixed with it for twenty fathoms, but never in much quantity, and the copper ever poorer. Indeed, as you know, 'twas only just alive. This is the first time there's been any rich indications.'

'Is there any size to the thing?'

'This is from a reg'lar bunch of ore, as you can tell by the weight. The

lode is narrower than 'twas, and generally comby; but this bunch is six feet
or more across, and we don't know how deep.'

Ross tilted his chair back and stared at his desk. 'I was in the process of
closing the books of the mine. Saturday is the end of it. The infidels from
Wheal Radiant are coming nearer to my price for the headgear. I have kept
them waiting two days as a business tactic, but I shall send over to-morrow
and accept.'

'And this?'

Ross turned over a piece of the rock with his foot. 'As we have spent
eighteen months and all our money seeking copper, you can hardly expect
me to become excited over the discovery of a small parcel of tin.'

'From the look of it below, I should say it was worth a second thought.'

'Do you want me to come down?'

'Yes. I'd like for you to.'

'Who found it?'

'Ellery and Green.'

'And they think they've discovered El Dorado?'

'They're keen enough, as you'd imagine. After so much wasted
effort. . . .'

'In their eyes it appears much bigger than it really is, eh?'

Henshawe said cautiously: 'I'd like for you to see it before we say more
about that.'

Ross got up and shut his ledgers. They went out and began to walk
across the valley. Low grey cloud was blowing across the sun, and the thin
smear of smoke from the mine chimney merged and blew away with it.
Farther west, rifts in the shifting canopy showed distant sky, blue and pale-
green and misty indigo. It was a quiet day and should have been mild, but
some northern air had infected it and the wind was chill. The trees in the
valley were still as black as mid-winter.

There had been silence all the way. As they neared the mine, Ross
looked up at the slow, measured swing of the balance bob. Trevithick had
said the engine would last fifty years, and no doubt he was right – given the
opportunity. Ross could tell that Henshawe was quietly very interested in
this discovery; but there had been so many bitter disappointments that in
self-defence he would not allow himself to perceive any novelty in this one.
And unless they had actually struck a bed of tin which needed the absolute
minimum of further outlay, with a quick return for what was raised, there
was no chance at all of keeping the mine in operation. In any case, tin was
basically less profitable than copper, the ore being so much more expensive
to extract at surface. There had been tin mines in this area before –
Grambler had begun as one in the seventeenth century – and there were
still a few alluvial workings, two- or three-man concerns eking out an
existence; but he had never seriously thought of finding or mining the
mineral in any big way. And the tin industry was still in a depressed

condition; no one would be willing to finance an exhausted copper mine on the strength of a few samples of rock.

They went down, and Ross inspected the find. Work had stopped in other parts of the mine – only the great engine still patiently sucked water out of the sump – and men were more or less taking it in turns to pick at the rock, weighing this lump and that in their work-seamed hands, bending over it and talking and nodding and comparing experiences of the past. Most of them were stripped to the waist, for the heat had much increased in the last twenty fathoms. Ross took the pick himself and worked away for a few minutes, while Ellery stood beside him pointing out the breadth and inclination of the lode.

Ross didn't say much; every one of the workers knew the state of things in the mine, but every one no doubt hoped this would just make the difference. He did not disillusion them, for that would come soon enough.

On the way up again he said to Henshawe: 'I agree. It is not unimpressive.'

'You said all along you had the feeling to go deeper.'

'Yes, but not for tin, man, not for tin. Anyway it may still be the merest pocket.'

As they reached the top and the now apparently bright day greeted them, he added: 'I'm glad Ellery found it. He and his partner are good men. We can get what little they have time to bring up stamped and dressed, and it will make a difference to their last earnings.'

'They'll take it some hard to be deprived of the chance to work a few weeks more. They would have given up more easier if there had been no such find. What we need's a breathing space to see what this means.'

'I agree, but where's it to come from? Who's to pay? I tell you frankly I haven't twenty pounds in the world.'

Henshawe said: 'I'd never much faith in you seeking the lodes at a greater depth. It's not been my experience in this district – they die on you. But this has a keenly look to me. And it's queer; copper under tin you expect – but not tin under copper.'

'Well, there's four days still to go. They'd be advised to work hard until Saturday.'

Ross did not tell Demelza of the discovery. There was no virtue in raising false hopes. But the whisper spread behind his back, and in no time she had heard of it and wanted to know what it meant.

'It means nothing,' Ross said. 'At best it would be a minor lottery prize. A few months ago we could have worked it as a side product; no one objects to an additional mineral, and the receipts from it would have kept us struggling awhile longer. But there is nothing more to it than that. It will be a blow to many families when the mine closes, and I suppose it is not unnatural that they should be hoping for the impossible.'

'So was I,' said Demelza, and after that nothing more was said.

Nothing more until Thursday evening, when Captain Henshawe called. He found them both at home, so the conversation took place before Demelza.

'I've just been down again, sur. They've opened of her up a tidy bit since Tuesday. More and more it look to me like a lode of value and not just a freak bunch. The stuff that's come up, as you know, is as rich as you'd want. It go more and more against the grain to let her fill with water at the present stage.'

Ross frowned his discomfort. 'It goes against the grain to let her fill with water at any stage. Let someone only provide the coal to keep the pump working. . . .'

'That's what I been thinking,' said Henshawe apologetically.

'What d'you mean?'

'I been thinking that if I'm eagerer than you, I'm also the more able to back my judgment. Leisure is doing a fine job for me and I've made savings. Not all that big, but I could see us through a month or more. I could put down a hundred pound if need be. It seem only right, and I'd be willing to do that.'

Ross stared at him. 'You would?'

'Yes, I would.'

Ross had known Henshawe for twelve years, since he was made mine captain at Grambler. He was an honest man and a clever one. His education, he sometimes said, had cost his father a penny a week for eight months. He had raised himself – at one time before the depression came – to a position of consulting manager to five mines solely on the strength of his own ability and acumen. His friendship with Ross had grown closer ever since the opening of Wheal Grace. But Ross had no fear that Henshawe was making this offer as a gesture of friendship or on a charitable impulse of the moment. Unlike certain other people who might be brought to mind, Henshawe had never disguised the fact that he felt his first duty to be to his own wife and family. He would perhaps have given five pounds to save a friend from prison; but nothing would have induced him to risk a further hundred pounds of hard-gleaned capital in a mining venture which had already absorbed so much unless . . .

Ross met Demelza's eyes across the room. He knew what she was thinking.

'Are you wholly satisfied, then, that this thing is worth pursuing? After all the other failures you feel so sure of this. . . .'

'Not sure, sur. But I thought to proceed slowly. In another week we shall know far more. If 'tis disappointing we can still close and I shall have lost twenty or twenty-five pound. If it go on as I think it will go on, I'll back it for a month longer. But we must move to-morrow. I thought with your permission I'd send over to Trevaunance or Basset's Cove for coal to carry on. 'Twill only just reach us in time.'

'Send over by all means,' said Ross, but neither his face nor his voice was easy to read. He was carefully combating a feeling within him which he was afraid to recognize as hope.

On the same day towards the evening George Warleggan went to see his father and mother at Cardew and told them that Elizabeth Poldark had promised to be his wife.

Chapter two

IN ALL PROSPERING human affairs there is a streak of hazard, a blending of good fortune with good judgment which gives the lucky man a sense of having earned his deserts and gives the deserving, if he is modest, an awareness of his luck.

That George Warleggan was able to break such startling news to his family came in part from events over which he had no control and in part from that sharp sense of timing which had stood him in good stead before as a man of affairs.

They met at Cusgarne on the Thursday afternoon, and Thursday was the last and most trying day of four which had been trying for Elizabeth.

First there had been the unpleasant scene with George Tabb, who had been a faithful servant of the Poldarks' all his life. As the last manservant, he had felt himself able to claim certain privileges even before Francis died; and since then he had become subtly less easy to handle. On Monday a trial of strength, and Elizabeth came out of it bitterly aware that she had let things slide too long. Now she must either accept his defiance or discharge her two remaining servants and take new ones who would not possibly get through the same amount of work.

The choice was temporarily but dangerously shelved. Then Mr Nathaniel Pearce arrived fresh from his gout, with new problems to face, the results of negotiations to report, and new decisions to be made for which only Elizabeth could be responsible. A tithe of £1 6s. 8d. per year on the seines of certain of the fishing boats in Sawle was payable to the Poldarks, and in the case of most boats this was long overdue. For the last four years catches had been poor. Should the fishermen be pressed for the money? Whose was the greater need now? A long-standing complaint from Garth, Mr Penvenen's agent, on the condition of the bridge over the stream behind Grambler village where the two estates ran together. Repair was Poldark responsibility, but now Mr Penvenen, newly returned from London, offered to pay one quarter of the cost of a new bridge if Mrs Poldark would meet the rest. Would she meet the rest? What about the pastureland to the west of the house? Ross advised her to have it ploughed; for now that war had come, corn growing would be likely to pay handsome dividends. But already it was late to do anything this year, and it would mean engaging and paying farm hands. Finally there was the making of a complicated dispute with some tinners who were claiming their age-old right under the Stannary Law to enter enclosed ground and prospect for tin.

She slept badly that night, and so in the morning in the very first light was the less strong to meet the news that it brought. A man from Cusgarne to say her mother had had an apoplexy and would she come at once. Elizabeth was in Kenwyn by eleven and found her mother paralysed in one arm and hardly able to speak. Over a silent meal with her father she faced up to the inescapable. There was now no choice for her. Already there was one bedridden woman at Trenwith, tended on unsatisfactorily by the village girl Elizabeth had been able to engage. The Chynoweths would bring a little money but trouble and difficulties out of proportion. Elizabeth looked into the future and saw it as one in which sickness and age and responsibility were her only companions.

Into this picture came George Warleggan, saying he had only just heard of her mother's illness and that he had come straight up from the bank, apologizing that he should be a little untidy, solicitous for Mr and Mrs Chynoweth, and more than solicitous for Mrs Poldark.

She told him all there was to tell, and without emotion told him what she proposed to do. While they were talking, her father shuffled out of the room, a man who for thirty years had accepted his directives from his wife and now without her was helmless, drifting as the first wind took him.

They talked on for a time. George seemed reluctant to go. He was watching Elizabeth with his attentive eyes. At length he said:

'Do you know what I wish?'

'No.'

'I wish, my dear Elizabeth, that you would allow me to make all the arrangements necessary, and that you would permit me to engage a separate establishment for your mother at Trenwith, so that no further burden would fall on you.'

'I couldn't let you do that.'

'Why not? You're so *frail*, Elizabeth. I fear for you. One does not expect the lily to stand the storms of winter. It needs protection. *You* need protection. I can only offer it you in this way.'

She glanced at him through her lashes, her face pale and withdrawn but not unfriendly.

'You're truly kind. But I'm stronger than I look. Now – just now – and perhaps for a few years, I shall have to be. I regret it – you don't know how much I regret it – but it has to be. One must take what life sends.'

'But one must not take what I send, eh? Is that it?'

She smiled at him. 'I have already taken so much.'

'Oh,' he made a gesture, 'a little for my godson, and that very reluctantly;

certain concessions in the matter of Francis' debts. But nothing for yourself. And now nothing for your mother. I should like to do it for your mother's sake.'

Always in the past he had found this the surest avenue to Elizabeth's sympathies, and it was so now.

'Oh, you know how very deeply I have appreciated what you've done for her in the past, George. Your kindness makes me ashamed to refuse you anything. But what you suggest——'

He said: 'If there was one thing you did not refuse me, it would solve everything.'

'What is that?' she asked, looking at him; and instantly knew.

'Yourself,' he said.

She turned a little away from him, with a sudden sensation of finding herself on the edge of a precipice. It was a precipice she had quietly known of for a long time but disregarded because she felt her balance so sure. There was no danger – except perhaps in allowing him to think there might be. Now suddenly the equilibrium was changed.

'Before you say anything,' he went on, 'let me add something to that one word. Although I've never spoken of it, you will be aware, I dare suppose, that I have loved you for ten years, ever since we first met. In that time I have served you only as I could, by paying back half Francis' card debts with my cousin Sanson, by waiving the interest on his ordinary debts to our bank, by allowing no thought of retaliation to be considered when he – persistently insulted me. All this I did willingly and would have done twice as much if the opportunity'd been present – as you also know. Since Francis' death I have served you in any way you would allow me, and will continue to without thought of anything *I* may gain by it.'

'Yes,' she said. 'I'm more than grateful – more than grateful.'

'But now I ask you to marry me. As I said, I love you. I don't think you love me. But I think you like and respect me; and I think – indeed I'm sure – that in time such liking would become something more than liking, something closer than a common interest.' He hunched his shoulders and stared at her. She had not moved any further away, and he could see her face. He thought there was a slight flush under her pale composure. He flattered himself that, considering all that hung on the outcome, he was putting his case well. 'I can't bring you breeding, my dear. But I can bring you a certain kind of gentility which is the more punctilious because it is only one generation deep. And so far as material considerations go——'

'Please,' she said.

'Oh, I know you would not marry me for my money or my possessions. If you did that, you wouldn't be the person I know you to be. But at the risk of offending you I want to tell you what I can offer.'

She tightened her lips, a little more tense, as if ready for another protest. The window through which she looked was full of trees and hedges, overgrown, overbranched, blowing in the wind.

He said: 'When I marry, my father has promised that he and my mother will vacate Cardew. That means I shall be able to take my wife to a house four times as big as Trenwith, everything in it almost new, twenty servants, in a park of five hundred acres. You've seen it. You know. If you marry me, Trenwith could be repaired and refurnished, kept as a second home where your father and mother could live with adequate servants, and where we could visit them as often as you chose. I already have my own carriage; you could have one also if you wanted it; or two or six if it pleased you. I could take you to London and Bath and introduce you into society there. Local society is already a thought provincial for me. I have undertaken to educate Geoffrey Charles. But as my son he would be differently placed from what he is now. I am heir to all Warleggan interests. So would he be. We're still young, Elizabeth, you and I. There's very little we could not achieve if we put our minds to it. For ten years you've lived in a cage. Give me permission to turn the key.'

'And the devil taketh him up into an exceeding high mountain and showeth him all the kingdoms of the world and the glory of them; and saith unto him: "All these things will I give thee . . ." ' It had been one of the lessons read last Sunday in Sawle Church, where Elizabeth sat alone with Geoffrey Charles in the family pew.

She picked up her bag from the table, fumbled in it without knowing what she wanted. She hadn't spoken and now he was waiting. The light was already poor in the room, as poor in its way as the worn furniture; but some reflection from the mirror above the sofa lit up his heavy, intent, contained face. She knew that every moment he waited his hopes of a favourable answer would rise. To her own astonishment, she realized that a favourable answer was no longer impossible for her. It was as if life were mesmerizing her into acceptance of a situation which at one time, and not so long ago, would never have been allowed to come into being. There was still enough critical detachment in her to notice the occasional gaucheries of his proposal; yet reason told her there was not one single statement he had made which was exaggerated or untrue. He *could* offer her all that. He, George Warleggan, very close to her now, known so long that easy familiarity led to an underrating of his achievements and his charm; but in fact formidable, wealthy, powerful in the county for good or ill, still young, not bad-looking, a person already become a personage, one of the few who counted and who would count still more as time went by; he was offering her all this as the price of marriage: her son lacking for nothing, *all* her problems solved. All except one, a new one, the problem of George.

'Elizabeth,' he said. 'Can I suppose that——'

She stopped him with a gesture, instantly, suddenly flushing into a rare colour and brilliance of expression. 'No, please, I don't want you to think . . .'

And there in her refusal she halted. Upstairs was her mother, crippled and fretful, and her father, indecisive and endlessly complaining. She had ridden over in the rain and to-night or to-morrow she must ride back to Trenwith, which would greet her unlighted and unheated and with all its problems still to solve. And years of loneliness and sick-nursing lay ahead. And on the other side was light and warmth and companionship and *care*.

'Oh, George——' she said, and put up her hands to her flushed face. 'I don't know what to say.'

Instantly he was beside her, one arm gently round her shoulders, aware of a startling triumph that he'd not dared to expect, but aware of how nearly it still trembled in the balance.

'Say nothing more now, my dear,' he urged. 'Nothing at all, please.'

'I am so depressed. Please don't ask me for an answer now.'

'I ask you for nothing. Only give me permission to give.'

'But if you give——'

'Don't say any more, Elizabeth.'

'But I must. It's the – loneliness. . . . What I'd not imagined – the lack of a person, a partner. But to pretend now, or to let you think . . .'

'I think nothing for the present. But I hope. Loneliness is not one-sided, Elizabeth. A man can feel it too, especially when he has loved anyone as long and as hopelessly as I have you.'

So they stayed for a time. And while she held her head down as if in defeat, he held his high in victory and looked over her bright hair at the wild, untended garden and the rain. He watched the water trickling in grey loops down the glass.

Though intention had not been in it, he suddenly found the prospect before him dazzlingly good – first because it gave him this woman whom he had loved and wanted for so long, second because by the same stroke it dealt what he knew would be the deadliest of blows at his bitterest enemy. It was not given to many men, he felt, to achieve so much by a single coup.

Chapter three

THE TIN LODE did not peter out. In a week they found that ore-bearing rock existed in a great mass at this point. No one knew how far it yet extended, but Ross began to feel himself infected with some of the general excitement. In another week they were raising the ore in quantity; and even allowing for the difficulties of dressing, there was the prospect of a return.

To keep down expenditure, all work on the copper lodes – such as they were – was suspended, and for the same reason other trying decisions had to be made. They were working an underhand stope, and already there was a worked-out open space above them. Very soon it would be dangerous to go on without timbermen and props for support. Already it was uneconomic, for no lode is constant in size and quality; and instead of eating at it in this unscientific way, they should have been making a series of right-angled shafts and levels to cut the lode at different depths and to create reserves of explored ground. That was the methodical way; but lack of capital forced them to live from hand to mouth.

No rumour of the momentous decision taken at Cusgarne reached the outside world. On a visit to Truro, Ross met Richard Tonkin, whom he had not seen for a year, and told him of the discovery of tin. Tonkin drew on his own experience to be encouraging, and, having at one time been manager of United Mines, his experience was considerable. He himself was no longer in mining, having six months before bought a small boatbuilding business in East Looe in partnership with Harry Blewett – another sufferer in the Carnmore Copper failure and one to whom Ross had lent money at the time of the crash. They were making a good living out of their venture.

Ross parted from him slightly encouraged by his comments. If one could just keep *going*, even with the most modest return, it would justify all manner of things within himself, it would maintain the men working on the mine, it would help everyone connected with the venture to a new self-respect. . . .

The following week end, Verity, Francis' sister, visited Elizabeth, She had not been to Trenwith since her brother died; but this was a long-dated invitation, and the ice had to be broken some time. Elizabeth too forced herself not to go back on the arrangement, though with so much milling in her heart and head. . . . Verity brought her stepson James Blamey who had arrived unexpectedly for a few days' leave. Young, noisy, warmhearted, attractively fond of his stepmother in a boyish, roughly gentle way, James helped to keep the spectres at arm's length.

They were much concerned when they learned of Mrs Chynoweth's illness and offered to leave at once, but Elizabeth would not hear of it. Her mother was well looked after – now. A nurse had been engaged and two new servants, and one could only wait and hope that in a few weeks she would be well enough to be moved. Verity wondered at the word 'now,' which seemed rather often to creep into Elizabeth's conversation.

James was openmouthed at Elizabeth's beauty – as young men so often were – and enjoyed himself cantering about the countryside on a borrowed nag. He joined Verity on several of her visits to old friends and went with her to Nampara for Sunday dinner and tea. Demelza was waiting for them, and she and Verity hugged each other while Ross shook James Blamey's hand. Then James had to kiss Demelza, so that it was some moments before she had the breath to ask the question Ross had forced himself not to ask.

'But – isn't Elizabeth with you?'

'No. She was to have been, but a severe headache came on. She's much worried, you know, over her mother. She sent her love as well as her apologies.'

They went in, and talked and laughed perhaps more easily than they might have done in Elizabeth's presence. While they were talking of Ross's mission to see Mark Daniel, Verity's eyes strayed out of the window and confirmed their earlier impression that the engine chimney was still smoking.

She said: 'But I see you have not yet given up.'

Ross explained.

'We exist upon a shoestring and everything's against us. But the quality of the ore this week is remarkable – fortunately, for every expense of development must be paid for out of what we raise and a single fault in the lode will see our end.'

'D'you know,' said James Blamey in his big voice, 'I have never been down a mine yet, though it is unnatural in me to be so neglectful. How deep is your bilge, Captain? Do you climb all the way or do you have one of these newfangled buckets?'

'Perhaps after dinner James would like to go down, Ross,' Demelza suggested.

'By all means.'

'Ha! so I should,' said James, 'though I've a fancy I shall get dizzy climbing the wrong way from usual. When you're in the foremast shrouds, 'tis most comforting to see the deck below you, even if 'tis only the size of a visiting card. In a mine I should expect to fly up to the surface if I lost my grip!'

Just before dinner Dwight came. A week ago Demelza had tackled him about the break-up of his plan to marry Caroline and so now felt a greater than ever responsibility for his welfare.

Nevertheless he was no damper on the party, being specially interested in James Blamey and medical conditions in the Navy. James laughed at his questions. When you were afloat, you didn't dare to be ill. If you were, you got dosed with a purge or an emetic according to where the pain was. Last voyage on his ship there'd been thirty deaths from scurvy alone. James had left the *Thunderer* and had joined the frigate *Hunter* in a squadron under Admiral Gell. They were at present in Plymouth Sound but under sailing orders for next week, destination yet unknown but probably the Mediterranean. James's concern, like Captain McNeil's, was lest the war should be over before he could have any part in it.

After dinner Dwight left and Ross took James off to the mine, so the two women were left alone.

At first they talked of Jeremy, and then quite suddenly Verity broke off the conversation to say:

'Tell me, my dear, have you noticed anything strange about Elizabeth?'

'In what way strange?' asked Demelza, her senses instantly alert. 'I've scarcely seen her.'

'Well, it's hard to define. But I think she has recovered quickly from her bereavement, has she not? Oh, I know it's six months, and no one would expect her to grieve for ever; it is not quite that – but she seems different in some way, a little on edge, as if innerly excited. Once or twice in conversation she has checked herself, as if afraid of saying too much.'

'To you? This week end?'

'Yes. I believe I am not imagining it. I know her quite well as we lived so long together. One gets the impression that she thinks her circumstances are going to change.'

They may already have changed, thought Demelza, remembering the six hundred pounds. 'You should ask Ross,' she said.

Verity looked at Demelza. 'That sounds a trifle bitter, my dear. Are you sure you have reason to be?'

Demelza looked up quickly, then smiled. 'Did it? It was not at all meant to be. I know Ross loved Elizabeth once; so when he goes to see her I'd not be human if I did not wonder what they say to each other. Would I? Ross does not tell me what they say, and 'tis not in my pride to ask, so I never learn.' She got up, looking down at Verity, now stooped and kissed her forehead. 'I should not have said that much if you hadn't asked me, but you did, and so I answered. Verity, would you care for a cup of tea? It is early, but all this talking has made me thirsty.'

'I'd like one. But just let me say – and I do not say this for your comfort – if Ross were——'

'No,' said Demelza. 'I do not think you should need to say that, whether for my comfort or no. Having a husband, it seems to me, is a small matter like going to church. Either you trust in something or you do not. If you do not, then there's no benefit in going to church at all, is there? But if you do believe in him, then you've no excuse to be asking for proofs all the time.'

'That's a very admirable outlook——'

'Oh, yes, and I am not always very admirable. Seldom, indeed. But it is true, isn't it; and that's more important than the feelings you feel sometimes. Verity, tell me about yourself for a change. You are happy, quite happy? I dearly love James. I should like Jeremy to grow up like James. He's like a west wind, gusty and clean and no breath of malice. I think he has quite fallen in love with you.'

Verity caught her smile and swiftly answered it.

'I love James like my own son. Yes, I'm happy, Demelza, or would be without the fear for Andrew's safety. So far there has been no trouble for the packets, and he says he takes a more westerly course to avoid possible attack. But he must come through the narrower waters between the Scillies and Ushant, and there is never any knowing now. You know what that feeling is.'

When they were in bed that night Demelza told Ross that Verity was going to have a baby.

'What?' Ross leaned up on one elbow. 'That is a surprise! Brave news. Are you sure?'

'She told me so herself. As yet it is a secret. Andrew doesn't know and she wishes to keep it to herself for the time. Isn't it good? I'm that pleased for them both.'

'So am I. When is it to be?'

'About October.'

'She will be thirty-five this year. I hope all will go well.'

'Oh, it is no age, Ross, though I believe she is a little anxious in that respect herself. It will be strange for Andrew with his daughter nearly twenty; but I know he'll be delighted and I urged her to tell him so soon as possible.'

'I have never noticed you overready with your own news. Indeed, it was my greatest complaint on both occasions.'

'Let's not go into that now,' said Demelza.

Later, in the darkness, her thoughts moved on to that other subject which had been nagging at her all afternoon. Why had Elizabeth given Verity the impression that her circumstances were soon going to change? In what way could her circumstances now change more than they already had done from the receipt of the six hundred pounds? It didn't make sense; and the more she went over the ordinary explanations, the less satisfied she was by them. At length Ross, who had been asleep, said:

'My dear, are you eaten by ants that you must toss and turn all night long? I have never known such disorder.'

'I'm sorry. It is something that will not let me sleep. I will be quieter now.'

'Are you upset or feeling ill?'

'No, no, in rudest health. Just can't settle. I shall be better now.'

Easy enough to predict. No sooner did her limbs compose themselves in momentary ease than the urge began to move them elsewhere. Even an inch. Even a half inch.

Were Ross and Elizabeth planning to run away together? Was *that* the change of circumstances Elizabeth foresaw? That would not bring any greater prosperity to her, but perhaps she did not refer to financial circumstances at all. Demelza would have taken this more seriously if Ross had not been lying beside her now, his breathing becoming deeper again as he went off to sleep. It was not at all improbable, she felt, that they would like to do that; but, knowing Ross so well, she was certain he would not do it this way. He was far too honest a person to do anything underhand. If he was going to leave her and go with Elizabeth, he would force himself to tell her.

Very well, but perhaps he would tell her when the time came. Perhaps Elizabeth had said: 'Keep it from her as long as you can – for her sake.' In the dark of the night Demelza could hear her say it. Yet even that did not tally with Ross's manner or moods. Yesterday he had been cheerful, more high-spirited than she remembered him since Julia died. That was because of the mine, not Elizabeth. Demelza would have staked her head that it was a mine-cheerfulness and not a woman-cheerfulness.

Then did George Warleggan come into Elizabeth's picture somewhere? Demelza suddenly went rigid. Something Sir Hugh Bodrugan had said, more than she had told Ross. A hint, no more. Did he know more?

Had Demelza been certain at this stage that the mystery she was trying to solve concerned only Elizabeth and George, she would have gone no further with it. But she was still by no means sure.

So to-morrow . . .

In visiting Sir Hugh Bodrugan she knew she was on thin ice. Ross strongly disapproved of her giving any encouragement to his attentions. In the second place Sir Hugh, though playful enough most times, was becoming less easy to keep at arm's length. The rumour was that he was deep in an affair with a woman called Margaret Vosper. If it were so, it did not abate his interest in Demelza. Perhaps having one easy conquest had made him less patient with young women who were too long on the hook.

To avert these twin dangers, or to reduce them, she waited until the Wednesday when she knew Ross would be most of the day down the mine, and she went in the morning when Sir Hugh's gallantry was likely to be at its lowest ebb.

In the event she was a little unfortunate, for Sir Hugh was out and was not expected back until dinnertime. Constance Bodrugan was also off with her dogs, so Demelza found herself drinking chocolate with the only member of the household able to entertain her and the one she least wanted to see.

She had not expected to meet Malcolm McNeil again, and she half expected him to show some resentment; but he greeted her like an old friend. His arm was still in a sling and he had put on weight from the enforced idleness. She always dressed her best to come to Werry House, and McNeil's eyes, she thought, were bolder than usual in his assessment of her. No doubt the degenerate influence of the Bodrugan household was having its effect.

When she was trying to think of the best excuse to leave, he suggested that as it was a fine morning they should stroll across the park and try to find Sir Hugh. It should not be difficult since he was rounding up his young deer and his gamekeepers would be with him.

They set off down the steps and along the path between the unkempt lawns. He found her long stride unusual in a woman.

'And how is Captain Poldark?'

'Brave, thank you. That busy with his mine.'

'I had hoped I should receive an invitation to visit you before I left.'

'. . . Last time you came without an invitation.'

'That was in the course of duty. This would be in the pursuit of plaisure.'

'Then come any time, please. I know Ross would be glad to see you.'

'And you?'

'And I, of course. . . . When do you expect to go?'

'Not for some weeks. That's if I continue to take notice of your doctor-smuggler friend.'

'He is a very good man to take notice of.'

'I still find it har-rd to understand his association with the smugglers.'

'Have you asked him about it?'

'Frequently.'

'If he has refused to explain, Captain McNeil, I don't think I should begin.'

They walked on in silence, passing a herd of about thirty deer who without exception raised their heads and watched suspiciously until the danger retreated.

'Captain Poldark was somewhere in the house that night, wasn't he?'

'How should you expect me to answer that?'

'You don't need to. I could tell that you expected him to be in that secret cellar when we opened it. I knew ye had seen him that night.'

After a moment she said: 'Is that Sir Hugh in the trees over there?

'No, he's on a chestnut horse. I thought it probable that if I posted a watch on your house long enough we should discover where he was hiding.'

'And did you – post such a watch?'

'No.'

'Why not?'

'Because I had too great a regard for you, ma'am.'

Demelza glanced quickly at him, expecting a conventional insincerity but not quite finding it.

McNeil went on: 'Or that is the half of the truth, to be honest. Had I conceived it my duty to do so, I would have. But I am a soldier not a spy and was already sickened of the affair. The men who were caught were caught and that was an end on it.' He screwed up his moustache. 'And now. Well, now it is all forgotten so far as I am concairned. I hold nothing against Captain Poldark except that he married so charming a wife.'

Demelza said: 'I don't hold even that against him – so far as it is true.'

'It is true.' McNeil stopped and she had to stop also. He smiled down at her. 'So I trust you hold nothing against me for my part in the affair?'

She gave him her very best smile in return. 'Far from it. I hold naught against you for what you did do, and thank you much for what you did not do.'

He bowed slightly. 'Would ye take my arm, ma'am? The good one, I mean. I think that is Sir Hugh in the distance now, and it would be more seemly to approach him in the proper manner.'

In the end Demelza got the information she wanted, though not without tactical manœuvre. She said she had come to see Sir Hugh about a new seed drill he had talked of on his last call. It was a poor story, but he was indulgent enough to break off his own work to show her the drill in operation. Fortunately it was to Sir Hugh's purpose as well as to Demelza's that they should get rid of McNeil, so in the end they managed it.

Sir Hugh said: 'Now you see the seed fed into the hoppers falls into the seed boxes fixed on the bottoms of the hoppers just as in Tull's old drill; but here's where the improvement is claimed—— Why d'you come in the morning, m'dear, when you interrupt my work, damme, when there's three evenings a week free, eh? Wednesday's not a good evening, for I'm often bespoke; but Thursdays, Saturdays, and Mondays I'd entertain you in a fashion proper for a young woman of your trim. Come Saturday; Connie's often away, and——'

'I should have thought 'twould have been a poor time to see a seed drill, after dark.'

'Oh, pooh, yes; but if you stop the night, I'll show you the drill Sunday morning. 'Twould be an excuse to stay from church.'

'And what do you suppose my husband would say?'

'What? Well, what would he say? Is he a spoilsport? Then come when he's from home and will not know the difference. I have an idea——'

'You were going to tell me, Sir Hugh, where the improvement in this seed drill was claimed.'

Sir Hugh grunted impatiently and told her. After a while she said: 'Do you remember when you called to see me last that you mentioned George Warleggan and Elizabeth Poldark, saying that George was paying her attentions? Do you know if it is true? What made you say that to me?'

Sir Hugh paused with his hand upon hers on the handle of the seed drill. His thick eyebrows crouched like furry caterpillars.

'Nay, rumour, that was all.'

'And what was the rumour?'

'What I told you. Now look ee——'

'What was the rumour exactly, Sir Hugh?'

'That he was paying her serious attentions. No more and no less. Indeed I was surprised you'd not heard it. Gossip is always a pleasant topic over tea, especially bawdy gossip. I'll tell you some when you come on Saturday.'

'About Elizabeth and George?'

'Nay, I know nothing more of them and misremember where I heard that. But stay, there was one other thing. I was in to Truro on Monday ordering some new cravats, and my tailor told me in confidence he'd just received an order for a wedding suit from George. 'Twas all secret at present, he said. So what George's relations are with your cousin-in-law, I'd not pretend to say. Either he's going to be legal about it or he's keeping her for the side door. I hope for your sake it is the first, for it would be a grand thing for the Poldarks to get George Warleggan in the family. I wish Connie would marry again and marry someone like that. We need the money. I'm always nagging her to, and she's always nagging me to, but I say I ain't a marrying man; and then without fail she says I'm a bedding man and what's the difference except for a service and a gold ring, and I say, ah, but the gold ring is just what I cannot face, for you can't turn your wife out to grass like a prize mare. Now, m'dear, when you come on Saturday——'

'I'm sorry, Sir Hugh, but I can't manage Saturday. You see——'

'Saturday sennight then. This army feller is accompanying Connie——'

'I'm sorry, Sir Hugh.'

He bent his eyebrows at her again. 'You're a damned unaccommodating minx, ma'am, if you'll excuse the familiarity. If I didn't like you so well, I'd like not at all.'

Demelza still had her hand in captivity. 'I'm glad you like me so well, Sir Hugh, for I like you well too and I should be grieved to think I displeased you. But you've told me you look on women as prize mares which can be turned out to grass just whenever you think. Then can you not forgive a woman for wanting to gallop off as she pleases with no hand to bridle her and no man to order her where or how she shall go? Isn't it good to have the exception as well as the rule? Must all women be just what you say so's to win your approval?'

He stared at the V of her collar, not bothering to follow her argument but liking the paling colour and gentle swell of her skin there.

'I'll tell you what, miss,' he said. 'It will be my birthday in a few weeks' time, and Connie and I are thinking of giving a party and a dance. Just a few friends – forty or fifty maybe. We get asked out here and asked out there, and I say to Connie it would be a good thing to push it through while the war's on. We'll do it in good style, though; not like that fellow Trevaunance who's too mean to spit. A band and what not. Now if I sat down and wrote a formal invitation to your stiff-necked husband, d'you think the two of you would come? Would that be right enough for you, eh?'

Demelza stared into his beady eyes trying to read what ulterior purposes might be there.

'Thank you, Sir Hugh. You're being that kind to me now. Much kinder than I deserve.'

'You can't judge what you deserve, ma'am. Leave that to me, and one of these days I b'lieve you will get it.'

She reached home without the necessity of having to tell Ross where she had been. She had discovered what she had gone to discover, but was unrelieved for knowing it. She knew at once that she could not break the news to Ross; she found she could not even hint at it. What his response would be, how he would act, she had no idea. All she knew was that she did not want to be the one to tell him or to be present when he was told.

Chapter four

WEEKS PASSED, and the primroses flowered and the first bluebells. Dwight's physician friend went home and Dwight made enquiries about joining the Navy as a surgeon. But he took no further action because the war was coming to an end. The optimists had been right and France was breaking up again. Defeated by the Austrians, who had at last moved, General Dumouriez followed Lafayette into the enemy's camp. Two thirds of the provinces were in revolt against Paris. The invasion of Holland had failed, and the British had taken Pondicherry and Tobago. For the second year running, Paris lay open to any army with the enterprise to take it. Obviously this time someone would, even if it had to be the grand old Duke of York.

Among the results of a general rise in spirits was a fall in the price of copper and tin. But the fall was not enough to make the difference. Success or failure at Wheal Grace still depended on their ability to eke out their finances during the change-over, to preserve a delicate balance between earnings and outgoings. Henshawe's hundred pounds was already gone, but they were existing on credit provided for them by Pascoe's bank against the next coinage. Trains of mules carried the black tin into Truro, where the bank issued its tin cheques on the quality and value of the white tin which would be extracted; and on the credit of these cheques the mine was able to continue.

Most of the economies they could make were eaten up aboveground, where a rearrangement and extension of the dressing floors had to be undertaken. Not only did it mean more dressers and spallers, it often meant new ones, for a good copper worker often did not understand how to treat tin. Much of the ore was sent out to the tin stamps of Sawle Combe.

On the second of May, Charlie Kempthorne's body was found floating in the sea off Basset's Cove. Dwight went to identify him.

The man had been in the water several days. There were no signs of violence, but the sea had not been kind to him. Dwight stared for a while at the remains of this person he had cured of miner's phthisis, one of his few real medical successes.

Traitor, informer, bridegroom for Rosina, sail maker, father, decaying eyeless flotsam; no ready-made deceitful smile now, only the black gape of corruption. Familiarity with death had not lessened Dwight's essential distaste. The more he saw of it, the less he understood it. The instant disappearance of personality, light from a candle, leaving nothing of value or interest except to the surgeon with his scalpel able to probe now at will. And it was not in his temperament to want to do that. *All* his preoccupation was with the living, even when the living lied and cheated and sold their friends.

Rosina Hoblyn came to see him at the Gatehouse. Dwight had avoided her since the night of his fight with Kempthorne.

'Is it true, sur,' she said, 'was it Charlie that was washed up?'

'Yes. . . .'

'Had he been – done to death – killed, afore he was dropped in the water?'

'Not so far as I could tell. It's possible. But he may well have fallen in.'

'Charlie wouldn't fall in, sur. 'Twasn't in his nature.'

Dwight knew in his heart that she was right. Rosina understood her man.

'Or he may have committed suicide – have done himself to death. He cannot have been very happy the way things turned out.'

'Nor me, sur.'

'You – are you very unhappy for him?'

She flushed sharply. 'Yes, sur. Or I don't rightly know. He was always that kind to me. . . . 'Tis part that and part the disgrace. It don't seem right, somehow, hard to believe; for it to have been the same man: him that was kind and him that played Judas. And I feel the disgrace so bad – as if I'd done it myself – like I'd known about'n all along. And I didn't, sur; I didn't; I never knowed a thing!'

'Of course not, Rosina; nobody could possibly suppose you did.'

'Sometimes folk *look*, so much as to say . . . They d'think if you're walking out with a man . . .'

'Be thankful at least that you didn't marry him. Has your knee been any trouble since that night?'

'No, sur. I'm that grateful. It seem funny, though, that if you'd never come t'elp me . . .'

He would be married, living in a strange town, Ross perhaps in prison or deported; much, so much, hanging on a single thread; three, four, five, countless people's lives altered by a single wanton circumstance. Here the girl at the centre of it all. Rosina's knee. Ludicrous. After Francis' death Ross had railed at the sudden changes of fortune that made nonsense of man's striving and contriving. So it had been once again, more outrageously than ever.

When Rosina had gone, Dwight felt the urgent need to talk to somebody. Other people discussed their troubles with him, but there was no outlet for himself. He repressed his own troubles and they festered and grew worse.

He knew now that he must get away. It was necessary to restore his self-respect. For no reward he must give up the things he had been reluctant to give up for Caroline. That was not the whole of it: the issue was not as simple as he sometimes tried to believe; but he knew he could not stay here with the memory of his failures.

There were only two people he could talk to, because they alone knew the truth – or part of it. But the opportunity had to be sought, the breaking of the ice. He decided to go at once, without more thought, before the old hesitations and the old embarrassments came. What mattered was the unburdening of his mind. Since his friend Wright went home, the long hours alone had become more than he could bear.

It was a rough, blustering evening for early May, with lowering cloud. The sea was as wild as winter, and between the white lines of breakers was a vivid oily green. In the distance the horizon was hidden in a pale grey mist, and he wisely waited a time in the porch. Sure enough the rain came, blinding in the stronger wind that brought it. It lasted some minutes and then as abruptly ceased, leaving everything guttering and dripping, and the sun flung a single sabre of green across the sea.

As he topped the hill, he could see both people he wanted. Demelza was brushing the water from her steps with the energy of one whose time is limited; and Garrick, nose on forepaws on the wet grass, was obviously waiting for some inner prompting or perhaps a fluttering jackdaw to set him galloping across the valley. Ross was just leaving one of the sheds of the mine.

Their tracks would not converge until near the house, and Dwight saw that Ross would be there well before him. He did not hurry. From this high ground he could survey the whole valley. Presently Demelza saw Ross coming and waved. Garrick, although through all his years at Nampara he had remained obstinately Demelza's dog, got slowly up and went to meet his master.

At that moment Dwight felt a slight tremor in the ground and a consciousness of noise which he could not specify and could not locate. It might have been an explosion far out to sea, but somehow he knew it was not. By the time the sensation was a few seconds old, he had decided it was some trick of his ears or an extra gust of wind.

Ross had paused to whack Garrick on the flanks; this was what Garrick really liked: pats were no use and he clearly despised anyone who attempted them. Demelza came down to speak to Ross and they were discussing something in the garden. Here Dwight went into the first ring of hawthorn trees, whose tops were bent at sharp angles by the prevailing wind. Between these and the apple trees was a clear gap; and as he came out into this, he saw a man running towards the house from the mine. He looked then at the mine and saw that, in addition to the ordinary coal smoke from the chimney, there had gathered about the engine house a sort of haze which gave the impression of being neither smoke nor steam. As he watched, the balance bob of the engine slowed and came to a stop.

Dwight also stopped. Other figures were emerging from the engine house. The man running had not yet reached Ross, but Demelza had seen him. They were walking to meet him. Dwight began to run towards the mine.

Casual accidents in Cornish mines were common enough – a man would fall and break a leg; blasting work was unreliable and hazardous – but major accidents were rare. In the five years of his being mining surgeon there had been none in these parts. Ross was running back now with the man and with Demelza a little behind him.

But Dwight would be there ahead of them. The first person he met was Peter Curnow, who, grey-faced and dirty, had just come out of the engine house.

'What is it, man, what is it?'

'A stull's run, sur, and filled all the bottom with deads! Jack Carter's just give the alarm. He'd say there's four, five trapped. The others is coming up now!'

'Some hurt?'

'Aye, half of 'em or more.'

'Look, will you do something for me? Run straight to the Gatehouse and fetch my bag and instruments. Tell Bone. He'll know what to bring.'

'Aye, sur. I'll do that!' He went off racing.

The stuff about the engine house was dust. The wind was clearing it now, but down below it would be still thick. Three or four more men had come out, but they waved Dwight away – nothing serious, scratches or bruises – and many had stayed below, some to tend the injured, others already beginning to dig.

As they spoke, Ross arrived. Dwight could see from his expression what he felt. Every day the great cavity above them created by the hasty mining of the tin had grown larger. It had not looked too bad a risk. There had been some hasty shoring up which might well have sufficed. Other mines had taken and were taking similar risks. Often such gunnies existed for twenty years without collapsing. But the luck had been against them and the work had caved in. With it had fallen perhaps thousands of tons of rock, burying the lode deep and the men as well.

Two men were killed by the fall and three seriously injured. All the work at the bottom of the mine had collapsed, carrying with it ladders, pumping gear, platforms; and nothing was to be seen in the flickering dusty light but a great pile of shattered rock, at which a dozen subhuman figures were frantically digging. The death roll would have been five, but the three who were recovered alive had heard the collapse begin and had run up part way and flattened themselves against the wall of rock as the stuff crashed down.

The most seriously injured were Ellery and Joe Nanfan, who were buried four hours before they were rescued.

Dwight went down for a time; but he soon realized that he could do more good aboveground, and he went up with the first seriously injured man to be recovered. The changing shed had been turned into a sort of hospital, with six men lying in it. Someone in the first panic had sent for Surgeon Choake, and he temporarily overlooked his dislike of his young rival. One man had his arm broken, and Choake had the arm off above the elbow almost before a sickened Demelza could turn her head away. Knife in hand, he looked round for the next victim and knitted his brows in disappointment when there seemed no more carving to be done. When Dwight came up, he was binding a head injury, and the two men exchanged a few cold words before concentrating on their common task.

Midnight was past before the last two survivors were brought up, and it was soon plain to Dwight that Joe Nanfan was near death. A beam had fallen on him; his right hip was crushed and a great bruise was spreading across the abdomen, which had suffered internal injury. He was wet with sweat and his breath came in agonized gasps. Dwight did what he could, administered laudanum, and bound up the abdomen to give it support.

Ellery was unconscious, with a deep wound in the temple. There was some prospect of a trepanning operation to remove bone pressing on the brain, and Choake said it was worth attempting anyway because he needed the practice; but eventually it was decided to see how the man went on unmolested.

Ross did not come up all night, and Demelza was not unaware of the dangers of a further fall. While others took it in turns to dig, he remained below. At four Demelza wanted to go down herself, but Dwight would not let her. Instead he sent Gimlett with a message asking Ross to come up. Ross sent word back that he would come when there was no more to do.

Light began to grow soon after four, but the black dawn sky was as torn and ragged as a beggar's coat. The sun rose in another flurry of rain and a rainbow arched its back across the head of the valley. The second vigil, Demelza thought, that she had spent in this engine house. But this time even the engine had stopped. Was Ross to be the final victim? In the cold morning light she shivered and stretched – tried not to yawn, aware of fatigue and ashamed of it. Sitting on the steps above her Daniel Curnow was quite motionless, as if a part of the engine he had stopped. Six others. The wife and sons of one of those buried; two sisters and a father of the other. Hoping for the impossible – or if the worst, then for a body to bear away.

At five o'clock Jim Ellery, having been wrapped in warm blankets and kept perfectly quiet, began to come round without any operation. By seven he was taking a little light broth, and at nine he was able to walk home.

At nine Ross came up, having been below thirteen hours. He had no energy and no speech left. They had been unable to recover the two others, and the water was slowly rising.

Contrary to Dwight's every conviction, Joe Nanfan lived the night and three days later appeared to be on the mend. Fascinated, Dwight compared him privately with one of those insects that you crush underfoot and which still contrive to move away as if nothing has happened.

On the seventh of May, Wheal Grace officially closed. There was nothing much else that could be done. It would take six weeks' work to remove enough of the debris to reach the lode again. Twenty fathoms of pumping gear had been destroyed. Two hundred pounds would not set it working.

Ross was not sure that he even wanted to see it working again. It had cost the lives of three men. It had been an ill-wished venture from the start.

On the ninth of May he received a letter from Elizabeth.

Chapter five

HE HAD BEEN in Truro all day, once again making arrangements with the venturers of Wheal Radiant for the disposal of the headgear of the mine. Half his life, it seemed to him, he was active in starting business ventures which he spent the other half winding up. Well, this was the end of them. From now on he farmed his land and, if he was allowed, lived on in debt-ridden poverty for the rest of his days. Now he had *no* mine, and no interest in a mine, and that was the way it would stay.

He was taking this failure very hard but not saying much about it. Looking back, he thought sometimes he had overdramatized his disappointments as a younger man. As one grew older one saw that no good came of kicking at the table like a hurt child. You took the bad luck and swallowed it and shook off the injury and pretended to yourself as well as to other people that it didn't matter.

That was a lesson hard to learn. It was particularly hard for Ross.

In the afternoon he met Richard Tonkin again and told him the news, receiving his sympathy with a better grace than most people's because they had once been fellow sufferers together. They had a meal in the Seven Stars, and it was nine before Ross arrived home.

There had been a faint suggestion of summer heat about the day, and Demelza looked very fresh and cool in the garden in a white ruched bodice and a cream poplin skirt with a little green apron. He got off his horse and she walked with him back to the house.

'You've supped, Ross? I thought you must have. I waited until a quarter after eight. Did that heavy shower catch you this morning?'

'No, I had none on the way.'

'Dry both in and out, truly surprising. These bull-horns are something terrible; I suppose it must be all the caudly weather. They eat my flowers and slime my stones; and if I *step* on them, it makes me feel sick. I have a lady's instincts where a snail is concerned. Funny, for I can wrap a bad wound or clean a baby or pick up a mouse without distaste.'

'You should train Garrick to eat 'em. Or perhaps if we're more reduced, we shall do it ourselves. I haven't seen that before. Is it new?' He touched her bodice.

'New?' She smiled.

'Well, I have not seen it, I'm sure.'

'I made it out of two of your old shirts which were far gone for patching. There is good material if you pick out where the wear does not come.'

'When I asked you to marry me, I did not suppose you would be driven to making your blouses out of the tails of my shirts.'

'Not tails: sides. And the lace I got from an old shawl. But I have been in much worse straits.'

Gimlett was not about, so she walked with Ross round to the stables.

She said: 'I'll unsaddle Darkie. If you go in, I'll follow so soon as he's comfortable. There's two letters for you.'

'Two? Who from?' Something in the lightness of her tone. 'No, Gimlett will be in soon, won't he? Have you read them?'

'The one that is addressed to us both. It's from Sir Hugh, inviting us to a party at his house next Saturday. He mentioned it when last I saw him. It's his birthday – I did not dare ask which – and he seems to be planning something to outdo Sir John Trevaunance.'

Ross thought that he had solved the slight peculiarity of her tone, and so forgot to ask about the other letter.

'I hope you'll not be disappointed if we answer no.'

She said: 'I would have thought it reasonable enough to go, as so many of our neighbours are likely to be there. But it don't matter if you'd better prefer not.'

He went in, glad that she'd so readily given up the idea and rather surprised that she had. Perhaps she was growing as tired of the man as he was.

He did not notice that she had not followed him into the house. He went through into the parlour and picked the two letters up off the spinet. The long twilight was ending and the light was very shadowy, so he took the letters to the window. Recently he had seen more of Elizabeth's writing, on documents and things, than at any other time, and he at once recognized it on the outside of the second one. He broke the seal.

My Dear Ross [Elizabeth had written],

I do not know how to write this letter; I do not know where to begin it or where to end it or how to tell you what I have to tell. I know it will upset you, and I, who gave you so much Pain once before, would rather do almost anything than hurt you again, and in the same way. Yet it seems that I must.

Oh, Ross, my life has been a very frustrative one; it has been an empty one and very cold. Never more so than in these lonely months since Francis died. Perhaps I am the wrong sort of person to be left alone. I seem to need the strength and protection that a man can give.

I have promised to marry George Warleggan.

It will be just ten days from now. We are to be married by Licence at St Mary's Church. At my insistence it will be very private, only our parents and the necessary witnesses. We will live mainly at Cardew, so that from now forward you will see little of me. I feel that is what you will wish.

Ross, I cannot give you Reasons for marrying George, for Reasons suggest I need justification, and I cannot begin my second marriage by being disloyal even in thought. If Affection has existed between us all these years, between you and me, I pray that you should use it now to reach an understanding of my position. For to understand all may be to forgive all. Or if not that, to excuse in part.

Your sincere and affectionate friend,
Elizabeth

While he read, it had gone dark. Or was the darkness in his heart and in his mind? He listened to the drumming of his own blood. After the first moments of utter incredulity, his brave, civilized thoughts of this morning were gone, completely swallowed up. You could not fight the imponderables of life, he had thought. But was this such? Was this something to be accepted with resignation and a sigh?

That was as far as recognizable thought went. Beyond was all feeling, all feeling. The thing struck at him two ways together, at his love and at his hate. Either by itself he could have mastered. Together they were overpowering.

He swung round and out of the room.

'Demelza!'

There was no answer.

He picked up his cloak and went through the kitchen, out to the stables.

'Demelza!'

No answer. Darkie was still saddled.

Jane Gimlett came hurriedly out of the stillroom.

'Can I help ee, sur? John'll be back any minute now.'

'No. Tell your mistress——'

'I'm here, Ross,' said Demelza, coming out from the shadow of the stables.

Jane Gimlett looked from one to the other. She could see little, but there was that in their voices which made her go quickly indoors again.

He said: 'Demelza, I'm going to Trenwith.'

She had been hiding from him, not because she was afraid of him but because she could not bear to see him receive this news. 'Do not go tonight, Ross.'

'I must. I have to see Elizabeth.'

'It will be better in the morning.'

'You – know something?'

'Is it about George?'

'How did you guess?'

'Something I heard.'

'You never told me.'

'How *could* I . . . ?'

'This . . . thing . . .' He found he was still holding the letter. He crumpled it into a ball. 'This thing must be stopped.'

'How can you stop it? You can't.'

'You think not. We'll see.'

'Ross, I don't want for you to go tonight.'

'Perhaps you don't want me to stop it at all.'

'I don't want you to – in the only ways you can,' she said distressfully.

New anger grew in him, one wave overtoppling the last. 'Please get out of my way.'

For a moment she did not move, watching him, striving to see. 'Always – always I had thought. . . . I had never thought it would be like this. . . .' There was anger within her too, responding to his, striving to form itself. But as yet she would not let it. 'Don't you see, Ross, that you cannot go. For if you do . . . Meaning what you do. . . .'

Although she barred his way, her white figure seemed already withdrawn, a little unreal. He tried to force himself to make some move, some affectionate gesture towards her. But for the first time he failed. The spectre of Elizabeth was immovably between them, more real, more tangible to his hurt than Demelza.

She saw that she could not stop him. He could not stop himself. This was something fundamental. She stepped out of his way. He mounted his horse and clattered out of the cobbled yard.

Trenwith House was in darkness, except for two lights on the first floor. From his close acquaintance with the house he knew that one was on the landing and one in Aunt Agatha's room. Elizabeth's room looked out upon the inner courtyard, as did Geoffrey Charles's. The Tabbs slept over the kitchens.

He slid off his horse and pulled at the bell beside the front door. Nothing now lingered of the dying day but a bluish tinge in the far west. Stars glimmered brightly, and as he looked a meteor flickered across the sky. The ride had cooled him but not altered his purpose. His resolutions were finer pointed, less unreasoning and impulsive.

The ring being unanswered, he pulled the bell again. After another minute or so he rapped at the door with his crop. Then he stepped back and stared up impatiently at the house. The Tabbs were most probably quite out of earshot. If they were asleep, he might ring till morning. And it would be easier to rouse Charles from Sawle churchyard than Aunt Agatha from her room. There was only Elizabeth and Geoffrey Charles.

He went back to the door and rapped very loudly on it. Was this a diplomatic retirement on Elizabeth's part? He had not asked what time the letter had been delivered, but perhaps Elizabeth had been expecting a visit from him all afternoon. She could hardly imagine that he would make no move at all. Perhaps as darkness fell she had bolted all the doors and gone up to bed, determined she should not see him to-night.

Well that was where she might yet be mistaken. He tried the door and found it locked. He stepped away again. The front of the house was impregnable, but he did not suppose it would all be.

He walked round to the east side, and an owl flitted away before his crunching footsteps. Here was the herb garden, much overgrown but doubly aromatic in the late evening. 'Larded with sweet flowers which bewept to the grave did go.' Words running through his head. Something was stirring in the bushes now besides himself, a rat or a stray mongrel, mute as he was mute, no business here.

Near the house a sycamore tree grew, some of its lesser branches brushing the window which had once been Verity's. Needed lopping. But it had not been lopped. He tested the lowest branch, then swung himself into the tree. At this stage he unhooked his cloak and dropped it over a bush below him. 'There's fennel for you and columbines – there's rue. . . . I would give you some violets but they withered all when my father died. . . .' He went on and up, a shadow moving it seemed with no great care, till he was level with the window.

A small-paned leaded casement. From below he had thought it an inch open, but this not so. Only a single tiny pane in the upper part of the window was open, too far from the catch. The one suitable thing he had was the key to the padlock on his own library door. He took this out and rapped against one of the panes until it broke. Then, almost before the glass had stopped falling, he had thrust in his gloved hand and lifted the catch. A minute later he was in the room.

He had made some noise but distinctly less than at the front door.

He came out in the east passage. At the end, towards the front of the house, a faint glimmer shivered on the panelled wall. It was the candle on the front landing, just round the corner from the great hall. He went towards it, and was nearly there when a door opened and Elizabeth came out.

She gave a scream half stifled, stepped back against the wall. They stared at each other. She looked as if she were going to faint.

'Ross! . . .'

'I came to pay my respects.'

'*Ross*, I thought . . .'

'That I was a burglar. So I am as to means of entry. But I could get no admittance by ordinary ways.'

She continued to stare at him with great eyes in a white face. She was wearing a green velvet frock, an old one and in better light shiny, but it suited her. Everything suited her. That was the trouble. 'I heard a noise. How did you get in?'

'I came to thank you for your letter.'

'I thought it was Geoffrey Charles. I – thought it was strange.'

'Is there somewhere we can talk?'

She knew him well enough not to be taken in by his even voice. There was no escape for her now, from this interview.

'Yes. . . . I'll get a candle. . . .'

She turned back into the room she had left. Irrationally suspecting she might be going to call someone, he followed her in and closed the door.

'This will do.'

It was her bedroom, and she lifted her hand from the candlestick. 'I don't think . . .'

'There's no one else to consider. I want to talk to you, Elizabeth, and now.'

A nice room. The brown draped curtains hung with cord, the gilt dressing-mirror, the rocking horse, the blue slippers, the white lace nightgown over a chair. He had never been in here before.

He could see the blood coming back to her face, to her lips. And some of the confidence.

'I so much hated sending you that letter, Ross. The *last* think I wanted – as I said. . . . But you can't come here like this, now. In the morning. . . .'

'The morning's too late. I want to know to-night.'

'To know what? What I've already told you in my letter? Is there anything more to say?'

'Well, yes.' He moved away from the door, pulled off his gloves and dropped them in a chair, came closer to her. She took a step away. 'I had a certain impression of how things stood. Tell me, Elizabeth, where I have gone wrong. . . . George Warleggan I have long thought of as my greatest enemy. You I have long thought of as my greatest friend. In which particular am I farthest adrift?'

She flushed. 'It isn't like that at all, Ross. But it has been a grievous position for me. Of course I'm happy and proud to think of *you* as my greatest friend——'

'Well, it was more than that, wasn't it? How long is it, not more than twelve months, since we met one evening at the Trevaunances. What did you tell me over the dinner table then? That when you turned me down and married Francis you made a mistake which you discovered a few months after and have regretted ever since. It was a – an astonishment and a humiliation to you, you said, that you should have made such a mistake. I remember the words.'

She stretched out a hand to the back of a chair. 'Your coming like this, Ross. . . . The shock has made me feel faint. . . .'

But he was not to be put off. 'That mistake you confessed to, Elizabeth, was one Francis suffered for all his life. And you suffered for it, and I. What sort of a mistake are you making this time?'

'No,' she said. 'What I told you that night – I'll not go back on it – though I should never have spoken if I'd thought anything was going to happen to Francis. Please, Ross, understand. I felt that some day I had to tell you, to let you know that if you were unhappy in those early days, it was not long before I was too. I thought it would please you to know that the mistake had been mine and not yours. It was too late, years too late to put things right; but I wanted you to *know*. As soon as I'd spoken I realized it was wrong to have spoken. And when Francis died . . . then more than ever.'

'It explains nothing. Where does George Warleggan come into this?'

'Not at all at that time, of course. Only now – much later. He's been so *kind*, Ross, so good——'

'Do you marry a man out of gratitude?'

'Not alone out of gratitude. But you're far wrong to think of him as your greatest enemy. I think – I *believe* – that I can bring you together, that truly you can and will be friends. He has no bitterness——'

'Are you marrying him for his money?'

She said nothing for a minute, her eyes narrowed in an effort to be calm. So far they had faced each other like adversaries, she content or able only to parry each thrust that he made, and with no time or thought for manœuvre. So far only the situation made the encounter worse than her imagining. She had known how bad it would be; and remembering her expectation of it, she took a grip of herself. She was injuring him, not he her; therefore she must bear his insults, try to lead him to reasonableness and perhaps later friendship again. To evade the issue wasn't possible. To give him detailed reasons for her decision to marry George was a waste of time. Each one she put up he would demolish in a moment.

'Please, Ross.' She smiled at him but avoided the searching blue-grey look in his eyes. Will you come to-morrow and we can talk more calmly and more properly than here? Believe me when I say I am not marrying George for his money. I have not been very clever with my life. But I've tried always to be loyal to the people I care for. What may seem disloyalty to you, isn't really that at all. What would you suggest for me, Ross? Thirty years of widowhood and loneliness? I might well live thirty years. Is that what you ask for the mistakes I've already made? Can you offer me anything else to hope for?'

He was silent, studying the curves of her brow and cheek and mouth.

'I'll go if you can answer me one thing. Do you love George?'

The clock struck eleven, accenting the other stillnesses. Far in the distance, communicated to an inner ear, was the sound of the sea.

'Yes,' she said.

That settled it. He took her by the shoulders, quietly but very firmly, so that her eyes flicked up quickly to his in surprise and alarm.

'This is a very similar imposture to the one just after you married Francis. You told me you loved him then, and you didn't mean a word of it. I was simpler then and believed you. I don't believe you to-night.'

She tried to free herself. 'Don't, Ross. You're hurting me.'

'You ask me if I'd condemn you to thirty years of widowhood. The answer's no. But with your looks you could have the pick of six men. I do not like this betrothal to George Warleggan. I ask you to wait awhile and try again.'

'Let me go. I'm my own mistress and shall please myself. I'm – sorry that you feel like this. But I can't help it.'

'You never *have* been able to help anything, have you? It has all been beyond your control. All your life you've drifted helplessly down a stream of good intentions. You can't help this either.' He kissed her. She turned her face away but could not get it far enough round to avoid him.

When he lifted his head, her eyes were lit with anger. He'd never seen her like it before, and he found pleasure in it.

'This is – *contemptible*! I shouldn't have believed it of you. To force yourself. . . . To insult me when – when I have no one——'

'I don't like this marriage to George, Elizabeth. I don't like it. I should be glad of your assurance that you'll not go through with it.'

'I'd be surprised if you believed me if I gave it you! You called me a liar! Well, at least I do not go back on my promises! I love George to distraction and shall marry him next week——'

He caught her again, and this time began to kiss her with intense passion to which anger had given an extra relish, before anger was lost. Her hair began to fall in plaited tangles. She got her hand up to his mouth, but he brushed it away. Then she smacked his face, so he pinioned her arm.

She suddenly found herself for a brief second nearly free. 'You treat me – like a slut –'

'It's time you were so treated——'

'Let me *go*, Ross. You're *hateful*, horrible! If George——'

'Shall you marry him?'

'*Don't!* I'll scream. Oh, God, *Ross*. . . . Please. . . .'

'Whatever you say, I don't think I can believe you now. Isn't that so?'

'To-morrow——'

'There's no to-morrow,' he said. 'It doesn't come. Life is an illusion. Didn't you know? Let us make the most of the shadows.'

'Ross, you can't intend . . . Stop! Stop, I tell you.'

But he took no further notice of the words she spoke. He lifted her in his arms and carried her to the bed.

Chapter six

DEMELZA STAYED AWAKE till four and then woke again at six to hear him come into the house. He did not come upstairs, and that confirmed what she already knew. For she had known it from the moment he left.

Jeremy woke soon after and began to play and crow in his cot. Jeremy didn't talk much yet, but his two favourite remarks were 'Aberdare' and 'No anemone,' which he employed in a system of his own to meet the varied circumstances of life. He had become a happier child recently as well as more robust, not so liable to fly off the handle if things didn't come his way, but as full as ever of intense nervous energy. It was one of Demelza's pleasures to wake early and lie in a drowsy contentment listening to the murmurs and chuckles of Jeremy in his cot.

Not so today. She got up at half past six, which was about the usual time, and went to the north window out of which she had climbed not many months ago. The sun had risen two hours ago, and the rhetorics of dawn were long past. The morning was cloudy but very still, the sea a shadowy slate blue and deeply calm, having fallen away in the night. Sometimes there seemed to be no movement at all, it was a stretched silk cloth, but every now and then an apparent ripple would form under the surface and at rarer intervals one of the ripples would topple over, betraying its size by the crackling roar with which it broke the stillness of the day. Gimlett was already up and about, tirelessly and persistently busy in the farmyard. Demelza often wondered at his quietness in the morning, for he never woke them with the clatter of pails or other untoward noise.

This morning there was in her a pain so deep that it derived from some part of her she had not known of before. She had never known such despair. *Everything* was in ruin and in ashes. Whatever consolation her brain turned to crumbled at the first touch. Nothing would ever be the same again, for she had lost faith.

Not long ago, talking to Verity, she had said that trusting one's husband . . . If one did. . . .

Well, now the faith was gone. Of course it was not so clean-cut as that really. She had lived with Ross too long not to know his faults, his weaknesses; if you thought of your husband as godlike and perfect, you were a fool and asking for disillusionment. But it was the principle of trust that mattered. All his life Ross had been in love or partly in love with Elizabeth. The discontent had been more active since Francis died; but all the same Demelza had known him in and out of love with herself, more in than out, and had felt that that intense sense of loyalties which was one of the faults and one of the virtues of his nature would preserve him to herself in the last resort.

It was more than that, of course. The loss was more than that. However sane and civilized she might be, however she might reason it out, Ross had always been one step more than a husband to her. From the moment when, a little over nine years ago, he had taken her into his kitchen as a starving miner's brat, he had represented a kind of nobility, not of birth but of character, a person whose standards of behaviour were always, and always would be, slightly better, surer than her own. Often she argued with him, lightly, flippantly, disagreeing with his views and his judgments; but underneath and on fundamental matters she gave him best.

So whether one expected complete fidelity from one's husband or not, there was so much else lost besides. Demelza's pride had been in him more than in herself. She had believed herself better than other women because a man like Ross had married her. In his visit to Elizabeth last night he had not only let himself down, he had let her down. It was a joint betrayal, something which destroyed the whole basis of her life.

Jeremy was waiting to be picked up, no longer content within the confines of his cot, becoming fretful. She ignored him and went to the other window while she brushed her hair. Somewhere within herself there was still a tiny thread of protest that perhaps this thing had not been; yet consciously she knew the truth. She had known it before he did, known what his purpose was before he rode away. And now? Why had he returned? Had he come to fetch his things and was he going to live at Trenwith with Elizabeth? Was the marriage between Elizabeth and George finally abandoned? Demelza was not a good hater, but she felt she could kill Elizabeth. Elizabeth had done her best to ill-wish the first years of their marriage. She had failed; but indirectly and innocently she was responsible for the death of Julia. *That* had been the first breach between Demelza and Ross. An estrangement, though barely perceptible, had grown from that day out of Ross's grief, and Elizabeth had made the most of it. Now, since Francis' death, she had had a free hand. One wondered if she had ever seriously meant to marry George, or if it had not been a gauntlet thrown down to provoke the reaction that she had in fact provoked.

Jeremy began to cry, and Demelza at last picked him up, changed him, and dressed him. Then she carried him downstairs. Jane Gimlett was in the kitchen.

'The master's 'aving his breakfast. I put on the cold gammon. I thought you was sleeping, and he says not to disturb you.'

'Is there tea?'

'Yes'm. Not made ten minutes. Shall I cut ee some bread and butter?'

'No. . . . Can you keep Jeremy for a few minutes . . . ?

She went into the parlour. Ross had changed his clothes and shaved, had almost finished his tasteless breakfast. He looked up and they looked at each other. In that moment she knew finally, and he knew that she knew.

'I thought you might be asleep,' he said. 'I thought I'd begin without you.'

She did not speak, but after a moment she came forward and sat at the table some distance from him. She poured herself out a cup of tea, added milk and sugar. The light from the window fell on her pale eyelids, the dark gloss of her hair.

'It won't be the last time, will it?' she said.

He didn't speak, but looked down at his plate and pushed it away.

She was suddenly visited with an overwhelming gust of anger. It came upon her and took her utterly by surprise. She had been afraid of crying, but now there was not a tear in her.

'Is–their wedding to go on?'

'I don't know. . . .' His scar was very noticeable this morning. Often it was as if that chance sword-thrust in Pennsylvania remained with him and had become a symbol of the nonconformity of his nature, the unabiding renegade.

She found her lips were trembling with anger.

'When are you seeing her – seeing her again?'

'I don't know.'

She swallowed, tried to control her voice.

'What time did you get back?'

'I think it was about five.'

There was silence between them then. She would not ask anything more, and he could not explain the unexplainable.

Trying hard to make talk, to be matter-of-fact, as if this was like any other breakfast there had ever been, he said: 'I called at Mistress Trelask's yesterday about the ribbons for Jeremy. She says she will have cheaper ones in a month or two.'

Demelza did not speak.

'I was with Harris Pascoe a good part of the morning and so did not have the opportunity to buy the other things you mentioned.'

She stirred the tea, took a sip, felt the hot liquid go down, stared out of the window with unseeing eyes. He picked up a fork, made twin marks on the tablecloth with it.

'I supped with Richard Tonkin. He has bought a boatbuilding business in partnership with Harry Blewett in East Looe. It has prospered since the outbreak of war.'

'Oh.'

'They have more orders, he says, than they know what to do with. Small craft. . . . At least it is satisfactory to hear of someone doing well.'

'Is it?'

Ross looked at his wife. 'You do not see that satisfaction?'

'No, I do not.'

'I'm sorry.'

'So am I.'

'You're spilling your tea, Demelza.'

'Yes,' she said and deliberately dropped her cup on the floor. The most frightening blazing anger was alive in her now. It was not only Elizabeth that she could have killed but Ross. She could have thrown every piece of crockery at him, and knives and forks too. Indeed she could have attacked him knife in hand. Fundamentally there was nothing meek or mild about her either. She was a fighter, and it showed now. She struggled with herself and gasped and met his grey gaze. Then she swung with her arm, knocking off teapot and milk jug and sugar basin and two plates, sweeping them all to the floor.

She went out.

Ross did not stir an inch until Jane Gimlett came running in.

'My dear life! What happened, sur? The teapot's scat all to jowds! And your rug. . . .' She bent to clear the mess.

'I caught my coat,' said Ross. 'It jerked the tablecloth. Pity.'

'Dear life, it is so. Where's the mistress?'

'She went out. She does not want breakfast this morning.'

All the week a great thunderbolt hung over the house. All her life Demelza's principle, though she did not know it as such, had been never to let the sun go down on her wrath. But she could very well have been buried with *this* wrath, because it came from a wound that knew no cure.

It was not that she could not forgive. She did not know that he cared about her forgiveness, or in any case that that was of importance. You can forgive someone for cutting down a tree, for smashing a precious vase, for burning a picture; it makes no difference to the thing destroyed.

They met only at meals, and then often contrived an avoidance by beginning early or coming late. When they had to meet they spoke little, and of things about the house or farm. Ross had a bed made up in Joshua's old bedroom, where Demelza had slept the first night she came. To him it seemed impossible after what had happened that he should force his presence on her upstairs; to her it seemed that one contact with Elizabeth had rendered his wife disgusting to him.

That so far he had made no effort to see Elizabeth again was rather a surprise, though of course he could have walked over every day for all she knew. At least he was continuing to eat and sleep in his own home. She would have died rather than ask him what he intended to do.

After that one outburst she was calm, though the anger had not left her. It had become a recognizable companion, colder, more deliberate, and she could not order it away. She didn't want to. Sometimes afterwards she thought it was only her anger during that week that kept her alive. It was her opium, to which she turned when ordinary thought became intolerable.

She knew he was busy all week over the sale of the mine gear. It was fetching about a quarter of what it cost. It would upset him when it began to go; but perhaps by then he would no longer be here. On the Thursday a letter came for him which he did not show her; but the following day he said:

'I shall have to be away tomorrow night. I am going to Looe and cannot be there and back in the day. Harry Blewett has written and wants to see me.'

'Oh.' So this was the excuse he must make. It lowered the relationship even further that he felt he had to lie about it. Why not say, I am going to Elizabeth.

'If you like to, you can read what he says.' Guessing perhaps, he pushed the letter across the table to her.

'No.' She pushed it back unread.

After a moment or two he said: 'I do not know what his motive is. Richard Tonkin must have told him I have no money to invest in his shipbuilding. I wish he would pay me back some he already owes me.'

She nearly said: 'Then you could give it to Elizabeth.' But at the last she had just too steady a sense of proportion to be petty.

On the Friday afternoon a man rode over from Werry House with a verbal message. Sir Hugh had received no answer to his invitation. Were Captain and Mrs Poldark able to accept? Demelza almost laughed. Sir Hugh and his party. Who felt like partying? Not she. And Ross would be away partying on his own. Partying with Elizabeth. Perhaps she should suggest that Ross should take Elizabeth and then she, Demelza, could pair off with George Warleggan.

She was not sure whether Ross intended to visit Looe at all, but she knew he would spend the last part of his week end at Trenwith House, in Elizabeth's arms. He would not want to be bothered with attending a reception and dance. Elizabeth's reception was all he cared about. Demelza wondered if Ross used the same endearments to Elizabeth as he sometimes had to her. No doubt she would be charmed with her new lover. She'd got what she wanted at last, at long last. In her own bed she was welcoming him. Slender as a lily in his arms. Patrician and well bred and distinguished in a way Demelza could never be. For a woman who traced her ancestry eight hundred years there were perhaps refinements of love of which a miner's daughter knew nothing. It was impossible after such a union that Ross should ever come back to common clay. Impossible. Impossible. He could go his own path while she drooped and languished at home, and drudged and cared for his child and tramped through the muck of the farm.

He could, could he? A light like a flame fell upon Demelza and illuminated all the dark places of her heart. Captain Poldark could not attend Sir Hugh Bodrugan's party. But Mrs Poldark could. An unrestricted Mrs Poldark. A Mrs Poldark bent on avenging herself upon her husband and salving her own hurt, on bolstering up her own pride in the only way she could at this time. Let Ross take the consequences, for the situation was of his creating.

She gave the appropriate message to the footman who was waiting, and saw him go off up the valley on his horse. The light was still playing in her mind and she knew it would not go out. She began to prepare for her visit on Saturday.

Chapter seven

WERRY HOUSE HAD been built at the time of Edward IV, when all the Bodrugan interests were at their peak. Later, when Richard's lust for power had ruined the Yorkist cause, the main Gorran Bodrugans had come crashing down; but the Werry Bodrugans had managed to find some favour at Henry's court and had preserved their inheritance. Now the stock was petering out of its own accord. Neither Sir Hugh nor his stepmother cared anything for appearances. They kept servants to wait on their needs but preferred to live in disorder. They liked to slop about the house in muddy boots and throw them anywhere when discarded, and Sir Hugh had been known to say that the sight of a tidy room or a polished floor put him in mind of his old grandfather, whom he was trying to forget.

But there had been some effort to better the place for the time of the party. The lawns were cut, some of the walls and ceilings brushed, and most of the menagerie of strange animals had been cleared out and herded into two rooms. If one were not too particular or took more notice of the company than of the chair one sat in, the whole thing passed muster pretty well.

Much the biggest room in the house was the hall, and this had a stone-flagged floor, a great fireplace, a raised dais at one end, and a high hammer-beam roof. The lower half of the walls, below the windows, was covered with moth-eaten tapestry, and above were numerous candelabra usually not lighted. It was in this room that the ball was to take place.

It was fortunate for Demelza that her decision to go, and to go in such a mood, was taken with so little time to prepare, otherwise she might have wondered a good deal what to wear. Problems of transport she had been quick-witted enough to solve before she dismissed the footman yesterday. Knowing that Ross would take Darkie, she had sent a message to Sir Hugh asking him to send over a groom and a horse; and this he did about five. So she arrived at Werry House in stylish manner, followed by a liveried man on another horse carrying her bag.

The drive of Werry House led out upon a coaching road, so most of the guests who came from central and southern parts of the county had arrived in their carriages. Six was evidently the fashionable time, for Demelza had to wait her turn before she could ride up to the front door, and she was the object of numerous raised quizzing glasses. She bore the scrutiny coldly, sitting straight-backed in her dark riding habit and tricorn hat.

Hugh and his stepmother were just inside the door, having been lured into the hall from an interesting discussion with John Treneglos on farcy in horses. Demelza came just on the heels of Mr and Mrs Nicholas Warleggan and heard Mr Warleggan's apology. George had very urgent business and presented his compliments and regrets. Following her were a couple whom she vaguely recognized as Lord and Lady Devoran. Lord Devoran was a friend of Ross's.

Sir Hugh came up to her and said: 'Ha! ma'am, so you've ventured to trust yourself to me care and left your husband by the fireside. Good. Good.'

'Yes, Sir Hugh. I thought 'twas not the weather for firesides.'

'Nor is it, m'dear. I'm with you there. But it is a very respectable gathering this week end, damme. Or most of it gives that impression at a distance. You'll be quite safe with us, ma'am, I assure you.'

'That's what I was afeared of,' said Demelza.

He chuckled dryly and looked at her with his beady black eyes.

''Tis comforting to hear you talk so even if you don't mean it. Respectability bores me to madness, and I fancy there'll be moments this week end when I shall be glad to slip away. Did I not promise you bawdy talk? Yes, I did, and you shall have it. We'll nip into a corner somewhere and——'

'Hughie!' called his stepmother. 'Miss Robartes is here with Dr Halse. Go and see 'em down. God damn it, I can't be everywhere!'

As Demelza was shown to her room along the floor-creaking corridor upstairs she reflected that she would have to be very far gone in drink before she could throw herself at Hugh Bodrugan's head. He had tried to make love to her in Bodmin, and even now her flesh crept at the thought.

That no doubt was always the trouble with wronged wives. The will to retaliate was there but not the object to make it possible.

The bedroom she had been shown into was big and low with heavy beams and panelled walls. When she was alone she at once went to the window and threw it open before beginning to unpack her dress. The window looked out upon the side of the house, across two sloping lawns towards a belt of beech trees. The trees were just in their first entrancing green, dappling in the sunlight like watered silk. Bisecting the lawns was a broad low-walled path sentinelled with statuary, much of it now showing the effects of wind and weather.

Coming along the path towards the house was Malcolm McNeil of the Scots Greys.

Sir Hugh's preferences seldom leaned towards the conventional; and since this was to be a dance, his view was that the thing should be got under

way as soon as possible and kept up as long as possible so that no one
should complain they hadn't had their money's worth. Also he wanted his
own money's worth out of the orchestra. Still further, he was no great hand
himself at these stately minuets and gavottes, so that if he could get them
disposed of before supper they could concentrate on the country dances
after and everyone could get hot and sweaty and enjoy themselves.

She deliberately kept her room for a time. A maid brought chocolate up
for her and she sat in her lawn morning-gown sipping quietly and enjoying
the view. She had no plans and no thoughts. Her mind did not go to Ross
and Elizabeth, nor did it to Sir Hugh or Captain McNeil. She was like the
captain of a ship just before an action, drained of emotion and free from
apprehensiveness, detached from what had gone and what might come.

About seven she began to dress, sponging her body and putting on clean
and flimsier underclothes. There was very little one could wear under this
dress which Ross had bought her for the Celebration Ball of '89 and which
she had not worn since. She had changed very little in figure since then,
but found it a little tighter in the bodice and a little less tight in the waist.
She put on her only pair of silk stockings – a present from Verity the
Christmas of '91 – liking the feel of the silk against her skin.

She decided to do her hair, or try to do it, the way the Warleggans' maid
had dressed it four years ago, piling it up and up, only allowing wisps to fall
in front of her ears and that bit of a fringe to curl on its own. No maid had
come to help, and she was grateful. Nor any patches on this dressing table,
but she had brought her own powder and rouge – present from Verity the
Christmas of '92 – and she used these very sparingly, and lengthened her
eyebrows about an inch each.

All that done, she at last began to struggle into her frock. It was curious
the warmth there was in fine silver brocade. Unimaginable contortions
were needed to fasten it, but at last it was done. She stared at herself in the
mirror and considered that she might have passed herself in the street
without recognition. But not without a second glance. Did not this
appearance proclaim her pretensions far too obviously? Did decent women
look like this? She decided after sober consideration that they did.

Out in the dusty, shadowy corridor the first strains of music came to her
ears. So she was not too early. The thing had begun. Dancing – or at least
music – before eight o'clock with the sun still in the sky and the birds
twittering. More suitable in high May to have dancing on the lawns. She
bitterly regretted not having included a bottle of port in her luggage. Facing
the company in cold blood.

In this house the stairs did not come down directly into the big hall but
into a smaller hall at the rear of the house, so she was saved the ordeal of
descending in full view. As she came down, John Treneglos was at the foot
of the stairs and immediately caught sight of her. Neighbour Treneglos,
eldest son of the master of Mingoose House and himself already almost

master of it; a clumsily built, sandy-haired, freckled man of thirty-five or
-six.

'Why, there, if it isn't Mistress Demelza! Tally ho! Where've you been
hiding yourself, eh?'

His trumpeting tones drew everyone's attention, and Demelza thought, I
must be careful. She had no particular affection for John Treneglos and
less still for Ruth, his wife, who always tried to take her down a peg; but she
well knew John's feelings for her. It would not do to repeat the
performance of four years ago at the Assembly Rooms when, in this very
frock and hair style, she had had four or five men nearly fighting for her –
and herself meaning *then* no more than to be polite and accommodating.

He came up a few steps and held out his arms. 'You'll allow me to escort
you into the ballroom, eh? And the first dance, eh? Same as once before,
egad. History repeats itself. 'Twould give me pleasure to spike your
husband's guns for once. Where is he?'

She gave him her hand. 'He was called away. Where is your wife?'

'In pup as usual. And 'tis near her time or she would have come whether
or no; you know her. This is all very well met. Damn it, I believe it was
arranged by Providence!'

'Damn it, I believe it was not,' said Demelza.

He laughed heartily, and they went into the ballroom.

Her impression of the first hours of the dance was hazy and confused.
Above all at the first she needed a stimulant to give her poise and
possession and to steady her nerves, but it seemed hours before anyone
offered her one. Then it was some dry-tasting wine and not enjoyable to
drink. But in the end it had the right effect.

Six in the orchestra, three violins, a tabor, a pipe, and a French horn.
The conductor, who was also one of the violinists, was the roundest man
she had ever seen, everything about him orotund, from his gold-rimmed
spectacles to his gold-fobbed belly. His coattails were never still; they beat
time metronome-fashion and were only subdued when he sat on them
during the negligible intervals.

All of fifty people in the room, which had been decorated with lilac and
daffodils. Sir John Trevaunance had come but not Unwin. Mr Ray
Penvenen was there, although he did not dance and looked very pale and
austere among it all. Robert Bodrugan, Sir Hugh's only nephew and heir
presumptive, had come, and she had two dances with him during the early
part of the evening. All the Teague family, and three of the Boscoignes,
and Richard Treneglos, John's second brother, and Joan Pascoe, the
banker's daughter – but not Dwight Enys; and William Hick, and Mr and
Mrs Barbary, and Peter St Aubyn Tresize, and the Hon Mrs Maria Agar,
and Lady Whitworth and her son, who was now a parson, and Lieutenant
and Mrs Carruthers, and dozens more.

One person very noticeable in the company was a tall handsome woman in black, with so many bangles and trinkets that she clinked every time she moved, and it wasn't until she was to be seen hanging on Sir Hugh Bodrugan's arm that Demelza placed her as the notorious Margaret Vosper with whom Sir Hugh had been going steady for twelve months. During the evening they came towards her and Sir Hugh said:

'D'you know my friend Mrs Vosper, ma'am? Mrs Ross Poldark. You two should have something in common; both pretty women and only need to crook a finger at a man, eh? Or have you already an acquaintance?'

Margaret laughed in a loud husky contralto: 'I don't know this one well, but I've had dealings one way or another with all the male Poldarks. Maybe we've more in common than you think, Hughie.'

Sir Hugh cackled and Demelza's soul went black within her. She didn't doubt the woman's insinuations; it all fitted in with Ross's perfidy.

'You have the advantage of me, ma'am,' she said, 'but I expect that would be before I was born.'

Sir Hugh's laughter became louder. 'I hope you're enjoying the dance, mistress. I confess I've not seen you sitting out much.'

''Tis a very beautiful dance, Sir Hugh, and I'd no idea there was so many handsome men in all Cornwall. 'Tis fortunate that you need not fear the competition.'

Sir Hugh took out his snuffbox and tapped it, hiding his expression from Margaret.

'Come, me lord,' Margaret said yawning. 'This fancy talk's giving me the vapours. I've buried two husbands and been straw widow to a number of others – naming no names – and I never see the point of beating about the bush. If you feel a taking for someone, go up and ask 'em yes or no and have done with it.'

'Twould be very businesslike,' Demelza said.

'Businesslike and honest,' said Margaret. 'A man knows where he is and so does a woman——'

'She knows where she's likely to be,' put in Sir Hugh with a rumble.

'Do you not think,' said Demelza recklessly, 'that there is a case to be made out for a thought more daintiness in love? I should better prefer to take my time in making up my mind. Even if it seem like beating about the bush to you, I should rather do that than get scratched and worn on every bush I see.'

Fortunately, John Treneglos came up just then and claimed Demelza, and Margaret drew Sir Hugh away and soon gained his attention again.

But it was Demelza whom Sir Hugh led in to supper.

She had not seen anything of Malcolm McNeil in the early part of the evening. He had not been in the room at all to begin; but when he caught sight of her, he at once hurried across, pushing his way between Peter Tresize and Lieutenant Carruthers, who were talking to her.

'Why, Mrs Poldark, I'd no idea! A glorious surprise on a man's last night! When may I have the favour of a dance? Are you engaged for supper?'

'Yes, I'm – that sorry.'

'And the dances before?'

'I'm five deep already.'

'Then after supper? The first?'

'Very well. The first.'

'Why,' said Tresize, 'that's unfair, ma'am. It was the one I'd just asked you for.'

'I'd been saving it for Captain McNeil. I'm that sorry, Mr Tresize. Perhaps the second?'

'The second then.'

'I want the third,' said Lieutenant Carruthers. 'I've heard the third is to be an *écossaise*. They are rare good sport and——'

'I think if 'tis that dance, I should dance it with a Scotsman. That is, if he would condescend to ask me.'

'Great plaisure, ma'am,' said McNeil, pulling at his moustache in agitation. 'And many more if I may have 'em.'

Demelza thought of Margaret's philosophy. 'What you care to ask for, sir, so long as you ask now.'

'The first, the third, the fifth, the seventh, and all thereafter, if there be an after.'

'I'm vastly religious,' Demelza said, 'and believe strongly in a thereafter.'

'I see it as naught but gluttony,' said Tresize. 'And you should not encourage gluttony, ma'am; it gives rise to other appetites.'

'Captain McNeil tells me he is leaving on the morrow. Or so I b'lieve. Perhaps he may be permitted special indulgencies on that score.'

'You're immensely kind, Mrs Poldark. I'm overcome by such marks of favour.'

Later, when Sir Hugh took her in to supper, she was aware that all the events of four years ago were being repeated, except that she was keeping a better control on them. The knowledge was headier than the thin French wine.

But to go on drinking in careful moderation, not enough to get drunk but enough to maintain her present condition, was vitally necessary not only for reasons of poise and confidence. In her spirit, in the very deep parts of her spirit, the desolation which had been there nearly a week was no different at all. *Nothing* she could do to-night could change it. Margaret could rub it freshly raw, but even that didn't vitally matter. She had already lost all there was to lose. To use her own simile, she was like a Christian who had lost God, a believer turned atheist, knowing relief and unexampled liberty, trying to rejoice over the outworn beliefs she had thrown away, conscious of the immense winds of freedom and utterly determined to make the most of them; but at heart lost, irretrievably lost.

Chapter eight

SUPPER WAS IMMENSE, and after supper, to shake the food down, the country dances. Full of good things and fumed with wine, even the most dignified members of the gathering unbent. Demelza was surprised at the way the upper classes let themselves go. Inherently she had felt that Lord This and the Hon Mrs That were by virtue of their titles only fitted for performing the minuet and the gavotte. That was not their view at all. Wigs bobbing and skirts swaying, they pranced about with the relish of Borneo natives. Some of the stouter women, following the low-cut fashions of the day, came very near to endangering their modesty; and if Demelza had been observing the thing from a distance, she would have been hot with anxiety for them. But instead she was in the fray herself, anxious from time to time that no clumsy shoe should step on her beautiful gown or clasping hand pull it from her shoulders.

She would not have denied that there was a sense in which she enjoyed it. She loved dancing; and now that Malcolm McNeil was her close attendant, she could encourage a man without hypocrisy – or without too much hypocrisy.

In a breathless fan-waving interlude between a galop and a Sir Roger de Coverley she said:

'You are truly leaving tomorrow, Captain McNeil?'

'Och, yes, I am truly leaving tomorrow. I should have been gone on Thursday but for an accident of post which I then abused but now believe the work of kindly heaven. As a special favour for to-night, would you consider calling me Malcolm?' McNeil had received such encouragement that he was taking the play out of Demelza's hands.

'Perhaps I'm mistaken,' she said, 'but was that not the name of one of the kings of Scotland?'

'More than one. You're very well informed on Scottish history – Demelza.'

'I read sometimes. I'm sure that surprises you. You think I do naught but milk cows and feed pigs and tend babies and bake bread.'

'No, no, I assure you.'

'Well, thank you for the assurance. Do you know, I b'lieve only two men have ever called me Demelza before: my husband and my cousin-in-law.'

'What of your father?'

'Oh, he did not, so far as I can recollect. When he liked me he called me "daughter," and when he disliked me he called me a name which being now a lady I have long since forgotten.'

McNeil laughed his big laugh and nearly stopped the band.

'Oh, you may laugh, Malcolm, but it is true. And now tell me something of yourself. How many ladies have called you Malcolm before?'

'What?' He stared at her, stared into her direct dark eyes, seeking the bubble of laughter but not finding it although he still suspected its existence. 'A few, I confess; but *few* conseedering the temptations of a soldier's life. I'm hard to please, as I fancy you are. I was brought up to like the best only, and it is a constricting circumstance as you'll agree. Nevertheless it has its rewards, for when the occasion arises——'

'What occasion?'

He laughed. 'To call a woman by her Christian name is the first endearment. It is like – like touching hands without gloves, like lifting her down from a stile, like receiving a smile that has more in it than friendship. I admire your name, Demelza. Where did you get it and what does it mean?'

'I got it where you got yours, I suppose, Malcolm – from my mother. I do not know where she came by it. An old gipsy who came to the door once told me that in the true Cornish tongue it meant "Thy sweetness." But he was an ignorant old man and I do not suppose he was right.'

' "Thy sweetness." Very apt. Though I think I should be more happy still if it were "my sweetness." '

'If I'd known so much was meant by this using of Christian names – that is, as you tell me – I should have trembled to let you be so free with mine.'

'But why so? Did you not say when we first met this evening that whatever I cared to ask for . . .'

She smiled into his eyes. 'I don't think there was an "ever" in it.'

'There is certainly an "ever" in my wishes.'

Neither spoke for a moment. Then, before she could frame the right reply, someone came towards them and said, 'I think this is our dance, ma'am,' and she was led away.

But McNeil, having advanced thus far, was not to be denied. He was in the cavalry and knew all the moves from now on. When it came time for their next, he suggested they should go upon the terrace for a breath of air. There were several other couples out there. The long twilight had at last faded and night had fallen blackly, without moon or stars. They paced up and down, her neck and shoulders showing palely in the dark. They talked for a few minutes, and then she shivered.

'You're cold, darling?' At once he put his arm round her shoulders. 'Forgive me, I'll get you a wrap.'

'I have none,' she said, very gently disengaging herself. 'I did not bring one, for I have never possessed one. But I am not cold; it was just – some feeling.'

'Describe it to me.'

'Oh, that I could not. There's an old Cornish word, shrims, which is nearest. But the feeling is gone, so we'd best forget it.' She had never had quite this *sort* of attention before, not even from Ross. It won her, though she tried to stay detached.

'What good fortune kept me here two days longer!' he said. 'I well see that you would not have gone unattended tonight; indeed the other men will snarl over you at the least excuse; but I fancy, I hope, that the others would not have suited you so well.'

'They would not have suited me so well,' she said. 'Are you quite recovered now from your wound? It is late to ask, but——'

'Quite recovered. Look.' He stretched his arm. 'It is as good as new. And the wound was worth the having. Just because of meeting you.'

They came to the end of the terrace and stopped. She moved to turn, but he did not. She thought, this is the first choice. He's bending his head to kiss me. Well, I've asked for it. I've often wondered what it was like, those moustaches . . . now I know. . . . Is this me, looking up at a strange man's hair, with his hands and lips on me? This is the moment to turn back; Judas, this is a long kiss, I like it and dislike it both at the same time. Oh, no, this isn't really me; I'm home by the fire with Jeremy asleep upstairs, and Ross . . . . Ross is in Elizabeth's arms . . . .

When at last he released her, she leaned back against the balustrade and glanced round rather belatedly to see if anyone was watching. But the night surrounded them. She took a breath, which was overdue, put a hand uncertainly to her hair. He was a big man, perhaps not as tall as Ross but heavier, stouter. And he was no beginner.

'Ever since I first met you,' he said, 'ever since that first time years ago, I've wanted to do that. Och, it is a very great thrill to me.'

'Och,' she said, 'I'm glad you enjoyed it.'

'Madam minx. But it is always the way with humankind, Demelza; the realization of an ambition leads on to greater ambition and greater ambition, until——'

'Until there is none left. What then, Malcolm?'

'What then? Why, then one achieves fulfilment of the most desirable kind. Were ye suggesting futility? It hasn't been my experience. And I am sairtainly convinced it would not be so in this case.'

'And for me?'

'I'd not be a disappointment. Do ye think it likely?'

Their heads were still close, within six inches of each other. The conversation had got completely out of hand, had run suddenly amok. Momentarily she did not know how to control it.

'I think we should go in. I think, I b'lieve, it is very warm out here and would be cooler in the ballroom.'

'Will you not give me a word of encouragement before we go?'

'It seem to me that there have been many words of encouragement. Or I don't know how else you would call them——'

'Encouragement yes,' said McNeil confidently. 'But will you not fulfil the promise of your looks, my darling? Perhaps later. Later tonight. Which is your room? Demelza. . . .'

Well, what was she waiting for? Was this not why she had come to the ball? Was this not the only way of getting back at Ross? Had she not a few hours ago been bitterly reflecting that no eligible man existed. Sir Hugh, in such a connection, filled her with repugnance. So did John Treneglos. But here was McNeil, off tomorrow, personable, quite attractive to her, eager and loving. What more could she ask? Unless the whole of her rebellion, the whole of her protest, was the empty breath of so many angry words, words spoken within herself and never seriously meant. A windbag, pretending to be daring. Bolstering herself up on glasses of wine so that she might reach the ultimate peak of wickedness by allowing someone to kiss her. How many casual carnal kisses had Ross given, not only to Elizabeth but to that bold coarse creature stalking about indoors? Margaret Vosper. Margaret Cartland, Margaret Poldark. Demelza Poldark. Demelza McNeil.

She lowered her head and said in a low voice: 'I am not well acquainted with this house.'

'I am. I have lived here many weeks.' His lips touched her ear, his hand on her arm. 'Thank you, my sweet, thank you. . . .'

When she got to her room much later that night, the conductor's coat-tails were still swinging. A few of the energetic younger couples were making the most of the emptying floor, but the majority of the guests had departed or were beginning the process of retiring for the night. Constance Lady Bodrugan had long since left them to it and was feeding her animals. Sir Hugh was drinking a last rum toddy with Lord Devoran, and Robert Bodrugan was making heavy going of a flirtation with Miss Tresize.

Demelza shut the door behind her and went across to the window and parted the curtains to look out. The heavy evening clouds had lifted and it was less dark. The silhouette of the trees bloomed against the lighter night sky. Light flooded out from the ground-floor window underneath her, reflecting back upon the ivy-covered walls. What she thought was a gargoyle upon the turret of the porch suddenly came to life and flitted silently past her window: a barn owl looking for prey.

She let the curtain fall and turned to warm her ice-cold hands at the single thick candle which burned like a beady yellow eye upon the table. She was now in process – in rapid process – of becoming what her father would have described as a whore-bird. She only wished she knew how whore-birds generally behaved. Did one wait in one's gown, presenting the exact picture which had enticed the man in the first place, but with all the hazards of a spoiled and crumpled frock? Did one undress first and put on one's morning coat, which was not one quarter so attractive but which had the merits of accommodation? Or did one get into bed in one's night shift – or even without it – and pull the sheet up to one's chin?

She wished now she had allowed herself to become a little drunker. If one felt dizzy and silly, it was all so much easier – one simply let him make the running and probably giggled one's way into infidelity. She had never felt less like giggling in her life. Of far more use to her now than wine was the mental picture she had of Elizabeth, with her pale fey face and golden hair flowing, lying in Ross's arms. The picture was extraordinarily vivid, as if it were painted and hanging on the wall of the room.

She wished her hands were not so cold. It was the only outward sign of nerves. She wished it all was not to happen so much in cold blood. He should have carried her off while they were on the terrace – got it over, like having a tooth out. No, that was unfair to him. It would all be better when he came. He was attractive, handsome, ardent. She should be flattered by his attentions, *was* indeed. She must think *hard* about *him*. It helped. It helped a great deal.

She decided that the morning coat was the thing and began hasty contortions to remove the frock. Eventually it slithered down in a beautiful shimmering heap, and she stepped out of it, long-limbed and black-stockinged and white. Well, if he came in now! She grabbed the morning coat and struggled into it. As she tied the cord, there was a just perceptible knock upon the door.

Only just in time! She picked up the gown and laid it hastily on a chair, then tiptoed to the door. In a moment Malcolm McNeil was inside.

Dressing gowns evidently were the correct thing. He looked bigger than ever in his, more down to earth, more *real*. Absolutely frighteningly real. And rather fat.

'My sweet, I was afraid I might have picked the wrong door and flushed some antique dowager. How adorable you look! How old are you, eighteen? If I did not know to the contrary, I should not suppose it to be more.'

'I'm forty-seven,' she said, playing for time with her own brand of humour, opposing it to her temporary sense of shock. ''Tis the light in here which is so becoming, Malcolm. I should not suppose you a day over twelve. Though, in truth, the candle has had a thief in it and has guttered half away. Did anyone see you come?'

'No one. The maids have gone to bed, and the guests that are left are yawning their heads off. But for us, my darling, the night is young——'

'What time do you leave tomorrow?'

'I catch the noon coach from Truro as it passes the gates——'

'And shall I then not see you again?'

'You shall if you wish. Only write me at Winchester. . . .'

He put his arms round her, still talking, and kissed her several times with great energy, allowing one hand to slip inside her coat and rest on her shoulder. I'm supposed to be *enjoying* this, she thought. What's the matter? Has it come too sudden, or doesn't he attract me so much as I believed? Am I liking being kissed like this? Not now. Not this way. But it will pass. I will try to forget everything. I wish I was drunk. Dear Malcolm; how he wants me. Soon I'll want him. Just surrender yourself up. It's naught but shyness that makes me all curled up and cold. Or am I really, truthfully, a prude and shocked at myself? . . .

'Malcolm,' she said, when she could get her mouth free.

'Yes, my angel,' he said, and gave her no time to reply.

For the moment at least she was able to keep his endearments within bounds, and while doing so she stormed at herself. Ross is unfaithful! Ross is unfaithful! He is gone from me as a lover for ever. Elizabeth has won him. He has even been with that *terrible* woman downstairs. What an insult, a *humiliation!* Ross has gone, I tell you. There is no more of him, nothing but desolation, and this: the furtive appointment in the bedroom; Malcolm is kind, upright, sincere, so much *more* than I might have expected, even if a little fat. I *wanted* him to make love to me; I almost asked him. Now am I not satisfied? Keep to your bargain. In a few minutes you will be enjoying it. It is just the beginning that seems so strange, so foreign, as if one had never been made love to before. Foreign, that was the word. Being seduced by a foreigner.

His endearments were becoming progressive.

'Malcolm,' she said breathlessly, part breaking away from him. 'Are you kind?'

'Kind? You will find me so,' he said, following her slowly backwards. He had exhausted his finesse downstairs.

'Then, Malcolm, I want you to listen to me. Please. Just for a moment or two. I – I want you to be kind and understanding. I want you to understand why I led you to suppose. . . . You see it is because of Ross. I thought because of what he has done that I wished to do the same. And of all the men I could have preferred to have chosen . . . *you* was here. . . . And it was not until this moment – a few moments ago – that I have begun to wonder——'

'Och, yes, darling,' he said. 'I quite see what you wonder. It is not an uncommon feeling at the last. . . .'

'No,' she said. 'Hear me out, please. It is of great moment. I——'

'Of course. Of course. No one is denying it. Have I told you how beautiful you are? I've rarely seen a woman so beautiful as you to-night. . . .'

She could retreat no further. She had her back against the wall.

Up to that moment there had been a strong element of doubt in her feelings. The terrible sick hurt within her goaded her on in spite of these very peculiar feelings which were attacking her now, which swept over her, wave after wave. Hurt pride and all the other things were working hard on Malcolm's behalf. But she knew then that she *must* have a breathing space, still a little time to relate one emotion with another, so that there should still be an ultimate freedom of choice, a rejection or an acceptance within her heart. Had he been a subtler man and given her time, she could have done this. But he did not give her time, and so the new feelings grew stronger than the old and his compliments slid past unheeded.

He stood smiling over her, a hand on either side of the wall, not touching her but about to. And suddenly, abruptly, knowing him and liking him, she breathlessly began to try to explain. Perhaps it was a lost cause but she went on, telling him of Ross's misconduct, of her own decision to come to-night, of his personal charm which had led her to the point where she was willing to do this thing; and then of her sudden humiliating recognition but a few moments ago that she could not go on. It was something quite fundamental, within herself, primal and entirely unrecognized until now, an adherence to one man however he might neglect her.

She did not use those words but she did her best, groping around to explain feelings as yet only half acknowledged. She had never felt so debased in her life, she said, not because of what had been proposed but because of the way she was behaving now. Only her absolute *certainty* that she could do nothing else gave her the courage to seem such a cheat and a prude. She didn't suppose he would like what she was saying; but they were not strangers; in a manner of speaking they were old friends, and she threw herself upon his friendship now, begging him to appreciate her position. . . .

She said these things at considerable leı.gth and hoped and prayed that he understood; and then she looked into his brown eyes and realized with a sense of shock that he wasn't listening.

'I quite appreciate your feelings, my angel. It does you cr-redit to be so scrupulous. But think of me a moment, who's been looking to this rendezvous as to a mortal's taste of heaven. I well know your tender heart. It would not, I know, deny me the privileges it has promised. Ye have two duties now, my angel; not one alone to your faithless husband. The first is to me. . . .'

He took her and began to kiss her again. She struggled, turning her head away, but not with great vehemence, hoping that her obvious reluctance would make an impression. It did not. He got hold of her morning gown and began to pull it off. She bit him.

He stepped back a moment, and she slid along the wall out of his reach. The look in his eyes changed. He glanced at the teeth marks in his wrist. The blood was beginning to come.

He said: 'Well, that is a pretty way of showing affection. I confess it surprises me in a lady. But perhaps it is the way you like it.'

'Oh, Malcolm, please, don't you understand . . . ?'

He came after her and captured her in a corner of the room. They struggled desperately for a minute or two. Then she broke away again, leaving a sleeve of her gown in his hands. They faced each other across the room. Her breath was coming in great gulps.

He took a deep breath himself. His intention had been so predetermined when he came into this room that no words of hers would have been sufficient to turn him from it. Nor would a solitary act of resistance. But this last struggle had shown him how much in earnest she was. And for all her slenderness she was as strong and lithe as a young animal. Of course he could still have his way if he chose. It was simple enough: you hit her just once on her obstinate little chin. But he was not that sort of a man.

He slowly rolled the sleeve of the gown into a ball and mopped his hand. Then he dropped the material to the floor.

'I like to think of myself as civilized,' he said; 'so I give you best, Mrs Poldark. I hope your husband appreciates such fidelity. In the peculiar saircumstances I do not. I like a woman who makes up her mind and has the courage and grace to stick to it. I thought you were such a one. My mistake. . . .' He walked slowly to the door and gave her a last glance. 'When admiration turns to contempt, it is time to go.'

He went out. At the last moment she almost spoke to him again, making a final effort to bring him to understand something of her feeling, so that, even though he might condemn, he would not despise. But as he moved she just did not dare to open her mouth.

And when he had gone, when the door had closed and she was alone again, she walked trembling to the bed and sat on it. All the tension of defence was moving out of her. She couldn't quite believe in her own vehemence. Every muscle in her body ached. Her arms and shoulders were bruised. Her teeth ached.

She didn't cry, but she put up her hands to her face. 'Oh, God, I want to *die*,' she said. '*Please*, God, let me die. . . .'

Chapter nine

ABOUT HALF AN hour later, as the big clock in the hall was striking three, when the band had finally worked itself out and peace was settling on the house, when those still up began to move more quietly for fear of disturbing those already retired, a short stocky man came slowly up the stairs and turned towards the east wing. It was Sir Hugh Bodrugan himself, and the exaggerated stealth of his movements showed not only that he was on illicit business but also that the spirits he had drunk had had the effect of making him abnormally sober.

Wine had been spilled down his red hunting coat, and the lace of one cuff had been torn in a skirmish, but that was all the obvious damage, and he was sure the ball had been a great success and that everyone had enjoyed themselves. Now to put the cap on the evening he was bent on enjoying himself in another way. He'd cunningly given Margaret the slip, and she no doubt was still pacing about in the library waiting for him. Presently she would get tired of waiting and would swear roundly and go to bed. That was as it should be. He was going to bed, he hoped, but not with her.

There were few guests in the east wing, and that naturally made his purposes easier, although the confounded floor creaked and moaned all the way. His choice of bedroom for the lady had not been undesigning, in case she should give him any encouragement. It was therefore with surprise and indignation that as he neared the door in question he saw another figure move towards it out of the shadows and peer at the handle as if to make certain of his bearings. As this figure stretched out a hand to open the door, Sir Hugh said:

'Hi, there! What the blazes . . .'

The other man straightened up sharply. It was John Treneglos. He said: 'Hullo! What?' and blinked. 'Oh, it's you, my friend. Is this my bedroom, did you say? I remember 'twas on the right-hand side as you turned up the stairs. This wandering great house of yours, it's worse than my own. Look ee——'

'You're not so foxed as that, sir,' said Bodrugan sternly. 'Oh, dear no, sir. One may make a mistake by a room or two, sir, but not by half a house.

That's your way, straight down the corridor; and I should be obliged if you'd take it.'

'Ah,' said Treneglos. 'Is that so? Yes, I see where I went wrong now.' He made a move and then stopped. 'Yes, I suppose 'twas all the jigging in the dance that put my bearings out. Thank ee.'

He waited. They both waited. Sir Hugh said: 'Well, good night to you.'

'Now, Hughie,' said Treneglos. 'Don't be a damned spoilsport. I never thought to think you a damned spoilsport.'

'You may think what you please, sir. That's your way to bed. This is Demelza Poldark's room, and well you know it!'

John Treneglos grunted. 'I'll confess if you want me to, though it's a thought unmannerly to need me to be so explicit.' He put his hand firmly on the other's shoulder. 'You know how it is on these occasions. Damme, you of all people shouldn't stand in a feller's way. You've done enough tile-walking in your time. The little bud was oncoming to-night. As good as invited me, y'know. Can't turn a good thing down. What with Ruth out of the way. Golden opportunity. I suggest you turn a blind eye and toddle off to bed.'

'Blind eye!' said Sir Hugh explosively. 'I was going in there myself!'

Treneglos stared at his host in startled fashion. 'What? What? You're joking. Damn it. Don't tell me she invited you too!'

Sir Hugh scowled. 'Not *invited* in so many words. But a nod's as good as a wink, man——'

'Ah, you put too much store by these nods, my dear. No doubt she wished to be polite, as any woman would to a handsome old war horse like you, but——'

'Well maybe she'll go on being polite. . . . And war horse be beggared!' said Sir Hugh, as the second half of the sentence registered. 'I'm inclined to suppose I'm just as good a man as you. What did she say to you – tell me that, eh? What did she say to you, sir?'

'I misremember the exact words, but 'twas plain enough in the meaning. And half of it was the look. She has a very suggestible look when she sets herself out to it——'

'Pshaw!' said Bodrugan. 'You've less claim to an invitation than I have. You thought to try your luck, that's all. Confess it, man. She's always been a tantalizing slut, and there must be an end of all things. How did you know which was her bedroom?'

'What? Oh, I squeezed that walleyed maid you have, and she gave off the information. Now look, Hugh, it is plain enough I was here first, if only by a short head, so I have a certain priority in the matter, even if we discount the exact manner of the invitation. After all, you have your own doxy here in the very house, which is more than Ruth would ever put up with. Don't be greedy. What do you say to giving me best? Then perhaps another time——'

'Rubbish!' The injustice of the situation welled up in Bodrugan. 'Who helped her in Bodmin two years gone and nothing for it but a few kisses? Who showed her how to use that new seed drill everyone's talking about? Who's sent her presents and called upon her regular? And who invited her here, sir? Whose house is this? Ecod, if 'twere in your house, I fancy you'd put in a substantial claim. . . .'

'Hush,' said Treneglos. 'If you argue in that tone, the whole house will be out in the corridor. . . . I grant that 'tis your house and welcome to it; but you're the host, Hughie, and it is your place to give way to a guest. Any book of behaviour will tell you that. The convenience of the guest should come first – always first. Damn it, you haven't a leg to stand on. Manners aren't what they were but——'

'I stand where I stand,' said Sir Hugh angrily. 'And if you go in that room, I go with you.'

John sighed, and wiped the back of his sleeve across his forehead. 'I don't fancy we'll win her that way. . . .' He was struck with a thought. 'It may be she meant the invitation to apply to us both and that 'tis just ill fortune we have come together. But if we go *in* together, that will finish it. What do you say to tossing a coin? Winner goes in right away. Loser chances his arm in an hour or so. Ecod, it seems the only reasonable argument. . . .'

Sir Hugh grunted. 'You're worse thoughted than I ever supposed, John. But no one shall say I wasn't a sportsman. If it is the only way to settle the matter peaceable, I'll accept it.' With some difficulty he fished a coin out of his fob pocket. 'Now if you'll toss, I'll call. . . .'

'Nay. Hold hard a moment. Let's see the coin. . . . Ah, just as I suspicioned: two heads. All's fair in love, but let's be fairer than that.' With equal difficulty John Treneglos fumbled another coin into his fingers and showed it to his rival. 'This one was born natural and has a top and tail. Now call, will you, while I spin.'

'Heads,' grunted Sir Hugh furiously, and at once bent and then went on his knees to see the result.

'Tails!' said John in triumph. 'Tails it is, by the beard of Moses. You've lost, Hugh, and the filly's mine!'

'It struck the edge of the carpet! Just as it fell I saw it. I demand we should toss again! Why, damn me——'

'Nay, fair's fair. You'd not go back on your word, I take it?'

On hands and knees they eyed each other, and Sir Hugh perceived that if he quarrelled with the fall of the coin he would have a fight on his hands. And Treneglos was the second-best amateur wrestler in thirty miles. Grumbling, grunting, sweating, he got to his feet. He bitterly regretted having agreed to any such hazard now. He knew, in his bones he knew, that things had been propitious for him to-night; and now this clumsy, bungling fool had come along to spoil it all.

With seething resentment he watched the younger man tiptoe to the door of Demelza's room, gently turn the handle, and slide inside. Unable to bear the sight of it, he turned sharply away and stumped off to the end of the corridor. But there he stopped. It would be a mistake to abandon his position too early. It did not after all turn entirely on the fall of a coin. There was the lady to consider. He flattered himself that she had a soft spot for him, and John Treneglos was the sort of bumptious ass who, given an inch, would assume a yard. He might well come out again at any minute with a cracked head. She was a quick-tempered girl and if his advances were unwelcome. . . . Sir Hugh decided to linger in the shadows at the end of the passage and wait a minute or two. To while away the time he took a pinch of snuff and dusted the loose powder away with the torn end of his cuff.

The sneeze that had been in gestation was stillborn with delight, for the very thing he had hoped came to pass. John Treneglos came sharply out of the bedroom with a dazed expression on his face and stared right and left. He spotted Sir Hugh and beckoned him. Preening himself, strutting, Sir Hugh came.

'Is this the room, Hughie? I've made no mistake?'

'Nay, of course not. She wants me——'

'Well, there's no one in it. See for yourself.'

'What!' Sir Hugh pushed past him. A candle guttered in the draught between door and window. The bed was not disturbed. A chair was overturned, but no articles of clothing were to be seen about the room. Sir Hugh went straight to the great wardrobe and flung it open. The cupboard was bare. He pulled the curtains further back from the bed. Then he went on his knees and looked under it. John Treneglos brought the candle over. United in adversity, they ransacked the room. All they found was a number of hairpins, some powder spilled before the dressing table, and the sleeve of a lawn dressing gown.

'She's maybe gone visiting herself,' said Treneglos. 'Ecod, I well call to mind a serving maid we had at Mingoose: you'd never be sure where she was to be found next. Once I remember——'

'I conceit it's different from that,' said Sir Hugh, scowling. 'Shut that pesty window, John; all the harmful night air's blowing in. . . . There's McNeil, now. He was making a mighty fuss of her after supper. . . . But he sleeps some way distant; and even if she went to him, she would surely leave some of her draperies behind.'

Treneglos had had his head out. 'I suppose she wouldn't be madcap enough to climb down this ivy, eh? What would be her purpose? Has it all been done to hoax us, d'you suspicion? I think she couldn't have done it, could she? Or would our noise have scared her? If you flush a hen pheasant, it flies farthest.'

Bodrugan put his head out tentatively and then quickly withdrew it.

'Bah, no, you're dreaming, man. Why should she go that way and risk her neck? 'Tis all very confusing and provoking too. I've never known a woman like her for promising much and performing little. I could put her over my knee.' He thought of that pleasurably for a moment, and then the long-delayed snuff-sneeze occurred. 'Shut the damned window, I say. We shall both have a distemper in the morning.'

The window was shut, and the two men returned disconsolately to the corridor. Sir Hugh was reflectively crumpling the gown sleeve in his fingers.

'It is a mortal pity,' said Treneglos. 'With Ruth away and all. . . .'

They tramped down the passage together, no longer on tiptoe or careful of creaking boards; the house might wake now for all they cared. In the distance at the head of the stairs a coat of mail armour glimmered in the light from below.

'When's her time?' said Sir Hugh, trying to take an interest.

'Whose?'

'Ruth's.'

'Oh . . . it was to have been last Wednesday, but she's always late in coming to the boil.'

'How many will this be?'

'Four. If she keeps up her rate of fire, we shall soon have our share of livestock. And you'd never have thought it to look at her before she was wed.'

They stopped at the great black banisters and looked down into the littered hall. A footman yawned in his hooded leather chair. Treneglos seemed to expect his host to walk with him into the west wing, but Sir Hugh stopped.

'You run along, dear boy. It will be daylight soon and the cocks crowing. The band'll be waiting for their settlement. I promised they should have it prompt. It was the only condition on which they'd agree to come.'

'Don't forget your Margaret in the library.'

'No,' said Sir Hugh. He brightened a little at the thought and his brow cleared. 'No, there is that. I'll call in there on the way.'

Chapter ten

Ross stayed three nights at Looe. Propositions were put to him, and he needed time to think them out.

Blewett, to Ross's infinite surprise, was in a position to repay him the £250 loaned when the copper-smelting company smashed. The small boatbuilding business had been a moderate investment when they bought it; but with war came boom conditions, and in six months they had doubled their capital. So £250 was there for Ross's taking. He had been invited to Looe because Blewett, well aware that Ross's loan had saved him from bankruptcy and prison, was keen to repay the unwritten debt as well as the actual one and was prepared to offer Ross a share in their business. In order to judge fairly, he must see the yard.

Ross saw the yard. It was plain that money was being made there. His £250 would double itself again in a year. As a business proposition it was first-rate.

But the yard was remote from where he lived. He could either find permanent lodging in Looe or he could allow the work to go on in his absence and look on the thing simply as an investment. Or he could take the £250.

And if he took the £250? Was he to put it aside for the emergencies of next Christmas? Was he to pour it down the bottomless drain where £1,500 of his had already gone?

Buried under twenty fathoms of rock and broken props was a lode of tin. He knew that. That much was not a speculation any more. Captain Henshawe had sacrificed a hard-earned £100 to prove it. But it had been an unlucky venture from the start.

During the last weeks Ross had bitterly blamed himself for taking the risks which killed the two men. He still did. He knew that whatever the inducement he would never take those risks again. But if he let it be known that he was thinking of restarting work on the mine, all the men who had worked on it would flock back, eager to go down. Not one of them would bother to enquire the number of timbermen he was likely to employ. For them it was the luck of the game.

Although much had been agreed for the disposal of the headgear, scarcely anything had yet been moved. £250 would by no means be an excessive sum to get the mine restarted. It might indeed be insufficient. He wondered what Henshawe would say. He knew what Henshawe would say.

He took the £250.

As he set out on the last stage of the journey home, his mind returned to the familiar devils, those which had occupied so large a part of his waking thoughts during the last week. He had not seen Elizabeth since his visit to her that night. He could not evaluate his own feelings yet and did not know hers. The only ones he was sure of were Demelza's, and as he neared home he knew that some personal decisions had to be made and faced quickly if his own attitude was not to go by default. But how could he explain or justify what he did not understand himself?

Ever since he left Elizabeth in the early hours of the morning he had been tormented with new problems. What he had done had brought Elizabeth very much down into the arena. That might have simplified everything. In fact, he found it had not. All his old values had been overthrown and he found himself groping for new ones. As yet they were not to be discovered.

This might have been a useful corrective had he supposed himself to be finding a solution when he broke into Trenwith House six nights ago, but in fact the thing had blown up like a squall in his brain; there had been no time for calculated motives or reasoned intentions. Reason came after and reason was still out of its depth.

When he got home, Demelza was out. She had been out all day, Jane Gimlett said in a peculiar voice. Ross had his supper alone, and then when the sun set he asked which way she had gone, and Jane said across Hendrawna Beach. He went to see if there was any sign of her.

It was a good two miles to the Dark Cliffs on the other side. The tide was high, and in the orange afterglow the sea had become an unusual willow-pattern blue, so full, so overflowing, that it looked as if the land would never contain it. Halfway across he saw her coming. She was walking slowly, stopping now and then to examine some offering of the tide or stir a pile of seaweed with her foot. She was in an old dimity frock, and her hair was beginning to curl as if it had been wet. He remembered there had been a heavy shower not long since.

He had to wait some time before she came up with him. At length they were within speaking distance, and she smiled in a brilliant brittle fashion.

'Why, Ross, how kind of you to come and meet me! Have you had a pleasant week end? Did it come up to expectations? Mine did not. I went to the Bodrugans, but 'twas nothing in my line so I left early. Have you had supper? Yes, I suppose you have. Jane will have seen to that. Jane's a rare good seer-to-things. I have been a long walk, miles beyond the Dark Cliffs. There's other sandy coves beyond there, but none with any deep water so I suppose they're no use to Mr Trencrom. Now——'

'They're no use to Mr Trencrom,' he said. 'You're wet.' He touched her arm, and noticed how she shrank away at his touch. 'That shower. You'll be taking a chill in the evening air.'

'How thoughtful of you to think of it! But 'twas only a surface wetting. I have been wetter than that today. One of the little beaches was so pretty that I swam in the sea. There was no one to observe but the choughs. And how is Elizabeth? Is she still to wed George or have you fixed another arrangement? I do not suppose she meant seriously to marry him, do you?'

'I haven't seen Elizabeth this week end,' he said quietly enough but the muscles tight in his cheek.

'Was there some hitch at the last moment? I thought 'twas all arranged.'

'I was at Looe,' he said, 'with Tonkin and Blewett. I don't lie to you, Demelza. When I go to Elizabeth, I will tell you of it.'

'Oh, but does that not constrain you unfairly, Ross? Might it not be thought even a little pompous? To have to tell one's wife every time one intends to visit one's mistress. . . . Is it not making a burden of one's enjoyments——'

'No doubt you feel entitled to these pleasantries. No doubt you are. Tell me when you have done, and then we can talk.'

'No, Ross; you tell me when *you* have done. Isn't that the way it should be?'

They faced each other. At that moment she hated him deeply – as she had done all week end – so *much* more deeply because she knew she was bound to him by apparently unbreakable chains, which he it seemed could cast aside at will; because she had discovered it at great personal humiliation to herself – greater than she had ever imagined possible.

Ever since her escape from Werry House with its valise-burdened five-mile trek across broken country in the dark; the desperate haste to be home before daylight to be spared the final humiliation; the bruised knees and scratched hands of her climb made worse at every gate and hedge – ever since then the knife had been in her, turning hourly, the *awful* degradation of her struggle with McNeil, the *utter* disgrace of her flight. Had she yielded to McNeil, she would not have felt one quarter as bad, not one tenth as bad.

Ross's adventures might have wounded her desperately, but the result of her own was not so much a wound as a goad.

Knowing nothing of this, he was taken aback by the hostility in her eyes, especially because it had not been present – or not so noticeably present – after his return from Elizabeth.

He said: 'You still think I've been at Trenwith this week end. I haven't. I never had an intention of going.'

'You must do what you think best, Ross,' she said. 'Go and live with her if you want to.'

They began to walk again. A shag flew across the surface of the brimming sea so close that it might have been skating on it.

Ross said: 'It is quite possible that Elizabeth's marriage to George will still take place.'

'Well, I'm sure you did your best to stop it.'

'No doubt I did.'

She said: 'Does she love George, then?'

'No.'

She perceived suddenly that not she alone was in torment.

'Did any good come of your visit to Looe?'

'Blewett has paid back what he owes.'

'What shall you do with it?'

'It is enough to restart the mine.'

She laughed. That startled him too, for it was not a winning laugh. He had never heard or seen her like this before.

'I can think of no better way to use the money. It is not enough by itself to discharge our liabilities.'

She would not answer.

'Oh, I know this mining is some taint in the blood, inherited, a fever. I shall make the excuse that I am doing it for Henshawe's sake, but it is not true. I do it for my own sake. If I did not do that, I should go to the war; and at the moment I have no special wish for that again.'

After a while they reached the stile which marked the end of the sand and the beginning of grass and meadow. She went over first. No one would have thought her dependent on anyone. Their words to-night had immeasurably widened the gulf between them. The fact that she had been wrong in supposing him at Trenwith did not seem to carry the weight it should. Acts had been succeeded by principles. Hostility by omission had become hostility by commission. They were both desolate people, needing friendship and sympathy and finding none.

As they reached the garden Demelza said: 'When do you want for me to leave, Ross?'

'Have I said that I wanted you to?'

'No. . . . But I thought 'twould be better for you – for us both. I can find work easy.'

'And Jeremy?'

'Jane can see for Jeremy, for the time being anyhow.'

'Do you want to leave?'

'I – think so. I want to do what's right.'

There was silence for a minute or two. He tapped some mud from his boot, his face half turned from her.

'God *knows* what's right, Demelza. And I don't believe there's anything to be gained by trying to do the right thing or the wrong thing in a situation such as this. We can only follow our own feelings so far as they lead and judge from day to day. I don't want you to leave if you're willing to stay.'

They had reached the door. She put her hand against the jamb, suddenly very tired. It was a long time since she had eaten.

'I'd like you to stay,' he said. 'That's if you feel you can.'

'Very well. It's as you wish. But what I said about you going to live with Elizabeth – please do that if you want. George can't marry her if you're there.'

He didn't speak.

'When will you know?' she asked.

'What?'

'About George and Elizabeth's marriage.'

'I can't tell. . . . We'll hear.'

'She didn't promise to let you know?'

'She didn't.'

It was going dusk. The afterglow had ended. Demelza stared out over her garden. A bat flitted before the fading face of the sky. A hundred times before she had taken a last look here before going in. But never like this. She had never thought it would be like this. The garden was nothing to her any more. Let it run to waste and let the giant weeds grow. It would match the desolation in her soul.

An hour before this George had come in haste to see Elizabeth.

He said: 'When I had your letter, I came straight away, Elizabeth. I knew if I didn't see you to-night I should not sleep. What's the meaning of it? I can make neither head nor tail of your reasons. Explain what it is that is troubling you.'

He spoke more sharply than he had ever done before to her, but she was far too caught up with her own feelings to notice it.

'All this week, George, I have been thinking, worrying. It seemed – somehow it came home to me that I was plunging into this marriage without due respect for Francis' memory. It isn't yet twelve months. Dear George, please try to appreciate my feelings. I've no one to advise me. I—— To be married in secret – oh, I know it was my own request – but in such haste does not look seemly. All this week I have been turning it over in my mind, and at last I plucked up courage to write to you——'

'Three days before the wedding——'

'It is only a *postponement*. Perhaps two months – or even six weeks – and I should feel better about it. I don't somehow feel I can go into it with relish so soon. People will say that I have married you for your money and——'

'People will talk if you sit all day by your own fireside. They concern me no more than the gnats on a summer pond. What is your real reason for asking a delay?'

Elizabeth's troubled eyes widened. She looked very lovely in her white dress against the dark wainscot of the room. 'I have given my reasons. Aren't they sufficient?'

He smiled. 'No, they are not.'

She made a little gesture of helplessness. 'I have no others, George; but they're sincere. Will you not humour me?'

'All the guests are invited.'

'Guests? But we agreed there were to be none! This was to be an entirely private wedding.'

'And so it is. A few of my closest friends would be hurt if they didn't come to the house afterward. I have had to notify them. I am proud, so proud of my bride. I would have asked five hundred if it had been left to me.'

'How many are there? What number have you asked?

'Oh . . . about twenty-five.'

From the way he spoke she knew it was more. She bit her lip. 'I feel so ashamed to be asking for a postponement; but . . .'

'But what?'

'I have promised to marry you, George, and I'll try not to go back on that promise. But it would – somehow, I feel it would not be fair to you – to either of us – to marry in such haste.'

He watched her with his careful, possessive eyes. She was more nervous than he had ever seen her, fine-strung; her eyes did not meet his but went anywhere about the room.

'Is it something to do with Ross?'

She instantly flushed. The colour came almost before he had stopped speaking. 'It is nothing to do with *anyone* but myself. That day you asked me – at Cusgarne – I was so beset with worry, not able to see which way to turn. I said I would marry you——'

'You regret it?'

Her head went up. 'Not in the very least. But time then seemed unimportant——'

'So it is.'

'Not altogether. I was forgetting Francis. It's only right to allow a decent interval to pass.'

'Many marry after three months – some less. You know that, my dear. No one would think anything of it at all. Ross has been here, hasn't he?'

'He came, of course.'

'You quarrelled?'

'. . . In a way.'

'He naturally does not like the idea of our marriage.'

'No.'

'And he is at the bottom of this change of heart on your part.'

She hesitated. George had so exactly stated the truth that she didn't know how to answer.

'Please. I don't want to discuss Ross. What we decide, you and I, is quite our own concern. I've asked as a great favour, George, that you would postpone the wedding. When I wrote you, I did not know it would inconvenience you so much, because of the guests. But I still request it. Believe me, I don't ask lightly or capriciously. It is a – a feeling I have.' She touched her breast. 'Please don't be angry with me. I – can't stand that. . . .'

George's fingers moved round the knob on the end of his stick. He was disappointed, angry, suspicious, and jealous. But fortunately he did not suspect the truth. He was jealous of Ross's influence and bitterly resentful of it, that was all. Thanks to Ross, thanks to something he had said or done, the prize that he, George, had coveted for so many years had slipped a little out of his grasp. No money could buy it, no power obtain it. At present he had no control over it at all. He must go carefully, walk gingerly, lest it slip away altogether.

He said: 'I want to be indulgent to your wishes both before and after marriage, my dear. It's a *bitter* disappointment to me. When I read your letter, I could hardly believe it true. I have the licence, the ring, the . . . But whatever you wish in the way of a postponement I will do – if you'll promise one thing.'

'What is that?'

'That you fix another date to-night.'

She hesitated again. Her impulse to postpone had been overwhelming. Whatever else, she was not a liar and a wanton. To go from one man's bed to another in the course of a few days – however disgracefully she had been taken advantage of. . . . Still less could she go from Ross's caresses to George's. Perhaps that was at the root of her feelings. Well now the postponement was achieved. George had given way.

But there was a sting in the tail. To gain her end she must bind herself for the future – to an exact day, not a vague time such as she had promised herself.

'A month from to-day,' he said. 'That's surely a sufficient concession.'

'Oh, no. . . .' She stopped. Did she want and need to marry him or did she not? If she did, she owed him some consideration. But in the meantime, what would Ross do? 'I had thought of August,' she ended lamely. 'That would then be almost the twelve months.'

He shook his head decisively. She knew that shake. It meant business. 'I may have to go away in August. Besides, that would upset other arrangements relating to Cardew – and to your own mother. Whom do you fear?'

'Fear? Why no one.'

'Whose opinion do you fear, then? Ross's?'

'No, no, of course not. It is entirely what I feel myself——'

He took her hand and tried to look into her face again. 'Come, my dear Elizabeth, let's not shy at bogies. And let us compromise in this arrangement so that we may both have something out of it. You disappoint me grievously by wishing to postpone our wedding at all. Give me the consolation of being able to fix it for this day month. I know you are not a changeable-minded woman, and I know you will stick to your word. Let me take something home with me to-night. . . .'

Elizabeth freed her hand, but not ungraciously, and walked to the table, stood turning the leaves of a book with beating heart. If Demelza had been in tribulation this last week, hers had not been much less. She had not seen Ross since the night he had called. In some moods she felt she never wanted to see him again. But those moods were by no means constant.

Not a changeable-minded woman! Was that what George thought her? All, all that had happened was a result of it. If she had not changed her mind, she would have been married to Ross these ten years and neither George nor Demelza would have been anything in their lives. But what had Ross to offer her now? A sudden wicked climbing in at windows, an incursion on her privacy, a violent taking of what was not rightly his. Demelza lived and would live. They had no money to run away. Ross had not proposed it. He had not even been near her since. That was the crowning insult.

'I know you will stick to your word,' George had said. 'I do not go back on my promises,' she had said to Ross that night. Were these things true? Yes, but the whole purpose of this postponement was that she should have time to think, to consider, and perhaps leave others with time to consider too. What was the good of time if she was bound at the end of it?

He had come up behind her. So far he had kept his attentions within the strictest confines. A half dozen times he had kissed her cheek; sometimes he held her hand. No more. She was not so foolish as to think him cold because of it. He disciplined himself to meet her varying moods. Only a man of his calibre could do it and she respected him for it. Now he lightly rested his fingers on her shoulder – in such a way as to make it quite clear that she was free to escape. She made no move to escape.

'Can I rely on you, Elizabeth?' he said. 'A month from today?'

'Very well,' she said. 'A month from today.'

At that he put his lips on her neck. She thought: other lips have been there. God, I am in a cage! Lost for ever! Why did Ross have to come? How I *hate* him for coming. And despise him. There'll *never* be any friendship between us again. Only *enmity*. I shall be George's heart and soul, his faithful wife and faithful friend. *Anything* I can do against Ross. *Why* did he have to come? God, I am in a cage. Lost for ever.

Book four

Chapter one

ELIZABETH AND GEORGE were married on the twentieth June. Contrary to her wishes, a big reception was held at Cardew at which more than a hundred guests were present. This had been George's intention all along. The bride and groom went away for their honeymoon and did not return to the county until late August. Then they took up residence at Cardew. Elizabeth found that Nicholas Warleggan and his wife had not yet moved out, which according to George they had promised to do, but which, also according to George, they were still preparing to do.

Cusgarne was sold and Elizabeth's father and mother moved to Trenwith, where two elderly gentlefolk and a number of servants were engaged to look after them. George wanted to have Aunt Agatha turned out so that Ross would be forced to look after her; but Elizabeth would have none of that and Aunt Agatha stayed.

Sale of the headgear of Wheal Grace mine was countermanded, and work rebegun on the fourth June. By July the debris was cleared and the lode was being worked again. Among the first miners to go down were Ellery and young Nanfan. The money ran out, but Ross borrowed another £50 from Blewett and then another £50, and that saw them through.

Life at Nampara moved on with the change of the seasons. The hay was gathered and ricked. The wheat and the barley turned from green to yellow, and deepened and grew ripe. This year they had sown close down to the back of the house, and the stalks whispered together all day long. Even when the sea roared you could still hear the other sibilant voice close at hand.

The Allied armies had still not taken Paris, and now it looked as if the opportunity had passed for yet another year. Perhaps it had passed for longer than that, for the latent energies of the revolution were at last beginning to work. General Custine had been thrown to the guillotine for the crime of being unsuccessful, and an unknown Burgundian, Lazare Carnot, had been appointed to organize victory. His first decree was a *levée en masse*, calling all Frenchmen to the colours and marshalling the services of France down to the last woman and child. It was a new conception of war, or an old conception revived, reversing the civilizing influences of a thousand years.

There had been no proper reconciliation between Ross and Demelza. Sometimes she wished she had left. Sometimes she thought of it even now. Yet she couldn't be sure of what he was feeling. Elizabeth was married to George. The thing had gone through in spite of his intervention. Therefore unless he was prepared to take Elizabeth from Cardew by force he had nothing to hope for from her. Therefore he would stay at Nampara married to Demelza. If she was prepared to be content with second best, then she could be of service to him.

But was she content with second best? Sometimes she thought yes, often emphatically no. Still the goad of her refusal of Malcolm McNeil worked in her. She, Demelza Poldark, had proved herself to be chaste and virtuous, that was what almost killed her. She had given up praying to die, but only just. The next time she met Sir Hugh Bodrugan he had questioned her peevishly on what had happened, and she had lied to him, telling him she never intended to stay the night and had slipped away soon after the end seeing him surrounded by friends and not wishing to intrude. She prayed that she would never meet McNeil again. That would be the crowning horror.

Ross still slept downstairs. He had never made any attempt to resume a normal relationship with her, and this was a second alienating influence – even though she would have refused him if he had made the approach. She supposed him to find her distasteful after the rare and delicate joy of Elizabeth's arms.

So two acids worked, both corroding to her self-respect, both in turn standing in the way of her customary impulses which always were to forgive and forget.

Often he was inscrutable to her, in a way he had never been since their marriage, though some days he was friendly and companionable enough within the limits of ordinary living. When news of Elizabeth's marriage reached them, he did nothing and said nothing unusual; only his face expressed strain for a time, but he changed the subject and did not mention it again.

The mine was his escape from his own thoughts. He buried himself mentally as well as actually, working longer hours than any of the men, and his face grew paler instead of browner with the summer's advance. The uncomfortable hours were in the evening, but usually Demelza contrived to be busy while the long days lasted.

As the nights drew in, the mine began to show a small profit. He worked it over twice with Henshawe to be sure there was no mistake. Henshawe proposed that they should frame the cost book which recorded it. They could none of them expect money back yet, but at this rate they would creep slowly away from the red line. With four months still to go before the next reckoning of Ross's personal account, he estimated that if he could see a hundred pounds clear, or a hundred and twenty, by the end of the year he might somehow, somewhere, scrape together enough to satisfy his creditors for another few months. His unknown well-wisher, being a well-wisher, could hardly foreclose on him for the sake of seventy or eighty pounds.

In September it became known that Mr and Mrs George Warleggan were staying at Trenwith House. This news served to incense Ross more than the news of the wedding, for which he had been in some measure prepared. For two days he contrived to spend all his time out of the house, and at mealtimes it was more than he could do to behave as if life were moving in a normal way. News soon followed that extensive repairs were being undertaken at Trenwith. One could not help but wonder at George's generosity in doing so much for Elizabeth's parents. If he was doing it for them. Both Ross and Demelza wondered, but neither spoke of it to the other. Speculation on such a subject was better not voiced.

Demelza received a letter from Verity.

My Dear Cousin,

Thank you for your warm and Affectionate letter, and for all your Warnings and advice, which, coming from one who used to seek mine, reads a little strange. Howsoever, I fully admit that in respect of Babies your experience has been greater than mine, and I defer to everything you say.

We had a great Scare last week when news spread through the Town that five French Privateers had been sighted, one of them but three miles off the Castlehead. Everyone was in a Consternation, and the Iris, Captain Soames, the Barbadoes Packet, which had just sailed, had a near escape of being taken. However, he put back in time, and an Officer was sent hot to Penzance to deliver a message by swift Cutter to Admiral Bell, who was cruising off Scilly. There is no doubt that he would have intercepted the Privateers, but a thick sea-mist came down a few hours later to Blanket our sight and theirs. Much Qui Vive all night lest the Privateers should take advantage of the Fog; but they did not and when morning came the Horizon was clear. But it has given us all, I believe, a salutary shock.

I hope Ross is prospering. I need hardly be told the effect Elizabeth's marriage to George Warleggan will have had on him, and now that they are coming to live beside you it will be an added Offence. Pray be patient with Ross at this time. I have not seen Elizabeth since the day of the wedding, but have had one letter from her. We went, of course, to the wedding, Andrew and I; for Elizabeth's sake we could not well refuse; she had Few enough of her own people about her. From the start I do not think I liked greatly the thought of this Union. I have no feud such as Ross has to support me, and I have nothing against the Warleggans because they are new rich. Most of our aristocratic families were founded by successful traders at one time or another. But George has never quite carried his money Rightly. None of them do, and when you see them in Aggragate, it is specially noticeable.

The wedding was a very brilliant Affair; St Mary's Church decked with lilies regardless of cost, a splendid Crimson Awning outside, and crimson carpet all the way up the aisle to walk on. The Rev Dr Halse performed the ceremony, and he used just the same voice that he uses on the Bench for malifactors. You will want to know what Elizabeth wore. Well it was a gown of heavy cream satin, with a crepe train decorated with small bouquets of white and purple lilac and a wide sash with a thick silver fringe. She told me afterwards when I admired it that it took twenty-six yards of material. Old Jonathan must have had a long stocking somewhere. But you will know without me to tell you that she looked very beautiful in it – like a queen – yet narvous, ill at ease, inclined to flush up and go pale at the least thing. George of course uas unruffled by anything, even when his great friend Paul Boscoigne dropt the ring; he was very swart in a rich gold-laced coat and a scarlet waistcoat with broad gold lace.

Andrew is due home on Wednesday. Only one packet, the Trefusis, *has had trouble as yet – what can a single ship do if she finds herself attacked by five? I ask myself that sometimes, in the night.*

Is it true, do you know, that Elizabeth is with child? She makes no mention of it in her letter, but Mrs Daubuz tells me that her mother had been saying so. It will be strange to have a family of Warleggans founded in the home of the Poldarks.

My dearest love to you both, and a special hug for Jeremy.

> *Your loving cousin,*
> *Verity*

Demelza did not show this letter to Ross. She had her own reflections on parts of it, but she thought it better he should not share them. As it happened he came home that day more than ever preoccupied, though earlier than usual. It was Lobb's day, but he did not even ask if there were any letters. Demelza began to feel she could not stand his silences much longer. They dined in silence and Jane cleared in silence. Demelza stuck on, determined not to be frozen out and more and more certain that a conflict must come. At length, her heart swelling, she said suddenly:

'Ross, if this is to go on you will have to eat alone. For days now you have scarce spoken and to-day has been the worst of all. I know why you are like this and cannot help you to a solution. Perhaps there is no solution any more. But there can be one for us. If I stay, if you want me to stay, then let us behave like human beings. But if you want for me to go, then say so, for go I shall if this be the way you expect us to live.'

Ross looked up, and the surprise in his face was a surprise to her. 'Has it been as bad as that?' He laughed. She did not remember when he had laughed before. 'I'm – sorry. I hadn't realized. I should explain——'

'Is that necessary?'

'Very necessary, considering I have not been thinking about Elizabeth and George this evening at all.'

She stared at him. 'Is there some other bad thing then?'

'No, good rather. I was hesitating yet whether to say anything of it because so often before. . . . I hadn't realized my face naturally set into such morose lines that——'

'What good thing?'

'But of course you're right – I have been in a mood all this week, and for that I . . . My feeling about Elizabeth's marriage need not be gone into now. That's something I've had to think out – fight out in my own way. But George's coming to stay at Trenwith and showing signs of remaining, that's a – a crowning indecency. Trenwith is part of the Poldark family. It is our *home*, if you understand. I cannot accustom myself at all to the idea of its belonging to George. I really can't, Demelza. It's – unnatural, a monstrous perversion of the right – or so it seems to me. That has been my trouble all this week. But to-day. . . .'

'To-day?'

'It is the mine. I thought it wiser not to tell you as yet. I have been almost afraid. The lode has split today. One half of it, the best half, is twice the size of the old lode. It appears to be over twelve feet thick. The first assays are very rich too. Henshawe says he has never seen richer ground.'

Demelza felt confused, as if she had braced herself to fight something that wasn't there. 'But – why not tell me? Why sit there. . . .'

'I'm *sorry*. I was so preoccupied, calculating. . . . Why not tell you? Because we've grasped at so many false hopes. I can't help having them, but I thought of saving you.'

'That I b'lieve is something you need not save me from. But will it mean so much? The mine is already paying its way, you said.'

He stared back at her and his face was no longer set in the old lines. She perceived that she had mistaken the tensions behind it.

'Let's wait,' he said. 'Let's hatch the chickens first.'

They waited. Ross kept his head down and would not allow his thoughts to progress beyond the day's work. Only Henshawe, with his more detached mind – having so much less at stake – would allow himself a jubilant tone. After another week Ross told Demelza that she need not worry about a debt settlement at Christmas. One month's work at this rate would pay all the interest. Two months would see part of the debt gone. They could already see two months ahead.

Demelza said: 'Do you mean – in any case?'

'In any case. The assay is as rich as the ground. It can't help but pay. There's little skill now in this part. We just have to get it up and dress it and sell it.'

'I can't hardly believe that.'

'No more can I.'

The flaw for them both was that success had been too long in coming. This venture had raised so many hopes before and then dashed them. It no longer seemed entitled to become a valuable property. Had mineral been found eleven months ago, it could have saved them dramatically from immediate bankruptcy. Thirteen months ago it would have saved Francis' life. Now, when hope deferred had made the heart sick, when everyone had grown past the stage of expecting anything any more, when bankruptcy was not quite so immediate a danger – though still existent – when a bare living from it was as much as anyone felt entitled to expect, now suddenly it began to give off riches.

Riches. That was the queer thing. Not just an income, not just a business return, but riches. This was quite different from Wheal Leisure, where cost books were still balanced and profits still calculated. The profits were here in lump sums. The money was here in lump sums. The gamble had come off. Ross felt he had to handle the coin sometimes. It was all very well to accept tin cheques and the rest, but gold and silver in bags was what he needed.

He also needed Demelza to help him savour it, for success after long tribulation can only be fully enjoyed if it is shared. They tried conscientiously to share it; but in that they failed. The division between them was too deep.

In late October, Dwight received a letter from Dr Matthew Sylvane of Penryn. It ran:

Sir,

One of my patients, Mr Ray Penvenen, of Killewarren, near Chasewater, has for some weeks been suffering from a wasting condition which has not responded to accepted medical treatment. After due consideration I have thought it desirable to have a Second Opinion, and Mr Penvenen has mentioned your name as a physician with some former knowledge of his physical condition.

Should you be willing to be called in Consultation, I suggest that you meet me at his house on Friday the Eighteenth at or about Five o'clock, when we can discuss the Symptoms privately before proceeding to examine the Patient.

Perhaps you will favour me with a Reply by the hand of my groom who has instructions to wait.

> *I am, sir, your obedient servant,*
> *M. Sylvane*

Dwight wanted to send word that Mr Penvenen could turn yellow and rot before he would enter his house again; but after a struggle he replied accepting the invitation. He had never met Matthew Sylvane, but knew of him as a man with small private means, like Choake, who practised among the gentry. At ten minutes to five Dwight rode in at the gates of Killewarren. Such a pang at the mere entrance, the gate posts, the droop of the pine trees, the long thatched house, even the servant who came to the door . . .

Dr Sylvane was in the big upstairs parlour over the stables. He was a narrow adenoidal man of forty-five or so who seemed to do nothing without the help of his nose. Dwight would have preferred to see Mr Penvenen first, but Sylvane was having none of that nonsense. The young fellow must enter the sickroom armed with the theories and observations of an experienced apothecary. Mr P. had gone down in the first place about ten weeks ago with what was clearly a spasm of the common gall duct, creating a low fever and slowing the circulation of the blood, dissolving the tissues and affecting the elasticity of the fibres. From that a wasting and possibly tumorous condition had sprung. The primary symptoms had given way to treatment: a little bleeding and a suitable draught: salt of wormwood and ammoniac, ginger powder, sugar candy, oil of cloves; jellies and broths to eat, beef teas, minced veal. No fish. Fish in this close weather smelled very quickly; Dr Sylvane was against giving it to sick people who smelt already.

But Mr P. had never lost his appetite. When the fever was brought off, he began to eat like a horse – still did. And white wine. Down it went, bottle after bottle, quite astonishing. There was slight pulmonary congestion of an edematous nature, and plenitude of urine; not surprising really. Bleedings, blisters, potions, he'd tried 'em all; but the patient remained very inert and was losing strength. A second opinion was really unnecessary, but sometimes a confirmatory diagnosis gave the patient confidence. . . .

Scarcely listening, his mind on earlier visits, Dwight followed his colleague along the passage to Mr Penvenen's bedroom. It was all horribly reminiscent. But his memories left him when he saw Ray Penvenen in bed, crouching like an injured weasel, grey-faced and dry. He had never been handsome but now . . . The skin was in folds upon his face and hands.

As Dwight came up to the bed, Penvenen said in his precise voice: 'I do not believe we parted very good friends, Dr Enys. I am the more obliged to you therefore for coming.'

Dwight bowed slightly but didn't speak. The man should have his attention but nothing more.

'I insisted on its being you, in spite of your youth, because I believe you have the courage not to be influenced by what other people say. Dr Sylvane has done his best, but his best does not appear to be good enough——'

'Well, Mr Penvenen, what I have done——'

'It is the first time for a great many years, Dr Enys, that I have been really sick. I have a feeling that unless something is quickly done it will be the last.'

'I trust not.' With a stiff face Dwight bent to examine him.

Certain symptoms at once. 'There's no fever now, Dr Sylvane.' 'No. as I told you, it has responded to treatment.' 'It did so nine weeks ago, Dr Enys. I have never had none since.' That acetose smell on the breath. He was almost too weak to turn himself. 'You drink a great deal, Mr Penvenen?'

'To excess. Nothing strong; a light canary.' 'Water?' 'Yes, even water sometimes.' 'And eat? 'And eat. Enough for four, yet I have become as thin as a shotten herring. Hitherto I have thought the gluttony of my neighbours a trifle disgusting.'

After a thorough examination Dwight allowed the curtain of the bed to fall and walked to the window. No Caroline to-day in her black riding habit and her flame-coloured hair. No little yapping pug. No Unwin Trevaunance with his great lion head. Only a sick man, sick to death.

'I have also considered,' said Dr Sylvane, following him nasally, 'the possibility of a cestoid worm in the alimentary canal. This ravening hunger. But I have examined the stools and have been unable to find any evidence——'

'And the urine?'

'Unusually sweet to the taste. But with all that unfermented wine. . . . Then again I have considered a tuberculous infection of an atmospheric-cosmic-telluric nature induced by the moist heavy weather in a county teeming with metals and minerals. There's a natural malignancy to the mineral effluvia, and folk here are hectic and consumptive at the best of times. Do you know, sir, it is fortunate there are few large towns in this county. Do you know, sir, that three thousand men living within an acre of ordinary ground make an atmosphere of their own steams seventy-one feet high. How much more dangerous then in a county——'

'It is surely the sugar sickness,' said Dwight.

'Ah?' Sylvane breathed out through his nose, a thin reedy sound. 'Ah.'

'A man – I've forgotten his name – Willis was it – years ago. And more recently. . . . And all these other symptoms, the hunger, the wasting, the sour breath——'

'Polydypsia,' said Sylvane warily. 'I had thought of it. It could be considered; but there are contradictory indications. The fever——'

'There has been no fever for nine weeks, he says. I believe it to be a mistake to consider it as a symptom now.'

'There is a gouty condition. And the pulmonary congestion——'

'Very typical and very dangerous.'

'I have not found it so.'

Dr Sylvane squinted suspiciously along his nose at Dwight, but Dwight was not giving way. 'I believe there is no other diagnosis.'

'Mr P. is fifty-seven. So sudden an onset in a man of his age . . .'

'It does occur. Anyway, that is my belief.'

'You cannot intend to tell him your views. It will be a serious shock. I'll not be answerable for the consequences.'

'I'll not be answerable if he goes on as he is.'

'How else can he go on? You do not suppose he will recover if that is his complaint!'

They talked for a few minutes in low tones, then Dwight turned back to the bed. Ray Penvenen watched his approach with red-rimmed eyes.

'Well, Dr Enys, is it to be the knife?'

'No, sir, no knife. I think possibly we can do something for you. And you can help yourself.'

'How?'

'By giving up most of the things you eat and drink. The wine especially.'

'But that is the only thing which relieves me! How shall I quench my thirst?'

'By cold water and some dilute milk. And you must eat very much less. I would urge the strictest possible diet. It will not be an easy treatment, for I know how hungry you will be.'

'You don't know how hungry I'll be for you've never felt as I feel! It's very well to prescribe these things. D'you mean I am to starve?'

'Not starve, though it may well seem like it. I'd also suggest warm baths and a greater amount of air in your room.'

Dr Sylvane was heard to mutter something under his breath, but when Mr Penvenen glanced up at him he was sniffing the perforated end of his gold-headed cane.

'You don't agree with this treatment, Dr Sylvane?'

Sylvane shrugged. 'We have talked over it at length, and I regret to differ from a colleague – but I positively cannot accept responsibility for a lowering treatment on one in such a weakened condition as yourself.'

'I am in an extremely weakened condition,' said Mr Penvenen, 'in consequence of twelve weeks' illness and ten weeks of your treatment of me. That suggests I am in need of a change of treatment. Can you cure me, young man?'

'No, sir.'

Mr Penvenen blinked and passed a tongue over his lips. After a moment he said: 'Well, that's honest anyway.' He motioned to his servant, who was standing by the bed, to pour him another glass of wine from the decanter. Then with a continuing gesture he stopped him. 'On second thoughts no, Jonas. The doctor advises me to take water.'

Chapter two

Dwight HAD NO patience with the view that because raw meat turned putrid when exposed to the air human beings necessarily did the same. And he was as much a crank in matters of food and drink. Fasting and fresh air had done good in several cases of bilious fever and the tertian ague, and he had tried a similar treatment on Charlie Kempthorne with his consumption of the lungs. Miraculously it had worked on him. Not on many others, but one success was something in a disease notoriously fatal. Then he had experimented with gout, to the annoyance of his few substantial patients.

Now Mr Penvenen. As a physic he prescribed Theban opium after each meal. It was all a shot in the dark and likely to kill or cure.

Mr Penvenen began to come round.

On his fifth visit he found his patient sitting up in a chair muffled in rugs and cloaks before a window open more than half an inch to the mild afternoon. After the usual examination Mr Penvenen said dryly:

'You said you could not cure me, Dr Enys, but you seem well on the way to having me out and about again. I'm very much in your debt.'

'It is partly your own doing.' Dwight had never unbent in his attitude. 'Without your will to deny yourself. . . .'

'The effort has been considerable. How much longer am I to deprive myself of the ordinary pleasures of life?'

'If by ordinary pleasures you mean ordinary food and drink, I should say for many months yet. Perhaps for the rest of your life.'

'And how long is that likely to be?'

'I can't tell you. Provided you take care of yourself, there is no reason why it should be short.'

Silence fell between them. Dwight took out his pulse watch, but Penvenen said:

'I trust you now feel able to overlook the unfortunate circumstances which attended my niece Caroline's last visit. No one regretted the situation more than I, or the measures it was necessary for me to take. Now that it is all past, I should like to assume that I may call on you when necessary; and perhaps sometime you will favour me with a social visit when we may dine together – assuming of course that your own diet will not be as strict as mine.'

It was a gesture of friendship, or as near as Ray Penvenen could get to making one. Dwight didn't answer. Penvenen went on:

'Perhaps I should tell you before you answer that Caroline will shortly be announcing her engagement to Lord Coniston, the eldest son of the Earl of Windermere. I hope the information will not now distress you.'

'I congratulate her,' said Dwight.

'Thank you. She was clearly predestined for such a match, and I should have been failing in my duty as her guardian if I had not prevented an unsuitable attachment from developing. I hope you understand it was no reflection on your personal capacities or that it showed a lack of esteem for them on my part.'

'Yes, I understand.' Dwight put his watch away. He did not know his patient's heartbeats and he didn't care. He went across the room and stood by the fire. 'When is the wedding to take place?'

'My sister does not say. I don't believe anything has been fixed yet. Caroline hasn't been well and that——'

'Not well?'

'One of the customary summer indispositions. She's quite recovered. But the wedding is not likely to be until after Christmas.'

'Will you give my wishes to Miss Penvenen. I'm sure it will be an entirely – suitable match.'

Dwight didn't deceive himself, but he evidently deceived Mr Penvenen.

'I'm glad you feel as you do about it. That is the attitude of a generous man. I was sure I could rely upon your good sense and understanding.'

Dwight felt like asserting that no one could rely upon either. 'Continue with the physic,' he said quietly. 'A little more exercise when you feel like it; but no overexertion. I'll be in again on Wednesday morning.'

He was going to leave then, but the older man said tentatively: 'I – hope I shall be well enough to travel up to London after Christmas. There is business I should attend to as well as the more social purposes.'

'We must see how you progress,' Dwight said.

He did not suppose that his patient's improvement would be maintained at its present rate. If his diagnosis was correct, there was nothing whatever he could do which would affect the underlying disease. However, there was no point in telling Penvenen so, and one never knew with the human constitution. Obviously the prospect of seeing his niece married into the nobility would be the strongest possible stimulus.

Verity had her child on All Hallows E'en, a boy of seven pounds, and both were well. He was called Andrew after his father, and Ross and Demelza went for the christening. Because there was a Coinage due that week, Ross rode there and back in the day; but Demelza stayed four days. She felt better then than she had done since May, and Verity's happiness was reflected in her. She was taken aboard Andrew Blamey's ship and went a trip up the river and to a reception in the town. She said nothing at all of her own trouble to Verity. For the first time this was something she could not discuss even with her. In any case she could not say anything without telling of things which she hoped nobody but herself and Ross and Elizabeth would ever know. With George and Elizabeth now so close, it seemed more than ever important to be absolutely silent about the events of the ninth of May.

The day after she returned home Ross received a note from George.

Dear Poldark,

As you are a trustee of Francis' estate, certain formalities cannot be gone through without your signature. Since June nothing whatever has been done, and it therefore seems necessary that we should meet. If you will come to Trenwith on Friday or Saturday morning next, I shall be there to receive you.

Yours etc.,
G. Warleggan

Ross replied:

Dear Warleggan,

As you are not a trustee of Francis' estate, I do not consider that the business concerns you. If you wish to see me on any other matter, I shall be at Nampara on Friday or Saturday morning next.

Yours etc.,
R. V. Poldark

George replied:

Dear Poldark,

It may have come to your notice that Elizabeth and I were married in June. In attending to Francis' estate I am only trying to take the burden off her shoulders. She has not been well this month, and it would be more convenient for her to meet you here. Perhaps you will let me know a time suitable to yourself.

Yours etc.,
G. Warleggan

Ross wrote that he would call on Saturday at noon.

As soon as he came inside the gates he saw the difference. In less than three months money had worked miracles. The undergrowth of ten years had been cleared, the hedges clipped, the unnecessary trees cut down, specimen trees newly planted; the pond had become a lake and bobbled with fish, flower borders were laid out and a few late flowers were still in bloom. Fat cattle grazed on the other side of the lake. Fresh gravel had been laid on the paths before the house.

When he went in, he saw that the great window of the hall had been repaired and long crimson satin curtains fitted. New rugs were laid, new hangings on the walls. Many of the old cracked portraits had been put away, and in the big parlour where he was shown by a liveried footman – no hasty, aproned Mrs Tabb – all had been changed. Even Elizabeth's spinning wheel and harp had disappeared.

No one was in the room, and he was allowed to wait ten minutes tapping impatiently at his boot before George came in followed by a tall, thin man with narrow shoulders and eyes too close together. George was in a fine buff-coloured suit with darker buff nankeen trousers. Then another, older man entered. Jonathan Chynoweth, Elizabeth's father.

They bade good day to each other distantly. George said: 'This is Mr Tankard, my attorney. You know Mr Chynoweth, of course. We need not take much of your time. Several papers have to be signed. Then you can go.'

'Where is Elizabeth?'

'Resting. We can complete the business without her.'

'I don't think so. She is the cotrustee of Francis' estate. I shall do nothing without her presence.'

'We anticipated that,' said George pleasantly. 'She has signed a power of attorney, so that I can act for her in these matters. Show the document to Mr Poldark, Tankard.'

Ross fingered the parchment, vaguely suspecting a sharp practice but unversed in law. He turned to Mr Chynoweth.

'It is true, my dear boy. There is nothing underhand about it, I assure you. I think you can acquit me of being party to any – hm – dubious expedient.'

'If you wish to know the truth,' said George, 'though it will not pleasure you, Elizabeth especially asked that I should do this on her behalf so that she shouldn't have to meet you. Her health is not perfect at the moment, but she is fully capable of transacting any business she wishes to transact. She wants to have nothing to do with you, so I'm helping her to avoid a meeting which would be distasteful.'

Ross returned the document to Tankard, who put it crackling back into his brief case. 'Is it true that she is with child?'

Tankard's head came up. George said: 'It is true. What is it to you?'

Ross shrugged. 'Let us get on with the business.'

There were various papers to discuss and sign. He had no intention of being amenable to their plans, but in fact there was little to query. Mr Chynoweth did not speak again but watched it all, fingering his thin little beard. George was honest enough in his day-to-day transactions. But when it was all done, Tankard said:

'Er, Mr Poldark, these shares, this half share in Wheal Grace – held on behalf of Mrs Warleggan's son – which was disposed of at the beginning of the year for a sum of six hundred pounds. Can you tell us how it came about? The transaction seems to have been irregular, and we are not satisfied that it was legal.'

'It was legal.'

'Well, sir, we have applied to Mr Harris Pascoe for details of the arrangement, but he tells us he is not at liberty to divulge them. We shall be glad of your explanation.'

'No explanation is necessary. Mrs Poldark – Mrs Warleggan received six hundred pounds on behalf of her son for a half share in a worthless mine.'

'Supposedly worthless,' said George. 'Who was so foolish as to pay her that sum?'

Ross put down his pen, dusted sand over the paper, shook it. 'I was.'

There was a moment's silence.

'Ah,' said George. 'I wondered if there was not some such explanation.'

'I understand,' said Tankard, 'that the mine is now into rich country – that it will be very shortly paying a high dividend.'

'It already is paying a high dividend.'

'Ah,' said George again. 'And no doubt at the beginning of the year——'

'I take exception,' Ross said, 'to your suspicions. I take exception to your lack of common intelligence. Good life, d'you suppose that if we had found rich ground in January, we should have waited until November to exploit it?'

'Why did you buy the other half of a worthless mine then?' demanded Tankard.

Ross gave him a look. 'Listen, man, I am not here to be cross-examined by out-at-elbow attorneys. Go back to your law books and speak when you're spoken to.'

Mr Chynoweth drew his spatulate first finger along the polished surface of the table. 'Come, come, I think we're getting a little heated, eh? No need for that, quite uncalled-for I assure you.' He stared at the tip of his finger. There was no dust. 'I don't doubt you had other and good reasons, dear boy. If you care——'

'In January,' said Ross, 'your daughter was in straits for money. I felt responsible for having persuaded Francis to sink his last six hundred pounds in a mine. I wished to give her the money back but knew she wouldn't accept it as a gift. So I devised a means whereby I could do so unknown to her. I thought the mine was a failure. I thought it as late as July.'

'A dubious story,' said George. 'No one——'

'What you think doesn't matter. But don't expect me to listen to your speculations.'

'Wait,' said George, as Ross seemed about to leave. 'I think we must give the devil his due. Eh, father-in-law? On certain conditions I am prepared to accept the explanation. It was a device – as you say – a thought cumbersome, no doubt, but one which would probably appeal to an unbusinesslike mind. Well meant. Eh, father-in-law? But cumbersome. The legality of the arrangement need not be questioned, for its moral aim was good. Indeed one views it as a gesture – a rather overdramatic gesture such as one would have anticipated – but let us accept it and wait for the following gesture which plainly will succeed it.'

Everybody waited as bidden. Mr Chynoweth had not followed George's meaning and blinked in perplexity.

'What following gesture?'

'Why to return the half share of the mine, now that it is successful, into the custody of Geoffrey Charles's trustees.'

Ross took up his gloves. They were still patched. 'Why d'you suppose I should do that?'

'Well, you acted to save Elizabeth in a difficult situation. Now that gesture is no longer appropriate because what you took from her has become worth more than what you gave for it. The situation's quite changed.'

'So have her circumstances.'

'Naturally. With her marriage to me. But in this you were acting for Geoffrey Charles. Francis' son has no claim on my generosity. All he has is a half share in your mine.'

'He *had* such a share. He sold it to me.'

'In fact what happened was that as Geoffrey Charles's trustee you sold this property to yourself.'

'Yes. Thinking it worthless.'

'We have only your word for that. And it's no longer true.'

'Fortunately for me, no.'

'It's obvious therefore that if you truly meant this transaction to be a gesture of friendship and affection in Geoffrey Charles's favour, it must in order to stand as such now be reversed. Otherwise it becomes a sharp practice.'

Ross continued to tap with his gloves. 'What is obvious to you, George, and what is obvious to me are two very different things. As cotrustee with Elizabeth of Geoffrey Charles's affairs, it was my duty to do the best I could for him and for such property as Francis left him. In January of this year I sold his half share in Wheal Grace for £600. That was *more* – far more – than the best I could do. Had the stock come on the open market, he would not have had fifty pounds for it. No; nor ten neither. You wouldn't have given me ten for my half share. The mine was finished. I thought so with the rest. By hook and by crook we kept her working through the summer. After an accident she closed, but we reopened her. And now we have struck tin. Tin when we were looking for copper. But tin in such abundance that it stretches out whichever way we go. Well, so now I deem the profit legitimately mine. I don't consider it belongs to Elizabeth or Geoffrey Charles or to Mr Chynoweth or to you. And if ever you had hopes of jockeying me into thinking otherwise, you'd best give 'em up for they will not benefit you.'

Tankard coughed and blew on his fingers and looked at George. George said:

'Since you've put your case so plainly, we can hardly do less. We shall contest the legality of the sale.'

'On what grounds?'

'You will get that information in due course.'

'I shall be waiting to receive it.'

'In any case, you will not come out of the litigation with a savoury character. A man who cheats his ward.'

'Up to now,' said Ross, 'I have offered you no violence. I don't want to spoil your vulgar new furnishings.'

'You would not,' said George. 'I have three servants within call.'

'Never stir without them,' said Ross.

George flushed. 'Go back to your scullery maid,' he said.

Chapter three

UNLIKE JULIA, JEREMY seldom prospered in his mother's absence, and Demelza returned to find him with a stomach upset. Dwight said Jeremy had a mild colic, and mixed him a sedative draught. When he had done and they went downstairs, Demelza said:

'You will stay to dinner? Ross has gone to Trenwith but will be back soon.'

'To Trenwith?'

'Yes. He is a whatever-they-call-it for Francis' estate and must visit them on some business matter.'

'Oh. . . . I see. Thank you, I'll stay, for I wanted to see you both sometime this week. I wanted you to be the first two to know my plans. I have put in for a post as surgeon in the Navy.'

'Oh.' Demelza stared at him, troubled. 'Is it final? Have you quite decided?'

'Yes, it will be for the best. I have a friend at the Admiralty, Sir Ralph Slessor, who has promised to use his influence. There's no trouble, of course, in getting a ship; but one wishes a good ship.'

'This is the second time you've threatened to leave us, and this time . . . Are you certain sure you are acting for the best?'

'Well, I cannot settle here. I've tried but it is useless. This – war is unsettling for one thing. I'm in a backwater. It is the wrong place for a young man. There's so much experience to be gained elsewhere.'

'Does it mean you must leave us altogether for a term of years, like going to prison; or shall you be able to come out when you are tired of it?'

'It will be for a term, but I've yet to hear how long. They're equipping the old ships as fast as they can press men to serve in them, but it is slow work. They say hardly more than forty thousand have been added since the war began.'

She went to the window and narrowed her eyes at the slanting sun. Sun fell and made luminous patches on her hair.

'And Caroline? Have you heard nothing from her?'

'After Christmas she's marrying Lord Coniston, whoever he may be. Her uncle told me last week.'

She knew now the final causes of his flight, for in a sense a flight it was.

'I'm that sorry – especially for the way it happened. It grieves me that much when I think——'

'Well it grieves me no longer. I am thankful for the escape. . . . Oh, I loved Caroline – still do.' He turned his eyes away from her. 'But we were not for each other.'

'Here is Ross now. 'Tis peculiar that I can tell Darkie's hooves from that of other horses. . . . Dwight, did you not go to see Caroline and explain? Did you not see her in London? I am unhappy to feel that this came about, whether for good or bad, because of what you did to save Ross.'

'No, I think she sensed it long before that, and in that respect I am to blame——'

It was not often that Demelza cried out, but she did so when Ross, leaving his mare to find her own way to the stables, came stooping into the parlour.

He had lost his coat entirely except for one cuff which hung round his wrist. His shirt was split up the back, and he had used his neckerchief to tie up his head. There was blood oozing through the improvised bandage.

'You have an aptitude,' he said to Dwight, 'for being in the right place at the right times.' Then he sat in a chair and so put himself on a level to be examined.

'You fell?' said Demelza. 'Have you broken any bones? How did it—— No, but you did not fall! Ross, who did this? You've been fighting at Trenwith! Oh, your head is so cut. Dwight, I'll get water. . . .'

She flew into the kitchen, and in a moment Jane Gimlett was flying too – for unguents and towels. When Demelza got back, Ross had already begun his explanation.

'– nor was the least thought of it in my mind. But it's no good. Every time I see him – and seeing him in Francis' old home; it has been almost as much my home as this; and his airs. . . . Then when he said that, I could stand it no longer and suddenly the respectable little scene broke up. My, but it did me a world of good! And his parlour——'

'Good!' said Demelza.

'And his parlour is in ruin. We batted to and fro across the room for three or four minutes, with that squint-eyed attorney crouching in a corner and Mr Chynoweth under the table. George is getting soft, I'll swear it; it is this city life or his wedding or something; I have never beaten him so easy before. But then three of his flunkeys came bursting in—— Ach! what are you doing, man?'

'Putting some stitches in your head. You don't want to be scarred this side as well.'

'And then three of his men came in and set on me. It was weighted the other way then, but two of them were puny fellows and had no real stomach for the thing. I threw one of them through the window. Then at the last they got me and threw me out after him. So I whistled for Darkie and she came trotting round. Even then I rode over their new flower beds. This eyetooth is loose; should it come out?'

'No, leave it. The gum is bruised, but the tooth is unbroken.'

'And where was Elizabeth during this?' Demelza asked quietly.

'I didn't see her. She was unwell or unwilling. You'd not believe the difference they have made to the place, with Turkey rugs and brocade curtains and new pieces of furniture. Already it's ceasing to be the home of the Poldarks and becoming the home of the new-rich Warleggans. I was impressed.'

'But what was it started it?' said Demelza. 'How did you come to blows when 'twas to have been just a business meeting and a signing of papers?'

Ross lifted his good eyebrow. 'He made an offensive remark.'

'What did he say?'

'Nothing I should wish to repeat to you.'

'Was it *about* me?' she asked, scenting as much from the expression of his face and thinking instantly of the Bodrugan party.

'It was about nobody I have any connection with.'

'Why then did you take offence over it?'

'Because I chose to.'

They stared at each other, and presently he laughed at her expression. It was as if the fight had done him the good that he claimed. She found herself warming to his attitude of mind.

When dinner was over and Dwight had gone, Ross told her what had passed at the meeting earlier. She was indignant and incredulous.

'I don't know if Elizabeth is party to such a manœuvre,' he said, 'but I must see Pascoe this week to know if the sale was watertight.'

'Not this week,' she said, looking at his head.

'Well, as soon as possible. George is marked too – that's some consolation. Until I see Pascoe, I shall not know what there is to be met.'

'I'm glad at least that you do not intend to return the share to Geoffrey Charles.'

'Well, I do not believe Elizabeth will have neglected Geoffrey Charles in any marriage settlement she has been able to arrange. He is the last person. If I see him short of money when he comes of age, I shall give him a share then. But not until then. I'm not having George with a finger in this pie.'

'I hope this new quarrel will not make things worse betwixt you and George.'

'I wouldn't wish it to improve them.'

'We live too close now for feuds, Ross. You may meet any time, accidental, about other business. Or he may attempt reprisal. Remember Jud. It will not do for you to be out at night alone.'

'Violent solutions seem to be the only ones that come natural to me at present. I'm very sorry, Demelza. It is an uncivilized attitude. But at least I can have no room for complaint if someone fires back.'

She did not reply, and he grimaced as he changed his position.

'You know the big parlour,' he said. 'They have a set of new chairs in there of fine polished – well, mahogany I suppose it would be, with delicate carved backs and satin-covered seats. I am not one with an expert eye for furniture, but they seemed to me as good a sort of work as any I've seen.'

'Oh, yes,' said Demelza.

'A great many things had been done to the room – some good, some bad. They have blue damask curtains with a broad gold fringe, and the new Turkey carpet is very thick, inweft with human figures. There were some considerable number of china ornaments on the mantelshelf – very rare no doubt – but these I did not care for. And they have a great candelabrum of cut glass suspended from the ceiling. And before the door, to shut off the draught, a Chinese screen.'

'You seem to have taken in a very fair number of changes.'

'I was kept waiting ten minutes, which naturally put me in a good mood to begin. One does not realize until one has seen it the variety of things money can buy these days.' He looked around, a man seeing his own house afresh. 'We're poverty-stricken here, aren't we?'

'Yes, I believe so.'

'Well, it need not be quite so much so any longer. What do you say to coming in with me, when I go to see Harris Pascoe, and we could buy a few new things for the house.'

He watched her as he spoke, but as always when the conversation took a personal turn she seemed to draw in from the natural response.

'It is just as you say, Ross. I'll come with you if you want me to.'

'Yes. I want you to.'

'The interest on our debts is due next month.'

'The south lode is twenty-five feet wide and still increasing. Our profit last month was £580. For a month only. If this goes on, we shall have no debts at all.'

Demelza got up, began collecting together the building bricks that Jeremy had left in a corner. 'I still can't hardly believe it.'

'Nor I. I shake myself twice daily. Don't do that, not just now. I saw the look in your eyes when I come in with a bloody head. I believe you still care for me.'

It was the first challenge, the first direct approach.

'Of course I still care for you, Ross. What a thing to say. . . .'

'Then listen to me, please. Tell me what you think we should buy. Women know better than men what are the first essentials. We need so much that I should not know where to begin.'

She came over to him. 'Suppose I make out a list and you take it in.'

'That was not what I suggested.'

'Well, there is so much to see to in the mornings. And Jeremy. . . .'

'That was not what you promised.'

'Well, there's only Darkie.'

'We've shared her before. We can buy a horse for you to return on if you dislike the proximity.'

She smiled, trying to release her hand. 'There are many things we need more badly than a horse. Let me fetch pen and ink.'

'And you'll come with me to get them?'

'Yes, Ross, I said I would. If you want me to.'

A fortnight passed before Ross's head was clear of its plaster, and then they went in together. He went first to see Harris Pascoe, before any purchases or extravagances were begun. Pascoe said:

'Th-they haven't a leg to stand on. The investment was legally transferred. I do not believe a civil court would waste time even on hearing their case; but if they did, there could be only one verdict, in your favour.'

'It may be George was making an idle threat. I thought that, but I came to you for reassurance.'

'You have it. I am sorry this quarrel has broken out afresh, though. With Warleggan your close neighbour on both sides . . . I don't b-believe feuds of this sort ever profited anyone.'

'What do you mean, a neighbour on both sides?'

'It is what I expected, but I don't welcome it all the same. Wheal Leisure is on Treneglos property, but the workings enter my land underground.'
Leisure is on Treneglos property, but the workings enter my land under ground.'

'I should not be astonished if the Warleggans soon gain a controlling part.'

'Well, George may organize his days as he thinks best. I shall seek no brush with him so long as he seeks none with me.'

Ross got up. Demelza was waiting for him in the room outside. He had often promised himself the pleasure of taking her out to spend money as she pleased, but the promise had gone sour with keeping.

'Oh,' he said, turning from the window; 'very soon I shall be able to clear off my debt to the man who saved my skin last Christmas. It's an agreeable thought. You should give me his name now, so that when I do pay him I shall be able to thank him in a suitable fashion.'

Mr Pascoe stroked his pen along the line of his cheek. 'The matter is one of confidence, as you know.'

'Which you are now entitled to break. D'you realize what he did? – but of course you do――'

'Yes, I do――'

'Without his timely help I should be in a debtor's prison with probably little hope of release. The mine would have closed. My wife and son would be paupers. It's no longer a question of confidence, Harris. It's one of common gratitude.'

'Oh, yes, I agree. B-but it does not absolve me——'

'I contend that it does. I owe him virtually everything and would wish to tell him so. What is his name?'

Pascoe wavered. 'I will write and ask his permission.'

'Nonsense. It was not *you* then?'

'It was not I. I said so at the time. I only wish my position would have allowed me——'

'Does he live in Truro?'

'No. In fact . . .'

'In fact what?'

'Well. . . . In fact it was not a man at all.'

'What?' Ross stared, thunderstruck. 'What do you mean? That it was a woman? A child?'

'A woman.'

'Who? Your daughter?'

'No. Dear me, I feel that I have already——'

'There cannot be many heiresses of my acquaintance. In fact I can think of none! I know no one, not one single woman with fourteen hundred pounds to put down for me. The thing's *impossible*! You're joking, Harris! Tell me you're joking.'

The banker looked upset. 'I feel I have already been guilty of a breach of confidence. Only the fact that you will soon be able to pay the capital back. . . . It was Caroline Penvenen.'

'Caro . . .' Ross swallowed and stared. After a moment he said: 'Oh, but I don't believe that!'

'It's the truth.'

'Caroline Penvenen? But I hardly know her. I spoke to her two or three times, no more. We said . . . How could she know? I don't go about confessing my financial situation to every slip of a girl. It's – monstrous. How did she approach you?'

'She came into this office one morning, said she was looking for an investment and that she considered the best investment she could make was loaning fourteen hundred pounds to you. She knew all about the bill, about the Warleggans possessing it, about the straits you were in. I felt it my duty – forgive me, but I felt it my duty to warn her what a risk she ran of never seeing her money again. She paid no attention to it. If I would not arrange it for her, she said, she would go elsewhere. Having done what I could to p-put her off, I was of course only too gratified to do what she insisted.'

'I positively can't believe it.'

'I don't know what she will feel at my having told you.'

Ross rubbed the new-healed scar on his head. As it healed it itched. 'Well, I have never been so upset with astonishment. *Never*. I can guess, I suppose, how she came by the information. But that she should choose to act on it. . . . No wonder I could not think who had helped me. God's life! What a strange creature! I – can't begin to understand. I must tell my wife. She too will be taken aback.'

'I'd appreciate it if you allowed the information to go no f-further,' said Pascoe. 'It is the first time I have ever broken an undertaking of that nature. I'm sorry that you forced it out of me.'

'I am not,' said Ross.

They bought several new items of furniture: a fine dressing table for Demelza's room, for which they paid £5 10s. od., another clock to replace the one they had sold two years ago, a new table – new secondhand – with a splendid polish on it and latest-fashion pedestal legs, two Turkey rugs at £4 each, fine calamanco cloth for bedroom curtains, and a rich cream silk paduasoy for the curtains for the parlour. Some cloths Ross bought because Demelza liked the feel of them – a piece of crimson velour and another of green satin – without an actual purpose in view for them, unless it was the purpose of tempting Demelza into a new attitude of mind. They bought six new-shaped wineglasses, which cost them 28s., and a dozen pewter tankards – cheap enough, these, at 4d. each – and new crockery and new cutlery – very expensive – and a cane-bottomed rocking chair.

Demelza bought two pairs of Dantzig shoes and some fine wool for a coat for Jeremy and a toy horse and a rattle. Ross bought neckcloths for himself and two for John Gimlett, and Demelza some striped muslin for Jane.

And in their minds the whole time, at the back of all their purchases, was the news they had learned about Caroline Penvenen.

By the time they had finished, the afternoon was well on, and it meant a long ride in the dark. So they went home as slowly as they came in, closer together physically than they had been for many months. In the old days when she was a child she had sometimes ridden on the pommel of his saddle, but that had been out of the question today. He found it pleasurable to feel her hand on his belt, and the occasional rub of her shoulder against his back; one could talk easily too, without raising one's voice or having it carried away by the wind.

He had not devised this shopping expedition with any motive other than the most obvious one; but on the way home he wondered if it had achieved a double end. Once or twice this afternoon he had noted a richness in her tone which he had not consciously missed until it came back.

Halfway home Demelza said: 'Ross, the more I think of Caroline the more I feel we have gravely misjudged her.'

'I know it. We're more in her debt than anyone has a right to be. I don't feel it should be left where it is.'

'No more do I.'

They were silent for a time. Demelza said: 'The more you think of it, the worse it gets. Caroline Penvenen saved us from the bankruptcy prison. Dwight saved us from another prison. There's no doubt he still loves her. There's no doubt that but for what he did that night they would now be married and living in Bath.'

'I cannot understand her doing it for us – unless it was with Dwight's connivance. He must have told her of our trouble and have pressed her to help, I suppose. But he seemed as surprised as we were when we told him of our good fortune – I don't believe him to be that good an actor. I'd like to go and see her, to ask her about it.'

'I think she is very impulsive, temperamental,' Demelza said slowly. 'She would jilt one man, or help another, because she has a sudden feeling that way. She has perhaps a strong liking for you——'

'For me? But we only met two or three times.'

'It would be enough. Oh, I don't mean to take away from her. But the good things and the bad things go together in her, and often I'm sure most for good, as Dwight found.'

They jogged on a little further. It was a mild evening but damp, and every now and then a flurry of rain would beat against their faces.

Demelza said: 'I think you are right, Ross; you should go and see her.'

'She's in London. I have her address from Pascoe and intended to write.'

'I think you should go, not write.'

He tightened his grip of the reins as a badger scuttered across their path. When Darkie had settled again, he said: 'I don't see we can do anything to bring Dwight and Caroline together again. She is engaged now to marry someone else – and in any case the very shortcomings which have helped us are precisely the reasons why she would not make a suitable wife for Dwight . . .'

'I'm not saying anything about bringing her and Dwight together. Dwight is going to sea, and she cannot jilt yet another man. But I do not think a letter from you would do, Ross. It – isn't enough. I think you should go'n see her in person – and tell her what we feel and how we should like to thank her. Maybe she doesn't know how much she's helped us, maybe fourteen hundred pounds don't count much to her; but it don't leave us any less in her debt.'

He couldn't question that. 'I'll go before Christmas. It will take a fortnight, but I can leave Henshawe in charge of the mine. I'll take the first year's interest with me and tell her I shall hope to repay the whole by Easter.' Already his mind was springing ahead to details of the journey. It was over ten years since he had been to London, and then it had been only to pass through.

'One thing,' Demelza said. 'I think you should do one thing about Dwight and Caroline, even if it is nothing to do with bringing them together. I think Caroline must have had some better reason for jilting him than just because he didn't turn up that night. She may be impulsive, but that's not the way a woman would be impulsive. Leastwise, she might well go off in an anger, but she wouldn't stay in an anger after he had come to explain.'

'And you think I should ask her?'

'Yes, Ross, I do.'

'All right, I'll tell her that my wife thinks it unfeminine to have acted as she did.'

'Tell her,' said Demelza, 'that we find we have a new debt and should dearly like to pay it any way we can.'

As they came to their own land, the lights of Wheal Grace glimmered over the valley. Mines, Ross thought, could wear expressions just like human beings. Or was it that men read their own thoughts into objects of slate and stone? Three months ago such movement as had existed seemed to be the motions of an animal already doomed and feeling the languor of death. Now everything moved with an invigorated air. Five lights burned where one had burned before. The steady rhythm of the engine was unchanged, but some new purpose had crept into it. Fifty new hands had been engaged this month, twenty for underground and thirty for the rapidly extending surface sheds. Some of the work of dressing was still farmed out, for the amount of mineral-bearing ore brought to the surface was still increasing faster than the dressing capacity grew. Young Ellery and his five partners were in the richest part of the lode, and Ellery had confessed to Ross that often he couldn't sleep at night for thinking of his work and wanting to get back to it. When men were on tribute, the percentage they received on what they raised was adjusted month by month and was reduced in proportion to the richness of the ground they worked; but Ross and Henshawe had been very generous in their bargains, and many of the miners were making big profits.

Once Demelza might have sighed for the disfigurement of a hillside and the south end of their pretty valley. The stream which ran beside the house was yellow with mud, and the bal girls worked almost on the fringes of her garden. But now she would have turned her flower-beds into ditches to dig out the tin.

When they got home, Gimlett was waiting for them, tireless, friendly, anxious to please. He took Darkie and his presents, it seemed, with equal gratitude. Presently he disappeared into the rear of the house. Demelza ran upstairs to see for Jeremy. He was asleep, looking more angelic, more frail than ever. Despite his vastly improved health, he clung to that look. He had a round, graceful head, dark hair, a slender neck, a wide, mobile mouth, a Poldark mouth. There was a look of distinction about him even so early – and an air of restlessness. Only in sleep was his energy dormant.

Hearing a movement, Demelza looked up and saw that Ross had followed her. He so seldom came in here now. He smiled without looking at her, nodded down.

'He has survived without you.'

'So it seems.'

'I wonder Jane has had no children of her own. We must get more help in the house now. Do you think Jinny would come back?'

'We could perhaps find someone younger. I only need another young girl.'

'Two would be better. You will have to grow used to giving orders instead of doing things yourself.'

She did not reply, and he thought perhaps his words had sounded like criticism. 'Soon, if the prosperity lasts, I want the library rebuilt. It has never been anything but a barn of a room. We need an extra room downstairs; and if that were in a proper state, it would transform the house.'

'At least we might fill in the cache.'

He smiled. 'I think it should be left as a warning.'

Jeremy turned over and breathed uneasily in his sleep.

'We should move,' he said, 'or we'll wake him.'

'Oh, no, that is past. He takes no notice of anything now.'

'Perhaps he's easier for my not being in the room.'

She looked up, half veiling her look with a swift glance away. 'I do not suppose that.'

'Some say children are jealous of their fathers. Jeremy has had little to be jealous of, of late.'

Demelza said: 'I think perhaps that's a subject we should sleep sounder for not discussing.'

There was silence for a few seconds. A shade experimentally, he put his hand on her shoulder. She did not move.

'I intended to have bought him some building bricks,' he said. 'I knew there was something else.'

'You'll be able to get them in London now.'

'Do you think you might come with me? Why not try? Jeremy is well enough with Jane.'

'Me? . . . Oh, no. No, thank you, Ross. Not this time. Though next time gladly. I think you should meet Caroline alone.'

'Why?'

'It is a feeling I have.'

'You could stay at the inn while I went to see her.'

'No. This time I'd rather not.'

He had moved a little closer to her. 'Demelza.'

'Yes.'

'There have been a lot of unhappy things between us these last months. Not said – but felt. I should be glad to think they are all forgotten.'

'Of course, Ross. I feel nothing now.'

He put his face against her hair. 'It is not nothing that I want you to feel.'

'I'm sorry . . .'

They stayed thus for a moment more. Although unable to feel any tautness within her, he knew it was there. He had not removed it, he had not defeated it. He knew he could take her if he wanted, and her resistance would only be token; yet the token was there, and while it existed the reconciliation would be ashes.

He kissed her abruptly on the hair, released her, went across to the north window, and pulled aside the curtain to look out. Her eyes followed him.

He said: 'Perhaps you're right; we don't ever regain what we lightly lose.'

'I don't think 'twas lightly lost on either side.'

'But lost.'

'Well. . . .'

It was so dark outside he could hardly see the sea.

'And lost to no good purpose,' he said, half speaking to himself.

'That I don't know.'

'Oh, there was a purpose, a good purpose served, if you come to think of it; though perhaps you would not agree. I don't know. . . . I have not wanted to talk of it.'

She stood by the cot watching him.

'Perhaps sometime it will have to be talked of,' he said, 'if we are ever to straighten this out between us. Yet I have a prejudice, a feeling that it is a bad thing. . . .'

'What is a bad thing, Ross?'

He turned from the window, let the curtain fall from his long fingers, said wryly: 'I think there is an etiquette even in adultery, and I cannot bring myself to discuss one woman with another, even when the second happens to be my wife.'

'You don't suppose I should want to hear it?'

'Yet it might not displease you.'

'I can't see how it would be likely to please me.'

'Then you are less perceptive than I suppose.'

' 'Tis very likely.'

There was another pause. Ross came slowly back from the window and after a moment's hesitation bent and kissed her on the lips.

'Yes, it is very likely,' he said, and went out.

She did not move for a time. Jeremy's breathing was a little more hurried now, as if he was dreaming. She turned him over expertly, firmly; as if knowing the touch of the familiar hand, he settled more comfortably after it.

She straightened up and went to the window herself. There were movements of warmth in her heart where she had not expected to have feeling again.

Chapter four

THE NEXT DAY Dwight received news of his appointment. He was to be surgeon of the frigate H.M.S. *Travail*, fitting out at Plymouth, and was to join her on December 20.

Ross said nothing of his intention to go and see Caroline, but he told Dwight of his discovery about the money. Dwight's face flushed up. He had known nothing of it, he said, and hid his other feelings behind a mask of apology for having spoken so freely of his friend's business affairs. Ross told him he had never been so much obliged to anyone for talking freely of his business affairs.

He left for London on the following day, dining at St Austell and spending the night at Liskeard. They crossed the ferry at Plymouth and lay the next night at Ashburton. Friday they dined at Exeter and slept at Bridgewater, and Saturday saw them eating at Bath and sleeping in Marlborough. The last day was a full one, for they were up early making a stage before breakfast. They dined at Maidenhead and reached London just before ten at night. The ground was snow-covered as they neared the city.

It was snowing the following day when Ross set out to find Caroline. Her address was No. 5 Hatton Garden, which he knew to be a superior residential district; but he had to ask many times on the way. The streets were more crowded than he remembered them, and people seemed to have no manners, pushing and thrusting each other aside to get along more quickly or to gain some temporary advantage. Twice he saw people knocked into the gutter. And there were enough in the gutter to begin: blind beggars, tattered ex-soldiers short of an arm or a leg, children with sore eyes, bent crones holding out acquisitive claws. Snow had made things worse, for there were a half-dozen pitched battles in progress between apprentices of one sort and another, and often the women joined in. In the middle of one fight a carriage came along, and suddenly everyone turned on it so that the coachman was nearly pelted off his seat. Whoever was inside knew better than to open a window to protest.

Ross bought a daily paper, but it was filled more with quacks' advertisements than news of the war. Anyway, since the execution of Marie Antoinette, people had become inured to the bloodstained horrors of Paris.

The French had gone mad, that was plain. But England was at war. That was the main thing. What fighting there had been had been disappointing and inconclusive, almost as if the combatants hadn't yet got their hearts in it. But even that was a relief to overburdened feelings. And more would follow. England was at war. Eventually the insanity would be purged. It was only a matter of time now.

Near his destination he saw two men suddenly come to blows; it was a dispute over a counterfeit ha'penny; they laid into each other with sticks, and he saw one man's nose caught under the full swing of the stick, saw the blood spurt all over his face. It was not only in Cornwall that these things happened, it seemed.

A liveried manservant opened the door of the house when he rang, stared petulantly at Ross's clothes, which he had not had time or patience to renew since his change of fortunes. 'Miss Penvenen?' said the manservant, after being stared down. He would enquire. A considerable wait. He came back. Miss Penvenen was in and would see Mr Poldark. Ross was shown into a fine rather empty, rather cold room overlooking the street. The manservant's heels clicked on the polished inlaid floor.

His eyes newly alive to decorations and furniture, he took note of the elegant walnut writing bureau with the claw feet, the inset oval-shaped cupboards displaying fine china on either side of the great marble mantelpiece. The panelling of the room was of carved pine, and there were few pictures but many miniatures and silhouettes. A fire burned in the grate but did not seem to warm the larger spaces of the room. Downstairs somewhere children were laughing.

The door opened and Caroline came in.

'Why, Captain Poldark, I could not believe it was you! But the name was so unusual. London is honoured. I have seen no flags out for your visit.'

'They don't put flags out when I come to a place,' Ross said, bending over her hand. 'They put them out when I go.'

He was quite shocked by the change in her. She had gone so much thinner and lost much of her beauty. She was a person whose looks would always be volatile, but just now they were at a low ebb. She wore a dress of a fashion Ross had never seen before, with the waist under the armpits and falling straight to the floor. It had short puff sleeves and a gold cord and tassel.

'You should have told me of your visit. How long shall you be staying?'

'Two or three days. I couldn't have forewarned you, for I didn't know of it myself until a few days ago.'

'Urgent business? You'll have sherry and biscuits? It's nearly time. The apothecary tells me I must have sherry every two hours, and I don't find it an unpleasurable remedy.'

He watched her sit and then took a seat himself at the other side of the fireplace while she talked on rather aimlessly and at some length. She was ill at ease in his presence.

'You've been ill, Miss Penvenen?'

'I am a little out of sorts, and the heat of a London summer has taken my energy. How is your wife?'

'Very well, thank you. We are all very well. And the mine has come into paying country, so that I am making money for the first time in my life. And all thanks to you.'

She looked quite convincingly surprised; then to give herself an escape from his heavy-lidded look, she turned and pulled the bell tassel beside her.

'I drew it out of Pascoe last week.' he said. 'Afterwards he was a thought repentant of his confidences, but I gave him your full absolution.'

'Indeed.'

'Yes, indeed. So it would be a pity to waste time denying the indictment. You are convicted, Miss Penvenen, of wilfully saving three people from the worst disasters that bankruptcy can bring. You had no possible excuse for doing it, no ties of friendship or relationship, and it is a very grave charge.'

'And what's the sentence?'

'To receive my sincerest gratitude for a selfless, kind, and Christian act that I shall never be able to understand and shall never forget.'

The colour came to her face, perhaps more at his tone than what he had said. She laughed and turned towards the door, glad before it opened of the interruption. When the sherry was on a table between them and the servant had left again, she said:

'You make altogether too much of it, Captain Poldark.'

'Ross,' he said. 'Christian names for a Christian act.'

'Captain Ross, then. You make far too much of it. I have always been used to indulging my whims, and that was such a one. Sherry?'

'Thank you. I disagree as to making much of it. You should have been in my shoes.'

'But I was not. And don't forget, spinsters are unreliable at the best of times. I might well have endowed a sailor's home instead, or indeed turned against you as easily——'

'I don't believe you.'

'In any case, the money is nothing to me. A few hundred pounds——'

'Dwight tells me your personal fortune is not large.'

At that she was silent a moment, took up a biscuit, and chewed it slowly. 'You have answers all ways. I see there is nothing for it but to accept the halo you offer me.' She put up her hand to her hair. 'I imagine it would look comic on a redhead, and in any case I shall surely tip it off at the first fence. But if it pleases you, Captain Ross, then don't let me interfere with any arrangements you wish to make. The canonization could be arranged for tomorrow at eleven.'

Ross sipped his sherry. 'My journey took me five days. I have been thinking a good deal about you on the way – Caroline.'

'I pray not for the whole five days. I do remember my ears burning once, but I thought it was the fever back.'

'I came to tell you – one thing I came to tell you is that I shall be able to repay the whole of the money very soon. I have with me a draft on Pascoe's Bank for £280, which is your interest for the year. But the capital should also be forthcoming within a few months.'

'There you are, you see. You elevate me merely for a shrewd stroke of business. I don't believe my uncles earned me anything near twenty per cent when the money was in their charge.'

'You talk of being a spinster, but I believe you're not to remain so very much longer. I heard of your engagement just before I left – to a Lord Coniston, is it?'

'Does that affect the safety of my investment?'

'No. It only points my interest in your future.'

She rose and poured him another glass of sherry. Her arm was slightly, pleasantly freckled along its outer curve.

'You were not about to make me an offer yourself, Captain Ross?'

He smiled. 'I'm not a Muslim. And have seldom regretted it before. . . .'

She curtsied slightly before she sat down. 'Thank you for being so gracious about it. But your compliments come a trifle early. I'm not promised to Walter.'

'Not? You mean you are not promised to Lord Coniston?'

'You look astonished. Does it matter – I mean, to you?'

'Well, yes. . . .'

'He has offered himself once or twice, the last time as recently as last month. He's personable enough, but I don't think I shall marry him.'

Ross stared at his wine. Her reply had taken him completely by surprise. All he had planned to say to her – and all he had planned not to say to her – had been built on this belief. He felt as if his attitude of mind suddenly needed rethinking, and he had only a moment or so in which to do it.

'Your uncle in Cornwall told someone I know that you had definitely promised to marry this man.'

'My Aunt Sarah – whom I live with here – is always premature. He's eligible and he had asked me; that was enough for her. But why does it upset you?'

'If it's not an impertinence, may I ask why you don't intend to accept?'

She smiled. 'Oh, the usual capriciousness of my sex.'

'And you do not love him.'

'As you say. I do not love him.'

'In fact it's probable that you are still in love with Dwight Enys.'

She took another biscuit. 'Could the impertinence be in that question and not in the other?'

'You know he has joined the Navy?'

She looked up quickly. 'What, Dwight? No, I did not.' For the first time he had got under her guard.

'He's joining his ship at Plymouth this week. There has been no settling him in Cornwall since you left.'

'How very unwise of him! I should have thought he would have behaved with the utmost common sense.'

'One does not always behave very sensibly when one loves a person as he loves you.'

'Did you really come to thank me for the money or to act as his ambassador?'

'He knows nothing of this. But he told Demelza last week that it was because of you he was leaving us.'

'And what am I supposed to do, go into a decline because of that? Would it suit you if I gracefully fretted away?'

'It would suit me if you told me why you left Cornwall when he failed to meet you that night. Oh, not that. I can understand that very well. Why you didn't later accept his very reasonable explanation.'

She got up and went to the window. 'What business is it of yours?'

'It has suddenly become my business. I've long had a sincere affection for Dwight. I'm now under the deepest obligation to you. I want to know.'

'It doesn't give you the least excuse to interfere.'

He came up beside her. 'I want to know, Caroline.'

Two young girls were just coming out of the house in the charge of an older woman, a governess. One girl glanced up at the window and saw Caroline and waved. She raised a hand in return.

'How is your cousin-in-law, Elizabeth Poldark?'

'She's married again. She married George Warleggan.'

'Oh. . . . That *does* surprise me. Are they living at Trenwith?'

'Yes. On my doorstep.'

'That will not be welcome to you.'

'It is not welcome to me.'

'And your mine? It's really paying?'

'We can't compute yet what the returns will be.'

'My uncle has been ill. Do you know if he's better?'

'At the moment, yes.'

She turned, her fingers still holding the curtain. He noticed the little amber specks in her eyes. 'Yes, I loved Dwight, if that's any joy to you. It's no joy to me, for I know we could not have been happy. I came to London with my uncle that day because I was vastly angry, piqued, disappointed – all the feelings you'd suppose. I did not know then that Dwight had been doing what he did for you – to help you. I knew that he had gone into Sawle, answering a medical call at the last moment from someone who needed him more than I did. The fact that *afterwards* he had involved himself in some scuffle with the preventive men and got himself knocked about and arrested did not really make the important difference which you seem to imagine. His going to see the Hoblyn girl was a – a symptom, a *symbol*. That is what you don't understand and what he surely must. At least I tried to tell him in my letter. Captain Poldark – Ross, as you say I must call you – did you see anything of Dwight during those last weeks when we had arranged to elope and live in Bath?'

'I suppose I did. I don't remember.'

'Well, he behaved as if he was preparing to do something *shameful* and underhand. Oh, yes, he was in love with me in his way, and that made him set a bright front on it; but underneath he was miserable! He thought he hid it from me, but it was plain to see. He was leaving his charge, his people, his cures, leaving them disgracefully, deserting them at dead of night and going to live in a fashionable and wealthy city. He may have had reasons for feeling that way – I don't say if it is the right attitude or the wrong attitude – but there could have been no happiness in it for me. You think me a fickle and capricious woman; but in fact I'm not quite so featherbrained as you suppose. At least I could see that we should have a miserable future if he spent the rest of his life blaming himself for the desertion and trying not to blame me! It is true; don't shake your head, it is true!'

'Yes, I see it; I'm not denying that. I didn't know. I didn't know it all. And you explained all this to Dwight in a letter?'

'As much as I was able.'

Ross took a turn about the room, and for a while neither of them spoke.

He said: 'The desertion as you call it was especially difficult for Dwight because of his affair with another woman years ago, a patient——'

'Yes. Keren Daniel. I know about her.'

'I am not defending him, but I suppose that gave him a bad background for any later move which might look a trifle sordid to himself. There would not be wanting people who would say he had married you for your money.'

'Oh, people! If you spend your life thinking what people will say, you will not stir from your own fireside.'

'I agree. And in principle I'm sure Dwight would. But he's a deeply sensitive and punctilious person. I see his point; and I see yours now. . . . But if you both loved each other, surely there was some other way out of the mess.'

'For me to live with him in three rooms at the Gatehouse, with my uncle kicking up a rumpus a few miles away and everyone in the district knowing of it?'

'*No*. . . . But would it not have been better to see him, when he had travelled all that way to speak to you?'

She looked at Ross with a little deprecating expression. 'I'm not made of iron, though no doubt you think that also.'

'No,' said Ross. 'I don't think so. I find you more and more a woman after my own heart.'

With a swift-flushing colour she said: 'I believe I shall have a proposal from you yet.'

'You may shortly have a proposal from me of a different nature. Do you still love Dwight?'

'Extravagantly.'

'No.' He put his hand on her arm. 'Tell me, Caroline.'

She shook her head. 'I find this a very embarrassing interview.'

'Dwight will be in Plymouth all this week and part of next. If you travelled with me when I return on Thursday. . . .'

She stared at him blankly, angry. 'You must be mad!'

'Am I? It depends what you feel for him.'

'It depends not at all on that——'

'Then on what? You could be in Plymouth Sunday. Don't you suppose it worth a final meeting? You've never talked over it sensibly together, in the presence of a third person, have you?'

'It's seldom possible to be sensible on such occasions.'

'I doubt that. Anyway, it's your last chance of seeing him.'

'I don't think you should appeal to my sentiment.'

'Well, you cannot ignore the facts.'

'That's just what you are doing. The facts have not changed since we separated. There's no better way out now than then.'

'But they have changed. You are not making him leave his friends in Sawle. He's doing it of his own free will. I didn't understand before why he thought that so necessary. I do now. If you meet him now, he will be free of all those associations.'

'And tied to the Navy.'

'Yes. There's no comfortable escape to Bath. The facts have changed both for the better and for the worse. They should be worth reconsidering.'

For a moment she seemed to waver. Then she shook her head emphatically. 'Impossible. . . .'

'Only one person can make it impossible and that is yourself.'

• 'Yes . . . you're right. You're wholly right, Ross. I have spoken as if all the weakness, all the shortcomings, were on his side. Do you think I've not had time enough since to look into my own? What happened, the way it happened, showed me up to myself. Do you know what it's like when your anger and bitterness are so great that you can only hurt yourself – and go on hurting yourself for ever and ever, it seems, so that there's no escape. That hasn't changed. The possibility of its happening again hasn't changed.'

'Why not?'

'Well, it may have lessened, but it doesn't disappear. How can it? If I had brought a different understanding to his feelings, I should be a different person. I am not a different person. I'm only myself. Not only did I expect too much of him, but he expected too much of me. I know less of married life than you, but I should have thought it the worst way to begin. The break went both ways – and *very* deep. I haven't such a plenitude of courage to hurt myself again, and him too.'

There was silence for a time. She said: 'Nor would what you think come out of a single meeting. I have done too much of it already – arriving to turn his life upside down and then leave again. Let him go – in peace.'

Ross took out his purse and unfolded a piece of paper. 'Here is my draft. Your banker will send a receipt.'

She took the paper. He did not like his defeat at all; not one bit.

He said: 'There's one other thing I should tell you. Your uncle is not altogether better. Dwight tells me the disease is held in check, but it's not probable that he will improve much from his present condition. When Dwight is safe at sea, I think you should come down.'

'Very well.'

The life had temporarily gone out of her, in a way he had not known before; the emotion had tired her. She asked him to meet her uncle and aunt that evening, but he refused, making the excuse of pressure of business. As he was leaving he said:

'If you should change your mind before Thursday, you'll find me at the Mitre in Hedge Lane. It is just off Leicester Fields.'

'Very well,' she said again. 'But I cannot.' And he went out into the crowded street.

Chapter five

WHILE ROSS WAS away Demelza had an unpleasant experience. She
received an invitation to tea from Mrs Frensham, Sir John's sister, who was
visiting him again; and, it being a fine day and Darkie in Truro, she
decided to walk. The shortest way took you along the cliff, dipping into
Sawle and across the shingle, then up the other side skirting Trenwith land
by way of the cliffs until you came to Trevaunance Cove.

On this journey Garrick decided to accompany her. It was funny about
Garrick. You could walk to the end of the combe of an evening and he
wouldn't lift an eyebrow from his after-rabbit sleep; but if you were *going*
anywhere, he knew instantly and it was the hardest thing in the world to get
started without him.

He followed perseveringly close beside her all the way, grumbling only
now and then in his throat. By now he was ten but bore his years like his
great size lightly. His black astrakhan coat looked more than ever as if the
moths had been at it, he had lost several necessary teeth in several
unnecessary fights, and he could not see much out of one eye; but these
were the ravages of battle not of time. Demelza sometimes suspected that
he was developing a middle-aged outlook. He had learned to distinguish
between a rabbit, which had to be galloped after before it escaped, and a
tossed bone, which lay where it fell until one came up with it. And he no
longer disappeared for days on wild rampages of his own. Jeremy loved him
dearly and pulled him about into improbable postures.

When he strayed from her today, she did not call him, knowing that after
a snuffle down some promising hole he would be back soon enough and
there was nothing he could hurt on this scrubland. When she heard the
shot, her mind had been far away and it took a few seconds for her to relate
it to the savage yelping which followed. Then she saw Garrick down,
rolling on the ground, and she ran across the heather towards him, alarm
and anger hardly fledged. In his anguish as she knelt down he bit her wrist,
but she forced his jaws open and tried to see where he had been hit. A part
of one ear had been shot away; a piece hung loose; blood was dripping over
his eyes and terrifying him. But there seemed nothing else.

There was a crackle of dry wood behind her and a voice said: 'That your
dog, Mrs?'

She looked up. A strange man, rough-dressed, carrying an old fowling piece under one arm. Another man of the same sort was coming over the heather.

'Did you fire that gun?'

'Aye, Mrs. Looks as if I only nicked 'im. . . .'

She got to her feet, blazing. 'Nicked him! You might have killed him! Judas God, you should be put in prison! What right've you to be firing your piece without looking if there's people about. Here, Garrick! Here, boy!' Garrick had jumped away from her and was running round, shaking his head then rolling over trying to stop the pain.

The man wiped a hand across his nose. 'Just obeying orders, Mrs. You'd no right to be on private land.'

'Private land! This is public land. Orders! Whose orders? What are you talking about?'

The second man had come up. He was another big fellow, older than the first, and there was a family resemblance.

'All right, Tom, I'll 'andle this. This is private land you're on, Mrs, and all dogs straying are shot. You ask whose orders. This is Trenwith land right to the sea——'

'Never!——'

'Oh, yes 'tis. And there's another thing. There's been too much sheep worrying of late——'

'Garrick doesn't do that sort of thing! You did ought to know it's young dogs——'

''E's cutting a fine caper now,' said Tom, snickering. 'Fair old dance he's doing, edn'e.'

'So would you, you great fool! I'll report you to Mr Warleggan. I'm Mrs Poldark, Mrs Warleggan's cousin, and I'll see she hears of this!'

Tom went on snickering. 'Oh, aye, we've heard tell of you, Mrs. A bit like your dog, ain't you: bit of a mixed breed, eh?'

If there was a characteristic for which Garrick was noted, it was his obstinacy rather than his intelligence; but at this moment he chose to show his insight into the situation by going for Tom's leg. Tom shouted and jumped away and swung his musket and missed. The other man stepped back and Demelza called to Garrick and in the confusion they were slow in seeing the horseman who was coming towards them across the heather. Trouble was saved by Demelza capturing Garrick, and then the older man said:

'Here's Mr Warleggan now. He'll see for you his self, Mrs. . . . Damnation take that great mongrel——'

They waited, all breathing sharply, for the arrival of the man who was to settle the dispute. To hide the pain in her wrist, Demelza bent trying to help the dog.

George came slowly. The ground was dangerous for riding, and he had no intention of being thrown. When he recognized Demelza, he took off his hat.

'Mrs Poldark in person. Were you about to call on me?'

'Far from it,' said Demelza, wishing her face would cool. 'I have an invitation to tea at Trevaunance House and was walking there when these two impudent louts first shot my dog and then insulted me! Look at my skirt! And they've sorely wounded my dog. I don't know what they think they're at. Judas, and my gloves too! 'Tis nothing less than disgraceful——'

'There's some mistake,' George said. 'They took you for a trespasser, which of course you are. But they exceeded their instructions——'

'I am not a trespasser! This has been open land ever since I came here——'

'Francis was overindulgent. Poachers and gipsies stray wherever they choose——'

'Do I look like a poacher? If I came within twenty feet of your window, I should not expect to be treated with such rudeness! Do you mean you *support* these men?'

'The Harrys were obeying orders. Have they been overzealous?'

'Overzealous! . . .' Demelza suddenly perceived that George was not going to help her. 'If that's how you feel, then there's no more to say.'

'I think your dog will recover. It will teach him not to stray.'

Trembling with anger, Demelza bent to pick up her other glove. 'We shall be poor neighbours, George.'

'Your husband has already shown himself to be that.'

She moved to go on her way, but young Tom Harry put out a hand like a plate. 'Not that road, Mrs.'

Demelza looked up at George. For a moment she could not believe that he would not allow her to go on after all this was said. Then she realized that even his permission now would be an insult. In any case she was in no fit state to go visiting. She whistled to Garrick and he came lolloping back, still shaking his head and keeping well clear of the men.

'Have a care, George,' she could not refrain from saying; 'I might send Ross to visit you.'

It was strange how Ross was always George's weak link. She saw that there was a mark on his face, under his chin, which had not been there before.

'If he comes on my property again, he'll be dealt with.'

'It will take more than two clodhopping bullies to do it.'

' 'Ere, you keep your insults to yourself, Mrs,' said Tom Harry. 'Else we'll send you 'ome with a clip out o' *your* ear.'

'Hold your tongue, Harry,' said George sharply.

She turned and left them; to retire with dignity is a hard and bitter thing, especially with three men staring after you and no doubt talking behind their hands. When she got home, she wrote an apology to Mrs Frensham and next day sent it with John Gimlett, telling him to go by way of the villages.

Dwight Enys was lodged at the Rising Sun, in one of the narrow streets off the Barbican. He had arrived in Plymouth to find the *Travail* much farther from being fully commissioned than he had expected. Captain Harrington was still in Portsmouth; the crew was barely a quarter of its full complement; and the first officer – a black-browed, long-jawed Welshman called Williams – said they were pitifully short of stores. *Travail* was a frigate of 860 tons burden, 46 guns, nine- and twelve-pounders, and her full complement was 314. When Dwight went below into what were to be his quarters, he found all Williams' gloomy views confirmed. His own tiny cabin next to the common wardroom was adequate enough, but the ship's medicine chest was bare of supplies and the stench below decks was already hard to be borne. It was his instinct to set about cleaning things up right away; but a feeling that it would be untactful to initiate any move without the permission of the captain sent him mute ashore.

He decided for the time being to stay ashore, although he made a daily visit to the ship, and for the next week spent much time wandering about the seaport, himself idle and restless and depressed. He kept thinking of Caroline and of his own failures and the constant futility which had dogged his efforts to make a recognizable and satisfactory pattern of his life. He knew that this act of his in going to sea would be regarded by most of his profession as a monumentally silly one. The pay was poor, the life arduous, his standing when he came out, nil. It might be patriotic to serve one's country; there were easier ways. What he had seen so far of the crew was the pick, the volunteers, from whom would be selected the petty officers, the top men. The remaining three-quarters would either be pressed men or debtors, rogues and ne'er-do-wells, the sweepings of gaol and port. It would be on such material, lice-ridden, diseased, that he would work for the next two years. For weeks on end it would be a monotonous round of purges and vomits, of rough-and-ready treatment with the minimum of medicinal scope. If there was an action, it would become a sudden blood-bath of brutal and hasty surgery in nightmare conditions deep in the heart of the ship by the light of a swinging lantern. Was this what he sought from life, this confined and disciplined escape? At least it was what he had chosen. He was not prepared yet to regret it.

On the Sunday, Dwight received a letter from Ross saying he was staying at the Fountain Inn overnight, having business in the town; would Dwight take dinner with him?

Dwight was surprised and pleased. He had had more than enough of his own company and had thought himself without a friend in the place. About six he walked over, and Ross was waiting for him in the front parlour of the inn.

When they had greeted each other, Dwight said: 'This is pleasant and unexpected of you. When did you arrive in the town?'

'This morning. I slept at Ashburton. When do you sail?'

'Heaven knows. Not before Christmas it now seems certain. How did you know where to find me?'

'Sent a boatman out to the *Travail*.' Ross eyed his friend speculatively. 'A handsome uniform, that. At least it must be some satisfaction to look the part. I've ordered dinner in a private room to-night; I thought it would be more comfortable. And what is your impression of the Navy up to now?'

'That everything is done in a very haphazard way,' said Dwight, following the other upstairs. 'It is plain that this lack of method must be an illusion, for they always produce the results; but at present I can't see how. *Travail* was to be one of a squadron of three for patrol work in the Channel; but the other two left last week. I suppose when Harrington does arrive, he will have fresh instructions from the Admiralty. . . . You're staying in very regal style, Ross. It must be a rare pleasure to have money in your pocket again.'

They had come into the private room where a servant was tending the crackling fire and a table was set for dinner for two. The curtains were drawn, and the warmth and comfort of the room contrasted with Dwight's bare lodgings.

Dwight said suddenly: 'Did you say you slept at Ashburton?'

'Yes. I've been farther afield and am on my way home. Sit down and I'll tell you of it.'

Dwight warmed his hands at the fire and accepted the glass he was offered. Ross went on talking, his long strong fingers running along the edge of the mantelshelf, curiously purposive, Dwight thought, though the conversation was idle enough.

'You said you had been farther afield,' Dwight prompted as the servant curtsied and went out.

'Yes. To London. I saw Caroline.'

Dwight did not move. When he was sure of his voice, he said: 'You went to see her about the loan, I suppose.'

'Yes, in the main. I went to thank her. Of course we had a considerable conversation on general matters also.'

'Indeed.'

'I found she was not engaged to marry anyone.'

'But her uncle said——'

'No. I asked her about that. The report was premature. She had not come to any definite decision.'

Dwight frowned miserably at the fire. 'It's hard to understand that——'

'We discussed you. I hope you didn't mind.'

'Naturally not,' he said in a voice that showed he did.

'What she said convinced me that it was worth while your meeting again. In fact, I tried to persuade her to come back with me, officially to visit her uncle, and to stop in Plymouth one night on the way.'

'Which she refused to do.'

'Which she refused to do. How well you understand each other! I visited her on Monday and used all my persuasions in vain. But on Tuesday I went to see her again. Possibly the effect of twenty-four hours' reflection – and the somewhat overbearing tone I used – had the effect of persuading her different. The fact that her uncle——'

Dwight got up: 'What do you mean?'

'The fact that her uncle was ill did, I think, make the project savour of respectability.'

Dwight said: 'Ross, what do you mean?'

Ross said: 'I mean she is here, Dwight. The servant has gone for her.'

'Good God, I—— She has come to see me? But I——' Dwight had gone pale.

'She has come, but very reluctantly. Very reluctantly, and with, I think, quite a new and sober attitude of mind. Let me emphasize that there's no settled idea of reconciliation in her mind, yet the fact that she *has* come makes reconciliation at least a possibility. The next move is with you, Dwight. And if I may offer advice——'

Ross broke off. Someone had tapped at the door.

Ross said: 'I have been explaining to Dwight that you are on your way to visit your uncle, are spending one night in Plymouth, and are here now at my invitation. I strongly feel you should both meet once more – as friends. It will probably be the last chance you'll have of meeting for some years – or the last ever. Sit down, will you? Here, Caroline. . . . You there, Dwight.'

He had the authority to impose his will on them as perhaps no one else could have done. Neither spoke. After a single glance they didn't for some time look at each other.

Caroline sat down by the fire and smoothed out the skirt of her travelling dress like a bird spreading its wings to the warmth. The tensions of the moment had given her back her colour.

Ross said: 'Believe me, I'm not by choice a tomfool meddler in other people's lives, especially in affairs which touch you both so close as this. The *last* thing. . . . But sometimes, however mistaken, one conceives it one's duty to meddle, and this is such a time. So far as I know you have never talked over your differences quiet-minded and without haste or anger or recrimination. I think you owe that much to each other – and in a degree to your friends. It took time to bring Caroline to my view. She positively felt that such a move on her part would be misinterpreted, and I undertook to explain to you – as I have done, Dwight – that this meeting is to be taken only for what it is, a gesture of common good will before you leave England. Of course, I believe it to be the only neighbourly way to behave.'

Dwight looked up and met a glance that wasn't in keeping with all this politeness. But in fact he was not inclined to disagree. His throat was dry.

'Nothing – would give me *greater* pleasure than to dine with Caroline – to talk with her again.'

Caroline looked at the table. 'You're staying, Ross? The meal is only set for two.'

'It was meant for two. I shall dine elsewhere. But I'll be back. You'll both wait here for me?'

It was an insidious request, ruling out as it did any angry breakup. After a second Dwight nodded and Caroline gave a little acquiescent shrug.

Dwight said: 'You have not been well, Caroline?'

'I am in good health, thank you.'

'I thought . . .'

'My complexion has always been poor. I am going off rapidly.'

'No, no; your uncle said you'd been ill.'

'Oh, I'm recovered. But I have found the prospect of this interview trying.'

It was plain that having been brought almost forcibly to make this first big move Caroline, being Caroline, would be defensive and prickly to begin. Dwight had started off on the wrong foot. She looked cool enough, a little disdainful, far more collected than Dwight, but Ross knew she was not. It was time Dwight discovered that. If he did not, he was lost and all would be wasted.

She had come in too soon, before he could say any of the things to Dwight that he had hoped to say, Ross wondered now whether to try to help still more or go, leaving them to struggle alone. He poured out a glass of sherry for Caroline and moved to take it to her. But Dwight quickly intercepted him. Ross watched him hand it to her and her quick, cool upward glance which betrayed nothing at all. But something in Dwight's look encouraged Ross. In ten months Dwight had suffered a lot. It had matured him in a new way.

Ross said: 'Before I go, I suggest that we take a glass of wine together. Nothing formal. No more than a friendly gesture. That's if you both still regard me as a friend.'

They drank. Caroline said: 'I do not know how Ross behaves to his own wife; but if he treats her one half so cavalierly as he has me this week, I shall call her very downtrodden.'

'You compliment me too highly,' Ross said, 'And yourself too little.'

Their eyes met. They had come to a queer understanding of each other, these two, among the conflicts of the last few days.

Ross said: 'But since you mention my wife, I'll mention her too, for she would have views on the situation to-night, though different in some particulars from ours. She would argue that if a man and a woman care for each other, then the obstacles which keep them apart *must* be substantial –

otherwise they are pretentious and unworthy or are contrived by one or the other with insufficient reason and should be disregarded. She puts emotion above intellect, and the result is what you'd expect.'

No one challenged him.

'I do not wholly agree with her; there's something to be said for both sides. But I think her side is worth the consideration along with any other. She would say that a man was a fool and a woman was a fool . . . that they were cowards too. She'd say life holds only two or three things worth the having, and if you possess them the rest don't matter, and if you do not possess them the rest are useless.' He went to the door. 'If you look round you, I suppose you would have to confess that her view works out in the majority of cases. It is sentimental; but by and large we're creatures of sentiment and cannot escape. Nor is it always wise to want to. You see people every day who take a chance and damn the consequences. Many of them suffer for it, but I do not think they come off worst. The people who come off worst are the people who draw back at the last moment and spend the rest of their lives regretting it. No, don't get up, Dwight, I'll see myself out.'

Chapter six

CHRISTMAS DAY WAS on a Wednesday, and the Tuesday came without any word at Nampara from Ross. Not that Demelza expected a letter, since letters travelled no faster than people; but she had hoped he would be back before this. She had not spent a Christmas alone at Nampara before, and this of all years would be most uncomfortable to bear.

Being in constant expectation of his coming was being on the constant *qui vive*, so she spent much of the day indoors, the first part of it casking some beer which they had brewed. Almost every footfall caused her to turn her head; but in the end she was out when he came, having gone to see Prudie Paynter, who was laid up with her leg and bitterly complaining of Jud's neglect and misbehaviour. When she came back, he was already in the parlour and she walked in unsuspecting.

She gave a squeak as he turned. 'Why, Ross, I didn't know. I was up at Prudie's. How did you come?'

He smiled as he kissed her – it was just a formal salute between them. 'On four legs and then two. Should I have brought the carol singers?'

'You're an hour or so early: they don't belong to be here before dark. When did you leave London?'

'Last Tuesday. In snow. They manage things more seasonably up there. I stopped at Plymouth and saw Dwight and left there yesterday afternoon.'

Conversation was broken by the arrival of Jeremy – but he helped to ease the constraint which now was sought by neither of them. Ross had brought him presents, and some he gave him now and some he saved until to-morrow. Over Jeremy's head, punctuated with squeals and shouts, he told her some details of the journey; but twenty minutes passed before he was able to say what he should have said at the start.

'Have you three extra bedrooms you could get ready for to-night?'

'*Three*? . . . Why, who is coming? What have you arranged?'

'I have brought Caroline back with me. Caroline and her maid.'

Demelza opened her eyes. 'Where is she? Do you mean at her uncle's?'

'She is with him now. But I invited her here to supper, and I want you to put her and her maid up over Christmas.'

'Over Christmas? Gladly. I'd lay special carpets for her if I had them. But it's *awful* short notice, Ross. And I don't quite understand. . . .'

'We stayed a night in Plymouth and then came on. The story of her engagement was overhasty. There was no truth in it. When I heard that, I felt most of our old misgivings should be set aside and I tried my hand as matchmaker. Of course I hadn't your skill, and at first she would have none of it. But on my second visit she decided to nibble at the bait. We saw Dwight in Plymouth.'

'Yes?'

'I believe they have made it up. He travelled back with us and, if we can fix him in, will stay here too.'

'They have? Oh, Ross, I'm *very* glad. More than glad. The longer I have thought of it. . . . But how did you contrive it? Can he get out of the Navy?'

'How did I contrive it? I thought, what would Demelza do, and I did it. That was all. It was really not very difficult once the first resistance was overcome.'

'And Dwight?'

'He's at the Gatehouse. There's been delay in commissioning his ship. The captain arrived only yesterday morning. He gave Dwight three more days ashore. That means he must leave here after dinner to-morrow and be in Plymouth Thursday evening. What's that on your wrist?'

She had put up her hand and the white bandage showed.

'It's nothing; a scratch. Ross, I'm delighted for what you did. Above all, 'twas *common sense*. There is so little of it in this world. What time are they coming? I must fly. If you'd——'

As she went past him, he took her arm and lifted the lace back from her sleeve again.

'It's nearly healed. What can I give them for supper?'

'Don't worry, I bought a goose in Truro and some ribs of beef and a fillet of veal. I have never known you tie up a scratch in your life. Who put this bandage on?'

'Jane. To tell the truth, it wasn't exactly a cut.'

'Then what was it?'

'Garrick bit me by accident, like. I must tell Jane at once——'

'Garrick bit *you*? Nonsense. What are you trying to hide?'

'It is the truth. Last week something happened to excite him. I'll tell you of it later. Just an unpleasantness. What time are they coming? Do you think it will work out right this time, Ross?'

'Right.' Ross still held her arm and was now untying the bandage. Seeing no way out, she suffered it without complaint, not entirely unflattered by his refusal to be put off. 'Yes, I think it will work out this time. It is a great pity they have no longer. At the best it can only be a reconciliation before he leaves.'

He took off the last bandage and the lint. The bite was healing cleanly, but the marks left no doubt as to what it had been. Ross looked up.

'Where's Garrick?'

'I left him asleep in the kitchen. You're not going to . . .'

'I don't know. How long is it since this happened?'

'Yesterday sennight.'

Ross was silent a moment. The dreaded rabies was ruled out. 'Has he been quiet since? Even if he is, I don't think we can run risks, for Jeremy's sake.'

'No. No, it's not that at all.' In defence of her beloved Garrick she found herself forced to tell him what had happened, though she toned it all down until it sounded like the merest accident for which no one was in the least to blame.

When the bandage was tied again, she said: 'Ross, which bedrooms shall they have? We have only two nice rooms, and I dearly wish they were not so shabby. And I cannot well get out of my own in so short a time, with Jeremy already settled there. I do not suppose Dwight will heed where he sleeps. But Caroline. . . .'

He went across and put on two fresh pieces of wood. 'You had best prepare her my room.'

'Yes,' she said after a moment. 'There are new curtains in there. And Dwight we can give the room over, though it is in poor shape.'

'You can set up my bed in the little room behind if you like.'

'Whatever you say.' Demelza fingered the bandage and glanced at him. When she pushed back her hair, the candles made of her movements a mystical confused replica on the ceiling. 'Jane and I could carry my new dressing table down. It would be nice for Caroline. And I'll fetch out the lace bedspread——'

'I'm sure she will appreciate anything you do. But I'm also sure that her pleasure will not turn on the newness of the furnishings. Demelza, it's not yet six-thirty. I thought to go out for an hour. You'll have a free hand then, and I shall be back well before our visitors arrive.'

'Will you go far?'

He smiled at her. 'I want just to drop over and see George.'

'I was *afraid* of that!' she said. 'Ross, you must not. You'll come back with your head all bloody – if you come back at all. Ross, I tell you, no!'

'Don't fret this time. I shall go in peace.'

'So you may, as you have before. But have you ever left in peace? It is very well for you to go to talk to him, but you know you will get thrown off his land – at the *very* least! Something worse happens every time you meet. You cannot mean to create more ill will just because of a silly mistake on the part of his gamekeepers! George as good as apologized for them when he came up.'

He did not answer, but she felt no awareness of victory.

She said: 'We have Dwight and Caroline coming. I do not wish to be bandaging your broken head, or – or talking to them, trying to be nice to them, and all the time waiting for your return. It's – a season of good will.

Let us be content for to-day and to-morrow.'

The new wood was hissing as flames discovered the moisture within it. Occasionally it sputtered a protest. Ross pushed one piece farther on with his boot.

'George seldom seeks violence – I introduce the violence, not he. As for his servants – they are nothing. I shall talk to him and come away. I'm *very* sorry, my dear. I very much want to please you to-night. I hope still to do so. But this is something . . . It is not wholly because of your brush with him. I have been thinking about him a good deal on the journey.'

George and Elizabeth supped at seven. It was early but a convenient hour for them both.

Immediately after Christmas they were to settle in town until after the baby was born. The one thing that irked George about his new country house was that no turnpike road existed. You could just get a coach through the last five miles, so long as the mud was not too deep, but it was a crazy lurching journey which shook you up more than travelling on horseback.

Elizabeth had kept well since her marriage, except for one or two diplomatic indispositions. In a looped-up polonaise gown of yellow brocade she looked as lovely to-night as she had ever done in her life, the extra fullness in her cheeks softening the fine-drawn classic oval of jaw and chin – that ultimate beauty of bone which would never fade. At Trenwith they always supped alone. George had let it be known early that he wanted his evening meal in the company of his wife, so the Chynoweths ate in their sitting room upstairs. The winter parlour had been transformed: much of the panelling ripped out and the walls hung with expensive flock paper; a new dining table with such a polish on it that the slightest thing left a mark; twenty extra candles; a liveried footman to wait on them. At the opposite end of the table George sat, full-bodied, self-possessed, well groomed. In the summer they would dine in the hall. George had plans for the hall.

Elizabeth had found life with her second husband a mass of contradictions. He lived, she found, more genteelly than the people of her own kind. Although he was putting on weight, he ate considerably less than Francis had done or her father did. Accustomed to a society in which men considered the courtesies observed if they didn't slide under the table before the ladies left, she found his sobriety attractive. He drank but never got the worse for drink. He never spat or blew his nose in her presence. His courtesy towards her was unchanged whether they were in company or alone.

But of course it was impossible to treat him as she had treated Francis. He was not one quarter so malleable, so mercurial, so easy to understand. She missed Francis' dry humour and easy sophistication. Somehow she never seemed able to meet George on equal terms. While she was absolute mistress of the small things, she found him absolute master of the large. She did not love him; she was not even sure that he loved her; but she felt herself to be a treasured possession, cared for and considered in every way. Often it was delightful to be so treated. It was what she had longed for during her widowhood. Occasionally she found it oppressive.

He kept all his other feelings under as good a control as his feelings for his wife. It seemed as if in climbing the ladder of society he had been so afraid of betraying the wrong emotions that he had grown afraid of showing any at all. He was morbidly sensitive about his humble beginnings, though even that he was clever enough to keep from her for some months. Then one day she made a remark that could be taken two ways, and she saw the instant resentment before he could hide it. After that she walked carefully, watching her own words when necessary so that no hint of condescension could be gathered from them.

To-night in the first part of dinner they talked about the news which had just come through to Falmouth of the fall of Toulon. Its surrender to the British in August, together with thirty battleships and great quantities of naval stores, had looked like the end of the war. Lord Hood in grateful astonishment had taken possession and had sent an urgent appeal for forty thousand troops to consolidate this magnificent opportunity. The government had sent two thousand British soldiers, some Piedmontese, and a few Spaniards. Now in December the Republic, freed of its other preoccupations, had sent a large force and reduced the town, led by a new young general of whose name the Falmouth news-sheet had three different spellings in the length of a column but of whose ability no one seemed in doubt.

George had always been for war as against Revolution. The Warleggans were founding their dynasty within the framework of a settled and ordered society. Anything which might undermine that society was to be resisted and condemned. War was far the lesser of the evils.

'. . . small forces,' he was saying, 'which we reduce to complete incompetence by distributing to the corners of the globe. Our campaign in Flanders is bogged in mud. The Vendeans have asked for our help in vain. This would bring about Pitt's downfall if there were anyone to replace him. But Dundas, Grenville, Richmond, none of them have the parliamentary command. . . . '

Elizabeth saw the door open just behind the manservant and Ross come in. So certain was she that it must be another servant with the wine that for a second she disbelieved her eyes. Then George saw her face and turned.

He instantly pushed back his chair.

Ross said quietly: 'I have not come to make a disturbance this time – unless you force it.'

George did not move his chair any farther.

'And *you*,' said Ross, as the manservant, catching some glance from his master, moved towards the bell pull.

'How did you get in?' George said.

'I want a word with you, George.'

The servant said: 'Shall I . . .'

'No,' said George, watching Ross like a snake.

'That's wise. There's no need to wreck your dining room: I have committed enough violence in this house. . . .'

Nobody spoke. Ross's eyes flickered across to Elizabeth. She met his gaze with bitter hostility. It was the first time they had seen each other since the night in May. He looked at her a moment longer, in surprise, a little in assessment. 'I am sorry to upset you, Elizabeth.'

'You don't upset me,' she said.

'I'm glad of that.'

'You may be glad or sorry. I'm not interested.'

George, gratified, said: 'Pray forgive me for exposing you to this intrusion, Elizabeth.'

'It need never happen again,' Ross said. 'I have no ambitions here. . . . But I'm tired of our relationship, George. Whenever we meet, we snarl like dogs – and every now and then it comes to the point of a scuffle, but inconclusive even then. It seems now we're to be neighbours, close neighbours perhaps, for years to come. A disagreeable prospect for me, but not one that I can alter. There are really only two ways out of it, and I have come to suggest that we should choose the better one.'

'Is there a better one?'

'Well, I think so. I'd suggest that we agree to avoid heedless provocation and live as peaceable as we can. What is your view?'

George looked down at his fingers. 'I should have thought your visit to-night a very heedless piece of provocation.'

'No, for I came to put the alternatives before you. I am law-abiding now, George, and prosperous. Think of that. Prosperous. That must gall you. But never mind. It surely must be in the interests of both of us that we should make the civilized choice.'

'And what other do you suggest exists?'

Ross listened to the sound of footsteps in the hall. 'I'm a little unsure as to details, because my wife would not supply them, but I believe an insult was paid her while I was away.'

'No insult was paid her that she did not invite.'

'I understand you're claiming the cliff path as your property between Sawle and Trevaunance.'

'It is my property.'

'I'm not sufficiently interested to dispute it, though there may be others who will.'

'I have already made sure of the legal position.'

'I thought you would have. But the possession of property doesn't entitle you to be affrontful to people innocently using a footpath which has been public for years.'

'Your dog was straying. In what way was your wife harmed?'

'She has left me in no position to argue about it. But I suggest that you take care she's not molested again.'

'The remedy is in her hands not mine.'

'That is where we differ, and differ beyond the point of peaceful enmity. As I say, I have no wish to come here again——'

'You will not, I'll see to that.' George took out his watch. 'You may have three minutes more.'

Ross said: 'I am trying *very* hard to put the choice intelligibly before you, and you asked me as to the other alternative. Well that is it. . . . Age has mellowed us both; but you must know of my ability to incite miners, for you once tried to get me convicted for doing so. It would not be difficult to bring three hundred, and you know what they are like. I don't wish to threaten or to dramatize a simple promise; but they would trample across your lawns and pull up your trees, and in a night it would look as if a hurricane had blown. And any bloodshed caused by trying to keep them out would certainly lead to more bloodshed. The law will not protect you; for it knows no way of offering protection except with a company of infantry, and soldiers now are scarcer than battleships.'

George turned as the door opened and Tom Harry put his head in.

'Begging your pardon, sir. The cook—— Ah. . . . '

He had seen Ross. Ross did not move. Harry sidled in and another man stood in the doorway.

Ross said: 'That's an alternative you'll have time to think over. The present alternative is before you.'

George hunched his shoulders. 'You've finished what you came to say?'

'Yes.'

Tom Harry said: 'Now, see 'ere——'

'Wait,' said George. 'Let him go.'

There was a pause. Harry's hands dropped to his sides.

Ross said: 'It is Christmas to-morrow and believe me, I have come in no carping spirit. We cannot be friends, but it's tedious to spend all one's life with one's hackles up. I certainly don't want to; and I hope you don't want to. In coming to live in my district, you have vastly annoyed me; but you have also offered up certain hostages for your own good behaviour.'

He glanced at Elizabeth. Seeing her had upset him in a new way. 'Explain to George, will you, that I'm in earnest.'

She said: 'I know nothing of any insult to Demelza. But I've complete faith in my husband's capacity to order his life as he thinks best.'

Ross stared at her. 'Then see to it that he appreciates the choice.'

He went out, pushing past Tom Harry, who only shifted an inch or so. The man in the doorway retreated more quickly, and Ross walked across the hall, half expecting some attack from behind. He glanced round that great hall which had been a part of his life ever since he was a child. Here he had come with his father and mother when he was just old enough to walk. He had played here in a corner with Verity and Francis while words from the sober elders grouped round the fire had floated across to his half-attending ears: Chatham's illness and the Wilkes controversy and the repeal of the Stamp Act. Here, returning from America, he had found Elizabeth celebrating her engagement to Francis. Here he had come for the christening of Elizabeth's child, for his uncle's funeral. . . . Something belonging intimately to his family had existed in this room.

But not any longer. The familiar wood and glass and stone were not enough.

Warleggan ground. George's influence was all-pervasive.

The bitterness of Elizabeth's tones and looks had only surprised Ross in their degree. He had expected her enmity. But he did not suppose all of it derived from the ninth of May. He was not proud of his adventure then, nor ever a man given to passing off his own behaviour with an easy excuse; but after the initial resistance that night there had been no particular indication that she hated him. Her attitude towards him during a number of years, and particularly the last two, was more than anything else responsible for what had happened, and she must have known it. Her behaviour that night had shown that she knew it.

But there had been other sins on his part. Over and over again during those first weeks following he had known he should go and see her and thrash the whole thing out in the light of day. It was unthinkable to leave the situation as he had left it; but that was precisely what he had done. He had behaved abominably first in going, then in not going; but he did not know what to say, and the impossibility of explaining himself had stopped him. If the history of the last ten years had been the tragedy of a woman unable to make up her mind, the last six months was the history of a man in a similar case. For a long time he had been quite unsure of his own feelings; then they had crystallized; and from that moment a private meeting with Elizabeth was impossible.

Now it was too late.

Chapter seven

HE WAS BACK in time to soothe Demelza's fears, and just before eight Dwight and Caroline came.

Caroline had been sobered by her visit to her uncle's. In spite of what they had agreed, she had been determined to tell him at once of her meeting with Dwight; but sight of her uncle had shown her how ill he was, and she was silent.

Demelza was nervous and excited too; and as dinner wore on, her attitude helped Caroline to an easier frame of mind.

Demelza said: 'But how long shall you have to be away, Dwight? Have you not heard yet? It is a matter of some importance to us all.'

'The naval surgeon is neither fish, flesh, nor fowl – but I'm told my appointment can be considered to be for two years or for the duration of the war, whichever is the shorter.'

'And if the war go on after that?'

Dwight hesitated. Caroline said: 'He will stay. I feel it in my bones he will not reconcile it with his conscience to retire.'

Dwight smiled. 'For once you overrate my conscience. Since Caroline came, my patriotism has been running out fast.'

Demelza said: 'But you will not have to wait until then, until you are out of it——'

'No. I think she will marry me – I believe she will – on my first shore leave. That may be in three months or six, no one knows. . . .'

'And until then?' Ross said to Caroline. 'What shall you do in the meantime?'

'Stay with Uncle Ray for a time. Then perhaps go back to London.'

'I'd prefer you to stay here,' Dwight said. 'The air is good and London hasn't suited your health.'

'Oh, yes, do you know,' Caroline said to Demelza, 'he spent the first morning of our reconciliation sounding my chest. Faith, I found it more embarrassing than any conjugal endearment!'

Dwight went very red. 'Nonsense, Caroline, you make it sound much worse than it was. I was less than half an hour, and your maid was present——'

'Oh, yes, my maid was present, which made it even more overfacing.

What allurement can a woman hope to have for a man who has already examined her tonsils and her teeth and has counted her ribs in the harsh light of day?'

Dwight took a draught of wine. 'Well, if you want to know that, let me tell you. You have every possible allurement for me that any woman could ever have. I love you and am fascinated by everything you do, and no amount of medical attention, either on you or on myself, will ever cure me of *that*!'

It was a change to hear Caroline getting more than she asked for, and to save them both Ross said:

'When Dwight has gone, so long as you stay with your uncle, I hope you'll come and sup with us once or twice a week. It will help the time to pass.'

'After Dwight has gone, I shall wake up sometimes and wonder if all this week has been a dream. I think I shall have to come here for reassurance. I hope my uncle improves so that I can tell him the truth.'

'If you are in any difficulty, come straight here,' Ross said. 'We will put you up for as long as necessary.'

Caroline looked at Demelza before replying. 'Your husband's committing you very deep.'

Demelza said: 'Well, no deeper than I'd want to go or be willing to go to-morrow.'

It was Caroline who eventually smiled and glanced away. 'I have told Ross. It was just a whim. Anyway, perhaps this war will be over next week and then I shall not need your kindness. In Plymouth the landlord's wife was whispering news of some sacrilegious feast the French have been celebrating in Notre Dame. It all sounds very decadent, and I trust the armed forces will be corrupted by it – especially the Navy.'

'Next year will see a change when I am at sea,' said Dwight. 'The lice at least will notice the difference.'

At half past nine the carol singers came from Sawle Church, and Demelza thought of the many other Christmases. . . . Six years ago at Trenwith, the Trenegloses had come unexpectedly with George Warleggan, and Elizabeth had played and she had sung, and she had tasted port wine for the first time and had loved the flavour of it and what it did to you in spite of feeling sick with Julia four months forward. And then two years later, when she was alone here and the same carol singers as to-night – though a much depleted stock – and she had asked them in and had sympathized with them over their ailments, nervous only for her new status and anxious to behave well, not thinking or dreaming that in two weeks more Julia would be dead and she a drawn and wasted invalid. And the wrecks that had come in on the great January gale, and Ross, like herself only worse, spiritually worse, bitter and lost, going down to the shore and the teeming, struggling miners.

The choir was at full strength to-night and in good form. Uncle Ben Tregeagle was in charge, ageless and gipsylike with his thin black curls, and Mary Ann Tregaskis, and Char Nanfan and Johnny Kimber and Betty Carkeek, whose husband had been killed in the tussle with the gaugers; and even Sue Baker got through the singing without going into one of her fits.

When they had gone, the four sat round the fire for another half hour drinking tea and eating homemade cake. Then Demelza excused herself and presently Ross followed, leaving the lovers to talk alone.

He went up to the mine and was gone some time. When he returned, Demelza was still in the kitchen and told him that Caroline had just gone to bed. He went into the parlour and found Dwight about to leave too.

Ross said: 'We thought you might like a few minutes alone.'

'Thank you. . . . And for so much else besides.'

'Little enough.'

'It isn't often that one man can retrieve another's mistakes for him. I want to tell you——'

'Don't try. Sometimes to be able to growl and bully is a signal advantage. And really it is very easy learned. Make the most of your happiness while it is here.'

'That I will do. Caroline . . .'

'The more I see of Caroline, the more I esteem her.' Ross poured brandy into a glass for himself and then put it down untouched. He wanted no more. 'Not until this week did I begin to understand her. You'll have a lifetime to do it, and that I imagine will not be too long. Always she will disguise her goodness as if ashamed of it. I congratulate you on your acumen in picking so exceptional a wife.'

Dwight shook his head. 'I only wish she were my wife. I'd give years of my life for a month ashore now. But she could not be rushed into it this time – in this way. . . . Demelza likes her?'

'Of course.'

'I asked for a particular reason. I hope it will not be so, but it may be that I shall not have a lifetime in which to appreciate Caroline. In war it's not uncommon for people to get hurt. I don't propose to sentimentalize on the possibility, but it might be that she will need all your friendship and the help you could give – even if we marry, then as a young widow. . . .'

'And do you suppose we should fail to give it?'

'No . . . no.'

The fire was burning low and needed more wood. Presently it would be made up for the night.

'There are many things on which I could not answer for Demelza. But in this I can.'

He went for the big logs into the storeroom after Dwight had gone. When he returned to the parlour with the logs, he found that Demelza had come in again. She was standing before the mirror, pinning up her hair. Her elbows were like wings.

She saw him in the glass. 'They're both settled?'

'Yes. All's well.'

'I hope Caroline won't want for anything. John left plenty of wood for her fire, but I expect she will not need it. Did you find London likeable?'

'Likeable enough for a visit. You must come with me next time.'

She lowered her arms and moved aside to let him put on the logs.

'I wonder why the weather is colder in London. It is four years since we had snow here. . . . If Julia had lived, she would have been near on six.'

He took up the poker and began spreading out and flattening the remnants of the evening's fire. 'I know. . . . And you. . . . Barely yet in your middle twenties.'

'Do I look that much older?'

'No. Often younger. But you began living so young, have experienced . . . Sometimes I feel you're as old as I am. Already in six and a half years we've shared so much.'

'And lost so much.'

'We've lost Julia. Nothing else irreparably.'

She lifted her shoulders. It was a shrug half abandoned, for she was watching him. This they both suddenly knew was the moment when he was going to force past the casual guards of companionship. Something in to-night had left a sudden gap.

She said: 'So you came away from Trenwith without a torn shirt.'

'Yes. . . . In recent weeks, more particularly since I went to London, I have come to realize how silly this constant enmity is, that its chief poison acts on the man who feels it. Not an original discovery, nor perhaps one I shall always be able to abide by, but worth a run. I put it as a proposition to George to-night that we should try to live without rancour.'

'And what did he say?'

'Nothing promising; but I hope when he gets over his astonishment he'll see the reason in it.'

'And Elizabeth?'

'Ah. . . . About even her I'm not sure.' He got the two logs firmly settled and then, still crouching, looked up at his wife. His lean introspective face was less guarded to-night. 'Demelza, I wanted to talk to you about her.'

'No, that I would rather not hear.'

'I think you must. Before I went away I thought not. But there's no other way.'

'Ross, I've forgotten it. *All* that time. It will do harm to bring it back now. I would much better prefer that nothing should be said of it.'

'I know but – in fact it can't be forgotten, can it? It is only – overlooked, set aside.'

She moved away from the fire to give herself breathing space, pulled a curtain straight, snuffed three candles on a side table so that the furniture at the end of the room slid its surfaces into an encroaching shadow. Absently she began to shake out a cushion.

Ross said: 'I want to tell you that Elizabeth means nothing to me any more.'

'Don't say that, Ross. I shouldn't want for you to say more than you feel——'

'But I do feel it——'

'Yes, at present. But then again sometime, perhaps next month, perhaps next year. . . .'

He said: 'Come here, Demelza. Sit down, will you? Listen to what I have to say.'

After a minute she came back.

He said: 'You're so desperately anxious to be fair, not to be self-deceiving, to make the best of what you have. . . . But what you have is all. . . . Will you try to believe that?'

'Have I call to believe that?'

Candlelight and firelight flickered over his face.

'Yes. I wish I could explain about Elizabeth. But in a way I think you must understand. I loved Elizabeth before ever I met you. It's been a – a constant attachment throughout my life. D'you know how it is when a person has wanted something always and never had it? Its true value to him may be anything or nothing; that doesn't count; what does count is its apparent value, which is always great. What I felt for you has always been assessable, comparable, something human and part of an ordinary life. The other, my feeling for Elizabeth, was not. So what I did – what happened in May, if it could only have happened in a vacuum, without hurt to anyone, I should not have regretted at all.'

'No?' said Demelza.

'No. Because from it I came to recognize things which no doubt I should have had common sense and insight enough to have known without the experience but did not. One is that if you bring an idealized relationship down to the level of an ordinary one, it isn't always the ordinary one that suffers. For a time, after that night, things were upside down – for a time nothing came clear. When it did, when it began to, the one sure feeling that stood out was that my true and real love was not for her but for you.'

She was very still, eyelids pale, brows straight with a hint of concentration at their inner ends. He received no hint that she was wrestling with strange demons, her mind and emotions split: on the one hand struggling against the too easy capitulation ready, so ready, within herself; on the other looking at the love that he now offered with both hands, and finding it, perversely, not enough – not of itself enough as a single isolated factor.

'May I ask a question?'

'Of course.'

'How did you come to feel that, Ross? What persuaded you of it? I mean, the experience itself can't hardly have been unpleasant.'

'What experience?'

'With Elizabeth.'

'No . . . far from it.' He hesitated, a little put out. 'But I wasn't seeking just pleasure. I was – I suppose in fundamentals I was seeking the equal of what I'd found in you, and it was not there. For me it was not there.'

'Perhaps it would have come in time. Perhaps you did not persevere, Ross.'

He glanced at her dryly. 'Would you have had me do so?'

'Well, I do not know the details of your – adventure, but it seems to me you are hardly quite fair on Elizabeth. At least . . . I do not very much like her, but she is not a light woman. You came upon her, I suppose, in surprise. I should not be astonished if at first she tried to be faithful to her new promise. I do not know how long you stayed with her or how much you made love to her, but I should think there could be times when she might show to better advantage.'

'Are you defending Elizabeth now?'

'Well, yes . . . or no. I think I am defending *women*. Truly, Ross, are not all women treated by all men like something inferior, like chattels you take up and put down at will? I – I'm very happy to-night that you prefer me and I hope you always will. But I think it is unfair to any woman to judge her, to condemn her, upon a chance encounter, like. I should not wish to be so judged. Though indeed I think I have been so judged, quite recently.'

'What do you mean?'

She hesitated, a little uncertain now of the chasm that gaped before her, then suddenly certain that – though all unplanned – this was the testing jump.

'If we have to talk of this, then there's something I must tell you. I have often thought I should, but it did not seem important if you did not care for me any more. But now if it is true what you say, if you really mean this. . . .'

'Of course I do.'

'Then I must tell you, before we go any further, that on my last visit to the Bodrugans I had an adventure – though it did not end in quite the same way as yours. I went – you will know the sort of mood I went in to that ball. It was but four days after you had gone to Elizabeth. I should dearly have liked to revenge myself on you in the only way I could. And as it came about, the opportunity was there. Malcolm McNeil was there.'

'McNeil?' said Ross. 'The——'

'Yes. We were something flirtatious during the evening. Then afterwards he came to my room.'

Ross looked at her.

She said: 'I do not want for you to blame him, for it was almost at my invitation that he came. But when he came and began to make love to me, I found him less attractive than I could tolerate. I do not know what standard I have created in you, but I know what standard you have created in me. And so at the last I would have nothing to do with him. The meeting did not end as happily as yours with Elizabeth. He was very angry.'

'My God. So I should think.'

'There, you see. You are taking the man's side, just as I took Elizabeth's——'

'I am not. If ever I meet with the profligate swine——'

'But it's not fair to rail at him. It is me you should be angry with, if anyone. . . .'

Ross got up and walked slowly across the room. He stood with his hands behind his back, seeing without reading the titles of books on his bookshelf. After a while he said: 'I don't *understand*. What occurred between you and McNeil? Have you ever had any feeling for him?'

'At one time I believe I had a little, but not now.'

'A little. . . .' Emotions disturbed his normal balance. 'Yet you allowed him the freedom of your room, of yourself——'

'Can you imagine how I felt at that time? You had just abandoned me for Elizabeth.'

'So you threw yourself at the first man available——'

'Not the first, Ross. At least the fourth.'

Their eyes met and clashed. There was an awful silence.

He said very bleakly: 'God in heaven, I don't admire your frankness after all this time.'

'Maybe I should not have told you, but I don't like to be dishonest. If there is to be something good and true between us again——'

'Good and true . . . How far did this – thing go between you and him?'

'Not any great way.'

'So I should think not.'

'Why should you think not, Ross? Should not the goose, if she chooses, be able to drink as deep as the gander?'

Anger was in him unencouraged. 'Well, I don't think I admire your attitude, either then or now. I take no pride in my visit to Elizabeth. But the thing was the outcome of a devotion which had lasted on my side for more than ten years. It was not some tawdry little passion worked up over the wine for a cheap satisfaction between dinner and supper!'

Her pulses began to beat suffocatingly. 'And Margaret Vosper?' she said.

'Margaret Vosper?'

'Yes. She was at the ball. Have you a ten-year devotion for her also?'

He could have struck her. 'The only dealings I ever had with Margaret Vosper were one night before I met you. I believe you would be twelve at the time. I can't swear to my faithfulness to you while you were in swaddling bands, and I don't propose to begin. Can you think of any other excuses to give a soldier licence of your body?'

'That was what I didn't do, Ross, as you would know if you had been attending instead of getting hot and angry about it. I *could* not. I found I had no love for him at all. I don't know if that gives you any gratification. . . . It gave him none.'

Ross said: 'How am I to know what gratification he received?'

'Oh,' she said, and stared at him blindly. 'Ross, what a thing to *say*! After you just told me. . . . That you should think . . .' She could get no words out.

He said: 'How am I to know anything any more?'

There was dead silence for a moment or two. 'No,' she said. 'How are you to know. . . .'

She ran from the room.

Upstairs in an impossible trembling state, part anger, part grief. In a cupboard the valise she had taken to Werry House. Out with it and a few things. Anything almost. A change of clothes, shoes, a few coins. She began to struggle out of her dress, pulling at the hooks, ripping the lace in one part. Then into her travelling clothes. Boots, crop, hat; it all took too long. Now and then tears fell on her hands. Now and then she took a breath as if there was no air left in the world. Jeremy stirred in his sleep. She must leave him now. Later she would send for him. She could not wake him, take him through the night.

Impossible end to the evening. Dwight and Caroline reconciled. They almost. It had begun so well. Ross could hardly have said more. Then her need of conviction. Then her mention of McNeil. McNeil. A test which had somehow recoiled upon herself, wreaking irreparable harm. She stared round, at this room which had been hers ever since they married. Never again. Not here. It was the end of all. Never again.

She got her hat on, pinned it, could not find gloves, must go without; picked up the valise. Handkerchief. She must go quickly or the sounds she was making would wake Jeremy.

Out in the passage and down the stairs. Ross. In the doorway of the parlour.

'Where are you going?'

She glanced at him, eyes like lamps, opened the front door, and went out. Round the house, stumbling, into the yard, the stables. She must take Darkie, no other mount of their own. The stables full to-night. Gimlett had left a lighted lantern. She stumbled, dropped her valise, almost fell, pulled herself to where the saddles were. Her own. Darkie whinnied. She carried the saddle to the mare and threw it over her back.

She had saddled horses many times, but now her fingers were all ways. The girth kept slipping through her hands. Darkie was restless, sensing her haste and frightened by it. The other horses pushed against each other, whinnied; a bat disturbed fluttered with futile wings among the rafters. The seventh Christmas of their marriage. What had Verity said in her letter? They were all so wrong.

A footstep. Ross said: 'Where are you going?'

She did not turn, tugged desperately at the girth, which had somehow got twisted and now would not release to begin again.

'Demelza.'

'I'm going away,' she said. 'What else can I do after . . .'

'Are you going to McNeil?'

'No, of course not.'

He came a little further into the stables. At last she got the strap free, but in tugging at it she slid the saddle over to one side.

'Then to-morrow would be more convenient for us all.'

'*No*. . . .'

He said: 'Here, let me,' and came up beside her and took the girth out of her hands and began to fasten it properly. In the lantern light his face looked like stone.

She turned sharply away to hide her own face from him and went for her valise, carried it to the horse. In silence he finished saddling the mare and reached for the bridle. Then he stopped, weighed it in his hands.

He said: 'Since you went upstairs I've been trying to think how this began, this quarrel, how it came so swiftly on us, and the cause. Perhaps you thought I was patronizing you by explaining myself in the way I did, by seeming to take your feelings for granted. Was that it?'

. . . 'Does it matter now?'

'No, plainly not. What I feel for Elizabeth now is of small importance; other things have come up. Still it was the truth, what I told you, all of it. When I saw her to-night, that confirmed it – it was like seeing a stranger. Queer. Like a stranger, even an enemy, sitting there. George's wife. I'm sorry that I did her an injury as well as you, but there's no way of recovering the past.'

'No. . . . I only wish there was.'

He fastened the bridle and bit and then looked at her. 'Shall I tie the case to the back of the saddle?'

'Please. . . .'

'Where are you going? It's very late.'

'I. . . . The Paynters for to-night. Prudie will find me somewhere.'

'Will you come back for the rest of your things, or shall Gimlett bring them over?'

'I don't know. I'll – send word.'

He said: 'Before you go, you should know that I don't seriously question your account of what took place between yourself and McNeil. You'll – perhaps see that what you told me came as a surprise – a shock, and in the first anger . . . perhaps you would call it the first jealousy. But of course I don't want you to think that that could be my eventual belief.'

Demelza turned blindly, took the reins, led Darkie to the door. Ross did not at once follow her but stayed in the stable picking up some things which had fallen from a shelf. She hesitated a moment, put her hand to the stirrup to steady it, but did not mount. He came out. Darkie pulled her a couple of paces forward and vigorously shook the bridle.

'Thank you,' she said. 'I'm – glad.'

'And there's one other thing I want you to know,' he added. 'That is how deeply sorry I am that I ever hurt you in the first place – in May, I mean. *You* were so undeserving of any harm. All these months. . . . I know how you will have felt. I want you to know that. If you had gone off with McNeil, I should have had only myself to blame.'

She dropped the reins and put up her hands and covered her face with them in a sudden gesture of capitulation. She wanted to say something but could think of nothing at all.

After a minute or two he said: 'Does it upset you now to be told that I love you? D'you still prefer McNeil? Is he still in the district? I'll go and call on him to-morrow.'

'No, Ross, he is gone; and I care nothing, nothing. Not a hair of his moustache.'

'Then why are you leaving? Are you not willing to overlook what I said?'

'I can't.'

'Why not?'

'Because it is the *truth*. That is what I had never realized till you had spoken it. Oh, I don't know why. A sort of blindness. The cheapness of what I did! 'Tis *quite* unbearable to think of. . . . Impossible to live with! I don't know what I shall do.'

He came out and stood beside her. He looped the reins over a peg.

'Should we not go inside and talk it over?'

'No. I can't.'

'You cannot forgive me, then.'

'I cannot forgive myself.'

'That was a favourite Poldark complaint at one time, but I judged you too wise to catch it. Look, supposing we go as far as the kitchen. I don't see that that need compromise either of us too deeply.'

He took the lantern and waited for her. She hesitated.

He said: 'You may leave in five minutes if you wish.'

She followed him into the kitchen.

He opened the side of the lantern and lit another candle from it. She resisted a sudden impulse to shiver.

He said: 'I've been giving good advice to two other people of late, but it's hard always to advise oneself. If——' He stopped and stared at the door leading to the stillroom. In the growing light they could see a black stain spreading under it. 'What is that?'

'Oh . . . the beer! . . . I casked it this morning.' She took the candle he had lighted. In the stillroom the cask was overflowing with froth, and beer and froth covered half the floor. She exclaimed and went back into the kitchen.

He said: 'Did you bung it too soon?'

'I don't know. The fermentation had ended – I thought.' She returned with a floorcloth and a pail. His impulse was to say, leave it, you'll spoil your dress; but in time he refrained.

' 'Twas the hops, I b'lieve,' she said. 'You remember you thought they smelled not quite right.'

He picked up the bung which had blown out and sniffed it.

'I should've waited till you came home,' said Demelza.

They cleared the mess. The place reeked of beer. He carried the bucket out twice and emptied it and after inspection replaced the bung. The fermentation was over now. Whether the stuff was drinkable must be decided at a later date.

When the job was done there seemed nothing more to do or say. The awful catastrophe of their quarrel had evaporated in a commonplace.

He handed her a towel and she dried her hands. There was beer on her cuff and on the hem of her dress. She did not look at him.

He said: 'There's not a drunkard in Cornwall smells worse than we do now.'

She took out a handkerchief and blew her nose, hiding behind it longer than she needed. Then she went to the window and opened it.

He said: 'My dear, I bought you something in London. I had intended giving it you to-morrow; but in case there is no to-morrow for us, it would be best perhaps for you to have it at once.'

She did not turn while he fumbled in his pocket, but then he came up beside her at the window and put a box in her hand. She was surprised to see that his fingers were not as sure of themselves as usual. She opened the box and saw a gold filigree brooch with a ruby in the centre.

'I could not get one just like the last. I believe this is French instead of Italian. The work is not quite so elaborate as the one we bought from the Jew.'

'It's lovely. . . .'

'I bought it in Chick Lane, near Smithfield Bars. Quite by chance, walking that way the second day after seeing Caroline. And this also. . . .'

She heard him fumbling again, and after a minute he put some tissue paper in her hand. She unwrapped a necklace of garnets.

'Oh, Ross, you'll break my heart.'

'No I shall not; not this way surely. If there——'

'Yes, you will. You do not know what is going on inside me. You make me feel so ashamed. . . .'

'Can't we agree to forget what has passed? I assure you I should be well pleased to do so. We can't go back, but we can go on. Is not *our* fermentation over too?'

'Truly, it isn't that I——'

'Think of this brooch as the payment of a just debt long owed, and this necklace as a Christmas present. Nothing more.'

'I have nothing at all for you.'

'See, the catch fastens this way.'

She had been fingering it, and he took it from her, showed her how it worked, then moved to put it round her neck. For a second she shrank away and he stood with the necklace. Then she straightened up and allowed him to put it on her. The acceptance had more than its own significance. She fingered the stones uncertainly.

'There's no mirror here,' he said. 'Come into the next room.'

'I don't think I want a mirror just yet. Until I can see myself in some less – less despicable light.'

'No such ill light exists. I assure you.'

'Ross, you know that I didn't need or expect a present like this——'

'I know. But if you suppose or suspect that in buying these things I was hoping to buy myself back into your favour, then you're right. I admit it. It is true, my dear, my very dear, my very dear Demelza. My fine, my loyal, my very sweet Demelza.'

'Oh, *no!*' she said, the tears overbrimming her eyes again. 'You *cannot* say that! You cannot say that now.'

'Do you know of any way to stop me?'

'Well you cannot *mean* it, for there is no truth in it. I have never felt so bitter for myself . . . so disgraced. If we are to make it up, if we are to live together, I think it will be a good thing if you are unpleasant to me for a little while.'

'Remind me next week. I could make a New Year resolution of it.'

'But seriously . . .'

'Seriously, Demelza,' he said.

She touched his hand as she turned away from the window. 'I – I wonder you had money to get home. So generous. I *wish* I had something for you. It is Christmas to-morrow and——'

'It's nearly twelve,' he said. 'Let us sit up awhile and call it Christmas to-night.'